Chicago's Greatest Sportsman

Charles E. "Parson" Davies

Mark Dunn

ISBN: 1453691588
ISBN-13: 9781453691588

Charles E. "Parson" Davies – About 1881 – Photograph courtesy of Christopher LaForce

CONTENTS

ACKNOWLEDGMENTS

There are a number of people who have made this book possible. My wife, Martha, supported my efforts in this project for ten years. She proofread a dozen or more drafts and traveled with me to ten different states to gather information. Without her support I would undoubtedly have abandoned the project long ago.

I communicated frequently with two scholarly men, Tracy Callis of the cyberboxingzone and Bob Peterson, a great teacher, researcher, and author from Australia who was interested in one of the best black heavyweights of all time, Peter Jackson. Parson Davies managed Jackson for about five years. Bob's book about Jackson, *Gentleman Bruiser, A Life of the Boxer Peter Jackson*, is a wonderful and scholarly account of Jackson's life. Tracy and Bob helped me find my way and provided me with information that was indispensable to my research.

Others provided me with information that I could never have collected, including Susan Schwartz, Jean Ward, and their mother Doris Cleary. Ken Gruschow, gave me a lead that was indispensable. Others who provided important assistance were Sister Anita Therese Hayes, BVM, Christopher Laforce, Mary Lou Eichhorn of the Williams Research Center in New Orleans, Nellie Martin, Executive Secretary at the Elks National Home, Margaret Mattison at the Amberg Historical Society and Museum Complex and well-known author Richard Lindberg from Chicago who has published fourteen books, several of which deal that city's history at the time Parson Davies lived there.

Work on this book began in the library at Illinois State University, where I viewed microfilm of the *Saint Louis Post Dispatch*, the *Chicago Herald*, the *Chicago Tribune*, the *New York Times*, the *Times of London* and the *National Police Gazette*. Night after night I would push through the newspapers, drop in my dime, and print the articles mentioning Parson Davies, boxing, or fighters that I knew Davies managed. I followed his trail in libraries in Bloomington, Illinois, including the public library and the McLean County Museum of History; the public libraries in Peoria and Chicago; Chicago's Newberry Library and its Museum of History library; the Illinois State Historical Library and the Illinois State Data Center; the beautiful old Carnegie library in Streator, Illinois; the Decatur, Illinois public library; the Cincinnati public library; the North Judson, Indiana, public library, and libraries in Indianapolis and Modesto, California. I also located Pinkerton files at the Library of Congress in Washington, D.C., and spent several days at the wonderful Williams Research Center in New Orleans. The Huntington Library in California refused to admit me despite recommendations from three university presidents.

I visited museums in Amberg, Wisconsin, Ogden, Utah, Carson City, Nevada and Sacramento, California and walked around small towns in northern Indiana to get a feel for the places where men were fighting in big matches more than one hundred years ago. When I had collected more information than I felt I needed,

I did nothing. In academic circles I would have been called ABD (all but dissertation). A period of guilt set in where I felt that if I did not write something, I might as well disown the past. Was I supposed to collect all this information and then just sit on it? Finally in 2009 as my professional career was winding down, I decided to write about Davies in the hope that I could call some attention to this truly self-made man and his important contributions.

PREFACE

At the end of the nineteenth century a Buffalo, New York newspaper wrote one of thousands of newspaper articles that mention Charles Edward "Parson" Davies. It wrote:

> "Parson Davies is one of the best known men identified with sport, particularly the fistic branch of the game. He is a born diplomat, a walking fund of fistic lore, a polished gentleman, as square a man as ever berated the ozone of any sphere: strong and courageous in his convictions, a splendid entertainer, and an all around good fellow."[1]

About nine years ago I decided to try to find out whether it was true that my great grandfather actually fought Jake Kilrain as claimed by one of my great uncles. When I began that project, I knew almost nothing about Kilrain except that he was a boxer and at some point fought John L. Sullivan. For weeks I poured over microfilm of local newspapers at the public library. Eventually I learned that my great grandfather did not fight Kilrain but that in 1884 he did fight a heavyweight named Patsey Cardiff. Cardiff would later fight to a draw with Sullivan.

Along the way, as I turned the crank on the microfilm machine, I saw the name of Charles E. "Parson" Davies. This man was everywhere on microfilm. In every newspaper I read there was Davies doing something in New York, Boston, Philadelphia, Pittsburgh, New Orleans, Buffalo, Cincinnati, San Francisco, Los Angeles, Chicago, England, Ireland, Paris, France, or Achen, Germany. For more than twenty years he was better known to the lunch-bucket working man than in their own state governors, U.S. senators, or the giants of industry.

Davies managed just about every important boxer who drew breath during the 1880s and 1890s. The list of fighters he managed at one time or another includes those known more than one hundred thirty years later and some known only to people who care about the sport: Paddy Ryan, Sullivan, James J. Corbett, Peter Jackson, Joseph Choynski, Tommy Ryan, and Jimmy Barry, among many others.

Davies was unquestionably the most important person in Chicago's sports history for more than twenty years, and then he disappeared. Who was this fellow? Where did he come from? What happened to him? Why has he virtually disappeared from human consciousness and become nothing more than a footprint washed out by time? I decided to try to answer these questions. Perhaps I should say that I felt somehow compelled to find the answers.

Of course, Charlie Davies had a father and mother, brothers and sisters. I doubt that I have located all of his siblings. He was a relatively private person on that subject and probably did not want to draw undue attention to family members who were not in the public spotlight.

My account of Davies' story begins with a shorter account of the life of his older brother, Henry W. Davies. Although Henry and Charlie were brothers, it seems as if their lives happened in two different generations. Henry helped protect Abraham Lincoln from a planned assassination and fought in the Civil War. Charlie was in the next generation of men for whom the war was more remote and during which fewer men were known as Captain, Major, Colonel and General. The President he knew was Teddy Roosevelt. Charlie never married, but for many years he financially supported his nieces and nephews when their parents had died. I suspected that Charlie was driven in part by a desire to live up to the standards of his older brother.

Most people live their lives and disappear as smoke from a candle blown out. Something lingers in the air when the flame dies, but it thins out and until it can no longer be sensed, like a last breath of an old man. You know something was there. Sniff the vacant air and you know that what was once seen is still really there, but it and he are gone to your eye. Parson Davies is gone, but his trace is there, and what he was deserves to be told of so that the past is not as obscure and mysterious as the future.

Some authors addressing events recorded in this book pay little attention to the men who managed and promoted prizefighters and wrestlers. When attention is given to such people, it is almost never in the context of their lives, the things they did or people they knew who were not professional athletes. My effort is to present Davies in a broader way, and I know for some this may be a distraction.

The nearest thing to a home for Davies was Chicago. It was clearly the hub of his operations for more than twenty years. He once told the *Chicago Tribune* that his home was under his hat. This was an accurate statement. Throughout most of his professional life, the primary method of long-distance travel was by train. Davies logged enough railroad miles during his career to make Casey Jones blush. He must have known railroad engineers, conductors, and porters by their first names and probably knew hundreds of other men and women who traveled by train frequently, including salesmen, businessmen, and actors.

Davies was a great opportunist. When the leading heavyweight would not fight Jackson, Davies took him to England, Ireland, France, and Germany. When that well was dry he took Jackson and Joe Choynski on the road with *Uncle Tom's Cabin*, and they made a substantial amount of money over the next year and a half.

When Sullivan was on the verge of bankruptcy and Paddy Ryan weighed over three hundred pounds, Davies made the two men the centerpiece of testimonials and benefits that helped them survive as older men. When Chicago police prevented boxing exhibitions within the city limits, Davies put on benefits for victims of a flood or for nuns operating an industrial school.

If a fighter signed with Davies, he was expected to work and work hard. There was no sitting back and waiting for the world to come to the fighter. The life of a fighter was not always glamorous, but the men Davies managed made money and became known all over the world before radios, televisions, the internet, face-book or twittering. Davies energy was unlimited, and it is hard to keep up with all of his movements even one hundred thirty years later.

We sometimes hear the declaration: "He was a self-made man." Davies was a self-made man of the nineteenth century. From the age of twelve he navigated the Bowery in New York and the saloon district of Chicago. He knew good and bad men and had personal and business relationships with both. Among his friends were Richard Crocker, Mike McDonald, Joe Mackin, Billy Pinkerton, Wyatt Earp, Bat Masterson, John L. Sullivan, Peter Jackson, Sir John Dugdale Astley, Lord Lonsdale, and Teddy Roosevelt. It is hard to think of some of these men as contemporaries, let alone as friends of the same person.

Although he was known best for managing prizefighters, he held many jobs during his life including waiting tables in a hotel, working in his brother's restaurant, operating a saloon, managing racewalkers and wrestlers, appearing on stage in legitimate plays and in minstrel shows, working as a newspapers writer, managing five theaters, operating a billiard hall, operating an off-track betting facility, managing two amusement parks, selling oil for a Texas oil company, managing an amusement park, and working as match-maker for sporting clubs. He even invented a board game.

What follows is my effort to tell Davies' story.

Chicago's Greatest Sportsman

Charles E. "Parson" Davies

Chapter 1

Curtain Going Up!

I was born in the city of Antrim in the north of Ireland, July 7, 1851. I lost my mother when I was 7 years of age. At the age of 12 my father and I came to New York and a year later he too died. I was an orphan and the world looked large to me.

I had gone to school little and my chances in life were anything but encouraging. Well, I just straightened up finally and said, Charles Edward (for that is my name) you must go to work. I applied for work in the old Putnam and was employed. I waited on table and worked in saloon for Lawrence Kerr. He had known my father and naturally took a little interest in me. I worked there a long time and finally Lawrence Kerr, Jr. took his father's place of business. I saved my money and for my education I read the newspapers as best I could, having been taught to read before father died. . . . I finally left the Putnam and got work around New York clubs. I had occasion to meet Richard Croker when I was 17. I was a gabby lad like most boys, but I had a good set of brains. The big politician talked to me and said: "I'll get you something good for you, Charlie" Finally, he came to me one day and said he had a place for me. "You are going to be a policeman," he said. My heart dropped into place. A policeman I was determined I never would be. I thanked Mr. Croker, but declined the position. . . . I never saw Croker after that, and he never gave me the job.[2]

♥

From Antrim to New York

Paul R. Davies and his twelve-year-old son, Charlie, came to the New York in 1863. A native of County Galway, Paul had moved to Antrim and lived there about two decades before coming to the United States. In Antrim Paul had been the clerk of the Petty Sessions Court and also worked as the clerk for the town's commissioners.[3]

Paul and Charlie left Ireland about five years after Charlie's mother died. Paul went to work in Chicago as the chief clerk for the Pinkerton National Detective Agency. He was well-suited for that work and his entrée to the job probably came through his son Henry, who had been a Pinkerton agent since at least 1861. Paul died on Christmas Day 1867 in Chicago. He was a beloved

Pinkerton employee, his funeral was held in the agency's offices, and he is buried in the Pinkerton plot at Chicago's Graceland Cemetery.[4]

Biographies of self-made men are often thin in chapter relating to family background. Self-made men were often forced to fend for themselves and reached their goals by negotiating the shoals of early life with little parental supervision. Charlie was then an orphan, but not alone. A younger brother, Vere, was about ten years old when their father died. An older brother, George Frederick ("Fred") Davies, was about nineteen, and he too was working as a detective for the Pinkerton agency in New York. There were three Davies sisters. One was Catherine Robinson, of New York. Another sister, Jane, married a man named Taylor, had three children, and lived in Chicago. One of his sisters, Annie Davies Suffren, remained in Ireland and lived with her husband Hugh near Belfast.

The Pinkerton spy

The most significant influence in Charlie's life was his oldest brother, Henry W. "Harry" Davies, who was born in Antrim in April 1843 and died on August 8, 1880, in New York after a life filled with excitement and adventure.[5] Henry was influential not so much because Charlie wanted to be just like his older brother but because he demonstrated through first hand example that fame and success could be achieved.

Harry had immigrated to the United States in 1858. He survived by selling stationery on the steps of the Sub-Treasury Building (formerly the Custom House) at the corner of Wall and Nassau streets in New York's central business district, then worked for a baker, John Gilbert, and by February 1861 was an undercover operative for the Pinkerton agency.[6]

Harry played an important role in discovering the "Baltimore plot" to assassinate Abraham Lincoln. Baltimore had strong secessionist elements and its mayor would soon be in a federal prison along with nearly twenty members of Maryland's legislature but the pro-slave snake was just beginning to uncoil in that city as Lincoln traveled from Illinois to Washington. In literature about the Baltimore plot, Harry is identified by a pseudonym. In her book *Lincoln and the Baltimore Plot 1861*, historian Norma B. Cuthbert identifies Joseph Howard as Harry W. Davies. In Allan Pinkerton's words, Howard had assumed the character of an extreme secessionist and then registered at a first-class hotel in Baltimore, where he and other operatives learned of the sinister plan to kill Lincoln before he could be inaugurated as president.[7]

When the Civil War began, Harry enlisted as a private in Company D of the Sixty-Ninth New York State Militia and was wounded at the first battle of Bull Run. He reenlisted as a sergeant in the same unit on May 26, 1862 and remained on active duty until September 3, 1862. Harry was offered a commission to serve with the new Irish Brigade, but he declined and instead went to work as the chief baker in various New York hotels until 1864, when he returned to the Pinkerton agency as a detective.[8]

Henry W. Davies – probably taken about 1861 –
Family photograph courtesy of descendants of Henry W. Davies

Harry's life as a Pinkerton agent and detective was full of excitement and accomplishment. In 1866 he played a key role in capturing a gang of train robbers who had stolen a substantial amount of money of the Adams Express Company from the Big Owl night train near Cos Cob, Connecticut. Harry managed that investigation on the ground, and his work led to the arrest of gang members who were all well-known thieves on the East Coast.[9]

Perhaps during that operation Harry met Catherine Driscoll of Hartford, Connecticut. In 1866 Harry and Catherine married and the following year they had their first child, a daughter, Sarah ("Sadie"), who was born in Chicago.[10]

His next important case involved the capture of a family of train robbers known as the Reno Gang. The Renos controlled the area around Seymour and Rockford in southern Indiana. Harry was in charge of the agency's operatives in Jackson County, Indiana, and opened a liquor store in Seymour to serve as a cover for agency operatives. In July 1868, Harry and other Pinkerton agents were involved in a gun battle that broke out inside a railroad express car that members of the Reno gang were trying to rob.[11]

In early 1869 Harry was named the second superintendent of the Pinkerton's New York City office. With Harry in charge in New York, young Charlie Davies probably could have worked for the Pinkertons, but he had already turned down Richard Crocker's offer of similar police work.

There was substantial pressure put on Harry to develop new business for the New York office and Harry generated new business by working as the Spanish spy and shadowing the Cuban junta in New York and American citizens who were providing aid to Cuban rebels in violation of the Neutrality Act. [12]

On January 12, 1870, Catherine and Harry had their second daughter, Anita. The family lived only a few blocks from the Pinkerton agency office in New York. Anita would later marry a Chicago librarian named Wilson.[13] In 1872, Harry and Catherine had their third daughter named for her mother. As an adult this Catherine became a Sister of Charity of the Blessed Virgin Mary and took the name Sister Mary Conradine Davies. She was well known as the mother superior of Saint Brigid's in San Francisco, where she provided help to Irish and Italian immigrants after the great earthquake in 1906 and the deadly 1918 Spanish flu epidemic. She was also a favorite of her uncle Charlie.[14]

In October 1872, Allan Pinkerton discharged Harry and appointed his son Robert to be the superintendent in New York City. Harry' termination was difficult for his family. In late November 1872, Robert Pinkerton wrote to his father: "I do not know where Davies is. The last time we hear [sic] of him he was in the West trying to get employment from the Ad. Ex. Co. . . . I feel sorry for Davies. I have not seen Mrs. Davies but understand that she is still here and about to be drummed out of her house for not paying the rent."[15]

Harry first went to Chicago and worked for his brother Fred in his restaurant on West Madison Street, just west of the Chicago River. This was an area packed with first floor businesses and apartments above those stores. People young and old were packed into the area and every block could be its own neighborhood. Harry later returned to New York and formed his own detective agency with Patrick Burns, an old army pal and another former Pinkerton agent.[16] They successfully obtained the business of the Spanish embassy and many other reputable clients.[17]

Catherine died on August 8, 1879. A coroner's jury found that she fell from the balcony of their flat at 250 West Twenty-Fourth Street in New York on the night of July 20, 1879. Her spine was badly damaged, she was left paraplegic, her kidneys were damaged, and she went into a uremic coma before she died on August 8, 1879. A brief mention of her death appeared in Chicago's *Inter Ocean* on August 14, 1879.

A year after her death the *New York Sun* reported that Catherine had jumped over the back-balcony with her baby in her arms and fell thirteen feet to the pavement below. The newspaper said she was suffering from hallucinations of burglars in her home and had become "crazed" after reading a newspaper account of the murder of a Mrs. Hull on West Forty-Second Street.

After Catherine's death, Harry's life was not what it had been. Dispirited and melancholy, he withdrew into himself and lost interest in all the things around him. He began drinking heavily almost immediately after Catherine's death. Irish men did this sort of thing when they lost the woman they loved. He suffered a stroke of paralysis, but the cause of his death on August 5, 1880, was cirrhosis of the liver. On the first anniversary of Catherine's death Harry was buried with her at Woodlawn Cemetery in New York. He left behind Sarah, Anita, and Catherine. Harry's little brother Charlie would financially support these young women for many years to come.[18]

Charlie in the Bowery

Charlie was without direct parental supervision from about the age of fifteen, but his brothers or sisters probably provided him with some support after his father's death. Charlie probably often visited them to hear about their lives and exploits. It was not an easy proposition for a young man to be on his own in New York in 1867. Tens of thousands of men who had been in sucked into military service until the spring of 1865 were spit out and washed onto New York's docks, main streets, side streets, alleys, and dives. These men found work where they could and looked for opportunity and entertainment wherever they could be found.

The city was loaded with gangs of footloose young men like the Fourth Avenue Tunnel Gang, which nurtured future Tammany Hall politician Richard Croker and brought him to prominence in New York. The code of the post war gangs was the same as it is of gangs now: discipline, loyalty to the gang, earning a reputation through successful criminal actions, making money and leading by force.

Charlie worked at the Putnam House hotel as a young man. The hotel at 357 Fourth Avenue (now called Park Avenue), between Twenty-sixth and Twenty-seventh streets, had a dinning saloon attached.[19] Croker and his Twenty-first Ward Tammany Association were based on Thirty-first Street near Fourth

Avenue, only a few blocks from the Putnam. Charlie's brother Henry and his family lived in the two hundred block of West Twenty-fourth Street, also close to the Putnam.[20] The hotel was a favorite spot for politicians and sporting men visiting New York City. It was owned by Lawrence R. Kerr, who was active in Nineteenth Ward politics in New York, and after his death by his son Lawrence Kerr Jr. Charlie said that the senior Mr. Kerr and his father had been friends, and Kerr took an interest in Charlie and gave him a job at the hotel waiting tables.

William Muldoon was about eight years older than Charlie and one of the more important sporting men of the era. Muldoon became a champion wrestler, athletic trainer, and the first commissioner of boxing in the state of New York. In his biography of Muldoon, *Muldoon-The Solid Man of Sport*, Van Every describes Muldoon's life in New York after the Civil War:

> He and his friends had the good fortune to fall into the graces of an obliging waiter who saw that they were not only accorded good service, but that their checks were surprisingly reasonable. It would seem that the waiter's arithmetic was rather poor and that his mistakes were always at the expense of the proprietor. Under the conditions, tipping as high as ten cents was not an undue extravagance. One day the friendly waiter was gone, but it did not take long to locate his new place of labor, though it was rather far uptown, up around 23d Street. The incident of the friendly waiter impressed itself later upon Mr. Muldoon, since the man I question was destined to occupy a place of some prominence in the sporting world. This waiter came to be known as Parson Davies, the same Parson Davies who managed Peter Jackson, the Negro heavyweight, estimated by more than one student of pugilistic values, as the best of all the heavyweight boxers, even though he never had the chance to become a champion.[21]

During those years Charlie went with the regularity of clockwork to a hall devoted exclusively to boxing exhibitions at 600 Broadway to watch Jem Mace, Tom Allen, Billy Edwards (ex-champion lightweight of America), Arthur Chambers, Peter Morris (English featherweight champion), Professor Johnny Clarke, Tim Collins, Abe and Harry Hicken, Barney Aaron, Johnny Keating, Dick Hollywood, Billy Madden, George Siler, Dooney Harris, Joe and Mickey Coburn, Professor Mike Donovan, George Sidons, Patsey Sheppard, and many others. His life in the Bowery amounted to an early education in the profession of boxing and the art of entertainment. There was no bright line dividing Charlie's childhood from his adult life. He started working when he could find a job and successfully navigated his way through the complicated life and society of New York's Bowery and then the reconstruction of Chicago.

Chapter 2 - (1871-1881)

Chicago

Well, I finally came to Chicago, where my brother George had a saloon at Peoria and Madison streets. So I went to work for him. Another brother, Harry was working for the Pinkertons in New York. He left them to go to the Spanish war.[22]

▬

Just after the great fire on '71 he came to Chicago, where his brother Harry and George were already located, and it was shortly after his arrival that he became so prominently identified with sports, though he had taken a lively interest in them all his life.[23]

▬

I finally saved up a little money and got interested in sports. John Ennis made me think he could beat Dan O'Leary in a 100-mile walking match. It was held in the old Exposition building on the lake front. Ennis proved a joke and quit after going fifteen miles and $500 I had saved and invested in the race was wiped away.

It was necessary to go to work again and I finally drifted back to New York and promoted a big walking match between O'Leary, Ennis, Charles Harriman, Charles Rowel and others. It was there I got my nickname of "Parson," and it was W. K. Vanderbilt who was responsible for it.

During the big matches I usually walked around dressed in a black frock coat and Mr. Vanderbilt would come in and sit for hours and watch the men walking. One day he called Frank Davidson, an old Times reporter, over and asked him who that minister was talking to O'Leary. When told that I was not a minister he said, he ought to have been a parson. That story was printed and broadcast and ever since then I have been known the world over as Parson Davies.[24]

▬

♦

Chicago and the Elks

Charlie came to Chicago after the 1871 fire. In the wake of that disaster, the city was a place of unlimited opportunity. Millions of dollars were being invested in creating a new central district and job opportunities abounded. Every place a person looked, hotels were being built, office buildings called sky scrapers were going up six and seven stories, railroads were unloading lumber, and ships were docking along the river to unload every imaginable thing from places as divergent as Syria, China and Duluth, Minnesota. Several years in the Bowery was an excellent prep-school for living in Chicago in the early 1870s, but prep-schools on the streets do not guarantee success in life. Charlie was interested in success and clearly wanted to make it big.

In Chicago, Charlie lived first on West Madison Street, west of the Chicago River where Fred had his business. His experience in the Bowery drew him to a similar area in Chicago, along Randolph Street east of the Chicago River and along Clark Street starting at West Lake Street and then for many blocks to the south. He made friends in Chicago with people who were working in the fast lanes. Some of his closest associates appear in public records in November 1876, when at the age of twenty-five he became a founding member of Lodge No. 4 of the Benevolent and Protective Order of Elks. Charlie loved the Elks and actively participated in their activities for almost forty-five years. In 1879 he became the Grand Exalted Ruler of the Elks, and he would live the last nineteen months of his life at the Elks National Home in Bedford, Virginia.[25] He is buried in Bedford with many fellow members.

In the summer of 1875, Joseph C. (Mike) Mackin, a young man who came to Chicago from Philadelphia just after the great fire, wrote to the Grand Body of the Elks in New York City expressing interest in forming an Elks lodge in Chicago. Joe had been a small-time politician in Philadelphia and a member of Elks Lodge No. 2 there before he came to Chicago.[26] The new Chicago lodge opened with Joseph Mackin, Cool White, Billy Rice, William Harrison, Fayette Welch, Harry Standwood, and John Hart as the founding members. Hart and Rice were well-known members of a minstrel team that often appeared at Hooley's Theater in Chicago. White was a stage manager at Hooley's.

When Lodge No. 4 was chartered, Mackin became its first Exalted Ruler and Charlie was the Esteemed Leading Knight. In its early days, the Elks club in Chicago was the home of many men involved in entertainment and theater business in downtown Chicago. The Elks was an active organization and held its first annual benefit on September 29, 1877.[27]

During Samuel J. Tilden's campaign for president in the fall of 1876, Sam Medill persuaded Charlie's friend Joe Mackin to form a Tilden club, and Mackin's efforts with that club attracted the attention of Mike McDonald, who was the source of the statement that "there's a sucker born every minute." McDonald and Mackin had a common friend in Charlie Davies. At about this time, McDonald began backing Charlie's efforts to promote sporting events, particularly racewalking and later boxing events. Moreover McDonald, Davies, and Billy Pinkerton were all close friends.[28]

Managing racewalkers

The lofty moral ends that propelled the abolitionists and energized the people at the beginning of the Civil War were dulled and fell limp as families learned that Johnny would not come marching home and that his body had been left in a farm field in northern Georgia. When the war ended, people all over America wanted something that could lift their spirits and good, accessible entertainment was one answer.

Walking matches and racewalking were among the first and most popular forms of entertainment in the 1870's. Other sports such as bicycle racing and sculling enjoyed some popularity too. Charlie was not a great walker, bike rider or oarsman but he found a portal to success by guiding those who were. For years to come Charlie was on the fast track both literally and figuratively

The participants in the early days of walking matches developed their reputations in the 1860's but became international stars in the 1870's. In 1877 Charlie began managing a Chicago racewalker by the name of John Ennis, and between May 1879 and March 1881 Davies managed the greatest American race walker of all time, Daniel O'Leary.

The contracts for racewalking events were called articles of agreement, and both sides in the contest had managers and stake holders. The articles included other terms designed to create betting opportunities for the public.[29] Articles of agreement became the staple of most athletic contests, including wrestling and boxing matches for many years to come. Typically contestants appeared on a specified date before a match for the reading of the articles. After the reading, the parties signed them, and the articles were often published in a local newspaper as a way of informing the public (and especially the gambling public) of the rules in effect. Of course, the meetings for the formal reading of the articles sometimes led to disagreements over things like forfeit money, the choice of umpires or referees, entitlement to gate receipts, and so forth, with the disputes often intended to gain publicity for the upcoming match.

In 1874 racewalking caught the interests of the huge immigrant Irish populations in cities like Chicago and New York. Daniel O'Leary, a native of County Cork, Ireland, came to the United States in 1861 and worked canvassing pictures and selling books door-to-door in Chicago.

The *New York Times* called O'Leary "a shapely racehorse" with a chest that was "finely developed" and a head "magnificently balanced." He walked "with the elasticity of a school-boy," and when he ran 'the first thought is of the antelope—of the young doe. But his resemblance to the young doe goes too far. He can run gracefully and swiftly, but not far, for his wind is not strong." [30] This stout little Irishman excited Chicago by walking one hundred miles in twenty-three hours and seventeen minutes, easily breaking the twenty-four hour barrier that had defeated many others who had tried to do the same.

The successes of the top racewalkers inspired others to become racewalkers and induced promoters to make matches between the lesser lights and "wannabees" of the walking world. In May 1876 another six-day match was scheduled at Chicago's Exposition building with a dozen local men and no famous pedestrians participating. One of the local walkers was George Guyon, who was identified as a Milwaukee brakeman. Another Chicago-based walker was John Ennis.[31] While this match did not have the big names of racing involved, the crowds were substantial and the promoters were perfecting the entertainment by offering bicycle races and shorter distance walking matches at $50 a side whenever the long distance walkers were off the track.[32]

As the years passed, racewalking and pedestrian events evolved into big business. Large halls were rented and substantial gate receipts collected. Bands were hired to provide entertainment. Policemen and Pinkerton agents worked venues to keep order and provide security. Beer, wine, liquor, and food concessions were set up and also generated large sums of money. Trainers and doctors were hired to work with contestants and keep them fit. Promoters of these events began to control the business, and in the United States many were the same men connected with wrestling and boxing.

Some of the men who became prominent in the pedestrian business were Tom Foley, who ran a billiard hall at 146 South Clark and had many boxing and wrestling connection in Chicago; "Professor" William Miller a well-known Greco-Roman wrestler who became a trainer for the walkers; and Joe Goss, another trainer who was from Northampton, England but lived in Boston. Another important man in racewalking was Al Smith, a well-known gambler and promoter. Harry Hill, the saloon owner, gambler, and fight promoter of New York who has been described as a centerpiece of the city's sporting culture was also prominent in pedestrian matters.[33]

Richard K. Fox, a renowned promoter of boxing matches and the owner and editor of the *National Police Gazette* was another person actively promoting racewalking. Others included Barney Aaron, who had won the light-weight championship of American in 1857 and was still fighting professionally into the late 1870s; Tom O'Rourke, who managed many fighters and was a close friend of Charlie Davies; William Harding, a New York promoter and lap-dog for Fox; and Mike McDonald, another close friend of Charlie's, who created the Chicago Democratic political machine and backed boxing and wrestling events for several decades.

A great advance occurred in the racewalking business in March 1878. Sir John Dugdale Astley, a well-known English sportsman and Conservative Member of Parliament, posted £750 and the Astley Belt for a sweepstakes to be held at the agricultural hall in Islington. The Astley prize money was equivalent to a prize of roughly $125,000 in 2007 dollars. The winner of the belt held it on conditions specified by Dugdale. The winner was required to defend the belt within eighteen months. The belt could be taken outside of England if won by a man from another country on the condition that security was posted for its return. The holder of the belt was required to accept all challenges issued for not less than $500 a side.

The first Astley Belt contest was staged in London on March 18, 1878.[34] Eighteen contestants started the race for the belt. Dan O'Leary almost missed the race when his entry fee was not posted properly, but it was determined that O'Leary should be allowed to compete. Other well-known walkers in the field included the English walker known as "Blower" Brown. The match was set up so that O'Leary would walk on a separate track from the English born competitors. If O'Leary could win this race he would lay claim to the title of world champion.[35]

Harry Vaughan, the leading British contestant, stopped walking on the sixth day of the match after he reached 500 miles. O'Leary continued to walk for over a half hour after Vaughan had conceded the match and stopped only when Astley went to him and declared him the champion pedestrian of the world. O'Leary had walked 520 miles. After the result was reported, the *Chicago Tribune* congratulated "our wiry little O'Leary" for his exhibition of Chicago brawn and brains in beating the English walker.[36]

In May 1878 Davies went to New York with George Guyon, a Chicago race walker. He took Guyon to the New York *Sportsman* magazine to issue a formal challenge to Charles Harriman for a thirty-six hour walking match for $250 a side, a champion's belt, and a trophy. Davies then backed and managed Guyon during July 1878 competition in Buffalo. Guyon walked against Ennis but sprained his ankle in the first ten miles. When he had walked another 260 miles, Charlie tried to haul him off the track. Guyon refused to leave and said he would stick it out to the end.[37]

O'Leary's defense of the belt was scheduled at Gilmore Garden in New York City at the end of September 1878 and on into the first days of October. O'Leary would walk against John Hughes for the belt and $500 a side. The Garden's owners received fifty percent of the gate. The other half was split two thirds to O'Leary and the balance to Hughes. An estimated thirty thousand people attended the event.

Hughes was another Irishman from Cork. He lived on Twenty-seventh Street, close to Gilmore Garden.[38] This contest was promoted as a battle between New York and Chicago. The match played out poorly. After the first day of walking Hughes drank a gallon of milk and almost immediately fell sick with cramps in his legs. It was suggested that someone had tampered with the milk, causing the cramps. A doctor attending Hughes said that he was "as pale as a sheet" and there were "grave doubts" about his ability to return to the track. When O'Leary left the track on the first day he had covered 103 miles and Hughes was laid up having gone only eighty-seven miles. Things were not entirely good for O'Leary, who had developed a small blister on one of his toes.

On the second day of the race Hughes periodically left the track to vomit, but he was still taking small amounts of lime water and milk. As the day went on Hughes gave up drinking milk and seemed to improve when he took beef tea and chicken broth. After sixty-eight hours of walking, running, and dog-trotting around the track, O'Leary was still thirty-five miles up on Hughes.

The next day Hughes' friends sent him a case of champagne and a dozen boxes of condensed meat to perk him up. His manager ruled against the use of the champagne, but when Hughes left the track to sleep, his manager decided to leave the building for a nearby saloon. In his absence Hughes and his wife began drinking some of the champagne. Hughes was soon drunk, and when he returned to the track he was wearing a white shirt and flesh-colored tights with blue silk trunks that were tipped with long gilt fringe. He was described as a "circus clown" but lacking the expected grace and dignity.

At the end of the day O'Leary was nearly seventy miles ahead of the tipsy Hughes, and the *New York Times* wrote that he was being denounced by the spectators as a fraud. Despite these circumstances the Garden was full all evening, with as many as seven thousand people in the building at any one time. In the end the match was called off when O'Leary had covered 403 miles and Hughes was more than ninety miles behind. O'Leary made about $5,000 for the race, and the besotted Hughes was said to have crawled off with $2,500.[39]

Riding the crest of the wave during the competition in New York, Davies published articles for a Guyon-Schmehl match at McCormick Hall in Chicago beginning October 9, 1878. This match was also well attended, and Mike McDonald acted in the official capacity as starter for this race.[40]

In late November 1878 the owner of the Gilmore Garden met with Charlie Davies at the Brunswick Hotel in New York and agreed to offer $3,000 in prize money for another Astley Belt competition if it would be held at the Garden. This offer served to demonstrate how profitable racewalking had become.

Parson Davies demonstrated his interest in the sensational side of sporting events in December 1878. This time he matched George Guyon against a stallion, Hesing Junior, owned by Cornelius Sullivan, for $500. The bet was that Guyon would walk farther in fifty-two hours than the horse. This contest was to take place at the Exposition Building in Chicago beginning on January 9, 1879, with the winner after expenses were paid to split the gate receipts 75/25.[41]

Charlie becomes "Parson" Davies

The third Astley Belt contest took place in Gilmore Garden in March 1879. The contenders for the belt were to include Ennis (Charlie's former man), O'Leary, Charles A. Harriman, and Charles Rowell, who was the most likely contender for the belt. Davies was the promoter for this match, and it was at this match that he earned the nickname "Parson" from William K. Vanderbilt.[42]

All classes of men attended the competition, including millionaires, mechanics, and laborers, tramps, and thieves. Among the wealthy were William H. Vanderbilt, Rev. Dr. Stephen Tyng, and Sir Edward Thornton, the British Minister to the United States. A young hustler, William A. Brady, was present and picked up some nice money during the event by establishing a messenger service between the Garden and New York newspapers. He hired a number of boys from the area of the Garden to run messages about the progress of the race.[43] Brady later managed two world heavyweight champions.

Davies said that Vanderbilt gave him the nickname "Parson". During the pedestrian events Charlie walked around in a black frock coat, and Vanderbilt sat watching the men walk for hours. Vanderbilt called Frank Davidech, a reporter for the *New York Times* and asked him who that minister was talking to O'Leary.

When told that it was not a minister, Vanderbilt said that the man in the frock coat ought to have been a parson. His remark was printed and the name stuck for the rest of Charlie's life.

Another account written in 1911 provided more detail: "O'Leary was the favorite, but broke down. In order to keep up interest in the race, Davies would walk miles with O'Leary around the track to induce him to remain in the race, as Dan was the card! The elder Vanderbilt noticed this and asked about the preacher-looking man walking with O'Leary. Someone answered: 'It must be the spiritual adviser.' From that time on he was known as the Parson."[44]

By the second day of this big match O'Leary was described as a broken man and out of contention in the race. By two a.m. on the third day, the record was Rowell 200 miles, Harriman 186 miles, Ennis 175 miles and O'Leary 168 miles. Soon after, O'Leary withdrew from the race, and it was said that he was fagged out and looked like a corpse. His doctor advised him that if he walked any more it would be at the risk of his life. Rumors circulated that O'Leary's handlers had been feeding him liquor and that he was simply drunk from being mishandled. Soon a rumor began that O'Leary had been poisoned by his trainers, Barney Aaron and William Harding (both members of the boxing crowd), and that they had been arrested for poisoning him.

Outside the Garden newsboys shouted that O'Leary was dead, and the rumor spread quickly so that thousands gathered to learn if it was true. Al Smith, O'Leary's backer, claimed that O'Leary was blind drunk even before the race began and claimed that he had been drinking since he returned to New York from England after winning the belt. Smith told the press that when O'Leary had walked against Rowell, it had been necessary to hire two men to watch him to prevent him from getting at whiskey. He claimed that in spite of his efforts, O'Leary had smuggled in two gallons of brandy and was blind drunk during the entire race.[45]

Interest in these ancillary matters was a terrific boost for attendance and of great potential benefit to Davies. The number of paid admissions on this day alone was said to be 20,000, exceeding the 18,600 tickets sold on the prior day. There were so many people in the Garden that part of the south end of the gallery gave way, injuring a number of people and causing a near panic. The race finished on the uptick with good sportsmanship demonstrated all around. Ultimately it was announced that the gate receipts alone were more than $60,000. It is highly likely that Davies earned a substantial amount for his work in promoting this event and was better fixed financially than ever before. He had also made his bones.

Toward the end of the last night Rowell had made 448 miles, Ennis 460 miles, and Harriman 440 miles. Harriman had been off the track to rest and when he returned, he was stiff and lame and could hardly continue, bringing into question whether he would share in the tremendous gate receipts. Then Rowell approached from behind and put one arm through Harriman's to help him continue to walk, and the Garden erupted in cheers at the great sacrifice and sportsmanship Rowell demonstrated. When Ennis appeared from resting, instead of complaining about the advantage being gained by Harriman, he took Harriman's other arm, and the crowd again went wild with yelling and cheering. The judges ruled this conduct to be illegal assistance and thereafter, Rowell walked in front of Harriman and Ennis behind to guide him along the path and to a share of the gate receipts. A few laps later, Ennis' three-year-old son, dressed in a black velvet suit, emerged from his father's tent. Ennis slowed down to take his son's hand, and together they took a slow turn around the track. Again the crowd went wild cheering the contestants.

On his last lap Harriman carried a red, white, and blue banner to signify his appreciation for the American crowd, and the entire place was frantic. Harriman, in appreciation for the crowd's support, took another lap, this time carrying the American flag with Rowell and Ennis walking together behind him. The drama of the event was said to be breathtaking. It seems certain that after the race concluded there were many sports from both New York and Chicago and all over the world who slapped Davies on the back and bought him a drink to congratulate him for carrying off such a tremendous success despite losing O'Leary early on.[46]

O'Leary, having lost both face and the belt, needed to do something to regain his reputation as a world class race walker. According to the *National Police Gazette*, it was at about this time that Davies formed a co-partnership with O'Leary.[47] In March 1879, O'Leary announced that he was creating the O'Leary Belt, which was valued at three hundred dollars and would be given as a prize in a seventy-five hour go-as-you-please competition that he would sponsor in the Exposition Building in Chicago. First prize would be the belt and $1,000 cash.

The O'Leary Belt was made of silver and gold. Its center was an oval shield of gold surmounted with branches of oak and laurel. Lettering on the shield in enamel read: "International O'Leary Champion Belt of the World." The upper part of the shield was decorated with the American, English, Irish, and German flags. An American eagle had three diamonds set as a trefoil. The idea of the O'Leary Belt probably originated with Davies as a way for the co-partnership to cash in on O'Leary's reputation.[48]

Charlie next backed Guyon in one of O'Leary's seventy-five mile races in Chicago, and then in May 1879 he backed Guyon in a match for the O'Leary Belt held in Chicago. Fame and fortune did not follow for Davies with Guyon as his client. Guyon started the event on May 28, 1879, but quit the race after only twenty-five miles with inflamed kidneys and failed to win any money. Chicago fans then gave their support in the race to a boy from Bridgeport named John Dobler.

The crowd attending the contest was greater than ever, with twelve thousand people in the Exposition Building on the final day. After seventy-five hours a walker named George Parry had completed 268 miles, and Dobler was second with 263 miles. Dobler entered a protest that Parry had been coached during the race and that one of his men had tried to dope Dobler on the second night of the event. The determination was quickly made that Parry had won the O'Leary Belt honestly and was entitled to the first prize of $1,000. Parry then skipped town without paying Fox $300 that he owed to Fox arising out of a lost wager. Soon after this race Dobler also came under the management of the O'Leary-Davies co-partnership.[49]

Then in early July 1879 Davies, O'Leary, and Guyon met in Chicago to discuss another competition. Charlie had been unable to secure a suitable venue in New York and thought that the best chance for a race might be in San Francisco; however, all of the men agreed that there had been enough racewalking for awhile and decided against another contest.[50]

It is interesting to recall that this event took place less than a month before the death of Catherine Driscoll Davies. As Harry Davies was about to lose his wife and die from his sadness, his little brother Charlie was at the beginning of a life of fame and sometime fortune.

Racewalking was the leading sport in America for many years. The competitions had an advantage over other sports because attendance was open to men, women, and children. All classes of citizens could attend. In *John L. Sullivan and His America,* Michael T. Isenberg wrote that "one colorful feature of this New York of 1881 was a social underclass, a collection of somewhat disparate groups whose activities were officially frowned on by the cultural elite, the 'better sort.' The underclass was bound together not so much by economic self-consciousness as by recreational activities."[51]

Pedestrian events as entertainment crossed cultural and class lines. Davies continued to promote walking events from New York City to San Francisco and from Buffalo to New Orleans. He took contestants to matches in London, but his future was in the sport of boxing, which in America primarily attracted those outside the upper class. Davies would spend many years trying to expand the audience for boxing.

Davies breaks with O'Leary

Davies' relationship with O'Leary broke down in March 1881. O'Leary had decided to walk again in a match at Madison Square Garden against Charles Rowell, Henry Vaughan, and James Albert. Both Rowell and O'Leary had posted $5,000 with the *London Sporting Life* as the stakes for the match. Albert broke down on the first day of the race and O'Leary began to suffer with nausea and cramps and didn't perform well. In addition, the rumor spread (probably fed by Albert withdrawing and O'Leary taking sick) that there was no real money riding on the match and the contestants had actually agreed to split the gate prior to the race starting. Both Davies and the *Sporting Life* were emphatic that there was no fix involved.[52]

On the second day of the race, under the handling of Davies and W. E. Harding, O'Leary had recovered, but he had lost too much ground and could not close the lead held by Rowell. On the fifth day of the race O'Leary split with his trainers over who was "boss" in the undertaking. Davies then returned to Chicago and promoted a match that included Harriman and four other walkers: Tracey, Krohne, Strucke, and Faber. Although expenses exceeded income and the match was not a financial success, Davies paid every bill connected with the event.

It seems that after this race, Davies' involvement in racewalking diminished.[53] His sense of responsibility and willingness to cover his expenses even when an event was a financial failure were unusual in his line of work and helped him earn a reputation as an honest businessman in a line of work where many managers would disappear on the midnight train rather than pay their bills.

O'Leary continued to walk until his death on May 29, 1933 at the Glendale Sanatorium near Los Angeles. On his sixty-sixth birthday at Cincinnati, he walked a mile each hour for one thousand consecutive hours. On his eighty-first birthday he walked sixty-two miles from the Philadelphia Post Office to Atlantic City, New Jersey. During his life it was said that he had walked over three hundred thousand miles[54]

By the age of thirty, Davies had built the perfect platform for his work over the next twenty-five years as the leading boxing promoter in the world. He had a good family life as a young man in Ireland. He had come to the Bowery of New York City as a young man and knew the leading sporting men such as William Muldoon, Harry Hill, Al Smith, and Richard K. Fox. His brother, Harry W. Davies, was a well-known figure around both Chicago and New York City and had a special knowledge of those who hung around with the "sporting" class. In the summer of 1871 Charlie had relocated to Chicago and created life-long friendships with men in entertainment, sports, politics and finance. As a result of his friendship with Joe Mackin and Mike McDonald, Davies had an entrée to the mayor of Chicago and would become nearly the only person who could promote major boxing and wrestling events in the city for nearly a decade.

Following an initial setback with Ennis, Davies became a leading promoter of pedestrian events and learned to make sporting contracts, prepare athletes for events, negotiate for gate receipts, make travel plans, and advertise and boom sporting events. When his brother Henry died in August 1880, he took charge of Henry's three daughters and provided for their financial support and education until they were adults and for Sadie even after she married. Many years later, one of his nieces would say that Charlie was the only father she had ever known.[55]

Chapter 3 - (1881-1883)

John L. Sullivan and the Law

Upon his return to the States he gave a number of varied pedestrian exhibitions, in the course of which he met John L. Sullivan, whose business he took charge of soon after Sullivan's victories over Flood of New York and Donaldson of Cleveland. The Boston boy's first exhibition in McCormick's Hall, in Chicago, was superintended by Davies.[56]

—

His first venture with the Sullivan-Madden combination at McCormick's Hall, about four or five years ago, realized a cool $2,000. It was he who induced M. C. McDonald to put up $5,000 on John L. Sullivan, then a rising young man, against the then champion, Paddy Ryan, but on account of a dispute about the stake-holder the money was withdrawn. The "Parson" estimate of Sullivan, then almost entirely unknown, was amply confirmed in less than a year. . . . After Sullivan won the championship the "Parson" took him to Chicago, Detroit and other cities.[57]

—

♠

Davies and Sullivan at the beginning of their careers

Sullivan's rise from obscurity to the heavyweight championship is well chronicled by many authors. Some of his career is retold here because it is important to his relationship with Davies and Davies' influence on Sullivan's early professional life. Many managers and promoters crossed paths with Sullivan at different points in their careers. Few men had careers and experiences as managers that paralleled Sullivan's as directly as did Davies'. He played a significant role in Sullivan's early career, spent six years managing pretenders and contenders, and then managed Peter Jackson the top heavyweight contender from 1889 through 1892. Sullivan used every dodge and blatant racism to avoid Jackson. After being on the outs with Sullivan for eight years, the two men reconciled, and beginning in 1895 Davies managed Sullivan's affairs for about a year and a half.

Sullivan had been fighting professionally for about seven years when he battered Steve Taylor at Harry Hill's saloon in the Bowery on March 31, 1881. During much of the period when Sullivan was honing his skills, Davies was rising in the ranks of athletic promoters, and the two men knew of each other. The important thing about Sullivan's fight with Taylor was that prominent members of the New York press were present for the mugging, and the newspapers quickly spread the word about Boston's bad boy and his brutal approach to boxing.[58]

There is something that stirs the primeval urges in a man when a heavyweight appears who is renowned for battering his opponent into a liquefied mass, and in the 1880s Sullivan clearly triggered those urges. In addition to his style Sullivan was a self-possessed egotist. In his early career people could hate him with great ease and hope that a more humble pugilist would come along and beat him to a pulp. Nevertheless, Sullivan captivated the public by the force of his personality and the way he destroyed opponents. At the end of his match with Taylor, Sullivan offered $50 to any man who could last four rounds with him fighting under the Marquess of Queensberry rules. There are several reports in newspapers from this period that Sullivan had a run-in with Fox at Harry Hills' place. Fox also had a huge ego, and was insulted by Sullivan's behavior and wanted to see the Boston brute laid low.

Sullivan's next fight was on May 16, 1881, against John Flood, the Bullshead Terror, for a purse of $750 on a moonlight barge that was taken north on the Hudson River. Flood had worked as an enforcer in Harry Hill's saloon and had also been a New York gang leader. Their fight was arranged in Hill's establishment and was held on the barge to avoid interference by the law. Harry Hill generally paid for "police protection" on his own premises, but not necessarily outside his neighborhood. Davies would have known Flood and had probably seen him fight several times. The brutal way that Sullivan beat-up Flood for eight rounds focused the attention of sporting men interested in such contests in the same way an artillery barrage catches the attention of lowly infantryman in a foxhole.[59]

On June 13, 1881, Sullivan participated in a three-round exhibition with Flood. According to Billy Madden, who was acting after Sullivan's manager, Madden then got the idea of a tour to show-off Sullivan using a $50-for-four-rounds challenge as the centerpiece of the tour. Sullivan's appearance in large and small towns was preceded by advance men to advertise the coming event. There was nothing unusual about such tours. In the short-run, the $50-four-rounds format used by Madden with Sullivan made excellent money and was emulated by many other fighters.

On July 11, Madden took Sullivan to Philadelphia where he knocked out Fred Crossley, a rank amateur. Sullivan then gave a three-round exhibition with Madden to make up for the brevity of the Crossley fight. Eight days later Sullivan knocked out a hapless fellow named Dan McCarthy (sometime reported as "McCarty") in another one-round pound.

After passing through Trenton, where he gave an exhibition with Madden, Sullivan headed for Chicago. Years later an article in the *Winnipeg Free Press* added some interesting insight concerning Sullivan's first appearance in Chicago. The facts as reported are that Parson Davies had written to Billy Madden and advised Madden that Davies had two heavyweights who could stop the Boston Strong Boy lined up in Chicago. Madden then went to Chicago without Sullivan in order to meet with Davies. While Madden was in Chicago Sullivan was visiting with his parents in Roxbury. Madden then wrote to Sullivan from Chicago and told him that the likely opponents there would be Captain James Dalton and Jack Byrnes (sometimes "Burns") of Michigan.[60]

On August 7, the *Chicago Tribune* reported that Sullivan had rented McCormick Hall to put on a sparring exhibition on August 13. Madden offered any boxer in Chicago $50 if that man could stay in the ring with the Boston Strong Boy, as Sullivan became known, for four rounds at his exhibition on August 13. Sullivan was asked his reasons for making so liberal an offer and said that he had already disposed of the best fighters on the East Coast, and no man had yet been able to stand for four rounds. Should anyone in Chicago win the $50, Sullivan said he would be happy to pay that man the money. The Chicago event included an exhibition by Madden against any interested local sparrer. Ed Dorney, a local pugilist, had lined up an unknown whom he intended to match against Sullivan. Davies was arranging the details of all the entertainment. In undertaking this job Charlie Davies found a profession that he would practice for more than twenty-five years.[61]

Sullivan meets Chicago's dark prince

Upon his arrival in Chicago, Sullivan was taken to meet Mike McDonald (the "Prince of Darkness") at his gambling resort on South Clark Street. McDonald took one look at Sullivan and exclaimed: "Holy smoke! Is this bank clerk the famous Boston Strong Boy?" McDonald thought that Sullivan had lost a lot of weight since he had defeated John Donaldson in Cincinnati. Sullivan responded with a smile: "I strip big." McDonald then said that Sullivan would not have a chance against Dalton and Byrnes. He was prepared to gamble on Sullivan, but he didn't like the idea of paying $500 of overhead for the hall and other expenses just to see Sullivan put down. Sullivan then offered to demonstrate his skills against any of the "husky birds" that McDonald could find working in Chicago's stockyards. He said he would lay them out inside of ten minutes.[62]

McDonald agreed to give this suggestion a shot, and the next day Sullivan, Madden, Tom Chandler, Davies, and McDonald met in a gym that Chandler operated above the Chicago Board of Trade. McDonald brought along the elite of Chicago's nightlife to watch as Sullivan was fitted out with skin-tight gloves. The first longshoreman was then put into the ring and lunged at Sullivan, who side-stepped, took one pace forward, and whipped out his right hand so that it landed with terrific impact on the man's chin. He crumpled to the floor spurting blood. The next man then climbed into the ring and Sullivan was on him in a flash. He banged this man under the left ear and stretched him out like a dead beef cow.

Sullivan began pulling off his gloves and McDonald cried: "Hey, wait a minute! There's three minutes left and one more of 'em you've got to whip."

Laughing, Sullivan replied that there wasn't anyone left to fight. "Number three is half way home now."

The crowd was excited, and McDonald was satisfied that he wouldn't be flushing away his money by backing Sullivan.[63]

On August 13, John Brucks was named to spar with Madden in a preliminary match. Brucks was a racewalker who had participated in several local walking matches promoted by Davies. It is likely that Charlie drafted Brucks to try out boxing with Madden for the evening and probably promised a decent remuneration for his efforts. On the night of the actual exhibition Brucks was described in introductions as the champion of California. The unknown who would take on Sullivan was Captain James Dalton.[64]

McDonald appeared as an aura around many of the leading matches in the ten years between 1880 and 1890. From the early 1870s until the early 1890s, McDonald was a powerful presence in Chicago. The press portrayed him as a dark, conspiratorial, brooding sort of man with enormous influence in Chicago politics and a hand in virtually all criminal enterprises in the city. The press was correct on all counts.[65]

Dalton was part of the sporting arm of McDonald's political machine in Chicago and a low-level political operative. Most men who were called Captain, Major, or Colonel were veterans of the Civil War. Dalton was a tug-boat captain, and all the male members of Dalton's family worked the port of Chicago and on the Chicago River. He was best noted for driving beer wagons in the pre-election parades because the beer wagons played a central role in garnering votes. In every city, north or south, there was a symbiotic relationship between sports and politics. Dalton was part of the Chicago sporting scene and a long-time Chicago-area heavyweight fighter who had developed a marginal national reputation as a man who could handle himself in a fight. He came from a sporting family. His mother's brother was Charley C. Gallagher, who had fought Tom Allen in St. Louis.[66]

It seems likely that Charlie had a little talk with McDonald about the money that was to be had if Dalton would serve as the local opponent for Sullivan, rather than hiring some unknown schlemiel. McDonald himself acted as master of ceremonies at the August 13 exhibition at McCormick Hall. This gave McDonald an up-close look at Sullivan against a real opponent.

The day after the entertainment, the *Chicago Tribune* reported that Dalton proved that he was "no mean opponent." For the first two rounds Dalton held his own, but in the third round Sullivan made one of his patented rushes smashing Dalton viciously until he had "considerably disfigured the ambitious tugman's countenance." Dalton was somewhat groggy by the time the fourth round was supposed to begin. He did come to time, but Sullivan then knocked Dalton stiff, and the tugman was not able to recover within the allowed time. Dalton was credited with a good showing, and Sullivan gave him $25 for the effort.[67]

The McCormick Hall production was good enough that an encore was planned. During the planning stage Sullivan headed off with Madden to his training quarters at Mt. Clemens, Michigan. On August 28 Davies announced that another exhibition would take place on September 3 at the same venue. McDonald would once again act as master of ceremonies. This time Dalton was to participate in a scientific exhibition with Sullivan (meaning not real), and Sullivan would fight another unknown. The *Tribune* concluded that Davies was in charge or planning the affair, and it was rumored that Paddy Ryan would be on hand. Ryan's presence was the real news because he was the reigning heavyweight champion of the United States, and the announcement that he would be present at a Sullivan exhibition presaged a coming challenge of Ryan by Sullivan.[68]

Davies continued to plug the encore event. He announced that Madden would spar a well-known local boxer and that Sullivan's opponent would be a "prominent Canadian athlete." Madden's opponent would be Duncan C. Ross, the champion all-around athlete of Canada. On the day of the fight the *Tribune* reported that Sullivan's opponent would be Jack Byrnes, who was born in Canada. Byrnes was twenty-nine years of age, six feet three in height, and weighed two hundred fifteen pounds. He was big enough to be in the ring with Sullivan.

Charlie was pulling out all the stops in ways that would characterize his future promotions. He also announced that E. W. Johnson, a celebrated wrestler, would put on two matches and that Ed Dorney's sons (called the Boy Wonders) would exhibit their skill in the manly art of self-defense. Child labor laws did not exist, and there is nothing like two little kids pretending to be grown men for a good laugh. The big news was that there had been no reply to McDonald's challenge made on Sullivan's behalf for a match against the heavyweight champion, Paddy Ryan, for $5,000 to $10,000 a side. McDonald sent $1,000 to the *New York Herald* in support of this challenge. Things were now getting serious, and McDonald was clearly impressed with Sullivan's fighting ability. Presumably, Dalton had told McDonald that this bad boy from Boston could knock out a cow because McDonald's reputation was that he would only bet on a sure thing.

The undercards for events Davies sponsored provided access to many lesser known boxers and wrestlers and some well-known sports. These men did not make the substantial sums that heavyweights earned in their headliner roles, but they made reasonable money, and Davies' promotions put their names before the public. Those who were successful over time often came back to Charlie for representation because as young fighters, they had seen what he could accomplish.

On September 3, the show turned out to be even more spectacular than promised and left no doubt that Davies had found his profession. The gate for the night was not less than $2,000. Abe Williams, a black fighter from Bloomington, Illinois, won a cup for defeating Charles Saunders in a three-round very scientific manner in a lightweight bout. There was a middleweight bout between Harry Clifford and Pete Gibbons. Then William Bradburn from Pittsburgh, who would in the years ahead become a class heavyweight contender, and Tom Doherty of Chicago fought three very fierce rounds with Bradburn prevailing.

There was an abbreviated heavyweight fight between William Owens and John Anderson that was cut short by an injury to Owens. Duncan Ross then wrestled a Greco-Roman match against Johnson, followed by a catch-as-catch-can match, and Ross won both contests. Catch-as-catch-can blended several wrestling methods so that throws were used but a variety of submissions holds were also permitted in an effort to pin an opponent to the mat or require him to submit.

The Sullivan match with Byrnes proved to be a short affair. Sullivan knocked Byrnes silly in twenty seconds, and when Byrnes foolishly stood up, Sullivan sent him flying off the stage into the audience. If nothing else, Sullivan threw a hard punch, and over the years he would be credited with knocking several other men out of the ring. To close the evening Sullivan and Dalton put on their scientific exhibition and thus concluded a fine and profitable event.[69]

Two days after this second Chicago exhibition word came from New York that "friends of Paddy Ryan" had covered McDonald's $1,000 deposit for a fight with Sullivan.[70] As it turned out, Ryan's backer was Richard K. Fox of *National Police Gazette*, who had given the sporting editor of the *Gazette*, William Harding, authority to put up $5,000 on Ryan to match him against Sullivan. Fox would spend much of the next fifteen years trying to locate any credible opponent for Sullivan in the hopes that someone could knock him down several pegs.

Making a heavyweight title match

Davies knew enough not to push too fast for a title match because there was money to be made leading up to such championship encounters. This cow had to be milked for what it was worth.

Davies first invited Paddy Ryan to come to Chicago for a scientific match with Dalton. This gave the public a chance to compare the American champion's performance with Sullivan's earlier showing against a common opponent. There was an undercard that included two wonders (i.e., "I wonder where these two guys come from?") named Little Mack and Japanese Tommy. An eastern newspaper donated a gold medal valued at $100 for heavyweight fighters from Illinois. Heavyweights interested in participating sent their entries to Davies at 221 East Randolph Street, which was the address of the Biggio saloon. Davies had not yet opened his own saloon. Davies soon left for New York to arrange the details of a proposed bare-knuckle Ryan-Sullivan match.[71]

The next day the news was that a Ryan-Sullivan fight for the heavyweight championship of the United States had been arranged for a stake of $10,000, and it would take place within fifty miles of New Orleans within four months. Charlie was back in Chicago on September 27, but a problem had developed in arranging the championship match.

Davies had arrived in New York on September 24 with McDonald's $1,000 check in hand. A representative of the *Gazette* also had a $1,000 check, and a tremendous crowd assembled at the *Gazette* offices to witness the final arrangements for the fight. Those present included Madden, Jack Styles, a noted gambler, Johnny Roche, a former noted fighter out of St. Louis, Owney Geogheghan, Harry Hill, and a host of others. Davies and Madden were said to represent Sullivan, and Ryan was there on his own behalf together with William Harding.

A dispute arose over the stakeholder. Davies pointed out that the articles called for a stakeholder to be selected at once. He suggested possible stakeholders from Chicago, Louisville, Philadelphia, and also Al Smith of New York. Harding suggested several other stakeholders and then insisted that if McDonald and Sullivan wanted a stakeholder agreed to that day, then only Harry Hill could act as the stakeholder. Harding also said that he would agree to no one other than Hill as the final stakeholder for the fight.

After additional conversation, Davies said that he would not act contrary to the instructions he had been given by McDonald, but that he would telegram McDonald to see whether he would agree to Hill as the final stakeholder. Following a second meeting at ten o'clock that night, Charlie explained that he would not agree to Harding's dictated stakeholder, but he would go to Chicago to meet with McDonald to discuss the entire situation. The parties were then scheduled to meet again in New York on October 5. Davies reclaimed McDonald's $1,000 check and headed back to Chicago.[72]

These were not good developments. McDonald was a stubborn man, and he was not about to be trifled with by the New York crowd of Fox, Harding, and Hill. Moreover, Ryan was fairly well-known for using almost any excuse to avoid a fight. Davies was to be commended for his conduct during these negotiations because he knew all the men in New York quite well, and he had known them from his childhood in that city. Charlie also knew that there was a huge gate at stake, and he was early in his career when money was especially important. Nonetheless, he held firm for McDonald and at the same time kept the door open for a possible fight.

Isenberg's book about Sullivan, *John L. Sullivan and His America*, is wonderful and well researched. However, he is probably wrong when he suggests that McDonald continued to back Sullivan after the first meeting in New York. It is much more likely that McDonald's instructions to Davies were to go back to New York and tell Fox to "shove it where the sun don't shine." This was McDonald's character.

A few days after things fell apart in New York, Ed Roche, Ryan's trainer, appeared in Chicago to make arrangements for the proposed Ryan-Dalton show. As part of that show Roche himself was going to fight an unknown and there would also be general variety entertainment as part of the show. Thomas Soap McAlpine, the California champion, was then named as Roche's opponent. In addition, a rumor circulated that Sullivan was in the city and would be present at the exhibition to gain some knowledge of his rival's skill and endurance in his contest with Dalton. There is nothing like a face-to-face confrontation of heavyweights to stir up the sports and gamblers and promote a coming championship fight. After all, the evening of entertainment was part build up of a real bare-knuckle fight between Sullivan and Ryan.

When the October 5 deadline arrived McDonald did not cover the $1,000 that had been posted by Fox because Fox would not agree to anyone other than Hill to hold the money. Sullivan and Madden still wanted a match with Ryan. They had already put considerable time and effort trying to boom the fight and did not want to lose the benefit of those efforts. Davies wanted a match, but he had lost his backer, and he too withdrew from the picture even though virtually all the hard work had been done.

As a consequence of McDonald's withdrawal the original proposal of $5,000 a side was reduced to $2,500 a side, and Madden and Sullivan put up some of their own money and persuaded James Keenan, a Boston man heavily involved in racing trotters, to put up the final $1,000. The Ryan-Dalton exhibition went well enough that a Ryan-Tommy Chandler exhibition was planned for October 15.[73]

The nationwide publicity about the events leading up to the February 1882 Ryan-Sullivan fight had some predicable consequences. On one side of the scale, small athletic clubs all over the United States began promoting local wrestling and boxing events that mimicked the success of the bigger shows being put on in New York, Boston, Philadelphia, Chicago, San Francisco and the other major cities. Men who were feeling emasculated in the industrial world decided to assert their virility by learning to box. Clerks, lawyers, grain traders, commission merchants, and other desk-bound types signed up for training at the local athletic clubs, and promoters and trainers who had lived their lives in the alleys and behind closed doors became the equivalent of today's personal trainers.

On the other side of the scale, local bookmakers created betting lines on local and regional sporting events as well as on the larger national events. Men would drop by the corner cigar store or hotel lobby to leave a little money with their bookmaker to be placed on Ryan whipping Sullivan or on some local equivalent display of Doe-Roe. In response to the huge interest in boxing and betting, religious organizations began to insist on the adoption of town ordinances or the enforcement of municipal laws to suppress the evil prizefighting crowd. Sullivan was referred to as "Thug Sullivan" (as opposed to "Tug" Wilson), and Hill was described as the man responsible for "the most bestial ring encounters of the period" and a prime person responsible for the evils of the fighting system. McDonald received similar treatment in Chicago.

The Sullivan-Ryan championship fight

State legislatures all over the country began passing statutes intended to suppress prizefighting. This was part of the class warfare that was being carried on in other ways in the United States. One view was that the Irish had infected America and its political structure with their pro-liquor and libertine policies. The immoral Irish were not only constantly drunk, but liked prizefighting. Sullivan and Ryan were archetypes of the perceived problems. Old line respectable families and solid citizens were not about to cede their towns and villages to these foreigners without a fight.

The most direct reaction to the upcoming Ryan-Sullivan fight was that the state of Louisiana, where their match was to be held, adopted a law providing that "it shall be unlawful for any persons to engage in prize fighting in the State, and any parties so engaging shall be guilty of a felony, and shall be fined in a minimum not exceeding one thousand dollars, and shall, upon conviction, be sentenced to the Penitentiary for a term of not more than five years, to pay such fine and undergo such imprisonment at the discretion of the Court."[74] This type of legislation made life miserable for promoters and fighters for decades to come. There were probably more "pay-for-play" contributions made to state and local politicians by boxing promoters over the twenty years after 1881 than had occurred during the first one hundred years of the existence of the United States.

With the enactment of the Louisiana statute, the state's governor, Samuel Douglas McEnery, a former lieutenant in the Confederate army, met with the representatives of Sullivan and Ryan and told them that he was the law in Louisiana, and they would be arrested if the fight went forward in his state. It was then widely reported that the Sullivan and Ryan match would take place just across the state line from Louisiana, in Mississippi.

In January 1882, Robert Lowry became the governor of Mississippi.[75] Lowry had been a Confederate major, and he surely had seen many boxing and wrestling matches around army camps in the slow hours during the war. However, the prominent citizens and legislators of Mississippi met with Lowry to impress on him the need for immediate action to suppress the Ryan-Sullivan match inside the boarders of that fair state, and Lowry went into consultation with the state's attorney general to ensure that the fight would not go ahead in Mississippi. Who needed these damn Yankees in Mississippi anyway?[76]

Although Davies was not able to conclude the arrangements for the fight on behalf of McDonald, he was retained to make the final arrangements for the match in New Orleans. He left Chicago for New Orleans on January 25 to wind things up in the Crescent city. As he left he told one of Chicago's leading newspapers the *Inter Ocean* that he expected $100,000 to be wagered the fight. He also thought that the match would take place before Mississippi could enact a law that would prevent the fight.[77]

Undeterred by their possible arrest, in early February 1882 a battalion of the prize-fighting impresarios poured out of northern cities on trains headed for New Orleans and from there to an undisclosed location for the match. Sullivan was to appear on Thursday, February 2, with Joe Goss to exhibit his sparring talents. As part of the show, Sullivan would award a massive silver goblet to the most talented sparrer of New Orleans as determined in preliminary matches. This performance had all the earmarks of a Davies'-planned affair.[78]

The *Chicago Tribune* sent a reporter to New Orleans to handle special dispatches to be wired back to the city. On February 4, 1882, a special was sent from New Orleans and appeared the following morning. It reported that many Chicago sports had arrived that evening including: Alderman James Appleton (a long-time protégé of McDonald), John Murphy (a self-described Chicago "capitalist"), James Peevey (a Chicago "cattle trader"), John Riordan (a Chicago "fur trader"), and Simon O'Donnell (a Chicago police captain). Others present for the fight from Chicago included McDonald, Davies, and Jere Dunne (a well-known local prize-fighter) who had already killed at least one man and would later kill a Chicago fighter named Jimmy Elliott.[79]

The big Ryan-Sullivan fight went forward in Mississippi. Sullivan beat Ryan into submission in nine rounds. Ryan was hit in the neck in the first round and went down like a dog at Sullivan's feet. Ryan said that his corner men partly revived him between rounds, and at the call of time he got up half dazed.

Things did not improve for Ryan during that match, and observers began to feel sorry for him. When it was over, Ryan had a plethora of excuses: he had a rupture or hernia that had existed from the time of his fight with Joe Goss and had become worse after the Goss fight; in the second round of the fight his truss failed and he was in great pain; his truss slipped in the second round, and from then on he was almost helpless; he had wrestled with his truss for hours to try to get it to fit correctly but it never really fit; his doctor told him that if he received a blow below the neck after the second round it would have been fatal; he was not in good condition, and his trainers had told him to lay back and not force the action, but he should have ignored that advice and taken the fight to Sullivan. Ryan also said that he doubted that he would fight again because his mother had made him promise to never again enter the ring. Ryan liked to invoke his dear old mother when it suited his purpose.[80]

The rupture or hernia that Ryan had was a hernia of the groin; his intestine was protruding between the muscles in the area of his groin. One can imagine how it would feel to be hit on an unprotected hernia and feel the small intestine break and begin emptying its contents where they were not supposed to flow. This would be something like being shot in the stomach.

Returning to Chicago

The day after the fight Sullivan, Madden, Davies, Pete McCoy, Bob Farrell and other hangers-on left New Orleans for Chicago on the Illinois Central express.[81] Chicago's *Inter Ocean* wrote that Sullivan was under Davies' management.[82] Even on an express train there were about twenty-five stops between New Orleans and Chicago. Those on the train included journalists, policemen, sports, and others who had attended the great fight. Sullivan was reported to be the hero of the day all along the railroad line, and whenever the train stopped, he was called to appear and acknowledge his assembled fans. He soon tired of this activity, and a Chicago gambler known as "Big Steve," wearing a heavy Petersham jacket, was pressed into service to go out and raise his hat, squirt out tobacco juice, and say: "Much obliged to yees, gentlemen," and then reenter the train to great applause from the assembled rubes.[83]

Reaching Chicago, Sullivan and the out-of-town members of his party took rooms at the Commercial Hotel and headed for The Store. Sullivan assumed his post by leaning on the bar, and held forth for several hours before escaping by a rear door down the alley. When interviewed by a reporter, Sullivan said that he intended to abandon the profession of prizefighting. However, he allowed that he might be induced to fight for a purse of $10,000 if a good man was found as an opponent. When asked what he intended to do in the meantime, Sullivan said that he would appear at McCormick Hall that evening, then go to Detroit the following Monday, then appear in Cleveland, Cincinnati, Buffalo, Philadelphia, New York, and Boston. After his road performance Sullivan said that he would stay home for about two weeks and then return to Chicago.[84]

That evening Sullivan appeared with McDonald as master of ceremonies. Sullivan and Madden pranced around with Sullivan mimicking moves that he had made during his bashing Ryan a few days earlier. There were no films at the time, so it was nice to give the locals an idea of how the execution in Mississippi had been administered with Madden playing Ryan's part. In addition, a local woman known as Miss Gray fought a man named Billy Malone and Dalton fought a local man named Paddy Golden. McCoy and Farrell put on a fair exhibition of scientific skill, but several expected performers did not appear. Goss, who was supposed to be present that evening, had been left behind at one of the stops as the train proceeded north from New Orleans to Chicago and had caught another train to Cincinnati. Ed Dorney was also supposed to show up to take advantage of Sullivan's $50 challenge, but he did not appear either.

The in your face behavior of McDonald and the sporting crowd in the wake of the big heavyweight championship fight was a challenge to the leadership of Chicago mayor Carter Harrison.[85] On February 21, fed up with McDonald, the mayor ordered the suppression of the gambling parlors. These raids were often coordinated with federal authorities and grand juries. At the time saloon operators were supposed to pay a federal excise tax in order to serve alcohol, but many ignored the law. When crack downs took place, the feds would obtain indictments of saloon operators, who would be fined $500 and court costs. Davies' brother Vere was operating a saloon and was one of many indicted and fined in this crack down. During the balance of February and March 1882, the police also conducted a series of raids on joints owned or protected by McDonald, who was in and out of the mayor's office day and night during this period. Harrison later said that McDonald was the smartest man he ever knew at finding out things.

After the big fight, Ryan left New Orleans a defeated man and headed back east to lick his wounds and offer excuses. Near the end of February he too headed for Chicago, where he had a so-called benefit at McCormick Hall. Benefits were a staple of fighting at the time. The idea was that the defeated fighter was out the prize money he had posted and therefore must be down on his luck. Promoters would then put on benefit nights where the vanquished could appear as part of the entertainment and receive part of the gate to help tide him over until he could pull himself together.[86]

In April, Ryan and his trainer Johnny Roche split up. It seems likely that Roche got tired of Ryan telling the press that Roche gave him bad advice before and during the Sullivan fight. To get even, Roche started telling the newspapers that Ryan had sold the fight with Sullivan.

Ryan and Sullivan were headed in different directions in February 1882—literally and figuratively. While Ryan was headed for Chicago, Sullivan was on his way back east, where he appeared at Harry Hill's place in New York on March 2 to pick up the balance of his prize money. He was clearly peeved with the substantial number of excuses that Ryan had ginned up over the three weeks after their fight. He offered to meet Ryan again at any time, but told the assembled throng that Ryan's whining was not going to help anything. He also claimed that Madden had been offered $5,000 to poison him before the fight, and in a dramatic manner he vowed to stick by Madden. While Ryan and his trainer were bickering and splitting up, everything with Sullivan and Madden was hugs and kisses. As with many things in Sullivan's life, one needed to be cautious when he Sullivan pledged his loyalty because when he was involved, money almost always outweighed spiritual inclinations such as loyalty.[87]

Finding someone to beat Sullivan

From February 1882 until 1892, the primary object of boxing promoters in the United States, England, and Australia was finding someone with enough real or manufactured credibility to stand up against Sullivan. Fox was notably active in trying to find and or groom any fighter to face Sullivan, but Fox was in no sense unique. Every promoter knew that the pot of gold would land in the lap of whoever could be matched to fight Sullivan. Every heavyweight fighter knew that fame and fortune were on Sullivan's doorstep. One road to that door was through the men Sullivan had demolished on his rise to the top. In that process challenges to men such as Ryan and Goss became common.

Davies was like the rest of the crowd when it came to Sullivan. As a promoter in the business of prizefighting he needed to find a heavyweight fighter who had some prospect of defeating Sullivan. Charlie's early experiences in this endeavor showed his lack of experience and the shallowness of the available pool of opponents. Unlike other managers and promoters, Davies learned from and persisted in his efforts with a diligence that marked his entire career.

Jimmy Elliott – strike one

The first heavyweight Davies found was two-time ex-con and former bare-knuckle champion, Jimmy Elliott, who had been released from prison in 1879 and then returned to prizefighting. In his first match after gaining his freedom, Elliott was beaten up by John J. Dwyer. Undeterred by that result, Elliott foolishly challenged Sullivan several times before showing up during one of Sullivan's self-promotions to call him out in person.[88]

On July 4, 1882, Elliott appeared at a Sullivan sponsored picnic at Brooklyn's Washington Park. Sullivan and Madden charged fifty cents for admission to the picnic, and some six thousand people appeared. They had also come up with two good ideas: First, they advertised the picnic as "ladies free," which would have been a serious breach of social etiquette had the primary purpose of the event simply been a prizefight. However, because it was staged as a picnic, they were able to open the gates to women. Second, they invited all would-be champions to appear and fight Sullivan with soft gloves. This notion was intended to put a stop to pretenders who complained that Sullivan was ignoring their challenges. Each of the complainers had a chance to show up at the picnic and enter the ring with Sullivan.

Elliott showed up. He was acting on his own and without a manager. The actual boxing was delayed by rain, which turned the park into a sea of mud until it let up at about five o'clock. A twenty-one-foot ring had been set up as the spot where Sullivan would meet all comers. This small ring was undoubtedly intended to help Sullivan to corner anyone stupid enough to try him out. When the rain let up, Sullivan transformed himself into a battering ram, charged like a locomotive and pounded Elliott down, blooding his mouth. When he got up, Elliott tried to avoid Sullivan's charge but "he might as well have tried to dodge a rain-storm in a 10 acre lot where there were no sheds." Sullivan knocked him senseless in the second round. Some reports claim that Elliott made it to a third round, but all reports are unanimous that Elliott had been totally mauled. With Elliott at his feet, Sullivan laughed heartily. The whole affair had lasted eight minutes. After Elliot regained consciousness, Sullivan stepped over and gave him $50 for his trouble, money that Elliot ill-naturedly accepted.[89]

When Davies picked up representation of Elliott, Charlie was working with seriously damaged merchandise, but at least he had a fighter with a name. Fortunately for Davies, he had already helped make a lot of money for Sullivan, and he had a chance to arrange something more formal for Elliott with Sullivan.

Within a month after Davies began representing Elliott, the *Post Dispatch* reported that Davies was in New York in the role of Elliott's manager and perfecting arrangements for a coming Elliott-Sullivan rematch. This was to be one of Sullivan's four-round affairs in which he would undertake to knock out his opponent before the end of the fourth round or be considered the loser. The stakes were $2,000 and the bout was to be with hard gloves, Queensberry rules. Davies also attempted to arrange a fight between Elliott and another has-been, Tom Allen.[90]

Davies took Elliott under his wing and had him in training for over a month to get Elliott into fighting trim. Elliott supposedly studied Tug Wilson's approach to Sullivan and worked on pulling, falling, and other dodges.[91] The *Tribune* followed up by writing that Sullivan was about to head for Chicago to fight Elliott. Davies also wanted to arrange an Allen-Elliott fight to take place after the Sullivan fight. In this venture Allen was represented by Fox, and it is likely that the Parson's trip to New York had more to do with arranging for Allen-Elliott fight than the Elliott-Sullivan match.[92]

Davies was only thirty-one years old. He had already been involved in some of the most significant sporting events in the United States. As he was working hard to arrange these new matches, Chicago's mayor Harrison had a far different agenda. The mayor elevated Austin Doyle to superintendent of the Chicago Police Department. Doyle then reorganized the police department to put Harrison's supporters in key roles. On November 23, newly promoted lieutenants led raids on the gambling dens. The mayor revoked the liquor licenses of McDonald's supporters. One of the first to lose his license was Dalton. These actions by the mayor and the police were making the going difficult for Davies, and he undoubtedly had to answer a lot of questions about whether he could continue to carry on boxing matches at the city's major venues.[93]

Ten days after the gambling raids, Davies posted $250 forfeit money with McDonald for the Allen-Elliott match. Supposedly Fox was on his way to Chicago to post Allen's money and finalize the arrangements inside a ten-day time limit set by Davies. The meeting with Fox was to take place at Davies' new saloon, which he had named the Champion's Rest. What followed was something of a joke.

No one showed up within the ten-day period, so it appeared that the fight was off. Local people said they had seen Allen in town the night before drinking heavily. Speculation was that he was too wiped out to walk. Allen said that he had been traveling for twenty-four hours straight and was too tired to do business. Then Fox arrived and said that Allen would soon be along to conclude the arrangements, so the fight was back on. Fox sat there for hours, but Allen never showed. A few days later both Fox and Allen were present in Chicago and were again reported to be on the verge of signing to fight Elliott. Again Allen did not show up when required, and Fox publicly repudiated Allen and announced that he had dropped Allen altogether. The forfeit money was then returned to Charlie by McDonald.[94]

Weeks later Allen returned to the Midwest to live in St. Louis. He had been in the East for six years, but St. Louis was his home, and he had become persona non grata in New York. Allen had his own story about why he didn't sign for the fight with Elliott. He told the *Post Dispatch* that he had received a rough deal in Chicago and that "the Parson and a few others wanted him to indulge in a hippodrome with Elliott, but he refused to be a party to any such affair."[95] Allen also blamed a reporter for the *New York Herald* for spreading a rumor that he had become a drunk.

Although Elliott's fight with Allen was off, his more important contest with Sullivan was still perking along. Originally, the fight was to take place on December 9, but Elliott sprained his right hand during an exhibition with Dalton (or at least he claimed he did), and the match was reset for December 23, originally in Pittsburgh but then in Chicago. On December 18, Chicago's *Inter Ocean* reported that Sullivan and his trainer Goss were both in Chicago and were staying at the South Park Hotel.[96] Two days later, Harrison's crackdown was directed straight at Davies and the proposed Elliott-Sullivan fight.

On December 20, the *Inter Ocean* published a proclamation issued by Doyle, the superintendent of police:

> To whom it may concern: The Grand Jury of Cook County, now in session, having been charged by the Hon. Elliott Anthony, Judge of the Criminal Court of Cook County, to inquire into and suppress sparring exhibitions under section 235 of chapter 38, Revised Statutes of Illinois; which reads as follows: "Whoever

> instigates, carries on, promotes, or engages in as a witness, any sparring or boxing exhibition, shall be fined not exceeding $500 or confined in the county jail not exceeding six months."
>
> [N]otice is hereby given that all persons who, either by advertising, leasing premises, attending as witnesses, engaging in or otherwise promoting such exhibitions will be arrested and prosecuted under the provisions of the law above quoted.
>
> Austin J. Doyle[97]
> General Superintendent of Police

The Elliott-Sullivan fight was off. Had Elliott fought on the originally scheduled date, the event would probably not have been interfered with by the police. The newspaper noted that the cancellation had caused regret among a very large crowd who had besieged the box office the day before and purchased tickets at $2, $3, and $5.

As a result of the cancellation Charlie suffered a loss of $800. The suggestion was made that the fight might be rescheduled for New Orleans during Mardi Gras in 1883. The *Tribune* contacted Davies, who explained that the fight was off and the janitor had been ordered not to open the hall. Charlie explained that he didn't want to become liable under the law and promised that all money would be fully refunded. He also explained that on December 19, he and Jere Dunne had been contacted by Doyle and told that he want to see Davies at the police station.

Davies and Dunne, Sullivan's backer for the fight, complied with the summons and met with Doyle. They had a courteous meeting during which Doyle told them about the action of the grand jury and explained the statute to them in detail. Davies explained that the exhibition could not be rescheduled in a place where it would be legal because Sullivan had a commitment with Joe Coburn for an exhibition in New York on December 28.

Charlie said that he was done with exhibitions of this kind in Chicago and that he intended to abide by the law. Dunne said that gate receipts collected in anticipation of the fight were already over $8,000, and he was sorry that he had become involved because he was personally out about $100 for printing and other promotional expenses. Sullivan said that he was disappointed that the fight was off and the match had always been only a planned scientific exhibition to determine the better man and not a real prizefight.[98]

That evening Sullivan and Elliott met at the Champion's Rest and healed their enmities over a bottle of wine. Sullivan remarked that he would back Elliott against any man in America and that Elliott was the best man that he had ever stood before. Of course, Sullivan made the same comment about many fighters. If a fight remained possible, there was no great benefit in panning the opponent. None of this helped Dunne recover his money.[99]

Two days after their meeting, Sullivan and Elliott met in Elliott's room at 119 East Randolph Street. From contemporary accounts it seems likely that

Elliott had been drinking for three days straight and had assumed a "sadly broken-up appearance." There is little doubt that Elliott was an alcoholic.

Sullivan was likely present to talk Elliott off the bottle, but being a poor counselor and a budding alcoholic himself, Sullivan instead decided to share several bottles of Veuve Cliquot with Elliott. Dunne told the press that after Sullivan's show with Coburn, they were going to Hot Springs, for six weeks of rest and then to California with Sullivan under Dunne's management. Sullivan obviously wasn't too worried about his exhibition with Coburn, which was scheduled for December 28 in New York, because his train didn't leave Chicago until five p.m. on December 25.[100]

Coburn had recently been released from six years in the state prison on an assault charge, and the New York sporting fraternity was using his match with Sullivan as a quasi-benefit for Coburn. All the New York luminaries were present for Sullivan's post-Christmas match. There were numerous preliminaries before Sullivan climbed into the ring. When the fight started, Sullivan and Coburn put up their soft gloves and began to play patty-cake with one another. The crowd yelled for them to go after one another. Both fighters then stopped and Coburn explained that he and Sullivan were friends and this was only gentlemanly set-to and not a prizefight. Sullivan then spoke and said that there would be no slugging tonight. He continued: "I'll kill someone for you people sometime. Perhaps, Mace's unknown." This declaration was met with great cheers from the assembled mass. If only Sullivan had donned a hockey mask and carried a chain saw![101]

Hebert Slade – Mace's unknown

The unknown mentioned by Sullivan was Herbert A. Slade, a man described in the press as a half-breed Maori whom they also called the Maori Giant. At this point Sullivan was not worried about the color line; he was more than willing to fight a man of color, and Slade was the first dark-skinned man Sullivan fought.

Slade had come to San Francisco from Australia on Christmas Day 1882 led by Jem Mace. He was the product of Mace's efforts to introduce a heavyweight who could stand against Sullivan. After the Tug Wilson fight, Fox had written to Mace and agreed to pay his traveling expenses if he would return to the United States from Australia with an unknown who could stand up to Sullivan. Mace had telegraphed Fox from the Palace Hotel in San Francisco on December 26, saying: "Mr. Richard K. Fox: I have arrived here with my unknown, who is the coming man, and await your orders."

Apparently, Fox thought that he might first try to match Mace against Sullivan if he could get him out of Australia. Mace had won the heavyweight title against Tom Allen in 1870. Like George Rooke, in 1882 Mace was well-past his best years. Compared to Sullivan he was a small man. Mace was only about five feet nine inches tall and weighed about 150 pounds but he was considered to be the most scientific fighter in decades.[102]

By 1882, reports were circulating that Mace had amassed a fortune in Australia as a keeper of a house of entertainment for men and beasts. He also taught many fighters how to box in the dominate style of the time. His method involved a relatively stiff-legged stance from the waist down with movement of the upper body from side to side. One foot was usually advanced ahead of the other, and this stance was complimented by even movements back and forth. All of these things were complimented by the use of a solid left jab. Good fighters would use the left jab followed by a right to the body, heart, or jaw.

Slade was a bigger fellow than Mace. He was six feet two inches tall and weighed 225 pounds, with an enormous chest and shoulders and arms like railroad ties, large powerful hands and enormous knuckles. He also had a huge nose, which made a nice target for his opponents.

Slade was twenty-eight years old and had worked on a farm in Auckland. Mace said that Slade was so strong that he could shear one hundred sheep a day for an entire week. This would have been a wonderful thing if Slade was going to enter a sheep-shearing contest in Montana instead of trying to fight Sullivan. Slade said that he had never had any professional training as a fighter and that he was not a half-breed anything but a full native-born Maori.

In early January 1883 Davies wrote to Fox about Slade. The most important element of Davies' letter was that Sullivan had asked Charlie to be his manager. The *Post Dispatch* claimed to have a copy of Davies' letter, which said: "I notice that to-day's papers, say that Jem Mace and his unknown, 'Slade,' intend stopping in Chicago on their way East. Will you tell Mace to drop in and see me? John Sullivan has made a verbal contract with me to go under my management. Jere Dunne, who was to look after Sullivan's interests in the Chicago affair, has nothing to do with him for some reason. I hear Mace has sparred with his pupil, Slade, in Australia, on his travels, and says of him that, in his opinion, he is a good man to fight Sullivan with the bare-knuckles. I want the public to know that Sullivan expresses his readiness to accommodate either for from $5,000 to $10,000 a side." [103] Sullivan's oral contract with Davies wasn't worth anything because Sullivan then wrote a letter to Davies dated January 9 saying that he regretted that other arrangements that he had made before he came to Chicago and which he was "duty bound" to fulfill would prevent him from abiding by his oral agreement with Davies.

The general idea was for Charlie to book a fight where Fox would back Slade and Davies back Sullivan. This event would not be a championship fight but rather another four-round match with gloves and under Queensberry rules for $2,500 a side. Sullivan would undertake to dispatch Slade before the end of the fourth round, or Slade would be entitled to Sullivan's money. This was the standard format that Sullivan was following at the time.

Mace arrived in Chicago on January 24 with Slade in tow. They checked in at the Palmer House (nothing but the best) and headed to the Champion's Rest at 219 Randolph Street, along with several reporters to document the events. This was the address where Fred Davies had done business with Henry Hart in

1882. Exactly how Charlie obtained the property is not clear. However, there was a lawsuit filed in May 1882 against Charlie and Fred to restrain them from taking possession of the saloon, but the Davies brothers did acquire the property.

Davies, the gracious host, met Mace, Slade and their entourage and took them to a parlor to meet Elliott, who basically spent his days either in his apartment one block west or at the bar in Davies' saloon. Davies and Mace were described as old friends who knew each other from their time in New York.

Mace was fifty-four years old in January 1883, and he had been in Australia and New Zealand for several years. He had lived in Chicago before the fire in 1871 but left when the city was in ruins. Finishing a cordial meeting with Davies and Elliott, the Mace and Slade party moved on to a meeting with Ryan and then finally went to McDonald's place at 176 Clark Street, where the great wizard was not behind the screen and they left somewhat disappointed.

During their stay in Chicago it was announced that Mace intended to spar with Slade at Madison Square Garden on January 29, and he then would take Slade on a tour of exhibitions around the country. It was part of their plan to take Slade to England for exhibitions in Liverpool, Manchester, and London.[104]

Jere Dunne kills Jimmy Elliott

It was time to leave Chicago for awhile. Davies was taking a show on the road in an attempt to make some money while avoiding the restrictions imposed by Harrison and enforced by Doyle. He planned to take Elliott, Fred Plaisted, R. H. Pennell, E. W. Johnson, and a vaudeville-type variety show to Omaha, Kansas City, Dodge City, Denver, Leadville, Cheyenne, Salt Lake City, San Francisco, and other points on the Pacific coast.[105] In years to come, similar tours became standard operating procedure.

Davies, with Elliott leading his combination of athletes, left for the West. They proved successful and made money as far west as Dodge City. However, Davies' well-laid plans went up in smoke in Dodge City, where Elliott started on a drunken spree that lasted several days.

Elliott spoke of his hatred for Jere Dunne and said that he was going back to Chicago and run Dunne out of town. Elliott disappeared on a night train headed for Chicago by himself. Davies learned of his departure and took the next train east. He arrived in Chicago close behind Elliott. He told a friend of Dunne's what Elliott had said in Dodge City. This information was duly reported to Dunne, who said that he would try to avoid trouble but would not stay away from his daily haunts in Chicago just to avoid Elliott. This was not the same old hype that often happened before a boxing match; it was the real thing between two men who would not hesitate to blow away an antagonist.

Elliott's enmity for Dunne supposedly started when Dunne had been promoting Sullivan and tried to arrange the Elliott-Sullivan fight. Like Elliott, Dunne had a bad reputation, and he had killed at least two men before March 1883. Dunne had invested significant money in making the arrangements for the proposed Elliott-Sullivan fight, but Elliott said that his hand was injured, and he was unable to fight and the proposed match had to be cancelled. Dunne then confronted Elliott at Davies' Champion's Rest and called him a coward and a poltroon.

Shortly after Dunne's promise to kill Elliott, the Davies-led sparring tour left town, but Elliott had returned to Chicago because he could not stand to have Dunne's threat linger.[106] On the night of March 1, Dunne was carrying a Smith & Wesson revolver when he stopped at McDonald's saloon at the corner of Clark and Monroe streets. He had armed himself in case of a confrontation with Elliott. McDonald saw the gun that Dunne was carrying and laughed. He told Dunne that the Smith & Wesson wouldn't hurt a fly. McDonald insisted on equipping Dunne with a Colt revolver. There were plenty of guns around McDonald's saloon, and it was well-known that his wife, Mary, carried a gun inside her dress.

Later that evening at the Trivoli restaurant operated by William Langdon, Dunne and Elliott confronted one another. Dunne later claimed that Elliott had no business at the Trivoli except to provoke Dunne. This affair involved bad sport, timing, and politics. Witness statements conflicted but it seems that Dunne entered the restaurant, raised his hand, and fired a pistol. The gun that Dunne fired was the Colt he had been given by McDonald.

Elliott stood up, having been shot in the arm and the two men then fought at close quarters with Elliott clubbing Dunne over the head with his revolver. There were four more shots before Elliott put his gun to Dunne's throat and pulled the trigger, but it misfired because the cylinder in the gun had been dislodged during the head clubbing. Dunne then shot and killed Elliott. McDonald's role in Elliott's death became widely known and this actually seemed to enhance McDonald's own reputation as a dangerous man.

Harry Hill then sent three telegrams to friends in Chicago asking them to spare no expense in getting Dunne out of trouble. Pat Sheedy was another pal of Dunne's, and he too went to great length to help Dunne. Davies testified that he was Elliott's manager and backer. He said that before the shooting, he had told McDonald that he was afraid Elliott would kill Dunne unless Elliott was shot in the back first by Dunne, which is what nearly happened.

Both Billy Pinkerton and McDonald testified on behalf of Dunne. They both said that Elliott's habit was to carry a revolver. McDonald swore that Elliott had a pistol in his possession only a short time before the fatal encounter. McDonald said he saw the revolver in Elliott's pocket an hour before the shooting. After the postmortem on Elliott's body, Davies ordered that the body be embalmed in preparation for return to New York to Elliott's mother and sister. This was a tragic end to Elliott's life, and Davies no longer had a heavyweight contender.[107]

By March 1883 in his short career Davies had lost Sullivan, Ryan, and Elliott as clients. Slade was not available because he was controlled by Mace and Fox. Another possibility, Charley Mitchell of England, was not available because he was working under the supervision of Madden. Many other heavyweights were too young, too inexperienced, or too old to be considered credible contenders. Without a legitimate heavyweight, Davies was in need of a fighter.

In early June 1883 the *Police Gazette* reported that Davies had published the following card: "I notice an interview with Mr. Frank Moran, who states, in reference to the glove match between John L. Sullivan and Paddy Ryan that Ryan does not mean business and is only 'bluffing.' In behalf of Paddy Ryan, whom I represent, I beg to state that Mr. Ryan does mean business, and when I approached Mr. Sullivan on the subject he referred me to Mr. Al Smith of New York as his business manager to arrange the details. I leave for New York for that purpose to-day."[108] Paddy Ryan was back; however, the entire heavyweight boxing system that had revolved around Sullivan for more than two years was soon upset by Al Smith, who effectively removed Sullivan from the equation.

Road trips to major cities and smaller towns were common. Al Smith proposed the Moby-Dick of road trips. He took Sullivan on the road for eight months, moving around the entire country beginning in September. Smith scheduled 195 performances for Sullivan during the trip. There were to be no exhibitions involving pounding but only exhibitions in the sublime art of sparring. Slade was to be part of the show for the first three months that it was on the road. Slade was paid $1,000 for his services. This operation involved a terrific amount of planning and promotion, with a cadre of advance men and a troupe of people to help stage the nearly daily events. In the meantime the big money that had flowed to anyone who could make a match with Sullivan was cut off for everyone except Sullivan and Al Smith. Before the tour began, it was announced that Sullivan would never fight again with bare fists and that he would retire for good at the end of the tour. Always humble, Sullivan likened himself to the president of the United States, who he said faded out of sight soon after he left office.[109]

Paddy Ryan – strike two

Davies' promotion of Ryan was delayed by Ryan's trouble with a woman. The problems began in late August 1883 with Ryan's Tiger Wood moment. It seems that Paddy, a married man, had been carrying on with a girl in Chicago named Sadie Wasserman, with whom he had attempted to break it off. Wasserman did not have the best reputation and was said to live in a "house" on Polk Court and she was referred to as a "soiled Amazon." Some stories said that Wasserman had taken a shot at Ryan with her own pistol and wounded him.

About seven o'clock one evening, Ryan was driven up to his saloon in a hack with a bandage on his head and lying on supportive cushions. He was then taken to a hospital. In the meantime, Wasserman unsuccessfully attempted suicide, being disconsolate over Ryan's rejection of her. Another story was that Wasserman actually killed herself and that Ryan was so chagrined that he tried to kill himself. In the midst of all of this, Ryan went missing.

Johnny Files, another old-time fighter, told the press that he had placed Ryan under "custody." Files was keeping Ryan out of sight to avoid Ryan's wife, his girlfriend, the press, the police, or some combination of these. Files was not the best company for Ryan to be keeping. He had become something of low-life around Chicago and was still fighting in stables and back rooms for $20 a show.[110]

In early September, Slade and his party stopped at Davies' place in Chicago on their way to New York. In the group were Johnny Brighton, his trainer, Jack Davis, Harry Montague, Mace, and Slade's agent Henry Rice. They were at Davies' to try to arrange a match between Mace and Mitchell and had expected to meet both Madden and Mitchell at Davies', but neither appeared. At the time the sticking point with the proposed fight centered on the location for the match. Mace was insisting on a fight within 100 miles of New Orleans. Madden and Mitchell wanted a fight somewhere in Mexico, near El Paso, Texas.

Madden sent a telegram to Davies: "Won't go to New Orleans. Mexico is the only place the fight can take place. You have no assurances at New Orleans or Kansas City. You have no conditions except what we agree on, and you know it. This is final." After several days of waiting, Rice and Mace left for New York and gave Davies the authority to conclude the negotiations if Madden and Mitchell ever arrived. This negotiation soon fell through because Rice and Mace refused to meet except at the places they had previously specified.

Faced with this unanticipated delay in the Ryan-Sullivan match, Davies began to promote a fight for the two men to take place in Boston in December. With little to do in the meantime, Davies arranged for Ryan to complete the tour that had been previously planned for Elliott. In late September, as Sullivan was departing on his grand tour, Ryan left Chicago on Davies' mini-tour headed for Leadville, Denver, Pueblo, Cheyenne, Ogden, Salt Lake City, Sacramento, Virginia City, San Francisco, and other cities in California. This trip was supposed to season Ryan for a December match with Sullivan.[111]

Records of Ryan's 1883 western swing show that he had a three-round exhibition with a fellow named Jack Waite, described as the champion of Montana, in Butte City on October 21, during which he knocked out Waite. Other matches were scheduled in Helena on October 23; Ogden, Utah, on October 25; and Salt Lake City on October 27. Finally in November, it was announced that Al Smith and Davies had met to arrange the details of the Ryan-Sullivan fight.

The Al Smith and Sullivan combination arrived in Chicago and put on their big show on November 16 at the Battery D Armory. Reportedly nine thousand people attended that evening with many luminaries present including Chicago aldermen, a Chicago police captain, McDonald, and Davies, who was sitting near the center of the hall with Ryan. This was supposed to be an admitted hippodrome—a show with no real sparring or fighting involved.

During the evening Sullivan had a scheduled bout with Slade using soft gloves. As their match progressed, Slade found Sullivan's nose and gave him a good bang on the button. Sullivan became nettled by this punch and began jumping at Slade. When Slade would duck these lunges, Sullivan would then fake with his right hand and give Slade a solid uppercut with this left. This caused great enthusiasm among the crowd, but it worried the promoters because of the large number of police present. After the third round, it was apparent that things were getting too serious between Sullivan and Slade and something needed to be done to prevent police action that might have an impact on other similar entertainment.[112]

At that point Davies stepped into the ring and was greeted with cheers from the audience. Charlie advanced to the ropes and said that Ryan had offered to meet Sullivan with soft gloves for fifty percent of the gate receipts. The match was to take place in San Francisco in one, two, or three months. Sullivan had agreed to give Ryan 100 percent of the gate if he did not knock him out within four rounds under Queensberry rules. Davies further announced that Sullivan had agreed to the fight.[113]

At the conclusion of the show that evening, Davies was mobbed by two or three hundred people wanting details of the fight. Charlie said that he had been assured that there would be no interference with a fight in San Francisco. The fight was to guarantee Ryan 50 percent of the gate. It was to be a four-round fight under Queensberry rules with articles to be signed at the Champion's Rest on the following day. If this match happened, Davies' reputation would be fortified, and he would be in for a big payday.[114]

On December 15, the *Police Gazette* provided some of the particulars of the upcoming fight. It would take place in the orthodox twenty-four-foot ring, with hard gloves, for four rounds. There was no stake posted that was dependent upon the outcome of the fight, but only a gate receipt division. Fighting without posting a stake made it easier for fighters to arrange a match because it was not necessary to find a backer and a promoter.

Davies was quoted as saying that the match would provide Ryan the chance to redeem the laurels that he had lost when he met Sullivan in February 1882. Supposedly Ryan was eager to meet Sullivan again. Al Smith said that the largest hall in San Francisco would not hold the sporting men who would travel there to witness this prizefight. The *Gazette* also reported that before starting for California, Ryan, under Davies' management, would travel to Pittsburgh, Wheeling, Columbus, Dayton, Cincinnati, Louisville, St. Louis, Kansas City, and then on the San Francisco.

The articles were published, and provided that the big match was to take place between January 10 and February 19, 1884, at Sullivan's specification. The articles were signed by Davies for Ryan and Smith for Sullivan. Estimates were published that Ryan would receive between $3,000 and $6,000 as his share of the gate whether or not he lasted four rounds with Sullivan.[115] Davies continued to work for Ryan arranging appearances in Minneapolis and St. Paul and at other places along the route of the Northern Pacific Railroad as they traveled to San Francisco in January 1884.[116]

Then Ryan showed the white feather and backed out of his written commitment. He left under cover of night on Christmas evening for Toledo, Ohio, and sent a telegraph to Davies: "I have to throw up everything at present." He said that his mother was seriously ill, and he needed to be with her. Ryan was the youngest of eleven children and the sole surviving child. His mother was nearly eighty years old and seriously ill. She had read about Sullivan and was worried that he little boy would be hurt, Ryan said. Davies offered another reason, probably the true one, that Ryan was afraid of fighting Sullivan. [117]

Davies sent a telegram:

> Friend Ryan – Your dispatch received about two hours ago. You do not explicitly state in it that you will not meet Sullivan. Let me know if you will – yes or no; and if yes, when you will be here and ready to leave for Frisco.
>
> There is much talk in this city about your not leaving for California via St. Paul and Minneapolis, and your forcing me to cancel engagements in those cities; also in Reno, Virginia City, Nevada City, Montana and other places, at a financial loss to myself.
>
> It is openly stated in Chicago that you are afraid to meet Sullivan, and are only screening yourself behind your mother's sickness as an excuse. Let me hear at once by wire, and give me an opportunity to refute the statements about your lacking courage. I telegraphed Mr. Muldoon to stop your exhibition, that, as you are aware, was to take place in San Francisco with Sheriff Jan. 5.
> /s/Chas. E. Davies[118]

Sports reporting on the development said that Ryan had been drinking heavily and was in no condition to fight. Sullivan was in Leadville when word reached him that Ryan was hiding out in Toledo. Sullivan was also drinking heavily, and he had been in a brawl in a bar with Pete McCoy. Pete had hit Sullivan over the head with a chair and Sullivan had retaliated by throwing a lighted kerosene lamp at McCoy before a local city marshal intervened. Sullivan commented freely when told that Ryan had backed out of the fight. He said that he was not surprised at all because Ryan had previously proved himself a cur and people would now see it clearly.[119] This ended the year of 1883.

Chapter 4 - (1884)

Finding Success

Davies has managed John L. Sullivan, Paddy Ryan, Alf Greenfield, Jack Burke, whose reputation he made, Jem Mace, Slade, the Maori, Tug Wilson, Arthur Chambers, Captain Dalton, George Holden, Jimmie Elliott, Charley Mitchell, Sheriff, the Prussian, Mike Cleary, Jem Goode, Jake Kilrain, Billy Edwards, John Files, Tom Chandler and a host of lesser lights. . . .

In personal appearance Mr. Davies is the picture of a saint, his resemblance to a doctor of divinity having given him the fitting cognomen —"Parson." He is tall and well built, always dressed quietly but in the height of fashion, and his voice is invariably low. In all his dealings he has a most excellent reputation for undeviating honesty and fair play, traits that have placed him in the front rank of managers of sporting events. Shrewd and quick witted, the "Parson" can "size up" a man at a glance, and that he rarely makes a mistake is evidence from the standing of all of the men he has managed have taken.[120]

♣

William Sheriff – strike three

When older boxers fade away, there are younger men waiting to take their place. In early 1884 William Sheriff, the "Prussian," was one of the oldest of the older fighters, and he was training in Chicago. Sheriff had fought Mitchell to a seven round draw in October 1883. On May 19, 1884, he would be knocked out by Mike Cleary at Philadelphia. But in February 1884 he was training in Chicago under the dual direction of James Connolly of Boston and Davies. Sheriff was another possible opponent for Sullivan.[121]

Sheriff expected to train for sixty days before issuing a challenge to some of the leading artists of the profession. He would make Chicago his headquarters while he was in the United States and had opened a sparring academy in the city enlisting eight pupils. He was training in the basement of Vere Davies' saloon at 219 Randolph Street, which had been fitted up for ball exercise. Charlie had turned over the Champion's Rest to his younger brother.

While Sheriff had some business relationship with Parson Davies in early 1884, Davies had decided to change gears and begin concentrating on a younger group of fighters who would be less likely to be murdered or to show the "white feather." For a younger promoter such as Charlie it may also have been easier to control a younger fighter. Men who had been fighting as long as Ryan, Elliott, and Sheriff were less likely to take instructions from a pup like Davies, who was still in his early thirties.

Mervine Thompson – another whiff

The fighters whom Davies managed and promoted were in the main from a generation that was born during or after the Civil War. The first man in this category was a fighter named Mervine Thompson. Duncan Ross had been involved in several wrestling matches that were part of Charlie's typical evenings of entertainment. Ross was a self-appointed talent scout who had found Thompson and named him the "Cleveland Thunderbolt." In April 1884 the Thunderbolt was a raw commodity. Ross had seen Thompson performing in a wrestling tournament and had promoted him as a wrestler. Soon Ross began to see greater possibilities in promoting him as a fighter rather than a wrestler. Ross then began arranging boxing matches for Thompson in the Cleveland area. By April 1884 the *Police Gazette* reported that Thompson had made $20,000 from his fights in and around Cleveland. This publication was never very clear about whether the amounts it published were net or gross figures.[122]

Seeing the possibilities presented by the Thunderbolt, Davies wrote to Sullivan asking whether he would be willing to meet Mervine in a fight under the London rules.[123] A London-rule fight could not take place in Chicago except in the back room of some building or in a barn. Davies went to Cleveland in late March 1884, and soon after Thompson said that he had deposited $5,000 with Davies for a fight with Sullivan to take place in Arkansas or Louisiana. Thompson was sometimes described as an "octoroon" and at other times referred to as a "malato." These are terms that have largely and thankfully left the American lexicon, but by way of explanation an octoroon means a person who is one-eighth black, a quadroon a person who is one-fourth black, and a mulatto a person who is one-half black. At the time most white Americans considered any black as all black.

The significance of this is that Davies attempted to match Thompson to fight Sullivan with no indication that a color line being asserted by Sullivan.[124] Thompson was the second man of color whom Sullivan was willing to fight. In his own reminiscences, Sullivan wrote that he "made several ineffectual efforts to induce Mervine Thompson, the Cleveland Thunderbolt, to meet me, and, failing in this, returned to Boston, thus ending the longest, most eventful, and most profitable tour of its kind on record, the total receipts being a little over $187,000, with expenses of about $42,000."[125] The possible fight with Thompson blew up when Thompson damaged a tendon in his right hand was unable to fight anyone.

Sullivan spent months prior to Thunderbolt's challenge waltzing through a series of phony matches with Slade and a journeyman named Steven Taylor. Both of these men were on Sullivan's payroll, and none of the participants in those fights can be credited with participating in a legitimate prizefight. In the process of sparring with Taylor and Slade during his grand tour, Sullivan had ballooned up to about 235 pounds, largely because the fights did not involve expending much energy, and he fed on a constant diet of hotel food: fried chicken, mashed potatoes and gravy, buttered rolls, apple pie, and uncountable steins of beer or ale.

Sullivan was in Los Angeles when he received Davies' telegram inquiring about the challenge from Thompson. Sullivan dictated that the conditions for the fight would be $5,000 a side and to the finish. As far as he was concerned, this could happen in a private room or in a ring. To avoid legal interference, there was also discussion of holding the fight in an amphitheater in New Mexico. Demanding $5,000 a side for a finish fight (a fight ending in a knock out or inability of one fighter to continue) could be enough by itself to shut up the most ardent pretender.

Jem Goode- not so good

Davies was also about to discover and bring to prominence another young fighter who would be a leading heavyweight for several years to come. Before that happened he had another misstep, this time with a heavyweight fighter named Jem Goode.

Some reports say that Davies brought Goode over from England as a possible match for Sullivan. Goode's first fight in the United States was with an excellent heavyweight prospect named Jake Kilrain. In 1885 Davies said that he had already acted as Kilrain's manager, so it may be that Davies represented Kilrain's interests for his fight with Goode before Davies began to manage Goode, but this is not clear.

Kilrain and Goode were matched in Boston on October 26, 1883, in a private room. Supposedly that fight was under Queensberry rules for five rounds, and it was declared a draw. This account seems improbable because matches held in private rooms were not usually fought under Queensberry rules, and they seldom resulted in a draw. Regardless of what really happened, it was significant that Goode could fight a draw with Kilrain in a five-round match under any rules, whether in public or private.[126]

Davies was impressed with Goode and brought him to Chicago to try to further build up his reputation. On May 1, 1884, he began promoting Goode by announcing that Goode had accepted Sullivan's challenge, offering to give $1,000 and the receipts of the exhibition to any man who could stand before him for four rounds.[127] Goode then fought a man named John Saunders (sometimes "Sanders"), a railroad brakeman, on May 10 in Chicago but was unable to knock out Saunders within the allotted four rounds. This was not the way it was supposed to happen.

In early 1884 Davies was trying to match Goode and Kilrain for five rounds at Battery D. The fight was to occur July 3, but it did not happen. Davies successfully matched Goode with the old, reliable Dalton at Battery D in Chicago on the evening of May 19. The political situation in Chicago had eased for Davies and other Chicago sports in early 1884, and this made it possible for Charlie to promote important sporting events once again. Carter Harrison was the Democratic candidate for Illinois governor; if elected, he would extend Chicago's influence throughout Illinois. His opponent was the Republican war horse and Civil War hero Richard Oglesby. Harrison needed McDonald help and the help of Mike's growing political machine in order to be elected, and so the pressure was off the sports and saloon crowds so long as they didn't get too carried away with their activities. Davies accommodated the mayor by avoiding London rule and finish fights. To test the waters Davies sponsored a May festival at the Battery D Armory. Before the festival Davies obtained a ten-dollar entertainment license directly from Mayor Harrison and began distributing posters promising a Maypole dance and the crowning of a May queen. The Parson (in a most un-Parson like fashion) was going to sell wine and liquor at this event. The mayor and certain aldermen said that they had been under the impression that Charlie was planning a wrestling match for the evening. But it looked as if there would be co-ed wrestling, and the aldermen became worried about just exactly what was going to happen around that May pole.

Chief Doyle was sent by the mayor to the houses of prostitution to tell the proprietresses to keep their girls at home because this May festival was not going to get out of hand with a bunch of loose women contending to be the May queen. Such an event might parallel a modern day wet T-shirt contest. Doyle next visited Davies and told him that his entertainment license did not cover the sale of liquor and if Davies wanted to sell wine and liquor it would cost him another $160. The chief also sent a large contingent of police to patrol Battery D and the surrounding area. While the May festival event was a flop, it did show that within reasonable bounds as outlined by the mayor and the police, Davies could get his shows produced. [128]

Four thousand people showed up at Battery D on the evening of May 19 for the Dalton-Goode fight. The sports of Chicago knew what Dalton could do in the ring, and therefore Goode was the big draw for the evening. The fight was with small, soft gloves for five rounds under Queensberry rules. Tom Chandler acted as referee for the event, and McDonald assumed the role of time keeper, giving him more control over the outcome than the master of ceremonies.[129]

Goode did not show as well as hoped. It seems that Dalton did not like Goode very much and did not play the anticipated flunkey role. It may be that Dalton saw an opportunity for himself if he could defeat Goode. Perhaps he thought he could move into the ranks of the nationally known heavyweights by putting Goode down. In the second round Dalton made a rush and fought Goode all over the platform. In the third round he made another rush and put Goode down and off the stage between the ropes, giving Goode a slight push for extra measure as he went over the edge.

As Goode climbed back in the ring, Dalton rushed at him again, this time with the two banging away at close quarters until Goode went down in his corner. While Goode was on the floor, Dalton swung at him again. When the fight was renewed, Dalton rushed for a fourth time, forcing Goode out of the ring and then grabbing his ankles to help knock him off the platform a second time and kicking out in Goode's direction. A foul was claimed by Goode's handlers. While Goode was trying to get back into the ring, the referee gave the match to Dalton on the ground that Goode was not on the stage within the allowed ten seconds.

McDonald, in his role as timekeeper, overruled Chandler, making the outcome of the event uncertain. The papers remarked that Goode was in better condition after the fight and that Dalton had a fearful cut on his left eye. The result of this fight was that Goode's reputation needed rehabilitation if he was ever expected to have a show against Sullivan or any other serious heavyweight contender.[130] Dalton said that except for Sullivan, his fight with Goode was the hardest fight he ever had.

Patsy Cardiff – a real possibility

Davies had the candidate he felt could help Goode get back to where he needed to be to merit a match with Sullivan. He had located a young fighter name Patrick Carda, who fought under the name Patsey Cardiff. Cardiff was only twenty-one years old in 1884. He was born in Gratton, Renfrew County, Ontario, in Canada's Upper Ottawa Valley northeast of Toronto. The Upper Ottawa Valley was lumber country and not much else besides ice and snow. Cardiff was reportedly six feet tall and weighed between 175 and 200 pounds during his career. He had made his way to Toledo, where there were many wrestlers and boxers appearing regularly. He then moved on to Peoria, Illinois, where a local man named Charley Flynn, a wrestler, was also operating a gym and athletic club.[131] For reasons that aren't clear that was a fairly strong connection between boxing and wrestling interests in Toledo and Peoria.

There were several good boxing and wrestling fraternities in central Illinois. Bloomington had a capable wrestler who went by the name of Colonel Johnson. Theodore George, known professionally as Greek George, was an excellent wrestler who frequently appeared in Peoria, where Flynn wrestled.

Cardiff was trained in Flynn's gym and had a promoter named William ("Billy") O'Brien. O'Brien was a reasonably well-know promoter who represented several boxers and wrestlers in what was called the O'Brien combination. On April 24, 1884, Flynn sponsored a tournament at Rouse's Hall in Peoria. The leading attraction was a wrestling match for three falls between Flynn and Greek George. Cardiff appeared on the undercard with a boxer from Pekin, Illinois, identified in the press only as Johnson who was offering $50 to anyone who could knock him out in four rounds. Cardiff won the fight in what was called a lukewarm performance, but it was evident to a reporter for the *Peoria Journal* that Cardiff could have easily knocked out Johnson. Knockouts were sometimes intentionally avoided because of the legal complications that could follow. O'Brien saw Cardiff fight that evening and liked what he saw.[132]

Ten days after the Peoria match, Cardiff appeared at the Durley Hall in Bloomington, where Sullivan had appeared about two years earlier and would again appear only six days later with his traveling road show including Steve Taylor. The Durley Hall was a beautiful theater that was well above the standard found in many other cities. It had been designed by a French-born architect named Alfred E. Piquenard, who also designed what is now the Illinois capitol. The hall was financed by David Davis, a justice of the United States Supreme Court. Judge Davis had been Abraham Lincoln's campaign manager in 1860 and had later been appointed by Lincoln to the Supreme Court. The Durley accommodated twelve-hundred patrons with upholstered seats bolted to a parquet floor that sloped downward toward the stage.

Cardiff was again part of a program that included Greek George, who was this time wrestling Colonel Johnson, Bloomington's prominent amateur wrestler. Cardiff's opponent for the evening was Richard T. Dunn, a Bloomington police officer who worked the west side Bloomington saloons and also taught boxing to men on the police force. Dunn's family came from County Wexford, Ireland, and he was its first member born in the United States. He was about six feet two inches tall and weighed 195 pounds in his prime. He had worked as an iron molder before being appointed to the Bloomington police department. Dunn and Cardiff were scheduled to show for three rounds with soft gloves. Although Dunn did quite creditable work, against Cardiff, the *Pantagraph* reported that in the second round, Dunn was knocked squarely off his feet and sat down on the floor with marked emphasis. In the third round he got a thump from Cardiff's soft cushion and was knocked through the curtain on the stage. [133]

Richard T. Dunn – Cardiff's second recorded opponent – Family Photograph

On May 26, one week after Dalton beat up Goode at Battery D, Davies took Goode to the Wigwam in Peoria for a big athletic night. There were one thousand two hundred in attendance, one measure of the growing interest in boxing throughout the country. Evenings of similar entertainment were taking place in second and third-tier cities all over the country. The featured event at the Wigwam was the Cardiff-Goode match.

Goode was accompanied by Davies himself. In a few well chosen words the "clerical looking advocate of sparring" thanked the crowd for their participation, stated that it was his party's intention to abide by the rules of the fight as advertised and hoped for fair-minded treatment of the local crowd. A referee and timekeeper were quickly selected. Davies took a moment to briefly explain the Queensberry rules, which would be applied during the fight. The match was with soft gloves with Cardiff to receive $100 if he could stand before Goode for four rounds.

Cardiff appeared first and took the northeast corner of the ring, and Goode followed taking the opposing corner. To those in attendance it was clear that Cardiff was the more powerful of the two men. Goode weighed 156.5 pounds and stood only five feet eight inches tall. Cardiff was 180 pounds and five feet ten and a half inches in stocking feet. Cardiff got in the first good blow of the fight on Goode's neck and successfully avoided most of Goode's counters. Cardiff then began a whirlwind style, forcing Goode against the ropes and using his superior weight to pin him there.[134]

A reporter from Bloomington observed that Cardiff knocked Goode through the ropes in the first round. Cardiff followed this successful style until the third round when he got in several good blows on Goode's left eye and then knocked Goode around the ring and back into the ropes before putting him on the floor. Some reports claim that Goode was knocked out in this fight but the local press does not agree, and the *Police Gazette* commented that Cardiff intentionally avoided knocking out Goode because he knew that if he did, it would "queer all future sporting events in that city."[135] This seems like a dependable contemporary account of what happened and why it happened. Cardiff claimed the prize money and received the great cheers of the Peoria crowd. In addition, he received sixty percent of the gate receipts as the winner's part under the terms of the articles. Davies seldom gave up sixty percent of the gate receipts without then pursuing management of the man who had taken his money.

Goode was almost washed up as a serious heavyweight contender. He had been whipped at the Battery D fight with Dalton and then trounced by the unknown Cardiff. God help him if he ever got in the ring with Sullivan. Davies was on the verge of losing yet another heavyweight. At the same time, Davies had found a great new prospect in Cardiff, and Charlie lost no time following up.

Two days after the Peoria affair ended, it was announced that Cardiff would go to Battery D on the following Monday, June 2, 1884 to stand for the heavyweight championship of Illinois. Davies was trying to keep both Goode and Cardiff busy, and it was also announced that a few days after the Battery D appearance, Cardiff and Goode would appear at Bloomington's fair grounds to put on a sparring exhibition.[136]

The contest at Battery D took place on Tuesday, June 3. Cardiff's opponent was a stiff named Ed Crooks of Chicago. Three thousand people were in attendance for the fight, and the crowd clearly favored the local man. Cardiff knocked Crooks through the ropes in the first round, but there was no decision awarded in the fight. Some reports say that Cardiff was awarded a technical knockout in the fourth round.[137] When Cardiff returned to Peoria, he said that he had a high regard for Davies but utter contempt for the idea of justice practiced in Chicago. He pointed out that his opponent had employed a number of tricks to kill time during the fight. He said that Crooks had successively lost his glove, his shoe, and then his belt, all of which came off in the most mysterious ways. Cardiff also said that the gloves used in the fight were so big and soft that no real damage could be done using them.[138] Cardiff had no prospects for future fights other than Sherriff; however, it was noted that Davies might bring over Goode's younger brother, Bill Goode, for a fight with Cardiff.[139]

A few days after Cardiff's June 3 fight, his manager, O'Brien, left Peoria for Chicago to travel with Davies to New York. They were going to attend the Sullivan-Mitchell fight scheduled for June 30. O'Brien thought that during the trip he might be able to reach an understanding with Davies regarding a traveling combination using all of the Peoria talent, including Greek George. O'Brien wanted Davies to agree to send Chicago area fighters on the road as part of O'Brien's combination.

While Davies and O'Brien traveled East, Cardiff came to Chicago, where Davies had arranged for a trainer to work with Cardiff so that he could learn more science and be in shape for a planed tournament in Chicago on July 3. The whirlwind style of fighting employed by Cardiff in Peoria was commonly seen on the playground and was a sure sign of an amateur who needed to learn to fight.

O'Brien and Davies attended the Sullivan-Mitchell fight at Madison Square Garden. The attendance estimates for that match vary from as high as thirteen thousand five hundred to as low as five thousand. When Sullivan finally showed up he was several hours late. Still dressed in a suit, he told the patrons that he was sick and not able to appear to box Mitchell. To most of those present, Sullivan was obviously drunk. Facing a substantial financial loss because of Sullivan's behavior, Al Smith quit as his manager.[140]

Back in Chicago, Cardiff was marking time waiting for another bout for the Illinois heavyweight championship. This time his opponent was a man named James McClarney (sometimes reported as McLarney) who was fifteen to twenty pounds heavier than Cardiff and three inches taller. Cardiff defeated McClarney in four rounds and was awarded the title, which had been denied him in his fight with Crooks.

While Cardiff had been set up for fights with local meatballs, Davies was trying one last time to promote Goode by matching him against a quality opponent. He was matched to fight a really top little fighter, Mike Cleary of New

York, at Battery D in Chicago on July 19. Cleary was five feet eight inches tall and weighed about 164 pounds. Unlike Dalton and Cardiff, Cleary was roughly the same size as Goode, who would not likely be pushed around the ring based on the sheer size and weight of his opponent. Fighting in the shadow of the debacle of the aborted Sullivan-Mitchell show in New York, this heavyweight fight in Chicago provided an opportunity to reclaim some positive buzz for prizefighting.

Cleary had already set himself apart from other heavyweight contenders. He had particularly enhanced his reputation in the months of April and May 1884. On April 18 he had defeated Sheriff at Germania Assembly Rooms in New York. Cleary was twenty-seven years old at the time of that fight, and there were estimates that Sherriff might be as old as forty-seven. Some reports said that Sheriff was only about five feet four inches tall but weighed two hundred pounds, a real fireplug. That fight turned out to be short. The result was recorded as a knockout at one minute and twenty seconds of the first round. Many claimed that Sheriff had been decked by a chance blow from Cleary, and the two men were matched for a second fight.[141]

On May 19, in front of about two thousand at the Industrial Hall in Philadelphia, Cleary and Sheriff met a second time. In 1884, prizefighters and their doctors paid little attention to such things as brain concussions, and rematches following a knockout were made quickly. Consequently, many fighters ended up with brain damage and died early. After only one minute and five seconds of the first round of their second fight, Cleary again tagged Sheriff and again dropped him like a log. That ended the lucky punch theory.[142]

To further enhance his national reputation, it was important for Cleary to fight in the West. In 1884 Chicago was considered the West. Davies had probably arranged for the Cleary-Goode fight while he was in New York attending the Sullivan-Mitchell catastrophe. Estimates were that two thousand five hundred attended the Cleary-Goode fight at Battery D. At fight time, Goode was still being described in the press as a protégé of Parson Davies.[143]

After the fight Goode would be a protégé of no one. For the third time, Goode was pounded but this time by a man of roughly his own size. Cleary knocked Goode down three times in the first round. This might not have been the type of fight that Davies was hoping for, but it was certainly another important step forward for Cleary, who was building a solid record and reputation as a significant heavyweight contender.

Cardiff, still waiting for a high profile fight, was matched to spar with McClarney for the *Sporting Journal* championship medal at the Buckingham in Chicago.[144] The *Peoria Journal* reported the fight as a draw and claimed that McClarney had the best of it, knocking Cardiff down once. McClarney had better science than Cardiff and used his size to his advantage.[145] Whatever the result, this match had no serious impact on Cardiff's career or the reputation he had been building, and it appears that Cardiff's performance was enough to further encourage Davies to promote Cardiff. From this time on, press reports no longer referred to O'Brien as Cardiff's manager and instead say that Cardiff was in the hands of Davies.[146] That situation would last until Cardiff injured his hand. After Cardiff had spent time in the big city, he began to realize that his future was not in Peoria with Charley Flynn and Greek George or even with a small-time promoter like Billy O'Brien.

William Bradburn – a better heavy

Soon after the McClarney fight, Cardiff was matched to fight Bradburn. They were to fight within a few weeks in Chicago. Bradburn was described as a two-hundred-pound giant and "big, active, powerful pounder." Scheduling a match with him led to the indefinite postponement of any further fights with McClarney.

Bradburn was a better-than-average heavyweight, and Cardiff's match with him was considered a build-up of Bradburn's career. Davies had kept Cardiff, in good condition but Bradburn was so confident that he agreed to articles providing that would stop Cardiff in five rounds, with small gloves, using Queensberry rules, a stake of $500 and gate receipts. If Bradburn failed to stop Cardiff, then Cardiff was to receive everything. Whoever cut this deal was either overconfident or a poor negotiator. The Cardiff-Bradburn match was scheduled for August 25 at Buckingham Hall in Chicago.[147]

Betting on the fight was heavily in Bradburn's favor. The contest was brutal and exciting from the start and was marked by the poor conduct of the audience. The police and seconds at the fight were forced to intervene between Cardiff and Bradburn several times because they were not following the Queensberry rules or the law. To the surprise of many, Cardiff knocked Bradburn senseless in four rounds and from that point on, the two men were bitter enemies.[148]

About one month later, on September 22, Cardiff fought a heavyweight named Jack King at Union Park in St. Louis. Tom Kelly represented King, and Davies was present in St. Louis for the fight on behalf of Cardiff. St. Louis papers observed that Cardiff's tactics were similar to those employed by Sullivan—perhaps not a good thing if a fighter lacked Sullivan's power. Cardiff won the first four rounds of the fight when the police interfered.[149]

Part of the consideration for the Cardiff-King match was that King was then matched to fight Captain Dalton in Chicago in early November 1884. However, the 1884 Chicago elections were over and substantial parts of the McDonald political machine had been indicted for trying to fix that election. Moreover, Carter Harrison had not been elected as Illinois governor as he hoped. About the only sporting events that could go forward in Chicago at that time were wrestling matches.

Chicago politics – the police appropriation

During his career, Davies dealt with the perpetually changing standards governing the presentation of athletic entertainment in Chicago. The standards generally changed to satisfy the political winds. Politicians would sometimes support prizefighting but later turn their backs on such entertainment just before elections to gain support at the polls. Then they would relax their strict standards for the proper consideration paid after taking office. It is no wonder that the major league cheating scandal with the Chicago Black Sox happened in the city where crooked behavior was a way of life. Chicago political figures provided ample examples of sport related dishonesty.

It could have been worse for Davies. One part of the November 1884 election in Chicago involved the so-called police appropriation. Chicago voters were asked whether they would support the city's expenditure of $100,000 to hire additional police officers. There was no civil service system in the 1880s and the police appropriation was politicized. Aldermen frequently controlled the appointment of the policemen assigned to their wards, and many of the aldermen were controlled by McDonald, who supported the police appropriation.

Doyle was anxious for the police appropriation to succeed and arranged for his police officers pass out pasters favoring the proposition. A paster was a sticker that a voter could put on his ballot to vote for a particular candidate or issue. The Republican ticket did not have a place to vote yes for the police appropriation. Nevertheless, in the second precinct of the eighteenth ward, one of McDonald's controlled precincts, the vote for the police appropriation was 694 in favor and none opposed.

This vote gives an idea of the extent of McDonald's power and ability to influence elections. Similar solid votes occurred in more than fifty precincts throughout the city. It was estimated that over sixteen thousand phony votes were tallied. The scope of the fraud with respect to the police appropriation was a barometer of the influence of McDonald. Ultimately, an Illinois state grand jury indicted nearly two hundred Chicago election judges for gross negligence in discharging their duties with respect to the police appropriation. Davies was one of the many election judges indicted, but he was later absolved of wrongdoing.[150]

Once again the political situation forced Davies to try to promote fights in venues outside Chicago. The town was no longer the best place for heavyweights like Cardiff. Davies therefore planned to make a match for Cardiff with either Jack Burke or Mitchell, both from England, and with Dominick McCaffrey, another fighter from Pittsburgh, with the winner to take 65 percent of the gate. Charlie hoped to make these matches in either New York or Pittsburgh.[151]

In the meantime, the nearest venue for a fight in Illinois was in Peoria at the Wigwam. On November 13 Davies took Cardiff back to Peoria to arrange an exhibition against a fighter named Tom Anderson. Anderson had fought Dalton in Chicago and had used up Dalton fairly severely during their fight. A grand jury in Chicago was investigating a charge that Anderson had used brass knuckles under his gloves during the Dalton fight.[152]

After the arrangements for the fight with Anderson were completed, Cardiff and Davies went to St. Paul for a fight with a man named Barnes, who was described as a "half-breed base ballist." Reports from that fight said that the friends of Barnes were so afraid that Cardiff would hurt Barnes that they decided to put extra padding in the gloves used in the fight.

As a consequence of the glove tampering, Cardiff was unable to close his hand to make a fist and therefore strained his left hand seriously. When Cardiff returned to Peoria to fight Anderson, it was announced that the match would only involve a display of science and no hard blows. [153] Cardiff was thereafter put out of commission while his hand healed, and in the meantime he went to Philadelphia to train and spar with Dominick McCaffrey, who was then under Billy O'Brien's management.[154] As a consequence, Davies no longer managed Cardiff.

Cardiff failed to follow instructions while in Philadelphia and engaged in some heavy hitting with McCaffrey and sprained his left hand a second time. Reports said that his hand was "badly swollen and quite tender." He was out of commission for at least another month, which meant that several matches had to be rescheduled and dates were then open to be filled by other men and events. Cardiff's loss would be some another fighter's gain and would unnaturally delay Cardiff's rise to national prominence.

Immediately after the Cardiff-Barnes fight, Davies returned to Chicago but then left for New York with several friends to watch the scheduled fight between Sullivan and Alf Greenfield, a thirty-one year old pugilist from Northampton, England, who had been brought over by Richard K. Fox to try to defeat America's great champion.[155]

When Greenfield arrived in America, the press commonly referred to him as the champion of England.[156] The Greenfield-Sullivan fight was scheduled for Madison Square Garden and took place before a crowd of from 5,000 to 7,000. Sullivan and Greenfield were both arrested before the fight began for planning to participate in a fight, but they were discharged. Their match was another post-election-day fight, and the politicians no longer needed to curry the favor of the sports in order to obtain votes. As a result, there was police interference in the fight after two rounds, and both Greenfield and Sullivan were again arrested. Fox posted bail for both fighters.[157] A few days later, all those connected with the Greenfield-Sullivan fight, including Fox and Harding, were indicted by a grand jury.[158]

Alf Greenfield – another small heavyweight

Davies went to the Greenfield-Sullivan fight to do business. Part of his business was to market Cardiff, but Cardiff's bad hand made it difficult to plan anything. Goode was under no one's consideration because of his dismal performances in Peoria and Chicago. Some reports said that Davies was representing Bradburn on his trip to the East. However, Davies had something bigger in mind. He had formed the idea that he could bring Burke to Chicago in early 1885 as part of a big athletic production that he was planning. To pull this event off, it would take work to convince Chicago authorities that the boxing portion of the program would not involve fighters injuring one another in any serious way.

There could be no London-rule fights or fights to the finish in Chicago. Because of these limitations, purists would refer to these matches as "fixed fights." That terminology did not always mean that someone was paid to win or lose. It sometimes simply meant that the fighters had agreed that there would be no knockout in order to comply with local law. Others would sometimes use terminology of the 1880s and refer to these fights as hippodromes. Fights were called fixed or hippodromes because the outcome in virtually every case would be a draw. At that time scientific points were generally not awarded by judges, and as long as there was no knockout the referee would declare the fight a draw. There were hundreds of fights during this time called fixed fights, but they were not fixed in the sense that a fighter was paid off in advance.

Davies knew that any fight he made for Cardiff would have to be delayed because of Cardiff's hand. Davies soon left New York to return to Chicago and the word spread that he had secured a match between Cardiff and Kilrain, who was probably the most prominent of the coming heavyweights.[159] Davies did not return to Chicago until December 5, and he then reported that he had made trips along the way to New York, Philadelphia, Boston, and other cities in the East. He confirmed that he had arranged a Cardiff-Kilrain fight that would probably take place in Boston in about February 1885.[160]

Even though prizefights in Chicago were hard to arrange, it was important for Davies to provide entertainment. In mid-December 1884 Davies announced that he had organized a wrestling show between Frank Whitmore of Chicago and a wrestler named James Faulkner. Charlie was backing Whitmore for this match and Billy O'Brien, Cardiff's original promoter, was Faulkner's manager. O'Brien also managed of Dominick McCaffery, an important young heavyweight contender.[161]

McCaffery and Faulkner were part of the traveling combination of athletes managed by O'Brien. This was to be a catch-as-catch-can match for $500 a side held at the Park Theater.[162] The large capacity of Battery D was not necessary for most wrestling events, and it was obvious that Davies' familiarity with theater managers through his participation in the Elks helped him find right-sized venues for his sports productions.

Faulkner defeated Whitmore, and a second match was quickly scheduled using alternate Greco-Roman and catch-as-catch-can formats.[163] Only a few days after these matches O'Brien's combination began breaking up because of continued police interference. O'Brien continued to manage McCaffery and another heavyweight named George Rooke. He planned to take the men to the Northwest, where the police would not confuse the situation, to give sparring exhibitions. When O'Brien dropped Faulkner, he was picked up by Davies, who began scheduling Faulkner for additional wrestling matches in Chicago.

O'Brien was not totally finished promoting in Illinois. On the evening of December 22, his full combination was scheduled to appear in Durley Hall at Bloomington, Illinois. Davies sent Cardiff along with O'Brien to provide sparring competition for O'Brien's men. Cardiff was well-known and admired in Bloomington and could draw a crowd.

Because of the impending break-up of the O'Brien combination, some of his advertised performers did not appear. Cardiff performed, but even his effort was described as "very ordinary." O'Brien then skipped town without paying for the hall rental. It was noted that none of O'Brien's combination had arrived without any baggage and that they were flying light. The hotels and saloons of the town were searched without success, and it was decided that O'Brien had played the town for suckers. The local paper commented that the "the sooner such a mob is taken off the road, the better for the reputation of Parson Davies and Cardiff, the latter of whom at least is a well-meaning and deserving fellow." [164]

O'Brien was not a pillar of society. In February 1885 he became involved in a bar fight with a wrestler named "One-eyed" Jim Connolly. O'Brien insulted Connolly and was then decked. O'Brien then grabbed an ale stein and hit Connolly with it above his right eye, creating a large gash. O'Brien grabbed Connolly and tried to gouge out his one good eye with his thumb. Connolly in turn bit O'Brien on the cheek, and they were pulled away with a "goodly portion" of O'Brien's cheek in Connolly's mouth. The *Chicago Herald* reported that early the next morning O'Brien slunk out of town and that his "cowardly attempt to destroy Connolly's one remaining eye was condemned on all sides, and Connolly was the hero of the hour."

In addition to sponsoring wrestling matches Davies took on a long-distance horseback rider named Charles M. Anderson. Davies financed Anderson's trip to New Orleans to challenge numerous Mexican equestrians who were present there. He was offering a stake of from $500 to $1,000 on Anderson.[165] There really was no limit to the events that Davies would consider sponsoring if he thought there was money to be made in the process. Whether the performers were racewalkers, prizefighters, wrestlers, sword fighters, child pugilists, or long-distance horseback riders, Charlie was ready to promote the event.

Despite Davies' indictment in connection with the 1884 police appropriation voting, 1884 had been a good year. During most of it he had been able to promote boxing matches in Chicago. His reputation as the "go to" promoter and manager in Chicago was solid. By the end of the year he had two credible young heavyweights: Bradburn and Cardiff. When boxing was temporarily suppressed after the November 1884 elections, he had found a way to make some decent income by sponsoring several wrestling matches in Chicago.

Chapter 5 - (1885)

The Irish Lad

Sport has always been popular in Chicago, and the main reason is because it has always been properly conducted. Charles E. Davies and the other managers to whom the athletic admiring public looks for entertainment in manly sports have prided themselves on the freedom from the annoyance so prevalent in the East, and it is that absence of the lower element that has made sparring exhibitions and other athletic entertainments so eminently successful here.[166]

An Early Depiction of Charles E. Davies – Photograph from the Biographic Review of Prominent Men & Women of Chicago - 1899

The wrestler Rabshaw

In early 1885 Davies picked up the representation of another wrestler, John Rabshaw, who was a collar and elbow wrestler. He matched Rabshaw for a bout with Faulkner for $300 a side at Hershey Music Hall on January 6. It was predicted that it would take the two men several hours of wrestling to determine a winner. Although Faulkner had split with O'Brien and his combination, they were still personal friends, and O'Brien backed him for the match with Rabshaw.[167] Like boxing in the 1880s, there was often a substantial disparity in size between the two wrestlers. Faulkner weighed only about 145 pounds and Rabshaw weighed 175 pounds. The referee for their match was the often present Dalton.[168]

The halls and audiences for wrestling matches in Chicago were generally smaller than for boxing matches, but there was still some money to be made. An estimated five hundred attended the Faulkner-Rabshaw match. Their match was in a mixed catch-as-catch-can and collar-and-elbow format. Rabshaw defeated Faulkner in three of the five bouts and was declared the winner. Davies promised the two men would meet again. In January 1886 this match was listed as one of the top fifteen sporting events in Chicago in 1885.[169]

One way of publicizing fighters and matches in the mid-1880s was to issue a "defy" (or challenge) in a newspaper. Defies made in Chicago were commonly published in the *Chicago Herald*, which seemed to have a special affinity for the boxing and wrestling news of the day. The "ethics" of the situation were that reputable newspapers were not supposed to publish challenges or defies unless the person making the challenge posted forfeit money with that newspaper.

A defy could be directed to a particular fighter or to several fighters at the same time. Often these defies appeared to be drafted by a promoter rather than the fighter himself. For example, in January 1885 Dalton issued a defy to McCaffrey to fight him a fair stand up fight with bare knuckles for from $1,000 to $2,000 a side at any place within 100 miles of New Orleans. The same day Tom Hinch, who styled himself the middleweight champion of Illinois, issued a defy to Tom Anderson, Frank Glover, James Connily, Harry Williams, Frank Ware, Paddy Carroll, Fred Sommers, Mike Kane, Bill Bradburn, Henry Burns, Patsey Cardiff, Billy Dalton and several others for a fight based on stakes of from $100 to $500 per man.

Many defies had no particular chance of success. It was unlikely that McCaffrey would fight Dalton with bare knuckles anyplace, and there was no particular advantage for McCaffrey to fight Dalton with gloves or bare knuckles. Hinch's defy was simply trying to find a fight and put his name before the public. His challenge was eventually accepted by Frank Glover, who wrote that he believed that Hinch didn't have the sand to back up his talk with an actual fight. Glover promised to knockout his opponent within four rounds or he would forfeit any rights to the take.[170]

Some defies published in the *Herald*, were probably written by the fighter himself. Bradburn issued a defy to Dalton. Bradburn had learned that Dalton had criticized him by saying that Bradburn could "only stand a punch or two" before folding up. He then challenged Dalton, but made sure that in his letter to the newspaper he insulted Dalton; and his insults provided interesting insights about some previous fights.

Bradburn wrote that when Sullivan fought Dalton, he allowed him to stand four rounds so that Dalton could "hold his reputation and open a saloon."[171] This may have been exactly what happened because Dalton used his take from his fight with Sullivan to open a saloon that was financed by McDonald. Moreover, there had been no real point in having Sullivan beat up Dalton because Dalton was a local man who was a reliable opponent for many fighters who came to Chicago.

Bradburn also commented that Tommy Chandler, a man twenty pounds lighter than Dalton, made him think he did not know how to fight, and Elliott knocked out Dalton with one blow and then "took him aside and gave him fatherly advice and told him to quit the business, for as a fighter he would be a failure." Bradburn proposed a fight with Dalton using kid gloves for $500 a side and the winner to take seventy five percent of the gate. The things that Bradburn wrote were not the type of thing that a promoter would likely include in his defy, but they certainly provided tabloid-like insight into the fight game at the time.

While Davies was busy in Chicago, promoters in the East arranged a Ryan-Sullivan rematch. Both of these men had fallen a long way in the public's estimation from the time of the championship fight in Mississippi. Ryan was considered by many to be a whining coward who was surrounded by a clique of sycophant friends. At the same time Sullivan was considered an overweight, pompous fool who had raked in huge sums of money on the fried chicken and mashed potatoes circuit and wasted most of it gambling, drinking, and making bad investments. Many people felt that Sullivan richly deserved all the contumely and bitter feelings that were directed toward him.[172] Strong feelings pro and con about Sullivan would exist even at the time of his death. However, in 1885 a Ryan-Sullivan match was still a big draw, and they were about to fight again, this time in New York.

The one minute rematch

Whatever his public perception, Ryan had earned a bad reputation with managers and promoters. After his championship fight with Sullivan in 1882, he had blamed his loss in part on poor advice from his manager. When Davies arranged a rematch with Sullivan, Ryan ran away to Toledo to hide behind his mother's skirts. For the proposed fight with Sullivan, Ryan was relying on Pat Sheedy, whom Ryan described as a personal friend who had always "used me square." This belief was somewhat naïve on Ryan's part because Sheedy treated people square when there was money in it for Sheedy.

Sullivan had taken on Sheedy as his manager after Al Smith gave up trying to control John L.'s alcoholic behavior. Sheedy was described as a "loud-talking, brassy promoter when he was not flicking pasteboards across a gaming table or betting on horses. . . . He was as tall as Sullivan and almost as heavy, his broad, smooth face continually creased in a smile. Sheedy was every inch a hustler and a dandy, his high forehead capped by long, wavy, black hair and his dress of the appropriate flash."[173] According to Ryan, Sheedy had offered him 50 percent of the gate receipts whether he won or lost if Ryan would agree to a rematch with Sullivan. Ryan then told Sheedy to go ahead and manage everything knowing that Sheedy was actually Sullivan's manager at the time.

The Ryan-Sullivan match went forward—at least in part—on January 19, 1885. Davies was in New York to see the match and to watch his former clients square off for their encore. Sullivan was seconded by his trainers Tom Delay and Dan Murphy. Ryan was seconded by Ned Mallahan and Jimmy Peterson. After about one minute of the first round the New York police entered the ring and intervened.[174] Although the receipts for the event were about $11,000, the Chicago press described the event as a "disgraceful exhibition" and this thing hardly qualified as an actual rematch. Ryan told the press: "I think without any bragging that I would have come out ahead." He felt that public confidence had been restored in him and that he could no longer be accused of cowardice.[175]

After the Ryan-Sullivan one minute rematch, Sheedy asked Ryan to promise him that he would not fight anyone else until he had met Sullivan again to finish what they had barely started in New York. Ryan agreed to Sheedy's request, and they shook hands on their oral agreement. This was a convenient arrangement for Ryan because it allowed him to avoid fighting anyone else and to rely on the high moral ground that he could not fight because of his promise to Sheedy. Sheedy probably insisted that Ryan should fight no one other than Sullivan because there was a substantial chance that many other fighters could beat Ryan and a loss would eliminate any chance for a rematch with Sullivan.

The day after their aborted rematch, Ryan and Sullivan met at the Coleman House in New York to divide up the gate money. Davies was present at this meeting. Several press reports including the *Post Dispatch* reported that Ryan slugged Sullivan while Sullivan was sitting at a table. It was said to be a "terrific blow on the nose," and it may have been the only time during their acquaintance that Ryan landed a clean blow on Sullivan. When questioned about it, Davies said, with his tongue firmly in his cheek: "I watched both men carefully and I am inclined to think that Ryan had the best of it. He met Sullivan from the word 'go,' and I know a place, and so does Sheedy, where they can meet either with or without gloves. There is from eight to ten thousand dollars waiting for Sullivan, and I will guarantee that the Sheriff of the county will not interfere."[177] The next day Ryan denied that there had been any conflict with Sullivan.

Davies wanted to take advantage of the excitement that was being generated by the Ryan-Sullivan affair. He returned to Chicago for a Faulkner-Rabshaw rematch at Hershey Hall on January 23.[178] Their rematch was also listed as one of the top fifteen sporting events of 1885.[179] That same evening Charlie announced that he was planning an athletic entertainment at Battery D that would be one of the best that Chicago had ever seen. He told the *Chicago Herald* that he began planning the event when he traveled east for Sullivan-Greenfield match, and he also announced that he had lined up Jack Burke to spar five rounds with Dalton under the Queensberry rules. He had also tried to line up both Mitchell and Greenfield for appearances in Chicago, but they had agreed to a private fight for some of their friends for a purse of $1,000. Ned Mallahan was Burke's manager at the time, and he and Burke both left New York for Chicago on January 29, 1885.[180]

The *Herald* noted that it had been months since Chicago had a really first-class evening of athletic sport and that the public was looking forward to a healthy revival of the manly sport. In order to make the performance acceptable to Harrison and Doyle, the program for the evening would include tamer things such as club-swinging, wrestling, bar exercises, and a broadsword contest. Cardiff was projected to be the likely referee for the Burke-Dalton match.[181]

The "Irish Lad" – Davies' first homerun

Jack Burke would be a tremendous attraction in Chicago, and Davies' representation of Burke marked at turning point in both of their professional lives. "The Irish Lad" was a Chicago promoter's dream. He was a good-looking young man of gentlemanly appearance. Burke was five feet eight inches tall, weighed about 156 pounds, and was broad shouldered. He was a natty dresser and always in the latest fashion. He always wore a brightly colored scarf at his throat. Although he was very young at the time, he knew how to draw a crowd.

Burke was born in Killarney, County Carey, Ireland, but had grown up in England. He was marketed as a man whom both countries claimed as their own. While living in England, Burke was educated at Saint Joseph's Catholic Academy in London. Jack had made his professional debut in England at the Ascot race course against Mitchell, who had become a well-known figure in America. His performance in that fight was often referred to in subsequent years as proof that Burke had sand. Their fight lasted an hour and forty-seven minutes with bare fists and was declared a draw. That fight was enough for any man to say that he had made his bones in prizefighting. Burke's success in Chicago soon eclipsed the less flashy Cardiff, and this was made possible because Cardiff had so thoughtlessly injured his hand sparring with McCaffery.[182]

Davies managed Burke with great skill and substantial financial success, marketing the fighter from coast to coast. In that process Davies outgrew the reputation of being a regional promoter and manager. He developed a national reputation and was known internationally. With Burke, Davies fully developed his template for promoting foreign fighters in America. In the process he made Burke a rich man. Fighters saw what Davies could do for them and the meant that he would attract the top flight fighters in years to come.

The event at Battery D was a great success and a big payday for Davies. This was the third Davies-sponsored event that would be listed among the top fifteen athletic events in Chicago in 1885, and it was only February.[183] Five thousand men were in attendance and three thousand others were left outside unable to get in. McDonald was among those present. Ryan made an appearance at the hall and was loudly cheered. He was introduced in the ring as the next heavyweight champion of America, and he told the crowd that he was ready to meet Sullivan, or any other man, at any time, at any place, and for any amount of money. This was typical Ryan bravado and certainly inconsistent with the promise he had allegedly made to Sheedy to fight no one else until after he had fought Sullivan. In most respects Ryan was a windbag.

After Ryan's appearance, the evening began with the broadsword competition between a Professor Monstery and his pupil Guy Rivers. The professor made six hits on Rivers and then with a flourish disarmed his opponent. Following this opening act, Glover and John Doherty fought a four-round match to a draw. Dalton's younger brother, Ed, had a three-round match with Fred Sommers. Several other matches appeared as part of the undercard, and they were followed by Burke's fight with Dalton.

Ryan acted as the referee for their match. Burke was no Jem Goode. The *Tribune* reported that Dalton was noticeably out of shape for the match and was entirely at the mercy of Burke. In contrast, the *Herald* reported that both men were in good shape. Although Dalton was the local man, the crowd was with Burke from the beginning, and he was noted to be a "clean, quick hitter, with plenty of science."

In the first round Burke delivered seven successive left-handers full on Dalton's nose and mouth and then drove him to the ropes where a right-hand put him down for an eight count. Burke stood at a distance and waited smiling at Dalton, who faced the music like a man. During the remainder of the fight, Burke did not use his right hand and controlled Dalton with his left alone. At this point in his career, Burke was known as a left-handed fighter who had a below average right hand. Even using one hand he was too much for Dalton, and the crowd cheered for the victorious Irishman.[184]

With the success of the Dalton match it was time for Davies to further capitalize on the Irish Lad, but to attract a crowd Burke had to be matched against a fighter of a better quality than Dalton. Davies arranged for Steve Taylor of New York to come to Chicago and spar with Burke. Taylor had been one of Sullivan's early victims, but he had then spent most of two years traveling around in the role of Sullivan's punching bag during his grand tour. Because of this exposure with Sullivan, Taylor was a well-known fighter around the country.[185]

Captain Dalton nearly buys the farm

In the meantime the world of boxing nearly ended for Dalton. After being soundly schooled by Burke on the evening of February 2, 1885, he traveled to Louisville for a fight with Mike Cleary. In making this move, the Captain was stepping out of his home territory and also out of his league. The Cleary-Dalton fight was held at Liederkranz Hall in front of two thousand paid spectators. It was again noted that Dalton was not in good shape. This time his physical stamina was not the issue. Dalton had a badly bruised and puffed-up eye and a severely cut lip from his earlier match with Burke. After two minutes and forty-eight seconds Cleary caught Dalton with a straight right, knocking him out.

It was more than four minutes before Dalton recovered consciousness. The *Cincinnati Enquirer* reported that when Dalton was hit, he "fell full length, his head striking on the bare stage with such weight that the sound produced was heard all over the large hall." Dalton's first words when he came to were: "I ain't knocked out, am I?"[186] He would not be the first or the last fighter to ask that question, and 100 percent of the time this is a question, a fighter's backers don't want to hear or answer.

Dalton limped back to Chicago with the news that he had been scheduled for a rematch with Cleary during the second week of March at New Orleans. This was to be a fight to the finish—as if he hadn't been finished in Louisville. This contest would be Dalton's third fight in about five weeks against high-quality opponents.[187] After packing his bags, Dalton headed for New Orleans to go into training for his rematch with Cleary. Ten days later, Dalton was returning to Chicago from New Orleans on the Illinois Central's New Orleans express train. A St. Louis express train had stopped on the track about nine miles south of Kankakee, Illinois, because of a broken wheel. Flares were set out behind the train to warn any following trains, but the New Orleans express was traveling too fast to stop and plowed into the sleeping car on the St. Louis train, telescoping it into the baggage car. One passenger was killed and a large number of passengers, including Dalton, were injured.

Little attention was paid to Dalton's injury in original accounts because it was learned that he was traveling on a pass that the railroad had issued to Alderman Gaynor of Chicago. Gaynor was one of the aldermen considered to be a sport and thought to be in McDonald's back pocket. The railroads regularly gave free passes to politicians for their personal use as a way of influencing their attitude toward railroad corporations. Every alderman in Chicago had a free pass from the Illinois Central. Politicians were not supposed to give up their passes to other people.

When asked what Dalton was doing with his pass, Gaynor said that Dalton had asked him whether he could help get him a pass. Gaynor had sent a friend to procure a pass, if possible, from the IC. According to Gaynor, the friend had misunderstood and procured the pass in the alderman's own name. He said that he was unaware of his friend's mistake, and he would never have abused a railroad pass. Chicago aldermen were and remain proficient at making such lying answers. The scheduled Dalton-Cleary fight in New Orleans had to be cancelled because of Dalton's injuries. Dalton would not fight again until May 1885, when he was matched to fight the heavyweight champion of Colorado, John P. Clow, another quality fighter.[188]

There was additional big news in mid-February 1885. Burke was moving from New York to Chicago, and his wife was coming along. Burke liked Chicago better than other places to which he had traveled during his career, and he said that he hoped to make a home there.[189] In addition, Davies announced that Burke's next opponent would be Greenfield.[190] As mentioned earlier, Greenfield had defeated Burke in a match for the championship belt of England, but Burke claimed that at the time he was only nineteen years old and weighed only 136 pounds. He said that he had been cheated out of the fight by a referee's decision for Greenfield and was anxious for revenge. This was probably just pre-fight drama.

Davies and Jack Dempsey

On the same day that Burke arrived in Chicago with his wife, Davies received a communication from New York asking him to arrange a meeting in Chicago between Johnny Files and Jack Dempsey, both of whom were then in the East. This was the first mention of the original Jack Dempsey—who is not the heavyweight Jack Dempsey later known to many people—in connection with Davies. Dempsey had knocked out nineteen successive lightweight fighters of greater or lesser reputation. Davies said that the match, if arranged, would take place within about two weeks.[191]

Dempsey was in Chicago by March 1, 1885, and met with Davies. Lightweight fighters seldom have the same cache as heavyweights. Dempsey was something different. He was born in Curragh of County Kildare, Ireland, on December 15, 1862, but had moved to Brooklyn when he was only four years old. Jack was a real fighter and not a cheap poser. He was another flashy dresser, favoring fine chinchilla overcoats, high silk hats, and fancy scarves. In early 1885 Dempsey was the lightweight champion of America. He would become one of the greatest fighters of all time, although his reputation was not that strong in early 1885. He was always a favorite in Chicago but did little fighting there.

Dempsey was another young fighter who was taking the limelight away from the old-timers such as Tug Wilson, Mace, and Ryan. He was a cooper by trade, which means that his was trained to make things such as barrels and buckets. His older brother was a collar and elbow wrestler, and when his brother needed a partner to put on a show Jack would go along to be the opponent. He and his brother appeared several times at Harry Hill's place to pick up five or ten dollars for exhibitions, and in the process he saw lots of sparring matches. Dempsey began fighting in April 1883 as a substitute for a fighter who did not appear as scheduled. He won that appearance by knocking out his opponent, Ed McDonald, in twenty-seven rounds and followed with nineteen consecutive knockouts.

Jack had an unusual fighting style for the 1880's. He took a position with his right side thrown considerably to the back, presenting only his left side to his opponent. He held his right hand straight out from his shoulder and high to cover his face. He was credited with having an unusually strong left arm, and he had great strength in his legs. He was sometimes called a wheeler, meaning that he circled his opponent constantly looking for an opening. By circling an opponent he was usually at an angle to his foe, thereby making him a more difficult target to hit. He was also quick as lightning, which can make up for most other shortcomings a boxer may have. Word was that Dempsey would stay in Chicago to see the Burke-Greenfield fight, and then he would head for New Orleans and a fight with a man named Jake Stearns.[192] Dempsey did not have much interest in fighting in Chicago, and Davies' plate was pretty full at the time. Although Dempsey and Davies had some common experiences in their background, they never seemed to hit it off very well.

Trouble with Ryan and Sheedy

Chicagoans wanted to see Burke matched against Ryan. Paddy had issued a general defy, and his friends said they would back him in a match with any man for $2,500 a side with hard gloves to the finish with $500 forfeit money. Ryan's primary backer was Colonel John P. Vidvard, the son of Peter Vidvard, a successful commission merchant and manufacturer of shirts and overalls from Utica, New York. Vidvard operated a saloon and restaurant at 336 State Street. He was a well-known sport and strong Ryan supporter. Apparently, Vidvard was not blessed with the soundest judgment.

When a Burke-Ryan match was suggested in response to Ryan's defy, Ryan asserted that he had made an oral promise to Sheedy not to fight anyone until after he had met Sullivan in another match that Sheedy would arrange. "I'd love to do it boys but I promised Pat and I have to live up to my word." This was obviously at odds with Ryan's public statement in the ring during the Burke-Greenfield match that he would fight any man, at any place, any time.

Ryan claimed that the matter of a fight with Burke rested with Sheedy and that if Sheedy would release him from his promise, he would agree to meet Burke. Ryan added that he hadn't heard anything from Sheedy since Sheedy had gone to New Orleans for the aborted Cleary-Dalton match. It must have occurred to Davies that Ryan had a somewhat flexible approach to his own promises because Ryan had never asked Davies to be released from a written promise to fight Sullivan when he decided to run off to Toledo to see his poor sick mother. It was also quite convenient that Ryan had no contact with Sheedy so that he could not ask for the release he claimed that he needed before fighting Burke.

On the evening of March 1, Davies' production entertained an overflow crowd estimated at between seven and eight thousand. This was going to be another great night for Davies, the fighters that he promoted, and the sporting fans of Chicago. The Burke-Greenfield match was the fourth Davies-sponsored sporting event that would be listed among the top fifteen events in Chicago sports in 1885.[193] It is likely that no other Chicago promoter has matched Charlie's production.

As sometimes happens, a preliminary match turns out to be a real bonus; and that happened on this evening in 1885. Glover, who was a relatively new fighter, met Tom Chandler, who was about as veteran as a fighter could be. This was the same Chandler who had been knocked out on the island in the Mississippi River thirteen years earlier. Chandler had been fighting professionally for about twenty years.

Dempsey acted as Glover's second during the fight, and he got a good show from his ringside seat. Their match was billed as for the heavyweight championship of Illinois. After a slow first round, Glover was pounding Chandler at a two-to-one punch rate. Near the end of the round, Chandler caught Glover with a blow on the neck and dropped him. Glover lay limp and motionless on the floor and then tried to rise but fell back again. He tried to rise a second time, and his legs gave way, but he was then saved by the bell for the end of the round. In order to revive Glover, Jack Dempsey bit Glover's ear so hard that he drew blood. Dempsey's action had the desired result and helped bring Glover back to consciousness. He recovered sufficiently to come out for the third round. [194]

Though groggy and weak, Glover held Chandler off and bought time. Glover then got his second wind, landed a big right hand on Chandler's left ear, knocking him out for good and winning the fight. A downstate paper reported that Glover's face was fearfully mangled during the fight and that the final blow administered to Chandler was thought to have killed him.[195] The *Tribune* reported that when Glover hit Chandler, old Tom "stiffened as though electrified, and the next moment crashed to the floor and lay perfectly motionless."[196] After their fight Chandler claimed that he had been robbed and that he should have been awarded the fight at the end of the second round when Glover could not rise within the count of ten. He thought Glover had been given a slow count in the first place and that the round was prematurely ended by the timekeeper.

Burke and Greenfield

Burke and Greenfield met at the end of the Glover-Chandler match. There was a dispute over the selection of the referee, but when that was resolved, the two fighters were introduced by Davies. Greenfield and Burke went to the center of the stage and then walked together to the ropes where Greenfield said; "If Mr. Burke beats me tonight I will say 'well done' and will shake 'im by the 'and afterwards. If I beat 'im I 'ope he will receive 'is defeat in a like manner." Burke bowed his assent and the two embarked on a highly scientific exhibition. After the five allowed rounds, both Burke and Greenfield were still standing, and both had done good work during the match. The referee declared Burke the winner of the fight and the *Herald* reported that "the shriek that went up was appalling. The Irish lad has many a friend in the city, and they couldn't do enough yelling for their favorite."[197]

Dempsey left immediately after the fight and headed for New Orleans, but as he rode south, he had to be impressed by the success that awaited fighters who participated in Davies-promoted events. About two weeks later Dempsey sent

Davies a letter from New Orleans declaring that he was anxious to meet Johnny Files, Tom Chandler, or any reputable light or middleweight in a five or six round glove contest managed by Davies.[198]

Davies gave a response that he may have regretted in years to come. As Tracy Callis has written, "Jack Dempsey is considered by many as one of the greatest boxers pound-for-pound who ever fought in the ring. He moved well and was extremely quick, agile and skillful. He was a two-handed fighter who could box or punch. His jab was quick and accurate. His right hand punch was stiff. He was game and cool under pressure. He could fight whatever style was needed to win. In short, he was a crafty boxer-puncher who was an excellent ring general."[199] Charlie told Dempsey that his hands were full at the time, but if Dempsey would come to Chicago then he would attempt to accommodate him. This was not exactly putting out the welcome mat.[200]

With Burke's success the effort to match Dempsey against the reluctant Ryan intensified and several other options were suggested. Mallahan said that after the March 2 fight he had promised Greenfield that he would have the first chance at another fight with Burke. He said that if he agreed to match Burke against Ryan, he would be breaking his word to Greenfield. Mallahan also said that he had received a telegram from Sheedy, who was in New Orleans wanting to know whether he would match Burke for a fight with Sullivan in that city. Mallahan said that he did not want to get too many irons in the fire at one time but that if Ryan wanted to stop hiding behind an alleged promise to Sheedy and really meant business about a fight with Burke, then the fight would have to be for $5,000 a side with deposits of $2,500 to bind the fight. Burke concurred in what Mallahan outlined.[201]

Burke and Sullivan proposed

The actual telegram from Sheedy and Mallahan's response to it were both published in the newspapers.[202] Sheedy proposed a ten-round fight in New Orleans between Sullivan and Burke. Ten-round fights were something unusual at the time. Mallahan responded that he would prefer to make the fight for four or six rounds if other terms could be agreed upon. The *Herald* reported that it had good word that "the match, if consummated, stands a most excellent chance of being fought in Chicago. It will be five or six weeks before there is any chance for the meeting to be held. It will then be too hot for a fight at New Orleans. I will have to be in the North."[203]

The word that Sheedy had proposed a Burke-Sullivan match in New Orleans upset Ryan, who had just a few days earlier described in great detail how much he trusted Sheedy to work in his best interests. It now seemed to Ryan that Sheedy was not working in his interest in the proposed Sullivan-Burke match. Ryan sent a telegram to Sheedy: "Chicago, March 5 – Pat Sheedy, 39 St. Charles Street, New Orleans: Your letter received. Did you telegraph Ned Mallahan to bring Jack Burke to New Orleans to meet Sullivan at a ten-round contest?"[204]

Sheedy responded by informing Ryan that he would not release him from his promise for any reason. Ryan was prohibited, Sheedy said, from fighting any person other than Sullivan until Sheedy could arrange their rematch. In this light Sheedy did not look like such a great friend after all.

As the drama played out—and with Ryan drama seemed a constant—preparation for a Greenfield-Burke rematch continued under Davies' supervision. Burke left for Racine, Wisconsin, to go into training with Chandler for the rematch. Greenfield went to Beloit, Wisconsin, to train under the supervision of Nobby Clark. Beloit was becoming a place commonly utilized by fighters training in the Chicago area. Davies had arranged for the match to take place at Battery D. It was to be another five-round affair with the same gloves as used in their first meeting in Chicago. Davies' entertainment on the night of the rematch would include a contest for a gold medal that he would award to the middleweight champion of Illinois.

Paddy Ryan shows the white feather

Both Burke and Davies had become annoyed with the situation that had developed with Ryan. It appeared that Mallahan was delaying making any matches for Burke, and their agreement that Burke would not participate in any matches without Mallahan's approval had prevented Davies from covering the forfeit money proposed earlier by Vidvard for a match with Ryan. Mallahan's foot-dragging could cost Burke a substantial amount of money, even though the proposed fight was to be a finish fight.

On March 9, Burke and Davies went to C. C. Corbet's office at 124 Clark Street to cover Ryan's forfeit money. After Davies deposited his money, he asked Vidvard where he proposed holding the match, and the he replied that he wanted the fight to take place in Chicago. Davies replied that this proposal was sheer nonsense and that any thinking man knew that a bare-knuckle finish fight to a finish could not possibly be carried off in Chicago without insulting the city's government. Vidvard responded that he thought if the fight were properly managed, it might take place in Chicago as anywhere else. Davies responded, "Oh, well, South State Street may possess more influence backed by a better reputation with the powers that be than East Randolph Street does, but I shall have nothing to do with it."[205] Davies promised that if Vidvard and his people insisted on having the match in Chicago, he would have nothing to do with it.

Vidvard then suggested that perhaps some other person would back Burke for the fight with Ryan, and Burke responded, "No, sir, Mr. Davies is handling my interests at present, and I will be guided wholly by him in this matter." Vidvard then asked where Davies proposed holding the fight, and the Parson answered that he would propose Butte City, Montana Territory. He pointed out that Pete McCoy had gone to Butte City to meet the Montana territorial champion by the name of Jack McDonald, and McCoy had received fair treatment. Moreover, Ryan had fought in Butte City when he was under Davies' management and had knocked out Jack Waite on October 21, 1881. Newspaper accounts of these events pointed out that given Ryan's unfortunate conduct over the past several years; he could not maintain his reputation and continue to quibble about the details of the proposed fight with Burke.

Burke was not the only fighter accepting Ryan's challenge. Sullivan had accepted the challenge and the *Police Gazette* wanted to know whether Ryan would accept Sullivan's counter-challenge. Vidvard sent a telegram to Fox advising him that Ryan would meet Sullivan after he met Burke.[206]

At a second meeting between Davies and Vidvard, Burke was not present because he was training in Racine.[207] Ryan, never a man to train too much for anything, was present for this meeting. It was agreed that McDonald would be the stakeholder for the proposed fight, but that if McDonald would not agree to serve then Alderman Appleton could be the stakeholder. Vidvard insisted once again that the fight should take place in Chicago.

At this point Vidvard was aware that his insistence on a finish fight in Chicago would kill the entire deal, and his motivation for doing that is not clear. Davies again said that he would agree to a fight within one hundred miles of Butte City for $2,500 a side and to a finish. He would also agree to fight at any other point where he felt assured that the fight could continue to a finish. Vidvard said that Ryan would agree to fight in the Montana Territory if Davies would increase the stakes to $5,000 a side; otherwise the fight would have to take place within 100 miles of Chicago.[208]

Ryan then proposed sparring ten rounds at Battery D. This was a marked departure from Ryan's claim that he wanted a finish fight. Davies said that the talking was through if Ryan and Vidvard were talking about a fight to the finish in Chicago. Vidvard replied that the talking was through if Davies insisted on going to Montana Territory for the fight. After heated exchanges it was agreed that no final decisions would be made immediately. In the estimation of the press it was clear that Ryan and his friends wanted to back out of a finish fight with Burke. Jack McDonald said that he was disgusted with Ryan's behavior but that he would follow the lead of Davies in whatever he decided to do.[209]

A series of telegrams passed between Ryan and Jimmy Patterson, another fight promoter referred to at this point as Ryan's New York representative. Ryan asked Patterson to schedule a fight with Sullivan for the last part of May. However, this telegram was followed by another from Ryan saying that he had decided that he would fight Burke with hard gloves to a finish for $2,500, either in Butte City or New Orleans.[210] It was nearly impossible to keep up with Ryan, as he bounced around in the wind like an old rooster weather vane, and all of this discussion with him took attention away from the scheduled Greenfield-Burke rematch.[211]

Another bounce by Ryan soon followed. He announced that he had been called out of Chicago and that he was sorry Vidvard had not been able to arrange for him to meet Burke.[212] He also regretted that he would not be able to meet Sullivan because having lost Vidvard's support he could no longer raise the $5,000 stake money that Sullivan proposed. Fox then stepped forward and said that he would back Ryan for a fight with Sullivan and that he would pay all of Ryan's expenses whether or not Paddy defeated Sullivan. The proposed match once again was to take place in Butte City.[213] About this time the *Police Gazette* had rated the heavyweights in March 1885: (1) Sullivan, (2) Mitchell, (3) George Fryer, (4) Burke, (5) Greenfield, (6) Kilrain, (7) Ryan, (8) McCaffrey, and (9) Cleary. Ryan was sure to drop out of this equation soon.[214]

Davies was doing little to line up matches in Chicago for Dempsey, who had been scheduled to fight Charles Bixamos on March 19, 1885 in New Orleans to a finish for $250 a side. But Dempsey was really interested in a match with Burke and sent a letter to Chicago dated March 13, 1885, in which he proposed to spar Burke for either four, five, six or eight rounds under Queensberry rules for gate receipts.[215] Dempsey's letter coincided with an article in the New Orleans' *Picayune*, in which Sheedy reported that Dempsey had come to him saying that he wanted to fight Burke. Sheedy spoke against the idea, saying that Burke was thirty pounds heavier than Dempsey.[216] The match with Burke was never made, and Sheedy's advice to Dempsey became part of strong enmity that would exist between Davies and Sheedy for many years.

Burke was dominating the Chicago prizefight news in early 1885, but Cardiff reemerged at the end of March. At this point Billy O'Brien purported to speak for Cardiff, who may have decided to go back under O'Brien's management because Davies was spending so much time promoting Burke's interest. Fighters can have tender sensibilities. O'Brien proposed to match Cardiff against the winner of the rematch between Burke and Greenfield.[217] It appeared likely that Davies would try to accommodate what Cardiff was proposing.

Burke and Greenfield part II

The Greenfield-Burke rematch on Monday, March 23, was another bout between well-matched heavyweight contenders. About seven thousand were present at Battery D for the six-round set-to. "High silk hats" predominated in the audience worn by businessmen who "adorn a pew, a counter, a drawing-room, or the outskirts of a prize ring with equal grace." Among those present were Vidvard, Vere Davies (Parson Davies' younger brother), Billy Pinkerton, police lieutenants Shea and Kipley (who would become best know years later in connection with Chicago's Haymarket riots), nearly every Chicago alderman, and numerous members of the board of trade. This was the fifth event sponsored by Parson Davies that would be listed among the top fifteen sporting events of 1885.[218]

The main event of the evening began with an announcement by Davies that the principals had failed to agree upon a referee. Burke's people suggested McDonald, among several others. Greenfield's people wanted a State Street businessman named Jack Miller, who had grown up in Birmingham, England, Greenfield's own home. Finally, they settled on two referees: Andy Hanley, for Greenfield's satisfaction, and Andy Hughes, to keep Burke happy. Two referees acting as judges of any prizefight is a dangerous and ill-advised thing.

The fighting began at about ten p.m. The blows came bang, bang, bang from both fighters, and punishment was dished out about evenly. At the end of the fourth round, Burke forced Greenfield away from a clinch and caught him with a heavy blow on the left side of his neck. Greenfield was staggered and looked as if he was about to drop when time was called from the direction of Greenfield's corner. As Greenfield regained his composure, the timekeepers yelled "Go on, go on!" Confusion reigned. The noise in the armory was so deafening that it took some time before it was realized that the round had lasted twenty-five seconds longer than three minutes. At the end of the sixth round referee Hughes shouted that Burke had done all the fighting and should get the win. Pandemonium followed until referee Hanley rushed into the ring shaking his fist in Hughes' face and announcing that the decision should be for Greenfield. Another round was proposed, and the men pulled their gloves back on. After a little cautious sparring, Greenfield landed a right on Burke's ribs and followed with a savage rush. Burke supposedly landed the greatest number of clean hits when time for the seventh round was called. Again there was a disagreement between the two referees. Finally, Davies brought Lieutenant Laughlin of the Chicago Police Department into the ring with two detectives, and they jointly stopped the fight. After discussion, Hughes insisted that the fight should be Burke's, and Hanley took the position that the match was a draw. The police said that they had interfered because they saw that the audience was becoming excited, and they feared a riot. The conclusion was that Davies had made several thousand more shekels than he possessed before the evening had begun.[219]

Immediately after the fight, O'Brien challenged both Burke and Greenfield to box Cardiff six or eight rounds for the net receipts of the house, with the winner to take everything if either man was stopped or knocked out. If both men were standing at the end, then the receipts were to be divided evenly. A match with Greenfield became unlikely because Alf announced that he was leaving Chicago to return to England.

To show their appreciation for the entertainment he had provided, the Chicago sporting crowd sponsored a benefit for Greenfield prior to his departure. Those who volunteered their services included Glover, Dalton, Bradburn, Clark, and many other local fighters. The press pointed out that Greenfield had left his wife behind in Birmingham and that she had given birth to a son who had died before Alf had ever seen him. It was time for Alf to return to England, his wife, and their five other children, and Chicago wanted him to leave with a decent sum of money for all his efforts.[220]

Little Casino – Tommy Warren

On the evening of the benefit, Greenfield sparred with Glover. Greenfield's appearance was met with a storm of applause and the orchestra present stuck up "God Save the Queen." Before the evening ended, Alf was presented with an elegant silk fighting shirt of a delicate pink tint and embroidered with the words "Merrie England." It was called "a tasty piece of work." Before he left the U. S., Greenfield went to Danville, Illinois, to participate in an exhibition there. Other fighters who went to Danville included Glover, Harry Franks, Nobby Clark, James Connelly and a kid named Tommy Warren.[221]

Warren, known as Little Casino, was a featherweight fighter who came to Chicago from the Wyoming Territory. He would turn out to be a streak of lighting in the prizefighting game for several years to come.[222] Today, Tommy would probably have been put on medication. He was a hyperactive kid with an apparent loose screw, but he managed to delight fight fans who witnessed his matches, and women loved his childish looks and diminutive size. While the Burke-Greenfield phenomenon was over in Chicago, the Ryan-Sullivan soap opera continued throughout March and April 1885.

As the national sporting world focused on Sullivan and Ryan, Davies continued to work with Burke. In mid-April 1885 he took Burke to Madison, Wisconsin, for an exhibition at the roller-rink.[223] Burke had been sick for some time and had been confined to his bed for over a week before going to Madison.[224]

Two days later, the Parson was at the Chicago Athletic Club, where he was a member. The C.A.C. was composed of about forty young businessmen, several railroad officials, and "men about town." The club's management had arranged a private fight between Warren, who was 112 pounds, and Andy Hanley, who was 123 pounds. The fight ended at the end of the first round when Hanley broke his right forearm.

Just at that time the Chicago police came charging up the stairs of the C.A.C. under the belief that a bare-knuckle fight to the finish was in progress. Davies kept his head and immediately called the officer in charge to one side. He then went with that officer to Doyle's home, where Davies explained that there was a misunderstanding about the nature of the fight. He assured Doyle that the fight was a glove match and was not a finish fight. After a few minutes with the remaining members being held inside the club by the police, Davies returned and told everyone that the matter was now "all right" and that Doyle had called off the dogs.[225]

Davies was a busy man. Four days after smoothing things over with Doyle, a meeting was held with Burke, Davies, Colonel C. D. Curtis, chief of the fire department at Helena, Montana, and his brother, J. H. Curtis, a prominent attorney at Butte City. Davies wanted to know whether there were any laws in the Montana Territory that would prohibit the Sullivan-Ryan fight from being staged at Butte City. Curtis assured the Parson that there were no laws that would bar the fight there. Both Curtis and his brother promised to telegraph Davies immediately if it appeared that any legal interference might be planned. This would be valuable information for both promoters and gamblers to know.

Mitchell comes to Chicago for the first time

Burke returned to Madison for a second exhibition on April 21, this time with Chandler.[226] Later in the month Burke and Chandler were scheduled to leave for a trip arranged by Davies to Oshkosh, Fond du Lac, and other cheese retreats to put on additional exhibitions.[227] Bigger things than exhibitions in Wisconsin were in store for Burke. On April 20, Mitchell showed up in Chicago. He was nattily dressed in a cheviot (or frock) coat with light checked trousers, a bark brown Derby hat and English walking shoes, and he was carrying a silver headed walking stick. Mitchell was on his way to California to meet Cleary and Mike Donahue before returning to the East. He stopped in Chicago to see whether he could arrange a match with Burke.

On arriving in Chicago, Mitchell went to Vere Davies' saloon, where he met with Parson Davies, Burke, Chandler, Charles Hoff, a New York friend of Mitchell, Nobby Clark, and Arthur G. Clampett, a champion swimmer who was accompanying Mitchell to California. Mitchell told the press that he didn't know whether a fight with Burke could be arranged because Davies hadn't offered him enough money to appear. According to Mitchell it was only a matter of money. Where money was concerned there was no "only" with Davies.

Davies told the press that he thought there would be a match but not for several weeks, given Mitchell's existing obligations in California. Mitchell said that he first had to deal with Cleary and that he thought more of Cleary's ability as a fighter than he did of Sullivan's. Mitchell spent a good part of his life trying to antagonize Sullivan. He said that he didn't think too much of McCaffrey, who had spent his time sparring with Cardiff and who had relied on Billy O'Brien to build up his reputation in the newspapers.

Davies posed a question: "Do you know where Sullivan got his reputation? Mike McDonald gave it to him. When Sullivan was out here a few months before he fought Ryan he hadn't a dollar in his pocket. He wanted in the worst sort of way to fight Ryan, but he couldn't get anyone to back him. Mike asked me what I thought of him, and I told Mike he was a good one, so Mike gave me a thousand to make a match for $5000. Our negotiations fell through, but the advertising Sullivan got then boomed him so that a few months later, he had but little trouble in getting the $2,500 they fought for. But it was Mike McDonald who first put John L. Sullivan to the front." [228]

The Store

That same week, the *Tribune* reported that Davies was taking over The Store at Clark and Monroe streets. Davies assumed operation of the saloon effective May 1.[229] Charlie and his brother Vere had operated the Champion's Rest for only about one year before Charlie took over The Store. He then gave Vere his interest in the property known as the Champion's Rest at 219 Randolph.

For his part, McDonald was retiring from the liquor business and taking a business office in the Montauk block. The terms of the agreement for Davies to assume the operation of The Store are not known. It seems likely that McDonald only leased the premises to Davies and continued to own the land, fixtures, furniture, and equipment. It also seems likely that McDonald simply told Davies that he would like him to operate The Store, and Davies agreed because this could be a profitable business and would provide a personal accommodation for McDonald. Charlie never liked operating a saloon because it tied him down too much.

McDonald and his wife Mary had operated The Store for many years. The building had a prime location just two blocks west of the Palmer House. McDonald ran games of faro, roulette, keno, poker, and hazard on the second floor, and Mary kept a rooming house above. Mike's brother Ed worked as a cashier in the pool room at The Store. It was a nice little family operation.

In addition, for many years the polling place for the Third Precinct of the First Ward was located in the blind alley just outside the back door of The Store.[230] After taking over The Store, Charlie had the place entirely refitted and had a grand opening on May 18. In 1907 Otto Floto, who had worked as Davies' assistant for several years, claimed that on the night Davies had his grand opening at The Store Charlie was forced to give One Eyed Connelly the worst beating of his life.[231]

The only exciting news in Chicago sports in May 1885 was Warren, who was described as the "pet of a large part of the local sporting fraternity." The *Herald* posted a challenge for any featherweight to fight Warren, but no one came forward and the challenge with taken down. In mid-May, it was announced that Warren had finally been matched to fight Chris Sommers, a St. Louis featherweight, at the Park Theater. Warren weighed 115 pounds for the match and Sommers 135. Warren won the match on a foul when Sommers hit him after he had slipped down, and Warren was awarded the fight. Warren was spending time with another Chicago promoter named Billy Lakeman, who operated a sporting establishment known as the Spirit of the Times at numbers 1 and 3 North Clark Street.

In early May there had been a lull in sporting entertainment in Chicago, but Davies intended to change that situation. Cardiff was no longer a factor in the city; he had relocated to St. Paul. Greenfield had returned to England. Dalton was injured and was no longer a creditable attraction, and Ryan had moved back to the East. Davies and William Emmett, the long-time manager of the Olympic Theater, then met at the business office of the theater. A few days later, Davies disappeared from Chicago.

Speculation was that Davies had gone to Madison and Oshkosh to arrange for additional exhibitions by Burke and Chandler. Charlie, however, did not go to Wisconsin. Instead he went east to try to arrange for a huge outdoor entertainment to take place at Chicago's Driving Park under Emmett's supervision. The program that Davies planned would consist of short distance walking and running matches, wrestling, club-swinging, sword and knife combats, jumping, sparring, and other exhibitions.

The wrestlers were to include Duncan Ross, Clarence Whistler, James Faulkner, and the great Muldoon. Money inducements had been offered to Sullivan and Burke to appear in a glove match. Burke had agreed to meet Sullivan, who indicated that he was favorably disposed to such a contest. [232] There was no sense in waiting on Mitchell to make his way back to Chicago. Although Mitchell was writing letters from San Bruno, California, telling Davies about his good intentions, those good intentions did not put bread on the table. A promoter could not let a single fighter clog up the process. Moreover, when Mitchell finally did fight Cleary, he was knocked down twice in the fourth round and very groggy when the police interfered and stopped the fight, saving Mitchell's bacon. Their match was declared a draw but Mitchell's stock slipped.[233]

A few days after the news about Davies' summer sporting spectacular, he revealed that Sullivan and Patsey Shepherd, John L.'s most recent manager, had signed articles for a four-round glove fight with Burke, Queensberry rules, with the winner to take 65 percent of the gate and the loser 35 percent.

Supposedly Sullivan had gone into active training for the fight, which probably meant that he was walking to the saloon rather than taking a cab. This fight would be a physical mismatch in terms of size. At the time the fight was made, Sullivan weighed about 232 pounds and Burke weighed about 160 pounds, and he was four inches shorter than Sullivan. Burke was the size of the heavyweight fighters that Sullivan preferred. He liked to pound on the little guys.

On the evening of May 28, Burke was in the Market Hall at St. Paul to spar John S. Barnes, a Wisconsin heavyweight who was a favorite of fight fans in the Twin Cities.[234] Their fight was Queensberry rules, with gloves for four rounds. Burke was to knockout Barnes in order to win the fight. It seems that Burke agreed to this fight only to further his training for his fight with Sullivan. It provided a reasonable tune-up for Burke, who might otherwise become stale. Barnes was afraid of Burke from the start and skipped around the stage "like a sore-legged hen" to stay away. Burke finally reached Barnes and knocked him off his feet. In the second round Burke caught Barnes with a right, and Barnes held on as the police stopped the fight. The referee then declared Burke the winner, giving him the receipts amounting to only $350. This was not a great deal of money and illustrated why a big payday in a town like Chicago was so important.

When Burke returned to Chicago, he and Davies learned that Mitchell was not going to show up in the city for a match with Burke. Mitchell telegrammed to say that he was going to stay on the Pacific coast for at least thirty days to see whether he could arrange a second match with Cleary. It was a good thing that Davies and Burke had not put all their eggs in Mitchell's basket.[235]

Burke and Sullivan meet at Chicago

Burke was in excellent form for the Sullivan contest. He had bulked up for the fight and raised his weight to about 168 pounds, while some reports said that Sullivan had trimmed down to about 205 pounds. Burke's best assets were his left hand and his nimbleness in the ring. He would need to be nimble to avoid the bull-rushes that characterized Sullivan's style. At some point Sullivan would use his weight to try to force Burke to the ropes, where Sullivan could pound away at the smaller man. Their match was to be five rounds, and it had been a long time since Sullivan had engaged in any match that lasted more than four rounds. Burke's best hope was that the fat boy would tire out.

Burke described his training routine for the fight, which seemed much more reasonable than the program Ryan had followed in preparing for his championship fight with Sullivan. Burke got up at about seven a.m. and took a short walk before eating a breakfast of rare beefsteak or mutton chops and a couple of soft-boiled eggs with dry toast and tea. After breakfast he took a fast walk with this trainer. After a rub down he ran a two hundred yard sprint and then had lunch. Following lunch he engaged in club swinging, used the bar bells, tossed the fighting ball for an hour or more, and then wound up with a slow walk of about twenty miles followed by a light evening meal. He also skipped rope every day.

As the fight approached, Sullivan repeatedly put off the time of his departure for Chicago. Sullivan's failure to come to Chicago had to be driving Davies frantic because he was well aware of Sullivan's mercurial nature. Finally, Sullivan left New York and was supposedly on the way to Chicago when word came that he had decided to stop in Philadelphia on personal business. He finally arrived in Chicago on June 12, with the fight scheduled for June 13. He went out on the evening he arrived in Chicago and stopped at The Store. A crowd gathered that was so large that the street cars could not make it down the road in front of the building. Sullivan then slipped out the back door and down the alley to probably drink somewhere else.

The personal business that Sullivan had been taking care of in Philadelphia involved liquor. He got drunk. The *Tribune* reported that when Sullivan arrived in Chicago he looked bad and was fat, with beefy proportions and a heavy expression and countenance – not 205 pounds. He appeared to be suffering effects from his long-continued dissipation and painful carbuncles on his back and neck. After the fight with Burke the gossip was that Sullivan held Burke cheaply and had not trained at all for their fight. He was not only fat but out of condition.[236]

On the night of the match, ten to twelve thousand people sat in and around the grand stand at the Driving Park—about twice as many patrons as could have been accommodated at Battery D. Ladies were usually not allowed at prize-fights, but they were quite numerous in private boxes that had been sold for the evening. The crowd included members of the board of trade and other businessmen who counted their wealth in the millions. The *Herald* reported that Davies was everywhere at once, full of business, but always ready with a joke or work for all his friends.[237]

The usual suspects attended, including Vidvard, Billy O'Brien, and Sheedy. Wrestlers such as Faulkner and Evan "the Strangler" Lewis were there. Fighters including Glover, Chandler, Bradburn, and McCaffrey were present. Billy Pinkerton, the head of the Chicago branch of the Pinkerton Detective Agency, was present. Lieutenant Shea led a squad of Chicago detectives, and Davies had hired a posse of Pinkerton men to help keep order.

The preliminary entertainment began about four p.m. The best match was provided by Tommy Warren, who battled Arthur Majesty of Bloomington, Illinois. Majesty was a graduate of Illinois Wesleyan University and taught court reporting and boxing in Bloomington. He was managed by Lee Cheney. The Magesty-Warren match was warm enough to catch the attention of the crowd. Warren was a mere boy in appearance but was heartily cheered by the huge throng and was awarded the victory.

The featured Sullivan-Burke match did not begin until about ten o'clock. Just as the orchestra stopped playing a movement, Sullivan appeared from the gates north of the clubhouse and walked two hundred yards to the ring. Imagine the sight of the big champion striding to the outdoor ring! He was the first man to appear for the match, and he was in a foul mood as he walked down the track to the ring with his people, including Sheedy, Patsey Sheppard, Arthur Chambers, and "Nobby" Clark. The boils he had on his back and neck were covered with a black plaster, and Sullivan was unsmiling and flabby. The *Post Dispatch* said that when he was weighed just before the fight, he was 237 pounds and was clearly not in the best fighting trim. He entered the ring and leaned back in his chair and coolly glanced about without acknowledging the audience.[238] The "Terminator" was in the house.

Burke appeared in the green and white colors that had become his trademark in Chicago and was greeted by a cheer from the crowd. He weighed 170 pounds just before the fight and was hard and firm. Davies, Chandler, and Mike Malloy acted as seconds for Burke. The referee was chosen and Lieutenant Shea stepped to the center of the stage and made a show by carefully examining the four-ounce gloves before pronouncing them all right for the match. Shea would obviously receive a few dollars for this service and for otherwise staying out of the way.

The fight went all Sullivan's way. His superiority was attributed to his bull-rushes and using his weight to advantage. As the two men faced each other in the center of the ring, the disparity in their height and weight was startling. Many observers thought Burke looked like a mere boy facing Goliath but without his sling or stone. After ten seconds of cautious sparring in the first round, Sullivan made his first rush, and Burke went down to the floor on his hands and knees having been pushed down by the sheer force of Sullivan's charge. Burke arose and avoided a second rush by Sullivan by springing to one side. Seemingly confident and alert, Burke was slowly backed toward the ropes before a right hand to his shoulder put him down a second time. Burke was not hurt so much as bulled over by the blow. He arose and dashed forward and landed a good left on Sullivan's ribs before Sullivan caught him in a clinch, with Burke striking Sullivan savagely as they separated.

In the second and third rounds, Burke fought more defensively. As the third round started, Burke stopped a rush by feinting and ducking a right from

Sullivan. This made the big boy boil over in anger, and he made another rush with Burke avoiding most of Sullivan's blows and stopping his advance with left jabs. Sullivan opened the fourth round with another patented rush and forced Burke to a corner, where he floored him with a heavy body blow. After a clinch Sullivan sent Burke to the floor for the fourth time with several right hand blows. The general impression was that Burke was going down not from the sting of Sullivan's punches but from the sheer size and weight of his being, but Davies and the referee were both expecting to see Burke laid out senseless at almost any moment.

In the fifth round Sullivan again forced the fighting and went at Burke hammer and tongs. Again he started with a rush with clenched teeth and an ugly scowl. Burke went down again and again—five times in the final round. It appeared to be a physical impossibility for Burke to keep his feet because of the tremendous difference in weight and height, and there was no real square knock down. Burke got in some good licks, but they seemed to have no effect on Sullivan. Burke stayed through the round and appeared to have a perfectly clear head, but the fight was Sullivan's and was awarded to him promptly. Burke walked away from the fight showing no sign of any punishment. The Burke-Sullivan fight was the sixth sporting event sponsored by Parson Davies that would be listed among the top fifteen events held in Chicago in 1885.[239]

The next day Sullivan was asked whether Burke was the cleverest of all the fighters from the other side. He replied: "Oh, he's clever enough but what good is his cleverness? He can't hit hard enough to hurt anyone." He said that he wanted to do Burke (i.e., clean his clock) so that the Chicago crowd couldn't call their fight a draw. As far as he was concerned winning the fight was all he wanted. Sullivan concluded: "Burke is a game one. I will say that for him." Sullivan quickly left Chicago and headed back to Philadelphia.[240]

Burke was seen the next day at The Store. He said he felt first rate except for a bit of swelling in his nose. His friends congratulated him as the first man who ever stood up to Sullivan for five Queensberry rounds. A few days later Burke was asked what he thought of Sullivan. He said that he had faced lots of good fighters on both sides of the Atlantic, "but not one of them can in any way compare with the champion." Burke said that he did not agree with those who claimed that Sullivan was not a clever man in the ring. He felt that Sullivan was both intelligent and quick on his feet. Burke concluded: "He is not only powerful, but his guard is fine, and it takes a man who has acquired a deal of skill in the business to stop or get away from his blows." He noted Sullivan's wicked smile, which could make a man a bit nervous, especially when an opponent saw the big man's eyes light up.[241] Sullivan's take from his fight with Burke in Chicago was said to be $4,800.

Burke and Mitchell

The Burke-Sullivan fight and particularly the associated big payday was enough to draw Mitchell back to Chicago. He arrived on June 22, 1885.[242] Final negotiations for a fight had not been completed, so Mitchell went to the Palmer House and then to The Store. Davies and Mitchell went out to Driving Park to meet Burke and arrange the fourth fight between the two men.[243] They had first fought a bare-knuckle draw in England and then faced each other in New York in a four-round glove match also called a draw. The third time Burke and Mitchell met, the police had interfered and there was no result recorded. Unlike Sullivan, there was not much difference between the height and weight of Burke and Mitchell, and their fight promised to be a more balanced affair.[244]

Mitchell and Burke fought at Battery D on the evening of June 29, 1885. Seven thousand patrons packed the house, and Davies acted as master of ceremonies. The first round was slow but the second was more heated with Mitchell leading the action and getting in several good body blows. At the opening of the third round Mitchell planted an "ugly blow" to Burke's stomach, and Burke claimed a foul that was not allowed. Burke was winded by the low shot and Mitchell controlled the remainder of the round.

The fourth round was much like the third with Mitchell seeming to have the better of the round. As the match drew to an end, things grew warmer. Burke reached for Mitchell's stomach and followed up with a blow to the chest that nearly dropped him. Mitchell then fought back to Burke's body and ribs. The sixth and final round was the best of the match. Mitchell put a right to Burke's ribs, and Burke countered to Mitchell's head. Mitchell made a rush, but was staggered by a left that appeared to daze him for a moment, after which he fought in a wild manner. After a clinch Burke knocked Mitchell against the ropes and then rushed in to force the fighting to the very end. At the end of this round, applause and shouts shook the place. It was one of the prettiest meetings ever seen in the city, the men being so evenly matched. The referee declared it a draw.[245]

June 29 was a big day for Davies, but the next day was bad for one of his longtime friends and close associates, Joe Mackin. They had been friends for years and were two of the founders of the first Elks Lodge in Chicago. Mackin was the closest protégé of McDonald and had tried to fix the November 1884 election in a way that would have given Democrats control of the selection of an Illinois U. S. Senator. A perjury indictment against Mackin for lying to a state grand jury came to trial on June 30. The trial lasted only two days. Two brothers were called and testified that Mackin had retained them to produce the fraudulent Republican Party ticket in November 1884 and that they had delivered the completed product to him at the Palmer House. A man named Fallis testified that he had engraved the head of the phony ticket. Members of the grand jury and court reporters were called and repeated the denials of these things that Mackin had made before them. Mackin made virtually no defense. He relied on the testimony of so-called reputation witnesses.[246]

Davies would not forget his friends, but it was imperative to keep things moving in the world of entertainment. After the Mitchell fight, it seemed that Burke had played out the string in Chicago. The two fights with Greenfield had been exciting and had broken a long layoff for pugilism in the city. The fight with Sullivan had been the biggest sporting event of its kind in Chicago history, and the battle with Mitchell was a terrific encore. But the public is always looking for variation in the tune being played and always wants something new.

In early July, Davies took Burke to St. Louis for sparring matches with Chandler at the Casino Theater as the "Parson Davies' Specialty Co."[247] The *Post Dispatch* was impressed and gushed that the men were not only able to take care of themselves but could afford first-class entertainment to lovers of the manly art. The sparring was part of a program that included a fine tenor, Wallace King and a quartet of singers and a juggler. Predictions were that a St. Louis fighter named Fred Zachritz might meet Burke at the Casino for a "friendly set-to for four or five rounds."

Friends of Zachritz were said to be meeting with Davies to see what could be arranged. This meeting was to be scheduled at the Union Base Ball Park in St. Louis.[248] Before that match, Davies arranged a match with an all-around Missouri athlete named Charles Effers (sometimes "Eiffert") on July 10. Between negotiations with the friends of Zachritz and Effers' Missouri backers, Davies made a quick trip back to Chicago to meet with Edward Hanlan about the possibility of managing five horse races in Chicago for Hanlan.[249]

Davies was back in St. Louis for the Burke's fight with Effers, whom he described as "a strong, finely built young duck." Effers weighed about 180 pounds and was in good physical shape, being a member of the local Turners' Society. Burke played with Effers for about one minute and then struck him a smashing blow in the ribs with his left, followed by a quick right to the face. Before Effers recovered, Burke threw a left to his face with such force that it lifted Effers off his feet and sent him to the floor. Effers stood up and declared that he had had enough. He went to the footlights in the Casino Theater and said: "I came here tonight for a friendly set-to, but this man has tried to kill me."[250] This brought a great laugh from the audience.

Burke then stepped forward and said that his professional reputation prevented him from letting any man stand before him without downing him if he could. To mollify the audience for the brevity of the match with Effers, Burke and Chandler agreed to demonstrate the art of sparring. A first rule of entertainment is never let the crowd go home disappointed. This appears to be the last of Jack Burke's matches that Davies personally managed for several months.

Davies' business at The Store was raided by the police on the evening of July 21. Before the raid the chief had ordered all gambling houses closed and had sent messages to all the proprietors of the gaming house telling them to meet him at Battery D armory on the evening of July 21. At their meeting he told all the proprietors that they were required to close up that night and to keep their gaming businesses closed.

Most of the operators complied. However, the police made a tour of the gaming houses and at 176 Clark Street could hear the rattle of chips. Employees of The Store were out on Clark Street and told the police that the noise that was heard was merely from putting away paraphernalia, but the police were not buying that line and knocked in the front door to carry out their raid.[251]

Burke tours Wisconsin

On July 24 Burke left Chicago with Glover for a tour of Wisconsin.[252] Just who was on the tour is unclear because articles published in Chicago refer to Burke and Glover as the prime participants, while articles published in other newspapers refer to Burke and Chandler. On July 25 Burke was in Milwaukee for a scheduled five-round bout at Stensby's Theater with a local athlete named Frank Witten. In the first round Witten hit Burke on the top of his head, severely injuring his right hand, and had to retire from the fights. Some articles incorrectly report this fight as a knockout for Burke.[253]

On July 28 and 29, Burke and Chandler were in Wausau, Wisconsin, on the Wisconsin River with a reasonable house each night. Burke had a friendly set-to with a local fighter known as Professor Lewis in soft gloves. Thirteen hundred people paid in Fond du Lac on July 31, and on August 1, they went on to Oshkosh, where The Oshkosh Rifles presented an exhibition at Nell's Hall on a very hot night.[254] They were in La Crosse on August 4, where Burke faced a heavyweight named Peter Nichols (sometimes recorded as Michaels) and stopped him in the second round.[255]

Burke moved on to Eau Claire's Opera House on August 7, where he knocked out a local fighter named John W. Curtis in three rounds and continued on to scheduled events at Stillwater, Minnesota, and St. Paul, where Burke appeared at the Music Hall on August 10.[256] Articles at the time said that when the Wisconsin tour wound up it would be extended through California. Then Jack received word that his wife, who had been sick before he left Chicago, was seriously ill and had taken a turn for the worse. He cut the trip short and returned to Chicago.

Burke goes to California

After Mrs. Burke recovered, Burke and Chandler started west to California. They sparred in Dubuque, Iowa, on August 17, and on August 28 were in Des Moines, where Jack knocked out Mike Haley in one round.[257] On Saturday, September 5, Burke was in Omaha, where he knocked out the state champion Mike Richie in one round using big eight ounce gloves.[258] From Nebraska the aggregation dropped down to Leavenworth, Kansas, on the evening of September 10 for an appearance there on Saturday, September 12 at the local opera house.[259] They then went to West Kansas City for appearances at Hanson's Opera House on Wednesday and Thursday, September 16 and 17.[260] Their stay was extended to Saturday, September 19 because Burke's offer to pay $100 to any man who could stay with him for four rounds had been accepted by a man named Cooke.[261] From Kansas City, Burke went to Denver, Colorado, where he was supposed to meet John Clow.

Road trips were a relatively easy way for a decent fighter to make good money and earn a reputation in more remote parts of the country. On the other hand they clearly were not calculated to keep a fighter ring sharp. While Burke and Chandler were traveling, the *Post Dispatch* reported that efforts to arrange a match in Chicago between Burke and Mike Donovan had failed "owing to the fact that Burke prefers to fight 'chumps.'"[262] As Burke continued west, Davies left Chicago for New York on August 16 to find new entertainment for Chicago during the fall of 1885.[263]

Davies had not been idle while Burke was touring through Wisconsin, Iowa, Nebraska, Kansas, and Colorado. With Burke on the road, Davies first turned his attention to managing a fight between Tommy Warren and forty-year-old Joe Morris of Chicago. The condition of the match was that Warren had to best Morris within four rounds or forfeit $50. The fight was to take place at the smaller venue of the Park Theater. Again Davies was able to put bodies in every available seat.[264]

With his first punch Warren caught Morris on his aging nose and bloodied it nicely. Warren forced the fighting and knocked Morris down in both the first and second rounds. Morris' age began to tell and before the second round ended, he threw a punch that carried his own body to the ground by itself. In the third round Morris commenced grabbing onto Warren to prevent the inevitable outcome. Nothing could induce Morris to loosen the grip he had around Warren's neck. The effort to throw off Morris winded Warren. The fourth round was a carbon copy of the third, except for the last minute when Warren dropped Morris for the third time with a right hand to the body and a quick left to his head. Morris was not knocked out and Warren lost the forfeit money but still made $350 as his part of the gate receipts.[265]

Three days after the Warren-Morris show, Davies went to Bloomington, Illinois, to watch Warren fight Arthur Majesty a second time.[266] These two fighters had been on the undercard on the night of the Sullivan-Burke fight and had impressed those present. In Bloomington the press referred to Warren as a midget whose claims that he was a fighter were likely to provoke a smile from those unfamiliar with this ability. The *Pantagraph* said that Warren was born in Shropshire, England, of Irish parents. Actually, he was born on June 7, 1865, in Los Angeles, California. He was described as the featherweight champion of the Pacific Coast. He was a very pleasant talker and a well-informed person and "slightly of the dude appearance."[267]

The Warren-Majesty exhibition took place in the Opera House in Bloomington. The night was intensely hot, and during the day it had been nearly 100 degrees. The crowd included a large number of sporting people but also a large representation of the most highly respected citizens, including several city officials. Richard Dunn, who had fought Cardiff more than a year earlier at Durley Hall, was matched with Rudy Schroder in a lively three rounds. He followed that up with a three-round exhibition with John H. Coyle, a local machinist whose father was a member of the Bloomington police department.

The Majesty-Warren wind up was the best ever seen in the town and even superior to the shows put on by Sullivan during his two prior appearances in town. For science, their match had never been equaled or surpassed anywhere. Warren was called a wonder and Majesty was credited for staying with him. The sympathy of the audience was naturally with Majesty, but Warren proved a strong favorite on the finish.

The next day Majesty announced that he was dissatisfied with the outcome and although he had no ambition to be a professional fighter, he challenged Warren to a finish fight at the Park Theater in Chicago. Of course, the presence of Davies and the proposed venue for a fight in Chicago strongly suggests that Davies liked what he saw in Bloomington, and he was the person who proposed a third match in Chicago.[268]

In July 1885 the Ryan-Sullivan mess emerged again. The story this time was that the two men would meet in Cincinnati in August. This was looking more like Charlie Brown with Lucy holding the football. Would this thing ever make it off the ground or would it once again be pulled back at the last moment? The task of arranging the fight was being undertaken on the East Coast, and it would once again fail.[269]

McCaffrey and Sullivan

Simultaneously, plans were being made for a McCaffrey-Sullivan fight in Cincinnati. O'Brien had been chasing Sullivan all over the country making challenges for McCaffrey. During the last week in July O'Brien was in Montreal, where he received a telegram from McCaffrey to get to Chicago at once to meet with Sullivan's representatives, who were coming there from Cincinnati.

On July 31, Billy O'Brien for McCaffrey and representatives from Cincinnati—referred to as the "Porkopolis authorities"—met at Davies' place in Chicago and signed articles. Billy Pinkerton was among those present during this meeting. His role was not clear, but it may be that the parties were going to use of Pinkerton agents in Cincinnati because of their acknowledged success as security during the Sullivan-Burke match. As first discussed on that day, the McCaffrey-Sullivan fight was arranged for six rounds, Queensberry rules, for all or nothing of the gate receipts. The match was to take place at Chester Driving Park, but the date not being definitely settled. It was to be on either August 18 or August 31, 1885. The parties were in telegraph communication throughout the day, and although McCaffrey and the Chester Park people had agreed to the terms, Sullivan had not responded to their proposals.[270]

The *Post Dispatch* reported that the original draft of the articles contained a clause that said "scientific points to count" but that Sullivan had insisted that this phrase be stricken, which it was. The original agreement also said that gloves were to be chosen at the time of the match, but Sullivan insisted that this also be stricken and replaced with the provision stating that three ounce gloves would be used. Both these changes favored Sullivan by increasing the chance of a knock out and avoiding the chance of McCaffrey winning on points. The day after the Chicago meeting McCaffrey telegraphed O'Brien, telling him that he needed three weeks to train for the match with Sullivan, and one week to get a man to run his business. O'Brien then telegraphed the Chester Park men who had returned to Cincinnati to tell them to have the date for the fight fixed for August 31, which was later changed to August 29.[271]

About three weeks after these arrangements had been made at The Store, McCaffrey sent a telegram from Far Rockaway, Long Island, to O'Brien, who was in Cincinnati. It seems that O'Brien had sent word to McCaffrey that he should come at once to Cincinnati, which irritated McCaffrey. He wrote:

> Dear Billy: I received your long "come at once" telegram. I don't see why you did not write me sooner. I did not know till this moment that I am to fight six rounds. It is all right, but I never dreamed of it and thought it was to be four rounds, just as the other was to be; but don't let it bother you. I will be there all O.K. but you should have posted me sooner. I was going to ask __________, but I thought he might think I was weakening, so I have been in the dark ever since. I would like my training quarters out in the country six or seven miles. Have a place fixed for a bath. Get an old cheese box, cut small holes in it, and fix overhead, so I can get a shower-bath. Have it in a barn, or inclosure of some kind. Now don't neglect this above all. I am feeling well enough, but I want to get four more days in here of hard work. I lost three days' training by going up to Shenandoah. I was treated to a reception – was met by a brass band; also had a carriage in front of the parade next day, headed by a brass band. I sparred Jimmy Ryan up there, three rounds, and got the dust, and returned at once. I will leave here the morning of the 21st at 6 o'clock and come through without stop. I must close to get at the ball. Yours as ever, D. McCaffrey.
>
> P. S. ______ _______ says the big fellow is drinking, but I don't take stock in that. I will try to be right.[272]

McCaffery's missive to O'Brien is interesting because it illustrates how quickly prizefighters of this period could become prima donnas, just as many athletes do today.

During the July 31 meeting, O'Brien was discussing McCaffery's ability, and Davies asked him whether McCaffrey would meet Cleary in Chicago. O'Brien said that McCaffrey would be there if the money was right. Davies told O'Brien that he would guarantee McCaffery $1,000 for his share of such a match with Cleary, to be held at Battery D in October 1885, and based on that guarantee O'Brien agreed to the match. That same day arrangements were made for Warren to appear on the undercard at the McCaffrey-Sullivan contest in Cincinnati.[273]

Two weeks after the agreement for the McCaffrey-Sullivan match, Davies left Chicago for New York to make arrangements to bring a good string of boxers back in order to put on first-class matches in Chicago. Davies returned from the East on August 24 and told the press that the feeling among the New York sporting crowd was that Sullivan would whip McCaffery with less trouble than he had beating Burke, Greenfield, or Mitchell. Davies felt that the length of the fight would depend almost entirely on Sullivan's condition at fight time. He thought that if it turned out to be a hot day and Sullivan was "a trifle out of sorts," he might adopt the rushing tactics he had with Burke, in which case the crowd would get its money's worth. Charlie said that Sullivan probably would be in condition for the fight, but that he would hate to see Burke or Mitchell go into any fight in the same condition that Sullivan considered to be good condition. Davies said that as a personal matter he did not like Sullivan, but he had high regard for his honesty and "sincerity of purpose." Davies felt that Sullivan had never participated in a hippodrome, and the Parson didn't think that any amount of money would induce him to throw a fight.[274]

Davies felt that if McCaffery went on the offensive in the fight, he would get thrashed soundly in a few short minutes. He also reported that while he was in the East, he had met with Ned Mallahan, who was bringing a heavyweight named James Smith over from England. If Smith showed well in the eastern cities, then he would come to Chicago under Davies' management.

Davies left Chicago on Friday, August 28, with a large delegation of men. As the years passed, such trips to remote sites to watch prizefights became a regular part of a promoter's business. Special trains were commonly chartered for round trips. Hotel arrangements were made at the nearest city to the site of the fight, and transportation to and from the site was also set up. In some cases hundreds of fans would travel together, like football fans who in our day rent a bus or airplane to attend college or professional football games.

Charlie also made arrangements to have the results of each round in the Sullivan-McCaffery fight telegraphed to Chicago and then bulletined to The Store so that his best customers could keep up with the action. This was as close to real-time coverage as was available in 1885 and was another new part of the promoter's business. Warren was included in Davies' Chicago delegation. Having active fighters under management remained the core of a promoter's business. Warren had been scheduled to fight a man named A. E. Duke of St. Louis at the Park Theater in Chicago on that same evening, but it seems apparent that the fight with Duke was not held because Warren instead went to Cincinnati.[275]

Warren made a big splash in his match with a fighter named Jack King, the "Hummingbird of Cincinnati." King was "a black-mustached frizzly-headed fellow that would pass for a Fiji Islander." In front page coverage, the *New York Times* wrote that King was much bigger than Warren but that Warren fought so furiously as to bring out repeated cheers from the crowd. The *Cincinnati Enquirer* said that Warren was a very little fellow and although King had the best in height and weight by at least thirty pounds, Warren did just about as he pleased with King, dodging all around King and occasionally delivering a stunning blow in a way that afforded great amusement to the crowd. Warren "was cheered to the echo, and is undoubtedly the best feather weight in the country," said the *Enquirer*. At the end of the fight the ladies crowded up and wanted to shake hands with the "baby" named Warren. Although not the main event, the fight was the best entertainment of the night.[276]

The main event was a real mess. McCaffrey stayed for the six rounds, but Sullivan was awarded the decision. McCaffrey showed that he lacked a backbone and was put down as many as twenty-five times during the fight. He had adopted the Tug Wilson method of fighting Sullivan: clinch, hold on, dodge, run away, and fall down when caught. Nevertheless, the fight was a huge economic success with a gate of more than $18,000.

Warren fought in Cincinnati on October 9 against a man named Quitman—not the best name for a fighter. It appears that this fight was probably not under Davies' management and that Warren acted without a promoter. Because of his good performance on the undercard of the Sullivan-McCaffrey fight, it may be that sporting men in Cincinnati invited Warren to come there and fight, and he went without supervision. At the end of the sixth round of the Warren-Quitman fight, the Cincinnati boy refused to continue. He claimed that Warren had bitten his hand through the gloves the fighters were wearing. Mike Tyson wasn't the first fighter who ever bit off part of an opponent, but not too many fighters could bite through a pair of boxing gloves.[277]

Davies' friend goes to prison

Difficult personal matters arose in late 1885 that occupied Davies' attention. In early September, attorneys for Davies' close friend Joe Mackin appeared before the Illinois Supreme Court to argue that Mackin's perjury conviction should be thrown out and that he should be granted a new trial. The court found none of the arguments persuasive and in mid-November his conviction was affirmed.[278] When the news reached Chicago about the adverse court decision, Davies was the first friend to see Mackin at the jail, where he was being held awaiting transport to the Joliet state prison. Charlie's appearance at the jail was closely followed by McDonald. "It may be true," Charlie told the *Chicago Herald*, "that Mike [Mackin's nickname] is a ballot box stuffer and a general fine worker in elections, but no man can accuse him of being a coward. His wife lamented and cried over his hard fate, but he was as brave and calm as any man could possibly be and took the matter philosophically. Some people say Mackin is a rascal, but I have always found him to be a true and honest friend."[279]

In addition to his friend's trouble, Charlie's brother, Vere, was seriously ill for several months with "brain fever" in mid-September but seemed to be recovering by mid-October. Ten days later Vere was again ill and confined to County Hospital.[280] A story on December 23 said that Davies had declined to serve as master of ceremonies during a prizefight because his brother had died. The *Trib-*

une reported that Vere had been very ill, but he was still alive, and the prospects of his recovery were good. Vere did recover and would eventually outlive Charlie, but his long illness in late 1885 must have made the management of everyday affairs difficult for Charlie.[281]

Management of The Store was difficult because the Chicago police had decided to crank up the pressure on the gaming houses. On September 28 the Tiger hunt started again when ten of the downtown gaming houses were raided. The Tiger was the gambling bank or the combined money of the syndicate of owners who operated gambling operations in the city. The Tiger hunt was organized attempt of law enforcement to close up gambling houses. No games were in progress in several of the houses that were raided. It was evident that scouts, which the gambling houses kept out on the streets, had learned in advance of the contemplated raids and had tipped off the owners in advance.

The police entered 176 Clark Street, McDonald's old lair and Davies' new place, by breaking open a door and going through a rear window. The raiders found thirty players, two faro tables, two stud-poker tables, two roulette wheels, and a chuck-a-luck table. Chuck-a-luck is a game played with dice in a wire frame cage rotated by the dealer. Bets are placed on the possible dice combination. It is not clear who ordered these raids. It may be that Doyle was acting on his own because less than a month after this raid, he was removed as chief, possibly as sanction for conducting gambling raids without the mayor's approval.[282]

In early October 1885, Davies began to discuss the revival of athletic events in Chicago during the winter season. Like the theater business, the prize-fighting business had a season that ran from late September through May. Davies felt that several important matches between men with international reputations would take place at Battery D during the coming months. He had word that Mitchell had authorized him to arrange a match with McCaffery. This match was to be for eight or more rounds with small soft gloves. Mitchell also wanted Davies to talk to Sullivan about a possible match. Sullivan was scheduled to visit Chicago with the Lester & Allen Minstrel Company within a few days.[283]

Things were also heating up with Burke, who had made it all the way to California. He wired back to Chicago saying that he wanted Davies to arrange a match for him with McCaffrey to take place in Chicago for any number of rounds or to a finish with kid gloves.[284] Last, but hardly least, Dempsey wanted Davies to arrange a fight with George Le Blanche. Le Blanche was a fine little pugilist. He was five feet six inches tall but weighed one hundred fifty four pounds with a forty inch chest. Le Blanche was described as a rusher in the style of Sullivan, and this usually made for an exciting boxing match. These possibilities were all important in their own right, and together they would light-up the Chicago athletic world.

Pat Killen a promising heavyweight

Davies had also taken on the management of another heavyweight fighter who had a better right hand than any of the others under consideration in 1885.

Pat Killen of Philadelphia was six feet tall and weighed 190 pounds. One day in late 1885, Killen had walked into Davies' place in Chicago and introduced himself saying: "I'm a fighter. Can you make a match for me?" In retort, Davies asked: "What can you do?" Killen responded: "Whip any fellow you can put up against me."[285] Davies found Killen's candor refreshing and scheduled him for a match against Jack Morris, who was six feet tall and weighed about 180 pounds. Killen and Morris were fairly matched in terms of height and weight, with Killen having an edge. Their match was to be a five-round affair with soft gloves.[286]

While the Killen-Morris fight was pending, Sullivan showed up with his minstrel company. Sullivan and the minstrels were to appear at Chicago's Columbia Theater. The Lester & Allen Minstrel Company were operated by a man named Billy Lester. Sullivan had signed a contract with his minstrel company to appear for $500 a week for twenty weeks, with possible extensions of the term of his contract. His role in the show was to appear from behind the theater's curtain wearing white tights with heavy white powder on his face and hands and then strike posses as the perfect form of a man. Somehow the thought of this brings a smile.

An advance agent for the minstrels visited the theatrical columnists of the Chicago newspapers to invite them to the opening night at the Columbia. It wasn't often that the theatrical columnists were asked to write about Sullivan. The advance man informed the columnists that Mr. Sullivan had an excellent stage voice and was thinking of giving up prizefighting and instead going into the dramatic profession as an actor.

Sullivan in drag

As he was for sporting events, Sullivan was also a terrific draw for theatrical events. The Columbia was sold out well in advance for his performance. Unlike prizefights, women and children could freely attend minstrel shows to get a good look at this Adonis. John L.'s first pose of the evening was described as "Ajax defying the lightning." He posed with his left leg thrust forward and his two arms pulled back parallel to one another to show off his chest and his back to greatest advantage. When this pose was announced, someone in the cheap seats yelled out: "Ajax refusin' a drink!" This made Sullivan grin and cracked the heavy powder that had been applied to his face to make him appear a statue.

He then struck a pose called: "Hercules at rest." In this pose he would lay down in stretched out and languid manner to give the impression of lazy strength. Then he struck the pose called "fighting gladiator." In this pose he held a shield in a raised left hand and a Roman sword thrust back in his right hand. The shield was said to look more like a wet lily pad. After he finished his routine there was great applause from the crowd with women calling out: "Wance more, darlin', come again!"

Sullivan appeared wrapped in a bed sheet to bow to his admirers and receive their accolades. He explained that he liked the statue thing first rate. He said:

"I don't have to put more than twenty minutes' work into it at each performance. The business seemed to take with the public whenever I appeared."[287] This whole thing was something that could legitimately drive any man to drink and many jokes were probably made at Sullivan's expense that evening at The Store and other saloons around Chicago.

Sullivan's arrangement with Lester & Allen lasted until January 22, 1886. At that point the company reached Boston, and a dispute developed between Sullivan and Lester. Sullivan claimed that he was owed $800.19, and he planned to expose Lester's unethical behavior when he appeared on stage in Boston. Lester bested the big man by instructing the crew not to raise the curtain for Sullivan's performance and simultaneously beating it out the back door of the theater leaving Sullivan behind in his white paste, powder and tights.

When Sullivan appeared in Chicago, he was still on good terms with the minstrel company and was raking in a nice weekly paycheck. Aware that Sullivan would be in Chicago, Ryan arrived on Thursday, October 8. Ryan said that he was there just to visit some friends in Chicago, but it seemed apparent that he was dogging Sullivan's trail to keep up the half-hearted efforts to make a match with him.

Ryan stayed with Colonel Vidvard on State Street. He said that he might be moving back to Chicago if he could make satisfactory arrangements. The local newspapers thought it nearly certain that before Sullivan left Chicago, the arrangements for a match with Ryan would be completed.[288] Sullivan later had a different account of his meeting with Ryan. He told the *Herald*: "When I was in Chicago I met Paddy Ryan and greeted him warmly with 'How are you, Paddy; I hear you want to fight me again.' He said, 'No, I'm in no hurry about it. Have a drink with me.' We had a small glass of ale together."

On the evening of October 9, Sullivan and Ryan attended the boxing matches held at the Park Theater. The crowd wanted them to act as timekeeper and referee, but Sullivan declined and explained that his contract with the minstrel company prohibited him from acting in either capacity. For Sullivan, contracts could be a helpful thing, but most of the time they were simply a nuisance.

While Sullivan was excusing himself from non-theater public appearances because of his contract with Lester & Allen, he was also talking to a man named John E. Cannon about entering into a three-year management contract that would take him to Europe and Australia. Cannon was not a hack in the promoting business. He crossed paths with Sullivan in Chicago while Cannon was producing a play at the Chicago Opera House at the same time that Sullivan was posing for Lester & Allen at the Columbia.

For many years Cannon had managed an act known as Harrigan & Hart during that team's successful run in New York City. Edward Harrigan and Tony Hart (whose given name was Anthony Cannon) led an important musical comedy and vaudeville act that had popularized several American comic characters.[289] On November 20, Sullivan and Cannon met again in Pittsburgh and signed a management agreement for a tour of Europe and Australia.[290]

At the same time that these things were happening with Ryan and Sullivan in Chicago, Burke was on his way back to the Windy City. While traveling to Chicago from the West Coast, he stopped in Colorado for a match with John P. Clow, who was called that state's heavyweight champion. Burke and Clow fought a four-round match with two-ounce gloves at the armory in Leadville. Neither Burke nor Clow did particularly well in this match; Burke said he was affected by the thin air. Leadville 10,152 feet above sea level, and many athletes have learned about oxygen deprivation in Colorado during their careers.[291] The question for Davies was whether he had enough available dates to schedule fights for Burke in Chicago, especially since Davies was then also managing Killen.

In Killen, Davies thought that he had discovered a very good and big heavyweight who could be a real contender and whom he could keep busy all winter long. On the evening of October 13, the scheduled Killen-Morris small-glove contest was presented at the Park Theater. The Park was well-filled, and a man named Mike Lawler was chosen as referee.

Killen virtually stopped the fight with his first punch. He caught Morris on the eye, which then ballooned up like a grapefruit. After that, every time Killen hit Morris, he would go down in a heap. It was clear that Morris was afraid of Killen and did not have sufficient science to deal with his crushing blows. It was later reported that Killen broke a bone in a finger on his right hand during the match.[292] Colonel Vidvard told the *Tribune* that he would be willing to back Killen against Cardiff, who had returned to Chicago from Minneapolis to watch Killen fight. This type of public offer could lead to bad feelings between Davies and Vidvard, especially because the two men had already been involved in some difficult meetings and because it appeared that Vidvard was poaching a fighter under Davies' management.

In the ring before the Killen-Morris fight began, it was announced that a heavyweight from South Boston named Joe Lannon was coming to Chicago to appear at the Park and meet another fighter named James Duffy in a five round match.[293] Lannon was a reasonably good heavyweight fighter under the management of Professor John S. Barnes. When Lannon arrived in town, he posted a $500 challenge to fight any heavyweight in Chicago. Glover accepted Lannon's challenge, and his agreement to fight was then published in the local newspapers.

On October 16, Lannon and Duffy met at the Park in front of an immense audience. Ryan acted as the referee for this fight. In the first round Duffy surprised the crowd by gaining the advantage and flooring Lannon. After that round it appeared that Duffy was out of shape and exhausted, and Lannon thereafter controlled the fight. He had not knocked out Duffy, who had simply stopped fighting and given up the effort due to his exhaustion.[294]

Killen and Lannon matched

The day after Lannon defeated Duffy, articles were signed between Killen and Lannon for a match to decide the championship of the Northwest. The championship of the Northwest appears to have been a title that simply made up by Davies. There was no recognized way to determine a champion of the Northwest, and no series of matches that led to a championship fight. But Davies liked to advertise his fights as for some championship or to offer cups and trophies to the winner. The Lannon-Killen match was scheduled for two-and-a-half-ounce gloves, and to take place on November 8, 1885 at a point within one hundred miles of Saint Paul, Minnesota.

When a fight was scheduled outside Chicago's city limits, there was an implication that it would involve something more than sparring. The articles for Killen-Lannon specified stakes of $500 a side, with the winner to take the entire stakes, the full net income from excursion earnings and gate receipts. This was a risky contract that could financially ruin a manager. Barnes posted the forfeit money for Lannon. In this case the winner would also receive a bell emblematic of the championship of the Northwest. Queensberry rules were to govern this fight. At the time the articles were signed, Killen weighed 195 pounds and Lannon 180.[295]

As soon as Lannon had signed to fight Killen, he began backwatering on his earlier challenge to fight anyone. His challenge had been accepted by Glover but Lannon apparently did not want to fight Glover. First, Barnes asked Glover to postpone the date when forfeit money was required for their match. Then Barnes said that he did not want to post money for a prospective match with Glover until after the match with Killen. He said that he thought he had an easy mark in Killen and that he expected to be flush after that fight and would then have no trouble making the match with Glover.[296]

When Cardiff was Chicago for the Killen-Morris fight, he talked to Davies about making a match with Killen.[297] While Cardiff was unable to schedule a match with Killen, Davies did schedule a match for Friday, October 23 in St. Paul between Cardiff and a heavyweight named James Brady. That fight took place at the Olympic Theater in St. Paul.

Brady was from Buffalo but was then fighting out of Valley City, Dakota Territory. He surprised Cardiff and forced the fighting throughout the match. Cardiff responded by fouling Brady, catching him by the legs and falling on him. The maneuver of falling on top of an opponent was fairly common in prizefighting, and it had long been a weapon in Sullivan's arsenal.

At the time of the Cardiff-Brady fight, Mitchell was in Minneapolis and challenged Cardiff. One account of Cardiff's match with Brady said that there was a kind of grim humor in Cardiff's view of a possible match with Mitchell: "If the latter ever cuts loose on him the pride of Peoria would find himself a mass of clotted gore."[298]

On Tuesday, November 3, Davies, Killen, and Chandler left Chicago for St. Paul and the meeting with Lannon. The press wrote that if Killen successfully defeated Lannon, Killen would have to meet Cardiff next.[299] This was because Cardiff claimed that he was the real champion of the Northwest. Davies came back to Chicago and on Saturday, November 7, led a large party of Chicago sporting men back to Minnesota for the fight.

The Killen-Lannon fight was not held within the St. Paul city limits but down the river six miles south, on the same ground where Cardiff had knocked out Billy Wilson in June. Wilson was selected as the referee for the fight. The St. Paul men were betting heavily on Lannon.

More than twenty years later, James J. Corbett wrote about this fight contending that he had heard the account directly from Davies. Corbett's account was printed in many newspapers including the *San Antonio Gazette* on January 6, 1906. He wrote:

> Parson Davies has been in the fighting game a long time and tells as many stories as any of the world's famous ring men. One of his experiences always comes to mind when I meet him. He was in charge of Pat Killen, the old pugilist, who had every quality of a great fighter but nerve. He had arranged for a battle with Joe Lannon, a pug of the late 80's, who also was no slouch. The fight took place on a barge on the Mississippi. Killen as the time for the battle drew near, began showing the white feather, and finally when the time for entering the ring came Killen was about sick. Davies had bet a lot of money on him and had a pretty good hunch that he could win.
>
> Finally after the fight had been delayed until spectators wanted to fight themselves, Davies grew desperate. Drawing a gun from his pocket be threatened to shoot unless Killen got on and did his best.
>
> When Killen saw the gun he got cold feet in another way and went to it. Well, that was as great a battle between second raters as was ever seen. After desperate fighting, in which both were badly used up Killen won with a blind swing that would have killed a mule. Parson Davies put his gun back in his pocket and Killen was hailed as the gamest man in the northwest where he belonged.[300]

The Killen-Lannon fight lasted nine rounds. Killen was visibly under the influence at the time of this fight. It could be that he was drinking for courage. In the second round Killen caught Lannon with a terrific right hand and broke his hand so badly that he was unable to use it during the remainder of the match. He continued the fight using only his left hand and his right elbow and forearm. Lannon had the best of the fight for the first three rounds, but then got winded and Killen seemed to gain his second wind. Killen floored Lannon several times. Some accounts say that Killen finally gained the advantage by backhanding Lannon across the throat cutting off his breathing. In the final round Lannon went down, struggled to his feet and fell over backward. Referee Wilson awarded the fight to Killen, who was said to take away about three thousand dollars as a result of his one-handed victory.

Lannon was badly served by Barnes during the fight. It seems that Barnes poured nearly a bottle of whiskey down Lannon's throat just before the fifth round. The use of liquor as a stimulant was common in the 1880s. It was not generally understood that alcohol is actually a depressant, not a stimulant, but it was not at all common to administer liquor in the volume that Barnes provided to Lannon. Press reports say that Lannon was affected quickly by the liquor, and began to stagger and lurch around from the effects. Presumably Barnes administered another bottle of liquor to himself after losing so much money to Davies' man.[301]

Killen and Davies returned to Chicago on November 9. The *St. Paul Daily Globe* reported that Davies was irritated with Cardiff and would bring Killen back to St. Paul when he was healthy and do-up Cardiff. Davies told the *Tribune* that he was satisfied with Killen as a fighter. He said that Killen had actually injured his right hand during the earlier fight with Morris and that he had broken one of the bones in his hand on the first punch that he threw during the Lannon fight. Davies acknowledged that Glover and Cardiff had both asked for fights with Killen. If Killen did have a broken hand before the fight started this too would explain his reluctance to fight Lannon.[302]

Burke and Cleary meet in San Francisco

On the West Coast, Davies' former heavyweight Burke had arranged a fight with Cleary to take place in San Francisco.[303] Nothing indicates that Davies was directly involved with their fight in San Francisco. Instead, Floto was with Burke acting as Davies' agent. Floto would later operate the Sell-Floto circus and earn great fame as the sports editor of the *Denver Post*. Floto was born in Cincinnati on January 12, 1863, and had been educated at a Jesuit school at Dayton, Ohio. He then left Dayton and began working for Parson Davies as his assistant. He was sent along with Burke to follow instructions given to him by Davies.

Corbett claimed that while Burke was in San Francisco in 1885, he was one of several fighters who sparred with Burke. Corbett wrote that he stood up eight rounds with Burke without a decision. Corbett claimed that years later he was told by Floto: "If you hadn't been such a 'kid' and had had more experience, you could have knocked him cold. You hit him more than once very hard and hurt him; but he covered up and 'kidded' you out of it."[304] In *The Fighting Man*, William A. Brady writes that Corbett's success in sparring with Burke in 1885 compelled the leaders of the San Francisco sporting world to begin to take Corbett seriously as a fighter.[305]

The Cleary-Burke fight took place on November 23 and resulted in an eight-round draw. The local police were present throughout the fight to see whether either man appeared to be going beyond the simple sparring that was permitted by California law. The police presence subdued both fighters, and there were no real exciting moments in the fight. The general opinion was that Cleary appeared to be the better fighter, but no firm conclusions could be reached. After the fight Dempsey posted a forfeit for a proposed match with Burke, who would soon be headed back to Chicago. It would be almost a year before they would fight.[306]

In Chicago, Davies was trying to fill his open dates by arranging a competition for a gold medal offered to any amateur who weighed less than 150 pounds and who had never boxed in public.[307] The medal was put on exhibit at The Store and consisted of a handsome gold tablet pendant from a gold bar inscribed "Davies." It had a raised figure of an athlete in a fighting costume with the inscription "Amateur Championship of Illinois."

Davies was looking for new lightweight, middleweight, and featherweight talent to replace Warren, who had left Chicago and was on the road. Davies also arranged a Glover-Chandler rematch for the heavyweight championship of Illinois. Glover held that title, but many remembered Glover's first match with Chandler, when Glover had been saved from a knockout by the bell at the end of the second round.[308]

The Glover-Chandler rematch on November 30 at Battery D was more flawed than their first fight. There were three thousand in attendance, which was well below the previous attendance for a prizefight at that venue. This was not the sparkling sort of event that Davies liked. In the first round, Glover knocked Chandler silly and had him so groggy that he could hardly keep his feet. Chandler's handlers began an argument with the referee claiming that Chandler had been fouled. This argument went on for seven minutes. Ned Dorney, Chandler's second, hit Captain Dalton, Glover's second, in the face, and the two had to be separated. The bickering went on until Lieutenant Shea of the Chicago police expelled Dorney from the ring. Shea dropped Dorney off the platform "like a huge mastiff shaking a snapping, ugly little terrier."[309] Chicago newspapers praised Davies for his promotional skill and Shea for his ability to control the ring.[310]

Charles Hermann, who lived through this era in Chicago, wrote: "Inspector John D. Shea had the last say when it came to issuing permits for boxing exhibition matches. The Inspector was a fearless, fighting police official, and a pronounced prizefight fan. Whenever a tough gangster or crook was arrested, the Inspector's orders were to bring him into his private office alone. Shea would then lock the door. If the offender would claim he was innocent and if the Inspector doubted the word of such gangster or crook, he would say to him, 'You are a liar and I want the truth from you. You are not giving it to me. Get up out of that chair!' It made no difference to Shea how tough they were, he would go at his man with his bare fists then and there. The offender nearly always came through with the truth and changed his plea to guilty."[311]

While the argument between the seconds was taking place, Chandler regained his senses and was able to last through the six rounds of the fight, which was then declared a draw. Despite the problems at the event, this was the seventh Davies' event that was later listed among the top fifteen Chicago of 1885.[312]

Burke and Cleary rematch in Chicago scheduled

Killen was sidelined by a broken hand, and Burke on the West Coast. Davies was short of the superior talent that he liked to promote. Hope for an end to the rather dull situation emerged when Davies revealed that he had scheduled a Burke-Cleary rematch for Battery D before Christmas 1885. Their rematch was to be managed by Davies, and it was certainly a lot bigger thing than a Glover-Chandler rematch. Davies was planning a twist to the evening's entertainment by adding the final match of an international billiard competition to the bill.

The champion billiard player in Chicago was George Slosson. The leading European billiard player was Maurice Vignaux, who played in Paris. Another top international player was Jacob Schaefer, who was backed by Dick Roche of St. Louis. Vignaux was on a tour of America and had been engaged in a long series of billiard matches, and Davies wanted their final match to take place at Battery D as a prelude to the Burke-Cleary fight. Boxing and billiards would normally be considered an odd combination in a single venue. It was something like playing chess on a roller coaster. Davies came up with some ideas for sporting events that seem fairly whacky. There was additional news that Killen was recovering faster than anticipated and was leaving for Louisville, Kentucky, for a December 21 five-round match with a heavyweight named George Gray.[313]

Burke arrived in Chicago on the evening of December 12 and was greeted at The Store by Davies and Billy Pinkerton.[314] He was asked about his San Francisco fight with Cleary. Burke said that he found Cleary a hard man to fight because he had both a hard blow and was as lively a man as he had ever fought. He noted that the affair had been little more than a sparring match because he and Cleary were required to wear big, soft gloves and that the first attempt at a knockout blow would result in the police stopping the fight in its tracks. Davies announced that he had changed the date of the Burke-Cleary match from December 23 to December 28. Davies said that the match was to be for six rounds, Queensberry rules, for a 75/25 division of gate receipts. This type of gate receipt split would normally allow the loser to recover his out-of-pocket costs and make a small amount of money.[315]

In mid-December, Davies received two telegrams about arranging fights with Dempsey in Chicago. Johnny Files wanted Davies to set up a match on his behalf, and a New York promoter named Billy Tracy wanted the Parson to arrange a match between an unknown and Dempsey. Davies responded to both telegrams saying that he would not make any matches with anybody and Dempsey until after Dempsey arrived in Chicago. There had been enough talk for over a year about Dempsey showing up to fight in Chicago, and Dempsey had always found something else to occupy his time in either New Orleans or in California.[316]

On December 19 Cleary came to Chicago and he too went immediately to Davies to make arrangements for the scheduled match with Burke. Cleary and Burke had engaged in draws in New York and San Francisco. However, the general feeling at the time was that outside of Sullivan, no heavyweight fighter in America could boast as good a record as Cleary nor could anyone approach him in the number of knockouts scored.[317]

Evan "the strangler" Lewis and Matsada Sorakichi

The same day that Cleary arrived in Chicago, Matsada Sorakichi, the champion Japanese wrestler, also arrived to fulfill a two-week contract with promoters known as Kohl & Middleton. Sorakichi was supposed to show his feats of strength with a 250-pound Indian club.[318] In 1882, C. E. Kohl and George Middleton had opened what some have called the first acknowledged vaudeville entertainment in Chicago at the West Side Museum. Arguably, the entertainment offered by Davies during racewalking, wrestling, and prizefights was either the first vaudeville or a close precursor to vaudeville. The business of Kohl & Middleton was so successful that in 1883 they moved to a higher rent district on Clark Street. The following year they leased the Olympic Theater and were doing well enough to get involved in backing men in sporting events.

Kohl & Middleton contacted Davies about arranging a match between Evan "the Strangler" Lewis of Madison, Wisconsin, (also called the champion of Wisconsin) and Sorakichi. Lewis had been letting it out that he could defeat the big "Jap." Lewis was backed by several men from Wisconsin who thought he could beat any wrestler in the world and saw Lewis as the Sullivan of the wrestling world.

Lewis was born on May 24, 1861, in Ridgeway, Wisconsin, a small village in Iowa County, near Madison. In 1881 Lewis moved to Butte City, Montana Territory, to work in the mines there. While in Montana, Lewis had learned Cornish wrestling and participated in several tournaments before returning to Wisconsin in March 1883. After about a year back in Wisconsin, Lewis began to learn the catch-as-catch-can style of wrestling. He had been wrestling for about four years before his Wisconsin backers approached Davies and asked him to promote Lewis. There were some significant differences between Sullivan and Lewis. Lewis was described as a quiet, modest and unassuming person without a bit of braggadocio about him in his private life. No one ever described Sullivan in those terms.

Davies began his efforts to arrange a wrestling match, but a dispute arose because Lewis wanted a Greco-Roman style match and Sorakichi wanted a catch-as-catch-can match. Davies took charge of things and within a day the articles were resolved and the terms called for a best three-out-of-five match in the catch-as-catch-can format. Sheedy was appointed to act as the representative of the stakeholder for the match, which was to be for $250 a side with the winner to have 75 percent of the net gate receipts. Davies was on a roll at the end of 1885.[319] On December 21, Killen met George Gray in Louisville before a crowd of one thousand paid spectators.[320]

The day before the Burke-Cleary battle at Battery D, Burke appeared at The Store. He stepped on a scale for the press and weighed 176 pounds. It was noted that he had grown more solid and compact since his arrival in the United States. Then he had appeared tall and gangly, but before the Cleary fight, his frame had matured so that he appeared well-built and compactly put together. There was considerable comment about the effort that Burke had made to improve his right-handed work. He had been working on his right hand for nearly a year and had intentionally developed a right-hand lead on his trip west so that he could become more comfortable throwing punches with that hand. Both Ryan and Dempsey were expected to appear at the fight.[321]

To the surprise of many, Burke stopped Cleary in the third round, knocking him unconscious for over a minute. Some critics of Burke claimed that Cleary had the stomach flu on the day of the fight. They asserted that Burke knew about Cleary's illness and pounded away at his stomach to take advantage of the situation. Many fighters have entered the ring suffering from an injury or illness, and there is no rule that prohibits an opponent from taking every advantage available. His defeat of Cleary was an important milestone for Burke and confirmed that Burke belonged among the top contenders.[322]

Cleary was gracious after the fight and credited Burke as the better man. Loud cheers greeted Burke's victory. This was the first-class entertainment that had marked Davies' past productions. Burke received $2,000 for the night's work and Cleary earned about $500 for his part. Burke was scheduled to leave Chicago within a day or two after the Cleary fight so that he could appear for a week in St. Louis with Killen. The appearances in St. Louis were put on by the "Jack Burke Specialty Company," rather than by Davies.

Cleary said that he would probably go back to San Francisco, but instead he went to Philadelphia to spend New Year's Day with his friends. Perhaps he was embarrassed to return to San Francisco, where many gamblers had lost large sums on the outcome of his third match with Burke. Before leaving, Cleary went to Davies' place and explained that he had got a punch in the neck that had knocked him silly but explained "any man in the business is liable to get that, you now."[323]

1884 and 1885 had been remarkably good years for Parson Davies. He was the dominate promoter of sporting events in Chicago and had earned that position with hard work, thousands of miles of train travel, and an ability to manage the big egos of prizefighters and wrestlers. His reputation had spread everywhere, and he had maintained the necessary political contacts that allowed him to continue to produce boxing and wrestling events. He also helped make fighters like Burke wealthy men. Burke had come to the United States with little money, and before he came to Chicago, his luck was not good.

After he came under Davies' management Burke's career took off. Some reports say that he had won $25,000 in the ring. By the end of 1885, he was worth about $18,000 (about $420,000 in 2009 dollars).[324] Virtually all of this money had been made as a result of Davies' promotional efforts during 1885.

Moreover, in the process of promoting sporting events, Davies had employed many fighters and wrestlers whose names have not appeared above, and countless other men and women who appeared in orchestras, vaudeville routines, or as singers, dancers, club swingers, swordsmen, marksmen, or other roles.

Davies had come a long way from waiting on tables in the Bowery of New York City. He was the successful, self-made man so idealized during the late nineteenth century. He was Horatio Alger.

Chapter 6 - (1886)

Donning evening clothes

"Parson" Davies looked his nickname. He was a fine looking man with gray hair and his clothes were always made by the best tailors, and always black. Whenever he was to introduce a pugilist to an audience in the afternoon, he would put on a black cutaway; when he presented the principals in the evening, he always donned evening clothes.[325]

♦

A difficult year

Chicago was a difficult place to promote sporting events on a year-around basis. There was no air conditioning in the 1880s except for the ultra rich, and during July and August, the theaters and armories were ovens and not good places for boxing and wrestling matches. This meant that in the off-season and during the dog-days, if sporting events were to be successful, they needed to take place outside. But outdoor venues were expensive to rent and were so large that only the best events could draw large enough crowds to turn a profit. In the winter, Chicago was frigid and frequent snow made travel difficult. In the 1880s, even indoor sporting venues could be extremely cold. The mid-1880s were some of the coldest years on record because the Indonesian volcano Krakatoa had erupted in May 1883 and continued to be active until a final huge explosion in August that year. Volcanic dust in the upper atmosphere cooled the entire planet, and January 1884 was six degrees below the average long-term temperature, with frigid temperatures carrying on for several years. Because of these conditions, during the worst part of the winter athletes tended to look for matches in places like New Orleans and California, where the sun was more than a memory.

The year 1886 was difficult for Davies and other Chicago promoters. Early in the year there was another crackdown on prizefighting and wrestling. Several factors led to the change of attitude about the sports, and some of the problems were created by people who participated in the events.

In early 1886 there were a series of national high profile wrestling and boxing matches that were particularly brutal. In March 1886 Dempsey defeated La Blanche. The last round of their fight was described in words such as: "The Marine was bleeding like a stuck pig, and Jack was puffing and blowing. The gloves of both were in tatters and covered with blood." On the wrestling side there were two significant matches in early 1886 at Chicago. During the first match, Lewis choked out his opponent. In the second match Lewis appeared to intentionally break his opponent's ankle. These and many other similar events played into the hands of that part of society (the Law and Order League types) that was opposed to prizefighting and wrestling.

Another factor that contributed to the crackdown was the practice of challenging local men to appear with a professional fighter and attempt to survive for four rounds for prize money. This format drew big crowds to traveling road shows but often resulted in a local man being knocked out. The shows contributed nothing to the idea that they were scientific sparring matches as required by law. When a local man survived against a professional fighter, his survival almost never resulted from skill but only because the local stiff spent four rounds running away and falling down to avoid being hit. These challenge matches were generally bad for the good name of fighting. Similar challenges were made by professional wrestlers with like results.

In Chicago the squeeze on prizefighting happened, at least in part, due to some major sociological issues. The so-called anarchists, socialists, and bomb throwers who threatened a reign of lawlessness were confronted by the Chicago police in what became known as the Haymarket riot.

The Haymarket riot is too big a subject to be addressed in a meaningful way here. Suffice it to say that among the leading citizens there was a prevailing opinion that the wage classes brought on their own poor living conditions by improvidence and misdirected efforts. This view was coupled with a low opinion of the "foreigners" that largely made up the wage classes and their trade unions and that gave rise to such entities as the American Protective Association. Without much analysis, prizefighting and wrestling were considered parts of the dissipation of the lower classes and needed to be stopped in order to prevent further lawless behavior. In large and small communities across the U.S., politicians were forced by the wealthier classes to take steps to suppress such sporting events.[326]

January 1886 in Chicago was marked by another failed effort to arrange a Sullivan-Ryan match. On the Sullivan front, the big man and his former closest friend, Madden, kissed and temporarily made up. Sullivan used the occasion as an excuse to break six weeks of alcohol abstinence. He wanted to properly celebrate the renewal of their friendship. Sullivan gave up alcohol about once a month. His twelve-step program was measured by the distance from the tavern door to the bar stool.[327]

Burke, Killen, and Floto left Chicago for St. Louis on January 2, 1886, to put on daily entertainment at the Casino Theater.[328] Some reports say that Killen fought a man named Pat McHugh in Chicago on January 6, but there is no discussion of such a fight in the major Chicago newspapers, and Killen was in St. Louis, not in Chicago, on January 6, 1886.

While Burke and Killen were in St. Louis, a match was arranged between old Tom Kelly's son, Ed Kelly, and Burke.[329] St. Louis had an excellent fighting community that included the formidable Daly brothers. The Dalys were extremely tough customers. Kelly had once been the middleweight champion of America, and because of their past experiences the people in St. Louis should have known how to put on a successful fight. Without Davies' presence, the contest between

Burke and Kelly was poorly managed and illustrated just how fouled up prize-fights can become without proper planning.

The Burke-Kelly fight took place before 1,500 spectators. Most of the paying customers supported the local boy. Burke posted a $100 forfeit on the condition that he would knock out Kelly within four rounds. Dick Roche, a St. Louis sport, was selected as the referee, but apparently no one bothered to tell Roche the terms of the match. Killen and Floto acted as seconds for Burke, and Kelly and Tom Allen acted as seconds for Ed Kelly. This was quite an aggregation of sporting talent for a simple exhibition.

Like the long-ago affair between Tug Wilson and the Thug Sullivan, Ed Kelly's plan was to go down often but never to go out. Kelly had practiced his role and went down nineteen times during the fight. Sometimes he dropped after only being touched by Burke. He fell down twice without being touched at all, but he apparently feared that a blow might soon be thrown. At the end of the match Roche called the match a draw! This was one of several similar events that put fighting in a bad light.

Amid the cheering of the local fans, Floto explained to Roche that the match could not be a draw because the terms of the fight were only that if Burke failed to knock out Kelly, then Kelly would be entitled to the posted money. Roche withdrew his original decision and announced privately that Kelly was entitled to the stake because Burke had failed to knock him out within four rounds. Burke didn't want to pay and claimed that the original bet should have been considered off because it was based on the assumption that the participants' would be using two-ounce gloves. However, just before the fight started, the two-ounce gloves had been removed and four-and-a-half ounce gloves were used in their place.

The bigger gloves were substituted because somehow one pair of the smaller gloves had been cut on the surface. The lighter gloves had probably been damaged intentionally to prevent young Kelly from being knocked out. Burke claimed that it was nearly impossible to knock out anyone with such big, soft gloves. The Kellys claimed that Burke was bound by the original agreement because he did not complain at the time the large gloves were substituted. In effect, they claimed that Burke had implicitly waived his complaint. Laughably, the *St. Louis Post Dispatch* ran a post-fight headline: "Kelly's Courage—He Stood Up Four Rounds Against Jack Burke!" After their show in St. Louis, Burke and Killen went to Philadelphia to spar together at the New Theatre Comique.[330]

In Chicago Davies was waiting for the big wrestling match between the Strangler and Sorakichi and, in addition, he was managing a Glover-Bradburn fight at Battery D on January 11.[331] Both Glover and Bradburn were better than average heavyweights, but they were not known as first-tier heavyweight contenders. Attendance for the actual Glover-Bradburn fight was not the best, with only about two thousand to twenty five hundred paid customers. Davies was concerned about the dwindling crowds, and smaller crowds would make it more difficult to attract the best fighters to Chicago in the future. Burke returned to Chicago from his road trip with Killen to pick up a few dollars acting as a second for Bradburn.

In the ring on the night of the fight, a dispute started over the selection of a referee. The bickering irritated Davies. Charlie had matured as a manager of sporting events, and he was tired of taking too much junk from fighters of the class of Glover and Bradburn. While the dispute was going on in the ring among the fighters' seconds, Davies went to the dressing-rooms of the two fighters and said to both men: "I will not have this, and the quicker you understand it the better."[332] Davies promised that if the fighters did not agree upon a referee immediately the he would take control of the gate receipts and give them to charity. The fighters seemed to know that the Parson was serious and quickly agreed on Sherman Thurston as referee. Two years earlier Davies might not have been able to control athletes in this manner, but he had earned a reputation and by 1886, even the toughest fighters and wrestlers avoided crossing Davies if possible.

In the first round of the fight, Glover sent out a wicked right and Bradburn ducked, catching Glover around his legs. Glover then raised both hands above his head to claim a foul and while his hands were raised, Bradburn hit him twice. Some would say that Glover got what he deserved because he was playing referee rather than sticking to his job of fighting. Bradburn was then warned not to repeat his behavior, but no foul was called.

In the second round Glover carried the fighting, but in a clinch he had his head cut. He claimed that Bradburn had head-butted him. The third and fourth rounds were relatively dull, but in the fifth round Glover sent in both hands time and time again. By the latter part of the fifth round Bradburn was groggy and could scarcely keep his feet, but he managed to survive. In the sixth round Glover resumed his work, and Bradburn's right eye was closed by Glover's assault. The seventh round started in the same way, and at that point Lieutenant Shea of the Chicago police went into the ring and ordered the fight stopped. For men betting on a fight, this is a dreaded event. Everyone thought the fight would naturally go to Glover because Shea had stopped the fight to prevent Bradburn for receiving additional punishment. Nevertheless, the referee called the match a draw, which enraged the crowd.

Prizefighting and wrestling would be suppressed for more than half of 1886. Nevertheless, Davies would promote five of the top ten Chicago sporting events that year. The Glover-Bradburn fight was the first of those five events.[333]

Immediately after the fight, Burke and Killen left for Philadelphia.[334] Within a few days Burke sent Davies a letter that was full of good news. He reported that the theater where he and Killen were sparring had been jammed to the doors at every performance. More importantly, he told Davies that Killen was making rapid improvement as a fighter and predicted he would turn out to be a leading heavyweight.[335] This must have sounded good to Davies, especially because Killen had the size that heavyweights such as Burke, Goode, Greenfield, Cleary, and Mitchell lacked. A fighter's ability in the ring is almost always measured by results.

Although Killen was a terrific puncher, he was raw and crude in his approach. He had not learned to jab or keep space between himself and his opponent. Building a record from fights that were won in the dressing room would not produce a champion. The test was whether a fighter was ready to face a real fighter and not just someone who was cannon fodder. The biggest payday in prizefighting would be the day that a clever heavyweight with science and size could enter the ring with the heavyweight champion of America. Many believed that prizefighting could not survive without a good class of heavyweight fighters. Certainly, pint size heavyweights like Burke, Goode, and Greenfield could not do the trick.

Lewis chokes Sorakichi

The Sorakichi-Lewis wrestling match was the next big event that Davies promoted. The match had been in the making for more than a month but delayed by the long period of preparation that the contestants demanded. Lewis's backers had sent the Strangler to New York to train with Edwin Bibby, who was known as the ex-world champion catch-as-catch-can wrestler. Sorakichi was training with another well-known wrestler, Joe Acton. The event was scheduled for the Central Music Hall on Wednesday, January 27, 1886.[336]

Sorakichi was conspicuously lithe and supple, and had tremendous strength in his arms but was a little light in the legs. Lewis was stronger in his legs, an overall powerhouse and "rough as a bear." A large crowd came to Chicago from all over Wisconsin, and there was a lot of money being bet on Lewis. Lewis insisted that the match be held on an empty stage without canvas or padding, but Sorakichi did not agree to this. Davies arranged for Glover to act as the referee for the match.

Shortly before eight-thirty p.m. on January 28, Davies stepped to the front of the stage and announced the terms of the match: best three out of five falls, catch-as-catch-can, for a stake of $500 and 75 percent of the net gate receipts. The Japanese wrestler was quick and agile but hardly a match for Lewis in strength. In overall skill he was thought to be a little superior to Lewis.

Lewis won the first fall in the match, and then in the second bout he applied the hold that made him famous. He used a neck-lock to squeeze Sorakichi's throat with "a vise-like grip" as he quietly waited for him to tap out. However, Glover ordered Lewis to break the choke. Glover ruled that a wrestler was permitted to use a choke-hold to work with, but he could not simply to choke a man into submission. There was no basis for this interpretation, but Glover was calling the shots. There would come a time when Lewis acted as a referee in one of Glover's fights, and Lewis would obtain his revenge.

After Glover's ruling, Sorakichi picked up Lewis in what was called the "tack-hammer-hang-lock" (whatever that is) and brought him to the ground. As the Sorakichi was trying to turn Lewis to his back, the Strangler was driven off the stage and fell into the orchestra pit. The crowd yelled for a foul and wanted Lewis to be awarded the fall, but Glover found that Sorakichi's actions were unintentional and the match continued. Lewis made a rush at his opponent and was knocked into the seats at the front of the stage. The crowd booed loudly and Sorakichi actually apologized, but Lewis was angry and rushed forward and knocked the "Jap" backward by twenty feet into the wrestling fans in the front row with Lewis on top of him. This time Glover gave the fall to Sorakichi based on Lewis' intentional foul.

In the third bout Lewis got Sorakichi in his favorite neck-lock, and Sorakichi tapped-out. When he was released from the hold, he had a mouth filled with blood from the "bear-like grip at his throat." He went to the front of the stage and told the crowd that he had wrestled all over the world and had never seen the strangle-hold allowed as a fair hold. Lewis said that he had learned the hold from Frank Whitmore and Tom Chandler, but to avoid controversy he would not use the hold again. Time was called for the fourth fall, but the Sorakichi failed to respond and the match was given to Lewis. This was the second Davies' event that would make the top ten Chicago sporting events of 1886. [337]

The complaints about Lewis' use of the strangle-hold and its fairness were heard all over the hall, and Lewis' financial backer stepped forward. He said that he would back Lewis in a rematch with Sorakichi at any time within the next two weeks for $500 to $1,000 a side and with the strangle-hold barred. The first Sorakichi-Lewis match had been big news in Chicago, and the post match publicity was not good for those interested in promoting sporting events in Chicago. There were many complaints made to Mayor Harrison about this match and Lewis' infamous choke hold.

As the events surrounding the big wrestling show were taking place, Mitchell came back through Chicago and met with Davies. Mitchell made several attempts to arrange another match with Burke but without success due to the conflicting commitments of the two principals. On Sunday evening, January 31, Davies headed for New York to see if he could find any new attractions to present in Chicago.[338] Sequels and reruns are seldom as popular as the original event, and Chicago needed some new faces. Before he left for New York, Davies wrote a letter to Burke asking him to contact Mitchell when Burke stopped off in Pittsburgh. Mitchell was scheduled to be in Pittsburgh, and Davies wanted Mitchell and Burke to meet and discuss a fight, apparently thinking that the principals might be able to agree to something if they met face-to-face.[339]

Davies headed east while Burke headed west and stopped in Cincinnati for scheduled appearances with Killen at the Vine Street Opera-House. This was Burke's first appearance in Cincinnati. Later in 1886, his career as a fighter would suffer major damage in that town, but on this occasion a local man named James Currier from Cincinnati's sixth ward accepted Burke's challenge to pay $100 to any man able to stay with him for four rounds. Currier, a raw-boned fellow, had little knowledge of the manly art. Burke stopped Currier in two rounds. On the evening of February 6, Burke met Mike Smith, another local man trying to capitalize on Burke's challenge. The *Cincinnati Enquirer* said that Smith put on the "baby act" and appeared to be scared to death. Burke had to coax Smith to try to hit him, and at the end of the second round Smith threw his gloves on the floor and refused to continue. It is really somewhat misleading to include such events as part of a professional fighter's record.[340]

There was a systemic problem with these tour-created challenge fights. Except for goofy affairs like the match with Ed Kelly in St. Louis, these fights were always won in the dressing room. Amateur fighters were not able to provide a serious challenge for a professional fighter such as Burke. Such fights unquestionably created local interest, but they did nothing to improve a professional fighter's skills, and if these fish-in-a-barrel shows continued, it was difficult to determine whether the professional was actually prepared to meet a fighter in his own class.

When Burke and Killen finished their exhibitions in Cincinnati, they headed to Indianapolis before returning to Chicago to see the Lewis-Sorakichi rematch.[341] Davies had also scheduled another match for Killen. This time he was to face a man named Dick Burke of the stockyards in a five-round match for a one-hundred-dollar forfeit. Their match was to take place February 19 at the Park Theater. Undoubtedly Davies wanted to see for himself whether Killen had improved as much as Burke had claimed.[342]

The Lewis-Sorakichi rematch was scheduled for February 15 at the Central Music Hall. Great interest existed because the strangle-hold had been barred, and the public wanted to see whether Lewis could handle Sorakichi without using his favorite hold. No wrestling match that had taken place in Chicago had created as much excitement. After their first meeting, Lewis told the press: "I didn't choke the Jap, that is, not hard. When a man's choked he can't stand up and he's as limp as a rag." Between the two matches Sorakichi's handlers brought in Edwin Bibby to help train him for the rematch. Bibby had been the trainer for Lewis before their first match. During the week before February 15, Bibby and Sorakichi appeared at the Olympic Theater every afternoon in practice sessions that were open to the public and drew good crowds.[343]

Lewis did not use the strangle-hold in his second match with Sorakichi. Instead, he intentionally broke the Jap's ankle. Actually, he didn't break Sorakichi's ankle, but that is what seemed to have happened during the match and what was reported in the morning newspapers. This match became another poster-event for those wanting to suppress boxing and wrestling in Chicago.

Lewis breaks Sorakichi's ankle - almost

On Monday, February 15, Davies stepped to the front of the stage at eight fifteen p.m. Every seat in the hall was filled and between two and three hundred standing room tickets had been sold. At this point the fire code in theaters wasn't strictly enforced in Chicago. Old-time wrestler Frank Whitmore was the agreed upon referee, but Sorakichi changed his mind about Whitmore and a man named Harry Palmer was substituted. Sorakichi made a dive for Lewis' legs, but was held off, and Lewis ended up on top. Lewis then sat down on Sorakichi, took his left foot and "twisted it back until he had his opponent helpless, when the big brute coolly wrapped both hands around the Jap's foot and deliberately broke his ankle, snapping it off like a dry faggot." Sorakichi lasted until his ankle snapped and then threw up his hands and permitted Lewis to roll him over on his back. The time for the fall was only fifty seconds. Billy Lakeman stepped to the front of the stage and asked whether there was a doctor in the house. Someone yelled out: "You don't need a doctor, you need a policeman!"

The crowd went mad, and no one could hear the referee. Davies stepped to the front of the stage, and at last the noise subsided. "Gentlemen," he said, "there are three thousand of you and only one referee. Give him a chance." With that, Palmer spoke. He expressed his opinion that there was nothing that permitted a man to intentionally break his opponent's leg. This brought yells and criticism from the audience. Then Palmer continued: "Catch-as-catch-can means catch wherever you can. Lewis, having won the fall, is ready to continue the contest; the 'Jap' is not, therefore, I give the match to Lewis." Not one person in fifty supported this decision, but it stood, and the violence of Lewis' conduct caused wrestling promotions in Chicago trouble for a long time to come.[344] It was another Davies' event, his third, listed as one of Chicago's top ten sporting events of 1886.[345]

After the match, Lewis stopped in a Davies' saloon to discuss future matches and to challenge Bibby for $500 to $1,000 a side. The press was more interested in what Sorakichi had to say. The big baby was in bed at the National Hotel on South Clark Street, surrounded by his wife and sympathetic friends. His ankle was black-and-blue and swollen to twice its normal size.

When asked about Lewis' style of wrestling, Sorakichi said: "Dat not wrestling." He said that he liked to wrestle in a clean way and did not use the choke hold nor twist his the ankles of this opponents. Although his assessment was anticlimactic, a doctor said that the ankle was not actually broken.[346] Other notables around Chicago were asked to express their opinions. Billy Pinkerton said: "It was a brutal way of winning, but the decision was right." Davies said that a catch-as-catch-can match is what the name implies and the referee's decision was correct.[347]

Sorakichi and Bibby came by The Store on Saturday, February 20 to discuss the match. Sorakichi carried a big cane and limped noticeably. When asked about his condition he said: "Legee all right, but knee vera sore." When asked whether he would wrestle Lewis again, he said: "Never wrestle Lewis again. Never, never." He said that over the summer he would go home and fetch back his brother to deal with the Strangler: "He wrestle Lewis and treat his leg same as Lewis treat mine." Sorakichi left Chicago soon after the Lewis rematch. He did not go to Japan, but instead went to St. Louis with Bibby to appear at the Casino Theater for the local sports. By the time he reached St. Louis, Sorakichi was no longer using his cane.[348]

In the early 1880s Davies had developed a set of rules for prizefights that were referred to as the C. E. Davies' Rules. Newspaper articles about fights that

Davies managed and promoted often state that the C. E. Davies' Rules were used for a given fight, but from descriptions of those fights it is difficult to see a difference between the Parson's rules and Queensberry rules. The result in the Lewis-Sorakichi rematch demanded some review of the rules applicable to catch-as-catch-can wrestling matches. In part this was necessary to demonstrate to politicians and police that they did not need to take action to shut down wrestling in Chicago. It was also necessary to take action to prevent serious injury to wrestlers, which could also have an adverse impact on the business.

With virtually no exception, professional wrestlers maintained that Lewis had done nothing wrong when he twisted and nearly broke Sorakichi's ankle. Others said that one of the rules of catch-as-catch-can wrestling applied to intentionally disabling an opponent. That broad rule said that "biting, gouging, or any other unfair act" could be penalized as matters within the referees' judgments. Davies decided to eliminate the ambiguity and prepared his own set of rules that would hence forth apply to catch-as-catch-can matches that he promoted. The new Davies' rules provided that deliberately maiming an opponent would be a foul and accompanied by the loss of the match and stakes.[349]

After the wrestling rematch Davies turned his attention to boxing and to promoting Killen and Burke. The two men needed to be treated differently. Killen needed matches to build his reputation and to develop his skill in the ring. Burke needed matches to stay sharp, but he was also expected to box some first-class heavyweights, and there weren't too many around Chicago at the time. A serious match between the two fighters would damage the reputation of one of them, so that was not in the cards.

Davies had matched Killen to meet Dick Burke at the Park Theater on February 19. With no immediate match pending, Jack Burke went to Tennessee for four days to continue his tour *sans* Killen. While Jack was in Tennessee, Davies scheduled a fight for him with Glover at Battery D to take place on March 8, 1886.[350]

Killen's fight with Dick Burke was a flop. The Park was crowded to the doors. The audience included Jack Burke, Davies, Paddy Ryan, Tom Chandler, Pat Sheedy, and other well-known sporting men. The press estimated that Dick Burke was at least forty-five or fifty years old. He had earned a reputation in the stockyards as a rough-and-tumble fighter, and he had participated in several battles while he was employed in the construction of the Erie Canal.[351]

Throughout his career Killen was known as a right-handed first-punch specialist. With his first punch in the Dick Burke match, he put his opponent down. Burke then played the "knock-down dodge" and went down several times without being hit. At the end of the second round everyone was disgusted and the fight was awarded to Killen. A few days after this match it was announced that Killen would meet Pat McHugh, dubbed the heavyweight champion of Wisconsin, at the Park on March 5.[352]

The Killen-McHugh match was another lemon. McHugh had the reputation for being a game man who never weakened. Killen had spent the two weeks before this match training in Madison and was in top shape for the event. To the disappointment of everyone, McHugh played the "baby act" during the fight. Killen failed to knock out McHugh, but this was due to McHugh's tactics. In the first round McHugh picked up Killen and tossed him through the ropes and into the footlights. When Killen returned to the ring, McHugh commenced dodging all around the stage and dropping to one knee to avoid being punished. In the second round, McHugh picked up Killen a second time and threw him as if in a wrestling match. While Killen was on the floor, McHugh tried to punch him. Throughout the remaining three rounds McHugh followed these tactics, and at the conclusion the referee called the match a draw. This was another fight that presented boxing in a poor light, and this type of match did not help to hone Killen's skills as a prizefighter.[353]

Killen and Jack Burke went to Cincinnati where they spared at opposing theaters with both drawing good crowds.[354] Then three weeks after the McHugh fight, Killen met James Brady, of Buffalo, in Milwaukee in a glove contest for $200 a side. A large crowd watched the match, and Killen hit Brady in the stomach so hard that Brady was stunned and unable to come-to in time for the second round.[355] Brady was described as Parson Davies' "unknown." On April 1, Killen was in Eau Claire to spar for four rounds using four-ounce gloves with a man named E. D. Stalker (sometimes "Stelker') who was described as a six-foot two lumberman. The fight took place before about eight hundred patrons at the Criterion Arena. One report says that Killen knocked Stalker through the ropes with the first blow, and his opponent quit. Another says that the fight lasted two rounds.[356]

On April 3, Pat left Chicago for Omaha, where he was to meet a man named Mike Haley, described sometimes as the champion of Iowa and at others as champion of Chicago. Accounts say that Parson Davies was not able to be present because there was an election taking place in Chicago.[357] Killen met Haley on the stage of the People's Theater with four-ounce gloves. Haley appeared to be afraid of Killen and went down every time he was touched. Finally, in the second round Haley stretched out full-length on the floor and gave up.[358] Not long after this fight Davies sent Killen to Mt. Clemens to "boil for five or six weeks."[359] Although there were hot springs at Mt. Clemens, this certainly means that Killen was drunk and needed to dry out and suggests that Davies was prepared to cut him lose if he didn't stop drinking like a fish.

In the 1880s, Mt. Clemens was known as the place to go for therapeutic hot mineral baths, and many prizefighters went there to take those treatments. It appears that Davies and Killen were in the process of a falling out because of Killen's excessive drinking. During his trips to St. Louis, Cincinnati, Philadelphia, Pittsburgh, and Indianapolis, Killen had developed his science, but he had also honed his fondness for alcohol, and Davies was not willing to promote a drunk. He sent Killen to dry out and put the fighter's development on hold until he put his liquor problem under control. Killen was unwilling to follow orders and instead he went to Duluth and opened a saloon, where he fought two or three local men a week and never failed to knock out his opponent. But drinking and fighting miners and lumber jacks provided no future for a heavyweight of Killen's quality, and he did not have a manager to find the best opponents. The great promise Killen held was lost at the rim of a whiskey glass.

About this time Davies was asked his opinion about the younger generation of prizefighters. He thought Burke and Mitchell were the two most promising of the group. He liked Dempsey, but thought Dempsey was too small. He felt that Cardiff was a good man. As for Killen, the Parson said: "Pat Killen would have been on top if he had kept up. I never saw a quicker man or a harder hitter, but whisky has knocked him." Killen left Chicago and went to Minneapolis. He claimed that the story about his drinking was planted by Davies. He called Davies a "shark" and claimed that his take from the fight with Lannon had been $34.50. About eight months later, the Parson received a letter from Killen asking him to act as his manager in the future and promising to take care of himself if Davies would agree. There is no real question that Pat Killen was a drunk, and it cost him dearly and would contribute to his death.

On March 7, in between the Killen-McHugh fight and the scheduled Burke-Glover fight, Davies went to Milwaukee to watch a wrestling match that he was promoting between Lewis and Charles Moth.[360] Moth was known as "The Pine Woods Terror," which was not the best nickname anyone every adopted. This match almost fell apart before it started. It was a best three-out-of-five falls, but there was a dispute over the style of wrestling to be employed. When that dispute was resolved, the wrestlers came to the ring and the crowd was against Lewis, even though he had been a favorite in his home state.

There was lingering bad feeling about the manner in which he had treated Sorakichi during their matches in Chicago. However, Lewis silenced his critics by winning the first bout in catch-as-catch-can format in just over two minutes. The second bout was in Greco-Roman style and Lewis won that contest in six minutes. Back in the catch-as-catch-can style for the third bout, Lewis again won in about two minutes.[361] This young wrestler was proving to be a marketable athlete, even if had cast himself as the bad guy.

Burke and Glover

The Burke-Glover fight was scheduled for six rounds. The terms were "all-or-nothing of the gate receipts." Burke was the quicker man and had better science, but Glover was more powerful, and although he had fought several draws, he had never lost a fight to that date.[362] The contest at Battery D on the evening of March 8 went the full six rounds. The crowd was better than it had been for many months, and there was apparent local interest in the fight. Every seat was occupied. Men holding standing room tickets were jostling for positions to better see the action. An estimated three-thousand five-hundred patrons had paid at the gate.

Glover's first mistake that evening was to agree to Evan Lewis as referee. Glover had ruled against Lewis at several key points in Lewis' first match with

Sorakichi, which was not a reason to expect an even hand from the Strangler. Moreover, Burke was Davies' fighter and Evan Lewis was Parson Davies' wrestler. Glover was giving up a lot for a chance to fight Burke. Davies brought the gloves for the match to the ring at ten fifteen p.m. and "the fun commenced." Glover seemed to dominate the fight from the beginning. Burke did not try to force the action until the fourth round, when he caught Glover on the nose and chin, but Glover countered with his right hand to the chin and then caught Burke square on his left eye, which began to swell and close almost immediately, making it difficult for Burke to see properly. Burke also caught Glover on the eye, and that blow resulted in a slight cut.

In the fifth round Burke went back on the defensive, and the crowd became irritated and started yelling for him to mix it up. These taunts from a crowd that had often favored Burke seemed to excite him, and he rushed toward Glover, who took the blows easily and banged away in return. The sixth round was similar to the fifth, and at the conclusion everyone supposed that the match would be declared a draw. To the surprise of many, Lewis awarded the fight to Burke. This outcome, absent a knock-out by Glover, might have been anticipated.[363]

Glover was angry about the treatment he had received and quickly issued a challenge to Burke for a fight to the finish within two weeks using London rules for $2,500 a side. The challenge appealed to sportsmen of the day who considered limited-round and Queensberry rule fights to be emasculated ring performances in which the managers controlled the likely outcome and nobody was really hurt.[364] People in the fight game would say that London-rule fights provided the only format in which a man's gameness and cleverness could really be tested. But London-rule fights could not be presented in Chicago, and there is no evidence that Glover knew anything about London prize-ring rules fighting.

Because a London-rule fight could not take place in Chicago, it would be necessary to find a remote place for a finish fight, such as Butte City, and it was impractical to think that a venue could be located and a fight promoted within two weeks. Burke's reply to Glover's challenge was that he could not risk his reputation for only $2,500. He proposed a finish fight within six to eight weeks for $5,000 a side, Queensberry rules, but with kid gloves. He wanted the fight to take place in Wyoming Territory. Burke then posted $1,000 with McDonald as his deposit for a rematch under the terms that he outlined.[365]

The typical dance between two fighters who might not really want to meet again but rather wanted to save face was under way in earnest. About one week after Burke's proposal, Glover's backer delivered $1,000 to Davies (no one could find McDonald) to bind a fight with Burke for $5,000 a side. Glover, however, would not accept Burke's terms. He refused to travel to Wyoming Territory, or any other remote place, and he continued to insist on a London-rule fight to the finish. Of course, this was only a counter-offer and did not bind either man to meet.

Glover gained enough notoriety from his match with Burke that promoters in other towns contacted him to appear in their communities. He agreed to appear in Minneapolis for a week at a local theater. While in Minneapolis, Glover hurt his arm but did not immediately seek medical attention. Instead, he applied liniment to the arm and went to Beloit to go into training for an eight-round rematch with Burke that Parson Davies was planning for May 3 at Battery D.

On March 10, Davies attended a banquet held by Chicago Lodge No. 4 of the Elks, the lodge started ten years earlier by Joe Mackin, Parson Davies, and a handful of other men. The banquet in was attended by some three hundred gentlemen. In addition, founding members of the Omaha, Nebraska lodge were present as that lodge was an offshoot of the Lodge No. 4.[366] The next day Davies, Lewis, and Lewis' backer Thomas Gill left Chicago together and went to St. Louis for a match that Davies had arranged between Lewis and Edwin Bibby at Pope's Theater. This was a match for $250 a side.[367]

The big news in prizefighting in early 1886 was the finish Dempsey-La Blanche fight that had been scheduled in New York City. This is one of the few major fights of the 1880s that Davies did not personally attend. The fight resulted in a thirteen-round victory for Dempsey and marked him as a preeminent fighter who would be emulated by many other fighters, including James J. Corbett. The finish nature of the Dempsey-La Blanche fight added fuel to the fire for those who wanted to shut down boxing. After he won the fight, Dempsey said that he next wanted to fight Burke. This sounded like the ring of a cash register.[368]

In mid-April 1886 Sullivan was in Joliet, Illinois, touring with the Lester & Allen Minstrel Company and while there, he went to the Joliet prison to meet with Joe Mackin. Joe had been the right-hand-man for Mike McDonald and had held numerous Democratic Party positions in Chicago and Cook County before his perjury conviction sent him up the river. Presumably Sullivan had met Mackin as early as 1881 when Sullivan was in Chicago with Parson Davies. It is likely that Davies prevailed on Sullivan to visit Joe to lift his friend's spirits. After meeting with Mackin, Sullivan then visited the prison shops, and his appearance created quite a stir among the prison population. Sullivan might have been the Johnny Cash of his day, but without a guitar.[369]

In late April, it became evident that the Burke-Glover rematch would have to be cancelled. Glover had hurt his arm much worse than he had suspected. While he was sparring in Minneapolis, he had put on big, soft gloves with John W. Curtis of Eau Claire, Wisconsin, whom Burke had defeated in August 1885. During his set-to with Curtis, Glover reinjured the arm. Weeks later he was still in pain and finally saw a doctor in Beloit. He then learned that he had fractured the radius in his right forearm and could not continue training or fighting until the bone healed. This meant that Davies had an open date to fill on short notice, and he immediately began trying to find an opponent for Burke.[370]

Matching Burke and Dempsey

Davies knew that Dempsey was in Pittsburgh as part of a theater tour. He knew that Jack had said publicly that he wanted to meet Burke. He wired

Dempsey and asked him to come to Chicago to fill the open date on May 3. Dempsey declined, saying that he had prior contractual obligations in Pittsburgh and that he would not make a match with Burke unless it was bare-knuckles fight to a finish for $5,000 a side. This was the same nonsense that Glover had tried earlier in the year. Anyone familiar with boxing at this point knew that making such a match between two well-known fighters was next to impossible. Davies next turned to Mitchell to fill the May 3 date, and Mitchell agreed. The shortness of the time before the scheduled fight caused the match to be pushed back to May 10. Mitchell immediately went into training with Tommy Warren at Beloit, Wisconsin.[371]

The Haymarket riot and prizefighting in Chicago

Several important events occurred in early May that had nothing directly to do with boxing but had a substantial impact on the presentation of athletic contests in Chicago and cities big and small all over the United States. A national organization known as the Federation of Organized Trades and Labor Unions had set May 1 as the date when the eight-hour work-day would either become standard or the unions would conduct a nationwide strike to support that objective. By Saturday, May 1, the eight-hour day had not been adopted and national strikes took place. In Chicago about forty thousand men went on strike, which whipped up tension in the city. Many of the strikers were part of the crowds that showed up for the boxing and wrestling shows that Davies promoted. New fighters came from their ranks. Sports like boxing and wrestling provided a way out of the so-called wage class.

The McCormick Harvesting Machine Company in Chicago had experienced labor conflict for over a year when in early May its president decided to give ten hours of pay to workers for eight hours of work, excluding members of labor unions. On the night of May 4, 1886 a sympathy strike was scheduled at the Haymarket Square in Chicago to support union pickets who had been roughed up by police and Pinkerton agents at the McCormick plant. About two hundred Chicago policemen were near the site of the planned Haymarket meeting of union, socialist, and communist elements.

The police decided to disperse protesters to avoid damage to nearby private property. They ordered the crowd to disperse, and someone threw a bomb. The police then fired into the crowd, and protesters and police were killed in the rioting that followed.

The entire country was on edge as a result of the general strike, and it was pushed over the edge by news of the Haymarket Riot. Every major industrial city thought that it would be the next one to face gunfire in the streets. A detailed and valuable account of the events in Chicago is provided in the 1946 book *Battle for Chicago*.[372] After these events virtually every politician in the country was told by the good people and leaders of their communities that prompt action had to be taken to prevent impending riot and disaster. Prompt action always included dealing firmly with those who scoffed at the law, which included gamblers, saloon owners, and sports promoters.

For Davies the next shoe dropped on the night of May 10, just before the Burke-Mitchell fight. Lt. John D. Shea was extensively involved in matters relating to the Haymarket Riot. He had searched the offices of the *Arbeiter-Zeitung* newspaper on May 5, shortly after the arrest of the anarchists Spies and Shwab. He had also questioned Spies after his arrest and then testified extensively about their conversation during a later trail.[373]

Shea appeared at Battery D to assume his customary role in overseeing the contest. "Seats were always reserved for Inspector Shea and his friends in the first row, and the show would never be started until the Inspector arrived. He was ostensibly present at such events to see to it that no 'brutal prize fighting' was being pulled off and that the law was being observed."[374] This should have been a fairly relaxing evening for Shea and a nice break from the problems and tensions of the prior week. It seems clear that Davies had been paying Shea to fill a quasi-official role at his boxing promotions because Shea's presence also prevented interference with Davies' sporting productions.

On May 10 Davies had arranged for extra security for the Burke-Mitchell fight. The violence in the city over the prior four or five days required a promoter to provide the best available security. As far as Davies knew the big crowd expected at an important prizefight might attract another bomb thrower. He had hired private security and a guard named Thomas Daly was working at the door and did not recognize Lieutenant Shea when he arrived. Daly asked Shea for his ticket. Of course, Shea didn't have a ticket. He never had a ticket. He had a badge. He explained to Daly that he was a lieutenant with the Chicago police and insisted on being admitted. Daly was not convinced. When Shea again insisted on entrance, Daly smacked Shea over the head with a night stick. Matters soon cooled down, but this incident clearly had an impact of the attitude of the police toward prizefighting in Chicago.

Others who were present for this match but were not clubbed at the door included: Sullivan, who was traveling with the Lester & Allen Minstrel Company; Dempsey, who had earlier insisted that his contractual obligations made it impossible for him to meet Burke; Tom Cleary; the injured Glover, who was supposed to have been Burke's opponent, and other notables. The Burke-Mitchell fight illustrated how the Chicago fans and its press corps had cooled toward Burke and had backed off of the adulation that he had enjoyed a year earlier. The headline in the *Chicago Herald* the next morning read: "Burke Again In Luck, This Time He Is Saved By a Draw."[375] The headline in the *Chicago Tribune* read: "An Unjust Decision. The Burke-Mitchell Glove Fight Declared A Draw." [376] This fight fit the idea that some had of a fixed fight without suggesting that anyone had been paid to achieve a particular result.

The referee was Bill Bradburn. He had been the referee for the Burke-Cleary fight at the end of 1885, and Burke had been a second for Bradburn during his match with Glover in January 1886. In this meeting Burke had the best of the fight up through the middle of the fourth round. In the fifth round Mitchell began to abuse Burke with regularity.

By the end of the sixth round Burke was winded, but then the timekeepers made a mistake and allowed a minute and thirty seconds to pass before ringing the bell for the seventh round. Thanks to this mistake, Burke was able to recover his wind. During the rest of the fight Burke continued to weaken, and Mitchell had the upper hand. In the eighth round the timekeepers called an end to the round after only two minutes, again providing Burke with an advantage when he appeared to be a goner. At the end of the allotted eight rounds, Bradburn said that he was unable to render a decision and the fight went on for two more rounds that were marked both by Mitchell's staggering Burke and also by continued "funny business" on the part of the timekeepers.

Four or five minutes after the end of the tenth round, Bradburn called the match a draw. The newspapers commented that the best proof that Bradburn's decision was wrong were the bruises left all over Burke, whose left eye was closed and his face was cut up terribly on both sides of his nose. Tom Kelly, whose son had been knocked around by Burke in St. Louis, said that Burke had landed only one square blow on Mitchell during the entire fight. Sullivan, who detested Mitchell, said that he thought that Bradburn's decision was correct. Sullivan took the position that no man should be counted as losing a fight until he gave up or was unable to come to time. This was a fairly well-accepted view among many heavyweights in the 1880s and the antithesis of the opinion that these were fixed fights. The Burke-Mitchell fight was Davies' fourth event listed as one of Chicago's top ten sporting events of 1886.[377]

Dempsey and Mitchell – two big egos

With both Dempsey and Mitchell in town, Davies tried to arrange a meeting between the two. They held a powwow at Davies' private office at six-thirty p.m. on May 13 with the intent of drawing up articles for a bare-knuckle or skin-glove contest for the middleweight championship of the world. This was preceded by a dispute between the two fighters about their weights. Dempsey bet Mitchell a bottle of wine that Mitchell outweighed him by twenty pounds. Along with Davies they went to Bathhouse Johnny Coughlin's Turkish bath and were weighed. Dempsey weighed 159 pounds and Mitchell 161. Mitchell won the wine and rubbed it in a little.

At Davies' offices Dempsey wanted the fight to take place within four weeks. Mitchell refused because he was scheduled to fight Sullivan but said that he would fight within eight weeks. A fight nearly broke out after Dempsey said that if everyone else would clear out he would "do-up" Mitchell in that room. This confrontation was prevented only by Davies and Burke.[378] Months later the *Chicago Tribune*, probably based on Davies' account of the events, reported that Dempsey became abusive and addressed Mitchell in vulgar terms. Mitchell, in a gentlemanly way, ridiculed Dempsey unmercifully and made him a laughing-stock. Dempsey, realizing that he was no match for Mitchell with his tongue, lost his temper and grew so abusive that Mitchell showed an inclination to fight him immediately and told Davies to close the door. At that point Davies and Burke interfered. Davies told the two that they could not fight in his house. No agreement was reached and Dempsey left late that same evening for St. Paul. Mitchell and Dempsey would despise each other for their entire careers.[379]

The hammer was hanging above Davies. The physical abuse of Lieutenant Shea and the perceived unfairness of the decisions in Burke's last two fights undoubtedly played roles in what happened next. On May 21, the new general superintendent of the Chicago police refused to grant a permit for a prizefight planned by another Chicago promoter. In addition, the police appeared on the stage of a Chicago theater and stopped a boxing match that was in progress as part of the regular entertainment.[380] The new chief announced that no more boxing or sparring exhibitions would be permitted in public in Chicago, and the order applied to all pending and advertised matches. This action was taken in part because of a letter that Mayor Harrison had received from a citizens' association demanding that he enforce the laws relating to prizefighting and the growing influence exercised by such citizens associations.

The *Chicago Tribune* published an editorial complementing the city authorities for suppressing the disgraceful and brutal wrestling, sparring, and slugging exhibitions. The use of gloves in a fight was called a "miserable subterfuge" and the paper hoped that in banning such matches the city would rid itself of the sporting characters, sluggers, and prizefighters found in virtually every saloon in the city.[381] Reportedly, the mayor had not wanted to prevent these sporting events and had argued against that action, but he was ultimately persuaded that the law should be enforced. About a year later, the city took the position that its ban was never intended to apply to wrestling matches but only to prizefighting, but that was not the way the prohibitions were first enforced when were announced in May 1886.

Wrestlers were already finding new places to put on their shows. Muldoon and Lewis appeared in Minneapolis on May 27. The terms of the match were that Muldoon was to throw Lewis twice in one hour. After forty-seven minutes Muldoon secured a contested throw but gave up the match because he was convinced that he could not get a throw in the time remaining.[382]

Two future hall of fame wrestlers

Ten days later Muldoon showed up in Chicago and went to see Davies at The Store. Muldoon was still disgusted by the outcome of the match in Minneapolis and wanted Charlie to arrange a legitimate wrestling match.[383] Davies went to see Lewis in Madison and when he returned told Muldoon that Lewis would make a match in a straight Greco-Roman format, there-out-of-five falls, for a 70/30 split of the gate receipts. Davies thought he could arrange a match in Chicago very shortly, but it wasn't at all clear why the Parson thought he could get a license for the match when Mayor Harrison had ordered such activity closed down.[384]

Muldoon sent a letter to the *Post Dispatch* in June 1886 contending that the efforts of Davies to schedule a rematch with Lewis had failed. Muldoon then issued a public challenge to Lewis to wrestle on the terms that he dictated. Davies was obviously irritated by Muldoon's characterization of why a rematch had not be scheduled, and the Parson publicly accepted the proposed match for Lewis on Muldoon's specified terms: best three-in-five falls, Greco-Roman style, winner to take a 75/25 of the gate. The rematch was to take place in Chicago on June 28.[385]

Many prizefighters who had been working in Chicago left town after the fight ban and went to St. Louis, where boxing was fairly wide open. Several of the lesser known Chicago fighters moved to St. Louis before the end of May. For promoters in the cities where athletic competitions were shut down, there were some unanticipated consequences. Many promoters were comfortable promoting boxing matches in their own towns and had become invested in their close relationships with local politicians and local police forces. They sometimes had significant influence over whether other promoters could obtain licenses for sporting events and often controlled which fighters were able to schedule the best matches and when those matches would take place.

Many fighters and wrestlers had become regional favorites and did not have the same national reputations as the prior generation. Fighters from England and Australia were about the only men who traveled from place to place for contests with local fighters. In addition, the best fighters and wrestlers were reluctant to appear outside the community where their backers and promoters had influence because the outcome of fights and matches could often depend on who selected the referee, who acted as timekeeper, and whether the police would interfere with a fight if things were going poorly for the local man.

Cutting off local sporting events forced promoters out of their comfort zones. Whether a promoter was in Chicago, Baltimore, Philadelphia, Boston, New York, or many other sporting centers they were forced to look for places where their events could take place and to consider making matches with fighters from outside of their own regions. All of these things would have an impact on Davies and the matches and fights he promoted during the last half of 1886.

Davies and J. B. Thorne of Chicago were in St. Paul on June 11 to watch the Cardiff-Mitchell fight. Unable to continue fighting in Chicago, Burke accepted a fight against a man named Peter J. Nolan at Chester Park in Cincinnati for June 12. Burke and Killen had appeared before large audiences in Cincinnati while they were touring earlier in 1886, and the city looked like a good place for prizefights and could be easily reached by sports from Chicago.

Nolan was a twenty-three-year-old Cincinnati boy of Irish heritage. He had been involved in local politics from the time he was a teenager. At twenty-one he had been appointed as engineer and elevator surveyor for Cincinnati's water department, earning the nice salary of $1,200 a year. Several years before 1886, a black fighter named Harry Woodson (the "Black Diamond") had been in Cincinnati for a fight with "Professor" Hadley of St. Paul. Their match was billed as the "colored" heavyweight championship of the world. Nolan challenged Woodson, who was an excellent fighter, and easily beat him in a gloved match. There was no color line drawn when Nolan fought Harry Woodson. Then in 1883 another fighter named "Professor" Brooks, described as the champion of the Pacific coast, passed through Cincinnati issuing challenges similar to Sullivan's famed challenges. Nolan accepted and on July 12, 1883, he defeated Brooks in two rounds at Cincinnati's Grand Opera House. Other than these two fights Nolan had no other ring experience.

Muldoon was the master of ceremonies for the Burke-Nolan match.[386] About two thousand paid patrons were on hand and squarely behind Nolan. Those who had been watching Burke's recent fights against Glover and Mitchell might have known that Burke's overall performance was slipping, but most observers would not have thought that he'd have trouble with Nolan. Burke drew first blood during the second round of the fight and forced the fighting. In the fourth round Nolan seemed to catch a second-wind and began to turn the tide of the fight. Nolan continued on the offensive through the end of the sixth and final round, and the local crowd was wild with excitement.

The referee for this fight was the wrestler Tom Cannon. He initially reserved his decision. While Cannon was undecided, local men rushed the ring and carried Nolan around on their shoulders as the victor. Burke was angry and insisted that Cannon make a decision immediately. The crowd too began to yell for a decision. Finally Cannon called the match a draw, which amounted to a victory for Nolan in the estimation of the Cincinnati crowd. Burke was embarrassed and demanded a rematch.[387] The two men were scheduled to meet again at Chester Park on July 5.[388] Burke went into training with Frank Ware, the lightweight champion of Illinois, at Waukesha, Wisconsin, and he did not return to Cincinnati until July 2.[389]

Burke's wife traveled with him for his training in Waukesha. While she was there she became ill and was required to undergo a severe surgical operation that nearly cost her life. Burke had to leave his wife in Waukesha to meet his commitment with Nolan. These events probably adversely affected Burke's performance and affected his training for the rematch. For many athletes it is difficult to perform at a high level under similar circumstances.[390]

After working the Burke-Nolan fight in Cincinnati, Muldoon went back to Chicago on June 24 and stayed at the Tremont House. He went to Davies' place, where he was questioned by the press. It is worth recalling that Muldoon had known Charlie Davies since Charlie had been a young man waiting tables in the Bowery, and now Muldoon was making deals for wrestling matches through Davies at his own famous saloon in Chicago.

Muldoon said that he had been in training for his rematch with Lewis at his farm at Belfast, New York, and that he had then gone to Cincinnati to warm up with Tom Cannon, who was the referee at the Burke-Nolan fight. Muldoon said that the hall where he had worked out with Cannon had been one hundred ten degrees, and he had lost ten pounds there. This statement helps explain why prizefights like the Burke-Nolan matches were held outside in Cincinnati in the summer of 1886. Muldoon also said that he wanted to find out whether Lewis really knew how to wrestle.

Davies chimed in, "He can't twist your ankle, but he can use the strangle just the same." "That's all right," Muldoon responded. "He's welcome to it if he can get it."

By the way, it was Parson Davies who coined the nickname "the Strangler" for Evan Lewis.[391]

Somehow Davies got a license for the Evans-Muldoon wrestling match when other promoters were getting nothing from the city fathers. In a town known for pay-to-play, it may be that he knew whom to pay to get a wrestling license. About fifteen hundred people appeared at Battery D for the match. This was not the kind of house expected at a good prizefight in Chicago. But the promotional costs for wrestling matches were not as high as for boxing matches and yet wrestling shows helped put bread on the table.

Duncan C. Ross, who had been in San Francisco for over a year, was the referee for the match. Muldoon weighed 195 and Lewis only 175. Shortly after the first bout began, the two wrestlers collided. Lewis got his famous strangle-neck-lock on Muldoon and took him to the floor in just two minutes and thirty seconds. Davies' prediction that Lewis would get Muldoon in the strangle hold had proved accurate.

The second bout was contested for twenty-five minutes before Muldoon asked for time to rub down and remove the sweat that covered both men. When they resumed after ten minutes, Muldoon picked up Lewis by a body lock and smashed him to the floor. He was able to throw Lewis over and take the second fall. Muldoon then retired to his dressing room to be rubbed down. Word was sent out from his dressing room that Muldoon was sick and could not resume the contest, so referee Ross gave the match to Lewis and then immediately read a challenge from Tom Cannon, who had been working with Muldoon in Cincinnati, to wrestle either Muldoon or Lewis for $500. Davies immediately accepted the challenge for Lewis.[392]

Burke gets ambushed in Cincinnati

The Burke-Nolan rematch took place at Chester Park on July 5. The articles specified Queensberry rules with two ounce gloves for $500 a side. The referee this time was Frank Kelly, a local deputy-sheriff. The crowd grew to about three thousand customers and included Cincinnati aristocrats and their ladies. Many observers thought that Burke would be prepared and demolish Nolan during their rematch. After their first match Jack claimed that he had not fought his hardest because he was afraid of police interference. This seemed like a plausible explanation because both Burke and Nolan had been required to post peace bonds before that fight began, and there had been a heavy police presence during the fight.

The battle went against Burke early. In the second round, Nolan caught Burke on his left eye and broke it open so that a rivulet of blood was oozing down Burke's face. Burke was clearly rattled and charged at Nolan but received a crack in the mouth for his effort. The *Cincinnati Enquirer* said that Burke was "bleeding like a slaughtered pig" and that at the end of the second round "his face looked as if his head had been dipped in a bucket of blood." The *Chicago Tribune* reported that Burke was bleeding from his nose, mouth, and eye at the beginning of the third round. Things like this often happened when fighters wore two-ounce gloves.

In the third round Burke caught Nolan on the mouth and bloodied his face. Nolan continued to carry the fight to Burke in the third, fourth, and fifth rounds. The sixth round was decisive. Nolan punished Burke with a left-handed crack to his chest and continued to do good body work throughout the round. The fight tapered off in the last two rounds, but the referee's decision was that Nolan had won the match, and it was generally agreed that the result was fair.[393]

After the fight Burke came back to Chicago for a day and then went to Waukesha where his wife was still in the hospital. The Nolan fight was Burke's first defeat in the United States to anyone other than Sullivan. After a few days in Wisconsin, he went back to Cincinnati and stood trial on a charge of participating in a prizefight. Several continuances occurred before the case finally went to trial on July 19 and resulted in a jury verdict of not guilty.[394]

As soon as the criminal matter was resolved, Burke challenged Nolan to a third match with soft or kid gloves, for eight, ten, or twelve rounds, to a finish, under any rules that Nolan wanted to name for $2,500 to $5,000 a side. Burke specified that the fight be held outside Ohio. Cincinnati law enforcement was becoming more aggressive, and prizefighting in Ohio was less attractive than a few months earlier. Burke claimed that the referee in the first match with Nolan had been intimidated by a gang of men who came onto the platform during the first fight. He said that the referee in their second fight, Frank Kelly, had been incompetent and unfair, and he thought that the overall circumstances demanded a third match on an even playing field. Nolan said he was looking for other opponents and could gain nothing more by fighting Burke a third time. Nolan left Cincinnati for New York City to try to arrange contests with Frank Herald and Dominick McCaffery. [395]

A *Post Dispatch* columnist had a different take on the fight and why Burke did not perform well. He felt that in his eagerness to make money, Burke had overworked himself by fighting almost constantly since coming to the United States. That writer felt that even if Burke were made of cast steel, the amount of work he had undertaken would have worn on him. This assessment may have been accurate given the significant fights and constant road trips that Burke had undertaken since January 1885.[396]

Billy Myer gets stiffed

The night after the Burke-Nolan fight, Billy Myer, a young fighter from Streator, Illinois, met Paddy Welch, the featherweight champion of Illinois, at Braidwood, Illinois. Welch had earned an excellent reputation among Chicago sports. The Myer-Welch fight was attended by sporting fans from all over Illinois because many of the other cities in Illinois had experienced the same problems that had arisen in Chicago, and prizefights had been shut down in their communities. The two men fought for $500 a side. Davies was the stakeholder for the match. In the third round Myer knocked Welch over the ropes and out cold. Welch was so badly beaten in the fight that his body had to be wrapped in tape and his left arm put in a sling. The fight caused a sensation in Chicago because there had been so little activity after Mayor Harrison had closed things down, and there had been far too little to talk about. Arthur Majesty, who had fought Tommy Warren on the undercard of the Sullivan-Burke fight, acted as Myer's trainer and as his second for this fight.[397]

After the fight Myer and his backer, Alf Kennedy, went to Chicago to collect their money from Davies. Charlie told them that he could not turn over the stake because Welch's backers had squealed and would not permit him to give up the money. There is no mention of what Welch's backers were squealing about. According to reports in the *Streator Daily Free Press*, both Kennedy and Myer were compelled to give bonds for $500 and costs of suit in the event they sued the Parson.[398] It is clear that Davies' connections in Chicago remained solid, but this result was widely criticized in the local press and, if true, their criticisms were justified.

Lewis gets the short end in Cincinnati

Davies left Chicago for Cincinnati on Tuesday, July 13, 1886 for the Lewis-Cannon match scheduled for July 15. Cincinnati was Cannon's home turf, and the match had resulted from Cannon's challenge at the end of the Muldoon-Lewis match in Chicago. The contest was for the best two-out-of-three falls, $250 a side and the net receipts of the house. Some sources say that the gate was to be divided 70/30. Davies had been unable to arrange this match in Chicago. Much to the Parson's disappointment, Cannon won the match, and it appeared that the loss could seriously impair Davies' efforts to promote Lewis.[399]

Dr. A. E. Heighway was the referee for the match. Davies was the second for Lewis, and a long-distance pedestrian known as Billy Gale was Cannon's second. As the match began, the contestants rolled off the stage. In the process Cannon landed on top with Lewis' back to the floor, which appeared to be a fall. The referee ruled that a fall had to take place on the mat. Cannon protested but that was not allowed. When the men went back to the canvass, they rolled to the edge of the stage. Lewis's legs hung out over the gaslights, the hair on his legs sizzled and the skin on his legs fried like a sausage. Pandemonium broke loose, and every individual spectator acted as a special committee-of-one to play maniac. Back on the canvas, Lewis got his strangle-hold, but Cannon rolled out of it and secured a half-Nelson on Lewis and put him to the mat.

During the intermission Cannon was in his dressing room spitting up blood because of Lewis' application of the strangle-hold. Lewis knew how to damage an opponent's throat. Cannon's seconds were frightened that he had internal injuries. Lewis went to his dressing room to treat his burned leg and to treat a spot where a "chip of flesh half as big as a butter cracker was knocked off just below the knee." When the men returned for the second bout, Lewis got his neck-hold once again, but it was broken by Cannon. Finally, "quick as lightning" Cannon secured a body-hold and in a half-flying fall got Lewis' shoulders to the mat. The referee declared Cannon the winner.

Amid the excitement Cannon turned to the audience and said: "I challenge any man in the world to wrestle me Greco-Roman style for $500 or $1,000 a side." Davies stepped forward on the opposite side of the stage and challenged Cannon to wrestle on the same stage, private or public, three out of five falls, the next evening for $500 a side. Cannon declined, saying he would not wrestle again until he could pull himself into good enough condition for a match.[400]

Cincinnati was not treating Davies' wrestlers and prizefighters well. Davies and Lewis returned to Chicago on July 16 on separate trains. When he arrived in Chicago, Charlie said that he thought Lewis had lost his head a little bit, but he was still convinced that the Strangler could defeat Cannon in a catch-as-catch-can format. Lewis was upset by his performance and vowed that he could not return to his home in Madison, Wisconsin, until he had thrown Cannon.[401] Although Cannon refused the public proposal made by Davies, he did reach an agreement for another Greco-Roman style match for two out of three falls. If Lewis won the rematch, then there would be a third match in another city, catch-as-catch-can style, for $250 to $500 a side. Davies was to prepare articles and notify Cannon when they were ready to be signed.[402]

Shortly after returning home, Davies was contacted by Sorakichi's manager, who was coming back for more of the good money available in Chicago. Sorakichi wanted to wrestle Lewis, provided the strangle-hold and wrenching of limbs were both prohibited. This was something like offering to participate in a prizefight provided neither of the fighters would use his left hand. Davies wrote in response that Lewis would wrestle and would bar wrenching of limbs and choking for $200 to $500 a side with the winner to take the entire gate receipts. With this sort of thing happening it was clear that promotion of sporting events was getting very slow compared to the five previous years.[403]

While articles about sporting events managed or promoted by Parson Davies are numerous, it is more difficult to locate information about Davies' day-to-day life. A series of articles published in the *Chicago Tribune* in early August 1886 provided some insight. The following account is a reconstruction that seems to make sense from what was actually reported in several newspapers, which seldom reported the events in the same manner.

Paddy Ryan and a knife fight at The Store

There were a series of fist and knife fights involving Paddy Ryan that took place in and around The Store on the evening of August 3, 1886. One of the fights led to the death of a Chicago businessman. It appears that the problems began with F. L. Willner, who was a stenographer and notary with an office at 107 Dearborn Street. Willner had gone to The Store after work for a few libations. Davies was present and was sharing a bottle of wine with some of his friends. One of the people drinking with Davies was Paddy Ryan.

Ryan had shown up that night at The Store. He and Davies had not spoken for two years. Paddy put out his hand and offered: "Can we be friends?" Davies responded "Certainly!" and shook Ryan's hand vigorously. Ryan continued: "I haven't been with you for two years, and I'm sorry I haven't, but now I am with you, and I want you to get me a meeting with Sullivan." Davies said he would try to help and sat down to the bottle of wine.

Davies heard loud and angry talk coming from the blind alley behind The Store. He opened the back door and saw Willner holding a Bowie knife and arguing with Duncan Ross. It seems that Ross and Willner had come to The Store with an unknown who was later identified as Mr. Harrison of Canada. Ross had brought Harrison because he wanted to arrange a fight under Davies' management between Harrison and Ryan. For some reason—probably alcohol—Ross and Willner started arguing and moved into the alley, where Willner had pulled out the knife. When Davies saw what was happening, he told Willner to put the knife away. Willner continued to flourish the knife and Davies then snatched Willner's arm and ran him out of the alley. In the process, Davies was cut on his right thigh.

Willner soon came back to The Store again flourishing a Bowie knife, but this time he was waving it in the faces of Davies and his friends and declaring loudly that he could whip anyone in the house. The knife was again taken away from Willner, and he was ejected forcibly through the back door into the alley where things had started. Ryan wasn't satisfied with this result and decided to follow Willner out into the alley, where Ryan beat him badly, adding a few kicks to the ribs to make sure Willner did not return. Ryan had an undefeated record with stenographers in the back alleys of Chicago. Willner later claimed that during all these events, Davies had taken a gun away from him, and he wanted his gun back.

After thumping Willner, Ryan returned to the bar where Duncan Ross and Harrison were waiting. Ross told Ryan that Harrison could whip Ryan in a fair fight, and Ross said that he wanted to make the arrangement for a match through Davies. This probably happened with dialogue something like this:

> ROSS: "Ryan, you're pretty good with stenographer with no experience but that's about all your good for anymore."

RYAN: "Maybe you'd like to step out back you SOB?"
ROSS: "I've had enough alley fighting for one night, but I have a fighter here with me who can lick you in a fair fight, if you'll let Davies schedule match I have $1,000 to put up."

Ryan then became angry and pounded his fists on the bar, saying that he could whip any man. A second brawl soon followed involving Ross, Harrison, Ryan, and several other men who had been sitting nearby. That second brawl also spilled out of the saloon and back out into the alley, which at the time seemed to be the best place in Chicago to see a real fight. The results of this encounter were not reported.

One of the men in The Store that evening was a Major William M. Durell, a prominent member of the Illinois Division of American Wheelmen and a well-known citizen of Chicago. Durell was financially interested in the World's Pastime Exhibition Company at Cheltenham Beach and had come to Davies' place with Duncan Ross. Durell got caught up in the general conflict and received several kicks and blows to his right side from the shoulder to the hip delivered by one or more of the participants. Who kicked Durell was not clear, but he had a large swelling on his neck that appeared to have been caused by a kick. Durell was able to make his way home. Later in the evening; however, he died of apoplexy, apparently brought on by the beating he had received earlier that evening at The Store. The term apoplexy is seldom used now, but Durrell essentially suffered a stroke caused by uncontrolled bleeding into his brain due to an injury he received during the brawl. The bleeding resulted in his sudden loss of consciousness, paralysis, and death.

Although less significant than Durrell's death, Ross was angry about his treatment by Ryan, and he posted $1,000 with Davies for a match between his unknown and Ryan. However, as usual Ryan did not show up to meet with Ross or try to come to terms for a fight, so Davies washed his hands of the whole affair. The next afternoon Willner, bruised but undeterred, still angry, came back to The Store and announced that he was going to "do up" Davies. He was then grabbed by Ross and Davies, and they disarmed him of a "very ugly 44-calibre pistol." For the third time Willner was physically ejected from the premises. Life in Chicago at the time was marked by men carrying big guns and knives. Perhaps it was not so different from the way things are today. At least Ryan was still willing to engage in fight—even if he was beating up a stenographer in a blind alley.[404]

Later in August 1886, responding to Ryan's pleas for a fight, Davies arranged a match between Ryan and Glover. Their fight was to take place on September 13 "*near* Chicago." They were to box six rounds with small, soft gloves for a 75/25 split of gate receipts. Exactly where the Ryan-Glover fight would actually take place was a challenge to be met by Davies. In the end Davies would regret that evening at The Store, when Ryan apologized and ask for his help.

The *Pinafore* and a fight at sea

On July 1, Malcolm McNeill, a Chicago businessman, opened the facility known as the World's Pastime Exhibition at Cheltenham Beach, which was located about twelve miles south of downtown Chicago between about 79th and 82nd Streets. This area is now part of Chicago, but in 1886 it was under the jurisdiction of Hyde Park Township. That township ran from 31st Street to about 138th Street, south of the city and was not part of Chicago. McNeill had invested over $40,000 in the construction of this park and the creation of an artificial lake on the property. The artificial lake was the home for a boat called the *Pinafore,* where special events could be held. By September 1886, this facility had been opened to the public for only about two months, but it had already developed a bad reputation.

As part of the opening of the Exposition, McNeill hired several prominent athletes to appear and perform. The main attraction during the opening weeks was Duncan Ross, who called himself the "world's greatest athlete." It was a humble appellation, but consistent with Ross' view of himself. Ross was in Chicago in the summer of 1886 because of his contract to appear for McNeill. Before coming to Chicago, Ross had been performing on the West Coast, but he entered into a contract with McNeill and had come east to Chicago. Late in July 1886 Ross filed a lawsuit against McNeill for nonpayment of the $1,500 that he had been promised for his appearances. Ross said that he had been paid only four silver dollars and that McNeill had told him that he could pay no more because he was broke.[405]

Davies decided that he could avoid Mayor Harrison and police interference if he put Glover and Ryan in a ring constructed on the deck of the *Pinafore.* He planned to anchor the *Pinafore* off the shoreline of McNeill's artificial lake. The little boat was jokingly called a warship. Grandstands were constructed so that those in attendance would have a clear view of the fight. In case of rain, the fight was going to be moved into a small pavilion on the Exhibition property. Davies had arranged a preliminary program that would include Cannon wrestling Faulkner.[406]

The fight took place on the evening of September 13, and it turned into a disaster. It had rained off and on all day, and the grounds were muddy and slippery. When a train from Chicago arrived at the site, it "looked like an inhabited swamp illuminated with electric lights." About two thousand men showed up for the fight, far too many customers to fit inside the pavilion. About ten p.m., with the rain still beating down, the crowd was told to take their seats in the outdoor stands erected along the shoreline. Just as the match was to start, the rain came down even harder, and the crowd headed back to the cover of the pavilion. Davies then appeared and told everyone to return to their shoreline seats because the main event was about to start.

Ryan appeared aboard the *Pinafore* followed by Glover. Ryan and Glover had not agreed on a referee, so two referees worked the match. After a few cautious leads, the two fighters clinched and began punching away while holding on to one another. While this sounds like an ineffective way to fight, some devastating punches can be thrown at such close range. Ryan did not have a great deal of skill or science as a fighter, but he could always grab and hold an opponent's arm or back and punch with his free hand better than most prizefighters.

One referee ordered the fighters to break their clinch, but Ryan would not break. At a point Glover raised his arms above his head, which was a common way to signify that he intended to break. For his effort he was hit in the teeth by Ryan. Perhaps, all of this amounted to repeated violation of Marquis of Queensberry rules. Ryan cut his teeth fighting under the London rules, and it was hard to break old habits. When the second round began, Ryan again threw himself onto Glover, trying to bear him down to the ground as if in a London-rule fight. Ryan forced Glover backward into the ropes, and the two men began to smash away at one another at close quarters. At this point a captain of the Hyde Park Township police stepped into the ring and ordered the match stopped. One referee immediately gave the fight to Ryan, and the other gave the fight to Glover. Eventually, the encounter was called a draw. Despite all of the problems with this match, it was considered one of the top ten sporting events of 1886 in Chicago, and it got Ryan thinking that he could still fight a good heavyweight.[407]

A Glover-Ryan rematch was immediately demanded and scheduled to take place at Battery D. There is no indication why Davies thought that he could obtain a license for a prizefight inside Chicago's own city limits. The fight was to be a seven-round match, Queensberry rules, with soft gloves, and to take place on October 25. A contingency was added that the fight would occur provided there was no police interference.[408]

In addition to the fight between Ryan and Glover, Davies began working to arrange a Burke-Dempsey match in San Francisco.[409] Ultimately, that fight would be another significant turning point in Davies' professional life, but it did not happen easily. As bad as the Ryan and Glover match had been, a Burke-Dempsey match would be serious business, and the possibility had been discussed for almost a year. At this time Dempsey was known as the middleweight champion of America, but Burke could have easily fought as a middleweight except that there was generally much better money fighting in the heavyweight class.

Months earlier, Dempsey had returned to the West Coast and married. There were suggestions that Dempsey's wife, who came from a wealthy family, did not want him to continue fighting and risk the money he had accumulated during his career. Dempsey abided by his wife's wishes for a few months. However, it was obvious that if a match could be arranged with Burke, there would be very good money for everyone who participated, and no one was going to lose anything except prestige.

Davies and Sheedy meet head-on

The proposed Burke-Dempsey match brought a simmering dispute between Davies and Pat Sheedy into public focus. The two were in competition for management of the best fighters and promotion of the most lucrative fights. In 1885 Dempsey had visited Chicago before continuing on to New Orleans. When he reached New Orleans, Dempsey had written to Davies expressing his interest in a match with Burke. However, Sheedy was already in New Orleans when Dempsey arrived, and he told Dempsey not to pursue a match with Burke because Sheedy thought that Burke was too big for Dempsey. Dempsey followed this advice was and cost Davies and Burke a big payday.

Sometime after Sullivan-Burke match in Chicago, Sheedy had proposed matching Sullivan and Mitchell for a fight to be held in Chicago. Davies was chapped because of Sheedy's interference with a possible Dempsey-Burke match and, he did not want Sheedy getting too far into the Chicago market. Davies used his influence with Chicago authorities and Sheedy was not able to obtain a license for the proposed Sullivan-Mitchell match. The *New York Sun* reported on June 13, 1886, that Davies and Sheedy got into a fight about who "had the best right to the 'pull' in the town," and this eventually was what caused the "tabooing" of fights in Chicago. These events resulted in a feud between Davies and Sheedy.[410] Their feud became more important after sporting events in Chicago were closed down because Davies needed to find other venues for the events he wanted to promote, and Sheedy had significant influence with officials in both New Orleans and San Francisco.

At the end of August 1886 Davies told the newspapers that Burke was prepared to meet Dempsey in San Francisco in an eight-round go for gate receipts.[411] In mid-September 1886 Davies and Burke signed articles and mailed them to Dempsey in San Francisco, where Burke hoped to meet Dempsey in an eight-round match scheduled for September 27.[412] Davies was no longer on his home court, and so he took along letters of introduction from McDonald, Billy Pinkerton, Alderman Whalen, and other Chicago friends introducing him to Chris Buckley, the leading politician in California.

Christopher Augustine Buckley, Sr.—known as the Blind Boss of San Francisco—had come to the city at the age of sixteen. His father was a stonemason and an Irish immigrant. Buckley operated a saloon and was active in Democratic Party politics in San Francisco and California government. By 1886 he was the virtual boss of San Francisco and controlled nearly everything that happened in that city, including who got licenses for boxing matches. He was also a good friend of Sheedy. The letters of introduction that Davies carried from McDonald would be similar to a letter of introduction from Al Capone to Frank Nitty, but they were not going to be enough to allow Davies to obtain a license if Sheedy wanted to cause trouble.[413]

As Davies headed to California with Burke, word came from New York that Sheedy was on his way to Chicago to put his affairs in order in anticipation of leaving the United States. He intended to travel with Sullivan and a supporting cast of miscellaneous pugilists for almost a year. Sheedy announced that he was first taking Sullivan to San Francisco, where he hoped to arrange a fight with Mitchell. Sheedy thought that if Mitchell was not available, then someone in California would find a man to fight Sullivan. He also said that he felt that Sullivan was a great favorite on the Pacific slope, and he was sure to draw big crowds.[414]

After making an appearance in San Francisco, Sheedy intended to follow that up with a road trip back to New York. Then Sheedy and Sullivan would leave for Australia. Sheedy's idea was that Sullivan would put on public boxing matches and "do the Grecian statute business" in both Australia and England. In addition, Sheedy suggested that Sullivan would commit to memory Marc Anthony's funeral oration, which he would deliver during his public appearances.[415]

Davies and Burke arrived in San Francisco on September 23 and learned that the municipal authorities would not issue a license. The entire matter had been referred to the mayor himself.[416] Finally, on September 30, the mayor said that he would not issue a license until after the statewide elections.[417] It would later turn out that Sheedy had contacted his friend Chris Buckley and asked him to prevent Davies from getting a license for the proposed fight.

Charlie quickly planned a tour for Burke around the West Coast that began on Wednesday, October 6, at the Turner Hall in Sacramento.[418] Advertisements were in the Sacramento press as early as October 4. That evening Burke fought a five-round match with a local man, Thomas Norton, who was described as the best Sacramento middleweight. Davies was in Burke's corner for this match and a "Professor" Simons worked with Norton. The local police had made it clear that a knockout would not be permitted and required the fighters to used big, soft gloves. The fight went the full five rounds. A result was not reported except to say that it was clear that Burke could have done what he pleased with Norton and several times had put his fist on Norton's face and held it there to show that he could hit Norton whenever he wanted.

From Sacramento, Burke's tour went to San Jose, Los Angeles, back to San Francisco, and from there to Portland, Oregon. During this tour Burke renewed his practice of challenging local California fighters to stay with him for five rounds, Queensberry rules, with small gloves. In Los Angeles on October 15, he met Jim Carr. Some reports say that he knocked out Carr in a four-round match. The *Sacramento Daily Record-Union* reported that the fight was stopped by the police in the third round, and everyone was surprised to see that the two men were so evenly matched. It was quite evident from the beginning, the paper reported, that Burke could not knock out Carr. During the tour Burke was coining money. [419] After completing this tour Burke went to the little town of Ocean View near Monterey, California, to train for his fight with Dempsey. Somehow Ocean View looked like a better place to train than Beloit or Madison.

With the tour laid out for Burke and after the match in Sacramento, Davies headed back to Chicago. He was ostensibly returning to prepare for the scheduled Glover-Ryan rematch, but he was really returning because Sheedy was coming to Chicago, and Davies would have to straighten things out with Sheedy before he could obtain a license in San Francisco. Sheedy was not finished messing around with Davies. He was a very bright man and during his lifetime he would operate gambling houses in New York, Chicago, Paris, London, and Cairo, Egypt. Sheedy would make and lose millions of dollars. His approach to being a manager was the antithesis of Davies' approach. Sheedy was well aware that Ryan had committed to a rematch with Glover. He had also learned that Mitchell was not available for a fight in California.

In Davies' absence, Sheedy met with Ryan at the office of the *Sporting and Theatrical Journal*, and they signed articles for Ryan to meet Sullivan on November 15 in San Francisco. The Ryan-Sullivan fight was to be for six rounds, Queensberry rules, with soft gloves and with the winner to take 75 percent of the gate. Sheedy added a supplementary clause to the standard contract providing that both Ryan and Sullivan agreed that they would not fight anyone else prior to November 15.[420] This supplementary provision was clearly intended to stop the scheduled match between Ryan and Glover in Chicago and hurt Davies. In modern legal language, this clause would be called direct and intentional interference with contract. Sheedy was clearly enjoying flexing his muscle and squeezing Davies every way he could.

Davies reached Chicago two days after Ryan had signed on with Sheedy to fight Sullivan. Charlie was in good health. He had gained a rich color and several pounds.[421] He said that he was aware of what Sheedy had been doing and denied that he was angry, but there is no question that he was. Glover was also upset. He had to be one of the most unlucky fighters of his time. Glover did everything he could think of to compel Ryan to live up to this agreement to fight Glover in October but to no avail.

Within two days Davies and Sheedy met to resolve their differences. Their meeting was arranged by McDonald, Billy Pinkerton, and Frank Flynn, who met at The Store and convinced Davies to participate. Frank Flynn was a prizefighter from Brooklyn. McDonald and Pinkerton were businessmen, and good business required a resolution of the differences between Davies and Sheedy as soon as possible. The Parson claimed that he had been wrongly accused by Sheedy and that he had done nothing to prevent Sullivan and Mitchell from fighting in Chicago. He also said that Sheedy had been wrong to interfere with the Burke-Dempsey fight, but Davies said that he was willing to have some third party arbitrate the matter. He suggested that Billy Pinkerton, who was described as Sheedy's best friend, could represent Davies and that Sheedy could select any other man, and the two would then selected a third person to try to solve the problems.

A messenger was sent to Sheedy, and he was invited to come to The Store to meet with Davies. Sheedy responded that he was willing to meet, but that he would not meet at The Store. He suggested a meeting at the Turf Exchange, a gambling establishment at 126 South Clark Street that was then operated by Paddy Ryan. Proposing a meeting at the Turf Exchange was simply a way for Sheedy to rub it in, now that he had Ryan under contract. Sheedy told the messenger that if he felt he had done anything wrong, he would go to The Store on his hands and knees to apologize.

When this word came back to The Store, Billy Pinkerton went to talk to Sheedy. Finally, McDonald dropped in at the Turf Exchange and arranged for Sheedy and Davies to meet on neutral ground at Wasserman's saloon at eleven forty-five p.m. At the appointed time Davies and Sheedy appeared with a number of other people. The Parson and Pat went to a corner table with Flynn, John Crawford, and McDonald and talked for about an hour. No matter how big Pat had become, he was not big enough to mess around with McDonald. At about one thirty a.m., Sheedy and Davies both left the table, and Sheedy told a reporter: "It's all settled now. We are just as good friends as we ever were, and I will do just as much for Davies as I think he will do for me." Davies added that he would do as much for Pat as Pat would do for him. How is that for two ambiguous declarations?

Davies told the press that everyone was going to California, and he expected to have the Burke-Dempsey match, with their fight to be followed by a fight between Sullivan and Ryan. He thought the entire group would not return to Chicago until after the holidays. He did not say, but it was nevertheless true, that if everything worked out in California, the entire group would come back to Chicago wealthy men, and 1886 would be a good year after all.[422] In addition to all of these events, while Davies was in Chicago, he was visited by the excellent featherweight fighter Tommy Danforth, who wanted Davies to arrange a match between him and Tommy Warren.[423] Charlie passed through Sacramento on Sunday morning, November 7 on his way back to San Francisco.

Sullivan and his troupe left New York on October 18 headed for San Francisco with the idea that they would be back in New York by March 1887.[424] After stopping in Chicago, they moved on from there on October 25.[425] Sullivan went to Milwaukee and put on a show at Chivas' Hall with a journeyman from Chicago, Tom Hinch.[426] One of their first stops after Chicago was in Minneapolis, where he signed articles with Sullivan to meet Cardiff for $500 a side in a six-round match, Queensberry rules, with the match to take place in Minneapolis in January 1887 and the winner to take 75 percent of the net gate receipts. Presumably Sullivan did not think a match with Cardiff would be much of a challenge, but simply a chance to shut Cardiff's yapping mouth and pay for his trip to California and back.[427]

Sullivan arrived in San Francisco on November 9 and was entertained by a carriage ride around the city accompanied by Chris Buckley and several other local politicians. Ryan was already in California training on the north side of San Francisco Bay. After Sullivan's arrival it was announced that Davies would be able to obtain a license for the Burke-Dempsey fight but only after the Sullivan-Ryan fight on November 13 was over.[428] This was not Davies' understanding when he left Chicago after the big meeting with Sheedy.

Many involved in prizefighting in 1886 would not consider the Sullivan-Ryan rematch as a match for the heavyweight championship. In the view of purists of the 1880s, a true championship fight had to be conducted according to London prize-ring rules, with bare fists, and had to be a fight to the finish. A fight under any other rules would not legally entitle the winner to claim a championship. Ultimately Sullivan would resolve these competing views by knocking Ryan cold in the third round of their San Francisco fight.

In the aftermath of the Sullivan-Ryan rematch, it was claimed that Sullivan and Sheedy had run a canard on Ryan. They told Ryan that they had inside knowledge that the police were going to stop the fight after two rounds. With Ryan's experience in New York and his most recent experience in Hyde Park Township aboard the *Pinafore*, Ryan apparently believed that police interference would occur. Consequently he fought aggressively in the first two rounds and wore himself out, expecting the fight would soon end. Then, when he came out for the third round, Sullivan took the fight to an exhausted Ryan and put him to sleep.[429] Sullivan supposedly knew that the police would not interfere because Sheedy's political friends had money riding on the fight and were not about to jeopardize their bets. The whole point of controlling the police was to make sure that the gamblers controlled the outcome of the fight as much as possible. Sheedy estimated that the receipts of the fight were about $12,000.[430]

Despite being cheated Ryan apparently liked what he saw in San Francisco, or perhaps he had burned his bridges back East. He certainly would not be welcome in Chicago after asking for Davies help and then stiffing him in favor of Sheedy. Sheedy offered Ryan $500 a week to travel with the Sullivan combination as it returned to the East, but Ryan turned him down. He may have been embarrassed by his performance and did not want to face his friends in Chicago or New York. He had double-crossed Davies by backing out of the rematch with Glover and would not be welcome in Chicago. Fighters often have big egos and avoid admitting defeat whenever possible. Given Sullivan's style, he would have harassed Ryan all the way across the country, and Ryan would have been the goat of the tour. Ryan used his share of the fight proceeds to purchase a saloon in San Francisco and also sold his saloon at 318 Clark Street to Bill Bradburn. He later improved the saloon by installing a gymnasium in the basement, which attracted many of the top fighters and wrestlers who visited Chicago.[431]

The Burke-Dempsey fight

After Sheedy had his own full loaf, Mayor Bartlett finally issued Davies a license for the Burke-Dempsey match. Their fight was scheduled for November 22.[432] Burke was in great shape for the fight, but Dempsey had done most of his preparation on the doorstep of Mike Smith's saloon with a huge Chinese cigar between his lips. Dempsey had contracted a cold and was coughing as if he had consumption. He had also been drinking heavily. All of this may have simply been hype to have an impact on betting, but the odds were still $100 to $75 on Dempsey.[433]

On the evening of the fight the excitement was not perceptibly less than it had been for the Sullivan-Ryan fight. A vast crowd was present, estimated to be at least eight thousand, amounting to a gate of about $10,250, with the winner to take 75 percent. Burke weighed 164 pounds and Dempsey 158 at fight time. After the fight Davies said the gate was $8,796. Both Sullivan and Ryan declined to serve as referee, and Frank Crockett was agreed on to serve in that capacity.

The fighting in the first five rounds was fairly even with both fighters working primarily on the body of his opponent. Months later Dempsey explained that he developed a strategy during the fight. It seems that after three or four rounds, Dempsey noticed that the ropes of the ring were drawn unusually tight. He described them as tight as drum cords. He decided that as he faced Burke, he would slowly retreat toward the ropes until his back was nearly touching them. Then he would purposely give Burke an opening at his head, and as Burke let fly with his left, Dempsey would duck under Burke's arm and wheel around to deliver a knockout blow. The plan worked up to a point. Dempsey retreated. Burke followed. Burke missed his left, was carried forward into the ropes and thrown back toward Dempsey. But Dempsey swung a little too early and caught Burke in the back of the neck. Dempsey noted that after that point Burke was wise to his tactic and avoided it throughout the remainder of the fight.[434]

At the beginning of the sixth round Burke looked fresh and Dempsey appeared to be winded. Burke landed a heavy right on Dempsey's head and followed that with a sharp uppercut. The fight was slower in the seventh round, but then picked up again in the eighth. In the ninth round, Burke pounded Dempsey's nose savagely and forced the fighting. George La Blanche, who hated Dempsey, was present and took great interest in Burke and loudly encouraged Burke to knock off Dempsey's head.

At the end of ten rounds, Burke took off his gloves believing that the fight was over, but Dempsey insisted that the two should keep fighting. Dempsey always wanted a finish fight. Burke put his gloves back on, but it was determined that the license for the fight was only for a ten-round fight, and everyone was legally obliged to stop. The referee then declared the match a draw, and the post-fight comment was that this was the best unfinished fight ever seen in California.

Sullivan thought it was a fine and very clever fight. The consensus was that Davies had taken much trouble to effect good arrangements for the fight and the punctuality of all the entertainment. The press wrote that Burke would soon start for Portland with Davies, and they would work their way back toward Chicago. The prediction in Chicago was that there would be a Dempsey-Burke rematch in that city, provided Davies could obtain the necessary approvals.[435] At this point it had been almost seven months since Chicago had hosted a decent prizefight, and there was no sign that the mayor or police force intended that situation to change. The fight in San Francisco was as good as the Ryan-Glover fight had been bad.

The trip back east

The combination that Davies led after the Dempsey-Burke fight included the two fighters and Dempsey's wife, Denny Costigan, a lightweight boxer from Brooklyn, Charles Daley, described as the champion of Iowa, James Bates, a middleweight fighter, and Jack Kennan, described as the ex-champion lightweight. Their tour left San Francisco for Portland on November 28 and weaved its way east appearing in Portland, Astoria, and Dalles, in Oregon; Walla Walla and Spokane Falls, in Washington Territory; Helena and Butte City, in Montana Territory; Salt Lake City; Cheyenne, Wyoming Territory; Denver, Colorado; Omaha, Nebraska; Council Bluffs, Iowa; Chicago, and Milwaukee.[436] In Portland on December 6, the troupe appeared before about seven hundred, and both Dempsey and Burke sparred a local athlete named Dave Campbell.[437] The group arrived in Salt Lake City on December 17 and stayed at the Walker Hotel. The next evening, they appeared at the Walker Opera House to a "fair audience" at prices of fifty cents for the gallery and one dollar for the dress circle.

The combination had appeared in Butte City and Helena to immense houses before reaching Salt Lake City. At Butte City, Jack McAuley, described as a big miner, accepted Dempsey's one-hundred-dollar challenge and attempted to stay five rounds. McAuley was knocked through the ropes in the third round landing on the floor and then failed to return to the ring.[438] In Salt Lake City on December 18, both Dempsey and Burke sparred with Charles Lange, who was identified as the heavyweight champion of Ohio.[439] They were far enough from Ohio that no one knew whether Lange ever fought there. On December 23, they appeared in Denver at the Annex Theater, and they were in Omaha on December 24, 1886. The *Omaha Daily Bee* described Davies as "a well built, handsome man, with regular features, which are strikingly like those of a Jesuit father. He has a mild blue eye that further carries out the comparison."[440]

In some places, such as Butte City, the group stayed two nights. In each of these towns a standing offer was made of $100 for any man to stand up against either Burke or Dempsey for five rounds. When the troupe was in Salt Lake City, Davies sent a letter back to Chicago reporting that the combination was doing magnificent business.[441] A fighter named Morrison tried Burke at Cheyenne and was knocked out in the fourth round. In Omaha, Dempsey was matched to fight a heavyweight named Hanley for $2,500 a side.[442] After spending Christmas in Chicago, Dempsey and his wife left for New York City, where Dempsey had many friends and might be able to make some money with his fists.[443]

Sheedy was leading his own combination back east from their successful appearance in San Francisco. The star of Sheedy's combination was, of course, Sullivan. Others in the combination were Duncan McDonald, called the champion pugilist of Montreal, La Blanche, and Steven Taylor, a former champion middleweight of the United States and a good friend to Sullivan, Jim Carroll, lightweight champion of New England, and Dan Murphy were also in Sheedy's group. Their combination first went to Portland, Oregon, then Helena and Butte City, and then on to Minneapolis. At Butte City, Sullivan was given a magnificent copper matte (a large ingot of molten copper sulfide) from the Parrott Smelter to commemorate his visit. The *Post Dispatch* reported that Sullivan had cleared $12,000 from his tour in Montana Territory.[444]

In Minneapolis, where Sullivan was scheduled to meet Cardiff, Patsey was considered among the better heavyweight pretenders. Sullivan was finally meeting and disposing of several of these pretenders. He also fought Cardiff because he was getting tired of Patsey's big mouth. Cardiff had fought to a draw with Mitchell, which indicated that he had developed fairly well since first fighting for Bill O'Brien in Peoria and then fighting under Davies' management in Chicago. After meeting Cardiff, Sullivan and the others in his combination were traveling to the Dakota Territory and then to Manitoba before Sullivan met Killen at an undetermined location.

Sullivan also agreed to a match with Killen. At the time a man named J. C. Murnane acted as Killen's manager.[445] The articles provided for a four round match at a location to be named by Sheedy prior to January 1, 1887. It was important to designate the location for the match so that it could be properly advertised in advance. The speculation was that the Sullivan-Killen match would be held in Milwaukee, which was the nearest city of any size where the match would not be prohibited. The winner was to receive 80 percent of the gate. In addition, Sheedy added his supplemental provision (the same provision he had added to Ryan's agreement) that prohibited Killen from accepting any other match before he fought Sullivan. Finally, the articles required Killen to post $1,000 with a stakeholder in Duluth; the money could be claimed by Sullivan if Killen violated any of the terms of the articles. Sheedy told the press that he considered Killen to be superior as a fighter to Cardiff, but the articles did not treat Killen as expected for a leading heavyweight contender.

It was obvious that Murnane had done a poor job of representing Killen, who had been taken advantage of under the terms of the articles. Murnane continued to represent Killen until mid-April 1887, when Killen finally decided to sell out his business and leave Duluth. When a reporter for the *Duluth Tribune* asked Killen why he was leaving town, Killen said that if he didn't get out of town he would probably slug Murnane and then get popped (i.e., shot) in return.

The year 1886 had been a mixed bag for Davies. When prizefighting and wrestling were closed down in May 1886, Davies was forced to find alternatives. His effort to promote a Ryan-Glover match was a dismal failure, even though it was listed as among the top ten sporting events in Chicago. His attempt to promote a Ryan-Glover rematch also failed because of the intentional interference by Sheedy. Nevertheless, he had successfully moved beyond Chicago to promote the Dempsey-Burke match. Their match had been a great financial success, and their tour back from San Francisco to Chicago had also done very well. Whether Charlie could continue to promote and manage Burke was an open question. If prizefighting were prohibited in Chicago, then it would be difficult to be in two places at one time, that is, planning sporting events in other cities, running his saloon, and also promoting wrestling events in Chicago.

Davies was very good at advancing the careers of athletes whom he managed. The list of racewalkers and fighters he had helped was already impressive: O'Neal, Ennis, Guyon, Sullivan, Cardiff, Killen, Burke, and Warren included. By the end of 1886 it was clear that he thought Evan "the Strangler" Lewis had what it took to be a championship caliber wrestler, and Davies spent many additional months helping Lewis gain his fame as a wrestler.

Chapter 7 - (1887)

Sullivan breaks his hand

When he {Parson Davies} laughs his eyes snap and sparkle, and he shows a fascinatingly white set of teeth. He can be very entertaining, for he has all the time most men spend in twisting their moustaches to give to being pleasant. . . . Mr. Davies doesn't mind answering questions, which is a great virtue in man.[446]

♠

In Duluth, Killen continued to flounder without Davies' guidance. Killen had defeated O. H. Smith, champion of Dakota, at Duluth, on January 4, 1887, by knocking him out in the first round.[447] Killen had agreed to a rematch with Paddy McDonald, a lesser-class heavyweight, who was styled as the champion of the Vermillion Range, an area of deep iron-ore deposits located roughly between the Minnesota towns of Ely and Tower. It was one of the several iron-ore ranges that were full of hard-working men and that were situated throughout the Upper Peninsula of Michigan, northern Wisconsin and northern Minnesota in the mid-1880s.

The Killen-McDonald match was scheduled for January 17, 1887, the night before the Sullivan-Cardiff fight in Minneapolis. Sheedy immediately complained that this match was a violation of Killen's contract with Sullivan and his promise not to meet any other fighter until after fighting Sullivan. He claimed that Killen had repeatedly violated his agreement. Moreover, Sheedy said that Killen had failed to post $1,000 forfeit money as required by the articles with Sullivan.[448] Killen and his backer claimed that he had not violated the articles because Sheedy had failed to name the location of the match with Sullivan before January 1, 1887. He claimed that Sheedy's prior breach of the articles freed him to agree to the match with McDonald. Killen knocked out McDonald in the seventh round of their match. He had ignored Sheedy's threats.[449]

Sullivan hits a hard head

All of this would soon be moot because of the outcome of the Sullivan-Cardiff fight, which became the beginning of the end for Sullivan. During this period Sheedy persisted in his attacks on Davies. He was interviewed by the *New York Sun* on January 23 about Jack Dempsey's claims that he was prepared to fight Sullivan. Sheedy said that Dempsey was the top fighter in his class but would have no chance against Sullivan. He compared Dempsey to Burke and said that Burke was not close to Dempsey's class. Then he claimed that the draw between Dempsey and Burke happened simply because Davies "fixed" things against Dempsey.[450]

On January 18, Sullivan met Cardiff at the Washington Rink in Minneapolis before six thousand customers. The Washington Rink was advertised as holding up to twelve thousand patrons, and the gate may have been affected by the cold weather that day. Sullivan broke the radius of his right arm in the first round of the fight. He continued for the full six rounds but was ineffective. He had to carry his right arm in a horizontal position because of the pain from the broken radius, and he could not make his famous rushes with only his left hand. Cardiff did not seem to realize that he could attack Sullivan and was generally content to spar at a distance. Their match was declared a draw, and because of his broken arm, Sullivan was effectively knocked out of the fighting business until after June 1887.[451]

Killen started to realize that he couldn't get back into the big-time by drinking and hanging-out in a bar in Duluth. It was winter and activity had slowed down in the far north to nearly nothing. Shipping on Lake Superior stopped and train travel was difficult due to heavy snows. Decent fighters were aware of the huge sums of money that had been made both by Sheedy and Davies during their trips to and from California in the last part of 1886. Killen's proposed match with Sullivan evaporated due to Sullivan's broken arm. Killen then came back to Chicago to talk to Davies about taking him on a trip under the Parson's management. He told Davies that he had not had a drink in six months and hoped to schedule a match with Bradburn at the Fifty-first Street Hall, which was outside the Chicago city limits. Presumably a Killen-Bradburn match near Chicago would be a big improvement over their pathetic effort several weeks earlier in the north woods.[452]

Davies and Killen did not come to terms, and Killen did not fight under Davies' management. This may have happened because Davies was not interested in another long road trip, and he couldn't promote Killen in Chicago. It probably happened because Davies was facing a choice. He could promote the wrestler Evan Lewis and stay in Chicago during most of the year, or he could go on the road and promote Killen. If he promoted Killen, it was likely that he would spend the year dodging the law, and he would have to back Killen with his own money or continually try to find backers. He would also have to worry about Killen falling off the wagon. If he promoted Lewis, he would not be interrupted by the law, and he would be promoting the best young wrestler in the United States. In addition, Lewis had a built in set of backers from his home town of Madison and did not drink like a fish.

Charlie was still trying to find a way around the prohibitions that had been enforced during the seven-month period beginning just after the Haymarket riot. This was not an easy because the Haymarket's aftermath continued to be an almost daily subject of discussion in Chicago. On January 18, 1887, Davies personally called on Mayor Harrison to ask for a license for an athletic tournament that would include a series of exhibitions of sparring and wrestling matches at Battery D in February.

Harrison sent Davies to the police department with word that he personally had no objection to the proposed exhibitions and intimating that it was the police department that had thrown up the barriers to sporting events.[453] Chief Frederick Ebersold then told Davies that the prohibition put in place in May 1886 had never extended to wrestling.[454] This was news to wrestlers and promoters, but it also served as a way for the chief to save face after the mayor sent Davies over to Ebersold.

Davies decided that he would make an effort to revive wrestling in Chicago. After he had gone to California, decent wrestling promotions in Chicago had virtually stopped. In part this happened because Tom Cannon had left the United States, but most of it was due to Davies' responsibilities for the tour to California and back. In mid-January, Arthur Chambers, the retired U.S. lightweight champion, was promoting Joe Acton, a wrestler known as "the little demon." Chambers indicated that Acton preferred to wrestle Lewis, with a match to take place in Chicago, New York, or Philadelphia, provided there was reasonable time to prepare for it.[455]

Family problems

In the middle of all of this wrestling, Parson Davies' older brother, George "Fred" Davies, was tried in federal court in Chicago for forging three one-hundred-dollar U. S. Treasury bonds. Fred seemed to have more than his share of problems.[456] In January 1876 he had been sued by John Sperry on a delinquent promissory note. In March 1881 Fred had filed bankruptcy. In 1882 he was doing business at 219 Randolph Street under the name of Hart & Davies. In May 1882 Hart had sued Charlie and Fred to restrain them from taking possession of 219 Randolph Street, but Charlie had the place within a few months after the lawsuit was filed.[457] Fred then disappeared from the Chicago directories from 1883 forward.

In late November 1885, Fred was arrested for allegedly trying to pass three forged one-hundred-dollar Treasury bonds. He was indicted in March 1886 by a grand jury on charges that he "feloniously did keep in possession three falsely forged obligations and securities of the said United States."[458] Testimony in his criminal trial in 1887 indicated that he had been away from Chicago for some time. He had returned to the city "broke" and said that he had found the bonds on the street and attempted to pawn them to give himself a stake.[459]

The jury returned a guilty verdict late on the evening of February 1, 1887. A bond in the amount of $2,000 had been posted on Fred's behalf by a professional bondsman Charles A. Winship and co-signed by Charlie. Fred failed to appear in court on the morning of February 2.[460] As a consequence a conditional judgment was entered against Charlie for the amount of the bond, which he would be required to pay if Fred was not in court for sentencing. In addition to being liable on the conditional judgment, Charlie paid several hundred dollars in court costs. Fred was later arrested on April 4, 1887, and a month later sentenced to one year of hard labor. Fred Davies seems to disappear from the records after he was sent to prison, and he may be a George F. Davies who died in New York in August 1900.

Back in the world of sports, the challenge posted by Chambers on behalf of Acton was the immediate reason why Davies had visited Mayor Harrison. The best deal financially for Davies and Lewis, who was training in Beloit, would be to hold a match in Chicago, but they needed to obtain a license first. Any time there was a championship at stake, it was important for a promoter to act quickly; a wrestler with a championship title was a bankable asset, and the collection plate could not be passed every Sunday.

Back to wrestling

Within ten days of Chambers' challenge, Davies sent articles to Acton for a match at Battery D to take place on February 7 under Davies' management. The articles provided a standard 75/25 split of the net receipts. Chambers and Acton agreed to a match and notified Davies on January 26 that they would both be in Chicago the following week for a match to take place Monday, February 7 at Battery D. The parties agreed that the strangle-hold would be allowed and that it was an appropriate hold in catch-as-catch-can wrestling.[461]

The referees for the Acton-Lewis match had not been agreed to, but they were to be selected from a galaxy of stars with connections to Davies: Dempsey, Burke, Cardiff, Killen, and Glover. Chief Ebersold confirmed for the sporting press that the prohibition against sparring matches had no application to wrestling and that his men would not interfere with a match. Ebersold explained that he could find no law prohibiting wrestling matches in Illinois and professed surprise that anyone thought he might take some other view.

When he arrived in Chicago, Lewis was accompanied by about two hundred supporters from Madison. It was this kind of support that made it easier to promote Lewis. He went to Davies' place to meet with the local press. Lewis said that he had great confidence that he would be successful against Acton. He said that he weighed 180 pounds to Acton's 158, but the betting still favored Acton and the gamblers were later proved to be correct.

About four thousand attended the match. Over one thousand patrons paid $1.50 each for reserve seats, and there were more than two thousand people who purchased tickets for $1 each. The two referees were Burke, who wore a Prince Albert coat, and Killen, who was in shirt sleeves. Lewis immediately went for his strangle-hold, but Acton successfully avoided his attempts. Lewis then executed a hip-throw, but Acton landed on his hands and knees and escaped. Acton then executed a flying fall by rushing at Lewis "like a man running for a train" and hitting him in the chest with a shoulder. Lewis went down and Acton executed a half-Nelson that Lewis escaped. Finally, Acton secured a full-Nelson on Lewis and slowly turned him for a fall. With this cries came from the crowd: "Ye ain't got no Chinee this time, Lewis." It was never hard to find ethnic or racial prejudice in the 1880s.

The second bout lasted about three minutes before Lewis secured a grapevine and turned Acton for a quick fall. At the beginning of the third bout it was clear that Lewis was winded and Acton still fresh. They achieved opposing standing-body-locks, but then Lewis attempted his strangle-hold once again. Acton slipped the hold and on the mat secured another half-Nelson, which he used to slowly turn Lewis and get the third fall. The fourth and final bout began again with opposing standing-body-locks. This time Lewis lifted Acton off his feet and slammed him to the floor, but Acton was able to turn from the bottom position and regain his half-Nelson until he turned Lewis and gained his third fall of the match.

Referee Burke announced that Acton was the winner of the bout and entitled to the stakes of $500 a side. The crowd cheered wildly for a minute or more. A rematch was scheduled in three weeks. Later that evening the champagne "flowed in bath-tubs at Davies' saloon" in honor of Acton's great victory. The *Chicago Tribune* speculated that Davies preferred that during the rematch they should be allowed to use of hatchets or axes. Acton would not agree to a match within three weeks, but articles were prepared that called for a match at Battery D on March 14, 1886. As it turned out, Chambers and Acton would not sign the articles and the Acton-Lewis rematch was delayed for more than three months. To stay fit, Lewis had several matches before his rematch with Acton.[462]

Davies' successful night was dimmed by the news that he could not obtain a license for a proposed Killen-Bradburn match.[463] All the arrangements for the match had been made and it was set to be held in the Town and Lake Theater.[464] Things were so bad that Davies was contacted by several local sports about sponsoring a six-day walking match in the Exposition Building that would feature Guyon and John Dobler and supplemented by a horse-shoeing contest. Davies must have felt as if he were walking five hundred miles backward. He would promote almost anything, but he was not a man who spent time on events that were out of public favor.

The 81 Tonner fails to fire

While the scheduling of wrestling matches moved slowly, Davies was about to receive a great gift from merry old England. Jem Smith and John Knifton (the "81 Tonner") were the two leading heavyweights in England. Knifton was of Scottish descent, born January 30, 1857, in Saint Cyrus, near Montrose, Scotland. He was a big man, about six feet-two-and-a-half inches tall and weighed 210 pounds when trimmed down for a fight. Knifton acquired his nickname because his punch had once been compared to the impact of a shell launched by an eighty-one-ton naval cannon. He was an all-around athlete who could run a fast one-hundred-yard dash and turn an easy handspring. History was establishing that several of England's top heavyweights were actually at their best when they were running in the ring.

Knifton had been attempting to corner Jem Smith for a heavyweight match for the championship of England. If he could get a match with Smith and win, Knifton could claim the championship title and become the leading contender to meet Sullivan. This meant that win or lose he would earn big money.[465]

Speaking of great runners, Charley Mitchell had turned himself into a quasi-manager and sports promoter by 1887. Some claimed that Mitchell had become a manager to create an excuse for avoiding a fight with Dempsey. Mitchell always had an excuse to avoid Dempsey. Whatever Mitchell's reason for turning to the management side of boxing, it was said that he would bring Jem Smith to the United States to challenge Sullivan and that Smith had no intention of meeting Knifton before leaving England.

On February 19 Knifton sent a cablegram to Parson Davies: "Will sail when you like. Challenge Sullivan or Smith."

It appeared that Davies was about to be at the top of the heavyweight heap once again. He replied to Knifton: "Sail immediately; wire your departure and I will meet you at New York." Davies had experienced mixed results with English fighters. Goode was a terrible bust under Davies's management, but Burke had been a highly successful and bankable asset. Davies told the press that he would first satisfy himself that Knifton would measure up to newspaper accounts, but if he was satisfied with Knifton's ability, he would back him against all comers. On the other hand, if Knifton did not show as advertised, then the Davies would not handle him at all.[466]

The possibility of managing Knifton went up in smoke. Knifton did not sail to the States, and Davies let it be known that he had no interest in managing a fighter who would not live up to his word. He sent a cable to Knifton: "To Mr. John Knifton, care Sporting Life, London, Eng.: I cancel your engagement as you have failed to sail as requested. Charles E. Davies." When asked to explain why he took this action, Davies responded: "I'll tell you why. Simply because I am a business man, and I don't propose to have a man flying all over England before he comes to me." Davies thought that Smith, Mitchell, Mace, Knifton, and company had entered upon a "love feast," and he wanted no part of whatever they were planning. Later during the summer, Davies' friend Pat Sheedy wrote to Knifton offering to represent him in the United States.[467]

A championship wrestler from the UP

Back on the wrestling front, Chambers had still not returned the articles for the proposed Acton-Lewis rematch.[468] Therefore, Davies scheduled a match between Lewis and Jack Carkeek, another good wrestler from the Midwest. Carkeek was born January 22, 1861, in the little town of Rockland in Ontonagon County in Michigan's Upper Peninsula. His father Thomas Carkeek came to Rockland from Plymouth, England, in 1855 and worked at a copper mine.

Rockland was settled in the 1840s when deposits of pure copper were discovered. The Victoria Mine had been opened about three miles south of Rockland, and the mine site is still open to the public. The Minesota (the correct spelling) Mining Company was then opened in 1847 and found a six-ton copper mass that was followed to a vein of copper. At its highpoint, this mine was producing up to four million tons of copper a year.

Carkeek had been wrestling professionally for ten years and was a specialist in Cornish style wrestling, which was popular among the Cornish miners who lived around Rockland. The Lewis-Carkeek match was for $1,000 a side, catch-as-catch-can, to be held in Milwaukee. When Chambers learned that Lewis was to meet Carkeek, he claimed that Lewis had breached the terms of the articles with "the little demon" and that Acton was entitled to the $500 forfeit money. Chambers said that Acton would appear on March 14 as proposed if Lewis would withdraw from his match with Carkeek.[469]

Lewis did not withdraw, and his match with Carkeek went forward at the Grand Opera House in Milwaukee on March 3. There was a good crowd, estimated to be at least four thousand. After about twenty minutes of exciting wrestling, Lewis put his right arm around Carkeek's neck, threw his body on his neck and chest and choked him out. A fifteen minute rest period followed, but Carkeek was not able to return and forfeited a second fall to Lewis in order to gain additional time before continuing. After another fifteen minutes, Carkeek returned to the mat, but it was clear that he was injured. Only one minute into the second bout, Lewis again secured his choke hold, and Carkeek tapped out.[470]

While this first match with Carkeek put Lewis back at the top of the wrestling contenders, Davies could not have been happy with his own personal circumstances. He needed to get back in the mainstream of boxing, and prospects were not bright. Kilrain was beginning to separate himself from other heavyweight contenders. In early March 1887 Kilrain had defeated Lannon in an eleven-round fight in Boston, which was Sullivan's home turf.[471] This was the start of Kilrain's surge forward in the heavyweight ranks. Within about eighteen months, Davies would play a leading role in Kilrain's career.

Davies arranged a Carkeek-Lewis rematch. He invited Carkeek to come to Chicago to meet Lewis.[472] After about three hours of discussion, they all arrived at an agreement. The match would be mixed Cornish and catch-as-catch-can wrestling for the best three out of five falls. No living wrestler had ever defeated Carkeek in a Cornish-style wrestling match.[473] The *Encyclopedia of Chicago* claims that Chicago's wrestling tradition began in 1887 at the Battery D Armory, where Lewis defeated Carkeek for the first recognized professional heavyweight wrestling championship in the United States.[474] This assertion is an obvious distortion, given the prior history of wresting events previously promoted by Davies.

The rematch was part of a bigger production typical of those sponsored by Davies. There was to be a club-swinging contest for a medal offered by the *Police Gazette*. Just before the match, a second meeting was held at Davies' office. Carkeek arrived with a large number of friends from Milwaukee, and the entire entourage met to resolve the issue of a referee for the match. Several wagers were also placed on Carkeek, despite his earlier poor performance in Milwaukee, and it was anticipated that the two men would have an exciting rematch.[475]

Despite all the preparations and build up, the actual match was well below average. There were only about one thousand patrons present for the entertainment, which was substantially below a typical gate. Carkeek won the toss and had the first choice of wrestling style. For unknown reasons he opted for Greco-Roman style wrestling rather than his Cornish specialty. This seemed to amount to a brain cramp.

Then to the surprise of the crowd Carkeek got the first fall in only about three minutes and ten seconds. The second bout was Lewis' choice and was conducted in the catch-as-catch-can style. The two men exchanged successive strangle-holds, and Carkeek appeared to be worn down when Lewis turned and pinned him with a back-hold in nine minutes and thirty seconds. The third bout was again in the Greco-Roman format. Carkeek forced Lewis to the ropes and attempted to throw him over before slipping backward. As Carkeek slipped, Lewis slammed his shoulders to the floor to claim his second fall. The crowd yelled that there had been a foul because Carkeek had attempted to throw Lewis over the ropes, which was a hold that was forbidden in Greco-Roman wrestling. Davies mounted the stage and addressed the spectators. He said that he and the referee agreed that Carkeek had committed a foul by trying to throw Lewis over the ropes; however, Lewis had not claimed the foul and should therefore be awarded the fall by pin. This was a fair resolution of the issue.

Before the fourth bout, Carkeek appeared and announced that he was out of condition and could not wrestle at his top form. He brashly said that within six weeks he would be in shape and would wrestle any man in the world for $1,000 a side. This sort of bluster was fine for show, but not so good for those who had their money on Carkeek. After those astonishing pronouncements the match went forward, and Lewis secured the fourth fall and was declared the winner three falls to one. Lewis' backer then announced that he received a telegram from Arthur Chambers proposing a Lewis-Acton rematch on April 11.[476] Carkeek soon left to wrestle in England and would remain there until late November 1887.

Davies was not entirely out of the boxing business. For several months Glover and Burke had been bickering over the terms of a possible rematch. Glover wanted a match for a smaller amount of money and a finish fight under London rules. Burke refused to fight for anything less than $5,000 a side and insisted on a finish fight under Queensberry rules. Two things seemed to breach the impasse between the two men. First, Glover agreed to fight under Queensberry rules for $5,000 a side. Second, Davies offered to post an additional purse of $5,000 so that the total amount at stake would be $15,000. On March 10 an agreement was reached. The prohibitions against boxing were to be avoided by having a private fight limited to one hundred spectators who were to pay $50 a ticket.

It seems that an argument could be made that a private fight did not require a license from the city for public entertainment, and the only remaining issue would be dodging the law.[477] But just as soon as the match had been made, the whole thing fell apart.

The failure of the match was attributed to John Dowling, who long before had been a partner of McDonald. Dowling backed out of his agreement to back Burke for $5,000. Supposedly this happened because when Burke posted his $1,000 forfeit he did it on condition that the referee would be selected on the day of the fight. Glover refused to post money on this condition and Dowling took down his money. It was not turning out to be a good year.[478]

Hope that the city of Chicago might let-up on prohibitions against prize fighting faded in March. The Haymarket affair was again front page news and resurrected the prior concerns about social order. On Saint Patrick's Day, the Illinois Supreme Court began hearing arguments on motions for a new trial filed for the defendants convicted in the Haymarket riot. One of the attorneys for the condemned anarchists was Leonard Swett, who was an old friend of Abraham Lincoln and who had helped represent McDonald's friend Joe Mackin in 1884.

Burke backed out of the proposed rematch with Glover and was dropped by Davies. The Parson had dumped Knifton a few weeks earlier, and he was obviously tired of fighters with big egos who would not live up to their agreements. It was hard enough battling the city and competitors like Sheedy without dealing with an unreliable fighter.

After the Burke-Dempsey match and the successful tour back to Chicago, Burke had been spending too much time in front of a mirror. He had a tendency to be his own biggest fan. He seems to have decided that it was a bad idea for him to fight the bigger heavyweights. He had done his best work over the prior two years against men that were undersized heavyweights like Greenfield, Cleary, and Mitchell, or former lightweights like Dempsey. In fairness, these were fighters who were in Burke's same weight range. He had not done well against either Glover or Nolan and would thereafter shy away from fighting men that big. In addition, Burke began to make a stab at managing fighters himself, and engaging in that activity was clearly poaching on Davies' territory.[479]

Burke walks away

Whatever happened between the two men, Davies stopped promoting Burke and within a few days, a man named Mike Breslauer was representing Burke and attempted to arrange a Killen-Burke match. Burke headed back toward the East Coast, making stops at places like Buffalo along the way.[480] It wasn't long before he said that he intended to make a trip to Australia to follow his fortunes there. He said that he was tired of Chicago because of the inability to arrange fights.[481] Prizefighting was not against the law in Australia, and a fighter was not going to be troubled there by posting peace bonds and facing a criminal prosecution, as Burke had faced in Cincinnati. Six months after his triumphant return from California Jack Burke had become irrelevant.

When the Glover-Burke match fell through, Glover attempted to arrange a fight with Bradburn. On March 15 the two fighters met at Davies' private office. Glover told Bradburn he would agree to fight if Bradburn would guarantee him $1,500 no matter the outcome. Bradburn was reluctant to guarantee that kind of money but said that he was confident that he could sell $3,000-worth of tickets at $20 a piece for a private fight. Davies opined that only about $2,500 could be raised from ticket sales, which would not be enough to guarantee Glover $1,500 as he had demanded.[482] To make matters worse, the Illinois legislature was in the process of adopting a law to force saloons to be closed all day on Sunday, and Chicago passed a midnight closing law that was directed against establishments in the levee area but was soon enforced against the downtown saloons too. These actions were additional factors that were killing the sporting life in Chicago.[483]

On the road with the strangler

The Lewis-Acton wrestling rematch was still on track. It is often reported that this match took place on March 14, but it did not. Both men arrived in Chicago in early April and met with Davies at ten a.m. on April 11 and selected Frank Whitmore as the referee.[484] Before the match there was such heavy betting on Lewis at John Dowling's saloon that some local sports began to suspect that the match was fixed. Dowling became concerned and got out his eraser, took the two wrestlers' names off his blackboard, and stopped accepting bets.[485]

Acton secured the first fall in the opening bout. Lewis took the second fall in just over three minutes and then won the match with a strangle-hold for his third fall and the match. In winning this match, Lewis was credited as the champion catch-as-catch-can wrestler of America. Davies had added another champion to his resume.[486]

From the sublime heights of first class wrestling, Davies next venture was to begin planning a sword fighting contest between Colonel Thomas H. Monstery, the self-declared champion-at-arms of America, and Masseur Trouchet, who called himself the master American swordsman. Davies planned to invite several other male and female personages involved in sword play and have the evening culminated with a championship Monstery/Trouchet duel.[487]

Lewis next wrestled for Davies in Pittsburgh. Davies and several men from Madison arrived in Pittsburgh on June 12. Lewis was there to wrestle Tom Connors, who was an experienced man and sometimes called the champion of England and America. Connors was born in Wigan, Lancashire, England, in 1861 and began wrestling when he was only eleven years old. He was only about five feet six inches tall and generally wrestled at about 150 pounds. Their match was for $500 a side, with a 75/25 split of the gate, and no holds were to be barred for this match. This meant that Lewis could use his strangle-hold, and Connors could use his own full-Nelson. Davies thought that Lewis would make short work of Connors, and the Madison men had brought $5,000 with them to bet on Lewis.[488]

The match went to Connors. A crowd or about three thousand was present at the Grand Central Rink. The entertainment started just after ten p.m. on June 13 and it was a brutal affair. In the first bout Connors head-butted Lewis and opened a vicious welt as big as a walnut and an inch long bloody gash under the Strangler's eye. Despite protests from Lewis' backers, the referee called the head-butting an unintentional act and not a foul. Even today the best weapon of some wrestlers is a well-directed head-butt, which can be as effective as hitting a man with a board. Some wrestlers are proficient at head butting without ever being caught.

Lewis kicked Connors wickedly in the thigh, and Connors ran at Lewis and butted him again, opening another bloody cut. Blood "flowed from the wound in streams, fairly deluging Connors's naked back." Again a foul was denied. After twenty-three minutes Lewis got his strangle-hold on Connors and was choking him out when Connors' brother entered the ring and began pulling Lewis away. The act of Connors' brother caused a near riot in the ring that lasted fully fifteen minutes. The referee once again saw no foul and the match continued. Lewis soon pressed Connors' head close to his breast and Connors began butting Lewis under the chin with the top of his head like a trip hammer. Finally, the referee saw a foul and gave the fall to Lewis.

The second bout was quick and won by Connors in three minutes with a leg hold and half-Nelson combination. This was followed by a bout that returned to heavy-fouling format. The referee awarded the fall to Connors. He said that Lewis was allowed to strangle Connors, but that he could not use his fingers to apply pressure to Connors' neck. No such distinction existed in the rules. This decision gave the match to Connors and resulted in the general feeling among the Chicago and Madison people that the referee had acted unfairly. One paper reported that Lewis could only have won the match by throwing Connors, his seconds, and the referee all at the same time. Davies called it "the most brazen piece of robbery he ever saw" and "worse than sandbagging." He felt that Lewis was deliberately robbed and said he would back Lewis for a rematch at $1,000 a side if a fair referee could be located.[489]

About one month after the unfortunate trip to Pittsburgh, Davies and several other saloon owners were arrested on charges that they had broken the new midnight closing law. It was common practice for saloon owners to use the back door of their establishments for serious customers. Many years later Davies' brother Vere said that he operated his saloon for twelve years and never had a key to the front or back door. Frank Glover was among the others against whom charges preferred.[490]

In mid-1887 Davies was trying to drum-up business for Lewis. He published a challenge offering to pay $100 to any man who could wrestle Lewis in the catch-as-catch-can format for twenty minutes without being thrown. A throw would require only two points down.[491] Frank Whitmore, a good professional wrestler who had previously thrown Ross, announced that he was accepting Davies' challenge, and Bradburn, who was then being called by the more gentile "William" Bradburn, was designated as the referee for their match.[492]

On July 30, Lewis and Whitmore met at the Casino before a large crowd. Davies introduced the men and announced that Lewis would not attempt to prevent Whitmore from throwing him because under the rules, a fall for Whitmore would not count toward winning the bet. The only question to be decided was whether Lewis could throw Whitmore within the prescribed twenty-minute period.

Bradburn, who had defeated Glover in Crown Point, Indiana, a few nights earlier, was met with ringing applause when he was introduced.[493] To the surprise of some, Whitmore was inclined to be aggressive rather than act on the defensive, and he laid out Lewis on two different occasions. After seven minutes of sharp wrestling they faced each other with opposing holds—a grapevine and a shoulder hold—but Lewis proved stronger. He bent Whitmore to his purpose and put both of his shoulders on the mat.

The crowd was upset and hissed the result, and Davies agreed to give Whitmore another chance. Davies had a knack for responding to a crowd in a positive way and enjoyed the limelight. After a five-minute rest, they resumed the match with more animated wrestling. Whitmore got a front headlock on Lewis and banged his head down to the floor making a sound loud enough to have broken a hole in the floor. Finally, Lewis slipped a double-leg-hold and pushed Whitmore over on his back, thereby saving the Parson $100.[494]

Finding other wrestlers to meet the Strangler on these terms was proving difficult. Within weeks, Davies wrote to Billy Madden and asked him to see whether he could find two men in New York who would be willing to wrestle the Strangler on the same evening for gate receipts or a stake, catch-as-catch-can, with the strangle-hold allowed. It would be six months before Davies figured out a format for promoting Lewis that would keep the customers buying tickets for his subsequent matches.

Cardiff and Killen in Minneapolis

On August 3, Davies and several of his friends left for Minneapolis to watch two of his former fighters, Cardiff and Killen, meet for the championship of the Northwest.[495] Their ten-round match was held on August 5. In addition to the delegation from Chicago headed by Davies, there were also delegations from Omaha, New York City, and Boston present for this fight. An estimated ten thousand customers paid. This was substantially more than had attended the Sullivan-Cardiff match in January 1887 and the largest crowd for many years after. The receipts for the house were said to be $11,185, one of the biggest ever in Minneapolis. The crowd howled to have Davies act as referee, but he declined.[496]

The fight was declared a draw. Asked for his opinion, Davies said that had he been the referee, he would have given the fight to Killen. After the fight it was learned that Killen had broken a small bone in his right hand in the third round. Killen and Sullivan had something in common: they had both broken a bone hitting Cardiff's rock head.[497] Davies had traveled to St. Paul with Lewis, and the Chicago contingent left St. Paul for Eau Claire, Wisconsin, where Lewis had a match with Charles Moth.[498]

Shortly after the Cardiff fight, Killen contacted Davies and asked him to arrange a rematch with Cardiff.[499] Killen often came back to Davies when things were not going well. He wanted the rematch to take place at Minneapolis as a fifteen-round affair using hard gloves. His big right hand had more of an impact in hard gloves. Killen then left Minnesota unexpectedly because his mother in Philadelphia had been seriously injured in a fall. On his way to Philly, Killen told the press in Pittsburgh that his backer was Davies, who would put up $2,500 a side for a rematch with Cardiff.

Killen had received injuries to both his back and his groin during the Cardiff fight. Cardiff had backed Killen to a corner of the ring where the ropes were supported by a steel post and then pushed him into the post while kneeing him in the groin. This caused a very bad contusion on Killen's back and a swollen groin that kept him in bed for several days after the fight. In the second round, Cardiff got his knee against Killen's throat at close quarters (although it is difficult to form a mental picture of this act) and this foul nearly ruined Killen. There are several reports during this time period accusing Cardiff of roughhouse tactics and attempts to throw or otherwise injure his opponent. Killen, who was apparently in a talkative mood after the fight, told the press that Davies was going to take Evan Lewis to England to wrestle and that the Parson wanted Killen to go along. However, Killen said that he had declined the invitation because of his mother's illness.[500]

Working with Kilrain

Perhaps the biggest surprise after Davies' trip to Minnesota was his announcement that he had arranged a twelve-round Kilrain-Nolan fight to take place at Cincinnati, on August 29. After that fight, Davies said he would take Kilrain on a foreign trip. If this announcement had panned out, then Davies would be back in the heavyweight game big time! However, none of this happened because Fox was not happy with Davies' messing around with Kilrain and quickly interfered.[501]

Fox had invested a lot of his time and money promoting Kilrain, and he sent his lackey William Harding to meet with Kilrain. Together Fox and Harding had de-belted Sullivan, and they were spending big money to send Kilrain to England.[502] Their message to Kilrain was that Fox was backing him in an anticipated fight against Jem Smith, and Fox did not want Kilrain fighting any other living soul before that match. If Kilrain planned to fight Nolan, then Fox would withdraw his backing for the Jem Smith fight. Kilrain soon caved in and backed out of the match with Nolan and also his deal with Davies.[503]

Unable to secure Kilrain for a match with Nolan and with Killen on the shelf in Philadelphia, Davies turned to his third choice. He posted a $250 forfeit with the *Cincinnati Enquirer* on behalf of Frank Glover.[504] Davies stipulated that skin gloves not to exceed two ounces were to be used in the proposed Glover-Nolan fight. Within a short time the forfeit money was returned to Davies with the comment that Nolan was not interested in a match with Glover. Frank then sent a certified check to the *Enquirer* proposing a fight for $1,000 a side within five or six weeks and spectators limited to five men each. This check was also returned.[505]

The Haymarket affair's impact on everyday life in Chicago continued into late 1887. The Illinois Supreme Court rejected the appeals of the seven condemned defendants, and they appealed to the U. S. Supreme Court. A large crowd appeared in Washington, D.C., for the October 27 hearing, and the parties were allowed three hours a side to argue their case. Arguments were not completed that day and continued on October 28.[506] Only four days later, the Supreme Court denied the writ of error in the case, and the sole remaining bar to the execution of the defendants was Illinois Governor Richard Oglesby.[507]

On November 10, the governor announced at the Executive Mansion in Springfield that he had commuted to life imprisonment the sentences of Samuel Fielden and Michael Schwab, but he had decided to uphold the death sentences for August Spies, Adolph Fischer, Albert Parsons, Louis Lingg, and George Engel. Later that same day Lingg took his own life in prison. He put a blasting cap that had been smuggled to him while in prison into his mouth and blew off part of his face and jaw. He lived six hours before dying in agony. The next day the four remaining defendants were hanged. They were all buried at Waldheim cemetery on December 18, and for the first time in almost two years, Chicago began to put the fear of a general uprising behind it.[508]

Many exciting things were happening in the world of prizefighting in the second half of 1887, but none of them seemed to involve Davies. He had been trying with no success to return to the mainstream. Killen was unwilling to go to England. Davies' proposed Kilrain-Nolan fight and tour in England had been interfered with by Richard K. Fox; he was unable to arrange matches for Glover, and then Bradburn retired from fighting to accept a position with Armour & Co. as its head of security.[509]

Kilrain is called the champion

While Davies was treading water, Kilrain had been awarded the title of champion of America by Fox, based on the assertion that Sullivan had failed to defend his title—even though Sullivan had broken his arm on Cardiff's hard head. Kilrain then left the United States and went to England to face the country's leading heavyweights with the ultimate objective of claiming the coveted title of heavyweight champion of the world.

Sullivan and Sheedy soon had a falling out. It would be difficult for two men with such strong personalities to stay together long. Many felt their split happened because Sullivan balked at going to England. Generally, Sullivan didn't like to be pushed around or out maneuvered by Fox, but Fox had clearly outplayed Sheedy. The Sheedy-Sullivan breakup was followed by the anticipated name calling between the two unprincipled egotists.[510] Observers suggested that Billy Madden might return as Sullivan's manager, but he said that Madden was the last man on earth he would have as his manager.

In Chicago, prizefighting had been replaced by other forms of entertainment. If you liked to watch long-jump contests, broadsword contest, the "hop-skip-and-jump" and a good old "tug-of-war," then you were in luck. Events such as these were being offered at many places around the city and, except for the tug-of-war, they were drawing little attention. Why would anyone leave their house or get off a bar stool to watch someone jump in a sand pit?

On October 10 a Whitmore-Moth wrestling match took place at Battery D. This was not Davies' event, but he was present near the ring with Lewis at his side. The match ended in a draw and at the end it was announced that Moth would wrestle Lewis, Greco-Roman style, strangle-hold barred, one week later, for $500 a side and the entire gate receipts.[511] Before that match could take place, Davies left Chicago for New York. He was supposedly going there to attend the funeral of one of his sisters, but there is no confirmation of such an event in New York newspapers.[512] Although not confirmed, circumstances suggest that Jane Davies Taylor had died leaving three children and that Parson Davies helped support Jane's children in addition Henry's three children after this point.

In mid-November 1887 Davies took Frank Glover to Minneapolis for a fight at the Washington Rink with John Clow, who had started fighting in Denver but was then fighting out of Duluth. Clow weighed 162 pounds for the match and Glover 187 pounds. Glover was trying to reclaim a position in the heavyweight ranks having been defeated earlier by Bradburn. Their fight with two-ounce gloves took place on November 14 and ended in a draw, but Clow was thought to have had the better of the fight.

Davies was credited with securing the draw for Glover by refusing to agree to a referee from the Minneapolis area. After six hours of arguing Davies got his way, and the parties agreed on two referees. Davies selection was Florrie Barnett, who had been working as Glover's trainer in preparation for the fight. Clow's handlers chose J. S. Barnes as their referee. Glover later said that his poor showing in this match happened because on November 11, he had stopped in Milwaukee to spar with Barnett and during that match he had injured his left hand. As might be expected, Barnett called the match for Glover, and Barnes called it for Clow resulting in a draw and a 50/50 split of the gate.[513]

Davies finally arranged a Lewis-Connors rematch in early December 1887.[514] The parties agreed to wrestle catch-as-catch-can under *Police Gazette* rules and the best two-out-of-three falls. The match was to be held at Battery D on the evening of December 19 for $250 a side and a 75/25 split of the gate receipts. Scheduling a match at Battery D suggested that Davies expected a big gate. The stakes were a grudging concession to Connors because the amount of money at issue was only half of the amount lost in Pittsburgh. Even if Connors lost the match, he was still going to end up ahead of the game.

In another concession to Connors, the strangle-hold was barred. This concession was necessary to persuade Connors to participate. The articles included the following interesting provision: "Each party shall have the right to have a man at the entrance gate, or gates, to see that all admission tickets are deposited in the box provided for that purpose. Charles E. Davies has been agreed upon to manage the above match."[515] Someone was worried that the entire gate receipts were not making it to the counting table. Along with many other false starts during the year 1887, this match fizzled because Lewis became seriously ill and was unable to appear for the match. It took almost two months for Lewis to recover.[516]

Chapter 8 - (1888)

Making the Big Match

"Parson" Davies – An 1891 drawing from the Decatur Republican

Thoughts about the role of prizefighting

In early 1888, public opinion about prizefighting included a broad array of ideas. James Parton, a well-known American historian and biographer, took a Darwinian view. He saw boxing as a way that Mother Nature preserved and improved the human species. He felt that the revival of prizefighting was natural reaction to the feminization of society evidenced by writers such as Ralph Waldo Emerson. To Parton, nature offset Emerson with Sullivan.

The Reverend Dr. Robert Collyer, a former Methodist minister turned Unitarian, served the Unitarians of Chicago from 1871 to 1879. Collyer had then become pastor of the Unitarian Church of the Messiah in New York. He was an author of several books on religious matters, including the book *Talks to Young Men* published in 1888—required reading for all young men aspiring to be boxers. Collyer said the sport existed because people generally nourished brutal instincts like those of the Romans. The brutal instincts of the modern man were overlaid by a thin veneer of civility. Collyer believed that the modern prizefighter took the place of the ancient gladiator. He thought it would be possible on careful examination to find some good in the sport. He conceded that knowledge of boxing might allow a man to trounce a brute soundly for insulting a woman or for some cruelty to a child, but it was good for little else. These possibilities obviously did not apply to Sullivan, who used his ability on occasion to trounce soundly both women and children.

Anthony Comstock, a Congregationalist and activist who founded the New York Society for the Suppression of Vice, was the leading anti-obscenity advocate of his era. Comstock said that those who found delight in pugilistic sport were people who frequented places providing brutal amusement for the excitement and the money they could make while gambling on such events. These low people, he said, did not represent any decent element of society. Comstock said that prizefighting had a brutalizing effect on the young people of America. He acknowledged that he believed in the culture of physical development, but not in physical development that degraded young men and caused them to lose their self-respect. Had Comstock executed a raid on a sporting event sponsored by Davies, such as those he led against local libraries, he and his fellows would have been beaten to a pulp. Comstock's view was shared by Senator John Sherman of Ohio, who hoped to be the Republican presidential nominee. Senator Sherman saw prizefighters as nothing more than dogs fighting in a cage and said that people attended such events for the same reasons that they liked to see a man throw knives all around a woman's head. In his view, prizefights were vicious and degrading and bad for the morals of the community at large.

Bill Nye, the great American humorist, said that prizefighting had enjoyed resurgence in the United States and England simply because the two countries had not had a full-blown war for some time. He suggested that it would be a good idea if politics could be turned over to the sporting world, where issues such as the tariff questions, international copyright, territorial boundaries and the Native American question would be solved in the prize ring without guns and swords. He suggested that men like Kilrain and Sullivan should replace the United States Army and meet the pugilists of foreign countries for final resolution of all similar questions. He had faith that U. S. fighters would win most such contests.[517]

Davies' view of prize fighting was quite different. He saw boxing as a legitimate form of entertainment that people of all social stations enjoyed. Above all prize fighting was part of the entertainment business. Davies treated the paying customer and fighters with respect and dignity and expected the same in return. He was a man who enjoyed some magnetism and drew people to himself without making an overt effort to influence others. He enjoyed interacting with people and the relationships that he had with leading politicians of the time.

Managing and promoting sporting events provided Davies with the income he needed to fulfill his obligations to the nieces and nephews he supported. The prizefighting business followed economic rules that remain common in Chicago. If one expects to sell or promote a product that has a public profile, then there are costs of doing business and those costs are paid without an invoice. After the production costs were incurred the entertainment should be first class and not phony.

More wrestling

The year of 1888 began as 1887 had ended: the early months were dominated by the promotion of wrestling events in Chicago. The wrestlers—Lewis, Carkeek, Muldoon, and Greek George—were among the top professional wrestlers in the world and champions of their particular styles of wrestling. While these matches did not result in the same big money generated by a quality prizefight, they did keep the wolf away from the door.

On January 5, 1888, Lewis wrote to the editor of the *Chicago Tribune* from his home in Barneveld, Wisconsin. He challenged his nemesis, Tom Connors, to sign new articles for a rematch of their earlier brutal encounter in Pittsburgh. Their rematch, previously scheduled for December 1887, had been cancelled because of Lewis's illness. Connors, however, went to England, and the rematch was indefinitely postponed.[518]

The Streator Cyclone

Prizefighting in other parts of the Midwest was not totally closed down. Billy Myer was one of the great lightweight fighters of his era and had developed an impressive record in central Illinois, Wisconsin, and northern Indiana. Myer put himself on the map by defeating Charlie Daly, who was one of the fighting Daly brothers of St. Louis. On February 2, 1887, he faced Paddy Welch in three rounds in a private fight before twenty-five men who paid ten dollars a ticket to witness the match. In the second round of that fight, Myer had his head pushed through the window but responded by knocking Welch out. Then on June 16, 1887, he knocked out Jack Gallager in Dana, Illinois, in only three rounds.

Myer moved well up in the ranks of lightweights with a fifth-round knockout of Harry Gilmore in Saint Croix, Wisconsin, on October 19, 1887. Gilmore was the lightweight champion of Canada and claimed that he had lost to Myer on a lucky punch. "Myer is a good little man, but it was by a chance blow that he knocked me out," Gilmore said. He demanded a rematch, and Myer obliged. Their second fight took place at North Judson, Indiana, on the morning of January 19, 1888.

One hundred Streator fight fans left their local depot at eight thirty on the evening of January 18, headed for the secret location of the match. Their train was in North Judson by about eleven thirty p.m. when another train arrived from Chicago carrying Davies, Floto, Bradburn, Glover, Mike Conley, the "Ithaca Giant," Tom Gallagher, and John Brannock. Floto was leading a delegation of men from "Blizzardville" (i.e., Minneapolis) who backed Gilmore. Billy Lakeman of Chicago acted as master of ceremonies, and Alf Kennedy of Streator was Billy's backer. Glover was the referee and Parson Davies held the stakes of $1,000 a side. Bradburn presented Gilmore with colors that had been sent to him by Richard Fox of the *Police Gazette*. Myer mocked this ostentation by holding up his colors, which consisted of an old glove with a husking peg that his mother had made many years before for use during the fall corn harvest.

The thermometer read six degrees below zero at fight time. A man with coffee and sandwiches showed up, and he ended up making more money on the fight than the contestants. The fight lasted twenty-eight seconds before Gilmore was out cold. Floto, who was one of the timekeepers for the fight, said that the official time, including the ten seconds allowed Gilmore after he was knocked down, was actually forty-two seconds. J. L. Black, one of Gilmore's backers, disparaged Harry for fighting a stupid fight. He said that he had told Gilmore to stay away from Myer's right hand.

Black remarked: "I believe Myer can whip Gilmore easier than anybody else, for he just takes advantage of Harry's weak spot—no use of his head."[519]

A week after the Myers-Gilmore fight the two contestants met in Davies' office. Others present included Muldoon, Lewis, and Colonel John D. Hopkins, who at the time was the manager of the Casino Theater in Chicago. Hopkins was a sometimes fight promoter, and he would later be the owner-operator of theaters in St. Louis, Chicago, Memphis, Atlanta, and New Orleans. He would also become a partner of Davies in several entertainment enterprises and a close friend in the years to come. Hopkins was a man who knew how to make money, and he did very well for himself and his associates.

That evening at Davies' office the men spent time talking about training for fights. Part of their conversation involved Hopkins' account of Sullivan's hateful attitude toward black fighters. These comments are interesting because some writers claim that Sullivan only drew the color line after Peter Jackson appeared in the United States, and Hopkins' account suggests that Sullivan was not simply a bigot of convenience but had honed his hatred for many years. If there was any doubt, this is part of what he wrote in 1905: "I want every negro to do well and my opposition to seeing white boxers meet colored boxers is not based on an petty feeling. But for a white man to meet a negro as an equal doesn't pull the negro up to the white man's level but rather pulls the blonde down to the brunette's." Sullivan's attitude was similar to the kind thinking that contributed to the extermination of millions of people between 1942 and 1945.

Hopkins said that he thought Jack Ashton was the best heavyweight outside of Sullivan, and in August 1887 he had tried to arrange a fight for $1,000 a side between Ashton and any of the other leading heavyweights, including the black fighter George Godfrey. Pat Sheedy was Sullivan's manager at the time, and Sheedy talked about backing Lannon to fight Ashton, but Sheedy would not post the required forfeit money. Then Sheedy offered to back an unknown against Ashton and Hopkins, and Sheedy agreed to meet at the offices of the *Boston Globe* to make the match. Sheedy failed to show, but Hopkins was tipped off that Sheedy's unknown was actually George Godfrey. Therefore, on behalf of Ashton, Hopkins issued a direct challenge to Godfrey.

As Hopkins recalled: "I said the other fighters and their backers would not make a match with a N_____, but neither race nor color would stop us."

Godfrey said he was willing to fight, but he could only raise $500. Hopkins told Godfrey that he should get the rest of the money from Sheedy, and a match would be made. At that point, "Sullivan made a kick to me about making Ashton fight a N_____ and wanted to know why I did it."

Hopkins told Sullivan that he had issued the challenge to Godfrey because Sheedy had tried to "ring in Godfrey as an unknown," thinking that Ashton would back out of a fight with a black man, and then Sheedy would keep the forfeit money. Hopkins had simply found out about Sheedy's scheme and called his bluff because neither he nor Ashton cared about Godfrey's color.

According to Hopkins: "I guess that settled Sullivan and Sheedy, for Sullivan got hot, and swore that a man who had done what Sheedy had could never act as his manager again. After that Sheedy, I think, handled Sullivan's benefit in Boston, and that was all."

The point of this was that Sullivan cut his ties with Sheedy because Sheedy tried to match the white Ashton against the black Godfrey. For Sullivan, matching his friend Ashton with a black fighter was unforgivable.[521]

A few days after the powwow at Davies' place, Myer was still in Chicago, and he indulged in a little catch-as-catch-can wrestling at the Athenaeum Gymnasium with Glover. Glover was too strong for Billy and outweighed him by about sixty-five pounds, but Glover said that Myer was strong and active and that he was "the strongest man of his weight I ever saw."[522]

With Myers' return to Streator, Davies' attention focused on promoting wrestling. In January 1888, Muldoon was performing with the Hallen & Hart specialty company doing the same living statuary business that had made Sullivan so happy, and Muldoon was also offering $25 to any man who would stand up before him for fifteen minutes under Greco-Roman wrestling rules. The specialty company was appearing at the Casino Theater in Chicago, which was managed by Colonel Hopkins, who saw that Muldoon's twenty-five-dollar offer was not bringing out challengers. Hopkins then offered $100 to any man who could stand up against Muldoon for fifteen minutes and not be thrown. Strangler Lewis accepted Hopkins' challenge.[523]

Lewis and Muldoon at the Casino

Lewis and Muldoon met on the evening of January 30 at the Casino. Glover was again selected as the referee. Lewis attempted to back out of the match at the last minute. He said that he had wrestled in Peoria a few days earlier and had discovered that he had not recovered his strength from being ill. Hopkins insisted, and Davies persuaded Lewis to proceed. After fifteen minutes of effort, Muldoon was unable to throw Lewis, and someone in the crowd yelled out: "It's a fake." This angered Muldoon, who came to the footlights and told the crowd that this was no put-up job and that he would have thrown Lewis had he been able.[524]

Muldoon was at the Casino a few nights later. This time the terms of the challenge were that a man would receive $25 if he could stand for fifteen minutes and an additional $2 a minute for every minute he could keep his shoulders off the floor after the first five minutes. Muldoon had developed a large boil under his left eye that had to be lanced that same morning. He entered the ring with two black eyes and a swollen face.

His challenger was an experienced Detroit wrestler named Thomas McMahon. Muldoon was unable to throw McMahon, and he was again hissed and booed. Muldoon again addressed the crowd and said that he thought it was unmanly for the crowd to hiss and ridicule a wrestler. He offered $100 to any man who had made a remark, plus $5 a minute for such man to come forward and see whether he could stand before him. The man who had made the most noise remained silent, and Muldoon was then cheered by the crowd.[525]

Davies then created the Parson Davies' Specialty Company and took Lewis and Muldoon on the road as his star performers. Charlie planned to take the company to Milwaukee and then work its way east through Chicago, Detroit, Pittsburgh, Buffalo, and other large cities. He planned to offer $50 to any man who could stand before Lewis for fifteen minutes catch-as-catch-can and $100 to any man who could throw Lewis within the allotted time. He made the same offer for Muldoon in the Greco-Roman style. Finally, Davies announced that he was forwarding a challenge to Jack Wannop, the English champion, on behalf of Lewis. Davies' off-and-on relationship with Wannop would continue into the year 1890.[526]

The specialty company's first night in Milwaukee did not go well. Carkeek showed up to challenged Lewis. The Strangler was unable to throw Carkeek within the allotted fifteen minutes. A professional wrestler named D. A. McMillan then announced his intention to challenge Muldoon on the second night in Milwaukee. This was not promising to be a good way to make money if the challenges had to be paid out every night.[527]

Two days later the specialty company was back in Chicago, and Davies added two prizefighters to his stable of athletes. First, he was representing Reddy Gallagher, who was from Tennessee but had learned to fight under Duncan Ross when he was operating out of Cleveland. He had also picked up a fighter named Martin Snee of Boston. On the evening of February 13, the specialty company was appearing at the Casino. Each of these fighters signed for twenty weeks under Davies' management.[528] The match of the evening was Muldoon-Carkeek in Greco-Roman wrestling.[529]

The following evening the wrestling bouts were preceded by a three-round sparring exhibition between Gilmore and Gallagher. How Davies was able to get away with a sparring exhibition in Chicago is not apparent, but he probably took the position that a license was not required because the match was not a prizefight. The Gilmore-Gallagher event was the first sparring exhibition inside Chicago city limits since one week after the Haymarket Riot. The exhibition was for scientific points. The crowd was starved for local boxing matches and even this tame exhibition brought down the house. The applause came from men who could have cared less what Anthony Comstock or Senator Sherman thought of prizefighting. Davies was riding on the crest of a vaudeville boom.[530]

Martin Snee came to Chicago to try to entice Billy Myer to fight. Myer was willing to fight any lightweight in America who would put up at least $4,000 in prize money. Snee did not have that kind of backing, and therefore a match between the two was unlikely. Within a few days Frank Ware came forward and announced that he would fight Snee. He offered to meet Snee at three p.m. on February 26 at Davies' office for the purpose of signing articles.

Across the Atlantic Ocean in London the announcement had been made that Sullivan would meet Mitchell for a fight that would probably take place in France. The typical build-up for the fight was lacing the newspapers. By March 6, the arrangements for the fight were complete, and Sullivan was claiming that he was going to settle the score with Mitchell, whom he called a non-fighting fighter.

On March 21, Davies was in Buffalo with Lewis serving as master of ceremonies for a match between Lewis and Dennis Gallagher. Over fifteen hundred people attended, and the condition of the match was that Lewis would have to throw Gallagher five times in sixty minutes. The match was for $500 and all of the gate money, which amounted to $2,000. This was a big risk, but Davies thought that Lewis was up to the task. The Strangler quickly obtained the first fall and then had Gallagher in a strangle-hold. As Gallagher's face turned black, the local police interfered, and the match was called a draw.[531]

Another possibility from England

The next day Davies headed back to Chicago, arriving on the evening of March 22. He left the wrestling tour because news had arrived that Wannop had agreed to a match with Lewis, and the terms needed to be resolved. For Davies, the Lewis-Wannop match would give him a chance to share in the international headlines being generated by prizefighters. If the champion wrestler of the United States could defeat the champion wrestler of England, then Davies' man could legitimately claim to be the heavyweight wrestling champion of the world—at least as the world was defined in the late 1880s.[532]

Kilrain had already claimed the heavyweight boxing championship of the world. The problem for Kilrain was that he had never defeated Sullivan in the ring, and in the opinion of the American public there was a cloud over Jake's title claim. Sullivan had failed to knock out Mitchell and was consequently in semi-disgrace. However, the issue for Kilrain was not whether Sullivan had faltered but whether Jake would be accepted as a champion without first defeating Sullivan.

In Chicago, Davies met with Wannop's backer. They agreed that the format for the match would be catch-as-catch-can, best three in five falls for two points down and that the match would be "bar nothing," which was something like agreeing to a London-rule prizefight. Wannop would not object to the use of the strangle-hold, which was Lewis' most formidable weapon. Each side posted $1,000 as forfeit money. Their championship match was to take place at Battery D on May 7, with the winner to get 75 percent of the gate receipts. Unofficially, Davies was willing to bet $5,000 of his own money on Lewis. The contest was also important because Lewis was not often an investment that paid well. A lot of money would be riding on a good night on May 7.[533]

The wrestling tour went on to New York City with Floto in charge in Davies' absence. On the evening of March 27, Floto and Lewis went to the London Theater, where Sorakichi was appearing. The Japanese wrestler had a defy up offering $50 to any man who could throw him within fifteen minutes. Floto and Lewis took seats near the ring. When the challenge was announced, Floto arose and said that Lewis would accept.

William Kellogg was handling Sorakichi at the time and said, "Who are you, sir?"

Then Lewis, who had not been recognized earlier, arose from his place beside Floto and said, "I am Evan Lewis. I am here for business."

Kellogg said that Sorakichi was engaged for every night that week and his opponent for the night, Thomas Scanlan, had already been chosen. Lewis said that he would wrestle both "the Jap" and Scanlan, and he guaranteed to down them both. The crowd was wild with excitement, but Sorakichi's backer refused the proposals on the grounds that the defy applied only to men local to New York, and Lewis was from Wisconsin.

Floto continued to argue the point when Sorakichi approached and told Floto that he talked too much. At that point Sorakichi's backer told him to "Shut up!" and claimed the issue was closed. This was good publicity for Lewis and that was probably the reason it happened. The Davies' wrestlers moved on to Williamsburg, Virginia, on March 26, 1888.[534]

In mid-April 1888 Lewis went to "Joe" Prendergast's hotel at Clifton, Staten Island, to begin training for his championship match with Wannop.[535] With so much riding on the upcoming championship match it seemed certain that the authorities would raise objections. Lewis arrived back in Chicago looking well and thinner than usual.

Another mayor and another fool

That same day Superintendent of Police George Hubbard notified Davies that no gambling of any kind would be allowed in Chicago. This action was taken to enforce a campaign pledge made by Mayor John A. Roche, who had been elected in 1887, and the police were acting on the mayor's orders. The mayor had instructed the police that his pledge went beyond poker and faro tables.[536] Therefore the $1,000 a side posted for the Wannop-Lewis match would have to be taken down. Davies argued that his wrestlers were not contesting in a game of chance but that their competition involved an athletic test of strength and skill.

Davies asked: "Well, will horse-racing for purses and stakes be allowed in Chicago?" In reply Hubbard said that an Illinois statute permitted horse racing, and the mayor was not challenging that statute. Davies asked about the proposed split of the gate receipts, but the superintendent had no response on that issue. More remarkably, Hubbard notified Davies that he had a further order from the mayor. There would be no "brutality" allowed in the match.[537] This meant that if Lewis used his strangle-hold, then the police would interfere. The police prohibition of the strangle-hold could have a significant impact on the outcome of the match and the betting on it. It would be interesting to know how much money the police themselves had bet on Wannop after the decision to bar the choke hold.

Roche's position was not consistent with what had been allowed in previous matches. It appeared to be arbitrary and made up on the spot. When asked why he had taken these new positions, the mayor said that he had seen flaming advertisements announcing a strangling match, which he would not permit. The mayor admitted that he could not prevent people from wagering on the outcome of this or any other match, but he said that he could prevent them from "flaunting their bets publicly in the face of the community." The mayor said that he remembered Lewis's brutality in damaging "the Jap's" ankle, and he would "not tolerate that sort of barbarism." Of course, it was that sort of thing that put people in the seats.

On May 5, Davies obtained his license for the Lewis-Wannop match. He gave assurances that everything connected with the match would be properly conducted and that the stakes had been taken down.[538] The match went forward on schedule. Captain Bonfield, of Haymarket infamy, was present with Detective Aldrich and a score of stalwart Chicago patrolmen to oversee the contest. Bonfield's presence suggested that in addition to paying for a license, Parson Davies probably had to pay-off Bonfield for the match to proceed.[539]

A world champion

Between two and three thousand attended the Lewis-Wannop championship match. The crowd included a mass of sportsmen, politicians, saloon-keepers, board of trade members, and rowdies. Davies' friend Colonel Hopkins issued a challenge before the match began. Hopkins had scheduled Matsada Sorakichi to appear at the Casino on the night after the championship match and said that he would give the winner of the Lewis-Wannop match half of the gate receipts if they would face Sorakichi and throw him within fifteen minutes. Hopkins and Davies thought alike on many subjects, and the championship match presented Hopkins with a chance to also make a buck.

Before the championship match Muldoon sent Lewis a telegram from Washington, D. C., that read, "Be cool, patient and determined. Nothing but the police can stop you winning." Joe Prendergast acted as Lewis's second during the match. Wannop was seconded by his backer John Hoare of New Cross, London. Lewis weighed 175 pounds for the match, and Wannop weighed 190. The match went better than expected for the Strangler and was considered a poor exhibition as far as Wannop was concerned.

In the first bout Wannop forced Lewis to his knees, but the Strangler broke away and secured a grapevine that he converted to a cross-buttocks. He then threw Wannop in only six minutes and twenty seconds. In the second bout, Lewis secured a headlock, but Wannop escaped and both men returned to the feet. Lewis again applied the grapevine, and a series of holds and escapes followed until Lewis turned Wannop with a half-Nelson, securing the second fall in a little over six minutes. Four broad-shouldered police officers then took up positions at the corners of wrestling platform before the third bout began. Black Jack liked to remind the public of his presence. The final bout lasted about one minute, and Wannop was thrown by a grapevine and shoulder-lock combination. Lewis was carried off on the shoulders of his fans and Wannop hobbled out with a bleeding ear and sore knee.

Davies had his first world champion! In less than a year he would have a shot of promoting a second world champion, this time in prizefighting. The long period dominated by wrestling was about over. [540]

Observers thought that Wannop had been drinking before the match began. They noted his red and flushed appearance when he came into the armory. After the contest, dudes gathered outside on the street and claimed that they too could have thrown Wannop in his drunken condition. His trainer, John Kline, emphatically denied that Wannop had anything to drink before the match began. His statement was contradicted by bartenders on Clark Street who said that they had seen him drinking at intervals on the afternoon before the match. The *Post Dispatch* reported that John Barleycorn had played a substantially part in helping Lewis win the match. More importantly, several newspapers reported that more than $20,000 had changed hands, and it is likely that Parson Davies was a big winner.[541]

On May 8, the night after the championship match, Lewis appeared at the Casino to meet Sorakichi, who was never anxious to wrestle Lewis and tried to back out of the match. After he was induced to appear, he made a good exhibition. Lewis was under instructions from Davies not to be in too much of a hurry and to go easy and give the people their money's worth. He was probably also concerned that the police would be present to prevent Lewis from beating up Sorakichi a third time. At twelve and a half minutes of the bout, Lewis secured a hang-lock on Sorakichi and turned him over for a fall. The call that Sorakichi was down was disputed because he claimed that he had bridged out. His backers said that they would bet the referee $100 that any twenty men in the place would agree that there had been no fall. Davies stepped forward and said that if they wanted to bet $100, then they should put it on the table and let Lewis and Sorakichi go at it a second time for that money. That ended the argument.[542]

The summer of 1888 moved on with some of Davies' former fighters involved in big matches outside of Chicago. Glover went to California and fought the champion of the Pacific slope, Joe McAuliffe. Glover did well in a forty-nine-round fight, but he was knocked out in the end.[543] This was the biggest fight of Glover's career and although he lost, he also proved that he was a talented heavyweight on a national level and not just a local Chicago fighter. Unfortunately for Glover, his health begin to fail soon after this fight and he never recovered.

Two of Davies' former heavyweights, Cardiff and Killen, met at Washington Rink in Minneapolis on June 26. In the third round Killen landed his terrific right hand on Cardiff's neck, and he went down like a log. There was no broken hand this time. It was sixteen seconds before Cardiff recovered. Killen had earned his revenge, and he also proved that he had the best right hand of anyone in that class.[544]

A fighter from Australia

Charlie was an avid reader of the daily newspapers. On June 30, the *Post Dispatch* carried the following short article:

> Boston, Mass., June 30 – Yesterday M. H. Haughton telegraphed from San Francisco to George Godfrey, the Black heavyweight pugilist, that the California Club had agreed to put up a purse of fifteen hundred dollars for a finish glove fight in August between Godfrey and Peter Jackson, the Australian Black heavyweight, the loser to take $300, and that $400 would be allowed Godfrey for expenses.[545]

Godfrey accepted these terms and Davies surely raised his eyebrows over this development. He may have been curious about why the men in California would be willing to put up that kind of money for a fight between two black heavyweights. There must have been something more than what met the eye going on here. The same article was reprinted in the *Chicago Tribune* on July 1.

Davies gave up his interest in The Store to a gambler named Harry Perry on September 1, 1888. The financing for this transaction is not clear, but it seems that Davies remained on the chattel mortgage he signed in early 1886 when he began operating the saloon. After this point Davies operated his entertainment business out of a saloon co-owned by his brother Vere and known as Corcoran & Davies. This place was located at 93 Clark Street, at the corner of the alley north of Washington. This was never an all-night saloon, but a resort for politicians who often stayed there drinking later than they should have to debate the chances of some candidate or speculate over the failure of another.[546]

In early September 1888 Davies received a letter from Australia. His former fighter Jack Burke wanted Charlie to know that he was thinking about making his home there. Burke said that money was flowing freely for boxers in Australia, and he was fighting with the European Circus. He had purchased an interest in the Castigan Mine and had made 700 percent on his money. Burke was also planning to build a gymnasium and had been offered $10,000 for a half interest. He wanted Davies to join him in this venture, but Davies had no interest in Australia, except for the good fighters who came from that continent.[547]

Killen returned to Chicago, and Davies saw an opportunity to make some hay out of his visit. He matched Killen for an exhibition with Wannop at Battery D. They met on September 17, and there were many Chicago aldermen present. Their presence probably kept "Black Jack" Bonfield quiet. He was present for the Killen-Wannop exhibition along with Captain Fitzgerald and Lieutenant Ross but did nothing to stop the match.[548]

In introducing the two men before the fight Billy Lakeman admonished them: "Gentlemen, I want you to understand that this will be a friendly set-to. There will be no slugging; the authorities (with a nod toward Bonfield) won't allow it."

The fight was to consist of only scientific fighting for four rounds. This declaration brought a great laugh from the crowd and a stern stare from Bonfield. The *Tribune* reported that before the men appeared on the stage Davies gave Killen a quiet lecture, admonishing him under no circumstances to turn his hands loose. This was the state to which prizefighting had fallen in Chicago by September 1888, but Davies was still making a good living.

The Killen-Wannop exhibition was better than most expected. The postmortem was that Wannop was a better boxer than wrestler. He was powerful and quick as a cat, and he fought with both hands. However, the consensus was that Killen had simply played with him in obedience to the prefight instructions from Davies. The Parson took note of Wannop's ability as a fighter and would have more business for him in years to come.[549]

Betting on the election

It appeared that the attitude of the Chicago authorities might be easing up until a good middleweight fighter, George Fulljames, was killed in a match at Grand Forks, Dakota Territory.[550] The fall election in Illinois was approaching, and the results of that election could change the political situation quickly. The Republican Party's candidate was "Private Joe" Fifer of Bloomington, Illinois. The Democrats were backing John M. Palmer, a former Illinois governor.

One good thing about an Illinois election was that it always provided the chance for a betting line. Billy Pinkerton offered to wager five-to-one odds that Fifer would beat Palmer. Was this gambling under Mayor Roche's theory? Pinkerton won $1,000 from William Fitzgerald. Davies made a savvier bet against Fifer. He bet an avid Republican that Fifer would not win by more the 20,000 votes. Fifer won the election, but Davies collected $100 when Joe's margin of victory was less than the specified spread.[551]

Throughout 1888 the sporting news was dominated by Kilrain and Sullivan. Fox had pushed Kilrain forward and then anointed him as America's champion while Sullivan was on the shelf unable or unwilling to fight. Fox had then financed Kilrain's trip to England to meet Jem Smith. After doing his part by defeating Jem Smith, Kilrain claimed to be champion heavyweight of the world. In the meantime Sullivan's fortunes had slumped with his failure to stop Mitchell and because of his several illnesses and continued dissipated lifestyle. Many of the leading heavyweights were getting brave and beginning to make bold challenges to both Kilrain and Sullivan. Everyone seemed to sense blood in the water. Kilrain was on a clay pedestal, and Sullivan was wounded but not dead.

Making the heavyweight championship match

The press was relatively quiet about Davies after Lewis won the world wrestling championship, and when the press was quiet, there was usually something simmering. On December 1, the *Herald* reported that Davies had left Chicago rather unexpectedly for New York, leaving no word of his mission.[552] The next day, many national newspapers reported that Kilrain had made a formal challenge to Sullivan for a heavyweight championship fight. Kilrain's backer was Fox, who would do anything and risk almost any amount of money to cut down Sullivan.

Davies left for New York because he had received word that Kilrain had challenged Sullivan, and this time things were serious. Fox understood that a match would never be pulled off if he and Sullivan met face to face; their personal animosity would complicate the situation. Davies was respected by Sullivan and had a reputation as an honest man and a peacemaker. He was exactly the intermediary that Fox needed to seal a deal. He would effectively act as the closing agent for Fox. In return, Fox allowed Davies to assume the management of Kilrain and Mitchell without interference.

When Davies arrived in New York, he went to Madison Square Garden to watch a racewalking contest, saying he had "to have a look at my old hobby."[553] When Sullivan arrived in New York on December 3, he was accompanied by Jack Barnett and Jack Hayes. Sullivan also headed for the Garden, ostensibly to support a racewalker named Dan Herty who was in the final day of a six-day race. Something was cooking with these heavy hitters gathering in New York.

During an interview, Davies was asked whether he had anything to report along the pugilistic line. "Well," he responded, "nothing definite yet, except that I have arranged to manage Kilrain and Mitchell in a tour of the West. I expect they will start very soon, and be in Chicago about the end of December."[554]

He followed this revelation by saying that Kilrain wanted to make an offer to Sullivan through Davies. He noted that Kilrain had once accused of being a coward for challenging Sullivan when Sullivan was sick. Davies noted that

Kilrain had since waited patiently for another opportunity to challenge Sullivan, and when Sullivan returned from England, he had challenged Mitchell. This clearly indicated that Sullivan had regained his health, and Kilrain felt that his renewed challenge was appropriate and beyond reproach. Kilrain said that he would fight Sullivan with bare knuckles to a finish under the rules of the London prize ring, the rules under which Sullivan won the championship from Paddy Ryan for $5,000 a side. He would "give Sullivan abundant opportunity to get into perfect condition, will not insist on fighting in five weeks, but will give him ten or twelve weeks." Davies noted that Kilrain was ready at any time and that he was anxious to arrange a fight.

The next day Sullivan said that he was ready to make a match with Kilrain.[555] A special to the *Tribune* reported that Sullivan had been asked, "Do you think a match can be arranged between you and Kilrain?"

"Yes," Sullivan replied. "I mean to force him to fight. I shall issue a challenge to the world and am ready to meet anybody, but am particularly anxious to fight Kilrain."

Sullivan said that he thought that Kilrain did not want to fight but would try in a gentlemanly way to force him into a fight. Sullivan was willing to "blackguard" Kilrain if necessary. This meant that Sullivan was willing to act in an unprincipled way if that is what it took to force Kilrain to fight. Sullivan said that Kilrain knew that he had no real claim to the title and that he would have to whip him before he wore any championship belt.

On December 8 Davies announced that he was managing Kilrain and Mitchell.[556] Both were in Chicago by December 12, and the *Post Dispatch* reported that Davies was planning to bring off the following fights in Chicago: Kilrain-Sullivan, Kilrain-Killen, and Mitchell-Sullivan. What a trifecta that would be![557]

Davies was asked about arranging these matches in Chicago. He said that Chicago was the best ground to make preliminary arrangements, but under the present Illinois law, even sparring matches were prohibited. But he wanted it on the record that Chicago had as many lovers of the manly art as any city in the country and that those who would like to see a fight in Chicago included representatives of the leading professions and mercantile pursuits. He acknowledged that any fight in Chicago would at best have to be for points and under police supervision. Old "Black Jack" Bonfield and his men would have to have their share too.

Taking Kilrain and Mitchell on tour

By mid-December Kilrain had accepted the Sullivan's challenge for a finish fight for $10,000. Mitchell would act as Kilrain's second. If there wasn't bad blood between Sullivan and Kilrain, then it would certainly be present with Mitchell in Kilrain's corner. On the afternoon of December 16, "C. Mitchell, N. Y." and "Jake Kilrain, Baltimore" registered at the Sherman House in Chicago. That same afternoon the two fighters met with Davies at his Clark Street resort. Davies put a nickel in a pay scale, and Kilrain registered as weighing 235 pounds.

"Just the right weight for a champion," Davies remarked.

In French, Mitchell commented: "I had the honor to procure a headache for Mr. Sullivan while in France!"

In a mutual love fest, Kilrain declared that Mitchell was the true champion, but Mitchell deferred and insisted that Kilrain held that distinction. Their preening was interrupted when a reporter asked: "Then what is the use of bothering the Boston man? If it's a question of championship why don't you two set to work and fight it out?"[558]

It was a reasonable question, but it seemed to puzzle Kilrain and Mitchell. Davies stepped in and explained that there was an ethical point involved, which made it necessary that Sullivan should stop quibbling and stand up to Kilrain, or quit the profession.

The next evening, Kilrain and Mitchell appeared in a friendly set-to before a large audience at the Casino Theater. Their exhibition consisted of three tame rounds. They were scheduled to put on similar demonstrations at the Casino every night for an upcoming week and then go on the road. Davies never let an asset sit idle if there was money to be made.[559]

Neither Kilrain nor Mitchell was well-received by the Chicago crowd. The people were clearly partial to Sullivan and Dempsey. With the curtain down behind him, Davies appeared on stage and explained that he had officiated at the Chicago debut of Sullivan, whose name was cheered, and he now asked fair treatment for Kilrain, whose name was met with groans.

Then the curtain came up and revealed Kilrain and Mitchell at the back of the stage. They were met with a rush of hisses from the audience. One boy in a corner yelled "Dempsey!" Then everyone in the crowd yelled "Dempsey!" They were all calling attention to Mitchell's actions over more than two years dodging repeated challenges from Dempsey, who was a favorite in Chicago.

Davies signaled for the men to begin their sparring. Kilrain hit Mitchell in the nose, which seemed to please the spectators but rile Mitchell. He then gave Kilrain a stinging blow to the midsection, which was returned by a vicious swipe to Mitchell's head. Mitchell returned in kind and Kilrain ducked when a spectator in a fur overcoat (obviously one of the professional types referred to by Davies) yelled out, "Fight, you chump."

Others began to taunt Mitchell yelling, "Run, Mitchell. Why don't you run?" and "Dempsey!" Mitchell, obviously irritated, gave Kilrain a good knock in the neck, which angered Kilrain.

This was followed by an admonition from Parson Davies: "Gentlemen! Gentlemen! Don't, I beg you. Don't hurt him, Jake. Oh, my! Remember what you are. Remember my position. The police." Then both men became more cautious until in the final round Davies whistled and their pace again picked up. After the exhibition Mitchell and Kilrain were followed to their carriage by the crowd that continued to hoot, "Dempsey! Sullivan!" Not a good start in Chicago.[560]

Mitchell and Kilrain appeared at the Casino again on December 18 and 19, but on the third night the police appeared before the match with orders to prohibit the exhibition. Nearly $500 in ticket money had to be returned to disappointed patrons.

Davies spoke from the stage and told those still present that he intended to speak to his attorney on the following day about whether sparring matches could continue. He also said that supporters of Sullivan had intended to invite him for a benefit, and Davies wondered whether that would be prevented. Chief Hubbard replied that the "Big Un" would not spar in Chicago if the police could prevent it. Davies replied that if Kilrain could not spar at the Casino, then he would arrange for him to appear as a wrestler.[561]

Davies saw his attorney and an affidavit was prepared seeking to enjoin interference by the Chicago police in the Kilrain-Mitchell sparing matches. A request for an injunction was considered a special remedy and heard in Chancery Court, where unusual and important cases where brought. In Chicago, this often meant that the biggest bribes were taken by the Chancery judges.

In the affidavit, Davies said that he was engaged in the business of giving shows in places of public amusement. He denied that Kilrain and Mitchell were acting as fighters but asserted that they were only acting as professors of sparring to illustrate the beauties of physical culture, a subject taught in gymnasiums and schools of physical culture. Judge John P. Altgeld granted an injunction restraining the police from interfering with the performances, and Kilrain and Mitchell were back at the Casino on the evening of December 20 with big, soft, pillow-like gloves.[562]

Davies punches out a theater manager

On the evening of December 22, Davies got into his own bare knuckle slugging match. That afternoon warrants had been issued for the arrests of Kilrain and Mitchell. Davies went to Andy McKay, the manager of the Casino, and asked him to post a notice at the theater that the two fighters would not be appearing that evening. It was Davies' view that no one should be drawn into the theater thinking that his two men would appear and then be disappointed. He thought this was part of running an honest business.

At about nine p.m. Davies sent Floto to the theater. Floto found that the house was already packed and the notice had not been posted as requested. Davies then sent instructions to collect 50 percent of the gate as the share he was entitled to if his fighters appeared. McKay at first refused to give up any of the gate receipts but finally gave Floto 25 percent. When Davies found out that McKay was shorting him on the gate, he went to the theater and confronted McKay, who tried to throw Davies out of his office. McKay outweighed Davies by 100 pounds, but Davies decked him with a punch and then pulled McKay up off the floor and sailed into him again. Davies gave McKay matching black eyes and a broken nose and left him with blood tricking between his teeth. Before he left, Davies gave McKay a couple of vigorous kicks in the rear end. That evening Mitchell and Kilrain hid out from the police and the next day they left for Fort Wayne, Indiana.[563]

Davies was able to beat the politicians and police force in court, but he had a harder sell in the court of public opinion. As Davies, Kilrain, and Mitchell headed out on the road, the two fighters were often booed and harassed. The *Cincinnati Enquirer* referred to them as Jake "English" Kilrain and "Blooming Bleeding" Charley Mitchell. The paper said that they were having a monkey and parrot time giving their looking-glass exhibition of "How to Be a Champion Without Winning a Battle."

On December 27, Davies, Kilrain, and Mitchell were in Cleveland and appeared at the Academy of Music. Rotten eggs were thrown at them when they first stepped on stage. Davies stepped forward and tried to calm the audience, but he too was greeted with howls and hisses. Only the presence of the Cleveland police prevented a riot.

After the Cleveland exhibition, Mitchell and Kilrain went to the Kennard House barroom with a number of friends, including Reddy Gallagher. When they arrived, Tom Costello, a notorious Cleveland gambler and friend of Sullivan's, was already there with a gang of Sullivan supporters. Mitchell ordered wine for everyone in his group including Kilrain, Gallaher, Davies, and two English sprinters who were competing in international track-and-field events.

An English middleweight fighter named Hugh Burns was in the bar with Costello's crowd. Mitchell knew Burns and invited him to join the festivities. Burns was not in a friendly mood and swore at Mitchell and threatened to slug him. He then walked over to Mitchell and took a swipe at him, which Mitchell ducked. One of the men in Mitchell's party told him that Burns was packing and would shoot him given a chance. Mitchell began backing away and accidentally stepped into the pool of a fountain in the center of the room. Burns pursued Mitchell then let go and laid him out. Meanwhile, Reddy Gallagher held Costello in a chair to prevent him from doing anything more. A call went up saying that the police were there, and Costello and his crowd disappeared.

Later Costello said, "When Americans go to England they get no show, and I believe in serving them as they serve us. These men, Mitchell and Kilrain, are not gentlemen and ought not to have been allowed to give an exhibition of sparring here at all, but as long as the police did not interfere I wanted revenge and that is the way I got it. We drove those fellows to their rooms and made them run like whiteheads."[564]

The next evening in San Francisco, an Australian heavyweight named Peter Jackson knocked out Joe McAuliffe.[565] From Parson Davies' point of view, the most important aspect of the Jackson-McAuliffe match was that over $70,000 had been wagered on the fight. If a black heavyweight from Australia and the Pacific slope champion could ring up those numbers, then it was likely that a huge payday awaited everyone when the Sullivan-Kilrain match was finally settled. That night Davies brought Kilrain and Mitchell to Columbus, Ohio, for a one-night stand before heading on to St. Louis. At Columbus, the local police prevented the appearance.

The year of 1888 was supposed to wind up at the Natatorium Theater in St. Louis with Mitchell and Kilrain again serving as the prime attraction at the top of the bill. However, James L. Blair, the vice-president of the St. Louis Police Board, claimed that it was his legal duty to prevent Kilrain and Mitchell from sparring. He read aloud from section 1508 of the Revised Statues of Missouri: "Any person who shall engage in any sparring or boxing exhibition, or who shall aid, abet or assist in any such exhibition, or who shall furnish any room or other place for such exhibition shall be deemed guilty of a misdemeanor."

Davies argued that the Kilrain-Mitchell meeting was simply for fun and that they would not hurt one another, but Blair was adamant. Davies was interviewed by a reporter from the *Post Dispatch* while he waited to receive word about whether the match could go forward. He said:

> I hear that the law here is opposed to things of this kind but it is a bad law and should be contested. We are afflicted with the same miserable code in Illinois and I intend to go back there and to contest it. There is no harm in sparring but back-room prize fights ought to be stopped. It is no doubt the abuse of the sport is responsible for the stringency of the statue. If the police do not want us to spar up there to-night, we won't spar; that is all. Thank goodness we have a little money left and we can stop at good hotels on our way. Now, I like the Southern. It's a nice little hotel, and they have treated us very courteously since we have been here. If we can't spar here this evening, we will stay in the town a few days and enjoy its beautiful scenery, and then go away again.

The newspaper was impressed with Davies' calmness in the face of adversity. It described Davies as "like Socrates, he is a bit ironical, but on the whole he is suave."[566] Thus ended the odd year of 1888.

Making the deal

Despite all the strange things that had happened that year and the constant pressure exerted to suppress prizefighting, 1889 would include some of the biggest prizefights of all time, and Parson Davies would be at the center of many of the most significant sporting events in both the United States and England. In 1889, Davies would also meet and assume the management of Jackson. This charming, intelligent man and terrific heavyweight would be managed by Davies for almost five years, and they would travel widely in the United States, England, France, and Germany.

Chapter 9 - (1889)

The Greatest Fighter Ever

I was standing in my brother's place, 93 Clark street, one afternoon when a big, tall colored man stepped up and handed me a letter. I read it. It was from Mose Guntz of San Francisco. It introduced the colored man as Peter Jackson. He wore a tall hat and he looked at least seven feet high. The letter said Jackson was all right and was anxious to get on some fights in the East. 'You can make no mistake with this fellow,' read Guntz' letter.

Just then someone asked Jackson to have a drink. In a manner which really won me because of his cleverness, Jackson refused saying he did not drink. I did not like the idea of handling a darky but I read the letter again and looked Jackson over. I finally said I would take him and handle him for half. Jackson accepted, and I became the manager of the greatest fighter the world has ever seen.[567]

All of which reminds me that Parson Davies always had the pugs sized up about right. When speaking of fighters he said: "They are, as a rule, an ungrateful lot, and in all my connection with the sport in the thirty years I have handled fighters I have found but one whose word was his bond and whose handshake was the shake of an honest man. And that man a colored man at that - I mean Peter Jackson. There was not a dishonorable hair in the head of that black fellow, and he couldn't do a mean or dishonorable thing if he even tried ever so hard to do it. It was against his very nature to do anything but what you could throw the limelight full upon it, and then you would find old black Peter standing forth like a marble statue in comparison with many others of his same calling. That is why I have quit the "fighting game." The trouble is not worth the result, and it is a continual performance of deception and knocking within the ranks. Let others have their inning. I have had mine."[568]

Peter Jackson was the greatest heavyweight ever, according to the Parson. The Parson managed Peter for five years, and, despite the differences in the color of their skins, the Irishman and the African were fast friends. Peter was under the Parson's wing when he fought Jim Corbett in San Francisco about a quarter of a century ago.

They went sixty-one rounds to a draw. According to the Parson, Jackson would have won it if he hadn't been injured by being thrown from a buggy a few weeks before the battle. Davies tried to get a postponement, but could not, and Jackson went through with it and got a draw.[569]

The quiet New Year's Eve Davies, Kilrain, and Mitchell spent in St. Louis was a short respite from a busy schedule and the quite before a storm of activity that would mark the coming year of 1889. They were due in Buffalo for appearances on January 4 and 5, 1889, and from Buffalo they would move on to Albany and Troy, New York. Between Buffalo and Albany, Davies traveled to Toronto, where he played a key role in arranging the infamous Sullivan-Kilrain heavyweight championship match.

On January 2, Davies was asked about his plans if a Sullivan-Kilrain match could not be arranged. He answered that if Sullivan would not show, then he would take Kilrain to California to fight the Australian heavyweight champion Peter Jackson who was already making a name on the Pacific Slope. What an odd twist of fate it would have been had Davies first encountered Jackson as the manager of Jake Kilrain. The years that Davies and Jackson would spend together as manager, fighter, and friends are discussed in great detail in subsequent chapters but in early January 1889 they had no relationship. Together Davies and Jackson would try unsuccessfully to secure a championship fight with Sullivan and then Corbett. In that effort they encountered the great evils of racial prejudice and discrimination. They would try to cross the color line that seemed to be drawn deeper as each year passed.

In January 1889 Jackson was of little consequence to either Kilrain or Davies. Neither Davies nor Jackson gave much truck to the so-called color line. From Davies' statements in early January 1889, he would have ranked the top heavyweights as: (1) Kilrain, (2) Sullivan, and (3) Jackson. If Sullivan was not going to fight, then Davies said that intended to match Kilrain to fight Jackson without regard to Jackson's color and despite the prejudice against blacks that infected much of the United States.

In reference to the Kilrain/Mitchell exhibitions being stopped first in Chicago, then Columbus and then St. Louis, Davies said that the sentiment of the better class of people was that such action on the part of the authorities was nearly malicious persecution. He noted that at Columbus the fighters had brought in a paying house, although the police knew much sooner that the men would not be allowed to spar and thought this action by the police mistreated everyone concerned. The melody playing in the background for Davies' entire professional career was the constant potential of interference with his sporting events.

On January 4, Kilrain and Mitchell appeared for their first night in Buffalo, where they were once again hissed and booed. Davies announced that evening that Sullivan's agents and Kilrain would meet in Toronto on January 7 to draw up articles for a fight for the heavyweight championship of the world and $10,000 a side.[570] After the Kilrain-Mitchell show in Buffalo, Davies headed off by himself to Toronto, where he took Room 137 at the Rossin House hotel and awaited the arrival of a throng of other men who would be there soon. The parties were meeting in Toronto to avoid the law in New York, which had threatened to arrest and prosecute them if they tried to arrange a fight in that state.

Sullivan arrived in Toronto on January 7, 1889 aboard the eleven fifteen a.m. train from Boston. He was magnificently dressed in a great fur-lined overcoat buttoned up to his chin and every inch the real king of the ring. He was accompanied by Jack Barnett of Boston, Charley Johnson of Brooklyn, Sullivan's backer, and W. H. Germaine, of the *Illustrated News*. They went to the Rossin House, where Davies was waiting with W. E. Harding, E. A. Plummer, James Wakely, James Lynch and Ed Hyar, all of New York, David Murphy of Boston, Steve Brodie, a famous bridge jumper (i.e., he jumped off public bridges), and J. R. Moyniehan, one the many former managers of Sullivan. While they were awaiting Sullivan's arrival, some of those present probably recalled September 1881, when they had met to try to arrange a Sullivan-Ryan championship fight.

With Sullivan's arrival at the Rossin House, Harding, Davies, Plummer, Sullivan, Johnson, Barnett, and Germanine were selected as the group to meet and make the final fight arrangements. Some accounts say that the group adjourned to Harding's room, and others say that they met in Davies' room. Perhaps factions were moving between several rooms to gain privacy during parts of the discussions. The true location may have been intentionally hidden because the Toronto police were nearby, and it was feared that they might interfere or make arrests. An account published in the *Nevada State Journal* in 1918 reports that as the terms of the match were being discussed, Davies remarked that the stakes would include the *Police Gazette*'s diamond belt, which Sullivan regularly and derisively called the "dog-collar." Fox had conferred the diamond belt on Kilrain when he was annunciated as heavyweight champion. Sullivan was sitting on Davies' bed when he shifted his position and asked what conditions would attach to the recipient of the diamond belt.

"If you win it," Davies replied, "why, you will have to defend it, as Kilrain has to now."

"If I win it," Sullivan said, "you can bet I'll give it to some bootblack. I don't want it."

"I would not do that John," Davies responded, "for there are eight big diamonds in it, and it is worth $2,500."

"I don't care if there are thirty diamonds in it," Sullivan said, "but I will fight Kilrain for it." [571]

"Parson" Davies – a drawing made about 1889

About three p.m. Harding came out and announced that an agreement had been drawn up, and its execution would take place at Bill Bingham's saloon later that afternoon. The articles were reprinted in newspapers all across the country.[572] Harding signed on behalf of both Kilrain and Allen. As soon as the articles were signed, everyone split town as quickly as possible. Sullivan was back in New York on Tuesday morning, January 8, with his supporters. A reporter asked him if he was satisfied with the articles. Sullivan said that he was happy with everything but the dog collar and that he had told them that he would put up the belt for the Bowery newsboys to fight for.[573]

On January 10, Kilrain and Mitchell were in Troy, New York, where rotten eggs were again thrown at them from the gallery.[574] An arrest warrant was later issued for a man named William Garvey, who was one of the egg throwers.[575] Davies said that Garvey had been put up to hiring several men to throw eggs, and the real culprit who plotted the incident was a man named McGraw, another friend of Sullivan. Davies said as soon as the eggs began to fly, the police had invaded the galley and cracked McGraw's skull and attacked the other miscreants with bare knuckles.[576]

After their appearance in Troy, the group began to split up. The long march from city to city to boom Kilrain and force Sullivan to fight was over. Kilrain headed for his home in Baltimore, and Davies and Mitchell went to New York City. Davies, Al Smith, and Mitchell were seen on the evening of January 14 at Bang's Broadway Palace. Mitchell was now the odd man out and on January 16 Mitchell left the United States aboard the steamer *Britannic* headed for his home in England. As he departed he explained that he was not afraid of fighting Dempsey, but that during his fight with Sullivan he had broken his left hand. Mitchell said he had consulted Professor E. L. Keyes, a noted surgeon with his office at 1 Park Avenue, who had told him that he could not fight anyone and that he needed to give up the ring for some time to allow his hand to heal naturally.[577]

Dr. Edward Lawrence Keyes was a prominent surgeon and, in particular, a specialist in modern genitor-urinary surgery. Some wag might have wondered what part of Mitchell Keyes had actually examined. Keyes issued a written statement that in his medical opinion, Mitchell's left hand had been injured to the extent that any surgical attempt to fix it would do more harm than good.[578]

The day after Mitchell sailed, Davies folded up his tent and returned to Chicago, arriving on January 17 on the nine p.m. train from New York. Naturally, all of the Chicago press wanted to know the news from the East Coast. Davies said that he felt Kilrain was one of the best two-fisted fighters he had ever seen. He thought that if the contest did take place, then the "wisdom" money would be on Kilrain. He had talked to his friend Al Smith, who was then one of New York's prominent bookmakers. Smith said that the odds would favor Kilrain. Charlie said that Kilrain was back in Baltimore and that Jake was convinced that Sullivan would never show up for a championship fight. Davies felt that Kilrain was one of the most modest men he had ever seen. He explained that Kilrain had told him that he never went into the ring with malice for his opponent. Kilrain's attitude was that if he could beat Sullivan, he would be the happiest man in the world; if he didn't, he would still be all right.[579]

Efforts were made over the next few months to change the location of the fight. Bat Masterson was the leading person behind an effort to move the fight to within one hundred miles of Denver. Masterson and Davies were close friends. Masterson was described as a man of rare courage and gameness, a desperate man in desperate emergencies, and a dead shot. He had been sheriff of several different counties in Colorado, and he commanded the respect of the fearless and sporting elements between the Mississippi River and the Rocky Mountains. He had been the sheriff of Dodge City in cowboy days and would later be sheriff of the mining town at Crede, Colorado. In 1888 he was manager of the Denver Cribb Club. He was also considered a man on the square. An example of Bat's fairness involved George Godfrey, who had fought McHenry Johnson to a standstill, although the referee had declared Johnson the winner on a foul. Masterson ignored the referee's decision and gave the purse to Godfrey.

Sixty-four rounds in North Judson

In early February 1889, many of the big-time names in sport went first to Chicago and then on to the little town of North Judson, Indiana, for the Myer-McAuliffe lightweight championship fight. The time seemed ripe of big matches.

Jack McAuliffe was an Irish immigrant who had been trained by and ran with some of the biggest fighters, including his close friend Jack Dempsey. He was an Irish-Catholic immigrant who had defeated anyone silly enough to climb in the ring with him. He was flashy, had a great left hand lead and left jab, and he was known for having good science. Dick Roche of St. Louis was McAuliffe's primary backer, along with the financial support of the East Coast boxing establishment. Alf Kennedy of Streator again acted as Billy Myer's backer. The fight was to be to a finish, with skin-tight gloves, under Queensberry rules. The parties were to weigh 133 pounds. The gloves had the end of their fingers cut off so that the fighters could make a tight fist.

On the evening of February 12, it was ten degrees below zero in Streator. About six o'clock that night, a special train chartered from the triple "I" railroad pulled up to the depot with four passenger cars and a freight car. The ring for the fight had been built by Myer himself in his father's carpenter shop. The ring was loaded into the freight car, and Myer and his closest friends boarded and went into a small compartment made for that purpose. Hundreds of Streator fight fans boarded the passenger cars, and the train departed for North Judson. It was an uncomfortable trip for the fans. The heaters in the cars did not work and the walls were not much help against the biting cold. In addition, the train engine developed an oil leak and had to stop every so often to re-oil the engine.

Special trains heading for North Judson were also being loaded at Chicago and St. Louis. The interest in Chicago was so great that the business of the city council came to a halt because alderman kept drifting out of chambers to catch the train. One hundred traders from the Chicago Board of Trade left for the fight. Five hundred fans were aboard a special Chicago & Atlantic R. R. train that loaded up at Fifteenth Street. One man tried to hop the train and stand between two cars. When the train stopped, he was found nearly frozen solid.

Among those in attendance were the luminaries of prizefighting in the 1880s, including Davies, Bradburn, Madden, Mike Corcoran (Vere Davies' future partner), and Condon. Some reports said that more than $100,000 was bet on the fight. Two days before the fight, a famous Canadian horseman was seen at Davies' in Chicago with $10,000 in new bank notes to bet on the fight at odds of one thousand to $800. Davies was holding $15,000, which he placed on the fight for several unidentified parties. In 1909, the *Salt Lake Herald-Republican* claimed that one newspaper man at ringside held $133,000 and that Davies held $70,000 at ringside.[580]

The Streator train arrived at North Judson at about eleven thirty p.m. and was met by the local sheriff, who said that he had orders from the Indiana governor not to permit the fight to go forward. This man needed some convincing. The fans were loaded back on their trains and pulled several miles down the track where they stopped and sat in the arctic night. About four a.m., the trains were pulled back into North Judson after the sheriff had "gone to bed." The ring was taken off the train and carried a block into town, where it was set up in the Old "Burch's" Opera House. The site of this great fight is now a beauty salon. Only an old caboose remains to mark the location of the railroad itself. It was not until seven a.m. on February 13 that the fight began. Mike McDonald was the referee for the fight. Sixty-four rounds and more than four hours later, McDonald declared the fight a draw. He had probably done more work that night than he had for several years.

There are many newspaper accounts of the fight, and they are not very consistent in their round-by-round reports. In the twenty-eighth round, McDonald called time when he saw the town marshal in the hall. General pandemonium reigned. Alf Kennedy attempted to throw the marshal off the stage, and intense excitement followed. The marshal used his billy club but was seized by several men and held before being thrown down the stairs and the door locked. A man in the gallery drew a revolver, and he too was seized and held.

Soon after these events, Davies announced that he had talked with the marshal, who had consented to allow the fight to continue, provided boxing was done while he was in the room. This decision by the marshal was greeted with cheers. Clearly the marshal had been passed a few bucks to disappear and had happily accepted, so long as he had plausible deniability.

All accounts seem to agree that Myer fought a very defensive fight and had some good success in the process. McAuliffe had the best left hand in lightweight prizefighting. Myer fought with an unconventional right-hand lead, and he was said to have the best right hand in the business for a lightweight. When McAuliffe would try to close, Myer would counter and seemed to be working hard on McAuliffe's left arm, trying to take-out his best weapon. The slowness of the pace probably became tiresome for McDonald, who was not a patient individual.

The fans too became restless. It had been a long, cold night. The crowd drifted out to the local grocery store, where they bought cheese and crackers to eat because nothing else seemed to be available. When they returned to ringside, the fight was still in progress with little to distinguish round forty from round fifty. During the fight Myer and McAuliffe conversed, apparently trying to psyche-out each other. When McDonald declared the match a draw, Myer supposedly told McAuliffe that the two of them should go alone into a twelve-by-twelve room and fight until only one could come out. McAuliffe declined. Myer was legitimately concerned because before McDonald declared the fight a draw, he consulted with Billy Madden but did not consult with anyone representing Myer. This was against accepted practice and the contest should not have been stopped unless both contestants agreed.

When asked his opinion of the fight, a man from the Board of Trade told the *Chicago Herald*: "Fight? What fight? I wasn't at any fight. I was down in Indiana to see a walking match, and on the side to demonstrate my qualities as a sucker. I've made a record in that line. It can't be beat. Look at it! In the first place I paid $20 for a ticket and had to tramp from saloon to saloon to get it. Since Saturday night I have hanging around downtown waiting for the 'tip.' I got it yesterday and telephoned my wife that I had business in Cincinnati and might not be back for two days. I sneaked down to the train last night and got a place near the stove. The train was hot, and the smell had nothing in its line to learn.

Everybody was smoking some kind of a nickel-movement cigar. We were three hours on the road. We got out at the junction town. The thermometer was 14 degrees below Baton Rouge." He concluded: "Who got the best of it? Well, I think it was about a stand-off. Myer was a little the more graceful walker but I think McAuliffe got a shade the best of the talk."[582]

The *Chicago Tribune* railed against the fight. It declared that Illinois should be humiliated because: "We selected Myer as our champion and he has not won us the lightweight glories of the world. It might be well for him to take in his sign." It wrote that the contest was disgraceful from the beginning to the end with "no bloodshed, no teeth gone, no eyes blackened."[583]

About a week before the fight Billy Madden had written to Bat Masterson to advise him that McAuliffe would win on the run. After the fight Madden sent a second letter to Masterson saying that Myer was the quickest man on his feet and the hardest to hit that he had ever seen. He said that Myer had a great right hand and didn't telegraph it either. McAuliffe knew how hard Myer could hit after the seventh round.[584]

The terms of the fight were supposed to be to the finish. Within a day, Alf Kennedy and Myer began to press McAuliffe to finish the fight. On February 15, Kennedy sent a telegram to Dick Roche in St. Louis asking for an early date to resume the contest. Myer and Kennedy then went to Chicago to press the referee to continue the fight. They contended that the fight was supposed to resume within seventy-two hours, but after meetings with Davies, who was the stake-holder, and finally with the McDonald, nothing could be done to persuade the New York men to resume the match.[585]

On February 28, Davies was asked to manage a skin-glove fight to the finish between Ike "the Spider" Weir and Frank Murphy, two celebrated feather-weight boxers. This would be the second of three championship finish fights held between mid-February and mid-July 1889. Fights of this importance would not happen again until 1892.

The Weir-Murphy fight

The Weir-Murphy fight was originally to be held within forty miles of Chicago, but that later changed because of difficulty finding a suitable venue.[586] This was another important fight that illustrated the sporting public's interest in fistic competition.

Davies went to Boston to conclude arrangements for the contest.[587] The goal was to have a fight take place between March 16 and March 23.[588] He returned to Chicago on March 9 with the fight booked and told the press that many of the big East Coast sports would soon be in Chicago for the contest. The articles provided that the contest would be a finish fight under Queensberry rules and witnessed by not more than 100 people in addition to press representatives. The stake was $2,000 and the match was to take place within 250 miles of Chicago. Davies added a purse of $1,500 to the stake money, and there was a side bet for

$2,000 between William Daly Jr., who was Murphy's backer, and Ed McAvoy, who was backing Weir. Tickets sold for $25 each. If the police interfered, then the fight was to be continued within three days. Dempsey was supposed to second Weir in this fight, but failed to show up.[589]

Jere Dunne nearly killed Sullivan in March 1889. On the evening of March 9, Sullivan and his friends Billy Bennett and Jack Barnett were bar-hopping in New York. Shortly after midnight Sullivan and his buddies entered a saloon known as Two Kellys, at the corner of Thirty-first Street and Sixth Avenue. Sullivan began threatening a small-time gambler in the saloon when Dunne appeared. Jere told Sullivan to leave the man alone. Sullivan quickly angered and said: "Dunne, I know you and I don't scare any. You are a thief and I can do you." Dunne pulled a revolver and with an oath, threatened Sullivan. Friends of Sullivan dived at Dunne and prevented him from letting loose, and then they quickly spirited Sullivan out the door.[590]

Ike Weir was in Chicago and on March 22 he went to Davies' place for an unofficial weigh-in and to meet the press. The details of the Weir-Murphy fight were issues exclusively in the hands of Davies, who was conducting his affairs out of Corcoran & Davies, the saloon the Parson had helped open after giving up The Store. On March 29, the saloon was crowded with men waiting for the tip about where the fight was to take place. Dick Roche was the stakeholder for the fight, and he arrived in town on March 29, raising suspicion that the contest was imminent. That same evening Murphy and Kline arrived in town starting a new rumor that everyone should be ready to move on short notice. When he reached Chicago, Murphy was put up at Mat Hogan's State Street Hotel.

Virtually all day on March 30, sports were in and out of Davies' place trying to pick up a tip about where the fight would be or where and when they could catch the train. At four p.m. word went out that customers should meet at the Polk Street Depot at nine p.m. to board a special train on the Chicago & Atlantic R. R. Men from the Board of Trade, lawyers, and politicians appeared at the gate of the depot and were escorted to the train. In addition, about fifteen armed Pinkerton men had been specially retained by Davies to accompany the patrons.[591]

Davies had received word that Connelly, the one-eyed ex-pugilist, was the leader of a gang of pug-uglies who were going to try to interfere with the fight by either boarding the train or invading the hall where the fight would be held. Over a thirty-year period, Connelly built a national reputation as a gate crasher, "moocher," and pickpocket. He had a special knack of boarding chartered trains without a ticket and then stealing money from the smashed ticket holders. Connelly also had an interesting habit of starting fights only after he first removed his glass eye and handed it to a bystander to hold for him.

The chartered train for the Weir-Murphy fight left Chicago slowly about nine thirty p.m. with the Pinkerton men riding the engine and stationed between the cars to deal with Connelly and his allies. Shortly after the train left the city limit, Weir passed through the cars to shake hands with his friends. He was singing the song "What the Dickie Birds Say," which would later be made popular by Frank Sinatra. The train went to Hammond, Indiana, without trouble, but Davies received a telegram there saying that Connelly was waiting a few miles outside of town to board the cars. The sports aboard the train were ordered to pull their blinds down, and doors on the cars were all locked. The train went on to Kouts, Indiana, a little town in Porter County south of Valparaiso and east of Crown Point. When the train steamed into Kouts, there was a crowd led by Connelly standing in the rain along the tracks. The Pinkerton men jumped off the train with their clubs and beat the invaders. All of the patrons were told to stay on the train while Davies and some of his Pinkerton agents scouted out the hall to make sure there was no sign of Connelly and his men.

Davies returned to the train, and the men were led by lantern-light along muddy streets to the second floor of O'Brien's Opera House, where a ring had been pitched. There was a piano in one corner of the room and a stove in another. All the windows had been covered with bed quilts. The referee for the fight was Billy Myer. His selection as referee helped contribute to the fight lasting more than six hours. Myer had just had his own fight with McAuliffe that was supposed to be a finish fight; however, McDonald had called the fight a draw. There was going to be no repeat of that experience with Myer acting as referee.

The fight began after one a.m. After about ten rounds the patrons could hear another fight going on outside between Connelly's gate crashers and the Pinkerton men. A pistol shot was heard and then the sound of the Pinkerton men rushing up the steps to the second floor of the hall to avoid a hail of stones being thrown at them. The fight inside the hall went on with Weir having the best of it. He pounded and bloodied both of Murphy's eyes and after awhile, it appeared that he would keep hitting Murphy's eyes, hoping that they would close and Murphy would either give up or be knocked out.

After sixty-eight rounds Weir's backers asked Murphy's side to agree to change the format to London rules, but Murphy's side would not agree. The owner of the hall telegraphed the county sheriff asking him to come stop the fight. He said that he had not rented the hall for a week-long contest. At six a.m. the men were about five feet apart facing each other, but with their hands down. This went on until the seventy-fourth round, when Weir resumed aggressive fighting. Finally, after eighty rounds, Myer was prevailed upon to postpone the fight to be resumed within three days. About seven a.m. the men headed back to the train and steamed off to return to Chicago. Before the train left town "Bad" Jimmy Connerton stole the badge from the town marshal, who then drew a big gun. The marshal's gun was then also confiscated and taken back to Chicago, and the marshal was told to run for his life. As the train pulled away, Connelly's men stoned the windows of the hall where the fight had taken place.[592]

Two days later, Myer went to Davies' place and told the contestants that the fight would continue. He instructed the men to meet him at a specific time to catch a train to another site. Everyone thought that Myer had lost his marbles. Davies said that if anyone tried to have the two men fight again, he would have that person arrested. Myers showed up at the train, but the fighters did not show. Instead, Captain Daly, Murphy's backer, and Ed McAvoy, Weir's backer, agreed that the match should be declared a draw and the stakes taken down. The $1,500 purse put up by Davies was split equally among the two fighters. They were paid less than ten dollars for each round that they had fought.

Murphy was in no condition to continue the fight. His eyes were black and swollen. His left arm was lame from having been hit so many times by Weir, and he had a broken rib. More than two weeks after the fight Murphy was still showing marks from it and still hiding out in his hotel room in Beloit. Weir would also have trouble continuing, because of a broken jaw and due to the condition of his hands, which were swollen and tender. The talk was that Ike's hands had given out after only ten rounds and that each time he threw a punch he had hurt his own hands worse than he had hurt Murphy. Three weeks after the fight one wag wrote that Ike's next performance would be in a dime museum as the man with both hands broken. It was said that Weir could never again fight a bare-knuckle or skin-tight glove match. There was no champion declared as a result of this futile fight, and the pay-off for Davies was probably not good considering the cost of the hall, renting a train and hiring Pinkerton men to deal with Connelly.[593]

Bill Muldoon had been wrestling under Davies' management until April 1888. The specialty company that Davies had formed featuring Muldoon and Lewis broke up after Lewis defeated Wannop. Muldoon then went back to the East Coast and continued to wrestle there. Muldoon and Sullivan had been friends for many years, and Muldoon seemed to be one of the few athletes who Sullivan actually respected.

Muldoon takes Sullivan to the wood shed

In May 1889 Sullivan continued his dissipated lifestyle, and his backers were getting concerned. The articles for the championship fight had been signed four months earlier and there was a lot of money at stake. At some point, it was important to make sure that Sullivan actually prepared for the fight, and the window was closing fast. On May 10, Sullivan left New York with Muldoon. They went to Muldoon's farm near Belfast, New York, in the Chautauqua Lake region, where Muldoon was to take charge of training Sullivan for the match.[594]

Sullivan remained on the farm for about three weeks, when he couldn't take any more of the cows and horses. About May 25, Muldoon, Sullivan, and Mike Cleary left Belfast on a tour that was supposed to go to Detroit, Cincinnati, Chicago, Philadelphia, and New York.[595] They appeared at the Grand Opera House in Cincinnati on May 28. Sullivan had lost twenty-six pounds since he began training with Muldoon.[596] Sullivan and Muldoon came to New York City to appear at the Metropolitan Opera House. Sullivan was supposed to wrestle Muldoon as part of an exhibition for the Actors' Athletic Club fund.[597] Their wrestling outfits did not arrive with the train, and they only appeared on stage. The consensus was that Sullivan was already looking as if he was in better condition.[598]

The same day that Sullivan and Muldoon were at the Met, events were taking place that involved fighters who would later occupy substantial parts of Davies' professional life. Peter Jackson started east to look up Joe Lannon and Jack Ashton. He had also called out Frank Slavin, the Australian heavyweight pretender, and was eventually planning to go the England.[599] The Halley's comet of Davies' life was arching over the Rockies and reaching across the plains toward the heartland.

A few days after Jackson left the Pacific Slope two young California fighters, Jim Corbett and Joe Choynski, finished a fight that they had started earlier. They fought on a barge before a small crowd of California sportsmen and Corbett ultimately prevailed. More than $35,000 had changed hands on their fight.[600]

The greatest fighter ever arrives in Chicago

When Jackson reached St. Paul, there was an incident that was all too typical of the boorish and insulting behavior that characterized some prizefighters but was simply a reflection of the common behavior of too many white people. This time the offending party was Pat Killen, who had already refused to fight Jackson because of the so-called color line.

Pat Killen was almost as big a bigot as Sullivan but lacked national influence. He had frequently made comments about black fighters and had said that he would not meet Jackson until he decided that he wanted to fight "pigs and N_______s."[601] Killen got the idea that he should start mocking Jackson before he arrived in town. Killen dressed up a large black man in a Prince Albert coat, silk hat, and gloves and provided him with a gold-headed cane. He then paraded this man through the streets of St. Paul, introducing him to the crowds as Jackson. The next morning, just after Jackson had arrived in town, Killen left town head for San Francisco to fight Joe McAuliffe. Jackson must have been impressed with his first impression of the sports of the Northwest provided courtesy of Killen.[602] This was only one of many similar experiences that Jackson encountered as a black man trying to make a living in the United States. Australia had its racial prejudices but not on the scale in this country. Such behavior was not familiar to Jackson but it would become the day-to-day fare served up in large regions of this country.

In June 1889 a middleweight fighter called "Sailor" Brown made his way to Chicago looking for help from Davies. Brown was a run-of-the-mine fighter and had participated in a finish fight in San Francisco in mid-March 1889. His opponent had been an excellent young pugilist named Jonathan L. Herget, who fought under the name "Young Mitchell."[603] Herget had obtained his nickname because he looked and fought like a young Charley Mitchell. To Herget's credit, he did not share Mitchell's big ego. He was a San Francisco boy born January 30, 1868. Smaller than Mitchell he stood only about five feet six and three quarters inches tall and weighed about 150 pounds. Herget would have a terrific career eventually retiring as one of the few unbeaten fighters of all time.

The Herget-Brown match was styled as the middleweight championship of the Pacific coast. Herget weighed 150 for the fight, and Brown weighed 155. The contest was for $1,500 and was held in the rooms of the Golden Gate Athletic Club. Brown was defeated in twenty-one rounds and shortly after his defeat had started back toward the East Coast ending up in Chicago.

When Brown reached Chicago in early June 1889, he became a beneficiary of an idea that Davies had developed and helped him stage prizefights in Chicago. Davies had figured out that he could present fights without police interference if the matches were styled as benefits for a deserving party. At the end of May 1889, over 2,500 people had died in Pennsylvania in the Johnstown flood. Substantial efforts were being made to assist the survivors, and Davies had the idea of putting on a benefit at Battery D for those survivors. Arrangements were completed for a benefit to take place on June 18, with one of the featured events a prize fight between Brown and a local pugilist, Jimmy Davies (sometimes identified as Jimmy Duffy). It was a vicious fight and was given to Brown in the fourth round on a foul. The entertainment netted $2,000 for the Johnstown relief effort, but it is not clear how the net was figured.

On June 28, Jackson arrived in Chicago. He was accompanied by three men who had traveled with him from California: W. W Naughton of the *San Francisco Examiner*, one of the great sport writers of all time, Sam Fitzpatrick and Tom Lees. When he arrived in Chicago, Jackson was under contract with the California Athletic Club but was on a five-month leave of absence provided so that he could enhance his reputation outside of the west.

Shortly after he arrived in Chicago, Jackson had his pocket picked and lost $300 in cash and a $700 draft drawn on the Nevada Bank of San Francisco. In somewhat naïve fashion, Jackson said that he would forfeit the money he had lost if whoever had or found his wallet would simply mail it to him in care of the Grand Pacific Railroad. He had also lost about $1,800 during the course of his tour from San Francisco to Chicago and was in poor financial shape.[604]

William Walter Naughton was born in Auckland, New Zealand, in 1854. He was a noted boxer and oarsman in New Zeeland and in 1886 had come to San Francisco, where he covered the Sullivan-Ryan fight that Sheedy promoted and the Burke-Dempsey fight that Davies had promoted. In 1888 he had joined the staff of the *Examiner* and was already considered one of the best sports writers in print.

Fitzpatrick was still a fairly young man. His real name was Samuel Fitch, and he had been born in Maitland, Australia. When he started fighting, he was known as "Young Fitz." He picked up that name when he moved to Sydney and started fighting on a regular basis. Fitzpatrick had come to San Francisco in 1887, and it soon seemed apparent that his real talent was as a trainer and fight instructor.

Tom Lees was a good heavyweight fighter from Australia. He was an ex-policeman who had defeated Bill Farnan in 1885 for the heavyweight championship of Australia. Lees had won by a knockout in the ninth with a controversial blow. In a rematch they fought for a period before the police interfered. Their second fight was resumed the following day, and Lees again knocked out Farnan.

Before the summer of 1889 Lees' career was fading, he too would work successfully as an instructor and trainer. Lees was traveling with Jackson to pick up some money sparring with him in places where no local fighter was willing or available to appear. He had some familiarity with the Chicago area, having been there to train Billy Myer.

When he arrived at Vere Davies' saloon, Jackson was carrying a letter of introduction from Mose Guntz addressed to Parson Davies. Morgan Arthur Gunst was a prominent San Francisco civic leader. He was an alumnus of Stanford University and during his professional life would be a San Francisco police commissioner, congressman, cigar magnate, bank president, big-time gambler, expert on horse racing and horse flesh and prizefight aficionado. Davies had met Gunst during his trip to California for the Burke-Dempsey match and the two men had become friends.

Jackson arrived at 93 Clark Street just when Parson Davies had several other pressing matters. Big money was being bet on the upcoming Sullivan-Kilrain fight and many of the bets were being taken in Vere's saloon in downtown Chicago. Next, only two days after Jackson's arrival in Chicago, Illinois' new governor, Joe Fifer of Bloomington, pardoned Joe Mackin, who had been one of Davies' closest friends, and Mackin was released after spending almost five years in prison.[605]

Davies was also arranging a special excursion train from Chicago to Louisiana for Chicago sports who wanted to see the Sullivan-Kilrain heavyweight championship fight. The Parson had lined up about fifty men who would travel with him to the fight. Among those in the Davies' party was Luke Short, a noted sport from Fort Worth, Texas, who had been in Chicago attending the races. They were supposed to arrive in New Orleans on Saturday, July 6, which would have given the party one day in the Crescent City before setting out for the unknown battleground.[606] Finally, Davies was arranging another benefit. This time the benefit was for the Braidwood, Illinois, coal miners, who were on strike at the time.[607]

An interesting story was told much later about an adventure that Naughton had in Chicago that summer. A writer for the *Oakland Tribune* provided an account in February 1890 based on what he was told by two eye-witnesses. It seems that when Jackson's party was in Chicago Naughton "happened into" a saloon. He stood at the bar and near him a burly man indulged in sundry uncomplimentary remarks regarding "the black N______" Peter Jackson. Another Midwest bigot who hated a man he had never met was at hand.

Naughton's dander got up. He had been something of a scrapper in Australia before turning to the writing profession. Naughton told the rounder that, if he did not dry up he would wipe the dirty sawdust oiled floor with him. Mr. Rounder immediately jumped Naughton, and "they had it rough and tumble for awhile." The result was that Naughton ended up with two black eyes "and a vague impression on his dazed brain that he had been monkeying with a new and aggressive kind of band wagon with a bull dog attachment."

The rounder turned out to be Billy Bradburn the former heavyweight, who at that point was an assistant buyer for Armour & Co, the great pork packer.

According to the account from the West Coast, the Chicago newspapers were "squared about the matter," and they all gravely stated that the man who was licked for being "sassy" to Bradburn was Sam Fitzpatrick, Jackson's trainer and that after being knocked down he was kicked in the face by Bradburn. But it was really Naughton who got the punishment.[608]

In the 1880s, Illinois was the home for many miners. A belt of coal stretched from the towns of Braidwood, Braceville, Godley, and Gardner, and then to the west through places such as Streator, LaSalle, Minonk, Ottawa and Seneca. The miners in these towns were making an average of about $380 a year and suffered long periods of unemployment when the mine owners closed their operations because of low coal prices. Unionization efforts were strongly supported in these towns, but owners suppressed these efforts by hiring Pinkerton agents to intimidate striking miners and protect scab laborers, who were often unwittingly brought in from impoverished mining towns in Europe. The new Illinois governor was opposed to unionization efforts and in 1889 called out the Illinois militia to suppress strike efforts in Braidwood. The militia members searched the homes of the Braidwood miners in a house-to-house effort to find weapons. Miners and their families were starving and in need of assistance.[609] These conditions gave rise to Davies' second planned benefit at Battery D.

Peter Jackson appeared at the perfect time to be featured as the star attraction of the Braidwood miners' benefit. His opponent was to be the diminutive Sailor Brown, who was still hanging around Chicago hoping to make a little more easy money.

Peter Jackson in boxing pose –1889 – believed to be a photograph by John Wood of New York

When Jackson arrived, Davies was on the cusp of the planned trip to the Sullivan-Kilrain battleground. McDonald declared that he would not be going because he was afraid that he might be appointed as referee. McDonald said that sixty-four rounds of Myer-McAuliffe was enough work for him. McDonald might have had other reasons for staying home. He was having marital problems at the time and within less than a month his wife, who had become something of a religious fanatic, would run off with a Catholic priest who was also a fanatic but perhaps not so religious. He may have suspected that if he left town for the fight, his wife would be gone when he got back.[610]

McDonald was also deeply involved in obtaining the franchise to build the West Lake Street (or Meig's) elevated railroad in Chicago. Supposedly, McDonald had been offered $750,000 dollars for his interest in the elevated railroad construction contract. In Chicago politicians salivate like Pavlov's dogs when a construction contract like this is mentioned.[611]

Davies recalled his first meeting with Peter Jackson many times during the later years of his life. His account generally included these elements. On June 28, he was standing in the saloon operated by his brother Vere at 93 Clark Street. A big, tall black man stepped up and handed Davies a letter. The letter was from Mose Guntz and introduced the man with the letter as Jackson. Peter wore a tall hat and to Davies he looked at least seven-feet tall. Guntz' letter said Jackson was all right and he was anxious to get on some fights in the East. Mose wrote: "You can make no mistake with this fellow."

Just then someone asked Jackson to have a drink. In a manner that impressed Davies because of Jackson's cleverness, Jackson refused the offer saying he did not drink. Davies said that he did not like the idea of handling a "darky," but he read the letter once again and looked Jackson over. He finally said he would take Jackson and manage him for half of the take. Jackson accepted, and Davies became the manager of the man he eventually considered to be the "greatest fighter the world has ever seen."[612]

When he arrived in Chicago, Jackson had only two exhibitions lined up. He left Chicago on the evening of July 2 for Milwaukee, where he appeared on July 3 in the Turner Hall with Tom Lees before a small crowd.[613] There were several other brief bouts during that exhibition including one with Tom Connors, the wrestler, who boxed a few rounds. In addition to the Milwaukee show, Jackson had a fight lined up during the second week in July with George Godfrey. That fight was to take place in Boston.

The *Chicago Tribune* described Jackson as a big and dark-colored man with pronounced "Ethiopian features." He was, however, a "mild mannered and intelligent" man who was just the reverse of the typical pugilist in every respect except size, strength, and science. Jackson had a forty-inch chest but only a thirty-inch waist. He was more than six feet tall. He weighed 195 pounds in July 1889.[614]

Davies invited Jackson to travel with him and his party to watch the Sullivan-Kilrain fight. The suggestion that a huge black man should travel with a bunch of Yankees to the soul of Mississippi to participate in illegal activity was at best naïve. Few people in the East and South had paid much attention to Jackson as a fighter at the time because the eyes of the sporting establishment were focused on the Sullivan-Kilrain fight. However, had Jackson been foolish enough to travel to the deep South in mid-1889, he might well have been killed along the way, in a place where large, well-dressed, black men had become a favorite target of some creeps that lived there and remained unwilling to give up their rights to abuse any black man in sight.

Davies' role at the Sullivan-Kilrain championship match

There are many books and articles that recount the matters leading up to the Sullivan-Kilrain fight and the fight itself, and only the broad outlines are provided here. About a month before the fight Kilrain turned over the "dog collar" to the stakeholder.[615] Then representatives of the fighters went to Louisiana to scout the exact site where the fight would be held.[616] Naturally, the legal authorities in every state between New York and Louisiana put out the word that the fight would not be permitted in their state.[617] The compulsory articles appeared in hundreds of newspapers, describing how Sullivan and Kilrain trained for their match and what they ate and drank. Many articles discussed how each fighter pickled the skin on their face and hands so that they would not be cut during the fight.[618]

Each fighter had a special train car prepared for their trip to Mississippi. Sullivan's car was equipped with a bathtub and shower attachment. He also had a heavy bag hung from the ceiling of the car along with various dumbbells and other exercise apparatus to help him keep fit during the trip. Kilrain was accompanied on his trip by Mitchell, Johnny Murphy, Pony Moore, and a Dr. Dougherty of Philadelphia, who was with Jake as his medical adviser.[619]

The fight took place on July 8 on a plantation outside of Richburg, Mississippi, about one hundred miles from New Orleans and just south of Hattiesburg. It lasted seventy-five rounds with Sullivan the victor. Before the fight Bat Masterson tried to persuade Luke Short, who was traveling with Davies, to bet $2,000 on Kilrain. Short consulted Davies, who told Short to keep his money in his pocket because Kilrain was not in good condition for the fight. Short took Davies' advice and was grateful for years thereafter.[620]

Mike Cleary and Muldoon were the seconds for Sullivan with Charley Johnson acting as bottle-holder. Kilrain's seconds were Mitchell and Mike Donovan, with Johnny Murphy acting as his bottle-holder. There were many men at the fight who were packing heat, and there was a reasonable fear that a gun fight might break out.[621]

In 1915 Davies, speaking to *The Referee*, described the situation just before the fight began as he remembered it: "It was a desperate crowd. 'Bud' Renaud, one of the gamest men I ever knew, walked to the center of the sand ring and said quietly: 'The first man who makes a false move at this ringside will ride home with his toes pointed at the stars.' And Bud meant what he said. The fight went on to the finish without any trouble. There aren't fight crowds like that anymore."[622] Two years before he died, Davies said that July 8, 1889, was "the most fearful day" of his life. He thought that the events on that day in the swamp near Richburg "did more to make an old man of me than anything else in the world. It turned my hair grey [and] made me hate myself to think that I had had anything to do with that awful battle."[623]

After the seventy-fifth round Mitchell crossed the ring and asked Sullivan's corner to call the match a draw. They refused and Donovan then threw in the sponge because Kilrain was unable to continue. Davies felt that if Donovan had not given up the match, there would likely have been murder in the air soon.

At that point the men began to scatter, and there was talk of leaving poor Kilrain in the ring by himself. He was a badly beaten man. His face was discolored and resembled mahogany more than anything else. His left eye was black and blue, and there was a large cut just under his right eye in the form of a crescent.

Sullivan had hired a special train on the Belt Road that took him across Mississippi to the Alabama state line.[624] The penalty in Mississippi for prizefighting was a fine of not more than $1,000 and not less than $500, or imprisonment for not less than twelve months, or both. All aiders and abettors were punishable by a fine of not less than $100, or imprisonment for six months, or both. Sullivan had no intention of spending a year in a Mississippi jail and had planned his escape. In Alabama he caught the regular train that took him north along the Louisville & Nashville line until he was arrested in Nashville. The next day Sullivan was freed, based on an order of a judge reviewing a writ of habeas corpus.[625] He would not be arrested again until July 31, when he was picked up in his room at the Vanderbilt House in New York City. Kilrain was better at dodging the police than he had been at dodging Sullivan. He was still on the loose when Sullivan was arrested.

Davies was one of three men who stayed behind to help Kilrain. Johnny Murphy, Mike Donovan, and Davies helped Kilrain through the ropes. When they reached the second set of ropes, Kilrain was unable to continue and Davies and Donovan lifted him over the ropes and helped him to a buggy owned by Colonel Rich, who also owned the plantation where the fight took place. Davies said that when Kilrain was placed in the buggy he broke down and cried. The buggy took Kilrain to a special train so that he could be taken back to New Orleans and from there begin his escape north. Mitchell, Pony Moore, William Harding, Billy Madden, and Dr. Dougherty were nowhere to be seen.[626]

Boarding the train proved more difficult than expected. The Davies' party, including Luke Short and Bat Masterson, had put up $500 for a special car comprising part of the escape train. When they arrived to board their car, the conductor told them that the engine had been secured by the Associated Press, which had apparently spent even bigger money to make sure that its members would be the first to carry word about the outcome of the historic match. Short, Masterson, and Davies were not men to be trifled with and along with eighteen others coupled their car to the Associated Press car. The press tried to pull the pin joining the cars but Masterson pulled his gun and that put an end to the attempted interference.

The telegraphic facilities were meager in the area, and two of the first telegrams to the East Coast came from Mitchell and Davies. Mitchell telegraphed his wife, who was staying with Mrs. Kilrain: "We are beaten." Parson Davies then sent a telegram to Mrs. Kilrain: "Jake is conquered, but not disgraced."[627]

Davies was seen in Nashville and then in Louisville with Mike Cleary and Bill Muldoon on July 11. Cleary and Muldoon had just evaded arrest in Nashville. Muldoon explained that he had been sitting on the train with Sullivan when the police entered the railroad car. He said that the police were about to arrest him when he said to them: "What do you mean, I am no prize fighter. Do I look like one?"[628] Muldoon said that he was simply a gentleman who should not be insulted in such a manner. The police then arrested Sullivan and Charley Johnson.

Davies, Luke Short, Muldoon, and Cleary all arrived in Chicago at seven a.m. on July 12 on the Monon train. The Parson, Muldoon, and Cleary went to breakfast together at the Richelieu, and at ten a.m. Muldoon and Cleary took the Michigan Central train for Detroit and then Canada, where they hoped to lay low and avoid arrest.[629]

During the trip to New Orleans and particularly as he returned to Chicago, Davies must have given serious thought to the situation in prizefighting as it would exist in the wake of Kilrain's defeat. As much as the Parson liked Kilrain, it was clear that he was a beaten man and that Jake's stock would soon fall like a rock. Back in Chicago a great gift had been delivered to Davies' front door in the form of Jackson, who was the champion of Australia.

Jackson had already acquitted himself well in the United States by defeating the black champion George Godfrey, Joe McAuliffe, the champion of the Pacific Slope, and Patsey Cardiff. The chance he had to assume Jackson's management was stunning. This man was far different from the string of Davies' past heavyweights, including Jimmy Elliott, Paddy Ryan, Patsey Cardiff, Jem Goode, Alf Greenfield, Frank Glover, Pat Killen, and many others. The Parson had proven his ability with Jack Burke, but Burke was small potatoes compared to Jackson. The only negative in the equation was that Jackson was black but Davies clearly thought that this obstacle could be overcome.

Davies had not returned to Chicago when Jackson met Sailor Brown on the evening of July 11. The Parson was aboard a train between Louisville and Chicago at the time of that match, which Ed McAvoy superintended in Davies' absence.[630] Under the terms of the contest, Jackson was to stop Brown in six rounds. On July 9, the day after the Sullivan-Kilrain fight, Sailor Brown came to Davies' place in Chicago to meet Jackson. Although Brown was only a little taller than Jackson's shoulder and forty-five pounds lighter, he told Peter that he would stay with him for six rounds because Jackson would not be able to hit him hard enough to do him up. Jackson laughed good-naturedly, and said, "All right."[631]

The accounts of this match are mixed. Some say that the men fought with two-ounce gloves, and others say four-ounce gloves. It seems more likely that four-ounce gloves were used, given the situation that existed in Chicago and that the newspapers had their own correspondents attend the match. There was no interference with the contest, but after all it was only a benefit! It may be that the curiosity of city officials about this huge black man outweighed their normal compulsion to interfere with a fight.

About four thousand attended the Jackson-Brown match at ticket prices ranging from fifty cents to $1.50 each. The numbers in attendance were probably high because sporting men in the city had been whipped up to a frenzy by the Sullivan-Kilrain match, and also because many other men would have thought that Jackson could play an important role in the future of heavyweight prizefighting. When Jackson appeared on the platform, he was met with a storm of applause. He was wearing a blue shirt and blue tights embroidered with the letters C.A.C. for the California Athletic Club, and black shoes. Queensberry rules were to apply to this fight.

Peter Jackson – classic pose

Some accounts say that the match was bloody and involved awful brutality, but this seems hyperbole and unlikely under the circumstances in Chicago at the time.[632] Such accounts seem more like the invention of a sportswriter who was echoing the news that was on the wires about the Sullivan-Kilrain match. The local reports say that in the first two rounds Jackson made no hard effort to hit Brown, being content to merely push him away when he would make a rush and then landing only a few light blows. Many of Jackson's fights include a similar approach. He was not customarily a man who rushed his opponent or tried to set the pace of the fight from the beginning. In the third round it appeared that Jackson was finally determined to dispatch Brown. It appeared that Brown was already very weak, and he went down twice before light blows from Jackson in obvious attempts to escape punishment.[633]

The *Chicago Herald* was critical of Jackson for not finishing the job in this round, but it seems likely that Jackson had been warned not to punch the Sailor's ticket too soon. In the fourth round, Jackson landed a stinging blow under Brown's left eye, knocking him down, and at that point it was apparent that Jackson was only playing with the Sailor. The match was brought to an end by the outcry of some of the spectators that Brown was being killed by the "giant Negro" from Australia. McAvoy stopped the match and awarded it to Jackson because Brown was no longer an active participant. It is probable that McAvoy too was under strict orders from Davies not to let things get out of hand. Charlie had worked hard to get to the point where boxing matches could be presented in Chicago without police interference and probably did not want to lose everything while he was away in the South.[634] Davies later sent $731 to Chicago's mayor for the miner's relief and benefit.

Jackson signs with Davies

After Muldoon and Cleary fled to Canada, Davies got down to business and signed a contract with Jackson to act as his manager during the remainder of his vacation from the C.A.C. Davies was going to take Jackson on a tour of cities on the East Coast and then to England where the hateful prejudices so prevalent in America were not generally shared.

Davies would sometimes move ahead to the rest of Jackson's party to make the necessary arrangements for his fights. Although Jackson was surrounded by advisers from Australia, that entire crew of Aussies must have been impressed that Davies was at the throbbing heart of the prizefighting world. At the time none of the men with Jackson was a fight promoter, and they had proved this by losing their shirts between California and Chicago. Naughton was a writer, and Fitzpatrick and Lees were fighters and trainers.

Every newspaper these men picked up in Chicago contained a story about the big championship fight and details of Davies' involvement. He was the man who had finally been able to bring the two sides together and to draft acceptable articles. He had shown his loyalty to the men he managed by sticking with Kilrain when others were fleeing to save their own skins. After the fight all the luminaries including Sullivan, Kilrain, Muldoon, Mike Cleary, and Mitchell came to Chicago, and they were accompanied by, or met with, Davies as part of their visit. For Naughton, Fitzpatrick, and Lees, signing on with Davies probably looked like a "can't miss" proposition, and they probably told Jackson that he should cast his lot with Davies. At the time Jackson was six feet one-and-a-half inches tall and weighed 206 pounds.[637]

Mitchell the tramp

The night that Jackson signed his contract with Davies, Charley Mitchell showed up at Davies' resort. Mitchell had traveled with Kilrain as far as Shelbyville, Indiana, southwest of Indianapolis, and then split off from the group. Kilrain was going to "lay-low" in Indiana before following Mitchell to Chicago. Mitchell left Shelbyville on the Big Four railroad, which had existed for less than two weeks and was the product of the merged Cleveland, Columbus, Cincinnati and Indianapolis Railroad; the Cincinnati, Indianapolis, St. Louis and Chicago Railroad; and the Indianapolis and St. Louis Railroad. Mitchell then traveled to Hammond, Indiana, where he acquired a disguise.

Usually a sharp dresser, Mitchell had taken on the appearance of a tramp. He was wearing a red-flannel shirt and an old pair of corduroy pants with a hole in the rear so that his shirt showed through. His face was covered with dirt and he had let his beard grow for several days. When he entered Davies' place, the bartender was about to throw him out when the tramp slid next to Parson Davies and whispered in his ear. Davies did not move a muscle. Mitchell asked for a whiskey, which he was served on the Parson's signal, and then downed a large sized glass. The two men retired to a secluded room to discuss Mitchell's wanderings. After explaining how he had traded his one-hundred-dollar suit to a tramp for his clothes, Mitchell said that he did not know what had happened to Kilrain after he left him in Indiana.[638]

Davies was of the opinion that Mitchell had treated Kilrain poorly, but he was willing to help him out and got him on the ten p.m. Lake Shore train in a second-class car. Davies said that he had not laughed so much in ten years as he had when he saw Mitchell "the tramp" and heard his story. He said he would give $100 for a photograph of Mitchell as he appeared at his place that night. The next evening Mitchell, was in Buffalo where he registered at the Mansion House as the Rev. Edmund Edwards of Westminster, England.

Kilrain hides out at Davies' home

Kilrain arrived in Chicago at six fifty-five a.m. on Sunday, July 14, 1889, aboard the Monon train. Johnny Murphy was with Jake, and their first move after arriving was to find Davies, who welcomed them and asked them to join him for breakfast. Jake and Johnny were happy for the invitation because they said they hadn't had anything to eat for the past thirty-six hours. Both Kilrain and Murphy downed a steak, and then Davies took them to his residence on the North Side and gave them a place to sleep. The two slept there all afternoon while Davies was making arrangements for them to take a night train east.[639]

At eight ten p.m. on July 14, Davies left Chicago headed for Louisville, Kentucky, where he hoped to arrange a match for Jackson. A new march from city to city, state to state and country to country was at hand. There had been enough time spent on the aftermath of the championship fight, and it was time to get busy on behalf of his newly signed client. Before his departure he turned Kilrain and Murphy over to his brother Vere, who at nine forty p.m. took them from the Parson's house to the Michigan Central Depot. The three men rode together to within a couple of blocks of the depot and then walked east on Randolph Street until they reached Central Avenue. Kilrain and Murphy then stood about a hundred feet apart so that they would not draw attention while Vere Davies went into the depot to buy tickets and sleeping-car accommodations for them to New York.

When he returned, Vere showed Kilrain and Murphy onto the train, where they entered the smoking-room of the sleeping-car. As Vere said goodbye, a *Chicago Tribune* reporter appeared. The reporter assured Kilrain that only Vere knew who the two men were, and Kilrain then agreed to an interview. One of the questions asked was: "Where is Pony Moore?" Kilrain hadn't see Moore for several days and supposed that he too was someplace in Chicago.

Kilrain told the reporter that his most serious injury as a result of the fight with Sullivan was a sunburned back. He said that his back and shoulders were roasted and that the skin was peeling off. Murphy showed the reporter the top of his head. He explained that he had taken his hat off during the contest and his head was cooked in the heat. Kilrain said that he was not seriously punished by Sullivan and that the hot sun had more to do with his poor showing than Sullivan's blows. "I just weakened and died away, and that is all there was to it," he said.[640]

Clearly, Davies had talked to Kilrain about the possibility of meeting Jackson because Kilrain told the reporter on July 15 that he might go to California to try for some of the big purses they offer there but that he wasn't yet sure whether he would fight Jackson.[641]

Sullivan takes out his bigotry on Sailor Brown

On the same day that Davies was helping out Kilrain and Murphy, Sullivan was in Chicago acting like a fool. In the dictionary his picture was next to the word bigot. He had been drinking for several days after his arrival and hiding out from the authorities in the Levee district south of the downtown, apparently sleeping at the flat of Tom Curley, a well-known Chicago sport, gambler, and saloon keeper. As reported by the *Chicago Herald*, on the evening of July 14, Sullivan was in Curley's saloon at 120 Fourth Avenue. He was celebrating with his former manager Sheedy, who had been won $1,500 gambling over the prior two days. Sheedy and Sullivan had both been drinking heavily when One-eye Connelly appeared with Sailor Brown in tow.

Connelly wanted to introduce Sullivan to Brown. When Brown extended his hand, Sullivan said: "You are the man that fights N______, ain't you?" He pulled himself together and squared himself in front of Brown and stared at him as a contemptuous sneer spread over his disfigured face. Brown shifted his feet uneasily and admitted that he had indeed fought Jackson. Sullivan's rejoinder was to hit Brown with a straight right and say: "Take that, you N_____ fighter!" Brown left town on the nine ten p.m. train for New York, about an hour ahead of the train carrying Kilrain and Murphy.

Connelly protested Sullivan's treatment of Brown, and Tom Curley then gave him a blow that started Connelly toward the door. At the time of these incidents, a half-dozen Chicago policemen were standing around, but did nothing to interfere. Sullivan was the king, and the police were not about to spoil his drunken pleasure. They may well have agreed with Sullivan's sentiments toward Sailor Brown. Sullivan later moved on to the Turf Exchange, where he was given a private room to accommodate his continued spree.[642]

Sullivan attitude toward Sailor Brown had a twisted logic. He had recovered from a broken arm and a long illness, only to be stripped of his title by the machinations of Richard K. Fox and the running-rabbit Mitchell. He had been goaded into a fight with Kilrain but it had just taken seventy-five rounds in the roasting, humid, swamp air of southern Mississippi to do up Kilrain, whom Sullivan considered a cut-rate bum. Sullivan was running from the law, and he was back to drinking heavily while waiting to collect $20,000 as the stakes of the fight.

Sullivan surely knew about Jackson—that Jackson had recorded impressive victories in San Francisco and that most sports now considered him a leading contender. Moreover, Sullivan knew that Jackson had signed on with Davies, who had represented Kilrain in drafting the articles and was known for his match making prowess. There would have been no doubt in Sullivan's mind that the next step would be a challenge from Davies on behalf of Jackson, who had said before the Sullivan-Kilrain match that he would be anxious to meet the winner. The last thing Sullivan wanted was another fight.

Sullivan and the color line

Sullivan probably wondered why it was taking Davies so long to demand a fight. Sullivan was sick-and-tired of training and fighting. He had plenty of money and was tired of tossing a ball with Muldoon on some god-forsaken farm in upstate New York. He and Muldoon were on the outs, and he clearly felt entitled to be treated as a king.

One sure way for Sullivan to avoid Jackson was to assert the color line. For Sullivan this involved deep thinking. Raising the color line solved a lot of problems for Sullivan and provided a credible excuse to refuse to arrange a contest with a real fighter and a threat to his re-minted championship. The color line excuse also fit well with Sullivan's own prejudices. That Sailor Brown had fought Jackson would only add fuel to the arguments by those who said that the color line was a sham in prizefighting circles. When Brown showed up with Connelly, it should have been no surprise that Sullivan would want to sucker-punch the Sailor—that's the way that Sullivan's mind worked.

Sullivan's attitude toward people of color was all too common in the late 1880s. Without intending to diminish the evil power of such hatred, racial prejudice was by no means universal. The *Las Vegas Daily Optic*, for example, commented on Sullivan's behavior toward Jackson by writing that "the keenest satire of late on race discrimination is the fact that John L Sullivan has drawn the color line on Peter Jackson . . . and refuses to fight him because of his ebony hue. The general opinion seems to be that Peter is a good deal more of a gentleman and a good deal less of a brute than the representative of modern Boston culture."[643]

The *Albuquerque Morning Democrat* wrote on July 16: "John L. Sullivan is a republican in politics and one of the staunchest kind. The idea that one republican by pugilistic lachrymose could degrade another is humorous in the extreme. Thus it is with most republicans of the whiter skin. They have no use for colored members of the party except to cast ballots for white republican candidates. It is the opinion of a great many people that Peter Jackson is quite as white a man normally and socially as John L. Sullivan, who practiced pugilistic exercises upon his wife."[644]

Jackson's own response was: "Since I came to the United States I have met a great many men of education, wealth, and high social and political position, and all have treated me most agreeably. I have no objection to Sullivan drawing the color line on me. That is his privilege."[645] Those who claim that Jackson suffered nothing but prejudice when he came to the United States should remember his own view that many educated, wealthy and positioned people had treated him well prior to mid-1889.

Putting Jackson to work

Davies always put his fighters to work and then kept them busy. He immediately went to work on Peter's behalf. On July 18, 1889 Jackson appeared in Grand Rapids, Michigan, and drew a top-heavy house at Smith's Theater. The event of the evening was the appearance of Jackson, who boxed three rounds with Lees. In addition, a couple of black lightweight fighters from the Grand Rapids area fought, and Sam Fitzpatrick put on an exhibition with Tim Quealy of Grand Rapids.[646]

On July 22 Jackson passed through Hamilton, Ohio, on his way from Chicago to Cincinnati. He attracted attention at the Cincinnati, Hamilton & Dayton Railroad station while on his way to Cincinnati, where a sparring match was scheduled with Lees on July 22. He had been advertised to appear in a sparring exhibition in an uptown theater, but the mayor issued a preemptory order to the manager of the theater not to permit it, and so the house was not opened. Newspapers in Cincinnati reported that Jackson had a deep feeling of disappointment over the cancellation but that he had left for Detroit on July 23.[647]

On July 24 Davies was already in New York City. The reporters guessed that he was there to arrange a Jackson-Kilrain finish fight. They also speculated that

Davies was there to see Bill Muldoon. It was noted that Davies and Muldoon were warm friends and that Muldoon had returned from his jack-rabbit flight from the legal authorities.

At Grand Central Station the Parson was met by Billy Madden, Dominick McCaffrey, and several others. He visited friends during the day on July 22 and then with a group of acquaintances went to the Hoffman House café where a man named E. J. Van Horn from North Platte, Nebraska, met the Davies' contingent. Van Horn had bet on Sullivan and began to taunt Davies about backing Kilrain. Van Horn reportedly said: "You're a fine sport, you are, to back Kilrain and that N_______, Jackson. Why can't you back a good man like Sullivan?" With that Davies hit Van Horn between the eyes, dropping him like a log to the sidewalk. The Davies' party continued on to the Morton House, where the discussion turned to Davies' fighting form.[648]

On July 25 Jackson appeared at Whitney's Opera House in Detroit. He was to spar with a man named George Peters, who was the black champion heavyweight of Michigan. Peters was much lighter and smaller than Jackson, and the disparity in size was amusing to the audience.

The tactics employed by the Michigan fighter were nothing new. He was a hit-and-run fighter, but he accomplished little except to keep out of Jackson's way. He was manifestly overmatched, and Jackson merely played with him until he was awarded a technical knockout in the third round.[649] In February 1890 Davies said that Jackson had cleared $1,000 on the night he appeared in Detroit. The *Kalamazoo Gazette* reported on July 26 that Jackson appeared in Grand Rapids on the evening of July 25 at the Smith's Opera House in an exhibition with Tom Lees. Their meeting was said to be one of several lively bouts presented that night.[650]

The same day that Jackson was in Detroit, Colonel J. Merwin Donahue, president of the California Athletic Club, was at the Hoffman House in New York City to meet Mike Donovan. Donahue was a millionaire and days earlier he had contacted Donovan to offer $5,000 if Kilrain would come to California to meet Jackson there. During their meeting Donovan announced that Kilrain would never meet for only $5,000, and Donahue then upped his offer to $7,000 for a finish fight.[651]

On July 26, Davies arrived in Cleveland. He had traveled there from New York to meet the rest of the combination as they came in from Detroit. At this point Charley Daly had been added to the group. When asked whether he would meet Kilrain, Jackson said that negotiations were underway for a match. The next day Kilrain was interviewed in Baltimore and said that he had been looking forward to a challenge from Jackson, and he had been expecting to meet with Davies for some time.[652]

On July 27, Jackson put on a four-round exhibition with Lees in Erie, Pennsylvania. Some reports say that Jackson appeared in Cleveland on July 27, but this would have involved the remarkable ability of bi-location. Two days later the group, which now included Davies, was in Buffalo, where Jackson was to meet a challenge with a local man named Billy Baker at the Lyceum Theater. On the afternoon before the fight Peter had a dust-up with Lees. It seems that the men were staying at the Tifft House Hotel in Buffalo, and Davies was using the hotel's office to pay those working on salary. When Lees appeared, he was paid for the period between July 13 and 27, but Lees said he was owed more. Lees said that he intended to leave the group and wanted to be paid off everything he was owed. He claimed that he was still owed for eight weeks work before Jackson signed with Charlie. Davies told Lees to take that issue up with Jackson himself because the amount claimed due was for a time prior to the Parson's management.

Lees then confronted Jackson in the corridor of the hotel and asked for the balance of the salary due him, again saying that he was going to leave the combination. Jackson said that he had no money and that if Lees was going to leave him in the lurch, then he would have to wait to be paid. Hot words followed, and then Peter shot out his left and caught Lees on the mouth. Lees jumped for him and downed him and would have severely mauled Peter as he lay on the floor if half a dozen bystanders had not pulled him off. Swearing he would get his money somehow, Lees was then put out of the hotel. Many newspapers played this event by asserting that Jackson had been beaten in a fight by Lees, but this is not what happened.[653] That night Jackson did meet Billy Baker as scheduled in a four-round match, and Jackson was credited with a win. Many local observers were not impressed with Jackson and thought that they had a local man, Tom Lynch, who was billed as "the Irish Giant" and would be able to stop Jackson. Several newspapers referred to Lynch as an "immense Negro."[654]

On July 30, Jackson met Lynch in Buffalo. Local reporters said that Lynch had more muscle than brains and had signed on to stand-up against Jackson for four rounds for a purse of $200. Somebody had put it into Lynch's head that he could down Jackson, so Lynch sailed into Jackson with the evident intention of doing him up. The two men began thumping each other with might-and-main as soon as they shook hands and the crowd yelled with delight. Lynch then began kicking at Jackson's legs. As reported by the *Post Dispatch*, Jackson asked the referee: "Is there kicking in this?"

Finally, in the second round, with a curse that could be heard for blocks (something to the effect of: "The black N_____! Let me at him. I'll kill him!"), Lynch grabbed Jackson by the legs, pulled his pins out from under him and then jumped on top of the prone man where he stuck fast. The local crowd immediately sprang onto their chairs, and every man yelled till the roof cracked. It required dozens of men to pull Lynch off, and just then the police put a stop to the fight. [655]

Whether the two incidents are connected is unknown, but that same night Davies sent a telegram to Billy Madden postponing a six-round glove contest that he had arranged between Jackson and Jack Ashton, whom Colonel Hopkins had been managing in 1887.[656] This fight had become the talk of New York City because many sports would be getting their first opportunity to see Jackson in the ring. It may have been that Jackson was hurt sometime during the day as a result of the conflict with Lees or from what happened with Lynch.

A week later Davies, wrote a letter to Madden canceling the fight with Ashton. Davies wrote that he had private reasons for not letting the affair go on. Madden was greatly put out, as he had three locations picked out for the men to meet and the financial success of the proposed contest seemed assured. Madden also intimated that Jackson was afraid to fight Ashton lest he have no reputation to carry across the water.[657]

It may be that Davies was afraid to match Jackson against Ashton, who was such a close friend of Sullivan. After watching what had happened in Buffalo, Davies could have decided that there were too many risks involved in a potential fight with Ashton, and the many Sullivan cronies who would likely appear ready to cause trouble for Jackson. There was no sense in having another fight result in a riot or worse before Davies could take Jackson to England. Someplace along the line the combination also appeared in Toronto and Jersey City, but the dates are not certain..

On August 5, Jackson met Paddy Brennan at the Genesee Hall in Buffalo. Brennan had undertaken to stand up before Jackson for four rounds for two hundred dollars, but he was a miserable failure. In the first round Jackson hammered Brennan unmercifully, breaking his nose, cutting a gash above the right eye, and nearly knocking the life out of him. He was so severely punished that the police interfered and stopped the fight. Jackson did not get a scratch.[658]

On August 6, Jackson fought another tame exhibition with Billy Baker in Buffalo and then left for New York City, where he had been scheduled to meet Ashton on August 8. Peter arrived in the big city accompanied by Davies and told the press that he would meet Sullivan if a match could be arranged between them. That night he went to Hoboken for a third match with Billy Baker, who seems to have replaced Lees in the lineup after the Tifft House problems.

Shutting up critics

This was Jackson's first time to show his skill to sports from the immediate environs of the big city. He appeared at Cronheim's Theater so that the locals could study his science. Sullivan had made his first appearance on the stage of Cronheim after he had broken his arm on Cardiff's head. Jackson's work that evening was judged to be tame, and Jackson had it all his own way. Local papers observed that fighters thought that Jackson was "weak in his pins" and that despite his reach, he could not impart strength through his blows. The critics also said that his "short arm" work was weak. In fact, they became so confident that Jackson was overrated that they lined up "Ginger" McCormick to face him on August 9 in the hope of collecting on Davies' offer of $100 to the man who could stand before Jackson for four rounds.

In the meantime, the price had already gone up for a Sullivan-Jackson fight. They had been offered a purse of $30,000 ($25,000 to the winner and $5,000 to the loser) for a finish fight to take place at the Carnival Palace in Ogden. Davies had many friends in Ogden and it was easily reached from San Francisco, Salt

Lake City, and Denver, so it offered some real possibilities and the city was not beset with the prejudice so easily found in the south, Midwest and east coast.[659]

Jackson knocked out McCormick in two rounds on August 9. The match was fought with four-ounce gloves, and Jackson used mostly left jabs that repeatedly rocked McCormick and avoided using his right hand. Accounts from the *Post Dispatch* contend that Jackson used both hands, but its reporter was probably not on the scene and may have engaged in some creative writing. Presuming that local accounts were more accurate, Jackson's use of his left hand may have been a hint that he had hurt his right arm when he was tackled by Lynch, and if that was correct, it might also explain why the match with Ashton was called off. Jack Fallon acted the referee for this contest.

Jackson finished McCormick with two short left hand jabs in the second round. Not bad for a man whose "short arm" work was supposed to be weak. Davies and Jackson were booked to sail for Liverpool aboard the *Wisconsin* on August 13, but they waited on the East Coast for additional matches with Joe Lannon and with Jack Fallon, the "American Strong Boy," in New York on August 19. The Lannon fight was stopped by local authorities.[660] In Jackson's appearances after Detroit and before New York City he cleared another $3,500.[661]

Jackson appeared to be a marvel to the *Brooklyn Eagle*. That newspaper described him as "straight as a plummet, a long armed loose hinged fellow who can sit in a chair and touch the ground with his hands. He is finely built and has a magnificent arm, but is so tall as to look slim. His face is good humored and dignified and his complexion as black as midnight. Agility more than anything else distinguished him. It showed in every loose, graceful, easy movement."[662]

Fallon was only twenty-one years old, but he was not a novice fighter. In February 1889 he had sparred Dominick McCaffrey in Hoboken. Jackson and Fallon met at Mike Shine's New York Circus at Fourth Avenue and Fourteenth Street (formerly Bowery Street) in the city. The New York police were present at this contest, and before the match Davies appeared and announced to the house that there would be no slugging that evening because of the police. It appears that this match was made at the last minute as part of an arrangement to enlist Fallon as a member of the group traveling to England. Lees was on the outs with Peter, and Billy Baker had not shown well enough to make a credible opponent.

Davies liked to travel with a decent fighter on the payroll because such a fighter could meet several needs. He provided a sparring partner for the star of the show. He could also fight on the undercard against local men, and he could spar with the star in public performances if no local man was available. Although Fallon was dispatched by Jackson in only two rounds, he seemed good enough to meet the Parson's needs, and there wasn't time to shop around. Jackson would later claim that on his trip east from Chicago, the combination had earned a profit of $8,500. This was probably a gross profit because there were no extraordinary expenses, and the Cincinnati appearance had been stopped by the mayor. After this match Jackson and Fallon had a beer together, and Fallon agreed to leave with the rest of the combination for London.

The general attitude of the eastern press toward Jackson displayed a good deal of racial prejudice on the part of the sport writers a group seldom bogged down by intellectual analysis. There was a persistent effort to find fault. Many articles said that he had good hands, arms and a powerful chest, but that his waist was too small, and he lacked good legs. Other articles claimed that he could hit hard enough to deal with run-of-the-mill fighters, but not to meet fighters of the top class. A common opinion was that Jackson's stance was wrong because he was not standing with one foot forward as expected, and he frequently stood up with his feet together.

Tom Lees told the press that Jackson would grunt whenever he was hit in the stomach and was more afraid of being hit there than any other man Lees had fought. Lees claimed that Jackson lacked variety and that he would draw in and then jump back every time if he thought his opponent could reach him. He was faulted for holding his left arm too far forward, and it was said that his left hand strikes were mere "laps." Others said he did not draw his arm back far enough to deliver a solid blow. Of course, he had already defeated many leading heavyweights despite all his alleged faults.[663]

There was also a general feeling that Jackson lacked "heart," which was a synonym for courage. This was a different thing than complaining about his stance or how he held his arms. This view reflected a common view among many whites that black fighters because of inherent racial inferiority were incapable of showing courage. Sport writers claimed that nearly all black fighters suffered from a lack of heart. One such writer claimed that on account of Jackson's phenomenal length of reach—his fingers touching his knees when he stood erect—he had been able to keep all of his antagonists so far at arms' length, but if he stood against a man who was able to break down his guard and get a few pile driving blows in on his stomach, he would be finished. All of this was pure nonsense.

On to England

On Wednesday, August 21, Davies and Jackson sailed for Liverpool on the Anchor Line's *City of Rome,* arriving in Ireland on August 28, and at Liverpool the next day. Some articles claim that they arrived on August 30, 1889. Both Fallon and his wife traveled with Davies and Jackson. Others on the trip included W. W. Naughton and Sam Fitzpatrick. Jackson was headed for England for the first time, and Davies was returning to England for the first time since his racewalking days nearly ten years earlier. Nevertheless, both men were well-known in England and had excellent reputations there. Davies had promoted many fighters from England with good success for most of them and with great success for Jack Burke. He had entertained such athletes as Jack Wannop in Chicago, and his role in the Sullivan-Kilrain match made him a recent celebrity.[664]

Even the trip to England was competitive, as a fleet of four steamships of different passenger lines left New York on the same day heading for Liverpool. Within the memory of the oldest steamship men, there has never been so much interest taken in a mid-August sailing day. The big racers were the *Teutonic* of the White Star line; *City of New York*, of the Inman Line; *Saale* of the North German Lloyd line; and *City of Rome* of the Anchor line. All the ships had a fair number of saloon passengers, and all were eagerly discussing the merits of the several vessels. Of course the *Teutonic* and *City of New York* were favorites, as they were the newer ships with the more powerful engines. The *City of New York,* the *City of Rome,* and the *Teutonic* all passed down the Hudson River within half an hour of each other. Among those who sailed were Davies and Jackson. What a sight this must have been! Clearly these two self-made men had hit the big-time.[665]

Reports sent to the United States said that Davies and Jackson were smothered with attention upon their arrival in England. James R. Moyle, a friend of Jackson's from Australia who had relocated to England, rented a coach-and-four (a carriage pulled by a team of four horses) to take Davies and Jackson to Anderson's Hotel on Fleet Street in London and then out for a night on the town. The primary interest was in Jackson and not Davies, but that was a fact of life if you were the manager of a great prizefighter.[666]

One of the first orders of business was to issue formal challenges. Through Davies, Jackson formally challenged Charley Mitchell, Jem Smith and Frank Slavin, the Australian champion who had arrived in England only ten days before Jackson.[667] Jackson and Slavin were well known to one another. Frank also had good size and stood about six feet one inches tall and weighed about 185 pounds. The target for both Jackson and Slavin was a match with Jem Smith, who was then considered the heavyweight champion of England. It would be important for Davies to arrange a Jackson-Smith match before Slavin and Smith were matched.

Both Jackson and Davies were treated like royalty. In late September they were invited to dine with two of England's prominent sportsmen, Edward Southwell Russell, the 24th Lord de Clifford and Sir John Astley, the president of the Pelican Club. Lord de Clifford held one of oldest titles in the United Kingdom, with his barony having been created in 1299 as the fourth on the list of English barons. He was the twenty-eighth de Clifford in the line of peerage, and the family owned thirteen thousand acres of land in County Mayo, Ireland, which was perhaps the county in Ireland most hostile to English rule. For an emigrant from Ireland to dine with Lord de Clifford must have been a remarkable measure of Davies' success.[668]

Beating the English champion

In late September 1889 Jackson and Jem Smith signed articles for a ten-round fight with small gloves according to *Police Gazette* rules for £1,000, £800 to the winner and £200 to the loser. The total was about $6,000, with $5,000 to the winner and $1,000 to the loser.

George W. Atkinson was designated as the referee. Smith had wanted a bare-knuckle fight but Jackson refused. Smith also wanted a finish fight, but Jackson's agreement with the C.A.C. limited his performances to eight-round contests with no finish fights. With the consent of the C.A.C. delivered by telegram to Davies, it was agreed that Jackson would fight ten rounds.[669]

The contest was to take place in the gymnasium of the new Pelican Club in November 1889 on a day to be named later. The articles required a fair, stand-up boxing-match and specified that the two men were to box in light boots or shoes without spikes or in socks with knickerbockers. Knickerbockers were knee length pants usually baggy at the knee. They articles further specified that "light or fancy points" would not count. This was probably a provision insisted on by Smith, as Jackson was the only fighter of these two who might score light or fancy points. Slavin was a banger and relied on rushes and heavy hitting. Finally, the articles specified that should the contest not be satisfactorily decided, the men would have the option of boxing another ten rounds within eight days, or if the men agreed to a draw, each was to receive £100. Davies had negotiated a terrific contract for Jackson. Jem Smith wanted a finish fight and that did not happen. Smith wanted a bare-knuckle fight and that too did not happen. Davies persuaded the C.A.C. to allow Jackson to fight more than eight rounds for the first time since he had left California, and the provisions of the contract relating to unspiked shoes proved extremely important in the ultimate fight outcome.[670]

There was a dispute about the gloves that were to be used in the match. Later, Davies said the trouble was that the gloves furnished Jackson were too small in the fingers, and when he closed his hands, they almost split. Consequently, Jackson could not fight with them. The Pelican Club eventually procured gloves that fit Jackson.

The new Pelican clubhouse in London was the leading retreat for English sportsmen. Membership was limited to 1,500 men, and its roles contained the names of some of the most prominent men in the country. Membership included professionals, theatrical men, and several leading English journalists. The club had billiard rooms and lounges, along with a steam bath, dressing room, and a large kitchen and dining area. The members met on Sunday evenings for sparring, wrestling, and fencing exhibitions in the club's basement, where a gymnasium had been set up that was electrically lit and provided seating for 700 men. These activities were under the supervision of John Fleming, who was also the backer and manager of Jem Smith. There was a side door entrance for the use of boxers and other visiting professionals. Prior to Jackson's visit to England, all the American boxers who had visited in London had boxed in the ring of the old Pelican Club. Lord John Henry Lonsdale was to act as stakeholder for the Jackson-Smith fight.

In preparation for Jackson's contest with Smith, Davies arranged for a series of exhibitions to take place in London. Some sources report as many as fourteen exhibitions between October 2 and 16 with a variety of opponents, including two matches with Fallon, four with Jem Young, two with Alf Mitchell, and one each with Jack Watson, Jem Hook, Jack Partridge, Coddy Middings, and Alf Ball.

On October 2, a Jackson-Fallon exhibition was given at the Royal Aquarium Theater before five thousand spectators anxious to see big Jackson "monkey with" the Brooklyn strong boy. Davies introduced the two combatants from the ring. The *Post Dispatch* wrote that his oration was: "Ladies and Gentlemen, I appear before you a stranger in a strange land. Since I have been in this country I have received the kindest treatment and courtesy. I am Jackson's manager, and I wish to state that in his travels every pugilist he has met he has defeated. This is the first time he has appeared before an English audience, and he will spar tonight with Jack Fallon, the Strong Boy of Brooklyn, and I hope they will both please you. In conclusion, I wish to state that Jackson is matched to box Jem Smith [champion of England] for 10 rounds for £1,000, given by the Pelican Club, and if defeated I shall be satisfied that the best man has won." Parson Davies was always impeccably polite to a paying audience.[671]

That night Fallon was so badly outclassed that the show was met with hissing of both the boxers. It was originally intended that Charley Mitchell would spar with Jackson, but Mitchell would not appear without a much larger share of the gate than Davies was willing to provide, and Fallon was substituted at the last minute. Only two months earlier Mitchell the tramp had appeared at Davies' saloon in Chicago looking for help as he fled the law. Mitchell either had a short memory or was something of an ingrate. Fallon agreed that he was "a mere baby in Jackson's hands." Newspapers in America said that as a result of the poor show at the Jackson-Fallon fight Davies had lost "caste" among a certain class of Englishmen of "sporting proclivities." The Jackson-Fallon presentation was particularly criticized because it reminded British fight fans of a recent and disappointing Smith-Wannop match that had been judged a hippodrome.

While preparations for the Jackson-Smith contest moved forward, Davies was attempting to arrange a Fallon-Wannop match. The first effort fell through, and when Davies began negotiating a second match Fallon objected to some part of the proposed articles. Fallon told the press that he was tired of England and that he was going to visit Ireland before returning directly to the United States.

Jackson was a strong favorite in betting on the Smith match, but on the day before the fight Smith became the betting favorite, selling six to four, with Jackson on the short end. Davies was said to be expertly playing the bookmakers and was called one of the shrewdest sporting men in America for the way he was playing public opinion and the betting line.

The Jackson-Smith fight was scheduled for November 11 at the Pelican Club, and the match was awarded to Jackson because of a flagrant foul by Smith. Prior to the match both men looked fit as they entered the sixteen foot ring. Jackson was about ten pounds heavier than Smith. Jackson's seconds were Jack Fallon and Sam Fitzpatrick. The seconds for Jem Smith were Jack Baldock and Jack Harper. The audience included men like Lord Mandeville, whom the Parson described as a good fellow generally and who had seen Jackson box with Cardiff in San Francisco.

The first round was a "quiet and tame affair" by most accounts, with each man trying to measure his opponent. Both men seemed nervous. The second round was decidedly different as Jackson started out quickly with an exhibition of confidence that showed he already decided that he could beat Smith. Jackson delivered terrific blows to Smith's head and body wherever he pleased. Jackson's extraordinary reach allowed him to avoid Smith's returns. Observers said that the "ruthless onslaught by the Australian" weakened Smith, who then resorted to dodging and slipping down to one knee in order to avoid additional punishment.

Finally, Jackson got Smith to the ropes and hammered him unmercifully with his left hand. Smith assumed an awkward position in which he held onto the ropes with his right hand and turned sideways to Jackson, attempting to defend himself only with his left arm. These were not the "light or fancy points" that Smith had apparently expected. After being battered heavily, Smith finally let loose of the ropes and escaped the pounding onslaught.

Smith made a rush at Jackson, grabbing him like a wrestler then back-healing and sending him to the floor by use of this flagrant foul. Smith's behavior was somewhat typical of an old-line London-rules fighter and demonstrated why it had been so important to prohibit the use of spiked shoes. Had Smith back-healed Jackson with spikes, Jackson might have suffered some long-lasting injuries. Injuries including slashed muscles or a damaged Achilles' heel were common in matches where spiked shoes were used. Some accounts describe Smith's move at the end of the second round as grabbing Jackson around the chest and then using a deliberate cross-buttocks move, which was a wrestling throw that essentially involved putting a leg behind an opponent and using a forearm to push that man over backward using the back leg as a tripping lever. While Jackson was on the ground, Smith hit Jackson in his testicles with his left hand.

Smith's conduct was met with a storm of hisses and yells that increased to a "deafening uproar." Davies, Fallon, and Fitzpatrick all jumped into the ring to raise their protests on Jackson's behalf. The referee agreed and then awarded the fight to Jackson on the foul. Smith began arguing with the referee, claiming that what he had done was within the rules. When the referee refused to change his ruling, Smith then became enraged and tried to resume the fight with bare knuckles. He pulled off his gloves and tried to make a rush at Jackson, who removed one glove but could not remove the other. Davies shouted to him to rip off the other glove to defend himself, but Jackson simply waived to Smith's handlers to let him lose. He apparently knew that he could handle Smith with one bare fist and one gloved hand. Seeing all of this, the police seized Smith and persuaded him to shake hands with Jackson.[672]

Smith was beaten at all points. He had sunken his chance of being a champion by his behavior at the end of the contest. Reporters said that it was beyond doubt that Smith would have been knocked out by Jackson had the fight been continued for another round. It was the common judgment that Smith was clearly overmatched by Jackson. When Smith was asked how it happened that Jackson bested him so quickly, he replied, "Dunno." This remark by Smith was probably honest. Fighters who are badly beaten often do not know what happened.

Immediately after the fight, Davies said that Jackson was open to a challenge from anyone in the world. The *Toronto Daily Mail* wrote:

> The Smith-Jackson fight will go down in history as one of the most extraordinary affairs of the ring. A stranger, and a man of colour, comes to a land many thousands of miles from that of his birth, with a manager whom he has known for less than a year and stands before a man who had long posed as the most dangerous fighter of the land, that has furnished hundreds of men who were his equals or superiors, and vanquishes that man in his own home and in the midst of hundreds of his partisans in one of the shortest fights on record. Among the patrons of prize-fighting in England to-day it is probable that Jackson has far more friends than Smith. None of the hundreds who witness Monday morning's affair will deny that he deserves to have more. England has had few champions who were vanquished so quickly and thoroughly as Smith.[673]

Davies sent a wire to a friend in New York: "Jackson is being lionized. The fight is considered a knock-out. The Pelican Club will give a reception to Peter. The English press acknowledge him the greatest fighter ever seen here. Will be home next month."[674]

Richard K. Fox attended the Jackson-Smith match and was excited that he had seen a champion who would put Sullivan down. Fox sent cards to Jackson that night and the next day praising him. It seemed apparent that he would be happy to take over Jackson if he could pry him away from Davies, but Jackson was more loyal than Fox had hoped.[675] Loyalty may have been easier because the combination was making so much money. Davies wrote to his assistant, Otto Floto, in Chicago on December 9, reporting that during the first two weeks of Jackson's appearance at the Aquarium in London they had netted more than $10,000 and that they had cleared another $7,744 on the Smith match.[676]

Jackson's defeat of Smith was one of several matches in 1889 that reordered the standings of several fighters. Big changes were in the offing in the ranks of prize fighting. Dempsey, who seemed indestructible, had been knocked cold by George La Blanche, then Killen had been knocked out by Joe McAuliffe, ending Killen's rise to prominence. In addition, a fight that crossed the color line took place between Godfrey and Sullivan's friend, Jack Ashton. This was the match Colonel Hopkins had tried to arrange in 1887 and that had enraged Sullivan and contributed to Sullivan's split with Sheedy. Godfrey knocked out Ashton to the surprise of many critics of black fighters. When Jackson defeated Jem Smith with such ease, the question naturally arose as to whether Sullivan would be the next man put down by a black fighter.

Sullivan says he will fight Jackson

Sullivan had finally been making noise about fighting again. His attitude toward fighting Jackson had changed somewhat. John L. had already blown his money from the Kilrain match and the it appeared that he would sell the color line for a price. Two days after Jackson defeated Smith, Sullivan told reporters that he would now fight Jackson, but only for a purse of $20,000. Sullivan had the opportunity to make his point again only a few days later when he received a telegram from L. R. Fulda, president of the C.A.C., asking whether Sullivan was willing to meet Jackson at the C.A.C. for $10,000. Sullivan's response was that he would fight white men for $10,000 apiece, but black men would be double that price.[677] When questioned about his apparent flexibility toward the color line Sullivan admitted that he had said that he would never fight a black man, but he rationalized that "they seem to think that Jackson is a world beater, and I am anxious to show them just where he belongs."[678]

Davies wrote to Fulda to tell him exactly what Jackson intended to do in the coming months. He explained that Jackson had no intention to challenge Sullivan, but he would fight him for a reasonable purse if the C.A.C. arranged the match. Davies said that Jackson would want five months from the date of signing the articles before meeting Sullivan in the ring. He explained that Jackson did not intend to leave for the States until January 20, 1890, and would then take two months in the East to fill arrangements that had been offered him there and could not fight Sullivan until the middle of 1890.

Neither Jackson nor Davies was ready to return to the United States immediately. Both of them seemed to understand that there was good money to be made in England, and within two days after the title match, Smith and Jackson agreed to give a sparring exhibition at the Aquarium. It is noteworthy that by early December 1889 Davies had already laid out Jackson's schedule through the end of March 1890.[679]

Davies was in the ring on the first night of the exhibitions at the Aquarium and introduced the contestants: "Ladies and Gentlemen, Mr. Jem Smith, champion of England, and Peter Jackson, the Colored Champion Boxer of the World, will engage in a scientific and friendly set-to." The title "Colored Champion Boxer of the World" was created by Richard K. Fox and bestowed on Jackson when Fox learned of the results of his contest with Smith.

The *Cyberboxingzone* reports that Jackson had five exhibitions with Smith between November 14 and 20. He then defeated Horace Horrigan in two rounds on November 21. The next day he defeated Charles Burgin in four rounds and then put on an exhibition on November 23 with Jem Smith once again. All of these matches were held at Westminster, England.

The group then moved southwest to Plymouth. At the Royal Amphitheater Jackson sparred in exhibitions with a man named Wolf Bedoff on November 25 through 27 and added a match with a man named Skinner, also on November

27. Fallon later reported that their matches in Plymouth were held in Saint James' Hall.

From the ring on November 26, Davies read to the audience a telegram from Luke Short, a prominent sportsman from Houston, Texas. The essence of the telegram was that Texas law permitted prizefighting and parties in Houston would guarantee $20,000 for a Sullivan-Jackson fight in that city. That was the price that Sullivan himself had set to fight a black man. Davies also attempted to arrange a meeting with Slavin but he refused to fight until after his match with Jem Smith.[680]

The combination then traveled to Portsmouth, where Jackson appeared six times between November 28 and December 1. His opponents included Jem Young, three times; Sailor White, the champion of the British Navy once, aboard the H.M.S. *Excelsior*; and Wolf Bendoff, twice. Their next stop was Brighton, where Peter met Scotchy Gunn of Sussex, considered the best heavyweight in South England, and a W. Woodhams. After a week-long rest they went to Leeds, where Jackson appeared on three nights for exhibitions with Jem Young and then went to London for ten more exhibitions with Young between December 16 and December 20. The exhibitions during this period were given at the South London Gymnastic School.

Fallon told the *Brooklyn Eagle* that after their last appearances in London the combination went to Paris, where they appeared for three nights at the Music Hall, the admission being two, three and five francs, and the French patrons taking great interest in the sport. According to Davies, Jackson sparred on an average of three times a night during their trip to England and Ireland, and he always took into consideration his superiority over his adversaries by not knocking them out. Davies said that this practice generally met with the favor of the British audiences.[681]

While working this busy schedule, Jackson was asked about meeting Sullivan. Jackson said that he had not been challenged by Sullivan and that he would pay no attention to him. noted that for a long time Sullivan had pledged that he would not fight a black man, and Jackson saw no reason why a black man should go out of his way to arrange a fight with Sullivan. He said: "I am going to stay in England awhile and make some money. Sullivan's talk of a match for $40,000 is nonsense."[682]

As if all of this work were not sufficient, the combination next traveled to Dublin for additional exhibitions: December 23, Jack Fallon and Jem Young; and December 24, Fallon and Young again. On December 24, Jackson also met Peter Maher, a coming Irish heavyweight, and knocked him out in two rounds. Some sources report this match as a three-round exhibition that took place on Christmas Day in Dublin. Maher would become a superior fighter who would contend for the heavyweight championship and fight for another twenty-five years. Many credit Davies as the man who persuaded Maher that he would be successful if he came to America to fight. If these claims are true Davies probably did the persuading in Ireland when at the Jackson-Maher match.

During their two days in Dublin, Fallon sparred six rounds with Jack Hickey, a middle-weight Irishman. Fallon told the *Brooklyn Eagle* that this exhibition was presented in the rotunda at Dublin and that ten thousand people attended. From Dublin they traveled to Belfast for two nights. One of Davies' sisters lived in Belfast with her family. Davies said that in Belfast the people came out in force and packed the hall. After appearing in Belfast, Jackson, Fitzpatrick, and Naughton returned to Bristol, England, for three more exhibitions with Jem Young on December 26, 27 and 28. After the conclusion of matters in Ireland the group began to split up for a month of traveling and recuperation. Davies remained in Belfast with his sister, Mrs. Hugh Suffern, and her five children.[683]

Fallon returned to Dublin with his wife. He was suffering from the grip and stayed at Costello's Hotel in Dublin for two weeks before becoming the first member of the combination to return home. The grip was a broad term which usually referred to a person suffering from influenza-like symptoms. Jackson went back to England and then to France. In Paris he was interviewed by a representative of the Press News Association and said: "I am not a person to boast, but I would like it to be distinctly understood that I am not afraid to fight any man in the world, bar none. There is one condition; however, I will always stick to, no matter with whom I fight. That condition is that anybody who wants to fight me must do so with gloved hands. I make that condition because bare knuckle fighting is looked upon as unscientific and inhuman. Those who engage in it are hunted down like beasts and made to appear as criminals before the law. I have no desire to be regarded as a criminal in any respect, and those who want to fight me must do so on purely scientific and legitimate principles."[684]

The King of the Canario Islands

An article published on June 22, 1904, in the *Sun* discussed a part of the trip to France when Davies, Sam Fitzpatrick, and Jackson were traveling together and visiting the famous sites in Paris. They stopped at a small café on one of the boulevards. While sitting at a table in the open they were approached by two distinguished looking Frenchmen who offered their hands to Jackson. One of the men spoke a little English and asked Davies to be formally introduced to Jackson. Davies referred the Frenchman to Fitzpatrick with a wink and Fitzpatrick took the hint that a joke was on.

Fitzpatrick took the two Frenchmen aside and told them that Jackson was actually a king. He named a mythical kingdom, the Canario Islands, in the Pacific Ocean as Jackson's regal domain. Davies, Fitzpatrick explained, was the prime minister of the Canario Islands, and due to his royal status Jackson was a very wealthy man. Fitzpatrick explained that both Jackson and Davies preferred to keep their true identities under wraps. Fitzpatrick warned the two Frenchmen that they needed to be discreet under the circumstances.

The Frenchmen believed this fanciful story and for several days they traveled around the city with the pugilistic party paying all the bills as they went along.

Jackson was lionized and the Frenchmen who bowed to him when in his presence. They tried to engage Jackson in conversation, but Davies and Fitzpatrick had told Peter that the two men were actually detectives operating in disguise and looking for a Negro who had shot a man in America. They warned Jackson to be careful of what he said to these two men because he might be mistakenly charged with a crime. With this warning Jackson made no effort to engage the two men in conversation and soon asked Davies and Fitzpatrick to get rid of their two tour guides.

A week later Davies, Jackson, and Fitzpatrick went out for a carriage ride around the city. As they passed a crowd someone yelled out, "Bravo! Bravo Peter Jackson!" This was followed by someone yelling in plain English: "Good boy, Peter, you did Jem Smith up brown!" Jackson acknowledged the shouts and about that same time the two Frenchmen who had been told that he was a wealthy Canario Islands king emerged from the crowd and stormed the carriage yelling that Jackson was a liar.

Jackson was surprised and did not know what was happening. Davies, sensing trouble, instructed the driver to speed it up and take them to their hotel. The two Frenchmen followed behind in another carriage, and when both rigs reached the hotel, the Frenchmen raised a row denouncing the travelers in French and broken English. Jackson still didn't understand what was happening. He was frightened and shut himself up in the hotel for three days thinking that the Frenchmen had mistaken him for the criminal that they were after and assuming that they wanted to arrest him. Fitzpatrick said that neither he nor Davies ever told Jackson the real story, fearing that he would be hot about the joke gone badly.[685]

Big dollars offered for a Sullivan-Jackson match

While the combination was in Dublin, Davies learned of the offer of the C.A.C. to sponsor a Sullivan-Jackson match for $15,000 a side. On December 24, he wired Fulda that Jackson had accepted the offer was greatly pleased to hear that Sullivan had also accepted. It is not clear why Davies thought that Sullivan had accepted; Sullivan had said that he would fight Jackson at the C.A.C. for $20,000 a side. Davies said that he would be sailing for America on January 15, 1890, with the apparent intention of pursuing arrangements for a match with Sullivan.[686]

Clearly there were many people in the United States who did not think that a match for $40,000 was nonsense. In Fargo, a new athletic club had been formed called the Dempsey Athletic Club. In early December 1889 the Dempsey club met and offered a purse of $40,000 for a Sullivan-Jackson fight. Such a purse would relieve both sides of finding a backer willing to put up $20,000.

The Dempsey club appointed a committee of five men to draft rules to govern the contest. In addition, W. H. Carmichael, a director of the San Jose Athletic Association, told the press that its agent had been authorized to offer $15,000 to Jackson and Sullivan but had been given subsequent instructions to increase the offer to $20,000 for a fight to the finish in their club rooms. The Santa Cruz Athletic Club telegraphed Sullivan that it would give $30,000 for a finish fight between John L. and Jackson, the fight to take place on the beach near Santa Cruz. At the end of November, with offers swirling in England and the United States, Davies was notified by Fulda that Jackson was required to hold himself in readiness to meet Sullivan at the C.A.C. in May for a purse of $10,000. Sullivan had agreed to nothing.

One reason that Sullivan would not agree to a fight was that his criminal conviction in Mississippi was still on appeal to the state's Supreme Court, and he did not want to do anything that would jeopardize his case. He had been sentenced to one year in jail in Mississippi and had good reason to be cautious. One can speculate whether his public derogatory comments about fighting Jackson were intended to appeal to the anti-black sensibilities of the legal authorities in Mississippi.[687]

For Davies, 1888 had ended quietly in St. Louis, where a local supernumerary had prevented a tame little Kilrain-Mitchell exhibition. He ended 1889 in Ireland with family members. No person could have anticipated what happened in 1889. Davies was unquestionably at the top of the heap. He had made a terrific amount of money during the year, and his reputation as an honest promoter and manager was sealed in England and America.

Chapter 10 - (1890)

Climbing Higher

I want to tell something right here that has never been told before. That is that John L. Sullivan once signed an agreement to meet Peter Jackson, and had it not been for an accident in which a boxer was killed at the Golden Gate Athletic club in San Francisco, which killed boxing for a time, these two great men would have met.

Major Frank McLaughlin came to us with a dispatch from President Fulda of the California Athletic club. It was after I had returned from Paris with Jackson and the big black had developed into the greatest fighter of the age, in my opinion. Fulda sent a telegram to John L. Sullivan, asking: "Will you fight Peter Jackson for $15,000 prize? Answer on back of telegram."

Sullivan wrote this answer: "Yes; I'll fight the n______, winner take all."

McLaughlin showed the message to Peter Jackson as the big colored fellow was laying sick in his bed. Jackson read it and said: "If Mr. Davies wants me to fight Sullivan I'll meet him in eight weeks. McLaughlin gave that telegram back to Mr. Fulda, and I understand he still holds Sullivan's signature to the querry.[688]

—

"Jackson is the squarest man with whom I have ever done business and his head can't be swelled."[689]

—

♦

Charles E. "Parson" Davies was thoughtful and reflective and there were important business matters to consider at the beginning of 1890. He would soon need to return to Chicago. As usual, Chicago politics and the influence of local politicians and the police department on his profession were issues that needed to be addressed. He was getting older and the faces in Chicago were changing. It was nearly impossible to travel and maintain necessary local relationships.

Another issue facing Davies was the ascendancy of the sporting clubs. The impact of these clubs on prizefighting was enormous, and they were springing up like toadstools in a forest after a month of heavy rain. The C.A.C., the Golden Gate Club, the Dempsey Athletic Club in North Dakota, the Pelican Club in London, and clubs in many others in places such as Denver, Houston, and New Orleans had changed the dynamic for managers and promoters like Davies. Sporting clubs tended to have local political influence, access to arenas and money. An individual such as Davies could seldom compete with these clubs unless he controlled the best fighters.

The 1889 Kilrain-Sullivan fight is often discussed because it was one of the last great bare-knuckle fights. It should also be noted because it was one of the last great fights of the period promoted by individual managers rather than an athletic club. Davies must have wondered about his future as the athletic clubs assumed the roles that had previously been filled by fight managers and promoters. Would there be a place for men like Charlie in a newly aligned sporting world? If he had a leading heavyweight contender such as Jackson, his position was probably secure. If he lost Jackson then it could be harder than ever to compete.

Davies and other prominent sportsmen soon formed the Puritan Athletic Club of Long Island City. That club was organized on March 21, 1890. The incorporators included C. E. Davies, George Blumer, Frank Stevenson, Gus Futhill, William M. Burke, and William and Frank Carroll.[690] Other members included Frank Brill, and William E. Harding. Prizefighting was still prohibited in New York, and all of the sportsmen who labored under that inhibition needed to devise a method for their own survival. The Puritan believed that it could secure protection from the police in Long Island City and thereby offer regular prizefights for its members. Securing a promise of protection implied regular payments to the police, as had become the custom in Chicago. The members of the new club would only exist on paper. Their sole duty would be to pay annual dues. In months to come, the Puritan would attempt to compete with the many other athletic clubs throughout America and England but without great success.

Davies left Floto in charge of his sporting promotions in Chicago while he was in England with Jackson. Floto was also branching out by acting as an agent for the Chicago White Sox baseball team.[691] The boxing business back in Chicago involved Billy Myer, who had changed his manager from Alf Kennedy to a man named Lee Cheney from Bloomington, Illinois. In an effort to get something going for Myer, Cheney had arranged a fight with Harry Gilmore. This contest was styled as another benefit. This time the benefit was given to aid the Servite Sisters, who operated two homes on West Van Buren Street. Davies had affection for religious orders. One of his sisters was reported to be a Catholic nun in Ireland, and his niece Catherine would soon become a Sister of Charity of the Blessed Virgin Mary.[692] However, apparently the Servites did not share the feeling because they refused to accept the money.[693]

The Myer-Gilmore contest was to be an eight-round contest at Battery D to take place on January 15, 1890, the same day that Davies was leaving England to return to the United States. Myer had made part of his early reputation by knocking out Gilmore twice, so the two men were familiar to the public. The announcement that Myer and Gilmore would meet again was welcomed and a crowd of five thousand was present for the fight. However, Captain Marsh of the Chicago police had determined that he would control prizefighting and sent a Captain Fitzpatrick and a large number of police officers to the venue.

Fitzpatrick started the evening's entertainment by announcing that the fighters would be required to wear nothing less than eight-ounce, circus-type gloves. He also stated that there would be no need for a referee in the fight because the contestants would only be allowed to score points for scientific style. There would be no heavy blows, knockdowns, or knockouts allowed. This charade went on for four rounds, and then Myer began to force the fighting. When Fitzpatrick saw what was happening, he jumped into the ring and stopped the fight. The only good thing about this match was that the gate receipts were not lost. However, if this was what the new administration had in mind for boxing in Chicago then the sport would be killed in a different way than under the previous administration. Government has many ways to kill a healthy business when politicians become involved. In Chicago becoming involved meant that the politicians wanted their share of the take.[694]

The group that left for England in the late summer of 1889 began to return to on January 1, 1890. Fallon had been away from the group in Dublin recovering from the grip. He and his wife left for the States and were the first to arrive. The *Germanic* made port on Sunday night, January 12. He had a stormy eleven day passage but was greeted upon his arrival by four hundred fans waiting to shake his hand and congratulate him. Fallon told the *Brooklyn Eagle*: "I never had so good a time in my life. Jackson became a favorite from the time we landed and the London swells fairly lionized 'Parson' Davies. I was in Jackson's corner when he fought Smith and don't exaggerate when I say the Britisher is entirely outclassed by Jackson. Jackson is certainly a wonderful fighter. His performances abroad were simply wonderful and he cleared above $30,000."[695]

Fallon said that after expenses his profits from the trip were $1,300 plus an extra bonus of $500 that Jackson gave him after he had defeated Smith. In addition, Davies and Jackson had gone together to buy Mrs. Fallon a five-hundred-dollar diamond ring in appreciation for her many kindnesses to the party while not feeling well more much of the trip.

A triumphant return to America

Davies left Liverpool on January 15 aboard the White Star line's *Britannic*. He was listed on the manifest as a thirty-eight year old male employed as a "Manager." He had already outlived his older brother Henry but was still a young man. While he was at sea, Charlie's niece, Sarah R. Davies, Henry's eldest child, married Robert H. Gruschow at Holy Name Cathedral in Chicago.

The *Britannic's* passage was to New York via Queenstown arriving January 19.[696] It was a clear day in New York with the temperatures in the mid-50's, a warm day for January. When the *Britannic* swung along the pier Davies was on deck, clean-shaven, smiling, and handsome. He was the first passenger to set foot on the gangway, wearing a plaid tweed suit, a blue English box coat (a heavy overcoat such as a coachman might wear), a high beaver hat and patent leather shoes. A number of his friends were waiting on shore to greet him.

As if a chorus, reporters shouted: "How did you leave Peter?" Davies replied: "I'm sorry to say that I left him considerably under the weather, but it is nothing serious." He explained that the climate of in the British Isles was so bad that Jackson couldn't stand it. He was confident that once Jackson was back in the United States he would be fine. Davies said that Jackson would arrive on the *Adriatic* within the coming week. In a later interview, Davies said that Jackson had been sick six days and had hemorrhages, but he thought that he had fully recovered and was in the pink of condition.

Reporters persisted: "Well, tell us all about it! Will he fight Sullivan and what kind of time did you have?" The Parson said that the whole combination had been treated first class and royally all around. He said that on the whole he was pleased with Jackson, who was one of the easiest men to handle he had ever met. Jackson had made friends wherever he went and had not been hissed but once, and then it was only because he refused to knockout a man with whom he was sparring with. Jackson had let up on the fighting and then the hissing started. Charlie said that didn't last more than a few moments. He described how Jackson had stepped to the front of the stage and explained that he would not punish his opponent anymore, in that he was satisfied that he had shown himself to be the better man. In a moment Davies said the hisses were turned to cheers.

First reports were that the combination had cleared $22,000 on the trip, but Charlie later said that amount had to be reduced by $1,500 of expenses incurred. He discussed Jackson's reception in Belfast. The Parson said that the people came out in force and packed the hall. He also reported that a number of members of the Pelican Club in London would be sending Peter a handsome souvenir that would not only be intrinsically valuable but an honor seldom conferred on any pugilist and that the club had engrossed a set of resolutions commending Jackson. The resolutions were being placed in a silver frame and would be presented to Jackson before he left England.

Concerning the fight with Sullivan, Davies repeated what he had written from Dublin: Jackson would fight Sullivan for $15,000 or more, just as soon as arrangements could be made. He remarked: "I am sorry about John L.'s Mississippi trouble, and hope he will get out O. K." Concerning the offer of the California Athletic Club for a Sullivan-Jackson fight for $15,000, the winner to take all, Davies said that Jackson, when shown the offer as cabled, replied that he was willing to fight for that sum or more so long as the California club was satisfied.

Davies was also asked about the stories that Slavin had been done up by a gang of toughs after his fight with Jem Smith in Belgium. He said that these stories were greatly exaggerated and that Slavin was only slightly hurt. Slavin had circulated the story as a play to gain sympathy.[697]

By the time he reached New York in January, Davies had scheduled Jackson through mid-1890. He explained that Jackson would make a tour of the country, meeting all comers in places where the contests were legal and boxing with a partner in cities where the laws would not permit the "all comers" format. He did not know what Jackson intended to do after the combination reached San Francisco. Jackson was a man of his own mind and had probably told Davies to make no commitments past San Francisco. Davies explained that Jackson needed a rest. He said, "Jackson is the squarest man with whom I have ever done business and his head can't be swelled."

Jackson had stayed behind in England for a few more days to recover from his illness. Jackson, Fitzpatrick, and Naughton were all passengers on the *S. S. Adriatic* out of Liverpool and arrived in New York on Monday, January 27. Peter was feeling and looking in splendid condition. He weighed 204 pounds, which was ten pounds over his regular fighting weight. He said that he never felt better in his life, that he had a fine trip and was not sick during the entire voyage. He said that he did not know where he would be staying in New York until after he had seem Davies, which suggests that it was part of Davies' practice to arrange accommodations for the party.

Fitzpatrick was asked about a fight with Sullivan and replied that he did not know when it would come off. Jackson told the press that he was satisfied with the purse that the C.A.C. had offered and that he had implicit confidence in that club. He also confirmed that the weather in England had not quite agreed with him, but he thought that after a little training he would be in fine condition. [698]

Jackson returns and is put back to work

It was a good thing that Jackson had recovered while traveling back to the States because Davies had lined up matinee appearances for him at Hyde & Behman's theater on Monday, January 27, the same day that Jackson disembarked, and then again on January 28, and 30, and February 1. All these appearances were with Jack Ashton. He was probably selected because Davies had cancelled the planned engagement with him just before the Jackson had left for England, and he wanted to make up for that cancellation. It was also clear that Ashton would fight a black fighter because he had recently been defeated by George Godfrey.[699] Six months earlier, men on the East Cost thought Jackson was afraid to fight Ashton. When Jackson returned writers thought that Ashton was ridiculously inferior and that Jackson could knock Ashton's head off within ten minutes.[700]

On Tuesday, January 28, 1890 the *Brooklyn Eagle* reported on Jackson-Ashton show. Davies was introduced to the audience by the editor of the *Brooklyn Eagle* and then Charlie introduced the contestants. Their match was a three-round diversion of a playful and harmless nature, tapping each other lightly and dancing away from each other with circumspection. Jackson was described as "a tall shapely negro with a long reach of arm and a good natured countenance." Ashton was described as a "hard headed" individual from Providence. The advertisement for their shows referred to the "Davies' Matchless Specialty and Athletic Combination" and stated that Jackson was willing to meet any pugilist against whom the C.A.C. might match him and with Ashton.[701]

On Wednesday, January 29, Davies took Jackson to Boston for the obvious purpose of showing Jackson in Sullivan's backyard. The exhibition in Boston on Wednesday night was sponsored by the United Athletic Club and was given at the Music Hall in Boston. Two thousand five hundred people attended. It involved four three-minute rounds and was described as tame. A police detail was in attendance and Sullivan himself was "an interested spectator." The *Boston Journal* reported that Sullivan's entrance touched off a large round of applause. He. would later say that he was satisfied that he could whip Peter.[702]

Two weeks after watching Jackson spar with Ashton, Sullivan was asked his opinion of Jackson as a fighter. Sullivan thought that the exhibition between Jackson and Ashton was poor but attributed that to Ashton being altogether too slow for Jackson. Sullivan said: "From what I saw of him he is the quickest man in the ring I ever saw. I never saw quite as much real science backed up by solid good sense." Later he said, "But I'll tell you what after all is more important still—it is hard hitting. Jackson hit hard, there is the whole point."[703]

About the time of the performance in Boston, Davies was asked his opinion of the top heavyweights and their proper ranking. Over the years he would often be asked to rank fighters in their class. In January 1890 he listed them as: (1) Sullivan, "away up at the top of the ladder," (2) Jackson, (3) Kilrain, (4) Slavin and (5) Joe McAuliffe. Two days after the exhibition in Boston the C.A.C. voted unanimously to empower the club's directors to arrange a Sullivan-Jackson match. In the East the friends of Fallon were arranging a benefit for him in Brooklyn. The attractions would include Jackson, Ashton, "Liney" Tracy, and Johnny Files.

After Jackson's appearance in Boston, Davies made a trip back to Chicago. He arrived there at five p.m. on February 5. He had been away since July 15, 1889. Charlie said that he was glad to be back. He said: "When I got to New York I felt good, but New York was not Chicago. There was no Clark Street there, and nothing else would satisfy me."[704] With Davies back on American soil, it was time to talk to his friends and protégés in the prizefighting business to get a better idea of where things were headed in the years to come. Two of Davies' former clients were busy. In February 1890 Kilrain and Muldoon were part of a combination that was on a tour in Texas. This combination was originally hatched as the idea of Muldoon, who hoped to take Sullivan, Mike Cleary, and the wrestler Ernest Roeber on the road with him. Sullivan backed out of the arrangement because of his legal problems in Mississippi. Then Muldoon's own arrest in connection with the Sullivan and Kilrain championship fight further delayed the beginning of the tour.

Kilrain, Mitchell and a kid named Corbett

In late January, Kilrain was elected instructor of boxing for the Southern Athletic Club for a term of four months with the hope that he might be given the position permanently.[705] On February 2 at New Orleans, Kilrain fought and defeated a huge heavyweight named Felix Vaquelin in only three rounds. Felix had been selected for the match because he had knocked out Lem McGregor, the "Saint Joe Kid," in early December 1889. After disposing of Vaquelin, Kilrain was critical of his ability, saying that "like all creoles, or other breed of Southerners, he hasn't got the stamina—he can't 'stand the gaff.'"[706] Kilrain then joined Muldoon's combination, and they left New Orleans on February 5 and traveled to Galveston for a show on February 7, and then on to San Antonio, Texas, to present an exhibition on February 8 at the Washington Theatre before eventually returning to New Orleans.[707]

When interviewed at San Antonio, Jake said he would challenge Sullivan just as soon as Sullivan's fight with Jackson was over. Interviewed by the San Antonio press, Kilrain said he would like to fight Sullivan again but it depended on what Sullivan would do about Jackson. He said: "I hear the negro has some skill, but I have never seen him." During his tour Kilrain sparred with Mike Cleary and was typically confronted by shouts from the crowd for "Sullivan!" The crowd was so noisy in San Antonio that Muldoon had to stop the Kilrain/Cleary bout and tell the crowd that Sullivan was thousands of miles away across the ocean and would not appear. At the end of their show in San Antonio both Kilrain and Cleary were arrested for violating the local anti-sparring ordinance and each of them had to post a two-hundred-dollar peace bond. Paying out that kind of money to the police could make it hard to make money.

On February 13, two weeks after Jackson had appeared in Boston in front of Sullivan himself, Kilrain and Muldoon reached Dallas. During their tour they had picked up a lightweight fighter named Louis Bezennah (variously spelled "Baznia," "Bezenia" and "Bezenak") as part of the combination.[708] While in Dallas, Bezennah fought a local bricklayer named Thomas James in a preliminary, or undercard, match. A $25 prize had been was offered for any man of about 140 pounds who could stand before Bezennah for four rounds. The house that night was crowded from "pit to dome." Bezennah delivered several heavy blows on James' neck when James collapsed.[709]

The circumstances that night are described by Edward Van Every in his book *Muldoon the Solid Man of Sport*: "The beaten man was removed to the dressing room still unconscious, and they went on with the show, after Muldoon had called for a doctor. . . . Word was brought to Muldoon that James could not be revived, and when he hurried back to the stage he found the doctor applying restoratives, but in vain. Kilrain peeled to his shirt and with tears streaming down his face, worked for fully an hour over the unconscious man under the physician's direction."[710]

A few minutes before midnight, James was pronounced dead. The entire Kilrain and Muldoon combination was held by the Dallas police while James' death was investigated. An inquest into James' death began at one thirty p.m. on Valentine's Day. A Dr. Leake testified that he had arrived at twelve thirty a.m. having been summoned by Muldoon, but when he arrived James was already dead. After all the testimony, the judge found no cause to hold anyone, and all the participants were released.[711] He said that no one from the gulf to the Rocky Mountains would believe that James' death was intentional. Kilrain was the most affected by the death and wept over the body of the dead man. No one doubted his sincerity. It was noted that Jake had a match scheduled in New Orleans on Monday and was worried that this affair might prejudice his case in Mississippi that was still pending on appeal. Only thirteen months later Bezennah too would be dead. He was fatally shot in a house of prostitution during the course of a fight over the affections of the woman who operated that place.[712]

With the trauma of the death of Thomas James on their minds, Kilrain, Cleary, and Bezennah all quickly returned to New Orleans. They did not leave Dallas until the evening of February 14, and Kilrain was committed to meet a young fighter from California, James J. Corbett, who had been working as the instructor of boxing for the Olympic Athletic Club of San Francisco on February 16.[713] Muldoon had selected Corbett as Jake's opponent. The Southern Athletic Club of New Orleans had asked for Muldoon's help, and he came up with Corbett without ever seeing Corbett fight. If Muldoon had known more about Corbett he might not have recommended him.

In *Muldoon the Solid Man of Sport*, Van Every claims that before the Corbett fight Kilrain wrote a letter to Davies saying that the upcoming contest was "with a chap named Corbett, from Montana."[714] In addition Kilrain's health was not good. He was reported to have advanced rheumatism so that he could not close his hands, his right shoulder was lame and his legs were very sore.

The Southern Athletic Club had offered Corbett a purse of $3,500 to appear in New Orleans the night before Mardi Gras. The purse was to be split $2,500 to the winner and $1,000 to the loser. Corbett agreed provided he would be paid $250 for his expenses. When the arrangements were made, Corbett left California and traveled to New Orleans by himself to meet Kilrain and try to make a reputation.[715] Corbett reached New Orleans on February 12 and spent time talking to the press. At the time Corbett's claim to fame was that he had defeated Joe Choynski, and Corbett said that he had accomplished the job with two broken hands.[716]

The Kilrain-Corbett match was not considered an important matter. For Kilrain his fight with Corbett would probably not be too much different from his fight with Vaquelin two weeks earlier. Corbett was so unknown outside of California that some newspapers referred to him as Mike Corbett. Kilrain and Corbett used large, five-ounce gloves and their contest was scheduled for only six rounds. To win Kilrain had to knockout Corbett. In retrospect, this seems like a very dumb agreement. However, a fight like this was only for show before a limited audience and had none of the indicia of a serious fight. Kilrain had done this sort of things many times.

On February 11 Sullivan's manager, Jack Barnett, told the press that Sullivan was offering to meet Jackson if Jackson would fight three rounds in Hoboken for gate receipts, which Barnett thought would amount to about $1,000. The *Boston Eagle* wrote that the offer was made through Parson Davies.[717] There was no chance that this match would actually happen with Jackson under contract with the C.A.C. and with the big numbers being circulated for a fight in San Francisco. Sullivan himself said that any man of sense knew perfectly well that

Jackson would not accept such a proposition. Sullivan said that he didn't intend to talk about any match until he returned from his appointment in the south. He said that Jackson was staying out of his way, and he intended to stay out of Jackson's way.[718] Jackson declined the proposal and said he was surprised that Sullivan should have made it. Jackson said he hoped to meet Sullivan in a fight after the Mississippi trouble was over.[719]

Sullivan's behavior with respect to Jackson opened him to criticism of the type found in the *Oakland Tribune*: "It is not so long ago since the champion sneered at the idea of fighting with the blankety-blank 'N_______' he talks differently, but names a big figure as the price of thus condescending to waive the color line. I, for one, would be unspeakably delighted were Jackson to make him bite the dust and cry whatever in the Bostonian's limited vocabulary may stand for _____. The color line forsooth! Why Jackson is a far bigger man today than nine tenths of the 'white trash' who have been Sully's chosen chums and boon companions, and he has done more to obliterate the color line than Fred Douglas."[720]

Davies put Jackson back to work on a tour that would take him from Hoboken back to Chicago in only a month. February 10 and 11, Jackson appeared in Hoboken at Cronheim's Theater. On the first night he appeared with a man named Billy Elluger from Jersey City and the following night with Jack Ashton. The next day Jackson moved on to Providence with Ashton.

As Davies was showing Jackson on the East Coast, the Kilrain-Corbett match took place in New Orleans. Mike McDonald, Davies' old mentor, was one of the only about five hundred people who were present to watch their fight. To the great surprise of almost everyone attending, Corbett soundly defeated Kilrain. Points were not kept, but Kilrain did not knock out Corbett as required. Moreover, he was clearly outclassed by Corbett and the young Californian reveled in his success like a school boy.[721]

Corbett had a lot of advantages. He was fresh for the fight. Kilrain had been on the road for weeks. Corbett had nothing to lose, and Kilrain had nothing much to gain other than a few more dollars. Corbett's mind was clear, and he was focused on this one fight. Only about forty-eight hours earlier Kilrain had been present at the death of a man in the ring and had been arrested. Corbett had trained for the match, and Kilrain had virtually no time to train and was in poor physical condition suffering from rheumatism. Nevertheless, Kilrain had far more experience in the ring than Corbett and a reputation to match.[722]

Muldoon described Corbett as something new in the ranks of heavyweights and a larger edition of Dempsey. Corbett had the style and speed of a much smaller man. Although the fight was with big gloves and for a limited number of rounds, Corbett shined. Even the sports in California who had previously seen Corbett fight thought that a draw was the best he could hope for in meeting Kilrain.

Sullivan never lost an opportunity to act like a gas bag, and he belittled the result of this fight. He expressed the opinion that in a finish fight with two-ounce gloves, Corbett would have been beaten soundly. Sullivan soon understood that Corbett's defeat of Kilrain created a plausible excuse for him to avoid fighting Jackson. After Corbett defeated Kilrain there was finally a white American heavyweight in the running rather than a bloom'n Brit or a black Aussie, and when that new option was weighed against to risks of fighting a black Aussie heavyweight, there was no question about whom Sullivan preferred to meet.[723]

The Corbett-Kilrain fight created a fault-line in the heavyweight ranks, but it was not yet a serious matter for Davies or Jackson who were busy with Peter's career. Beginning on February 17, Jackson and Davies' combination appeared in Washington, D.C., at Kernan's New Washington Theater on Eleventh Street, south of Pennsylvania Avenue, with ladies matinees on Tuesday and Thursdays.[724] On February 20 Jackson met "Soldier" James Walker at Keenan's Theater. Three thousand people were present for the fight and cheered Jackson when he appeared on the stage to meet the blacksmith. The matchless specialty company appeared to be raking in some matchless money.

James Walker was a powerful man and had accepted a challenge issued by Jackson offering $100 to anyone whom he failed to knock out in four rounds. This type of contest involving knocking a sub-par opponent unconscious was not something that Jackson enjoyed. Big eight-ounce gloves were used for the fight to reduce the chance of serious injury. At the outset Walker appeared cautious, but confident when he first stepped forward. Jackson then hit him with a hard left hander in the stomach and followed that left with a right-hand blow. Walker went to his knees. As he arose, he received another hard stomach blow that dazed him, and he announced that he had enough. The fight occupied just forty seconds.[725]

On February 21, Jackson fought a man called "the Herculean Gypsy" in a four-round contest for the Gypsy to earn the $100 offered by Davies. The Gypsy was described as a "Maryland fighter, weighing 250 pounds." He got in one savage blow that nearly took Peter off his feet before being put away in the second round.[726]

Davies left Washington and made a quick trip back to Chicago to conduct some business there. He told the *Chicago Tribune* that his next big undertaking would be to arrange a huge athletic carnival at the time of the World's Fair in Chicago. He planned to invite athletes from every country and have them compete for prizes. He had laid up $20,000 as a nest egg to finance his idea. This certainly demonstrated that Davies did not intend to rest on his laurels and also indicated how financially well Davies had done since taking on Jackson.[727] While in Chicago a large group of Chicago's black residents met with Davies and told him that they wanted to arrange a large reception for Jackson with Davies' cooperation. The Parson said that he would consult with Jackson and let them know Peter's disposition toward the idea. Davies started back for Baltimore on February 26 to catch up with the rest of the combination.[728]

Jackson had gone north from Washington to Baltimore, where he arrived on the evening of Monday, February 24. The large black population of Baltimore gave him a rousing welcome and almost worshiped Jackson every night that he was in Baltimore. It required a squad of police to keep back the crowds that gathered in front of the theater where he appeared nightly. The black population took the theater by storm at every performance and nearly crowded out the white customers. On the streets, in the theater, and whenever the opportunity existed, members of the black population were taunting the white sports with comparisons between Jackson and Sullivan or Kilrain.

This situation led to some white toughs seeking retribution against Jackson, who was the innocent target of their displeasure. The whites decided to retaliate and waited outside the stage entrance of the theater. After his performance on February 27, 1890 an immense crowd of blacks gathered about the stage entrance to the theater. As Jackson emerged with several people in his combination, one of whom was probably Davies, a shower of rotten eggs filled the air. Jackson was hit with the eggs along with several other men, and a race riot was prevented only by police action.[729]

On March 3 the Davies' combination starring Jackson appeared in Jersey City. Those who arrived in the city that morning included: Jackson, Ashton, Naughton, Fitzpatrick, Johnnie Kohn, and Davies. When Jackson was still in Baltimore, particulars were released about the benefit to be given for Fallon. The show was to take place at the Palace Rink on Grand Street in Brooklyn on the evening of March 4. Other boxing matches that evening would include Billy Myer-Jack Fogarty, Johnny Files-Jimmy Lynch, and Jack Hopper. This was a great list of fighters appearing for the Fallon benefit.[730]

On March 4 the combination was in Brooklyn. Davies and Frank Stevenson of New York managed the event. Stevenson was a founding member of the Puritan Athletic Club. About fifteen hundred people were present for the show. Included in the audience were Police Inspector McLaughlin and Captain Short, together with several city officials, politicians and sporting men from neighboring cities. After the preliminary fights George Dixon was introduced. Dixon was a black featherweight from Boston who had recently fought and defeated "Cal" McCarthy of Jersey City. Dixon held great promise and was an exciting fighter.

Jackson and Fallon

After Dixon's introduction, there was supposed to be a friendly Ashton-Fallon match. For reasons that were never explained, Fallon told his friends before the exhibition that he intended to knock out both Ashton and Jackson. When the exhibition with Ashton started, Fallon deliberately back-heeled Ashton and then fell on him with his entire weight. Not satisfied, Fallon hit Ashton several times while he was still on the floor. Ashton realized what was happening and he began fighting for blood. Amid great excitement, Captain Short jumped into the ring and forced the pugilists apart and escorted Fallon off the stage as the crowd hissed his behavior.[731]

Jackson was to spar Fallon next, and they started out their appearance with the intended light sparring. However, Fallon soon started making vicious lunges at Jackson. Fallon finally got in one or two blows that irritated Jackson, and he then shot out his right staggering Fallon. In the second round, Jackson went after Fallon and pounded him heavily with several "rib roasters." Fallon was hopelessly beaten, but persisted in his efforts to try to injure Jackson. Fitzpatrick and Captain Short jumped into the ring and stood between the two men. Jackson had traveled at considerable inconvenience to appear at this benefit for Fallon, and the general conclusion was that Jackson had received very bad treatment at the hands of Fallon. At the end of this mess Jackson and Ashton sparred two rounds in what was described as "a beautiful exhibition." Jackson received a perfect ovation from the crowd, and Fallon lost many friends that evening.[732]

A fat man named Lambert

The next night at Troy, New York, Davies had arranged a show with a local heavyweight named Gus Lambert, a powerful man who weighed about 220 pounds and was sometimes called the champion of Montreal, Canada. He was considerably shorter than Jackson and appeared to be fat, but he had appeared professionally as a fighter and a wrestler. Davies made the introduction that evening and said it was his intention to have Jackson spar four rounds with Ashton, but he knew that many people wanted to see Jackson's real skill and explained that he had offered Lambert $100 if he would spar four rounds with Jackson.

At the outset Lambert seemed to be afraid of Jackson, but then he began to rush at Jackson and grab him around the waist. Before the second round was over, the crowd was screaming, and Lambert followed the same approach he had adopted in the first round. Jackson soon saw that Lambert had no intention of fighting. Lambert then picked up Jackson and ran across the platform and tried to throw him over the ropes, but Ashton caught him. Finally, a little fighting took place, but it appeared that both men were winded. Some reports say that Lambert staggered Jackson. Whatever happened, Lambert stayed the four rounds and earned $100. This news then went out on the wire with claims being made that Jackson had been knocked out by Lambert.[733]

Other stories circulated that Jackson had been drinking quite heavily during the preceding afternoon. The story was that on March 4, several friends had given a reception for Jackson that began at midnight. This reception could not have happened until after Jackson's appearance at the Fallon benefit. At the party "champagne flowed like water from a spout on a rainy day" and Jackson emptied his glass often, forgetting that he had to meet Lambert.[734] Jackson slept little on March 5 and barely had time to catch the train to Troy for the match with Lambert. Still others claimed that Jackson has been "crooking his elbow" too often and that he had "developed a fondness for the juice of the grape and late hours."[735]

The matches for Jackson continued at a dizzying pace. On Friday, March 7, the combination including Ashton, Fitzpatrick, Davies, and Jackson all took lunch at Syracuse, New York, on the way to Buffalo. That evening they reached Cleveland where Jackson denied that Lambert had nearly knocked him out, and Davies said that Lambert was a professional wrestler who trained for weeks only to run away.[736]

Davies was quoted in the *Philadelphia Inquirer*: "He didn't fight! He only grabbed Jackson around the waist and tried to throw him. In fact, all Lambert did was to run around the stage trying to keep away from Jackson, and when he failed in that he would duck his head, rush in and catch Peter around the waist."[737]

Davies pointed out that Lambert would agree to no one for referee but a saloon-keeper friend and then insisted on eight-ounce gloves. He asked: "Now, what can anyone do with pillows?"[738] The whole affair with Lambert would often be raised to criticize Jackson's ability as a fighter but that was a baseless claim.

On Saturday, March 8, Jackson appeared for an exhibition with Reddy Gallagher, who was one of Davies' former clients. They did not spar until after midnight and then only for two rounds, so the match technically happened on Sunday, March 9. It was reported that Jackson "kept that energetic young Irishman continually guessing" about his whereabouts. When he left the ring, Gallagher said, "That chap is away out of sight."

On Sunday evening, a reception was given Jackson by many of the black people of Cleveland. Jackson had hundreds of callers who assured him that they were satisfied that he could defeat Sullivan in a finish fight. Jackson was always humble in the face of such assurances. The only place a heavyweight could win a fight was in the ring and all the hype and assurances would not change that simple reality.

Curious crowds followed Jackson around the streets of Cleveland and were said to have given "the mysterious countersign necessary to pass the outer door of a Cleveland dram shop on a Sunday," but Jackson politely declined. From Cleveland Jackson went to Mt. Clemens, Michigan, for a week of rest.[739] The *St. Paul Daily Globe* reported on March 16 that Jackson was about to return to the road for shows in Columbus and Dayton, Ohio, and Louisville, Kentucky.[740]

Davies and the others reached Chicago on March 24, and Jackson took a room at the Briggs House on the northeast corner of Randolph and Wells Streets, just west of the courthouse and not far from the McVicker's Theater. The combination had spent a few days in Mt. Clemens taking hot mineral baths and just relaxing.[741] The Chicago Fishing and Hunting Club wrote to Davies to say that they wanted to give Jackson a reception on his arrival in the Windy City. Jackson then sent a letter ahead declining their offer.[742] Peter said he was personally opposed to ostentatious display (he had already been given many such displays), and furthermore thought "such receptions entirely out of place when greeting a man in my profession." Perhaps he was tired of receptions because he had been the object of many for the last six months.

A few days before Davies returned to Chicago, the Mississippi Supreme Court reversed Sullivan's conviction on the grounds that the statute under which he was charged was too vague to be fairly applied. Sullivan would not spend a year in a Mississippi prison, and his excuses for avoiding a fight with Jackson were disappearing.[743]

Davies kept Jackson working. On Tuesday, March 25, Jackson appeared at Battery D and sparred with "Professor" Thomas Chandler and then three rounds with Ashton.[744] There were more than five thousand customers for this exhibition. With Ashton, Jackson ducked, countered, and landed with both hands in a way that showed him to be one of the cleverest heavyweights who ever appeared at Battery D. It seemed that Ashton was allowed to stay with Jackson only on his sufferance. The match was described as clever, and Peter made "an exceedingly good impression. His superior reach told against Ashton, but he was clever on his feet and quick as a flash in avoiding his opponent's blows." Ashton too showed cleverness and "gave a good exhibition of scientific movements, but his cleverest motions failed to catch Jackson off his guard." Stories published before the exhibition reported that Jackson was also going to spar a big "Stock-Yards boxer" named Mike Queenan, but that did not happen.[745]

Additional engagements followed. Jackson was spotted at the train depot in Dayton, Ohio, on his way to Louisville, Kentucky,[746] where he met a man named Dick Keating and knocked him out in one round. On the morning of March 29, while the combination was in Louisville, a large tornado struck the central part of the city, and more than one hundred fifty people were killed. The fate of the Davies' combination was not known, but around midday it was learned that Davies, Jackson and the rest of the company were all right. From Louisville they went to Cincinnati, where Jackson appeared at the People's Theatre on the afternoon of April 1.[747]

The *Cincinnati Commercial Gazette* wrote: "Long before the curtain went up for the first act at the theater last night the house was filled, and as the time approached for the modern wonder of the prize ring to appear there wasn't standing room." The newspaper also reported that Davies said that he had witnessed all ring battles of any prominence in America and that if Sullivan and Jackson came together it would be a terrific fight. The appearances in Cincinnati were limited to punching a ball for points against local challengers. Another large audience filled the People's Theatre on April 2, and Jackson "displayed even greater cleverness than on the previous night and when he wound up his performance he was warmly applauded."[748] The combination continued to appear though April 7.[749] Local papers reported that Jackson's stay in Cincinnati was marked by one continual debauch that continued into the early morning hours with many cracking bottles of champagne provided by his numerous friends.[750]

Before the engagement in Cincinnati ended, the local police notified Davies that they would prohibit even the ball-punching exhibitions. While discussing this development with Davies, the Australian offered to bet Davies a seventy-five-dollar suit of clothes that the Parson would not punch the ball in front of a crowd. Davies agreed to the bet and donned a set of tights and appeared on the stage before two thousand spectators. Jackson came to the footlights on stage and announced: "Charles E. Davies, the famous pugilist, will now fight four rounds." Davies went to work on the punching ball and didn't hit it very often, but the crowd caught on to the joke and greeted the Parson with a big round of applause for his effort. Jackson paid off the $75, and Davies then contributed that money to fund for the victims of the recent Louisville tornado. The manager and his fighter were getting along well and had turned into a good pair of entertainers.[751]

Corbett's impact

In fact, the entire troupe was making a good impression and a lot of money, but there was a cloud growing over their efforts. Articles began to appear contending that Jackson's sun had been eclipsed by the beautiful California boy, Jim Corbett. Predictions based on Sullivan's nature and disposition were that he would fight Corbett—if only because of his color—much sooner than he would fight Jackson.[752] Two years later these predictions would come true. Some claimed that the prospects of a Sullivan-Corbett ten-round glove contest were actually bright.

Davies, working through the Puritan Athletic Club, was attempting to alter the tide. On April 11, 1890, the Puritan agreed to put up a purse of $20,000 for a Sullivan-Jackson match. The purse was to be deposited with Richard K. Fox for a fight to take place within three months after signing the articles. Davies may have felt comfortable working with the Puritan Club because Jackson's contract with the C.A.C. was about to expire. Certainly, his membership in the club put him in a position of perceived conflict with the C.A.C.'s offer. Davies may have felt relieved of this conflict because the C.A.C. had refused to raise its offer to meet Sullivan's demand. He may have believed that his obligation to Jackson trumped his obligation to the C.A.C.[753]

Jackson did not return to California on schedule. April 19 found Davies and Jackson in St. Louis at the Olympic Theater at the invitation of Pat Short. When they arrived, a large crowd of black citizens of St. Louis were awaiting their arrival. One of the men leading the delegation was Henry Bridgewater, a saloon owner who was also a large contributor to an industrial school for black children in Kirkwood, Missouri. Henry had been the manager of a black baseball team known as the Black Stockings. These were distinguished people anxious to see a man of their own color who was rising to the top of his profession and proving that a black man could succeed at the highest levels of athletics.[754]

The Parson's experience with Kilrain and Mitchell at the end of 1888 had taught him that a sparring exhibition would likely be prevented in St. Louis. So he made plans for Jackson and Ashton to appear at Brotherhood Park, a large outdoor theater. They were to give exhibitions of hitting the light bag, at which they were both experts. Davies spiced up the performance by offering $100 to any person who could hit the ball more times than Jackson could in a prescribed period of time. The appearance was part of a program including the 100-yard dash in heats, 200- yard hurdles, the hammer throw, and a baseball toss. There was also a baseball game between the Home Comforts and the St. Louis Reds.[755] The gates opened at twelve thirty p.m. with the sporting events starting at three o'clock. The *Police Gazette* reported that nearly fifteen thousand spectators assembled for the appearance but that the local police prevented a Jackson-Ashton exhibition. It is likely that this was a misunderstanding of what happened. It is true that Jackson and Ashton did not spar, but that was not planned in the first place.[756]

On April 22, 1890 Corbett passed through Chicago on his way from New York to San Francisco. He was asked about Kilrain's repeated demands for a rematch and said that he would pay no attention to Kilrain, having already bested him. "Denver" Ed Smith had challenged Corbett, who said that he would fight Smith only if the Olympic Club agreed to the match. Most of the attention during the interview was given to Sullivan. Corbett said he would fight Sullivan either for a limited number of rounds or to a finish if the Olympic Club would consent to the match.[757]

Jackson was not in Chicago when Corbett passed through but had returned to Mt. Clemens, where he had stopped a month earlier. On April 24 Davies received a telegram from Jackson saying he would accept the C.A.C. offer to fight Sullivan for $20,000. This was nothing new. Jackson had agreed to accept the offer several times before late April 1890.[758] Publishing Jackson's acceptance was probably only an effort to shake something loose, but it may have been Jackson's personal response to the proposal of the Puritan Club. If his club matched the price of Davies' club, then he intended to sign with the C.A.C. Before coming back to Chicago, Jackson and Ashton went back to Buffalo for a three-round exhibition on May 3.[759] Some reports say that he was given a reception in Philadelphia on May 2 before returning to Buffalo.[760]

Although Davies was keeping the combination employed and making excellent money, it seems that he was getting irritated about the failure of the C.A.C. to conclude arrangements for a match with Sullivan. Davies did not have the control he liked to exercise. He probably had a better understanding of Sullivan and what it would take to get him into the ring with Jackson than the directors of the California club. Davies told the *Police Gazette* that the C.A.C. was holding a mortgage on Jackson (as if he were chattel property) and blocking other matches that could be made until Jackson first met Sullivan.

The dynamic of the situation had to be difficult for Davies. Jackson had been sent to him by the C.A.C., but there was string attached because he remained under contract to the club. Davies had promoted Jackson's career and helped make him world famous beyond what anyone might have hoped, but he could not finish the job. Davies was described as "a cool, calculating business man."[761] He was given credit for having "piloted Jackson successfully over the 'breakers' which always are ahead of pugilists, both in England and in this country." However, when push came to shove, it seemed that Jackson remained more committed to the C.A.C. than to Davies.

Denver "Ed" Smith – a rough customer

Davies had a final night of work in Chicago for Jackson before they started back to San Francisco. This job was arranged with the Parson's friend Muldoon. During the year after the Sullivan-Kilrain championship fight, Muldoon had enhanced his reputation as a trainer by taking charge of "Denver" Ed Smith, a fighter out of Birmingham, England. Smith had shown promise and had worked for Bat Masterson. In 1889 Smith's career was moving up the ladder. In February of that year he showed well in a fight with George LaBlanche. They fought in Denver, Colorado, but there was no result before the police stopped the match. Smith had then knocked out Patsy Daley in New York City and Mike Cleary in Hot Springs, Arkansas. Cleary had demanded a rematch, and Smith agreed and went into training with Muldoon as his mentor. On Thursday, April 3, 1890, Smith met Cleary a second time in Hot Springs. The combatants used four-ounce gloves and this time Smith knocked Cleary out in the first round. These achievements marked Smith as a comer, and his relationship with Muldoon, who was a close friend of Davies, formed the basis for a Smith-Jackson match at Battery D in Chicago on May 19.[762]

Reports of this Smith-Jackson fight say that between four thousand and six thousand people attended. There is no question that Jackson could draw a big gate. Police were present for the fight, and based on Davies' past experiences there was probably a good chance that they would stop the match with the slightest excuse. To remind everyone that nothing too rough should take place, Captain Lewis of Chicago's Central District sat at ringside. Because of these circumstances it is likely that Davies had cautioned Jackson before the match about getting too aggressive with Smith. He had given this type of instruction in earlier matches in Chicago.

Charles Hermann attended this match and recalled that evening:

> In 1888 a great match was arranged by "Parson" Davies between "Denver" Ed Smith and one of the greatest boxers of all time, Peter Jackson, for whom no match could be arranged for the World Championship because John L. Sullivan said he drew the color line. It was staged in Battery "D" and the house was packed. Young lads even climbed on the rafters above the audience. I didn't have the price of admission, and anyway the house was sold out. That's the only time that I ever crashed a gate. I knew "Parson" Davies was a friend of Tom Connors. The "Parson" was outside at the entrance. I walked up to him and said I had a message for Tom Connors, that he was inside, and that I must see him. The "Parson" looked at me suspiciously, thought for a while, and then gave me a hard push through the gate and said for me to hurry out. Well, I forgot to "hurry out" until the fight was over. I even found a good seat and everybody had to wait until Inspector Shea arrived. He was on time and as he walked down the aisle, the great crowd gave him a hand. It was a good fight.[763]

Hermann provided an interesting follow up. Although he did not provide a date for the events described below, they probably took place sometime about 1895:

> A few years later "Parson" Davies and I became good friends. I was with him, Tom Hanton, and Smiley Corbett one day at the old Schiller Cafe in the basement of the Schiller Building. "Parson" Davies ordered a quart of champagne. When the "Parson" wasn't looking, I paid the bartender for that bottle. When the "Parson" placed a five dollar bill on the counter it was pushed back to him by the bartender with the remark that I had already paid for that bottle. Then, the "Parson" looked at me and asked, "Why did you do that?" I then explained how in 1888 at Battery "D" he had been "soft" enough to let me put it over on him and crash the gate to the Jackson-Smith fight. Tom, Smiley, and I gave the "Parson" the laugh. The "Parson" then said, "Let me see; that was seven years ago. How about the amount of interest due on that debt?" I was then obliged to buy another quart.[764]

The Smith-Jackson match was to be for five rounds with four-ounce gloves. Interest in the match was enhanced because Smith had been trained by Muldoon, who had been Sullivan's trainer and also because Smith had knocked out Cleary. Stories circulated that some of the horse hair had been taken out of the gloves before the match. If that happened, it would have been done secretly because fighting with less than four-ounce gloves was prohibited in Chicago.

In the first two rounds Smith was badly hammered. He dropped to his knees two or three times in the first round, depending on which newspaper account is reviewed. No one thought that "Denver Ed" would actually face Jackson for the third round, given the severe punishment he had received in the first two. The press noted Jackson's long reach and ability to deliver left-hand jabs without being hit by his opponent. Smith did come out for the third round, and to the surprise of observers, Jackson appeared to be winded. He was heavy and not in good shape. He continued to hammer Smith, who got in some good blows too. Both men were groggy when the contest ended, and the referee announced that although Smith had made a wonderfully good fight, he must give the battle to Jackson on points. Muldoon did not lose the opportunity to make news and offered to back Smith for $5,000 against any man in the world, barring Sullivan, McAuliffe and Jackson. The performance at Battery D had to be a disappointment for Davies, who had become a cheerleader for Jackson and had developed admiration for him as a fighter.[765]

On the evening of May 21, Davies, Jackson, Ashton, and Fitzpatrick left Chicago for California with scheduled stops at Omaha, Denver, Salt Lake City, and Ogden via the Chicago, Burlington and Quincy Railroad, commonly called the Burlington Route.[766] The night that the combination left Chicago, Tommy

White and Billy Brennan fought on a pleasure boat named the *Josie Davidson* on Lake Michigan. Their match was with skin-tight gloves. Harry Gilmore and Mike Queenen (the stockyards man who was supposed to spar Jackson) were seconds for Tommy White. A man named Bill Richards was behind Brennan. The match went forty-eight rounds in the pouring rain before White's seconds threw up the sponge. During the match, Brennan knocked out four of White's teeth and broke his nose. From the twenty-third round forward, the bone of White's nose was sticking out through his skin. Davies had nothing to do with this match, but the accounts of the match and its brutality fueled the anti-prizefighting element. Billy Brennan, the man who administered the beating to White, would soon play an important role in Davies' life.

In Denver on May 25, 1890 Jackson appeared at the Grand Opera House, where he and Ashton sparred for three rounds before a number of black members of the Denver population. The next night they were in Salt Lake City, where Jackson appeared at the Golden Gate Athletic Club. The *Salt Lake Tribune* reported that the club's rooms were crowded, and the best of the sporting element of Salt Lake City were on hand to see the Jackson-Ashton exhibition. Neither Jackson nor Ashton went there to knock each other out, but they did some pretty sparring.

The typical western tour route – Map prepared by Jill Thomas

The full entertainment that night would have made Davies proud. It began with Professor James Messenger, the champion cannonball tosser and club swinger of the world. How many people were in competition for that title is not known. Messenger held down the audience for twenty minutes, and they were perfectly satisfied to watch him while Jack Ashton and a fighter named Strader donned their tights and had a four-round set-to for points. Ashton won, but Strader was credited with doing some good work and scored well. Then Sam Fitzpatrick sparred with a man named Jim Williams. Other matches included a fellow named Frank Fitzgerald, who had a match with an unknown, and by Davis and Black, two local lightweights. Colonel Ed Kelly officiated as master of ceremonies, but then gave way to Parson Davies, who, "in a neat little speech, recalled his past visits to Salt Lake, and paid a deserved compliment to its sporting men. Then he introduced Jackson and Ashton, and both were received with applause, their records were known, and it required nothing more than an amateur, to see that they were built like fighting men from away back."[767]

A reporter from the *Salt Lake Tribune* attempted to interview Jackson but without much success, as Jackson seemed to display one of his rare instances of petulance:

> Q: Well, I suppose it's right that you are willing to meet Sullivan anywhere or any time?
>
> A: Yes, that's what I said, but then I have nothing to say.
>
> Q: How about Joe McAuliffe, will you give him that return match?
>
> A: I meet him once, you know that don't you— well, I have nothing to say about any man.
>
> Q: But will you meet him on the same terms?
>
> A: I told you once and you ask me again. I've, got my hands full. Now you can say anything you like and I won't contradict it.

That ended the interview.

After his appearance at the Golden Gate Athletic Club, Jackson was tendered a reception by the black population of Salt Lake City (presumably a small group). Along with Davies, Ashton, Fitzpatrick, and the rest of the combination, Peter found his way down to the Elks Club. Of course, Davies had a long relationship with the Elks. Jackson was given the seat of honor at the reception and was entertained by the Salt Lake Glee Club. Wine "flowed freely, speeches were made, songs were sung and toasts were drunk too until an early hour this morning, when the party broke up to give the champion a chance to sleep before leaving for Ogden where he will appear this evening. On behalf of the colored ladies of Salt Lake, he was presented with a handsome floral design, and in a neat speech returned his thanks, and expressed a wish to meet all his Salt Lake friends again."[768]

Jackson returns to San Francisco

On the night that Jackson was in Salt Lake City, Sullivan sent a telegram to Muldoon, who was in Chicago, asking him if he would return to New York and take charge of him for an expected contest with Jackson. Muldoon answered that he would do so and immediately packed up and headed east to make arrangements. That same night Davies probably used his time to make arrangements for his return trip from San Francisco. On his way back to Chicago he would be accompanied by Ashton. It is likely that Davies knew that as soon as Jackson's contract with the C.A.C. expired, he intended to return to Australia.[769] Ultimately Jackson would leave on the *Mariposa* headed for Sydney via Honolulu on July 28. Davies' relationship with Jackson ended at this point and was not renewed until months later.

After appearing in Ogden on May 27 at the Novelty Theater,[770] the combination took the train on to Oakland. They arrived there at three o'clock on the morning of May 29.[771] In a beautifully written story, the *Oakland Tribune* reported that the "wind whistled dismally thru the telegraph wires at Sixteenth Street station this morning and the fog rolled overhead in great sheets and banks and a dozen or more sports stood on the platform with their hands in their pockets and wished that they had not dressed in summer clothes and spring overcoats. There were a substantial number of colored sports dressed in the lightest of light spring suits. They buttoned their coats tight around their throats at the expense of their many colored vests and gathered to discuss the great Peter who they were there to meet."[772]

When the train had stopped, the crowd boarded and proceeded to a Pullman sleeper where Jackson was waiting with Davies, Ashton, and Fitzpatrick. Jackson was wearing a black Prince Albert coat, striped trousers and a black vest plentifully speckled by red. He was met by many directors of the C.A.C. who had come to welcome him as a committee.

The questions immediately began about a possible match with Sullivan. Jackson replied: "I don't know anything about the date or the arrangements. I will do just as the California club wants me to in those matters."

The questions persisted: "But is the fight coming off?"

He answered with a smile: "Sometime."

"Has any agreement been reached, or any articles signed?"

"I will tell you the way the affair stands," said Jackson. "Sullivan hasn't got that Mississippi affair off of his hands yet, and he won't have, for some little time yet. When he does it will be time enough to talk about our fight. Sullivan can do nothing until his troubles over the Kilrain fight are ended. After that I am to have the first fight with him."

"Has any date been set?"

"Sometime in the future," replied Jackson with an expansive smile.[773]

That night Davies and Jackson attended an fight between Bob Fitzsimmons and Billy McCarthy at the C.A.C. Bob knocked out McCarthy in nine rounds.[774]

The situation with respect to prizefighting in California had deteriorated in the year that Jackson had been away. He and Ashton had put on nearly twenty sparring exhibitions after Peter had returned to the United States. The tour with Jackson had been a good thing for Ashton, whose stock as a contender had tumbled earlier when he was defeated by Godfrey. Jackson and Ashton expected to put on another tame show in San Francisco on June 1 at the Grand Opera House, but police interfered and prevented the exhibition from taking place.[775]

After the meeting between Jackson and Ashton failed, the C.A.C. met to discuss its business. Parson Davies attended the meeting and told the directors that he intended to bring a number of wrestlers west to show on the Pacific Coast. In particular, he intended to bring Evan Lewis. Davies said he thought that wrestling would be popular in the West. In addition to the Jackson-Ashton exhibition, the C.A.C. planned a La Blanche-"Young" Mitchell match for $3,000.[776] Sam Fitzpatrick was chosen as trainer for Mitchell and was considered a sure-thing in preparing him for the match. But that fight too was in question because of La Blanche's weight. Jackson had visited with La Blanche in Chicago, when he weighed more than 180 pounds. For his contest with Mitchell, George had agreed to appear at only 154 pounds.[777]

West Coast newspapers had joined a chorus questioning Jackson's ability and his status as the leading heavyweight contender. On June 6, the *Oakland Tribune* questioned his ability to be a champion. It noted that on his return to California, Jackson had not received anything like the welcome he had expected. This happened even though while touring, he had always been loyal to the C.A.C. and lived up to all his contractual obligations.

The *Tribune* noted in particular reports of Peter's dissipation from alcohol and of his "comparatively mediocre" showing against "Denver Ed" Smith. The *Tribune* opined that Jackson's stock had "bearded" and outside those of his own race, most people thought that even if given a chance, Jackson could not defeat Sullivan. Later the *Tribune* agreed with statements made by Frank Slavin that Jackson was the most scientific and prettiest of boxers, but he could not hit hard. Slavin referred to Jackson as "Punch," and said that he was a "bad stayer if a fellow gives him trouble."[778] Two years later the man who could not hit hard did up the man with the big mouth.

With these disappointing opinions circulating in prizefighting circles, a serious and tragic event that had a long-lasting impact on prize fighting in California occurred on the evening of June 9. Two waiters, Harry McBride and Frank Larue, quarreled over a girl. To settle their differences they decided to go to the Golden Gate Club to fight it out. This was not done on the spur of the moment; many people were involved in producing this fight, and eventually more than sixty arrest warrants were issued in connection with it. The match was to be with three-ounce gloves. The two men fought twelve rounds and worked with a referee and seconds. At the end of the twelfth round, McBride was unconscious and blood was flowing from his ears, nose and mouth, and his face and body were terribly bruised and mauled. A physician was called and determined that McBride had a broken blood vessel in his head. McBride died the next night, and several club directors were among those arrested. His death effectively ended fighting in California for months to come.[779] Within a few days, Davies exchanged good-byes with Jackson and went back to work. Peter did not leave California until July 27 as a cabin passenger aboard the *Mariposa*, reaching Sydney on August 21.[780]

Immediately after delivering Jackson back into the hands of the C.A.C., Davies' attention turned back east. On June 2, he telegraphed from San Francisco saying that he and Ashton would be back in Salt Lake City on June 12.[781] Ashton would then engage in a friendly glove contest for points with a man named George Williams who defeated Steve Wilson in Salt Lake City on June 6 for the privilege of sparring with Ashton.[782] On June 11 a notice was published in the *Salt Lake Tribune*: "Owing to a misunderstanding 'The Parson Davies' Combination' could not secure the Theater or Opera House for their exhibition. Saturday evening. We therefore wish to announce to the public that we have rented the Golden Gate Club rooms for the occasion on the above date. Respectfully, Edwards and Burton, Managers." [783] June 13 found Davies and Ashton both in Salt Lake City registered as guests at the Walker House as C. E. Davies of Chicago and J. Ashton of Providence. That day Ashton would meet an "unknown." The *Tribune* said that the unknown was from Des Moines, Iowa and that Mike Conley had refused to meet him. This last statement was meant to infer that the mystery man was a dangerous customer. The fight was for $250.[784]

Davies put on a great show on the evening of June 14. The *Tribune* reported that: "Parson Davies managed the affair, and that is equivalent to saying that everything was on the square and above board. The Parson has a reputation that he couldn't afford to monkey with, and he didn't monkey with it last night but gave what he said he would, a first class exhibition." Ed Kelly, who had been the master of ceremonies a few weeks earlier when Jackson was still with the combination, served in the same capacity on this evening.

Several local fighters appeared along with Messanger the cannon ball juggler. The featured event of the evening was the contest involving Ashton and the two-hundred-fifty-dollar purse that had been put up for anyone who could stand before him eight rounds. Ashton was introduced along with the unknown, who turned out to be a man named Noble. He hailed from Iowa and had a good record in that state. The two men were of even weight. Noble showed well, but he tired and was knocked out by Ashton in the fifth round. After reporting on this fight, the *Tribune* noted that "Evan Lewis, the strangler will be here in about a month. Parson Davies will manage him."[785]

Davies sent a telegram back to Chicago on June 20 saying to expect a match in mid-July between Ashton and a "well-known" heavyweight.[786] The first speculation was that Ashton would meet Denver Ed Smith, but others said that Davies would not allow Ashton to meet Smith. The story then circulated that Ashton was matched to fight Glover and that their contest would be under Davies' management.[787] Frank Garrard and Billy Brennan were to fight in a preliminary match.[788]

The Parson Davies' International Vaudevilles were at the Bijou Opera House in St. Paul beginning June 22. The show included "Champion Athletes!" and Evan Lewis, the wrestler, as well as a big specialty show. It did not include

Ashton. Matinees were offered on Wednesday and Saturday with the last show on Sunday, June 29.[789]

Davies and Ashton were in Chicago on June 21 to meet with Glover and conclude arrangements for his match with Ashton.[790] The *Chicago Tribune* reported that Davies was planning entertainment for July 3 that might include a match between Frank Garrard and Billy Brennan, as well as an Ashton-Glover match. Garrard and Brennan were to box for a prize offered by Davies.

In early July 1890 the weather in Chicago was extremely hot and all the fighters stopped training a few days before the match. Davies revealed that he intended to have Dempsey present on July 3 to act as referee for the match. When that information was published, Reddy Gallagher came to Chicago to challenge Dempsey. Davies had probably asked Dempsey to referee and then told Gallagher to be at the contest to challenge Dempsey in order to increase the gate for the night. He also announced that Gerrard and Brennan were to fight first, to be followed by Ashton and Glover.[791]

Billy Brennan is killed

The evening of entertainment on July 3 ended abruptly with the death of Billy Brennan. This was the second death in the ring within three-and-a-half weeks. The Gerrard-Brennan match was supposed to be a five-round contest with four-ounce gloves. Gallagher acted as referee, Sailor Brown was one of the two seconds for Brennan, and Harry Gilmore was a second for Gerrard.[792]

There was bad blood between Brennan and Gerrard well before they fought. This bad blood existed because Brennan had half-killed Tommy White in their fight on May 21. Some wrote that the Brennen-White fight had been a seventy-eight-round battle and after its conclusion uncomplimentary words passed between Garrard, who was White's friend, and Brennan. But there was nothing unusual about uncomplimentary words between fighters before a match.[793]

Brennan was no match for Gerrard. In the second round Gerrard sensed Brennan's weakness and rushed him, hitting him at will. Brennan then grabbed Gerrard's legs and threw him heavily. No foul was allowed. In the fourth round Brennan came to scratch quickly, but Gerrard continued to pound him around the ring. Brennan then rushed Gerrard in an attempt to hold on and avoid punishment. Gerrard tried to shake him and in the effort to throw off Brennan, the two men fell off balance, and Brennan's head hit the floor. He did not move a muscle and was counted out.[794]

Brennan was carried from the ring and placed on a rug in one of the parlors in Battery D. Some reports say that a doctor was in the audience and jumped into the ring to attend to Brennan before he was taken away, but this probably did not happen. It does appear that Davies summoned Dr. Francis R. Sherwood, and when he arrived, Brennan was ashen with heavy, labored breathing. The doctor gave Brennan injections of brandy and administered aromatic spirits of ammonia without results. Strong coffee was also administered.

While Brennan was dying, two friendly preliminary matches were taking place. Word then came to the ring that Brennan had died and the proceedings were stopped. The crowd quietly left the building. Both Gerrard and Sailor Brown were placed under arrest, and the police stood guard outside the room where Brennan lay dead. Paddy Carroll, who had acted as master of ceremonies, Gilmore and the wrestler Jack McInerney were all locked up. Captain Lewis placed Davies under only nominal arrest. Dempsey left town quickly and went to Saint Louis, where he appeared at Brotherhood Park the next day for a sparring match that was stopped by the police.[795]

Brennan's body was taken to an undertaker and an autopsy was performed by Dr. Ludwig Hektoen, who regularly performed autopsies in Chicago. He was later head of the McCormick Memorial Institute for Infectious Diseases, founded in 1902 by Harold F. McCormick in memory of a son who died of scarlet fever. The autopsy showed that Brennan had suffered a brain hemorrhage and an inquest was scheduled.

Ashton and Davies were supposed to leave that same night for a match before the Buffalo Athletic Club with Jim Brennan on the Fourth of July. Ashton begged Davies to leave Chicago as planned. Davies' response was: "Not for a thousand. That boy (pointing to Brennan) can have my time, my money, and my company. I'm not running away." Ashton left for Buffalo alone and Davies remained to face the music and foot the bills. Ashton arrived in Buffalo on July 5 and agreed to serve as the referee in a fight there.[796]

Gerrard was locked up at the Harrison Street Station. He had broken down and was crying like a child. Davies came to the station the following day. He told Gerrard to be of good cheer and that all would turn out well. On Davies' order, an excellent restaurant dinner was sent to Gerrard at the jail.[797]

The coroner's jury convened on July 5 concluded that Brennan's death was caused by an accident and was not intentional. Davies occupied the front seat at the hearing. He was described as having "a sad smile of resignation" and told reporters that he would consider himself under arrest even though he had not been charged. Davies was given permission to sit next to the deputy coroner and suggest questions to be asked to witnesses. The *Chicago Tribune* reported that he "took advantage of this privilege to make light of the 'accident' and to diffuse about him an apologetic sentiment to the effect that 'accidents will happen.'" Gallagher and Paddy Carroll had first refused to testify, but after Davies voluntarily told of the events leading to Brennan's death, they both changed their stance and confirmed the Parson's explanation. The autopsy suggested that Brennan had some preexisting injuries that contributed to his death. It is likely that these injuries had been sustained during his forty-eight round match with Tommy White only about five weeks earlier.[798]

No one seemed to know anything about Brennan's family or what to do with his body after his death. Before the fight Brennan had been described as coming from Brooklyn. After his death Davies went to Brooklyn and searched for a week without finding a trace of Brennan's relatives. Davies then paid for his burial in Chicago. Months later, in mid-December 1890, it was learned that Brennan was actually Jacob Adams of Cleveland. In 1888 Adams had left his home and gone to Battle Creek, Michigan, then to Latin America and California before assuming the persona of Billy Brennan from Brooklyn and drifting back east to Chicago.[799]

The day after the inquest ended, the *Chicago Tribune* published an editorial sharply critical of prizefighting in general. It was typical of that newspaper to have little in the way of human response to any tragedy: "It is absurd longer to claim that these affairs, with which this city has been disgraced so often, are contests of skill and endurance. They are in point of fact prize fights." The *Tribune* found that Brennan's death was of no special account to the community at large. Decent people, it said, would show no remorse over Brennan's death and concluded that he had been murdered. It concluded by demanding that Mayor Creiger and Chicago's Chief of Police take action.[800]

The next day the mayor announced that no more sparring matches will be allowed in Chicago. The year between July 1889 and July 3, 1890, had been exciting professionally and had greatly enhanced Davies' reputation. He had also been very successful financially. That period seemed to end for awhile with Jacob Adams' death.

While fighting in Chicago was again brought to a standstill, there were important events taking place in the profession. A young man from New Zealand by way of Australia and named Bob Fitzsimmons had arrived in the United States. He was a middleweight and had developed a strong reputation. Soon an effort began to match Fitzsimmons with Jack Dempsey.

Sullivan had removed himself from the boxing world. Some might say that Sullivan had shown the white feather. In August 1890 he began memorizing lines to appear as the blacksmith in Duncan B. Harrison's play "Honest Hearts and Willing Hands." The play would debut in September, and Sullivan contracted to appear at least two years as an actor. After the play opened, he earned $1,200 a week and had no need to either train or fight.

After Brennan's death, Davies did not remain idle. If he could not offer entertainment in Chicago, he would find another place to work. Although Jackson was gone to Australia and Ashton had returned to the East Coast, there was always wrestling. Evan Lewis had been wrestling in St. Paul with good success. He wrestled "Professor" Frank Lewis of Minnesota on June 23, and Tom McInerney at the Bijou in Minneapolis on June 27 before traveling to Chicago, having been summoned by Davies.

Taking wrestlers west

In mid-July, Davies, Lewis, and McInerney were in Denver, where Davies offered $500 to any local man who could stay with Lewis for fifteen minutes without being pinned. By July 20 the *Morning Call* of San Francisco hailed Parson Davies, who had returned to the coast with his troupe of neck twisters and carpet tumblers. This aggregation included Evan Lewis and McInerney, who had been arrested with the others at the time of Brennan's death. McInerney was styled as the champion wrestler of Ohio. At this point Jackson and Sam Fitzpatrick were still in San Francisco but about to leave for the voyage to Australia. Davies brought his wrestlers to fill the void in athletic entertainment on the West Coast and was on hand when Jackson and Fitzpatrick left for Sydney.[801] Somehow, Charlie also agreed to appear on stage in 'Frisco in the role of Gaston in a musical burlesque of Camille at the Baldwin Theater in San Francisco on August 7.[802]

Joe Acton had been in San Francisco working with a traveling troupe organized by Jimmie Geogan and featuring Young Corbett. Just before Lewis arrived Acton and the others had left for a tour to Seattle, Washington, and Astoria, Oregon. However, Acton had said that he would be back and prepared to meet Lewis for $1,000 a side for the best two out of three falls if Lewis would drop his weight to 165 pounds. Lewis said that he could not possibly drop below 170, but the press sized this all up as "press play" designed by the athletes and managers to get the crowd interested in the coming match.

During their first week on the West Coast, Davies put both of his wrestlers to work meeting "raw recruits" who were willing to roll around on the carpet to see whether they could avoid a fall for fifteen minutes. In each case the wrestling matches would be preceded by a short dissertation on wrestling for the San Francisco fans, who were not as familiar with the sport as those in the Midwest. One particularly interesting match was staged at the Olympic club between Lewis and a local man named Dan S. "Angus" McLeod, who was sometimes described as the club wrestling champion and sometimes as the Scottish wrestling champion. Apparently, Lewis could have obtained a fall several times early in the match with McLeod but would let him up at the last second to continue the suspense of the match. Davies would continue to promote both of these wrestlers through 1892.[803]

Over the next several months Lewis appeared in matches in and around San Francisco. On August 26 Parson Davies' Big Specialty Company was at the Orpheum Theater in Oakland, headed by Lewis for a rematch match with McLeod. The stakes for their match were $400 a side, and Lewis was required to throw McLeod three times, catch-as-catch-can style, within one hour, which he accomplished eighteen minutes to spare. The *Morning Call* said that there was a "large attendance of gullible sports" at this match. Betting was heavy on McLeod, and after the match it was said that Davies raked in several thousand dollars in bets and that Lewis won $800 in prize money and about an equal amount in gate receipts.[804]

Having dispatched the local talent and with Acton in Oregon, Lewis left San Francisco in mid-September and went back to Chicago for about three weeks. Davies told the Chicago press that he thought that wrestling deserved a higher position in the world of sport and had enjoyed greater success on the Pacific Slope (meaning California, Oregon and Washington) than he anticipated. However, Acton's departure had slowed the progress of his efforts to promote the sport.[805]

While his wrestlers were in Chicago, Davies sponsored a tournament that was an apparent effort to find some new faces who could wrestle and who Davies could take back to California.[806] In early October 1890 Davies finally arranged a Lewis-Acton match with the California Athletic Club for in a bout for $500 a side. The gate receipts were divided 65/35. Under the terms of the match, Lewis agreed to throw Acton twice within an hour. Davies also wrote to his friend Ed Kelly in Salt Lake City that he planned to bring Lewis and Acton there for an exhibition for "blood." Lewis returned to San Francisco, and he and McInerney began training in Sausalito. They could be seen almost every day doing road work in San Rafael.

In October Davies also wrote to his brother Vere in Chicago regretting the death of Dion Boucicauit. Dion was born in 1822 and came to United States in 1853. He had died in New York in mid-September 1890. Dion had written many popular plays. Charlie had given him $500 to write a play, *A Bunch of Fives*, that he wanted to use as the centerpiece of a vaudeville tour featuring athletes under his management. Before his death Boucicauit had given Davies an outline for the play, and Charlie hoped to find someone who could complete the project. Charlie wanted to bring Lewis on a tour beginning in Portland and returning Chicago. When he reached Chicago, Charlie planned to form a vaudeville company and start back west with *A Bunch of Fives* serving as part of the entertainment. He intended to feature Jackson in the play when he returned from Australia, along with Corbett.[807]

The C.A.C. was attempting to work itself out of the bad situation caused by McBride's death. They took several actions to change their management and the rules applicable to prize fights. In addition, after fighters, their seconds, and bottle-holders were arrested, the C.A.C. challenged police interference in the local court[808] The arrests had been made on September 12.[809] It took two months for the cases to come to trial, but on November 18, 1890 a jury returned a verdict of not guilty for all the defendants and that seemed to settle the question of police interference with C.A.C. events in the club's favor.

In late October it was learned that Jackson would return to the United States about November 6 and make a tour under Davies' management. Jackson would star on the tour with Corbett.[810] As odd as this prospect sounds in retrospect because of the later enmity between these two men, it was a real possibility. Davies was familiar to fighters on the West Coast, but his connections went far beyond San Francisco. Corbett was not as well recognized outside of California. He had been on the national scene only after defeating Kilrain in New Orleans in February 1890. Taking Jackson and Corbett on tour would be similar to taking Kilrain and Mitchell on tour, which Davies had done in 1888 and early 1889.

The speculation about when Jackson would arrive proved to be off by about seven weeks. In early November, another story was published that Jackson would remain in Australia for matches with a man named Joe Goddard, who was calling himself champion heavyweight of Australia, and with Frank Slavin.

What those in San Francisco did not know was that on October 20, Jackson and Goddard fought an eight-round draw at Melbourne. Eight days later, United States newspapers were reporting that Jackson was training for that fight.[811] This information was not reported in the San Francisco newspapers until November 23. The explanation for his failure to defeat Goddard was that Jackson was in poor condition for the match. It did seem that Jackson had trouble staying in top condition. Jackson had knocked down Goddard in the second and third rounds, but as happened with "Denver Ed" Smith in Chicago, Goddard had rallied and the two men staggered through the fourth round too exhausted to knock each other out. In the fifth round, during heavy countering, Goddard got in a number of clean blows on Jackson's face and head. A ringing left-hander forced Jackson across the ropes, and he showed signs of distress.

The blows were pretty evenly distributed during the sixth round. In the seventh, while the referee was parting the combatants after a clinch, Jackson received a blow that his seconds claimed was a foul. Their claim was not allowed, and Goddard forced the pace, planting his left on the jaw and his right on the ribs. Jackson fought more warily and got in some good body blows. In the eighth and last round Jackson tried hard to wind his man, but neither man had a clear advantage.[812]

After time was called, the referee announced that one of the judges had decided in favor of Jackson and the other in favor of Goddard, so he declared the contest a draw. At best this was a disappointing result. Given the earlier outcomes with "Denver Ed" Smith and Gus Lambert it appeared that Peter had lost his edge. In each instance his conditioning was an issue that was attributed to a lack of dedication. It was becoming more difficult to maintain that Jackson was the top heavyweight contender. If he fell into a group of several contenders who had plausible claims to the top spot, then he would have no chance to force Sullivan to fight.

Writing to the *Chicago Herald* from California in early November, Davies described several of the key athletic events that would be happening over the coming months. He wrote about the wrestling matches he had scheduled in San Francisco, the planned match between Fitzsimmons and Dempsey, and Corbett's schedule through June 1891. The Parson was irritated by statements of Sullivan to the effect that Davies and Jackson had not made as much money in England as had been reported by the press. Davies wrote: "I was not aware that Sullivan was doing my bookkeeping. Jackson and myself were satisfied with our trip in every respect."

Jackson returns to Australia

On November 28, Jackson left Australia and sailed for the United States.[813] After he reached arrived, he was asked about the fight with Goddard. He said that he was astonished about what had been reported in America about that match. Peter said that when he had reached Sydney he had been asked to box in order that his old-time friends could judge his improvements. He originally resisted making any matches, but he said that his friends were so persistent that he consented to spar eight rounds with Goddard. Jackson said that he presumed that this match would only be such rounds "as two men commonly box without especial preparation." He said that he was having a good time and continuing to indulge the social pleasures with no thought of a serious match. However, when the match began he found that Goddard had trained hard and was in the finest condition. During the match he had confined himself to scoring clean, scientific points and made no effort to put up Goddard.[814]

Davies was still promoting Evan Lewis on the West Coast when Jackson returned. While Charlie was with Lewis he became a great uncle. His niece Sarah Gruschow gave birth to her first daughter, Anita Katherine Gruschow, on November 15. Charlie was probably notified by telegram of Anita's birth and gave a little smile to know that the Davies' family lived on.

On November 22, the Lewis-Acton match was staged at the New Republican Wigwam in San Francisco before two thousand five hundred spectators. To defeat Acton, Lewis had to throw him twice within an hour. Lewis appeared on stage in a loose-fitting parlor ulster and Action in a pea jacket. Joe appeared to be as round as a cannon ball, and Lewis seemed to tower over him. After twenty-five minutes Lewis thought the referee had awarded a fall and let Acton go. But the referee said he had been misunderstood and the match continued. Lewis got Acton in his choke hold and blood began to pour out of Acton's nose. After thirty-five minutes Lewis was awarded his first fall. After a five-minute break the action resumed. For the remainder of the hour Lewis was unable to secure the second fall, and Acton was declared the winner.[815]

On Thanksgiving Day, November 27, Davies had his wrestlers on the road. They appeared at Clunie's Opera House in Sacramento for one night "for ladies as well as gentlemen." As a special announcement the advertisement for the match said: "Evan Lewis will meet any local athlete or wrestler under the following conditions: for every minute the local man succeeds in wrestling Lewis without being thrown, Parson Davies will pay him three dollars per minute, limited to thirty minutes."[816]

A Lewis-Acton rematch was agreed to on November 30, best three out of five falls for $500 a side. On the evening of December 9, the catch-as-catch-can world championship match was held in San Francisco. Lewis took three out of the first four falls. The West Coast newspapers concluded that from the start it was evident that Acton was too small to struggle with a powerful opponent such as Lewis. Acton was credited with making a very clever showing, even if he did lose the championship.[817]

On December 19, Davies and Lewis passed through Ogden without stopping to put on a show. They were headed east and the Ogden paper said that the town got the "blow-by" because Davies was no fish, and he knew he could get no match on there. Some reports said that Davies was planning a big wrestling tournament in Chicago in February and that it would be catch-as-catch-can style and open to the world. The winner would receive $3,000 and a championship belt.[818]

Jackson returns in bad condition

Jackson returned to San Francisco on December 20, but he was in poor condition.[819] He quickly left the city to visit Byron Hot Springs, twenty miles west of Stockton. Davies reached Chicago on December 21, 1890 and told the Chicago press that Jackson was in the hospital and had been ill with rheumatism since his fight with Ed Smith.[820] It is likely that the hot springs were another favorite spot for Davies. A trip there would take Peter out of the wet, cold air of San Francisco.

Before he left he explained that his match with Slavin at Melbourne had been cancelled, explaining: "Corbett never said anything to me about a fight. I shan't discuss Corbett at present. All that I have heard about him was through the papers while I was in Australia. When I get over my present illness you can rest assured the people of America will hear from me."[821]

Despite his illness Jackson was leading a liberal lifestyle, even after reaching California. The term "liberal" was a polite way of saying that Jackson was eating and drinking too much and not keeping in condition. It also infers that he enjoyed spending time with women and visited them when possible. What Jackson said about his knowledge of Corbett could not have been completely forthright because most sports had known something about Corbett after his fight with Kilrain in New Orleans and subsequent tour under Davies' management.

Despite Jackson's condition and his claimed lack of familiarity with Corbett, the C.A.C. was anxious to arrange a fight between the two men. Three days after he disembarked, he was matched to fight Corbett for $10,000, with $8,500 going to the winner and the rest to the loser. Corbett signed articles on December 29, and Jackson signed the next day. The fight was to take place on May 21, 1891, to give the men adequate time to get into condition. Years later Corbett took credit for arranging the match and for demanding the purse of $10,000. Davies's role was in arranging this fight is not clear, but later events seemed to indicate he influenced the financial terms. It would be five months before Jackson and Corbett fought, and for Davies those months were crowded with activity on behalf of athletes other than Jackson. [822]

One of Corbett's reasons for agreeing to fight Jackson was that Corbett had lost his job with the Olympic Club.[823] The club had about one thousand five hundred members and was one of the strongest members of the Amateur Athletic Union. In late 1890 it began building a new facility at a cost of about $25,000. It was to be a 137-square-oot, three-story brick building with each floor having fourteen-foot ceilings. Its gymnasium was to be fitted with all the modern appliances. There was to be a swimming pool with running salt water. Corbett had been employed by the club as a boxing instructor at $200 a month for two-hours-a-day of actual work. He claimed that he resigned from the job, but there were many newspaper reports that said he was fired for appearing drunk several times. Without his regular job Corbett concentrated on fighting. Moreover, Corbett found a backer who advanced $500, paid him a salary, and hired "Professor" John Donaldson to train him for the Jackson match.

At the end of 1888, Davies had been in St. Louis with Mitchell and Kilrain. They were in the midst of their tour leading up to the Sullivan-Kilrain heavyweight championship fight. At the end of 1889 he had been in Dublin with members of his family and near the end of the great tour of England, France, and Ireland. At the end of 1890 Davies was in San Francisco with Jackson, who had agreed to fight the future heavyweight champion of the world, James J. Corbett. No other person in the world could claim to have played such important role in prizefighting during those years.

Chapter 11 - (1891)

Jackson and Corbett to a draw

Fitzsimons destroys Dempsey

The big news in early 1891 involved a Dempsey-Fitzsimmons match scheduled to take place at the Olympic Club in New Orleans. La Blanche had knocked out Dempsey and proved that he was vulnerable. Rumors circulated that Dempsey was suffering from consumption and was substantially weakened. Fitzsimmons was considered the best man that Dempsey had agreed to fight. Bob was a terrific hitter and a big, powerful, raw-boned, middleweight fighter. Hitting Fitzsimmons was like hitting a wire cable. Before he left San Francisco with Evan Lewis, Davies bet $500 with Mose Gunst on Fitzsimmons. Mose favored Dempsey.[824] Months later Fitzsimmons claimed that Davies had sold his bet for $75 and did not actually win the money.

Nearly everyone involved in boxing in the United States was present for the Fitzsimmons-Dempsey fight. Conspicuous among the spectators were Davies, Bat Masterson, Tommy Warren, Kilrain, Muldoon, Mike Conley, the Ithaca giant, and Mike Cleary. Sullivan was performing in Chicago on the night of the match.[825] This was the only time that Jackson went to the Deep South. The Olympic Club refused to admit him to their premises to watch the fight. He then refused to agree to appear at any contest in New Orleans.[826]

Vere Davies took a group from Chicago on a special car and had made arrangements to wire round-by-round accounts back to his saloon in Chicago. Men traveling from Chicago included Malachi Hogan, Alf Kennedy, Billy Myer, Thomas Curley, and George Clark. Other sporting men from Beloit, Grand Rapids, and Minneapolis also traveled with them.[827] Those present from St. Louis included Tom Allen, Tom Kelly, the Daly brothers, the McManus brothers, Bob Farrell, and many others.[828] Tammany Hall politicians including Ed Kearney traveled to New Orleans. Men also came from Hot Springs, Memphis, Buffalo, and San Francisco. Other contests were slated at the Olympic Club.[829] One welterweight glove contest was to match Doc O'Connell and Eddie Conley. Jim Corbett had agreed to second Conley with Jimmy Carroll behind O'Connell.[830]

Dempsey arrived in New Orleans on January 13, 1891. Unlike the Sullivan-Kilrain fight, the Dempsey-Fitzsimmons fight would take place under police protection with a cordon of blue coats to preserve order. Corbett was in New Orleans on the day of the fight and sent a telegram to San Francisco predicting that Fitzsimmons would defeat Dempsey.

Fitzsimmons did not simply defeat Dempsey. About five thousand spectators watched him beat Dempsey to a pulp in thirteen rounds. Dempsey was outclassed from the start and was left crying at ringside as Jack McAuliffe tried to console him. Davies declared Fitzsimmons nothing short of a phenomenon and wasted no time trying to sign him and his trainer, Jimmy Carroll, to a contract.[831] The *San Francisco Morning Call* reported that Davies had won $3,000 on the fight.[832]

What happened after the Dempsey-Fitzsimmons match with respect to Davies and his management of fighters is the most complicated puzzle of his entire career. It is possible that Davies had direct and indirect interests in promoting Corbett, Fitzsimmons, Jackson, and Jim Hall at the same time. This part of the story begins with the end of the Dempsey-Fitzsimmons fight in New Orleans.

The *Post Dispatch* reported that on January 15 Carroll and Fitzsimmons had signed a contract with Davies by which "the clever money-maker will manage them. He is to tour them through this country, and then take Fitzsimmons to England and match him against Ted Pritchard, the English middle-weight champion. If Fitz whips Pritchard, as it is generally believed he will, Davies will tour Carroll and the New Zealander through Europe, return to this country and finally visit Australia. The pugilists expect to realize enough money by their exhibitions and Fitzsimmons' fights to make them independently rich, and their intention to finally return to San Francisco and go into business."[833]

Many newspapers reported that Davies quickly left New Orleans on January 16 to begin arranging the tour to Europe.[834] Advertisements were being placed in Rochester, New York, for Fitzsimmons appearance as part of Parson Davies' Specialty Company on January 17. Davies himself sent a letter to the *Chicago Herald* saying that at the request of Fitz and Carroll he was making arrangements for them to tour the United States, Great Britain, and Australia.[835] Finally, on January 25 the *New York Sun* reported that Davies was acting on behalf of Fitzsimmons.[836] This sounded like the same format that Davies had followed with Jackson.

Later reports said that Fitzsimmons would be paid $500 a week and all his hotel and traveling expenses for himself, his wife, and child, to spar three rounds each night with some boxer who would be engaged to appear with him. When Bob reached England, he would fight before the Pelican Club and meet either Pritchard or Jack Burke, whoever was on top of the heap at that time. About a week later the same newspaper repeated an earlier story that Corbett was going to go on a sparring tour across the country under Davies' management and with Jackson as part of that tour. What happened after the Fitzsimmons-Dempsey fight is complicated because it follows the divergent paths of these fighters from coast to coast.

Corbett described his movements after the Fitzsimmons-Dempsey fight in his book. He wrote: "Then I took a trip down to New Orleans to see Jack Dempsey and Bob Fitzsimmons, and after that contest went to New York. On my way back to San Francisco to train for the Jackson fight I stopped off at Chicago where John L. Sullivan was appearing in a melodrama called 'Honest Hearts and Willing Hands.'"[837]

The awkward looking Bob Fitzsimmons in 1902 - Photograph of the Chicago History Museum

Corbett's account of his movements provides an inaccurate impression of the sequence of events. Corbett was in New Orleans on January 15. He put on an exhibition on that evening with Donaldson. Bob Fitzsimmons attended this show. Charles J. Stenzel, Corbett's manager, Corbett and Donaldson had all traveled (but not together) to New Orleans, and Stenzel claimed that he paid all of the expenses for their trips because he had a contract with Corbett. In addition to paying the expenses for their trips to New Orleans, Stenzel said that he gave Corbett $500 "on account" and paid both Corbett and Donaldson liberal salaries between January and May 1891.

Corbett is introduced to Sullivan

On the evening of January 18, Corbett was in Chicago, where he met Sullivan. Local papers said that he would soon be appearing in Davies' new play, *A Bunch of Fives*.[838] On January 19, several newspapers reported that Corbett met Sullivan for the first time on the evening of January 18, 1891."[839] In an age of train travel, it is next to impossible to conclude that Corbett went to New York City after exhibiting with Professor Donaldson on the evening of January 15 in New Orleans and that he then traveled from New York to Chicago by the afternoon of January 18. It seems much more likely that Corbett went directly to Chicago from New Orleans.

In his own book, Corbett provides his own description of his Chicago meeting with Sullivan and explains how he was then pressed into bar-hopping spree with John L. He remembered Sullivan asking: "You're matched to fight that N_____?" Corbett nodded that he was so matched. Sullivan then said: "Well, you shouldn't fight a N_____!" Corbett recalled that at the saloons they visited Sullivan would introduce him: "This young fellow's Jim Corbett. He's going to fight that N_____ Jackson." Corbett said that on that evening he met Mike McDonald and Billy Pinkerton, among other luminaries.

He also recalled an indirect challenge that he made to Sullivan that caused Sullivan to back down in front of a crowd of his friends. Corbett wrote that he left Chicago the next day to begin training for his match with Jackson, but this too seems unlikely because Corbett appeared on the East Coast in New York and Brooklyn and did not return to the West Coast until early March. The real sequence was that Corbett traveled from New Orleans to Chicago, then to New York, and then back to San Francisco.

Armond Fields wrote that at the beginning of 1891, Corbett went to New York without his wife Olive. Fields writes that "Parson Davies, Jackson's boxing manager" wanted to find out whether the better class of theatergoers would react favorably to a prizefighter appearing in a theatrical production. Therefore, Davies took "a young, trim, handsome, charming, tasteful, and urbane Jim Corbett" to New York with John Donaldson to appear at the Eighth Street Theater during the last week of January.[841] Their performance was presented to standing-room-only crowds of customers of high-class variety shows. On February 1, the *Brooklyn Eagle* carried the following summary the performances to take place during the coming week at the Hyde & Behman's Theater:

> The performance promised for this week will include the specialties of Parson Davies' boxers and wrestlers, James Corbett, John Donaldson, Evan Lewis and Thomas McInerney: Harry Kernell, monologist; George K. Wood, "the somewhat different comedian;" the four Adonis in their medley; John E. Drew, singer; the Carles in grotesque dances; McCann, concertina player; the Coulson sisters in song and dance; Leonzo, juggler; Harry La Rose, juggler, and R. M. Caroll in his "Mortar and Bricks."[842]

On February 3, the *Brooklyn Eagle* reported that the audiences' approval of the performance of the athletes at Hyde and Behman's Theater was so loud that it could be heard by the public on the streets outside.[843] Armond Fields wrote that seated in the audience during one of these East Coast appearances in early 1891 was William A. Brady, a theatrical manager who was then appearing at the Standard Theater.[844] Brady's presence could be compared to a virus that would poison Jackson's chance to ever fight for the heavyweight championship. From

Brooklyn the Davies' performers went back to Chicago for a two-week engagement, first at the Olympic Theater and then at the Madison Street Opera House.

Jackson, Muldoon, Kilrain, and Godfrey went to San Francisco after the Dempsey-Fitzsimmons fight. They were all present at the C.A.C. on January 29. At that meeting Kilrain and Godfrey signed articles for their fight on March 14.[845] Davies and Jackson were on opposite coasts while Corbett was working with Davies. This was happening about sixty days before the Jackson-Corbett match.

Davies managing multiple champions

Who employed Fitzsimmons during the first few months after the Dempsey fight is not clear, but it seems likely that Davies probably had at least an indirect interest in Fitzsimmons. Within two days after the fight, he and Jimmy Carroll signed a contract with Davies in New Orleans. Fitzsimmons and Carroll then had an argument and split. Fitzsimmons said that Carroll had shorted him on money. Carroll claimed that Fitzsimmons was angry because he incorrectly thought that Carroll had opened a personal telegram that had been sent to Fitzsimmons.[846] Carroll left New Orleans and went to San Francisco. This effectively trashed the contract with Davies. It may be that Davies himself cancelled his arrangement with Fitzsimmons after Carroll left because he had already assumed the management of Corbett and Donaldson and therefore did not have the time to personally handle Fitz. It is also possible—perhaps likely—that Davies assigned his contract with Fitz to his friend George R. Clark (sometimes spelled "Clarke") or simply told Clark that Fitz was "available."

Fitz entered into a new contract with Clark as early as February 6, 1891.[847] Some reports at the same time claimed that Fitzsimmons had signed with Frederick Reynolds, manager of the Australian Theater Company, but those accounts were not accurate.[848] Stories reported years later say that Fred M. Bishop, a saloon owner from St. Louis, also had a part of Fitzsimmons' management at this time. However, neither Clark nor Bishop had any substantial experience managing fighters outside of Chicago, except that Clark was referred to as the backer of Tommy Ryan.[849] Clark then placed Fitzsimmons under the supervision of Floto, who was purportedly acting as Clark's agent. The most detailed account of Floto's work on behalf of Clark is found in the *Times-Picayune*.[850] Of course as Davies' personal assistant, Floto had considerable experience managing fighters and conducting promotional tours outside Chicago. Floto was working on behalf of Fitz before February 12 because Floto had contacted Richard K. Fox before that date.[851] On the morning of February 13 Fitz arrived in Chicago in the company of Billy Woods. They left for the East Coast on the same night after spending the early evening in George Clark's home.

When Fitz reached Chicago, Corbett was supposed to be there along with Donaldson, appearing in a show produced by the "Parson Davies' Vaudeville Co."[852] However, Corbett had caught a cold while visiting New Orleans and was under the weather. He had gone to Mt. Clemens to recover.[853] It is likely that Davies had sent him to one of his favorite places to recover.

The press reported that for the following fifteen weeks Fitz would be "engaged in extracting the dollars from the pockets of the American public in the interest of George R. Clark. In this he will be assisted by Billy Woods, who will appear and spar with him Fitzsimmons who was looking fresh and well."[854] Some reports say that Fitz' engagement was for eight weeks, but it seems more likely in view of subsequent events that the fifteen-week contract first reported was correct. Floto handled the Fitzsimmons-Woods tour over the next ten weeks from February 14 through the middle of April.[855] It is possible that Floto was working for Clark but that Clark had a business arrangement with Davies.

On February 16 Floto, Fitz and Woods were all in New York City, where the fighters appeared at the newly rebuilt Bowery Theater, operated by Henry Miner, and also at the Eighth Avenue variety theater. That day the *Post Dispatch* reported that Jim Hall had arrived in San Francisco and had already issued a challenge to fight Fitzsimmons. Hall's real name was Montague James Furlong. He was born in Sydney on July 22, 1868, and had worked in Australia as an apprentice plasterer before pursuing a boxing career. The *Post Dispatch* claimed that Fitz was "pleading his theatrical engagement as a bar to his negotiating with Hall for a fight," and it also reported that Floto was working on an advertising boom for Fitzsimmons by having Richard K. Fox telegraph to London to make a match for Bob in England.[856]

The telegram that Fox sent at Floto's request was published in several newspapers:

> New York, Feb. 12, 1891.
> George W. Atkinson, Sporting Life, London:
> Bob Fitzsimmons, the middle-weight champion of America and holder of the "Police Gazette" middle-weight championship belt, is eager to fight Ted Pritchard, Jack Burke, Toff Wall, or whoever is the middle-weight champion of England. He has requested me to correspond with Lord Lonsdale to ascertain how large a purse the Pelican, National or Ormonde clubs will offer for a contest between him and the winner of the Burke-Pritchard fight or Toff Wall. Will you find out and cable reply.
> Richard K. Fox.[857]

On the evenings of March 5 and 6, Fitz and Woods appeared at the Standard Theater in Syracuse, New York. At the end of the regular evening performances, the two sparred for a three-round contest. The *Evening Herald* of Syracuse wrote that "it doesn't take more than a minute or two to discover that 'Bob' Fitzsimmons is all that is claimed for him. He is quick and full of tricks, and a great 'ducker,' while inclined to save his right for emergencies."

Fitzsimmons described Hall for the *Evening Herald*: "He has the advantage of me in class as I do not think he can train down to 160 pounds, even. I gained four or five pounds since my arrival in America, and Hall will perhaps gain more. I have no desire to go against Sullivan. I am ready to meet any man in the world in my class, but will not make a bloomin' fool of myself by going against men who have the advantage of me in weight. A man's weight thrown into his blows without extra exertion on his part would win for him; that is, I mean a heavy-weight fighting a lightweight."[858]

Plans for a match with Hall were improving. Clark had deposited $2,500 with the *Chicago Inter-Ocean* to bind a match with Hall at the Astoria (Oregon) Athletic Club. A man named Jim Ryan of Portland, Oregon, then had telegraphed Clark that would cover the deposit for Hall. A few days later the *Post Dispatch* reported that Hall's money was up but that Fitz was insisting that the Astoria Athletic Club should deposit a match guarantee of $5,000 with either Parson Davies, Dick Roche, or Mose Gunst.[859]

After stops in Baltimore and Buffalo, Fitz opened on April 5 at the People's Theater in Chicago in the play *Fashions*. The People's Theater was managed by Colonel Hopkins. Fitz appeared clad "in full dress, with a snowy expanse of immaculate linen" and acknowledged the thunders of applause from the audience. In the last act of the play *"Mrs. Manhattan's Reception*, Fitzsimmons and Woods proceeded to pound each other within the limits of the city ordinances. Clothing a sparring match as if it was part of a play was another device that allowed prizefighters to appear in public performances without police interference. Fitzsimmons was interviewed in his dressing room after the show and said that he was ready to meet Hall and was within a pound of making weight. He predicted that the fight would take place in July. He and Woods continued to appear in this production for another week.[860]

In mid-April Clark fired Floto. The *Post Dispatch* reported that Fitzsimmons had been paid $500 a week under the terms of his contract with Clark but that the shows featuring Fitz and Woods had been playing constantly to business of a few thousand dollars a week. For some reason Clark had become dissatisfied with Floto's management and discharged him, assigning the Fitzsimmons contract to a Mr. Sellers.[861]

For his part, Davies was more than busy. Jackson had little professional management between December 1890 and May 1891. He was on the West Coast preparing for a match with Corbett and was not splitting his money with a manager. One paper reported that Davies had given up Jackson's management and was Corbett's manager.[862] It was easy to see how someone could draw this conclusion. Corbett and Donaldson were under Davies' management from about January 18 through early March 1891, when Corbett began preparing to fight Jackson. Although Fitzsimmons was nominally working for George Clark under the supervision of Floto, that arrangement may have been a ruse, and it may have been that the real party in interest was actually Davies.

There is no question that Davies was also personally managing Jim Hall and Billy Woods from April 9 through the end of 1891. In addition, from February 9 to 13 the Davies' wrestling tournament featuring Evan Lewis and Tom McInerney was staged at the Olympic Theater in Chicago. Davies was trying to find a credible wrestler to take back to California with Lewis and McInerney. The big name drawn to his tournament was the Cleveland Thunderbolt who had started his career as a wrestler. Davies was also negotiating to match Lewis for a contest on the West Coast with an unknown. In addition, as early as February 7, Hall's backers Barney Allen and Joe Harris had published a challenge to Fitzsimmons and stated that "all arrangements can be made with Parson Davies who is our authorized agent in the matter."[863]

Corbett comes to Chicago

Corbett and Donaldson were to appear in Chicago beginning about February 8, 1891. Corbett had caught a cold in New Orleans' wet and clammy weather. He had also been losing weight and decided to stop in Mt. Clemens for a week of hot mineral baths before continuing to Chicago.

After recovering his health, he came to frigid Chicago swept by cold north winds and appeared between February 15 and February 22 at the Madison Street Opera House as part of the Parson Davies' Vaudeville Co.[864] The production featured an original play written by Frank Livingston called *Sawdust Bill*. The cast for the play included Davies, Corbett, Donaldson, Stenzel, and several others. Incidental to the show Corbett and Donaldson boxed a few rounds to show off the young thoroughbred.[865]

While they were there, a man named Patrick Daly challenged Corbett.[866] Davies sent a card to the local newspapers in response to the challenge:

> As Mr. Daly is aware no doubt Mr. Corbett is under contract with me to spar Professor Donaldson at both matinee and evening performances at Madison Street Opera house this week and therefore has his hands full. Furthermore the terms of his agreement with the California athletic club will not allow him to enter a contest with any one until after his fight with Peter Jackson. But if Mr. Daly is anxious to try and win $500 I will bet him that amount that I will produce a man by no means Mr. Corbett's equal as a pugilist who will stop Mr. Daly in private in four rounds. Yours truly, Charles E. Davies.[867]

Davies planned a typical trip west that would keep Corbett busy at every opportunity. He laid out appearances in Omaha and Denver and continued to travel ahead of the others to make the necessary arrangements. The combination departed on the Rock Island line just as a cold snap hit the Midwest. Snow was falling from Illinois through Iowa and Nebraska. It was a nineteen-hour trip to Omaha over endless Illinois flatland and Iowa's rolling hills.

Corbett remained the featured star of the aggregation. Other members were the erratic Weir and Donaldson. Davies knew that Corbett was under Stenzel's management, but Stenzel probably had no financial stake or income from the performances that Corbett and Donaldson put on in New York, Brooklyn, Chicago, Omaha, and Denver, and he was likely not paying either Corbett or Donaldson while they were touring with Davies.[868]

After completing arrangements in Denver, Davies went to Ogden on February 27. He stayed at the Pacific Hotel with a view of the snow covered Wasatch Range on the western edge of the Rockies. There were trains every hour to the therapeutic hot springs located north of downtown Ogden and he spent several days using the therapeutic waters shake off the ever increasing pain in his legs.[869] The *Salt Lake Herald* reported he was in the city on the evening of February 28 and met with a reporter to discuss his travels with Corbett.

Davies said the combination had traveled all over the east and everyplace they stopped they met with "flattering success." He said that the company appeared in Omaha on February 28 and would appear at the Coliseum Hall in Denver on March 2. The article concluded: "Mr. Davies is thirty-nine years of age and remarkably well preserved for a man of his age and especially for a man who has followed the pugilistic business for as long as he. He is a very pleasant man to meet, and the reporter's conversation with him, was wholly an enjoyable one."[870] Davies appreciated the importance of having good relationships with the press; he generally liked reporters and enjoyed telling tales about the exploits of his fighters.

Early in the morning on March 4, 1891 Davies was at the Union Pacific depot in Ogden. This large stone and masonry building had been completed two years earlier and angled and swept north and south from a central clock tower. It was located south of the Ogden River and east of the Weber River on the west edge of downtown Ogden. It was Romanesque in style with many elegant decorations and provided comfort for travelers equivalent to the best depots in the United States. Ogden's served as the western terminus of the Union Pacific's line and the depot was a corporate beacon signaling the growth and expansion taking place in Utah and the strength and power of the Union Pacific. From Ogden the Central Pacific ran west across the Great Salt Lake and salt flats before a four hundred plus mile run through the sage brush of Nevada to Reno, up and over the Sierra Nevada mountains and into the central valley of California and on to Sacramento and then Oakland.

A reporter for Ogden's *Standard* was with Davies at the depot as they waited for the train carrying Corbett. During the reporter's time alone talking with Davies he was clearly captivated by Charlie's pleasant manner and storytelling. He wrote the following about their time together:

> Yesterday morning at 4:05 James Corbett, the famous pugilist, arrived over the Union Pacific, and accompanied by his wife. At an invitation from "Parson" Davies, a *Standard* reporter was at

the depot to meet the fighter. The train was due at 3:20 but was behind, and during the wait the "Parson" and the representative made themselves comfortable in the Pacific hotel office and chatted away the time. Mr. Davies told of his many amusing experiences, among which was an account of the great John L. as an actor. This "famous tragedian" plays the blacksmith in Loving Hearts and Willing Hands, and thinks he makes much of the part. The "Parson" is an interesting story teller and the reporter was almost sorry when at last the incoming train whistled its approach. As the passenger drew up at the platform, the *Standard* man was taken into the Pullman sleeper by Mr. Davies and after the latter had aroused Corbett from his slumbers, was introduced to the great exponent of the manly art.

Corbett arose with good grace and entertained the reporter for nearly an hour. The pugilist is a handsome fellow, the picture of manly strength dark hair and eyes, clear complexion, good firm month filled with a beautiful set of pearly teeth, large expressive eyes, strong wrists, medium sized hands which are long and well shaped, six feet in height, and weighs, dressed as he was last night, about 195 pounds, he is twenty-four, years of age and is quick and seems a fluent and interesting talker. His trainer thinks he will be able to keep him at his present weight as soon as active training begins.

After Corbett had had time to collect his scattered senses the reporter asked him how he felt and when he would commence training for the coming match. . . . Corbett is accompanied by his wife, a pretty little lady, about twenty-two years of age, a decided blonde. "Parson" Davies also obtained a berth on board and will go as far as the Coast with the fighter and then return to the East until the May match comes off. He thinks Ogden the most beautiful City in the West and declares that the waters at the Springs have helped him a great deal.[871]

Davies departed on the Central Pacific with Corbett early on March 4. The Central Pacific's track between Ogden and Oakland was the last long stretch of the transcontinental trip. The *Standard* reporter wrote:

The more a person becomes acquainted with the great sporting authority the more he likes him, and during the short stay he made in Ogden many friends have been added to his already long list.

The Parson attended the opera last evening and was as much disappointed as anyone on account of the long delay but he said to the *Standard* reporter while chatting with him in the hotel office,

"I feel sorry for the troupe because I have been in the same predicament myself several times. I remember when I was managing the Paddy Ryan combination we left Ogden for Butte on time and. by the way, that did not last long. A little further north the depth of the snow increased and as we passed the Idaho line the engine tried to buck great banks of snow. We were booked for the night in Butte and did not arrive there until too late to show. The people would take no excuse and the managers paid back over $900. Those who desired got tickets for the next night. Then we had more trouble. The hall for the next night was rented to Prof. McAllister, a magician, and I offered him $200 to cancel his engagement, but he refused. We were forced to take a little out of the way place and took in about $400. The Professor had a $36 dollar house.

During my experience I have had numerous delays in getting from one point to another and the company members usually fret and worry so and declare that the season's business will be ruined, that they nearly drive a manager silly. In the end the troupe suffers most."[872]

Corbett later related some of the events that happened while he and Davies were traveling from Ogden to San Francisco. Corbett wrote:

Peter Jackson's manager was the picturesque "Parson" Davies, who had also managed Charley Mitchell, Jack Burke, "the Irish lad," Frank Glover, and a host of other celebrities. Oh, what a credit to pugilism Davies was, and how different from some of our fight managers of today!

"Parson" Davies looked his nickname. He was a fine looking man with gray hair and his clothes were always made by the best tailors, and always black. Whenever he was to introduce a pugilist to an audience in the afternoon, he would put on a black cutaway; when he presented the principals in the evening, he always donned evening clothes.

I was very fond of "Parson", and although he was managing Jackson when I was matched to fight him, that didn't interfere with our friendship. He believed Jackson had a "walk-over" and felt sorry for me; and I used to "kid" him considerably about this confidence which to me was decidedly misplaced.

During one of these chats, he showed his friendship by asking me if I wouldn't agree to have the loser take $3,000, and the winner $7,000, of this $10,000 purse, thus increasing the defeated man's end. I knew he was doing it just through his liking for me,

> because, as I said before, he thought it was a "cinch" for Jackson to win. But I refused.[873]

Davies and Corbett arrived on the West Coast about midnight on March 4 to much warmer weather with temperatures in the mid-sixties and light rain. For the Parson and his rheumatism, the mid-sixties was a vast improvement over the ten-degree temperatures in Chicago.

Between mid-January and early March, Corbett and Davies were probably exploring options they might have in May, after the Corbett-Jackson fight. Corbett was probably reluctant to rush into a long-term agreement because his manager, Stenzel, was paying all of his training expenses, and an agreement with Davies might cause Stenzel to withdraw financial support. After all, Stenzel mistakenly expected to be Corbett's manager for years to come. It was more than two months before Corbett would meet Jackson, and training expenses could be substantial.

It seems likely that Corbett had decided he should break away from Stenzel's management because there would be better opportunities available if he showed well with Jackson. Corbett had seen the big cities, and it would be difficult to keep him down on the farm. He must have known that Davies was only one prospective manager, and he also knew that Davies was unlikely to put Corbett at the top of the list of fighters he managed because he was expecting Jackson to trim Corbett's sails.

San Francisco's *Morning Call* reported the arrival of Davies, Corbett, and Donaldson noting that Corbett had had been traveling with Davies in the eastern states and had lost fifteen pounds after leaving California for New Orleans. Corbett attributed his weight loss to the constant travel and a touch of malaria that he picked up while in the South.

Davies said he was working on arranging a match featuring Muldoon, Roeber, and Lewis but had not come to the West Coast on wrestling business but simply to get out of the cold weather and spend a few weeks in "God's own country, and there you are." The last phrase he used, "and there you are," had become Davies' hallmark manner of speaking. The catch phrase became his way of ending discussion on a particular matter: "and there you are." [874]

Davies becomes Jim Hall's manager

Davies' claim that he was only in San Francisco for the weather seems an understatement. He was likely in Frisco because Jim Hall and his backer Joe Harris were there and the next big match, at that time thought to be bigger than Jackson-Corbett, would be Hall-Fitzsimmons.[875] He clearly wanted to size up Hall and do a little business with another Australian fighter, if possible.

A week after Davies and Corbett arrived, Davies went to the Oakland Theater for a light play entitled *The Honeymoon* starring a Ms. Wainwright as Julia. The theater and stage seemed to be the Parson's real passions. He shared a box at the theater that night with J. J. Guttlob, manager of the Bush Street Theater in San Francisco. George B. Heazelton of the San Francisco Press Club was also at the theater that evening.[876]

From December 9, 1890, through March 11, 1891, Davies had been moving at a hectic pace. He had traveled from San Francisco through Salt Lake City to Chicago. From Chicago he went to New Orleans and back to Chicago before traveling to New York and Brooklyn and then returning to Chicago and then to Omaha, Denver, Salt Lake City, and Ogden, then back to San Francisco. During that time he had acted on behalf of a constellation of the top fighters of the 1890s, including Jackson (heavyweight champion of Australia and England), Corbett (future heavyweight champion of the world), Fitzsimmons (middle weight champion of the world and future heavyweight champion of the world), Hall (middle weight champion of Australia), Woods, and Lewis (catch-as-catch-can world wrestling champion). It is unlikely that any other fight manager has ever matched the pace Davies set during this three-month period. At corner saloons and club meetings, sportsmen read about Davies' exploits and discussed what the Parson might do next.

On March 13, Kilrain, one of Davies' former clients, met Godfrey at the C.A.C. for a stake of $5,000, with $4,500 to the winner. They drew a large but select crowd that included Davies, Corbett, Harris, the Australian bookmaker who was backing Hall, Joe Thompson, another Australian bookmaker, and millionaire Lucky Baldwin. Kilrain's seconds were Hall and Muldoon, who was in the process of trying to woo Hall away from Harris. Jackson seconded Godfrey. Kilrain won the match in the forty-fourth round, and some reports said he unnecessarily punished Godfrey for the final eleven rounds.[877] There is little doubt that Davies met Hall on this evening and probably said just enough to let him know that opportunity was knocking, and Charlie was at the door.

On the afternoon of March 16, Davies was at the Richelieu with several others, including W. D. English, the former California State Harbor Commissioner and Democratic Party leader in San Francisco. English stood with a glass of Shasta water in his hand and explained to Davies, Tom Clunie, P. D. Baker, "and a little knot of true-blues" how he had been doing up the redoubtable Jackson. Peter was one of the men present, and he smiled approvingly as English spun his story. English announced he had beaten Peter at throwing darts, playing billiards, casino and pool.

"Then what do you think he wanted to do?" English asked.

"Take a drink?" suggested Parson Davies.

"No," said English, "to put on the gloves with him."[878]

This story illustrates the degree to which Jackson had been accepted among some of the highest society of San Francisco.

Within a few days Davies left the West Coast and did not return until May 16. He probably would not have left unless he thought that Jackson's preparations were in good shape and had done what he could to get Hall's attention. He returned to Chicago with Godfrey. He liked Godfrey and may have seen some business possibilities if he needed someone to travel with Jackson.

On March 20 in the Variety Theater at Salt Lake City, Godfrey put on a sparring exhibition with Davies present. On the morning of March 21, Davies again passed through Ogden.[879] He was going to Chicago to arrange a match on behalf of Hall on the same bill with Fitzsimmons. In so far as the public knew, Hall was backed and managed by Harris, who had named Davies as his agent to arrange a match with Fitz. However, it seems likely that Hall had already decided to split with Harris and go under Davies' management, although Hall not yet told Harris about his intentions.

For several weeks, Harris had been negotiating with George Clark in an attempt to arrange the Hall-Fitz match. It may be that Harris did not know that he was actually negotiating with a straw figure when he was communicating with Clark and that the real wizard behind the screen was Davies. The negotiations between Harris and Clark suggest that Harris never had a real chance to make the final arrangements for a Hall-Fitz match.

For example, when the issue of posting forfeit money arose Clark designated Davies, Dick Roche, and Gunst as the three persons who could accept Harris' forfeit money.[880] Gunst and Davies were close friends. Harris took his deposit money to Gunst who initially refused to accept it, saying he wanted nothing more to do with prizefighting. Harris then telegraphed to Clark asking him to designate someone to replace Gunst and this resulted in another delay.[881] During that delay Hall came under Davies' management and Harris was left on the outside looking in. It isn't totally clear that Davies and Clark were working together; however, if they were, the ethics of this course of dealing are questionable.

Davies arrived in Chicago on the evening of March 26. He looked healthy and better than when he left. Chicago had warmed up to the high thirties, and mayoral election politics were in full swing. He held court for the Chicago press and answered questions about the events on the West Coast. He was full of praise for Godfrey and for the C.A.C.[882] The California club had an important business alliance with Davies, and he stroked that relationship when possible. Godfrey was a prospective client and there was no harm in building him up after his defeat in California. The intrigue with Hall had been simmering for a few weeks and would soon boil over.

On March 30, Hall was in San Francisco with Harris. Together they went to the Associated Press and disclosed that Harris had posted $2,500 to bind a match with Fitz.[883] The *San Francisco Chronicle* held $1,500, and Gunst had relented, and he held another $1,000. On the afternoon of March 31, Hall arrived in Ogden on the Central Pacific. He was traveling with a combination of Australian fighters under the immediate supervision of J. J. Ryan, who was working for Harris as the day-to-day manager of Harris' combination of fighters.[884]

Ryan moved on from Ogden to Salt Lake City on April 2, 1891. However, Hall went back to San Francisco, where he again met with Harris. He had probably received a wire in Ogden asking him to come back to Frisco immediately because an offer relating to Fitzsimmons fight seemed imminent. Instead, on April 3, both Hall and Harris received word from the Astoria Club that it had secured a purse of $17,000, but it was not satisfied with money being held by third parties and wanted both Hall and Fitz to deposit $1,000 directly with the Astoria to bind the match.

The next day the *Salt Lake Tribune* reported that Torn Hennesy of Colorado was matched to stand before Hall for six rounds on Friday, April 10, at Ogden's Novelty Theater a short walk from the railroad depot up Twenty-Fifth street. The Novelty was originally completed in the summer of 1889 but was burned to ground by an arsonist on September 14, 1889 and then rebuilt. It was a favorite venue for boxing in Ogden Tom Hennesy was described as a rattling fighter, a long-winded, plucky, and scientific boxer, and their fight would be worth seeing.[885] J. J. Ryan had probably arranged this fight.

On Tuesday, April 7, Hall passed through Reno on his way back to Ogden and his match with Hennesy.[886] The train was an hour and a half late, but a large crowd waited at the Reno depot. Some were there to see Hall but others to see the secretary of war, who was aboard the train.

He returned to Ogden at ten a.m. on April 8. Harris had been in Ogden for two days when Hall arrived.[887] This suggests that Hall had been left alone in San Francisco, which gave Hall plenty of opportunity to exchange telegrams with Davies and explore his options. Hall and Harris visited the Ogden office of the *Salt Lake Tribune* and asked the newspaper to publish the following defy:

I Joseph Harris, as the backer of Jim Hall, who defeated Bob Fitzsimmons in three rounds and a half in Sidney, take this method of challenging Bob Fitzsimmons to a boxing contest before the California Athletic Club at such time as may be decided upon by the said club and the parties concerned. I hardly anticipate an acceptance of this challenge from Fitzsimmons being thoroughly assured that he full well understands that Hall is his master in the art of boxing. However, as an earnest of my good intention, I have this day deposited with the sporting editor of the *Chronicle* my check in the sum of $500 to bind the match.[888]

Hall was given the royal treatment in Ogden. It was a bustling city of about fifteen thousand residents and a hub of many of the great railroads. It was not unusual for six passenger trains to be switching in Ogden at the same time. On his arrival in Ogden, Hall was met by a large group of sporting men who escorted him to a room at the Pacific Hotel and later in the day gave him a grand tour of the city. The *Standard* reported that Hall and Harris were on their way to Chicago to make final arrangements for a match with Fitz.

On Friday, April 10, Hall appeared with Hennessy and their show began at midnight. Ed Kelly, another good friend of Davies, acted as timekeeper, and George Lewis was chosen as the referee. Hall put on a good show. He bloodied Hennessy's nose in the first round. In the fourth round Hall made a little hop in the ring, as if to kick Hennessey. Hennessey in turn became riled by this behavior and gave Hall a sound rap, which in turn irritated Hall, who then proceeded to punish Hennessey severely, cutting up his face. Finally, the round ended good-naturedly.[889]

Hall left Ogden on April 11 on the train for Denver. The next day the *Salt Lake Herald* reported that Hall had dissolved his relationship with Harris in Ogden on April 11 because Hall was afraid that Harris was taking him to Chicago to sell him to another manager. Hall said that while in Ogden he had received generous offers from both Muldoon and Davies. The claim that Harris was going to try to sell Hall was probably spin applied to the story by Hall to explain his actions.[890]

On April 12, Hall was in Denver, where he received a telegram from Harris in San Francisco. Harris advised that he was withdrawing his financial support of Hall. On April 13, the *Post Dispatch* confirmed that Harris was in San Francisco—no longer on his way to Chicago—and had sent the telegram withdrawing his backing and accusing Hall of leaving Salt Lake City with the proceeds of the show before splitting the take with Harris. For his part, Hall said he was in communication with Davies, who had agreed to back him in the anticipated match with Fitz.

Masterson joined Hall in Denver for the trip to Chicago. Davies and Masterson were tight friends. Masterson had given up law enforcement and was running the Olympic boxing club out of the Palace Theater in Denver. Charlie probably enlisted Masterson to accompany Hall. He didn't need to take any chances that someone else would sink their claws into Hall before the Australian reached Chicago.

The *Saint Louis Post Dispatch* reported that Hall's tour along the Pacific Coast under Harris' management had been a financial failure.[891] This information was probably provided by Hall and was an important reason for the Hall-Harris split. This was Hall's second explanation for dumping Harris. About ten days after the split, Hall said that Harris was "all right" but never bet a dollar unless it was on a sure thing. Hall also claimed that Harris tried to persuade him to participate in a fake fight, which was really the cause of their split. This was Hall's third explanation for dumping Harris, and it might be interpreted to mean that Harris wanted Hall to engage in a fixed fight with Fitz. Hall continued: "I'm in this country to fight, and I'll tell you whenever I get back here again, if I don't get a 'go' before I leave, I'll fight, not box, mind you, any man, no matter what his weight, in the town, and all the proceeds I'll give to any charitable institution in the city."[892]

Harris' withdrawal of financial backing probably made no difference for Hall because Davies was already arranging Hall's schedule. This appeared to be a case similar to Jackson's: an Australian fighter had made a name but was not making money commensurate with that name. Hall, like Jackson, came to Chicago seeking Davies' management. In both cases Gunst played a key role in Davies assuming the fighter's management. It was important to have influential friends, and Davies had them from coast to coast.

Hall and Masterson arrived in Chicago on April 17. It was early spring in Chicago with a warming southerly breeze in the air. Hall was probably impressed to find local papers heralding him as the "wonder from Australia."[893] The next day the *Tribune* reported he had signed a contract to travel under the management of Davies. Hall then appeared at Battery D on Monday, April 27.

Given all these circumstances, it seems likely that while they were in Ogden, Hall told Harris that he had already entered into an agreement with Davies. Consequently, there was no reason for Harris to go to Chicago. Harris probably tried to persuade Hall not to follow through with that plan. When he failed to sway Hall, Harris returned to San Francisco and Hall continued on to Chicago to sign on with Davies.

On his part, Davies had probably talked to Clark about a new arrangement between Hall and Fitz that would cut out the Astoria Club and would move the fight in a different venue. Sensing trouble, the Astoria Club notified Harris that it would not sponsor the Hall-Fitz fight unless Harris was involved. But the Astoria was too late in acting and its insistence that money had to be deposited directly with that club had probably queered its chances.

In Chicago, Hall said he and Harris had parted on the best of terms. He said he did not take any money from a performance in Salt Lake City because he had never been in a performance there. According to Hall, when they were in Ogden, Harris had asked him to return to San Francisco instead of going on to Chicago, and Hall insisted on continuing on to Chicago. This account was at odds with the original story—that Hall believed that Harris was taking him to Chicago to sell him to another promoter. Sometimes when a story is made up it is hard to keep track of the misrepresentations made.

The "fixed" fight problem

The *Tribune* also discussed the stories that had been circulating about a fixed Hall-Fitz fight in Australia. The allegation was made by Fitz, whom Hall had been defeated. Fitz said he did not really lose to Hall. He claimed he was approached by Hall's people and asked to take a dive. Fitzsimmons said he had agreed to go down because he was hurting for money, and even with a loss to Hall, he would be paid more money than he had ever made in his life up to that point. Hall denied that the fight in Australia was fixed. He said he was thunderstruck on arriving in America to hear that Fitz was making this claim. He said he was anxious for a return match to prove he could whip Fitz, just as he had done in Australia. If this was prefight hype it was a dumb approach.

Some sports became suspicious about what was going on between Hall and Fitz. On the East Coast, men speculated that the coming Hall-Fitz match would be another fixed fight. Hall himself fed the suspicion when he told the press he split with Harris because Harris wanted Hall to engage in a fake fight. All the circumstances created honest doubts about the proposed fight. Some thought that Davies had both sides of the proposed Hall-Fitz match. After all he had just spent several months traveling with Corbett, who was about to fight Jackson.

While working on the Hall-Fitz match, Davies brought Dixon to Chicago, where he appeared on April 20 at Battery D. Many people think that Tom

O'Rourke was Dixon's only manager. But Davies too managed several fights for Dixon. Three weeks earlier, Dixon had defended his featherweight title by defeating Cal McCarthy in Troy, New York. Davies matched him with Martin Flaherty, who had received local notoriety by defeating Link Pope of Streator, Illinois. Pope was part of the strong group of Streator fighters and was a close friend of Myers. Dixon defeated Flaherty in a six-round match.[894]

Davies was in Chicago on April 21 and met with Clark and Colonel Frank Shaw, who was the president of the Twin City Jockey Club of Minneapolis-St. Paul. Shaw was the club's proprietor and had offered a $12,000 purse for a Hall-Fitz finish fight to be held on July 22. Hall was reluctant because the Astoria had offered $17,000 for a match there. Davies and Clark sent a telegram to the Astoria to determine whether its $17,000 offer was still good. By the following day, the participants had decided that the Astoria's offer was not firm enough to be relied on, especially in light of the Astoria's declaration that it would not sponsor the fight unless Harris was involved. In order to gain Harris' participation he would have to be paid off, and that meant the net amount Hall earned would be less than the net from a fight in Minneapolis.[895]

On Monday, April 27, Hall and Fitz appeared as part of the entertainment Davies offered at Battery D. Chicago police Lieutenant Alex Ross was present at ringside. After the usual entertainment the main events of the evening involved both Hall and Fitzsimmons—but not against one another. Hall was to spar Ed Niland for two rounds, Fitz was to spar Abe Cougle for two rounds, and then the opponents were to be switched.

Cougle was a local heavyweight employed by the South Water Street commission in Chicago and only two weeks earlier had been "badly used up" in a fight with a north side heavyweight named Jimmy Dohoney. He was in no shape for a serious match with Ruby Bob. All of this activity was to take place with big eight-ounce gloves to keep the authorities happy. The problems started because Niland did not show up, and Woods substituted for him and sparred with Hall in place of Niland.

After the Woods-Hall show, Fitz met Cougle. Fitz had been told that the match with Cougle was a set up. Cougle was going to try to hurt him so he would not be in condition when it came time to box Hall. Fitz therefore insisted that Cougle should be instructed to "go easy" in their match.[896]

They started off slow as Fitz "fiddled and played" with Cougle. For two minutes of the second round the sparring was tame as Fitz had insisted, but the crowd grumbled. Then Cougle delivered a vicious (and unexpected) swing at Fitz's lip. He clearly was not happy with Cougle's blow and gave him a straight shot to the stomach and a right and left to the head, knocking him down. When Cougle got up, Fitz hit him four more times until he was knocked out cold. At that point, Lieutenant Ross jumped into the ring and stopped the show.

Cougle was so wasted he could not spar with Hall, and a three round Fitz-Woods show finished the entertainment. This little exhibition did nothing to quell the rumors that any Hall-Fitz fight was going to be fixed. Two nights later

Hall and Woods were in Cleveland for a three-round sparring exhibition. Woods had stopped traveling with Fitz and hooked up with Hall.[897]

Peter Jackson is injured

Meanwhile, on the West Coast, the coming Jackson-Corbett fight was the big story. There was no doubt that both men were good fighters and reasonably matched in terms of size. Jackson was a little taller, about twenty-five pounds heavier and had far more experience than Corbett. A general view was that Corbett hit harder than Jackson. There was a real question about whether Jim could reach Peter to deliver a blow.

Jackson's fighting style was to reach way out with his long arms and stab his opponent with his left hand. This approach tended to keep opponents away. No one wanted to put his head down and try to bore in on Jackson because the cost was too high. Peter also kept his left leg bent pretty well and would stiffen that leg at the point he delivered his blow. He would then take a little slide or hop backward to avoid a body blow, which again prevented a response by his opponent. Jackson repeated this movement so often some described it as ambling or shuffling.

Jackson was thin in the stomach area, but at the same time not many men had been able to land there effectively. It took an exceptionally good man to hit Corbett anywhere because of his quickness with his hands and feet. Corbett was constantly on the move and bouncing around. He was not a standstill, slug-it-out fighter. Sporting men on the West Coast thought that Corbett had the advantage in speed over Jackson but he lacked experience.

On April 4, Jackson was injured. There were conflicting stories about what happened and whether his leg, foot, or ankle was injured.[898] Three days later it appeared that Jackson was more seriously injured than first supposed. He was confined to his bed, and predictions were that it would be several days before he could continue his regular daily exercise.

Stenzel, Corbett's manager, said that the story about Jackson's ankle injury was phony and circulated only to affect the betting line, which was then two to one in favor of Jackson.[899] Years later Corbett claimed he had a spy watching Jackson every day. This assertion may say something unflattering about Corbett's character. Corbett claimed in his autobiography that Jackson's injury happened one day less than a month before the fight, but he was wrong because the injury actually happened forty-six days before the contest. Corbett also said that his spy told him that the injury amounted to only a little sprain and that within a week Jackson was out doing road work and training for their fight.[900]

It seems that both Stenzel's claim that Jackson had never been injured and Corbett's claim that Jackson had only a little sprain were both wrong. On April 14, a wire story said that Jackson was on crutches but confident he would be in condition for the Corbett match.[901] Jackson finally discarded the crutches on April 21, one month before the big fight. From the beginning, Corbett was concerned that Jackson's injury might taint the fight's outcome. There was no glory in whipping a cripple. It was always in Corbett's personal interest to assert that Jackson was not hurt but rather perfectly fit at the time that they met, and it continued to be in his best interests after the fight to insist that Jackson was not really hurt.[902]

Corbett said he began playing mind games with Jackson about two weeks before the fight. He always thought he was smarter than his opponents. He began speaking disparagingly about Jackson whenever his name was mentioned. He said he made these disparaging comments to get Jackson's goat because he thought that this would make Peter a little bit afraid of him. According to Corbett, he was successful in getting into Jackson's head, and this was evidenced by the fact that Jackson sent Naughton to see Corbett to tell him that the verbal agreement that Davies had offered about splitting the fight purse no longer applied.[903]

From about March 20 until May 21, Davies had no personal contact with Jackson, nor did he try to supervise Jackson's training. Moreover, Davies did not manage Jackson for many months after the Corbett-Jackson match.

On May 9, Davies chartered a special train and chaperoned a party of his personal friends, including Hall, to a match between George Siddons and Tommy White held at Fort Wayne. The group that went to that fight included men from the Chicago board of trade and several "solid business men" and aldermen from Chicago. Davies was maintaining his roots and relationships with the sporting fraternity in Chicago.[904] The ability to move easily between the local sporting crowd and the upper crust was a facility that Davies had developed from his youth and important to his success. He left on evening of May 9 for the West Coast and the Jackson-Corbett match.[905]

On May 10, the *Salt Lake Tribune* reported that Ed Kelly of Ogden had received a telegram from Davies advising him that his combination of Hall, the Australian wonder, and Woods, "the clever Denverite," would be in Ogden for an exhibition on May 16 and that Hall would offer $300 to any pug who would stand before him for six rounds.[906]

On May 11 the Davies' combination appeared in Omaha, where Hall and Woods spared at the Opera House. Jack Davis, an Omaha heavyweight, had an interesting match with Hall followed by a match between Woods and Jim Hightower. Danny Daly and Young Gallagher fought, and then Hall and Woods sparred for three rounds.[907]

They appeared in Ogden on Friday, May 15, at the Novelty Theater, where Hall and Woods sparred three rounds before a large crowd and impressed the audience. It is likely that between Omaha on May 11 and Ogden on May 15, the combination also appeared in Denver, but that is not confirmed.

On Saturday, May 16, 1891 the Davies' combination was in Salt Lake City at the Electric Hall, where Hall and Woods sparred ten rounds.[908] There were about one hundred fifty sporting men present to witness their meeting and several preliminary bouts. Billy Manning acted as master of ceremonies and introduced Hall and Woods. The local press said Hall was on his way to the West Coast to train for his $12,000-fight with Fitz in Minneapolis. However, it is obvious that Davies was taking Hall to San Francisco for the Corbett-Jackson fight and was making some money for everyone along the way.[909]

The *Morning Call* reported on May 15 that Davies was on his way to San Francisco with a group of fighters for the Corbett-Jackson fight.[910] Woods attended the Corbett-Jackson fight on May 21, and newspaper reports the following day included an interview with Woods and his personal observations about their fight. Davies, Woods, and Hall could not have arrived in San Francisco more than forty-eight hours before the Corbett-Jackson fight.

The Corbett-Jackson fight led to an unsatisfactory result. After sixty-one rounds the referee declared the match no contest. Davies was not present at the end. Many years later he said that after fifty-four rounds he got hungry and went out to find something to eat. The referee said he stopped the fight because both men were so weak that it was plain to everyone neither fighter could go on with the match and still be expected to throw effective blows. Accounts said that the first half of the fight was one of the most scientific matches ever seen on the Pacific slope. But the last thirty rounds were simply a walk-around.[911]

The C.A.C. first decided that because the fight was called no contest it had no financial obligation to either fighter. This was so evidently unfair that the directors met and decided that each man should be awarded $2,500.[912] Again, this outcome was considered an insult to both fighters, and Jackson initially refused the money. Against the advice of Stenzel, Corbett accepted the money but pledged never again to fight at the C.A.C.

Corbett's decision to accept the $2,500 caused a break up in his relationship with Stenzel, who likely received $1,250 for all his prefight expenses with Corbett.[913] This undoubtedly caused Stenzel a substantial financial loss. Corbett said he was thinking about accepting an offer to work for San Francisco's Olympic Club or, as an alternative, an offer to travel with a minstrel company.

Post-fight reports said that Jackson's chief financial backer was Gunst, and he had backed Peter to win for $5,000, with most of his bets being made early at odds of 100 to 80. Davies had risked $1,000 on Peter, and Masterson had wagered an equal amount. After the fight Jackson's ankle was severely swollen and pained him to walk. Within ten days after the fight, Jackson said he was prepared for a rematch with Corbett, but Jackson would not fight in the South due to the prejudice against him in that part of the country.[914]

Shortly after the fight, reports appeared that Davies was about to assume the position as king pin of the American Athletic Club, a new sparring club in San Francisco. The *Post Dispatch* said that there would be enough money behind the new club to build a line of steamships.[915] The *Morning Call* on June 12 said that the club would be called the Great American and would be devoted entirely to prizefighting. The prime movers behind the club were John D. and Adolph Spreckles, sons of Claus Spreckles, the sugar king, and California's ex-senator, James G. Fair. Three hundred men had agreed to purchase stock in the new club.[916]

One account said that as soon as the Hall-Fitzsimmons match was over, Davies was going to marry a San Francisco woman and settle down.[917] But Davies did not hang around San Francisco long and never assumed management of the club. Instead he went to Tacoma, Washington, and Portland, Oregon, with Hall and the rest of his new combination.[918]

At Portland, Davies acknowledged he had been offered the opportunity to head the new club, but he had declined the honor. He also said that rumors about a possible marriage were not true. He said he had twice asked women to marry him, and in each case he had been turned down. He had not yet worked up the nerve to try a third time.[919] It would have been a challenge for any woman to have married Davies. He liked his independence, traveled constantly, and used substantial sums of his money to support his nieces and nephews.

Many years later, Davies wrote that he was first man who put Corbett on the stage. His account was published in the *Chicago Tribune* on December 10, 1899. Davies explained that just after Corbett's fight with Jackson, Davies, and Nick Long induced Corbett to appear on stage as part of a benefit for Long, an actor and a resident of San Francisco. Charlie explained he had talk to John Russell the manager of a famous group of comedians known as the "City Directory" and to the manager of the Bush Street Theater and suggested that they should ask Corbett to appear on stage as part of the benefit. Corbett agreed to appear on the condition that Davies would also appear. Davies "somewhat reluctantly" agreed to "make myself ridiculous" and also appear as part of the benefit.

The first part of the Long benefit included a minstrel show. Minstrel shows were almost always presented as black-face comedy. The show included Maurice Barrymore and J. B. Stoddard, and a burlesque on "Camille." The cast also included: "May Irwin; Armond, Charley Reid; Count de Varville, Corbett; Mme. Prudence, Alf Hampton; Gaston, Davies. Bert Haverly, Laura Biggar and other notables were also in the cast." Corbett wore a borrowed dress suit that was three inches too short in the sleeves and trousers at least four inches about his shoe tops. Davies wore a borrowed song-and-dance costume from an actor who was not much larger than the great featherweight champion Jimmy Barry.[920]

The Davies-Hall combination heads for a showdown with Fitzsimmons

Less than a week after the Corbett-Jackson affair, the newspapers in Winnipeg and in cities in the United States were reporting that Hall would be in Minneapolis by mid-June 1891 along with Woods, who was coming to the Northwest prepared to stop any man there, preferably Killen. Of course, the combination remained under Davies' management.

On their way to Minneapolis, the combination stopped in Seattle, Portland, Tacoma, Missoula, and Butte, taking the Southern Pacific's northern route at a time when weather would not interfere with travel. In Portland, Hall met a 180-pound heavyweight named Jack Flaherty at a baseball park before one thousand seven hundred fans. He defeated Flaherty easily.[921] In Butte the company ran into the kind of trouble that plagued prizefighting in those days. They were putting on a sparring match at Fred Riche's Comiqué Theater when the local police chief appeared and placed Davies, Hall, and Wood under arrest for violating a newly adopted city ordinance. The crowd had paid a dollar each for admission. They complained, Davies complained, and Riche complained, but the police were obstinate. To be released each man had to pay $150 as security, which was all the money they had taken in at the box office.[922]

With a bad taste from their experience in Butte, the combination moved on to Minneapolis for the showdown with Fitz. The Minneapolis-St. Paul area was a refuge for many sports who had previously lived and worked in Chicago. When Chicago cracked down on gambling and prizefighting these men had settled in the twin cities. The twin cities had not formally cracked down on prizefighting in the same way Chicago had turned the screws.

Fitz began training on June 1 in the country outside of St. Paul using Needham as his trainer. The tireless Davies and his combination arrived in St. Paul on June 13, and Fitz was in the city on that day.[923] Hall and Fitz met in a saloon where "several hot words passed between them, and they would have come to blows had not friends interfered."[924]

That evening Hall and Woods appeared at a venue called the Pence. Woods fought a black fighter named Burt Liverpool, who would win $100 if he could stay four rounds. Woods pounded Liverpool viciously, and he laid down in the ring and quit in the second round rather than receive additional punishment. After a ten-minute break, Hall and Woods sparred four rounds. The local press noted that Hall was fast, clever, and stronger below the waist than Fitz but lacking the same large chest and shoulders. The common expression that evening was, "Fitz can carry my money."[925]

Woods was matched on June 15 in St. Paul with wrestler Charles Moth. Davies had a long-running grudge against Moth arising out of his mistreatment of Lewis. He instructed Woods to give Moth a good drubbing. Following Davies' instructions Woods had Moth out on his feet in the third round but continued to pound him even after Moth had slipped between the ropes. Woods then gave Moth a few extra whacks after he had been counted out by the referee.[926]

Davies then sent Lewis a telegram after the match to let him know that the deed had been done. When Davies and Lewis next met, it was reported that Lewis had hugged Davies with delight.[927] This little bit of vengeance involving Moth may have cost Davies dearly in the long run; the Woods-Moth contest was held up as evidencing the type of prizefighting brutality that should be stopped by the authorities.

Davies, Hall, and Woods all went from Minneapolis to Beloit, where Hall went under the supervision of John Kline, who had successfully trained several fighters and wrestlers managed by Davies. Hall trained daily with Woods, who was then fighting at about 187 pounds. This training was done to get Hall ready for dealing with the heavy-hitting Fitz.

Davies went back to Minneapolis about a week later to arrange a match between Woods and Godfrey for $3,000 a side to be staged at the Twin City Club of Minneapolis. Davies had probably discussed such a match with Godfrey when he traveled with George to Salt Lake City a few weeks earlier. Charlie was also arranging a match for Woods with Kilrain and had received a telegram from Gunst saying that Dempsey wanted to work in Hall's corner for his fight with Fitz.

The do-gooders interfere

The *Post Dispatch* began to raise questions about whether the Hall-Fitzsimmons fight would be on the square. It reported that Davies and George Clark, Fitz's manager, had been seen "hob-nobbing" together and thought this "looked decidedly strange when it is considered that Hall and Fitz were just previously to that speaking most disrespectfully of each other." The *Post Dispatch* wrote: "It is known that Parson Davies likes to make a dollar about as well as any man on earth, and Fitzsimmons has confessed his participation in a fixed fight with Hall in Australia before coming to this country, in which he allowed the latter to stop him. In view of all these things it would be well for outsiders to let the meeting between the men next month severely alone."[928]

Davies said that all rumors that the fight would be a fake were absurd and suggested that people should judge the fight on its merits. Davies hated fake fights and saw them as a great threat to the business. The *Post Dispatch* later backed off its criticism, writing that Davies was "far from being a fool" and knew that the American people had no use for "fakirs" (meaning beggars) and would not be part of such an event. Subsequent events involving both Davies and Hall would demonstrate that it was unlikely that a fake fight was being arranged by Davies.[929]

When Davies reached Chicago he talked about the combinations trip East and some of the events during their tour. He was asked about rumors that that he might be getting married. He told the *Chicago Herald*: "No! No one has so far popped the question to me, and I am not sufficiently imbued with my own benedictarian qualifications to take the initiative, so that the prospects of getting married are as remote as ever."[930]

The articles for the Hall-Fitz match were published on July 2. The match was to take place at the Minnesota Athletic Club in St. Paul, for a purse of $12,000, with $11,000 to the winner and $1,000 to the loser. Four-ounce gloves were to be used and Queensberry rules governed. It was stipulated that neither fighter would weigh over 156 pounds. This provision was to protect Fitz, who claimed that Hall was more of a heavyweight than a middleweight. Davies was to receive half of the winner's purse if Hall won the contest.[931]

Unlike the situation with Jackson when he was preparing to meet Corbett, Davies took a personal interest in Hall's preparation for this fight. He trusted Jackson. He didn't know Hall's habits, and there was a lot riding on this match.

The Parson superintended every movement and was putting in his own hard work directly with Hall.[932] By early July, Hall had trained down to 152 pounds, and felt he would have no difficulty making the fighting weight.

Davies told the press in Chicago he was pleased with Hall's preparation and was confident of his winning the match. He said that Hall was in excellent condition and that the match was no fake. "Hall is in excellent condition, just lovely, looking elegant and feeling splendid. He could not be in any better condition than he is now. Hall will fight to win. His chances rest entirely upon Fitzsimmons' behavior. The latter is a fine man and a great fighter. I have nothing to say against him." [933]

While the preparations for the fight continued Jimmy Carroll—who held Davies in part responsible for his split with Fitzsimmons—sent a letter to the *Boston Police News* suggesting that Davies had engaged in a conspiracy to fix the fight. He asserted that Davies had traveled from San Francisco to St. Paul with the designated referee for the fight and implied that Davies had paid off the referee during that trip. When asked about this suggestion, Davies merely laughed and said the only conspiracy he was involved in was preparing Hall to be in his best possible shape for the fight.[934]

In addition to working with Hall, Davies was enjoying his own thespian efforts. *The Tramp*, a comedy-drama, was presented at the Beloit Opera House on July 5. Hall, Woods, and Davies respectively played the parts of Robert Lee, Richard Mason, and Judge Graham.[935] The *St. Paul Daily Globe* noted that "Mr. Davies had appeared on the boards many times, so that the sensation will be nothing new to him, but as neither Hall nor Woods have ever been in any speaking part it will be curious to note how they deport themselves."[936] The last act of that play included a three-round set-to between Hall and Woods so that the ladies could see them perform.

Davies was also in active training for the Elks Lodge No. 4 production of *As You Like It* to be staged at Burlington Park on July 28. The heavily wooded park in rural Naperville featured a central pavilion and a lagoon with row boats for the amorous. The park had aspects of an amusement park with a steam carousel and a ball toss at baby dolls. On summer days thousands of Chicagoans would take the one-hour ride on the nine, ten, and twelve a.m. and one p.m. trains out of the crowded city to enjoy the great outdoors. Businessmen wore white linen suits and panama hats Their lades wore shoulder capes of light flimsy materials such as lace and chiffon and veils from their feathered hats.

This was the lodge that Charlie had helped establish, in which his long-time Chicago friends were active. Davies played the role of Charles the Wrestler. He appeared for his wrestling scene clad in a horse blanket and a scowl. He "stripped big" for the match, and twitched his shoulders up and down in imitation of Sullivan, spit over his shoulder and charged at Orlando. He was finally laid out in the second round by a neck lock. The crowd loved the production and broke down the ropes to get closer to the ring and encourage the participants.[937]

Davies was normally at ringside, but he clearly loved the applause he received for his effort inside the ropes.

In world of real sports, the prospects for the Hall-Fitz match were not doing well. It is too much to chronicle all of the events that led to interference with their St. Paul match. The sale of seats at the fight began ten days before the contest; they were expensive, costing $10, $15, and $20. Preliminary fights were arranged for the evening before the featured contest. Betting on the match picked up and favored Fitz. Rumors circulated that Corbett was going to serve as referee, which pleased Fitz but upset Hall. Davies left Beloit on July 18 to make the final arrangements for quarters for the Hall party.[938]

On July 21, there was a preliminary bout in Minneapolis that was not interrupted by the police. This was a finish fight between Joe Ellingsworth of New York and Harris Martin, better known as the "Black Pearl," of Minneapolis. Several sports were already in the Twin Cities for the big fight and attended the preliminary match. Those men included Billy Pinkerton, Billy Lakeman, Bud Renaud of New Orleans, and Masterson. Martin won the fight, knocking out Ellingsworth in the fifth round.[939]

In the meantime, those who know best for their fellow men (i.e., Christian ministers of Minneapolis and St. Paul, the YMCA, and the chamber of commerce) appealed to the mayor of St. Paul and the governor of Minnesota to stop the fight. They argued that members of the athletic club were inflicting injury on the "fair fame of St. Paul" and throwing a mantle of propriety over a disgraceful and brutal sport, making it for more dangerous in its immoral tendencies. The mayor took no action on the protests. The religious elements of the city called for mass prayer meetings, and the Law and Order League of St. Paul was formed to support a popular uprising to stop the fight.[940]

St. Paul's *Pioneer Press* attacked the Minnesota Athletic Club and the YMCA, pointing out the latter maintained a gymnasium in which it had staged sparring matches for years. In the end the governor issued a proclamation enjoining the local authorities to do their duty to enforce state law.[941]

On July 21, when Fitzsimmons arrived in St. Paul, he was arrested and compelled to post a peace bond that would be forfeited if the fight went forward.[942] Hall was not arrested, but it was sure he would be when he arrived in town. On the day of the fight, the governor sent the First Regiment of the Minnesota National Guard to occupy the Minnesota Athletic Club. Davies was not a man to force the issue when the law intervened, and the match was called off. Each fighter was paid $2,500 for their effort, which they agreed to accept. They made the same amount of money for doing nothing that Jackson and Corbett made for fighting sixty-one rounds.

Corbett jumps ship and signs with William Brady

Davies was back in Chicago on July 25 and said he was satisfied that there would be no fight in Minnesota.[943] Less than two weeks after the disappointment in St. Paul, Davies had arranged a Corbett-Hall four-round set-to at the aging barn called Battery D. There was a full evening of preliminary entertainment offered before the important exhibition. More than two thousand five hundred men appeared in ninety-degree-plus temperatures for the entertainment on August 5. Corbett weighed 200 pounds, and Hall 160 for the show. Hall was credited with quickness and good-straight-hitting ability, but Corbett was the impressive man. His style was called "showy, clean cut, and his own."[944]

Corbett left Chicago for the East Coast, where he had agreed to a appear in an acting role for theatrical producer William A. Brady, who had first seen Corbett under Davies' management at the Eighth Street Theater in late January 1891. As late as July 31 Corbett had written a letter to his brother saying he was going to appear on stage with Hall in productions managed by Davies, but something changed in the following week.[945] Perhaps Corbett was afraid he would play second fiddle to Hall or Jackson if he was managed by Davies. Corbett had a huge ego and wanted to be the center of attention. It would not be long before Brady would gain control of Corbett's career and fill that role for many years to come. Brady would repeatedly block efforts to arrange another Jackson-Corbett fight. He was the dark side of the force and stroked Corbett's basest urges.

In his book *The Fighting Man,* Brady wrote that after Corbett's match with Jackson, Corbett started out from California with a minstrel show. Brady wrote: "At this time I was playing the leading part, 'Old Tom,' in *After Dark*. I was making a great feature of the music-hall scene in the play and I wired Corbett, offering him an engagement to appear in that scene. After some negotiations, I got him to join my company, paying him one hundred seventy-five dollars a week."[946] He had a contract to manage Corbett by August 12.[947]

Brady's lack of experience in managing a fighter showed early. By mid-September 1891, Brady was in New Orleans at the Olympic Club where he announced that Corbett would not fight either Choynski or Jackson. This was the first time that Brady blocked a fight with Jackson. Brady described matches with those two fighters as "dead issues" and said that Corbett had his sights on Mitchell. From Jackson's standpoint, the influence of Brady on Corbett was extremely negative.

Corbett's decision to accept an engagement with Brady must have been disappointing for Davies, who had worked hard to develop a relationship with Corbett. However, the Parson probably did not foresee a long-term relationship between Corbett and Brady because Brady had had never managed a prizefighter. After the evening's entertainment on August 5, both Hall and Davies planned to travel to Mt. Clemens to enjoy the hot baths there and regain their footing.

Davies slits Hall's throat—literally

Before leaving for Mt. Clemens, Davies and Hall attended a fight on August 9 in Richardson, Illinois, a milk station on the Chicago, St. Paul & Kansas City R.R. The fight was between Tommy Ryan of Chicago and Billy McMillan of

Washington, D.C. Ryan was a welterweight. He was born in 1870 at Redwood, Jefferson County, New York, and his true name was Joseph Young, although some places he is called Joseph Lajeunesse and others Joseph Juvenal. After his father's death Ryan left home and lived in Syracuse and then Detroit before moving on to Chicago. Tommy took the name "Ryan" because his backer was Colonel Thomas Ryan of Syracuse, a congressman from the area and a wealthy brewer.

Hall acted as a second for Ryan in his match with McMillan. McDonald was present and was asked to referee, but he declined in favor of Malachi Hogan. Ryan was nearly knocked out in the first round, but survived and knocked out McMillan in the third round. Davies bet $100 to $20 on Ryan before the fight but admitted that Ryan benefited from a long count in the first round. It helps to have a friendly face making the count when you have bet on the fighter who is down. The gate for the fight was $2,300 and Ryan received 75 percent. Three hundred men attended paying $12 each, which probably included the round-trip train ride.[948]

After reaching Mt. Clemens, Davies and Hall stayed at the Avery Hotel. Two weeks later, they were in the hotel bar and engaged in an argument that almost ended in Hall's death. The Avery was three stories with a mansard roof, spacious verandas, and 385 rooms capable of accommodating five hundred guests. The hotel offered mineral baths on its premises.[949] It was a favorite vacation spot for both athletes and the wealthy of Detroit.

About noon on Sunday, August 23, a large crowd of sports had gone to McSweeny's clubhouse, about four miles from Lake Saint Clare. Hall was drinking champagne heavily and demanded $25 from Davies, which he gave. Later he demanded another $50, but Davies refused to give him the money. The reason for Davies refusal is not known but probably apparent. Hall was drunk, and giving him more money was only to going to make things worse. Hall began to berate Davies with all sorts of names, and a shooting was only prevented by friends who intervened.

About eight p.m. Davies returned to the Avery's bar and was drinking with friends when Hall entered the room. Davies invited Hall to join the group, but Hall refused and demanded that Davies settle up with him immediately. Name calling again ensued, and trouble was again prevented by Davies' friends. Both Davies and Hall then went to their separate hotel rooms. After midnight, the group returned to the bar, and Hall again showed up to demand that Davies settle up with him. Davies told him it was impossible to settle up and also told Hall he was drunk and didn't know what he was doing. One of the people present was Dick Fails a 122-pound fighter.[950]

At that point, Hall grabbed a bottle and swung it at Davies, missing him but hitting another man in the stomach. Hall continued to threaten Davies and described the harm he was going to do to him.

"If you do I will make you get down on your knees," Davies responded.

Hall then grabbed a heavy piece of iron to throw at Davies. Davies grabbed the lemon knife and slashed Jim's throat. Hall dropped to the floor bleeding like a "stuck hog."

What followed was a rare moment of panic for Davies. He apparently initially thought he had killed Hall. He turned to his friends and said: "What will I do? Hadn't I better skip?" He was encouraged to stay, and Hall himself assured Davies he had done nothing wrong and was only acting in self-defense.

Davies offered Hall the lemon knife and said, "You use it on me just as I have on you." Hall declined.

The doctor and sheriff were then summoned. Both Davies and Hall must have been drunk if this account is accurate. Ultimately, the sheriff concluded that Davies had acted in self-defense.[951]

The reasons for their fight were not certain. In 1916 the "Romances of the Ring" series carried in several national newspapers asserted that Hall was a hard man to manage and had an ugly disposition when he was under the influence of alcohol. According to that account, the reason for the fight was that Hall threatened to beat the Parson within an inch of his life, which seems reasonably consistent with contemporary accounts.[952]

In 1920, the *Referee* provided a different account. It reported that what had happened that evening confirmed Davies' reputation for honesty. Hall and Davies were said to be discussing a prospective match when Hall suggested he and Davies wager a large sum of money on Hall's opponent, and then Hall would lie down.

"That way we can make more money losing than winning," Hall reportedly said.

Davies replied, "You want to fake do you? Well, you take this." He then slashed Hall with a lemon knife that the barkeeper had left on the bar.

That account does not correspond with contemporary accounts but tends to glorify Davies' actions. It is an unlikely scenario.[953]

Another account is provided by Jack Marx in his book entitled *Australian Tragic, Gripping Tales from the Dark Side of Our History*:

> While touring Detroit with his fighter, Davies found Hall drunk one morning and angrily told him to go home and sleep it off. Hall didn't take the advice, appearing later in the evening, drunker still, in a bar in which Davies was entertaining associates. A boisterous argument ensued, Davies keeping his cool while Hall raged and abused, poking his finger into Davies' chest and generally making a prize nuisance of himself. Frustrated by Davies' composure, Hall threw a haymaker and Davies snatched a lemon knife from the bar and stabbed Hall in the neck, missing his jugular by millimeters, growling at the stunned Australian, "Next time I'll make a sure job of it." Hall responded by opening his shirt and daring Davies to plunge the knife into his heart,

> then accused the Chicagoan of cowardice as Davies escorted the drunk and bleeding fighter to the local hospital. It was the end of their association.[954]

This account too seems unlikely given the seriousness of the neck wound inflicted by Davies. It is also particularly kind to Davies given the more contemporary accounts of the incident.

Briefer accounts said that Hall and Davies had stopped at the Avery House and got into a quarrel in the bar room at eleven o'clock on August 24. After a word or two, Hall struck viciously at Davies with a bottle. His arm was then caught by a bystander. When Hall attempted to repeat the first blow, Davies grabbed a lemon knife off the bar, dodged Hall's blow, and lunged at him striking him in the throat and cutting a terrible gash from the chin to the ear on the right side of his face, narrowly missing Hall's jugular vein.

The two men were then separated and Hall said, "You've done me, Charlie, but stay by me."

After the fight the room looked like a slaughterhouse. Everything in the bar was said to be covered with blood. Davies led Hall away to see a surgeon. Initial reports were that Hall would recover and was considered to blame in the matter, Davies having acted in self-defense.[955] The account seems like a dime novel version of the events and is probably not accurate.

Davies sat at Hall's bedside all night long. An initial physician's report said that the wound was ugly, but not necessarily fatal. A full week after this incident Hall was still confined to his bed, and his physician opined that his condition was still critical. Davies told the press he would make no statement about what had happened. It would be seven weeks before Hall returned to the ring to fight again. He carried the scar from the stabbing until his dying day and never afterward trifled with Davies. During the seven subsequent weeks there is little information about Davies, who had probably stayed with Hall until he had recovered and was left alone by the press.[956]

After his slashing with a lemon knife, Hall surprisingly remained under Davies' management. In late September, the *Post Dispatch* reported that Madden was negotiating with Davies for Hall's appearance at Peter Maher's reception at Madison Square Garden in October.[957] In addition, on September 28 Hall gave a quiet exhibition with Ryan in Chicago for about one thousand five hundred customers.[958] All this suggests that Hall had recovered from the knife wound.

Davies arranged a fight for Hall in Milwaukee on October 8. He was to stop a local fighter named Ed Kenney (sometimes "Kinney") in four rounds. Davies acted as master of ceremonies and William Slavin, Frank Slavin's brother, acted as referee. During the first three rounds, Kenney had his way with Hall. Near the end of the third round however, Hall woke up and landed twice on Kenney's jaw and put him down each time. In the fourth round Kenney went down three more times but saved himself from a knockout. Finally, a local police inspector stopped the fight without a decision.[959]

In this process, Hall regained the confidence that he could return to the ring against more substantial opponents. He had several other fights during October. Not long after, Hall issued a challenge to spar Maher, the Irish heavyweight champion, six rounds or a fight to the finish. Madden who was representing Maher said in response that Maher had come to the United States to fight either Jackson or Corbett and he would pay no attention to challenges from middleweights.[960] Unfortunately for Maher, Madden later changed his mind and matched Maher with Fitzsimmons, who was still a middleweight but moving toward being a heavyweight.

Pat Killen dies

Three days after Hall fought in Milwaukee, Pat Killen fought a man named Bob Ferguson for the heavyweight championship of the northwest and a purse of $2,000. Their fight was at Richardson, Kane County, Illinois, where Ryan and McMillian fought. As customary, a Chicago contingent attended the fight.

Killen weighed 195 pounds, and Ferguson 198 at fight time.[961] Siler provides a detailed account of this affair in book *Inside Facts of Pugilism*. He says that Ferguson was backed by the toughest group of stockyards men that could be found, and Killen had his own group of plug-uglies. At the end of the second round, a brawl erupted in the ring between the two contingents, with men on both sides keeping guns and knives at the ready. Siler was the referee for the match, and said that one of Ferguson's backers kept a ten-inch blade on the ropes, and whenever Siler got close enough the man would poke him in the back with the knife and promise he would put it through him if Ferguson did not win. Killen put Ferguson down in the sixth round and although he wasn't knocked out, he refused to get up within the allowed time. After the match Ferguson's supporters took three pistol shots at Siler as he was walking to the train.[962]

Less than ten days later Killen died of erysipelas, an acute infection of the skin, accompanied by high fever and often complicated by blood poisoning and pneumonia. Although it is a highly contagious disease, it is now controlled by antibiotics. As the result of the bruises sustained in the Ferguson fight, some carelessness and exposure, and more dissipation after his victory, the disease had attacked Killen quickly.

His obituary in the *Chicago Tribune* treated him poorly. It noted that after he came under the guidance of Davies, his career took off with victories over Joe Lannon, Dick Burke, John Hughes, Pat McHugh, and several others. However, on "the edge of a long spell of dissipation, for which Parson Davies discarded him," Killen made a match with Mervine Thompson, the "Cleveland Thunderbolt," who defeated him. The *Tribune* said that for the last year Killen had operated a saloon on Clark Street under the Cosmopolitan Hotel and had almost dropped out of sight.

He was described as "one-handed" with a swinging right hand that tore many a punching bag from its moorings. It concluded by saying that Killen "had none of the qualities of a champion. He was heady, a poor trainer, rather clumsy, and not stout-hearted."[963] The *Chicago Herald* wrote that Killen was a pretty good second-rate fighter and that his erysipelas was complicated by mania. His saloon had been closed after he was forced to bed and sold before he died.[964]

In late October or early November, Davies went to the West Coast to see Jackson, who had apparently decided to return to the world of the living. With Sullivan back from Australia, the heavyweight logjam might be breaking loose.[965] On November 7, Davies was back in Chicago, where he met with Jack Barnett, Sullivan's manager. Barnett came to Chicago after landing with Sullivan's party in San Francisco. He was on his way to New York. He said Sullivan weighed 240 pounds, and that the trip to Australia was bum. Barnett told the Chicago press that a new play was being written for Sullivan in which he would be the leading character. Barnett offered Davies $400 a week and his expenses to star with Sullivan in the new production.

Jackson challenges Frank Slavin

Charlie declined Barnett's offer because Jackson had authorized him to challenge Frank Slavin, which the Parson planned to do within a few days. He said he would also start to stir up some of the eastern fighters on behalf of Hall. Jackson's agreement to fight Slavin was a tacit admission he no longer had a superior claim to a championship match with Sullivan.[966] However, if he defeated Slavin, then Jackson would again be in the top contender position without question.

Jackson notified the C.A.C. he would fight Slavin as early as mid-October.[967] On November 10 Davies issued the challenge for Jackson.[968] This was said to be the first time in his career that Jackson had challenged any fighter. However, when Jackson first went to England Davies made challenges on Jackson's behalf. In any case, the challenge issued to Slavin illustrates Jackson's sincere effort to get back into the prizefighting game. Jackson had effectively been idle after his sixty-one-round draw with Corbett. For most people interested in prizefighting in America, Jackson had fought only once in two years. He had put himself on the shelf preferring to operate a saloon in San Francisco.

It did not take long to get a response to Jackson's challenge. He was a marketable athlete in England, and on November 14 the National Club of London wired an offer of $10,000 for a fight there.[969] Davies wrote to Jackson to determine whether the C.A.C. would follow through and offer the same amount for the contest. Before receiving a response from California, Davies received a telegram from the National Club saying that Slavin had signed articles for a fight with Jackson and that the articles had been forwarded to Davies for Jackson's signature. The articles provided for a twenty-round fight, using four-ounce gloves, at catch-weights, for a purse of £2,000 with £1,750 to the winner. The contest was to take place at the National Club on Monday, May 30, 1892.[970] Jackson liked the conditions and the location.

Slavin's backer was George Piess, the head of a large perfumery house in London. Piess was the largest stockholder in the National Club, where the match was to take place. Slavin later said he agreed to the fight at the National because he thought a match there would benefit Piess. Jackson wrote to his friend Lord Lonsdale in England and advised Lonsdale he would sign the articles for the match with Slavin. Before leaving San Francisco, Jackson sold his saloon. All these decision showed a recommitment to prizefighting. He had made the important choice to get back to a serious boxing career, and this was good news for Davies.

While Barnett was in Chicago, Davies announced he intended to promote a tug-of-war tournament in Chicago. It is this type of event that made Davies unique among most prize fight managers. He enjoyed the unusual and being a showman. He saw the opportunities that unique entertainment provided and seemed to know what the public liked. Davies noted that a similar tournament had just closed in San Francisco and was a great financial success. He intended to offer prizes of $2,000 and give Chicago a taste of this exciting form of sport.

The tug-of-war and a killer horse

Davies was in San Francisco around the first of November because a big tug-of-war tournament occurred there in the last week of October and first week of November. San Francisco newspapers noted that Davies had watched the show. The San Francisco tournament included teams from the United States, Canada, Germany, Italy, Norway, Denmark, England, Sweden, Scotland, and Ireland pulling against one another in contests that sometimes lasted more than two hours. This entertainment drew immense crowds and was later mimicked by many smaller tournaments. For example, the Olympic Club arranged a tournament at its gymnasium and asked nearby communities to send teams on behalf of their towns. Tournaments were also arranged among school children and trade unions as well as police and fire departments.

After beginning to organize the tug-of-war show in Chicago, Davies went to New York, Boston and Philadelphia to arrange a fight for Hall and to plan another tug-of-war contest in Boston.[971] He returned to Chicago on November 21 and explained he had retained the Mechanic's Hall in Boston, a structure with seating of up to ten thousand, and the Industrial Art Building in Philadelphia for tug-of-war tournaments in those cities. He had tried to rent Madison Square Garden for Christmas week, but it was already booked.

The tournament in Chicago began on Monday, December 7, 1891.[972] Davies made a flourish by depositing $2,050 with the Globe National Bank in Chicago as the prize money to be paid to the winning teams. Rules for the tournament were issued, and Davies invited virtually every nationality in Chicago, except for the Chinese, to be represented by a team.[973] At the time the Chinese were considered lower than low and a physically small and weak nationality.

The tournament at Battery D included ten teams denominated as America, England, France, Germany, Scotland, Ireland, Bohemia, Italy, Africa, and

Canada. In addition to the international teams there were other contests between a military team from Fort Sheridan and teams of policemen, firemen, and letter carriers. When the competition began, one of Davies' best clients played a role: Evan Lewis, who served as a judge. Unfortunately, the competition in Chicago proved to be less than successful, and many spectators from the upper classes who had watched the same event in San Francisco did not attend.[974]

The next great entertainment that Davies sponsored in Chicago involved "Julius, The Ghost." Julius was a "man-eating" Norman-Percheron stallion that weighed 1,800 pounds. Percherons had been the mainstay draft animal for Midwestern farmers. Downstate farmers like George White frequently traveled to France and imported Percherons directly from that country.

Julius was a bad-tempered representative of his breed, but he was not insane or horse-trainer proof. J. Goldsmith of Pontiac, Illinois, had imported Julius from France at a cost of $2,000. As his thanks, Julius bit off Goldsmith's thumb and finger. Unwilling to risk additional digits, Julius was traded to F. H. Poundstone of Grand Ridge and then sold to C. S. Heagy of La Salle. Some reports said that Julius had killed three men and disabled five others, but this seems unlikely because the horse was obviously not destroyed.

Julius came to Chicago on the Rock Island line in a reserved car and wore a massive leather and iron muzzle to keep his mouth closed and sported an array of hobbles to control his movement. He was unloaded at the Chicago depot with great fanfare and was met by Davies and his owner. Julius was then escorted through the city streets from the depot to the Palmer House stable by several Pinkerton agents and men specially trained to operate his hobbles. Over one thousand people visited the stables on December 18 to view the vicious Julius for a fee of twenty-five cents.

The great Julius was in Chicago to meet Professor Oscar E. Gleason, a famed trainer. Davies had a contract with Gleason promising him $1,000 if he could subdue Julius in a twenty-four foot square ring that was not more than nine feet high on its sides. Judges were appointed to determine whether Gleason accomplished the task. Julius was set loose inside the enclosure without any harness, and Gleason was allowed sixty minutes to work his magic without using a strap, rope, or harness. Once Julius was subdued, the smaller ring was removed and Gleason was then required to drive him successfully inside a ring seventy feet by forty feet. He was allowed another hour to accomplish that goal.[975]

Approximately $7,500 was collected from the four thousand five hundred spectators who came to Battery D on December 18 to watch the Gleason-Julius match. The *Tribune* said that Davies was "getting even for the tug-of-war frost of last week and thawing out in the glow of the dollar pile in the adjacent ticket office."

When the entertainment began, Julius lay down and plunged about wildly in the pen's saw-dust shavings. Gleason appeared in a "black silk blouse, cords, long boots, and slouch hat." He instructed the crowd to remain quiet as he entered the small enclosure holding a large pistol "of mammoth proportion and shot it off twice." Julius jumped back and stared at Gleason, who then seized a whip and snapped the stallion on his rump. He then proceeded to chase Julius around the enclosure with the whip snapping his rump until the horse's eyes bulged out. Gleason then grabbed Julius by the forelock and told the crowd: "You may make as much noise as you want; the horse is mine!" Every time Julius looked at Gleason, he would produce the pistol again and fire it under the horse's nose. In the end the arena came down and Julius was hitched to a buckboard that the professor drove around the arena.[976]

Back to prizefighting

Two days after the great horse-taming extravaganza, Davies hosted a sparring match between Hall and Killen's final opponent, heavyweight Bob Ferguson. Hall was required to stop Ferguson in six rounds. Hall weighed 160 and Ferguson 210 pounds. Hall accomplished his goal by knocking Ferguson out in the fourth round. The match was billed as the last time that Hall would fight in Chicago, as he and Davies planned to leave immediately on a sparring tour of the eastern states followed by a trip to England with Jackson.[977]

Despite signed articles, Jackson's fight with Slavin was soon called into question.[978] The problem started with Sullivan and his backers. The great windbag instructed his backers to tell Slavin he would agree to a match with him only on the condition that Sullivan could withdraw from any fight if Slavin first lost to Jackson. Slavin's representatives wanted to make the match whether their man lost to Jackson or not, but Sullivan would not agree. Slavin agreed to Sullivan's stipulation and delivered $2,500 to Arthur Lumley of *The Illustrated News* to cover Sullivan's earlier conditional deposit.[979]

After the agreement was reached, Slavin's backer sent a cable to the United States saying he would no longer back him for any match in America. This meant that Slavin would not have backing for a match with Sullivan if he backed out of his match with Jackson.

Slavin was riled by this development and reminded the press he had only agreed to meet Jackson because of his friendship with Piess. Slavin said he intended to pull out of the fight and remain in the United States to fight Sullivan. Slavin said Piess had posted a $1,000 forfeit to bind Slavin's appearance, but Slavin felt justified in backing out of the match with Jackson because Piess had previously promised to back him in America. Piess' breach of his promise supposedly justified Slavin's breach of his promise to fight Jackson. Slavin saw no obligation to Jackson even though Peter had not part in causing the problems that Frank had encountered.[980]

Jackson wrote to Slavin, saying that Frank could not escape fighting him and that if he continued to talk about backing out of their match, then Peter would come east and force him to fight. The C.A.C. was anxious to secure the Slavin-Jackson contest and offered a $12,000 purse, $2,000 more than the National Club, to have the contest moved to San Francisco. The Pacific Club, another San Francisco boxing club, then offered $12,500 for the fight. All of this demonstrated that matches between top black and white fighters could be financially successful.

For the first time in four years Davies was in Chicago for the new year, which he had celebrated in St. Louis in 1888, Ireland in 89 and San Francisco in 90. Charlie had been on the road almost constantly during that period representing the world champion catch-as-catch-can wrestler, the top-ranked heavyweight contender, the champion heavyweight of Australia, the future heavyweight champion, and the champion middleweight of Australia. He probably indirectly handled the middleweight champion, Fitzsimmons. After eighteen months of only slight contact with Jackson, Davies resumed Peter's active management and would soon devote some of the best years of his professional life in an attempt to promote Jackson.

Chapter 12 - (1892)

Staying on Top

Peter Jackson was matched to fight Frank Slavin in England – a momentous fistic event indeed. "Parson Davies took Jim Hall and me to England to help train Jackson and second him. . . . Slavin was a powerfully built fellow with a head like a gargoyle. Both he and Jackson were trained to the minute.[981]

▬

Most boxers, outside the ring, remain boxers, tough, truculent, and considerably on the uncouth side. Choynski, to the contrary, was a polished man of the world, who invariably wore beautifully tailored clothes and manifested the manners of a cultured gentleman.

He was an intelligent conversationalist in almost every field, and he was a witty, clever and much sought after dinner speaker. When he came to Cincinnati, approximately eight years ago, he had difficulty in convincing persons that he was, or had been a fighter. . . . He was especially well informed about the stage and one of his hobbies was the study of the great masterpieces of painting.[982]

▬

Soft spoken, quiet and scholarly both in appearance and manner, there was little in Choynski to suggest his pugilistic past. Described by close friends as an esthete at heart, he had a penchant for beauty – be it a painted picture, the subtle turn of a phrase or the glory of a sunrise. An intense student of the stage, he appeared at conversational ease whatever the subject and was an accomplished after dinner speaker.[983]

▬

♣

Charles E. "Parson" Davies – About 1890 – Photograph courtesy of Dan Cuoco of the International Boxing Research Organization (IBRO)

Jackson left San Francisco on the evening of January 2, 1892, headed for Kansas City to link up with Davies.[984] The *Chicago Tribune* reported on January 3 that Jackson would arrive in the Windy City about January 10 and that arrangements were being made for him to appear at Battery D with a well-known heavyweight in a four-round contest.[985] In an article about the big money being raked in by prizefighters, one newspaper wrote that Jackson hailed directly or indirectly from the Congo and was raking in $500 a week for sparring in halls and theaters.[986] On January 4, Jackson and Con Riordan arrived at Ogden on their way to Chicago and then on to London. That evening Jackson and Riordan gave a four-round exhibition and he proved himself "quite equal to the occasion."[987]

On January 7, Davies left on the evening train for Kansas City to link up with Jackson and Riordan before they reached Chicago. Hall went as far as the Chicago depot with Davies to reinforce his position that it was again time for Davies to arrange a fight with Fitzsimmons. The news was circulating that Fitz intended to fight Mitchell, and Hall was hot under the collar. With a true heavyweight coming his way, the Parson's interest in the unpredictable Hall may have been slipping. Jackson and Riordan were to show on Saturday, January 9, in Kansas City and then in on the following Monday in Chicago.[988] Davies undoubtedly arranged the events in Ogden and Kansas City; he believed in making money wherever the opportunity presented itself.

The same day that Jackson and Riordan were in Ogden, Slavin and Mitchell opened at the People's Theater in Chicago for evening performances and Wednesday and Saturday matinees running through January 9.[989] They appeared in a sparring bout at every performance as part of a comedy entitled "U and I," and they had a successful run. The following week they appeared at the New Windsor Theater in a play entitled *The Struggle of Life*, which ran through January 16. Part of their success in Chicago was attributed to the fact the Mitchell refrained from his usual cheap boasting.[990] In his two previous appearances in Chicago at the end of 1887, Mitchell had appeared disguised as a tramp and had then been booed off the stage.

On January 7, there was good news for both Slavin and Jackson from a representative of the National Club of London. He stated that after the police interfered with the Slavin-McAuliffe contest, the club had determined to resolve the questions of legality in court. After two separate juries found in favor of the club in two different lawsuits, the prosecution agreed that it would no longer interfere with London prizefighting events.[991]

Jackson arrived in Chicago early in the morning on Monday, January 11, 1892. He never liked Chicago much, probably because of its cold weather. When he left San Francisco it was sixty-nine degrees. When he reached Chicago it was overcast, snowing and fourteen degrees. Nevertheless, arrangements were in place to give him a reception by his black friends there. That evening he appeared at Battery D to an overflow crowd. He was matched against the journeyman Jack King, and as part of the agreement he was to stop King in four two-minute rounds.

Floto was a timekeeper for the contest, and Hall acted as Peter's second. King appeared diminutive compared to Jackson, and for two rounds Peter took pity on him. In the third round Jackson went after King and almost frightened him to death. King was put down and quit the fight even though he was not knocked out. He was hissed off the stage for his cowardice.

That night, Tommy White sparred four rounds with another Billy Brennan, and Con Riordan performed with Henry Baker of Michigan. Davies had hired Riordan to travel with Jackson. The windup was a contest between Jackson and John Dalton, who was described as "late of Philadelphia." This was not Captain James Dalton, who had fought Sullivan ten years earlier. Again, the terms of the contest required Peter to stop Dalton within four two-minute rounds. After two active rounds, the "crisis was reached" in the third round, when Jackson knocked out Dalton. When Dalton came to, he claimed he wanted to finish the fight with bare knuckles, but his friends, having better sense, drew him away. Dalton then did a handspring to show he remained strong.[993]

Slavin, Mitchell, and Gallagher all came to Battery D to watch Jackson and were given a warm reception. Jackson and Slavin met socially but likely had little to say to one another. The next evening Hall, Jackson, and Davies all returned the favor by attending the performance at the New Windsor. After that performance, Jackson and Slavin met to talk over their match on May 30.[994] They must have had a good conversation because after this meeting Slavin stopped talking about pulling out of their match.

The new Davies' combination did not stay long in Chicago. They left on Saturday, January 16, after depositing $1,000 in the Globe National Bank to secure Jackson's appearance against Slavin. They opened at Hyde & Behman's Theater in Brooklyn on Monday, January 18.[995] The *Brooklyn Eagle* reported that "Peter Jackson and Con Riordan, professional sluggers" would fight at every performance.[996]

Davies' Athletic & Specialty Co. appeared in Brooklyn through January 23, with a matinee offered every day. After they appeared in Brooklyn, the fighters moved on to Boston and put on a show on January 25 at a benefit given for Dixon. Davies acted as master of ceremonies for this event.[997] From Boston, Jackson and Davies made a long trip to St. Louis to meet with Slavin on the morning of February 6.[998]

That day in New York, Corbett signed articles of agreement to meet the winner of the Jackson-Slavin match in New Orleans. Corbett confirmed for the press that the match would have to take place in New Orleans. This was simply a show by Corbett because he knew that Jackson had said as early as May 1891 that he would not fight in New Orleans. Brady and Corbett knew full well that Jackson had already said he would never return to New Orleans[999] Whatever had happened to Jackson in New Orleans in January 1891 had soured him on the Deep South, and he never returned there.[1000] Corbett didn't want to fight Jackson, and he proved it, repeatedly using every dodge he could to avoid Jackson.

On February 14, Jackson responded to Corbett's proposal to fight the winner of the Slavin-Jackson fight but only in New Orleans. He was quoted in Omaha's *Morning World Herald* as saying: "I have said before I will not fight in New Orleans, not that I don't think I would get fair play, but because of the feeling there against my race. As to signing an agreement, I will say that I shall sign nothing. I will finish the fight I have on first, and then look after the others. If I win this fight with Slavin, then I will be glad to meet Corbett and give him the first chance if he wants it, but before this fight is over I will not do anything."[1001] Jackson's statement was somewhat ambiguous. He seemed to be taking a stance that was based solely on the treatment of his race in the South. However, in other circumstances he did not take such a strictly principled position.

Jackson and Davies went to Philadelphia, where Jackson appeared at the Lyceum Theater to meet all comers for points, i.e., he was not required to knock out his opponents. He appeared at the Lyceum to packed houses every night. His recorded exhibitions there included: February 15 three lame rounds with Al "Fish" Carter, whose antics were not appreciated;[1002] February 16 with Professor Billy McLean of Philadelphia (McLean was reported to be 59 years old but didn't look a day over 40), who put on an interesting show;[1003] February 17 with Joe Butler; and February 18 with a person named Milton.

The *Philadelphia Inquirer* reported that Jackson had made a good impression during his week there. The *Boston Globe* reported that he had a flattering offer to continue on stage and was considering whether to accept and remain in the states rather than traveling to England.[1004] In Philadelphia, Jackson was also asked to appear before a black political club known as the Edwin H. Fitler Republican Association. Davies left Jackson to return home. He passed through Pittsburgh on the evening of February 16 headed for Chicago.[1005]

During the time between the benefit in Boston and the appearances in Philadelphia, Hall also went back to Chicago for an appearance on the evening of February 1 at Battery D with Jack King. Hall was to stop King within three two-minute rounds. Poor King was being pummeled on a regular basis by Australians. Hall made a mark of King and from the call of time he beat King ruthlessly. King was knocked out to stay in the third round.

After several other matches, the windup for the evening was Hall's attempt to stop Mike Boden of Philadelphia in four Queensberry rounds with four-ounce gloves. Malachi Hogan was the referee for the match, and Floto was the timekeeper. The *Tribune* said that Boden presented a curious sight in the ring because he was short and thick set and carried his right hand forward with his left held in front of his stomach. He apparently fought in a style similar to Tom Sharkey but he could not "fight a particle and from the beginning resorted to all kinds of unfair tactics to stay four rounds." Between "clinching, kicking and biting" he managed to stay the four rounds.[1006]

Another Hall-Boden match was scheduled for Wednesday, February 17, at Battery D in Chicago.[1007] This match was to be a five-round affair, and Hall was to meet an unknown heavyweight that evening in a four-round match. However, two nights earlier the Chicago police stopped a match at the Second Regiment Armory between John Dalton and Harry Baker, and then the police again interfered during the planned windup between Andy Bowen of New York and Jimmy Murphy of Chicago and ordered the men off the stage in the third round.[1008] This led to the cancellation of the entertainment scheduled for the February 17. Chicago was not a place that welcomed prizefighting.

Jackson and Riordan leave for England

Jackson and Riordan reached New York on February 23 and the next day set sail on the *Britannic* of the White Star line to disembark at Liverpool on March 4.[1009] The immigration manifest that was required for ships bringing passengers into the United Kingdom listed them as the last two persons on the eight-page form and shows both of their occupations as "Lawyer."[1010]

Jackson had spent five months training for his match with Corbett. Except for the exhibitions with Riordan that began in Ogden and his matches with lower-level fighters, he was not in shape for a serious fight with Slavin. He apparently did not want to continue on the exhibition circuit, where it was too easy to drink and too hard to stay in shape, but he did want to go to England with Riordan and seriously prepare for his match.

The *World* reported that Jackson had gained ten pounds of flesh during his voyage and would go into training at Brighton the following week. Jackson told the press he wanted to "take ample time about training," and wanted "to be in perfect condition to fight Slavin." A delegation of about four hundred London sluggers and sporting men met Jackson on his arrival at Euston Square Station near King's Cross in London. Representatives of the National Club took him to College Inn on Portland Street, where he stayed until going to Brighton. He was taken to his hotel in a coach and four. This was a far cry from the treatment a black man would receive in New Orleans.[1011]

The departure of Jackson and Riordan left Davies' combination short on talent. Hall had no confirmed matches in either the United States or England, and his scheduled appearance with Boden in Chicago had been canceled. These circumstances created a lull in activity that was filled, in part, by a trip to New Orleans, which had become a Mecca for pugilists. The big news was that two important fights had been scheduled there for early March. Needham was to fight Ryan, and Maher, considered a coming heavyweight, was matched to meet Fitz, the champion middleweight.

A special train was chartered from Chicago to take sports to New Orleans. The train was to leave on Saturday, February 27, ten minutes after the departure of the limited on the Illinois Central Line. At that time, the limited left Chicago at two p.m. and arrived at New Orleans at four fifteen the following afternoon. Those traveling to the match would arrive late in the afternoon on Sunday, February 28, in time for the Ryan-Needham fight the following evening at the Metropolitan Club. Passengers on the special train included Davies, his brother Vere, McDonald, Billy Pinkerton, Clark, Alf Kennedy, Myer, Sol Van Praag, a Chicago politician, Hogan, and other leading sportsmen in Chicago. Hall also went to New Orleans, where he and Myer were to act as seconds for Ryan.[1012]

New Orleans was a wide-open city at the time. Italian crime syndicate murders were rampant, and even the police chief had been assassinated. Gambling of all kinds was available. Live horse racing and off-track betting were available from tracks such as Ascot and Oakland, California.

The Ryan-Needham fight was canceled because Ryan fell ill and was taken to the Charity Hospital earlier on the day or the fight. A doctor certified that Ryan had tonsillitis and would be unable to fight that evening and for at least two weeks.[1013] The Fitzsimmons-Maher contest was scheduled for the next day, so many sports from around the country were left to enjoy the city of New Orleans.[1014]

One of the fighters present in New Orleans was the heavyweight Joe Choynski of San Francisco, who was hoping to make a match with the winner of the Fitzsimmons-Maher fight.[1015] Choynski was well known on the West Coast, having participated in a battle with Corbett that stretched over two days. Joe had also traveled to Australia, where he made a good impression and then returned to San Francisco on the same ship with Sullivan and his huge party.

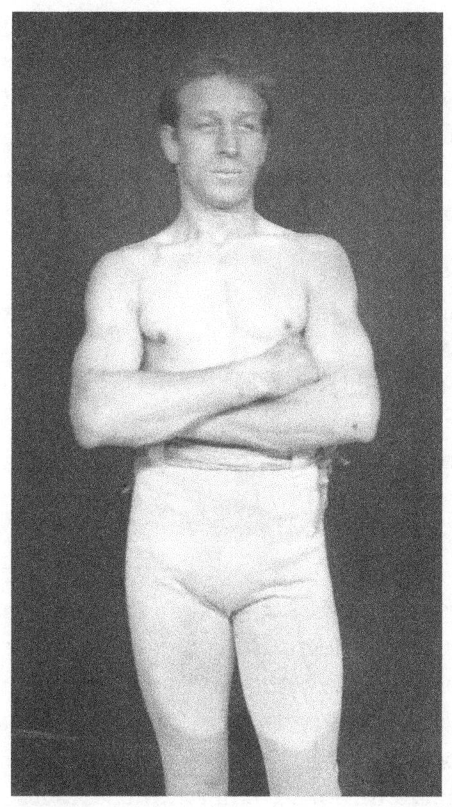

Joe Choynski in 1909 at the end of his great career – Photograph of the Chicago History Museum

Davies finds Joe Choynski

Choynski was the kind of fighter Davies favored. He liked to fight and fight often, and he was not too picky about his opponents. After returning to the United States, he had knocked out Woods in thirty-four rounds on December 17, 1891 at San Francisco and sparred in an exhibition with Sullivan three days later to help Sullivan make some quick money. Joe had traveled to Bay Saint Louis, Mississippi, and helped train Fitz for his contest with Maher.[1016]

Choynski was born in San Francisco on November 8, 1868. A Jewish-American, his father Isidor was a Polish Jew and his mother was born in England. An article in the *California Historical Quarterly* provides some insight into Joe's background:

> Clearly, the Choynski household was highly literate and politically oriented. Joe's father was one of the founders and leaders of the Hebrew Young Men's Literary Association, established in the 1850s in San Francisco. His leadership, atypically, was a product of his intellectual brilliance, rather than the result of economic success. The highest office in the community structure of Jewry of the western states was the presidency of District Grand Lodge No.

> 4, Independent Order of B'nai B'rith traditionally had German Jewish leadership, and I. N. Choynski was a Polish Jew, he held the District Grand Lodge presidency in 1874 and was re-elected for 1875. Joe's father also had been an editor for the *Alta California* and a reporter for the *Evening Post*; he was known in literary circles for his Antiquarian Bookstore and press.

Joe's mother was also highly educated. The former Harriet Ashim "had been a pupil in the 1850's of Rabbi Julius Eckman, of San Francisco. Her father was Jewish, her mother a convert to Judaism."[1017]

During the Fitzsimmons-Maher fight, Hall sat in front with Davies. Choynski acted as one of Fitz's seconds and later received credit for helping Bob survive the first round so he could stop Maher in twelve rounds. Actually, Maher quit in the twelfth round because he was badly beaten and had simply been taking punishment since the seventh round.

In the first round Fitz bashed Maher's lip causing a fairly serious cut which bled throughout the match. This cut riled Maher. He made a rush at Fitz and staggered him with a right hand to Bob's neck. That blow nearly knocked out Fitz, but at the call of time he was rescued by Choynski. When Fitz came up for the second round, he had recovered his faculties. He had a remarkable ability to recover after a near knockout.

The day after the Fitzsimmons-Maher fight, Davies said that if it had not been for the cut lip Maher suffered during the first round he felt that Maher would have won the match. He thought that Maher had been badly handled by his people during the match. Davies and Hall also met with the leadership of the New Orleans' Olympic Club in an effort to arrange a Hall-Fitzsimmons match.[1018] Unable to arrange something in New Orleans, Davies decided to take Hall to Europe.[1019]

Reports circulated on March 3, 1892 that the San Francisco sports in New Orleans were trying to arrange a Hall-Choynski match.[1020] President Noel of the Olympic Club contacted Hall and offered a purse of $5,000 for a fight with Choynski, and Warren Lewis posted $1,000 with the *New York World* on behalf of Hall for a finish fight with Fitzsimmons before the club that would give the largest purse.[1021] Reports also circulated that "Denver Ed" Smith had issued a challenge to fight Hall in a finish fight to take place near Pittsburgh in May for a purse of $5,000.[1022]

The day after his arrival in England, Jackson was being treated like a king by the English while back in American one of the most detestable events in sporting history occurred. A man who could have changed sporting history chose the low road. Sullivan issued a challenge from St. Paul. His challenge was addressed: "To the Public in General and Frank P. Slavin, Charles Mitchell and James Corbett in Particular." He was willing to fight anyone who would put up their money for match at the Olympic Club. He concluded his challenge: "In this challenge I include all fighters, first come first served, who are white. I will not fight a negro. I never have. I never shall."[1023] Corbett's manager rushed to make the deposit required. He was not disturbed at all by Sullivan's overt prejudice and was always quite proud of himself for beating everyone else to the starting line.[1024]

Choynski remained in New Orleans through March 10, sparring with Fitzsimmons.[1025] Soon after, Choynski was touring with Davies and Hall. He joined the Davies' combination because he was short on money. He had traveled to Mississippi to help train Fitz for his match with Maher. Fitz wanted a heavyweight to work with before meeting the Irishman, and Joe thought he could get a match by being near the action. Joe acted as second for Fitz during the Fitzsimmons-Maher fight. At the time it was customary for the winning fighter to make a substantial payment to his seconds; however, Fitz bought breakfast for Choynski the next morning and gave him nothing else.[1026] Davies needed a fighter and picked up Joe, and by March 16 Joe was in Chicago.

While all these boxing events were in progress on March 19 one of Davies' nieces entered the Sisters of Charity of the Blessed Virgin Mary. Kittie was one of the three orphaned daughters of Charlie's brother Henry W. Davies, and Charlie once told a newspaper reporter that Kittie was his favorite niece. You see, even grizzled boxing managers have a heart and in years to come, newspaper articles would mention visits that Charlie made to San Francisco to see Kittie or Kittie's sister Sarah (Sadie) working with the Parson in New Orleans, or her other sister Anita carrying for her aging uncle at Anita's home in Chicago.

Hall and Choynski tour the East

An important chapter in Davies' career was about to start. Once again he was taking a star combination on the road for nightly appearances in theaters on the East Coast. These tours were important; however, to be a true success in this line of work theater appearances needed to lead to a real fight that would make international headlines, draw a crowd, and return a substantial payoff. Before the tour started, Davies, Hall, and Choynski went to Mt. Clemens, Michigan to recharge their batteries in the mineral baths.[1027] On Friday, March 25, 1892 the *Post Dispatch* reported that "Parson Davies started on an exhibition tour with Jim Hall and Joe Choynski yesterday."[1028]

On March 29 they gave an exhibition in Detroit. On Wednesday, March 30 all three were spotted by a reporter for the *Daily Times* of Lima, Ohio. They were traveling from Detroit to Louisville to appear there on the evening of March 31.[1029] After a night in Louisville, all three men went to Chicago to take part in entertainment on Saturday, April 2, 1892 and then go east, together with Evan Lewis, the wrestler. They intended to sail for England after their appearances on the East Coast.

At the end of March, Jackson, and Riordan quarreled, and Riordan decided to return to the United States.[1030] No reason was given for this problem, but it probably related to Riordan's heavy drinking. His departure concerned Davies because it left Jackson without a sparring partner. Charlie wanted Jackson in England because he was the load star around whom Hall and Choynski would orbit when they reached the British Isles, but Davies preferred that someone be with Jackson.

The Hall-Choynski sparring match in Chicago was scheduled for Saturday, April 2.[1031] The "Saint Joe Kid" and John Dalton had expressed interest in meeting either of the two international stars. During the Hall-Choynski match, the Chicago police kept a close watch to assure that no "rough work" took place. Hall out pointed Choynski, who appeared to be more of a rough fighter than a sparrer. Hall also sparred with Jack King that same evening.[1032]

George Siler provides an account of these matches in his book *Inside Facts on Pugilism*. He places the King-Hall match in the fall of 1901, but his recollection seems to be wrong. He writes that King had an overblown view of his ability and saw himself as championship stock. King had approached Davies and asked for a chance to spar a full four rounds with Hall. Davies agreed to put King on the program and to allow King to stand the full four rounds.

Davies told Siler about the agreement and Siler went to King and decided to stir him up by saying he had learned that Davies' secret plan was for Hall to knock him out. King replied that if this was Davies' game then he was going to use his right hand and get some good licks in on Hall before he knew what was happening.

Siler wrote: "Jack demonstrated he could not fight enough to keep warm by connecting his head with every one of Hall's leads, and before the second round his was on the floor taking the long count." When Siler asked King about his failure to use of his right hand, Jack said he had decided to hold it back until the third round, and he guessed he had waited too long.

Another account of this match discusses what happened between Davies and King after the fight. King hunted up Davies to complain he had been told that the "gazook from Australia was going to let him stick." Davies loved a good joke and told King that Hall had intended to let him go the distance but that Jim had suffered from St. Vitus dance as a child and that sometimes his right arm would jerk involuntarily. He said that Jim had suffered a relapse during the match, and his right arm had snapped out and struck King.

"Say Parson, I never heard of a guy having what you said," King replied. "But if you don't mind, do you think you could find me one of them dancin' schools in America?"[1034]

The combination left Chicago late in the evening on April 2 because Hall was scheduled to meet Billy Leedom on April 4 in Philadelphia for a four-round go.[1035] The run to Philadelphia by way of Pittsburgh was made on the Pennsylvania limited in about twenty-four hours. The limited provided Pullman sleepers and a buffet car. There were six double bed rooms in each sleeping car complete with clean, pressed sheets, and private wash rooms. Meals in the buffet car included choices of a large assortment of regional cuisines with linen table clothes and fine crystal china made especially for the railroad. Four men could sit in a booth on high quality cushions while a black steward served beverages on a sliver tray. This wasn't exactly roughing it.

They all arrived in Philadelphia late in the evening on April 3 in excellent health and condition. On April 6, while Davies, Choynski, and Hall were in Philadelphia, Sullivan arrived in Bloomington, Illinois, on the Big Four train. He had played in Peoria the previous night and appeared at Bloomington's Grand Theater in *Honest Hearts and Willing Hands*, along with Jack Ashton. During the fifth act of the play Sullivan and Ashton sparred. Sullivan said he was fond of Bloomington, having visited there "on a number of occasions in past years." He was accompanied by his wife, and they stayed that evening at the Windsor Hotel only about a block away from the theater. While the fighters turned actors were in Bloomington, Ashton was mysteriously injured. He supposedly went for a horseback ride and came back with "a well developed limp." It is likely that Ashton slipped off to some unknown location for a secret set-to with a local fighter, who may have been the same Richard Dunn who met Cardiff early in Patsey's career. After Bloomington the company left for Decatur, Illinois.[1036]

Throughout April and the first few days of May, Davies, Hall and Choynski were on the East Coast working the theaters and building a reputation with local sports and newspapers. They were in Philadelphia at the Aerial Athletic Club for Hall's April 4 match. Some sources say Jim's intended opponent was Billy Leedom, but others say Jim Glynn. Most reports say that Glynn failed to show and Jack Flood (sometimes "Floyd") of Richmond was substituted at the last moment. Hall put Flood out in one round.[1037]

The combination stayed in Philadelphia for a week. Two nights after meeting Flood, Hall met Jack Houghey of Port Richmond, and after two hard rounds Houghey sank to his knees unable to continue. The club's manager instructed the two fighters to continue for two more rounds but with no additional hard hitting.[1038]

On April 8, Choynski was scheduled to meet Jack Martin, but that fight was canceled. On April 9, Hall knocked out Mike White in one round, and Choynski defeated Joe Godfrey in one round.[1039] Hall told the press he was leaving for New York to meet Fitzsimmons face-to-face.[1040] Stories circulated that the Chicago Athletic Club wanted to hire a sparring instructor, and the two leading candidates were Billy Myer and Choynski. The *Chicago Tribune* noted that both "Myer and Choynski belong to the better grade of pugilists, are quiet and unassuming in their ways, and amply qualify to fill the position acceptably."[1041]

While in Philadelphia, Davies made a push to reschedule a Hall-Fitzsimmons match. The Jackson-Slavin fight was important to keep Peter on the map as the leading heavyweight contender, but a Hall-Fitzsimmons match could result in Davies having two champions at the same time and give him enormous leverage with other managers. Hall said that his backer, Davies, was prepared to put up $5,000 for the fight. He belittled Fitz's claim that he would only meet if Hall trimmed down to 154 pounds. Hall pointed out that Fitz had given Maher fifteen pounds of advantage and offered to bet $5,000 of his own money in addition to the posted stakes if Fitz would agree to fight. Hall concluded, "The controversy between us has reached a point where he has either to fight me if he dares or crawl like the coward he is."[1042]

The entire Davies' combination moved to New York and took rooms at the Metropolitan Hotel. On April 11, Hall and Choynski sparred three rounds in an exhibition at Niblo's Theater in conjunction with the Henry Burlesque Company.[1043] The next afternoon Fitz, his trainer Jimmy Carroll, Davies, and Hall held a business meeting.

The best account of this meeting was provided by the *Picayune* several days later. Essentially, Fitzsimmons' side wanted to fight in New Orleans, and Davies wanted to fight before the club that offered the best purse. Davies also had some trouble with his own fighter, who pressed for a meeting at the Olympic Club in New Orleans.[1044]

After meeting for an hour the group published an agreement that they had already signed. Fitz and Hall agreed to a glove contest to a finish, at catch weights, before the one of three possible clubs that were offering a purse of $12,000 or more. The three clubs specified were the Olympic in New Orleans, the Pacific in San Francisco, or the C.A.C. They also agreed to a side wager of $5,000 with the match to take place no earlier than November 1 and no later than December 30.[1045] The three clubs were to bid for the fight with bids to be accepted before April 25. Davies probably wanted a specific date for bids because the group was planning to leave for England. It seems likely that the November 1 date was directly related to his plans for Hall, Choynski, and Lewis in England and an anticipated tour to France and Germany.

After signing the agreement, Hall went to Niblo's, where he and Choynski put on their nightly show. Later, the entire group went to the Metropolitan Hotel's café, where they celebrated into the early hours of Wednesday, April 13. Agreeing to a Hall-Fitzsimmons match was a very big deal, and that match would frame the combination's work over the next seven months. Moreover, Hall and Choynski's time in England would enhance their international reputations, and when they returned to America the prizefighting world would hopefully focus its attention on Davies' fighters. At least, that was how it was supposed to work.

Davies does up "Pug" Connors

Eight men were present for the celebration at the Metropolitan: Fitzsimmons, Carroll, Davies, Maher, Brodie (the bridge jumper), Madden, Jere Dunne (who had killed Jimmy Elliott), and an ex-fighter named Eddie Connors, better known as "Pug." Connors had been the sparring partner of Jimmy Carroll and then worked as a bouncer in the gallery of the London Theater. About three a.m. on April 13 and after forty-two quarts of champagne, a dispute occurred.

Maher was wearing a religious medal and Connors made a derogatory comment about the religious symbol. Maher objected to Connors' remark, and Connors called Maher a "bloody coward" for giving up in the twelfth round of the Fitzsimmons fight. Maher made a lunge at Connors, who was carrying a dirk knife. He pulled the knife and jumped for Maher, but Davies grabbed Connor's arm.

"I'll kill you for that!" Connors said to Davies.

"Oh, will you?" the Parson replied, and with two blows broke a champagne bottle over his assailant's head.

Although Charlie had earned his reputation as being among the upper crust of fight promoters, he knew how to handle himself. Whether pulling a gun to get Killen into the ring, using a Bowie knife in the alley with Ryan, slashing Hall with a lemon knife, or bashing Connors with a champagne bottle, Davies was familiar with weapons and defending himself in a heated situation.

A few days later Davies told the *Philadelphia Inquirer* that the whole story was exaggerated. It bothered him that some newspapers had reported the story as if Connors was a consumptive when he was really a Bowery bouncer. Davies said that Connors had forced his way into the small group that was meeting together quietly and then had tried to dominate the conversation. Davies said that when the fight started it was clear that if he did not intervene Connors would kill Maher. Davies asserted that the owners and clerks at the Metropolitan had thanked him for preventing a murder in their place.

When Connors was laid low, Hall stayed behind as a good samaritan. He had been done up by Davies about a year earlier at Mt. Clemens and could sympathize with Connors. Hall took Connors to a nearby drug store, where his wounds were cleaned and dressed. Davies left for Philadelphia that day, and Hall and Choynski continued sparring at Niblo's that evening although they both must have had healthy hangovers.[1046]

Hall and Choynski continued their nightly sparring at Niblo's and took matches with other fighters who would show up to fight.[1047] The matches were not particularly interesting.[1048] On several occasions Hall and Choynski alternated opponents. On April 22, 1892, at New York, Choynski knocked out Tom Ryan (not the Tommy Ryan of Chicago) in another two-round match.[1049] Hall and Choynski then went back to Philadelphia, where Hall met Billy Leedom on April 23, and Choynski sparred four rounds with "Denver Ed" Smith on April 25.[1050] Their match was stopped by the police and the referee declared it a draw.[1051] There were claims that Smith got the better of Joe and that Davies sent out false information about the match to protect Choynski.[1052] The "false" information was that Parson Davies had cautioned Joe to go easy with Smith during the first three rounds because Smith was a dangerous customer. This advice caused Joe to lie in the weeds until the fourth round, when the fight was stopped.[1053]

Toward the end of these shows, Davies arrived back in Chicago on April 25. He confirmed that Hall would accept the offer of the Olympic Club for a Hall-Fitzsimmons match. The Olympic increased its offer from $10,000 to $12,000 for the match but insisted it take place on September 5. However,

Davies insisted that Hall would appear there only in November or December. He said that Hall would not appear before November 1 because he was taking his fighters to England. He said that while he was in England Warren Lewis would look after Hall's affairs.[1054] The Olympic issued a response in the form of an ultimatum, which was unfortunate because Davies did not respond well to ultimatums.[1055] Nevertheless, it was Hall who was criticized for his refusal to agree to a fight in New Orleans.[1056]

In 1927 Choynski wrote a series of articles about his life and career for the *Winnipeg Free Press*. About the days at Niblo's Garden he wrote: "Jim and I alternated in the pummeling. One night I would mall some aspirant and the next night Hall would be the executioner, except when some particularly formidable-appearing foe would be scheduled; then Hall would plead illness." Joe recalled one evening when a "gigantic colored fighter, C. C. Smith, who had more than a local reputation as the 'Black Thunderbolt' [appeared]. It was Hall's turn to save the one hundred dollars, but Jim developed an illness. The management was panicky and was for having the 'Black Thunderbolt' blackjacked in the alley or arrested, or what you will—anything to save the money. I suggested they give me a chance and wait until the third round before starting the 'win the wrangle' stuff. I knocked Smith out in the first round."[1057]

The Olympic wanted the Hall-Fitzsimmons fight to be part of a planned boxing carnival in New Orleans. Davies insistence on the November or December fight date specified in the original agreement jeopardized the club's plan.[1058] The Olympic was going to hold three consecutive nights of championship matches: Sullivan-Corbett, Myer-McAuliffe, and Hall-Fitzsimmons. They were offering $10,000 each for the latter two. As exciting as this was for most of the sporting world, it did not fit in with Davies' plans. He wanted the attention of the sporting world on the Jackson-Slavin fight in London, and then he planned to make a lot of money in England before coming back to America for the Hall-Fitzsimmons match.

At that point it wasn't clear what would happen. On April 28, Carroll and Davies met at the Metropolitan in New York and decided to hold to the original agreement that they had made two weeks earlier, which provided for a Hall-Fitzsimmons fight no earlier than November 1.[1059] Despite an agreement that they would not meet until November 1, by the time Fitzsimmons and Carroll reached Philadelphia on May 1 they had changed their minds.[1060] Fitzsimmons, Hall, Carroll, and Davies were all at the Continental Hotel in Philadelphia and again met to discuss a possible fight in New Orleans. Fitz then took the position that if Hall did not appear on September 5 then Fitz would ignore him in the future.[1061] The *Post Dispatch* wrote that Hall would not accept the Olympic Club's offer because it would upset his future plans and cause him to miss the Jackson-Slavin fight.[1062]

Hall and Choynski stayed in Philadelphia into early May, and the two fighters continued to perform. On the afternoon on May 4, Davies, Hall, and Choynski all left New York aboard the *Germanic*, of the White Star line, on their passage to England and a new part of the long-range plan. Hall, twenty-three years old, and Choynski, twenty-four, were both described as "Gentlemen" on the ship's manifest.[1063]

Davies and Jackson in England again

On May 10, a dispatch from Liverpool reported that over two hundred representatives of English sporting circles would meet the three travelers, who would also receive a royal reception when they arrived in London. From London the men went on to Brighton, where Jackson had trained for his match with Slavin. Peter's fellow black heavyweight George Godfrey also went to England at the end of May to watch Peter fight.[1064] Davies said that he and his aggregation intended to stay in England for four months.[1065]

Davies' relationship with Jackson had clearly changed. When Jackson first visited London, Davies had played a controlling role in scheduling and training. When Jackson returned to San Francisco from Australia, Davies had played virtually no role in Peter's preparation for his fight with Corbett. In England a second time, Jackson was again largely on his own while Davies gave his attention to Choynski and Hall.

Upon arrival in England, Davies was stunned by Jackson's apparent loss of weight and wasted appearance. He was told that Jackson had been doing a lot of swimming in fresh water baths, which Davies thought to have contributed to his changed appearance. He insisted that Jackson give up the swimming routine, and Peter quickly recovered his weight and appearance.[1066] Between May 23 and May 29, 1892, Hall and Choynski put on sparring exhibitions at London's Novelty Theater while waiting for the Jackson-Slavin match on May 30.[1067]

Davies and Hall split

The next day Davies learned that the situations with respect to his management of Hall had changed. Davies did not use written contracts with the fighters he managed. He considered a fighter's word his bond and thought that something in writing would not improve the situation. On May 30, Davies was in the ticket office of the Novelty Theater, where Hall and Choynski were appearing. Choynski called him aside and asked to talk with him after the performances ended, and Davies agreed. At the meeting, Joe told Davies that Charley Mitchell, with the backing of George Washington Moore, who was known in sporting circles as "Pony" Moore, had arranged a match between Hall and Pritchard. Moore was a long-time boxing manager, the founder of the Christy Minstrels and also Mitchell's father-in-law.

Davies went to Mitchell and Hall and asked for an explanation. Hall discounted the situation by saying he had no intention of fighting at 160 pounds, the weight Pritchard had demanded. Davies told Hall he hoped he had not agreed to a match with Pritchard because it would imperil a $15,000 purse that was waiting for him in America for a match with Fitz.

The following Monday, a group including Hall, Mitchell, Moore, and Davies met at the offices of the *Sporting Life*. Mitchell produced a written contract for the Pritchard fight and wanted Davies to sign it as a witness. This was an insult because Davies was Hall's manager and not simply a witness. In reply, Davies said he wanted nothing to do with the affair. Mitchell smiled "in a smooth sort of way" and said that if the Parson would only sign as a witness it need not interfere with his management arrangement with Hall. This last remark was an implicit threat that if Davies did not sign the agreement then Hall would drop Davies and use Mitchell as his manager. Davies declined and told Mitchell that one manager was enough for a fighter. A few days later he paid off Hall with a large check and had nothing to do with his management after that point.

The Hall-Pritchard match that Mitchell arranged was originally supposed to take place on August 22. Davies went to Belfast to visit with his family, and the date for the fight was then changed to August 20, so Davies was not present for the match. He had been invited to the fight by Pritchard's backer but contended that even if he had been in London he would not have attended. Both Davies and Hall said that they parted as friends.[1068]

The Slavin-Jackson fight

The Slavin-Jackson contest began about eleven twenty p.m. on the evening of May 30, 1892, at Covent Garden under the auspices of the National Club in London. The audience was composed of the aristocracy of England, including royalty. The spectators were in evening clothes. Davies and Choynski were the seconds for Peter. Most accounts list Harry Smith of London as another second for Peter, who had trimmed down to 193 pounds for this important fight. Slavin weighed in at 185. The referee for the evening was B. J. Angle, who had refereed the Sullivan-Mitchell contest in France.

Jackson knocked out Slavin in ten rounds. Choynski recalled in the *Winnipeg Free Press* that "Slavin was an aggressive fighter but Peter was too clever for him. Jackson would jab his left to the head and follow with a hard right to the body. As Slavin rushed, the clever black man would step away as easy as if he were showing a new dance step to a pupil."[1069]

Of the active fighters at the time, Slavin's style was probably closest to Sullivan's, and Jackson handled Slavin easily. Throughout the fight Jackson kept his long left hand in Slavin's face. Through the third round he prodded Frank in the mouth and left eye, which was soon swollen shut. By the fourth round it seemed that Jackson had measured his man and was confident of victory. Time after time Jackson banged his left in Slavin's face and avoided his opponent's rushes. In the tenth round Slavin came up quickly but appeared weaker. Jackson went after him and landed a hard right and then a left on Slavin's jaw. From that point on, Slavin was clearly a beaten man and simply trying to hold on and avoid punishment.

As he often did, Jackson appealed to the referee indicating that Slavin was a beaten man, but the referee told him to fight on. He then continued to pummel Slavin until he knocked him cold.

Choynski said that from "the seventh round to the end Slavin was groggy. . . . A groggy man is often harder to knock down than one in good shape. I advised Jackson to work Slavin to a position near the ropes, wallop him with everything he could put into a punch, then push him hard against the ropes and step back. My expectation was that Slavin would fall on the rebound. This is exactly what happened."[1070]

After the fight, the *Chicago Tribune* reported that Davies had been a big winner in the betting. The gossip was that Davies had won a combined $50,000 on bets placed in London and the United States. In addition, many black friends of Jackson had bet heavily on him, and they also won good money for their support. The odds in Chicago were said to be ten to seven or eight on Slavin. Mitchell bet on Slavin and lost over $1,000.[1071]

Sullivan wasted no time in commenting on the outcome of the Jackson-Slavin fight. He said he was surprised when told of Jackson's victory. He repeated that any "white man who fights with a N______ ought to be whipped." He claimed he was disappointed with the outcome; he wanted to fight Slavin for purely business reasons because he knew that Slavin "would be dead easy picking for me." He concluded that Slavin's defeat had cost him $50,000.[1072]

In England Davies remained busy on behalf of his two remaining fighters. Jackson had defeated Slavin, and no reasonable or fair person could claim that Jackson was not the top heavyweight contender. Choynski challenged Ted Pritchard, but the English sports laughed at his presumptuousness. Davies issued a challenge to Jem Smith on behalf of Choynski for a fight for $2,500 and an undetermined purse.[1073] Smith waited to answer that challenge until after Davies and Choynski sailed for New York.

Other news out of England was not so good. Davies was becoming concerned about Jackson's health. If his health failed and that became apparent, he would not remain the top contender. Davies wrote to his friend Al Smith in New York: "I don't like Pete's looks."[1074] Davies was not considered a tipster, and it was well known that if he had a fighter in the pink of condition, the most he might say was that his fighter was "well and confident."

Not long after his match with Slavin, Peter discovered that he had broken a small bone in his hand under his little finger.[1075] The injury required Jackson to stop fighting for about two months.[1076] Davies' concern about Jackson's health proved to be well-taken. After the Slavin match, Jackson never again fought a top heavyweight while he was a healthy man.

Many years later Choynski recalled that "Jackson became a popular idol in England, and enjoyed himself so well that he undermined his health."[1077] This conclusion was somewhat unfair because the tuberculosis that eventually killed Jackson can strike the healthiest person.

In August, Davies went back to Ireland by himself to see his family.[1078] His sister Annie and her husband lived northwest of Belfast. On June 25, Charlie's niece Kittie took her final vows and was received into the community of the Sisters of Charity of the Blessed Virgin Mary, and from that point forward she became known as Sister Mary Conradine Davies.

After the match with Slavin, Davies, Choynski, and Jackson went to France and then Germany. A special to the *Herald* in Salt Lake dated London, June 20, 1892, said that Davies and Choynski were going to France for a couple of weeks and that Jackson was going to Hamburg, Germany.[1079] After those trips the group intended to come together in Paris. On July 9, they were all in Achen, Germany.[1080]

On July 11, Davies wrote to Chicago from Berlin that "Jackson is slowly improving, but will not be able to fight again for some time. He says that Hall and Pritchard are both getting ready for their match."[1081] Choynski also wrote to a friend from Germany and reported that Jackson's hand was still in bad shape.[1082]

While in London, Choynski appeared at the Novelty Theater, in a play called *Punch and Judy*. The play included a barroom scene that allowed Joe to show his boxing prowess. Each night the management offered £20 to any man who lasted three rounds with Joe during the play's barroom scene.[1083] Jackson was said to be "gathering in the queen's good shekels on his starring tour."[1084]

The Hall-Pritchard contest finally took place on August 20 in the rooms of the National Club for a purse of $10,000. Pritchard was stocky, only five feet nine inches tall, but he weighed 160 pounds. He was twenty-two years old and an undefeated fighter before meeting Hall. However, he was no match for the Australian champion.

Mitchell was one of Hall's seconds. When the fourth round started, Pritchard landed two quick lefts on Hall's mouth, but Jim only smiled and soon caught Pritchard with a right to the cheek that put him down for a seven count. When he arose, Hall sailed in and landed repeated lefts to Pritchard's head and chin and then smashed his right on the point of that chin. Pritchard went down on his back, rolled over to his stomach and laid motionless as the count of ten expired.[1085]

Record time between London and New Orleans

Davies and Choynski wanted to clear out of England quickly for several reasons. Jackson's hand was injured, and he was not performing. Hall was under Mitchell's management, and there was no reason to stay with him. Some reports say that they actually left before the Hall-Pritchard match.[1086] Finally, an influenza epidemic had spread from the European continent to England, and quarantines were being thrown up in the United States to prevent the spread of the illness.

Quarantines could last for months, preventing anyone from traveling. Many accounts described the epidemic as an outbreak of cholera.[1087] Warren Lewis, who was backing Hall, and several other English sports wanted to try to sail to New York and then travel to New Orleans in time for the championship fights there.[1088] Jackson wanted no part of New Orleans, and he remained in England.

In 1927, Choynski recalled the events during the late summer when he and Davies decided to return to the United States because of the flu epidemic. When they arrived at New York passengers were being held in quarantine at Fire Island. Davies and Joe wanted to be in New Orleans for the Corbett-Sullivan fight.

The quarantine, ordered by the U.S. president and imposed by federal authorities at the port of New York, was supposed to last twenty days.[1089] Davies sent word to friends in New York who chartered a tug called the *Black Bird*, which then came out to their ship. Davies, Choynski, Lewis, and a few others slipped off the *City of Rome* without the approval of federal officials. The *Inter Ocean* wrote that the New York doctor responsible for enforcing the quarantine let Davies and the others off their ship because of Davies' influence with Tammany Hall.[1090]

The group chartered a Pullman car and started for New Orleans. At Washington, D.C., the car was hooked to Corbett's private train.[1091] The Corbett special was a train of the Piedmont line chartered by Brady for Corbett's exclusive use that traveled from Asbury Park, New Jersey, to New Orleans in forty hours. The parlor in Corbett's car was beautifully upholstered in blue silk-plush with cushions on a special sofa designed to soften the motion of the train. His private car had been partitioned into two staterooms. One room held Corbett's bed—the one he had been using all summer—and a washroom. A library separated Corbett's bedroom from the parlor, and there was an observation platform so that Corbett could appear for the public wherever the train stopped. There was a training car in front of Corbett's special car, which was followed by a well-appointed dining car.[1092]

In Washington, D.C., Davies' Pullman car was attached at five minutes after nine p.m. on September 3. The train passed through Salisbury, North Carolina at noon, and headed to Charlotte where it arrived at one p.m. on September 4.[1093] In the morning Corbett took his exercise in his private gym, and Davies and Warren Lewis were invited into the car to watch.

About eleven a.m. Choynski came into the training car. The *Inter Ocean* explained what happened:

> "Parson" Davies preached an able sermon on pugilism and succeeded in converting both Corbett and Choynski, so they shook hands and buried the hatchet, although they have been bitter enemies for many years. They fought three bitter and bloody battles, Corbett winning all. At Salisbury a large crowd gathered around the train and yelled like Indians for Corbett to show himself and they were more than surprised to see Corbett and Choynski make their appearance together chatting pleasantly. . . . Choynski presented Corbett with a wishbone, stating that it was brought from Europe with him, and he hoped it would bring him good luck.[1094]

During this trip Davies' made an offer for Jackson to meet Corbett, regardless of whether Corbett won his match with Sullivan.[1095]

Corbett wanted to arrive in New Orleans after Sullivan and his train laid over in Spartanburg, South Carolina. Other reports say that Corbett stopped in Charlotte and not Spartanburg. Perhaps, he stopped at both places, but his train did not reach New Orleans until seven a.m. on September 6.[1096] At Spartanburg Davies' Pullman car was separated from Corbett's express and the Davies' posse rushed on to New Orleans to attend the Myer-McAuliffe lightweight championship fight.[1097]

Davies' brother Vere was on a specially chartered train from Chicago. Others traveling with Vere included Floto, Kline (the trainer from Beloit), Bradburn (who had again retired and was a cattle buyer), Henry Glickauf (who would become Parson Davies' assistant when Floto left for Denver), and many other Chicago politicians and businessmen.[1098]

The three fights finally scheduled in New Orleans were: (1) September 5, Myer-McAuliffe for the lightweight championship; (2) September 6, Dixon and Jack Skelly for the featherweight championship; and (3) September 7, Sullivan-Corbett for the heavyweight championship.

Davies and Choynski arrived in time to see the Myer-McAuliffe match, which Jack won in fifteen rounds. Choynski served as a second for McAuliffe and was paid $1,000 for his work.[1099]

They were also present for the Dixon-Skelly match. Choynski acted as a second for Skelly and earned $500 for that work.[1100] Joe earned something else during the match. According to Tom O'Rourke, Dixon's manager, Choynski yelled racial slurs at Dixon during the match, which upset Dixon and angered O'Rourke. Tom pledged to find a way to get even with Joe for his behavior, and eight years later arranged a match between Joe Walcott and Choynski with the special intention of having Walcott beat the devil out of Joe. Walcott was a little man standing only five feet one-and-a-half inches. Like George Dixon, Walcott was managed by O'Rourke.

The next evening Corbett stopped Sullivan in twenty-one rounds and turned the world upside down. Choynski sat in the front row at the heavyweight match along with Fitzsimmons. Joe was wearing a loud English cap. Davies was present and probably felt he had done the right thing to offer Corbett a fight with Jackson whether or not Corbett defeated Sullivan. In the years after this match there were many reports published that said Davies bet heavily on Corbett and won a small fortune on this fight. If this is true, Davies was probably at the top financially, having also cleared a large sum of money on the Jackson-Slavin fight in England.[1101]

After the fights in New Orleans, Davies and Choynski went back to the East Coast with Warren Lewis. He was opening a new saloon known as the Alhambra on Eighth Avenue in New York. His establishment had its grand opening on September 12. Davies and Choynski were among noted guests such as William Harding, James Wakeley, Brodie, and Gus Tuthill. The next day Davies met with the Coney Island Athletic Club, which offered a purse of $25,000 for a Corbett-Jackson fight.[1102] That day, Charlie went to the offices of the *Police Gazette* and reported the club's offer.[1103] Davies then returned to Chicago on September 25. His purpose there was to make the preliminary arrangements for a show at Battery D between Jackson and Choynski after Peter returned from England.[1104]

Davies was looking hard for other matches for Choynski. He and Joe went to New Jersey and engaged training quarters near Navesink.[1105] Joe was getting into condition for a fight with George Godfrey to take place at the Coney Island club in October. When Choynski signed on with Davies, he had been out of money, stuck in New Orleans and looking for a fight. After he signed on with Davies he had traveled extensively around the eastern half of the United States and appeared in major venues there. He accompanied Davies to England, met the country's high society, appeared in theaters all over England, traveled to Ireland, France, and Germany and then returned to the United States, where he earned another $1,500 acting as a second in two big fights.

For reasons that are not clear, Lewis withdrew as Hall's backer in early October.[1106] Lewis may have been busy with his new saloon, or he may have had a confrontation with Hall, who had remained in England, where he was leading a dissipated life. One story was that Lewis withdrew because of the ungrateful way Hall treated Davies when he switched to Mitchell.[1107] A few days later the Olympic in New Orleans announced that articles had been signed for a Hall-Fitzsimmons fight in February 1893 for a purse of $15,000. It was claimed that these articles were sanctioned by Davies, who was referred to as Hall's backer, but this seems unlikely.

Frank Glover dies

Frank Glover, another of Davies' former fighters whom Choynski had defeated in February 1889 in California, died at home at 123 Hudson Avenue in Chicago on September 22. His death was caused by tuberculosis of the stomach and bowels.

Not long after returning from his several fights in California, Glover, whose real name was Frank John Heisenberg and had been born September 29, 1863, in Chicago, suffered a hemorrhage of his lungs and then gradually wasted away. In May 1892, Chicago fighters including White, Myer, Dalton, and Gilmore put on a benefit for Glover. Davies wired $50 to Chicago to help out with the benefit. In July, Glover returned to the Pacific coast, hoping that the climate would help, but his disease had progressed too far, and he returned home only one week before he died. Glover was a member of the De Molay, Knights of Pythias, and his wake was held in their club rooms. He joined Killen among the fighters previously managed by Davies who died very early in their lives.[1108]

The athletic clubs in California had been preempted by the athletic clubs in New Orleans. Davies and Jackson had their strongest support in London and San

Francisco. Joe Goddard, who was still calling himself the champion of Australia had drifted to California and had a few fights there of no great significance. He had defeated Joe McAuliffe in fifteen rounds on June 30 and Australian Billy Smith on August 25. Goddard then came east in September so that the sports there could have a look at him and he could find some decent matches. In New York, he put on an exhibition on September 12 against Herbert Goddard and on September 13 against Tom Moore, whom he knocked out in two rounds. He then went to Philadelphia and had three more matches between September 19 and September 24.[1109]

On September 27, a wire from Philadelphia revealed that Davies, acting for Jackson, had accepted an offer of the Pacific Athletic Club of San Francisco for a match with Goddard and a purse of $10,000.[1110] As if to define the problem that existed in New Orleans, the president of the Olympic Club stated on October 1 that his club would not offer any purse for a Jackson-Goddard fight "because the Southern people do not like to see contests in which a white man is opposed by a negro." Apparently, they objected to Dixon beating the tar out of Jack Skelly during the big boxing carnival.[1111]

The Godfrey-Choynski fight

Godfrey had gone to England to see his friend Jackson defeat Slavin, and it seems likely that Godfrey-Choynski match was arranged by Davies in London. Charlie had a lot of respect for Godfrey and considered him a clever fighter who could hit "pretty hard." Still, Godfrey was toward the end of his career, and Choynski was an up and coming young man. Davies hired Martin "Buffalo" Costello and Jim McVey to train Joe for the match. McVey was a wrestler who had helped train Corbett for his match with Sullivan.[1112]

This group of fighters trained at the Highlands, where they occupied a two story cottage on the Shrewsbury River. While Joe was working, Davies often visited the training facility, as he had done when Hall trained in Beloit.[1113] Choynski's daily routine included morning bicycle riding of a dozen miles or more, which was something of a novelty for fighters at the time. He also used a punching bag and dumbbells and walked fifteen miles a day. The press obviously liked Joe, and it was seldom critical of him. He was described as a fighter who was "rapidly climbing the ladder that leads to championship distinction" but held in check by his astute manager, Davies. Godfrey was known as "Old Chocolate," and it was acknowledged that Joe would have a fight on his hands.[1114]

Jackson kept in contact with Davies. In late October, Davies received a letter informing him that Jackson had engaged in a fight in England, but it was not a prizefight. It seemed that Jackson was in a restaurant in Dorcaster, Yorkshire, and four "ruffians were insulting a barmaid." Jackson asked them to desist, and they then turned their attention to him. In the ensuing fight Jackson "struck out but four times and the four toughs were stretched senseless and bleeding on the floor. For his chivalrous action the sporting men presented Jackson with a valuable gold watch and chain."

After storing his Superman cape, Jackson hurried back from England to be in the United States in time to watch his two friends fight. He arrived in New York as a saloon passenger on the *Teutonic* on October 27.[1115] On the manifest, he identified himself as a pugilist. Among the other passengers were John W. Mackay, a millionaire from California; United States Senator George F. Edmunds; Agnes Huntington, a famous singer of the time; Joseph Howard Choate who would be United States ambassador to England from 1899 to 1905; and Marshall Field Jr. of Chicago with his family and servants.[1116] Jackson headed to New Jersey to help put the finishing touches on Choynski for the Godfrey fight, which was to take place on October 31.

Joe's seconds were McVey, Jimmy Carroll, Davies, and Dominick McCaffery. Dominick O'Malley of New Orleans acted at Joe's timekeeper. A reported seven thousand spectators attended the fight. Godfrey went at Choynski like a bull and cut Joe's eye in the sixth round. The cut bled profusely throughout the remainder of the match. Later in the fight Choynski closed George's left eye. Old Chocolate was knocked out by young Choynski in fifteen rounds by a right hand blow to his jaw just below his ear.

The fifteenth round was described in these words:

> Godfrey rushed at Choynski like a blind bull and got a straight jab in the closed eye that made him stagger about three feet. He was totally blind in the left eye and thus placed at a great disadvantage, as Choynski kept on his left side, and the more Godfrey rushed him the harder Choynski got on that damaged eye. The knock-out blow was a swinging right on the damaged eye, which knocked the colored man completely out.[1117]

The *New York Times* said that after Joe's final blow the "colored man's legs seemed to lose their power, and he fell like a log, and, finding his head did not rest upon the floor, he raised his right arm and used it as a pillow. He was not knocked out, but quit, and was counted out by the referee."[1118]

In 1927 Joe wrote in the *Winnipeg Free Press* that in the fifteenth round of the match Godfrey began cursing him and calling him vile names in the hope that Joe would lose his head. But a few seconds later he knocked George out.[1119] George may have been angry because Joe had been laughing at him during the last two rounds when he had Godfrey at his mercy. Two of the biggest winners on the fight were Gunst and Goddard who each won $7,000.

Hall and Fitzsimmons finally agree to meet

Hall had remained in Brighton, England, and was biding his time until he could be matched with Fitz. He returned to the United States aboard the *Majestic*, which arrived at New York on December 7.[1120] Jim had become a good friend of Mitchell, who had taken over his management. Hall's return had been delayed because Mitchell had assaulted a man twice his age and had been sentenced to two months in jail. Charley's legal issues had to be resolved before he could travel with Hall.[1121] As described by Choynski, Hall was a handsome fellow, a fine dresser, and a Valentino with the women. He seemed to enjoy the high life in London and had also befriended Squire Abingdon and patched up his problems with Warren Lewis. If Hall could secure a match with Fitzsimmons, he had no particular need for either Davies' management or backing.[1122]

Fitz had expressed his willingness to fight Hall for a long time. There seemed to be a real dislike between the freak of nature and the Valentino-like Hall. The sticking points between Hall and Fitz always revolved around Hall's weight and when the fight would take place. The issue of weight related to the question of whether the match could be considered a championship fight or whether they would be fighting outside the weight class. Several major clubs began bidding to sponsor the fight, and the price that they were willing to pay for it spiraled above the amount paid for the Corbett-Sullivan heavyweight championship fight.

As soon as the Choynski-Godfrey fight ended, Davies took Jackson on the road. On November 1, Peter appeared at the Academy of Music in Philadelphia, where he sparred three rounds with big John McVey before one thousand five hundred patrons.[1123] After exhibiting in Washington, D.C., and Baltimore, Jackson and Davies arrived back in New York on November 13 and went on to Philadelphia that day. In both New York and Philadelphia Jackson told the press that fighters seemed to have become scarce in the United States but that actors had multiplied at a remarkable rate. In New York, he said that black actors in the United States were not as successful as white ones, and he would just stick to the ring. However, in Philadelphia he said he was thinking about taking to the stage.[1124]

Jackson continues to work without a championship fight in sight

In mid-November, Peter had a pleasant meeting with Corbett. They shared glasses of lemon and seltzer water and discussed their respective circumstances. This was reportedly the first time that they had met since their May 1891 match at San Francisco. During the meeting, Jackson told Corbett that he was expecting to take a speaking part in a production in the near future.[1125] Several reports said that the Newton Beers production company had secured Jackson to appear in a play called either *Alone in London* or *Lost in London*.[1126] The idea of putting Jackson on stage was more than a possibility as early as November.

On November 25 Jackson was at a hotel in Birmingham, Connecticut, when he was approached by a man named Bunnel from New Haven. Bunnel told Jackson of doubts about whether Peter was really anxious to meet Sullivan, and wound up by saying: "Why, there are plenty of N______s in Webster street that can whip you." With that Peter hit Bunnel on the jaw and knocked him out.[1127]

A more substantial prejudice, however, existed in the newfound unwillingness of any of the leading heavyweights to agree to fight Peter. He was the leading contender for the championship, but he could not get a decent fight. On the other hand, the Coney Island Athletic Association was offering up to $45,000 for a Choynski-Goddard fight. Jackson too could have agreed to fight Goddard, but the risks for Jackson were too great; a loss or a draw would likely knock him out of top contender status.

Jackson appeared in Philadelphia at the Lyceum Theater.[1128] On November 28, he sparred three rounds with Denny Kelliher.[1129] On November 29, he sparred with "Professor" Billy McLean who was described as a very active but old man.[1130] Jackson had an exhibition at the Lyceum with Bob Caffrey on November 30, a three-round exhibition with Billy Leedom on December 1, a four-round exhibition with Jack Fallon on December 2, and another exhibition with Joe Butler on December 3.[1131]

Choynski was doing most of his work in Philadelphia at the Ariel Club. On November 18, Davies returned to Chicago and left his fighters behind. He was already discussing his plan to take them all on a tour of the Pacific Coast, and he had to be thinking about what changes he could make that would keep the public interested. Both Jackson and Choynski were well known there and would not draw curious fans like those on the East Coast. On November 21, Joe had another match with the "Black Thunderbolt," C. C. Smith, and this time Joe knocked Smith out in four rounds. Two nights later Choynski met Denny Kelliher and disposed of him in two rounds. On Saturday, November 26 Choynski was to spar in an exhibition with Joe Butler, who failed to show. Choynski then knocked out Fallon in four rounds. More than four thousand people were on hand for the match with Fallon, who had put on considerable weight after returning from England two years earlier.[1132] After the match Fallon challenged Choynski to meet him again in six weeks for $1,000 a side.[1133]

Some newspapers say that Joe was scheduled to spar with Buffalo Costello on November 30; however, two nights earlier Joe had been a second for Costello at the Coney Island Athletic Association. That night Costello and Alex Greggains fought an eighty-round draw, and Costello was probably in no condition to spar with anyone for several weeks after that marathon. At this point Choynski too was discussing the possibility of becoming an actor. On November 30, the *Post Dispatch* reported that "Joe Choynski, the fighter, believes that he is built for an actor. He intends, it is said, to have a play written around himself, and to star under Parson Davies' management."[1134] The seed of what was to come had been planted, and Joe would get his wish much sooner than he anticipated.

After they finished in Philadelphia, Jackson and Choynski returned to Chicago. On December 5, Peter sparred with "Professor" Tom Chandler and Jim Douglas at Battery D, but the show was a dud.[1135] That day, Davies wrote to Colonel Kelly in Salt Lake to explain his plans. Davies said he was leaving for New York on December 6 to take in the Goddard-Maher fight, and then he would return to Chicago before coming west. He explained that Choynski would not be on the first trip but would follow about two weeks later. He told Kelly he expected to put on a show in Salt Lake but would not appear in Ogden during the second trip and asked Kelly not to make any arrangements in that venue.[1136] On the evening of Monday, December 10, Davies, accompanied by Jackson and a party of other pugilists, left for the West Coast. Sunday morning they passed through Omaha, where it was a frigid 16 degrees, headed for Denver, where Jackson was scheduled to exhibit with Woods.[1137] Davies had arranged appearances on December 12 and in Salt Lake on the fourteenth before he went on to Frisco.[1138]

The party arrived in Salt Lake on the evening of December 13, and everyone seemed to be happy and in a good mood. They registered at the Knutsford Hotel. The Knutsford was a two-hundred-fifty-room hotel that had just opened in June 1891. They took a suite of rooms with a northern exposure. Davies controlled the visitors to the room and permitted only the newspaper reporters into their quarters.

The stage beacons Davies, Jackson, and Choynski

A representative of the *Desert Evening News* met with Jackson and wrote that Peter was an "intelligent, quiet and unassuming man, with apparently none of the characteristics of a person who follows the brutal business of besting his fellow men for a living."[1139] The reporter for Salt Lake's *Herald* noted that it had been three years since Jackson had last visited that community, and the passage of time had resulted in a few changes in Peter's appearance. He was much stouter and dressed in an immaculate fashion. He wore a dark diagonal-striped Prince Albert coat, gray trousers, and a pair of galoshes over calfskin boots. Jackson also wore a finely cut cameo pin tucked in his necktie, and a ring encircled his finger but "there was an absence of the big flashy solitaire diamond which most sports consider an indispensable part of their gear."[1140]

Davies was "as young and fresh as a cucumber and his comedian face all aglow with humor and mirth." He was excited about having met Julia Marlowes' manager, John Stetson, in Denver. Charlie said he wanted Stetson to remain in Salt Lake City so that Charlie could help him out by playing the part of Charles the wrestler in *As You Like It*. Davies was still excited about his stage appearance in Chicago in 1891 and pointed out he had played the role of Charles the wrestler to as many as six thousand people at a single performance. He seemed to speak "with a tinge of pride of his theatrical powers."[1141] Davies, Jackson, and Choynski were all thinking about the stage with different degrees of interest.

Peter was also asked about the possibility of appearing on the stage.

"When are you going on the stage?" asked the reporter.

"I'm going on tonight," Peter answered.

He was referring to an exhibition planned that evening with Woods. They later sparred three rounds to a large audience and cheers all around.

"It is the kind of acting that suits me best," Peter said. "I want to hold off until I make one more fight and that the fight of my life when I will retire from the ring."

Davies said that Jackson had three playwrights who wanted to furnish him with a drama suited to show off his histrionic abilities but that whenever the stage was mentioned Peter would back clear across the room to avoid the idea of becoming an actor. It is clear from this statement that there had been more than casual discussions about possible stage appearances well before mid-December.

Of course, Jackson was asked the obligatory questions about fighting Corbett. He "drew his extended chin down on his shirt front contracted his eyebrows but loosened up this severity of countenance by smiling out of the corner of his eyes and rolling the lower lip away from his ivories in a playful manner. 'You'll have to ask Corbett that question,' he replied."

Davies wanted the *Herald* to say that he would back Peter Jackson to fight James Corbett for a $10,000 side wager and the largest purse obtainable.[1142]

From Ogden a wire was sent to Naughton informing him of Jackson's impending arrival. Naughton went to Reno to meet Davies and Jackson. It seems likely that Davies did not go on all the way to the West Coast and simply handed Peter over to Naughton at Reno.[1143] Having delivered Peter back to a friendlier part of the United States, Davies turned around and headed back over the snow covered Great Plains to Chicago. He was in Ogden on December 21 and was questioned by the press about many issues including the prospect of a Hall-Fitzsimmons fight. Charlie said he preferred not to talk about Hall because he had split with him in London. He preferred to have Choynski fight either Hall or Fitzsimmons and was highly complementary of "Mysterious" Billy Smith, the welterweight, and of Dick Burge, who was scheduled to fight McAuliffe. Davies planned to leave from Chicago with Choynski on December 29 and go to Denver and from there to Salt Lake and then San Francisco, where he would put on a monster show on January 7, 1893. The "genial manager" promised the athletic promoters in Ogden he would do all he could to secure good talent in the east for the Utah Athletic Club. His parting request was that the Utah club should "not to tolerate any scrub or fake matches."[1144]

Davies was back in the Windy City by December 23.[1145] He had planned a big show for December 29 at Battery D featuring Choynski.[1146] Davies was in Chicago for Christmas for the first time in more than five years. The show on December 29 was well attended and a great success. However, Davies was hauled into court that day to respond to a warrant that had been sworn out by a Chicago contractor named Michael McCarthy, who was the deputy South Town assessor. As politicians do in Chicago, McCarthy had asked Davies for free tickets to the show at Battery D and had been turned down. He then filed his complaint to retaliate. That McCarthy had asked for special concessions was confirmed by Captain Shea of the Central Station, who said he too had been pressured by McCarthy for passes to the event. The charges were dismissed.

That evening Choynski sparred with Bob Ferguson, the Chicago stockyards champion and the man who had been Pat Killen's final opponent. Joe knocked Ferguson down in the second round, again in the third round, and then dealt four upper-cuts to Ferguson's face in four seconds of the fourth round. Ferguson got up, shook Joe's hand, and staggered away before the end of the round. There were other spirited matches that night including Jack Dalton, of Philadelphia and Jack King and Henry Baker, both of Chicago, and Mike Fitzpatrick, of St. Paul. One article reports the last two fighters as Denny Hurley and "Nick of the Woods" Fitzpatrick.[1147]

As the conclusion of the show Choynski met Boden, and they fought four savage rounds. Joe knocked Boden down in the second round. Boden was dropped to his knees in the third round and was saved only by clinching. In the fourth round Joe belted Boden at will. No decisions were given in any of the matches because the shows were billed as involving scientific set-tos. The night after the Choynski-Boden match both Davies and Choynski left for San Francisco to participate in a testimonial that the friends of Jackson and Choynski were to tender them on the January 7, 1893. As he was leaving, Davies said he wanted to match Choynski with Jim Daly, who was Corbett's former sparring partner.[1148]

A few days later a reporter for the *Standard* of Ogden asked Joe about his experience in Chicago, and he said that the experience was not pleasant: "Two men, and such men as Ferguson and Boden, in one night is not an easy task. Boden has never been knocked out. In fact, he is Chicago's best man, but I handled him so easily that he got mad and bit me severely on my right bleep. But everything goes in my business, I suppose."[1149]

The fights presented at Battery D at the end of December were some of the last fights held before the place was entirely redone. Dr. Florenz Ziegfeld leased Battery D before the Columbian Exposition began and then remodeled the building and installed a stage to present classical music productions for those attending the fair. Ziegfeld's son would later develop the famous Ziegfeld Follies.

As the New Year arrived, Davies was where he seemed most comfortable. He was on a train traveling on behalf of the fighters he represented and probably somewhere near Denver, Colorado. The plan had been to stop in Omaha on the evening of December 31, so that Choynski could spar, but no opponent could be located.

The year 1892 had been good in many respects. Davies had managed three of the ten highest paid fighters in the world: Jackson, Hall, and Choynski. When he took Choynski under his management in mid-March, Joe had been virtually penniless. Davies also managed the world champion catch-as-catch-can wrestler, Evan Strangler Lewis. However, there were troubling matters afoot. Hall had teamed with Mitchell and Pony Moore and was arranging a fight with Fitz without Davies' participation.

In addition, many top fighters had turned themselves into actors. Corbett was traveling with Brady, causing young women to either swoon or hop in bed with him. He had told the national press he did not intend to fight for a year.[1150]

Sullivan was on the road in a new play and appearing at the Windsor Theater in the Bowery in *The Man From Boston.* Fitz was on Broadway. Myer had appeared on stage. McAuliffe and Woods had both signed on with Duncan Harrison, and even Goddard had been signed to a short-term acting role. The *Post Dispatch* repeated earlier stories that Choynski was talking about becoming an actor.[1151]

It was also becoming almost impossible to find anyone who would fight Jackson other than a black man. When Sullivan and Corbett fought in New Orleans, by rule of the Olympic Club the only black man allowed to attend the match was Jackson. Of course, he stayed in London and did not attend, making it an all-white affair. The new Pelican Athletic Club was formed in New Orleans. The club hired agents to live in Brooklyn and San Francisco and be on the lookout for fighters who could appear in New Orleans, but it had also announced that no black man would be allowed to fight in the club.[1152] Moreover, every leading fighter had some excuse for not signing for a match with Jackson.

Chapter 13 - (1893)

The Stage and Uncle Tom's Cabin

♥

On January 1, 1893, Ed Kelly at Salt Lake City received a telegram from Davies confirming he and Choynski would arrive the next morning and would appear that evening at the People's Theater.[1153] Davies had laid out the plans in a letter to Kelly on December 5, 1892. The group was in Ogden on January 1 and Salt Lake City on January 2 and took a tour of the city visiting Fort Dodge.[1154] That evening Choynski sparred with Frank Fitzgerald, who was credited with being the cleverest man with the gloves in Utah.

The local paper noted that Choynski was "the coming man" and that the "Parson is just the same as he always is—affable, cheary and sociable—and spent a pleasant day renewing the acquaintances he has made and the friendships he has formed during his several visits."

The *Ogden Standard* wrote: "Of Choynski only pleasant words can be written. Quiet, modest, gentlemanly and sociable, he won many admirers who will watch his career with interest. While babies will never be thrown into spasms by his face, it is also a sure bet that the girls will never rave over his beauty. His countenance has a decided Hebraic cast, and like his old time opponent Jim Corbett he wears his hair *a la* Pompadour."

Choynski discussed his match with Goddard when he was in Australia and said he had Goddard beaten several times during their contest and that on one occasion Goddard was out for sixteen seconds. However, the referee, instead of remaining where he was at the time of the knockout, came across the ring and only began counting after he reached Goddard and then at the count of nine the gong sounded. Choynski said he would put up $5,000 of his own money for a match with Corbett. Davies was not as enthusiastic. The Parson said: "Choynski is desirous of again meeting Corbett. I know he is willing, but I do not encourage it. You know he'll fight anything, but I believe in going slow."

Choynski was asked his opinion about a proposed Corbett-Mitchell match. He responded that Corbett would beat Mitchell, but he wanted to say a word for Mitchell, whom he found to be "a decent man, a staunch friend and a good fellow all around." Joe said that Mitchell had never been in better condition. He reiterated, "As I said, however, Jim can best him."

In his interview with the reporter for the *Standard*, the Parson said: "The more I come to your town the better I like it and the people. . . . Jackson was also well pleased with his reception and treatment here, and will come again when the opportunity offers."

About his plans, Davies said: "What am I going to do? Well, I go to San Francisco to-night, and as soon as the benefit is over I will return to the East for the purpose of arranging a match for either Jackson or Choynski."

Concerning Jackson's prospect for a fight in the near future Davies was not so sanguine. "You see, Peter has a right to expect another chance with Corbett but he will not give it to him it will be a difficult matter to find a man for him."[1155]

On the evening of January 2, at least one thousand people enjoyed the entertainment at the People's Theater. Davies was introduced, and the usual neat speech resulted. He announced that Ed Kelley would act as master of ceremonies. Kelly introduced Choynski and Fitzgerald, and they gave "a rattling good exhibition." Joe, who was called "the fair-haired Hebrew," was a favorite in Salt Lake City.

According to the *Standard*, "Choynski gave his sparring partner numerous openings which he never failed to take advantage of. The wind up was most interesting and as the final handshake took place the pleased crowd broke into cheering." Loud calls were made persistently for Choynski. Joe had retired to his dressing room, and Davies finally sent for him, and "the coming" man made a neat little speech of thanks that was very acceptably received.

Choynski and Parson Davies left for San Francisco immediately after the exhibition, but before leaving Choynski said: "Set me right on that Corbett fight. I've never had but one battle. It started in a barn, as you know, and being interrupted by the police, was afterwards concluded on a barge in the Sacramento River. It was really one fight, and it was the only one I ever had with him."

After passing through Reno the two men arrived in Oakland in the late afternoon on January 4 and attended a match at the C.A.C. that same evening.[1156]

Jack Ashton dies

Two days later another fighter Davies had managed died. Jack Ashton was last managed by Davies on the evening that Billy Brennan died.[1157] Ashton then went to Buffalo, New York, without Davies. Charlie stayed behind in Chicago to cooperate with the authorities and see that Brennan got a proper burial. Ashton did not return to Davies' management after that evening. Jack had spent most of his subsequent professional life traveling and sparring with Sullivan.

As with Killen, Ashton died of erysipelas. His death occurred about nine fifteen p.m. on January 6 in the annex of Bellevue Hospital in New York. One month before he died, he had been with Sullivan when the big man broke down crying and despondent about his loss to Corbett. Jack had attempted to console Sullivan, but John L. told Jack he would kill him if he did not leave him alone.[1158]

Ashton had been appearing with Sullivan in the new play *The Man from Boston*. They had packed houses numbering in the thousands each day.[1159] Somehow Ashton cut his arm. Some reports said he had cut it on a nail backstage at the Windsor. Other accounts said he had been carousing with friends and had put his arm through a window. Jack apparently thought nothing of the cut and had continued to fill his engagements with Sullivan. They played to an enormous house at the Windsor up to Saturday, December 31, 1892. Aston sparred during the play with increasing difficulty, and on Sunday, January 1, 1893, he stayed in bed at the Vanderbilt House. On the following Monday and Tuesday, Jack grew rapidly worse until his friends took him to the hospital. Doctors diagnosed the condition, and Jack was listed as critical. Jack was Roman Catholic and was administered the last sacraments on January 5.[1160]

Jack's wife was with him before his death. She was an actress with the stage name of Louise Dempsey. In reviews of Jack's career he was said to be "too good-natured a fellow to fight." Ashton's funeral was on January 9 at Saint Agnes Church, and he was buried at Calvary Cemetery as a temporary matter until his body could be move to his hometown of Providence, Rhode Island.

Jackson was in California but wired instructions that $50 should be used to purchase flowers. He also sent a letter of condolence expressing his regret in not being able to attend Jack's funeral.[1161] Sullivan did not attend Ashton's funeral although Jack was considered one of his closest friends, but he too sent flowers and a letter of condolence.[1162] Although he had many friends and earned large sums during his career, Jack left his widow in poor straits.[1163]

The *Uncle Tom's Cabin* saga begins

Davies and Choynski were in Frisco on the morning of January 4. Joe had been ill in England and treated for a stomach ailment. He said that Jackson stood ace high in England and anyone traveling with him was treated royally. Joe thought he would stay on the West Coast for about a month and then go to New Orleans.[1164]

The big party for Jackson and Choynski was given at the Orpheum on January 10.[1165] All of the local sporting men were present for the show, which included scientific boxing and wrestling bouts and concluded with a ten-round bout between Choynski and Jackson. Both men showed well, and it was noted that Joe had made tremendous strides during the year he had been away.
The day before the exhibition at the Orpheum, the Pacific Athletic Club of San Francisco offered $5,000 for either a Maher-Choynski match or a match with Jim Daley. Davies said he thought the proper protocol was for either Maher or Daley to indicate a willingness to fight in California before any commitment was made on Joe's behalf.[1166] Less than a week later, the Olympic of New Orleans upped the ante by offering $6,000 for a finish fight between Choynski and Daley.[1167]

Goddard, who had been moving around the East Coast, returned to San Francisco in late January. Davies thought that when Goddard reached San Francisco, he would surely challenge Jackson, Choynski, or both. This would create an awkward situation because arguments could be made that Davies' fighters should fight Goddard. Davies did not want either of his men to fight Goddard, so he arranged a fight for Jackson in Los Angeles with a relative unknown by the name of Frank Childs and took Choynski along for the trip. San Francisco can be raw in January, and it may have been that all three men simply wanted to go someplace where it was a little warmer and stay beyond Goddard's immediate reach.[1168]

Childs had been fighting for about five years, and he was no pushover. He was smaller than most of the leading heavyweights of the 1890s—about five feet nine inches tall and 165 pounds—but he could hit hard and take punishment. Child's claim to fame was that about eleven months earlier, he had knocked out George La Blanche in three rounds.

Davies, Jackson, and Choynski arrived in Los Angeles on January 19 and took rooms at the Hollenbeck Hotel. That night, Jackson put in four rounds in the Turnverein Hall with Childs before a packed house.[1169]

When they arrived at the Hollenbeck, a telegram was waiting:

> Will you accept engagement for yourself and Peter Jackson, commencing February 6, for two weeks, at 'Stockwell's' in the mammoth production of 'Uncle Tom's Cabin,' Jackson as Uncle Tom and yourself as auctioneer; will give you certainly two thousand five hundred dollars for two weeks.
> -s- Alf Ellinghouse.

Lincoln R. Stockwell was the owner and manager of the Alcazar Theater in San Francisco and a man well-known to Davies. Ellinghouse was Stockwell's agent. Stockwell promised to provide a company of twenty performers and to route them all the way to Chicago if the show was a success in San Francisco. Three days later the group was back in San Francisco, and Davies was leaving soon for Chicago to get the new production scheduled there during the Columbian Exposition.[1170]

In 1927, Choynski explained how he had learned of the idea that he, Jackson, and Davies might appear in *Uncle Tom's Cabin*. Joe recalled that the subject was first introduced in Chicago, and it may be that the idea originated with Davies in December 1892 and that he then discussed his idea with Stockwell in January after he, Jackson, and Choynski reached San Francisco.[1171] But how did Davies come up with the idea?

Well before January 1893, there were articles in national and international magazines about the possibility of Jackson taking an acting role. Before July 1890, Davies guaranteed Dion Boucicauit $500 to produce a play entitled *A Bunch of Fives*. Jackson and Corbett were the intended stars of that play, but Boucicauit died before finishing the project.[1172] In November 1892, there was discussion of Peter playing Othello and in Newton Beers' play *Lost in London*.[1173] Three playwrights were interested in producing a drama that would feature Jackson.[1174] Choynski had also said he wanted to become an actor. His interest in performing had been reported in newspapers on the East Coast and in the Midwest in November 1892. Davies loved the stage and had performed in San Francisco, Beloit, and Chicago. Perhaps he had been thinking about a creative way for Jackson to get into the theatrical business.

The idea to produce a version of *Uncle Tom's Cabin* may also have been inspired by news in Chicago that a special exhibit was going to be prepared for the Columbian Exposition. Supposedly, Uncle Tom's cabin, the real cypress wood cabin, or so its owner claimed, was to be exhibited there.[1175] In addition, a bust of Harriet Beecher Stowe was featured in the women's pavilion at the exposition. The word was out that prizefighting would be suppressed in Chicago because the grand high leaders of the fair did not want the evil boxing boys around to spoil their lily white production. It may be that when Davies heard that the Uncle Tom's cabin was going to be exhibited at the fair, he formed the idea of producing the play as a vehicle for getting two prime prizefighters in front of the large audiences that were visiting the exposition. Davies may then have discussed his idea of producing *Uncle Tom's Cabin* with Stockwell, who had a theater company that could be used to test the idea.

As early as 1887, an article in the *Omaha Daily Bee* described Davies' passing involvement with the play. The credit for using live dogs in the production of *Uncle Tom's Cabin* was attributed in that article to Jay Rail, a theater manager from Rochester, New York, and later a theater manager in San Francisco. According to the story, in the 1870s in Rochester a newspaper man, Davies, and Rail were standing in front of the Opera House talking about Rail's plans to take a production of *Uncle Tom's Cabin* out on the road. A young boy came by with a large dog on a leash. Rail asked the boy what he was doing with the dog, and the boy said he was going to drown it. Rail bought the dog from the boy for a quarter and then wondered out loud what he would do with the animal. The newspaper man suggested he should buy another dog and take them on the road to play the bloodhounds in the production. Rail liked the idea, and purchased a second dog, had both trained, and took them on the road with great success.[1176]

Choynski recalled the first mention of the play: "In Chicago 'Parson' Davies got Peter Jackson and me together and told us we were to become actors. 'We are going to play *Uncle Tom's Cabin*, said Davies. 'Peter will be Uncle Tom, Choynski will play George Shelby and I will play the auctioneer. We will write a prologue to introduce a boxing match, and Uncle Tom will put on the gloves with Shelby.'"

Joe recalled that Jackson thought that Davies had gone "balmy." Choynski almost fainted, and Peter drank two quarts of Scotch. This probably did not happen in Chicago because Jackson and Choynski were not in Chicago together at the end of 1892. Jackson and Davies went west in early 1892. Davies then came back to Chicago and went west with Joe just after his show at Battery D.[1177] Nevertheless, Joe's recollection is otherwise consistent with contemporary accounts.[1178]

The unfair condemnation of Peter Jackson

Scholar Susan F. Clark has written about the decision to cast Jackson in the role of Uncle Tom. Her 2000 article "Up against the Ropes: Peter Jackson As

'Uncle Tom' in America" contains factual mistakes and a fundamental misunderstanding of the relationship between Davies and Jackson:

> When Jackson, a novice to American culture, allowed his manager to convince him to be "whipped to death" nightly before packed houses as Uncle Tom in a touring production of *Uncle Tom's Cabin*, his battle in America was all but over. Never again would he be taken seriously as a heavyweight contender. Literally and figuratively, Jackson had become America's most famous Uncle Tom.[1179]

Clark contends, for example, that "despite his best efforts to break the color line, Jackson's first significant fight with a white boxer did not happen until he was in America for nearly nine months."[1180] Clark writes that this happened on December 28, 1888, when he defeated Joe McAuliffe. But this is inaccurate.

Jackson's ability and his fighting record were not well-known in America when he arrived in San Francisco. Most articles about him relate to his efforts to challenge Jack Burke during February and March 1888, when Burke was fighting in Australia. Burke had issued a challenge to all Australian fighters but refused to fight Jackson because of his prejudice against black fighters. While this made little sense, it was Burke's excuse.

There is no evidence that when Jackson arrived he was trying to break the color line. He told London's *Sporting Life* he was coming to America to wipe out the fighters there starting with the colored fighters. Then he intended to go to England to meet Jem Smith. In addition, there is substantial evidence that many black fighters in all weight classes were fighting top quality white fighters in California both before and after 1888. Jackson was greeted favorably when he arrived in San Francisco, and he was treated well by many, though not all, black and white residents there.

In 1890, when Jackson became the top contender for the heavyweight championship, Sullivan raised the color line against him. There is plenty of evidence that Sullivan hated black people. Jackson was aware that Sullivan had said he would not fight a black man, even before the Sullivan-Kilrain match.[1181] However, Sullivan fully embraced the color line only after Peter became the top contender and in particular after Jackson's defeat of Jem Mace in London.[1182]

It is true that there were far too many sporting men who subscribed to Sullivan's evil prejudices. It also seems apparent that after their sixty-one round draw, Corbett wanted nothing to do with Jackson because Corbett knew that Jackson could beat him. It was Jackson's ability and not his color that frightened Corbett. Brady wanted to make money and saw no financial advantage if Corbett met Jackson, so from the beginning of his management Brady poisoned the well.

There is also no fair implication to be drawn from the fact that nine months passed before Jackson actually fought McAuliffe. At the time Jackson came to the United States, Jem Smith, who was white and a very good fighter, had agreed to fight Jackson, and it was thought their match would take place in the United States.[1183] When Jackson arrived he said at various times that he wanted to meet Godfrey, fight the winner of the Glover-McAuliffe match, and meet all comers.[1184]

The Glover-McAuliffe fight was a brutal forty-nine round match that McAuliffe won.[1185] McAuliffe wasn't likely to be in another significant fight quickly after that battle. Jackson went six rounds with Con Riordan, who was white, on June 18, 1888, and created a very favorable impression with the C.A.C.[1186] Contemporary accounts said that Riordan was the best person available for a match with Jackson. He was the boxing instructor at the Golden Gate Athletic Club and forced Jackson to show what he could do.

After that fight boxers were not opposed to fighting Jackson because of his color but because of his demonstrated ability as a fighter.[1187] He knocked out M. J. Sullivan (white) in two rounds on June 20, 1888, had a four-round exhibition with Choynski (white) on June 26, 1888, and fought nineteen rounds with the excellent heavyweight Godfrey (black) on August 24, 1888.

Godfrey demanded favorable financial conditions for his fight with Jackson. This happened not because Jackson was black but because he was good.[1188] If Godfrey was going to travel from Boston to San Francisco he had to have money to show for the effort. To get Godfrey to meet Jackson, the articles of agreement required payment of $400 for George's expenses, $300 if Godfrey lost and a $1,500 purse with no side bets.[1189]

Despite being undersized compared to Jackson, Godfrey put up a terrific and bloody fight that ended only after nineteen grueling rounds.[1190] After the Godfrey-Jackson fight the two men began a tour that took them to Portland, Astoria, Spokane, Tacoma, and Seattle.[1191] It would be hard to fight McAuliffe while touring with Godfrey. In addition, the C.A.C. announced within a few days after the Godfrey fight that it would put up $2,000 for a match between Jackson and Mike Conley (white), the Ithaca Giant.[1192] Then a few days after Conley signed to fight McAuliffe and McAuliffe quickly signed to fight Jackson but two months after his match with Conley.

The issue is not when a Jackson-McAuliffe match took place but rather when the match was made. To illustrate this point, almost two months passed between the time the Jackson-Godfrey match was arranged and when it took place. Jackson's match with Corbett was made in late December 1890, but the fight did not take place until May 21, 1891. There was a similar delay between the time that Jackson and Frank Slavin agreed to fight and the actual date of their fight. There is no implication that can be drawn from that five-month delay between the agreement to fight and the actual fight.

The economics of such delays seem obvious, but this was also explained by the *Pittsburgh Dispatch* in 1892.[1193] Long delays gave the participants the opportunity to make money, as illustrated by Corbett's performance tour under Davies' management between the time the Jackson-Corbett fight was made and the end of March 1891. Because of his poor health Jackson did not engage in a tour but tried to regain his strength and stamina and recover from his injury.

There was real evidence of prejudice in the process of negotiating the terms of the Jackson-McAuliffe. This prejudice was exhibited by McAuliffe's backer. However, the white officials of the C.A.C. came to Jackson's defense during those negotiations.[1194]

With respect to the Jackson-McAuliffe match, the two fighters took their match seriously and wanted time to prepare. As soon as Jackson defeated Godfrey, a quality and well-known American heavyweight, then the offers for other good matches with quality white opponents came quickly. This doesn't sound as if white men in San Francisco were raising the color line. After Jackson defeated McAuliffe, he engaged in contests with white heavyweights including Cardiff (April 26, 1889), Lees (June 15, 1889), and "Sailor" Brown (July 11, 1889). Then Jackson went to England and fought white heavyweights there.

It is apparent that Jackson did not make and keep much money until after he was managed by Davies. Jackson is not the only fighter who did not make money until he was managed by Davies. Burke (white) made his big money after he was managed by Davies. Hall (white), an Australian fighter, had performed at a loss in America before he went under Davies' management. Choynski (white) was virtually penniless and stuck in New Orleans, until he went under Davies' management. The idea in the fighting profession is to make money. The profession is not like college football, where only the university cleans up. Davies knew how to help his fighters make money whether they were white or black.

It is also inaccurate to say that Jackson's demise began when he agreed to take the role of Uncle Tom. Peter's last important fight was in England on May 30, 1892, with Slavin, and this happened nine months before his decision perform as Uncle Tom. It was Jackson's decision to become an actor. He was not forced into the role any more than Sullivan, Corbett, Fitzsimmons, Ross, or Myer were forced onto the stage. Acting offered good money with less effort than constant fighting.

Contemporary sources indicate that Jackson's physical condition deteriorated after the Slavin fight. Sam Fitzpatrick said Jackson took punishment that damaged his constitution. This is not to say he was a wreck, but many sources comment on his deteriorating physical condition, which undoubtedly explains why Davies was anxious to arrange a match with either Sullivan or Corbett as soon as possible. The window of opportunity was closing. The longer Jackson went without meeting the champion, the more his chances of success diminished. It reached the point in early 1894 that many people, including Davies, were saying that Peter had one more good fight left in him.

Clark writes that "after an unwelcome three-month layoff, Jackson defeated Irish-American Patsy Cardiff handily in 10 rounds."[1195] Suggesting that a three month delay before fighting Cardiff involved an unwelcome delay is inaccurate. When a heavyweight is in a real fight, it generally takes time to recover and to schedule another match. Within five days after the McAuliffe fight, the C.A.C.

had offered $8,000 for Kilrain to meet Jackson. Within two weeks they offered $5,000 for Smith to meet Jackson. None of these white fighters raised the color line.

Kilrain's problem was not that Jackson was black; it was finding financial backing. Even after he lost to Sullivan, Kilrain wanted to fight Jackson and did fight the black heavyweight Godfrey. On the other hand, Jackson had all the financial backing a fighter could want; however, he just wasn't keeping the money he earned. The articles for the Jackson-Cardiff match were signed only one month after Peter defeated McAuliffe.[1196] That was quick work for 1889.

Finally, Clark is incorrect when she writes that Cardiff was Irish-American. He was born in Canada, came to Toledo, and then as an adult traveled on Peoria, Illinois, where he began fighting.

Clark writes that after Jackson defeated Cardiff in San Francisco, he "hired the Chicago-based Charles E. Davies as his personal manager . . . [whose] chosen dress, a black topcoat with a high white collar around his neck, gained him the nickname 'Parson,' implying the owner's trustworthiness in a sport not known for high levels of integrity."[1197] This too is substantially incorrect.

It was several months after Jackson defeated Cardiff before he showed up unannounced in Chicago with Fitzpatrick (white Australian), Lees (white), and Naughton (white) and a note from Gunst (white) vouching for Peter's character. Jackson did not hire Parson Davies. He asked Davies to assume his management and brought references along from California to support his request.

Davies was not immediately "alert to Jackson's moneymaking potential" but was initially reluctant to take him on as a fighter. Instead, Davies left Jackson in Chicago and traveled to Mississippi before returning after the Sullivan-Kilrain fight and agreeing to represent Jackson. His decision to take on Jackson was driven by Kilrain's defeat in Mississippi. Before he lost to Sullivan, Kilrain was at worst the top contender and Davies had traveled extensively promoting both Kilrain and Mitchell another top contender. After Kilrain was pummeled by Sullivan, Jake's market value dropped like a rock and thus Jackson arguably became the top contender. If Kilrain had defeated Sullivan it seems less likely that Davies would have agreed to represent Jackson. Finally, Davies had been given his nickname by William Vanderbilt, and he never liked the name. He was given the name when he was managing racewalkers and before he became involved in managing prizefighters. His reputation was not implied or inferred from his nickname. His reputation was earned from the time he was a sixteen year old orphan through his years waiting tables, working in hotels and saloons and becoming a leading theatrical and athletic manager. The name stuck because it fit the man so well.

Clark also claims that *Uncle Tom's Cabin* was rewritten to accommodate Jackson's lack of acting experience and that Uncle Tom's appearance in the first act of the play was deleted because of his lack of experience.[1198] This too is incorrect. Uncle Tom's appearance was removed from the first act of the play because Jackson and Choynski put on their sparring exhibition between the end of the first act and the beginning of the second act. Vaudeville activities between acts were not uncommon. Putting the boxing after the first act kept people in their seats and got them involved in the show. It was not practical for Jackson to put on his makeup and costume as Uncle Tom, and then them to change into boxing tights after the first act and then be made up again in time to appear in his role.[1199]

I mention all of this to refute the conclusion that some shame should be associated with Jackson's decision to play the role of Uncle Tom—unless that judgment is based on preconceived notions and mores formed a century or more after the events.

In January 1893, Jackson, Choynski, and Davies had just completed nine financially successful months on the East Coast and in England. Jackson wanted to fight Corbett and had earned the right to expect a fight. Choynski wanted to fight either Fitzsimmons or Corbett. However, Corbett had put himself on the shelf, and Fitz was also on the stage. Davies, Jackson, and Choynski were simply trying to make money before the public lost interest. This is a time-honored tradition of sportsmen of any race.

Davies loved vaudeville and acting. As mentioned earlier, in 1890 he hired Boucicauit to write a play to be the featured as part of a traveling athletic-vaudeville show. Boucicauit had written the play *After Dark* in which both Myer and Corbett starred. Unfortunately, Boucicauit died after preparing only an outline of the new play.

Davies himself had appeared in productions of *The Tramp* in Beloit in 1891 and *As You Like It*, put on by the Elks' club in Chicago and in which he had appeared before an audience of six thousand.[1200] He had also appeared on stage with Corbett in San Francisco and been involved with actors and theater managers his entire life beginning at the age of twelve.

In the late 1890s, Davies would give up managing fighters as his primary profession in order to manage theaters in New Orleans, including the St. Charles, Academy of Music, Baroone, and Lyric. In addition, he was the southern agent for the Shubert brothers' theater syndicate. He was also part owner of a theater in Pittsburgh.

Choynski, another well-educated man, also loved the stage and had expressed a desire to act. Joe married an actress, Louise Miller. He acknowledged that his profession was fighting and that he was a better fighter than actor. But in his later life Joe was an acknowledged expert and after-dinner speaker on matters related to the theater. According to Jackson, Davies had been working with Peter for almost a year to improve is oratorical skills. In mid-December 1892, Davies told the press in Salt Lake City he had offers from three different playwrights to create a play that would feature Jackson.

Davies had arranged countless events in which his fighters appeared with jugglers, marksmen, singers, dancers, comedians, magicians, animal acts and other vaudeville performers and actors. He loved the entertainment end of the business as evidenced by such events as the May Pole affair, the great tug-of-war event, and the taming of Julius the killer horse. At heart he loved the show and was happiest when the people in the seats went home happy. Nevertheless, Davies was practical and knew that no one would survive long as a promoter unless there was net income after expenses. For several years he had been working to put his fighters on the stage. He wanted them to appear with higher class acts. Putting fighters like Jackson in a classic play that was known to most Americans and was being featured at the Columbian Exposition was logical. Finally, a guarantee of $2,500 for a two week acting gig in San Francisco was good money and beat the idea of more prizefighting or fighting Goddard.

Although Peter admitted he was concerned about embarrassing himself in public, this is a common feeling for most people new to the stage, regardless of race. Peter accepted the adulation of black Americans on many occasions, but there is no evidence he ever sought out their recognition.

Jackson was polite to everyone, whether black or white. He made friends with black and white men alike. But Jackson did not want to be a hero to black Americans. After about a month in the acting profession, he told the *Salt Lake Tribune* he was not an idol of America's black population. "I never go with them, seldom meet them," he said. "They can do nothing for me except go out in the street and hollow or yell—and I'm not after that."[1201]

Jackson was also not interested in being an American citizen. He never applied for U.S. citizenship, and he was more than happy to be an Australian. At best, the United States would have been his fourth choice for a home, after Australia, England, and Hawaii (not yet a U.S. territory). He told the reporter for *Omaha World Herald* that the United States did not comprise the whole world and that a black man or foreigner had no show in America because class distinction was drawn too tightly.[1202]

Davies thought there was no reason why Jackson could not succeed on the stage. If he did well as Uncle Tom, then perhaps his next role would be Othello. As Davies pointed out, Peter's qualifications were as good as Sullivan's and Corbett's. For his part, Jackson told the *Referee* that "There's a whole lot about this acting that I don't know anything about." However he had decided he was going ahead with the project. One newspaper wrote: "It is a great relief to know that at last we have something that will knock out the donkeys and the Siberian bloodhounds."[1203]

Another big show in New Orleans

In early February 1893, Davies challenged Corbett to a match on behalf of Jackson for $10,000 a side.[1204] He also announced he would match Choynski against the winner of the upcoming Hall-Fitzsimmons fight.[1205] Davies said he intended to be in New Orleans on March 2 for the Lewis-Roeber wrestling match he was producing.[1206] Choynski was in Lewis' corner for that match.[1207] This wrestling match was part of the run-up to the Hall-Fitzsimmons fight. It is clear that at the start of presenting *Uncle Tom's Cabin* there was no intention that anyone would be getting out of the businesses of either prizefighting or wrestling. Without fighting there was no reason for anyone to attend the theater to see Jackson, Choynski, or Davies.

Before the new production began, Davies took Choynski to Portland, Oregon, where he used the Pastime Athletic Club's rooms for a match between Tommy West and Choynski. West was a welterweight. He was a relative novice when he met Choynski. The terms of the match provided that West would win $100 if Choynski didn't stop him within four rounds. Davies charged one dollar for admission to the show. West did what he could to fall down and dodge Choynski's blows but was put down in the third round.[1208] Later in his career West would defeat some excellent fighters such as Joe Walcott, Billy Stift, Billy Hanrahan, and Paddy Purtell. He would also participate in several fights that were considered to be fixed affairs.

Less than a month after receiving Stockwell's initial telegram, Jackson, Choynski, and Davies held their first regular rehearsal of *Uncle Tom's Cabin* with the full company. Peter as Uncle Tom was a little nervous, but he did well. Davies in the role of the auctioneer was even better and acted like he was a veteran. After the first dress rehearsal, the play appeared for two nights with a matinee at Macdonough Theater in Oakland.

On February 25 and 26, *Uncle Tom's Cabin* was presented at the Metropolitan Theater in Sacramento.[1209] During these productions, Jackson sparred with a Professor Johnson of Marysville, California, and his acting was panned. The local press said that a phonograph could have done as well.[1210]

Davies and Choynski were not in Sacramento because they had started for New Orleans.[1211] During the early days of the San Francisco performances, Davies and Choynski were in New Orleans. The *Ogden Standard* reported that Choynski, his manager and two lightweight fighters passed through Ogden on the morning of February 24 headed east on the Union Pacific and then on to New Orleans.[1212] The manager referred to in this article was not Davies. Joe was traveling with Ed Graney the champion amateur lightweight of California.[1213] While passing through Chicago on his way to New Orleans, Choynski was asked about Peter's acting skills and said that Peter took naturally to the part and seemed to enjoy acting.[1214] Choynski was away from the *Uncle Tom's Cabin* production through almost mid-March.

The play without Davies and Choynski opened at Stockwell's Alcazar on Monday, February 27, to a full house and played there for three weeks before moving on to Ogden.[1215] The big city newspapers said Jackson was better in the third and fourth acts. One commented that "Jackson will never make an emotional or sentimental actor. It's not in him. He has looked at life in the sterner aspects for too long."[1216] However, the show did draw well in Frisco.[1217]

There was a lot going on in the world of prizefighting and wrestling in February and March 1893, and most of it was happening in New Orleans. Both Davies and Choynski were involved, but Jackson stayed away as he had said he would after his one and only visit there.

The hopeless attempt to arrange a match with Corbett continued. Corbett had a way of distorting the facts, which is generally called lying. Corbett decided that his first title defense would be against Charley Mitchell. He said he would fight Mitchell because he was the first man to issue a challenge after Corbett defeated Sullivan.[1218] Davies then ordered Jackson's money taken down.[1219] He also pointed out that he had personally attempted to arrange a Jackson-Corbett match while traveling on the Corbett special to New Orleans before the fight with Sullivan. Corbett admitted Davies' attempt to make a match but said he discounted that challenge because it had not been repeated immediately after the end of the Sullivan fight. Of course, there is no logic involved in such an explanation, but only an attempt on Corbett's part to rationalize why he would not meet Jackson.

Next, Davies announced that Jackson would not meet Corbett if Corbett first fought Mitchell. Corbett responded by telling Brady to deposit $10,000 for a fight with Jackson to take place within seven months after the Mitchell fight. Corbett said that the amount Jackson would have to post would be entirely up to Jackson, and he added the additional provision that if he failed to defeat Mitchell, then Jackson could take down his money without penalty.[1220] While this sounded good, Brady quickly added the additional provision that the fight would have to take place at one of two clubs in New Orleans.

Both Corbett and Brady knew that Jackson would not fight in New Orleans and that some of the New Orleans' clubs were already prohibiting fights between black and white fighters. If they read the newspapers at all, and both of them admitted to being avid newspaper readers, they knew that Jackson might well be murdered if he fought for the heavyweight championship in the South. Therefore, they both knew that the rest of their proposition was pure newspaper talk. Moreover, the opportunity to fight in California had evaporated because California athletic clubs had stopped sponsoring prizefights after another death in the ring. A fighter named Billy Miller had been killed by Dal Hawkins at the Pacific Athletic Club.[1221]

After the bluff by Corbett and Brady, Davies made his own bluff and proposed that Jackson would be present at ringside for the Corbett-Mitchell match, and if Mitchell failed to appear, then Jackson would step in to fight Corbett. He offered to post $5,000 a side as a forfeit that would be due only if Mitchell failed to appear and either Davies or Jackson were unwilling to fight on that evening. Corbett would not agree to this proposition.[1222] He likely sensed that Davies might pay Mitchell not to appear so that Jackson would have his championship shot.

Davies was in New Orleans as early as February 19 and was still there as late as March 2. He represented Lewis in his match with Muldoon's man, Roeber. Davies apparently attended the Hall-Fitz fight because years later he talked about the fight when discussing Jack Johnson. He thought Johnson was fortunate to be champion at a time when there were few good heavyweights. He commented: "I don't believe he [Johnson] would have had a chance with Bob Fitzsimmons when the later knocked out Jim Hall in 1893. Hall was a wonder at the time, a splendid boxer and terrific hitter, but he was easy for Fitz. If Johnson loses his title in the ring it will be from the effects of body punching, and in this sense Fitzsimmons had no equal."[1223]

Choynski arrived in New Orleans on February 27. When he arrived his public position was he thought Hall would defeat Fitz, but he said he would challenge the winner of their match, whoever that might be. He appeared at the Olympic club on March 1 on behalf of Ryan, who was scheduled to meet George Dawson of Australia.[1224] The Ryan party was trying to gain a postponement of the Dawson fight. The Metropolitan Club had lost substantial money when Ryan pulled out of his earlier fight there because of tonsillitis, and the Olympic was not anxious to repeat that money-losing experience. It refused Ryan's postponement request.

Another scheduled match in New Orleans involved the lightweight fighters Austin Gibbons of Paterson, New Jersey, and Mike Daly of Bangor, Maine. This was a thirty-one round match held on March 7 for a stake of $20,000 and a purse of $3,500, $500 for the loser. Gibbons was the winner of this fight and Choynski was one of the seconds for Daly.[1225]

The next evening Hall and Fitz met, and Hall was knocked out in four rounds.[1226] Choynski was also present at this fight. An interesting description of this fight was provided in the *Nebraska State Journal* on August 1, 1909, by Billy Bunt, who said that Hall was out pointing Fitz for the first three rounds, and Fitz' backers were squirming in their seats. Joe then told Fitz he would have to fight better, and then:

> In the fourth Hall was peppering Bob at will with lefts and rights. He edged him over to a corner, slammed away for dear life and although Fitz tried to cover-up, the effort was futile. It looked like a sure finish, and so it proved, but not for Bob. Fitz was stooping over awkwardly to get away from the punishment, both feet on a line. Here it was that his ability to hit from an angle served him well and saved him from certain defeat. Hall had drawn back momentarily to harden-up for a wicked right hand punch. That fraction of a fleeting second served to turn the tide of battle. Bob's left foot shot forward and almost simultaneously, his right went swishing through the air with the speed of a comet it moved so quickly that the eyes of but few of the spectators could followed its course. It was an overhand swing that landed fairly on the jaw. No human being could have withstood its force without succumbing. Hall crumbled like a stricken deer and was unconscious before he reached the ground, it was the hardest blow I ever saw delivered my life.[1227]

After defeating Hall, Fitzsimmons said that Choynski was the greatest light-heavyweight of the day. Bob said that Joe was not as clever as Hall or himself, but Joe could "hit as hard as any of us." Davies, acting for Choynski, again challenged Fitzsimmons to a match for $5,000 a side and the biggest purse obtainable with the men to fight at catch weights. But Bob said he would not meet Joe because he was not again going to go out of his own weight class.[1228]

Uncle Tom's Cabin takes to the road

In early March, the *Ogden Standard* knew that *Uncle Tom's Cabin* would open there on March 29[1229] The *Standard* noted all of the variations that had taken place in presenting the play over the years after its original production. It suggested the idea that "when in the play the slave driver Simon Legree, raps the aged Uncle Tom over the shoulder, and the faithful servitor dies, Uncle Tom should instead of falling and dying strike out a vigorous right hander knocking Legree off his feet. Legree should then rise and have a nine second mill with Uncle Tom, an innovation that would be decidedly relished by modern audiences." The newspaper further suggests that in the final act Little Eva should "hover as an angel referee while Uncle Tom and Legree have a four-round 'set-to.'"[1230]

This suggestion would likely have pleased contemporary annalists such as Susan F. Clark. In years after he lived, some want Jackson to have been not only a great professional fighter but also a modern-day black activist.

Noting also that James Corbett was to appear as an actor in Ogden, Utah on May 1, the *Standard* suggested that Jackson should wait until then to open in Ogden and then have Corbett play the fight scene with Jackson.[1231]

Before the final performance in San Francisco, Davies had returned from New Orleans. He stepped forward to the footlights and made a little speech that was reported in the *San Francisco Call* on March 20:

> When Peter Jackson came to this country five years ago he came with the determination to reach, it he could, the top of the ladder as a—that is in, let us say, athletics. He was already the champion of Australia and brought with him a reputation of which he might well be proud. Although a black man the California Club of this city gave him an equal show with other aspirants for honors in his line and they never had cause to regret it.
>
> After meeting many good men in this country and defeating them he went to Europe, where he defeated Frank P. Slavin, who claimed the championship of Australia. The man who held the heavy-weight championship of the world for twelve years always said at all times and in all places that he would not fight with a black man, and he never did. It was a matter of principle with him and that was enough for Jackson. I believe that, no matter what a man's color, if he is a good man, an honest man and trying

> to climb up, it is the man who takes the ladder away from him who should he criticized. When Sullivan was defeated Jackson asked his conqueror to meet him and has been refused, because, the champion says, Charley Mitchell claims the right to meet him first. I have already deposited $1,000 which I will forfeit if the statement about Mitchell's claim is not untrue. We are going away to-night and take with us one of your boys, a good one, Joe Choynski. We hope to return within twelve months with honors, but one thing is sure, neither Jackson nor Choynski will do anything to disgrace themselves or you. Jackson will ever keep his eye on his home, San Francisco.[1232]

Uncle Tom's Cabin was scheduled to open at the Grand Opera House in Ogden on Wednesday, March 29, under the management of Ellinghouse. Advertising said that Jackson and Choynski were to spar three "friendly and scientific rounds" between the first and second acts, and they were to be introduced by Davies.[1233]

Before the performance one Ogden newspaper explained to its readers:

> A novel sort of show will be "Uncle Tom's Cabin" Thursday night. This company is built around Jackson, and naturally the great colored pugilist is the central attraction. In order to make a good performance, as well as to show off the noted athlete, a strong company has been put around him: Stockwell, the veteran San Francisco comedian and manager of the beautiful Stockwell's Theater, playing Marks, and Parson Davies, Jackson's backer, the part of the auctioneer. Bessie Carr, familiarly called the black Lottie Collins, will do the "Ta-ra-ra-boom-de-aye" song and dance.

Ogden was a good place for the company because the three principles, Davies, Jackson and Choynski had all been well-received there and each of them had previously said how much they enjoyed that community.

After the show in Ogden the newspaper reported:

> Peter Jackson and his company appeared at the "Grand" last night in "Uncle Tom's Cabin." Jackson and Choynski were the figures of interest. Parson Davies failed to make connections and Ogden people were denied the pleasure of seeing the noted pugilistic manager in his stage attire as the auctioneer. The house was partly filled with people who didn't want to see "Uncle Tom's Cabin" and went to see Jackson, partly people who didn't want to see Jackson and went to see "Uncle Tom's Cabin." The combination is a good one so for as 'attraction' is concerned; but take away Jackson and Choynski and there is no more "Uncle Tom's Cabin."[1234]

From Ogden, the case moved on to Salt Lake for two nights, March 31 and April 1. Posters depicting Jackson appeared in the following way:

***Poster of unknown origin advertising* Uncle Tom's Cabin**

The *Salt Lake Herald* was critical saying that the downstairs part of the house (i.e., the whites only area) was sparsely populated while the upper tier (i.e. the blacks allowed area) was packed. It described the performance as one of the sickest, rottenest plays presented in a respectable theater in some time.[1235]. The *Salt Lake Tribune* also described a top-heavy house. It wrote:

> Critical ability could not do justice to the performance last night. The upper portions of the house swallowed with greedy appetite the treacle ladled out for their benefit. While Jackson is by no means an accomplished actor, common honesty compels

> the statement that he tried faithfully and intelligently and was not so much a burlesque in his part as was John L. Sullivan in his. He didn't throw the sporty slang and swig into his work as Sullivan did into his; but after all, the difference was but the difference of the men themselves. "Parson" Davies took the role of the auctioneer. The clever comedian L. R. Stockwell, who generally does Marks, was disgraced by a wooden substitute. Stockwell was recalled to San Francisco by urgent business, but may possible return to-day.[1236]

It is fortunate that the review of the performance was followed with an excellent interview with Jackson and Davies at their conducted hotel by a *Salt Lake Tribune* reporter. This article is as near as possible to a first-hand account of how Jackson thought and discusses issues important to understanding Jackson's positions on several important subjects.

> On the fifth floor of the Knutsford Hotel Peter Jackson and his manager, "Parson" Davies, have a suite of rooms. A *Tribune* reporter called upon the colored pugilist at these quarters last evening to learn the impressions of the stage life upon the new aspirant. Every ring hero seems disposed to go before the footlights at the present time. Sullivan was the first to make his bow in regular drama, followed successfully by James J. Corbett, Peter Jackson, Choynski and Ed Smith.
>
> The colored pugilist was found dressing for the evening, with a quandary agitating his mind as to whether he should put on a plaid lavender or a pale maroon tie.
>
> When asked for some expression as to his new calling, he was very reticent. "Holding up the mirror to nature" was an art in which he was too much a novice to venture many opinions and he frankly said so.
>
> "I have to earn a living, so I have turned my mind to this. I like the business fairly well, and have worked pretty hard at it."
>
> "Don't you see a different class of people from those you have been accustomed to see?"
>
> "No. I have had ladies and gentlemen at my boxing exhibitions and see no difference between them and my present audience."
>
> "Do you think the people come to see you as an actor or from curiosity as a pugilist?"
>
> "As an actor. I think they come to see the play, not me." answered Jackson. Later, however, when in a more communicative mood, he said that he thought the present crowds come to see him because of his reputation as a pugilist. "But that can't keep up," he continued. "I and all the other pugilists must build up a

reputation as actors, or else, with first curiosity satisfied, people will quit coming to our performances."

"Do you expect to remain on the stage?"

"I can't tell—it depends all on circumstances. I am like a piece of paper, whisked around wherever the wind may blow me. I may stay on the stage – I may not. I may stay in this country – I may not. I try to do the best I can on the stage, the public must judge me. I have to earn a living some way, and that's why I am acting now."

Jackson, in all his talk on the matter of theatrical venture, was extremely reticent and ill-at-ease. His manager, "Parson" Davies, who is extremely suave, genial and ready in conversation, came frequently to his "star's" rescue with statements of the large business and enthusiastic receptions. The "Parson" and his star had just made a present of a silk umbrella to Mrs. Ed Kelly, the wife of Salt Lake's patron of sport.

TALK OF BOXING

Having attired himself Jackson sat down and entered into a running conversation with the *Tribune* man on the topic of boxing and fighting. Entered upon this, he seemed at home once more and talked in a most intelligent manner. He is above the run of the usual sports, uses little slang, employs well-chosen language, and shows that he has ideas of his own. Not for once does he boast of his own abilities, or even take credit for anything he has done. Modesty seems his cardinal virtue.

Referring to Sullivan's career as a pugilist and actor he said: "Sullivan lacks manly courage. Yes," (this reflectively) "that is it—those words express it exactly. He was the idol of the Irish-American people: in fact, was the pride of this country as a splendid specimen of physical development. No one ever had a chance like his. But he threw away his opportunities, he was not true to his friends. Had he been a manly, honest, courageous man, it would have been a million times better for himself, for me, for every pugilist. He injured the whole profession."

"Are you the idol of the colored people much as Sullivan was the idol of the Irish?"

"Idol of the colored people? No! Why should I be the idol of the colored people? I never go with them, seldom meet them. They can do nothing for me except go out in the street and hollow or yell—and I'm not after that."

> "But don't the colored people rally round you, look upon you as a prominent representative, and back you as far as they can?"
>
> "No! Assuredly not!"
>
> Here Ed Kelly interpolated a remark by way of corroboration, that during the Jackson-Slavin fight, when he cold [?] pools, the colored people bet more freely on Slavin than on Jackson.
>
> "Corbett has treated you better than Sullivan, has he not?"
>
> "I don't personally know Corbett, or at least I have only met him once—at Philadelphia last year."
>
> "But Corbett don't bar you in fighting as Sullivan?"
>
> "He might as well, for he won't fight me. He wants to wait till I'm older—twenty years or so older. Then he'll be willing to meet me," that sarcastically.

Jackson said that the company supporting them was Stockwell's, and that they would play through to Chicago. It was uncertain whether they would continue during the summer or not. Fighting, he said, was an unnatural profession, a man could only do it successfully for a few years, and no one could look to it as a permanent business. Neither could the present pugilists who are on the stage make a continued success of it unless they could develop sufficient ability as actors to compete on an honest level with other actors.[1237]

Jackson's attitude toward the black population of America changed over time. In 1898, the *Boston Globe* reported Jackson was then enjoying himself with the black citizens of San Francisco, but it contrasted that circumstance to his earlier attitude toward his black supporters. According to the *Globe,* several years before 1898, Jackson had been loath to associate with the black people in America; however, Parson Davies insisted that Jackson acknowledge their attentions. The *Globe* reported that in Washington, D.C., Jackson had received an invitation to participate as the guest of honor at a ball held by the city's black population. Jackson did not want to attend, but Davies insisted and accompanied Peter. During the ball, they were seated on an elevated platform and the rest of crowd filed by one at a time to shake Jackson' hand and express their support. After this part of the evening ended a large crowd gathered around Jackson to ask him questions. It was a warm evening and the perspiration ran down his face until he finally leaned over to Davies and said: "For heaven's sake get me out of here!"

At that point Davies said to the assembled party with great sincerity, "Mr. Jackson tells me he is delighted with your attentions and would be glad to remain longer, but he has forgotten something—he came away without a razor."

A response came from a half dozen guests who reached into their pockets and withdrew their own razors to offer them to Peter: "Take mine!" With this result Peter glared at Davies for an instant and then thanked each person and declined their razors saying that they were too small for his immense hand. He then stalked out of the hall in offended dignity.[1238] It seems highly likely that this story was related to the *Globe* by Davies himself. It is the kind of story telling that endeared Davies to many reporters.

In 1893, the great American humorist Bill Nye wrote about Jackson and his participation in the acting profession:

> Peter Jackson, I had been led to believe, would elevate the stage. People told me that he resembled Salvini on the stage. He does not. They belong to two different schools of acting. Salvini is more *en rapport* with the audience.
>
> I have never seen Corbett act, but I judge that he will rank with Jackson and Sullivan, whose rankness is noticeable even from the back seat.
>
> Race prejudice has nothing to do with my criticism. When I begin to criticize, I do not let those things interfere: neither do I care to attack a man without cause who has chosen the great field of art as his profession.
>
> I simply wish to say that the pugilist depends for his success outside the ring on the man who managers him and how well he obeys his manger. When he begins to think, he is lost.
>
> But the question arises, Has the pugilist who has succeeded a right to star in a play? Of course he has. Anybody has the right to avail himself of even accidental notoriety to exhibit himself in answer to the public demand, and then the public must decide whether it is worth a dollar or not.
>
> Peter Jackson is a good looking man *anatomically.* More so than he is uncle-tomically, I may say. He has long arms, with rather slender wrists and small hands and feet. He is well arranged for fighting purposes, but his interpretation of Uncle Tom won't do.
>
> If he would punish Lagree profusely, I would agree to rewrite the play so as to give him a chance. Then if I could name the man to play Lagree I would be almost too happy.[1239]

In a book of essays entitled *A Question of Manhood: A Reader in U.S. Black Men's History and Masculinity, vol. 2, The 19 Century: From Emancipation to Jim Crow*, author David K. Wiggins claims that Jackson entered into the *Uncle Tom's Cabin* project "reluctantly" and he was "totally inept" in the role.[1240] This assertion does not seem to be supported by contemporary reviews his performance. The *Salt Lake Herald* wrote: "The cast is a very powerful one and Peter Jackson who plays Uncle Tom, displays an earnest intelligence and self-possession that is a surprise in an actor of a few weeks' experience. He speaks his lines distinctly and audibly and seems thoroughly imbued with the spirit of his part."[1241] Peter had many positive reviews, and Bill Nye's is one of a handful of negative assessments of Jackson's acting.

The cast of *Uncle Tom's Cabin* moved northeast from Salt Lake City to Cheyenne, Wyoming, where they appeared on April 4, and they were in Kansas City by April 10 and in Omaha for three nights from April 20 through April 22.[1242] After Omaha they headed for Sedalia, Missouri.[1243]

About that time, a rumor was circulating that Chicago would soon become prize ring headquarters during the 1893 World Colombian Exposition and that Davies was the moving spirit behind the idea that would involve a new athletic club similar to the New Orleans and San Francisco organizations. The actual result was the opposite. Prizefighting was banished in Chicago, and the Columbian Athletic Club was formed and then set up shop at Roby, Indiana, with a man from New Orleans, Dominick O'Malley, operating both a race track and prizefight pavilion.

While they were in Kansas City, Davies and Jackson were each asked about reports that Mitchell intended to give up the ring for the pulpit and become a minister. Several newspapers reported: "The grin peculiar to Peter Jackson overspread his face when he was informed of the New York dispatch. He thought it possible that it might be true. He also has a slight inclination in that direction. The scriptural passages in *Uncle Tom's Cabin* and the general religious air that surrounds that character, he says, are seriously affecting him."[1244]

The show opened in Omaha on April 20, 1893 for a three night stand at the Farnam Street Theater. The party including Jackson stayed at the Paxton Hotel the most elegant structure in Omaha with 175 guest rooms, a large dining room, and a comfortable bar. Presidents Wilson and Roosevelt were among the many distinguished people who stayed at the Paxton.

On the first night of the show, the Farnam was packed from top to bottom. The *Omaha Daily Bee* noted that Jackson had a talent for the part:

> But to Peter alone does not belong all the credit for his co-laborers in a common cause, the well-known "Parson" Davies, gentleman and sporting caterer, and Joseph Bartlett Choynski, one of the exemplars of the prize ring, come in for an abundant measure of praise. The Parson is extraordinarily clever, as he is in the ordinary rut of every-day life, and he supports the Brobdignagian Peter in his histrionic ambition with the same zest he urges his claims on being the best man with his dukes on the top of the earth.[1245]

Choynski played the part of the slaver driver with discrimination and judgment that suited the part.

At the end of April, the cast reached St. Louis to make its appearance at Pope's Theater from May 1, through Saturday, May 7, with matinees on Wednesday and Saturday and seats sold at twenty-five cents and fifty cents apiece.[1246] The production would return to St. Louis in March 1894. The *Post Dispatch* reported that the show opened to an immense audience. Jackson had always been well-received in St. Louis.

While in St. Louis, Peter was "the object of adoration by the pugilistic fraternity" and was the recipient of the social attentions of such organizations as the Gentleman's Athletic Club.[1247] Davies continued his efforts on behalf of Jackson and Choynski to bring Corbett and Fitzsimmons out of hiding. Choynski had no trouble agreeing to fight in New Orleans, but Fitz remained uninterested in that proposition.[1248] Both Davies and Jackson said that they had about concluded that Corbett would never agree to a fight with Jackson and was simply doing everything possible to avoid Peter.[1249]

In the second week of May the production reached Chicago. Davies was planning for the upcoming summer, and the *St. Paul Daily Globe* reported that he had summoned Lewis to Chicago to discuss a summer wrestling tour or a tournament in Chicago.[1250]

Jackson and Davies left Chicago with different goals. Peter was going to the West Indies and then to England for about three months. Davies was going to spend a few days on the East Coast.[1251] On May 30, Davies and Jackson both arrived at the Grand Central Depot in New York and were met by a crowd of some five hundred friends and admirers. Charlie was described in the *World* as Jackson's "good looking and decidedly shrewd manager." Peter appeared to be considerably heavier than when had left New York, and he said that his health could scarcely be better.[1252] Jackson was asked his opinion of the Corbett-Mitchell match but begged off because of lack of familiarity with Mitchell's ability, having never seen him fight.[1253]

Davies—called the "smooth-faced Chicagoan at Jackson's elbow"—agreed with Peter's statement that the outcomes of glove contests are very uncertain. According to the *World*, Davies was more talkative than Jackson, but Charlie seemed to be more interested in the route of the big *Uncle Tom's Cabin* company. Davies announced he would be assuming the management of the company in the coming season.[1254]

It was suggested that Stockwell wanted out of production because it had been a financial failure during its first season. The *San Francisco Call* wrote that the production fell flat after the company crossed the Rocky Mountains and that people in the East had no interest in the production.[1255]

Davies was asked about the proposed Choynski-Fitzsimmons match. Referring to Fitz he said he did not care to hound a man. He also remarked that "so long as Fitz doesn't care to fight the Californian there is nothing more to be said. I do not want to be understood as looking upon Joe as a sure winner. Fitz is a great fighter, but I'll back Choynski against him for $5,000 and I think Joe would put up a better fight against him than he has ever had. Of course, Joe cannot fight at the middle-weight limit, but Maher and Hall were a trifle over 158 pounds."[1256]

Davies confirmed that Jackson would leave on May 31 for the West Indies to visit his brother, whom he had not seen in years. Then after a stay of two weeks, Peter planned to go to England and spend a month. Meanwhile, Davies said he was working on booking the *Uncle Tom's Cabin* show.

Jackson left New York at the end of May on the White Star Line's *Teutonic*. He did not go to the West Indies but arrived in Liverpool on June 7, 1892, listed on the manifest as a twenty-seven-year-old "pugilist." He said he wanted to make the most of his vacation while in England.[1257]

Making plans while Jackson was in England

Davies was in New York for several weeks after Jackson's departure for England. Once again rumors circulated that he was thinking about managing a sporting club. Now the story was that Davies might join the Coney Island Athletic Association as one of the its leading officers. Choynski was also in New York, and the rumor was that he would be challenged for a rematch with Godfrey. In Salt Lake City, Colonel Kelly said in mid-June he had received a telegram from Davies saying he would like to manage Mysterious Billy Smith who was then in Utah.

Davies also took on the management of another Australian fighter, Alf "Griffo" Griffith, the featherweight champion of his homeland. Griffo was in New York at the time and was anxious to get on a match with any man of his weight.[1258] Only a few weeks later, Davies decided to leave the management of Griffo to Ed Alexander, who had brought the Australian over to America. Davies said he considered that two stars like Jackson and Choynski were enough to handle.

In late June, Davies and Choynski made several demonstrations of signing articles of agreement and posting money in an effort to induce Fitz to sign for a match.[1260] In early July, the Coney Island Athletic Association offered a purse of $15,000 for a Choynski-Fitzsimmons match. Davies responded, saying he would agree to fight at 165 pounds before the club offering the largest purse. At the time the Columbia Athletic Club had an eastern agent who was in New York trying to arrange a fight involving Fitz.[1261] After the Coney Island offer, the Columbia Club's agent offered a purse of $17,000 for the fight. Davies left New York and returned to Chicago without reaching any agreements for such a fight.

Prizefighting in Chicago had been banned inside the city limits, and the sports from the Windy City had opened a big pavilion in Roby, Indiana. Roby was on the New York Central R.R. line, not far past South Chicago and Hammond-Whiting stops but before Gary, Indiana. A race track had been operated at Roby by John Condon, one of Chicago's most important bookmakers. Northwest Indiana has frequently benefited from various prohibitions in Chicago, and things were no different in 1893.

Corbett agrees to fight Jackson

On July 10, the big match at Roby was between Johnny Griffin and Solly Smith for a purse of $6,000. Eight special trains left Chicago with men wanting to see the fight. Among those in attendance were Davies, Jackson, Choynski, Corbett, Wyatt Earp, Sam Fitzpatrick, Ryan, Griffo, Gilmore, and many others. O'Malley was the master of ceremonies. Corbett showed up at about nine thirty p.m. and was given a warm reception. Earlier in the day a number of Chicago firemen had lost their lives in a fire at the Columbian Exposition. O'Malley appealed for aid for the families of the lost firefighters and then Corbett entered the ring.[1262]

What motivated Corbett's actions is not totally clear, but the implication from available sources is that he and Davies had a private argument before Corbett made their differences public. A good record of what happened in public is provided by the *New York Times*:

> The conqueror of Sullivan jumped over the ropes and silence having been secured, Corbett announced:
>
> "There is a colored pugilist by the name of Jackson [a yell, 'You are afraid to meet him!'] who wants to fight me. Jackson is not here to talk for himself, but his manager is here. I want to say that I will fight him, and that I have a check for $10,000 in my hand that I will whip Peter Jackson at any time or place."
>
> At this moment 'Parson' Davies cleared the ropes amid mingled applause and hisses, and from the centre of the ring he proclaimed that Jackson had months ago posted a forfeit of two thousand five hundred dollars for a fight with Corbett and that the later only required to state the time.
>
> "Put up your money," shouted Corbett. "You know I have to fight Mitchell in December."
>
> "Our money is up," responded the 'Parson,' with an uproar of shouts and hisses. "By _______, I want a forfeit," roared Corbett.
>
> "Here is another forfeit," shouted the 'Parson,' producing a big roll of bills from his trousers pocket and handed it to O'Malley. "That is satisfactory," answered the latter, and then the announcement was made amid a torrent of cheering that Corbett and Jackson would meet in November for a fight to the finish.[1263]

The *Chicago Tribune* wrote that "Davies and Corbett stood talking at each other like mad men while the crowd yelled like a crazy mob."[1264]

This declaration that Corbett would meet Jackson in November was later corrected to say that Corbett and Jackson would meet in June 1894, it being apparent to everyone that Corbett had already agreed to meet Mitchell in December.[1265]

Two days later Corbett and Davies met at Chicago's Press Club and signed articles for a fight to take place between June 20 and 30 "before a club north of Mason and Dixon's line," offering the best purse for $10,000 a side and the championship of the world. Corbett withdrew the $10,000 check he had waived around the ring and substituted a check for $1,000 as his forfeit money.[1266] Jackson cabled from London on July 11 and said he would sail July 19 for America to sign the articles.[1267]

Jackson had planned to go to the West Indies before returning from England to the United States, but he again scrapped that plan for that trip. He was greeted at the port of New York by an estimated five hundred people as he disembarked from the *Teutonic* in the afternoon of July 27.[1268] Jackson was accompanied by the twenty-nine-year old Ambrose Preece, who was a master horse trainer in England. When he disembarked, he was dressed to the height of fashion and seemed to be in good condition, but thinner than when he left. He said he always lost weight during an ocean crossing. He also said he was happy to meet Corbett, "barring the South." Plans were he would spend about two weeks in Chicago, then travel to San Francisco, and then return to the East for the new season of *Uncle Tom's Cabin*.[1269]

Jackson wasted no time reaching Chicago. He was there on the day after he arrived in New York.[1270] Exactly what happened with respect to the articles of agreement is not clear, but whatever document Corbett signed at Chicago's Press Club may not have been final articles. Reports said that Jackson and Davies were awaiting a meeting with Corbett to sign the articles, but earlier reports said that Corbett had already signed the articles.[1271] Some stories said that Davies, Jackson, Young Mitchell, and Dempsey were planning to be at Roby to witness a contest between George F. Green (known as, Young Corbett) and Paddy Smith.[1272]

The reason for their planned trip was likely to give Peter a first-hand look at the venue where he and Corbett would probably meet. However, Jackson left for San Francisco before the Smith-Young Corbett fight, and at that point Jackson had not signed the articles but had empowered Charlie to arrange all that details and then Davies planned to follow within a week.[1273] Whatever the parties agreed to there were still changes being made to the proposed articles as late as September 4, when the conditions for posting the stake were changed to require successive postings: January 25, 1894, $1,000; March 26, $2,000 April 26, $3,000 and May 17, $3,000.[1274]

West Coast newspapers said that Jackson was back in San Francisco late on August 2, which means he must have moved on from Chicago without attending the fight at Roby because no train could have made the trip from Chicago to San Francisco that quickly.[1275] Corbett was present at the Roby fight and sat in Young Corbett's corner, but there seems to be no record of a meeting or confrontation between Davies and Corbett.

That night there was a riot outside of the Roby stadium between a crowd of South Chicago and Whiting toughs and Pinkerton agents who had been hired as security. Gunshots were fired, several men injured, and a man named Dan Slavin was killed. Corbett, his wife, and Brady left Chicago on the morning of August 1 to begin training at Asbury Park.[1276] Word of this riot and the killing at Roby would work its way to the Indiana state capitol and be bad news for future Roby activities.

It appears that soon after the Smith-Young Corbett fight, Davies went to San Francisco. In *Gentleman Bruiser*, his terrific biography of Jackson, Bob Petersen wrote:

> On Friday the 11 [of August 1893] there was "a road party." In a carriage pulled by four grays, a dozen of Peter's buddies went on an excursion along El Caimno Real out Millbrae and San Mateo way, about where the San Francisco International Airport is today. Davies, Naughton, Choynski, George Dawson arrived from Australia with his trainer Teddy Alexander, Fitzpatrick, Jack Miles and others. They consumed boiled chickens, oysters, big yellow peaches and lots of alcohol, they sang as they went along, they sang themselves hoarse. Peter and Herget "supplied the clown comedy portion of the outing." It was a happy day. A photograph of the party, each holding his hat, which was taken at Barney Farley's roadhouse in San Mateo.[1277]

Davies, Choynski, Fitzpatrick, and Gunst probably left San Francisco on the evening train on August 11. They were racing back to Chicago to attend another fight at Roby, and were there on the evening of August 14 to watch Dan Creedon of Australia and Alex Greggains. All of them occupied a box at the Roby match. Fitzpatrick was Creedon's trainer and was at ringside. Lewis and Myer were also present for the fight that Creedon won in fifteen rounds.[1278] Outside the Roby arena was a mob of one thousand or more identified as stockyard men, iron workers, and railroad hands who wanted free admission and pelted the outside of the arena with rocks while firing blank cartridges throughout the match. At one point the mob broke into the arena and attacked the paying customers.[1279]

The second season of *Uncle Tom's Cabin*

Jackson left San Francisco on August 14 and arrived in Chicago on August 17 – another trip of over two thousand two hundred miles. He was on his way to Mt. Clemens. The *Chicago Tribune* said that Jackson would remain in Mt. Clemens doing light work before going into active training for Corbett. However, the real reason for going to Mt. Clemens was to meet Davies and the cast for the new season of *Uncle Tom's Cabin*.[1280]

About this time Davies and Billy Myer were on one side of a bet that a few months later received national notoriety. Two young college graduates, Fred Julian Sydney, a twenty-five-year-old Yale Law School graduate, and J. Francis Payne, a nineteen-year-old University of Michigan graduate, had been working as newspaper men but were laid off during the financial crisis in 1893. Sydney and Payne made a bet with Davies and Myer that they could travel six thousand miles through the South and all the way to California in one hundred days with only one cent in their pockets but posing as newspaper reporters. If they could successfully accomplish this goal then Davies and Myer would lose the bet and pay them $5,000.

The two young men nearly accomplished their goal using false newspaper credentials that they created and then posing has reporters for the *Chicago Tribune*, *Century Magazine*, the *Chicago Times*, and the *Brooklyn Eagle*. They traveled for free and lived a high life until they reached Los Angles in December, where Fred Sydney was stricken by a guilty conscience. Payne continued on San Francisco and then Ogden, Utah, and was in Salt Lake City on December 14. A few days later, Sydney disclosed the sham they had been running. Their story made that national newspapers, but no one said what became of the bet or whether anyone ever paid.[1281]

At Mt. Clemens in the late summer of 1893 Choynski met the woman who would become his wife for almost fifty years to follow. He related the story in January 1927 for the *Winnipeg Free Press* explaining that romance came to his life in September 1893, when the company gathered at Mt. Clemens to rehearse for their second season. Several new faces were in the cast and the hotel management as Davies to arrange some entertainment for its guests.

One of the new cast members was Louise Anderson Miller who came aboard to play Topsy. She sang during that Mt. Clemens performance, and Joe thought she had the most beautiful voice he had ever heard. Joe and Louise married at Cincinnati during the second season of *Uncle Tom's Cabin*. Joe said that as an actor he was a great middleweight, and he preferred the ring. However, he thought he was at least as good as Sullivan, Fitzsimmons, Jeffries, or even Corbett.[1282]

The new season of Davies' *Uncle Tom's Cabin* opened at the Music Hall in Newark, Ohio, on Wednesday, August 30. Prices for seats were twenty-five, fifty, and seventy-five cents. The newly composed cast featured Davies as auctioneer and as George Harris, and Choynski as George Shelby.[1283]

The opening night crowd was not "as large nor as enthusiastic" as was expected by Newark, Ohio's *Daily Advocate*, but the sparring match at the end of the first act was an occasion for a "momentary outburst of enthusiasm." The *Daily Advocate* wrote that "Jackson's manner was as near like that of the original Uncle Tom as possible for a man of his towering figure and wonderful muscular development" and that Peter "succeeded quite well in laying aside, momentarily, the air of the pugilist but there was a fullness in his voice and a suggestion of reserved force in his movements that could scarcely find any connection with the popular idea of aged, wrinkled and decrepit Uncle Tom."[1284]

It is difficult to follow the exact route that the production took after leaving Newark. Choynski and Jackson were in Cincinnati on September 5, 6 and 7, at Havlin's Theater with a two p.m. matinee and an eight p.m. evening show on September 6.[1285] While there Jackson was asked by the *Cincinnati Enquirer* about a recent match between Hall and Slavin won by Hall. The fight was widely thought to have been fixed. Jackson said the fight had hurt Hall more than if he had lost the match. He said that Hall had been shunned in London after the match. He further commented: "It was a job fight. Slavin was to lose it. He didn't have the gall to do it, so he got drunk before he went in the ring."

The cast stayed at Cincinnati's preeminent hotel, the Gibson House on Main Street between Fourth and Fifth streets, just south of Fountain Square. On September 7, Davies received a telegram from his new assistant, Harry Glickauf: "There are parties here who say they are willing to back Fitzsimmons against Joe Choynski at 160 pounds. Can Joe get to that weight?" Davies responded by telegraph that Choynski could not do justice to himself or his friends and fight at less than 165 pounds, but that at that weight Glickauf could make a match for as much as $10,000 a side.

After sending the reply, Davies and Choynski went to the *Cincinnati Enquirer* to share the news with the press and answer questions:

> "Isn't it about time Fitzsimmons should do something for the big purses that are given him?"
>
> "All the fights he has had in America have been gifts," Davies responded. "Dempsey is the only man who gave him half a fight. He has had great marks in all the others, and he owes the American people at least one fight. I see he caught another sucker. Poor Hickey! I knew him in Ireland. He is only a 140 pound man. Then I see he is matched to fight O'Donnell a limited number or rounds. It is a case of one Australian against another. The American people have had enough of this sort of thing. . . . It is funny that Fitz won't take on Choynski. The Roby Club has offered us a purse of $17,000 for such a fight and the Coney Island Club $15,000. If Fitz doesn't want a fight to a finish we will make the match for a limited number of rounds."[1286]

Fitzsimmons continued to avoid facing Choynski.

It is likely that the cast and stars of *Uncle Tom's Cabin* went northeast from Cincinnati and visited such towns as Columbus, Steubenville and Pittsburgh. On September 13, the company was in Bradford, Pennsylvania, just south of the New York state line toward the northwest corner of Pennsylvania. The next evening it was in Olean, Cattaraugus County, New York, which is northeast of Bradford and toward the southwest corner of New York. The Olean newspaper described Davies as the famous promoter of athletic exhibitions. Given the railroad routes, it is likely that the company also went to Elmira and Ithaca before being presented on September 18, 19 and 20 in Syracuse.[1287]

The *McKean Democrat* of Smethport, Pennsylvania, noted that several representatives of the black citizens of Smethport had traveled to Bradford to see Jackson.[1288] Smethport is about twenty miles from Bradford, and it is likely that black citizens from smaller surrounding towns often traveled to see Jackson appear in towns near their homes.

After opening night in Syracuse, the *Herald* wrote that Jackson attracted a large audience and did creditable work as an actor. It concluded that "he is not a wonder in his new line, but he plays 'Uncle Tom' with a fair conception of its requirements. His supporting company is of a first rate order and the mounting of the piece is better than 'Uncle Tom' has had here. Some of the scenes are exceedingly pretty."[1289]

Other places where they appeared were Kingston, New York, on October 2, New York City from October 15 through October 22, Lawrence, Massachusetts, on October 24, Bangor, Maine, on October 27, New Brunswick, Maine, on November 3, and Lowell, Massachusetts, on November 4.

Davies continued to try to find someone creditable and willing to be matched with Choynski. Steve O'Donnell appeared to be a possibility. He had been fighting in Australia as early as 1886 and was considered a technician who moved, had science, and a good jab. Corbett employed O'Donnell to work with him as his sparring partner. In late August, Davies issued a challenge to O'Donnell to meet Joe at the Coney Island club, but O'Donnell too wanted no part of Choynski.[1290]

Those who know what is best strike again

While the Davies' company was touring, legal authorities across the United States began an all-out assault on the leading boxing venues. Many of Chicago's sports had contributed more than $30,000 for the construction of the facility in Roby. Barred from offering events in Chicago, they had moved across the state line and hired O'Malley to operate the club. Over the years he would be the man responsible for carrying off such fights as Fitzsimmons-Dempsey, Fitzsimmons-Maher, Fitzsimmons-Hall, Smith-Goddard, and Corbett-Sullivan. Several fights were held at Roby without interruption until a scheduled fight between Lavigne and Griffo was advertised by O'Malley as a finish fight and posters were also plastered all over Indiana's capital.

It was a blunder to advertise any match as a finish fight because that violated a law that had been pushed through the Indiana legislature. Davies had lived with that problem for many years in Chicago. It was silly to push advertising posters in the face of Indiana's government. Soon Governor Claude Matthews announced he would stop the Lavigne-Griffo match, and all other boxing at Roby.

A company of the Indiana National Guard known as the Fort Wayne Rifles was ordered to proceed directly to Roby to prevent any and all boxing. On September 4, the Fort Wayne Rifles went to Roby equipped with a Gatling gun and ten experienced artillery men. Within two days there were seven hundred national guard soldiers surrounding Roby "fortified with swords, bayonets, rifles, and 27,000 pounds of ammunition."[1291] That was it for Roby.

O'Malley went to Indianapolis to meet with Matthews to explain how much money the club members had invested in the operation and the financial benefits that were accruing to northern Indiana. The governor told him that there would be no more prizefighting at Roby, and he didn't care if one thousand Chicago toughs got killed in the process.[1292]

Of course, the demise of Roby would have a substantial impact on many fights, including the Jackson-Corbett contest. In addition, the governor sent writs to New York seeking the arrest and extradition of several fighters, including Choynski for participating in prizefighting in Indiana in violation of state law. Joe's only participation at Roby had been as a referee. Creedon, who was being managed by Davies' friend Hopkins, was arrested in New York and brought back to Indiana for trial on a charge of prizefighting.[1293] Joe was not arrested.

One potential result of barring fights in Indiana was that many of the big fights might be pushed over to Coney Island, where local officials seemed willing to allow prizefighting. Less than two weeks after the governor of Indiana shut down Roby, the effort to prevent fighting at the Coney Island began in earnest. New York Mayor Thomas Gilroy met with the *New York Times*—a newspaper with a long anti-prizefighting record—to say that there would be no prizefighting on Manhattan Island if he had anything to say about it. In defiance of the mayor, the club sponsored a match between Dixon and Solly Smith.[1294]

The mayor's statements about closing down Coney Island fueled an all out effort to prohibit prizefighting in all of New York. Citizens' petitions were published almost daily in the *New York Times*, and more than one hundred ministers petitioned the governor. The YMCA joined in the anti-fighting effort and the do-gooders seemed to multiply like fungus. Mass meetings and rallies were organized let by the Reverend Dr. Lyman Abbott of the Plymouth Church in Brooklyn and the Reverend Dr. Charles H. Pankhurst of the Madison Square Presbyterian Church.[1295] None of this was good for promoters such as Davies, but he was still busy on the stage.

While *Uncle Tom's Cabin* was in Kingston, New York, Jackson was asked on September 30 about the upcoming Corbett-Mitchell match and about his own sixty-one round no contest with Corbett. Jackson said he was not in shape at the time of that fight because of his lame leg. He also said he thought that the C.A.C. had acted incorrectly by declaring the match no contest instead of allowing it to continue to a finish.

On Sunday, October 8 Davies, Jackson and Choynski were all spotted in New York, and they all had money to burn. The *Post Dispatch* wrote that Jackson was "taking pretty good care of himself" and using only an occasional glass of champagne, "instead of several pints an hour, as in former years."[1296] The good news was that "Mike" Haley of Norfolk, Virginia, who was the backer for O'Donnell, issued a challenge to fight any man in England or America for $2,500 a side and the largest purse offered by any club. Davies soon accepted this offer on behalf of Choynski.[1297]

Uncle Tom's Cabin opened at the Park Theater at the corner of Thirty-Fifth and Broadway on October 15 and ran for a week.[1298] The *World* reported that it was playing before a full house. Commenting on the sparring between Jackson and Choynski between the first and second acts the reporter stated that in "one round of less than a minute the black 'un tapped the white pugilist just sixty-nine times by actual count." It reported that Davies "as the auctioneer showed much sprightliness as a comedian."[1299]

On October 18, the play was in Lewiston, Maine. Applause was frequent and there were many encores given in response to the enthusiastic audience. Davies appeared in multiple roles: as the introducer, George Harris, leading juvenile and then the auctioneer. The house was full and the "colored contingent" was out in full force.[1300] The local press wrote that "those who went to see the character burlesqued by an ignorant, incompetent, or brutal giant, were sadly disappointed because the character was never played in a more meek and humble manner than by Peter Jackson."[1301]

During mid-November in a saloon late one night after the show had closed, someone slipped Choynski a "micky" of chloral hydrate, and Joe had $1,500 stolen from his wallet. The suspected thief was a man named George Stevenson. Choynski was found wandering the streets, and Davies was summoned and told that one of his men was on a bender. This news "rather staggered the Parson, knowing that Joe was not addicted to strong drink." Davies collected Joe from the authorities and learned what had happened. He then discovered that Stevenson had sailed for England before anything could be done to recover Joe's money.[1302]

As *Uncle Tom's Cabin* moved through the east, questions about where the Corbett-Mitchell fight would be carried off grew more serious every day. At the end of October, a new possibility emerged as a syndicate of men from Jacksonville, Florida, offered $30,000 to have the match held there.

By November 13, Davies, Choynski, and Jackson were all back in New York, where the Grand Horse Show was opening at Madison Square Garden with over one thousand entries. *Uncle Tom's Cabin* was on a second run in New York at that time. They were spotted by a reporter for the *World*, who noted that the horse show was also attended by "more bewitchingly pretty girls, by more bewildering fine gowns, by more exclusives of the very most exclusive society folks" and all superseded by "the most noticeable figure was a gigantic negro Peter Jackson with shoulders of Hercules and the face of a Roman gladiator in ebony."[1303]

Davies' company appeared in Holyoke on November 14 and New Haven on November 15.[1304] Harriet Beecher Stowe lived in a small cottage in Hartford, Connecticut. As a courtesy Davies sent her an invitation to occupy a box at the production. Some of her friends in Hartford were scandalized by what they considered the corruption of her play by including a sparring match. They attempted to organize a protest and to circulate a petition in opposition to the show, but their efforts came to nothing.[1305]

As the Corbett-Mitchell fight grew nearer, every person with even a remote connection with prizefighting was asked about Corbett or Mitchell or Sullivan, or who was likely to win the match. In early December, Jackson went beyond his usual polite declination. He was asked why Corbett and Fitzsimmons were not the same popular idols that Sullivan and Dempsey had been when they were champions. Jackson said that the American people were slower to forget a favorite than any other people, and he thought they cherished a bit of animosity toward Corbett and Fitzsimmons for defeating Sullivan and Dempsey. He noted that in England, this state of affairs did not exist and that Britons liked their sports of its own sake and not for the sake of the champion. Consequently, when a good man was beaten in England, then that man was not scorned nor the victor despised. Jackson's insight is typical of his thoughtful approach and marked him as a man of intelligence, so different from many contemporary prizefighters.[1306]

On December 4, *Uncle Tom's Cabin* began a week-long run in Philadelphia.[1307] "As Uncle Tom, Peter Jackson made a very favorable impression," the *Philadelphia Inquirer* wrote, "although with the massive figure of the pugilist before one it was difficult to separate him from his real character."[1308]

Eight days later the company was still in Philadelphia appearing at the National Theater. Mitchell was also appearing in Philly, putting on sparring matches with Woods. Mitchell came to the National and bought a private box at the play's matinee. He told the press he thought the sparring between Jackson and Choynski was very clever. After the show Mitchell stayed behind and visited with Jackson and his old friend Davies.[1309]

The next morning Jackson was asked about the conversation with Mitchell. "I saw more of Mitchell today than I have ever seen before," Peter said. "I have never seen him box except in Chicago and that was some time ago. I can hardly form an opinion of his ability from that. He looks well now and should be in good condition for the fight. Corbett will have age, height, length of reach and quickness, and I rather fancy his end of it."[1310]

On December 13, Davies, Jackson and Choynski all went to Philadelphia's Walnut Street Theater to watch the Mitchell-Woods performance and then back to Worcester, Massachusetts, where they appeared on December 14 and 15.

The *Worcester Daily Spy* wrote that "Mr. Jackson appeared remarkably well in his impersonation of Uncle Tom in the play. He was always at his ease, spoke his lines well, and in short, showed himself thoroughly well fitted for the part."[1311]

On December 23, Davies, Jackson, and Choynski were in New York, and it was predicted that all three of them would be in Jacksonville for the Corbett-Mitchell match. In addition, Joe had finally been matched with O'Donnell for a fight to a finish at catch weights, Queensberry rules, within five to eight weeks for the best purse. Davies represented the interests of Choynski and Hall represented O'Donnell.[1312] Hall wired the Duval Athletic Club in Jacksonville suggesting that their contest should be presented the night before the Corbett-Mitchell fight.

Both Davies and Jackson were optimistic about his promised mid-year championship match. Davies felt that if the Corbett-Mitchell fight was carried off successfully, then a club would come to the front with a good offer. Davies promised to post the final $2,500 deposit for the Corbett match. Jackson's immediate plans were not certain. Davies said that in the event Corbett lost to Mitchell, then Jackson would still be willing to meet Corbett, but he wasn't sure that Jim would want to meet Jackson. Davies noted that the public hadn't considered the possibility that Mitchell might win. He concluded that "it will be time enough, though, to talk of that after the contest."[1313]

As 1893 ended, prospects for the year 1894 were excellent. *Uncle Tom's Cabin* had been a great financial success in its East Coast tour. All three men seemed to enjoy their acting work, and prospects for productions in the future were good. Most importantly, a world championship Jackson-Corbett fight seemed highly probable, and Choynski had been matched with O'Donnell. It appeared that Davies, Jackson, and Choynski were all at the top of their professional lives.

Chapter 14 - (1894)

Disappointment

The American people, and particularly the Southern section, would never accept gracefully a black champion. If Peter Jackson ever becomes champion of the world the American people will likely turn from pugilism in disgust.[1314]

—

Peter Jackson has surprised all by his intelligent and sympathetic interpretations of Harriet Beecher Stowe's famous character, and the unanimity of the critics in according him unlimited praise is exceptionally marked. Parson Davies, the no less celebrated manager and promoter of athletic events, is also credited with a most emphatic hit in the part of the auctioneer, in which he succeeds in arousing no end of uproarious merriment.[1315]

—

♦

Drawing from the St. Louis Post Dispatch September 19, 1894

Before the Corbett-Mitchell match, Davies, Jackson, and Choynski continued to travel together. On the evening of January 14, they passed through

Pittsburgh on their way to Baltimore, where they were scheduled to appear at Baltimore's Academy of Music in *Uncle Tom's Cabin*.[1316] Peter had given up his effort to be neutral about the predicted outcome of the Corbett-Mitchell fight, and both Jackson and Davies said that they thought Corbett would be the dead-cinch winner.[1317]

Peter was also angry about statements Corbett had made that the only reasons he had not whipped Jackson in California were that the official of the C.A.C. and the referee of the match were all against him and defrauded him of his victory. These statements were palpable lies, and Jackson correctly said that they were lies. He pointed out that Corbett was born, bred, and raised in San Francisco and suggested that there was no logical explanation of why officials of a San Francisco club would turn against the hometown boy to favor a black fighter from Australia. Peter was also riled about advertisements for the Corbett-Mitchell fight that billed Mitchell as the heavyweight champion of England. Jackson correctly pointed out he was the champion of England, having earned that title by defeating both Jem Smith and Slavin. Mitchell had no claim to that title.

Davies was in Baltimore on the evening of January 21 and the morning of January 22. Beginning on the evening of January 21, Davies and members of two other theater companies that were working in Baltimore at the time began a long celebration. The group included Misses Cecil Eeissing, Bessie Cleveland, and Katie Reid as well as Davies, Tim Fraley, and Will Carelton.

At about midnight they all left Harris' Academy of Music in downtown Baltimore and headed by stage to the Halstead Road House near Pimlico for an evening of eating and drinking. They left the roadhouse about three a.m. to return to the city, and Davies sat on the top of the stage with the driver. About six a.m. the stage was at the corner of Centre and Cathedral streets in Baltimore when it took the corner too quickly and overturned. Davies and the other passengers were thrown from the stage and Davies had his hand badly sprained and mashed, and a large chunk of flesh was torn out of one of his knees.[1318]

Despite his injuries, on January 24 Davies arrived at Jacksonville, Florida, but he was not accompanied by either Jackson or Choynski.[1319] Davies again said he expected Corbett to win his match, and reaffirmed that without regard to the outcome, Peter would fight Corbett.

In Jacksonville on the evening of January 26 Davies sent a telegram to his brother, Vere Davies, in Chicago, to post an additional $1,000 for Jackson in the hands of the stakeholder, Will J. Davis. Davis was the dean of all the theater operators in Chicago and for many years managed the Columbia Theater.

Davies told the press, "They say I'm too foxy to let Jackson go up against Corbett, do they? Well, they can say what they please, but this second deposit going up just on the heels of Corbett's victory looks like I meant business, don't it? I've got a wonder and people will see it when Corbett and Jackson meet."[1320]

Two days after the Mitchell fight, Davis, the stakeholder for the Corbett and Jackson fight, received $1,000 deposits from both Brady and Davies [1321]

Corbett had defeated an old, bloated, dissipated fighter when he won the heavyweight championship of the world. Fitzsimmons said on the night that Corbett defeated Sullivan, "any well man ought to have whipped Sullivan as Corbett did."[1322] To add to his reputation, in January 1894 Corbett defeated Mitchell, a man who was six years older, four inches shorter, and weighed only 156 pounds at the time of their fight. Corbett did not just defeat Charley but knocked him out to the extent that Mitchell had to be carried to his corner and administered ammonium salts before he finally began to recover consciousness.

The referee gave Mitchell a slow ten count, but Charley lay motionless in the ring. Pony Moore, Hall, and O'Donnell carried Charley's limp body to the corner, and it was only then that Mitchell began to revive.[1323] Very soon after defeating Mitchell, Corbett and Brady renewed their nearly repulsive efforts to avoid ever fighting Jackson.

With the fight in Jacksonville ended, spectators scattered. On the evening of January 27, Davies was in Louisville and sent a telegram to St. Louis. The telegram was intended to intercept "Denver Ed" Smith, who was also returning from Jacksonville but headed for Colorado. Davies' wrote that he was considering matching Jackson with Smith sometime before the Corbett match in order to properly prepare Peter for his match with Corbett.[1324] Tom Allen, who had been providing financial backing for Smith, declared that if the Parson was in earnest, he would have the money for a match within one week.

From Louisville Davies went to Indianapolis and met with Governor Matthews to discuss the prospect of obtaining a license for a Jackson-Corbett prize fight at Roby. It is not clear whether Davies was talking to the governor on behalf of O'Malley, Alf Kennedy, who was managing the Roby for the new ownership, or simply speaking on behalf of Jackson and his hope to meet Corbett at Roby.[1325] The governor bluntly told Davies that there would be no prizefighting at Roby. In addition to losing the chance for a championship match at Roby, the proposed Choynski-O'Donnell fight had been called off because no club had offered a purse.[1326]

Despite the negative news reports not everything was bleak. A telegram arrived from the Washington Athletic Club of Tacoma offering a $40,000 purse for the Jackson-Corbett match.[1327] Soon after, the chamber of commerce in West Superior, Wisconsin, offered $50,000 to have the fight staged there.[1328] It was well known that the governor of Wisconsin would not permit prizefighting in that state, but there was an area of ground near Superior known as Wisconsin Point that was reserved to the federal government for a military station. Wisconsin did not have jurisdiction over Wisconsin Point, and the West Superior chamber was proposing to hold the fight on federal ground. Davies also said that in the coming week he would meet with Brady to discuss arrangements for the contest.

On February 3, Davies was traveling alone when he passed through Chicago on his way to Milwaukee. The entire company was not far behind because there were afternoon and evening engagements in Milwaukee on February 4. After appearing in Milwaukee, the company was scheduled to appear successively in Elgin, Joliet, and Niles in Illinois, and Jackson, Michigan, on February 9, followed by an appearance in Battle Creek.

The *Omaha Daily Bee* wrote that Jackson on stage had been a greater drawing card and had earned more money than Corbett had in his theatrical ventures. However, after defeating Mitchell it was expected that Corbett's money-making potential on stage would be much greater, and this fact was part of the problem in persuading Corbett to reenter the ring to fight Jackson.[1329] Why should Corbett rush into a match when he could collect money for appearing on stage? The only thing that could really damage his money-making potential was a loss to Jackson. This could mean that he would be known as the man who lost the title to a black man.

Questions persisted concerning Jackson's health. There were so many during the first six months of 1894 that it seems likely that Jackson was not well. When asked about Jackson's health, Davies told the *Chicago Tribune* that Peter was not in poor health and he "had one good fight left in him if not more."[1330] This is not exactly a ringing endorsement. When Jackson passed through Chicago on the morning of February 4, he was asked about his health and replied he had entirely recovered his health and would be ready to meet Corbett in June.[1331] This certainly suggests that Jackson had previously been ill but thought he had recovered.

As the prospect of a Jackson-Corbett match seemed to be moving toward fruition, opposition to their match along racial grounds emerged. On February 12, the *Chicago Tribune* wrote an article referring to the "woolly head of Peter Jackson" and expressing its opinion that the American people, and particularly the South, would never accept gracefully a black champion. "If Peter Jackson ever becomes champion of the world, the American people will likely turn from pugilism in disgust. There is no real reason why they should, but they probably will."[1332]

As if designed to illustrate that the *Tribune's* prediction was true, on February 20 the League of American Wheelmen held its general assembly in Louisville and by secret ballot without any debate voted to amend its constitution to prohibit black men from joining the association or participating in its cycling events.[1333] Within the same week the Knights of Labor, which had prohibited black men from joining their organization for several years, adopted a scheme that proposed sending black Americans to Liberia and to pay them twenty-five dollars apiece to leave.[1334] There is no doubt that Jackson had good reason for not wanting to fight anywhere in the South.

On February 13, the *Uncle Tom's Cabin* company was in Kalamazoo. The *Kalamazoo Gazette* wrote that of the three heavyweights on stage—Sullivan and Corbett being the others—Jackson came the nearest to being an actor.

Davies was interviewed concerning the Corbett-Jackson match. He said he was going to travel from Kalamazoo to Mt. Clemens, where he understood that a large purse had been offered for the fight. Davies noted that a number of proposals were being received, but "it is one thing to offer a purse for the fight and another to post a $10,000 guarantee that the club making the bid is able to pull the fight off." Charlie said he had also written to Lord Lonsdale in England about the possibility of a fight there and expected to hear from him soon.[1335] Davies was working hard to assure a contest would occur, but there was little or no effort being made by either Corbett or Brady.

The press sought out Fitzpatrick, Jackson's former trainer who was visiting Chicago in February, to ask his opinions about whether Jackson had "a good fight left in him." Once again, there seemed to be an opinion that Jackson was no longer capable of fighting at the top of his class. Fitzpatrick told the *Chicago Tribune* that Peter was a "willing worker" and Sam thought that Peter would be ready and fit when the time for a fight arrived. Fitzpatrick remarked that Peter had the practice of not breaking retreat from any fighter. "Even with a great hitter like Frank Slavin he stood and punched while the fight lasted. He got quite a grueling in that fight, and I guess it did not do him any good."

Corbett shows the white feather

About March 1, Corbett began to show the white feather. To put it more bluntly he appeared to be a coward. Writing about Jim's career, Brady describes what may have been happening in 1894. He wrote that Corbett got "ring fear":

> Naturally, every man hates to risk the crown he has won. It is a one-sided affair at best. He has everything to lose and nothing to gain. Corbett was earning anywhere from $25,000 to $100,000 a year, he was living on the fat of the land, it all looked mighty good to him, and he hated to take a chance of losing it. We were all in clover, for that matter; everything was going swimmingly. But victory has its worries no less than defeat. Every triumph brings its apprehensions.[1337]

Corbett issued a statement claiming that he was in the dark concerning the contest and announcing that he was going to go to England in April to see whether a match could be made there. It was a lie that Corbett was in the dark concerning the contest; he could learn everything he needed to know about a possible fight in England without leaving the United States. Corbett also wrote "I think the event will be postponed."[1338] From Baltimore on March 5 he declared he favored England as a location for the fight.[1339] Jackson said that basically he only wanted a chance to fight for the championship.[1340]

In early March, Jackson and the *Uncle Tom's Cabin* production was in Washington, D.C., where the *Washington Post* noted that "some very complimentary things have been said of Jackson's impersonation of the old slave," and added that a "contingent of colored singers and dancers add to the realism as well as the amusement of the plantation scenes, and the company carries a car load of special scenery for this production."

From Washington, Jackson went to New York on March 9 to meet with Davies and hear about his meeting with Brady and Corbett. Probably because of the recurring questions about Jackson's health, Davies arranged for a thorough physical examination of him by Dr. John W. Gibbs. The *Brooklyn Eagle* commented that reports had circulated that Jackson "was afflicted with a weakening disease and he was subject to hemorrhages."[1341] These reports may have indicated some early sign of the tuberculosis that would eventually take Jackson's life when he was still a young man.

Gibbs reported that except for a slight cough Jackson was in good health. He could inflate his chest to a size that was two and a half inches greater than Corbett. Gibbs noted that Jackson could dive and swim seventy yards underwater in fifty-eight seconds. Although most Americans did not know it, Jackson had been swimming his entire life and was a champion in the water too.[1342]

On March 9 Corbett was in Baltimore, where he learned of the reports about Jackson's health and said that if Peter would add another $10,000 to the stakes it would convince him of his good health.[1343]

Davies was in Baltimore on the evening of March 11 and was asked about Corbett's statement that he expected the contest with Jackson to be postponed and also about Corbett's suggestion that the fight should take place in London. In a meeting with Brady, Davies agreed that the fight could undoubtedly be arranged in England within the next sixty days.[1344] In response to Davies, Corbett would only say that he believed the fight would be postponed until August or September and that it would probably be staged at the National Club in London[1345] This was the beginning of the end of any prospect of a championship fight.

Four days later, on March 15, Davies was in Richmond, Indiana, appearing with *Uncle Tom's Cabin*. He said he had no reason to believe that a fight would take place within the time specified in the articles. He had heard nothing from Brady and thought that the Corbett side of the contest did not seem anxious to arrange anything.[1346] The company left Richmond and went to Decatur, Illinois, but Davies himself skipped Decatur and went ahead to St. Louis, where the play was to be presented after its Decatur stop.[1347]

In St. Louis, a representative of the *Post Dispatch* visited with Davies, who pointed out that it was Corbett himself who had made the original challenge publicly at Roby and that Corbett had specified that the fight was to take place between June 20 and June 30. Davies stated the obvious. With Corbett leaving for England, it seemed impossible that the champion would live up to the terms of the articles he had signed. Nevertheless, Davies said he would continue to post the stake money with W. A. Davis in Chicago, as specified in the articles.

Unlike many others involved in prizefighting, Davies had a keen sense of practical issues involved with proposed fights. He took time to explain some of the problems caused by Corbett's behavior. Davies noted that he was employing a company of twenty-five people to put on *Uncle Tom's Cabin* and that they had been making money right along. He intended to break up the company at

St. Louis so that Jackson could go into training for the championship fight, but that now seemed premature. Why stop the tour if Corbett was not going to fight? Charlie noted that the company had received many good offers to perform in other towns but had turned them down in reliance of Corbett's promise to fight in June.

Davies candidly said he was not sure what to do under the circumstances. He pointed out that if Jackson accepted additional acting work as the featured player in the production, then Corbett might try to spring a trap and demand a fight on short notice. Davies concluded: "I must say I was dumfounded when he told me in the presence of Brady and Al Smith that it did not suit him to keep his engagement."[1348]

While Davies was in St. Louis awaiting the Sunday, March 18, opening, both Jackson and Choynski were performing in Decatur. Interviewed there, Jackson provided insight into the world of the traveling theater company. After the play ended that evening, he answered a few questions for the *Decatur Daily Review*'s reporter, who had followed him to the St. Nicholas hotel. "This thing of jumping from one town to another is not the snap some people might think it is," Jackson told the reporter. "Now I have to hustle around and get ready to leave for St. Louis tonight."[1349]

Davies seemed to thrive on jumping from place to place and making his home under his hat. He had decided that he was not going to wait for Corbett to commit himself and continued to look for a venue for the championship contest. Davies sent an agent—probably Glickauf—to Cripple Creek, Colorado, to scout the possibility of a fight there. When the governor of Colorado got wind of this possibility, he announced he would not permit the fight in his state.[1350]

While Davies, Jackson, and Choynski were in St. Louis, Brady left for England aboard the German Lloyd steamship *Spree* and was treated in royal fashion in London. Moreover, the National Club announced that it would offer a substantial purse for the Jackson-Corbett fight. Almost as soon as Brady arrived in England, the National Club agreed to host the match. Writing in his capacity as a "special correspondent" for the *World*, Brady expressed his delight with that proposal.[1351]

In an astonishing turn of events, Corbett issued an official statement from Cincinnati attacking both Davies and Jackson and concluding he would not be forced to fight outside of the United States. He asserted that as champion, he alone had a right to decide where the fight would be held, and he had determined that it must be held in the United States.[1352] Davies reiterated that Jackson simply wanted a fight and Corbett should say whether he would or he wouldn't fight.[1353]

"Corbett refers to me as Jackson's cheap and bluffing manger," Davies said. "I most respectfully ask Mr. Corbett, when he ever knew me to fail to back my talk with the support of my money?"

When Corbett reached England, he was treated like a king. He waited until after he left England and had traveled to France and Germany to say he would not fight in England because the National Club would only promise a twenty-round match with Jackson. Corbett insisted he would only meet Jackson in a finish fight.[1354] Corbett continued to ignore the articles he had signed with Jackson. Finally, near the end of April he unilaterally declared them "null and void." He said he would deal with Jackson when he returned to the United States and concluded, "In view of what has passed in pugilism, Peter Jackson, on account of his color, ought to feel flattered that I ever recognized him for a fighter."[1355] There walked a true hypocrite.

On April 19, Davies was in Boston working behind Tom Tracy in his fight with Joe Walcott. Although Walcott was reported the winner in sixteen rounds, in February 1938 a story circulated in the *Oshkosh Daily Northwestern* claiming that Tracy had won the fight after fifteen rounds but O'Rourke told Davies that a fan would give $1,000 for five more rounds and gave Davies $500 in cash if Tracy would only continue. The fight then resumed, and Walcott knocked Tracy cold in the sixteenth round.[1356]

The company traveled from Cleveland to Boston to present the final performance of *Uncle Tom's Cabin* on April 29. The season had been extended beyond St. Louis because Corbett refused to fight, and Peter was winding up his acting career with good reviews.

The *Boston Daily Globe* wrote: "The public refused to believe he could so easily lay aside his qualifications as a fighter and assume the dignified role of an actor. By dint of sheer perseverance and hard work he has successfully surmounted all obstacles, and on the stage today is said to be the living personification of Uncle Tom."[1357]

Jackson and Davies were at the Quincy House in Boston, where Peter was asked about Corbett's declaration that the articles were null and void. He understandably let loose: "This man Corbett is the two ends of the darndest liar the world ever saw, and the reason why I am not training is simply that I am awaiting something definite from the bluffer across the water."

Davies was asked about the articles that had been signed in Chicago in July 1893. He simply shrugged his shoulders and remarked: "Corbett is champion, and he is white. I'm afraid it's a case of 30,000 men marched up the hill and down the hill."[1358]

Davies was looking very weary when he explained he had posted $7,000 for a fight with Corbett sometime between June 20 and June 30. He continued: "When Corbett says that Brady, Corbett and myself had a quiet talk and agreed that the fight would not take place until the autumn, he deliberately lies."

Corbett had been telling the press that the articles allowed for three months' training before a fight. Davies had shown the articles to the press and pointed out that "there is not a word in the agreement to that effect."[1359]

Davies then said that Jackson should be entitled to the money posted by Corbett, but Corbett refused that and insisted that the fight should take place in New Orleans or Jacksonville, places he knew what Jackson would not go and that were both below the Mason-Dixon Line. Given all these circumstances

Davies announced that Jackson would be leaving for the Pacific coast on Wednesday, May 9.[1360] Jackson, Davies and Choynski all left New York and went to Chicago. They arrived there on May 9.[1361] The *Chicago Tribune* noted that Davies, Jackson and Choynski would stay in Chicago for about two weeks before leaving for California.[1362]

Davies and Jackson split

Davies was still trying to arrange a Choynski-Fitzsimmons fight but was not having much luck. Then only a few days after the group reached Chicago, the arrangements were made for such a fight at catch weights for a purse of $15,000.[1363] For Fitz this signaled a decision to move up in weight class and would ultimately lead to his heavyweight championship.

Jackson left Chicago for San Francisco on May 22.[1364] The possibility loomed that he might never fight again. In many respects when Davies said goodbye to Jackson, their parting could be viewed as the end of several important episodes in the history of prizefighting. It was the end of Jackson's career as contender, and as a practical matter it was the end of a long business and personal relationship between Jackson and Davies. As he reached San Francisco, Jackson heard wire stories that Davies wanted to take down the $20,000 posted for the Corbett fight. Jackson said he knew nothing about such a possibility.[1365]

Choynski and Davies left on June 2 for Boston, where Joe and Fitz were to fight on June 18.[1366] Joe trained at Lake Quinsigamond, outside of Worcester, Massachusetts. The lake had eight privately owned islands, good roads, and excellent hotel accommodations, which was something that Davies always set as a priority. Training in the country also kept a man away from the distractions of the big city. The *Brooklyn Eagle* claimed in 1895 that Davies and Choynski intended to train their in the future.[1367]

This five-round fight ended in a draw because it was stopped by the police. The newspaper coverage heavily favored Fitzsimmons. In 1927 Choynski provided his account of the match. He had watched Fitz fight several times, acted as his second, and knew the typical tricks that Fitz used in a fight. He knew that Fitz would lead short of his opponent to draw an opponent closer and they lay the wood to him when he was inside Fitz's real range. Joe wrote:

> The bell finally rang and we began feeling each other out. I saw Bob was as cautious as I. The first and second rounds were fairly even. Both of us had been shaken by punches, but no real damage had been done. Once Fitz stung me with a left jolt to the nose.
>
> "'Owd you like the smell of that 'oof?" he asked pleasantly. It was the only time I had ever heard him speak to an opponent in the ring.

> "Do you think you're shoeing horses now, Fitz?" I retorted.
>
> Then came the third round and the fireworks began. We fiddled and fiddled, trying to pull one another out. Fitz began shuffling his feet, edging his left foot steadily forward, a characteristic Fitzsimmons maneuver. Instinct told me he was setting the stage for a lightning double lead, a left for the boxer's head followed by a darting good right crusher to the jaw.
>
> Quick as a flash I decide to follow it up with an offensive. I started with a swishing right high, stopped it suddenly as Bob worked the Jem Mace shift, then hooked a terrific left to his ear. He fell flat on his back with a thud as if thrown from the rafters.
>
> Captain Jack Dalton, the referee started to count: "One, two—back up Choynski—three, four—there will be no more counting while you are close, and so on, the old army game once again. Just before ten was reached the bell rang with the just one minute and forty-five seconds old according to my timekeeper.
>
> Several days after the fight I met Fitz on the street, and we began discussing the battle like a couple of lawyers chinning over a tilt in court.[1368]

One story said that Choynski was able to reach Fitz with his big blow because Fitz was looking around periodically trying to count the number of people in the house. He didn't trust the promoters to give a fair count and liked to check things out himself. Davies had noticed Fitz looking around and told Joe between rounds to lay into to Fitz the next time he started looking at the crowd. Years later Fitz said that the blow he received from Choynski was one of the hardest blows ever visited upon him. In 1917 Bob said:

"Choynski?" Said Fitz, one day in response to a question—"Why, he was a great fighter. The time he hit me on the chin in Boston I was knocked out. Only one thing saved me, I was lying on my back in the middle of the ring, watching everything whirl around. I thought all the gallery chairs were falling over on me, and I was trying to dodge. I didn't know I was down or that I was in a fight, until I heard Choynski's manager, Parson Davies, say: "I told you Joe would knock Bob out." All of a sudden I remembered, and got up. If Davies hadn't said that I would have been counted out sure."[1369]

The day after the fight in Boston, Davies and Joe met at the office of the Associated Press, and Joe said that Bob had promised him a rematch.[1370]

The slow beat of the battalion's drummer grew even slower as the agreed time for the Jackson-Corbett match passed. In early August, a group of business men from Sioux City, Iowa, agreed to sponsor a fight for $40,000.[1371] Most of the particulars were absent: Where would the fight take place? When was the fight to take place? What type of match was it to be? Were there any financial guarantees? As time passed some of these questions were answered in odd ways.

The Sioux City group proposed to hold the fight on an island in the Missouri River at the conjunction of the states of Nebraska, South Dakota, and Iowa, where no state had jurisdiction. This site was selected because prizefighting had been prohibited by all three states and by the local officials of Sioux City.[1372] Concerning Corbett's idea of holding a match in New Orleans, the *Times-Democrat* of New Orleans published an editorial on August 6, coming out squarely against the idea of any fight between a white and a black man in New Orleans. The newspaper wrote that "the general opinion is decidedly against a repetition of the miscegenation idea."[1373]

In early August, both Brady and Corbett had returned to the United States, and Corbett began asserting he was ready to make the final arrangements for a match with Jackson. About August 8, Jackson left San Francisco traveling to New York and a showdown with Corbett.[1374] He reached Chicago on about August 11 and met with Davies. Jackson would later admit that while in Chicago he had "a little scrap" with Davies. He said that the Parson saw little chance of any match with Corbett being made and did not see the use of going on to New York. Jackson did not agree with Davies and went on to New York alone. He was a man who could make his own decisions.[1375]

Jackson arrived in New York at one forty-five p.m. on August 13 and was met by Davies' friend Tom O'Rourke, who managed Dixon and Walcott. Jackson and O'Rourke went to the Grand Union Hotel and took a room there. On the day he arrived, Corbett and Brady were at Brady's office meeting the press, with the champion declaring he intended to force Jackson to fight or shut up.[1376] Word was brought to Jackson at his hotel room that Corbett was waiting for him at Brady's office. Jackson said he had spent five days traveling 3,000 miles for a meeting with Corbett and to tell Brady and Corbett he would meet them at eleven a.m. the next day. He reiterated he would not fight in the South and had made that clear from the beginning.[1377]

When word was carried back to Corbett and Brady, the champion made a big show. He charged out of Brady's office to hail a cab and said he was going to Jackson's hotel room to settle matters. Corbett reportedly said: "I'll nail that man yet!" Corbett with the press in tow barged into Jackson's hotel room and their conversation was recorded by the press:

> Corbett: How are you, Jackson? I want to fight you right away, and I came up to see you about it.
>
> Jackson: Oh, you're nothing but a bluffer. You've been bluffing all along.
>
> Corbett: You've always been a bluffer yourself. I don't want to call you a liar.
>
> Jackson: Well, it wouldn't be gentlemanly. I will not go South.
>
> Corbett: I will not go to England. I do not believe I will be treated fairly in England. I feel about England just as you do about the South.

> Jackson: Well, I won't go South. If I were a white man, Jim, you know it would be a different thing.
>
> Corbett: Well, I won't fight in England under any circumstances.
>
> Jackson: You won't listen to common sense.
>
> Corbett: The deuce I won't! Well, I'll fight you anywhere to a finish fight, although you might last the twenty rounds which you have all along urged as the limit.
>
> Jackson: No. I won't fight except in England, and a twenty-round go at that. You could have had a fight with me in the North long ago if your battle with Mitchell at Jacksonville had not killed pugilism in this country.[1378]

Jackson then offered to give Corbett an American referee if Corbett would fight in England. Corbett consulted Brady and refused to accept the proposal.

The possibility of a match was declared off. The *Post Dispatch* commented that it must have cost the swell-headed Corbett a spasm to have to admit he could not whip Jackson within twenty rounds. Jackson had the best end of the argument with Corbett and had captured the New York sporting editors bodily.[1379]

For those of our time who may doubt the real risks associated with Jackson accepting a fight in the U.S. South in 1894, note the following incident that occurred near Memphis, Tennessee on September 1, 1894 as anecdotal evidence. There is plenty of non-anecdotal evidence too.

Six black men, all alleged to be members of a gang of arsonists, were arrested, handcuffed and placed in leg shackles. They were being transported to jail when the officers in charge were stopped and surrounded by a mob of fifty men armed with Winchesters and shotguns. One black man stood up in the wagon and raised his hands above his head to show he was shackled. The mob immediately began shooting. Volley after volley was poured into the bodies of the shackled men. Then the mob took the bodies out of the wagon, threw them into the road, and continued to fire volley after volley into their dead bodies. Some of the mob hid their faces but others were recognized by the police. After a coroner's inquest the verdict was that "the deceased came to their death at the hand of unknown parties."[1380]

About ten days later Jackson told the *Post Dispatch*:

> "This business of a fight between Corbett and me has been going on for three years now, ever since we had that draw out in San Francisco. I've been trying to get a fight ever since, and I've done everything in my power. And now the truth is out. Corbett don't want to fight. Why? Well I'm no mind reader. Of course I think I know. But what is the use of saying what you think when you don't know? I don't want to lose the advantage I now have with the public by giving out opinions when I don't have facts. . . . He is the champion of America and I am the champion of

> England and Australia. The battle between us would have been the first battle to decide who is champion of the world. Nobody can claim that title now and it seems to me the sporting public demands that the two men who could decide it should come together."[1381]

Jackson did not return to Chicago until the last day of August. He was finally satisfied that Corbett did not want to meet him in the ring. He noted that his forfeit money was still being held by W. A. Davis in Chicago and said he would not draw it down until he was satisfied that all possibility of a match had evaporated. Jackson said he would stay in Chicago for nine days, and he was willing to meet with the Sioux City contingent that was supposed to also be in Chicago. Jackson said he had heard the O'Rourke was to be his manager in the future, but no such arrangement had been made.[1382]

The Sioux City group went to New York without seeing Jackson and secured Corbett's signature on their ambiguous contract.[1383] They returned to Chicago to try to get Jackson's signature. Davies was several hundred miles away, in West Baden, where a new casino with hot mineral baths had opened, and he was not present when the Sioux City boys showed up with their Corbett-signed document. Davies was meeting at West Baden with Hall and was arranging a Hall-Choynski eight-round match for gate receipts to be staged at Tattersall's in Chicago on October 1.

Vere Davies, Charlie's brother, took the news to Jackson that the men of Sioux City were back in town and looking for him. Vere told the press that "Jackson was around here for two or three hours this afternoon, waiting for these people but they did not show up." Davies returned to Chicago from West Baden and met with the Sioux City folks on September 11 at the Briggs House, where Peter had been staying.[1384]

The Iowa group produced the papers that Corbett had signed and wanted Jackson to sign the contract at once.[1385] Davies asked whether the fight would come off within the next three months. No date had been set for a fight in the contract signed by Corbett. Davies pointed out that this was a serious flaw and under the circumstances merely allowed Corbett to gain free advertisement during the theater season without committing himself to anything. Davies continued to pick flaws with the contract. He pointed out that the contract did not say whether the contestants would fight ten rounds or to a finish, and this too was a fatal matter. Jackson joined in and asked whether the fight would be in a clubhouse and explained he did not want to fight in an open field or under a tent.[1386] Jackson was insulted that the Sioux City contingent had tried to force him into a corner by going to Corbett and having him sign articles that neither Jackson nor Davies had approved.[1387]

The Sioux City group had no response except to claim that they were insulted by Davies' questions. The whole idea fell through, and Jackson announced he would be leaving Chicago and traveling to New York, the West Indies, and then to England. He had experienced enough. The next day the $10,000 posted with W. A. Davies was taken down.[1388]

The impossible fight was off. When he passed through New York on his way out of the United States, Jackson was asked about the remaining prospects for a Corbett fight.

> "I cannot see that there is any," he responded. "Corbett may have it all his own way now, for I'm off to the West Indies on Saturday. I am glad it broke up Brady's scheme. That will always be a source of satisfaction to me. I leave the whole field to the great champion. He can talk. I will not reply. . . . I shall think some when I am away of that island in the Missouri River where the fight was to have been held. They say the tides are wonderfully strong out there. What if we had been squaring off at high tide? 'Both Drowned,' would have been a newspaper headline. I shall never again answer anything Corbett may say. He has the field to himself." [1389]

Corbett issued a statement bitterly denouncing Jackson as a cur whom he said was seeking notoriety at his expense. Davies responded bluntly. He said that Corbett was a dirty dog for referring to Jackson in such terms. Davies said that in his mind, Corbett had removed all doubt that he had a streak of yellow in his makeup.[1390]

In October, Corbett said he had driven Jackson out of the country and that he had engaged in a humiliating back-down.[1391] Two months later he wistfully told the *Chicago Tribune* he was occasionally asked about Jackson. "Really, Peter is but a memory of the past now, and I seldom think of him," Corbett said.

He pointed out that Jackson had gone to England and might fight Slavin there. He felt that Jackson would defeat Slavin but that would likely be Peter's last fight. He thought, "Peter is towards the farther end of his life, and there are but few fights left in him."[1392] A month later Corbett again talked of Jackson in the past tense: "In Jackson's day he was a better man than Fitzsimmons ever was or will ever be, but I think that Jackson has now played out and is no longer any good."[1393]

Life goes on without Peter Jackson

Although Corbett's relegation of Jackson to a mere memory was harsh, it carried an element of truth, and Davies could not stop thinking about what might have been. Nevertheless, prizefighting was beginning to be reborn in the Chicago area and the business did not abide too much regret.

On September 15, a fighter named Casper Leon from New York met and was defeated by another young fighter of Chicago named Jimmy Barry in a twenty-round fight held at Lemont, Illinois. Many of the old-time Chicago sports were present for this match, including McDonald, Myer, and Hogan.[1394] McDonald had become the king of Lemont. He owned the stone quarry there and had turned the town into sin city. Davies rode on the engine of the train for the short ride from Chicago to Lemont perhaps enjoying a late summer night or just grabbing a little solitude where it was possible.

After the fight night in Lemont, on September 17 Davies sponsored a boxing tournament at Tattersall's in Chicago. Before Chicago authorities closed down boxing there had been five places that hosted most of the boxing in Chicago: Tattersall's, Tommy White's Triangle Club, McGurn's Court, the Pelican Club, and the Chicago Athletic Association. Davies favored Tattersall's and had his own ring there with all the modern requirements for safety, such as well-padded posts and floor and excellent lighting. About two thousand spectators paid to watch the matches at Tattersall's. Choynski was matched to stop the tough Boden in three rounds. Joe and other top fighters had met Boden before, but no one had ever stopped their durable opponent within the allowed time.

Choynski appeared, looking slim and bony compared to his bulky opponent. Boden's hands were hardly up when Choynski commenced pounding him. He drove a right to Boden's nose and put him down for a nine count. With his fists working like trip-hammers, Joe delivered a series of heavy uppercuts to the crouching Boden, who was bleeding and staggering when time was called to end the first round. In the second round Boden "rolled around the ring" while receiving a cannonade of blows. Choynski landed thirty-two blows in two minutes without a return from Boden, who then fell against the ropes, where he hung helpless and was counted out. The press reported that Boden had been hammered "into an astonished jelly."[1395]

A few days after this fight, Joe nearly ended his career. He was in Jackson, Michigan, preparing to spar ten rounds with Joe Tansey when he shot himself in the hand with a forty-four caliber pistol. Davies was with Joe at the time and had just finished preparing articles of agreement for a fight between Choynski and Hall at Tattersall's on October 8.

Joe was rummaging around in a drawer when Davies heard a loud noise, and Joe yelled: "I am shot!" He had discharged the gun accidentally while looking for something in the drawer. His injury prevented Choynski from fighting for several months.[1396] He was not able to return to training until the first week of November.[1397] Davies kept him busy by having him work as a referee, sparring with Ryan, and training Woods for a planned match with Hall.[1398]

Colonel Hopkins, Dan Creedon, and Tom Tracy

Other than the failure of Corbett-Jackson match, the most significant news in the fighting business concerned Fitzsimmons and the Australian middleweight champion Dan Creedon, whom Fitz had agreed to fight before the Olympic Club of New Orleans in late September. Creedon and another Australian fighter, Tom Tracy (sometimes "Tracey"), had come to the United States and were being managed by Colonel John D. Hopkins. Tracy was sometimes referred to as Creedon's foster-brother. Hopkins had relocated from Chicago to St. Louis, where he operated a theater in addition to managing fighters. It is likely he left Chicago because fighting had been killed there during the Exposition.

Creedon left for New Orleans for his fight with Fitz via the Cairo Short Line and Illinois Central R.R. The Cairo Short Line put a special train at his disposal. The party on the trip included Hopkins, Tracy, Davies, representatives from St. Louis newspapers, and a delegation that Davies brought from Chicago including Condon, Kennedy, the gambler Harry Varnall, and Houseman. Tom Allen and Charley Daly were part of a delegation from St. Louis.[1399] At ringside on the day of the match Davies was present and described as "a staunch friend of Creedon" who was anxious to see him win.

The promise was short-lived. Fitz knocked out Creedon in the second round. In many of Fitz's matches the first round was slow, as he seemed to be measuring his opponent. The same was true in his fight with Creedon. Between the first and second round Fitz told his corner men, including Dempsey, that he would finish Creedon in the second round, which he did.[1400]

As soon as the match ended, Fitz challenged Corbett to fight in New Orleans. This challenge became realistic only because Jackson was out of the picture. If Jackson had not dropped out then Corbett would have claimed that he would fight Fitz if he had first defeated Jackson. It is likely that Fitz wanted no part of the bigger Jackson but had concluded that if he could handle Choynski he could handle Corbett.

Fitz said he had backing of up to $50,000. He sent a letter to Corbett, "I am well aware of the fact that although I have earned more money than you at fighting since I have become middleweight champion, you can buy and sell me financially no doubt, your faculty of saving being better than mine."[1401]

Corbett's initial response was classically evasive. He would not accept a match with Fitz unless he first proved himself a champion heavyweight and not a middleweight. He suggested that Fitzsimmons should start with Steve O'Donnell.[1402]

After Creedon was knocked out by Fitz, Hopkins issued a challenge to any other middleweight to fight Creedon for $2,500 a side.[1403] Soon negotiations began between Davies, acting on behalf of Hall, and Hopkins for Creedon.[1404] Hall had lived the high life in England after his defeat of Pritchard. He hung around lived on his reputation and making wealthy friends. When he returned to the American he had a big-money match with Fitz but had turned his back on Davies.

It is perfectly clear that after being knocked out by Fitz, Hall's career tumbled. Although he had beaten Slavin in England virtually everyone thought it was a fixed fight. Davies took Hall back under his management probably under the theory that even a bad penny had value. He wanted to match Hall and Creedon, and also arranged an evening of entertainment featuring Hall in separate matches against Baker and Woods on the same evening.[1405] Davies' renewed representation of Hall did not last long, and Hall soon went under the management of L. T. Curtis.[1406]

Davies returned to Chicago by way of St. Louis. The *Post Dispatch* noted that although he had gone to New Orleans with the St. Louis party, he was far too diplomatic to be numbered among them during the fight because he was on best of terms with Fitz.

The *Post Dispatch* said that while he was in New Orleans, Davies was continually interviewed by the local press. He was asked about Jackson's reluctance to meet Corbett in New Orleans. He told the *Post Dispatch*:

> Everything would go along nicely down there as long as Corbett was winning, but we know too well what result would follow should it be the opposite. White men can get an even break in New Orleans, but in my opinion the Negro that fights there is very foolish. The Dixon-Skelly battle nearly brought about a crisis, and the next black that gets the best of a fight down there is sure to receive the worst of it from the crowd. To illustrate the feeling against black fighters in New Orleans, I will mention a little incident that happened in the Olympic Club, on the night of the Corbett-Sullivan fight. George Dixon had defeated Skelly the evening previous and he was on hand with some friends to witness the big contest of the carnival. None of the local residents would countenance his presence near themselves, however, and the little featherweight was changed around five or six times, before he finally secured a seat from which he could view the fight without being requested to move on.[1407]

Davies begins to manage new fighters

Soon after his return to Chicago, Davies began picking up new fighters. He had virtually limited his representation to Choynski and Jackson for almost three years. Jackson had left America, and Joe was out of commission with an injured hand.

On October 5, Davies sent $1,000 to New Orleans to bind a match between Tommy Ryan and Dempsey at 154 pounds.[1408] A few days later Ryan came back to Chicago from Syracuse to prepare for the fight.[1409] This appears to be the first time that Davies acted for Ryan; although he had employed him as a sparring partner for other fighters. Davies worked directly with O'Malley on the Ryan-Dempsey match. In years to come Davies would have several important business relationships with O'Malley and be killed by one of O'Malley's political enemies.

In early October, he completed his arrangements for a night of athletic entertainment at Tattersall's that would feature Hall, Woods, and Baker. Hall trained for this match in Mt. Clemens, where he had become the victim of Davies' lemon knife. Davies began representing a good bantamweight fighter from California named Joe Bertrand.[1410]

In early November, Davies went to Mt. Clemens to check on Hall's conditioning. When he returned to Chicago on November 10, Davies reported that Hall was in condition and did not underestimate either of his opponents. Jim weighed 166 pounds, but could easily gain more weight, which would make him stronger for the dual task awaiting him.

Tommy Ryan was training with Hall in Michigan and was boxing with him daily. Ryan was preparing for a fight in New Orleans on December 12 with Dempsey.[1411] Davies was addressing his disappointment at Jackson's departure by taking on new fighters. Jackson had left Davies twice, and life could not stop because Peter was now living in England. However, there is no question that the one fighter Davies admired throughout his life was Peter Jackson.

Hall met Baker and Woods as scheduled, but he failed to stop either of them within the allowed four rounds. He smothered Baker from the call of time and jabbed him at his pleasure. Baker was fairly slaughtered. Hall punched him into a helpless lump, thought he had won, and walked away rather than delivering the final blow. The *Chicago Tribune* announced that "Hall's humanity cost him the decision."

Tired from his hard work with Baker, Hall was less effective against Woods, who slowed things down by incessant clinching. In the first round it looked as though Hall would settle Woods before the bell, but Woods clinched from the start so that the match began to look like wrestling. Finally, Woods came out of his shell in the fourth round, and Hall was so tired then that the two men fought on a nearly even basis in that round.[1412] Immediately after the entertainment, Davies learned that Mayor Hopkins and chief of police Brennan intended to stop local boxing sometime during the coming week and boxing would again be effectively killed in Chicago.[1413]

Then on February 16, Fitz killed his sparring partner Con Riordan during the first round of an exhibition at Jacob's Theater in Syracuse. The killing blow was a right-hander that caught Riordan squarely on the chin. Riordan did not fall from the force of the blow but "sank slowly until he measured his length on the stage." Fitz said that "after a little sparring I tapped him on the cheek with my left hand, and he made motions with his right and left, and then asked Capt. Glori to call time. He staggered and fell, and I thought when he fell, that was all there was of it."[1414]

Riordan had been drinking heavily before he showed up for the exhibition. He was removed from the theater, taken to his hotel about two hours later, and died early the next morning. When given the news Fitz said: "My God! You don't mean to tell me Connie is dead. I cannot believe it. I did not hit him hard enough to injure a child."[1415]

Cornelius "Con" Riordan joined Killen, Glover, and Ashton as fighters whom Davies had managed and who met an early death. A coroner's jury determined the cause of his death to be a hemorrhage of the brain caused by an accidental blow struck by Robert Fitzsimmons while he and Riordan were engaged in a legal sparring exhibition on the stage of the H. R. Jacobs Opera-House. The jury exonerated Fitz of any criminal intent.

Riordan had been fighting professionally eleven years. He had traveled to England with Jackson and Davies in 1892 and while there, he fought Slavin's brother Jack.[1416] He was a Roman Catholic, but charity is not a hallmark of the American clergy. Influential members of the clergy in Syracuse refused to conduct his funeral and denied his body a resting place on consecrated ground, asserting he was not in "good standing" with the Catholic Church.[1417]

Davies commented that Riordan was a clever boxer but a heavy drinker. He said that when Riordan had traveled with Jackson, he would often show up for the entertainment just in time to go on stage and be full of liquor when he arrived. Davies thought that Riordan's death was an accident, but he also reminded the press that stepping into the ring was always dangerous. He noted that this accident was a hard blow to boxing, and it would be months before the public would forget the affair.[1418]

Asked about Riordan's death, Hall said that there should be medical supervision of boxing—an idea well ahead of its time. Choynski said he had heard that Riordan was suffering from "fatty degeneration of the heart." He also said that Fitz "hits too hard in play, and without intending to hurt people. He is too awkward and too powerful to gauge a blow and reduce its force, but he is not naturally brutal."[1419]

Despite the favorable corner's jury verdict,[1420] Fitz was arraigned in the police court on a charge of manslaughter and an inquest scheduled. Bail was set at $10,000. Although the corner found no fault on Fitz's part, the Law and Order League of Syracuse and the district attorney pressed for a grand jury indictment.[1421]

Ryan ends Dempsey's career

After talking to the press about Riordan's death, Davies went to Detroit to personally supervise Ryan's training for the upcoming Dempsey fight. To train with Ryan, Davies hired Kid McCoy, a young fighter with great reach and a lot of speed and potential. He was also a quick learner and eager to get experience with a world-class fighter like Ryan, who did not spare McCoy during their daily workouts.

While Ryan was put up in the best hotel, McCoy was assigned to a cheap boarding house. He was also forced to do all the dirty work, and in the presence of visitors every afternoon Ryan gave McCoy some awful beatings. McCoy submitted to all this abuse without a complaint because he was anxious to learn the trade. He picked up all of Ryan's cleverness, and Davies would have many future encounters with McCoy after first using him as Ryan's punching bag.[1422]

The Ryan-Dempsey match was supposed to be one of several fights presented in New Orleans as part of a carnival of entertainment, including Barry-Jimmy Connors and Kid Lavigne-Andy Bowen. Lavigne was being trained by Fitzpatrick, and his fight with Bowen was to take place at the Auditorium Club of New Orleans on December 14.[1423]

When Davies was in Detroit making sure that Ryan was ready for the fight with Dempsey, he also met Sullivan by chance, and the two men buried the hatchet. The reconciliation would lead to a financially beneficial relationship that would save Sullivan from imminent destitution.

The *Chicago Tribune* reported that Sullivan and Davies had buried the enmity that had existed between them for eight years. Sullivan and his theatrical company happened to be in Detroit on the same day that Davies was there. Sullivan was "standing in a hotel corridor talking with friends when the Parson, accompanied by Hall, Joe Choynski, Tommy Ryan, Steve Brodie and a number of other sporting men, came upon him. The Parson hesitated a moment and then thrust out his hand. Sullivan grasped it warmly." After shaking hands, Sullivan and Davies adjourned to Sullivan's room, where they continued their friendly conversation.[1424]

On December 8, Davies, Ryan, and Choynski all arrived in New Orleans, where Ryan and Choynski sparred together at a local theater.[1425] Dempsey was expected to arrive the following day. As the parties were gathering, the Auditorium Club declared the Barry-Connors fight off because of Connor's illness. It also spread the word that Connors was afraid to fight. Jack Madden of New Orleans was substituted as a last minute replacement for Connors.[1426]

The second shoe dropped on the evening of December 14, when Kid Lavigne killed Andy Bowen in the ring of the Auditorium Club. Bowen was carried from the ring limp and senseless and taken to the Charity Hospital, where he died several hours later. At about seven a.m. Bowen's wife leaned over and said: "Oh, Andy, say something to me." Bowen shivered, groaned, his body shook, and he died.

The knockout blow was a right hand. Bowen had ducked a punch, and Lavigne caught him on his chin with his elbow. As Bowen straightened up, Lavigne caught him on the jaw and Bowen fell back, striking his head on the floor. Head injuries from striking a hard floor were common at the time. Lavigne and his entire party were arrested. Bowen was only thirty years old at the time of his death. The other matches scheduled in New Orleans were canceled immediately.[1427]

The third crisis happened three days later, but had begun on the evening of November 11, when Tommy White defeated Dannie Daly of Omaha at the city's Triangle Club.[1428] Several years earlier, Daly and White had fought a ninety-one-round draw in South Omaha. This time they had fought a six-round match that was described as clean, pretty, and scientific, with White doing all the leading and getting the decision on points. On December 17, news broke that Daly was dying from injuries suffered in that fight. White had broken Daly's jaw early during their match. Daly did not know his jaw was broken and fought on for six rounds. After the fight the extent of his injury was discovered, and he was taken to a physician. His jaw was set and he was asked to go to the county hospital but refused. He stayed in Omaha but failed to take care of himself. About two weeks later his health began to decline.[1429]

Davies, Ryan, and Choynski went back to Chicago. A week after Bowen's death, Davies tried to arrange an exhibition between his two fighters. The Chicago police refused to allow the two men to box. Davies then had them demonstrate their training techniques, including skipping rope, dumbbell exercises, and punching the heavy bag. Their demonstration was frequently applauded and at least saved the gate receipts.[1430]

When Davies saw that the ability to make matches in the United States were slim, he wrote to the *London Sporting Life* offering to back Ryan for $2,500 against any 142-pound man in England, give or take two pounds. He also offered to put up $2,500 for Choynski against any heavyweight in England except Jackson, Fred Craig, the "Harlem Coffee Cooler," preferred. He also deposited $1,000 with Will Davis to secure these challenges.[1431]

Just before Christmas Davies had almost completed his arrangements for the trip to England when the Atlantic Athletic Club confirmed that it would sponsor the Ryan-Dempsey match for fifteen rounds with the winner to take 60 percent of the gate and $500 expenses allowed for each of the fighters.[1432] This match would take place in mid-January 1895.

Two telegrams concerning the match preparations were reprinted in the San Francisco newspaper the *Morning Call*: "Brooklyn, N. Y., Dec. 25—Dempsey agrees to box Ryan fifteen rounds January 14. We expect both contestants to post five hundred dollars. The club will do the same. Answer if acceptable. Will do anything you suggest. Ed Stoddard, Match-maker, Atlantic Coub." The Parson responded: "What weight agreed to if Ryan is too fat January 14? He will weigh 148, but if Dempsey prefers it he will fight at catch weights."[1433]

Davies left for New York on the evening of December 28.[1434] On Sunday, December 30, he sent a telegram to Stoddard advising him that the he would arrive in New York on the evening of December 31. He told Stoddard that if he was interested in making a Ryan-Dempsey match then Stoddard should meet him in New York.

On Monday at about four p.m. Stoddard received a second telegram from Davies advising him that he had checked in at the Grand Union Hotel in New York and was ready to meet for the purpose of signing articles to bind a match. Davies said he would only remain in New York for a few hours. Stoddard rounded up officers of the club including its treasurer and secretary. In addition, he contacted James Kennedy, the matchmaker for the Seaside Athletic Club on Coney Island, and several other club officers, and together with Jack McAuliffe and a reporter for the *Brooklyn Eagle*, the entire group rushed into New York to meet with Davies.

When the entire group met at the Grand Union Hotel, Davies said he was ready to make a match with the Atlantic but it had to be scheduled before January 20 because he and his fighters were planning to leave for England soon after that date. The Sea Beach Palace was still under construction, and Stoddard and the officers of the Atlantic said they could not get adequate heating installed in time for the proposed match.

Jimmie Kennedy of the Seaside was then called into the meeting with Davies, and he agreed that the Seaside would take the three bouts that the Atlantic had hoped to present and run them on January 18, the night before a big

Dixon-Griffo match. Davies was satisfied with this proposal, signed the articles on behalf of Ryan, and promptly caught a train back to Chicago to gather up Ryan and prepare for the match.[1435]

At the end of 1894, Davies was again on a passenger train traveling on behalf of one of his fighters. One year earlier Davies, Jackson and Choynski were all in New York. Corbett was about to fight Mitchell, and Jackson had a signed contract with Corbett. At that time it looked as if Choynski might be meeting O'Donnell the day before the Corbett-Mitchell fight.

The prospects for 1894 had been excellent. *Uncle Tom's Cabin* was coining money on its tour. A world heavyweight championship fight between Jackson-Corbett seemed probable. All three men seemed to be at the top of their professional lives.

But most of the exciting prospects for 1894 fell apart. Choynski did not fight O'Donnell, and Corbett unconscionably backed out of his match with Jackson. The season for *Uncle Tom's Cabin* had ended well, but then Jackson left the United States in disgust over Corbett's behavior. There was no play without Jackson, so their life as actors was over. Finally, Choynski shot himself in the hand with a revolver and put himself out of commission.

Chapter 15 - (1895)

Tommy Ryan Becomes the Champion

Tommy Ryan after his fighting days

Davies did not long mourn the losses of 1894. His new fighters, particularly Barry and Ryan, showed great promise, and Davies continued to hustle on behalf of Choynski. Davies likely preferred traveling with the theater company and managing two great heavyweight fighters, but that was yesterday and this was today. A new year had begun and for the first two weeks of it, Ryan and Choynski sparred on the East Coast in order to keep Ryan sharp for the upcoming match with Dempsey.

The Ryan-Dempsey match was billed on the East Coast as a contest for the welterweight championship of America. Participating in a championship match was not a bad way to start 1895. Before leaving for Chicago, Davies sent a wire advising Ryan that the match had been made for the Seaside Club for fifteen rounds at catch weights to be held on January 18.

Chicago reporters asked Ryan if he was afraid of police interference in any fight held on Coney Island. "Not with Parson Davies in charge," Ryan responded.

Even before the Ryan-Dempsey match, stories were circulating that Dempsey was not mentally stable. Before his fight with Fitz, Dempsey had thought of himself as invincible. But he was beaten so thoroughly that even he knew he was not the boxing god he had imagined. This broke his mind and spirit. Several sports who had seen him in New Orleans reported that Jack seemed to be "deranged" and was a "fit subject for a hospital or some private asylum."[1436]

Parson Davies left Chicago on January 10 with six others for the match. Vere Davies had bet $1,400 on Ryan to $1,000 on Dempsey. Friends of Ryan sent substantial amounts of money along with the men traveling to New York, to place on Ryan when they reached the East Coast.[1437]

Ryan, accompanied by his trainer Choynski, arrived on Monday, January 14. He would be fighting at 147 pounds, and the match would be decided on points unless there was a knockout before the end of fifteen rounds. Ryan's friends were enthusiastic about the probable outcome and were worried only that Dempsey had so much more experience fighting than Tommy.[1438]

Unfortunately, the actual fight was a near disaster. Early in the evening before the match began, Dempsey sent word that he would not appear unless he received a guarantee of $2,000. Of course, there was no such provision in the articles. Dempsey's backers went into consultation with Davies and club officials. Davies was seen leaving his private office and hurrying along through a side aisle to Ryan's dressing room. Apparently a deal had been struck by which Davies agreed to give Dempsey's side a larger share of the gate than called for by the articles. This was a compromise that virtually guaranteed Jack more money, though it did not promise a specific amount.

At this point Davies probably had a fairly good idea of the gross gate receipts and was willing to cut a deal rather than lose everything. Flexibility was a trait of Davies that allowed him to succeed where others failed. Ryan agreed to the altered split, and word went back to Dempsey's side. Ultimately, the gross receipts from the fight were $5,100, half of which went to the fighters. Instead of taking 75 percent of $2,550, Davies took only half. Dempsey did not receive the full $2,000 he wanted, but his holdout did get him some additional cash.

Dempsey showed up at the club in a private carriage and was taken to his dressing room. He seemed drunk when he arrived, and some in attendance said they had seen him drinking heavily earlier in the evening.[1439] The actual match was awful, as Ryan hammered Dempsey at will. This would be Dempsey's last professional fight. He would show only once after this, during a benefit in June 1895.

Ryan was the first man to enter the ring and took the lucky corner. It was considered lucky because all the fighters in the preliminary matches who had worked from that corner had won their fights. Ryan's seconds were Choynski, "Harry" Pigeon of Chicago, Mick Dunn of Australia, and George Siddons of New York. Jack was seconded by his brother Martin, Frank Patterson, and

Jimmy Carroll. The two men simply tapped each other in the first round, but it appeared to spectators that Dempsey was fat and drunk. The crowd began to yell to take Dempsey out of the ring: "Dempsey's drunk. Take him off!"

In the second round Ryan began to pound Dempsey at will, working mostly to Jack's body, and then floored him with a blow to the jaw. The crowd yelled louder: "Take him off! It's a shame. Take him off!" In the third round Dempsey seemed to get mad and went after Tommy, but he was stopped cold and battered to the ropes, where Ryan was once again hitting him at will. After letting this go on for more than two minutes, the referee stopped the fight and declared Ryan the victor. Dempsey protested vehemently, but the police captain present also refused to let the match continue.

Many people blamed Dempsey for being drunk and failing to train properly. Others said that the fault should be placed with backers, trainers, and seconds who were cognizant of Jack's physical and mental condition but permitted him to fight. Davies had experienced other difficulties with Dempsey over the years, and he commented that even in his best days Jack would not have had a chance with Ryan. Davies said that Ryan was the quickest man on his feet he had ever seen and was a marvel of cleverness with his head and hands as well as being a thorough tactician.[1440]

Three weeks after Ryan was declared welterweight champion of America, the London Club proposed a match between Choynski and the "Harlem Coffee Cooler." Joe accepted their proposal with the proviso that a large side bet be arranged in addition to the $2,500 purse. At the time, Davies and his fighters were traveling with Herbert Beerbohm Tree's road company and appearing in Washington, D.C. The new champion appeared each evening hitting the heavy bag and the speed bag for those in attendance. Their trip from Washington back to New York was prevented by a huge East Coast snow storm, and Davies' steamer trunk and Ryan's boxing platform and rigging used in his exhibitions were all lost in transit.

In early February, Davies was also trying to arrange a match between Choynski and Mitchell.[1441] At this point Joe was newly married to Louise Miller, an actress who had been a cast member of *Uncle Tom's Cabin*.[1442] Davies said he was willing to back Joe for any amount between $5,000 and $10,000 a side if Mitchell would come out of hiding. Moreover, for months William Brady had been claiming that Jackson should fight O'Donnell.

Davies called Brady's bluff and arranged a meeting in New York. Davies told Brady he had authority to agree to a fight between the two men at the London Sporting Club. Brady immediately began to crawfish—he always did—and Davies told him: "You are all right, Mr. Brady, but you talk too much." This match was never arranged. Davies had other propositions in mind.

He proposed a boxing tournament that would exclude only Corbett and Jackson. He proposed a sweepstakes format and would enter Choynski in the proposed tournament. The fighters would be set up in brackets with each of the matches lasting five rounds, but with a final match of eight rounds. Davies said that Hall, O'Donnell, Maher, "Denver Ed" Smith, Slavin, Frank Craig, David St. John, and Mitchell would be other contestants. The winner of each match would get 75 percent of the gate receipts for that match. Davies said because of his notoriety he would give Mitchell a larger percent of the gate receipts.[1443]

The political landscape of Chicago changes

On February 13, Davies returned to Chicago from New York.[1444] The first letter he received on his return was from "One-eyed" Jimmy Connolly putting the "touch" on Charlie for money. Davies wrote the words "Marble Heart" across the face of the letter and returned it to Connolly.[1445] He planned to stay in Chicago for about ten days and then sail for England along with Choynski and Ryan. Ryan was going to England with the idea of getting a match with Dick Burge. Davies was also trying to arrange a carnival-like exhibition that would include Corbett, Choynski, and Ryan in a bag-punching contest for prize money. Corbett refused to participate, and the idea was abandoned.[1446] It seems that Davies was doing everything he could think of to devise athletic events or carnivals that would include Corbett. He seemed to be making these propositions knowing that Corbett would not participate, hoping to embarrassing Corbett and Brady by making them refuse every proposal that involved fighting.

Within three days of his arrival in Chicago, Davies met with Mayor Hopkins and received assurances he could make arrangements for a Ryan-Choynski exhibition and for two local boxers in limited-round matches. This would be the first boxing entertainment to take place in Chicago for more than eight months.[1447]

Davies arrived in St. Louis on the evening of February 21 to meet with his friend Hopkins. He wanted Hopkins to agree to match Tracy with Ryan in Chicago on Monday, February 25. Hopkins refused to make a match on such short notice, and Davies then returned to Chicago on the midnight train.

After Davies left St. Louis, Nelse Innes of Boston sent him a telegram asking whether Davies would agree to have Tracy and Ryan meet in Boston on March 25. Davies declined this proposal because he planned to leave for England with his fighters before March 25. When Davies reached Chicago early the next morning, he had another telegram waiting. This wire was from Hopkins offering to make two fights: Creedon-Choynski and Tracy-Ryan within two weeks. With this proposal from Hopkins the idea of leaving for England was moved toward the shelf.[1448]

Davies decided to delay his departure for England to see whether he could arrange the dual matches proposed by Hopkins. Both Davies and Hopkins felt that they could do better financially by holding the two matches in Chicago rather than on the East Coast. Davies wanted the Tracy-Ryan match to be eight rounds and Creedon-Choynski match to be six. He had proposed that if he could not clear the necessary hurdles in Chicago these matches should take place at the Seaside Club on Coney Island. Davies wrote to Hopkins saying he was confident that Mayor Hopkins would allow a permit for the two contests.[1449]

Davies wanted his two fighters to keep busy. On the evening of March 5, he had both Choynski and Ryan appear at the Triangle Club in Chicago to keep them tuned up. Choynski sparred three rounds with a black fighter named Jack Douglas. Choynski toyed with Douglas, inducing Douglas to chase him and avoiding every rush while tagging Douglas with some heavy leather. Ryan's opponent for the evening was "Shorty" Ahern. They sparred four two-minute rounds.[1450]

The dual matches with Hopkins' two fighters were arranged for March 20 at Tattersall's. On March 6 Davies, Ryan, and Choynski all traveled to Kansas City to appear along with Tommy White and Barry at a benefit for a fighter named Billy Williams. This benefit took place on March 10, 1895. The feature of the affair was a four-round bout between Ryan and Emmet Mellody, a local fighter.

That evening, Choynski was matched with local named Mike Madden, but the event was dull because Madden was not in shape for their contest.[1451] When everyone returned to Chicago, Choynski and Ryan went to Lyons to finish preparing for the matches with Tracy and Creedon.[1452] The day that Ryan and Choynski left for Lyons, Davies received a telegram from the Seaside Athletic Club asking him to agree to a twenty-five round match between Ryan and "Mysterious" Billy Smith. Finally, Davies sent $500 to Richard K. Fox, who was in London. This money was to be used as a forfeit for a Ryan-Burge match for the world's welterweight championship if Burge would agree to fight.[1453]

Shortly after their party returned from Kansas City, Davies was approached by five citizens of Chicago's twenty-fourth ward who offered to pay all of his expenses if he would run as an independent for alderman. Davies told them he was compelled to turn down their offer because all of his time was taken up in the management of Choynski and Ryan.[1454]

According to the *Post Dispatch* Davies became Barry's manager on March 15. Barry was a remarkable fighter.[1455] Choynski wrote in 1927: "Barry, by the way, I consider the greatest fighter I ever saw. He had everything: speed, science, stamina, ring generalship, courage and uncanny punching power. There were many great bantams in that day, but Barry outclassed them all, even the great Casper Leon."

In addition to picking up Barry's management, Davies arranged a match between Frank Childs and Rufus Sharpe, a fighter from St. Louis, to take place in Chicago. It is not clear which fighter Davies represented in arranging this match. Sharpe was generally under the management of Hopkins, and it appears that Childs worked for Davies and traveled with his fighters to spar with Bob Armstrong.[1456] It seems likely that Davies contacted Childs and asked him whether he was willing to appear opposite Sharpe as an accommodation to Hopkins, and perhaps as part of the consideration for bringing Creedon and Tracy to Chicago. Childs appeared in Chicago many times and would later play an important role in Armstrong's career.

The first Tracy-Ryan match in Chicago took place on March 20 at Tattersall's. The fight was supposed to last eight rounds but was stopped in the eighth round and called a draw. The fight was stopped to prevent Tracy from being knocked out by Ryan. Davies and Hopkins had agreed that the match would be called a draw, and there would be no winner. Agreeing to this outcome was probably necessary for Davies to obtain a license for the match. A finish fight would not have been allowed and a knockout might have prevented future fights in Chicago. Vere Davies acted as a timekeeper along Sol Van Praag. Choynski was a second for Ryan, and Tommy White was a second for Tracy.[1457]

In years to come Van Praag would have a saloon at 2226 South Wabash Avenue known as the Tammany Athletic Club. His place was later called the Four Deuces and frequented by the mobster "Little" Johnny Torrio, sometimes called "The Brain," who is credited with teaching Al Capone everything he knew. Still later Van Praag would have a tobacco store next to the Four Deuces, and Capone was his partner in that business.

On March 21, Choynski met Creedon at Tattersall's. There was a crowd of three thousand five hundred for the fight. Again Vere Davies acted as a timekeeper and no decision was rendered. Before the main attraction Barry met Bertrand in a six-round match. Their preliminary match was given rave reviews compared to the later Choynski-Creedon match.

Creedon and Choynski fought evenly through the first three rounds, and then Choynski started the fourth round by jabbing Creedon. Joe fought off some good blows by his opponent and then closed the match with a hard right on Creedon's face. The fifth round was also Choynski's, and he opened the sixth with a rush and landed hard with both hands. He raised Creedon off the ground with an uppercut and then landed repeatedly in the rally that followed. While no decision was given, the Chicago press reported that Choynski had the best of the match.[1458]

Strychnine nearly kills Davies

On the evening of March 24, Davies nearly died. At about six p.m., he was home at 216 State Street and was dictating to his secretary, Glickauf. The dictation involved a telegram to the Seaside Club on Coney Island. Davies was sitting on a nearby chair when he suddenly stopped dictating. Glickauf turned and saw Davies' body grow rigid and his spine stiffen. It was later discovered that Davies had been accidentally poisoned with strychnine.

Davies had been suffering with the grip during the prior week. The Parson had visited his physician, Dr. Francis McNamara of 277 State Street. McNamara was the physician for several fighters, including Choynski, and he would later be the physician for the Cook County Jail. For the uninitiated this means that McNamara was politically connected.

McNamara gave Davies a prescription for phenacetine. This drug was used as an anti-neuralgic to relieve nerve pain. It is no longer marketed because of its carcinogenic properties, but it was commonly used in the 1890s. Davies had exhausted the original prescription and went to a drug store to have it refilled. Someone at the drug store made a mistake and filled the prescription with strychnine. For almost a hundred years strychnine in small doses had been used by some American medical practitioners in treating nervous system issues. Davies had taken the strychnine at about four thirty p.m. believing that it was phenacetine.

The rigid appearance noted by Glickauf was caused by the effects of the strychnine, which is a potent stimulant of the spinal cord; it increases the secretion of gastric juices and heightens sensory awareness. Poisoning by strychnine is characterized by violent convulsions and prevents the proper operation of the chemical that controls nerve signals to the muscles so that the victim suffers severe, painful spasms. Although the person who is poisoned remains conscious and alert, he will be in great pain. Eventually his muscles will tire, and he will not be able to breathe. Rigid arms and legs, such as those noticed by Glickauf, are often a symptom of this malady. Long-term effects of strychnine poisoning may result from damage caused to the brain from low oxygen levels or kidney failure.

When Glickauf saw Davies' go rigid, he tried to help him up and to have him exercise by walking across the room. This was the wrong thing to do, as Davies should have been kept quiet. Glickauf soon summoned a Dr. Smedley of 213 Chicago Avenue, who began to administer emetics to force vomiting and hot mustard plasters to ease the pain in Davies' muscles. Davies was comatose for nearly an hour. Accounts say that Glickauf also summoned a nephew of Davies, identified as Harry Taylor, who was a son of Davies' sister Jane.

McNamara was summoned to Davies' home and after examination, determined that the Parson was suffering from strychnine poisoning. The two doctors stayed with Davies until eleven p.m., when they pronounced him out of danger of death. It is likely that during the remainder of his life some of the illnesses Davies suffered were caused in part by the long-term effects of this poisoning. In retrospect Charlie's poisoning was another watershed event in his life. He did not know it at the time, but the effects of the strychnine would last for the rest of his life. Within less than two years his hair had turned snow white, and it would not be long before rheumatism became worse, and he began experiencing trouble with his sight.[1459]

The day after he nearly died, Davies was working again. Ryan was a hot commodity, and offers and counteroffers were coming from all sides. On March 25, he sent a wire to Kansas City setting out his terms for a Ryan-Paddy Purtell match for about April 15.[1460]

Two days later Davies received a wire from Fox saying Burge had accepted Davies' proposition for a Ryan-Burge match for $5,000 a side. Burge wanted the fight to be at 140 or 142 pounds on November 25 in England. Davies was holding the high cards said that the match would have to take place on September 25 in England or November 25 in the United States.[1461] The date proposed by Burge conflicted too much with other plans that Davies had for Ryan. On March 29, Davies signed articles between Ryan and "Paddy" Smith, a brother of

"Denver Ed" Smith, for a match at the Seaside Athletic Club in New York on April 29.[1462]

Bathhouse John Coughlin sticks it to Davies

On April 1, it was announced that Jack Wilkes, a St. Louis welterweight, had been scheduled to box Ryan at the Second Regimental Armory on Friday, April 5.[1463] The deal was that Ryan was required to stop Wilkes in eight rounds or give up a forfeit of $600. The length of each round had been extended from three to four minutes. Ryan again went to Lyons to tune up for the match. The two men had fought once before at the Omaha Athletic Club in a seventeen-round match that was stopped by the police with Ryan winning handily.[1464] Ryan had admitted that Wilkes had given him the hardest fight of his life. Several other matches were scheduled for the evening, including Childs fighting a man named Will Mayo.

What happened next was a lesson in Chicago politics of the kind that caused Davies to leave town. The situation had been building for several years before 1895. "Hinky Dink" Kenna and "Bathhouse" John Coughlin were in the process of taking over Chicago's first-ward politics and controlling the city's gambling, burlesque, and prostitution houses. The big money in Chicago was in the first ward. There were several reasons for this. The depots for the major railroads such the Illinois Central, state and federal governmental offices, La Salle Street with its banks and exchanges, and the key hotels and clubs were all located in the first ward. Coughlin was elected alderman in 1892 as McDonald was pulling out of active politics.[1465] Kenna was elected alderman in 1907, but he was the brains behind Coughlin from the beginning.[1466]

Coughlin had one principle, and it has been followed in Chicago by many aldermen. Coughlin owned the first ward and nobody did business in his ward without first coming to Coughlin. Between 1973 and 2010 thirty-one Chicago aldermen were sentenced to prison, thus keeping a long legacy in tack.

In early April, Hopkins was still the mayor, but George B. Swift was the mayor-elect. Van Praag was still a force in Chicago politics and had enough power that in 1896 he was able to secure an appointment as a deputy U. S. marshal.

Sol and "Big" Sandy Walters, Sol's first-ward henchman, had obtained a license from Hopkins for a boxing exhibition in Coughlin's ward. Van Praag and Walters sold the license to Davies for $500, a price well above the actual cost of the license. This was part of the cost of doing business in Chicago and was a practice that Davies had probably accommodated in many instances.

Coughlin didn't like the idea of another politician making money off an event held in his ward. If money was to be made from selling a license, then that money was supposed to go into Coughlin's pockets and not to Van Praag and Walters. In retaliation for the impertinent behavior of Van Praag and Walters, Coughlin pushed through the city council an anti-prizefight ordinance that he hoped would prevent the exhibition. The ordinance was specifically directed at fights to be held on April 6 and 7 at the Second Regimental Armory.[1467]

The new ordinance could not become effective without the mayor's signature. Coughlin learned that Hopkins had no intention of signing the ordinance until after the Ryan-Wilkes match. Coughlin therefore hired two men to appear before a Judge Foster and obtain warrants for the arrests of Ryan, Wilks, Mayo, and Childs on charges of prizefighting. Coughlin took the arrest warrants to the general superintendent of police, Michael Brennan, who passed them along to Inspector Shea, who gave them to officers Myer and McKeogh. The two officers went to visit Davies at Vere's saloon on Clark Street and gave the Parson the bad news.[1468]

Davies met with Brennan and learned the details behind the issuance of the warrants. He called off the entertainment, rather than collecting gate receipts from seven thousand people and then having the fighters arrested before the show could take place. Davies told the press: "I could have gone ahead, but trouble would have resulted and thousands of people who had paid their money to see the contest would have been defrauded, as the police would undoubtedly have served the warrants and arrested the men in the ring." [1469]

Davies felt that the situation might have been avoided had he met with Coughlin. But he stated his position: "If my business is legal, the spite of the alderman ought not to affect it; if it is against the law, I shall not induce any alderman to legalize it."[1470] This statement can be fairly translated: "I could have gone to Coughlin and paid him off for this match. I could also have paid him off to drop his anti-prizefighting ordinance but I am not going to be extorted by Coughlin. I paid Walters and Van Praag for the license and that is far as I am going."

Coughlin was candid about the situation. He told the press with a cheerful grin he had stopped Davies' fights all by himself. He said bluntly: "I did it because I thought certain people interested in the affair had no right to presume to run a show in this ward—such people as Sol Van Praag and Big "Sandy" Walters. I have no spite against Mr. Davies, who is a good fellow, but I did have a personal spite, with plenty of reason, against such fellows as Van Praag and Walters—fellows that are no possible good on earth. They have no right to bring off a prize fight or anything else."[1471]

Van Praag described Coughlin's conduct as a contemptible trick. He said: "It is particularly dirty because it hits an innocent man, Mr. Davies, who never did anything to Coughlin, a great deal harder than it does us, who only had a friendly interest in the Parson's show."

Walters said he had read in a natural history book that the lowest form of life was an animal called a bathybius. He thought that term fit Coughlin well. A bathybius was a gelatinous substance found in mud dredged from the floor of the Atlantic Ocean while laying the trans-Atlantic cable. It was named by Professor Huxley but later discredited as a real organism.

There were aspects of this incident that promised long-term trouble. Another generation of crooks was taking over Chicago politics. Davies had known and been good friends with the former generation, including men such as McDonald, Mackin, Van Praag, and their puppet Mayor Carter Harrison. However, Davies' own success had moved well beyond Chicago as he had promoted many fights and fighters all over the world. Davies was internationally known and had promoted matches in such divergent places as San Francisco, Los Angeles, Boston, New York, Coney Island, New Orleans, Belfast, Dublin, and London. He had traveled to Paris and Berlin. But the hub of his wheel had also been Chicago.

Davies' ability to produce fights in Chicago played a part in making him a fixture in international prizefighting and wrestling circles. He did not have the same relationship with Kenna and Coughlin he had with the post-Chicago-fire generation. Unless he started paying off these new men, his ability to promote in Chicago would be seriously impaired and diminish his own significance. If he did make the necessary payoffs, then he would ultimately lose control of his own future.

The year 1895 was turning out to be difficult. Davies had been poisoned and had nearly died. His ability to promote in Chicago was thwarted by Coughlin and Kenna. He was still attracting and managing good fighters and was playing a major role in the prizefighting game, but the problems confronting the Parson were real.

On April 8, Hall and Choynski were matched to meet sometime after June 2 before the best club and for the largest purse possible.[1472] At the end of April, Bob Armstrong was matched to meet Will Mayo in a private, six-round contest.[1473] Armstrong was Davies' newest heavyweight.

Armstrong's family moved to Washington County, Ohio when he was about three years old and later moved to the area around Davenport, Iowa. As a young man he grew to be six feet three inches tall. He weighed between 185 and 217 pounds during his career in the ring. He was a left-handed fighter with a good left jab and a strong right hand and considered to be the next best thing to Jackson that Davies could find. But he was not Jackson. Because of the differences in their lives before prizefighting, Armstrong's experiences with race relations were much different than Jackson's. The United States was Armstrong's home, and he had not known a society where men were treated equally regardless of race. Armstrong gave Davies the management of a full-fledged heavyweight.

Davies takes his fighters east

With no prospect for further contests in Chicago—short of paying off men like Coughlin—Davies took Choynski, Ryan, Barry, and Armstrong east with him. They took quarters in Asbury Park, New Jersey, on a farm owned by Colonel Russell Rulick.[1474] Asbury Park, where Corbett had trained for his contest with Sullivan, had become the summer rendezvous of many in the prizefighting fraternity. Corbett and his girlfriend occupied a painted cottage on Seventh

Avenue, the town's prime thoroughfare. O'Rourke and Davies had a place across Deal Lake called The Farm, where there were sometimes as many as twenty or more fighters training. During May Choynski and Ryan sparred frequently at Deal Lake, and their matches apparently added to the animosity the two felt for one another.[1475]

Davies was not a fan of Corbett's manager, Brady. After the failure of the proposed Jackson-Corbett match, Davies missed no opportunity to torment Brady wherever he could. On May 13, Davies sent a letter to the editor published in the *Brooklyn Eagle* offering to match Choynski against O'Donnell "for $2,500 a side, nine or ten weeks from the time of signing articles, the contest to take place before the club offering the largest purse."[1476]

The Seaside Athletic Club hosted a fight between Ryan and Mysterious Billy Smith on May 27.[1477] This was the fourth time that Ryan and Smith faced each other, and the match was billed as for the welterweight championship of the world. Davies was in Ryan's corner for the fight and was later credited with great work in supervising his seconds. Smith had been battering Ryan all over the ring in the eleventh round and had Tommy in a semi-conscious state. Ryan was so dazed he went to Smith's corner at the end of the round not knowing where he was.

The police came into the ring to stop the fight. During this distraction Davies had Ryan lifted into his chair and told the seconds to go to work on him to bring him around. He then proceeded to argue with the police contending that Ryan was fine and able to continue without any danger. In the meantime Smith was celebrating in his corner thinking he had won the fight. Billy took a pint of whiskey out of the bucket in his corner and drained the bottle.

As the argument went on Ryan was revived and when the police looked over to his corner he appeared to be in good shape as Davies claimed. The fight was then allowed to continue. Davies had seen Smith consume all the whiskey and instructed Ryan to go for Smith's stomach. Ryan made a remarkable recovery in the next two rounds, and two minutes into the eighteenth round had Smith almost unconscious on the ropes when the police stopped the fight. Although the match was called a "no contest" Davies had saved Ryan from a certain defeat, and he thereby retained his title.[1478]

While Choynski was preparing for his match with Hall, Davies arranged a warm-up bout for Joe with a fighter named Jack Cattanach out of Providence to take place at Baltimore on June 3. Their match proved to be a disappointment for the spectators, as Joe slugged Cattanach at will to the point that the crowd was yelling at the end for the Providence man to be taken off the stage. Some reports say that Joe knocked out Cattanach in two rounds.[1479] At some point McCoy was invited to Choynski's training camp and sparred three rounds with Armstrong. In the process he trounced Armstrong thoroughly.[1480] On June 8, Joe had a three-round exhibition with Armstrong in New York. This match was primarily intended to show Armstrong to interested New Yorkers.[1481]

The Hall-Choynski contest did not take place as scheduled. On June 15, the Seaside Athletic Club sponsored several matches. The first match was between George Green of San Francisco, better known as Young Corbett, and Eddie Pierce of New York. In the third round Young Corbett knocked out Pierce, and the police then entered the ring and arrested the fighters: "Wake up Eddie, you're under arrest!"

Dixon and Frank Erne were to fight in the next match that night. When the fighters came through the ropes, the police announced that if the match began, they too would be arrested. The Seaside suspended its operations, canceling the Hall-Choynski match.[1482]

Sullivan renews his relationship with Davies

On June 27, Davies took Choynski and Armstrong with him to put on a six-round exhibition as part of a huge benefit planned for Sullivan, who sparred three rounds with Corbett as the central feature of the show.[1483] This was the start of Davies' business relationship with Sullivan, which lasted almost a year and probably hurt the Parson's relationships with the fighters he was managing. Sullivan had fallen on hard times, so a benefit at Madison Square Garden was held to help him back on his feet.

Davies had buried the hatchet with Sullivan and organized the benefit. Sullivan's hard times provided both an opportunity for Davies and an income for Sullivan. It gave Davies a vehicle for keeping his athletic combination employed. All Davies' fighters were involved in the production, which included bag-punching demonstrations and other similar activities. This was the first of many benefits that Davies arranged for Sullivan over the last six months of 1895.

In his book *John L. Sullivan and His America*, Michael T. Isenberg incorrectly reports the dynamic of what happened. As a result of his apparent misunderstanding of the events, Isenberg implies that Davies somehow took advantage of Sullivan, when actually the opposite is the case.

One of Sullivan's many creditors was the Metropolitan Job Printing Company. The printing company had obtained a money judgment against Sullivan and an attachment of the receipts from the benefit. Metropolitan had arranged for a deputy sheriff to serve the writ of attachment on the benefit's promoters, ordering the proceeds due to be Sullivan to be turned over to sheriff to satisfy Metropolitan's judgment.

When the deputy appeared to serve the writ, he was confronted by an attorney named Max Hirsch, who produced a bill of sale dated June 25. Under the terms of the bill of sale, Sullivan had already sold his rights to the proceeds of the benefit several days earlier to Davies for $5,300. Because Davies was a good faith purchaser for value without notice of Metropolitan's judgment, the printing company had no way to collect its judgment because Sullivan was no longer owed any money. With Davies the owner of the proceeds, the attachment was ineffective.

"I bought all the privileges of this show from John L.," Davies said. "And if I make any profit on the deal I can use my own judgment as to the disposal of it."

A device like this was used in later years by Tommy White to avoid paying a debt he owed to Davies. It was a way to avoid Metropolitan's judgment, but not a way to make money off of Sullivan when he was down and out.

Because he misunderstood the events, Isenberg implied that Davies had taken advantage of Sullivan, but the opposite is true. A deal probably had been cooked up between Davies and Sullivan's lawyer. Sullivan would have been well aware of the outstanding money judgment; he had many creditors on his tail at the time. When Davies began planning the benefit, Sullivan's lawyer probably suggested that the proceeds of the benefit be sold to Davies in advance. The lawyer likely did not mention Metropolitan's judgment specifically because that would have given Davies knowledge of what was happening and prevent him from being a good-faith purchaser.

Davies was not naïve and certainly had an idea of what was happening. Isenberg writes that the "Parson therefore walked away with most of John L's share of his 'benefit,' after paying off the writ." This is simply wrong. First, Davies did not have to "pay off the writ." He didn't pay a dime to the deputy sheriff. The writ was enforceable against Sullivan and not against Davies. Unless Metropolitan could prove otherwise, Davies was a bona fide purchaser for value without notice. This was a common method of creditor avoidance. The prime beneficiary of this device was Sullivan, not Davies.

Davies' relationship with the fighters he managed changed in the last half of 1895. Instead of keeping his fighters training together at Asbury Park or taking them on the road or into theaters, the fighters were allowed to disperse and in some cases participated in exhibitions or matches that were not arranged by Davies. There were several reasons for this change in format.

Prizefights, exhibitions, and sparring matches were being suppressed by authorities just about every place the combination tried to appear. Their only relatively stable activities were the Sullivan benefits that began in New York and continued in other cities for many months thereafter. In addition, Choynski and Ryan did not like each other, and this made it difficult to keep the two of them in close contact. Choynski felt that Ryan had a swelled head considering his accomplishments, and Ryan felt that Choynski was overrated. It was better to keep the two men apart. It is also possible that Davies was having physical problems as a result of his strychnine poisoning and simply wasn't able to do as much as he had before he nearly died.

In early July, another of Davies' former fighters died. Alf Greenfield had been brought to the United States by Fox at the age of thirty-one to try to defeat Sullivan. After he flopped in that effort, Davies brought him to Chicago and matched him against Jack Burke. At one point Greenfield had been rated by Davies as the fifth leading heavyweight in the world. In addition to his fights with Sullivan, he also met Jem Smith in Paris and fought Kilrain when he was a relative unknown. Greenfield was only forty-two at his death. He joined Killen,

Glover, Ashton, and Riordan as a fighter formerly managed by Davies who had died at an early age.[1484]

Dempsey went back to Portland, Oregon, in July a broken man. He was dying of consumption and wanted to be home with his wife before he died. He passed out on the train several times and nearly didn't make it home. His life was saved by a female doctor who happened to be traveling on the same train. A physical shadow of his former self, Jack hung on to life until November 1.

News stories at the time of his death said that his heart had been broken by his loss to Fitz, and he had lost his will to live. Dempsey had attributed his condition to a blow he received from Fitz during their title fight in New Orleans. It seems likely that both of these possibilities may be true. He was broken by his loss to Fitz, and he did absorb a lot of punishment during their fight—more than many heavyweights whom Fitz later defeated. Jack was only thirty-two years old at the time of his death.[1485]

The focus of virtually all prizefighting news in the second half of 1895 was a proposed Corbett-Fitzsimmons fight. For much of the year it appeared that the fight would take place in Dallas in a stadium that had seating for more than fifty-two thousand spectators. For the first time, the articles of agreement addressed the distribution of royalties from the sale of an Eidoloscope of the contest.

The Eidoloscope, created in 1894 by a man named Woodville Latham and his sons, was an early form of motion pictures, a medium that was in its infancy. Motion pictures and prizefighting would soon be closely associated. Movies provided a way to show prizefights to a large audience while earning additional income for fighters and promoters with little extra effort or expense. In effect motion pictures would kill the road trips that Davies so often conducted. In addition, motion pictures provided an alternative use of local theaters without dealing with the New York theater syndicate.

Davies had been promoting testimonials for Sullivan, and many believed Davies wanted to manage Sullivan in 1896.[1486] Sullivan appeared before six thousand people at Halifax in mid-July and claimed he was going to challenge the winner of the Corbett-Fitzsimmons fight.[1487] On July 22, Davies was in Bangor, Maine, where Sullivan had another testimonial and sparred three rounds with Paddy Ryan.[1488] Two days later they were in Bar Harbor and put on another exhibition as part of a benefit.

In between those engagements Davies met on July 23 in New York with the promoters of the Corbett-Fitzsimmons fight and agreed that Tommy Ryan would meet "Mysterious" Billy Smith in Dallas on the night before their heavyweight championship.[1489] There was also an effort to persuade Davies to accept the job of referee for the Corbett-Fitzsimmons fight, but he would not agree.[1490] Of course, the fate of the Ryan-Smith match depended entirely on the fate of the Corbett-Fitzsimmons match. If that contest failed or was prevented, then the Ryan-Smith fight would go down in flames too.

Davies renewed his efforts to arrange a Hall-Choynski match despite the failure of their match at the Seaside Athletic Club. On July 31, Choynski received word from Davies that he had accepted a fight for $2,500 a side. No other particulars were provided, and Choynski said he was doubtful that Hall would ever show for the match.

Davies sent a letter to Glickauf advising he had arranged an evening of athletic entertainment for August 19 at the Academy of Music in New York. As part of this show Ryan would spar with O'Rourke's man Walcott for five rounds. The match would be supplemented with a ball-punching competition for a gold medal and a limited-round match for Barry, whom Davies was hoping to match with Billy Plimmer.[1491]

In early August, Davies again wrote Glickauf to tell him he had arranged a Choynski-Godfrey match for August 28. Davies wanted Joe to return to the East Coast and go into training at Asbury Park immediately. He also told Glickauf he was still trying to arrange a match for Barry. Billy Plimmer was out, and the likely candidate was then Billy "Kid" Madden.[1492] However, the prospects for additional productions in New York dimmed when Davies and several others were arrested on August 19 at the Academy of Music. Davies and O'Rourke were making big plans for the rest of the year, and they were even discussing a tour to the South and then to South Africa. None of this happened.

Davies and O'Rourke spent substantial time preparing for the entertainment that August evening. They had organized the program under the name of the National Athletic Club of America. Davies arranged a bag-punching exhibition that went off without a problem. The contestants included Armstrong, Ryan, Dixon, Joe Elms, and Harry Pigeon. That exhibition was followed by wrestling, weight lifting and preliminary boxing.[1493] Then before the featured boxing began, O'Rourke entered the ring and announced that Inspector Cortright was present to watch the boxing and if anything in violation of the law happened, he would stop the match.

Nothing in particular happened until the Dixon-Leonard match. These two men were the star attractions for the evening and because the police were present, it was anticipated that no heavy action would take place. However, when the match began, Leonard did not attempt to fight but instead rushed at Dixon, grabbed him around the neck in a headlock and smashed him in the face with his free hand.

The referee rushed in to separate the fighters, but Leonard again grabbed Dixon in a wrestling hold and threw him to the floor. Dixon got angry and began smashing Leonard (who was called "the fashion plate") all over the ring until Leonard put both arms around Dixon to prevent himself from being hit. Dixon got his hand free and slugged away at Leonard until the police entered the ring and arrested both men.

O'Rourke then led Davies to the center of the ring. Davies began to explain that the fighters had been warned about inappropriate behavior, but in the midst of his pronouncement a police officer tapped Davies on the shoulder saying: "That'll do." Davies, O'Rourke, Leonard, and Dixon were all taken to the station and released on bond. It was several days before the charges against O'Rourke and Davies were dropped.[1494]

CHARLES E. DAVIES.
(The "Parson.")

Drawing from the September 4, 1895 Chicago Inter Ocean – Courtesy of NewsBank - Readex

The drawing above was created from an amateur photograph of Davies taken in early September on the iron pier at Coney Island. The photograph was unusual because Davies was not wearing his customary necktie and was caught off guard staring out at the Atlantic Ocean. Davies refused to pay for the negative and the photograph was then sold to an East Coast newspaper.

Davies returned to Chicago on September 25.[1495] He left there soon after his experience with Coughlin and did not return for five months. He probably came back because his niece Sara gave birth to her second daughter Adele Sarah Gruschow on September 23, and Davies wanted to see the latest addition to his extended family. It seems clear that in matters of business Davies was letting go of his ties to the city of Chicago. His nieces had grown to adulthood, his brother Vere had married in 1892 and operated a good business. Charlie had become odd-man-out, and there was little left to hold him in Chicago because he could not sponsor athletic entertainment without paying off Coughlin.

The *Chicago Tribune* noted that things had not run smoothly for Davies while he was away from Chicago. The planned Hall-Choynski match at the Seaside had been stopped by the police. The Choynski-Godfrey match could not be carried off because Joe was ill and unable to fight. In addition, a planned Barry-Madden fight had been prevented by the authorities. In each instance Davies lost substantial time and money. In particular, with respect to the Choynski-Godfrey affair, the Parson was forced to pay a $150 forfeit to the Farragut Club, where the contest was to have taken place. At the time he paid the money, Davies was not aware that the authorities had told the club that it could not go forward with the match. Davies felt that the club had played him an unsportsmanlike trick.[1496]

Davies remained in Chicago for three days before he left for Philadelphia to arrange yet another Sullivan benefit, this time to take place at the Grand Opera House on October 3.[1497] The show did not take place because the theater owner withdrew his agreement to rent the house. However, Davies took the two pudgy old men to Cleveland, where they were to appear on October 5. That appearance was also canceled because of interference by Cleveland's mayor.

Davies returned to Chicago on October 7 but stayed only two more days before again leaving for Detroit, where Ryan was training for his fight with Smith.[1498] The newspapers were interested in Davies' opinion concerning the prospects of the Corbett-Fitzsimmons contest. Davies said he had not heard from Dan Stuart, who was president of the Florida Athletic Club, the entity trying to promote the fight in Texas. He explained that after visiting Ryan in Detroit, he was going to Toledo to manage yet another benefit for Sullivan on October 9. The two old war horses Sullivan and Paddy Ryan would spar a few friendly rounds during the Toledo benefit.[1499] Choynski also appeared at the Sullivan testimonial in Toledo.[1500]

After this appearance, the entire Sullivan benefit combination went to Pittsburgh to appear on Friday, October 11, and then took in the Griffo-Lavigne fight at Maspeth before putting on another Sullivan show in Jersey City on October 14.[1501] It is likely that all along the way Sullivan was paid directly by Davies and that Davies was assigned the proceeds of each benefit in advance so that John L.'s creditors could not glom onto the money.

While in Pittsburgh for the Sullivan benefit, Davies met with J. J. Quinn, who was Maher's manager, to try and arrange a Maher-Choynski match. In the meantime the appearance in Philadelphia did not happen because the manager there had refused to rent the house for a boxing show. Davies said this happened only after he had been promised use of the house and had gone to considerable expense to advertise the show.

During this time there was virtually no mention of Jackson in the newspapers. Hopkins' fighter Creedon had traveled to London, where he was matched for a fight on October 14 with Craig in a twenty-round bout. The newspapers noted that Jackson was present for that fight, and he was wildly cheered by the crowd when he entered the area. There is little wonder that Jackson enjoyed spending his time in England rather than the United States.[1502]

After its appearance in Pittsburgh, Davies took the Sullivan-Ryan group to Jersey City to appear at the Oakland Rink before the Hudson County Athletic Club on October 14. About this time Davies finally arranged the Barry-Madden match.[1503] The two bantams then met at Maspeth, New York, on October 21, and Barry completely outclassed Madden and continued to add to his reputation.

Their fight was scheduled for twenty rounds, but Barry was awarded the fight after only four rounds.[1504]

As Davies was traveling with the Sullivan testimonial aggregation, the Corbett-Fitzsimmons fight was moved from Dallas to Hot Springs, Arkansas, to avoid interference by the Texas governor. It seemed that the fight would take place in Hot Springs, and therefore the call went out for the contestants. Smith showed up in Hot Springs by October 17.[1505] On October 25, Ryan stopped his training in Detroit.[1506] Davies was in Rochester with Sullivan and Ryan.[1507] The Parson was doubtful that the Corbett-Fitzsimmons fight would happen in Arkansas, but he told Ryan to get to St. Louis, where Davies had planned another testimonial for Sullivan. Davies originally planned to feature Tommy Ryan as part of the Sullivan event in St. Louis, but he also wanted Tommy nearby in case he would have to scoot off to Hot Springs on short notice.[1508]

Davies and his combination were all in Chicago on the morning of October 30. They met at the Wabash R.R. Depot on Polk Street at eleven a.m. to travel to Corbett-Fitzsimmons match. The word on the street was that the match could not be carried off at Hot Springs but nothing was certain. Davies said his combination planned to stay the night at the Imperial Hotel in St. Louis before going on to Hot Springs to see firsthand how things stood. Davies, Paddy Ryan, Tommy Ryan, Harry Pigeon, and a number of "camp followers" were part of the group traveling together to St. Louis.[1509] As it happened, the group stopped in St. Louis for only about one hour before catching the Iron Mountain Cannon Ball to Hot Springs.

The Davies' group arrived in Hot Springs at noon on October 31 and went to their quarters at the Arlington Hotel.[1511] Davies and his stars, including Sullivan and the two Ryans, went to dinner and created an instantaneous furor. Everybody wanted to see the redoubtable Sullivan, and "between dignified citizens and big-boned, wiry individuals who came in from valley and mountain, the ex-champion's right arm was pretty severely tested for nearly an hour. Then he was piloted about the town with crowds of admiring men and boys following in his wake."[1512]

Davies met with Smith's backer, J. Westcott, to talk about the prospects for the preliminary match between their fighters.[1513] The managers learned that the match had been officially declared off by the Florida Athletic Club, but there remained a slim possibility that the Hot Springs Athletic Association might sponsor the fight between their welterweights, provided both Davies and Westcott agreed.

The next morning everything that had been planned for Hot Springs fell apart because Fitz withdrew from the fight in the face of threats of prison time and failing financial support. Bob had already engaged in a long battle with the law after the death of Riordan and knew that determined local authorities could make his life a living hell. Although he had been exonerated in Riordan's death, he was in no mood to spend time in an Arkansas prison and said he would not fight there because of the threats of Arkansas officials. When Fitz dropped out, everyone began to scatter and the entire program of entertainment was declared off. Without the spectators to watch there was no money in the fights for any boxing club.

By November 3 Davies' group was back in Chicago and most of the travelers were staying at the Imperial Hotel. The trip from Detroit to Hot Springs and back had cost Davies about $500.[1514]

Sullivan said in an interview that he was disgusted with the whole affair: "It's pretty tough to haul a man all over the country for a fizzle. I guess prizefighting is dead." He thought that Corbett wanted to fight, but Fitz didn't have any money and that settled it.[1515]

The *Galveston Daily News* quoted Sullivan as saying: "I'm that sick and sore of this fighting burlesque that I'm compelled to stay over and rest. It ain't so very long that I used to be in this business myself, and, say, I could always find a way to fight any fellow that wanted to fight. I ain't saying which of these fighters didn't want to fight, but it's a sure thing one of them was scared. You can pick him out if you like. I won't tell the one he is."[1516]

The Sullivan based combination was scheduled to leave for the east on a three p.m. train on November 4.[1517] They appeared in Buffalo on Monday, November 18, for another testimonial. In Buffalo Sullivan's comments were more explicit. He told a reporter there that it was all Fitz' fault that there was no fight at Hot Springs.

Following the failure of the Corbett-Fitzsimmons match, Davies and O'Rourke made plans to leave for England in mid-November. Choynski had been matched for a twenty-five round match with Slavin, and O'Rourke had matched Dixon with England's featherweight Billy Smith. However, Davies did not go to England. Instead he continued to promote the testimonials for Sullivan and arranged a six-month tour with for Sullivan and Paddy Ryan. It was sometimes hard to dismount a winning horse and the public was still paying good money to see the two old heavyweights.[1518]

A six month road tour with Sullivan, Ryan, and *The Wicklow Postman*

The last 1895 testimonial was scheduled for Chicago on December 10 at Battery D but was rescheduled for Saturday, December 14, at the Alhambra.[1519] The promotional material said that after his appearance in Chicago, Sullivan would go into mercantile life and would never appear in ring costume again. Truth in advertising was not too important because Davies was already planning a six-month road tour featuring Sullivan and Ryan. The Chicago event was the first entertainment that Davies promoted in Chicago after Bathhouse John Coughlin had engineered the cancellation of the Ryan-Wilkes contest. It seemed unlikely that even Coughlin would take on Sullivan.

Interviewed before his benefit, Sullivan told the *Post Dispatch* that between 1881 and 1895 he had made $2,000,000. However, he contended he was the same "honest" John that people knew at the beginning of his career. The reporter also asked about Jackson, and Sullivan launched on a discussion of black fighters generally. He was quoted as saying: "No man of principle will fight in a ring with a colored man. No man can say I ever refused to fight when the time came for a fight, but I would not fight with a N_____."

Despite these stupid comments, the American public loved Sullivan. In the midst of this discussion Sullivan drifted to the subject of religion and said he was a Catholic according to the directions he had received as a child.

"When I die they'll put me in a steel coffin and burn me to a cinder; and I won't have no use for championship belts then," he concluded. [1520] At that time, burning a Catholic to a cinder was not exactly what the church condoned. Apparently, honest John was not paying too much attention during catechism class.

The Chicago newspapers noted that there was a tremendous call for tickets in advance of the Sullivan benefit, and it was expected to be a smashing success. Tickets were selling at "fabulous prices," and standing-room-only tickets were at a premium. The theater was filled from pit to dome, and hundreds of people were turned away.[1521] The actual event was as good as the buildup.

As a result of the reception that Sullivan received, Davies decided to have additional exhibitions at the Academy of Music on the following Thursday, Friday, and Saturday nights. In addition to the testimonial gimmick, Davies began to offer the services of Sullivan and Paddy Ryan as potential referees, which he did first in connection with the Corbett-Fitzsimmons match and then for a proposed Maher-Fitzsimmons fight. A few days before the Sullivan testimonial, Davies sealed a deal for a real fight between Choynski and Hall in New York on January 13, 1896.[1522]

Davies' sister is reported murdered

On Saturday, December 21, the body of a woman was found in the yard behind 432 East Fourteenth Street in New York. Her nose had been broken and her eyes crushed inward. Her face was swollen and blackened to the extent that she seemed unrecognizable. It appeared that she had been beaten severely. The woman's body was taken to a morgue as the investigation of her identity and cause of death began.[1523] The next day the *New York Times* reported that she had been recognized by police as a dissipated frequenter of the neighborhood saloons but that no one knew her background or relatives. The day after Christmas 1895, the *Chicago Tribune* published a special sent from New York on Christmas Day. According to the *Tribune*, the woman who had been murdered was identified by a man named William Hollinger as Mrs. Cassie Davies Robinson, a sister of Parson Davies.[1524] This report conflicted with an earlier report published in the *World* stating that the murdered woman had been identified by Patrick J. Horan as his wife Maria H. Horan.[1525]

The sensational story carried by the *World* and repeated by the *Tribune* asserted that Hollinger had seen the body of the murdered woman at the morgue and recognized her as Carrie Davies Robinson, a sister of Davies. Hollinger said he had never met Davies, but he had known the deceased for ten years and knew that she said that Davies was her brother. Hollinger said that Mrs. Robinson had often received money from Davies and that she occasionally received small amounts of money from Ireland as her share of distribution made from a decedent's estate. He said that she also received a handsome present at Christmas time from her brother.

The *Tribune* contacted Davies at Joliet, where he was on the road managing Sullivan and Ryan in *The Wicklow Postman*.[1526] Davies was asked about the possible murder of this Mrs. C. D. Robinson and replied that he had not seen his sister for four years. At that time they had been together in Ireland. Charlie confirmed he had given money regularly to his sister, who he said was fifty-years-old and living by herself on West 38th Street.[1527] Whether the woman who died was Davies' sister is not totally resolved. She was probably not his sister but rather Patrick Horan's wife, as originally reported.[1528] There was a death certificate issued by the state of New York for a Mary Horan, who died on December 20, and there are no additional stories identifying the murdered woman as Davies' sister.

Chapter 16 - (1896-1897)

Times Changing

I shall go to New York Tuesday. Live there? Well, hardly. The Parson's home is under his hat.[1529]

♣

The first two months of 1896 were setting up to be busy and would involve Davies managing his fighters and going on the road with a production of *The Wicklow Postman*. This comedy was on the same bill with a boxing show that featured Sullivan and Ryan. The play opened in Chicago during the second week of December 1895 without Sullivan and Ryan as part of the production.[1530] They were quickly added to the show, and a few days later Davies met with the play's production manager to work out the formal arrangement.[1531]

By December 20, 1895, the play was advertised as featuring Sullivan with Ryan, who were to be introduced by Davies.[1532] After Sullivan and Ryan joined the cast, the show stopped in Joliet at the end of 1895 and then went on the road to other cities including Milwaukee; Rockford, Sterling, LaSalle, Springfield, and Rock Island, Illinois; and Davenport, Iowa. The show headed to Texas for performances in Dallas and San Antonio and a big athletic carnival that Dan Stuart was putting on near El Paso.[1533]

In early January, Davies left Chicago for New York to make final preparations with the Empire Athletic Club at Maspeth for the Hall-Choynski match.[1534] The build-up and promotion of that match included a Ryan-Lavigne fight at the Grand Central Palace. However, in early January, Ryan moved from Chicago to Syracuse, parted company with Davies and began handling his own affairs. His departure was probably a result of the growing animosity between Ryan and Choynski.[1535] Ryan might also have known that Davies was going on the road with Sullivan and Paddy Ryan, and he possibly felt that this would distract Davies from promoting his prospects. What was the point of keeping a manager who spent his time traveling with two has-beens?

Ryan told the press he was in good condition: "I am ready to box any 154 pound man in the world. I will never fight less than that in my life again, for to reduce lower has a tendency to weaken me."[1536]

Davies was presented with the problem of being in two places at one time. He needed to manage the Hall-Choynski match, but he also needed to supervise Sullivan and Paddy Ryan.[1537] He first dealt with this problem by sending Glickauf along with Sullivan and Ryan and going in person to New York with Choynski. Davies had big plans for Choynski, and the general idea was that if he beat Hall then he would go to England and challenge the winner of the Creedon-Smith match.[1538] Davies himself stayed in New York until the end of January.

Choynski defeated Hall in thirteen rounds at Maspeth before three thousand five hundred enthusiastic spirits who "shook the great amphitheater with their yells and their cheers at the achievement." According to the *Brooklyn Eagle* "Choynski's body was a perfect mass of knotted muscles, piled up above each other like ridges." It was a sensational fight because Joe had been badly beaten several times before he polished off Hall. "From the ninth round there wasn't a man in the building who would have given 10 cents, barring an accident, for Choynski's chances and after that it was simply Joe's magnificent form united with his well known hard hitting powers that bore him to triumphant conclusion."[1539]

Years later Joe explained he had entered the match with Hall with two broken ribs courtesy of an amateur fighter named Dody Schwangler. Joe recalled that Schwangler had been a favorite pupil of Mike Donovan. In 1896 Professor Mike Donovan was the boxing instructor for the New York Athletic Club and had previously been an instructor of Choynski. According to Choynski he was sparring with Schwangler before the Hall fight and "letting him make a showing, pulling my punches and offering no defense when he landed a crazy heave that broke two of my slats." Choynski wrote that when he reached the Empire Club, Hall was the most confident fellow in the club. He said he had to pass Hall's corner to get to his dressing room, and as he went by he heard Hall call out to an admirer in the audience: "I'll make a monkey of Choynski. He couldn't hit me in a million years."[1540]

Davies and O'Rourke were in Joe's corner that night, and Jackson's former trainer, Sam Fitzpatrick, was one of the men in Hall's corner. Joe recalled that because of Hall's decisive victories over Slavin and Pritchard, he had been made the betting favorite. However, articles written at the time of the match in 1895 said that Choynski money was so plentiful that odds of $100 to $50 on the Californian could be had. Apparently those betting on the fight were not aware that Joe entered the match with two broken ribs. In the ninth round Hall floored Joe for a count of nine and then put him down twice more in that round. Joe came back fighting and in the thirteenth round landed a tremendous right on Hall's jaw, putting him out cold for more than fifteen seconds. When Hall came to, Joe was standing over him and extending his hand to help Jim up off the floor. Two days after the fight Joe returned to Chicago from New York.[1541]

This was Hall's last important fight. His professional life was essentially over, and his natural life ended in a sadder way. In March 1913, the *Oshkosh Daily Northwestern* wrote the following about Hall's condition before he died. He was living in a shack the paper described as "a miserable, cold, dirty hovel—in Neenah, Wisconsin" and struggling for every breath he took.

The writer found Hall shortly after four o'clock Saturday afternoon. He was in bed with his clothes on in a small room with no ventilation. Hall was lying on a bare mattress and was covered by a thin, dirty blanket. He was sober, clear-headed, and gasping for breath. He had a "death rattle" and on the brink of the grave that "long since would have claimed him were it not for the great physique with which nature endowed him."[1542] He also had a nasty scar on his neck.

One of Hall's obituaries noted incorrectly that after the Fitzsimmons fight, Hall joined forces with Davies for a time. Actually, Davies had managed Hall before his match with Fitzsimmons. The obituary went on to note that "while at Mt. Clemens, Mich. Hall got into an argument with the famous Parson, and, as a result of it he carried a mark inflicted by the Parson to his grave. Hall had a few matches, but finally gave up the game and became a traveling salesman and was also interested in other ventures, being very successful for a time. He kept straight for a long while, but getting back to wine was the beginning of the end."[1543]

Choynski wrote in 1927: "What a tragic finish the once elegant and rugged Jim Hall had. A few years ago he died of tuberculosis in a Wisconsin farmer's pig-pen where he had dragged his emaciated body from the roadside."[1544]

While in New York, Davies attended a match held at Madison Square Garden between George Dixon and "Pedlar" Palmer that ended in a draw.[1545] On Palmer's arrival from England for the match with Dixon, he was asked about Jackson's condition. Palmer said that Jackson had broken down and would never fight again. He said that when Corbett refused to fight Jackson, it had broken Peter's heart. But Jackson's popularity in England had not waned one bit, and he was the only fighter who had free access to the National Sporting Club.[1546]

Sullivan is nearly killed

Davies stayed in New York scouting out possibilities for Jimmy Barry. Soon after the Dixon-Palmer match ended, the Parson heard bad news about Sullivan and went to St. Louis, where he intended to intercept Sullivan and escort him to El Paso. The rest of the company was already in Texas appearing in Dallas, Houston, and San Antonio before going on to El Paso to perform during Stuart's boxing carnival. Davies' bantamweight Barry was going to fight Johnny Murphy as part of the athletic carnival near El Paso.[1547]

All the boxing matches in Texas were to take place outside during the day, and it was expected that there would be large crowds in El Paso in the evenings looking for entertainment that Davies would provide via Sullivan, Ryan, and *The Wicklow Postman*. This road show featuring Sullivan and Ryan was to then go west from El Paso before looping back to the north and then east. It was to last about six months, but the entire idea was nearly foiled by an injury to Sullivan that almost killed him.

Sullivan and Ryan appeared in *The Wicklow Postman* at Davenport, Iowa, on the evening of January 28, at the beginning of their six-month road tour. The play was Eugene O'Rourke's own production and presented novelties incidental to the plot, including singing and dancing by O'Rourke himself and a company of eighteen supporting cast members.

The leading lady was known by the stage name of Bettina Gerard, a daughter of General Albert Ordway, a famous Civil War officer. Gerard was a handsome and beautiful woman, but was also a hard drinker who was often not in condition to take her part.[1548] She would not be alone at the bottle because even after she left the company, Sullivan drank hard from Chicago to El Paso, through San Francisco, and back to Pittsburgh. In conjunction with and after the conclusion of O'Rourke's play, Sullivan sparred three friendly and scientific rounds with Ryan.

The morning after the performance in Davenport, Sullivan boarded a train at five minutes after eight in the morning from Rock Island to Peoria and then on to Springfield. The weather was relatively mild for late January and light precipitation hovered between rain and snow. Even at this early morning hour Sullivan had been drinking. He was standing in one of the cars on the train talking with Ryan and some other men when he was struck by the urge to urinate.

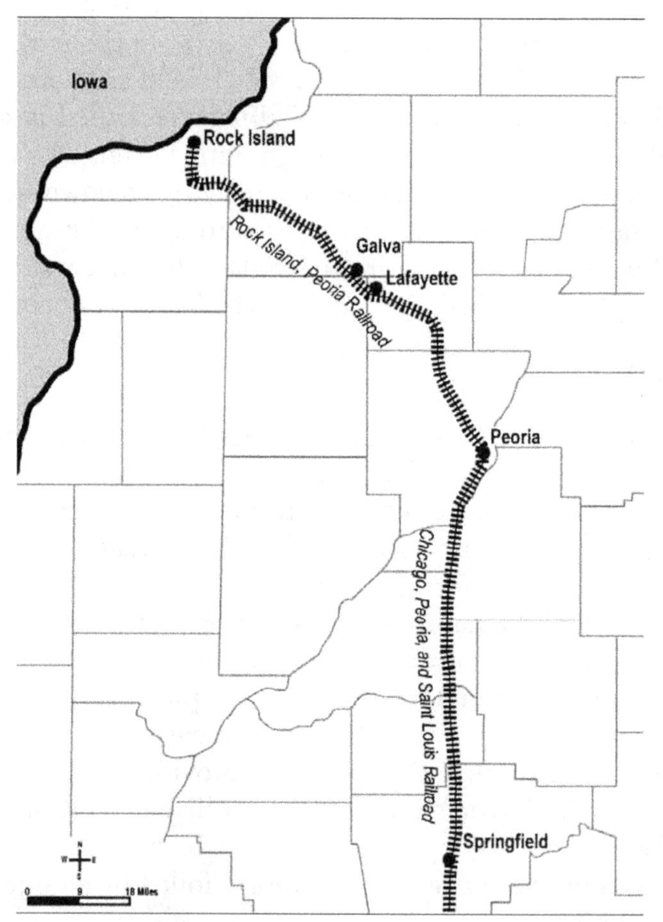

General Route of Sullivan's Trip in January 1896 – Map by Jill Thomas of Illinois State University

For men of Sullivan's age, the urge to go required a reasonably quick response. He left the company of the men with whom he had been talking and headed toward the back of the train where the bathroom was strategically located. When he reached the bathroom he discovered that it was occupied. He then went out the back door on the last car of the train where there was a narrow platform used in boarding. He stood on the platform and unbuttoned his trousers so he could relieve himself off the back of the train that was traveling between thirty and forty miles per hour.

For obvious reasons, Sullivan did not have a grip on the railing when the train jerked hard as it went around a curve. It was ten a.m. and the train was about halfway between Galva and La Fayette, Illinois. These two towns were on a spur of the Rock Island line and roughly halfway between Rock Island and Peoria. When the train lurched, Sullivan lost his balance and fell or was thrown off the platform. He tumbled into a ditch that was about ten feet deep and landed at the bottom in a mix of mud and newly frozen water.

Some reports said that other passengers on the train saw Sullivan fall and alerted the conductor. Other reports said that John L.'s friends began to wonder where he was and sent Glickauf to look for him. Glickauf discovered that Sullivan had been thrown off the train. The train stopped about a mile beyond where Sullivan was ejected and began backing up to try to find him.

Sullivan was ultimately spotted in the ditch. Ryan picked him up and brought him to the baggage car. He had a bad cut on the back of his head, several smaller cuts on his face and scalp and was severely bruised. His clothes had caught fire when matches he had in his pocket ignited in the fall. When the train arrived in Peoria at eleven forty-five a.m., a doctor was summoned to sew up the gash in the back of Sullivan's head and clean up his other wounds. Sullivan was still in a dazed condition when he left on the Chicago, Peoria, and St. Louis line headed for Springfield. The troupe was scheduled to appear there on January 29 at Chatterton's Opera House.

Sullivan did not seem to understand what had happened. About five p.m. he started to come out of his daze and at about six p.m. after the troupe had reached Springfield he asked Glickauf what had happened. When Glickauf told him he had fallen off the train, Sullivan thought he was being made fun of and couldn't believe what he was being told. Glickauf and others then began to think that Sullivan might have fractured his skull in the fall.

J. N. Dixon, a doctor in Springfield, was called to the Hotel Palace, where the party was staying. Dixon worked for an hour picking dirt and gravel from Sullivan's wounds and cleaning them. The *New York Times* reported that Sullivan cried like a baby when his head was sewed up.[1550] The doctor ordered him not to appear in the performance at Springfield and confined him to bed. Glickauf sent a telegram to Chicago for Choynski to come immediately. Joe had only been back from New York and his fight with Hall for a few days. He was asked to catch up with the production's troupe to take Sullivan's place.[1551]

The play was presented Wednesday night in Springfield. On Thursday morning the rest of the cast left headed for Texas but without Glickauf, Sullivan, and his wife. That morning, Sullivan was able to sit up in his bed, but his face had started to swell, and he had a large infected mass around the gash in the back of his head. By eleven a.m. he was in acute pain and a Dr. Walter Ryan was summoned.

Ryan then lanced "a gathering which had formed on the back of his head, where he was injured, and from which a large quantity of matter was taken, much to the relief of the big fellow." By that evening the swelling in Sullivan's face had gone down considerably, but the doctor explained he still was at risk of erysipelas and had to stay quiet and in bed. The possible outcome of erysipelas was well-known to Sullivan because his friend and former sparring partner, Jack Ashton, had died from it. Throughout this crisis both Glickauf and Sullivan's wife stayed by his side.

By February 1 Sullivan's condition was improved, and his fever broke. Dr. Ryan told Sullivan and Glickauf that if Sullivan's condition remained stable, he should be able to leave Springfield on Tuesday, February 4. But when the day arrived, Sullivan had not recovered enough to leave and had to stay another day in Springfield. Sullivan said he intended to catch up with the rest of the troupe at Fort Worth and wanted to start resuming his boxing role with Ryan within a few days.

At four p.m. on February 5 Sullivan left Springfield on the Chicago and Alton Limited headed south. A large crowd of people was at the station in Springfield to see him off and wish him good health. He arrived in St. Louis at about eight p.m. but left on the nine p.m. train for Fort Worth.[1552]

On the evening of February 1, Davies passed through St. Louis trying to catch up with the rest of troupe. Apparently, he had concluded that Glickauf had things under control in Springfield, and Davies needed to take charge of the rest of the company that was already in Texas. To make the trip to St. Louis, Davies must have left New York on the night train immediately after the Dixon-Palmer fight. In the meantime, Choynski, who had been summoned by Glickauf to fill in for Sullivan, had also ill and had returned to Chicago.[1553]

In St. Louis, Davies was asked about Joe's condition and said that Choynski had an abscess in his ear and would not be able to fight for four or five months. This may have been a convenient time period for Davies because he knew the play would last about five months. He did not mention Joe's broken ribs. "The trouble with Joe is he is trained to death," Davies said. "He is a fellow who insists on training all the time."[1554]

At this point the tour had been laid out at least as far as San Francisco. On February 2, a notice appeared in the *San Francisco Call* that Sullivan was on his way west and would be appearing at the Columbia Theater there.[1555]

Despite Sullivan's condition, the show had to meet its commitments. On February 1, the production arrived an hour late in Dallas for an appearance at the Dallas Theater. The show did not begin until nine seventeen p.m., and only a small audience was present, in part because of predicted inclement weather.[1556] A date in Galveston was cancelled because of Sullivan's illness but the Dallas press noted that Davies was in the city and had received a telegram that Sullivan was improving and would rejoin the company at Fort Worth.[1557] On Tuesday, February 4, the troupe, sans Sullivan, appeared at the Grand Opera House in San Antonio, Texas.[1558] That same day, Davies sent Sullivan a telegram asking the ex-champion to meet him in St. Louis on Wednesday, February 5, so that they could travel together to El Paso.[1559]

The El Paso mess

On Sunday, February 9, Davies, Sullivan, and Ryan spent the day with other sports in Fort Worth and then left that evening for the long haul to El Paso, arriving there on the morning of February 12.[1560] In El Paso Sullivan and Davies teamed up to offer personalized letters written by Sullivan to one major newspaper in the large U.S. cities describing the preparations for the big fight. Sullivan was paid $200 a letter. Sullivan wrote the letters, and then Davies translated them into readable English and arranged for their distribution.

Barry was already waiting in El Paso when Davies arrived. Jimmy was training with Jack Everhardt and Billy Smith. He had made a favorable impression on the sports who were gathering at El Paso, and considerable money had been bet on Jimmy to best Murphy.[1561] On February 8, 1896, all the managers of the fighters participating in the carnival issued a press release attesting that they were convinced there would be no official interference with the matches and that the contests would be offered in comfortable surroundings.[1562]

As the day of the championship match neared, the predictable legal assault began. On February 7, the United States Congress passed and President Grover Cleveland signed the Carton anti-prizefight act, making it a felony for a prizefight to take place on land that was under the exclusive jurisdiction of the federal government. The law was aimed directly at the matches scheduled to take place near El Paso because one of the most likely places for the carnival's fights was on federally owned land. Many sports had been through the scenario before and had been traveling to increasingly remote places to watch matches. With the delay caused by Maher's eye problems, many men began to leave El Paso expecting the worst.[1563] On February 17, it was finally agreed that the Maher-Fitzsimmons fight would take place on February 21, but all of the ancillary matches, including the Barry-Murphy match, were called off.

With all the spectators already leaving town, it had become increasingly difficult to generate enough money to pay what had been promised to the fighters, and it was cheaper for the promoters to simply pay forfeit money rather than to spend more for the fights.[1564] During the next few days the fighters, sportswriters, and fans began to leave Texas.

On the evening of February 17, Sullivan and Ryan and *The Wicklow Postman* production appeared before the remaining boxing figures and fans. Sullivan was "loaded to the gunnels" and was barely able to participate in the fake fight. Later that evening he was found lying prone on the sidewalk outside the Grand Central Hotel.

On another night during the week, Sullivan was so drunk he entered the wrong room in his hotel and tried to get into bed with a George Ade, a young Chicago sportswriter for the *Chicago Record.* George was a quiet young man from Brook, Indiana, and would later author the play *Sultan of Sulu.* Ade did not drink alcohol but was a friend of almost everyone in Chicago involved in sporting events.

Ade woke up when Sullivan entered his room and then watched as Sullivan started to take off his pants. He was muttering to himself unaware he was in the wrong room. Ade got up as Sullivan was about to pull back the covers and then guided him back to his own room where, like Lyndon Johnson many years later, Sullivan wanted to display his scar and the wound in his scalp. Ade said that Sullivan's head appeared to have been sewn up with piano wire.[1565]

While they were in El Paso, Sullivan and Ryan were standing in a bar getting their "sea legs on" when a gun fight erupted outside the bar's entrance. Fearing stray bullets Sullivan and Ryan hid together behind the ice box in the bar. Ryan had been wearing a tall silk hat, which he removed before peeking out from behind the ice box to see how things were going. Sullivan eying Ryan's silk hat said: "That's it! I knew it would come off. I was told for years they always shoot those kind of dicers full of holes. What in the hell did you wear it in Texas for?" Ryan believed for some time thereafter he was the cause of the shooting and from that time on during the tour he wore only a cap and got rid of his silk hat.

Fitzsimmons and Maher finally meet—for a few seconds

Fitz and Maher finally fought on February 21. A ring was erected inside canvas tarps that had been hung like a cloth fence designed to shield the ring from non-paying spectators. The site of the match was south of the Mexican border and across the Rio Grande near the small town of Langtry, Texas. The location was almost four hundred miles from El Paso. Davies was present for the match, and held a watch for Maher. Only 185 men attended at $20 a head. Others in this select group included Naughton, O'Rourke, Siler, Masterson, Hopkins, Buffalo Bill Cody, Floto, and Sheedy. After all the effort associated with making this fight, it ended quickly with Fitz knocking out Maher in the first round so that the whites of Maher's eyes were the only thing showing from his blinkers.[1566]

A prefight argument between the two fighters involved the use of a kinetoscope. This was another early effort to capture a prizefight on film. This device had been invented by Thomas Edison and William Dickson in 1891. Edison's company had made a 37 second film of an indoor staged match between Mike Leonard and Jack Cushing in 1894. Because the Maher-Fitz match took place outside and lasted such a short time, the efforts to put the contest on film failed. Reports said that if a film had been successfully produced it would have been worth $500,000.[1567]

The Wicklow Postman troupe did not leave El Paso until February 19. Although most of the sports had left town, the production had no scheduled dates because they had intended to be working in El Paso. Sullivan refused to leave because he was having too much fun. When the production company finally hit the road it first went north to Albuquerque and left Davies behind to act as a timekeeper at the fight.[1568] After Albuquerque the company went west and appeared at the Phoenix Opera House on February 22, 1896. The next day the *Arizona Republican* noted that Sullivan had aged a great deal over the last few years. Davies finally caught up with the rest of the company in Los Angeles, which was their stop after Phoenix. From Los Angeles the company worked its way north through California toward San Francisco.[1569]

Davies probably did not intend to supervise the Sullivan-Ryan tour. While in El Paso the told the *San Francisco Call* he intended to return to New York in April, when he and Sullivan would meet with O'Rourke with the idea of forming a national sporting league.[1570] The Parson undoubtedly wanted Glickauf to travel with the production. However, the experiences of Sullivan falling off the train in Illinois and his continued dissipation and drunkenness including the several incidents in El Paso made it apparent that Davies would need to personally manage the situation. In addition, when he decided to go with Sullivan and Ryan, Davies was under the impression that Choynski was out of commission for four or five months because of his ear problems and that may have played a part in his thought process.

As the production continued its West Coast swing, it was financially successful, which undoubtedly made it difficult to leave the tour. The decision to travel and stay with Sullivan and Ryan had consequences with the fighters that Davies managed because they reasonably expected their manager's personal attention. Davies had made a choice and continued traveling with *The Wicklow Postman*.

The troupe was in Sacramento on March 6, San Jose on March 7, and San Francisco on March 9.[1571] The *San Francisco Call* on March 7 carried a long article about Davies' arrival:

> "Parson" Charles E. Davies arrived in San Francisco yesterday and was immediately surrounded by a host of friends and old admirers of his interest in the "manly art." His last visit to this City was three years ago, when he took Peter Jackson the colored pugilist, round the country in "Uncle Tom's Cabin." This time he is the manager of John L. Sullivan and Paddy Ryan, who will appear next week in "The Wicklow Postman," at the Columbia. Sullivan is expected to arrive here Sunday afternoon.

Davies said that Sullivan had met Ira D. Sankey, a famous gospel singer, on the train near Sacramento and Sankey had told Sullivan, "You're a good man Mr. Sullivan, people like you. John, leave the bottle alone."

Davies said he had Choynski at home in Chicago with his wife: "If all the boxers were like Joe they would be an honor to the profession. I may make a match between him and Maher on my return."[1572]

The company appeared at the Columbia Theater on March 10, 11, 12, and 13. The Dry-good's Men's Association of San Francisco contracted with the production company to assist with a benefit for charity. Anyone purchasing tickets through that association could attend any performance during the four-day run at the Columbia. The *San Francisco Call* wrote that the theater was filled only enough to satisfy the management and that there was considerable seating room to spare. However, a large crowd of people waited outside on Powell Street to catch a glimpse of the former champion. When Davies introduced Sullivan each evening, he was greeted by cheer after cheer from the audience. As Sullivan waddled to the front of the stage, he was met again with cheers that could be heard outside on the street. He was said to weigh 277 pounds at this time.[1573]

Sullivan was drinking heavily throughout *The Wicklow Postman* tour. Davies warned John L. to take better care of his health because he seemed to be in the early stages of dropsy. The term *dropsy* was used to describe the accumulation of fluid in a person's lower legs and feet. This edema was generally linked to congestive heart failure and the inability of the person's heart to circulate blood sufficiently to prevent the edema. Sullivan's knee was swollen, and he was scheduled for an examination while he was in San Francisco, but he denied he had any form of dropsy and said that the never felt better in his life.[1574]

Charles E. "Parson" Davies as depicted in a drawing from the* San Francisco Call *on March 7, 1896, in San Francisco

While they were in San Francisco, a young fighter named Tom Sharkey met Alex Greggains in an eight-round match for charity at the Bush Street Theater. The match was called a draw, but Sharkey was a fresh face and held in high regard on the Pacific coast.[1575] Davies saw this match, and then arranged for a Sharkey-Choynski match by substituting Sharkey for Greggains as Choynski's opponent. The original articles of agreement included a paragraph that required Choynski to stop Greggains in eight rounds. This provision was not changed when Sharkey's name was substituted for Greggains.[1576] Davies wired Choynski telling him that Sharkey was a "dangerous man," "strong as a carthorse," and game.[1577] Choynski wired back that he was satisfied with the agreement as written.[1578]

After the cancellation of the Barry-Murphy contest, Barry returned to Chicago and began teaching boxing in a gymnasium on Chicago's North Side. While illustrating a punch with one of his students, he broke his hand and was put out of commission for several months.

Although in California with Sullivan and Ryan, Davies had scheduled a six-round match between Choynski and Kid McCoy at the Grand Central Palace in New York for March 21.[1579] The match was part of a boxing tournament including other six-round matches between Jimmy Handler and Joe Harman, Skelly and Jack Downey, and Solly Smith and Godfrey Burnett. Only a few weeks earlier McCoy had surprised the sporting world by knocking out Ryan in the fifteenth round of their fight at the Empire Athletic Club in Maspeth, New York.[1580] For Choynski, this was a quick recovery from a couple of broken ribs and an ear problem that was thought to be so serious that it would keep him out of the ring for four to five months.

On the evening of fight, after several preliminary bouts, the featured Choynski-McCoy match was announced, but the police immediately notified the managers that both the fighters would be arrested if they did anything more than spar. The crowd jeered and hissed as the two fighters began tapping one another. The fighters finally stopped sparring and Choynski stepped to the front of the stage and told the audience that the situation was not McCoy's fault and the crowd quieted down. The two men gave up the farce after three rounds. After this debacle Choynski left New York and went to Frisco for the scheduled six-round match with Sharkey. Davies was on the West Coast with Sullivan and Ryan.[1581]

Tom Sharkey in 1906 – Photograph of the Chicago History Museum

Barry was out of commission and after defeating Hall, Choynski was ill for several weeks.[1582] Moreover, Choynski's return to the ring to meet McCoy was a failure. Davies was on the road with Sullivan and Ryan and would not be back until mid-June. Matters did not seem to be going that well when a ray of sunshine appeared.

In April, New York passed the Horton law, which made it legal to hold sparring exhibitions conducted by a domestic incorporated athletic association in a building leased by that association for athletic purposes. In addition, the building had to be leased for at least one year, or it had to be owned and occupied by such the association. The fighters had to use gloves of not less than five ounces. The law opened the door in New York for legal matches without police interference and breathed life into clubs like the Coney Island Athletic Association. In addition, newly organized clubs sprang up like mushroom in the woods after a heavy rain and places where fights had previously been held in back rooms began to assume a respectable visage.[1583]

On April 16, Choynski and Davies were at San Francisco for Joe's match with Sharkey. Sharkey managed to last the eight rounds and was given the decision. This outcome was generally considered crooked. Sharkey hit Choynski with a low blow in the first round, and the police stopped the match. Joe was offered the match, but refused to accept. After twenty minutes he resumed the fight and was the aggressor throughout.

Choynski knocked Sharkey down multiple times and repeatedly drove him to the ropes. At one point, with Sharkey on the ropes Choynski landed a left on the Sailor's jaw and knocked Tom through the ropes. In the last round Sharkey fell and clinched a number of times in order to avoid punishment. He was almost out when the round ended, and the call of time saved him. Nevertheless, the referee awarded Sharkey the match because he lasted the eight rounds. This was one of several fights in 1896 in which it appeared that the referee had been fixed. The fight did not damage Choynski's reputation because the result was widely considered a put up job. Such fixed fights were potentially damaging to the whole business of boxing.[1584]

Mercifully, *The Wicklow Postman* draws to a close

After touring through California, *The Wicklow Postman* started back east. It is difficult to trace the route of the return trip. The troupe was in Butte and closed there on Wednesday, April 15. Sullivan was drunk and got into a dust up with Ryan and an innocent local man whose beard seemed to offend the former champion.[1585] They were in Brainerd on April 21 and at Ironwood in the Upper Peninsula of Michigan on April 27, and this suggests that they probably followed the northern railroad route through such towns as Ogden, Butte, Brainerd, Duluth, and Superior, Wisconsin, and then on to Ironwood. From Ironwood the troupe traveled south and then east. An article in the *St. Paul Daily Globe* on April 30 said that Sullivan had stayed there on April 29 after appearances in Duluth and La Crosse, Wisconsin.

On May 4, 5, and 6, 1896, the play was offered at the Grand in St. Paul with a matinee on Wednesday the sixth. On May 11, 12, and 13, the production was at the Bijou in St. Paul giving two performances each night.[1588] By May 16 Davies, Sullivan, Ryan, and company were at the Temple Theater in Alton, near St. Louis.[1589]

On May 24, the troupe was in Kansas City and then on June 1 and 2 at Boyd's Theater in Omaha, where the local paper reported that "from start to finish" it was well worth seeing.[1590] The production then moved on to Sioux City, Iowa, on June 3, to Des Moines, where it was presented at Foster's Theater on June 4 and 5, and then to Moline, Illinois.[1591] In Sioux City, Sullivan stayed in Room No. 57 at the Garretson Hotel, the same room that Jackson had occupied in 1893 when traveling with *Uncle Tom's Cabin*.[1592]

The *Davenport Daily Leader* reported on Sullivan's night in Moline:

> John L. Sullivan visited Moline last Friday night with the Wicklow Postman company and treated the city to one of his old time genuine drunks. From the time he struck the city until he left Saturday morning for Joliet excepting the time he was at the Auditorium and while he was asleep there was very little time that he wasn't swilling down beer at the Keator hotel saloon and is said to have left quite a little account there unpaid.
>
> Once during the afternoon Perry Merryman got the three renowned sports, Sullivan, Paddy Ryan and Parson Davies into a carriage and took them up to the Pump company and showed them the Westaway punching bag. As soon as they returned John L. was the first to alight from the carriage and he made straight for some liquid refreshments. During the afternoon and also in the evening John used language that was strange to the ears of Moline people, but it is needless to say that no Moline policeman particularly cared for the job of making an arrest, although we have some able officers who could have done a good job of it if it had seemed expedient.
>
> The Auditorium wasn't overcrowded, at the production of the Wicklow Postman and during the performance John occupied a place behind the scenes and consoled himself with a bottle. Sullivan made his appearance upon the stage with Paddy Ryan at the close of the play in a three round friendly match in which the principal part of the match depended on Paddy Ryan. Ryan would hit Sullivan with his right hand and catch him with his left in such a manner that few in the audience were on to the racket. The company left early Saturday morning for Joliet.[1593]

The play finished with a one-night-stand at the Haymarket in Chicago on June, 7. The theater troupe stayed at the Tremont Hotel in Chicago. Sullivan was interviewed there and was "in a state of comparative sobriety."[1594]

The entire thing wound up on June 13 in Pittsburgh, where the troupe was disbanded. A wire service article commented: "Five nights out of six, however, the ex-champion of the world has been so much under the influence of the ardent that the bout has been little more than a farce, calculated to bring out groans, hisses and ironical ejaculations from the audience rather than applause."[1595]

A few years after *The Wicklow Postman* tour under the management of Davies concluded, reports said that Sullivan netted $13,000 for his efforts during the run. As late as 1957 the *Hammond Times* claimed that Sullivan earned $85,900 on this tour, but this seems to be an implausible number.[1596] Whatever Sullivan actually earned, by the end of the tour he was said to be dead broke. There was talk of setting him up in the saloon business in Chicago, but it did not take any definite shape. Paddy Ryan, on the contrary, had been frugal and there was "no immediate prospect of the wolf being at his door." Davies' second tour with a full-theater company and two famous heavyweight fighters was over.

Choynski goes it alone

In late June, Davies posted $3,000 as a guarantee for Choynski-Sharkey rematch. He was also negotiating with O'Rourke to have Choynski meet either "Denver Ed" Smith or Maher in a limited round bout at Madison Square Garden and talking with Hopkins about a Choynski-Creedon match.[1597] On July 1, it was learned that Maher's manager had matched him to fight Choynski before the National Sporting Club of San Francisco for an eight-round fight and a purse of $6,000 with the contest to take place on August 3.[1598]

Six days later, Choynski left to go into training for his match, but before he left, he told the press that Davies would have no finger in his match with Maher. Choynski said: "I have no complaint to make against Davies, but I want to make a few matches for myself and not have to split the money with anybody if I win. I simply mention this because I saw in one of the papers that Davies was expected in San Francisco shortly to attend to my end of the arrangements. I am looking after my own business this time, and it was a mistake to suppose that the Parson was coming here to direct me."[1599]

The *Cedar Rapids Evening Gazette* reported that when asked about Choynski's decision Davies said: "I have known Joe a long time and have always found him upright and conscientious in every way. If he can better himself no one wishes him more success than I do."[1600]

It is probable that Choynski decision to go it alone was motivated by several factors. After *Uncle Tom's Cabin* had folded its tent Joe did not have steady income but was simply fighting for a living. He was a married man and probably felt he could not afford to give up half of his income to a manager. In addition, his manager had been gone for six months with the two fat, old has-been heavyweights. Finally, with new clubs opening in New York under the Horton law Choynski may have felt that it would be easier for individual fighters to make matches for themselves.

As Choynski was leaving for California, Hopkins introduced the Vitascope to Chicago. The Vitascope was Edison's most recent invention. He had finally developed a machine that could deliver a quality film product. The Vitascope opened in Chicago on July 5 at Hopkins' South Side Theater, where it was used in conjunction with the standard vaudeville shows for twenty consecutive weeks. This was the beginning of the end for vaudeville as it was steadily replaced by motion pictures.

The *Chicago Tribune* explained that the Vitascope was a combination of "electrical forces" that reproduced actual occurrences from real life that were distinct and accurate in detail. The pictures were shown on a canvas screen set up on the stage of a theater. "At first focus the view suggests the stereopticon, but in an instant it is given life, motion, and coloring. Figures begin to move symmetrically, and the bustle of activity of real life are before the observer." [1601]

The value of the Vitascope became apparent quickly. Just three weeks after the Vitascope opened, Hopkins said that in the prior week the volume of attendance and receipts was the heaviest ever known in the ten-twenty-thirty style of entertainment in the country.[1602] The phrase "ten-thirty style of entertainment" refers to admission prices that ranged between ten and thirty cents. Later in the summer the Hopkins sabotaged the opposition. The Great Northern Roof Garden attempted to offer a show using the Phantoscope. Hopkins had one of his electricians operate the machine and make sure that it didn't work.

Choynski soon found out that trying to arrange a match without a manger was no easy task. Maher's manager had trouble obtaining a license for the match in California, and Maher said that if the proposed fight was not concluded soon, he was going back East.[1603] Soon after these events stories said that the Maher-Choynski match might be moved from California to New York in a new club that might be opened there. Choynski's interests might be protected by his friends in San Francisco; however, if the match was moved to New York, he could be hung out to dry.

It was learned later that Maher wanted out of a fight in San Francisco because Corbett had interfered. Corbett had gone to Maher and told him that Choynski was a close friend of Guntz and there would be no way Maher would be given fair treatment on the West Coast. Maher believed him and refused to fight there.[1604] On July 29, Joe and Maher met at the Baldwin Hotel to talk about the prospects for a fight. Ed Greaney was present as a friend of Joe's but not as his manager. Maher's manager said that there was a good prospect for holding the fight in New York at a new club being organized there.[1605]

The following day, according to the *St. Paul Globe*, Davies participated in a meeting of prominent sporting men held in New York. to discuss the formation of the American Sporting Protective League which was intended to promote professional athletics by taking in representatives of every prominent sporting club in the United States.[1606] It seems probable that the group also talked about more practical business, including how to best map out Sharkey's future.

Sharkey comes to Chicago

Sharkey arrived in Chicago on July 31, traveling there from Butte. Davies returned to the Chicago from the East on August 1, and it seems apparent he came back to meet with Sharkey and his manager. Subsequent events suggest that during the first week of August Davies, Sharkey, and Tom's manager mapped out Tom's activities for the next two months. The sequence of events was complicated, but it is typical of the energy and planning that Parson Davies devoted to his business.[1607]

On August 2, Armstrong fought Will Mayo on Kimbal's Island near Davenport. Creedon acted as referee for this fight. The fight was for a winner-take-all $400 purse, and Armstrong knocked out Mayo in the second round. At the end of the fight, Armstrong took up a collection for Mayo to help pay his way back to Chicago.[1608]

When Davies returned to Chicago on August 1 he was asked about the impact of losing Choynski. He told the *Chicago Tribune*, "I still have Bob Armstrong, who defeated Will Mayo so decisively last Sunday, and will match him against this man [Jim] Jeffries as soon as he reaches town."[1609] Tommy Ryan was gone. Barry was on the shelf, Choynski was on his own, but Davies still had big Bob Armstrong under his management.

"This man Jeffries" who Davies mentioned in August was another young heavyweight who had started making a name. James Jeffries was born on April 15, 1875 at Carroll, Ohio. In August, he had only four or five professional fights under his belt. Three of those fights had taken place in Los Angeles and one in San Francisco, but his reputation was already spreading across the county. Both Armstrong and Jeffries were big heavyweights, and there were few others at the time that would match up physically with either of them.

Soon after Choynski ended his relationship with Davies, the Parson began booking business more rapidly than ever. He picked up the management of the Chicago featherweight Tommy White and arranged a match with Eddie Santry. Originally scheduled for New York, that match took place in Lemont, Illinois, where White knocked out Santry in eight rounds.[1610] This match was followed by the arrests of White and Santry by Lemont police.[1611]

On August 3, Sharkey left Chicago for Mt. Clemens to train for a match with Corbett. Davies also left Chicago, but he went to New York and met with O'Rourke. As part of their business they matched Tommy White to meet Dixon in New York for the featherweight championship of the world at the newly organized Broadway Athletic Club, but they were clearly also discussing Sharkey and how to market him in Chicago and New York.[1612]

Davies with O'Rourke's help was planning a mammoth production that would include both Sharkey and Sullivan in New York at the end of August.[1613]

Davies also booked Sharkey's appearances in Chicago before he moved on to the big New York production. Sharkey was to be paid $1,200 for a week's work in Chicago in conjunction with a "high class vaudeville company." It was originally planned that Sharkey would appear at the Haymarket Theater, beginning Sunday, August 23. As part of his appearance in Chicago, Sharkey and his trainer Needham put on a three-round sparring exhibition.[1614]

After meeting with O'Rourke, Davies went to Mt. Clemens to meet with Sharkey and his manager to conclude the arrangements for the Chicago and New York performances before returning to Chicago on August 13 so he could leave with a troupe of fighters for a tour of Indiana.[1615] The day after booking Sharkey, Davies also announced he was taking an athletic combination on a week-long tour through Indiana with appearances at Richmond, Elwood, Fort Wayne, Logansport, and Dayton, Ohio. That combination included Tracy, Armstrong, White, Murphy, and Bertrand. Finally, Davies announced that Sullivan had dried himself out, walked the straight and narrow, and he was going to resume John L's management. At the conclusion of this tour John L. would come to New York to spar with Sharkey.[1616]

Sullivan gets stuck in a window

On Saturday, August 22, Davies' Boxing Carnival featuring Sullivan was presented at the Princess Rink in Fort Wayne.[1617] The prior evening the combination had appeared at Logansport. The bill that night included Creedon sparring with Tracy, Armstrong sparring with Tom Chandler, Murphy and White, and then White and Bertrand. All matches were three rounds, and the price of a ticket was fifty cents. Only a small crowd saw the show at Fort Wayne, but it was pleased with the performances. The *Fort Wayne News* reported that the combination had made a week's tour of Indiana and played all over to losing business. It noted that the backer of the show was a man from Richmond who settled his bills in Fort Wayne at fifty cents on the dollar.[1618]

Three years later the *Post Dispatch* carried an account of one night on this Indiana sojourn. The newspaper's story must have been provided by Davies:

> The troupe reached Kokomo and it was discovered that the only place available for their purposes was the skating rink. The building was a large one and had but one drawback—there was no dressing room where the athletes could prepare for their respective exhibitions. Finally it was decided to dress in the engine room of the fire hall which stood next door. In order to obviate the disagreeable method of walking through the street to the entrance of the rink it was necessary to crawl through the upper window of the rink, which opened into the fire hall, thence gaining the upper gallery and so down to the stage.

> Wrestlers McBride and Billy Murphy were the first to essay the task. Clad in their tights, they slipped through easily. Then came Joe Bertrand, who also passed without any difficulty. Tommy White's attenuated carcass slid through with delightful ease, and Australian Tom Tracey followed him. Matters looked more serious when Dan Creedon's broad shoulders filled the narrow opening but he made it all right. Tom Chandler and Bob Armstrong squeezed through with the aid of a few choice oaths. Sullivan had not finished dressing.
>
> The show was proceeding merrily, when the audience and exhibitors were startled by the prolonged, hoarse bellowing of a voice which called down execrations upon the heads of everyone in general and the Davies' combination in particular. Armstrong and Creedon rushed up to find half-way in the window, the portly form of John L., clad in full ring costume.
>
> The twain laid hold of John's arms and pulled vigorously, but their attempts to release him by main force only brought forth fresh howls of rage from the veteran gladiator. He was there for "keeps" and could not be moved an inch backward or forward. Armstrong rushed down and communicated the startling news to Davies. The Parson rose to the occasion. Procuring an ax he rushed to the rescue and after half the window sash had been chopped away John L. was released from the pillory and waddled indignantly to the stage.[1619]

Sharkey did not return to Chicago from Mt. Clemens until August 26 and then appeared at the Alhambra on Chicago's south side.[1620] Davies was so busy he asked O'Rourke to make Sharkey's arrangements on the East Coast. Davies and O'Rourke then arranged another fight for White with "Dal" Hawkins as a preliminary match to Sharkey's appearance at Madison Square Garden.

Davies took Sullivan, Tracy, Creedon, and Armstrong to New York to be part of Sharkey's introduction.[1621] In addition, Armstrong and O'Donnell were scheduled to give a four-round exhibition, and Sullivan himself agreed to spar a few rounds with Sharkey. Learning of all of this Choynski must have wondered why he had pulled out of his arrangement with Davies. If he had stayed with Davies the match with Maher would have gone forward in California and Joe would have had a big role in this big New York production.

The New York production featuring Sharkey took place on August 31 at the Garden.[1622] The culmination of the night was the Sullivan-Sharkey set-to. Many fans thought that Sharkey was a natural bare-knuckle fighter and considered him a modern-day Sullivan. Consequently, an exhibition between the two brawlers from different generations was of great interest.

Some stories about that evening say that Sullivan weighed at least three hundred pounds for their encounter. He was dressed in black breeches and was naked above the waist, which must have been quite a sight. Sharkey wore green trunks fastened with a red, white, and blue scarf. At the start of their exhibition Sharkey went into his trademark crouch and danced in on Sullivan, bobbing and weaving as was his custom. He then led at Sullivan's head and Sullivan gave him a return chop with his left, which seemed to surprise Sharkey. Tom then moved away as if to size up the situation, and as he moved backward on his toes, Sullivan followed quickly and tapped Sharkey once again. Sharkey hit back, and then Sullivan hit Tom often and came away with a big grin on his face.

Accounts of their exhibition said that Sullivan hit Sharkey five times for every time that Tom hit Sullivan. After the fight Sharkey said that Sullivan was a fat old man, and he himself was simply taking it easy. Tom said that had he done anything else but play around gently with Sullivan, he would have been chased out to the Garden.[1623]

By September 21, Choynski was back with Davies. Apparently Joe had learned that that it was not so easy to make money in the fight game without a manager.[1624] Davies then went to New York for the White-Dixon championship match on September 25 at O'Rourke's new club, and Choynski went back to Cincinnati. On the evening of the White-Dixon fight, Davies was in White's corner. The fight went the distance and was declared a draw. The *Brooklyn Eagle* said that Dixon never had such a fight in his life as he was given by White. There was a huge galaxy of stars present as spectators, including both Corbett and Sharkey. While he was in New York, Davies arranged a match for Choynski with Maher.[1625]

Tommy White jumps ship

A few days after the White-Dixon match, Davies and White returned to Chicago, but the two had already terminated their brief business relationship. While he managed White, Davies had arranged a championship fight, but White was not very grateful for being given that opportunity. The reasons for their split were discussed in several newspaper articles.

On Saturday afternoon September 26, Davies and White met to divide the net receipts of White's match with Dixon. White said that when they met, Davies handed him $472 as White's share of the purse and then kept the same amount for himself. An equal division of the net proceeds of a match was the typical split at the time between a manager and a fighter.

When Davies kept $472 White said that he nearly fainted, then he departed without saying a word. Later White said: "That settles me with managers in future. When the manager receives as much money for saying a few words in regard to a match as the man does who does the boxing, then it's time to quit them."

White said that managers were too expensive and that Davies would never again get the chance to make matches for him. Tommy said he felt capable of making matches for himself and transacting his own business. When Davies was asked about White's comments, he said: "I wouldn't walk ten feet with a pug who would refuse to split his money with me."[1626]

In fact, an equal division between Davies and the fighters he managed was his practice. Floto worked as Davies' assistant for several years and was one of a small number of people who was in a position to know about the Parson's business practices.

In January 1907, he told the *Denver Post* that "Parson Davies would never think of handling a fighter for less than 50 percent of his earnings. He received that amount from Jackson when Jackson was champion of the world. And here are a few others: Charlie Mitchell and Jack Burke and Frank Glover and Barry all gave Davies 50 percent of their winnings."

Davies' practice was common. Floto reported that O'Rourke always shared and shared alike with George Dixon and Joe Walcott and that George Lavingne did the same with Fitzpatrick.

White continued to complain about the split from his fight with Dixon. After he reached Chicago, White told the *Chicago Tribune* that the venue had been sold out and that there were between four and five thousand men present. He recalled that seats had been sold at prices ranging from one to five dollars.

"I expected my share would be considerably larger," he said. [1627] The hard feelings between White and Davies festered for many years after 1896.

In 1920, almost twenty-five years later, Tommy White told the *Racine Journal News*: "I never had a manager but one. I did allow Parson Davies to call himself my manager for a short time, but I did this only because I could not get bouts any other way. But Davies did a lot of things I did not like. He put everything on a cold business basis, and I believe many times prevented me from advancing in my work positively the Bolshevik of the sport. Unless they are curbed the game will hit the rocks. It cannot last under such conditions."[1628]

Similar comments were made about Davies by Tommy Ryan in 1910, many years after he moved away from Chicago to Syracuse and fifteen years after he ended his business relationship with Davies. Ryan told the *Syracuse Post Standard*:

> Then he staggered me with the claim that I owed him $1,800. I couldn't see it and asked him for particulars. I finally gave him $200, though I never owed it. Afterward I met Tommy West in New York and I had a guarantee of $2,500, win or lose. I heard luckily, that a scheme was on foot by which Davies was to grab the money. A deputy sheriff was to be on hand as the club's manager hand the cash to me. It was supposed to be in settlement of that mythical account of Davies', which I never owed him anyway, but for which I had paid him $200 to get rid of the bother. Well, I was primed for Mister Smarty, and I took along down to the fight a young Syracuse man, now a leading insurance dealer here had a right good friend of mine. And when I got down there I said to the club manager: "That money goes into the hands of my friend

here before I step into the ring." Did it go? Sure it went. What could he do? And Davies never worked me out of another cent.[1629]

Davies matches Choynski and Maher

Although the Choynski-Maher match in California fell through, with Davies' assistance it was arranged for New York. The *St. Paul Globe* reported on November 1 that Davies had invented a board game. The game used a board with two sets of railroad tracks. Little wooden blocks represented two railroad trains that had to be moved around on the board to the best advantage using switches that were placed at strategic points on the board.[1630]

On November 14, Davies and Choynski arrived at the Colonnade Hotel, near the Broadway Athletic Club's facilities. Davies told the press that Joe had been in training for three weeks in Palos, Illinois, under the supervision of Barry and Al Schrosvee. The Choynski-Maher match was described as the best match made in New York that fall.[1631] The final agreement for the Maher-Choynski match called for a six-round fight to be held at O'Rourke's Broadway Athletic Club.[1632] Tickets were expensive, ranging between three and five dollars each depending on location.

Davies and Teddy Roosevelt talk prizefighting

One of the men in attendance that night was Theodore Roosevelt, then the President of the New York Police Board and a long-time boxing fan. T.R. was also a long-time admirer of Parson Davies. Roosevelt occupied a box seat close to the ring. He told the press that evening: "Boxing is a manly sport, and I can see no good reason why the contests between well-trained and evenly matched men should not be conducted in this city. I think the Maher and Choynski contest was a grand struggle and I could find nothing brutal in it. Both were well trained athletes and did not display the slightest particle of blood or bruises until the climax came."[1633]

In January 1900, Davies provided insight to his interaction with Roosevelt on that evening. His comments were published in the *Chicago Tribune* on January 14, 1900. He explained he and O'Rourke met with Roosevelt when he was police commissioner. Their purpose was to determine why or on what authority Inspector Cartwright of the city's police force had stopped the Dixon-Leonard contest that was to have taken place at the Academy of Music.

Charlie said Roosevelt had expressed "without hesitation" his belief and conviction that good clean boxing was a healthy thing and should be promoted. He told Davies and O'Rourke that he had attended the Sullivan-Mitchell match at the Garden. He thought that the police had acted correctly in stopping that match because if the fight had "been extended beyond the limit it was permitted to reach it might have bordered on the brutal." Roosevelt also thought that the police should refrain from entering the ring and arresting the contestants.[1634]

Maher was the betting favorite at odds of 10-6 and came into the ring at 173 pounds, and Choynski at 167. When the bell rang for the final round, both men were in good condition. Choynski had the best of the fight throughout the first five rounds. He rushed Maher and forced him to the ropes in heavy work by both fighters. He then staggered Peter with a blow on his chin. Maher squared himself and retaliated by slugging Joe until he dropped to the floor. Choynski was up immediately, but knocked down once again. He stayed down several seconds but then got up again at which point Maher delivered a knock-out blow. After he was counted out, Joe recovered quickly and was able to walk to his dressing room without assistance.

This match helped restore some of Maher's lost credibility and hurt Joe's standing as a top contender. After the fight, Davies said that Choynski was a wonderful fighter but had failed to follow instructions. He said: "We told him not to mix it up with Maher, but to keep away and jab Peter with his left in the face and wind. He lost his head, however, and the result was that Maher crossed him with his right and Joe went out. He did a foolish thing when he mixed it up with a strong two-handed fighter like Maher."[1635]

Nine days after the Choynski-Maher match, Armstrong fought Slavin before the Union Park Athletic Club in New York. This match had also been arranged by Davies and became one of Armstrong's finest hours. At this point Slavin still had a name, but was on the down side of his career. He had lost to Hall in London, to Maher in New York, and to Steve O'Donnell and was no longer fighting with the top heavyweights. A reported two thousand spectators were in attendance for the match. In the fourth round of the fight Armstrong put Slavin on the floor with three left jabs on Slavin's face. Then he caught Slavin with a hard right and pounded him so hard that Slavin finally threw up his hands and quit after two minutes and fifty-six seconds of that round.[1636]

Davies stayed in New York with Armstrong, and on December 14 they were part of another old-timers production at the Broadway Athletic Club. The entertainment that evening featured Jem Mace, the 65-year-old ex-champion heavyweight, who sparred six rounds with Mike Donovan. Donovan was only 49 years old.

Choynski wrote of these two men in 1927, "Mike Donovan was the greatest of all boxing instructors in America, while Mace was undoubtedly the greatest boxing teacher of all time, as well as perhaps the most perfect boxer."

Sullivan attended the performances and was welcomed with warm applause. Davies was the honorary referee for the Mace-Donovan match. Earlier in the evening Armstrong put on a three-round exhibition with Tommy Kelly, a lightweight fighter from Hoboken, New Jersey.[1637]

In 1927, Choynski wrote that after their performance Mace received $2,000 as his share of the proceeds with tears of gratitude; however, Donovan's attitude was not so grateful. Mike was given his share along with a record of showing receipts and disbursements. He then wanted to know what the disbursements were for and was sore that money was taken out for the costs of the production.[1638] This seems to have been the attitude of many fighters who thought that things like travel expenses, theater rentals, advertisement, ticket takers, security, and printing expenses were somehow provided for free.

Corbett and Fitzsimmons are matched

On December 17, Davies was one of the men present at the offices of the *Police Gazette* for a meeting with James "Jaw" Corbett (as some critics were referring to him) to attempt to arrange a Corbett-Fitzsimmons fight. In order to avoid charges of conspiring to arrange a prize fight in the state of New York, the entire crowd took a ferryboat to Jersey City and went to Taylor's Hotel, where a large room was rented for all those present to witness the discussions. The movement to New Jersey probably reminded Davies of his meeting in Canada with Sullivan to arrange the championship fight with Kilrain.

When Corbett agreed to the terms for a match, a telegram was sent to Fitz in San Francisco. Bob told the press on the West Coast: "I have not signed articles of agreement for a fight with Corbett, but I expect them to arrive any day now. As soon as they get here I will sign them. I am ready to meet Corbett for any amount. I have $20,000 to put up on the side. I understand that the articles call for a meeting on March 17. I am ready to fight at any time, any place, and for any amount."[1639]

Davies continued to promote Armstrong on the East Coast in an attempt to impress others with the talent of his big heavyweight. On December 21, Bob was matched with Charley Strong of Newark. Once again their match was held at O'Rourke's Broadway Athletic Club. Strong was described before their match as "at best a second rate fighter." They were to meet in a twenty-round contest.

Davies told the press he saw a great future for Armstrong and that eventually Bob had the chance of surpassing Jackson. Through Davies' efforts this match was styled as for the title of black heavyweight champion. The claim was that Jackson had secured that black heavyweight championship title eight years earlier by knocking out Godfrey in nineteen rounds. However, Jackson had forfeited the title by failing to defend it. By some sort of fiat this Armstrong's match was supposed to fill the lapsed title.[1640] Davies pointed out that big Bob was only twenty-two years old, but despite his tender years, the Parson was willing to back him against Maher or O'Donnell. Armstrong was six inches taller and twenty-five pounds heavier than Charley Strong. Choynski was in Bob's corner for the fight. Armstrong finally stopped Strong in the nineteenth round of their match but showed poorly. He was slow, and he showed little knowledge of scientific fighting.[1641]

After over a month in New York, Davies left for Pittsburgh. He had arranged a show for the evening of December 26. The two drawing cards for that evening were Choynski and Maher, who sparred three friendly rounds. Davies said he intended to remain in Pittsburgh for about one week to finalize a match between Barry and Sammy Kelly.[1642] For Davies the year 1896 came to an end in

Pittsburgh. On Saturday, January 2, 1897 Choynski boxed a local man named Frank Dwyer and defeated him in four rounds and a new year began.[1643]

The year 1896 had included a six-month tour through the West and Midwest with Sullivan and Ryan. That trip was punctuated by a stop for the Maher-Fitzsimmons heavyweight championship fight in Mexico and by the near death of Sullivan when he fell off the boarding platform of a moving train near Galva, Illinois. The Sullivan and Ryan tour was followed by six months of matchmaking, primarily in New York, made possible because of the passage of the Horton law. In almost all these endeavors Davies worked closely with O'Rourke, and he often used O'Rourke's Broadway Athletic Club as the venue for his fighters.

The Parson had signed and then lost Tommy White during the year. He had lost Barry to a broken hand, but at the end of the year the Davies was again actively promoting Barry. After working with Choynski from March 11, 1892, through mid-1896, Joe had tried it on his own, but then returned to Davies' management by September 1896. In addition, Davies was promoting Armstrong. Finally, by the end of the year Davies was once again representing Sullivan, albeit on a limited basis.

New York's Horton law improves the prospects for 1896

Because of the Horton law, the prospects for 1896 were bright. If fights could be made in New York, there was no reason to run off to remote venues such as the hills of Mexico. Finally, Teddy Roosevelt was the president of the Board of Police Commissioners, and he had a good opinion of both Davies and boxing.

The adoption of the Horton law and similar statutes in other states adopted after the enactment of the Horton law changed the landscape in prizefighting circles.[1644] Individual managers formed their own athletic clubs, where fights would be legally conducted. This took the fighters out of the theaters and multipurpose venues. In order to compete on a national scale it became important for managers to own or operate such clubs.

Another consequence of the Horton law was that traveling combinations that appeared with vaudeville shows became less necessary to financially support fighters. When it became clear that matches could be made in qualified New York athletic clubs on a regular basis, it was no longer necessary to travel around pretending to be part of vaudeville entertainment such as ball shooting, club swinging, acrobatics, and the like. These road trips had been a staple of Davies' success as a manager.

There was another factor that was changing the prizefighting landscape permanently. Methods had been developed that allowed prizefights to be captured on motion picture film. As this process was perfected the need for fighters to travel from big cities to small towns quickly disappeared. Instead, the film of a fight could be shown in local theaters and the price of admission could be shared with fighters with little cost to promoters, managers, or fighters. This too killed the traveling show format for prizefighters.

Davies' home base was Chicago, but Illinois had not adopted a law that allowed boxing clubs like those sanctioned in New York. Consequently, only with the right political circumstances could fights be held in Chicago in the old theater or armory-based format, but managers could not be sure that a fight would be allowed. The right political circumstances in Chicago meant that the mayor of Chicago had to be willing to allow licenses to issue for prizefights, and the proper aldermen and police officials had to be paid off so that they would not interfere with the proposed entertainment. In order for a manager to sponsor or promote fights in Chicago, he had to be prepared to pay off the correct politicians. In most cases the geography of the city was such that Coughlin and Kenna were the aldermen to be paid.

While he was in Pittsburgh, Davies had Barry, who was styled as the "premier bantamweight of the world," sparring against all comers at the World's Theater. Davies offered $100 to anyone who could stay four rounds with the hard-hitting Barry.

A month or so after this event Davies talked to the *Chicago Tribune* about Barry: "When in Pittsburgh I had a tournament for local boxers. Barry would stand in the aisle and when a good little fellow showed up and won his bout he would say, 'Say, boss, let me have a crack at him.'"[1645] Davies said that throughout the entire trip Barry would be sneaking off to work on a punching bag to spar with someone on the sly.

On Saturday evening, January 2, O'Rourke presented a match at the Broadway Athletic Club between two bantamweights, James Duffy of East Boston and George Justus. Dick Roche was the referee for this match.[1646] This was a ten-round bout that went the distance. Duffy had been fighting for five years and had many professional fights on his resume.

After the fight ended Duffy collapsed and was taken to Saint Vincent's Hospital. The next day a hospital spokesman said that Duffy had ruptured a blood vessel in his head during the fight with Justus and was dying. O'Rourke, Roche, and Justus were all arrested and arraigned in Jefferson Market Court on suspicion of homicide. At the preliminary hearing, a police inspector testified he had been present during the match and saw no blows struck that appeared to be hard enough to result in such an injury. Nevertheless, Magistrate Flammer held all three men on separate bonds of $2,000. Predictions were made that Duffy's death would be the death knell for pugilism in New York for some time to come. This would have had a substantial impact on Davies because he had promoted so many events at that club.

On January 4, James Duffy died. An autopsy was performed and physicians found no fracture of the skull. Trepanning of his skull (drilling a hole in the bone) disclosed a meningeal hemorrhage, which might have been caused by jarring his heart by the blow or by a fall in the ring. There were no bruises on the head or face, but there was a slight abrasion on the shoulder. The autopsy showed that Duffy was not strong and was afflicted with thickening of the muscles of the heart, and an inquest was scheduled.[1647]

The inquest was completed on January 7 and the coroner's jury issued a verdict "that James Duffy came to his death, on the 4th of January, 1897, in the St. Vincent hospital, by meningeal hemorrhage super-induced on January 2, 1897, at the Broadway Athletic club, by excitement following a boxing exhibition with George W. Justice and accelerated by hypertrophia [or enlargement] of the heart, and we exonerate from all blame the said club, Thomas O'Rourke, manager, Richard Roche, referee, and George W. Justice, principal."[1648] This of course was a great relief for everyone involved in prizefighting on the East Coast.

The biggest news of January was that Fitz signed the articles that had previously been signed by Corbett and witnessed by Davies. Their championship match would dominate the boxing news for the first part of 1897. In January, O'Rourke arranged a six-round match for Dixon with Australian Billy Murphy, fighting out of Cincinnati. Murphy's backer was Frank Marrow, who felt he had a new champion. Morrow bet Davies $1,000 that Murphy would defeat Dixon, but lost his money when Dixon knocked out Murphy in the fourth round of their match.[1649]

There was comparatively little published about Davies in early 1897. The *National Police Gazette* carried a report that Davies was trying to promote Armstrong and had posted a $1,000 forfeit for a match between Bob and any heavyweight including Maher, O'Donnell, or Sharkey. The *Gazette* reported that Davies had "taken quite a stand on the race question and believes that if there is to be a class distinction between pugilists there should be a championship match to decide who is entitled to the distinction of being the black champion. He thinks an Armstrong-Jackson match would draw very well in view of the fact he has received letters from England which tend to confirm the belief that the stories about Jackson have been grossly exaggerated."[1650]

About this time Armstrong married a woman named Henrietta, and this added another person to the equation when decisions were made about Bob's career.

Davies returned to the Broadway club with Barry on January 29. The contest that evening was between Barry and Sammy Kelly of New York. Roche, who had been arrested as the referee of the Duffy-Justus bantamweight fight, was also the referee for this match. The Barry-Kelly fight was well attended and went the full twenty rounds. Barry was knocked down in the fifth round and hung on to save himself. He recovered for the sixth round and knocked Kelly down in the twentieth round before Roche decided the match as a draw. After the match Davies said that Jimmy's trouble was he fought like Harry Gilmore, his teacher, and was fighting too open and dropping his right when he led with his left.[1651] This was the same style that cost Gilmore in his matches with Billy Myer. Davies said that Jimmy still had a lot to learn but always wanted to fight.

Three days after the Barry-Kelly fight another testimonial offered for Sullivan was announced. This whole bit was getting tiresome. The event was to take place on February 17 at the Arena, at the corner of Broad and Cherry streets, in Philadelphia. The central feature of this performance was a four-round go between Sullivan and Ryan.[1652] By this time they could do this stunt in their sleep.

After the Barry-Kelly fight but before the Sullivan testimonial, Davies went to Chicago to make plans for the Corbett-Fitzsimmons fight. It seemed clear that the heavyweight championship fight would be held at Carson City, Nevada, a city of three thousand five hundred citizens located a few miles from Lake Tahoe and east of the California-Nevada state line and on the main line of the Virginia and Truckee Railroad, which then connected at Reno with the Southern Pacific. It was the key link between East and West.

Davies began planning a fistic carnival of his own to be held just over the line from California, near enough to Carson City to attract the crowd that would be traveling to the heavyweight championship match. He hoped to have Maher, Sharkey, and Choynski there along with Barry as part of the production. At one point he discussed holding the event in Reno on March 15 and 16, the two days before the Corbett-Fitzsimmons fight. He thought he could secure a purse of $10,000 for the Maher-Sharkey fight if he could bring these two men to time. However, New York clubs were competing for a Sharkey-Maher match, and wanted it held on the East Coast. In addition, Davies had his brother Vere preparing a train excursion from Chicago to Carson City. At one point there were one thousand men that were to travel from Chicago to Carson City for the fight. Their Davies' special was in competition with other trains being arranged from Chicago by the referee for the match Siler and by Hogan, Houseman, and Joe Ryan.

Attempts to arrange a Maher-Sharkey match were not working out, and Davies' next tried to arrange a "Denver Ed" Smith-Choynski match to take place at Carson City on the same day as the Corbett-Fitzsimmons match. The basics of the match were agreed to by February 20, 1896, but the details were to be resolved in person on the East Coast.[1653] This match was moved back and rescheduled for New York. Davies also matched Barry to fight Jack Ward before the American Sporting Club of New York on March 1. Two days after the match was arranged, Davies announced he had matched Armstrong with a fighter known as "Muldoon's Thunderbolt" (a.k.a. Joe Butler) in Buffalo.[1654]

Barry met Ward on March 1 in New York. Davies, Choynski, Armstrong, and O'Rourke were all in Jimmy's corner that night. This match again went the full twenty rounds, but the decision was given to Barry, who had dominated the last seven rounds of the match. Then on March 6 the Armstrong-Butler match at the Broadway club took place before two thousand spectators. Armstrong slaughtered Butler. The fight was stopped in the sixth round after only forty-five seconds because Butler was staggering around the ring and "virtually out of service from a series of awful punches."[1655]

As soon as the Armstrong-Butler match ended, Davies returned to Chicago, but at ten p.m. on March 8 he left for appearances in Denver (March 11), Colorado Springs (March 12), and Victor and Cripple Creek, Colorado, where Barry, Armstrong, and Choynski were to appear to give a sparring exhibitions before they continued on to Carson City.[1656]

Davies, Barry, Choynski, and Armstrong then met Masterson in Salt Lake City, and then all of them went on to Ogden. They were all in Ogden most of the day on March 14, but Davies and Masterson left on the two thirty p.m. train for Carson City while the three fighters waited for the Davies' special and then went the rest of the way with the Chicago sporting crowd.[1657] Davies and Masterson would have reached Carson City around midnight on March 14. Davies had Armstrong along on the trip to spar with Choynski and with the expectation of making a match with Jim Jeffries and Barry in the hopes of matching him with a fighter named Anthony. Davies told the press he wanted to match Armstrong against the winner of Jeffries' April 9 match with Theodore Van Buskirk (the "Marysville Hercules"). Armstrong said he was also interested in a match with Steve O'Donnell.[1658]

The Davies' special heads to the big fight in record time

The Davies' special under the supervision of Vere Davies and Glickauf left Chicago at five thirty p.m. on Saturday, March 13. A delegation from the National Sporting Club of London had been added to those traveling. Other luminaries included Alf Kennedy, Billy Myer, Jere Dunne, O'Rourke, Sullivan, and a delegation from the Chicago board of trade.

The train, traveling on the Rock Island line, included three sleeping cars, a dining car, and a baggage car well-stocked with "wet goods."[1659] It passed through Davenport at ten thirty that night, when over seven thousand were on the local platform watching. Before Davenport the train had stopped briefly in the Illinois towns of Joliet, Morris, Bureau, Geneseo, and Rock Island. At Davenport, local people were permitted onto the train to catch a glimpse of the famous sports on board. W. H. Harrison, a personal friend of Glickauf who lived in Davenport boarded to shake hands with his friend, and then had to leave almost immediately because the train was pulling out of the station.

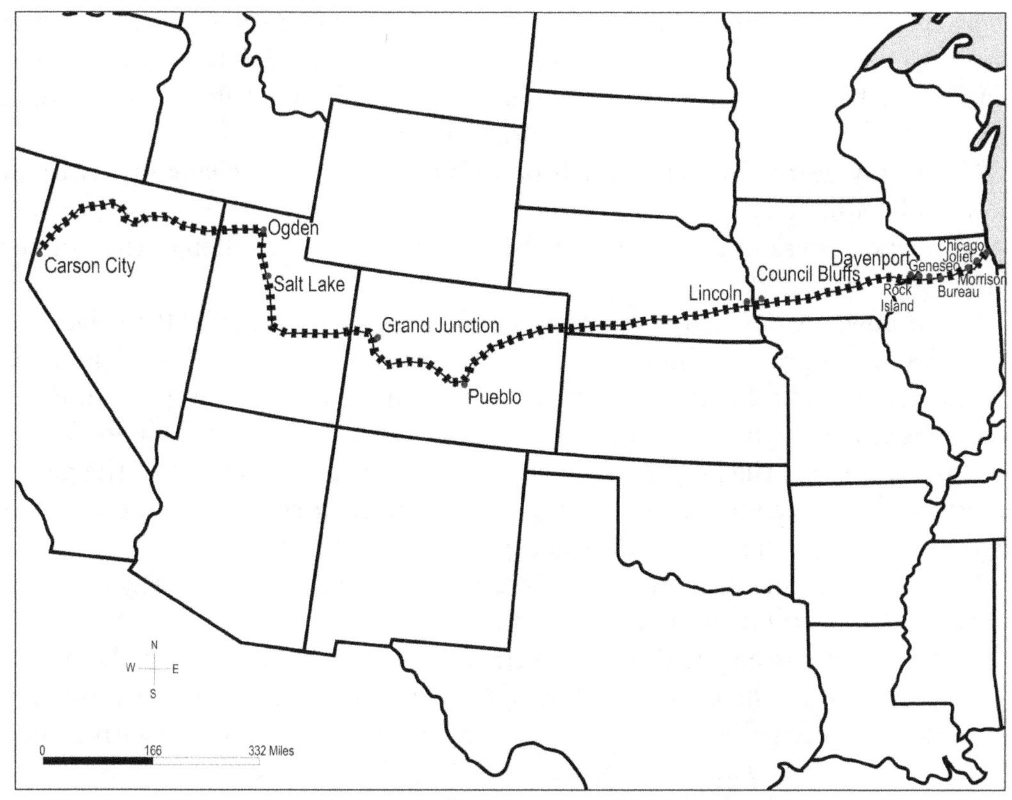

Jill Thomas map of the route of the Davies' Special

The train left Davenport before eleven p.m. and rushed through Council Bluffs and Lincoln, Nebraska, which it reached on the morning of Sunday, March 14.[1660] From there it headed across snow-covered Nebraska through Denver and the south to Pueblo, Colorado. The special continued via the Denver & Rio Grande through Leadville to Grand Junction. From there by the Rio Grande it continued west to Ogden, where it linked up with the Southern Pacific.

Sixty-three men used this special train, which set speed records on several legs of the trip to Carson City, Nevada. National press reports said that it left Pueblo at one thirty-eight a.m. on March 15 and reached Grand Junction at twelve twenty-five p.m. that day, crossing ten miles over the Grand Canyon in only eleven minutes. It made the 222-mile run from Grand Junction to Salt Lake City in just over eight hours, arriving there at nine thirty-three p.m. It stopped for ten minutes and then made a "phenomenal run" to Ogden, arriving there about ten twenty p.m., in time to connect with the regular Southern Pacific train to Carson City, arriving there about midnight on March 16.[1661] The Davies' special was more than four and a half hours ahead of one competing Chicago special and thirteen hours ahead of the other. That evening the governor of Nevada entertained Davies at his mansion along with ex-Senator Ingalls of Kansas, Davies' old friend Muldoon, Sharkey, Donaldson, and many other men prominent in pugilistic circles.

M. J. Geary, a reporter for San Francisco's *Morning Call*, met with Davies in Carson City during the afternoon before the special arrived. The reporter noted that Davies' hair had turned as white as a snowball. He asked about this change, and the Parson responded in his own pleasant way.

"Well, my dear fellow, all animals of high or low creation change to white in snow-clad countries."

The reporter asked about reports that Jackson would challenge the winner of the fight.

"Well now, my dear fellow, that is absurd," Davies responded. "Peter Jackson in his day was a grand fighter, but like poor, old John L., the colored gladiator has run his race, and I am certain he will never enter the prize ring again. Peter Jackson is too wise a man to issue a challenge unless it is back up with good hard coin, and if some of the pugilists who are always writing challenges to the newspapers would send a money order along to back up their statements there would be more fighting and less talking among the alleged champions."[1662]

"One-Eye" Connelly showed up at the fight. He had stolen his way onto the Houseman-Ryan train from Chicago and was suspected of stealing $800 from one of the other passengers during the trip. A story told twenty years later said that at the gate to the championship fight a big sign read, "Free list entirely suspended." Supposedly, Connelly heaved a brick inside the fence with a note addressed to Davies wanting to be admitted.

"Let him in," said the Parson to the gatekeeper, "or he'll bean you with the next brick and come in over you senseless body."

To the surprise of many including Davies, Fitz defeated Corbett.[1663] Before the fight Davies was asked why he had not visited Fitzsimmons' camp to watch him spar. Davies replied that he did not want to see Fitz. He had concluded that Corbett would be the winner. "I expected to see Jim with a down face, but he is simply perfect," he said. [1664] He felt that the fight would not last long and that Fitz would not be in it.

This is one of the first fights for which a substantial video record exists. The originals of these pictures were produced by a kinetoscope, and it is readily available on the internet at sites. These videos and many others show several of the men discussed in this biography of Davies' life.

One man clearly visible in the video was Davies' friend Masterson who is the timekeeper for the match. In particular, video is available of the prefight, first round, sixth round (when Corbett knocks down Fitz) and the fourteenth round, when Fitz delivers the famous solar plexus blow. Another man who clearly appears in the video is Siler, the referee. Siler was wearing a suit in the first round but removed his suit coat before his next appearance on the film. Houseman, Fitzsimmons' timekeeper, is also seen with his back to the audience. He sometimes raised his hat toward the end of a round as if to scratch his head. This was actually a signal to Fitz that there were about ten seconds until the end of the round.

Another California swing but with Armstrong, Barry, and Choynski

Davies, Armstrong, Barry, and Choynski went to San Francisco immediately after the championship fight. They arrived in San Francisco on the nine p.m. train on May 18.[1665] Others who arrived at the same time included Masterson and Wyatt Earp. One reason Davies went to California was to see Jeffries' match with Van Buskirk. In addition, Barry was there looking for a match with a fighter of or near his weight class.[1666]

Davies called Barry a natural fighter and always ready to fight. "In fact, almost too anxious to put on the gloves. The sight of a bantam causes Jimmy's blood to circulate, and his remark always is, 'I'd like to fight him.'"[1667]

By the end of March, the news from San Francisco was that Barry and Australian Jimmy Anthony had signed articles for a twenty-round fight at the National Athletic Club in San Francisco for a fight on April 23.[1668] Davies was trying to pair that match with a fight between Armstrong and another heavyweight. Then on April 5 Choynski was matched with "Denver Ed" Smith for a twenty-round fight at the Broadway Athletic Club on May 11.[1669] Articles said that Davies was representing Sharkey in connection with a match with Maher to be held in Pittsburgh.[1670]

Davies remained in San Francisco to supervise Barry's training for Anthony.[1671] Barry, Armstrong, and Davies had training quarters six miles outside of San Francisco. Davies called it an ideal spot for work and sleep:

> I used to get in bed by 8 p.m. and then be up at 5 in the morning. The man that owned the place kept hundreds of chickens, and Jimmy, Bob and I ate four eggs each and every morning. I never saw such a fiend for work as Barry. I am trying to get him to build up to 116 or 117 pounds, as at such weight he would get more matches. He always has stuck to the system taught by Harry Gilmore – the old English style, don't you know! – that tells of a chop, a bit of bread, and a half cup of tea for breakfast. Now I want him to eat a big steak, eggs and drink a mug of ale or claret.[1672]

Davies finally matched Armstrong to meet a local fighter named Sam Pruitt (sometimes spelled "Prewett"). Sam weighed 237 pounds, and was a piano mover by profession.[1673] There seems to be no doubt that by 1897, the prejudice against black fighters had intensified and spread.

For managers such as Davies and O'Rourke who handled black fighters, it was becoming ever more difficult to find matches with white fighters. The Supreme Court added to the problem with its *Plessy* v. *Ferguson* decision in 1896. The court held that a Louisiana law requiring "separate but equal" railroad accommodations for blacks and whites on intrastate railroads was constitutional. The court's ill-considered holding became the legal justification for segregation until the decision was overturned almost six decades later in *Brown* v. *Board of Education*. The decision provided the cover for legalized discrimination and lent itself to such things as separate black and white prizefighting championships and baseball leagues. Fighters such as Corbett, McCoy, Jeffries, and Sharkey all asserted the color line at some point in their careers. Though Jeffries and Sharkey gave up the practice and later fought black fighters, others maintained their discrimination their entire careers,.

Before the Barry-Anthony match, the *Chicago Tribune* published a story that Davies was going to assume the management of a prominent boxing club in San Francisco and had started arranging matches for it.[1674] This was an overstatement of the reality. George Green had assumed the management of the Occidental Club in San Francisco and had contracted Davies to help him locate and arrange matches. Davies also issued another defy to Fitz for a match with Choynski and promised he would meet Fitz in New York on May 8 or at any other time or place that Fitz would name to sign articles.[1675]

The agreement with Green may have looked like a conflict of interest to fighters whom Davies managed. It might also have spoiled his relationship with O'Rourke, and it may have put Davies at odds with the managers of other fighters. His own fighters might have wondered whether Davies was arranging matches in their interests or in the interests of Green's club. In addition, if Davies approached fighters managed by other men, then those other managers might have thought he was poaching or trying to beat them out of the manager's share of a contest.

More than five thousand attended the Barry-Anthony match in San Francisco on April 23. Anthony was described as the champion bantamweight fighter of Australia and Barry as the champion of that class in America. Barry won the fight on points earning the decision at the end of twenty rounds.[1676]

Armstrong's match with Pruitt was a preliminary to the Barry-Anthony match, and did not receive kindly attention from the press. If one wonders about how the prejudice against black fighters was spread so thoroughly in the 1880s and 90s, one need look no farther than the men who were writing, editing, and publishing U.S. newspapers at that time. For example, the headline in the *Post Dispatch* read: "Two Smokys Put Up A Farce."[1677] In addition, the story is full of stereotypical descriptions of black men. According to the paper, Pruitt seemed to be full of sorrow or something else as he came forward in the first round. When the two came to scratch Armstrong hit Pruitt in the face with several lefts, and Pruitt then looked mournfully at Armstrong. After a few more blows Pruitt walked to his corner and said he had had enough. The whole thing lasted about five seconds and was of such a comical nature that the spectators roared with laughter.

From California to New York again

Davies, Barry, and Armstrong left California for New York on April 27 because Davies wanted to be ringside for the Choynski-Smith fight.[1678] But there were likely other reasons for the trip. Through Davies, Choynski had challenged Fitz, who had responded that he would not fight Choynski until Joe had beaten Corbett and Maher. Speculation was that Davies was really going east to meet with Corbett to arrange a Corbett-Choynski match.[1679] On their way back to Chicago, Armstrong and Barry appeared in Denver and in Omaha on the evening of May 4, 1896. Armstrong stopped in Iowa to visit his family there.[1680] Davies and Barry reached Chicago on May 6. Davies continued on to New York. Barry's plan was to stay in Chicago for several weeks because the prime part of the prizefighting season in New York had ended, but Davies went to New York on May 8. Davies said that if Choynski defeated Smith, then he had a club in San Francisco lined up to offer a purse of $13,000 for a Choynski-Fitzsimmons match. Davies also went east as a representative of the National Sporting Club to try and arrange a Choynski-Corbett match to take place in San Francisco. These two purposes seemed to be in conflict, but both clubs were aware of what Davies was doing, and there were no objections or complaints.[1681]

The Choynski-Smith fight was at O'Rourke's Broadway club and was one of the last big fights of the season. Smith had been out of the fighting business for a period of time, but had returned to fight Joe Goddard in South Africa before twenty thousand spectators.[1682] The best account of the Choynski-Smith fight is provided by Choynski himself and includes an excerpt from an article written by Langdon Smith in the *Winnipeg Free Press*.[1683]

After Choynski's victory over Smith, Davies went back to Chicago.[1684] Choynski was looking for work and agreed to train Sharkey for his upcoming match with Maher.[1685] While sparring with Sharkey in late May, Joe sent a letter to Davies in Chicago telling him: "Armstrong paid a visit to our training quarters a few days ago. He boxed four hard rounds with Tom Sharkey, and I must say I was agreeably surprised and pleased at the improvement Bob showed. He is very fast and clever, and he more than held his own with Sharkey."[1686]

As soon as he received this letter, Davies arranged a match for Armstrong with Childs at Chicago's Alhambra Theater. When he needed an opponent for a black heavyweight, Davies seemed to call on Childs.[1687] In addition, plans were in the works to match Armstrong with C. C. Smith (the "Thunderbolt") at the Broadway club. Also, Brady had offered a Jeffries-Armstrong match at his New York club, and Jeffries was expressing interest. This was unexpected because Jeffries had joined the Sullivan-Corbett clan in drawing the color line.[1688] Both Barry and Armstrong appeared at the Alhambra at the end of May. After that appearance the press said that Armstrong was in some respects a copy of Jackson.[1689]

The good things that had been happening in New York went sour before Sharkey and Maher met. The mayor of New York wrote to the new head of the Board of Police Commissioners and petitioned that board to direct the police to close down all prizefighting in the city, and it was done. The halcyon days of business-like matchmaking were suspended.

At the end of June and in early July, Davies took both Barry and Armstrong on a tour through Wisconsin. They visited Oshkosh, Watertown, Racine, and

Kenosha, and Waukegan, Illinois. Although not specifically mentioned, it is likely that Childs was on this tour to spar with Armstrong. Their goal was to be back in Chicago for a presentation on July 4. This would be one of the last boxing tours that Davies personally managed. On the trip through Wisconsin, Armstrong was sometimes pitted against local fighters. On one occasion, a local fighter put up a pretty stiff defense until Armstrong began to pound him and moved him back toward the ropes. At that point Glickauf and Barry realized that Bob's opponent had a cork leg under his tights, and they shouted out for Armstrong to ease up rather than suffer the embarrassment of injuring a one-legged man.[1691]

Jack Burke dies in England

On June 29, 1897, another of Davies' former fighters, Jack Burke, the "Irish Lad," died in Cheltenham, England,[1692] at age thirty six. Jack had retired from boxing in 1894 and operated a tavern in Islington for about a year between November 1895 and November 1896.

After giving up the tavern business, Jack developed peritonitis, an acute inflammation of the membrane that lines the abdominal cavity. He contracted it after a cycling tour. The condition is often caused by bacterial agents or by foreign matter that invades the membrane because of a rupture of an internal organ caused by such things as appendicitis, ulcers, colitis, or rupture of the gall bladder. Severe abdominal pain, vomiting, prostration, and high fever follow. Jack probably ruptured an old boxing injury while on the cycling tour. Today peritonitis is successfully treated with antibiotics, which were not available in 1897. Jack underwent an operation but died at the Bellevue Hotel. Six months later reports were published that when he died Jack was sipping a glass of champagne.[1693]

He was buried at Norwood a few days later, leaving behind a wife, daughter, and sister. A campaign was then started to fund the erection of a memorial to Jack. Mitchell announced that if the fund did not receive enough subscriptions, he would personally pay for Jack's memorial. There is no record whether Davies contributed to the memorial. A granite obelisk was eventually constructed to mark Jack's grave. His daughter, Florence Gertrude Armitage was a passenger in the *Lusitania* when it was torpedoed by a German submarine off the coast of Ireland on May 7, 1915.

July brought the eighth anniversary of the seventy-five round Sullivan-Kilrain championship fight at Richburg, Mississippi.[1694] At the time of that fight Davies was approaching the top of his game. He played a key role in getting Sullivan to agree to the fight's terms, and he had managed Kilrain and Mitchell until Kilrain went into his final training for the Sullivan match. In addition, Jackson had appeared in Chicago just before the championship match, and then had begun working for Davies as soon as Charlie had returned from Mississippi. In the intervening years Davies had stayed at the top of the fighting game. However, change was in the wind, and that change included one reality for all men in the 1890s.

In 1897 the average life expectancy of an American male was only about sixty-three. Davies was forty-six and nearing the end of his best working years. He had been suffering from rheumatism for at least ten years, which he had often treated with mineral baths at Mt. Clemens, West Baden, Ogden's hot springs, or at Hot Springs, Arkansas. All of these places were also popular training sights and had ample gambling establishments. No detailed description of Davies' rheumatic condition exists, but he probably had a form of arthritis causing inflammation of his joints, and given the medical treatments in the late 1890s the condition was not likely to improve. The constant train travel and sleeping in hotels must have often aggravated his condition. In addition, he suffered from chronic ataxia, which was probably a result of his strychnine poisoning in 1885.

Other circumstances suggested that Davies' future would not be more of the same. In early July, Choynski accepted a position with a cigar manufacturer promoting their product. This job reportedly paid Joe $5,000 annually and provided him some financial security, which meant that Joe did not have to constantly travel and put on exhibitions in order to put food on the table.[1695] Next, Barry went to England in 1897 without Davies. Even worse, he was accompanied by Tommy White, who had left Davies' management and publicly criticized Davies.[1696] Finally, Charlie's friend Hopkins was continuing to acquire vaudeville theaters throughout the southern United States, and the management of those theatres was becoming difficult for the Colonel. In early July, Hopkins acquired a vaudeville theater in Louisville, adding to his operations in St. Louis and Chicago, and he would soon add theaters in Atlanta and New Orleans.[1697]

In late July, Davies was at West Baden taking mineral bath treatments. This was probably not simply a medicinal trip because West Baden also provided off-track betting, gambling, and the company of other sportsmen. He was interviewed there and told the press that he and O'Rourke were contemplating forming a partnership for the limited purpose of putting on a boxing carnival in Reno. Davies said he and O'Rourke would enter all of their fighters—Armstrong, Choynski, Barry, Walcott, Dixon and Everhart—in the carnival. Other promoters were working on similar plans, and there was no certainty that this could be carried on in the face of competition from other promoters such as William Brady.[1698] It is hard to distinguish sometimes between what was real and what was talk for the newspapers. In this case there was no boxing carnival held in Nevada.

Illinois was in the midst of additional strikes during the summer of 1897. Many of the state's coal miners had gone on strike and were being locked out by mine owners. Miners and their families were facing starvation, and Davies agreed to sponsor a benefit featuring Choynski and Armstrong at the Gaiety Theater in Chicago on August 6 to aid of the starving miners.[1699] In sponsoring a benefit Davies was probably able to avoid making the typical payoffs that would have been expected in Chicago. The evening of entertainment netted $600 for the miner's fund.

Throughout the summer Davies continued to talk about Armstrong as the next Jackson. But Armstrong had done little to earn a position among the top heavyweights or to earn the valid comparison to Jackson. Jackson was interviewed in early August by the *London Sporting Life* and that interview was reported in several American newspapers. Peter said he was about to return to the United States. He spoke fondly of Parson Davies and said he longed to see his old manager.

"You have never seen a manager like Davies," Jackson said. "He is as far in front of other managers as the moon is from the earth. We have been separated three years—three years too long. No one knows Davies better than I do."[1700]

As the fall approached, it was important for Davies' men to get in shape for the heart of the boxing season. Jeffries had refused to fight Armstrong, but he had agreed to meet Choynski in San Francisco.[1701] This meant that Joe had to be fine tuned for the match; Jeffries was a huge man compared to Choynski. Joe had been training during the summer at the Catlin Boat club near Lake Michigan on Chicago's North Side.[1702] Armstrong had gone to Syracuse to help train Ryan for his upcoming fight with McCoy.[1703]

Davies went to Syracuse to watch the Ryan-McCoy match, but the outcome was another black-eye for professional boxing. The match was widely considered a fixed affair that involved a payoff to the Syracuse police by Ryan's backers to induce them to stop the fight after Ryan had taken the lead by pouring it on in early rounds.[1704]

Davies begins working with Colonel Hopkins

On September 13, both of Davies' heavyweights participated in another exhibition as part of a second miners' benefit that was held at the Second Regimental Armoury in Chicago.[1705] Choynski sparred in a friendly bout with Al Schrosbee and then went to St. Louis for a big exhibition on September 16 with Creedon. This was part of a benefit for Creedon that was sponsored by Hopkins.[1706] Armstrong fought an eight-round match with Jack Douglas at the Chicago miner's benefit before going to St. Louis for a four-round exhibition with Douglas, and then he went on to Pittsburgh to meet Jack McCormick on September 25. In early October, Joe went to Galveston, Texas, and defeated Herman Bernau in a four-round match.[1707]

As all of these things were happening, the United States was about to go to war with Spain and was sending out its warships toward Havana, Cuba. Teddy Roosevelt was then assistant secretary of the Navy and expressed his view that the United States was on the verge of war with Spain. Sullivan wanted the United States to annex Cuban and install its own government. In addition to the impending war, yellow fever was spreading throughout the United States, particularly in New Orleans and other southern cities.[1708]

At Hopkins' request, Davies planned the benefit for Creedon in St. Louis. Davies was in St. Louis for several days in mid-September making the preliminary arrangements for the entertainment. In addition to bringing along Armstrong and Choynski, Davies had arranged a bag-punching contest for the championship of Missouri with a gold medal to be awarded by Creedon to the winning man. He also had arranged for two different wrestling matches. No one could plan an evening of athletic entertainment like Davies.

While he was in St. Louis, Davies explained that Choynski had shaved off his "Paderewski locks" and had returned to looking like a fighter. He said that Joe might already be on his way to California to meet Jeffries. But because Joe's wife had been ill, and he was reluctant to travel far from Chicago, Joe had not left for California. Davies explained that after the McCoy-Ryan fight in Syracuse he had stopped in Pittsburgh to meet with Corbett.[1709]

After the miner's benefit in Chicago but before the Creedon benefit in St. Louis, Jackson came to Chicago on a long trip from London to San Francisco. The *Chicago Tribune* noted that Jackson was a man of means and held "varied financial interests, stocks and mortgages." Jackson had been operating a boxing school in London known as the Harmony Club, which was frequented by the English nobility. He was thirty-six years old and said he weighed 210 pounds.

While in Chicago, Peter was introduced to Armstrong and was favorably impressed. There was some talk of a Jackson-Choynski match if Joe defeated Jeffries in San Francisco. Joe noted that as soon as he was finished with Jeffries, he was committed in New Orleans for a ten-round contest with Greggains but felt he could do something with Peter after filling that commitment.[1710]

Jackson was still looking for a match with Corbett, but the bigot (or coward) in Corbett led him to announce he would not cross the color line and would never fight Jackson again.[1711] In early October, Sharkey joined the side of the racial bigots and announced he too had drawn the color line and would positively refuse to meet Jackson or any other black man.[1712] To give them their due, it is true that both Sharkey and Jeffries later softened their positions and agreed that they would fight Jackson. However, they changed their positions only after it became apparent that Jackson was a shadow of his former self. Sharkey later said that men who made distinction based on color made him tired.

Late in September, the second Mayor Harrison, Carter Henry Harrison, Jr., of Chicago met with the *Chicago Tribune* to discuss policies of his new administration. He told the *Tribune* he saw no reason why boxing exhibitions should not take place in Chicago so long as they were conducted with proper restrictions. These restrictions would have to include a limitation on the number of rounds that could be fought, which effectively counted Chicago out as a place for any championship fight. In addition, Harrison said that "no slugging" would be permitted in any boxing exhibition in Chicago, which also seemed to doom any real match in that city.[1713]

On September 27, Barry left Chicago headed for England. He had exhausted all his opportunities in the United States and hoped he would be able to book a world championship match in London. Davies did not travel to England with Barry. Instead, Davies went to St. Louis in late October to meet with the St. Louis Press Club and arranged a series of "Olympic games" to be presented in the new coliseum that had been built there. The entertainment was to set for November 17. Hopkins indicated he would join with Davies in developing a satisfactory program that would include races among sprinters and distance runners, wrestling matches, and exercise exhibitions by Turners.[1714]

As part of this program Davies hoped to also arrange a Maher-Armstrong match. He had already talked to several railroad agents, who had promised to run special trains to St. Louis if the match could be arranged. A few days later Maher issued a statement that he would fight no one other than "Tut" Ryan. Davies was incensed by this statement because, he said, he had been working for months to arrange the Maher-Armstrong match with no indication from Maher's side of any such limitation on Maher's availability.[1715] As a substitute for the heavyweight fight he arranged for Griffo to meet Tracy as the centerpiece of the show.[1716]

While Davies was appearing in the newspapers frequently, his direct association with fighters he managed had substantially diminished. Barry was in England. Davies was not making a move forward with Armstrong, primarily because so many heavyweight fighters were asserting the color line and would not give him a chance. Davies did not travel with Choynski to his match with Jeffries in San Francisco (he thought Joe would win easily) or to Joe's fight in New Orleans. Instead, he stayed behind in St. Louis to arrange the Press Club entertainment.[1717]

Davies' short stint with Griffo

A year after the St. Louis show, the *Post Dispatch* recounted Davies' interaction with Griffo in the week before the big match with Tracy. Griffo and Tommy Warren had a lot in common in that the both needed serious medication. According to the *Post Dispatch* when Davies brought Griffo down to St. Louis from Chicago, he asked a friend where he could take Griffo to train for his match. His friend suggested that Griffo could prepare at the South Side Park, and Davies took Griffo there.[1718] Davies then went back to Chicago that night.

A week later Davies returned to St. Louis and asked his friend:

> "How's Griffo coming?"
> "Dunno."
> "Why?"
> "Haven't seen him since the day you left."
> "Hasn't he been training?"
> "Heard he was. Down at the brewery they say he broke all records."
> The Parson was furious and he hunted Griffo up.
> He found him at the Standard Theater bar, fondling a schooner.

> "You're a pretty fellow," said the Parson.
> "That's wot me mother used to call me," said Griffo.
> "I hope Tracy knocks your blooming head off," said the Parson
> "E'll not do that," said Griffo. "He'll blow the bleedin' works first. 'Ave a drink with us Pawson, 'Ere's to Albert Griffths, wot some folks call Griffo, and wot others calls old boy Griff. 'E as ust to be a foighter, but who 'as retired on 'onors 'onestly won."
> The Parson grew white in the face.
> "Yes," continued Griffo, "retired. 'E doesn't call this 'ere mill with Tracy a fight. It's only a wee bit of a bout. 'E never trains for that sort of a dickey. It would take away 'is speed to train and so 'e does nothink but take things heesy and heat and drink as 'e pleases."

Davies left Griffo in disgust.

"I don't care what happens to him," said the Parson. "I'll not worry my head about him any more."

The big show that Davies had worked so hard to promote had a bad ending. Armstrong boxed three friendly rounds with John Holtman of St. Louis before the featured Griffo-Tracy match.[1719] About ten thousand people were present on the evening of November 18. As the time for Griffo to go on, Johnny and Charley Daly, who were supposed to be keeping track of Griffo came to Davies and told him that Griffo was missing.

"Find him!" said Davies. "Fetch, him into the coliseum. If you can't bring in all of him, bring in a leg or an arm. I'll have to have some kind of evidence to prove up my case. Hire a hack and keep going until you land him."

The Dalys then hired a hack and went looking for Griffo and found him in front of a bar shadow boxing for a crowd. The Dalys grabbed Griffo, put him into the hack and directed the driver to go like mad for the St. Louis Coliseum. The driver took off but ran into a cable train and threw Griffo and the Dalys into the street. Nevertheless, following Davies' instructions the Dalys gathered up Griffo from the street and continued to the event with Tracy.[1720]

When he arrived Griffo was drunk. He was so drunk he could barely walk. Griffo and Tracy boxed about only one minute before Griffo quit fighting, threw his arms in the air and then climbed up on the ropes to address the crowd. Tracy had no idea what Griffo was up to and just stood back with a puzzled expression on his face. Griffo told the crowd that he had been hurt when the hack he was riding in had collided with a trolley car. He said he was in severe pain and bruised and could not possibly continue. It was true that Griffo had been injured in a collision, but no one believed his claims because he was also plainly drunk. Cries of "fake!" went up from the crowd and near pandemonium reigned.

A substitute was quickly found. The substitute was Paddy Smith, who was "Denver Ed" Smith's younger brother. Smith was able to spar two rounds with Tracy. Davies did not pay Griffo, and Griffo then complained about being shorted by the Parson. Griffo's manager had him arrested for vagrancy the next day and then left town without paying his bail. Griffo did not have a cent of his own because Davies too had not paid him.[1721]

For about six months Davies had been working with Green, the Occidental Club's manager in San Francisco to help arrange matches there. As part of that work he had lined up Griffo to appear there against Lavigne, and Davies was obviously worried about Griffo's drunken behavior in St. Louis.[1722] It wouldn't exactly being doing George Green a favor to send Griffo out to California. While in Chicago, Davies and Hopkins decided that they had to do something to straighten out Griffo. Davies found Griffo and wanted to give him his ticket for San Francisco, but Griffo was again dead drunk. In fact, Griffo was so drunk he would not even agree to sleep it off in a hotel room. He had work to do because there were a few gin mills in Chicago he had not yet visited.[1723]

Hopkins then had an idea. He told Davies to keep Griffo occupied as Hopkins slipped out to a nearby drug store, where he purchased a bottle of a substance called "shoo-fly." Hopkins then arranged for the bartender to spike Griffo's drink with the shoo-fly. Hopkins gave the substance to the bartender, who apparently misunderstood his instructions and put the dope intended for Griffo's drink in all three drinks. The Colonel and Davies realized the bartender's error and declined their glasses. Griffo then took all three glasses and gulped down every portion. He became so ill he later took the pledge never to drink again and swore off alcohol forever.[1724] "Forever" turned out to be shorter than most think because Griffo was drinking heavily again by the time he reached San Francisco.

Davies arranged a boxing event at Battery D for the last day of November. The prime attractions were to be Ryan and Billy Stift, who were matched to box in a twelve-round event.[1725] Davies returned from Omaha on November 29 bringing along O'Rourke, Tracy, Walcott, and Dixon. Davies acted as the master of ceremonies for the Battery D event. That day, he also announced that Walcott and Tracy had signed articles for a match.[1726] In addition, O'Rourke, who had been in San Francisco for the Sharkey-Goddard contest, brought back word that Goddard was willing to schedule a match with Armstrong. Australia fighters did not share the prejudices toward black fighters.[1727]

The fight at Battery D was good while it lasted. Ryan was normally a cautious fighter, but he went after Stift early and was clearly winning the fight when it was stopped by the police after six rounds. Ryan was awarded the victory by the referee.[1728]

That night in San Francisco, Choynski fought Jeffries[1729] in one of the classic fights of all time, but Davies was not present. His failure to travel to California may have indicated that his relationship with Joe was once again slipping. Joe was outweighed by Jeffries by more than fifty pounds, but reporters said that Joe's judgment and ring generalship that night were flawless. In addition, he seemed to have changed his style of fighting from the Australian format of keeping his arms tight to his body with his left up guarding his face to a much more open style of exposing his body but allowing him to move faster. Joe was still using this new style when he trained with Jeffries for his fight with Jack Johnson, and film of those sessions shows how he fought. The day after the Choynski-Jeffries contest, the *Chicago Tribune* wrote that "few will now dispute Jeffries' claim as a possibility for the world's championship."[1730]

Jimmy Barry in 1906 – He was undefeated when he became world champion – Photograph of the Chicago History Museum

Less than a week after the Choynski-Jeffries match in San Francisco, Barry met Walter Croot of Newcastle, England, for the bantamweight championship of the world at the National Sporting Club. Barry knocked out Croot in the twentieth round of their match with a right to the heart and then to the jaw. When he fell, Croot's head struck the floor hard, and later that day he died from the injury. At this point in his career Barry had fifty-six wins, no losses, and two draws with thirty-eight knock outs. Although Barry was declared the world champion and exonerated of any culpability in Croot's death, he was never quite the same fighter after that evening.[1731]

The Parson had scheduled a match at Battery D between Tracy and Walcott for December 21. However, he first went to New York for the McCoy-Creedon fight and quickly returned to Chicago for the Tracy-Walcott match.[1732] That was stopped by a court. The reason it was stopped was not the typical argument that

Illinois law prohibited prizefighting. Instead, the court enjoined the city from renting out Battery D because of recent court ruling on long-running litigation over the occupancy of the land by any building. The litigation had been filed by a famous plaintiff, A. Montgomery Ward.

The facts of the litigation were complicated, but the essential claim was that the land where Battery D stood had been originally reserved as open space for public grounds that would lie east of Michigan Avenue and between Randolph and Madison streets, fronting on Lake Michigan. The land had been given to the city, subject to a prohibition in the deed that the city had accepted. The prohibition specified that the ground would be kept free of any buildings. In addition, the city had passed a resolution in 1844 accepting the land as part of the city on the specified terms. However, in 1881 the city had granted permission to Battery D to build and occupy one hundred twenty five feet of land north of Monroe Street for an armory building, and it had also given permission to a cavalry regiment to erect a similar building just north of Battery D. Both buildings were erected as one-story structures extending nearly back to the Illinois Central tracks.

In 1890 Montgomery Ward had filed a suit against the city to prevent the continued use of Battery D and to compel its demolition. A Chicago judge had ruled in Ward's favor, but the city had appealed to the Illinois Supreme Court. On November 8, 1897, the Supreme Court affirmed the decision of a Chicago judge ordering the city to cease using Battery D. When the city rented to property to Davies for the Walcott-Tracy fight, Ward had gone to court to enforce the order of the Illinois Supreme Court, and the Chicago judge enjoined use of the facility for any purpose.[1733] In October 2010 Chicago recognized the value of Montgomery Ward's efforts to protect the lakefront by name a park for him at 630 N. Kingsbury Street on Chicago's near north side.

In the presence of Creedon, Choynski, Tracy, Hopkins, and several others who gathered to talk over the postponement, Davies said: "Boys, I knew this was going to happen. I woke up this morning around 10 o'clock, and when Harry Glickauf came into my room I said: 'something is going to happen. Things are coming too easy.' I had a hunch and went down to the Battery and there were the men fixing chairs, and it struck me it was all for nothing, and the next I heard was about the injunction. Judge Brentano told me it was not a fight against boxing, but simply an attempt to see that the court decree regarding the Battery was carried out."[1734]

The Tracy-Walcott match was rescheduled for December 27 at the Winter Circus in Chicago. Every time a fight was rescheduled, it cost the promoter money.[1735] The Tracy-Walcott match had been considered a cake walk for Walcott but ended in a draw. Choynski had returned from California and was a second for Tracy along with Stift and Billy O'Donnell. Walcott had Armstrong and O'Rourke in his corner. The fight generally involved Walcott setting the pace and pressing in on Tracy, who would retreat and make an effective stand. Walcott looked as happy and jolly as one could be throughout the match, and

Tracy was as equally good natured. The fight was met with general praise and was ranked as one of the fastest and hardest ever seen in Chicago. This was a good way to wind up the year 1897.

Between two preliminary bouts Davies mounted the platform and was greeted with a degree of applause, indicating he was a popular man with the sporting public. He took the occasion to thank, tongue-in-cheek, "our liberal city government, which permits of harmless boxing events of this character." Davies also announced that additional matches were planned in January 1898 at the same location. The press noted that Davies had made sure to cover all the bills incurred with the failed match at Battery D. Although the rescheduled match was successful, Davies lost about $1,800 because of the additional bills incurred when the match had to be rescheduled.[1736]

Chicago's police and the Pinkertons battle

Another event that evening illustrated why putting on fights in Chicago had become so difficult. About the time the crowd had taken their seats, a "great crowd of policemen almost caused a riot by trying to force their way into the Walcott-Tracy fight without paying admission. They were turned down at the door, but stood around and finally made a rush to get in." Davies had hired Pinkerton agents to act as security for the match, and the Pinkerton agents got into a battle with the police.

"My, but you should have seen that Pinkerton man baste those policemen," O'Rourke said. "It's an outrage that all the trouble we had in Chicago should have come from the police officers themselves. Think of having to hire Pinkerton men to protect us against the city's guardians of the peace!"[1737]

In the days when McDonald controlled the first ward, the police would not have tried to break into a sporting event sponsored by Parson Davies for had they tried, they would have been walking the Chicago streets looking for work. Davies no longer enjoyed that kind of influence, and he no longer had friends in the police department or on the city council who would protect him from such abuses.

This was the first time in many years that Davies spent the year end in Chicago. He had continued working as if he were still a young man. He announced on December 30 that he had arranged a McCoy-Choynski match in New York with a side bet of $5,000. McCoy had promised Davies right after he defeated Creedon that his next match would be with Choynski, and he had stuck to his word.[1738] The best news reached Chicago on New Year's Eve. Barry was acquitted of all charges in connection with the death of Walter Croot.[1739]

Chapter 17 - (1898-1908)

New Orleans

Parson Davies is one of the best known men identified with sport, particularly the fistic branch of the game. He is a born diplomat, a walking fund of fistic lore, a polished gentleman, as square a man as ever breathed the ozone of any sphere; strong and courageous in his convictions, a splendid entertainer, and an all around good fellow.

The "Parson" is universally popular among the members of the sporting fraternity, and he has friends by the hundred among the newspaper and theatrical professions. His opinion on all matters pertaining to the boxing game is always sought after in times when important prize-ring affairs are pending, or when such events are concluded in a manner such as to cause any complications or controversy over the outcome. Conversation is one of Parson Davies' chief characteristics. While he always receives members of the press courteously he only expresses decisive opinions to writers with whom he is well acquainted.[1740]

▬

{Kid} McCoy, though, would not meet them. They are black, and he draws the color line. Say, but this drawing of the color line makes me tired. It is not the color these fellows are afraid of, but the men.[1741]

▬

Ordinarily, the world has little consideration for "has beens." The moment a public man, whether he be a pugilistic star, a great warrior, or a brilliant statesman, shakes hands with defeat, his usefulness is destroyed and he disappears from public view.[1742]

▬

♥

Davies went to St. Louis on January 2, 1898 to see Hopkins. The two men were starting to negotiate a business arrangement that would change the next twelve years of Charlie's life. Along with Dominick Call O'Malley, they were about to lease two theaters in New Orleans for which Davies would be the on-site manager.

In early January, the press did not know what Davies, Hopkins, and O'Malley were doing and was more curious about boxing matters. "Have you concluded arrangements for the fight between Choynski and McCoy?" "If the fight is arranged where do you propose bringing it off?"[1743] These were the same questions that Davies had been fielding for almost twenty years.

Davies and Hopkins traveled to New Orleans and registered at the Cosmopolitan Hotel on January 9. This time the press thought that Davies was there to arrange a Corbett-Fitzsimmons rematch in Jefferson Parish. In response to inquiries Davies said he did not even know where Jefferson Parish was located.[1744]

The press said that Hopkins was in New Orleans to close a business arrangement for either the St. Charles Theater or the Academy of Music with a lease to begin after March 1. Hopkins told the *Picayune* he was anxious to have Davies give up the ring and manage one of the theaters in New Orleans, but Davies said he was too old to change professions.[1745]

The St. Charles Theater was on the east side of St. Charles Street near Poydras and had long been a centerpiece of New Orleans entertainment. It was built in 1835 by James H. Caldwell. That version of the St. Charles had four tiers of box seats, huge galleries and accommodated four thousand people for a single performance. When it was constructed only three theaters in the world were larger. In 1842 the St. Charles burned down and a smaller theater was built using the surviving front wall of the old building. Caldwell also owed the smaller Academy of Music on Camp Street.[1746]

These two theaters were later owned and operated by David Bidwell, who was born in New York but became a legendary figure in New Orleans entertainment history. Over time Bidwell found it more difficult to book quality talent for his venues and wanted a booking agency in New York that would supply regular fresh talent for New Orleans productions. Bidwell retained two young men, Marc Klaw and Abraham L. Erlanger, and persuaded them to open a booking agency. They formed the firm of Klaw & Erlanger and eventually grew that business until they controlled 90 percent of the traveling theater business in the United States and became founding members of the New York theater syndicate.[1747]

There was nothing hidden or secret about the syndicate, especially after March 1898 when the agreement between its members became public in a New York civil suit. The syndicate was nominally created in August 1896 and controlled a huge number of theaters. Klaw and Erlanger controlled, by ownership or lease, more than five hundred theaters primarily in the South. Their co-conspirators Al Hayman and Charles Frohman controlled about three hundred theaters from New York to California; and their other co-conspirators Samuel Nirdlinger and Z. Frederick Zimmerman controlled theaters in Ohio and Pennsylvania. As part of their agreement, Klaw & Erlanger controlled talent bookings for all members of the syndicate and prohibited actors and performers they controlled from appearing in any theater in a city where the syndicate operated. Performers who did not cooperate were blacklisted. The syndicate's purpose was to control ticket prices and salaries paid to performers in the United States and Europe and to enrich its owners.[1748]

After Bidwell died in December 1889, his widow personally managed the St. Charles and Academy of Music for three seasons.[1749] She then leased the theaters directly to C. B. Jefferson and Klaw & Erlanger.[1750] When Bidwell's widow died in May 1897 she left all her property, valued at nearly $120,000, to Dr. George K. Pratt, his wife, and the Pratts' seven children.[1751]

Pratt had been the Bidwell's personal physician and close friend for many years, and he was attending Mrs. Pratt at the time of her death. Although Mrs. Bidwell's last will was challenged as having been written under undue influence by Pratt, the doctor prevailed, and he was appointed by the Louisiana courts to serve as tutor for his minor children. Under Louisiana law a tutor was a person appointed by a court to act for the benefit of his minor children. Pratt controlled the St. Charles and Academy of Music from that point forward.[1752] He did not like either Klaw or Erlanger and thought that it was not in the best interests of his children to renew the lease for the two theaters with the syndicate.

In New Orleans the *Daily Item* was the newspaper that wrote most critically about the syndicate and strongly supported local independent theater managers and owners. O'Malley was the owner and editor of the *Daily Item* and a friend of both Hopkins and Davies. It seems likely that O'Malley was the person who alerted Hopkins to the pending availability of the St. Charles and Academy of Music and Pratt's hostility toward the syndicate.

Hopkins first met with Pratt as an agent and employee of the Tri-State Amusement Company. It appears that Klaw & Erlanger had entered into an agreement with Tri-State to sublease the two theaters if Hopkins could negotiate an acceptable primary lease from Pratt. Klaw & Erlanger were apparently trying to use Tri-State as a shill to obtain indirectly what they could not obtain directly. However, that secret plan did not pan out. Instead a new corporation was created that was known as J. D. Hopkins & Company. This company, owned in equal shares by Hopkins, Davies, and O'Malley, obtained the lease for the two theaters.[1753]

Klaw & Erlanger decided not to give up their position in New Orleans but to compete for that market. It purchased the site of the old Tulane College at Dryades and Common and tore down the building there. They then built two new theaters targeted to open for the fall theater season. The two new theaters were known as the Tulane and the Crescent.[1754] The Tulane was the smaller of the two and designed to compete directly with the Academy of Music. The Crescent competed directly with the St. Charles. Because Klaw & Erlanger controlled the theater talent, their new theaters could offer superior entertainment in New Orleans and block Hopkins, Davies and O'Malley from bringing top acts to the city.[1755] During the negotiations for the theaters, there was speculation that Davies would be the manager of a new athletic club to open in Saint Bernard's Parish.

Davies and Hopkins left New Orleans and went back to St. Louis. The St. Louis press continued to nose around about what Davies had been doing in the South. He told them he would act for New Orleans parties bidding on fights and hoped that good matches could be arranged. Davies noted that Choynski had been matched to fight Billy Stift before the new American Athletic Club in Chicago for a six-round match. He also said that a big party was being planned to welcome Barry back from England. Davies had no hard feelings toward Barry and was always thoughtful when a death in the ring was involved.[1756]

The situation in Chicago continued to twist. Mayor Harrison said he would permit limited-round matches; however, by mid-January the mayor changed his mind and said he wanted a system in which one man would have control of all boxing matters. He specified that the new system must provide a physician who would examine the contestants before boxing matches to see that the fighters were fit.[1757] These were good ideas, but putting one person in charge of anything in Chicago generally meant that person would have to be paid off to do business there.

In January, Davies was managing Tracy's interests. He had arranged a fight for Tracy with Walcott, and a Tracy-Douglas match to take place at the Oriental Theater in St. Louis in early February.[1758] Douglas was from one of the best families in St. Louis. He had learned to box in a high-class club there, but had been induced to appear in Chicago before the Chicago Athletic Club, where he had beaten the best Chicago welterweights. Douglas was considered a clever fighter and a good match for Tracy. He had never been beaten and was six pounds lighter than Tracy.[1759]

Davies was also attempting to match Armstrong with a big new heavyweight named Gus Ruhlin. Finally, Davies was also trying to arrange fights for the New Orleans Mardi Gras on behalf of the new Saint Bernard Club. He wanted to match Lavigne and Dixon as the featured fight. If this happened, Davies would be putting a thumb in the eye of New Orleans sports, who had hated Dixon for years because he had beaten the Skelly so terribly in 1892.[1760] Davies knew what he was doing and probably thought he would get a huge gate if he could make that fight. But Dixon would be taking a great personal risk if he returned to New Orleans.

On January 20, Hopkins returned to St. Louis from a second trip to New Orleans, and Davies came down from Chicago to meet Hopkins.[1761] Before leaving Chicago, Davies had some adverse comments to make about Martin Julian, whom he described as "a sleek fat creature" who survived by using Fitzsimmons as his meal ticket.[1762] These strong words were prompted by what Julian had told the press a few days earlier. He claimed that Davies and O'Rourke were working together to steal the management of the proposed Corbett-Fitzsimmons fight from Dan Stuart. Davies said that Julian had concocted this story after a meeting held two weeks earlier between Julian, Davies, and O'Rourke.

Davies said that after McCoy announced he would fight anyone, he and O'Rourke thought that Fitz might be a likely opponent and that Choynski and Walcott were other possible opponents. Davies and O'Rourke then decided to meet with Julian to discuss the situation. The three men met in a hotel room with a newspaper reporter present. Davies said that during their conversation the discussion turned to the chances of a Corbett-Fitz rematch.

Charlie suggested that if the contestants were not too tied up with Stuart then managers like Brady and Julian could handle the match. Davies said to Julian, "If you have no such desire, O'Rourke and myself will look up the matter, and possibly we could handle the carnival and give as big purses as anybody else." Davies was irritated that Julian had twisted this discussion by claiming he and O'Rourke were trying to rob Stuart of the Corbett-Fitz rematch. He concluded, "For the life of me, I cannot understand how a sleek fat creature like Julian would tell such an absolute falsehood unless it was to curry favor with Stuart who seems to have a mortgage on him."[1763] These comments clearly show Davies' growing disgust with the prizefighting business.

On January 22, the *Post Dispatch* reported that Davies and Hopkins had met at the Planters' House and that Hopkins "wants Davies to quit the prizefighting business and manage his new theater in New Orleans." Davies was asked about becoming a theater manager and said he had grown too old in one line of work to enter another. He said he had Choynski, Armstrong, and other pugilists under his management and he would hate to quit them.[1764] This wasn't exactly a firm refusal of what Hopkins was purposing and may have made his fighters nervous that their manager was about to fly the coup.

Hopkins made a third trip to New Orleans at the end of January. When he came back to St. Louis, he told the *Post Dispatch* that Davies was going to become the manager of a new club to be called the Saint Bernard Club and that he had already arranged for matches to be staged there during Mardi Gras. The matches he had lined up were Tracy-Lavigne and Pedlar Palmer-Sammy Kelly. Davies had also received a telegram from Athens, Pennsylvania, asking him to match Armstrong with Maher.[1765]

Davies and Armstrong split

By the end of January, Davies and Armstrong had split, though the reasons for it are not all clear. Armstrong and Choynski had not been getting along for several months. It might have been that Armstrong felt Davies was spending too much time in St. Louis and New Orleans or that Davies was more interested in Choynski's future. It might have been that Armstrong and Choynski knew that Davies would soon be leaving Chicago to live in New Orleans, and Bob had no interest in following his manager south, where life could be dangerous.

Whatever the exact reasons for their disaffection, while Davies was away from Chicago, Armstrong agreed to fight Childs on January 29. The Armstrong-Childs contest was held at the Chicago Athletic Association in front of about five hundred spectators with Siler acting as referee. Childs was paid only twenty dollars to appear.

Childs had been working with Armstrong as his sparring partner, and Van Praag (Al Capone's future cigar-store partner) somehow persuaded Armstrong to meet Childs and to go easy with Childs so he would not hurt him. However, no one told Childs he was supposed to go easy with Armstrong. One man was fighting a friendly match, and the other was out for blood. It may be that Armstrong was set up and that the whole affair was designed for people on the inside to make money betting on Childs at long odds. On the other hand, given the way some white men in Chicago thought, it may be that they just saw this as a way to have a little fun with two black men, or it may simply have been a fraud to make money betting on Childs to win.

Armstrong was knocked out by Childs in the second round. He was out on his feet and wandered around the ring at the end of the second round wobbling dangerously. He came to Childs' corner by mistake, and when Childs saw Armstrong's condition he helped ease the big fighter down to the ground, where he stayed sitting in a daze.[1766]

This fight effectively killed all the effort Davies had made to promote Armstrong as a coming heavyweight champion. Siler wrote in *Inside Facts on Pugilism* that "To see Frank and Bob fighting different opponents it was any kind of odds that Bob could make Frank appear like a novice, but put them in the ring together and Frank, with his awkward style of milling, would trim Bob like breaking sticks. This could never be accounted for, as Armstrong was as scientific as they turn them out."[1767]

After this match, Armstrong was tainted merchandise. Although it provided little solace for Davies, it turned out in that Childs was a much better fighter than he was considered to be in 1898.

Davies was angry when he learned that Armstrong had been knocked out by a second-rate fighter in a contest that happened without his knowledge. He told the *Tribune* he was happy that Armstrong had been beaten by Childs. Charlie said that it "served him right." He felt that in the future Armstrong would not "permit himself to be used by others in his manager's absence." Davies was satisfied that Armstrong could easily handle Childs and said he had managed both of them on the road, where they boxed at least seventy-five times. Davies pointed out that Armstrong had always had his way with Childs. He also said he had word "from a trustworthy source in Chicago" that Armstrong had been double-crossed.[1768]

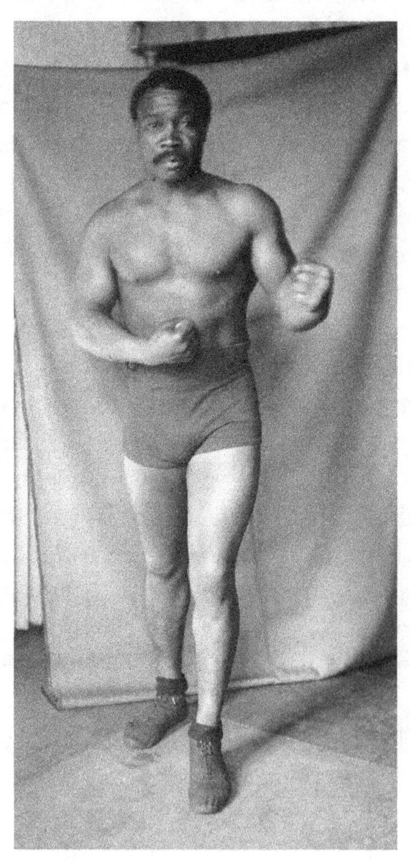

Frank Childs who fought Peter Jackson and defeated Bob Armstrong – 1902 Photograph of the Chicago History Museum

Davies downplayed the situation, but he managed Armstrong in only twice after January. In the summer of 1898 he arranged an Armstrong-Jeffries match, and in the summer of 1902 he took Armstrong to London with Larry Temple. At the time of their split the *Post Dispatch* quoted a well-known Chicago sport as saying that Armstrong had been right to leave Davies because "the latter kept him around town carrying bundles for the past year, and when he had a chance to make a little money his manager objected to him risking his reputation. He finally decided to go against the Parson's orders and take on Childs."[1769]

Less than a week later Choynski again withdrew from Davies' management.[1770] This time their split was somewhat bitter. Davies told the press he had written to O'Rourke to take down the $1,000 forfeit he had posted for a McCoy-Choynski match and said that Choynski would have to back himself in the future. Davies also said that when he took over Joe's management he had paid Joe $100 a week for thirty-seven weeks to act as Jackson's sparring partner. Choynski shot back that Davies had never paid him a cent he didn't earn, and Joe said he had made a mistake in having a manager. Joe felt that with the anticipated 75-25 split with Sharkey he would be "in velvet" because they would draw a huge crowd in San Francisco. In New Orleans, "Mack's Melange" wrote that Davies had stood by many fighters with his money and his brains and that Choynski should quickly renew his friendship with his old manager.[1771]

Charlie no longer had a heavyweight under his management, and managing heavyweights had been his hallmark for more than fifteen years. A good heavyweight fighter would make far more money than the world champion bantamweight. Choynski left Chicago for San Francisco, where he thought he would be matched with an Australian fighter known as Tut Ryan. After that match fell through, Choynski wired O'Rourke in New York authorizing O'Rourke to represent him in arranging a match with McCoy. Asking O'Rourke to manage his interests was adding insult to injury because Davies and O'Rourke had worked so closely in the past. From Choynski's standpoint he was simply eliminating the middle man[1772] McCoy refused to fight unless Choynski dropped his weight to 158 pounds. Later McCoy claimed he refused to fight because O'Rourke and proposed putting on a fake bout.[1773]

The Tracy-Douglas match in St. Louis was another surprise.[1774] Their fight was called a draw, but many spectators thought that Douglas actually had the best of the fight. After the match Tracy was not in good shape and his face had been cut up by the St. Louis gentleman boxer. This dimmed Davies' chances of making good money by promoting Tracy.[1775]

Trying to establish a boxing trust

With all of these issues to address, Davies left Chicago and went to New York to meet with several managers to discuss something he thought was more important than his own situation and that related to the future of the business of boxing. In the late 1890s many businesses were controlled or influenced by some kind of trust. Andrew Carnegie, J. Pierpont Morgan, and John D. Rockefeller were pictured in dictionaries that defined the word "trust." Business trusts controlled everything from the sale of bananas to the control of the railroads.

In simple terms, the trusts were agreements among the owners of otherwise competitive businesses to stop competing and to sell their products or services on prearranged terms and for specified prices in order to control their markets. The trusts were also successful because United States tariff policy protected American companies from the importation of foreign goods and that policy helped keep prices for American-made products artificially high. Professional baseball and American theaters had both organized as trusts or syndicates, and Davies thought boxing should do the same. Through his friend Hopkins and his own theatrical background Davies knew first-hand about the New York theater syndicate.

A sad profile of the great Joe Choynski taken in 1929 – Photograph of the Chicago History Museum

He argued that the managers of prizefighters should enter into a trust agreement. He pointed out that the movement of baseball players between professional teams was controlled by the club owners. Even today baseball acts as a trust and is exempt from the antitrust laws. Charlie saw no reason why prizefight managers and club owners could not do the same thing, thereby controlling how much fighters were paid and where matches were held. However, it wasn't simply a question of money. He was interested in cleaning up the sport, and he felt that the power to control it would help cleanse it of fraud.

Davies wanted O'Rourke, Brady, James A. Kennedy, and other managers and club owners to join a beneficial association. He proposed that Corbett and Fitzsimmons be excluded from the aggregation of fighters who would be controlled by the prizefight trust because the two fighters had already achieved too much prominence on their own. But other fighters such as McCoy, Maher, Choynski, Jeffries, and Ruhlin would be put into a competition controlled by the managers. He proposed that the managers should sell stock by public subscriptions to purchase a suitable championship belt that would be awarded to the winner of a bracketed heavyweight tournament. The belt would become the winner's property if he defended it successfully three times. The winner of the tournament would be entitled to a purse of $5,000.

"With a trust it would be business and not 'chin music,'" Davies said. "If a man did not keep his engagements he would be blacklisted, as would one who did any crooked work. . . . Boxing should be on a business basis."[1776]

Two years later in a special to the *Chicago Tribune* Davies explained he had talked to O'Rourke and other leading managers and promoters about forming a boxing league "modeled after the different baseball leagues of the United States." He took the position that great benefits would accrue from a boxing league, and he thought that the men he had spoken with were "greatly impressed" with its arguments. He acknowledged that nothing had come from his suggestions, but he had at least planted the seed. Much to the Parson's disappointment, the other managers did not buy into his proposal, and the idea of a boxing trust was dropped.

Davies was disgusted with prizefighting because it was no longer operating as a real business but more like a crooked scheme (or Chicago government). This has been a nearly constant problem for the sport. Davies believed that prizefighting was a real business, and he had sliced Hall's throat when Hall suggested fixing a fight. Davies moved away from the business of managing fighters. For a short time he negotiated with Dave Shafer to take over the management of James Michael, who was then the world's champion bicycle rider.[1777] Bicycle racing had become an extremely popular sport, and getting into this racket would have been something like returning to the early days of managing racewalkers. Davies offered $10,000 and 10 percent of Michael's winnings to Shafer to assign his management rights, but the two men could not reach an agreement and the idea fizzled.[1778]

Interference with fights in New Orleans

He left Chicago on March 13 and went to New Orleans, where he hoped to make the final arrangements for a McCoy-Bonner fight to take place on March 28 at the new Saint Bernard Club.[1779] The former Saint Bernard *Athletic* Club had fallen apart at the end of 1897 because of disputes over its management. The new Saint Bernard Club had dropped the *Athletic* and was made up of part of the old club's membership. The new president was Joe Catalanotto, a wealthy wholesale butcher in Saint Bernard Parish. Catalanotto hired Davies to act as the club's manager. However, some of the disaffected members of the old club were politically connected and threatened legal action if the new club went ahead with any prizefighting. As a consequence the McCoy-Bonner match was not a sure thing. It is remarkable how quickly Davies left the politics of Chicago behind and entered headfirst into the cesspool of New Orleans politics.[1780]

McCoy and Bonner had agreed to fight for 50 percent of the gross receipts with a guarantee of at least $2,000. Each was also guaranteed $250 for expenses if the fight was prevented. This was a long limb for Davies to be on because it put the financial burden of a successful venture on a new club that had also spent a large sum remodeling the venue. He wanted to produce a financially profitable contest in a town where he had no strong connections.

While he was in New Orleans, Davies went to the race track. He had never shown any particular interest in horse racing, but he explained that Hopkins gave him a pass and thought he would see what it was about. In addition, his friend O'Malley was active in horse racing in New Orleans and his brother Vere was a daily patron of the Chicago tracks.

Charlie was optimistic about having a successful show in New Orleans. He obtained a permit from Albert Estopinal, president of the Police Jury of Saint Bernard Parish. In August 1897, the parish had raised the price of a license to $500 per fight in order to discourage future applications. The new club paid the higher fee, and the license seemed to be the only legal prerequisite for the match. A chart of reserved seats was published and tickets went on sale about ten days before the fight with a good response. Advertisements were placed in several New Orleans newspapers. Box seats were $5, reserved seats $3, and general admission $2. Choynski was coming to New Orleans to challenge the winner of the fight at ringside.[1781] It may have cost a few dollars to have Joe appear, but it was good for ticket sales. Joe told the press that Davies and he were still friends and that even though the Parson was no longer his manager, Charlie would back him in a fight against McCoy.

Only two days before the match, Louisiana's governor, acting under pressure from editorials in the *Picayune* and the angry members of the old club, announced he would stop the fight and arrest the participants.[1782] Two days before the fight the attorney general filed a civil complaint in Plaquemine Parish for a writ to enjoin the fight as a violation of Louisiana law.[1783] The writ was issued ex parte, and the sheriff served five copies of the court's order on Davies and the others.

The next day a justice of the peace in Saint Bernard Parish issued criminal warrants for the arrest of Catalanotto, Davies, McCoy, Bonner, and several other members of the new club charging them with conspiring to engage in an assault and battery. The sheriff went to see Bonner and told him he would let him go if Jack would get on a train and leave town. Bonner said he didn't have the money for a ticket, and the sheriff offered to pay half the price. But Bonner resisted and was then arrested and jailed. Davies and the club finally called off the fight at a substantial financial loss. McCoy got word that the sheriff was looking for him, and he escaped Louisiana on a northbound train headed for St. Louis after collecting $250 from Davies. When the sheriff learned that McCoy had skipped town, he went home without arresting anyone else. Estimates were that Davies may have lost as much as $10,000 when this fight fell through, but much of this loss probably fell on the club members.[1784]

The second week of April found Davies in Detroit making a cameo appearance in the famous Gay Nineties musical-comedy, *A Trip to Chinatown*.[1785] This play had been the longest-running musical in the history of Broadway, where it had opened in 1891. It had returned record profits at the World's Fair and had been presented in London, Saint Petersburg, Russia, and in France. It was a comedy that featured the story of Mrs. Guyer, a chaperone who is retained to guide several young couples on a trip to San Francisco's Chinatown. Uncle Ben, their wealthy guardian, is accidentally led into a romance with Mrs. Guyer believing that she has invited him to a liaison at a famous restaurant. Davies' longtime friend John R. Considine was presenting the play in Detroit, and he persuaded Davies to take the part of the proprietor of the Cliff House, where the central action took place. After visiting with Hopkins in St. Louis, the two men traveled to Chicago where they parted, and Davies left for Detroit on April 12 for a week-long part in the play. This was at least the third personal theatrical venture for Davies and clearly was his avocation.[1786]

War with Spain

Just as his appearance in Detroit ended, war broke out between the United States and Spain. The headlines over the next few weeks were of a type that had not been seen since 1865,[1787] which Davies would have remembered from his days in New York when he was between twelve and fourteen years of age: "War Has Begun – Spain Throws Down the Gauntlet at Madrid by Dismissing the American Minister! Illinois Ready to Respond! Call of President McKinley on a Basis of 100,000 Men Would Take the Prairie State's Entire Militia. English Snarl At Americans! Madrid Shouting for War! Ready to Join The Army – Assistant Secretary Roosevelt To Resign Within A Week! Spain Now Declares War! Russia Stands By Uncle Sam."[1788]

On the day that Spain declared war, Davies postponed the boxing bouts scheduled for Tattersall's in Chicago. He thought continuing as usual would be inappropriate, and he said that some of the boys scheduled to fight might want to join the Army instead.

Hopkins showed his patriotism by changing the programs in his theaters to feature panoramic photos military and naval incidents, such as the sinking of the *Maine* and the U.S. Army's camp at Tampa, Florida. The panoramic presentations were on huge wall-sized boards and proved to be a popular way for people to obtain news of the war effort, foreshadowing the later theater-based newsreels.[1789]

Davies rescheduled his athletic entertainment for June 2 at Tattersall's.[1790] He had matched Kid McPartland to box six rounds with Tom Tracy and was also hoping to arrange a match between Billy Stift and a fairly new fighter named Jack Moffatt. He was also negotiating with Corbett to appear in Chicago on June 2, offering Corbett a $5,000 guarantee or a percentage of the total gate receipts.

Davies' plan was to bring in McCoy, Ruhlin, or Jeffries if he could get Corbett to sign on.[1791]

On May 19, Davies was in Syracuse to watch the McCoy-Ruhlin fight with the idea of bringing the winner of that match to Chicago to appear with Corbett.[1792] He traveled from Syracuse to St. Louis, where he met with Hopkins on Monday, May 23.[1793] In retrospect, it should have been obvious he and Hopkins were "doing business" and that the business they were doing related to the theaters in New Orleans.

A message to either play ball or get out of Chicago

The next day Davies returned to Chicago to complete arrangements for the Tattersall's show. He was never able to sign Corbett or any other leading heavyweight to participate. The postponed show at Tattersall's was sabotaged. Someone tampered with the dynamo, the electrical generator that powered the theater's lights, and it blew out after only one bout, leaving everyone in the dark and forcing the postponement of the entertainment. This was not an accident. The electrician hired by Davies to repair the dynamo said he had never before seen such damage and that it was no ordinary burning out and. There was a clear message being sent to Davies, and it was probably being sent by Coughlin and Hinky-Dink Kenna: "Don't get the idea you can put on shows in Chicago without paying us off! If you do, you'll be sorry. We are the syndicate here, and we control what happens here. McDonald can't protect you anymore. Van Praag and Walters can't help either."

Charlie rescheduled the bouts for the following evening at Tattersall's. About two thousand five hundred people attended, but doing everything twice ended up costing him $1,800. The *Tribune* wrote: "A feature of the evening was the demand made for 'Parson' Davies, who was noisily received on entering the ring. In a short speech he said suggestions reflecting on him had been made as to the sudden termination of the show on the previous evening, and 'money could not purchase the satisfaction he now felt because he had kept faith with the public.'"[1796]

In July, Davies picked up a new fighter, Jack Root. Root was born in May 1876 in Fryhelge, Bohemia. A large immigration of Bohemians came to Chicago in the early 1890s, and many of them lived in and around the Levee district, just north of the Chicago River. Root lived until June 10, 1963, and his life spanned several generations of remarkable changes in the United States and the world. He was not a true heavyweight because he weighed between 155 and 170 pounds, about the same size as Jack Burke when he first came to Parson Davies. Root's first fight was in November 1897. As late as March 1898 he was still being referred to as an "unknown" from Chicago. In May, he defeated Jack Moffatt in six rounds, and his accomplishment drew Davies' attention.

If Root was going to amount to anything, he needed to be shown outside of Chicago. Davies scheduled Root to meet Tom Lansing of Louisville at the Lenox Athletic Club in New York in late July. Lansing had been McCoy's sparring partner. Jack was classed as a middleweight and was considerably smaller than Lansing; however, he knocked out Lansing in six rounds and impressed the New York fight fraternity.[1797] Less than two weeks later Root fought at the Lenox club, this time beating up on a Jim Watts, a black fighter from Louisville. Root smashed Watts at will, and it was noted that Watts had little knowledge of how to fight and was simply a target for Root's fists.[1798] Root stayed on in Philadelphia to work as Sharkey's sparring partner.[1799]

In early November, Root had a rematch with Lansing in Chicago and knocked him out in five rounds. Within a few days Lansing was critically ill at his home and almost entirely paralyzed. His doctor thought Lansing had a blood clot and offered slight chance of his recovery. In late January 1899 Lansing died from the injury sustained in the Chicago fight.[1800]

Davies decides to leave Chicago

Davies' heart was no longer in his work. Something had knocked the pep out of him and that "something" probably related to a series of events that included his own health, the loss of star fighters, interference with his shows in Chicago and New Orleans, the ever-growing number of crooked fights, political payoffs, and the loss of his own political influence in Chicago. Losing the McCoy-Bonner fight in New Orleans was expensive.[1801] The sabotage in Chicago was expensive. Both Ryan and White had walked out on Davies after he had brought them to the top of their professions. Then Barry went to England with White and without Davies. This too would have been a hard thing to swallow. Finally, Choynski and Armstrong left his management.

Davies had picked up Joe in New Orleans when Choynski didn't have the train fare to leave town. He had managed Joe longer than any other fighter, including Jackson. Charlie had then picked up Armstrong as an unknown black fighter with no record and had tried to bring him to the top of the heavyweight ladder before Armstrong double-crossed his manager by fighting Childs while Davies was out of town. Finally, Davies' health was not good. He had been poisoned, his rheumatism was not improving, and he had been diagnosed as having chronic ataxia. It is reasonable to suppose that doctors had told Davies that his condition would only get worse if he continued to travel constantly and did not slow down.

Late in July or in early August, Davies had a brief reconciliation with Armstrong. Jeffries was making a swing on the East Coast to impress the fight fans there with his undefeated record and potential as a heavyweight champion. Jeffries' handlers agreed that their man would appear at the Lenox Athletic Club in New York and box two heavyweights, Armstrong and O'Donnell, on the same night. He was to box each man for ten rounds with the idea that he would stop them both.

Jeffries' first match of the evening was with Armstrong. Jeffries had dropped his earlier assertion of the color line because and had already fought and defeated Jackson in March 1898. Newspapers credited Davies with arranging Armstrong's participation in Jeffries' show. Jeffries broke his left hand in the first round of the match. This was reminiscent of Sullivan's match with Cardiff in Minneapolis, where Sullivan broke his hand on Cardiff's head in the first round. Jeffries said he had broken his hand on Armstrong's hard head. Later accounts imply that Jeffries had not really broken his hand, but he had been taxed so much by Armstrong that he could not continue with O'Donnell. Supposedly, after this match Ryan taught Jeffries his famous crouch, and this change in approach launched Jeffries success.[1802]

Davies bet $200 to $500 that Armstrong would last the entire ten rounds with Jeffries, and he cleaned up on his bet. Jeffries hand was examined after the bout, and the house doctor refused to let him continue with the second match with O'Donnell.[1803] The *Philadelphia Inquirer* saw Jeffries as a fighter with foot work like an elephant and equally as graceful with his hands. It said that Armstrong's "think tank" was not of the luminous variety and that Armstrong could have won the match if he had only let himself out a little bit.[1804] Whether or not it was fair, this match with Armstrong damaged Jeffries' reputation for a long time after August 1898.

Jack Root – One of Parson Davies' last fighters before leaving Chicago
1903 Photograph of the Chicago History Museum

Davies stopped managing fighters, and many of his former clients were thereafter managed by Lou Houseman, the well-known sporting editor of the *Chicago Inter-Ocean*. Houseman was a native of New Orleans and relocated to Chicago by way of Cincinnati. He was already replacing Davies in Chicago. He came to Chicago at the time of the Haymarket affair and began working as a police reporter for the *Inter Ocean*. After a few years Houseman became the sporting editor for the *Inter Ocean* and then became associated with Tom Hanton and Harry J. Franks in operating Tattersall's.[1805]

Hanton had worked in a rolling mill before taking a half-interest in Coffee & Hanton, a Randolph Street saloon just east of Clark Street. It was a popular place and patronized by city and county officials, politicians, professional ball players, and many theater people. Hanton promoted several matches in Chicago in the late 1890s. He had the political pull necessary for Houseman to successfully promote events and obtain licenses in Chicago.

Hanton was also a bigot who set out to cleanse prizefighting in Chicago of what he considered the stain of black fighters. Houseman was also active in political affairs and a friend of the Cook County sheriff. These were all prerequisites for success in Chicago. Houseman and Hanton were part of the new generation of Chicago sporting promoters. These men along with many others such as Smiley Corbett and Cap Anson were all friends of Davies, but part of the next generation. Charlie was neither part of their generation nor did he have the influence he had exercised for the prior twenty years.[1806]

On August 31, the *Chicago Tribune* published a one-paragraph article noting that Davies had left for New Orleans to assume the management of the two theaters there: "He is interested in the theaters as a partner of Colonel John Hopkins. Davies will return to Chicago in two weeks to arrange special trains to the Corbett-McCoy fight."[1807] This was small notice for the greatest sporting man Chicago had ever seen.

On September 1, the *Picayune* noted the arrival of "C. E. Davis" as a guest of the St. Charles Hotel on the prior day.[1808] It carried a short article: "Mr. Chas. Davies, called the 'Parson' by those who dare to be familiar with him arrived in the city last night, to assume the local and personal management of the St. Charles Theater and the Academy of Music of Colonel John D. Hopkins, the new lessees of the playhouses on St. Charles street. Colonel Hopkins will be here a week later."[1809]

Life begins in New Orleans

There was a strange duality in the reaction of the New Orleans press to the theater situation in that city. The leading newspapers carried articles almost every day asserting the need to enforce an 1892 Louisiana antitrust statute. That law made it unlawful for any individual, firm, company, corporation or association to enter into, continue or maintain any combination, agreement or arrangement of any kind, expressed or implied, to create or carry out restrictions in trace, to prevent competition, or to limit or reduce the prices of merchandise, produce or commodities.

On the other hand, it was common knowledge that Klaw & Erlanger controlled 90 percent of the traveling theatrical performers and intended to drive independent managers and owners out of business. Nevertheless, their investment in New Orleans was lauded by the *Picayune* and their near monopoly ignored.[1810]

At the end of June 1900, the *Post Dispatch* referred to an article in the *Police News* that provided an explanation for Davies' move to New Orleans:

> "Parson Davies'" departure from fistiana for the legitimate fields of livelihood removes the picturesque figure from the fistic ranks. Davies at various times made money, but never could hold any, and was glad to grab the chance offered him by Col. Hopkins. Davies was a good impresario of a fighter—in fact, his own individualism entered into the combination, no matter whom he was starring. . . . Davies is a good story teller, a good liver, but his days of precedence in the sporting world have been supplanted by men like O'Rourke and Brady, who know no scruple and who would stop at nothing to attain their ends. In Davies' days sporting men had one thing which was better than money—their word. Today the general sporting man's word isn't worth 30 cents—it's a case of money with a capital "M."[1811]

The claim that Davies could not "hold any" money was not true as events over the next ten years would demonstrate. The more subtle idea that Charlie's own individualism entered into the combination with his fighters no matter who was starring is on the mark. Fighters who were willing to let Davies mold their careers did well with Davies. However, many fighters have huge egos and those men found it difficult to submit to Davies' control.

About two weeks before Davies left Chicago, the *Post Dispatch* carried the following article about Jackson:

> San Francisco, Cal., Aug. 18 – Peter Jackson's plight is sad. He is spending his days and nights in saloons. What money he had when he came to California, it is said, has been spent. It is believed he has drunk it up, in addition to the money which he earned in England.
>
> "Jackson hasn't a cent," remarked an old sporting man yesterday. "He has gone through every cent he had, and I don't know what is to become of him. I can see his finish. He lives in a saloon near Turk and Market streets and not a night goes by but he goes to bed drunk. His is a pitiful sight.
>
> "If there ever was a perfect specimen of manhood, he was. His great body was symmetrical and he carried it so gracefully you

were bound to admire him. Whiskey had made him a toddling wreck. He is even worse than Sullivan."[1812]

That last phrase—"even worse than Sullivan"—was quite a condemnation because for years Sullivan was the poster child for the American drunk.

For the balance of 1898 Davies was busy with the two theaters in New Orleans. Davies, Hopkins and O'Malley wanted to get the jump on the syndicate's theaters by opening their season earlier than usual. Between September 1 and September 11 the auditorium, foyer, and lobby of the St. Charles were all painted, new carpets and curtains installed, and electric footlights and proscenium lights added. The prices for seats were set to cut the prices charged by the syndicate: ten, twenty, and thirty cents versus fifteen, twenty-five, and thirty-five cents.

The St. Charles opened with a stock company but added vaudeville performers between acts.[1813] Use of a stock company was required because the New York syndicate controlled the traveling theater companies and had blacklisted the St. Charles and Academy of Music. Davies' niece Sarah (Sadie) Gruschow came to New Orleans to assist with the Academy of Music. She lived in apartment above the theater and during the season became well known around New Orleans.[1814] The new Crescent opened on September 25, and in the first few months of competing Davies, Hopkins, and O'Malley made good money.[1815]

On October 5, the *St. Paul Globe* reported that the president of the Hawthorne Club in Buffalo wanted Davies to take charge of a proposed Corbett-McCoy match, but Davies refused.[1816] He needed to deal with the day-to-day problems of keeping the stock company talent happy, offering decent productions for theater-goers, and providing advertising that worked. In many respects he was an old hand at this type of thing and did well for his partners.

In January, an important match was scheduled at the Lenox Athletic Club between Sharkey and McCoy.[1817] Sporting men from all over the world flowed into New York, and advance ticket sales brought in $42,000. Davies headed a large delegation from New Orleans that made the trip to New York. The *Picayune* reported "that one would think that all that were interested in the winter racing in New Orleans had, by some magical force, been shipped suddenly to Gotham" to watch Sharkey knock out McCoy in ten rounds. Davies also had a special telegraph service arranged at the Academy of Music and many New Orleans sports gathered there to hear the round-by-round account as wire transmissions were received.[1818]

Davies did not return to Chicago until January 27. Van Praag asked him to return to produce a show at Tattersall's. He had probably run into Sol at the McCoy-Sharkey match in New York, and Van Praag likely convinced Davies that it was possible to present a meaningful show in Chicago under his sponsorship. It would be up to Sol to make sure that the Coughlin-Kenna duo didn't interfere with the production. When Davies arrived in Chicago, the *Tribune* noted that "the South has apparently done [Davies] good and he looks in the best of health."[1819]

The show at Tattersall's was to feature a Sharkey-Corbett match. Corbett had declared he would fight the winner of the Sharkey-McCoy match. Articles were signed for that match, but then Mayor Harrison, always the weathervane, said he would not allow this type of fight in Chicago.[1820] This was the type of thing that killed boxing in one of the greatest venues in America. The timing for the Sharkey-Corbett match was bad because the mayor was facing reelection within a few months. One sure way for a Chicago mayor to attract votes was to get tough with boxing. History established that beating up on prizefighting was an appropriate pre-election tactic.[1821] Stories circulated that the city council would petition the mayor to permit the fight, especially because Von Praag had secured the license and assigned it to Davies. If the mayor prevented the fight, it would cost Davies the $1,000 he had posted as his personal bond to protect the fighters from financial loss in the event of a cancellation.

Some noted that O'Rourke, who was handling Sharkey, would probably not stick it to his friend Davies, but it seemed likely that Corbett would insist on his share of the posted money. In the end the mayor would not relent, providing another example of how Chicago politics worked and confirming that Davies had made a wise decision when he got out of the business. After the failure of the match with Corbett, Sharkey was suffering from rheumatism and went to Mt. Clemens for three weeks to take the mineral bath treatments.[1822] Davies did make something out of the situation by booking Sharkey to give sparring exhibitions with Armstrong at the Academy of Music in New Orleans for three weeks beginning at the beginning of May.[1823]

In April, Davies was one author of a guidebook published to interpret the Queensberry rules. Others given credit for the guide were O'Rourke, Billy Madden, and J. B. Angle, who was referee of the National Sporting club of London.[1824] These books were made available to patrons of the Lenox and Broadway athletic clubs in New York. Both clubs subscribed to the interpretations provided in the guidebook, which specified a point system and required the referee for a boxing match to award a maximum number of five points (or marks) at the end of each round and a proportionate number to the other contestant. The points were awarded when fighters were on the attack for direct, clean hits with the knuckle-part of the gloves and for defense including effective guarding, stopping, and getting away. If in the referee's judgment the points were otherwise equal, the referee was required to give a preference to the contestant who did the most leading or displayed the best style.

The guide also allowed contestants to use soft bandages, if necessary. The use of bandages under the gloves was considered to be an innovation. Some fighters, such as Jeffries, never bandaged their hands. Jeffries first used bandages when he fought Jack Johnson. Other provisions included: (1) all contests were to be decided in a roped ring of not less than twelve feet or more than twenty-four feet square; (2) the limit to the number of rounds was either twenty or twenty-five rounds of three minutes, with intervals between the rounds of one minute; (3) the gloves were to be a minimum weight of five ounces each; (4) contestants were entitled to the assistance of three seconds, but the names of the seconds were required to be submitted to the committee for approval; (5) the referee was allowed to disqualify a contestant for delivering a foul blow intentionally or otherwise, for holding, butting, shouldering, falling without receiving a blow, wrestling, or for a boxglove (using the inside butt of the hand, the wrist or elbow), or for roughing it at the ropes; (6) if, in the opinion of the referee, a deliberate foul was committed by a contestant then that contestant would not be entitled to any prize; (7) breaking of any of these rules by a contestant or his seconds would render a contestant liable to disqualification; and (8) the referee would decide any question not provided for in the rules and the interpretation of any of the rules.[1825]

An arsonist burns the St. Charles to the ground

After his failed effort in Chicago, Davies went back to New Orleans and resumed managing the two theaters. Catastrophe struck on June 4 when the St. Charles was burned to the ground.[1826] When the fire started Davies was eating supper with O'Malley at Leon Lamothe's restaurant on St. Charles Street near Common.

The fire started in the back of the building around midnight. The St. Charles had a seating capacity of two thousand seven hundred while the Academy of Music only accommodated about one thousand four hundred patrons and was intended for higher-class entertainment. The *Picayune* published several articles about the fire, one of which provides insight into the impact of the fire on Parson Davies:

> Last night a few minutes after 11 o'clock a tall, heavy-set man, with a straw hat and a light suit of clothes, rushed up to the main entrance of the St. Charles Theater. The perspiration was standing out on his face. He was excited, hot and apparently rattled. He rushed down St. Charles street toward Commercial alley and in a moment came back only to see the flames eating out through the main stairway.
>
> C. E. Davies, better known [to] the sporting world over as "Parson" Davies, had for once lost his self-control. He backed out across the street on the opposite side of St. Charles street and under the shed of one of the string of saloons. There he stood like a marble statue and watched the total destruction of the Old Drury.
>
> "Parson" Davies was broken up. He mopped his face with a handkerchief, and he could scarcely speak.
>
> "Charley, there is no need to take it so hard," said his partner, D. C. O'Malley, who came up and stood by his side. "Breaking down won't put out that fire."
>
> "No, but everything was staked on the St. Charles. If it had to be one of them, why couldn't it have been the Academy?" was the reply. . . .

> "This is not the first time the St. Charles has been on fire—this is the third time." Said Mr. Davies. "No one can make me believe that the first was accidental. No, sir. The last time, which was about four months ago, one of our men got badly burned in trying to extinguish the blaze, which he finally did. It is too evident to my mind that the fire is incendiary."[1828]

Davies was particularly upset by the loss of the St. Charles because of its huge seating capacity. He said that on a Sunday night they could pack three thousand people into the house with standing room to the point that they wondered where all the bodies came from. Sunday night at the St. Charles was the big lift for weekly expenses and was the thing that made the New Orleans operation profitable.

Pratt stated publicly that the fire was the work of an arsonist and offered a reward of $1,000 for evidence leading to the discovery of the culprits. The watchman for the St. Charles had been placed under surveillance and arrested for a spurious reason so that he could be questioned. According to Pratt, the theater had been making money for the lessees during the prior season. He said their books showed "a very handsome balance on the right side." However, later information showed a different picture.

Pratt was asked what effect the fire would have on the lease and he said: "None at all, except that pending the rebuilding of the theater the lessees are exempted from rental, and are entitled to any moneys paid me in advance for such rent." Asked about insurance he said: "I carried very little insurance on the theater; in fact only enough to replace the old building as it stood before the fire, having had an estimate from a contractor on that point. The high rate of insurance, 3 ½ per cent, did not justify my carrying any more." Davies, Hopkins and O'Malley carried $15,000 of fire insurance as lessees. O'Malley claimed that their loss was $7,500, which would have amounted to a $20,000 loss each for Davies, O'Malley and Hopkins.[1829] An article published in 1908 suggests that after the St. Charles burned, Parson Davies gave up his interest in the two theaters.[1830]

The same night that the St. Charles burned, another fire was found burning in the Academy of Music. An alert observer noticed that fire, which had been set on one of the upper floors above the stage. A captain of the New Orleans fire department extinguished the fire and summoned Davies to show him the obvious evidence of another attempted arson. That fire's loss was only about $50. In November 1903, Hopkins' theater in Louisville, which was the largest one in town, also burned to the ground in a mysterious fire that destroyed half a city block, including the Masonic Temple.

The cause of the fire was never precisely determined, but it soon became known to Davies and Hopkins that Pratt thought that O'Malley had arranged to burn both theaters because their new corporation was losing money. Losing money was particular a problem for O'Malley because he had personally signed a large bond to secure payment of the rent.[1831]

The Chicago papers noted that Davies' assistant, Glickauf, had relocated to New Orleans and was concerned with the St. Charles Theater. Glickauf made the interesting comment that Davies had abandoned his scheme to start boxing in Havana, Cuba, for the time being.[1832]

There was a tremendous amount of commerce between Cuba and New Orleans, and some of the biggest New York banks were starting to work with the New Orleans banks to expand business with Cuba. After the fires in New Orleans, the St. Louis newspapers reported that Davies would soon start a boxing club in St. Louis and would probably give two or three shows during the hot weather season as a way of introducing the club. While making his plans, Davies went to West Baden for the hot baths.[1833]

An unsuccessful attempt to open a boxing club in St. Louis

Although the St. Charles had been burned to the ground, Davies did not stop working. Three weeks after the fire he wrote to a correspondent in Chicago that he had learned that New Orleans might legalize boxing and if that happened, he hoped to pull off some big matches there. He also reported that the Olympic Athletic Club, where Corbett won the championship from Sullivan, expected to become active again and would be offering big purses for important fights.[1834]

Davies and Hopkins also began negotiating to open an athletic club in St. Louis so that prizefights could be staged there under a new Missouri law similar to New York's Horton law, which allowed boxing in a club format. Theater owners who could not resist the syndicate were anxious to rent their venues for almost any profitable use. In early July, Hopkins and Davies agreed to rent the Fourteenth Street Theater in St. Louis from its owner C. W. Whitney. The theater was rented for a series of "pugilistic entertainments."[1835]

C. W. Whitney had attempted to promote boxing matches in St. Louis, and in 1898 the state of Missouri filed a complaint against him to prevent his use of Whitney's Fourteenth Street Theater.[1836] That litigation was resolved when Judge Willis Clarke set the legal requirements to establish that a match was illegal. After Judge Clarke's ruling, the city attorney issued an opinion that bona fide athletic clubs could hold exhibitions for club members without police interference.[1837]

These two things had induced Davies and Hopkins to make a stab at opening a new athletic club. Under the terms of their lease Davies had two thirds of the obligation for its payments. Both Whitney and Hopkins also had an interest in the profits and like obligations for the losses from the fights to be staged. It is probable that none of this would have happened had the St. Charles not been burned down.

Dixon and Eddie Santry were scheduled to meet in Chicago in mid-July.[1838] On July 12 Davies announced another Dixon-Santry match in St. Louis on July

31 at the Fourteenth Street Theater.[1839] Davies' prizefights in the city were offered by an entity called the Commercial Athletic Club and were in competition with fights being produced by the West End Athletic Club of St. Louis, which had also been reorganized after Judge Clarke's decision and the opinion by the city attorney.[1840] The West End Club was not happy that Davies was capitalizing on its hard work by forming a new competitive athletic club and that he had secured the proposed Dixon-Santry match as his club's opening show.

After announcing his plans for the match in St. Louis, Davies went back to New Orleans.[1841] By July 16 Davies was again in St. Louis, and both Dixon and Glickauf were with him. He took Dixon to Bridgeton, near Barney Schreiber's place, to rest up and train for his reprise with Santry. Davies was planning to return to New Orleans in a few days. Glickauf was to stay in St. Louis to take charge of the operations at the Fourteenth Street Theater. Charlie then met with Hopkins at the Forest Park Highlands, Hopkins' outdoor theater. On Tuesday evening July 18 Davies left for New Orleans and did not return to St. Louis until Sunday, July 30.[1842]

At the end of July, trouble was in the wind. Rumors circulated that the Dixon-Santry match would be stopped. On Saturday, July 29 C. W. Whitney issued a statement to the press: "Regardless of reports to the contrary, the entertainment next Monday night will take place as previously stated in the public press, and George Dixon, champion featherweight of the world, will meet Eddie Santry in a 20-round scientific boxing contest."[1843] Davies could not have approved of this declaration because throughout his career he had been careful not to promise that entertainment would take place when police interference was threatened. Whitney's unconditional declaration was incorrect because he and Glickauf were ultimately not successful in obtaining a permit for the fight.

"The West End club appears to be running things in this town," Davies commented.[1844]

The Dixon-Santry match was then moved to the Lenox Athletic Club in New York and drew more than five thousand spectators. Davies' loss was O'Rourke's gain. For his part Santry had to get out of a prior commitment with Houseman to fight Tommy White at Dubuque, Iowa, in order to have a second chance at Dixon.[1845]

Davies and Glickauf remained in St. Louis and did not go to New York for the fight. Davies told the *Post Dispatch* he was staying in town to investigate why the police had barred the fight. He also announced that the box office at the Fourteenth Street Theater would be open from nine a.m. to five p.m. to refund tickets to the Dixon-Santry fight.[1846]

Davies and O'Rourke then took in the races at the Fair Grounds on August 1.[1847] By mid-August Davies left St. Louis and went back to New Orleans. He left Glickauf in St. Louis to handle the arrangements for a Tracy-Smith match being advertised for Monday, September 11.[1848]

Davies opens the Crescent billiard hall in New Orleans

Over the years Davies had run into interference many times in St. Louis. He apparently decided to take his life in a different direction. On August 19, several newspapers reported that Davies would abandon the idea of opening an athletic club in St. Louis. He had just agreed to lease the historic Crescent billiard hall at New Orleans.

The Crescent was at the intersection of Canal and Royal streets. Originally constructed in 1826, it was converted to the Merchants' Hotel in 1856. Colonel A. W. Merriam had then converted the hotel to a billiard hall in 1865. A 1904 *New Orleans Guide* identified this intersection as the center of the city.[1849] Davies paid $12,000 for the lease, good will, and fixtures of the hall. He intended to give the club a thorough overhaul, putting in twenty new tables of the highest quality and making other changes that would make his establishment equal to the best in the United States.[1850]

O'Malley had a 50 percent interest in the new billiard-hall venture.[1851] Davies said he intended to reopen the Crescent on October 2 and would invite the top billiard champions, including Frank Ives and Jack Schaffer to appear during the coming winter. Davies also hired Charles E. Parker, a Chicago billiard manager, to manage the Crescent. Unfortunately, on October 30, a few weeks after the Crescent had reopened, Parker had a stroke while reading a newspaper in a restaurant and died the next morning.[1852]

Davies arrived in St. Louis on the evening train on Monday, August 21, to meet with Glickauf. He stayed until Wednesday, August 24, when he left for Chicago where he bought furnishings for the billiard hall in New Orleans. Before he left he said he expected the Tracy-Smith match to go forward and predicted that it would be a great fight.[1853] Davies passed through St. Louis on his way back to New Orleans on August 27.[1854]

A modified boxing trust

In late September, the New York managers adopted a modified form of the boxing trust that Davies had suggested in January 1898. What the boxing club managers did was to follow "the example of theatrical managers" in the belief that they could better themselves, make more money and improve the business of boxing in the process. The boxing promoters candidly stated that they "also desire to keep rival managers out of the field and have united for protection." Those joining the trust included the George Considine's Broadway Athletic Club, Brady's Coney Island Athletic Club, and O'Rourke's Lenox Athletic Club. Martin Julian, Fitzsimmons's manager, was a stockholder in the Coney Island Club. Considine was Corbett's manager and O'Rourke had Sharkey under his management. The group began to call itself the Greater New York Boxing Clubs and planned to rule the pugilistic world.[1855] In the long run the trust failed because of its members' big egos and the repeal of the Horton law discussed in more detail below.

In addition to business trusts, patriotism was a hot commodity in late 1899, and Hopkins took advantage in several ways. His theaters were sponsoring a panoramic of the Rough Riders, who had become the greatest heroes of the time. In addition, Hopkins brought a trainload of Texas cowboys to St. Louis to display the riding and roping techniques of T. R.'s favorite soldiers. On October 2, the cowboys went to Chicago to appear at the Fair Grounds, and Davies arranged a "Wild West Show" featuring fancy and trick roping and riding techniques to be held at Tattersall's on October 29 and 30.[1856]

Davies is caught in the middle of a gun battle

Davies was in New Orleans and writing a regular Sunday sporting column for the *Chicago_Tribune*.[1857] On October 10, he was nearly killed in a gun battle. His closest business associate in New Orleans was O'Malley, who was the owner and proprietor of the *Evening Item* and also a well-known sport promoter. This was the same man who had been hired to run the Roby enterprises during the Columbian Exposition.

O'Malley was another Irish immigrant. His family emigrated to Cleveland when Dominick was only thirteen. When he was sixteen O'Malley spent eight months in jail for stealing iron bars from a Lake Erie loading dock. He had then traveled to Boston, Pensacola, and Mobile before arriving at New Orleans in the summer of 1878.

In New Orleans, O'Malley worked on the levee for a dollar a day before obtaining a job as a watchman for a shipping company. He eventually operated a detective agency and employed as many as twenty-seven people before going into the newspaper business. He also built up his own impressive criminal record by being arrested more than forty times for various offenses.[1858]

O'Malley had a long-running feud with Colonel C. Harrison Parker, a Louisiana tax collector for the First District of Orleans Parish and chairman of the Democratic State Campaign Committee. This enmity arose out of Parker's opposition to the Louisiana lottery, which O'Malley supported. Parker was also editor-in-chief of a newspaper called the *Delta*, which was an anti-lottery newspaper that wanted to stop the famous Louisiana lottery. He had previously been an editor of the *Picayune*. On Sunday, October 8, O'Malley's newspaper carried a political cartoon mocking Parker and depicting him as a little dog led by a string held by Louisiana's governor. Parker was offended by the cartoon.

The business office for the *Evening Item* was located on Camp Street between Poydras and Commercial Alley and only about a block from the Crescent Billiard Hall. The *Picayune's* office was on Camp Street between Gravier and Poydras. All of this was near the wholesale cotton and wholesale grocery houses and not far from the current site of the Harrah's New Orleans Casino. According to the *Times-Democrat* Davies had gone to the business office of the *Evening Item* to obtain O'Malley's signature on some documents related to their theatrical business.

About two thirty in the afternoon, the evening papers were just hitting the streets. With the newspapers being wrapped up, O'Malley signed the documents Davies had brought to him and asked Charlie to go with him to a place on St. Charles called McCloskey's to get coffee. The two men left the *Evening Item's* office together and someone briefly spoke to Davies, which resulted in him falling a few paces behind O'Malley as they walked down Camp Street toward Commercial Alley, where they were going to cut through to St. Charles.

Parker was standing across the Camp Street conversing with some friends as O'Malley and Davies exited the front door of the *Evening Item*. Parker turned and saw O'Malley. He started toward O'Malley from across the street. Eyewitness accounts differ about what happened next. Davies said he had never met nor seen Parker before that day, but he did notice a man coming from the other side of Camp who was well-dressed, and this attracted his attention. Davies said that the stranger yelled, "Now!" At that, O'Malley exclaimed in surprise and then, according to Davies' version, Parker drew his pistol.

Davies cried out, "Stop; this is cowardly!" Parker turned and looked at Davies as if he would shoot him, but then turned back toward O'Malley and shot twice. After the second shot Davies saw O'Malley's leg twitch, and then O'Malley drew his weapon, slid behind two adjoining telegraph polls, and returned Parker's fire.[1859] The telegraph polls were directly in front of the entrance of the *Picayune*. Davies said he was in the middle of the street and kept busy dodging.

At some point a woman began to run between the combatants, and Davies grabbed her and held her back. She fell back into the crowd and was never identified. Both pistols were emptied. Two shots hit an unfortunate newsboy who was selling the afternoon paper about one hundred yards away. He was hit in the foot and the head, but no serious damage was done as the head shot was only a glancing impact.

Parker was known to be a crack shot, and observers said he handled his pistol like an experienced marksman. He moved forward through the street and from side to side as he came closer in order to get a clear shot at O'Malley, who was moving in a circular way in order to keep the telegraph polls between himself and Parker.

When Parker reached the sidewalk in front of the *Picayune*, he fired his last shot and then went in through the front door of that office and slumped to the floor. Some accounts say that both men were using .45s, and others say that both were using .38s. It seems likely that Parker was using a .38 caliber six-shot known as the "improved" Colt revolver. It is likely that the improved Colt being used was the model M1900, a semi-automatic pistol with short recoil such as the one depicted below.[1860]

Likeness of Colonel Parker's "improved" Colt .38
Photograph courtesy of Bob Adams

Tranter .450 caliber pocket revolver. Factory engraved dealer marked on barrel
"Wilkinson & Son, Pall Mall London" – Photograph courtesy of Collectors Firearms

O'Malley was firing a Tranter that had "W. A. Pinkerton" engraved on the handle. This had obviously been a gun previously owned by Billy Pinkerton, who was a close friend of Davies and also a friend of O'Malley. Pinkerton had probably given the gun to O'Malley as a gift. O'Malley's gun was probably a .45 but older and not semi-automatic.

O'Malley customarily kept his gun in the left back pocket of his trousers as evidenced by his several arrests for carrying a concealed weapon. By the time the firing stopped, the two men were only about thirty feet apart. Parker received a bullet in the right breast just under the nipple and another in the shoulder. The bullet that hit Parker in the shoulder actually passed through him and hit a globe on the front of a saloon at the end of Commercial Alley.

O'Malley was seriously wounded in the abdomen and also received a bullet in the leg. The *New York Times* noted that O'Malley "has been in several shooting affairs, and Parker had wounded Mayor E. A. Burke, then state treasurer, in a famous duel in 1882."[1861] Davies was not hit in the exchange of gunfire. The *New Orleans States* wrote that some claimed that O'Malley had started the shooting, and others claimed that Parker had fired the first shot.[1862]

When the shooting stopped Davies ran down Commercial toward the Crescent Billiard Hall on Canal at the corner of St. Charles Street because he knew that O'Malley was wounded. Davies wanted to get Tom Shaw to take him to a Dr. Levy's office. Levy was not in, and Davies went looking for another doctor. He finally went back to O'Malley's office, where O'Malley was already receiving medical attention.

Later Davies was quoted as saying:

> "I just spoke to O'Malley," said Mr. Davies, "and asked him the cause of the shooting. He said: 'I don't know; God knows I don't.' Now about a month ago, I heard talk of O'Malley being killed in this election, and I went to him and told him he was getting along nicely and he should let elections go. He told me that his enemies were now his friends, and everything was all right. He said, however, that he had made up his mind that if any one took a crack at him he meant to crack back. He did that. Now I know of no trouble between the men. I remember when the theaters were opened I wanted a license for six months, instead of a year, and asked O'Malley about it, and he referred me to Mr. Parker. I sent Tommie Shaw to him and he did just as we expected—he was nice in the matter. I have often heard of the man, but never saw him before to-day."

The Tom Shaw that Davies was looking for on the day of the big gun fight later became a famous New York bookmaker. Shaw broke into that profession as a young man at Davies' Crescent Billiard Hall. "Long" Thomas J. Shaw became known as the Dean of the Bookmakers, and he was the best-known and the most spectacular of the bookmakers in the 1930s. It was said that Shaw had never been known to refuse a bet, no matter how large.

Shaw was the son of a New Orleans confectioner who owned trotting horses. He had been an amateur bicycle rider of some national prominence, but he never turned professional. He was also something of a boxing aficionado and was just the type of young man Davies would like to help get started in the business.[1865]

Both Parker and O'Malley were charged with attempted murder. After several delays Parker's case was the first to be tried on December 28. The District Attorney agreed to a bench trial – which is an indication that the fix was probably in. Sixteen witnesses were called. General E. H. Lombard, was the first witness for the prosecution. He was a close friend of Parker and had been talking with Parker before O'Malley left his office. Parker left his conversation with Lombard and turned and started toward where O'Malley was walking.

Calling Lombard as the State's first witness was a second indication that the fix was probably in. Lombard testified that O'Malley fired the first shot and that Parker did not begin shooting until after he had been hit in the leg. The D. A. called only one other witness, who said he saw what happened and that witness said that Parker shot first. Oddly, the defense called six witnesses and four of them testified on cross-examination that they saw Parker fire the first shot. The State's failure to call four witnesses who said Parker fired first is another indication that the fix was in.

At the end of this mess, the D. A. declined to provide any final argument. The judge asked only to have someone to repeat what Lombard had said. When Lombard's testimony was repeated, the judge found Parker not guilty. It appears that the State then dropped O'Malley's prosecution. This is the type of justice that still haunts New Orleans, but it was also a measure of how disliked O'Malley was by old-line New Orleans people.[1866] It had been apparent from the outset that there was more than a reasonable doubt about who fired the first shot but the D. A. had kept O'Malley under indictment for months while virtually planning to present a case that would result in a not guilty verdict against Parker and absolve him of liability.

Davies as a sports columnist for the *Chicago Tribune*

Just three days after the gun fight Davies provided another article in a series of his specials to the *Chicago Tribune*. He suggested that those in control of boxing needed to give specific attention to the roles that should be fulfilled by the official timekeeper and the referee. This was not particularly breathtaking stuff, but Davies wanted to propose several questions: Why do you appoint, and probably pay, an official time-keeper? What are his duties under the present system of conducting ring contests? He acknowledged that some men in the business thought that the timekeeper should be eliminated as an unnecessary part of a match. On the contrary, Davies wrote that the timekeeper was the most important man at ring side, and he should be the sole judge of time. Charlie felt that a referee who had no watch but counted with "long sweeps of his arm" rendered an unreliable count

99 out of 100 times. Davies thought this practice did not reflect good judgment and should not be permitted. He concluded that "it is not the duty of the referee to count, but to listen to the official timekeeper's call and predicate his decision on that."[1867] If his advice should be followed, then presumably quick counts and long counts could be eliminated.

Siler, the most famous referee of the day and also a regular columnist for the *Tribune*, wrote a column two weeks after Davies' column agreeing with Charlie's opinions. Siler concluded that Davies was right about how the count should be made in the event of a knockdown. However, Siler wanted to point of that "I was fortunate in my count at the Maher-Fitzsimmons fight in Mexico, and Lou Houseman, the official timekeeper, told me after the fight that every count I made up to nine was correct, and that I lost a fifth of a second between the count of nine and ten."[1868] Davies had been holding a watch for Maher during that fight, and Siler thought the Parson would confirm that his count had been fair.

The biggest fight of the year was the Jeffries-Sharkey battle at the Coney Island Athletic Club on Long Island.[1869] Attendance at this match was estimated to be ten thousand, which was a far cry from the 185 souls who had seen the Maher-Fitzsimmons match in Mexico a few years earlier. Davies led a delegation from Chicago that included Houseman and "Benny" Falk.[1870] Others at the match included the heavyweights: Sullivan, Corbett, Maher, and McCoy. This was the last important fight of the nineteenth century, and Jeffries retained the heavyweight championship when the referee Siler awarded him the decision after twenty-five hard rounds.[1871] Siler's decision was hotly debated and was studied and criticized because a complete film of the match was available.[1872]

After watching the Jeffries-Sharkey fight in New York, Davies went to Buffalo and stayed at the Iroquois Hotel as a guest of the house. A reporter for the *Buffalo Courier* conducted a long interview with Davies. The principal topic discussed was the championship fight, the respective merits of Jeffries and Sharkey, and Siler's decision. Davies thought that Siler should have called the fight a draw, but Charlie said he personally favored Sharkey because Sharkey had been the aggressor for nineteen rounds of the fight. Davies also discussed his recent meetings with Sullivan and Corbett and predicted that Corbett would be Jeffries' next opponent. Asked whether he could account for Siler's decision, Davies responded: "I really think Siler should have called it a draw, and at that he really would have been favoring the champion somewhat."[1873]

Peter Jackson nearing his death

On November 6, Davies wrote an article for the *Tribune* in response to several reports about Jackson's poor physical and financial condition. He wrote of Jackson's fondness for Dixon, and said that it was never said of Peter that he took advantage of any opponent, "for his heart was unquestionably in the right place."[1874]

A few days later another story about Jackson's deteriorating condition was on the news wires. The reports, out of Victoria, British Columbia, said that

Jackson's health was broken, that he was a wreck without a dollar to his name, and was trying to raise money to return home to Australia.[1875] Some articles referred to Jackson as the greatest heavyweight who ever lived and noted that in 1894 Jackson and Davies had divided profits of $30,000 from touring the United States with the *Uncle Tom's Cabin* productions.

Many stories talked about Jackson's generosity and used the following story to illustrate the type of man he was. Davies explained that Jackson was generous to a fault. He recalled a meeting with McAuliffe and his backer, Barney Farley, that took place at the C.A.C. with its president Fulda when reaching the articles of agreement for the Jackson-McAuliffe match. As Farley had said, "I have come to the conclusion that I won't let Joe fight the N_____ unless he agrees that the winner shall take all."

This was throwing cold water on the proceedings, and Peter and Fulda looked amazed at the new turn affairs had suddenly taken. Finally Fulda said:

> "I don't really believe that proposition is fair, Barney," said Fulda. "You cannot reasonably expect this man to make a fight and receive nothing for all the time he loses in preparing himself for it. To say the least, it looks very unsportsmanlike to me."
>
> "I can't help how it looks," replied Farley, "those are our conditions, and you can accept or leave them. Joe is the card, and he ain't going to give everybody that comes along a chance to make money out of his reputation."

Peter then pointed out he was a stranger in the United States and thought Farley was asking too much. Farley was adamant that the match would be called off if Jackson would not agree. Fulda then intervened and said that the C.A.C. would pay for Peter's training expenses and passage back to Australia if he was defeated in the match.[1876]

Peter put Joe down in the twenty-fourth round. He stood over Joe and said to Farley: "There's your loser's end, Mr. Farley." Then when Peter received the winner's purse he found McAuliffe and gave him $1,500, saying, "Mr. McAuliffe, you are entitled to this, as I would not have been able to secure the contest had it not been for you."[1877]

A few days later a squib in the *Tribune* said that Jackson was in a hospital in Victoria and had written his friend Elijah ("Lafe") Smith, the superintendent of the Polk Street Bridge in Chicago, to tell him of his circumstances. Smith had started raising a subscription to help Peter out financially.[1878] Just before Christmas, Davies received a letter from Lafe asking him to contribute to the fund for Jackson.

Prior to receiving Smith's letter, Davies had heard from Bud Renaud that Jackson was in bad shape physically and financially and had been given the address of the hotel where Peter was staying. Davies had written to Victoria and asked the owner of the hotel to let him know about Peter's condition. After Lafe's letter, Davies wrote to Corbett, O'Rourke, the Considine brothers, and several others in New York to solicit their financial assistance on Peter's behalf. Davies felt that Corbett would likely be one of the first men to help Peter financially and said that Jim always "speaks in the highest terms of Peter, both as a man and as a pugilist."[1879] Davies did not say specifically he sent money to Jackson, but it would be unusual had he not because he had been generous with others under similar circumstances.

On December 1, Davies' special to the *Tribune* carried the report that he had been asked to accept the position of matchmaker for the Southern Athletic Club and then had been asked to fill the same position for another Louisiana club. It is not clear whether he accepted either position. About this same time Hopkins announced he would rebuild the St. Charles Theater, which suggests he had purchased the property from its former owner.[1880]

Hopkins also paid Siler for the rights to exhibit the Sharkey-Jeffries fight films and also the still pictures of the match. Siler had paid $8,000 for the film, which the Colonel then exhibited in his theaters around the country. The movie was a huge drawing card. By obtaining the rights to the film from Siler, Hopkins was able to put quality entertainment into his independent theaters, and this entertainment was not controlled by the New York syndicate. This new use of his theaters helped Hopkins beat back the syndicate.

Glickauf acted as an advance man for the Sharkey-Jeffries motion pictures. He traveled to the cities where the pictures were going to be displayed next to advertise the coming novelty.[1881] In addition, Hopkins paid Siler to come to the St. Louis for the opening of the exhibition of the still pictures and to watch the film.[1882] Part of this was intended to let Siler see on film what he had judged in person and to then be questioned about his decision in favor of Jeffries. It was not exactly an instant replay, but it was the first time a referee had been able to evaluate his own work.

Davies came up from New Orleans on that occasion to watch the match on film. There were seven and one-quarter miles of film, or 285,000 feet of actual pictures of the fight. More than four hundred arc lights were used to create enough light inside the club to make the motion pictures.[1883] This entire record of the fight has been lost, but about four-and-a-half minutes of a pirated film of the match still exists that was created by a camera hidden in a box. That partial film of Jeffries-Sharkey championship match is available on YouTube.

While he was in St. Louis, Davies, and Siler went to dinner with Hopkins. Charley Haughton, the president of the West End Club of St. Louis, was eating at the same restaurant. Davies and Haughton had been considered enemies from the time that the West End had interfered with the Dixon-Santry match and Davies' attempts to open the Fourteenth Street Theater as a private club. However, Hopkins, acting as the diplomat, introduced Davies to Haughton. The two protagonists shook hands and after a few minutes of conversation buried the hatchet.[1884]

After watching the films of the Sharkey-Jeffries fight in St. Louis, Davies returned to New Orleans. On December 29, he sent a telegram to the manager of the Cincinnati Reds baseball team, Francis Carter "Bannie" Bancroft. Davies asked Bancroft to come to New Orleans at once, as he had a job for Bancroft for the balance of the winter. Speculation was that Davies wanted Bancroft to fill a position at the Academy of Music in New Orleans. It was noted that in 1898 Bancroft had worked as a press agent for the theatrical enterprises controlled by Hopkins and Davies.[1885] Somehow Davies also persuaded the Reds to spend their winter season in New Orleans under Bancroft's leadership.[1886]

Davies ended the century in New Orleans. His life had changed dramatically since leaving Chicago. He had managed two of the leading theaters in New Orleans, renovated and operated the city's largest billiard parlor, attempted to open a fight club in St. Louis, worked as manager for the Saint Bernard Club, explored the possibility of opening up prizefighting in Havana, produced a few shows in Chicago, and become a special correspondent for the *Tribune.* For the most part Davies had given up the direct management of prizefighters and seemed content with his decision.

The new century began with another big heavyweight fight at Coney Island. On January 1, 1900, McCoy met Maher and knocked him out in the fifth round.[1887] It was a decisive victory for McCoy and moved him back toward the top of the heavyweight contenders. Several other important heavyweight matches were quickly scheduled that had the New York clubs not been created would have taken months to arrange. Brady, Jeffries' manager, announced that big Jim would fight Corbett within thirty days and Sharkey within two weeks after the Corbett match. In addition, McCoy agreed to meet Choynski about two weeks after his fight with Maher.[1888]

On January 9, 1900, a fight for the featherweight championship of the world was held in New York between Terry McGovern and the great George Dixon.[1889] This was no fake or fixed fight. Both men fought hard and fast, but McGovern won in eight rounds to capture the title. McGovern received $9,000 and Dixon about $3,000 as his share of the gate. Shortly after the match a benefit for Dixon was planned to ease the financial pain of losing the championship. The *Brooklyn Eagle* noted that Davies had contributed $500 as his subscription for George's benefit.

The motivation for trying to schedule these matches quickly was that Theodore Roosevelt, who was then governor of New York, had sent a message to the general assembly urging the repeal of the Horton law on the grounds that "when any sport is carried on primarily for money—that is, as a business—it is in danger of losing much that is valuable and of acquiring some exceedingly undesirable characteristics."[1890] A few university presidents might consider what T.R. opined on this subject.

Davies agreed with only part of what the governor had written. He believed that boxing was a business and should be conducted as strictly as possible on a businesslike basis. In mid-June 1900, in a special to the *Tribune* the Parson wrote: "Pugilism is a business, and it should be conducted in a methodical and businesslike manner. The position fighters occupy in the sporting world is much akin to that occupied by the solid money men in financial circles."[1891]

By 1900 many other sports had become businesses. However, Davies clearly agreed with the governor that boxing was in danger of losing much of what made it valuable and was taking on undesirable characteristics—particularly in New York—because of political interference and fixed fights.

McCoy frequently engaged in fights that were suspected of being fixed. After his fight with Maher, many stories circulated that McCoy had intended to throw that match. Supposedly McCoy had made an arrangement with his friends to bet heavily on Maher, who was getting odds of six to ten, and then McCoy would lay down and split the winnings with his pals. This scheme had allegedly been prevented only because McCoy's pals could not find people willing to take their bets.[1892]

Before the Jeffries-Sharkey fight another issue arose concerning the choice of an appropriate referee for heavyweight fights. Siler had become the acknowledged leading referee in the United States. However, he was a German from Chicago, and the Irish sports in New York saw no value in bringing in a German from Chicago to referee fights in the big New York clubs. The enmity toward Siler increased when he declared Jeffries the winner in his fight with Sharkey. After that fight, New York politicians, including state Senator Ahearn, Richard Croker, and "Dry Dollar" Sullivan, got behind O'Rourke's efforts to ban Siler from further appearances in New York and insisted on the selection of Charley White as the referee for all the city's big fights.[1893]

Sullivan engaged in public denunciations of Siler and accused him of being a sworn member of the American Protective Association (A.P.A.) and anti-Irish.[1894] This was a serious matter in 1900. The A.P.A. was a particularly strong secret association that, although it sometimes equivocated, was primarily an anti-Catholic society. The influence of Catholics in the United States had increased exponentially in the late 1800s. In 1776 there were only twenty-five thousand Catholics out of a U.S. population of three million. By 1830 there were still only six hundred thousand, immigration had increased the estimated Catholic population to about twelve million by 1894. That year, Catholics were operating 172 high schools for boys, 668 high schools for girls, and 3,772 parochial schools nationwide. The A.P.A. oath was one Protestant answer to the Catholic menace that these numbers reflected:

> I do most solemnly promise and swear that I will use my influence to promote the interests of all Protestants everywhere in the world; that I will not employ a Roman Catholic in any capacity if I can procure the services of a Protestant; that I will not aid in building, or in maintaining, by an resources, any Roman Catholic church or institution of their sect or creed whatsoever, but will do all in my power to retard and break down the power of the Pope,

> in the country or any other; that I will not enter into any controversy with a Roman Catholic upon the subject of this order, nor will I enter into any agreement with a Roman Catholic to strike or create a disturbance whereby the Roman Catholic employees may undermine and substitute the Protestants; and that in all grievances I will seek only Protestants and counsel with them to the exclusion of all Roman Catholics, and will not make known to them anything of any nature matured at such conferences; that I will not countenance the nomination in any caucus or convention, of a Roman Catholic for any office in the gift of American people, and that I will not vote for, nor counsel others to vote for, any Roman Catholics; that I will endeavor at all times to place the political positions of this Government in the hands of the Protestants. (Repeat) To all of which I do most solemnly promise and swear, so help me God. Amen.[1895]

Of course, in 1900 an oath denouncing Roman Catholicism was virtually equivalent to an oath denouncing the Irish, and for "Dry Dollar" Sullivan to accuse Siler of being a member of the A.P.A. was a serious matter, something like calling a person racist in our time.

Many of these problems came to a head in a dramatic way when Choynski lost to McCoy on January 12, 1900. Siler had been barred from acting as the referee for that fight and Charley White, who was the choice of the New York politicians, served as referee. Choynski knocked McCoy down four times in the second round and had seemingly knocked him out. White then engaged in a slow count and finally the timekeeper, believing that McCoy had been counted out, rang the bell to signal the end of the match. White then said he had not counted out McCoy and that the bell had only signaled the end of the second round. White sent both fighters to their corners, and there was a two-minute break between the second and third round. This was exactly the behavior made the contest look fixed, and two of the biggest suspects, McCoy and White, seemed to have worked together to make sure that McCoy would win. The McCoy-Choynski fight was in some respects the death knell for the Horton law.

Choynski described the circumstances of that match:

> At the end of the first round I knew I had McCoy. . . . I tore in again at the opening of the second round. . . . Down went McCoy lifeless with an impact that loosened O'Rourke's diamond shirt stud.
>
> Instantly the place was a madhouse. McCoy had been the favorite in the betting and the betting was heavy. The fast pace made me blow, but I had plenty of fight left.
>
> As the referee, Charlie White started counting over the prostrate McCoy, I smiled at my seconds. That smile was premature. . . . Of the hectic round Bob Edgren wrote: "Choynski got a vicious

> right over to McCoy's jaw. He was down 13 seconds. But the referee was there to see McCoy win, not lose. He counted in a most peculiar manner: 'One – two – Choynski, get back there, three – Choynski, go to your corner or I'll stop the count. You've got to stand further away – four – I told you to go to your corner – five, and so on. When the count was finally up to ten, McCoy got up. Choynski went after him, eager to give him the finishing blow, McCoy went down two or three times. Once he stayed down 12 seconds by the timekeepers' watch. It had been the custom at the Broadway club to ring the bell after a knockout, just as it is rung at the end of a round. Thinking he was finished the timekeeper rang the bell. McCoy was dragged to his corner after only two minutes of the third round had passed. McCoy was given the benefit of the other minute and the regular minute as well."[1896]

Davies continued to operate his billiard hall in New Orleans and hosted several good tournaments and professional performances there. In late January, Charlie brought Willie Hoppe, a brilliant young star in American billiards, to New Orleans and attempted to match Hoope and another young billiard player, "Young" Malone, for a prize of $1,000.

Hoope was only twelve years old and came to New Orleans with his father, who was also a well-known billiard and pool champion. While in New Orleans he took on all challengers and defeated every player with whom he was matched. His appearance in New Orleans decidedly increased the interest in billiards in that city. In one of his articles for the *Tribune* Davies wrote that before he left New Orleans, Hoppe told him that Corbett was one of the few amateurs who had ever defeated him. Hoope said he had beaten Corbett in New York, but after considerable effort Corbett had finally bested Willie after several attempts.[1897]

During his ten years in New Orleans, Davies lived at the St. Charles Hotel at 211 St. Charles Avenue—just a short walk from his billiard hall and the theaters he managed. One attraction of the St. Charles was its variety of baths, which included electric, Turkish, Russian, Roman, plain electric light and electric water, and massage. The baths were offered to relieve rheumatism, cure colds and serve as a nerve tonic. The availability of in-house treatment for his rheumatism was important to Charlie's general well-being. The St. Charles was one of the largest hotels in the United States, with accommodations for over one thousand guests and featured its famous Palm Garden and open-air terrace promenade. Davies had spent thousands of nights staying in hotels all over the United States, England, Ireland, France and Germany, and the St. Charles in New Orleans could compete with any of them.

Sharkey lost his heavyweight championship fight with Jeffries in November 1899 and as a result, moved down the ladder of the top heavyweight contenders and became the target of upcoming heavyweights who wanted to climb over him and catapult off of Tom's fading career. On the evening of February 19, Sharkey was in Detroit, where he knocked out Jim Jeffords in two rounds and thereby put down one of the more prominent young heavyweight rivals.[1898] Davies had traveled to Detroit to watch the fight. The next day Sharkey, accompanied by Davies, left Detroit and headed for New York. At Albany, Governor Roosevelt got on their train and rode in the same parlor car with Davies and Sharkey for the three-hour, 150-mile ride to New York.[1899]

In 1907 Davies recalled the events during that train trip for the *Atlanta Constitution*:

> The governor recognized me in the parlor car, and sent Mr. Young, his secretary, to me, saying he wished to speak to me. We engaged in conversation on the merits and demerits of boxing in New York on our ride to the city. At that time I thought the Legislature would vote favorably to [up]hold the Horton law, but the Governor thought differently, and said he was sorry to have to sign a bill against boxing, as he was so much in favor of the sport, but he said it had got to be a nuisance the way the clubs were carrying on boxing and the way they were managed at the time, paying me a compliment by saying that if they were managed the same as I had managed them, he would have no fault to find.
>
> I tried to convince him that he had probably taken his information from the press, which is sometimes wrong, but he convinced me before we arrived in the city that he knew more about the doings of the various clubs than I did. It is like everything he has done during his career—he always knew from his own knowledge what was doing before he attempted to abolish it.[1900]

Davies did not record all the particulars of his meeting with Roosevelt, but it seems likely that they discussed and the Choynski-McCoy fight and the gun fight between O'Malley and Parker. T. R. loved that kind of excitement and danger.

It should be acknowledged that O'Rourke got even with Choynski in February, when he matched Choynski to fight Walcott at the Broadway Athletic Club.[1901] Even though Choynski had briefly used O'Rourke as his manager the two men never liked each other. Tom claimed that his dislike for Choynski stemmed from the Dixon-Skelly match in New Orleans in 1892, when Joe acted as a second for Skelly. O'Rourke claimed that Joe had hurled racial slurs at Dixon throughout the match, and because of Joe's behavior, O'Rourke swore to himself that he would get even by having one of his fighters knock the tar out of Choynski. He thought there was poetic beauty in having a black fighter administer the beating. He claimed he arranged this match so he could finally do up Joe and that his plan worked like a charm.

There are many accounts of this match, but it appears from a distillation of all the information that Walcott caught Joe in the first round and knocked him silly. For six rounds after that, Walcott pounded Choynski from pillar to post, and Choynski thereby lost much of the good will he had built up as a result of being jobbed by Charlie White in the McCoy match.[1902]

One of Davies' friends from Chicago was a man named Big Jim O'Leary who was a descendant of the family whose cow was said to have kicked over the lantern that allegedly stated the Chicago Fire. Together O'Leary and John Condon nearly controlled the pool rooms in Chicago. Condon also controlled the Harlem track that was located just outside the city limits. *Pool room* in this context did not mean billiard tables with pockets, but rather off-track betting operations. In most cases the pool room operators and track operators were hostile to one another because the pool rooms downtown allowed men working in the city to place bets without going to the track and thereby hurting the take at the track. Many pool rooms would be open year-round taking bets on races from all over the country and receiving race results by wire.[1903] A lot of funny bets could be made just before the race results reached the pool room if a man had better connections with the track where the races were being run.

In early April, Davies leased part of the Crescent Billiard Hall for a pool room known as the Orleans Turf Exchange controlled by O'Leary and operated by a local gambler named Curry. The room rented to O'Leary was fitted out in first-class style and supposedly accommodated one thousand persons, although this is likely an overstatement. O'Malley had a 25 percent interest in the Turf Exchange, which paid the Davies-O'Malley partnership that owned the building 25 percent of its monthly net revenue as rent. The decision to rent to O'Leary brought a big time Chicago gambler in direct competition with the New Orleans tracks and off-track betting houses in New Orleans, including the Louisiana Turf Exchange, Behan & Duffy, and Jack Farrell's pool rooms.[1904] Competition with a Chicago gambler was probably not welcomed by local sports.

Beginning in January 1900 and continuing into March, several newspapers reported that Davies was planning to take a large aggregation of American fighters to Europe in 1901. The fighters who would travel with Davies were primarily men under contract with O'Rourke. If Davies was successful in negotiating an agreement with O'Rourke, then he intended to match the American boxers with foreign boxers from all over the world. The American fighters mentioned as those who would travel to Paris with Davies included Sharkey, "Mysterious" Billy Smith, Walcott, and Dixon. Davies said that to entice other fighters to come to the Paris Exposition to participate in the matches there, he would put up purses and open the show to all comers. Davies suggested he might also take McGovern, McCoy, and some good wrestlers to meet first-class wrestlers from other countries. Brady told the press that the entire matter was settled and was a certainty, but nothing actually happened.[1905]

The failure of anything to develop may have been because of Davies' physical problems. In early March 1901, New York's *Evening World* reported that Davies was going blind. He was under the care of the finest eye doctors in New Orleans, and each day had to have a probe inserted under his eyeball, which caused great agony. He was supposedly having trouble with his optic nerve, and the probe was supposedly releasing pressure under his eye. A friend who had just returned from New Orleans said that the Parson was "a wreck of what he once was."[1906]

It seems likely that his eye problems, his hair turning white by early 1897, and his increased rheumatic pain were all associated with his chronic ataxia. All of this was compounded by his strychnine poisoning in 1895. Davies left New York, and when he arrived in New Orleans on March 15, 1901, his sight and health were fine. But from this time forward his health was unstable.

The Horton law was finally repealed in early April, just as T. R. predicted when he talked to Davies in the parlor car of the train from Albany to New York on February 20.[1907] Boxing in New York was then thrown into a cocked hat, but Davies always had an idea how to accommodate change. When boxing was shut down, he suggested that the fight club managers use their facilities for wrestling matches. He suggested that a wrestling tournament take place in New York, Philadelphia, Boston, Buffalo, Cleveland, Pittsburgh, or Chicago with contestants paying an entry fee that made them eligible for a substantial prize. He even suggested that Muldoon take an interest in promoting such a tournament and endeavor to keep the project honest. Davies felt that there was a world of money to be made if his suggestion was accepted. His suggestion that Muldoon was the man who could keep athletics honest may have been a factor that later led to Muldoon's selection as the first chairman of the New York State Boxing Commission.[1908]

In early April, Davies took the train from New Orleans to Memphis to meet with "Dry Dollar" Sullivan and his friend Masterson. The race track in Memphis had its dates in April each year and many sports gathered there for the races. Sullivan had been the political patron for O'Rourke and probably knew that it would not be possible to pass legislation that would restore boxing in New York. Much of their discussion likely centered on an upcoming Jeffries-Corbett fight and the advantages and disadvantages of each fighter. Davies also talked to Masterson about a story that had been circulating that Hall had knocked out Masterson during a bar fight. Masterson just laughed at the story and said it was too utterly absurd to even discuss.

On April 9, the Parson was seen in San Antonio getting off of the westbound Southern Pacific train. He spent a few hours in San Antonio, where he met several friends. They spent that time spinning yarns of the squared circle of days gone by. Davies was reportedly on his way to California.[1909] It may be that Davies was on his way to Marlin, Texas, for the mineral baths or actually on his way to Denver because later O'Rourke and "Dry Dollar" Sullivan attempted to open an athletic club there to provide a place where big fights could be staged.[1910] This may have explained why Masterson and Sullivan were meeting with Davies in Memphis. They may have been discussing plans for the future club in Denver. Otto Floto had relocated to Denver and opened his own athletic club. Floto was in the process of forcing Masterson out of town, and Davies and Floto were close friends.

In mid-May, Davies, O'Rourke, Madden, Brady, and Al Smith were identified as the principals behind a political interest group to be formed in New York, to lobby in favor of prizefighting and candidates who were pro-prizefighting. They planned to accept memberships and support candidates who favored the legalization of prizefighting something like a modern political action committee. Davies said he felt that a minimum of 350,000 men in New York state would subscribe to such a body. Davies was clearly frustrated with what was happening to the sport that had been his life for twenty years.[1911]

On June 17, he wrote in a special to the *Tribune*: "The history of pugilism is replete with injurious blunders and examples of asininity, and it is exasperating to think these might have been prevented had the proper remedies been applied." Davies pointed out that in many of his letters to the *Tribune* he had tried to impress on all levels of the profession that the business needed some radical changes in the way it conducted its business. Charlie noted that while he had planted the seed for change, it had borne no fruit.[1912] However, the state of New York would eventually adopt most of Davies' suggestions.[1913]

Charlie went to New York in early July. Several newspapers noted that a few days before a scheduled Griffo-Gans match, Davies had watched Griffo in training and said he was surprised by Griffo's excellent work.[1914]

Paddy Ryan dies

One of Davies' early clients, Paddy Ryan, died on December 14, 1900, at Green Island, New York. Paddy was two years younger than Davies. During 1895 Ryan and Sullivan had participated in numerous testimonials for Sullivan that had been produced by Davies. Then those three old warriors spent six months traveling together, beginning at the end of 1895 and continuing through June 1896. After that tour ended, Ryan returned to Albany and had then taken a job in a factory at Laurel Hill, Long Island. He had been working up until about two months before his death. However, in early December 1900 stories appeared that Paddy was destitute and that a subscription was started for his benefit.[1915]

Ryan died from complications of Bright's disease, which was named after a Dr. Richard Bright and in 1900 was used as a general classification for various kidney diseases. At the time, kidney diseases were frequently called nephritis. Bight's disease had severe symptoms that included back pain, vomiting, and edema that could extend to the whole body. Ryan lost his ability to speak sometime before his death. Reports said that on the morning of his death he had a convulsion, and he died later in the afternoon. Ryan was survived by a daughter.

Jack Johnson and Joe Choynski go to jail

In January 1901, after Ryan's death, newspapers began to mention a new man in the ring, John Johnson.[1916] Johnson was a black heavyweight who was appearing in second-tier venues. He had been fighting for six years, but virtually all of his matches had taken place in Galveston, Texas, against third-rate opponents. In May 1899, Johnson traveled to Chicago and lost a match to another black heavyweight, John "Klondike" Haines (sometimes "Haynes"), in six rounds. However, Johnson had been given another shot at Haines in Memphis at the end of December 1900 and had made up for his earlier defeat. Johnson then issued a challenge to fight any black heavyweight in the world for a side bet of $1,000.[1917] Frank Childs' manager immediately accepted the challenge, but another fighter beat Childs to the mark. Choynski had been looking for a fight because prizefighting was at a near standstill in almost every venue. With few alternatives available, Joe went to Galveston in February 1901 to meet Johnson on his home territory and collect on his side bet. Joe had no truck with the color line.

On the night of February 25, 1901, at the Galveston Athletic Club, Choynski met and knocked out Johnson in three rounds with a solid right hook to the jaw. This should have been no disgrace for Johnson because in his day Choynski had leveled Fitzsimmons, McCoy, Jeffries, and Sharkey among many others. All of these stars would say that the hardest blow they ever received was delivered by Choynski. Immediately after Johnson's knock out, a squad of Texas rangers dashed into the ring and arrested both Choynski and Johnson and took them off to jail to await a bond hearing. The two remained in jail for twenty-four days until after two separate grand juries had refused to issue a true bill, and they were then released on bond.[1918]

In April 1901, Davies was awarded a Past Grand Exalted Ruler's jewel by the Grand Lodge of Elks. The award was presented at the New Orleans Elks Lodge. The Grand Lodge of the B. P. O. E. had decided to honor their past Grand Exalted Rulers, and Charles E. Davies had held that position in 1879. The jewel he was awarded was pictured in the *New Orleans Item* and described in the *National Police Gazette* as "a splendid specimen of the goldsmith's work and is adorned with an elk's head and a clock, the hands of which are pointing to 11 o'clock, the significance of which is understood by every member of the order. But Mr. Davies knows that his faithful services while he presided as Grand Exalted Ruler were such as to leave such pleasing memories behind that it does not need the reminder of eleven strokes of the clock to recall him to the minds of those who in years gone by honored him by calling him to the highest position in the order." The jewel included three good-sized diamonds set in a pendant medal on which was an inscription and the elk's eyes set as rubies. For some men, serving as the Grand Exalted Ruler of the Elks would be the ultimate achievement of a life. For Davies it was part of the beginning of public life that never ended.[1919]

Charlie went back to Memphis in April 1901 for the races at Montgomery Park. He saw Creedon at the track, and they talked about Dan's unexpected defeat of Jimmy Handler.[1920] Early that summer Charlie was working on behalf of the Southern Athletic Club of New Orleans to arrange a wrestling match between Sharkey and "Professor" Schoenfeldt of New Orleans.[1921] With prizefighting shut down in New York, some fighters were participating in wrestling matches to keep the wolf away from the door. Sharkey participated in several wrestling matches including one with Dan McLeod in early July in Buffalo. Schoenfeldt was a legend in New Orleans. He ran the gymnasium for the Southern Athletic Club, was an expert on the parallel bars, taught fencing, and taught physical education at Harvard. In addition, the Professor was a first-class wrestler. He also opened the first athletic club for women in New Orleans.

Davies agreed to arrange a New Orleans wrestling match between Sharkey and Schoenfeldt for the Southern Athletic Club but to be staged at the Academy of Music.[1922] He went to New York, to look over Sharkey's training quarters and watch Tom's preparation for a fight with Maher. After his match with Maher, Sharkey was to come to New Orleans to do his final preparation for the wrestling show. Davies was about to leave for England and Ireland, and he put Harry Glickauf in charge of the final preparations for the wrestling match. However, Schoenfeldt suffered a serious injury before his match with Sharkey. He stepped into a porcelain basin that was elevated off the ground to sponge off. The basin broke under his weight and the cuts on his legs required forty-two stitches. The Sharkey-Schonfeldt show was then cancelled.[1923]

The summer of 1901 in London

In mid-July 1901, Davies went to England. He arrived at Liverpool on July 23, 1901 aboard the *Minneapolis,* a ship of the Atlantic Transport Line.[1924] He had probably had enough of the long hot summers in New Orleans and wanted some relief. The baths at the St. Charles hotel could go only so far to escape the stifling weather. Before he left, a newspaper story said that Davies had established himself as an outside dealer in oil shares.

Davies was greeted warmly in London. In mid-August, the *Picayune* reprinted an earlier article from the *London Sportsman*:

> "Not so very long ago sporting men in the old country received a painful shock by a report published to the effect that Mr. Davies was losing his sight; in fact, that he was on the high road to total blindness. Fortunately, this proved to be but a hysterical paragraph, for the genial manager called at the Sportsman office last evening in the best of health, sound in wind and eyes, and looking hardly a day older than he was when he brought the Black Diamond over to astonish us with his power and skill. Jackson's old guide, philosopher and friend was accompanied by Mr. A. B. Chivers of New Orleans [Arthur B. Chivers was a young newspaper manager], and with the two visitors a member of the Sportsman staff passed a very pleasant half hour. For some time past Mr. Davies has devoted the best part of his time to theatrical business, and, as manager of the Academy of Music, New Orleans, he presided over one of the finest buildings in the southern states."[1925]

Davies did not arrive in England in time for the Victoria Cup, which was held at the end of June. His childhood patron from New York, Croker, had the race's winning horse, Sweet Dixie.[1926] The power that Croker wielded in 1901 is described in *Tigers of Tammany, Nine Men Who Ran New York*. The book points out that after resigning from a $25,000-a-year job as New York's chamberlain in 1890, Croker held no paying job; however, shortly after the 1890 election he purchased an eighty-thousand-dollar brownstone in the East Seventies and remodeled his new home for $100,000. In 1891 Croker purchased a five-hundred-thousand-dollar stock farm near Utica. He later bought a stud farm in the South for $250,000 and owned a home in Florida, in addition to his string of horses in England.[1927] This was not bad work for a fellow who had a job without a salary.

While in England, Davies met David Nagle, a well-known English turf man who was also Croker's right-hand man there and responsible for the care and training of Croker's several dozen thoroughbreds.[1928] Croker had been generous with Nagle, and in May 1901, Nagle had purchased an eighty-thousand-dollar tract of land near San Diego. He had acquired the land through Christopher Buckley, the blind California politician who controlled San Francisco when Davies was trying to get a permit for Jack Burke's fight there with Dempsey.[1929]

Davies and Nagle traveled together in Europe for five weeks and went as far as Wiesbaden in southwest Germany.[1930] Davies let his whiskers grow and over time had a long, white beard that he wore for several months. During their tour of Germany, Nagle contracted pleurisy. He returned to London for treatment in September and was described as being near death. Accounts say that Nagle was attended by a Dr. Jenkins, Croker's brother-in-law, and by Davies. Croker came to London to see his old friend and when he returned to New York, he left Davies in charge of Nagle's care. Davies stayed with Nagle night and day after Croker left for New York, and several of Nagle's relatives from Ireland came to London to await his death.

In mid-September 1901, Davies told Nagle he should have a lawyer draw up a last will. Nagle told Charlie, "Just write out that I leave everything to Richard Croker to dispose of as he thinks best." Davies drew up the will as directed, and it was signed and witnessed. Fortunately, Nagle did not need it, but recovered to the extent that he was able to return to New York in December 1901.[1931]

During the fall of 1901 McCoy was also in London operating a boxing school there. Davies had known McCoy from the early days in Detroit when he hired the Kid to spar with Ryan in preparation for Tommy's championship fight with Dempsey. McCoy had made and lost a fortune in the intervening years. He had also divorced and remarried his wife and then was once again the respondent in a divorce action. During that second divorce action his wife filed an affidavit with the court stating that the Kid was earning $1,000 a month running a boxing school in England. Some newspapers speculated that Davies would soon assume McCoy's management and that McCoy would take on all comers in England, providing they were middleweight fighters.

On December 2, 1901, McCoy fought three heavyweights with the assignment that he would knock each of them out within four rounds. He disposed of Dave Berry of Philadelphia in two rounds, Jack Scales of England in twenty seconds, and Jack Madden of Boston in four rounds. Davies was present for these fights, but it is not clear that he had a role as manager of McCoy, and he did not assume the Kid's management. Some reports said that Davies was trying to arrange a match for Walcott with Jack O'Brien, but that did not happen.[1932]

Davies wrote a special to the *Tribune* from London dated December 10, 1901, just before he returned to the United States. He predicted that there was a fortune to be made in England for any man who could develop a truly English heavyweight champion capable of competing with the leading American heavyweights. He felt that the English people would hail such a champion with delight, and the existence of an English champion would give a wonderful impetus to the whole pugilistic sport. Davies noted that McCoy had been fighting in England and also mentioned that the wrestler Carkeek, who was an old opponent of Lewis, was wrestling the English champions throughout the British Isles. Davies had seen Carkeek at the Tivoli, one of the leading London music halls, in evening dress and delivering a clever speech to the crowd there.

In his special Davies noted he had spent five weeks in Germany, where he had seen a company of American boxers and wrestlers led by Jack Lewis. He said that these men were having "a successful tour of that country, dealing out hard knocks and knockouts to the German athletes. At Berlin, Hamburg, Copenhagen, and other cities Lewis says he found the Germans strong but slow, showing but little evidence of boxing ability." Davies said that Lewis had told him that just the opposite was true with German wrestlers, who were adept in any style of wrestling entertainment. Charlie also reported he had it on good authority that a first-class boxing club would soon be opened in Paris.[1933]

Davies returns from London

The Parson took the *Campania* back to the States and made the ocean crossing in five days and seven hours. While on the trip he cut his whiskers and returned clean shaven.[1934] On December 24, Davies landed in New York in time for Christmas.[1935] The New Orleans newspapers called attention to his impending return and wrote that as soon as he landed he intended to try once again to line up Sharkey to wrestle Schoenfeldt in New Orleans.[1936] The *Salt Lake Herald* reported on January 1, 1902, that Davies had been in Europe on behalf of a Texas oil concern but had played the boxing game on the side and consequently returned with considerable cash.[1937] An article dated January 7 in the *Semi-weekly Interior Journal* of Stanford, Kentucky, said that "Davies, acting for a Texas oil company, has obtained contracts from people in London and Manchester, England, calling for 10,000,000 barrels of Texas oil."[1938] The *Dallas Morning News* reported that Davies had gone to England as the foreign representative of the Lone Star and Crescent Oil Company. On his return Davies said that

England was going to be a big market in the future because within a few months all the railroad were converting their engines from coal to oil.[1939]

While in New York, the Parson had another dust up, this time with a young comedian named Louis Harrison. The difficulty took place in the bar of the Delevan Hotel, where Charlie was meeting with O'Rourke and some of his other old friends. The Delevan was operated by O'Rourke and was a favorite haunt for sports. It seems that Harrison had been drinking heavily and became abusive toward Charlie, who attempted to cajole and then ignore the young man.

Finally, O'Rourke got so tired of Harrison's abuses toward Davies that he told Charlie he would have to break off their friendship if Charlie didn't put the young man in his place. Davies protested that the fellow had no training in fighting. Then Harrison approached the table where the Parson and O'Rourke were sitting. With a cigar between his lips he continued to insult the Parson until finally Charlie grabbed the lighted cigar and jammed the hot end of it into the fellow's face. He then grabbed Harrison by the color and carried him to the door and threw him out into the street. Charlie then calmly returned to the table to resume his conversation with his friends. No lemon knife was apparently in the area, which was a good thing for Harrison.[1940]

He returned to New Orleans on January 4, 1902, and again took up residence at the St. Charles Hotel.[1941] Interviewed by the *New Orleans Item* Davies said that all of England was paralyzed by the Boer War and that many citizens were turning against the conflict.[1942] It wasn't long before the Parson had returned to ringside and being asked his opinion on fights and fighters. In this case fights were being stage by the New Orleans' Young Men's Gymnastic Association but Davies saw the featured fight has only a staged affair.[1943]

In the first few months of the year he received good and bad news about some of the men he had formerly managed. In early January, Hall had been confined to the City Hospital in Cincinnati after suffering a violent lung hemorrhage. The doctor told Jim he was in no immediate danger of death. Jim only smiled and said: "I know better; I know when the referee is counting ten."[1944]

Unfortunately, it was a slow count for Jim as he suffered for more than a dozen years after his first hospitalization. In fact, Hall visited New Orleans in early February, and was thought to look well and healthy, and Davies was telling humorous stories about incidents involving Hall during their visit to England.[1945]

In mid-January, Barry began his campaign to be elected alderman for Chicago's twenty-second ward. Barry was then working as a member of the firm of Barry & O'Neil, proprietors of a handball court and boxing academy at 206 East Division Street in Chicago.[1946] Matters had gone from bad to worse for Griffo, who was found with his hands and feet frozen while standing near the gate of the Bridewell Prison at Twenty-Sixth and California streets in Chicago. Griffo was taken to the County Hospital, where doctors thought he might have to have his hands and feet amputated. He did not lose his limbs, but a few days later was adjudicated as insane and confined to the Jefferson Insane Asylum.[1947]

In late April, Davies talked to the press about the color line:

> I see that "Kid" McCoy is the latest to draw the color line in pugilism by refusing to box "Denver" Ed Martin in the Century club at Los Angeles, which desired this attraction for "Festival" week in lieu of the Jeffries-Fitzsimmons contest, which fell through owing to Fitz's refusal. The "Kid's" decision is peculiar, in as much as during my visit to England last summer I saw a challenge issued by him and published in the London papers in which he stated that he would box any one, size or weight not barred.
>
> Can it be possible that the pugilists who draw the color line do so through fear of defeat? It seems strange that McCoy and others of his class take refuge behind "the color line," while such great fighters as Jeffries, Fitzsimmons, James Corbett, McGovern, Young Corbett, Jack O'Brien, Frank Erne and others have fought colored men. John L. Sullivan frequently stated he would not box a negro, yet in the face of these declarations he was stripped and prepared to box George Godfrey in a room in Boston, when the police appeared and prevented the contest taking place. Another time, in Boston, at the Music hall, at an athletic entertainment, both Sullivan and Godfrey being present, John L. offered to box the negro then and there, but the colored pugilist declined. Sullivan also signed with the California Athletic club of San Francisco to box Peter Jackson for a $20,000 purse, winner take all, but the 'Frisco authorities shortly after stopped all boxing and the match was declared off.[1948]

Jimmy Barry in 1910 – Photograph of the Chicago History Museum

Another summer in London

The coronation ceremonies for Edward VII were set for June 26, 1902, and London's National Sporting Club decided to hold a series of boxing matches in late June and July to honor the new King of Great Britain and Ireland.[1949]

Davies decided he would prefer another summer in England rather than New Orleans and decided he could take some fighters with him to participate in the shows. In April, the big match in the making was between Jeffries and Fitzsimmons.[1950] Jeffries had been training with his brother Jack and with Armstrong as his sparring partners.[1951] Fitz also wanted to secure Armstrong as his sparring partner if the match with Jeffries could be arranged, and Fitz sent word to sign Armstrong offering the job.[1952]

Armstrong was a favorite sparring partner of most of the big heavyweight fighters. He had moved from Chicago to New York and was living with his wife on West Fifty-First Street. He worked with Sharkey when the Sailor trained for his contest with Jeffries, and he was with Fitz when he prepared himself for his fights with Sharkey and Ruhlin. Armstrong had also been Jeffries' sparring partner when the champion trained for Ruhlin. However, Bob was tired of being poorly paid for the honor of being pounded on by the white champions. Siler said that Armstrong had told him he "was tired of getting battered around by the topnotch big fellows for a small amount of money and concluded that he could fair no worse with 'Denver Ed' Martin, whom he is to fight for a good chunk of English money, hence his trip across the Atlantic."[1953]

Instead of singing with either Jeffries or Fitz, Armstrong decided to go to England with his former manager Davies.[1954] This was a good alternative to being punched around by a white heavyweight who was about to become rich. Armstrong probably hoped he would enjoy some small measure of the acceptance and success in England that Jackson had enjoyed.

Another black fighter who traveled to England was Larry Temple. He was also known as the "Quaker City Terror." Born in 1882, Temple was more than thirty years younger than Davies and fought well into the 1920s. The newspapers in 1902 said that O'Rourke had taken Temple out of his Delavan kitchen and molded into a middleweight fighter.[1955] For most of his career Temple would fight as a welterweight. The plan in taking Temple to England was to match him against the best middleweights in London. During his years in the ring Larry Temple fought such good fighters as Johnson, Walcott, "Young" Peter Jackson, and Sam Langford.

At the end of May, reports said that the coronation tournament had been agreed on. The matches were to be held at the National Sporting Club beginning on the afternoon of June 21, when there would be boxing competitions between representatives of Yale, Oxford, Cambridge, and the English public schools.[1956] That evening "Spike" Sullivan (American) and Jabez White were to compete for the 134-pound championship of the world, and "Denver" Ed Martin was to fight Armstrong for the black heavyweight championship of the world.

Other matches in June were to include Walcott and Tommy West competing for the welterweight championship of the world, and Frank Erne and Pat Daly, the English lightweight champion, to decide the lightweight championship of the world. The final event was to be a Sharkey-Ruhlin bout with the winner to meet the winner of the Jeffries-Fitzsimmons match. One of Davies' former advance men, Leonard B. Schloss, promoted these fights, and this may have played a role in Davies' decision to participate in the show.[1957]

Davies' friend Masterson and his wife Emma left Denver in April 1902, looking for a new home. Masterson had tired of a long-running feud with Floto, who was then the editor of the *Evening Post* in Denver. Masterson stopped in Chicago to visit friends and worked as the referee in a six-round contest between Santry and Kid Abel. Masterson called the match a draw, which dissatisfied most of the spectators. In Chicago, Masterson was running with James C. Sullivan, a gambler from Oregon, Leopold Frank, a Chicago gambler, and J. E. Sanders a Denver bookmaker. He learned that Davies was planning to spend the summer in England and the word circulated that Masterson was going along with his old friend to participate in Davies' undertakings. Masterson himself said in mid-June he had come to New York with Davies with the intent of traveling to England with Charlie.

Masterson's hope of traveling to England went up in smoke in early June. He and his gambling friends had traveled to New York and were arrested on a charge of running a crooked faro game. George L. Snow, a wealthy and diamond-studded Mormon from Salt Lake City, lost $17,000 in one night and then went to the police claiming he had been cheated. Masterson, Sanders, Frank, and Sullivan were all released by the police without charges, except that Bat had to pay a ten-dollar fine for carrying a concealed weapon. Masterson then filed a $10,000 law suit for slander against Snow.[1958] These legal troubles prevented Masterson from attending the big fights in London, and Davies traveled alone.

Davies left New Orleans on May 20 and was in New York with Masterson on May 23. He arrived in England June 3 once again aboard the *Minneapolis* of the Atlantic Transport Line. Armstrong and Temple traveled aboard the *Etruria* of the Cunard Line, but they did not reach England until June 21. This is probably why Armstrong did not fight "Denver" Ed Martin on June 21 as had been scheduled. Instead, Martin defeated Sandy Ferguson of Boston in five rounds. Martin was then matched to fight Armstrong on July 25. Armstrong lost a fifteen-round decision to Martin, and there is no record of him fighting again in England. The next record of Armstrong in the ring was on December 10 when he fought a "no decision" with Martin at Philadelphia. In early August, Temple was matched for a ten-round bout with a fighter named Dido Plumb. But opponents were scarce, and Davies ended up sending the two black fighters back to New York before the end of August.[1959]

Before he fought Martin in London, there was still considerable interest in Armstrong as a contending heavyweight fighter. However, the Chicago papers were skeptical and said that men there who had seen the two men fight many times were putting their money on Martin.[1960] The Armstrong-Martin contest took place at Crystal Palace and attracted a large crowd. Reports said that Bob began as the favorite, but his performance did not justify it. Martin, proving to be the cleverer of the two from the outset, never gave Bob a chance of being declared the winner.

There is surviving film that includes a few frames showing Armstrong. In 1932 he worked in Max Baer's corner during Baer's fight with King Levinsky. Approximately one and a half minutes into the film clip and just before the first round of the fight starts, Bob is seen standing on the apron of the ring talking to Max Baer.

Davies left England about August 20 and arrived at New York aboard the *Majestic* on September 2.[1962] In mid-September, he said he was disappointed about the results of his renewed managerial stint. One newspaper remarked that Davies was bewailed by his inability to stir up any interest in England for prize-fighting and was sorry to find the English sports more interested in golf, cricket, polo, and ping-pong. What happened to Briton's manliness?[1963]

Davies assumed the management of Kid Broad in October and went to Chicago to take care of Broad in his match there with Buddy Ryan.[1964] He continued to handle Broad until January 1904. A report in the *St. Paul Globe* at the end of October explained Davies' unsuccessful efforts to arrange a match for Broad with Terry McGovern.

Davies was in New Orleans at the end of 1902. News of his activities had considerably diminished after his return from England with Armstrong and Temple.[1965] One report said that in 1903 Davies was considering traveling with a vaudeville troupe that would feature him delivering a monologue.[1966] The *Washington Times* wrote on January 3 that its reporter had spoken with Davies, and the Parson had confirmed his intention to return to the stage as a monologue specialist. He said that a monologue entitled "Consolation" had been written for him by Con T. Murphy, and if a business opportunity he had been working on did not pan out then he would be on the stage.[1967]

The business proposition involved Davies' continued efforts to arrange a fight between Broad and Young Corbett. The *Salt Lake Tribune* reported that Davies had posted $2,500 with "Honest" John Kelly for the Broad-Corbett match to be held in Salt Lake City. Davies had a backer, a bookmaker named Kid McMahon from Buffalo, who was prepared to back Broad for $10,000, but Young Corbett had not agreed to anything.[1968] Corbett wanted to meet Terry McGovern and not Broad. His opinion was that Board was nothing more than a hard man to beat and did not have the makings of a champion.

"Mack's Mélange" in the *Picayune* wrote: "Davies is a capable, well-traveled man. He has toured the world and has many friends in every part of it, and he will certainly prove a drawing card and a valuable attraction to the theatrical stage. If the Parson would but tell a tenth of the hundreds of things he has seen and heard while in the universe, he'd be recalled at every performance until he was tired out."[1969]

Kid Broad in 1901 – The last fighter that Parson Davies managed
Photograph from the Chicago History Museum

On April 25, an article was published in the *Galveston Daily News* about a New Orleans reunion of the United Confederate Veterans.[1970] An *Atlanta Constitution* article said that the chairman of the entertainment committee for the reunion, A. R. Blakely, had enlisted Davies to act as the manager of the entertainment. Another member of the reunion committee was Henry Lehman, who for the next several years would be involved in multiple business ventures with Davies. The Parson probably did not tell Mr. Blakely or Lehman that his brother Henry had helped foil the Baltimore plot to assassinate Abraham Lincoln and had fought and was wounded in the cause of the Union. Davies, the article said, was arranging a mammoth carnival of boxing, wrestling, fencing, and other athletic features to increase the receipts for the entertainment portion of the reunion. He was "endeavoring to arrange for the heavyweight champion Jim Jeffries and Bob Fitzsimmons to appear in a scientific exhibition along with other boxing and wrestling celebrities."[1971] The carnival was to be held on May 15 the Stadium building, located at New Orleans' fairgrounds. That structure had a seating capacity of more than seventeen thousand.

The United Confederate Veterans reunion in New Orleans was the organization's thirteenth reunion and by far its largest veterans' assemblage. An estimated two hundred thousand people visited the city for the event. Virtually all the passenger railroads ran special trains at reduced prices from every part of the country. Decorative arches were built over the downtown streets. Camps were established in city parks for men assembling from the various southern states. The opening services were held at the city's Jefferson Davis Memorial, and there was a great memorial service for the sons and daughters of the Confederacy.[1972]

General John B. Gordon spoke at the largest gathering of the reunited veterans. Davies was probably an observer because he clearly enjoyed such ceremonies. Gordon asked the veterans not to indulge in bitterness but to draw the curtain over the regretful and unseemly things of the past. He asked them as Americans to cherish the valor and noble deeds of both armies and recognize that North and South were joint heirs in the inheritance of freedom. These were indeed noble things to say under all the circumstances.

"We are growing old," he concluded, "but we still stand firm on this narrow strip of land that separates us from the boundless ocean."[1973]

By the late spring of 1902 Davies was again affiliated with the Southern Athletic Club of New Orleans. While working with that club, he assumed the management of Ned "Kid" Broad.[1974] The Kid had been fighting for many years before he was managed by Davies and was an active fighter, not a tomato can. He had defeated Joe Bernstein, fought to a draw with Benny Yanger, lost to McGovern in six rounds, and was defeated by Young Corbett in ten rounds. However, before losing a decision to Young Corbett, Broad had knocked him down and was the only man who had accomplished that task.

In early April, Broad had a six-round bout with Billy Maharg at the Washington Sporting Club in Philadelphia. Davies was in Philadelphia at the time of this fight according to the *Philadelphia Inquirer*.[1975] A month later Broad fought twenty fast rounds with Benny Yanger of Chicago at Louisville. This match was arranged by Davies and Bob Gray, the club's manager, and was to complement the Kentucky Derby. Yanger got the decision, but both fighters showed well.[1976]

Davies first brought the Kid to New Orleans to meet a local fighter named Ben Schneider, who was handled by Jack Everhardt.[1977] Jack had been one of the people on Canal Street in 1899 when O'Malley shot it out with Parker. He was a popular sport in New Orleans and told the press before the fight that he was enthusiastic over Schneider's improvement and expected him to show well against Broad. It was predicted that this match would rival the old days of the Olympic Club.[1978]

The Broad-Schneider fight took place on May 8.[1979] In the first round Broad landed a stiff right hook on Schneider's "short ribs" directly under the heart and sent him to the floor. Ben staggered to his feat after a six-count and received another blow that laid him out full length on the floor. The sponge was thrown in and Broad declared the winner. The crowd was somewhat stunned by the quick end. The *Picayune* said that the public knew that Broad was up in the ranks of well-known fighters but also thought Schneider was a hard hitting man and would put up a real fight. They were wrong.[1980] One paper reported that Schneider quit after being hit in the stomach one time and that the crowd put up such a howl that the club officials had to apologize.[1981]

Tommy Mowatt of Chicago had notified Davies he would fight the winner of the Broad-Schneider fight. In addition to having that fight on the books, by May 12 Davies had scheduled the Kid to fight Aurelio Herrera as part of the Miners' Day celebration at Butte, Montana. They were to fight on June 13 at the Broadway Theater in Butte.[1982]

The Montana Athletic Club was one of two competing prizefighting clubs in Butte in 1903, and both clubs were scheduling matches for the Miners' Day. Davies thought that the fight would be a big financial success because Miners' Day was a holiday and there were many boxing fanatics in Montana. Davies and Herrera's manager both expected a ten-thousand-dollar house for the contest, which would be possible, in part, because Herrera was a charismatic and popular fighter in that part of the country. This was like the good old days, but out under a big Montana sky.

Sometime after his fight with Schneider, Broad went to Cincinnati to have a bone removed from his nose that had been impairing his breathing. It was hoped that removal of his nasal obstruction would improve his chances against future opponents.[1983] On May 29, only two weeks after the surgery, Broad fought Mowatt before the Southern Athletic Club in New Orleans. Mowatt was called the "fighting conductor" because for many years he had been a street car conductor in Chicago. He was a well-educated young man who had trained to be a Jesuit priest before finding he lacked the vocation. Mowatt and Broad had fought twice previously and both matches had been called draws. In New Orleans the two fighters "fought ten of the fiercest rounds ever witnessed in New Orleans before an immense audience."[1984] The referee decided the contest as a draw. Broad would return to New Orleans later in 1903.

Davies went to Butte with the Kid for the Herrera fight.[1985] While discussing the final arrangements on the day before the match, the two contestants started slugging one another in the lobby of the Butte Hotel. Herrera hit Broad on the chin and when the Kid rushed at Aurelio, "friends and managers interfered."[1986]

The next evening before a crowd of three thousand spectators Herrera knocked out Broad in the fourth round and then did an Indian war dance in the ring to celebrate. It was Broad's 106th professional fight and the first time he had ever been knocked out.[1987] When he awoke in the ring, the Kid asked: "Did I win, or was I knocked out?"[1988] When he was told he had been put to sleep, Broad burst into tears and said he had thought there was not a fighter alive who could knock him out.[1989]

Davies noted that Butte was at an altitude of 5,800 feet, and the experience of fighting in that air had been difficult for his man. Newspapers reported that Davies lost $2,500 of his own money betting on Broad. Charlie said that if more people had been interested in betting on Herrera, they could have cleaned him out of all the money he had because he was so convinced of Broad's ability. Davies said that Broad would be in Chicago by June 17 and then go to New York. Davies went to Chicago and then back to New Orleans.[1990] After the Herrera fight, Broad's career went downhill rapidly.[1991]

On the evening of July 2, there were additional prize fights held at the Southern Athletic Club in New Orleans arranged by Davies. Mowatt defeated Tom Cody. Their match was another ten-round contest that went the distance. According to newspaper accounts, "Mowatt had Cody on queer street as early as the seventh round, and only the gong saved him. Again in the ninth Mowatt had his man going, but was unable to deliver the clinching blow." Additional comments about this match said that when Mowatt fought Broad to a draw some weeks earlier at the Southern Athletic Club "the devotees of the game who were present admitted that they had seen the best fight since the days of the Olympic club. Last night they declared the Mowatt-Cody mill better than the one which has taken place between Mowatt and Broad."[1992]

While all of this was going on, Davies, Henry Lehman, and a secret investor had obtained a ten-year lease with an option to purchase the building previously known as Wenger's Theater at the corner of Iberville (formerly Customhouse) and Burgundy streets in an area below Canal Street.[1993] The secret investor was Jake Wells, president of the Bijou Amusement Company, of Richmond, Virginia.

Wells, Lehman, and Davies had formed a new entity known as the Southern Amusement Company. Wells was president, Lehman was vice-president, and Davies was secretary and treasurer. Early reports said that Hopkins, who was Davies' old friend, would be given preference in case it was determined to use the theater for stock productions. Hopkins would present stock and vaudeville productions at popular prices. The new theater would ultimately be called the Lyric.

The Parson left New Orleans on July 4 for St. Louis, Chicago, Buffalo, and New York. Davies, Lehman, and Wells had all decided that they did not have the time to manage the Lyric themselves and would be renting it for the season to one of the northern theatrical syndicates. Davies was going to interview the potential managers in order to close a lease of the theater for the season.[1994]

On July 21, Davies was in New York. He had been there for a few days and was about to travel to Chicago and then back to New Orleans. He spoke to the press at the Delavan House:

> "You know every man is a crank on some subject, and I have my little hobby. I want to see a boxing league formed, or rather a boxing and wrestling league. I want to see all the fakirs and crooks run out of the business, and the only way you can do it, as I see, is to form an association in every city where boxing is allowed, all the associations forming one big league. Then, when a fighter breaks his agreement he will be down and out for good. Each association should have its own lawyer and its physician, but the referees should be appointed by the league, just as the baseball umpires are selected by the presidents of the baseball leagues."[1995]

Davies was proudly showing off his life membership card in the B.P.O.E., and he pointed out that Lodge #4, which he helped form in Chicago was about to build a new club house at a cost of $175,000.

During the second week of August Charlie took a special fifteen-car train from Chicago to San Francisco to watch the Jeffries-Corbett heavyweight championship fight. Others on the special train included Siler, Nat Goodwin, the actor Dennis O. Sullivan, and many sporting men of national repute. During the two previous years Davies had spent his summers in London, but because of his activity with Broad, the Southern Athletic Club, and the Lyric theater, he did not return to London in 1903.[1996]

Davies was back in New Orleans in September in time for the theater season. He had also arranged a fourth Mowatt-Broad match as the opening show of the fall season in New Orleans. This match was scheduled for October 16, but Mowatt refused to fight because he said he had injured a thumb in a fight with Charlie Neary. However, after backing out of his New Orleans fight Mowatt went ahead and fought Tom Callahan at West Baden on October 13.[1997] So much for his Jesuit training in ethics.

Kid Hermann, another Chicago fighter, was substituted for Mowatt and the fight delayed until October 28. Less than twenty-four hours before the fight, Hermann also refused to appear offering no excuse. No fighter other than Sullivan would have dared pull such stunts when Davies was in his prime as a manager. The club tried to arrange for Joe Bernstein to fight Broad, but he wanted too much money. They tried Kid Able next, but he was unavailable.[1998] Reports said that Davies had been in New York trying to arrange a McGovern-Mowatt match to open the fall boxing season, but McGovern refused the fight on short notice, and they went back to Tom Callahan.[1999]

On November 13 en route to New Orleans, Davies stopped in Richmond, Virginia. He met with Wells, Charlie McKee, and a man named James Baccigalupo.[2000] It seems probable that the last two men were part owners of the Bijou Amusement, and Davies stopped to report on his efforts to lease the old Wenger's Theater to a third party. Charlie was back in his room at the St. Charles Hotel on November 24.[2001]

At the beginning of December, the *San Francisco Call* reported that Davies had new tenants in the pool room he had installed in the Crescent Billiard Hall—Riley Grannan, who was supposed to be working with Davies, Benny Falk, and George Boles. The exact business relationship between these men is not clear. It seems likely that Grannan paid rent to Davies and that Davies, Falk, and Boles were financial backers who shared in the profits of Grannan's business. In 1903 there were six pool rooms operating in New Orleans, and those six had entered into an agreement with respect to the odds they would pay on certain bets. Grannan almost immediately set out to attract customers by offering better odds so that horses that won at even money were paying off at three or four to one. The local pool rooms considered Grannan to be an interloper and complained he would either run them out of business or go broke trying.[2002]

Davies also revealed in September he was attempting to arrange a Corbett-Fitzsimmons bout in New Orleans. However, the best he was able to achieve was a ten-round fight on November 9 between Broad and Callahan. Broad took the decision in that match. He then went to Boston, where he fought and lost a brutal fifteen-round match to Jimmy Briggs on November 18 at the Criterion Athletic Club.[2003] Davies was back in New Orleans on November 24 after spending several weeks in the north.[2004] He had arranged another Mowatt-Broad fight on November 25 and Mowatt was awarded a ten-round decision.[2005] This was not the highest quality stuff, but it certainly was not just club fighting.

It seemed that other fight managers were boycotting the Southern Athletic Club because betting on the matches was illegal. Finally, Davies arranged a match for the Kid for December 18 in Milwaukee with Charles Neary. Board lost the six-round match, and this seems to be the last time that Davies directly managed him.[2006]

Louisville Tommy West takes Kid Broad to San Francisco

Six weeks later Broad was in San Francisco for a match with Eddie Hanlon at the San Francisco Athletic Club. Articles at the time refer to Davies as the Kid's manager for this fight, but also say that Davies was communicating with Broad and West about fight arrangements by telegrams sent from New Orleans. It appears that "Louisville" Tommy West had arrived in New Orleans during the winter of 1903. His trip had been financed by J. P. Morgan, who had befriended Tommy during an earlier passage from New York to Liverpool. Tommy was in financial distress and was hired by Davies to work in his pool room and to look after Broad. In his book *The Long, Long Trail in the World of Sports*, West described both Davies' pool room in New Orleans:

> I became the outside man for Parson Davies, who conducted one of the largest poolrooms and gambling houses in the Crescent City. . . . At this time New Orleans was a wide-open town. Everything went, from racing to the "tiger." The Parson's place was the headquarters of every follower of Dame Chance that lived in or came to New Orleans. . . . The races were on at New Orleans that winter, and after they were concluded every afternoon the racegoers would crowd the Parson's poolroom to play the ponies at Ascot Park and Oakland, Cal., which were running full tilt. There was a bunch of fighters and jockeys that always mixed with our crowd, including [Kid] Broad, Roscoe Troxler, Barney Furey, Monk Sheehan, Freckles O'Brine and "Shang" Paretto.[2007]

Tommy also described his work with Broad:

> In addition to the Parson's big business he had several boxers under his management, one of whom was Kid Broad, at that time about the toughest scrapper in the lightweight division in America. The Parson named me as his agent to look after Broad, both in training and out. Broad was a hard boy to handle, but

> he was a good-hearted fellow. That the Kid's education had been neglected was always a source of annoyance to both himself and friends. The Kid could not read, but had been taught to sign his "John Hancock," and that was about as far as his literary talents went. . . . In addition to Broad's meager education he was afflicted with an impediment in his speech, so that at times none but his closest intimates could understand what he was talking about.

Davies sent West with Broad to California for the Hanlon fight. Charlie had been there only three months earlier and probably did not look forward to January in Frisco. Traveling over the Sunset Route, West took the Kid to the Hanlon fight. West explained that Broad was always a big draw, but he was not in good shape for this match.[2009]

After fourteen rounds of fighting that heavily favored Hanlon, West threw in the sponge.[2010] Broad's share of the take was $1,235 paid in gold coin. Tommy returned to New Orleans by way of Albuquerque and then Kansas City. They stopped there to visit with "Syracuse" Ryan, who operated a billiard hall, and to recall old times. From Kansas City they went back to New Orleans. Tommy writes that Davies then sent the Kid to New York, to be handled by O'Rourke.[2011]

The National Boxing Association

When Davies had arranged the Neary-Broad match in Milwaukee in November 1903, he likely met with Thomas S. Andrews, the author of annual boxing record books and a Milwaukee newspaper editor. He was also the matchmaker for the Badger Athletic Club. Within a few weeks after the Neary-Broad fight, newspaper articles stated that a movement was underway to create a national boxing association "to classify weights, etc." The earliest articles said that the movement had been started by Davies and Andrews in early January 1904. The *St. Paul Globe* reported on January 10 that one of the concerns discussed by Davies and Andrews was the differences in weight classes in various parts of the country.[2012]

Andrews was interested in the project as a sports writer, and he said that Davies thought that it was the time for interested parties to get together at a central place and reach a resolution. Davies had long been interested in some way to control prizefighting to diminish the fraud that had crept into the sport. It seems that Davies and Andrews sent out letters to the major boxing clubs and newspaper writers around the United States asking them to indicate whether they were interested in participating in the creation of such a national organization. Favorable replies were then received from all over the country.

A meeting of the club managers and newspaper writers was called for February 6 and 7 in Detroit. Articles at the time said that the "promoters of the plan to form a National Boxing Association" were Andrews of Milwaukee and Davies of New Orleans, and a large attendance was expected at the meeting in Detroit.

Fifteen boxing clubs met at the Oriental Hotel. The number of sportswriters that appeared does not seem to be reported.

On February 8, many newspapers published articles announcing the creation of the National Boxing Association and explained that it was intended to regulate and promote the interests of boxing throughout the United States. The officers and directors were reported: President, William H. Considine of Detroit; Secretary-Treasurer, Thomas S. Andrews of Milwaukee; Directors, Charles E. Davies of the Southern Athletic Club of New Orleans, E. H. Bigham of Indianapolis, Dr. J. H. Message of Chicago's Battery D Athletic Club; James Manon of the Pittsburgh Athletic Club; and A. R. Bright, of the Milwaukee Athletic Club.

The new association would require all professional fighters to register with the association and pay a twenty-five-cent fee. Non-registered fighters would not be permitted to fight in clubs operated by association members. The association also agreed to enforce all contracts between fighters and member clubs—although they did not say how—and would be able to suspend fighters for infractions of association rules. The association was also going to establish and maintain a "blacklist" of referees who were thought to have engaged in fixing a fight.

As one of its first acts, the association established a uniform set of weight classifications that were to govern all fights in the United States. The new classifications were special (or "minimus") class, 105 pounds or lighter; light bantamweights, 110 pounds; bantamweights, 115; featherweights, 122; heavy featherweights 127; lightweights, 133; light welterweights, 140; welterweights, 148; middleweights, 158; light heavyweights, 175; and heavyweights, all men over 175. These classifications were to hold until the association's next meeting, when the officers and directors would review suggestions provided by prominent men interested in the boxing game in America.

The fate of the National Boxing Association is not clear, but the same idea was pursued many times after 1904. Other such associations were created in 1921 and in 1927, and it was not until 1927 that an organization was created that survived for a long period of time.[2013]

Acquiring the Lyric Theater and Southern Amusement

Davies' activities at the end of 1903 and most of 1904 with respect to the entertainment industry were some of the most complicated business transactions of his professional life. His associates in these ventures were Wells and Lehman. As mentioned above, Wells was from Richmond, Virginia, and was president of Bijou Amusement Company. Bijou Amusement operated a Bijou theater circuit in Southern cities including Richmond, Norfolk, Nashville, Atlanta, Birmingham, and Memphis.[2014]

Lehman was part of a New Orleans' family that operated a large dry goods house known as A. Lehman & Co. The head of the Lehman family was Gustavo

Lehman Sr. Other members of the family included A. Lehman, Henry Lehman, and Gustavo Lehman Jr. Henry Lehman was active in Democratic party politics in New Orleans and Louisiana and had served as the president of the Citizens Protective Association of New Orleans and as a member of the committee that planned the great Confederate soldiers reunion in the city in 1903.[2015]

At the end of 1903, Lehman agreed to completely remodel the old Wenger's Theater so that it could be leased to Bijou Amusement with the new facility to be known as the Bijou.[2016] The new theater would seat 1,600 patrons arranged so that each would have an unobstructed view of the stage. In addition, the theater would have eight separate entrances and wide isles to comply with the latest fire codes in America's largest cities. The second and third tiers were to have six boxes each, three to a side.

In early 1904, Southern Amusement secured a six-year lease to provide summer entertainment at the New Orleans Athletic Park. The Athletic Park was on Tulane Avenue between South Carrollton Avenue and South Pierce Street and was leased by the Young Men's Realty Company. Southern Amusement intended to spend $10,000 to construct a Luna Park patterned after the famous Luna Park on Coney Island. Admission to Athletic Park was free, but patrons would pay between five and ten cents for each of the amusements that were used.[2017]

Athletic Park included a theater know as the Casino owned by Hart D. Newman, who was the sole owner and president of the New Orleans baseball franchise known as the Pelicans. The Casino was also leased directly from Newman for six years, and it was remodeled and rearranged from front to back. The theater was to provide live vaudeville and musical entertainment. Southern Amusement also constructed an eighteen-gauge miniature railroad that circled the entire park and was a great attraction, and it also installed a roller-coaster, toboggan slide, loop-the-loop, shooting gallery, Katzenjammer castle, café, restaurant, ice cream stands, and other similar attractions.[2018]

Then in mid-February, Southern Amusement secured a lease from the New Orleans Railways Company to provide summer entertainment beginning on the first Sunday of May at another park, West End, located on the shore of Lake Pontchartrain at the entrance to a canal known as the New Basin, which opened in 1900. There were several structures along the levee at the mouth of the canal including a lighthouse, and the Southern Yacht Company was directly across from West End. The New Orleans Railway Company ran an electric railroad with its terminus at West End, so the site was easily accessible from other parts of the city.[2019]

Southern Amusement agreed to provide vaudeville every night at West End with four complete turns each evening and with new talent every week. They also provided a first-class, handsomely uniformed military band of not less than thirty pieces, with a complete repertoire of popular and classical compositions. In addition, they were to provide motion pictures to be changed weekly. Wells made several trips to New Orleans before the scheduled opening of West End and said he found everything satisfactory at both the Athletic Park and West End.[2020]

The Athletic Park opened on May 2 to large crowds. The central feature was a lagoon that was lit at night with colored lights. The Casino was filled at its eight thirty p.m. opening and people were entertained by attractive young women who performed exceptionally high kicks in a program that included Gibson Girls and German comedians known as the Otto Brothers.

In the midst of all this activity Davies' niece Sadie died in Brooklyn on Friday, April 29. Sadie was a daughter of Henry Davies. Her mother and father had died when Sadie was a child. She had been with uncle Charlie in New Orleans when he first took over the management of the Academy of Music. After becoming a popular figure in the city, Sadie had returned to Chicago and divorced her husband for desertion before moving to Brooklyn. Davies traveled to New York, to attend Sadie's funeral in early May.[2021]

By the end of July 1904 rumors were circulating that Southern Amusement would attempt to lease West End directly from the city and circumvent the sublease it had obtained from the New Orleans Railways Company. If Southern Amusement could obtain a direct lease for West End, then it intended to install a roller coaster, loop-the-loop, carousals, dance platforms, and a Venetian way for gondolas, pagodas, and similar attractions. At the same time the New Orleans Railways Company wanted the city to grant it a fifty-year lease for West End and intimated that it would relocate its railroad to the other side of the canal if it could not get what it wanted.[2022]

Davies had a tongue-in-cheek idea that he made public in August. Some promoters had been talking about hold fights on the ocean outside the three-mile limit to avoid prosecution. Davies saw many potential problems with this suggestion but said he thought one possible alternative was to fit an air ship up with a twenty-four foot ring surrounded by mesh suspended below the air ship. Spectators would be transported in other airships that would hover around the suspended ring and have a clear view of the fight. He suggested that all the airships could be chartered for a normal excursion, and then the promoters could laugh at the police who could not possibly reach them. He thought this idea might need to wait for additional testing of airships at the St. Louis Fair that summer.[2023]

Trouble for Southern Amusement began in August, when the Casino Theater burned. Smoke was seen coming from the roof of the theater, and an alarm was raised. The night watchman attached a hose to the fire-fighting equipment on the site and climbed to the top of the soda fountain and began spraying the roof of the Casino, but nothing could be done to abate the fire, and part of the building was lost. Trunks with costumes were saved and the stage remained in tack.[2024] After the fire Jake Wells came to New Orleans and let it be known he would not do business in New Orleans in the 1905 summer season under the circumstances. Southern Amusement had not obtained a lease on West End for the next season, attendance at the Athletic Park and West End had been "only fair" in 1904, and Wells was angry because the Bijou that Lehman was supposed to be working on had still not been completed and opened for the fall season.[2025]

Then early Sunday morning September 25 the entire Athletic Park burned in a spectacular fire that destroyed all the improvements and what was left of the Casino. Davies said that the second fire had been set. He noted the earlier fire at the Casino and pointed out that on the Saturday before, the stage carpenter at the Casino had made a report he had found two bottles of oil with some rags and paper overturned with the contents spilled on the floor. He said that pieces of paper nearby had been burned to ashes but had not caught the oil on fire. Davies explained that the Casino was a total loss. He noted that the Southern Amusement had spent about $25,000 repairing the Casino and making additions to the Athletic Park, and everything was a total loss. All that Southern Amusement had left was its lease on the ground where the Casino had stood. Davies said he had an idea about who might have started the fire and had given his information to the police.[2026]

It appears that Wells withdrew from Southern Amusement after the fire at the Athletic Park. He had been unhappy because Lehman had not finished the Bijou, and Bijou Amusement later filed suit against Lehman for defaulting on a promissory note in the amount of $7,500.[2027] Whatever happened with Wells, the theater finally had its grand opening on November 20 as the Lyric. Its opening was about eight weeks after the season began. The *Picayune* described the Lyric as "a little beauty." It wrote that the idea that people would not go below Canal Street to attend a theater was thoroughly set at rest with the opening of the Lyric. Its seating arrangement, with two large aisles on each side of the central section and leather upholstered seats, was described as the best in New Orleans. The boxes on opening night were filled with well-known people from every part of the city. Two weeks after the Lyric opened, it was learned that Southern Amusement intended to build a new theater on the site of the burned-out Casino Theater.[2028]

In September, John L. Sullivan became affiliated with a saloon in St. Louis. It was twelve years after he had lost the heavyweight championship to Corbett when he began working in a Market Street bar in St. Louis. Sullivan had been ill for a protracted period earlier in 1904, but had recovered somewhat. St. Louis newspapers noted that Sullivan's condition was poor and that he was gray and worn-looking, not showing the traces of his recent illness but showing the marks of his advancing age. Sullivan still had "the same thunderous voice, the same positive utterances when referring to men of the ring, and he is still the same authority on matters pertaining to pugilism, that he always was." The St. Louis saloon did a terrific business with John L. at the tap, and this gave Davies an idea.[2029]

About ten days after Sullivan started working in St. Louis, Davies said he had decided to open a booking agency in New Orleans to represent prizefighters of both the past and present vintage, to be sublet to saloons à la Sullivan. He said that for saloons where the business had run down, he would find a current or past champion fighter to appear and infuse new life into the business. He would conduct his agency along the lines that usually governed vaudeville-booking agencies. His idea was judged to be "plausible" and perhaps profitable. Of course, modern agents for athletes often schedule such personal appearances, but Davies' idea seemed to be well ahead of its time.[2030]

Exploring Havana

In January 1905, Davies traveled from New Orleans to Havana, Cuba, to investigate the possibility of opening a theater there. He returned to New Orleans on January 6 aboard the *Chalmette.* A brief story in a Galveston, Texas, newspaper explained why Davies went to Havana: "Charles E. (Parson) Davies got back from Cuba the other day, where he had been prospecting on a theater deal."[2031]

The *Picayune* said that the Empire Theater circuit of Cincinnati intended to invade the South and take over the Lyric. It speculated that Davies had gone to Cuba because the Empire circuit was considering jumping the Florida Straits and opening a theater in Havana. The guess was that Davies had gone to Cuba to scout out theaters behalf of the Empire circuit.

Davies was asked: "Would the Empire circuit take in Cuba? Is that the scheme?"

"No. I hardly think so," he replied.

"Were you figuring on a theater in Havana?"

"Not myself, no: but I might have something in a few days." Davies thought that Havana was truly a wonderful city.[2032]

The rumor that Davies was trying to obtain control of a theater in Havana was revived in April. The Parson had scheduled a performer known as The Great Lafayette to appear at the Lyric beginning April 9.[2033] The Great Lafayette was appearing in New Orleans, but he was scheduled to then go to Havana with his company of fifty people, which included a twenty-member orchestra. It was reported that Lafayette's trip to Cuba was the opening gun in an American theatrical circuit that would be backed by Davies and his associates. It was said that Davies would be returning to Cuba on the next boat.

A reporter for the *Picayune* asked Davies whether he was arranging a Cuban theater circuit and he replied: "This whole matter is embryonic as yet. I cannot discuss it further than to say that Lafayette has sailed, and I will probably go in a week. I would rather talk about a Cuban theatrical circuit after I return."[2034]

In mid-April, an attempt was initiated to resurrect the rivalry between Sullivan and Mitchell. Willis ("Willie") Green, sporting editor of the *Tacoma Daily News*, attempted to match Sullivan and Mitchell for a twenty-round bout, Queensberry rules, that he hoped to schedule in May 1905. The protagonists then engaged in their age-old prefight mating dance of charge and countercharge. Mitchell was in the United States acting as the manager of Jabez White. Mitchell's presence apparently made Green think he had an opportunity to match the two relics. Green proposed presenting the fight at Recreation Park in Tacoma and filming the match for later resale. To help the two old battlers survive, the rounds were to be two minutes each with a four- minute break between rounds. Green estimated that the motion picture privileges alone for this exhibition would be worth $40,000, and it was noted that both Sullivan and Mitchell needed the money.[2035]

Charley Mitchell in 1904 – Photograph of the Chicago History Museum

Reports circulated at the end of April that Davies and Lehman had received an offer of $100,000 from people in Chicago to purchase their interest in the Lyric. A race-track owner in New Orleans, D. H. Barnes, was identified as the contract person for the Chicago people. This was interpreted to mean that a higher price might be obtained for the Lyric through negotiations. Nothing came of this proposal and it appeared that neither Davies nor Lehman was interested in selling his position in the theater.[2036]

In mid-May, Sullivan and Mitchell met in Seattle to conclude the arrangements for a match.[2037] This sounded like a bad dream, but it had some elements of reality. They met in Sullivan's hotel room with Tom Considine, the theatrical manager and former manager of Corbett, representing Mitchell and Frank Hall representing Sullivan. As usual, Sullivan and Mitchell nearly got in a fist fight, and the police had to be called to settle down Mitchell. The only argument concerning the proposed contest concerned timing. Mitchell wanted a match within two weeks of signing, but Sullivan said he needed four months to get in shape for the fight.[2038] (He must have been planning to visit Lourdes in the hope of a miracle.) They ultimately agreed that the match would take place on September 19, 1905.

A news story dated August 5, 1905, reported that Mitchell had selected Davies to look after his affairs and attend to the details of the proposed match. It had been sixteen years since Charlie had represented Mitchell and Kilrain. The article noted that Davies had already written to Willie Green with a view of completing all arrangements relative to the match. It noted that Mr. Davies was a believer in posting forfeits, and the purpose of his communication with Green was to take up that matter of forfeits. Sullivan was in San Francisco in August and was said to be training with Jim McCormick, who was preparing for a match with Gus Ruhlin. The Tacoma parties had assured everyone that the fight could take place without police interference. One writer speculated that the Tacoma people would need to make some special arrangements for the fight; i.e., they would need a derrick to hoist Sullivan into the ring. Many had speculated that the fight would never happen and was only a show, but one writer noted that Davies was a pretty careful sort of man who did not jump hastily to conclusions and that his involvement suggested that the exhibition might actually happen. Less than a week before the two old men were to meet, articles discussed a planned weigh-in, but then Sullivan went on another vaudeville tour and the proposed match fell apart.

John L. Sullivan in 1904 (notice his big hands) a year before the plan to fight Charley Mitchell – Photograph of the Chicago History Museum

In September 1905, the *Salt Lake Tribune* reported that Davies had sent a telegram to Greggains on the West Coast advising him that Mitchell would agree to meet Sullivan in October. However, it also noted that the former champion had blown out of town. As a noted monologist he could not abandon his habit of talking and was exercising his voice in the role of vaudevillian has-been.[2040] On the date set for the match, Sullivan was with his vaudeville company in Butte, Montana, and Mitchell returned to England in November.

In the early summer several newspapers reported that O'Rourke, the proprietor of the Delavan at Broadway and Fourteenth Street in New York, was being forced to sell his leasehold interest in the hotel and that the putative buyers were Corbett and Parson Davies.[2041] One article claimed that the purchase price for the hotel property was $50,000; other articles said that the buyers were really purchasing O'Rourke's interest in a lease for the hotel and that lease had nine years remaining in its term.

O'Rourke denied he was being forced to sell and offered several explanations. He said that the prizefighting business was not returning income as it should and he was getting out of it and going to Europe.[2042] O'Rourke said he was not a hand shaker and that a person operating a hotel had to like people and like mingling with the clients. Tom said he did not have the personality to be in the hotel business.[2043] O'Rourke also said he had invented a pneumatic drill, which he was selling to the hotel to generate income to promote his new invention. Tom said the drill was going to make him a rich man. He had given up the human pneumatic drill known as Joe Walcott.

If Davies and Corbett had purchased the hotel, it seems likely that its day-to-day management would have fallen to Davies. He had spent a substantial part of his life living in hotels and knew the area of Broadway and Fourteenth Street. He probably intended to operate the Delavan as a modern-day Gilsey House, where sporting men visiting New York would want to stay.

The possible sale of O'Rourke's leasehold interest was not simply newspaper talk, but an injunction by a New York Supreme Court judge prevented the closing of the transaction. The injunction was requested by the Henry B. Harris Theatrical Company, which alleged that it had an enforceable contract with Corbett that prevented him from lending his name to any other business. O'Rourke, Davies and Corbett met on June 15, 1905, to conclude the sale, but their meeting was interrupted when they were served with a restraining order. As a result, Corbett and Davies did not purchase the hotel, and O'Rourke said he would be forced to continue operating. He said that the hotel would not be closed, but he had no other prospective purchasers at that time.[2044] One newspaper commented that the theatrical managers who kept Corbett from going into the hotel business must have had a grudge against the theater-going public by leaving James J. Corbett on the stage.

Davies returned to New Orleans in mid-August and was looking over the theater situation. Davies and Lehman had decided to lease the Lyric to Henry Greenwall and his associate Walter S. Baldwin for the 1905 season. Neither

Davies nor Lehman could find the time to manage the Lyric themselves. Greenwall had several theaters in Texas and before May 1904 had managed the Grand Opera House in New Orleans for about twenty years. He also had his own theater called the Greenwall. While he was the manager of the Grand Opera House, Greenwall had often employed the Baldwin-Melville Stock Company to provide entertainment there, and Greenwall and Baldwin planned to provide entertainment at the Lyric during the 1905 season using Baldwin's stock company with Lester Lonergan as the leading man.[2045]

Davies and the Shubert brothers

When the Lyric was leased to Greenwall and Baldwin, the *Picayune* reported that Davies had met with the Shubert brothers about adding the Lyric to the circuit of theaters they were developing across the United States. Davies said he had suggested that the Shuberts should wait to lease the Lyric in 1906.[2046] In the summer it had become public that the Shuberts along with David Belasco and Harrison Grey Fiske, Minne Maddern Fiske, David Warfiled, and others were developing a circuit of theaters extending all over the country to compete with New York syndicate. They were being financed by Henry Huttleston Rogers of the Standard Oil Company, who was one of the wealthiest men in America.[2047]

The Shuberts explained their reasons for forming their own circuit. Lee Shubert said that when the Shuberts had taken over the management of the Herald Square Theater in New York, Klaw & Erlanger agreed to book it but then demanded 25 percent of the profits for their services. This money was paid, but then the syndicate began to demand the same tribute at all the Shuberts' theaters. In addition, Erlanger had met with Sam Shubert and demanded he close all his theaters to talent managed by David Belasco. When the Shuberts refused this demand, the syndicate promptly canceled all of the talent scheduled for the Shubert theaters. The Shuberts said this behavior forced them to begin forming a competitive circuit.[2048]

By October 1905 the Shuberts had control of theaters in London, New York, Brooklyn, Newark, Philadelphia, Pittsburgh, Syracuse, Rochester, Buffalo, Cleveland, Chicago, St. Louis and Washington, D.C. Davies had personally supervised the construction of a new Belasco theater in Pittsburgh during the summer. He made at least five trips to Pittsburgh to make sure the theater was in proper condition. Both Davies and Lehman owned interests in that new Pittsburgh theater. In addition, Davies was working on behalf of the Shuberts to acquire additional theaters in Atlanta, Memphis, Birmingham, Louisville, and Mobile.

Beginning in 1906 the Shuberts leased the Lyric for five years. Davies was asked about rumors that there would be a new theater built in New Orleans. He said he thought that the construction of another theater in New Orleans would be a poor investment with the St. Charles Orpheum devoted to vaudeville, the two syndicate theaters occupied by syndicate talent, Greenwall's own theater devoted to burlesque, and the Lyric booked by the Shuberts.[2049] Not only did this situation create a lot of competition for the theater-going public but it diminished the quality of the talent available to put people in the seats.

In December 1905, Greenwall told the *Picayune* that the Shuberts would not be taking over the Lyric, but would instead take over Greenwall's theater in New Orleans.[2050]

Davies responded: "I will bet anyone $1,000 that Lehman and Davies have a contract on the Lyric Theater for five years to book the attractions of the Shuberts and also the attractions of David Belasco and Harrison Gray Fiske." Davies was described as the Shubert brothers' representative in the South.

He was asked about his recent trip through several Southern states and replied: "I went to Mobile and arranged for the building of a new theater, which will be ready next season. In Montgomery the arrangements made practically assure the Shuberts control of a house. In Chattanooga all arrangements have been made for the building of a new theater. In Birmingham negotiations are still under way, but the outlook is very promising that we shall have a theater in that city. In Nashville we have capital interested, and the outlook is more than favorable."

He also explained that the Shuberts had closed on a property in Atlanta, Denver, San Francisco, and Oakland and had representatives working on houses in San Antonio, Houston, Fort Worth and Dallas, and Los Angeles.[2051] The Parson was correct when he said the Shuberts would lease the Lyric, and by March 1906 it was listed as part of the Shubert circuit.

On September 20, 1905, Charlie was in Philadelphia to watch a fight between Dixon and Kid Murphy, a.k.a. "Harlem" Tommy Murphy. This was about the last real fight for Dixon, and he was knocked out in the fifth round.[2052] The match was similar to the Ryan-Dempsey fight. McGovern, an old foe who respected George's courage and ability jumped over the ropes after George was KO'd and carried him from the ring. McGovern's attitude toward Dixon is in great contrast to the attitudes of Sullivan, Corbett, and Brady to Jackson.

There was no cheering when George went down, the silence was like a funeral, as everyone seemed to know that the career of a great champion was over. Accounts noted that others at ringside for this match included Davies, O'Rourke, Young Corbett, Abe Attel, Joe Humphreys, Dick Barnard and many others who knew "Little Chocolate."[2053] During his career Davies had seen many great fighters emerge from obscurity, climb to the top of their profession, and then fall back to their former state. However, Dixon had been a special fighter who achieved and sustained his great success despite the color line that had prevented Jackson from becoming world champion.

By February 1906 a new corporation had been formed to replace Southern Amusement, which had gone defunct when Jake Wells withdrew his support and sued Henry Lehman and when the Athletic Park had burned. The new company had capital of $50,000. The incorporators were Davies, Arthur B. Leopold, J. Loyocana, Anthony Patorno, Jr., Gus Lehman, Jr., W. Swartz, S. Clollna, and

Captain Lewis, who was a promoter of an amusement park in St. Louis called the "Boer War."

The new company had obtained a lease on the Athletic Park for the coming season and intended substantial improvements including the Baldwin airship called the California Arrow, a new show called Fighting the Flames, an exhibit called the Naval Show, which portrayed a battle at sea, and an exhibit of baby incubators (complete with premature children) that had been popular at Chicago's Columbian Exposition.[2054] But the Athletic Park venture failed to produce a profit and litigation followed.

Davies reported to be losing his sight

A short squib in the *Palestine Daily Herald* of Palestine, Texas, on February 26, 1906, said that Davies was going to manage the New Orleans baseball team.[2055] The *Sun* reported that Davies was at the head of syndicate that had purchased the New Orleans franchise in the Southern baseball circuit. However, other news about Davies was published on February 23, and it was not good. Stories said that Davies had been stricken with paralysis of the eye and that total blindness would probably result. His condition was labeled serious.[2056] The *Evening World* of New York reported on February 23 that Davies had been stricken with Bell's paralysis while attending a meeting of the Athletic Park Amusement Committee.

One account quotes Davies:

> I was sitting at my desk with a pen in one hand signing some papers. Suddenly, and without any warning, my eyelids dropped shut and everything was a blank. I was stunned. A dizzy feeling came over me. I put my hands up to my eyes and found the lids closed, without a particle of life in them. They seemed dead. I tried to open them but they fell back perfectly lifeless. Then the thought came to me, "Have I gone blind?" and it was the most terrible thought I ever can recall, and I was stunned with the sensation the mind sent over the nervous system. I again put my hands to my eyes and the lids were perfectly lifeless. I lifted one lid and it fell back like a piece of flesh which had lost all of its functions.[2057]

The next morning, Davies' physician found swelling around his temples and made the Bell's paralysis (i.e., palsy) diagnosis. The doctor planned to open Davies' left eye in a few days by using an electrical shock from a battery. Michel Faraday had discovered the use of aspects of electricity and magnetism in the treatment of various medical conditions, and these uses came to be called faradic electricity. The electricity was applied to stimulate the facial nerve that was causing the palsy. It is interesting that in long standing cases of Bell's palsy the practice at the time included the administration of small doses of strychnine.

Charlie went to Hot Springs to meet with a doctor who had expertise with eye-related problems.[2058] The *Evening World* reported on March 26 that Davies' condition was improving and chances were good that he would be able to see again. Over the next few years Davies suffered several similar events as his health continued to decline.[2059] His eye paralysis may have been a form of peripheral neuropathy caused by systemic damage to his peripheral nerves. This all may well have been a nascent effect of the strychnine poisoning he had suffered in March 1895.

At about the time that Davies was stricken with eye paralysis, several stories said that Jere Dunne was dying of cancer in San Francisco. Dunne's story was described as "dimenovelish and gunpowdery" in that he had killed three men during his life including Jimmy Elliott, who was one of the Parson's earliest fighters. Sullivan used the reports of Dunne's and Davies' illnesses as an occasion to reflect on the past. In his typical gracious way, Sullivan illustrated his unlimited ego and unbounded prejudice when he wrote:

> Jere Dunne is reported to be dying of cancer in 'Frisco. I supposed that his trouble with Jimmy Elliott could be traced to Jere's anger at Elliott ducking out of a match with me after Jere nearly went broke paying out money to arrange for the battle. News comes from New Orleans that Parson Davies was stricken with blindness not long ago in his office in New Orleans. It seems strange that some of the men who were the best of my advisers and who used to predict what was going to happen to me if I didn't watch out are taken, while my career keeps rolling on. . . . Peter Jackson was the best of all the smoked-pugs, and I say this in spite of what has been said about my being afraid to meet him. I was never for one minute afraid of Jackson, or any other fighter, but I never would go into the ring with a negro, and my record is clean in this respect. My course in meeting only white men in the ring, if followed by others, would have kept a lot of fakes out of the history of the ring, and all who size up the same for the past dozen years will agree to this.[2060]

Perhaps Sullivan should have paid more attention to the Parson's advice; Charlie ultimately outlived John L. by two years.

Davies' eye paralysis put him on the shelf for only a short time. Late in March, he was described as the head of a group of New Orleans' promoters who were trying to bring McGovern and Oscar Mattheus Nielson, known as "Battling" Nelson or the "Durable Dane," to New Orleans for a contest to be held in May 1906.[2061] The group proposed a ten-round match in an arena seating ten thousand. McGovern would not agree to the proposed fight, and it ultimately did not take place. Nelson was a rough fighter who had fought a six-round, no decision with McGovern in mid-March 1906.

Their proposed match in New Orleans was called the most important glove contest that would be held in New Orleans since Corbett beat Sullivan for the heavyweight championship on September 7, 1891. Davies had contacted Nelson's manager, Billy Nolan, and had a telegram from Nolan that Nelson had agreed to meet Aurelio Herrera in a twenty-round contest before the Pacific Athletic Club on either May 7 or May 12 for a purse of $20,000. Nolan wrote he would return to New Orleans immediately after the Herrera fight to begin preparation for a match with McGovern. Once again this fight did not happen.

Charlie wrote back to friends in New Orleans that he would return to the city on April 25, 1906. His sight had improved substantially while undergoing painful treatments at Hot Springs. He had picked the twenty-fifth as his target return date because that was the date that the Athletic Park was to open and also because he intended to attend the big Confederate reunion. Charlie was described as the head of a group that had leased the Athletic Park for the summer season.[2062]

On April 18, a great earthquake and subsequent fire nearly destroyed San Francisco, including the shanty homes of many Italian and Irish Catholics of that city. Within a few days after the catastrophe, the Catholic archbishop mobilized the forces of the church to assist the dispossessed. Sacred Heart Convent was turned into a hospital, and the Catholic technical school operated by the Sisters of Charity became a shelter for the homeless. The city's engineering department also constructed temporary buildings in Golden Gate Park to accommodate the homeless, and the Sisters of Charity played a prominent role in caring for the families housed in the ensuing encampment. Charlie's niece, Sister Mary Conradine, had been working in San Francisco for four years at the time of the earthquake and played an important role in the relief efforts on the West Coast.[2063]

Davies and Teddy Roosevelt meet again

The *Los Angeles Herald* reported on June 10 that Davies was in New York. The article said that a few months earlier the Parson's sight had failed him, and he had traveled to Hot Springs to obtain treatment for his sight. He had recovered his vision and then traveled to New York. There he met with the vaudeville company of Rich, Plunkett, and Wesley and entered into a contract with them to appear on stage as a monologist telling stories from his own life experiences.[2064]

On the lighter side, in 1906 Oscar Hammerstein constructed the Manhattan Opera House, a popular new attraction of the big city. Maurice Guest, Hammerstein's theatrical agent, had seen a Russian giant named Feodor Alexiovitch Machnow on display at a hippodrome in London and got the idea of bringing Machnow to New York to shake hands with people on Hammerstein's rooftop garden. Guest arranged to bring Machnow to New York, where he arrived on board the Hamburg-American liner *Pretoria* in mid-June.[2065] Arrangements were also made by to have Machnow come to Washington, D.C., to meet President

Theodore Roosevelt. The giant Russian had previously met many of the kings and queens of Europe and was anxious to meet the U.S. president.

On his return to New Orleans, Davies explained that in New York he had met a friend who was the sponsor for the Russian giant. This was probably Maurice Guest. Davies learned that the giant and his wife wanted to meet President Roosevelt.

Davies promised, "I will take you to him."

Davies was scheduled to meet his old friend Teddy Roosevelt on June 21, the same day that Machnow came to the White House. The meeting between Davies and Roosevelt occurred with the assistance of Bat Masterson, who had written to Roosevelt asking him to meet with Davies. In February 1905, Roosevelt had found Masterson steady employment by appointing him a deputy U.S. marshal of the district of New York. Bat was just the kind of man Roosevelt admired, and when Masterson asked Roosevelt, he happily agreed to see Davies.

When Davies arrived at the White House, he brought along the nine-foot-three-inch tall, 360-pound Russian giant. He drove up to the White House and called for Secretary Loeb, whom Davies had known for many years. Loeb came out and said that Roosevelt was meeting with Secretary Root and would be available presently. Davies soon introduced the giant and his wife to the President. However, they became panicky and tried to run away. They were headed off and embarrassment was avoided.

Davies and Roosevelt had several things in common in 1906 in addition to their love of boxing. The President had been suffering increasing difficulty with his eyes, and both these warriors were suffering more each year from their chronic rheumatism. A special published in the *New York Times* on June 21 described their meeting:

> President Roosevelt to-day gave an audience to Machnow, the Russian giant but declined to let the nine-foot specimen of humanity kiss his hand. The giant, compromised by addressing him as the "King and Emperor of All the Peoples of the World," but as Mr. Roosevelt does not understand Russian, he missed this, and the interpreter was so rattled he did not interpret it until after the audience.
>
> The visit to the President was brought about through two well-known sporting men, Bat Masterson and Parson Davies, prize fight promoter. Masterson wrote a letter to the President, asking him to receive the Parson, and the Parson carried along the giant and his wife, the press agent for a New York theatrical manager, and a score of newspaper men. The Parson had immediate entree at the White House. The various secretaries and guards were not in evidence, and when the President appeared in the room of Secretary J. Loeb he stepped quickly to the Parson and warmly shook his hand. Then the Russian was introduced, trembling like a leaf.

> He was picturing his finish if he did anything objectionable to this new World Czar, and the thought made him shiver.
>
> Machnow tried to kiss the President's hand, but was headed off by the vigilant Parson. Mr. Roosevelt bent his head back to take a view of his towering visitor's face, and then backed away from the Russian, who, balked in his effort to kiss the President's hand, seemed meditating some other demonstration of reverence.
>
> "Come in, Parson," the President called to Davies, "it's you I want to talk with." The Parson went into the President's office and official business went by the board while the Executive talked of fighting with his visitor. Mr. Roosevelt was evidently very glad to see Davies, for he put his arm over his shoulders and beamed upon him.
>
> "Has Jeffries really retired?" the President asked.
>
> "Yes," said, the Parson," "and I believe you have also. When Croker said he had retired from New York politics it was a long time before the people believed it. But he was a man of his word. I know that you are, and you have done enough to have made a young man old. You have had plenty of honor and all that."
>
> "Oh I'm done; I'm done," the President replied.
>
> Mr. Davies said afterward that he would stake his last dollar that this country would not see Roosevelt a candidate for President again, and added that he felt he was sure as a betting man in saying that Bryan would fill the chair he had been sitting opposite just a few moments before. Davies said that the President asked about the existing conditions of the sport of boxing in New York. "He looks a bit thin," said the fight promoter of the President, "but I would say that he would be good for an hour on the mat with any wrestler, and then be able to take on an easy mark."[2067]

After talking to the press outside the White House, Davies lit up a cigar and ambled off toward his hotel.[2068]

The next evening Masterson was at the Waldorf Astoria in New York, where he confronted Colonel Dick Plunkett, the former sheriff of Tombstone, Arizona, and a man named Dinklesheets, who ran a Texas newspaper and was sitting with Colonel Plunkett. It seems that the former sheriff and the Texas newspaper man had been hanging around the bar at the Waldorf and casting aspirations on Masterson.

It is not clear whether Plunkett and Dinklesheets were aware that Masterson was at the Waldorf, but word of their talk reached Bat, who went to the hotel's bar to confront Plunkett. Dinklesheets, who must have been drunk to do it, then butted in and took a swing at Masterson but fell over a table loaded with glassware. Masterson slugged Dinklesheets and then stepped over his prone body. As Bat stepped toward Plunkett, he slipped his hand into his coat pocket where

Masterson was thought to be carrying his revolver. Someone yelled out, "Look out! Bat's gonna flash his cannon." The Waldorf bar emptied out quickly. At this point, the incident ended without further violence. Because Davies had just seen the President the prior day based on Masterson's importuning and because the two men were such friends, it is likely that Davies was somewhere nearby when all these events happened. The incident provoked articles in New York newspapers, which claimed that one in every five men in New York in 1906 carried a gun.[2069]

When Davies returned to New Orleans from his visit with the President, he announced that the Shuberts had leased both the Baronne and Lyric theaters for a period of ten years and that high-class attractions would be offered at the Baronne with a stock company working at the Lyric. The *Picayune* reported that upon his return from the East, the Parson was looking much better than he had looked for several months and his friends were glad to see him after a two-month absence.[2070]

Davies must not have recovered his full health because in early August 1906 he traveled to Marlin, Texas, for a two-week rest. Hot mineral water had been found in Marlin in 1892, and a health industry sprang up like those at Mt. Clemens, West Baden, Hot Springs, and Ogden. Davies returned to New Orleans on August 25. He announced that the Lyric would open on September 10 with the Brown-Baker stock company and denied another rumor that he was about to become a married man.[2071]

Then Davies was in an accident that nearly took his life. Less than a week before Christmas of 1906 he was hit by a street car in New Orleans.[2072] The *Washington Times* said that Davies had been crossing a busy street when he was hit and seriously injured. The Parson was knocked out, and it was thought originally that his injuries were fatal. Davies' poor sight had led to several recent injuries; however, in this case it was believed that after several days for recovery he would be all right. He suffered a big gash on his leg, and a large chunk of flesh was taken out of one elbow. He had saved himself by rolling out of the way of the street car. Witnesses said that but for his quick evasive action he would have been cut in two.[2073]

Early January 1907 found Davies meeting with the press to complain about the excessive fees being charged theater managers in New Orleans when compared to other major cities. He pointed out that New Orleans required theater owners to have a fireman on duty at every performance, but in New York owners merely paid an annual fee of $500 and the city provided the fireman. He thought the new ordinance was merely a device for extra jobs that the politicians would control at great expense to businessmen. In addition, theater owners in Louisiana paid a higher annual license fee to the state than saloon owners; the annual license in Louisiana was $900 compared to only $500 in New York.[2074]

Charlie also sponsored what was probably that last boxing show of his career. He had Maher appear between acts of a show at the Lyric to put on an exhibition with Sammy Phillips. Maher was called an old time friend of Davies.[2075]

Davies was away from New Orleans for most of February and March meeting with the Shuberts in New York, to schedule the coming attractions for the season at the Lyric and the Belasco Theater in Pittsburgh. In addition, the Shuberts were planning to redecorate the Baroone Theater during the summer to make many improvements there.

In 1908 this theater was converted to the largest vitagraph theater in the world. Davies told the New Orleans press that a big fight was brewing in New York, to control vaudeville performers and the opposing parties would be going at it hammer and tong. However, he was excited about the big crowds that were being drawn by the Shubert theaters in New York and optimistic about the coming season.[2076]

During the third week of April 1907 Davies left New Orleans to spend three weeks at Hot Springs. This was another sign that his health was poor. After his stay in Arkansas he said he would return to New Orleans and then travel to San Francisco to spend some time with his niece.[2077]

The White City amusement park

On May 4, a White City amusement park was opened in New Orleans by promoter Charles C. Mathews. After the 1893 Columbian Exposition in Chicago, the name White City was frequently associated with large amusement parks. There were White City copy-cats were found in Syracuse, Washington, D.C., Atlanta, Cleveland, Trenton, and many other cities and towns. New Orleans' White City featured a boardwalk lit with more than one thousand five hundred electric lights and opened with a performance of *Kismet* presented by the Olympia Opera Company. Attractions included flying horses, a Figure Eight, a side friction toboggan roller coaster, and a Katzenjammer Castle. For a brief time Parson Davies was the manager of New Orleans' White City.[2078]

The Parson visits Sister Davies

Davies was staying at the Saint Francis Hotel in San Francisco on June 23. He said he was on a pleasure trip and had come west for his health and to see the Britt-Nelson and Squires-Burns fights on July 3 and 4. Certainly San Francisco was a more pleasant place to be in June and July than New Orleans. Charlie said he was in Firsco in particular to meet and visit with his sister. However, he was undoubtedly misunderstood and was probably referring to his niece Sister Mary Conradine Davies. He also said he was going to Byron Springs to take treatments for his rheumatism, but he would make frequent trips from there to San Francisco for social visits.[2079]

On June 25, Davies was in San Rafael, California watching Bill Squires train for his upcoming match with Tommy Burns to take place at Colma, California. Davies was asked about Bill Squires and said he could "tell whether or not a man can scrap by the way he combs his hair." After Davies watched Squires skip a rope and spar, the Parson said he was convinced that the Australian was a really great fighter.

"Never in my life have I seen so great a piece of fighting machinery concentrated in 180 pounds of human being," Davies said. "When I say that I mean that every ounce of flesh on the Australian is there for a purpose and will be used in his fight against Burns. Usually with heavyweights, there are from 6 to 10 pounds of natural coarseness that all the training in the world would not reduce. This is not the case with Squires, however. A more cleanly built big athlete couldn't be found in any man's country."[2080]

Davies was not at all right about Squires' chances because on July 4 Burns knocked out Squires in the first round. Undoubtedly Squires looked something less than a fighting machine while the referee was counting to ten. Later that month the *San Francisco Call* reported that Davies was still in California and representing a 350 pound heavyweight named Joe Rogers, who was under O'Rourke's management. Davies was trying to arrange a fight between Rogers and a fighter named Al Kaufman.[2081]

Illness begins cutting down Davies

Only two weeks after the last report from California, Charlie was again sick. The *Picayune* published an article with an August 7 Chicago dateline reporting that Davies had arrived in Chicago, but had been forced to take to his bed, suffering from acute rheumatism.[2082] The Parson had probably visited with Floto in Denver on his trip from San Francisco to Chicago because in mid-August, Floto wrote a retrospective about Davies that was published in several newspapers. In the article Floto wrote he knew that Davies' niece had become the superior of her community in San Francisco, and because that was unusual information Otto probably learned it directly from Charlie.

On August 14, Charlie was still lying ill at the Sherman House in Chicago. He was not so ill, however, that he was isolated from the press. He visited with a Chicago reporter and was questioned about various charges that continued to circulate about Siler and his competence as a referee. Charlie told the press: "Siler's record so plainly speaks for itself that there is no need of indorsing him. There never was and probably never again will live a man quite so honest as old George."[2083]

In mid-August, Floto wrote an article for the *Denver Post* that was republished in the *Salt Lake Telegram* with the headline "Parson Davies Is Near Death." Floto was a man who knew Davies well and had worked for him for many years. In his article Floto said that Davies "was one of the most wonderful men I ever met." Floto wrote about the Parson's relationship with Croker. "To this day exists a great bond of friendship between the pair, and never does Davies go to Europe that he is not the guest of Croker, and then the talk always drifts to days of long ago."

Floto however made some unusual claims. For example, he claimed that Davies had cleared $133,000 from the walking match at the Garden with Ennis, O'Leary, Harriman, and Rowell. This seems unlikely at best. If this claim was true the money that Davies earned would convert to nearly $3,000,000 in current value. He also claims that Davies had three brothers: James, George, and Vere. This is wrong. His brothers were Henry, George, Vere, and perhaps William. Floto also writes that George Davies was dead before 1907. This may have been true but has not been verified. Finally, Floto wrote: "Financially, he has plenty of the world's goods. He never married because he supported and educated his brother's children. One of them is now a mother superior in San Francisco, and the rest of them are well married and the finest young ladies you would care to meet." [2084]

In another article from Floto's pen he wrote that that Davies "was one of the most wonderful men I ever met. As a fight promoter and manager of big sporting events there is not at the present before the public a man following the business who could be mentioned in the same class with him, unless, perhaps it be James W. Coffroth, in San Francisco. Coffroth comes near being the man that Davies was than any other I can think of. . . . I could sit for hours and write about Davies, for we were together a long time. The greatest advice I ever received was from the Parson, and he certainly was a man who knew right from wrong."[2085]

Davies was not ill for long because by mid-September he was visiting his friend O'Rourke in New York. Tom, it was reported, had taken Davies to his summer retreat in Summit, New Jersey, where Davies was going to begin a dietetic treatment known as the milk cure.[2086] This process, described in a 1922 article entitled "The Genuine Milk Cure," included the following elements: "The general rule is six quarts of milk a day (with no other food) for six weeks. In extreme cases the length of time is extended to eight, ten and twelve weeks." The steps in the cure were: (1). twenty-four hours before starting on the milk take a dose of castor oil, (2) for one day eat fruit only, except no bananas are permitted, (3) on the second day start at once on the six quarts a day by slowly drinking a one-half pint glass of milk every half hour from seven in the morning till seven at night with a little lemon or grapefruit juice after each glass, (4) an enema every night, and (5) a quick hot bath every night. No food is allowed during the process.[2087] This is not a cure that Davies was likely to stick with, and it seems more like slow torture than a cure.

In mid-February 1908, the *Los Angeles Herald* reported that the famous sportsman Frank Kelly had returned from New Orleans, where he had visited with Parson Davies, who had returned there from a trip to London. Kelly and Davies discussed the relative abilities of wrestlers that Davies had seen during his trip to England.[2088]

The *Atlanta Constitution* reported on March 26 that Davies had announced in New Orleans that he had signed a contract to serve as "middleman" for a minstrel company during the next theater season.[2089] A middleman is a performer in a minstrel line who acts as the interlocutor and engages the others in conversation to set up a punch line. The interlocutor introduced jokes to the end men who then delivered the punch line to a seemingly innocent question posed by the middleman. For example:

Interlocutor: "Joe, I heard you bought a cow farm?"

End Man: "Why, yes I did. I bought 100 cows, but the other day somebody came by and cut off all their tails and now I am going to have to sell them all wholesale."

Interlocutor: "Why do you have to sell them wholesale?"

End Man: "Well I can't retail them!"

Frequently, particularly in the South a minstrel show would involve black face "comedy" routines. It is unlikely that Davies ever appeared with the minstrels because his health took a turn for the worse before the season began.

Davies closes up shop in New Orleans

In mid-September, the *Washington Times* reported that Davies had left Chicago, having recovered his health, to return to work in New Orleans.[2090] However, on October 2, 1908, the *Picayune* reported that "Charles E. Davies, the famous sporting man, known wherever sports are known as 'Parson' Davies, has closed out his business here, folded his tent and is preparing to abandon New Orleans as a place of permanent residence." This article noted that Davies had a half interest in the Lyric in along with Henry Lehmann. He had lived there for over ten years, having taken up residence there just before the theater season opened.[2091]

The *Los Angeles Herald* of October 6 said that Davies intended to take a tour of the world and then retire in either Los Angeles or San Francisco.[2092] The *Picayune* said that when "he came here a little more than ten years ago Mr. Davies had determined to retire permanently from connection with sports." That was probably what Charlie had told the reporter, but he had not retired permanently. In fact, he spent most of his ten years in New Orleans working at numerous business ventures at a frantic pace.

The paper reported that the New Orleans climate did not agree with Charlie and that on three different occasions he had the "distressing experience of being stricken totally blind. On each occasion he had recovered, but only after many days of pain and anxiety. Not very long ago Mr. Davies suffered from a relapse of this malady, but it was not so serious as on the three former occasions . . . ."[2093]

Davies said he had not been troubled by experiences with blindness while traveling and thought that relocating would help his condition. He had just closed his billiard hall and sold the furniture and equipment in preparation for leaving. He told the *Picayune* that his plans for the future were not definite, and he would probably initially go to New York and perhaps take a trip to Europe. After that, he was considering living on the Pacific coast near his niece, who was a Sister of Charity. Despite his intentions to leave, Davies was still living in the St. Charles as late as March 30, 1909.[2094]

Anita Gruschow Cleary (b: Nov 15, 1890) in Chicago, Cook County, Illinois. – Parson Davies' grandniece

Davies may have decided to leave New Orleans because of increasing legal entanglements there. In January 1908, the Lehman family had gone into receivership and recorded a deed of trust for all of the family's real property and given for the benefit of the family's creditors. Gustavo Lehman Sr., Henry's father, had committed suicide by drowning himself in the Mississippi River. The family's receiver was going to sell all of their property to pay off a committee of creditors. In addition, a lawsuit had been filed arising out of the failure of the Athletic Park venture in 1906.[2095] Several contractors had sued the amusement company, and in October 1909, the court fixed Davies' share of the liability as $9,600. Henry Lehman was found liable for $6,500 and Gustavo Lehman Jr. for $3,500. A receiver was ordered to collect the amounts determined due and pay them to the several creditors.[2096] These judgments may imply that the Lehmans together owned about 51 percent of the company. Charlie returned to New Orleans in December 1909 to go duck hunting with some of his friends, but by that time he was only a visitor there.

Chapter 18 - (1909-1920)

It's a Great Country - Ours

Time is hanging heavily over the head of Parson Davies, for years a character of the sporting world. Broken in health and having practically lost the use of one leg, the promoter of athletic events and backer and manager of some of the most famous prize fighters of a few years ago is confined to his room at 3320 Flournoy street, where he has been for weeks.

Only the rumbling of the elevated trains past his windows relieves the monotony of the long days and sleepless nights. His little grandniece, Edith Wilson, aged 7, cheers up the dark moments now and then as she trips in quietly, says "Hello, Uncle Charlie" and plants a kiss upon the whiskered face of her granduncle.

"There's an angel if there ever was one," he said as the brighteyed little girl patted his hand and slowly moved toward the door.

"Were you ever married," was asked.

"No," he said, with emphasis. That's one of the things in life I did escape, but I've raised a family of six children which were left practically homeless when my brothers died.

"Yes, he's the only father I have ever known, and he's been a good one to me," said Mrs. Harry G. Wilson, with whom the Parson now makes his home.

"Well, if I am through with life I go with the satisfaction of knowing that I lived honestly and spent my money in a just cause and brought up from childhood six boys and girls, every one of whom I am today proud of," continued the veteran sporting man."[2098]

—

Sitting in a big chair in the lobby of his hotel, with his crutches across his knees, and an expression of resignation on his countenance, Parson Davies, once known as king of American sports, talked of old times and old-timers. Probably the greatest manager of fighters and professional walkers who ever lived was the old "Parson," and beyond doubt the most thoroughly sportsmanlike character in the history of sport. Tears swelled the old man's eyes as he talked of better days - better ones for him and for the boxing game.[2099]

—

♦

On May 26, 1909, many newspapers reported that Parson Davies was in Chicago and in his last illness at the home of his sister in this city.[2100] Charlie was actually at the home of his niece Anita Wilson. Anita was the second daughter of Charlie's older brother, Henry. She had married Harry G. Wilson who worked for the Chicago Public Library and lived at 3320 Flournoy. Anita was Wilson's second wife and they had a step-daughter Edith, who was six years old.[2101]

In mid-June 1909, nationally syndicated news stories reported that Charlie had seen his first fight as a child at Killarney and had bet $25 of his father's money on the fight. It is possible that Charlie's father took him to a prize fight before they immigrated to the United States, but it is probably not true that he bet his father's money. To publishers who wanted to market the story of his life, the Parson invariably said, "After I'm dead you can write that. My story is not concluded while I am living." The *San Antonio Light & Gazette*, June 8, 1909 is one example of the syndicated story.[2102]

Charlie was not dying. By August 1 he was again in New York and talking to reporters. He had been there for several weeks before being interviewed and the papers there said he "looks as young as he did a dozen years ago, is enjoying good health and if it weren't for a rheumatic limp in one of his legs, you wouldn't think there was a thing in the world the matter with him. Unless there is a big unexpected change in his health for the worse, the former manager of Peter Jackson, Choynski and Tommy Ryan is good for years to come. He always has been a man of, exemplary habits and the reports that he was so low really surprised his friends."[2103]

In February 1910, Charlie was back in Chicago, where he was again interviewed. A reporter for the *Denver Times* saw him at Anita's home and then wrote the passages found at the beginning of this chapter.

The six children he referred to were the three daughters of his brother Henry and the children of his brother George. Davies also discussed his early life in New York and his career as a promoter and heaped praise on Jackson.

Sometime after February 1910 Charlie left Chicago and went back to New Orleans and then on to Coney Island. While in New York, he suffered a relapse and was again critically ill.[2104] The newspapers said he had a second stroke. He had his first stroke while he was in New Orleans and then a second stroke at Coney Island. Again the accounts of Charlie's condition appear to have been overstated. With a Chicago dateline of February 22 the *San Francisco Call* reported that Davies had returned to Chicago and was staying with relatives recovering and not in immediate danger.[2105]

After recovering his health at Anita's home, Davies went back to New York. He was there into July, and that summer he told the press he was through with boxing for good.[2106] One report said that Davies could no longer walk.[2107] On July 18, the newspapers said that the new claims that Charlie was dying were overstated. The articles said that the dire predictions "seemed to make the veteran sportsman rather more cheerful than unusual tonight. 'No,' he said, 'I'm not dying. I'm only going to Chicago next Wednesday.'"[2108]

Charlie had been staying with his friend, Sam Gompertz, at Coney Island. He was convalescing from an illness and said he was much better and could not imagine how the rumor of his impending death got started. Gompertz was the general manager of Dreamland, the huge amusement park with a long iron pier at Coney Island. Dreamland had been opened in 1904 by Leonard Schloss, who had worked as an advance man for Davies in 1893.

On Saturday, July 23, Davies returned to his niece's home in Chicago (a long way from Dreamland) and he was visited there on July 27 by Billy Delaney and Matt Larkin.[2109] They had come to Chicago to meet with Charles Comiskey and passed most of their day with members of the Chicago White Sox. They found time to call on Charlie, whom Delaney had known for thirty years. Shortly after their visit, newspapers reported that the Parson was "slowly sinking and on July 29 he had suffered another relapse, and was in a worse condition than when he arrived in Chicago from New York." Charlie was not confined to bed and was able to sit up in an easy chair.[2110]

Charlie recovered from his lowest point and returned to New York, where he took a room at the Hotel Albany located on West 41 Street and Broadway, at the southeast corner of Times Square.[2111] The Albany had about two hundred fifty permanent guests and most of them were members of the theatrical professions.[2112] It was within a block of the Hotel Murphy, the Calvert Hotel and the Knickerbocker. The Astor was at Forty-Fourth and Broadway, and the Rossmore not far away. The Broadway Theater was across the street from the Albany.

The head clerk of the Albany was the first man convicted of violating a new state law prohibiting anyone from acting as a stakeholder for bets on prizefights. He held the stakes for a neighborhood black barber who bet $1,000 on Jack Johnson when he defeated Jeffries. This was just the kind of place where Davies could live among friends. He started his adult life in New York working at the Putnam. The city had changed substantially in the years between 1870 and 1911, but he was back close to his starting point.

An article in March 1911 said that Davies was found lying on a bed alone in a small room on the third floor of the Albany. He could not get around by himself and was visited frequently by McCoy, who would help him stand and move around some. The writer said that it was like going back a lifetime to talk with Davies, who in the old days had managed such men as Mitchell, Choynski, Jackson, Ryan, Kilrain, and Hall. He told the reporter he had watched the Jackson-Corbett fight for 54 rounds, but it looked like it would last a week, and he had left to take a nap before the fight ended. Charlie felt that Jackson should never have taken the fight because he was a cripple at the time of the match. He said he tried to have the contest postponed but Peter had insisted on going forward.[2113]

Despite renewed reports he was about to die, in early May, he was healthy enough to sail from New York to England aboard the *Caledonia* of the Anchor line arriving at Glasgow, Scotland, on May 7.[2114] The press said that Davies and John R. Rogers, a well-know actor and theatrical manager of the time, were going to Europe to locate a Great White Hope. Rogers was seventy-three years old but "looked much younger." He said that they were not coming back until their quest for a champion was successful.

"I am going to talk things over with Hugh McIntosh in Paris," Rogers said, "and between us we are going to find some way to beat Jack Johnson." This story was simply a joke played on the press by two old showmen. In a more serious story Charlie said he was going to Belfast to see his sister. He said he that started out to see her six years earlier but had suffered a stroke of paralysis in London. The Parson said that after six years of medical treatment he was giving up on the doctors.[2115] He and Rogers would be gone until late October 1911.

On October 30, 1911, the *New York Times* reported that Davies had returned aboard the *Caledonia* after spending six months with his sister Annie, Mrs. Hugh Suffern, who lived near Belfast.[2116] The *Caledonia* left Londonderry on October 21.[2117] The first two names on the manifest of the *Caledonia* are Charles Davis [sic] and John Rogers. The home for both Rogers and Davies was recorded on the manifest as the Hotel Albany. The *New York Tribune* noted that when Rogers had left his hair was white but upon his return it was brown. They questioned him about the change and Rogers said that during the trip he had met a mysterious Egyptian who had entrusted him with a secret hair restorer.[2118]

A census performed in Antrim in 1851 identifies a farmer named Hugh Suffern who lived near Antrim. He lived in Ballyclan Townland, County Antirm, Ireland. There were several Sufferns who lived in and around Antrim. The Hugh Suffern identified in the 1851 census was forty-six years old and was born in the town of Antrim. Hugh and his wife, Sara, had a two-month-old son also named Hugh. This two-month-old Hugh Suffern was undoubtedly the person who later married Charlie's sister. A 1911 census shows a Hugh and Annie Suffern (both aged sixty) and their daughters Annie, age twenty-six, and Nettie, age twenty-five, living in 16 Glenburn Park, Clifton, County Antrim, Ireland. The entry shows that Annie and Hugh had five children in total. One of their other children was a daughter named Lillian. Their home address was a few miles northwest of Belfast.

When he returned to New York Charlie was using crutches to walk, and his complexion was very pale. He told the *Times* that until his trip he had thought he was fifty-eight, but he had inspected his birth records at Antrim and learned he was actually sixty years old. Charlie also said that Mrs. Suffern was his only remaining relative in the world, but this certainly was not the case as his brother Vere was alive and well, and he had many nieces and nephews. He said that his sister had five children, and he expected to return to Belfast in the spring of 1912 and live there for the rest of his life.

On Sunday, May 26, 1912, the *Oakland Tribune* wrote that one of Charlie's friends in San Francisco had reported that "that Charles E. ('Parson') Davies, the noted manager years ago of pugilists like John L. Sullivan and Peter Jackson and later connected with amusement houses in the South, particularly in New Orleans, is now dying in Ireland with relatives broken in health." The *Tribune* repeated the story that Davies "had a quarrel with Sullivan once and the latter threatened to strike him. Don't you do it, John, for I'll kill you in your tracks coolly replied the Parson as the two men eyed each other; and John did not do it."[2119]

However, Charlie did not die and New York newspapers reported on August 7 that he was back in New York "seriously ill in this city and 'broke.'"[2120]

After Jack Johnson beat Tommy Burns and then cut up Jeffries in a surgical fashion, the tensions between white and black fighters were worse than ever. Davies had managed black fighters including Jackson, Armstrong, Childs, and Temple. On January 3, 1913, at Chicago, Charlie was asked about what he thought would happen between the black and white fighters in the future. He said that that in the future the white and black boxers would conduct separate championships battles among themselves without a unified title. He thought that black and white fighters would continue to be matched in non-title contests, but felt that on account of the prejudice that prevailed, championships would be segregated.

"Boxing promoters have the example of baseball mangers before them," he said. "It is true that there is no rule of organized baseball that would prevent a negro becoming a member of a national agreement club, and there is a tacit understanding that negroes shall not be signed. The boxing authorities are apparently following out that idea and it will result in the elimination of the negro from pugilism within a few years."[2121]

He also told the *Winnipeg Free Press*: "However, if all the negro boxers conducted themselves as Peter Jackson did there would not be the prejudice that now exists in the public mind. Jackson was an exceptional negro in all respects. He was remarkably intelligent, fairly well educated, could converse on any subject and was quiet and unobtrusive in manner. In my opinion he was not only the greatest heavyweight boxer of the day, but I question whether any of his successors possessed the class that Peter possessed when he was in his prime."[2122]

Davies noted that the current "white hope" Luther "Luck" McCarty had drawn the color line but he felt that it was a foregone conclusion that both Langford and Joe Jeannette would defeat McCarty. Charlie was clearly correct in that opinion. The Publishers Press syndicate and Jeff Thompson of the *Atlantic Constitution* picked up Davies comments and published their own stories a few weeks later, agreeing with Davies.[2123]

According to an article in the *New Orleans Item* Charlie made a visit there in March 1913. He came to New Orleans following another trip to Ireland. He said he had gone there to visit an old friend in Antrim but that the whole place was "shot to hell" and he did not meet his friend as he intended. As late as this 1913 article Charlie was reported to own a half interest in the Lyric theater property.[2124] The property was sold in a court ordered auction in 1915 for only $22,000.[2125]

When Hall died in March 1913, several newspapers recalled his career and noted that his old friends Davies and Mitchell were both also critically ill.[2126] The *Fort Wayne Journal-Gazette* reported: "Parson Davies Awaits the End." In an article that was more informative than most, the newspaper described a man who seemed to becoming dejected and bitter:

> All day long in the lobby of a prominent Longacre square [now Times Square] hotel, in New York, you'll find propped up in a big easy chair the man the world once was pleased to call "king of American sports." Charlie (Parson) Davies has come back to look up his old cronies. The Parson has long been a cripple, and when he talks of the old days he looks down sadly at the crutches that rest across his knees. "They're all gone—all the old faces," he said. "I sit here all day and not a friendly face among the thousands that I see here. All dead, all dead. Poor Johnny Considine, he's gone. Jimmy Considine, he's gone too. I sit here all day and wonder why I'm not taken along with them. Tom Gallagher and Dick Roche are the only two old timers that I've run across. They came in arm and arm yesterday, and, my, what a lot of old scandal we did dig up.
>
> "Go to the fights? I wouldn't go across the street to see one round. I've got enough set aside to keep me till the time comes to toe the mark for the final bell."
>
> "No. I'm through. I'm willing to let the younger fellows have their time."
>
> "Who was the greatest fighter? To my last breath—Peter Jackson, with a black skin, but the whitest man through and through that I ever did business with. He would have whipped the world in his day."
>
> And speaking of Peter Jackson, Davies told a story that showed the class in Jackson. Peter went into a cafe in San Francisco and asked for a drink. Beer constituted Peter's simple wish. "That'll cost you $20." said the bartender sneeringly. Without batting an eye Peter went down in his pocket, put two twenty dollar gold pieces on the bar and said pleasantly, "Have a drink yourself."[2127]

Davies said he could not understand the fuss that had been made about Johnson beating Jeffries: "After all, the best man won didn't he?" He was asked about Corbett and said that Corbett had always liked flattery, and when he couldn't flatter another man he preferred to say nothing.

Nearly one year later, on January 10, 1915, the *Oakland Tribune* carried a similar article. It seemed that at the end of each year the newsmen would look around to see whether Charlie was still alive. The *Tribune* found Charlie:

> Sitting in a big chair in the lobby of his hotel, with his crutches across his knees, and an expression of resignation on his countenance, Parson Davies, once known as king of American sports, talked of old times and old-timers. Probably the greatest manager of fighters and professional walkers who ever lived was the old "Parson," and beyond doubt the most thoroughly sportsmanlike character in the history of sport. Tears swelled the old man's eyes

> as he talked of better days - better ones for him and for the boxing game.[2128]

Charlie said he was frightened by all the new faces that appeared in front of him each day with none of them even exchanging or offering a smile. As he was talking to the reporter, "Kid" Broad who was the last fighter he had managed back in 1903 and 1904 "stole up behind him and patted his silver white head fondly and said: 'The good old Parson – they can't count you out, can they?'"

Davies wanted Broad to confirm for the reporter he did not owe the Kid any money, and Charlie insisted he did not owe any man money. He said; "I'm not down and out. I've got plenty to carry me to the end of the journey. It can't be too much longer, and I'm ready."

As had become the custom, he was asked his opinion about various fighters. He said that Young Griffo was the most scientific fighter he had ever seen, and George Dixon was the greatest all-around fighter he had known. He said Joe Gans was another great fighter, but as for Jackson: "He was the man of them all. There wasn't an unfair thought in his whole nature."

"Teddy Roosevelt is my ideal man," Charlie said. "He's the greatest we ever had. I've met him twice [actually three times]—once as commissioner of police at the Maher-Choynski fight and at the White House while he was President. It's a great country—ours. . . . Tell them the 'Parson' sends his blessing—to all old friends who might read this little talk of ours. Tell them I'm dying game—that I'm just sitting around ready to go when He calls. Let the young fellows have their swing. I'm through and nobody knows it better than the old 'Parson.'"[2129]

The *Referee* of January 27, 1915, discussed Davies and his work with "the greatest of the glove fighters." The *Referee* wrote that Davies, "once known as the 'King of American Sports' has returned to America after visiting his sister and other relatives and friends in Ireland, and now his only home is a leading hotel in Long Acre Square, New York. Here you will find him all day long propped up in a big easy chair in the lobby."[2130] It appears that this was probably stale reporting recycled from stories that were more than a year old.

Charlie's last promotional venture involved an Elks benefit given on July 6, 1918, in Chicago. The benefit was a barbecue give at the Chicago White Sox baseball park to help support a war fund. President Woodrow Wilson and his wife had agreed to sign three baseballs that would be auctioned at the benefit. Davies had charge of the entertainment at the benefit, which would include a boxing and wrestling show by the Great Lakes Jackies. Chicago's Mayor Thompson, who was opposed to boxing shows, had not agreed to permit the proposed boxing exhibitions.[2131]

With the end of his life approaching, Davies turned back to some of his family to assist him in his lowest moments. His youngest brother by about six years was Vere A. Davies, who had played several supporting roles in Charlie's Chicago business ventures. Vere had married Carrie L. Morley on April 13, 1892, at Chicago. He was thirty-five when he married, if he recorded his age correctly.

Carrie was twenty-six, and about 1896 they had a son, Leroy C. Davies. Sometime before 1905 Vere and Carrie separated and both of them left Chicago. At the time of the 1910 census Vere was living in Amberg, Wisconsin, where he operated a candy and cigar store, and Carrie and LeRoy were living in Mt. Clemens, where LeRoy was working as a newsboy.[2132] A book entitled *Amberg–The First 100 Years–1890–1990*, published by the Amberg Historical society provides some information about Vere's life there and includes a fuzzy photograph taken in about 1919. This book also provides an oral history obtained from a man named John Downing, who as a young man had known Vere. Downing's account is wonderful and illustrates that Vere had emulated many of the characteristics of his brother Charlie:

Vere Davies – Amberg, Wisconsin - 1919

Mr. Vere R. Davies came to Amberg from Chicago in the early 1900's. He used two canes to walk. His legs were quite useless. [Apparently Vere suffered from medical issues similar to his brother Charlie's problems.]

He started a pool room and ice cream candy shop up on the hill in the front of Riddlers Hall. There also was a barber shop in the front. At that time most of the social activities were held at the back of the building. There were also basketball games held there, and many dances. . . .

As a kid, I found Mr. Davies quite interesting to talk to. He told lots of his history in Chicago. He operated a tavern in the Loop of Chicago. Generally there were 8 bartenders on duty. He

> never had any keys for either the front door or the back in 12 years he was there. He was a man who went to the horse races every day, bet and lost, day after day. He and a brother hired a special train coach and took their friends to the west coast to a famous prize fight. They would charter a boat in Chicago and go to Milwaukee up the river to a famous place in Milwaukee named The Little Bohemia Club, bring their own orchestra with them and party for days.
>
> His piano player was a man named Charlie Harris who later became famous for his popular song of that time named "After The Ball Is Over."
>
> He told me many tales and later on when I was employed in Milwaukee I found the tavern, Little Bohemia, at the same address he had told me, the southeast corner of Wells Street Bridge.
>
> He finally lost his wife and had one son whom he thought a lot of. In later years the son was shot to death.
>
> Later years in Amberg, Mr. Davies gave dances at the Town Hall, hired the best orchestra, sometimes made money, sometimes lost money. But he sure had beautiful clothes and he could dress up like a millionaire. At the dances they would always announce that dinner would be served at 12 o'clock at Mrs. Young's Hotel. At that time and for quite a few years, Mrs. Young operated Woods Hotel. Some claim Vere R. Davies operated a saloon, but he never served booze in Amberg and he did not drink. His last drinking was done in Chicago. He was very well educated and surely a name in Chicago as long as it lasted.[2133]

It may be inferred from this account that Vere's marital problems stemmed from bad habits of the type that plague many men. He loved to bet on the horses, lost money every day, and he seemed to have had a problem with alcohol. These two things probably caused his wife to leave him and led to Vere's decision to get out of Chicago for his own good and to start over in a small town where the vices of the big city were not readily available.

On September 18, 1918, the *Referee* published another article about Charlie. It described his departure from Chicago on July 21. A nephew had picked up Charlie to take him by taxi to the train for Amberg. At the time Charlie was engaged in a discussion with Al Spink and Dan O'Leary. He told them he was only sorry he lacked the pep and ginger to be in Europe helping the boys fighting the First World War and expressed his views about fighters past and present. He concluded by saying: "'Send me a paper at Amberg. I don't know how long I'll be there, but keep on sending it unless you happen to hear I've cashed in.' He was then gone from Chicago for the last time.[2134]

When Charlie went to Amberg, the town was served by a fine railroad that connected as far north as Champion in the upper peninsula of Michigan. Vere probably met his brother at the Amberg train station, which was only about one hundred yards from Vere's store. These two old men supported by their canes and crutches probably exchanged a firm handshake as Charlie was helped off the train and onto the station's platform. A porter probably lifted Charlie's steamer trunk out of the baggage car onto the luggage wagon and bid these two old gentlemen good bye. The trunk would have been delivered by the stationmaster to Vere's place later in the day, and these two old shadows of their former selves would have walked slowly together across the dusty summer street of this little town in northern Wisconsin that was so far from where their lives began in Antrim, Ireland.

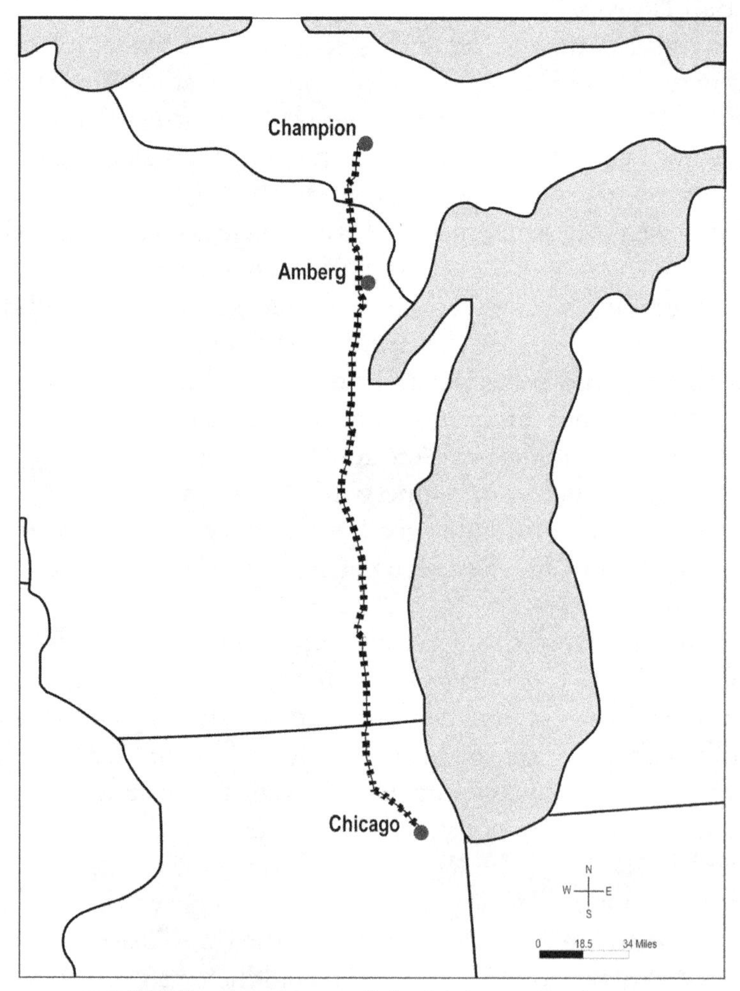

Jill Thomas Map of the Trip to Amberg

And there you are

Except for reminiscing with Vere and reading the newspapers, there was little for Charlie in Amberg, and staying there for a frigid winter in northern Wisconsin was not a good idea. By October 10 Davies was back in Chicago.

That day he prepared an application for admission to the Elks National Home in Bedford, Virginia, and his application was accepted.[2135] He entered the home on November 13 listing his occupation as: "Theatrical & Boxing." His religion was recorded as Episcopalian. General remarks about the state of his health said: "Health poor. Heart bad. Paralysis on rt. side of body. Locomotion ataxia. Walks very poorly on crutches."[2136]

Charlie probably liked the Elks National Home. The Elks had purchased the Hotel Bedford in 1902 from a bankruptcy sale and dedicated its National Home on May 21, 1903. Originally, the home was intended for indigent Elks that were supported by contributions from Lodges across the United States. The old hotel was demolished in 1915 and in 1916 the new home and outlying cottages were dedicated by Warren G. Harding, who was then a United States Senator. A railroad line ran in front of the home about a quarter of a mile away, and it seems that the Parson used it from time-to-time. In August 1919, he was in Binghamton, New York, where he commented on Tex Rickard's promise to give Willard a $100,000 guarantee to appear against the new Jack Dempsey. The Parson thought that Rickard's guarantee would ruin boxing for years to come. The *Wilkes-Barre Times* reported that Davies was leaving for England to spend his final days with his family.[2137]

Charles Edward Davies died at the Elks National Home at nine thirty a.m. on June 28, 1920. Two days earlier, he had suffered a cerebral hemorrhage that wiped out his memory.[2138] Without those memories there was nothing left for him. Charlie held on to life for two days before passing. He was buried on July 1, 1920 at the Elks Rest Oakwood Cemetery. On the death certificate issued by the Commonwealth of Virginia, the occupation of the deceased was listed as "Theatrical & Boxing Mgr." His death was reported in the *Chicago Tribune* the next day. His obituary was shot through with factual mistakes that should have been an embarrassment to a leading newspaper in the town where he spent most of his career.[2139]

W. A. Phelon a writer for the *Cincinnati Times* wrote on June 28, 1920: "His acquaintance was international—in fact he was an international figure, of much prominence, mingling with the underworld and the upper circles. . . . He was like King Arthur's 'bold Sir Bedivere—first made and latest left of all the knights.' Older than any of the men he managed, he outlived them all. It is said he never married—never forgot the memory of a lost love in Ireland. His was a strange and fascinating character, and one that would well adorn a novel or a play."

It isn't clear why Mr. Phelon thought Davies had lost a love in Ireland.

A month after Charlie's death Al Spink, a columnist for the *Reno Evening Gazette* who had interviewed Davies in 1918, wrote more lines about the Parson's last days in Chicago:

> Old-timers read with regret the news the other day of the passing of Charles Edward Davies, known the world over as Parson Davies. It seemed the irony of fate that the Parson should have

passed away before the annual reunion of the Elks in Chicago, for the Parson was a member of the first Elks lodge established in the Garden City.

The Parson was a guest at the Elks club in Chicago until about a year ago, but getting tired of the confinement, there, he left for the Elks home in Elkton, near Bedford, Va., intending to pass his last days here. But before leaving he told his Chicago friends he would be back for the Elks' reunion at Chicago this month. . . . Just before bidding his Chicago friends good-bye a year ago the Elks thought of making the departure of the Parson a red letter occasion by giving him a banquet and all that, but the old master preferred to depart quietly and without noise or ostentation.

"At that" said the Parson at that time, "there is not much to leave. The boys that I loved the best have nearly all cashed in and the old place doesn't seem like it used to. When I joined the Elks' lodge there were just five members. Joe Mackin was one and I was another. I think Roland Reed, the actor, was the third and Billy Emerson and Harry Armstrong, the minstrel boys the fourth and fifth. But I would no swear to the last two.

"Now this Chicago lodge has 3,500 members and is growing like a green bay tree. But nearly all its members are strangers to me, and I break few hearts by pulling my freight. Still I hate to leave the old town and the few dear friends I have left."

Spink concluded, "and then the Parson shook hands with me and Dan O'Leary, who was with me, and bade us a last good-by. That was the last view we had of one we had known and thought well of for fifty years."

As Charlie would have said: "And there you are."

Appendix

Some racewalkers, fighters and wrestlers Charles E. "Parson" Davies managed or promoted, the dates of his management, and the athlete's highest titles during their careers:

John Ennis: November 1877-May 1879

George Guyon: May 1879-September 1881

Daniel O'Leary: May 1879-March 1881 (All-time greatest American racewalker)

John L. Sullivan–August & September 1881, and June 27, 1895–June 13, 1896 (Heavyweight Champion of the World)

Paddy Ryan: April 1882–December 1883, and January 1, 1896–June 13, 1896 (Heavyweight Champion of America)

Jimmy Elliott: November 1882–March 1883 (Heavyweight Champion of America)

Jem Goode: May 1884–July 1884 (Heavyweight Champion of England)

Patsey Cardiff: June 1884–December 1884 (Heavyweight Champion of Illinois and the Northwest)

Alf Greenfield: March – April 1885 (Heavyweight Champion of England-disputed)

Jack Burke: February 1885–August 1885, and December 1885–March 1887

Tommy Warren: March 1885–October 1885 (Featherweight Championship of the World)

Pat Killen: October 1885–April 1886 & November 1887–December 1887 (Heavyweight Champion of the Northwest)

Frank Glover: October 1887–December 1887 (Heavyweight Champion of Illinois)

Evan "the Strangler" Lewis: January 1886–July 1886, January 1887–June 1888, July 1890–February 27, 1891, and January 1, 1892–February 20, 1893 (Catch-as-Catch-Can Champion of the World)

William Muldoon: January 1888–June 1888 (Wrestling Legend – Wrestling Hall of Fame)

Reddy Gallagher: February 1888

Martin Snee: February 1888

Jake Kilrain: December 1888–July 1889 (Heavyweight Champion of the World)

Charley Mitchell: December 1888–January 1889 (Heavyweight Champion of England)

Peter Jackson: April 1889–June 2, 1890, and November 1, 1891– September 11, 1894 (Heavyweight Champion of Australia & England)

Jack Flood: August 1889–December 1889

James J. Corbett: January 18, 1891–March 4, 1891, and August 5, 1891 (Heavyweight Champion of the World)

Jack Ashton: January 27, 1890–July 3, 1890

Jim Hall: April 9, 1891–December 31, 1892, and October 1, 1894 (Middleweight Champion of Australia)

Billy Woods: April 1891–July 22, 1891

Con Riordan: January 1, 1892–August 20, 1892

Joe Choynski: March 11, 1892–July 3, 1896, and September 21, 1896 – December 31, 1897 (Amateur Heavyweight Champion of the Pacific Coast)

Tommy Ryan: October 1894–January 12, 1896 (Welterweight Champion of the World)

Joe Bertrand: November 1, 1894–December 31, 1895

Jimmy Barry: March 15, 1895–September 27, 1897 (Bantamweight Champion of the World)

Robert Armstrong: April 20, 1895–December 31, 1897, and

June 21, 1902–September 30, 1902 (Black Heavyweight Champion of America)

Tommy White: July 31, 1896–September 27, 1896 (126-pound Championship of the World)

Tom Tracy: November 18, 1897–December 31, 1897 (Lightweight Champion of Australia)

Jack Root: July 1898-August 1898 (Light-Heavyweight Championship of the World)

Larry Temple: June 21, 1902–September 30, 1902

Ned "Kid" Broad: April 4, 1903–December 1904

Other activities conducted by Parson Davies – 1898 – 1908:

Manager of the St. Charles Theater: September 1, 1898–June 4, 1899
Agent for Lone Star & Crescent Oil Co.: June 1901 – December 1901
Manager of the Academy of Music: September 1, 1898-1903
Co-Owner and Proprietor of the Crescent Billiard Hall: 1899–1908
Match Maker for the Saint Bernard Club: 1898-1899
Match Maker for the Southern Athletic Club: 1903-1905
Co-Owner of the Lyric Theatre: 1903-1908
Manager of the Lyric Theatre: 1903-1908
Manager of the Baroone Theatre: 1906-1908
Co-Owner of the Southern Amusement Company: 1903-1904
Co-Owner of the Athletic Park Amusement Company-1905-1906
Manager of the New Orleans White City–1907
Agent for the Shubert Theatre Syndicate-1905-1908
Director of the National Boxing Association-1904-1908

Endnotes

Preface

1. "Parson Davies, The Astute Diplomat of Fistiana in Buffalo," Buffalo Courier, November 11, 1899.

Chapter 1 - Curtain Going Up!

2. "Parson Davies Recounts The Incidents Of His Sporting Career As Life Ebbs Away," *Denver Times*, February 25, 1910.

3. Thom, *Thom's Almanac and Official Directory*, Antrim County, 1862; *Belfast/Ulster Street* Directory *1861*, Provincial Towns, Antrim.

4. "Died," *Chicago Tribune,* December 27, 1867, 4; "A Detectives Resting Place," *Brooklyn Eagle*, August 31, 1884, 9. This article lists Davies as an employee buried in the Pinkerton employee Plot; "Mrs. Pinkerton's Funeral," *Chicago Herald*, January 25, 1887, 4. This article also lists Davies as employee buried in the Pinkerton employee plot. Graceland Cemetery's records are available at the cemetery's office and several web sites also discuss the Pinkerton's employee plot.

5. US Census Bureau, New York, Ward 9, District 5, New York County, New York City, New York (2nd Enum.), 1870 U.S. Census, January 7, 1871, page 40. Henry Davies and family appear in this census. Henry's wife appears as "Kate"; US Census Bureau, New York, New York County, New York, (Manhattan, 19th Electoral District, 13th Assembly District, 6th Ward, 1880 U.S. Census, June 1, 1880. Henry W. Davies is shown as a widower. City of New York, Certificate of Death No. 355970, Henry W. Davies, August 5, 1880.

6. "Detective Harry Davies," *New York Sun*, August 8, 1880, 3; "A Detective's Exploits," *Stevens Point Daily Journal*, September 11, 1880, 12.

7. Cuthbert, Norma, *Lincoln and the Baltimore Plot 1861, From Pinkerton Records and Related Papers* (San Marino: Huntington Library, 1949), 20; Pinkerton, Allan. *The Spy of the Rebellion: Being a True History of the Spy System of the United States Army During the Late Rebellion* (New York: G. W Carleton and Co., 1883), 55; Rowan, Richard W., *The Pinkertons: a Detective Dynasty*, (Little, Brown & Company, 1931), 84-95; Mackay, James, *Allan Pinkerton The First Private Eye* (John Wiley & Sons, Inc., 1996) 98-99; "The Baltimore Plot to Assassinate Abraham Lincoln," Harper's New Monthly Magazine, Vol. XXXVII, Jun. to Nov. 1868, 123-128; Moffett, Cleveland, "How Allan Pinkerton Thwarted the First Plot to Assassinate Lincoln," McClure's Magazine, Vol. III, No. 6 (1894), 522; "How Abraham Lincoln Went to

Washington Through Baltimore," *Brooklyn Eagle*, February 16, 1879, 1; James, Marquis, *They Had Their Hour* (The Bobbs-Merrill Co., 1934), 144-156.

8. US Civil War Service Records: Davis [sic], Henry, N. [sic], Company D, 69 N. Y. State Militia, Induction Rank: Private, Discharge Rank: Corporal; Allegiance: Union; Davies, Henry W., Union, 69th Regiment, New York State Militia; New York: Report of the Adjutant-General: Henry W. Davies, Enlisted as a Sergeant on May 26, 1862, Enlisted in Company D, 69th Infantry Regiment New York, Mustered out Company D, 69th Infantry Regiment New York on September 3, 1862 in New York; U.S. Civil War Soldiers, 1861-1865; Film Number: M551, roll 33; "Detective Harry Davies," *New York Sun*, August 8, 1880, 3. Other information relating to the 69th New York State Militia includes: Claire Morris, "History of the 69th New York," 69thnewyork.co.uk/69history1861.htm; "The Military Furore-The Sixty-Ninth Off to War," *New York Times*, April 23, 1861, 8; "The Sixty Ninth," *New York Times*, May 20, 1891, 1; "The Irish Brigade, *New York Times*, September 26, 1861, 1; "Letter from Col. Corcoran," *New York Times*, November 20, 1861, 3; "The Irish Brigade," *New York Times*, October 26, 1861, 5; "Letter from Col. Corcoran," *New York Times*, December 21, 1861, 5; "Col. Corcoran Coming," *New York Times*, August 18, 1862, 8; "Gen. Corcoran's Movements," *New York Times*, August 24, 1862, 5; "Sixty-Ninth Home Again," *New York Times*, August 27, 1862, "Letter from Secretary Seward," *New York Times*, August 28, 1862, 8; "Progress on Enlistments," *New York Times*, September 5, 1862, 3.

9. "Great Robbery-Safes of Adams Express Company Robbed of Half a Million of Dollars," *Sun*, January 8, 1866, 1; "The Adams Express Robbery Discovery of the Robbery and Recovery of a Large Portion of the Money," *Boston Journal*, January 11, 1866, 2; Pinkerton, Allan, *Bucholz and the Detectives*, (G.W. Dillingham Co., 1880), Ch. XVIII, 185-204; Margaret Pinkerton Fitchett, "The Early Pinkertons," Ch. 13 (November 1999), freepages.genealogy.rootsweb.
ancestry.com/~pinkerton/the_earlypinkertons_main.htm.

10. *1867 Edwards New Chicago Directory*: Davies, H. W., chief clk. Pinkerton's police agency; *1867 Bailey's Chicago Directory*: Davies, H. W., chief clk. National Police Agency; US Census Bureau, Hartford City, Hartford County, Connecticut, 1850 U.S. census, page 194, Family No. 841, David Driscoll and family; US Census Bureau, New York, Ward 9 District 5, New York County, New York City, New York (2nd Enum), 1870 U.S. census, January 7, 1871, page 40. Henry Davies and family. Henry Davies' wife appears as "Kate".

11. Horan, James Davies and Swiggett, Howard, *The Pinkerton Story* (Putnam, 1951, 31; S. Y. Asher and M. Wilson, "The First Big Train Robbery," Lexington (circa 1975); Moffett, Cleveland, "The Destruction of the Reno Gang: Stories from the Archives of the Pinkerton Detective Agency," McClure's Magazine, 1895, 549; Bell, W.,

"The Reno Gang's Reign of Terror," *Wild West Magazine*, February 2004; Alan J. Garbers, "The Legend of the Reno Gang," Reporter-Times (1999); "The Seymour Thieves," *New York* Times, July 31, 1868; "The Re-Arrest of Frank Reno," *New York Times*, August 12, 1868, "Express Robberies," New York Times, August 17, 1868; "The Adams Express Robbery, *New York Times*, August 22, 1868; "A Statement by the Lawyer," *New York Times*, August 26, 1868; "The Adams Express Robbery Investigation in Canada," *New York Times*, September 13, 1868; "The Reno Express Robberies," *Brooklyn Eagle*, September 21, 1868, 4; "The Reno-Anderson Case in Toronto," *New York Times*, October 7, 1868; "The Indiana Express Robbers," *New York Times*, October 16, 1868; "The Indiana Lynching and the Extradition Treaty," *New York Times*, December 19, 1868; "The New Albany Tragedy, *New York Times*, December 21, 1868; "Canada: Affairs at Toronto," *New York Times*, December 21, 1868; "Canada: Affairs at Toronto,: *New York Times*, December 22, 1868; "Proclamation of the Vigilance Committee," *New York Times*, December 26, 1868; "The Seymour Express Robbery," *New York Times*, January 2, 1869; "An Incident at the Funeral of the Renos," *Herald and Torch Light*, Hagerstown, Maryland, January 6, 1869; "Adams Express Robbers," *Petersburg Index,* August 11, 1868, 3; "Lynch Law in Indiana-Four Men Hanged by a Mob - Desperate Struggle of One of the Victims, *Petersburg Index,* December 15, 1868, 3; "The Lynching in Indiana–Statement of an Eye-Witness," *Petersburg Index,* December 17, 1868, 3; "The Seymour Express Robbers–Their Former Character–Touching Scene," *Petersburg Index,* December 18, 1868, 2; Old Rockford, Jackson County, Indiana, 1860 U.S. census, Age: 23 (b. abt 1837), (Frank Reno); Redding Township, Jackson County, Indiana, 1870 U.S. census, Age 69 (b. abt 1801), (Wilkinson Reno); Seymour, Redding Township, Jackson County, Indiana, 1860 U.S. census, Age 58, (b. abt 1802), (Wilk Reno).

12. Records of Pinkerton's National Detective Agency, 1853-1999, ID No.: MSS36301, (Employees-Gangs "A-Z," Individuals "A-E," Box 39, Davies, Harry, Pinkerton Operative: Davies, Harry W. (Jos. Howard an Opr.) Secret Opt. AFC, Investigated Baltimore Plot, Became Sup. of N.Y. Office); Ledgers of employee time, payroll, and uncollected accounts, Box 37, Library of Congress; Letterbooks of the New York Office, George Bangs, General Superintendent, Library of Congress. Key letters include: George Bangs to Allan Pinkerton, No. 5, February 12, 1869; George Bangs to Allan Pinkerton, No. 7, February 12, 1869; George Bangs to Allan Pinkerton, No. 24, February 28, 1869; George Bangs to Allan Pinkerton, March 1, 1869; George Bangs to Allan Pinkerton, No. 36, March 16, 1869; George Bangs to Allan Pinkerton, No. 41, March 17, 1869; George Bangs to Allan Pinkerton, No. 43, March 18, 1869; George Bangs to Allan Pinkerton, No. 45, May 26, 1869; George Bangs to William A. Pinkerton, No. 71, July 16, 1869; George Bangs to H. W. Davies, August 24, 1869; George Bangs to J. D. Bingham, September 15, 1869; H. W. Davies to George Bangs, No. 133, June 2, 1870; George Bangs to Supt. of NDA, Chicago, Ill., No. 137, June 2, 1870; George Bangs to H. W. Davies, No. 210, December 20, 1870; George Bangs to H. W. Davies, No. 212, December

20, 1870; George Bangs to Allan Pinkerton, No. 221, December 23, 1870; George Bangs to J. W. Sherwood, Esq., No. 240, December 24, 1870; George Bangs to George Smith, Esq., No. 276, December 30, 1870; George Bangs to H. W. Davies, No. 114, January 18, 1872; George Bangs to H. W. Davies, No. 108, January 18, 1872; George Bangs to H. W. Davies, No. 115, January 18, 1872; George Bangs to H. W. Davies, No. 121, January 18, 1872; George Bangs to H. W. Davies, No. 130, January 20, 1872; George Bangs to H. W. Davies, No. 153, January 20, 1872; George Bangs to H. W. Davies, No. 154, January 21, 1872; George Bangs to H. W. Davies, No. 132, January 28, 1872; George Bangs to George B. McClellan, No. 204, February 4, 1872; George Bangs to George Smith, No. 347, May 11, 1872; George Bangs to Allan Pinkerton, No. 352, May 14, 1872; George Bangs to Allan Pinkerton, No. 389, May 31, 1872; George Bangs to Allan Pinkerton, No. 50 unknown date.

13. In many instances it was Harry and his New York based Pinkerton operatives who gave the Spanish government the information to prevent military assistance from reaching the Cuban rebels. In June 1869 two revenue cutters captured three tugboats, the H. D. Coole, Jonathan Chase, and W. H. Webb, located near Cobb Dock on Long Island. The *New York Times* described Harry as the reputed "Spanish spy" and referred to him as a Deputy United States Marshall. In January 1871 Harry played a key role in the capture of the Hornet out of New York that had landed at Punta Brava, southwest of Havana. Then in mid-June 1872 the Fannie out of New York was captured and all but five crew members killed based on information supplied through Harry Davies: See, "Affairs in Spain," *New York Times*, January 18, 1869, 5; *New York Times*, "Affairs of Spain," January 30, 1869, 5; "The Cuban Ringleaders, *New York Times*, July 7, 1869, 8; "The Cuban Captives," *New York Times*, July 8, 1869, 8; "The Neutrality Laws Enforced," *New York Times*, August 4, 1869, 8; "The Gunboat Seizure," *New York Times*, August 5, 1869, 2; "Affairs of Cuba," *New York Times*, August 9, 1869, 5; "The Pinkerton Conspiracy, *New York Times*, August 24, 1869; "News of the Day," *New York Times*, August 29, 1869, 4; "An Absolute State of Barbarism, *New York Times*, October 19, 1869; "A Cuban Privateer in Charleston, *New York Times*, January 7, 1870, 1; "Mr. Sumner on Cuban Recognition," *New York Times*, January 10, 1870, 5; "Cuban Affairs," *New York Times*, January 16, 1871; "Cuban-American Relations, *New York Times*, July 3, 1872; :The Fannie's Expedition," *New York Times*, July 5, 1872; "The Dunn Homicide," *New York Herald,* September 5, 1872, 6; "The Nathan Tragedy," *New York Times*, September 8, 1872; "Forrester's Fate, *New York Times*, September 27, 1872; "District Attorney Phelps and Wesley and Martin Allen," *New York Times*, March 31, 1873, 4; "The Mercer Street Burglars," *New York Times*, April 1, 1873, 8; "A Remarkable Will Case, *New York Times*, April 10, 1876, 8; The Steamer Estelle's Boiler, *New York Times*, December 12, 1877; "The Suspected Yacht Estelle," *New York Times*, December 15, 1877; "The Suspected Estelle," *New York Times*, Decem-

ber 16, 1877; "The Steamer Estelle's Boiler, *New York Times*, December 17, 1877; "The Suspected Estelle," *New York Times*, December 18, 1877.

14. US Census Bureau, San Francisco, San Mateo County, California, 1920 U.S. census, Sister M. Conradine Davies, Age 48; Anita Therese Hayes, BVM, Mount Carmel Archives, e-mail to author, September 15, 2009.

15. Records of Pinkerton's National Detective Agency, 1853-1999, ID No.: MSS36301, Letterbooks of New York Office, George Bangs, General Superintendent, Library of Congress: Robert Pinkerton to W. A. Pinkerton, No. 74, November 23, 1872. Other relevant letters include: Allan Pinkerton to W. A. Pinkerton, No. 122, September 22, 1872; Allan Pinkerton to George Bangs, No. 131, September 20, 1872; Allan Pinkerton to George Bangs, No. 144, September 17, 1872; Allan Pinkerton to George Bangs, No. 169, October 9, 1872; Allan Pinkerton to William A. Pinkerton, No. 211, November 1, 1872; and Allan Pinkerton to Robert A. Pinkerton, No. 222, May 22, 1879.

16. Frank Morn, *'The Eye That Never Sleeps:" A History of the Pinkerton National Detective Agency* (Indiana University Press, 1982), 61; "Captured the Forger," *Daily Chicago Inter Ocean*, July 18, 1874, 5; US Census Bureaur, New York, New York County, New York City, 13th Electoral District and 11th Ward, 1870 U. S. Census, June 17, 1870, page 40; US Civil War Service Records: Patrick Burns, Enlistment Date: 26 May 1862; Rank at enlistment: Private, Enlistment Place: New York City, NY, State Served: New York, Service Record: Enlisted in Company D, New York 69th Infantry Regiment on May 26, 1862, Mustered out on September 3, 1862 at New York, NY. Sources: New York: Report of the Adjutant-General.

17. Harry was involved in another important case for the Spanish government and recovered a part of a religious painting by Bartolomé Esteban Murillo known as "The Vision of St. Anthony of Padua" that had been stolen from the Cathedral of Seville. Harry captured the thief in Havana. There is no question that Harry was well-known in New York and Chicago to men at both ends of the social ladder. See, "The Stolen Murillo," *New York Times*, January 13, 1875; "The Stolen Murillo," *New York Times*, January 28, 1875; "The Stolen Murillo at Cadiz," *New York Times*, February 19, 1875.

18. "Inquest Into Death of Catherine Davies," *Chicago Inter Ocean*, August 14, 1879, 2; City of New York, Certificate of Death No. 326388, Catherine Davies, August 8, 1879; US Census Bureau, Chicago, Ward 32, Cook County, Illinois, 1900 U.S. Census, Sadie Graschow, Age 31; US Census Bureau, Chicago City Part, Ward 13, Cook County, Illinois, 1910 U.S. Census, Anita D. Wilson, Age 39 Enum. Dist. 661, Sheet #9A; US Census Bureau, Chicago, Ward 13, Cook County, Illinois 1920 U.S. census, Anita D. Wilson, Age 49, Enum. Dist.786, Sheet #13A; State

of Illinois, Department of Public Health, Division of Vital Statistics, Certificate of Death No. 18275, Anita Wilson, July 10, 1924; "Brief Messages of Comfort," *New Orleans Daily Picayune*, April 25, 1906, 3; "Charles Davies Leaving," *New Orleans Daily Picayune*, October 2, 1908, 5.

19. See note 2 above; "Marine Court," *New York Herald-Tribune*, February 13, 1866, 7.

20. "The Charter Election, Review of the Field," *New York Herald-Tribune*, December 6, 1869, 5; "Political Intelligence, Irish Republican Third Assembly District," *New York Herald*, August 3, 1870, 8; Advertisement, *New York Herald,* October 2, 1870, 12; "Tammany and the Young Democracy-Speculations on the Fall Campaign-Probable Nominations for State and County Offices," *New York Herald*, August 28, 1870, 7; Connable, Alfred and Silberfarb, Edward, *Tigers of Tammany: Nine Men Who Ran New York*, (Holt, Rinehart, & Winston, 1967), 197-224.

21. Van Every, Edward, *Muldoon-The Solid Man of Sport*, (New York: Frederick A. Stokes,. 1929), 33- 34.

Chapter 2 – Chicago – (1871–1881)

22. See note 2 above.

23. "Athletes of Chicago," *Chicago Herald*, November 8, 1885, 3.

24. See note 2 above.

25. Ellis, Charles Edward, *An Authentic History of the Benevolent and Protective Order of Elks*, (Publisher: The author, 1910); Ellis, Charles Edward, *The Official History of Chicago Lodge No.4, B. P. O. E.* (Publisher: The author, 1910), 5-50; "Annual Elections to the Elks," *Chicago Tribune*, November 2, 1876; "Initiated into Lodge No. 4," *Chicago Tribune*, November 19, 1876; "The Elks' Rest," *Chicago Tribune*, August 14, 1882, 3; "Grand Lodge of Elks Present Davies With a Past Exalted Ruler's Jewel," *National Police Gazette*, April 20, 1901; "Origin and History of Elks," *Washington Post*, September 25, 1910, 4; Commonwealth of Virginia, Department of Health-Division of Vital Records, Certificate of Death No. 14781, Chas. E. Davies, June 28, 1920.

26. *Chicago Herald*, Dec. 6, 1884, 2; *Chicago Herald*, Dec. 14, 1884, 1;

27. "The Elks' benefit," *Chicago Tribune*, October 11, 1877.

28. Dunn, Mark, *Fraud, Perjury, Prison & Pardon-Joseph C. Mackin and Michael C. McDonald*, 27-35 (Author Published: 2009).

29. One of the early American race walkers was Edward Payson Weston who walked 453 miles from Boston to Washington, D. C. to attend Lincoln's inauguration to pay off the bet and he reportedly received a handshake from Abe for his efforts. After the war's end, Weston gained national attention in 1867 when he walked from Portland, Maine to Chicago in twenty-six days to win a prize of ten thousand dollars. A man such as Weston doing challenging things is interesting, but two men competing for a prize in the same sport is usually more exciting. The stage was set for more than a decade of insane walking competitions began in earnest in early 1868 when George Topley, the leading English race walker, came to the States and a Topley/Weston challenge match was arranged. See, Cumming, John, *Runners and Walkers* (Book Sales, 1981), 82-96; "Pedestrianism," *Wilkes' Spirit of the Times*, May 30, 1868.

30. "The Hughes-O'Leary Walk," *New York Times*, October 1, 1878, 5; "The Walk," *Brooklyn Eagle*, March 15, 1879, 4; "Who the Men Are," *Brooklyn Eagle*, March 16, 1879, 4; "Depictions of O'Leary and Rowell," *National Police Gazette*, March 19, 1881, 4 (providing additional biography of Daniel O'Leary); "O'Leary's Antecedents," *Chicago Tribune*, March 26, 1878, 7.

31. "Pedestrianism," Inter Ocean, October 5, 1875, 5; "Pedestrianism, The Tournament," *Chicago Tribune*, May 16, 1876, 2; "John Ennis published a challenge, *Chicago Tribune*, October 15, 1876; "John Ennis and Guyon," *Chicago Tribune*, November 26, 1876; "Ennis undertakes 400 miles," *Chicago Tribune*, March 25, 1878; "Ennis successfully walks 400 miles," *Chicago Tribune*, April 20, 1878; "Davies Memories," *Chicago Tribune*, April 13, 1900; "Ennis & O'Leary," *New York Times*, March 9,1875; "The Ennis-Guyon Walking Match," *New York Times*, July 22, 1878.

32. On November 10, 1877, Dan O'Leary and John Ennis began a one hundred mile walking match at the Exposition building for five hundred dollars a side. Ennis had persuaded Charlie Davies to back him in this contest for five hundred dollars. Davies was only twenty-six years old at the time, but still remembered the result of that race thirty-five years later. As he put it in 1910 with only slight overstatement: "Ennis proved a joke. He quit after going fifteen miles." See, "O'Leary/Ennis in a 100 mile walk," *Chicago Tribune*, November 10, 1877. Charlie recalled that as a result of losing his money, he had to go to work again and that he drifted back to New York to promote other walking matches before he returned to Chicago. Both Charlie and John Ennis were becoming well known in such contests.

33. Gorn, Elliott J., *The Manly Art* (Cornell University Press, 1886), 183.

34. Entrants in the contest paid ten sovereigns each. The match was "go-as-you-please" for six days and nights. Contestants could run, trot, walk or proceed at whatever gait they chose. The man who covered the greatest distance received the Astley Belt

and first place money of £500. Second place received £100 and third £50. Other prizes were provided for anyone who walked over 460 miles, with larger prizes for anyone walking over five hundred miles. See, "Pedestrianism, Six Days' Competition," *London Times*, March 19, 1878, 11; "America Loses the Belt, *New York Times*, March 16, 1879, 1.

35. "Pedestrianism," *London Times*, March 20, 1878, 13.

36. O'Leary's achievement was particularly important because he had defeated Vaughan "in the very class of exercise for which the later has always been famous; and Chicago will congratulate herself that she is ahead again as usual, however much it may add to the discomfort of St. Louis and her other suburbs. At the same time, the tension has been so great that we are glad it is removed." See, "Sporting Intelligence," *London Times*, March 21, 1878; "O'Leary 16 Miles Ahead at Midnight," *New York Times*, March 23, 1878; "Daniel O'Leary the Champion," *New York Times*, March 24, 1878; O'Leary's Antecedents, *New York Times*, March 26, 1878; *Chicago Tribune,* "Daniel O'Leary, *Chicago Tribune,* March 24, 1878; "O'Leary's Walk," *Chicago Tribune,* March 24, 1878; "Pedestrianism," *London Times*, March 23, 1878; "Pedestrianism," *London Times*, March 25, 1878.

37. "Long Distance Walking," *New York Herald*, May 14, 1878, 4.

38. "John Hughes Background," *New York Times*, January 7, 1881.

39. "O'Leary's Latest Feat," *New York Times*, September 9, 1878, 1; "The Great Walking Match, *New York Times*, September 13, 1878, 8; "The Hughes-O'Leary Walk," *New York Times*, October 1, 1878, 5; "The Big Walking Match, *New York Times*, October 2, 1878, 5; "O'Leary Thirty-Two Miles Ahead," *New York Times*, October 3, 1878, 2; "O'Leary Leads. Progress of the Walking Match between O'Leary and Hughes," *Inter Ocean*, October 2, 1878, 2; "The Hardy Pedestrians," *New York Times*, October 4, 1878, 5; "O'Leary's Contest With Hughes," *New York Times*, October 5, 1878, 2; "Hughes' Heels," *Inter Ocean*, October 5, 1878, 3; "O'Leary Again A Victor," *New York Times*, October 6, 1878, 2.

40. "The Races," *Inter Ocean*, October 9, 1878, 5; "Sporting News," *Inter Ocean*, October 10, 1878, 5; "Pedestrianism, Guyon v. Schmehl," *Inter Ocean*, October 11, 1878, 5.

41. "Sporting News, Homo-Equine Race," *Inter Ocean*, December 30, 1878, 12.

42. "Contest for the Astley Belt," *New York Times*, March 1, 1879, 3; "The Astley Belt Contest," *New York Times*, March 4, 1879, 3; "The Contest for the Astley Belt, *New York Times*, March 6, 1879, 8; "Contest for the Belt," *New York Times*, March 9, 1879, 1; "The Six Days' Tramp Begun," *New York Times*, March 10, 1879, 1; "Extraordinary Excitement Attending the Contest at New York," *New York Times*,

March 10, 1879; "Walking," *Chicago Tribune*, March 10, 1879, 2; "The Champion in the Rear," *New York Times*, March 11, 1879, 1; "The Big Walk," *Chicago Tribune*, March 11, 1879, 5; "The Englishman Leading," *New York Times*, March 12, 1879, 1 (discussing William Vanderbilt and friends); "O'Leary Out of the Race, *New York Times*, March 13, 1879, 1 (additional discussion of Vanderbilt and his box); "Defeat," *Chicago Tribune*, March 13, 1879, 5; "Ennis Gaining on Rowell," *New York Times*, March 14, 1879, 1; "Rowell Still Leading, *New York Times*, March 15, 1879, 1; "America Loses the Belt, *New York Times*, March 16, 1879, 1; "The Next Contest for the Belt," *New York Times*, March 21, 1879, 8; "Walking For a Belt," *New York Times*, May 30, 1879, 1.

43. Brady, William A., *The Fighting Man* (Bobbs-Merrill Co., 1916), 10-11.

44. "Athletes of Chicago," *Chicago Herald*, November 8, 1885, 3; "Parson Davies, Now Ill and Forgotten, Talks of Old Times In Fighting Game," *Trenton Evening Times*, March 5, 1911, 27. William Vanderbilt attended the race; however, in 1911 he was referred to as Cornelius Vanderbilt.

45. "Defeat," *Chicago Tribune*, March 13, 1879, 5.

46. "O'Leary Out of the Race, *New York Times*, March 13, 1879, 1; "Rowell Still Leading, *New York Times*, March 15, 1879, 1.

47. "'Parson' Davies," *National Police Gazette*, November 11, 1882, 5.

48. "The O'Leary Belt," *New York Herald*, April 4, 1879, 10; "The O' Leary Belt the Long-Distance Pedestrian Challenge Championship of America Chicago, Ill., March 31, 1879," *Cincinnati Commercial Tribune*, April 6, 1879, 13. When a leading English walker named Crossland entered the Chicago competition for the O'Leary Belt, he was backed by Richard K. Fox, who would be in frequent competition with Parson Davies for more than two decades. Hearing that Crossland was in the race, O'Leary announced that he too would participate in the competition. The blow-back from his declaration was strong and Dan soon withdrew his own entry, explaining that he had only entered the race because he wanted to settle a score with Crossland. See, "Arrival of Crossland," *Chicago Tribune*, March 17, 1879, 7; "Crossland, the Pedestrian. An Englishman Who Wants to Win the O'Leary Belt-Winer in Many Exciting Contests," *New York Herald*, May 15, 1879, 5.

49. "The Seventy-Five Hour Walk," *Chicago Tribune*, May 28, 1879, 7; "The Seventy-Five Hour Walk," *St. Louis Post Dispatch*, May 28, 1879, 1; "The O'Leary Walk," *Chicago Tribune*, May 29, 1879; "Guyon Gone," *St. Louis Post Dispatch*, May 29, 1879, 1; "Progress for Pedestrian Contest for the Seventy-Five Hour Belt," *Chicago Tribune*, May 30, 1879, 5; "Walking For A Belt," *New York Times*, May 30, 1879, 1; "An Immense Crowd," *Chicago Tribune*, May 31, 1879; "The Walking Contest,"

St. Louis Post Dispatch, May 31, 1879, 1; "The O'Leary Belt," *Chicago Tribune*, June 1, 1879, 7.

50. "General Sporting News," *Inter Ocean*, July 3, 1879, 2.

51. Isenberg, Michael T., *John L. Sullivan and His America* (Illini Books Edition, 1988), 3.

52. "The Walkers," *Chicago Tribune*, March 7, 1881, 3; "The Walkers," *Chicago Tribune*, March 10, 1881, 3; "A Fizzle," *Chicago Tribune*, March 11, 1881, 3; "O'Leary Still in the Rear," *Chicago Tribune*, March 12, 1881, 3; "The International Match," *Chicago Tribune*, March 13, 1881, 2.

53. "The International Six-day Pedestrian Contest," *National Police Gazette*, May 19, 1881, 14.

54. "O'Leary, 81, Hikes 62 Miles," *New York Times*, April 16, 1922, 16; "Dan O'Leary Dead; Famed As Walker," *New York Times*, May 30, 1933, 15; "Great Walkers," *New York Times*, May 31, 1933, 16.

55. See note 2 above.

Chapter 3 – John L. Sullivan and the Law – (1881–1883)

56. "'Parson' Davies," *National Police Gazette*, November 11, 1882, 5.

57. See note 25 above.

58. "Steve Taylor Whipped," *New York Herald*, April 1, 1881, 4.

59. "Prize Fight at New York," *Duluth News-Tribune*, May 17, 1881, 1; "Prize Fight," *Philadelphia Inquirer*, May 18, 1881, 1; "Prize Fight on a Barge," *Kalamazoo Gazette*, May 18, 1881, 1; "The Life of John L. Sullivan," *Winnipeg Free Press*, April 2, 1927, 82.

60. "The Life of John L. Sullivan," *Winnipeg Free Press*, April 2, 1927, 82; "The Life of John L. Sullivan," *Winnipeg Free Press*, April 9, 1927, 66.

61. "Pugilistic," *Chicago Tribune*, August 7, 1881, 16; "Sparring," *Chicago Tribune*, August 13, 1881, 2.

62. See footnote 61 above.

63. Hermann, Charles H., *Recollections Of Life & Doings in Chicago, From the Haymarket Riot to the End of World War I*, (Normandie House, 1945), 34-35.

64. "The Sparring Match," *Chicago Tribune*, August 14, 1881, 6.

65. In the fall of 1873 McDonald was successful in backing and electing Harvey D. Colvin as Mayor of Chicago. Colvin had been a general agent for United States Express Company and was putty in the hands of McDonald. Colvin's predecessor Joseph Medill had attempted to suppress gambling. Colvin had no such inclination; and saloons, gambling and prostitution were wide open, with the result that McDonald would become an unparalleled power broker with access to Mayor Colvin and the police department. The parts were being laid out for construction of his political machine in Chicago. McDonald was the man who really controlled the sporting action in Chicago from the mid 1870's until the mid 1890's with periodic interruptions necessary to get politicians elected. See, Asbury, Herbert, *Gem of the Prairie*, (Alfred A. Knopf, 1940), 146-148; Dunn, Mark, *Fraud, Perjury, Prison & Pardon-Joseph C. Mackin and Michael C. McDonald*, 27-35 (Author Published: 2009), 21.

66. *Chicago Tribune*, Nov. 2, 1884, 14. James Dalton was the oldest child of William and Kate Dalton. Bill Dalton operated a dredge on the Chicago River. He and Kate had eight sons and two daughters. His son Jim was part of the sporting arm of the McDonald/Mackin machine and a low-level political operative. He was noted for driving beer wagons in the pre election parades. All of Bill Dalton's boys worked on dredges or tugs. Captain Jim Dalton had been a long time Chicago-area heavyweight fighter and who had developed a marginally national reputation.

67. "The Sparring Match," *Chicago Tribune*, August 14, 1881, 6.

68. "Pugilism," *Chicago Tribune*, August 28, 1881, 6; "Athletic," *Chicago Tribune*, September 1, 1881, 7.

69. "Pugilistic," *Chicago Tribune*, September 3, 1881, 3; "Athletic," *Chicago Tribune*, September 4, 1881, 8.

70. "Pugilistic," *Chicago Tribune*, September 6, 1881, 6.

71. "Pugilistic," *Chicago Tribune*, September 25, 1881, 7; "A Prize-Fight Arranged," *Chicago Tribune*, September 26, 1881, 8.

72. "Pugilistic," *Chicago Tribune*, September 28, 1881, 3; "Pugilistic, *Chicago Tribune*, September 29, 1881, 3; "Pugilistic," *Chicago Tribune*, October 1, 1881, 7; No headline, *National Police Gazette*, October 8, 1881, 14; "The Prize Ring," *National Police Gazette*, October 22, 1881, 14; "Ryan and Sullivan," *National Police Gazette*, October 29, 1881, 11; "The Fistic Gladiators," *National Police Gazette*, November 5, 1881, 10; "The Prize Ring," *National Police Gazette*, December 10, 1881, 11; *National Police Gazette,* December 17, 1881, 14; *National Police Gazette*, December 24, 1881, 14.

73. "Athletic," *Chicago Tribune*, October 15, 1881, 6.

74. "Ryan's Training Ground Advantages of Mississippi City for the Purpose in Excellent Condition," *New York Herald*, January 18, 1882, 8.

75. "Lowry Inaugurated etc.," *Vicksburg Daily Commercial*, January 9, 1882, 1.

76. "Sullivan and Ryan-Their Flight From Mississippi to Louisiana-Their Quarters in New Orleans," *New York Herald*, January 24, 1882, 9; "Prize Fighting in Mississippi," *New Haven Register*, January 19, 1882, 1;

77. "Battle of New Orleans Not That of 1812 but the Forthcoming Knockdown," *Inter Ocean*, January 25, 1882, 5.

78. Advertisement, *Times-Picayune*, January 31, 1882, 2.

79. There were hundreds of newspaper reports of the fight: Sample articles include: "The Prize Fighters," *Chicago Tribune*, February 5, 1882, 5; "The Ryan-Sullivan Prize Fight," *Bloomington Daily Bulletin*, February 4, 1881, 4; "Ryan-Sullivan," *Bloomington Daily Bulletin*, February 7, 1882, 1; "The Scrap," *Peoria Journal*, February 7, 1882, 1; "Plug Uglies," *Chicago Tribune*, February 7, 1881, 2; *National Police Gazette*, February 18, 1882, 14.

80. "Sullivan Wins The Fight," *New York Times*, February 8, 1882, 1; "Poor Paddy Ryan," *Chicago Tribune*, February 12, 1882, 3; "Ryan on the Fight," *Chicago Tribune*, February 14, 1882, 5; "Extra, Sullivan Wins!," *National Police Gazette*, February 18, 1882, 1; "Paddy Ryan in Chicago," *Chicago Tribune*, February 24, 1882, 6.

81. "Pugilists Returning Home," *New York Times*, February 10, 1882, 1.

82. "At New Orleans The Fight Still the Sole Topic" *Inter Ocean*, February 9, 1882, 2.

83. "The Hero of the Day," *Chicago Tribune*, February 11, 1882, 5.

84. "The New Champion, Sullivan, the Champion of the American Prize-Ring, Returns with His Party to Chicago, *Inter Ocean*, February 13, 1882, 6; "Sullivan to Give an Exhibition in Cleveland," *Chicago Tribune*, February 15, 1882, 6.

85. Pierce, Bessie Louise, *A History of Chicago, Volume III, The Rise of a Modern City* (Alfred A. Knopf, 1957), 355-365.

86. "Paddy Ryan," *Chicago Tribune*, February 26, 1882, 7); "Sporting," *Chicago Tribune*, March 11, 1882, 5.

87. "Sullivan," *Chicago Tribune*, March 3, 1882, 5.

88. "Eager for a Fight," *Bloomington Bulletin*, June 4, 1882, 1.

89. "Pugilists at a Picnic," *New York Times*, July 5, 1882, 8.

90. "Sporting Sundries," *St. Louis Post Dispatch*, November 28, 1882, 8.

91. "Sporting Sundries," *St. Louis Post Dispatch*, December 1, 1882, 8.

92. No Headline, *Chicago Tribune*, December 3, 1882, 11; "The Ring," *Inter Ocean*, December 4, 1882, 6.

93. "Knocked Out of Time," *Chicago Tribune*, November 25, 1882, 8. This fight was an insult to the Mayor Harrison and his attempt to crack down on vice – which by definition included boxing. The next day Mayor Harrison pulled Dalton's liquor license. The alleged offense was that Dalton ran a variety show that included private boxes where members of the audience could meet the performers face-to-face.

94. "The Ring," *Inter Ocean*, December 4, 1882, 6; "Gossip," *Inter Ocean*, December 9, 1882, 9; "Walk Up, Allen," *Inter Ocean*, December 12, 1882, 3; "The Elliott-Allen Fizzle," *Reno Evening Gazette*, December 12, 1882, 2; *Chicago Tribune*, December 12, 1882, 8); "The Prize Ring," *St. Louis Post Dispatch*, December 13, 1882, 8; "Notes," *St. Louis Post Dispatch*, December 15, 1882, 8; "Notes," *Inter Ocean*, December 18, 1882, 12; "Sporting Sundries," *St. Louis Post Dispatch*, December 21, 1882, 8.

95. "At the Old Stand," *St. Louis Post Dispatch*, December 30, 1882, 8;

96. "Notes," *Inter Ocean*, December 18, 1882, 12; "The Grand Jury," *Chicago Tribune*, December 31, 1882, 12.

97. "Chief Doyle vs. Sparring," *Inter Ocean*, December 20, 1882, 4.

98. "The Law Steps In," *Chicago Tribune*, December 20, 1882, 6.

99. "Notes," *Inter Ocean*, December 22, 1882, 5; "Elliott and Sullivan," *Chicago Tribune*, December 22, 1882, 8.

100. "Sporting Notes," *Inter Ocean*, December 26, 1882, 5.

101. "Events in the Metropolis," *New York Times*, December 29, 1882, 8; "Grab-Bag," *Inter Ocean*, January 6, 1883, 4.

102. "Mr. Mace in America," *New York Times*, December 27, 1882, 8; "Jem Mace," *Inter Ocean*, December 27, 1882, 7.

103. No Headline, *National Police Gazette*, February 10, 1883, 11.

104. "Sporting Chronicle," *Inter Ocean*, January 25, 1883, 3.

105. "Sporting Matters," *Inter Ocean*, January 29, 1883, 5; "Sporting Notes," *Inter Ocean*, January 31, 1883, 7.

106. Sprogle, J. L., "A Reporter's Recollections," *Lippincott's Monthly Magazine*, Vol. LXIII (Jan.–Jun. 1899), 136; "Jere Dunn, Boots Off, Dying Game," *Washington Post*, March 5, 1906, 6; "Pugilist Elliott Killed," *Sun*, March 2, 1883, 1.

107. "Elliott's Great Funeral," *Sun*, March 12, 1883, 1.

108. *National Police Gazette*, June 30, 1883, 10.

109. "The Esthetics of Pugilism," *New York Times*, September 19, 1883, 8.

110. "Paddy Ryan Shot," *Daily Pantagraph*, August 24, 1883, 4; "Crimes And Casualties. An Unexplained Report That Paddy Ryan Has Been Shot," *Times Picayune*, August 24, 1883, 8; "The Paddy Ryan Mystery," *Salt Lake Herald*, August 25, 1883, 7; "Paddy Ryan in Trouble," *Sun*, August 24, 1883, 1; "Paddy Ryan on a Spree," *New Haven Register*, August 24, 1883, 1.

111. "A Slugging Tourist," *Daily Pantagraph*, September 22, 1883, 1; "Paddy Ryan's Western Tour," *Wheeling Register*, September 24, 1883, 1.

112. "Sullivan to Fight Paddy Ryan," *New York Times*, November 17, 1883, 1; "The Prize Ring," *National Police Gazette*, December 8, 1883, 10.

113. Ibid.

114. "The Prize Ring," *National Police Gazette*, December 15, 1883, 10.

115. No Headline, *National Police Gazette*, December 22, 1882, 10.

116. "Paddy Ryan," *National Police Gazette*, December 15, 1883, 14.

117. "Day Dispatches," *Daily Miner*, December 29, 1883, 2.

118. "The Prize Ring," *National Police Gazette*, January 19, 1884, 10.

119. "The Boss Slugger," *Daily Pantagraph*, December 31, 1883, 1.

Chapter 4 – Finding Success – (1884)

120. See note 25 above.

121. "How a Pugilist Trains," *Fort Wayne Sunday Gazette*], February 3, 1884, 6; "How a Pugilist Trains," *Piqua Morning Call*, February 6, 1884, 3. These articles are republishing articles from the *Chicago Herald*.

122. No Headline, *National Police Gazette*, April 5, 1884, 10; No Headline, *National Police Gazette*, April 12, 1884, 10.

123. "Where are You, John L.?," *Daily Miner*, March 18, 1884, 1.

124. "Sullivan Will Stand by His Colors," *Daily Miner*, March 18, 1884, 1.

125. Sullivan, John L. and Sargent, Dudley A., *Life and reminiscences of a 19th century gladiator*

(J.A. Hearn & co., 1892), 156.

126. "Another Soft Glove Match," *Daily Evening Bulletin*, January 10, 1884, 1.

127. "Interesting Slugging in Prospect," *Manitoba Daily Free Press*, May 2, 1884, 1; "Sporting Matters," *Chester Times*, May 2, 1884, 4.

128. "The May Festival," *Chicago Tribune*, May 3, 1884, 5.

129. "Mill at Chicago," *Salt Lake Herald*, May 21, 1884, 4.

130. "The Manly Art," *Peoria Journal*, May 20, 1884, 1; "The Prize Ring," *National Police Gazette*, June 7, 1884, 10.

131. "Patsy Cardiff," *National Police Gazette*, July 19, 1884, 3; "Charles Flynn, Champion Wrestler of Illinois," *National Police Gazette*, March 4, 1882, 10.

132. "The Wrestlers," *Bloomington Bulletin*, April 25, 1884, 4.

133. "The Peoria Athletic Combination," *Pantagraph*, May 5, 1884, 4; "Peoria Athletes," *Peoria Journal*, May 5, 1884, 4.

134. "The Boxers," *Peoria Journal*, May 27, 1884, 4.

135. "Cardiff Wins," *Pantagraph*, May 27, 1884, 4; "Patsy Cardiff [With Portrait]," *National Police Gazette*, July 19, 1884, 3 with drawing 13.

136. "Sporting," *Peoria Journal*, May 28, 1884, 4.

137. No Headline, *Pantagraph*, June 5, 1884, 3.

138. "Pugilistic," *Peoria Journal*, June 5, 1884, 4.

139. "More Boxing," *Peoria Journal*, June 2, 1884, 3.

140. "In the Ring," *Peoria Journal*, June 21, 1884, 4; "Extra! Sullivan Knocked Out-In Preparatory Round with King Alcohol he is Completely Floored," *National Police Gazette*, July 12, 1884, 2.

141. "The Prize Ring," *National Police Gazette*, June 7, 1884, 10.

142. "A Jug-Handled Glove Fight," *Sun*, May 20, 1884, 1.

143. No Headline, *Atchison Glove*, July 22, 1884, 2; Pictorial Page, *National Police Gazette*, August 9, 1884, 8.

144. "In the Ring," *Peoria Journal*, June 27, 1884, 4.

145. "Patsy Cardiff," *Peoria Journal*, July 22, 1884, 4; "Cardiff," *Peoria Journal*, July 28, 1884, 4.

146. "Peoria's Pugilist," *Peoria Journal*, July 30, 1884, 4; No Headline, *National Police Gazette*, September 6, 1884, 10.

147. "Pugilistic Bravado," *Peoria Journal*, August 14, 1884, 4; "A Fight arranged," *Daily Pantagraph*, August 16, 1884, 1;

148. "Sluggers," *Peoria Journal*, August 26, 1884, 1; "Pugilist Patsy," *Daily Pantagraph*, August 26, 1884, 1.

149. "The Cardiff-King Fight," *St. Louis Post Dispatch*, September 23, 1884, 5.

150. No Headline, *Chicago Tribune*, January 13, 1885, 7; No Headline, *Chicago Tribune*, January 15, 1885, 6; No Headline, *Chicago Tribune*, January 25, 1885, 11; "A Struggle in Illinois," *New York Tim*es, October 5, 1884, 5; "The Republican Seated," *New York Times*, December 3, 1884, 1; "The Chicago Election Frauds," *New York Times*, December 4, 1884, 4; "Ballot-Box Frauds," *New York Times*, December 9, 1884, 3; "Charged With Fraud," *New York Times*, December 12, 1884, 3.

151. "General Sporting Notes," *Chicago Herald*, November 9, 1884, 5; "Looking After Patsey Cardiff," Chicago Herald, November 16, 1884, 9; "Sporting," *Wheeling Register*, November 2, 1884, 2.

152. "The Match," *Peoria Journal*, November 13, 1884, 4; "Another Glove Fight between Pugilists," *Critic-Record*, November 13, 1884, 1.

153. "The Men of Science," *Peoria Journal*, November 22, 1884, 4.

154. "Cardiff Back from the East," *Chicago Herald*, January 16, 1885, 3.

155. "Looking After Patsey Cardiff," *Chicago Herald*, November 16, 1884, 9.

156. "To Knock Out Sullivan," *Chicago Herald*, November 9, 1884, 5.

157. "Police Spoil the Fun," *Chicago Herald*, November 19, 1884, 1.

158. "Prize Fighters Must Go," *Chicago Herald*, November 23, 1884, 5; "The Thumpers in Legal Trouble, *Daily Pantagraph*, November 24, 1884, 1.

159. "Cardiff will Tackle Kilrain," *Daily Pantagraph*, November 26, 1884, 3; "Telegraphic Briefs," *New Haven Register*, November 23, 1884, 1.

160. "Trying to Arrange a Sparring Match," *Chicago Herald*, December 6, 1884, 3.

161. "Whitmore to Wrestle Faulkner," *Chicago Herald*, December 10, 1884, 3.

162. "General Sporting Notes," *Chicago Herald*, December 21, 1884, 7.

163. "Whitmore and Faulkner to Meet Again," *Chicago Herald*, December 17, 1884, 3.

164. "A Failure and a Fraud," *Daily Pantagraph*, December 23, 1884, 6; "A Pugilistic Fraud," Peoria Journal, December 24, 1884, 4.

165. "Anderson Defies the World," *Chicago Herald*, December 14, 1884, 11.

Chapter 5 – The Irish Lad - (1885)

166. "Why Sport is Popular Here," *Chicago Herald*, December 6, 1885, 6.

167. "Rabshaw and Faulkner to Wrestle," *Chicago Herald*, December 28, 1884, 5; "Rabshaw to Meet Faulkner," *Chicago Herald*, January 4, 1884, 6.

168. "The Rabshaw-Faulkner Match," *Chicago Herald*, January 6, 1885, 3; "Won By the Flip," *Chicago Herald*, January 7, 1885, 3.

169. "Local Sport of the Year," *Chicago Tribune*, January 1, 1886, 2.

170. "A Sweeping Challenge to Chicago Boxers," *Chicago Herald*, January 11, 1885, 6; "Sharp Talk at M'Caffrey," *Chicago Herald*, January 11, 1885, 6; "A Few Words to Tom Hinch," *Chicago Herald*, January 17, 1885, 7.

171. "After Captain Dalton's Scalp," *Chicago Herald*, January 11, 1885, 6.

172. "Great Days for Sport," *Chicago Herald*, January 17, 1885, 7.

173. See note 54 above at 174.

174. "A Disgraceful Exhibition," *Chicago Tribune*, January 20, 1885, 3.

175. "Sullivan Slugged," *St. Louis Post Dispatch*, January 21, 1885, 2.

176. "Paddy Ryan, A Chat with the Pugilist," *Chicago Tribune*, January 26, 1885, 8; "General Sporting Notes," *Chicago Herald*, February 14, 1885, 7; "Ryan's Reply to Burke," *Chicago Herald*, March 1, 1885, 5.

177. Ibid.

178. "The Next Rabshaw-Faulkner Match," *Chicago Herald*, January 17, 1885, 7.

179. "Local Sports of the Year," *Chicago Tribune*, January 1, 1886, 2.

180. "Jack Burke on His Way to Chicago," *Chicago Herald*, January 30, 1885, 4.

181. "Setting the Ball Rolling," *Chicago Herald*, January 25, 1885, 7.

182. "A Revival of Sport," *Chicago Herald*, February 1, 1885, 7; "Cardiff Back from the East," *Chicago Herald*, January 16, 1885, 3.

183. "Local Sports of the Year," *Chicago Tribune*, January 1, 1886, 2.

184. "Dalton Knocked Out," *Chicago Tribune*, February 3, 1885, 5; "Burke Is A Good One," *Chicago Herald*, February 3, 1885, 3.

185. "In The Arena of Sport," *Chicago Herald*, February 8, 1885, 6.

186. "Cleary Knocks Out Dalton," *Cincinnati Enquirer*, February 7, 1885, 7; "Dalton Knocked Senseless," *Chicago Herald*, February 7, 1885, 1.

187. "Dalton Matched Again," *Chicago Herald*, February 14, 1885, 7.

188. "Wrecked At Midnight," *Chicago Tribune*, February 26, 1885, 3; "How Dalton Rode," February 27, 1885, 8; "Captain Dalton to the Front," *Chicago Herald*, May 10, 1885, 9.

189. "Pugilistic," *Chicago Tribune*, February 24, 1885, 2.

190. "Greenfield and Burke Matched," *Chicago Herald*, February 15, 1885, 4; "They're Hard to Beat," *Chicago Herald*, March 1, 1885, 6.

191. "The Hard Hitters," *Chicago Tribune*, February 26, 1885, 6.

192. "Under-Cuts," *Chicago Tribune*, March 1, 1885, 3.

193. "Local Sports of the Year," *Chicago Tribune*, January 1, 1886, 2.

194. "Pugilistic," *Chicago Tribune*, March 1, 1885, 6.

195. "A Brutal Prize Fight," *Daily Pantagraph*, March 3, 1885, 4.

196. "The Glove Fight," *Chicago Tribune*, March 3, 1885, 6; "Sporting Matters," *Chicago Tribune*, March 14, 1885, 6).

197. "Burke Is The Winner," *Chicago Herald*, March 3, 1885, 1.

198. "Burke and Ryan, The Latter's Stand Causing Comment," *Chicago Tribune*, March 11, 1885, 6.

199. Callis, Tracy, "Nonpareil" Jack Dempsey (John E. Kelly), cyberboxingzone.com/boxing/non-jack.htm.

200. See note 202 above.

201. "Ryan's Bold Defiance," *Chicago Herald*, March 5, 1885, 3.

202. "Pat Sheedy Is Heard From," *Chicago Herald*, March 6, 1883, 3; "Eager for the Fight," *Chicago Herald*, March 8, 1885, 6.

203. "Ryan's Bold Defiance," *Chicago Herald*, March 5, 1885, 3 (declaration at end of article).

204. "Pat Sheedy Is Heard From," *Chicago Herald*, March 6, 1885, 3.

205. See note 202 above.

206. "Patsy Sheppard Defends His Friend, Mr. Sullivan," *Chicago Tribune*, March 8, 1885, 14.

207. "Burke and Greenfield to Go Into Training," *Chicago Tribune*, March 8, 1885, 14.

208. "Burke Covers Ryan's Forfeit," *Chicago Tribune*, March 10, 1885, 3.

209. "Paddy Ryan Says No," *Chicago Herald*, March 11, 1885, 2; "Burke-Ryan-Prospects of a Contest Doubtful," *Chicago Tribune*, March 13, 1885, 2.

210. "The Ryan, Sullivan and Burke Fights," *Chicago Tribune*, March 15, 1885, 11.

211. "The Ring," *Chicago Tribune*, March 15, 1885, 11.

212. "Exit Paddy Ryan," *Chicago Tribune*, March 21, 1885, 2.

213. "Sullivan, Ryan, and Burke," *Chicago Tribune*, March 16, 1885, 6; "Fox Egging Paddy Ryan," *Chicago Tribune*, March 26, 1885, 6; "The Fox-Sullivan Challenge," *Chicago Tribune*, March 27, 1885, 6; "Paddy Ryan to Meet Fox and Arrange a Fight with Sullivan," *Chicago Tribune*, March 29, 1885, 14; "Ryan's Answer to Fox," *Chicago Herald*, March 29, 1885, 3.

214. "The Nine Best Fighters in the World," *Chicago Herald*, March 22, 1885, 6.

215. "Jack Speaks to Jack," *Chicago Herald*, March 17, 1885, 3.

216. "Sporting. The Prize Ring. Dempsey After Jack Burke," *Times-Picayune*, March 12, 1885, 8.

217. "Patsey Cardiff Challenges the Winner," *Chicago Tribune*, March 18, 1885, 3; "Tomorrow Night's Glove Contest," *Chicago Herald*, March 22, 1885, 15; "Naming The Winner," *Chicago Herald*, March 22, 1885, 6; "Burke and Greenfield at Battery D Tonight-The Program," *Chicago Tribune*, March 23, 1885, 2; "You Take Your Choice," *Chicago Herald*, March 24, 1885, 1; "Couldn't Tell Which Was Best," *New York Times*, March 24, 1885, 5.

218. "Local Sports of the Year," *Chicago Tribune*, January 1, 1886, 2.

219. "The Glove-Fight. Seven Thousand People Pay a Dollar Each to See Two Men Pound One Another. Heavy Blows Struck, but No Blood Drawn--Seven Hot Rounds Fought etc.," *Chicago Tribune*, March 24, 1885, 2; "An Old Sport's Opinions," *Chicago Tribune*, March 25, 1885, 8; "Monday Night's Glove Contest-Greenfield Dissatisfied," *Chicago Tribune*, March 26, 1885, 6.

220. , 2; "Chicago's Greeting to Alf Greenfield," *Chicago Herald*, April 5, 1885, 6; "Greenfield's Friends to the Front," *Chicago Herald*, April 10, 1885, 3; "General Sporting Notes," *Chicago Herald*, April 12, 1885, 6; "Alf Greenfield to Leave for England Today," *Chicago Tribune*, April 22, 1885, 2; "Greenfield Starts Back Home," *Chicago Herald*, April 26, 1885, 6.

221. "Alf Greenfield and Party to Spar at Danville, Ill., Tonight," *Chicago Tribune*, April 7, 1885, 2.

222. "Sporting New, Afraid of the Wyoming Champion," *Chicago Herald*, May 8, 1885, 2 (listing Warren's prior matches).

223. "General Sporting Notes," *Chicago Herald*, April 12, 1885, 6.

224. "Sporting," *Chicago Tribune*, April 15, 1885, 2.

225. "Other Events," *Chicago Tribune,* April 12, 1885, 11.

226. "Burke and Chandler to Spar at Madison, Wis.," *Chicago Tribune*, April 21, 1885, 2.

227. "Burke and Chandler to Spar Through Wisconsin," *Chicago Tribune*, April 26, 1885, 10.

228. "Mitchell and Burke," *Chicago Herald*, April 21, 1885, 4.

229. "A Report that 'Parson' Davies Is to Assume Control of 'The Store' May 1," *Chicago Tribune*, April 22, 1885, 2; "The Ring," *Chicago Tribune*, May 3, 1885, 14; No Headline, *Chicago Herald*, May 17, 1885, 10.

230. It was said that a patent polling booth was operated there. That is, there was no other polling place like this in Chicago. A voter at this poll would come to the end of the alley and pass his ticket through a slot located above his head. The voter was unable to see the person inside who took the ballot or even to know what happened to the ballot after it was passed through the slot. It's probable that ballots that McDonald didn't like were put in the trash can. Many of the voters didn't really care what happened to the ballot so long as McDonald was happy. See, Lindberg, Richard, *The Gambler King of Clark Street: Michael C. McDonald and the Rise of Chicago's Democratic Machine* (SIU Press, 2008), 139.

231. "Parson Davies Is Near Death," *Salt Lake Telegram*, August 16, 1907, 8.

232. "The Ring," *Chicago Tribune*, May 3, 1885, 14; "Athletic," *Chicago Tribune*, May 17, 1885, 14; "Sullivan Is Coming," *Chicago Herald*, May 17, 1885, 10.

233. "The Mitchell-Cleary Fight," *Chicago Tribune*, May 23, 1885, 2; "Mitchell and Cleary," *Chicago Herald*, May 23, 1885, 1.

234. "Burke and Mitchell Matched," *Chicago Herald*, May 27, 1885, 2; "No Hippodromes Here," *Chicago Herald*, May 29, 1885, 1.

235. "Athletic, Coming Events," *Chicago Tribune*, May 31, 1885, 17.

236. "The Ring," *Chicago Tribune*, June 5, 1885, 2; "Sullivan Will Be Here Soon," *Chicago Herald*, June 6, 1885, 3; "The Sullivan-Burke Meeting," *Chicago Herald*, June

7, 1885, 6; "Sullivan and Burke," *Chicago Tribune*, June 7, 1885, 14; "Sporting Notes," *Chicago Herald*, June 9, 1885, 3; "Sullivan to Arrive Wednesday," *Chicago Tribune*, June 9, 1885, 3; "Sullivan Detained," *Chicago Tribune*, June 11, 1885, 5; "John L. Sullivan Is Here," *Chicago Herald*, June 13, 1885, 3; "Sullivan Arrives-Today's Contest," *Chicago Tribune*, June 13, 1885, 2.

237. "In An Ugly Temper, Sullivan Tries to Knock Burke Out," *Chicago Herald*, June 14, 1885, 6.

238. "Sullivan Bests Burke," *St. Louis Post Dispatch*, June 15, 1885, 4.

239. "Local Sports of the Year," *Chicago Tribune*, January 1, 1886, 2; "Burke Stays Five Rounds With Sullivan," *Chicago Tribune*, June 14, 1885, 10.

240. "Macon's Gossip," *St. Louis Post Dispatch*, June 15, 1885, 4; "Sullivan In Philadelphia," *Chicago Herald*, June 17, 1885, 1.

241. "Burke Bobs Up Serenely," *Chicago Herald*, June 16, 1884, 3; "Athletic," *Chicago Tribune*, June 21, 1885, 14.

242. "Mitchell to Arrive Today," *Chicago Tribune*, June 21, 1885, 14.

243. "Mitchell and Burke Matched," *Chicago Herald*, June 23, 1885, 2; "Mitchell and Burke Matched," *Chicago Tribune*, June 23, 1885, 2.

244. "The Ring-Tomorrow Night's Contest," *Chicago Tribune*, June 23, 1885, 18.

245. "Jack Burke and Charlie Mitchell," *Chicago Herald*, June 30, 1885, 2; "The Ring," *Chicago Tribune*, June 30, 1885, 2; "Charley Mitchell and Jack Burke. A Tame Six-Round Contest Ends In Another Draw," *Aurora Daily Express*, June 30, 1885, 2.

246. McDonald was present when the jury retired. Mackin was permitted to remain in the court room. His attorneys left about twenty minutes after the jury retired. They apparently thought they had time to catch up on other matters while the jury deliberated. The jury reached their guilty verdict quickly and the defense attorneys were not present when the jury verdict was read in open court. The jury found Mackin guilty on all counts of the indictment and then announced the penalty to be imposed of five years imprisonment. Mackin was placed in custody and taken to Cell No. 25 in the county jail. This cell had earned fame as the place where Jere Dunne had been held after he had killed Jimmy Elliott in March 1883. See, "Mackin. Members of the Special Grand Jury on the Fine-Worker's Testimony Which Caused Them to Suspect Perjury on Joseph's Part--The Printers' Evidence. Argument Begun by the Prosention--Mr. Storrs to Talk for His Client Today. The Witness. The Printers' Testimony. The Arguments," Chicago Tribune,

July 1, 1885, 7; No Headline, *Chicago Herald*, July 1, 1885, 4; "Mackin Offering No Defense," *New York Times*, July 1, 1885, 1; No Headline, *Chicago Herald*, July 2, 1885, 4; "Mackin's Second Conviction," *Chicago Tribune*, July 2, 1885, 2; "No Insane Man on The Jury, *New York Times*, July 7, 1885, 2; "Mackin Sentenced. Judge Moran Overrules Mr. Storrs' Objections, but Allows Fifteen Days to File Exceptions," *Chicago Tribune*, July 8, 1885, 8.

247. "General Sporting Notes," *Chicago Herald*, July 5, 1885, 6; Advertisement, *St. Louis Post Dispatch*, July 6, 1885, 5; "Amusement Notes," *St. Louis Post Dispatch*, July 6, 1885, 8.

248. "An Interesting Sparring Contest," *St. Louis Post Dispatch*, July 8, 1885, 7.

249. "'Parson' Davies at St. Louis," *Chicago Herald*, July, 10, 1885, 3.

250. "Jack Burke's St. Louis Experience," *Chicago Tribune*, July 15, 1885, 2.

251. "Superintendent Doyle Closes All The Houses At Midnight," *Chicago Tribune*, July 22, 1885, 2.

252. "Sporting Notes," *Chicago Herald*, July 23, 1885, 2; "General Sporting Notes," *Chicago Herald*, July 25, 1885, 6.

253. "Glover and Burke at Milwaukee," *Chicago Tribune*, July 26, 1885, 10; "Pugilistic," *Daily Pantagraph*, July 27, 1885, 1.

254. "Short Notes," *Oshkosh Daily Northwestern*, July 30, 1885, 4; "Wausau Items," *Oshkosh Daily Northwestern*, July 31, 1885, 1; "Short Notes," *Oshkosh Daily Northwestern*, August 1, 1885, 4; "The Ring," *Chicago Tribune*, August 2, 1885, 8.

255. "Sullivan and M'Caffery," *Chicago Herald*, August 1, 1885, 3; "The Ring, Chicago Tribune, August 2, 1885, 4; "Physical Ability," *St. Paul Daily Globe*, August 3, 1885, 1.

256. "Athletic Notes," *Chicago Tribune*, August 10, 1885, 6; "Burke-Cardiff," *St. Paul Daily Globe*, August 10, 1885, 1; "Notes About Town," *St. Paul Daily Globe*, August 11, 1885, 3.

257. "Burke Knocks His Man Out," *Chicago Tribune*, September 6, 1886, 12; "Sporting Notes," *Chicago Herald*, August 14, 1885, 3.

258. "Pugalistic Notes," *Cleveland Plain Dealer*, September 8, 1885, 5.

259. "Leavenworth," *Kansas City Star*, September 11, 1885, 2.

260. Advertisement, *Kansas City Star*, September 15, 1885, 8; "Sporting Notes," *Kansas City Star*, September 15, 1885, 1. This article says that Burke was in Wayandotte, Kansas on that date for appearances at Harrison's Opera House.

261. "General Sporting Notes," *Kansas City Times*, September 19, 1885, 1.

262. "Sporting Sundries," *St. Louis Post Dispatch*, August 22, 1885, 9.

263. "General Sporting Notes," *Chicago Herald*, August 16, 1885, 5.

264. "General Sporting Notes," *Chicago Herald*, July 12, 1885, 6; "Tom Warren to Stop Joe Morris," *Chicago Herald*, July 17, 1885, 3; "Warren and Morris to Meet Tonight," *Chicago Tribune*, July 17, 1885, 2.

265. "Warren and Morris at the Park," *Chicago Tribune*, July 18, 1885, 6.

266. No Headline, *Bloomington Bulletin*, July 19, 1885, 4.

267. "The Midgets," *Daily Pantagraph*, July 20, 1885, 4.

268. "Sparing for Points," *Daily Pantagraph*, July 21, 1885, 4; No Headline, *Bloomington Bulletin*, July 21, 1885, 4; "With Soft Gloves," *Chicago Tribune*, July 21, 1885, 2; "Will Try Again," *Daily Pantagraph*, July 22, 1885, 3; "Magesty Will Challenge Warren," *Bloomington Bulletin*, July 22, 1885, 4.

269. "Will Ryan Meet Sullivan," *Chicago Tribune*, July 23, 1885, 2; "Sporting Affairs-Ryan and Sullivan," *Chicago Tribune*, July 27, 1885, 2; "Where Paddy Ryan Shows Good Sense," *St. Louis Post Dispatch*, August 15, 1885, 9; "Sullivan and Ryan Will Fight," *Daily Pantagraph*, August 21, 1885, 1; "Sullivan and Ryan to Meet at Baltimore," *Chicago Herald*, August 29, 1885, 3; "The Sullivan-Ryan Set-To," *Chicago Tribune*, September 9, 1885, 2; "The Sullivan-Ryan Match," *Chicago Herald*, September 9, 1885, 3; "Paddy Ryan Is 'Sore'," *Chicago Tribune*, September 12, 1885.

270. "McCaffery to Meet Sullivan at Cincinnati and Cleary at Chicago," *Chicago Tribune*, August 2, 1885, 4; "Sullivan And M'Caffrey," *Chicago Herald*, August 1, 1885, 3.

271. "The Ring," *Chicago Tribune*, August 2, 1885, 4; "Sullivan and Ryan," *Chicago Herald*, August 2, 1885, 6; "Physical Ability," *St. Paul Daily Globe*, August 3, 1885, 1; "Sullivan and Ryan," *Chicago Herald*, August 2, 1885, 6; "The Sullivan and M'Caffery Contest," *Chicago Tribune*, August 15, 1885, 2; "Sullivan Training in Maine," *St. Louis Post Dispatch*, August 19, 1885, 5; "Sullivan-M'Caffrey [This name is often spelled "frey" but more often "fery"], *St. Louis Post Dispatch*, August 21, 1885, 5; "McCaffrey's Mettle," *St. Louis Post Dispatch*, August 24, 1885, 8: The Brute Drank as Usual," *Newark Daily Advocate*, August 28, 1885, 1.

272. "The Sullivan-M'Caffrey Fight," *Chicago Tribune*, August 21, 1885, 2; "The Sullivan-McCaffrey Fight," *St. Paul Daily Globe*, August 22, 1885, 1.

273. "Sullivan and M'Caffrey," *Chicago Herald*, August 1, 1885, 3.

274. "What The 'Parson' Thinks of the Coming Contest in Cincinnati," *Chicago Tribune*, August 25, 1885, 2.

275. Ibid.

276. "The Fight," *Cincinnati Enquirer*, August 30, 1885, 1.

277. "Defeated By a Foul," *Chicago Herald*, August 30, 1885, 1; "Hard Hitters," *Daily Pantagraph*, August 31, 1885, 1; "Sullivan Did Not Want to Kill Him," *Chicago Herald*, September 2, 1885, 3.

278. *Mackin v. People,* 115 Ill. 312, 3 N.E. 222 (1885).

279. No Headline, *Chicago Herald*, November 15, 1885, 1; No Headline, *Chicago Herald*, November 16, 1885, 1; "Joseph Mackin. While Awaiting the Penitentiary Trip He Will Not Talk For Publication," *Chicago Tribune*, November 17, 1885, 3; "Joseph C. Mackin," *Chicago Tribune*, November 18, 1885, 2; "Mackin's Departure," *Chicago Tribune*, November 19, 1885, 2; "The End of Mackin. He Must Serve His Time. Just Like Any Other Criminal," *Atlanta Constitution*, November 20, 1885, 1.

280. "Sporting Notes," *Chicago Herald*, October 13, 1885, 3; "Sporting Notes," *Chicago Tribune*, October 24, 1885, 11.

281. "Sporting Notes," *Chicago Tribune*, December 23, 1885, 6.

282. "Tiger Hunt By Doyle," *Chicago Herald*, September 29, 1885, 1. The other gaming houses raided were: Nos. 125, 126, 176, 91, 134 and 148 Clark Street; Nos. 103, 110 and 113 Madison Street, and No. 5 Calhoun place.

283. "Athletic-What the Winter Promises," *Chicago Tribune*, October 5, 1885, 2.

284. "Sporting Notes," *St. Louis Post Dispatch*, October 10, 1885, 11.

285. "May Whip Sullivan, The Champion's Dangerous Rival, Pat Killen, the Only Fighter in the Country Who Can Hit Hard Enough to Knock John L. Out," *Chicago Herald*, December 5, 1886.

286. "Two New Sparrers to Meet To-Night," *Chicago Herald*, October 13, 1885, 3. Under the terms of the fight Killen was to best Morris in the allotted number of rounds or forfeit $100.

287. "John L. Sullivan Makes a Sensational Dramatic Debut at the Columbia-A Poser," *Chicago Tribune*, October 6, 1885, 5.

288. "Ryan and Sullivan in the City," *Chicago Herald*, October 19, 1885, 3.

289. "Sullivan to go Round the World," *Chicago Herald*, October 11, 1885, 2.

290. "Sullivan Going Across the Water to Fight," *Chicago Tribune*, November 21, 1885, 6; "Sullivan Under Contract," *Sacramento Daily Record-Union*, November 21, 1885, 1.

291. "The Burke Clow Fight," *Chicago Tribune*, October 12, 1885, 3.

292. "Killen Finds Morris a Soft Mark," *Chicago Herald*, October 14, 1885, 3; "Local Sporting Events," *Chicago Tribune*, October 14, 1885, 3.

293. "Lannan to Stop Duffy," *Chicago Herald*, October 16, 1885, 3.

294. "Lannan Stops Duffy," *Chicago Herald*, October 17, 1885, 3.

295. "Killen and Joe Lannon to Fight at St. Paul," *Chicago Tribune*, October 18, 1885, 11; "Killen and Lannen [sic] Matched to a Finish," *Chicago Herald*, October 18, 1885, 3.

296. "John S. Barnes Taken to Task," *Chicago Herald*, October 18, 1885, 3.

297. "Sporting Notes," *Chicago Herald*, October 13, 1885, 3.

298. "Patsy Cardiff Thumped," *Daily Pantagraph*, October 26, 1885, 4. Cardiff and Brady were matched a second time on January 4, 1886 at the Opera House in Fargo, Dakota Territory. Their second fight was fairly even with Cardiff having the slight advantage until the seventh round when he caught his arm in the ropes and sprained his elbow. By mutual agreement their second fight was declared a draw. It was beginning to appear to some promoters that Cardiff was an injury prone fighter or that he lacked "sand." See, "Declared a Draw," *St. Paul Daily Globe*, January 5, 1886, 5; "Cardiff-Brady Fight," *Peoria Journal*, January 6, 1886, 1.

299. "The Killen-Lannon Fight, Local News," *Chicago Tribune*, November 1, 1885, 10; "Killen Off For St. Paul," *Chicago Tribune*, November 4, 1885, 6; "Sporting Notes," *Chicago Tribune*, November 17, 1885, 2.

300. "Corbett's Gossip of the Fighting Game," *San Antonio Gazette*, January 6, 1906, 3.

301. "Pat Killen's Second Wind," *Chicago Herald*, November 9, 1885, 1; "Sporting Sundries," *St. Louis Post Dispatch*, November 9, 1885, 7.

302. "Sporting Affairs," *Chicago Tribune*, November 10, 1885, 3.

303. "Burke and Cleary to Fight," *Chicago Tribune*, November 17, 1885, 2.

304. Corbett, James J., *The Roar of the Crowd* (Grosset & Dunlap, 1925), 27-28.

305. See note 45 above at 60-61.

306. "The Glover-Chandler Match," *Chicago Herald*, November 29, 1885, 3; "The Glove Contest," *Chicago Tribune*, November 30, 1885, 5.

307. "Parson Davies' Amateur Medal," *Chicago Herald*, December 13, 1885, 2.

308. "Chandler and Glover to Meet Again," *Chicago Herald*, November 19, 1885, 3.

309. "Tom Chandler in Luck-His Match with Glover a Draw," *Chicago Herald*, December 1, 1885, 3; "The Glove Contest," *Chicago Tribune*, December 1, 1885, 2.

310. "Why Sport is Popular Here," *Chicago Herald*, December 6, 1885, 6.

311. See note 66 above at 30.

312. "Local Sports of the Year," *Chicago Tribune*, January 1, 1886, 2.

313. "General Sporting Notes," *Chicago Herald*, December 13, 1885, 2;

314. "Sporting Notes," *Chicago Tribune*, December 10, 1885, 3; "Burke to Arrive This Evening," *Chicago Tribune*, December 12, 1885, 6; "Jack Burke Arrives for his Meeting with Cleary," *Chicago Tribune*, December 13, 1885, 12.

315. "Sports for December," *Chicago Herald*, December 13, 1885, 2.

316. "Sporting Notes," *Chicago Tribune*, December 18, 1885, 2.

317. "Mike Cleary in Chicago," *Chicago Herald*, December 20, 1885, 2; "Athletic, Cleary Arrives, Other Notes," *Chicago Tribune*, December 20, 1885, 10.

318. "The Japanese Wrestler in the City," *Chicago Herald*, December 20, 1885, 2.

319. "Wrestling-The Parson's Man Against Matsada Sorakichi," *Chicago Tribune*, December 18, 1885, 2.

320. "General Sporting Notes," *Chicago Herald*, December 20, 1885, 2; "Pat Killen the Victor," *Chicago Herald*, December 22, 1885, 1; "Killen Knocks Out a Bricklayer," *Chicago Tribune*, December 22, 1885, 6.

321. "It Will Be a Great Entertainment," *Chicago Herald*, December 25, 1885, 3.

322. "The Burke-Cleary Meeting Tomorrow Night," *Chicago Tribune*, December 27, 1885, 11; "Burke and Cleary," *Chicago Tribune*, December 27, 1885, 2.

323. "Three Times and Out," *Chicago Herald*, December 29, 1885, 1; "Cleary Knocked Out," *Chicago Tribune*, December 29, 1885, 2; "Sporting Affairs, Mike Cleary, the Pugilist, Says 'That Punch in the Neck was a Tough One'," *Chicago Tribune*, December 30, 1885, 2.

324. "Sports Gossip," *Boston Daily Globe*, June 5, 1886, 13.

Chapter 6 – Donning evening clothes – (1886)

325. See note 309 above at 124.

326. Bogart, Ernest Ludlow and Thompson, Charles Manfred, *The Centennial History of Illinois, Volume Four, The Industrial State 1870-1893* (Illinois Centennial Commission, 1920), 162-177; Andrews, Wayne, *Battle for Chicago* (Harcourt, Brace and Company), 127-149.

327. "Sullivan and Ryan," *Chicago Herald*, January 10, 1886, 2; "The Match Between Sullivan and Ryan off Because the Latter Can't Raise the Cash," *Chicago Tribune*, January 17, 1886, 11.

328. Advertisement, *St. Louis Post Dispatch*, January 4, 1886, 5; "Notes," *Chicago Tribune*, January 3, 1886, 10.

329. "The Burke-Kelly Match," *St. Louis Post Dispatch*, January 5, 1886, 7; "Pugilistic Notes," *Chicago Tribune*, January 7, 1886, 5; "The Kelly-Burke Contest," *St. Louis Post Dispatch*, January 7, 1886, 7.

330. "Kelly's Courage," *St. Louis Post Dispatch*, January 9, 1886, 2; "Sporting Affairs, Jack Burke Meets a St. Louis Pugilist Who Adopts Cowardly Tactics," *Chicago Tribune*, January 9, 1886, 3; "The Burke-Kelly Fight," *St. Louis Post Dispatch*, January 12, 1886, 7.

331. "Glover and Bradburn," *Chicago Herald*, January 10, 1886, 2; "Sporting Affairs," *Chicago Tribune*, January 11, 1886, 8.

332. "Sporting Matters," *Chicago Tribune*, January 12, 1886, 6.

333. "Local Sports of 1886," *Chicago Herald*, Januayr 1, 1887, 2.

334. "General Sporting Notes," *Chicago Herald*, January 17, 1886, 6.

335. "Sporting Notes," *Chicago Herald*, January 22, 1886, 3.

336. "Giants in the Ring," *Chicago Herald*, January 24, 1886, 2; "Wrestling for Big Money," *Chicago Herald*, January 28, 1886, 2.

337. "Lewis Downs the Jap," *Chicago Tribune*, January 29, 1886, 3; "An Exciting Contest," *Daily Pantagraph*, January 29, 1886, 1; "Local Sports of 1886," *Chicago Herald*, January 1, 1887, 2.

338. "Sporting Notes," *Chicago Herald*, February 2, 1886, 3.

339. "About Burke and Mitchell," *Chicago Herald*, February 7, 1886, 2.

340. "Jack Burke to Meet a Noted Scrapper To-Night," *Cincinnati Enquirer*, February 5, 1886, 2; "Jack Burke Makes Currier Quit in Two Rounds," *Cincinnati Enquirer*, February 6, 1886, 2; "Mike Smith Makes a Holy Show of Himself," *Cincinnati Enquirer*, February 7, 1886, 2.

341. "General Sporting Notes," *Chicago Herald*, February 7, 1886, 2.

342. "Pat Killen to Stop Dick Burke," *Chicago Herald*, February 14, 1886, 2; "Pat Killen Returns to Chicago," *Chicago Herald*, February 17, 1886, 2.

343. "In Sporting Circles," *Chicago Herald*, February 7, 1886, 2; "The Wrestlers Put Up Their Money," *Chicago Herald*, February 11, 1886, 2; "Wrestling for Blood," *Chicago Herald*, February 14, 1886, 2.

344. "Over in One Minute," *Chicago Herald*, February 16, 1886, 1; "Brutal Sport," *Chicago Tribune*, February 16, 1886, 1.

345. "Local Sports of 1886," *Chicago Herald*, January 1, 1887, 2.

346. "Burke in Training, The Jap on His Feet," *Chicago Tribune*, February 22, 1886, 3.

347. "Opinions of Sporting Men on the Recent Wrestling," *Chicago Tribune*, February 17, 1886, 2.

348. "Wrestling at Pope's," *St. Louis Post Dispatch*, March 6, 1886, 10.

349. "Wrestling Will Be Improved," *Chicago Herald*, February 21, 1886, 2.

350. "In the Sporting World," *Chicago Herald*, February 24, 1886, 2; "Burke and Glover at Work," *Chicago Herald*, February 28, 1886, 2; "Sporting Notes," *Chicago Tribune*, February 28, 1886, 15.

351. "Pat Killen's Soft Mark," *Chicago Herald*, February 20, 1886, 2.

352. "Killen to Stop Pat McHugh To-Night," *Chicago Herald*, March 5, 1886, 3.

353. "Pat McHugh Plays the Baby Act, *Chicago Herald*, March 6, 1886, 2.

354. "Sporting Notes," *Chicago Herald*, March 21, 1886, 2.

355. "Killen Wins in One Round," *Chicago Herald*, March 28, 1886, 1; "Lively Knock-Outs," *The Marion Daily Star*, March 29, 1886, 3.

356. "Here and There," *Eau Clair Daily Free Press*, March 30, 1886, 3; "General Sporting Notes," *Chicago Herald*, April 4, 1886, 2; "A Hippodrome at Eau Claire," *St. Paul Daily Globe*, April 3, 1886, 4 The *Globe* reports a first blow KO.

357. "General Sporting Notes," *Chicago Herald*, April 4, 1886, 2 (Champion of Iowa); "Pat Killen the Pugilist," *Omaha Daily Bee*, April 5, 1886, 8.

358. "Dropped at the Touch," *Omaha Daily Bee*, April 7, 1886, 8.

359. "General Sporting Notes," *Chicago Herald*, April 11, 1886, 2.

360. "General Sporting Notes," *Chicago Herald*, March 7, 1886, 2.

361. "Won By the Strangler," *Chicago Herald*, March 8, 1886, 1.

362. "Sport with the Mitts," *Chicago Herald*, March 7, 1886, 2; "The Burke-Glover Meeting," *Chicago Herald*, March 8, 1886, 2.

363. "Burke in Great Luck-The Referee and He Best Glover," *Chicago Herald*, March 9, 1886, 1.

364. "Glover Challenges Burke," *Chicago Herald*, March 12, 1886, 2.

365. "General Sporting Notes," *Chicago Herald*, March 14, 1886, 2.

366. "Chicago Lodge B.P.O.E. Banquet," *Chicago Herald*, March 12, 1886, 1.

367. "Sporting Notes," *St. Louis Post Dispatch*," March 12, 1886, 5; "Bibby vs. Lewis," *Chicago Tribune*, March 14, 1886, 10.

368. "Whipped By Dempsey," *Chicago Herald*, March 15, 1886, 1; "'The Marine' Mangled," *St. Louis Post Dispatch*, March 15, 1886, 1; "Won by a Foul-How La Blanche Explains his Knockout by Jack Dempsey," *St. Louis Post Dispatch*, March 18, 1886, 8; "La Blanche's Bluff," *St. Louis Post Dispatch*, March 20, 1886, 10.

369. "Slugger Sullivan Calls on Joe Mackin," *Chicago Herald*, April 20, 1886, 2; "Sporting Notes," *St. Louis Post Dispatch*," April 20, 1886, 7.

370. "Glover's Arm Hurt," *Chicago Herald*, April 25, 1886, 2; "Jack Dempsey," *St. Louis Post Dispatch*, May 1, 1886, 11.

371. "The Burke-Mitchell Match," *Chicago Herald*, May 2, 1886, 2.

372. Andrews, Wayne, *Battle for Chicago* (Harcourt, Brace and Company, 1946), 132-140; "A Reign of Riot, *St. Louis Post Dispatch*, May 5, 1886, 1.

373. *Illinois v. August Spies et al.*, Trail transcript, Volume J [Witnesses for the State, July 22-24, 1886], Testimony of John D. Shea, July 22, 1886, 50.

374. See note 66 above at 31.

375. "Burke Again In Luck," *Chicago Herald*, May 11, 1886, 1.

376. "An Unjust Decision," *Chicago Tribune*, May 11, 1886, 1; "Mitchell-Burke," *Daily Pantagraph*, May 11, 1886, 4.

377. "Local Sports of 1886," *Chicago Herald*, January 1, 1887, 2.

378. "Dempsey and Mitchell," *Chicago Herald*, May 12, 1886, 2.

379. "Here and There," *Chicago Tribune*, October 17, 1887, 6; "Moment for Jack Dempsey," *The St. Paul Globe*, December 29, 1901, 9.

380. "Prize Fighters Must Go," *Daily Pantagraph*, May 22, 1886, 1; "War on the Pugs," *St. Louis Post Dispatch*, May 22, 1886, 10.

381 ."Reluctant Suppression of the Sluggers," *Chicago Tribune*, May 23, 1886, 4.

382. "General Sporting Notes," *Chicago Herald*, May 23, 1886, 2; "Muldoon in Hard Luck," *St. Louis Post Dispatch*, May 28, 1886, 12.

383. "Sporting Notes," *St. Louis Post Dispatch*, June 5, 1886, 12.

384. "Muldoon and Lewis," *Chicago Herald*, June 6, 1886, 2.

385. "Muldoon Mad," *St. Louis Post Dispatch*, June 11, 1886, 8.

386. "No Interference Looked for by the Police at Chester Park To-day-Pete Nolan and Jack Burke Will Spar," *Cincinnati Enquirer*, June 12, 1886, 4; "Chester Park-To-day-Grand Glove Contest Between Jack Burke and Pete Nolan," *Cincinnati Enquirer*, June, 12, 1886, 1.

387. "Burke and Nolan in the Ring," *Chicago Herald*, June 13, 1886, 2; "A Grand Contest," *Cincinnati Enquirer*, June 13, 1886, 1; "The Burke-Nolan Fight," *St. Louis Post Dispatch*, June 14, 1886, 7.

388. "Burke and Nolan," *St. Louis Post Dispatch*, June 26, 1886, 10.

389. "Burke's Condition," *St. Louis Post Dispatch*, July 4, 1886, 5.

390. "Jack Burke Feels Rather Sore," *Chicago Herald*, July 17, 1886, 2.

391. "Records of the Two Wonders," Chicago Herald, January 30, 1887, 3 (Davies christened Lewis as "the strangler,"); "Muldoon Will Come Here at Once," *Chicago Herald*, June 23, 1886, 3; "Champion Muldoon Arrives," *Chicago Herald*, June 25, 1886, 2; "Evan Lewis, The Strangler," *Chicago Herald*, June 27, 1886, 3; "The Muldoon-Lewis Match To-Night," *Chicago Herald*, June 28, 1886, 4.

392. "A Hard Man to Down," *Chicago Herald*, June 29, 1886, 3.

393. "Miscellaneous," *Cincinnati Enquirer*, July 5, 1886, 2; "It Was a Fight," *Cincinnati Enquirer*, July 6, 1886, 1; "Jack Burke Is Bested by Pete Nolan in Eight Rounds," *Chicago Tribune*, July 6, 1886, 2; "Plucky Pete, How Nolan of Cincinnati Whipped Jack Burke in Eight Rounds," *St. Louis Post Dispatch*, July 7, 1886, 7; "Nolan the Pugilist-He Does Up the Black Diamond and Stops Prof. Brooks etc.," *Chicago Tribune*, July 12, 1886, 2.

394. "Jack Burke Feels Rather Sore," *Chicago Herald*, July 17, 1886, 2.

395. "Arrival of Jack Burke," *Cincinnati Enquirer*, July 15, 1886, 2; "Burke and Nolan Found Not Guilty," *Chicago Herald*, July 20, 1886, 3; "Burke Ready to Meet Nolan," *Chicago Herald*, July 26, 1886, 2; "Sporting Notes," *St. Louis Post Dispatch*, July 27, 1886, 5.

396. "Jack Burke Give His Version of the Fight With Nolan at Cincinnati etc.," *St. Louis Post Dispatch,* July 30, 1886, 7; "Afraid of the Mob, Why Jack Burke Did Not Use His Right on Nolan's Neck," *St. Louis Post Dispatch*, July 30, 1886, 7.

397. "Fragments," *Daily Pantagraph*, July 6, 1886, 4; "Myers-Welsh," *Streator Daily Free Press*, July 7, 1886, 3; "A Knockout-The Result of the Myers-Welsh Hard Glove Contest-Five Coaches and a Base Band," *Daily Pantagraph*, July 7, 1886, 4; "Paddy Welch Knocked Out," July 7, 1886, 2; "Welch Worsted," *St. Louis Post Dispatch*, July 7, 1886, 7.

398. "General Notes," *Streator Daily Free Press*, July 14, 1886, 3.

399. "The Sporting World-The Cannon-Lewis Match To-Night," *Cincinnati Enquirer*, July 15, 1886.

400. "'The Strangler' Downed," *St. Louis Post Dispatch*, July 17, 1886, 11.

401. "Lewis Has It In for Tom Cannon," *Chicago Herald*, July 17, 1886, 2.

402. "Cannon and Lewis to Wrestle Again," *Cincinnati Enquirer*, July 17, 1886, 2.

403. "The 'Jap' and Lewis to Meet Again," *Chicago Tribune*, July 24, 1886, 2.

404. Stories on which the author's reconstruction above is based include: "Duncan C. Ross' 'Unknown," *Chicago Tribune*, August 4, 1886, 1; "Who Was 'Licked' By Ryan?," *Chicago Tribune*, August 5, 1886, 3; "Paddy Ryan's Row," *St. Louis Post Dispatch*, August 6, 1886, 5; "No Match Made Between Paddy Ryan and Duncan C. Ross' Unknown," *Chicago Tribune*, August 6, 1886, 3; "Mysterious Death," *Montreal Daily Witness*, August 6, 1886, 6; "What Killed Durrell?," *Boston Daily Globe*, August 7, 1886, 2; "Met His Death," *Daily Kennebec Journal*, August 7, 1886, 1; "General News Notes," *Syracuse Daily Standard*, August 7, 1886, 1; "Beaten to Death in a Rum Shop-Untimely because of Major William Mr. Durrell," *Boston Journal*, August 6, 1886, 1.

405. "The World's Pastime-Formal Opening of the Great Exposition at Cheltenham Beach Yesterday, *Inter Ocean*, July 4, 1886, 7; "Duncan Ross Defeated in a Broadsword Contest at Chicago," *Cincinnati Enquirer*, July 15, 1886, 2; "All Night on the Lake," *New York Times*, July 5, 1886, 1; "Chicago's Vesuvius. Development on the Lake Front of an Innocuous Form of Volcano," *Inter Ocean*, July 8, 1886, 3; "Ross Wins the Medal," *Chicago Herald*, July 13, 1886, 2; "Cheltenham Beach a Statement Mad That it Has Failed Duncan Ross Story," *Daily Inter Ocean*, July 21, 1886, 6; "Disgusted Athletes, Who Were Lured to Chicago on False Pretenses," *New York Times*, July 21, 1886, 1.

406. "A Meeting Arranged Between Paddy Ryan and Frank Glover for Sept. 23," *Chicago Tribune*, August 22, 1886, 11; "Philly's Fighters," *St. Louis Post Dispatch*, August 21, 1886, 11; "The Big Fiasco," *St. Louis Post Dispatch*, September 4, 1886, 11; "Ryan and Glover," *Chicago Herald*, September 5, 1886, 2; "Ryan and Glover in Pinafore," *Chicago Herald*, September 10, 1886, 3; "The Glover-Ryan Match," *Chicago Herald*, September 12, 1886, 2; "Paddy Ryan Fights Again," *The Los Angeles Times*, September 14, 1886, 1.

407. "Fighting in the Rain," *Chicago Herald*, September 14, 1886, 1; "Glover's Gameness," *St. Louis Post Dispatch*, September 16, 1886, 5; "Is I Shot?" *St. Louis Post Dispatch*, September 18, 1886, 5; "Local Sports of 1886," *Chicago Herald*, January 1, 1887, 2.

408. "Ryan and Glover to Fight Again," *Chicago Tribune*, September 24, 1886, 2.

409. "Burke Wants to Fight Dempsey," *Chicago Herald*, August 20, 1886, 3; "Dempsey and Burke Matched," *Chicago Tribune*, August 27, 1886, 3; "Dempsey and Burke," *St. Louis Post Dispatch*, September 14, 1886, 8.

410. "Gossip About the Boxers," *Sun*, June 13, 1886, 7.

411. "Dempsey and Burke to Meet in San Francisco Before Oct. 1," *Chicago Tribune*, August 29, 1886, 3; "The Burke-Dempsey Fight," *Chicago Tribune*, August 29, 1886, 7.

412. "Telegraphic Ticks," *Evening News*, September 16, 1886, 1; "Burke to Meet Dempsey," *Chicago Tribune*, September 17, 1886, 2; "Sporting Items," *Chicago Tribune*, September 18, 1886, 2.

413. "Mayor Bartlett Gives Himself Away," *Sacramento Daily Record-Union*, October 1, 1886, 4; "Burke Promises to Meet John L.," *Chicago Tribune*, October 1, 1886, 2; "The Burke-Dempsey Match Postponed," *Newark Daily Advocate*, October 1, 1886, 1; "Burke and Dempsey Not Allowed to Fight," *Chicago Tribune*, September 24, 1886, 2; "Burke Ready to Meet Sullivan," *Syracuse Daily Standard*, October 1, 1886, 1.

414. "Sporting Miscellany," *Chicago Tribune*, September 27, 1886, 2; "John L. in the Role of a Gentleman," *Chicago Tribune*, September 28, 1886, 2.

415. "Pat Sheedy Will Pilot the Champion Around the World," *St. Louis Post Dispatch*, September 25, 1886, 9.

416. "I Told You So," *St. Louis Post Dispatch*, September 25, 1886, 10.

417. "Sporting Miscellany," *Chicago Tribune*, October 27, 1886, 6.

418. "General Sporting Notes," *Chicago Herald*, October 3, 1886, 2.

419. "The Freedom of the City is His," *Sacramento Daily Record-Union*, October 1, 1886, 4; "Jack Burke; Jim Carr; Los Angeles," *Evening News*, October 16, 1886, 5; "Sporting Miscellany," *Chicago Tribune*, October 17, 1886, 13.

420. "Sullivan and Ryan to Spar in San Francisco," *Chicago Tribune*, October 11, 1886, 6.

421. "The Burke-Dempsey Match," *Chicago Herald*, October 13, 1886, 2; "Sporting Miscellany," *Boston Daily Globe*, October 26, 1886, 3.

422. "They Have Made Up," *Chicago Tribune*, October 13, 1886, 6.

423. "In the Sporting World," *Chicago Herald*, October 21, 1886, 3.

424. "Sullivan's Western Experience," *Chicago Tribune*, October 18, 1886, 2.

425. "John L. Sullivan Calls on Ryan," *Chicago Herald*, October 20, 1886, 2; "Sullivan Talks About Fighters-His Opinion of Ryan," *Chicago Tribune*, October 21, 1886, 2; "Chicago Admirers of John L. Sullivan," *Chicago Herald*, October 24, 1886, 2.

426. "Sullivan on His Travels," *Chicago Herald*, October 31, 1886, 2.

427. "Sullivan Starts for the West," *Chicago Herald*, October 26, 1886, 3; "Sullivan Combination at St. Paul," *Chicago Tribune*, October 31, 1886, 11; "Sullivan and Cardiff to Fight," *Chicago Tribune*, November 4, 1886, 7; "Sporting Notes," *St. Louis Post Dispatch*, November 8, 1886, 7; "To Contest In The Ring. Meeting of Featherweights to Take Place Today. Kilrain and Hearld to Spar etc.," *Chicago Tribune*, November 8, 1886, 3.

428. "Sullivan in San Francisco," *Chicago Tribune*, November 11, 1886, 5; "License Issued for the Sullivan-Ryan Fight etc.," *Chicago Tribune*, November 12, 1886, 2.

429. "Sully 'Sold' Him-He Expected the Police to Stop the Fight in the Second Round, etc.," *St. Louis Post Dispatch*, November 20, 1886, 9; "Paddy Ryan This He Was Imposed On," *Chicago Tribune*, November 17, 1886, 3.

430. "Sullivan Whips Ryan," *Chicago Herald*, November 14, 1886, 1; "Champions in the Ring, The Sullivan-Ryan Fight at San Francisco," *Chicago Tribune*, November 14, 1886, 10; "Ryan Knocked Out Again," *Saint Louis Post Dispatch*, November 15, 1886, 5; "Paddy Does Some Good Fighting at First, but the Champion Knocks Him Senseless and After the Decision Carries His Fallen Foe to a Chair," *Daily Pantagraph*, November 15, 1886, 1; "Ryan Knocked Out," *The Weekly Bulletin*, November 19, 1886, 2.

431. "Exit Paddy Ryan-Having Bought a Saloon in San Francisco He Will Not Return to Chicago," *Chicago Herald*, November 28, 1886, 2.

432. "In the Field of Sports," *Chicago Tribune*, November 16, 1886, 2 (Sheedy withdrew all opposition to granting of a license.).

433. "Burke and Dempsey," *Chicago Herald*, November 21, 1886, 2; "The Dempsey-Burke Fight," *Chicago Tribune*, November 22, 1886, 3.

434. "Dempsey's Tact-An Incident of the Middle-Weight's Fight With Jack Burke," *Saint Louis Post Dispatch*, April 22, 1887, 8.

435. "They Fought A Draw," *Chicago Herald*, November 23, 1886, 1; "Neither Won the Fight," *Chicago Tribune*, November 23, 1886, 2; "A Draw," *Saint Louis Post Dispatch*, November 23, 1886, 8; "Opinions of Experts on the Burke-Dempsey Match Favor the Later," *Chicago Tribune*, November 24, 1886, 2.

436. "The Sluggers at San Francisco," *Chicago Tribune*, November 28, 1886, 10; "Sporting Notes," *Saint Louis Post Dispatch*, December 1, 1886, 7; "Burke Wanted Money Not Glory," *Chicago Herald*, December 11, 1886, 3; "Jack Burke Sails for Portland," *Oregonian*, November 29, 1886, 4; "The Pugilistic Revival," *Salt Lake Daily Tribune*, December 16, 1886, 6 (setting out route of Davies' tour with Burke and Dempsey; "Burke-Dempsey Combination," *Salt Lake Daily Tribune*, December 17, 1886, 4.

437. "Scientific Sparring," *Morning Oregonian*, December 7, 1886, 8.

438. "The Sporting Events," *Salt Lake Daily Tribune*, December 18, 1886, 4.

439. Advertisement, *Salt Lake Herald*, December 18, 1886, 4; "At the Opera House," *Salt Lake Herald*, December 19, 1886, 8.

440. "Davies, Burke and Dempsey," *Omaha Daily Bee*, December 24, 1886, 8.

441. "In the Sporting World," *Chicago Herald*, December 21, 1886, 4. It was expected that when the troupe reached Chicago, Davies would arrange a Dempsey/Burke rematch. But the authorities were still barring all prize fighting events in Chicago. See, "To Match Dempsey and McCaffrey," Chicago Herald, December 22, 1886, 2.

442

443. "Will Meet Sullivan," *Chicago Herald*, December 26, 1886, 2; "Dempsey Want War," *Saint Louis Post Dispatch*, December 29, 1886, 5; "Two Rattling Prize Fights," *Chicago Herald*, December 30, 1886, 2 (Dempsey and his wife left yesterday); "The Champion Middle-Weight Pugilist and His Wife in New York," *Saint Louis Post Dispatch*, January 1, 1887, 8.

444. "Sullivan's Tour," *Saint Louis Post Dispatch*, December 18, 1886, 10.

445. "Fun at the Comique," *St. Paul Daily Globe*, November 13, 1886, 3; "Sporting Gossip," *St. Paul Daily Globe*, November 15, 1886, 3; "In the Orthodox Ring," *Omaha Daily Bee*, December 31, 1886, 2.

Chapter 7 – Sullivan breaks his hand - (1887)

446. "Woman's Curiosity," *The St. Paul Daily Globe*, July 26, 1891, 1.

447. "Killen Knocked Him Out," *St. Paul Daily Globe*, January 5, 1887, 1.

448. "Pugilistic Pointers," Omaha Daily Bee, January 11, 1887, 8 (Sullivan says he things Killen will back out of their Milwaukee fight); "Minnesota Globules," *St. Paul Daily Globe,* January 12, 1887, 4; "Sheedy Talks," *St. Paul Daily Globe*, January 15, 1887, 2; "Killen and Sullivan," Chicago Herald, January 15, 1887, 2; "Minneapolis Sports," *St. Paul Daily Globe,* January 17, 1887, 7.

449. "Killen-McDonald-The Big Boy Does up the Latter in Six Rounds and One Blow in the Seventh," *Lake Superior Review and Weekly Tribune*, January 21, 1887, 1

450. "Pat Sheedy's Opinion of Dempsey and Ryan," *Sun*, January 23, 1887, 7.

451. "Sullivan in St. Paul," *The Minneapolis Tribune*, January 18, 1887, 1; "A Broken Arm," *The Minneapolis Tribune*, January 19, 1887, 1; "Neck and Wrist Met," *Chicago Tribune*, January 19, 1887, 3; "Sullivan's Wrist Broken," *Saint Louis Post Dispatch*, January 19, 1887, 5; "Sullivan Fights Six Rounds With a Broken Arm," *Daily Pantagraph*, January 19, 1887, 1; "That Fight-In Which Cardiff Held His Own Against Sullivan," *National Police Gazette*, February 5, 1887, 10.

452. "Pat Killen in Chicago-Glover's Challenge to Cardiff-In General," *Chicago Herald*, January 25, 1887, 2.

453. "'Parson' Davies Referred to the Police," *Chicago Herald*, January 19, 1887, 2.

454. "Joe Action and Evan Lewis to Meet at Battery D," *Chicago Tribune*, February 6, 1887, 7.

455. "A Wrestling Match To-Night," *Chicago Herald*, January 5, 1887, 2; "Sporting Gossip," *Saint Louis Post Dispatch*, January 13, 1887, 5; "Sporting Gossip," *Saint Louis Post Dispatch*, January 20, 1887, 5; "Lewis v. Acton," *Inter Ocean*, January 23, 1887, 4; "Club Swinging," Inter Ocean, April 4, 1887, 3; "The Lusty Lewis Madison's "Strangler" Surprises Acton by Throwing Him Three Times in Succession," *Inter Ocean*, April 12, 1887, 1.

456. "Before Judge Blodgett," *Inter Ocean*, February 1, 1887, 7.

457. "The Court Record-Superior Court-New Suits-Case No. 60-396," *Inter Ocean*, January 25, 1876, 3; "The Court Record-U.S. Courts-Bankruptcy No. 4-494" *Inter Ocean*, March 2, 1882, 6; "The Court Record-Circuit Court-Case No. 41-166,"

Inter Ocean, May 8, 1882, 6; "The Court Record-'Parson' Davies' Brother Sentenced," *Inter Ocean*, May 12, 1887, 10; "The Court Record-Superior Court-New Suits-Case No. 82-596, Brady v. Hart and Vere R. Davies," *Inter Ocean*, May 15, 1882, 6; "The Court Record-Superior Court-Case No. 82-596, Bardy v. Hart and Vere R. Davies," *Inter Ocean*, May 17, 1882, 12.

458. *United States v. George F. Davies*, Gen. No. 1102, Docket Sheet and Court File.

459. "George Davies Defense," *Daily Inter Ocean*, February 2, 1887, 2.

460. "Davies Convicted But Missing," *Inter Ocean*, February 3, 1887, 7; "The City in Brief Official Cognizance to be Taken of the May Corn Deal," *Inter Ocean*, April 5, 1887, 7.

461. "Acton and Lewis Matched," *Chicago Herald*, January 23, 1887, 2; "Acton and Lewis to Meet," *Chicago Tribune*, January 23, 1887, 7.

462. "Records of Two Wonders," *Chicago Herald*, January 30, 1887, 3; "Joe Acton and Evan Lewis to Meet at Battery D," *Chicago Tribune*, February 6, 1887, 7; "The Demon and the Strangler," *Chicago Herald*, February 6, 1887, 6; "Won By The Sly Demon," *Chicago Herald*, February 8, 1887, 1; "Strangler and Demon," *Chicago Tribune*, February 8, 1887, 1; "Catch-As-Catch-Can," *Daily Pantagraph*, February 8, 1887, 1.

463. "Of Interest to Sports," *Chicago Herald*, January 20, 1887, 1; "Patsey's Prattle," *Saint Louis Post Dispatch*, January 23, 1887, 10.

464. "Daly the Only Delay," *Chicago Herald*, January 27, 1887, 3; "The Killen-Bradburn Fight," *Chicago Tribune*, January 27, 1887, 7; "The Killen-Bradburn Match Is Off," *Chicago Herald*, February 11, 1887, 2.

465. "English Pugilist Coming," *Chicago Herald*, February 6, 1887, 6.

466. "Trying to Arrange a Fight-The English '200-Tonner,'" *Chicago Tribune*, February 20, 1887, 6; "Smith, the English 'Champion,' and Knifton," *Chicago Tribune*, February 27, 1887, 6.

467. "Jack and 'The Parson,'" *Saint Louis Post Dispatch*, March 9, 1887, 8.

468. "Sporting Notes," *Chicago Tribune*, February 17, 1887, 3; "Lewis and Acton," *Chicago Tribune*, February 27, 1887, 6.

469. "Lewis and Carkeek Meet To-Night," *Chicago Herald*, March 3, 1887, 3; "Sports Looking Up," *Chicago Herald*, March 2, 1887, 3.

470. "Badly Choked by Lewis, Carkeek and the Strangler Have a Bout at Milwaukee," *Chicago Tribune*, March 4, 1887, 2.

471. "Kilrain Defeats Lannon in Eleven Rounds," *Chicago Tribune*, March 9, 1887, 3; "Have at Him, Jake," *Saint Louis Post Dispatch*, May 23, 1887, 8.

472. "Carkeek to Meet Lewis Again," *Chicago Tribune*, March 9, 1887, 3; "Lewis to Wrestle Carkeek Next Monday Night," *Chicago Tribune*, March 10, 1887, 3.

473. "There Will Be No Fight," *Chicago Herald*, March 10, 1887, 3.

474. Grossman, James R., Keating, Ann Durkin, Reiff, Janice L., Newberry Library, Chicago Historical Society, *The Encyclopedia of Chicago* (University of Chicago Press, 2004), "Wrestling."

475. "Lewis and Carkeek Meet To-Night," *Chicago Herald*, March 14, 1887, 2.

476. "A 'Cooked-Up' Contest," *Chicago Tribune*, March 15, 1887, 3; "Lewis at Battery D, Defeating Carkeek in Four Bouts," *Chicago Herald*, March 15, 1887, 1.

477. "General Sporting Gossip," *Chicago Herald*, February 20, 1887, 3; "What 'Jack' Burke Has to Say," *Chicago Herald*, March 4, 1887, 2; "Glover and Burke," *Saint Louis Post Dispatch*, March 4, 1887, 5; "Glover and Burke," *Chicago Tribune*, March 5, 1887, 3; "Plenty of Fights in Prospect," *Chicago Herald*, March 6, 1887, 2; "Frank Glover Is Anxious to Meet Jack Burke," *Chicago Tribune*, March 9, 1887, 3; "Burke and Glover Still Jawing Each Other," *Chicago Tribune*, March 10, 1887, 3.

478. "Glover and Burke Still Far Apart," *Chicago Herald*, March 12, 1887, 2.

479. "A Fight Arranged," *St. Paul Daily Globe*, April 14, 1887, 5; "Tonight's Fight Between Bradburn and McGregor," *Chicago Tribune*, May 16, 1887, 3; "Won on a Foul," *Daily Evening Bulletin*, May 19, 1887, 2; "Sporting Notes," Saint Louis Post Dispatch, June 7, 1887, 8.

480. "Sweeping Challenge," *St. Paul Daily Globe*, April 16, 1887, 5; "Among the Pugilists," *Chicago Herald*, April 16, 1887, 2; "Among the Fighters," *Chicago Herald*, April 17, 1887, 2.

481. "Jack Burke-He Will Try His Luck With Australia Sluggers," *St. Paul Daily Globe*, June 3, 1887, 6; "Chandler Roasts Burke," *Chicago Herald*, May 26, 1887, 3; "Burke's Reply to Chandler," *Chicago Herald*, May 27, 1887, 2.

482. "Bradburn and Glover," *Chicago Herald*, March 16, 1887, 3; "Glover and Bradburn-To Fight with Skin Tight Gloves at an Early Date," *Inter Ocean*, July 11, 1887, 6.

483. "Closing the Saloons-One of the Features of the Proposed Sunday Law," *Chicago Tribune*, June 12, 1887, 10.

484. "The Lewis-Acton Wrestling Match To-Night, etc." *Chicago Herald*, April 11, 1887, 4; "The Match Tonight-Carkeek and Greek George," *Chicago Tribune*, April 11, 1887, 2.

485. "Lewis and Acton," *Chicago Tribune*, April 12, 1887, 7.

486. "Lewis is Champion," *Chicago Herald*, April 12, 1887, 1.

487. "A Retired Athelte," *Inter Ocean*, May 8, 1887, 2; "Miscellaneous," *Inter Ocean*, May 16, 1887, 8; "Walsh v. Ross," *Winnipeg Free Press*, May 21, 1887, 4.

488. "The 'Strangler' and Tom Connors to Wrestle for $500," *Chicago Tribune*, June 13, 1887, 3; "Wrestling," *Inter Ocean*, June 13, 1887, 2; "Wrestler Lewis Complains. Alleged Unfair Treatment by the Sports of Pittsburg," *New York Herald*, June 16, 1887, 10; "The Champion Loses," *Wisconsin State Journal*, June 17, 1887, 8.

489. "Tom Connors Defeats Evan Lewis in an Exciting Contest," *Chicago Tribune*, June 14, 1887, 3; "Lewis Rather Badly Used Up," *Chicago Tribune*, June 16, 1887, 7; "Wrestler Lewis Complains. Alleged Unfair Treatment by the Sports of Pittsburg," *New York Herald*, June 16, 1887, 10.

490. "Saloonkeepers Who Defy Mayor Roche's Orders Arraigned Before Justice Lyon," *Chicago Herald*, July 13, 1887, 2.

491. "All Kinds of Sports," *Chicago Herald*, July 24, 1887, 2.

492. "Pugilistic and Wrestling Challenges Issued and Accepted," *Chicago Herald*, July 27, 1887, 3; "Frank Whitmore, the Athlete, to Wrestle Evan Lewis," *Chicago Tribune*, July 29, 1887, 3.

493. "Glover Knocked Out, Bill Bradburn Whips Him Badly," *Chicago Herald*, July 28, 1887, 1; "Bradburn Knocks Out Glover in Nine Rounds," *Chicago Tribune*, July 28, 1887, 3; "Bradburn Won," *Saint Louis Post Dispatch*, July 28, 1887, 5.

494. "Tom Chandler's Cowardly Assault," Chicago Herald, July 29, 1887, 3; "A Lively Bout Between Evan Lewis and Frank Whitmore," *Chicago Tribune*, July 31, 1887, 3; "Fine Wrestling," *Saint Louis Post Dispatch*," August 1, 1887, 5.

495. "All Sorts of Sporting Squibs," *Chicago Herald*, August 4, 1887, 3.

496. "The Crowd Howled," *St. Paul Daily Globe*, August 6, 1887, 2.

497. "Killen and His Trainer," Chicago Tribune, August 4, 1887, 3; "The Cardiff-Killen Fight Settles Nothing-Patsy's Foul," *Saint Louis Post Dispatch*, August 6, 1887, 9; "The Killen-Cardiff Fight Minneapolis Declared a Draw," *Chicago Tribune*, August 6, 1887, 3; "Pat Killen Badly Injured in the Cardiff Fight," *Chicago Tribune*, August 13, 1887, 3.

498. "From Chicago," *St. Paul Daily Globe*, August 5, 1887, 6; "Lewis Won With Ease," *St. Paul Daily Globe*, August 7, 1887, 7.

499. "Some Observations on the Killen and Cardiff Meeting," *Chicago Tribune*, August 8, 1887, 5.

500. "Sporting Notes," *Saint Louis Post Dispatch*, September 22, 1887, 8. Killen also wanted Davies to arrange a ten-round fight with Sullivan. If Killen really wanted to fight Sullivan, he would have soon found him in England because circumstances finally shamed Sullivan into going there to fight. See, "From Pat the Pulverizer," *Bismark Daily Tribune*, October 8, 1887, 1.

501. "Parson Davies to Take Kilrain to Europe," *Chicago Tribune*, August 6, 1887, 3.

502. "Kilrain Wears the Belt," *Chicago Herald*, June 5, 1887, 2; "The Champion Pugilist Presented With a Big Diamond Belt," *Saint Louis Post Dispatch*, August 8, 1887, 5.

503. "Kilraine [sic] Called Off by R. K. Fox," *Chicago Herald*, August 8, 1887, 1.

504. "Pat Killen Wants to Fight Cardiff Again," *Chicago Tribune*, September 9, 1887, 3.

505. "Glover After Cincinnati Heavyweight," *Chicago Tribune*, September 9, 1887, 3; "After Clow-Glover Willing to Meet Him on His Own Terms," *St. Paul Daily Globe*, September 19, 1887, 5.

506. "Beginning of the End-Proceedings in the United States Supreme Court in the Case of the Anarchists," *Inter Ocean*, October 28, 1887, 1; "The Anarchists, Their Case Opened Yesterday before the U. S. Supreme Court," *Boston Journal*, October 28, 1887, 2; "In the Supreme Court Appeal of the Chicago Convicted Anarchists," *Philadelphia Inquirer*, October 28, 1887, 1; "Justice is Done-Destroying Factors of Republican Institutions Pay the Penalty with Their Lives, *Inter Ocean*, November 12, 1887, 1;

507. "'We Deny the Writ.' The Decision of the United States Supreme Court in the Anarchist Case," *Inter Ocean*, November 3, 1887, 1.

508. "Nearing the End-A Habeas Corpus is Relied upon to Save the Condemned Men," *Inter Ocean*, November 10, 1887, 1; "Justice and Mercy. The Governor Says Spies,

Parson, Engel, and Fischer Must Pay the Extreme Penalty," *Inter Ocean*, November 11, 1887, 1; "His Own Executioner, Louis Lingg Cheats the Gallows by Committing a Terrible Suicide," *Inter Ocean*, November 11, 1887, 1.

509. "Sporting Notes," *Saint Louis Post Dispatch*, August 16, 1887, 8; "Sporting Miscellany," *Chicago Tribune*, October 6, 1887, 3.

510. "Sullivan Ready for the Trip to England," *Chicago Tribune*, October 10, 1887, 6; "Sullivan's Arrangements for His European Tour," *Chicago Tribune*, October 16, 1887, 13; "Dude and Plug Ugly," *Chicago Herald*, October 17, 1887, 3; "Farewell, John L.," *Saint Louis Post Dispatch*, October 28, 1887, 8; "John Lawrence Sullivan on a Steamer Bound for Europe," *Chicago Tribune*, October 28, 1887, 6; "Sullivan's Send Off," *Chicago Herald*, October 28, 1887, 6; "John L. Sullivan In London," *Chicago Tribune*, November 6, 1887, 14.

511. "Neither Took A Fall," *Chicago Herald*, October 11, 1887, 1; "Moth and Whitmore Contest Unavailing for Three Hours," *Chicago Tribune*, October 11, 1887, 3.

512. *Chicago Herald*, October 16, 1887, 5.

513. "The Glover-Clow Fight," *Chicago Tribune*, November 13, 1887, 14; "It Was A Drawn Battle," *Chicago Tribune*, November 15, 1887, 6; "Clow the Better Man," *Chicago Herald*, November 15, 1887, 1.

514. "Tom Connors and Evan Lewis Matched," *Chicago Tribune*, December 4, 1887, 5.

515. "Lewis and Connors Matched," *Chicago Herald*, December 8, 1887, 3; "Evan Lewis in Fine Shape," *Chicago Herald*, December 11, 1887, 2; "Englishmen In The Ring," *Chicago Tribune*, December 12, 1887, 9.

516. "Evan Lewis Sick," *Hamilton Daily Democrat*, December 20, 1887, 1; "Evan Lewis Sick," *Decatur Weekly Republican*, December 22, 1887, 12.

Chapter 8 – Making the Big Match - (1888)

517. "Slugging Symposium," *Chicago Herald*, January 8, 1888, 3.

518. "Evan Lewis to Tom Connors," *Chicago Tribune*, January 6, 1888, 5.

519. "Myers Whips Gilmore," *Chicago Herald*, January 19, 1888, 1; "Twenty-Eight Seconds," *Saint Louis Post Dispatch*, January 19, 1888, 8; "Another Victory-Billy Myer The King of the Light Weights," *Streator Daily Free Press*, January 19, 1888, 3; "The Little Wonder," *Daily Pantagraph*, January 20, 1888, 4; "What Gilmore

Says," *Daily Pantagraph*, January 20, 1884, 4; "The Prize Fight," *Streator Daily Free Press*, January 20, 1888, 3; "Notes," *Chicago Tribune*, January 27, 1888, 6.

520. "Jolts From John L.," *San Francisco Call*, May 28, 1905, 7.

521. "A Chat With Pugilists," *Chicago Tribune*, January 26, 1888, 6.

522. "Miscellaneous Notes," *Chicago Tribune*, January 28, 1888, 15.

523. "Muldoon and 'The Strangler' to Wrestle," *Chicago Tribune*, January 30, 1888, 5.

524. "Muldoon Fails to Throw Lewis," *Chicago Tribune*, January 31, 1888, 3.

525. "Muldoon Threw His Man," *Chicago Tribune*, February 3, 1888, 3.

526. "Parson Davies' Big Scheme," *Chicago Herald*, February 5, 1888, 3; "Evans and Muldoon. To Start out under Parson Davies Auspices with Special Offers to All Comers," *Cincinnati Commercial Tribune*, February 6, 1888, 2; "Muldoon on Wrestlers," *Chicago Tribune*, February 5, 1888, 14; "Miscellaneous Notes," *Chicago Herald*, February 5, 1888, 14.

527. "'Strangler' Lewis Loses A Bout," *Chicago Herald*, February 10, 1888, 3.

528. "Jack Fogarty Says That Gallagher Fears to Fight Him," *Cleveland Plain Dealer*, February 24, 1888, 6.

529. "Money Talks, Mr. Muldoon," *Chicago Herald*, February 11, 1888, 3; "Two New Sports In Town," *Chicago Herald*, February 12, 1888, 3; "Muldoon and Carkeek," *Chicago Tribune*, February 14, 1888, 3.

530. "All Kinds of Sports," *Chicago Herald*, February 19, 1888, 3; "Lewis Downed M'Mahon," *Chicago Tribune*, February 15, 1888, 6; "Lewis Thows M'Mahon," *Chicago Herald*, February 15, 1888, 2. Other matches in Chicago included: "The 'Strangler' Was Not Thrown," *Chicago Tribune*, February 17, 1888, 3; "Lewis Makes A Good Show Against a Big Cornish Champion," *Chicago Herald*, February 17, 1888, 3; "Muldoon and McMahon Met," *Chicago Tribune*, February 18, 1888, 2; "Muldoon Had Hard Work," *Chicago Tribune*, February 19, 1888, 11.

531. "Lewis and Gallagher Wrestle," *Chicago Herald*, March 22, 1888, 3;

532. "The English Champion, Jack Wannop Coming to America to Make a Match with the Strangler," *Inter Ocean*, February 3, 1888, 3; "Sporting Notes," *Logansport Journal*, February 11, 1888, 6; "Comes To Meet The 'Stangler'," *Chicago Herald*, February 16, 1888, 2; "A Match Between Lewis and Wannop," *Chicago Tribune*, March 23, 1888, 6.

533. "After Wannop's Wealth," *Inter Ocean*, February 19, 1888, 7; "A Match Between Lewis and Wannop," *Chicago Tribune*, March 23, 1888, 6; "For $1,000 a Side-Evan Lewis and Jack Wannop Matched for a Catch-as-Catch-Can Wrestling Match, *Inter Ocean*, March 24, 1888, 2.

534. "Oscar [sic, Otto] Was There, And So Was His Friend, Evan Lewis 'The Strangler'," *Saint Louis Post Dispatch*, March 27, 1888, 8.

535. "General Sporting Notes," *Chicago Herald*, April 21, 1888, 2; "Miscellaneous Sporting Notes," *Chicago Tribune*, April 22, 1888, 11.

536. "Barkeeps In A Flutter," *Chicago Tribune*, April 7, 1888, 12; "Mayor Roche's Annual Message," *Chicago Tribune*, April 10, 1888, 3; "Getting Good," *Saint Louis Post Dispatch*, May 4, 1888, 8.

537. "The Chief Of Police's Latest Edict," *Chicago Tribune*, May 4, 1888, 6; "The Coming Wrestling Match," *Chicago Tribune*, May 5, 1888, 6; "The Coming Wrestling Match-There Must Be Neither Money Nor Brutality in the Contest," *Chicago Tribune*, May 6, 1888, 6.

538. "General Sporting Notes," *Chicago Herald*, May 5, 1888, 5; "Scraps of Sport," *Chicago Herald*, May 6, 1888, 2; "Tonight's Wrestling Match," *Chicago Tribune*, May 7, 1888, 6; "The Wrestling Match To-Night," *Chicago Herald*, May 7, 1888, 2.

539. "Black Jack" Bonfield was not a nice man. He earned his nickname because of his brutality using a black jack when enforcing the law. His motto was: "The club today saves the bullet tomorrow." Bonfield and Davies had something in common. As a young man Bonfield had been an engineer on the Ohio & Mississippi line that passed through southern Indiana and the home ground of the Reno family. Davies' brother Henry had played a key role in capturing the Reno gang. Bonfield had punctuated all the events relating to the Renos in an odd way. After vigilantes had hung the Reno boys, their father Wilk Reno became drunk and wandered onto the Ohio & Mississippi railroad tracks where he was struck and killed by Bonfield's train. In 1888 Black Jack was the Captain of the Desplaines Street police station in downtown Chicago. From this station he could play havoc with the theaters, sports and saloons and coerce them to make payoffs to remain in operation. His personal agenda and purposes were on the surface consistent with what Mayor Roche wanted. Black Jack could threaten suppression of the saloons, houses or prostitution, gambling joints and even sporting events and then turn his head for the proper amount of money. In February 1889, about nine months after the Wannop/Lewis match, Mayor Roche removed Black Jack from all his positions with the police department. Along with Bonfield the Mayor removed Michael J. Schaack, a Captain of Police in charge of the East Side Precinct and a detective named Lowenstein. The Mayor took these actions because of a report in the Chi-

cago Times showing that Bonfield had permitted gambling and prostitution to continue in Chicago (including the operation of the Louisiana Lottery) in return for payoffs from saloon keepers and gambling operators. However, in May 1888 Bonfield was still in charge, and Davies surely would have had to keep Bonfield happy or risk losing his biggest payday in almost a year. See, "Bonfield's Latest Bomb. The Inspector Yanks Two Editors on a Charge of Criminal Libel," *Inter Ocean*, January 5, 1889, 7; "Bonfield Talks Back. Another Civil Suit to be Instituted and More Criminal Ones Threatened," *Inter Ocean*, January 8, 1889, 7; "Inspector Bonfield Resigns. In a Letter to the Mayor He Tenders His Resignation," *Inter Ocean*, February 14, 1889, 1; "Bonfield and His Gun. The Ex-Inspector Challenges Mr. James J. West to Mortal Combat," *Inter Ocean*, April 13, 1888, 1; "Moving Day at City Hall. Mayor Roche's Last Official Acts Are Those of Kindness," *Inter Ocean*, April 16, 1889, 9.

540. "Champion of the World," *Newark Daily Advocate*, May 8, 1888, 1; "Wannop An Easy Mark," *Chicago Tribune*, May 8, 1888, 1; "Lewis Downs Wannop," *Chicago Herald*, May, 1888, 1.

541. "Wannop Worsted," *Saint Louis Post Dispatch*, May 8, 1888, 8.

542. "The 'Jap' Goes to the Carpet," *Chicago Tribune*, May 9, 1888, 6; "Fun For the Onlookers. Jack Wannop and the 'Jap' Wrestle and Perspire," *Chicago Tribune*, May 13, 1888, 3.

543. "M'Auliffe The Victor," *Chicago Herald*, May 22, 1888, 3; "Glover's Plucky Fight," *Chicago Herald*, May 23, 1888, 2; "McAuliffe Gets the Best of Glover etc.," *Daily Pantagraph*, May 23, 1888, 1; "P. Jay's Comment on the McAuliffe and Glover Pugilistic Chat," *Saint Louis Post Dispatch*, May 27, 1888, 8.

544. "Killen & Cardiff," *Saint Louis Post Dispatch*, June 24, 1888, 6; "Cardiff Knocked Out By Killen," *Chicago Herald*, June 27, 1888, 2; "Killen Against All Comers," *Chicago Herald*, June 28, 1888, 2.

545. "An Offer to Pugilist Godfrey," *Saint Louis Post Dispatch*, June 30, 1888, 8; "A Pair of Colored Fighters," *Chicago Tribune*, July 1, 1888, 15; Doherty, W. J., *In the Days of the Giants* (George C. Harrap & Co. Ltd., 1931), 47-55.

546. Lindberg, Richard, *The Gambler King of Clark Street: Michael C. McDonald and the Rise of Chicago's Democratic Machine* (SIU Press, 2008), 139.

547. "Miscellaneous Matters," *Chicago Tribune*, September 9, 1888, 14; "General Sporting Gossip," *Chicago Herald*, September 9, 1888, 6; "Jack Burke's Australian Ventures," *Saint Louis Post Dispatch*, September 9, 1888, 8.

548. "The Battery D Entertainment," *Chicago Tribune*, September 15, 1888, 3.

549. "Killen and Wannop Have A Set-To," *Chicago Tribune*, September 18, 1888, 6; "Easy Work For Killen," *Chicago Herald*, September 18, 1888, 2.

550. "Killed In A Prize-Fight," *Chicago Tribune*, September 24, 1888, 3; "The Death of Fulljames," *Saint Louis Post Dispatch*, September 25, 1888, 8; "Fact About Fulljames," *Saint Louis Post Dispatch*, September 27, 1888, 8.

551. "Five To One On Fifer," *Chicago Herald*, October 16, 1888, 3.

552. "Kilrain's Offer to Sullivan," *Chicago Herald*, December 1, 1888, 2.

553. "Gossip About The Pugilists," *Chicago Tribune*, December 1, 1882, 5.

554. Ibid.

555. "Sullivan Sizes Up Mitchell," *Saint Louis Post Dispatch*, December 2, 1882, 7; "Sullivan Looking for a Fight," *Chicago Tribune*, December 2, 1888, 14.

556. "Parson Davies On Pugilism," *Chicago Herald*, December 9, 1888, 15.

557. "Sporting Notes," *Saint Louis Post Dispatch*, December 8, 1888, 8; "Sporting Notes," *Saint Louis Post Dispatch*, December 11, 1888, 8.

558. "Mitchell and Kilrain, Arrival in Chicago of the Celebrated Pugilists," *Chicago Tribune*, December 17, 1888, 3; "To Meet in Canada," *Saint Louis Post Dispatch*, December 17, 1888, 3; "Kilrain Will Fight," *Saint Louis Post Dispatch*, December 17, 1888, 3; "Kilrain Has Accepted," *Chicago Tribune*, December 23, 1888, 15.

559. "Kilrain and Mitchell," *Chicago Herald*, December 18, 1888, 3.

560. "The Guyed Mitchell," *Chicago Tribune*, December 18, 1888, 7; "Kilrain and Mitchell," *Chicago Herald*, December 18, 1888, 3.

561. "Kilrain and Mitchell," *Chicago Herald*, December 20, 1888, 3.

562. A Master in Chancery, who was not a judge but more like an appointed insider who was a step above a justice of the peace, reviewed the application and supporting affidavit and recommended that the application should be granted. See, "They Are Not Fighters," *Chicago Herald*, December 21, 1888, 3; "Kilrain, Mitchell and the Law," *Saint Louis Post Dispatch*, December 23, 1888, 16.

563. "Parson Davies a Slugger the Redoubtable Sportsman Makes His Debut at a Chicago Theatre," *Omaha Herald*, December 24, 1888, 2; "Pugilist 'Blazing Mad'.

Mitchell and Kilrain in Biding from the Chicago Police, *New York Herald*, December 23, 1888, 14.

564. "Bloody Barroom Work," *Galveston Daily News*, December 29, 1888, 1; "Mitchell Driven to Bay," *Chicago Tribune*, December 28, 1888, 6; "Charley Mitchell In A Row," *Chicago Herald*, December 28, 1888, 5; "Charley Mitchell Assaulted by Roughs In Cleveland," *Toronto Daily Mail*, December 31, 1888, 2; "Fight Without Stakes," *Boston Daily Globe*, December 28, 1888, 10.

565. "Jackson Wins A Fight," *Chicago Herald*, December 29, 1888, 2; "Jackson As A Fighter," *Chicago Herald*, December 30, 1888, 11; "Cardiff and Jackson May Meet," *Chicago Herald*, January 5, 1889, 6.

566. "Mitchell and Kilrain," *Saint Louis Post Dispatch*, December 31, 1888, 3.

Chapter 9 – The Greatest Fighter Ever - (1889)

567. See note 2 above.

568. "About Davies and Prize Fighters," Oakland Tribune, June 29, 1905, 11.

569. "The Parson," *Atlanta Constitution*, April 23, 1916, 40.

570. "Mitchell and Kilrain Hissed at Buffalo," *Chicago Tribune*, January 5, 1889, 3; "Sullivan on His Way to Toronto," *Chicago Tribune*, January 6, 1889, 11: "May Arrange A Fight," *Chicago Herald*, January 6, 1889, 11.

571. "Made A Match At Last," *Chicago Herald*, January 8, 1889, 5; "Sullivan and Kilrain," *Saint Louis Post Dispatch*, January 8, 1889, 1; "Sullivan and Kilrain," *Chicago Tribune*, January 8, 1889, 6.

572. "Articles of agreement entered into this 7th day of January, 1889, between Jake Kilrain, of Baltimore, Md. and John L. Sullivan, of Boston, Mass: Said Jake Kilrain and said John L. Sullivan hereby agree to fight a fair stand-up fight, according to the new rules of the London prize ring, by which said Jake Kilrain and said John L. Sullivan hereby do agree to be bound. Said fight shall be for the sum of $10,000 a side and the belt representing the championship of the world, and shall take place on the 8th of July, 1889, within 200 miles of New Orleans, in the State of Louisiana, the man winning the toss to give the opposite party ten days notice of the place; said Jake Kilrain, and John L. Sullivan to fight at catch weights. The men shall be in the ring between the hours of 8 a.m. and 12 noon, or the man absent shall forfeit the battle money. The expenses of ropes and stakes shall be borne by each party, share and share alike. In pursuance of this agreement the sum of $5,000 a side is now deposited with the sporting editor of the New

York Clipper, who shall be stakeholder. The final and last deposit of $5,000 a side shall be made on the 13th day of April, 1889, in New York City, where the final stakeholder shall be agreed upon, if not agreed upon before. The referee to be appointed at the ring side and the toss for choice of battleground to be on the 8th day of June, between the hours of 8 p.m. and 10 p.m. at Charley Johnson's store on Fulton street in Brooklyn, N. Y., by the participants or their representatives. Said final deposit must be put up not later than the day aforesaid, and either party failing to make good the amount due at the time and place named shall forfeit the money down. In case of managerial interference, the referee, if appointed, or the stakeholder shall name the next time and place of meeting, if possible, on the same day or in the same week, either party failing to appears at the time and place specified by that official to lose battle money. Stakes not to be given up unless my mutual consent or until fairly won or lost by the fight. Due notice shall be give to both parties of the time and place for giving the money up. In pursuance of this agreement we hereto attach our names. s/John L. Sullivan, s/Jake Kilrain, per W. E. H. Witnesses, L. B. Allen, John W. Barnett." "Pugilists Use Pens," *St. Paul Daily Globe*, January 8, 1889, 1; "To Meet Near New Orleans," *Sun*, January 8, 1889, 3.

573. "Sullivan Eager to Fight," *Chicago Herald*, January 9, 1889, 5.

574. "Notes," *Chicago Tribune*, January 12, 1889, 7.

575. "Kilrain and Mitchell Egged," *St. Paul Daily Globe*, January 12, 1889, 5.

576. "'Parson' Davies Back," *Chicago Herald*, January 18, 1889, 3.

577. "Charley Mitchell Off For Home," *Chicago Herald*, January 17, 1889, 5.

578. "In The Arena of Sport," *Saint Louis Post Dispatch*, January 18, 1889, 5.

579. "'Parson' Davies Back," *Chicago Herald*, January 18, 1889, 3.

580. "M'Auliffe Lives on Easy Street," *Salt Lake Herald-Republican,* September 12, 1909, 7.

581. "Myers and McAuliffe," *Streator Daily Free Press*, January 31, 1889, 3: "Billy Myer In Shape," *Chicago Herald*, February 1, 1889, 2; "M'Auliffe In Training," *Chicago Tribune*, February 3, 1889, 13; "The Cyclone," *Streator Daily Free Press*, February 5, 1889, 3; "McAuliffe the Favorite," *Saint Louis Post Dispatch*, February 5, 1889, 8; "The Pedigree, Career and Record of Fighter Jack M'Auliffe," *Saint Louis Post Dispatch*, February 6, 1889, 8; "Meyer's [sic] Condition," *Saint Louis Post Dispatch*, February 8, 1889, 8; "Ready For The Battle," *Chicago Tribune*, February 8, 1889, 2; "Both Are In Condition," *Chicago Tribune*, February 9, 1889, 8; "Ready

For The Fight," *Chicago Herald*, February 9, 1889, 3; "Myer Takes A Rest Over Sunday," *Chicago Tribune*, February 11, 1889, 8; "Ready For The Battle," *Chicago Herald*, February 11, 1889, 2; "Will Fight To-Night," *Saint Louis Post Dispatch*, February 12, 1889, 2; "The Date of the Fight," *Chicago Tribune*, February 12, 1889, 3; "Money To Back Myer," *Chicago Herald*, February 12, 1889, 2; "Myer Is In Fine Form," *Chicago Herald*, February 10, 1889, 11 (Parson Davies is holding $15,000 in bets on the fight); "Extra - 4:30 A. M. Myer-M'Auliffe Fight," *Chicago Tribune*, February 13, 1889, 1; "Extra - 7:30 O'Clock A.M. Both Men In the Ring," *Chicago Herald*, February 13, 1889, 1-2; "Latest Edition-Declared a Draw-Unexpected Result of the Much Talked of Light Weight Fight," *Saint Louis Post Dispatch*, February 13, 1889, 1; "A Draw," *Streator Daily Free Press*," February 13, 1889, 3; "It Was Called A Draw," *Chicago Herald*, February 14, 1889, 2; "Extra! Drawn Battle," *National Police Gazette*, February 23, 1889, 6.

582. "They Fought To A Draw," *Chicago Herald*, February 14, 1889, 1.

583. "A Mockery Of A Prize Fight," *Chicago Tribune*, February 14, 1889, 4.

584. "Sporting In The West," *Chicago Tribune*, February 24, 1889, 3.

585. "Myer Anxious To Fight," *Chicago Tribune*, February 16, 1889, 1; "Billy Myer Is In Town," *Chicago Herald*, February 16, 1889, 6; "Echoes Of The Fight," *Chicago Herald*, February 17, 1889, 11.

586. "Weir and Murphy May Fight Out West," *Chicago Herald*, February 28, 1889, 3; "Weir and Murphy May Fight Near Chicago," *Chicago Tribune*, February 28, 1889, 3.

587. "Sporting Notes," *Chicago Tribune*, March 4, 1889, 6.

588. "Weir and Murphy Will Fight," *Chicago Herald*, March 4, 1889, 3.

589. "General Sporting Notes," *Chicago Herald*, March 9, 1889, 3; "Among the Fighters, *Chicago Herald*, March 10, 1889, 11; "The Weir-Murphy Fight," *Chicago Herald*, March 11, 1889, 2; "The Weir-Murphy Fight," *Chicago Tribune*, March 20, 1889, 3; "Notes," *Chicago Tribune*, March 21, 1889, 5; "Ike Weir in Fine Form," *Chicago Herald*, March 23, 1889, 2. Isaac O'Neil Weir, the "Belfast Spider," was born in Lurgan, County Armagh, in Northern Ireland. He was five feet five and three-quarters inches tall and weighed about one hundred eighteen pounds. He began fighting in 1883 at Liverpool and had moved up the ranks in a deliberate fashion. He had bested such fighters as William Snee, Martin Burns, Young Sullivan, Jack Farrell and Tommy Danforth. He had also fought draws in 1887 with Tommy Murphy and with Tommy Warren in fights for the featherweight championship. His fight with Murphy was his second fight for the featherweight cham-

pionship of the world. Frank Murphy was from Birmingham, England. He was somewhere between twenty-one and twenty-four years old and stood five feet four inches tall and weighed one hundred twenty six pounds. By 1887 Frank had been fighting for five years. In August 1888 Murphy fought a forty-nine round draw with Jack Havlin at New York. In January 1889 he had defeated Jimmy Hagen of Philadelphia in a ten-round match and that same month beat Johnny Griffin in an eighteen round glove fight in Boston. Murphy was reputed to have big fists for a little man and was a hard hitter. He was to train at John Kline's place in Beloit.

590. Less than a month after the incident with Dunne, Sullivan was back at the Two Kellys, where this time he nearly slugged an eighteen-year-old actress Gracie Waite. Ms. Waite was the daughter of a prominent New York dentist, who had died several years earlier. When she reached the age of sixteen, the legal age for independence, Gracie went out on her own as a performer at the Casino theatre in New York. She was between jobs at the time and she was out for a night on the town, which included a visit to the Two Kelly's. Sullivan became interested in Gracie and attempted to open a familiar conversation with her. She became frigid and dignified and wanted Sullivan to mind his own business. Sullivan approached her as if he intended to slug the 100 pound Gracie when she hit him above the belt. Sullivan was apparently astonished that this little girl would hit him, and he quietly turned away. However, the next day he was roasted in the press for attempting to assault a 100 pound teenager. See, "Tried To Kill John L. Sullivan," *Chicago Tribune*, March 10, 1889, 9; "Sullivan Makes Trouble," *Chicago Tribune*, March 11, 1889, 3 (Sullivan drunk again at the Two Kelly's); "John L. Is Very Drunk," *Chicago Herald*, March 12, 1889, 2; "Sullivan Knocked Out," *Chicago Tribune*, April 7, 1889, 26.

591. "Ike Weir and Murphy," *Sunday Herald*, March 31, 1889, 12.

592. "Extra! 7:15 A. M. The Weir-Murphy Fight," *Chicago Tribune*, March 31, 1889, 1; "Weir and Murphy Met-Eighty Rounds And No Decision," *Chicago Herald*, April 1, 1889, 2; "Another Draw," *Daily Pantagraph*, April 1, 1889, 1; "The Weir-Murphy Fight," *Chicago Tribune*, April 1, 1889, 2.

593. "Will Not Fight Again," *Chicago Tribune*, April 2, 1889, 3.

594. "Sot Sullivan Hustled Out of Town," *Chicago Tribune*, May 13, 1889, 3; "Sullivan In Training Quarters," *Chicago Tribune*, May 19, 1889, 13; "A Talk With Sullivan," *Chicago Tribune*, May 19, 1889, 31; "Progress of Sullivan's Training," *Chicago Tribune*, May 22, 1889, 2; "Sullivan on Pugilism-John L. In Training For the Mill With Kilrain," *Streator Daily Free Press*, May 29, 1889, 3.

595. "Sullivan, Muldoon and Cleary," *Salt Lake Herald*, May 26, 1889, 1.

596. "John L. Sullivan at Cincinnati," *Chicago Tribune*, May 29, 1889, 3.

597. Advertisement, *World*, May 31, 1889, 5.

598. "Knights of the Knuckle," *Chicago Tribune*, June 2, 1889, 28.

599. "Kilrain's Bereavement," *Chicago Tribune*, June 1, 1889, 3.

600. "Twenty-Seven Fierce Rounds," *Chicago Herald*, June 6, 1889, 5.

601. "Sporting Notes," *Pittsburg Dispatch*, January 17, 1889, 6; "Killen Talks Back," *St. Paul Daily Globe*, June 11, 1889.

602. "Pat Killen's Profitable Joke," *Chicago Herald*, June 18, 1889, 5; "Killen Wants the Earth," *Chicago Tribune*, June 1, 1889, 3; "Killen and McAuliffe Will Fight," *Chicago Tribune*, June 3, 1889, 6; "General Sporting Notes," *Chicago Tribune*, June 4, 1889, 6.

603. "Sailor Brown Knocked Out," *Chicago Herald*, March 14, 1889, 2.

604. "Jackson, The Colored Fighter," *Chicago Herald*, June 29, 1889, 3; "A Talk With Peter Jackson," *Chicago Tribune*, June 30, 1889, 1.

605. "A 'Fine Worker' Pardoned; Joseph C. Mackin Set Free," *New York Times*, July 3, 1889, 2; "Joe Mackin Set Free," *Chicago Herald*, July 3, 1889, 1; "Mackin Surprised At The News," Chicago Herald, July 3, 1889, 1; "Why Mackin Was Pardoned," *Chicago Herald*, July 3, 1889, 2; "Five Years For Perjury, The Crimes for Which Mackin Was Sent to Joliet-His Career," *Chicago Herald*, July 3, 1889, 2; "Joseph Mackin Free," *Chicago Herald*, July 3, 1889, 4; "Mackin Pardoned," *Pantagraph*, July 3, 1889, 4; "Joseph's Welcome Home," *Chicago Tribune*, July 4, 1889, 9; "The Pardon of Joe Mackin," *Chicago Tribune*, July 8, 1889, 4.

606. "Will See the Fight," *Chicago Tribune*, July 1, 1889, 3; "Luke Short Going to the Fight," *Chicago Tribune*, July 3, 1889, 2; "Nearer The Ring Side," *Chicago Tribune*, July 3, 1889, 2.

607. "A Braidwood Benefit," *Daily Inter Ocean*, July 3, 1889, 7; "Will Spar for the Miners' Benefit," *Chicago Tribune*, July 3, 1889, 6.

608. "Fistiana," *Oakland Tribune*, Feburary 6, 1890, 4.

609. "Strikers Remain Firm-Braidwood Miners Will Not Accept a 10 Cents Reduction, but Will Compromise," *Inter Ocean*, June 1, 1889, 9; "Starving at Braidwood-Terrible Result of the Miners' Strike at That Point," *Saint Louis Republic*, June 22, 1889, 3; "Hunger At Braidwood," *Daily Gazette*, June 28, 1889, 4.

610. Mrs. M. C. M'Donald, *Inter Ocean*, October 11, 1889, 1. This just one of many articles relating to McDonald's marital issues provide as an example.

611. "M. C. M' Donald's Money, The Democratic Leader on the Lake Street Elevated Road's Bond. *Inter Ocean*, February 27, 1889, 8; "The Great Conspiracy," *Inter Ocean*, June 8, 1889, 6.

612. See note 2 above.

613. "Peter Jackson at Milwaukee," *Chicago Tribune*, July 4, 1889, 6; "Jackson and Lees Spar," *Saint Louis Republic*, July 5, 1889, 3; "Jackson Please Milwaukee," *St. Paul Daily Globe*, July 5, 1889, 1.

614. "A Talk With Peter Jackson," *Chicago Tribune*, June 30, 1889, 12.

615. "General Sporting Notes," *Chicago Tribune*, June 7, 1889, 7; "Jake Kilrain Visits Boston," *Chicago Tribune*, June 8, 1889, 7.

616. "Please With Abita Springs," *Chicago Tribune*, June 26, 1889, 3; "The Clash of Arms," *Salt Lake Herald*, June 30, 1889, 1.

617. "Planning For The Fight," *Chicago Tribune*, June 28, 1889, 6.

618. "Kilrain Is Full Of Confidence," *Chicago Tribune*, June 24, 1889, 3; "Sullivan Is Training Hard," *Chicago Tribune*, June 24, 1889, 3; "Jake Kilrain At Work," *Chicago Tribune*, June 2, 1889, 9;

619. "What Jake Kilrain Says," *Chicago Tribune*, June 28, 1889, 6; "On To New Orleans!," *Chicago Tribune*, July 1, 1889, 3.

620. "A Talk With Luke Short," *Chicago Tribune*, July 12, 1889, 2.

621. "Arrangements For The Fight," *Chicago Tribune*, July 7, 1889, 10; "In The Ring," *Chicago Tribune*, July 9, 1889, 2.

622. "John L. Is Up Against More Trouble," *San Francisco Call*, March 21, 1910, 9.

623. "Dempsey Like Cardiff-Old Ones and Those of To-Day: Chat With Parson Davies," *Referee*, September 18, 1918, 1.

624. "John L. Leaves Hurriedly," *Chicago Tribune*, July 11, 1889, 2.

625. "Sullivan Is Free Again," *Chicago Tribune*, July 12, 1889, 2.

626. "'Parson' Davies On The Fight," *Chicago Tribune*, July 13, 1889, 2.

627. "Mrs. Kilrain Hears The News," *Chicago Tribune*, July 9, 1889, 2.

628. "How Muldoon Escaped," *Galveston Daily News*, July 13, 1889, 1.

629. "Sullivan Is Here," *Chicago Tribune*, July 13, 1889, 1.

630. "Sullivan Is Here," *Chicago Tribune*, July 13, 1889, 1.

631. "General Sporting Notes," *Chicago Tribune*, July 10, 1889, 6.

632. No Headline, *Cleveland Gazette*, July 27, 1889, 3.

633. "Jackson Plays With The 'Sailor'," *Chicago Tribune*, July 12, 1889, 6.

634. "To See A Dusky Giant-An Immense Crowd At Battery D," *Chicago Herald*, July 12, 1889, 2.

635. "Sporting Notes," *Chicago Tribune*, July 23, 1889, 3.

636. "The 'Parson' Will Manage Jackson," *Chicago Tribune*, July 13, 1889, 3.

637. "Junior Cup," *Observer*, July 20, 1889, 13. Jackson's other measurements in 1889 were: neck 16 ½ inches, length of arm and hand 33 inches, biceps 15 inches, upper one third of forearm 12 ½ inches, middle third 9 ½ inches, lower third 8 ½ inches, Chest 40 inches, Waist 32 inches.

638. "Charlie Mitchell As A Tramp," *Chicago Herald*, July 14, 1889, 9.

639. "Kilrain's Pretty Mug," *Chicago Herald*, July 14, 1889, 9; "Kilrain Visits Chicago," *Chicago Tribune*, July 15, 1889, 2.

640. "Kilrain Says He Wasn't Hurt-He Just 'Weakened Away' and Couldn't Fight Any Longer," *Chicago Tribune*, July 15, 1889, 2: "Kilrain's Condition," *Reno Evening Gazette,* July 15, 1889, 2.

641. "Kilrain And Peter Jackson," *Salt Lake Herald*, July 16, 1889, 1.

642. "Sullivan Buys A Jag," *Chicago Herald*, July 15, 1889, 2; "The World's Champion," *Sandusky Daily Register*, July 15, 1889, 1.

643. "No Use Debating It," *Las Vegas Daily Optic*, July 15, 1889, 2.

644. "Democrats to Organize," *Albuquerque Morning Democrat*, July 16, 1889, 2.

645. "Sullivan Still Here," *Chicago Tribune*, July 16, 1889, 3.

646. "Peter Jackson's Sparring Tour," *Chicago Tribune*, July 19, 1889, 5.

647. "The Australian in Cincinnati," *St. Louis Post Dispatch*," July 21, 1889, 16; "Prohibited Jackson's Exhibition," *Chicago Tribune*, July 23, 1889, 3.

648. "Parson Davies As A Slugger," *Chicago Tribune*, July 23, 1889, 3.

649. "Peter Jackson at Detroit," *Chicago Tribune*, July 26, 1889, 6. This theater where Jackson appeared had been built by C. J. Whitney of Detroit and was used for a wide variety of theatrical entertainment.

650. "State Briefs," *Kalamazoo Gazette*, July 26, 1889, 5.

651. "Donohue's Generous Offer-A Purse of $7,000 for a Finish Fight between Kilrain and Jackson," *New York Herald*, July 26, 1889, 8; "Kilrain May Meet Jackson," *Sun*, July 27, 1889, 6; "Kilrain and Jackson," *Salt Lake Daily Tribune*, July 27, 1889, 1; "Wants Kilrain to Fight Jackson," *Omaha Daily Bee*, July 27, 1889, 2; "John L. Sullivan," *St. Louis Post Dispatch*, July 28, 1889, 1. Kilrain says that he talked to Jackson at the Hoffman House and asked him if he would fight Sullivan. Jackson responded: "Well, I'm off on vacation now, [but] . . . The California Club makes all my matches."

652. "Peter Jackson at Cleveland," *Chicago Tribune*, July 27, 1889, 3.

653. "Peter Jackson at Buffalo," *Saginaw News*, July 31, 1889, 3; "Peter Jackson's Bad Luck. Jumped on by an Irish Giant and Thumped by Tom Lees," *Oregonian*, July 31, 1889, 1; "Peter Jackson Downed," *Inter Ocean*, July 31, 1889, 6.

654. "Peter Jackson Thrown," *Wheeling Register*, July 31, 1889, 1; "An Exciting Fight," *Inter Ocean*, July 31, 1889, 6.

655. "Jackson Slugged," *St. Louis Post Dispatch*, July 31, 1889, 8;

656. "Will Not See Peter Jackson," *St. Louis Post Dispatch*, August 1, 1889, 8.

657. "Sporting Notes," *St. Louis Post Dispatch*, August 9, 1889, 8; "Boxing And The Boxers," *Chicago Tribune*, August 11, 1889, 5.

658. "Jackson Was Not Touched," *Daily Pantagraph*, August 6, 1889, 4; "Sporting Notes," *St. Louis Post Dispatch*, August 6, 1889, 8.

659. "Peter Jackson's Program," *Chicago Tribune*, August 7, 1889, 6; "Peter Jackson vs. Billy Baker," *Chicago Tribune*, August 9, 1889, 3.

660. "Jackson and Lannon-Prevented from Fighting by the Boston Chief of Police," *Wheeling Register*, August 19, 1889, 1.

661. "Took Two Rounds," *St. Louis Post Dispatch*, August 10, 1889, 8.

662. "Fallon Was Astonished," *Brooklyn Eagle*, August 20, 1889, 5; "Jackson Easily Bests Fallon," *St. Louis Post Dispatch*, August 20, 1889, 8.

663. "Peter Jackson vs. Billy Baker," *Chicago Tribune*, August 9, 1889, 3; "Sporting Notes," *St. Louis Post Dispatch*, August 9, 1889, 8; "They Think Jackson No Good-Even Hoboken Fighters Laugh at Him, To Meet Ginger M'Cormick," *New York Herald*, August 9, 1889, 8; "About Peter Jackson," *Pittsburg Dispatch*, August 18, 1889, 6; "Sporting Notes," *Evening Herald*, August 9, 1889, 7; "Boxing And The Boxers," *Chicago Tribune*, August 11, 1889, 5; "Jackson As A Fighter," *St. Louis Post Dispatch*, August 20, 1889, 5; "No Flies On The Parson," *Chicago Tribune*, August 25, 1889; "General Sporting Notes," *Chicago Tribune*, August 26, 1889, 3.

664. "No Flies On the Parson," *Chicago Tribune*, August 25, 1889, 1.

665. "Off for an Ocean Race-Crowds Watch the Starts of the City of New York and the Teutonic," *New York Herald*, August 22, 1889, 3.

666. "Sports of Different Sorts," *New York Herald*, August 31, 1889, 8; "Peter Jackson-The Black Pugilist is Being Lionized in London," *Evening News*, August 31, 1889, 2; "General Sporting Notes," Chicago Tribune, September 10, 1889, 6.

667. "General City News," *Cedar Rapids Evening Gazette*, September 2, 1889, 1; "Smith to Fight Jackson and Slavin," *Boston Globe*, September 9, 1889, 11; "Jem Smith and Frank Slavin Matched-Peter Jackson's Debut Arranged For," *New York Herald*, September 8, 1889, 11; "Peter Can Box with Jem," *San Francisco Bulletin*; September 10, 1889, 1. Slavin left Australia in July 1889 and arrived in England on August 11, 1889. Like Jackson, Slavin was anxious to arrange matches with the top heavyweights there, with the ultimate goal of securing the title of heavyweight champion of England and thereby creating the circumstance that would force Sullivan into a fight.

668. "Peter Jackson Wined and Dined," *Wheeling Register*, September 9, 1889, 1; "Peter Jackson; England; Lord DeClifford; Sir John Astley," *Savannah Tribune*, September 21, 1889, 2; "The Color Line-Is Not Drawn So Close In England As In America," *Sacramento Daily Record-Union*, September 17, 1889, 1; "Anglo-Colonial Notes, *Te Aroha News*, October 26, 1889, 6.

669. "Jem Smith and Peter Jackson," *Sacramento Daily Record-Union*, September 27, 1889, 1.

670. "Sporting Notes," *Evening Herald*, September 27, 1889, 8; "Sporting Notes," *Decatur Daily Republican*, September 28, 1889, 2; "Conditions of the Battle," *Pittsburg Dispatch*, October 5, 1889, 6. In the event of the contest falling through, the men will be awarded £100 each for training expenses. In the event of either man failing to appear, he would be required to forfeit £100.

671. "In The Arena of Sport," *St. Louis Post Dispatch*, October 5, 1889, 16.

672. "Jackson Whips Smith," *Chicago Tribune*, November 11, 1889, 1; "Jackson Whips Smith," *Chicago Herald*, November 11, 1889, 1; "Smith Slaughtered," *St. Louis Post Dispatch*, November 11, 1889, 3; "Pugilistic," *Wanganui Herald*, December 2, 1889, 2; "Jem Smith Used As An Exercise Bag By Jackson," *Toronto Daily Mail*, November 11, 1889, 2.

673. "The Ring-Nothing But Praise For Jackson," *Toronto Daily Mail*, November 12, 1889, 2.

674. "Congratulations," *Desert News*, November 14, 1889, 1.

675. "Jackson After The Battle," *Chicago Herald*, November 12, 1889, 3.

676. "Parson Davies A Prime Favorite," *Chicago Tribune,* December 23, 1889, 6.

677. "John L.'s Fighting Price-List," *Chicago Herald*, November 16, 1889, 2.

678. "John L. Insists On His Price," *Chicago Herald*, November 22, 1889, 3; "Another Offer to Sullivan," *Daily Nevada State Journal*, November 22, 1889, 2.

679. "Peter Jackson In Clover," *Chicago Herald*, December 5, 1889, 7.

680. "Anglo-Colonial Notes-London, November 2, 1889," *Te Aroha News*, December 18, 1889, 6.

681. "Jack Fallon," *Brooklyn Eagle*, January 13, 1890, 1.

682. "Jackson Ignores Sullivan," *Cleveland Gazette*, November 30, 1889, 2; "Slugger Sullivan-He Is Willing to Fight Pete Jackson," *Decatur Daily Dispatch*, November 15, 1889, 1; "Pete Jackson or Any Other Man," *Boston Daily Globe*, November 30, 1889, 17; "How Jackson Would Fight Sullivan," *Chicago Herald*, December 10, 1889, 6.

683. The 1911 Census of Belfast, Ireland shows a Hugh & Annie Suffern (both aged 60) and their daughters Annie (26) and Nettie (25) living in 16 Glenburn Park, Clifton, Co Antrim. The entry shows that they had 5 children in total.

684. "Must Wear Gloves," *Daily Nevada State Journal*, January 18, 1890, 2.

685. "The Royal Peter Jackson," *Sun*, June 22, 1904, 12.

686. "Will Fight In 'Frisco," *Chicago Herald*, December 29, 1889, 12; "Jackson Will Fight Sullivan," *Daily Pantagraph*, December 31, 1889, 4; "Peter Jackson Coming Back," *Chicago Tribune*, January 8, 1890, 6.

687. "Sullivan's Sentence Is First," *Chicago Tribune*, December 30, 1889, 3.

Chapter 10 – Climbing Higher - (1890)

688. See note 2 above.

689. "Parson Davies Arrives," *Chicago Tribune*, January 20, 1890, 3.

690. "The Young Men of Muscle etc.," *New York Times*, March 23, 1890; "The Jackson-Sullivan Match," *Chicago Tribune*, April 4, 1890, 2; "Several Propositions and Challenges Posted at the Puritan Club," *Chicago Tribune*, April 17, 1890, 6; "General Sporting Notes," *Chicago Tribune*, June 5, 1890, 6.

691. "Shugert's Future," *Burlington Hawk-Eye {from the Chicago Times}*, August 19, 1890, 4.

692. "Billy Myer And Harry Gilmore," *Chicago Tribune*, January 6, 1890, 3; "Will Myer Meet M'Auliffe?," *Chicago Tribune*, January 7, 1890, 5; "Myer, Gilmore, and M'Auliffe," *Chicago Tribune*, January 8, 1890, 6; "Jack M'Auliffe In Town," *Chicago Tribune*, January 12, 1890, 7; "Billy Myer Ready to Fight," *Chicago Tribune*, January 13, 1890, 5; "Sporting Notes," *Chicago Tribune*, January 22, 1890, 3. Davies benefit earned $727 for the Servite Sisters.

693. "Michael Davitt on Disunion," *New Zealand Tablet*, March 21, 1890, Page 19.

694. "General Sporting Notes," *St. Louis Post Dispatch*, January 16, 1890, 3.

695. "The Strong Boy's Account of His Trip Abroad," *Brooklyn Eagle*, January 13, 1890, 1.

696. New York Passenger Lists, 1820-1957, Charles E Davies, Arrival Date: January 19, 1890, Port of Departure: Liverpool, England and Queenstown, Ireland, Destination: United States of America, Port of Arrival: New York, Ship Name: *Britannic*, Passenger Ships and Images' database, Line: 48, Microfilm Serial: M237, Microfilm Roll: M237_543, List Number: 71.

697. "Parson Davies Arrives," *Chicago Tribune*, January 20, 1890, 3; "Parson Davies Home Returning from His Trip Abroad," *Chicago Herald*, January 20, 1890, 2; "Notes of Numerous Sports," *Philadelphia Inquirer*, January 20, 1890, 6.

698. "Peter Jackson Back. Arrival at Quarantine on the Adriatic-What He Thinks of John L. Sullivan," *New York Herald*, January 27, 1890, 10; "Pete Jackson Arrives Ready to Fight John L. Sullivan," *Chicago Herald*, January 27, 1890, 1.

699. Advertisement, *Brooklyn Eagle*, January 27, 1890, 3.

700. "Jackson's Return," *Pittsburg Dispatch*, February 02, 1890, 6.

701. "Hyde and Behman's Theater," *Brooklyn Eagle*, January 28, 1890, 4.

702. "The Australian Pugilist in Music Ball," *Boston Journal*, January 30, 1890, 1; "Telegraphic Brevities," *San Antonio Daily Light*, January 30, 1890, 1.

703. "Jackson Estimate," *Salt Lake Herald*, February 15, 1890, 1.

704. "'Parson' Davies Home," *Chicago Tribune*, February 6, 1890, 3.

705. "Jake Kilrain Gets a Job," *Chicago Tribune*, January 21, 1890, 6.

706. "Jake Kilrain Heard From," *Chicago Tribune*, February 6, 1890, 3.

707. "Kilrain Wins The Fight," *Chicago Tribune*, February 3, 1890, 3; "The Prize Ring-The Kilrain-Muldoon Combine," *Time Picayune*, February 5, 1890, 2;

708. "Bezenah's Cincinnati Record," *Chicago Tribune*, February 15, 1890, 2.

709. "Met Death In The Ring," *Chicago Tribune*, February 15, 1890, 2; "A Member of Kilrain's Company Kills A Tenderfoot in the Ring," *St. Paul Daily Globe*, February 15, 1890, 5.

710. Van Every, *Muldoon, the solid man of sport: his amazing story as related for the first time by him to his friend* (Frederick A. Stokes Company, 1929), 176-177.

711. "Bezenah Set At Liberty," *Chicago Tribune*, February 16, 1890, 4; "Funeral of Thomas James," *Chicago Tribune*, February 17, 1890, 3.

712. "The Wounded Light-Weight," *St. Louis Post Dispatch*, March 24, 1891, 10.

713. "Corbett To Meet Kilrain," *Chicago Tribune*, February 12, 1890, 5.

714. See note 724 above at 178.

715. "Corbett Coming to New Orleans to Fight Kilrain," *Times Picayune*, February 8, 1890, 2.

716. "Corbett In Town," *Times Picayune*, February 13, 1890, 3.

717. "Sullivan's Offer To Jackson," *Brooklyn Eagle*, February 12, 1890, 5.

718. "What Sullivan Says of Jackson," *Salt Lake Herald*, February 14, 1890, 1

719. "Peter Declines With Thanks," *Chicago Tribune*, February 12, 1890, 5; "Peter Jackson Declines To Spar Three Rounds With Slugger Sullivan," *St. Paul Daily Globe*, February 12, 1890, 1.

720. "Fistiana," *Oakland Tribune*, February 6, 1890, 4.

721. "Corbett A Wonder, The Young Californian Surprises Kilrain and the Crowd," *Time Picayune*, February 18, 1890, 2; Corbett Wins The Fight," *Chicago Tribune*, February 18, 1890, 3; "James J. Corbett 'Does' Kilrain," *National Police Gazette*, March 8, 1890, 10.

722. "Kilrain to Retire Temporarily," *Chicago Tribune*, February 22, 1890, 6.

723. "General Sporting Notes," *Chicago Tribune*, February 21, 1890, 3; "The Ring. Sullivan on Corbett's Victory," *Times Picayune*, February 25, 1890, 8.

724. Advertisement, *Washington Bee*, February 15, 1890, 3; "Peter Jackson," *Salt Lake Herald*, February 21, 1890, 1.

725. "A Fight That Lasted Forty Seconds," *Chicago Tribune*, February 21, 1890, 3.

726. "Knocked Out by Peter Jackson," *Chicago Tribune*, February 22, 1890, 6.

727. "General Sporting Notes," *Chicago Tribune*, February 22, 1890, 6.

728. "Grand Tour," *Pittsburg Dispatch*, February 26, 1890, 6.

729. "Eggs and Bricks," *Pittsburg Dispatch*, February 27, 1890, 1; "Peter Jackson Rotten-Egged," *Sacramento Daily Record-Union*, February 27, 1890, 1.

730. "Jackson and Fallon to Box," *Chicago Tribune*, March 4, 1890, 3.

731. "Hissed Off Of The Stage," *Brooklyn Eagle*, March 5, 1890, 1.

732. "Fallon's Peculiar Actions," *Chicago Tribune*, March 5, 1890, 6.

733. "Jackson's Equal-An Amateur Named Lambert Spars Four Rounds With the Colored Australian," *Bismarck Daily Tribune*, March 6, 1890, 1.

734. "Jackson's Fiasco at Elmira," *Chicago Tribune*, March 10, 1890, 5.

735. "Sporting Notes," *Syracuse Daily Standard*, March 17, 1890, 4.

736. "The Jackson-Lambert Bout," *Bismarck Daily Tribune*, March 8, 1890, 1.

737. "Jackson's Bout With Gus Lambert," *Philadelphia Inquirer*, March 8, 1890, 6; "The Colored Fighter's Tour," *Daily Nevada State Journal*, March 8, 1890, 2.

738. "Jackson's Scrap With Lambert," *Chicago Tribune*, March 8, 1890, 7; "Parson Davies' Plaint," *St. Paul Daily Globe*, March 08, 1890, 5.

739. "Jackson on the Road," *St. Louis Republic*, March 16, 1890, 14; "Sparring at Batter D," *Daily Inter Ocean*, March 16, 1890, 6.

740. "Jackson Will Go On The Road Under Davies," *St. Paul Daily Globe*, March 16, 1890, 6.

741. "Peter Jackson's Appearance," *Chicago Tribune*, March 25, 1890, 6.

742. "Sporting Notes," *Syracuse Daily Standard*, March 21, 1890, 6.

743. "Sullivan Escapes Prison-The Indictment Against the Champion Quashed by the Supreme Court," *Chicago Tribune*, March 18, 1890, 6.

744. "Jackson Will Box for Points," *Chicago Tribune*, March 16, 1890, 3; "The Parson Will Offer Medals," *Chicago Tribune*, March 17, 1890, 3; "Peter Jackson's First Appearance," *Chicago Tribune*, March 24, 1890, 6.

745. "Lively Sparring At The Battery," *Chicago Tribune*, March 26, 1890, 1.

746. "Pungent Points," *Hamilton Daily Democrat*, March 20, 1890, 3.

747. "Parson Davies' Experience," *Chicago Tribune*, March 30, 1890, 2; "Awful Work-Digging the Dead From Louisville's Ruins," *Brooklyn Eagle*, March 29, 1890, 6; "Loss of Life and Property," *Cincinnati Enquirer*, March 31, 1890, 1; "Pete Jackson Arrives," *Cincinnati Commercial Gazette*, April 1, 1890, 3.

748. "Peter Jackson-The Famous Colored Pugilist Appears at the People's," *Cincinnati Commercial Gazette*, April 2, 1890, 2.

749. "The Australian Champion," *Cincinnati Commercial Gazette*, April 3, 1890, 2; Advertisement, *Cincinnati Post*, April 4, 1890, 3; "Jackson Protests," *Cincinnati Commercial Gazette*, April 4, 1890, 2; "Connors' Bad Break-Mellow with Booze-He Is Unable to Punch the Ball etc.," *Cincinnati Commercial Gazette*, April 5, 1890, 6.

750. "Jackson On A Bender," *Cincinnati Commercial Gazette*, April 7, 1890, 2.

751. "Peter Jackson's Joke," *St. Louis Post Dispatch*, April 8, 1890, 10.

752. "Sullivan and Corbett," *Cincinnati Commercial Gazette*, April 4, 1890, 2; "Ready To Meet Sullivan-Jim Corbett is Willing to Make a Match with the Big Fellow," *Chicago Tribune*, April 3, 1890, 6; "Wants To Meet Corbett," *Chicago Tribune*, April 5, 1890, 3; "Handsome Corbett," *St. Louis Post Dispatch*, April 9, 1890, 10.

753. "Davies' New Athletic Club," *Chicago Tribune*, April 9, 1890, 6; "Planning For Some Fights," *Chicago Tribune*, April 17, 1890, 6.

754. "The Ring," *St. Louis Post Dispatch*, April 13, 1890, 18.

755. "An Athletic Exhibition," *St. Louis Post Dispatch*, April 18, 1890, 5.

756. "Peter Jackson," *National Police Gazette*, May 10, 1890, 11; "The Australian Giant," *St. Louis Post Dispatch*, April 19, 1890, 8; "The Jackson Exhibition," *St. Louis Post Dispatch*, April 21, 1890, 2; "Peter Jackson at St. Louis," *Chicago Tribune*, April 21, 1890, 6.

757. "Jim Corbett Arrives in Town," *Chicago Tribune*, April 23, 1890, 5.

758. "Jackson Willing," *St. Louis Post Dispatch*, April 24, 1890, 1; "The Sullivan-Jackson Fight," *Chicago Tribune*, April 26, 1890, 6; "Will Fight In San Francisco, Sullivan Agrees to Meet Jackson Before the California Athletic Club," *Chicago Tribune*, May 25, 1890, 3.

759. "Sullivan and Jackson," *St. Louis Post Dispatch*, May 10, 1890, 16 (Jackson's return to the East from Mt. Clemens puzzles his friends here).

760. "A Reception to Jackson," *Salt Lake Herald*, May 4, 1890; "Welcoming Peter," *Sacramento Daily Record-Union*, May 02, 1890, 1.

761. "Chas. E. Davies," *National Police Gazette*, May 10, 1890, 11.

762. "Smith and Jackson," *St. Louis Post Dispatch*, May 18, 1890, 16.

763. See note 66 above at 31-32.

764. Ibid.

765. "Jackson 'Bests' Smith," *Chicago Tribune*, May 20, 1890, 2; "Two Lively Encounters," *National Police Gazette*, June 7, 1890, 10.

766. "Jackson Coming Home," *Arizona Republican*, May 22, 1890, 1.

767. "Peter Jackson Here-The Exhibition Last Night-A Champagne Banquet Given," *Salt Lake herald*, May 27, 1890, 5; "Sporting Notes," *Salt Lake Tribune*, May 26, 1890, 5.

768. "Meet at the Golden Gate," *Salt Lake Tribune,* May 27, 1890, 5.

769. "Jackson to Leave for Australia," *Chicago Tribune*, July 1, 1890, 6.

770. "The City In Brief," *Salt Lake Herald*, May 27, 1890, 3; "Peter Is Coming," *Morning Call*, May 26, 1890, 2.

771. "Peter Jackson Menagerie," *Morning Call*, May 29, 1890, 8.

772. "The Black 'Pug'," *Oakland Tribune*, May 29, 1890, 1.

773. Ibid.

774. "Fitzsimmons Knocks McCarthy Out in Nine Rounds," *Sacramento Daily Record-Union*, May 30, 1890, 1.

775. "Getting Good," *Arizona Republican*, June 02, 1890, 1; "Latest Telegraph," *San Antonio Daily Light*, June 2, 1890, 1.

776. "Gloves and Fists," *Morning Call*, June 03, 1890, 8; "The Field of Sport," *Morning Call*, June 08, 1890, 3; "Young Mitchell Makes His Final Deposit," *Morning Call*, June 10, 1890, 2; "The Field of Sport," *Morning Call*, June 15, 1890, 3.

777. "General Sporting Notes," *Chicago Tribune*, June 7, 1890, 5.

778. "Fistiana," *Oakland Tribune*, June 6, 1890, 3.

779. "The M'Bride Slaughter," *Oakland Tribune*, June 11, 1890, 1; "Fatal Result of a Fight-Harry McBride Dies From Injuries Received in the Ring," *Chicago Tribune*, June 11, 1890, 6; "Has Pugilism Seen Its Palmiest Days in Frisco?," *Morning Call*, June 15, 1890, 3; "The Attorney General on Slugging," *Oakland Tribune*, June 19, 1890, 8.

780. New South Wales, Australia, Unassisted Immigrant Passenger Lists, 1826-1922 [database on-line]. Provo, UT, USA: Ancestry.com Operations, Inc., 2007. Original data: New South Wales Government. Inward passenger lists. Series 13278, Reels 399-560, 2001-2122, 2751. State Records Authority of New South Wales. Kingswood, New South Wales, Australia; "Jackson Leaves for Australia," *Chicago Tribune*, July 27, 1890, 3.

781. "Notes," *Salt Lake Tribune*, June 7, 1890, 5.

782. "Sporting Notes," *Salt Lake Tribune*, June 7, 1890, 5.

783. "Rumbles of the Railroad," *Salt Lake Tribune*, June 11, 1890, 5; "Monday's Contests," *Salt Lake Tribune*, June 11, 1890, 8;

784. "The Manly Art," *Salt Lake Tribune*, June 13, 1890, 5.

785. "Sports and Sporting News," *Salt Lake Tribune*, June 14, 1890, 2; "Ashton vs. Nobel," *Salt Lake Herald*, June 15, 1890, 8.

786. "Will Spar at Battery D," *Chicago Tribune*, June 20, 1890, 6.

787. "General Sporting Notes," *Chicago Tribune*, June 20, 1890, 6.

788. "Garrard Want to Box Brennan," *Chicago Tribune*, June 25, 1890, 6; "General Sporting Notes," *Chicago Tribune*, June 26, 1890, 6.

789. "Amusements," *St. Paul Daily Globe*, June 21, 1890, 3; "Bijou Opera House," *St. Paul Daily Globe*, June 22, 1890, 10; "Amusements," *St. Paul Daily Globe*, June 23, 1890, 3.

790. "Glover and Ashton to Meet," *Chicago Herald*, June 22, 1890, 13.

791. "The Ashton-Glover Match," *Chicago Tribune*, July 2, 1890, 7; "Ashton Ready for Clover Hard Thumping Contests Promised for the Battery D Show Tomorrow," *Inter Ocean*, July 2, 1890, 6.

792. "His Final Battle-Billy Brennan Fatally Injured in a Set-To at Battery D," *Chicago Tribune*, July 4, 1890, 7; "Pugilist Brennan Dead," *St. Louis Post Dispatch*, July 4, 1890, 4; "Knocked Senseless," *Chillicothe Constitution*, July 3, 1890, 5.

793. "Desperate and Brutal," *Chicago Tribune*, May 22, 1890, 6; "The Loser Won," *St. Louis Post Dispatch*, May 22, 1890, 12; "General Sporting Notes," *Chicago Tribune*, May 24, 1890, 6.

794. "The Fatal Fall," *Chicago Tribune*, July 4, 1890, 1.

795. "Stopped by the Police," *Chicago Tribune*, July 4, 1890, 1.

796. "Give the Mayor His Share," *Inter Ocean*, July 8, 1890, 4.

797. "Fatal Sparring Match," *Chicago Tribune*, July 5, 1890, 3; "The Brennan Killing," *St. Louis Post Dispatch,* July 5, 1890, 5.

798. "Frank Garraard Is Free," *Chicago Tribune*, July 6, 1890, 1.

799. "Where is Jack Adams. His Father Believes He Was Killed In An Illinois Prize Fight," *Cleveland Plain Dealer*, December 7, 1890, 3; "Brennan's Identity," *St. Louis Post Dispatch*, December 12, 1890, 8.

800. "The Tragedy of Battery D," *Chicago Tribune*, July 7, 1890, 4.

801. "The Ring," *Morning Call*, July 20, 1890, 3.

802. "The Pacific Coast Notes," *Inter Ocean*, August 10, 1890, 14.

803. "Carpet Sports," *Morning Call*, August 14, 1890, 7.

804. "Budget of Sport," *Morning Call*, August 27, 1890, 2.

805. "The 'Parson' on Wrestling," *Inter Ocean*, September 14, 1890, 3.

806. "A Wrestling Tournament, *Inter Ocean*, October 22, 1890, 2; "The Parson's Wrestlers," *Inter Ocean*, October 28, 1890, 2; "Higgins and Whitmore Defeated," *Inter Ocean*, October 30, 1890, 3.

807. "Sporting Notes," *Inter Ocean*, September 8, 1890, 2; "The Oleaginous Parsom [sic]," *Inter Ocean*, October 15, 1890, 2.

808. "The Police Interfered," *St. Louis Post Dispatch*, August 27, 1890, 5.

809. "Sloggers Held," *Evening News*, September 19, 1890, 2; "Effort to Renew Prize Fighting," *San Francisco Bulletin*, September 22, 1890, 2; "Prize-Fighting, an Encounter at the California Club. Arrests Made and the Case to be Tried in Court," *San Francisco Bulletin*, September 22, 1890, 2; "On Trial for Prize Fighting," *San Francisco Bulletin*, November 17, 1890, 3; "Parson Davies Chats. Letter on Sporting Topics," *Chicago Herald*, December 16, 1890, 7.

810. "Parson a Davies' Chat-Writing the Herald from Frisco," *Chicago Herald*, November 9, 1890, 27.

811. "Australia Pugilistic News," *St. Louis Post Dispatch*, October 28, 1890, 5; "Salvin and Jackson Matched," *St. Louis Republic*, October 28, 1890, 5; "Salvin and Jackson to Box in Australia," *Plain Dealer,* October 29, 1890, 5.

812. No Headline, *Taranaki Herald*, November 1, 1890, 2.

813. "General Sporting Notes," *Chicago Tribune*, November 22, 1890, 6; "Sporting Notes," *St. Louis Post Dispatch*, November 28, 1890, 3.

814. "Jackson Vanquished," *St. Louis Post Dispatch*, November 23, 1890, 24; "Jackson and Goddard, An Eye Witness Describes the Recent Glove Fight," *St. Louis Post Dispatch*, December 1, 1890, 10; "Jackson on Goddard," *St. Louis Post Dispatch*, December 30, 1890, 8.

815. "Brief Mention," *San Francisco Bulletin*, November 22, 1890, 4; "Lewis Did Not Defeat Acton," *Sun*, November 24, 1890, 1; "Joe Acton Is Champion," *Morning Call*, November 23, 1890, 2.

816. "Clunie Opera House," *Sacramento Daily Record-Union*, November 27, 1890, 2; "The Wrestlers," *Sacramento Daily Record-Union*, November 28, 1890, 2;

817. "Lewis Is Champion," *Morning Call*, December 10, 1890, 2; "Lewis Defeats Acton," *Chicago Tribune*, December 10, 1890, 6.

818. "Personal Mention," *Salt Lake Tribune*, December 20, 1890, 8.

819. "Peter Jackson, Arrival of the Colored Champion from Australia," *Morning Call*, December 21, 1890, 11.

820. "'The Parson' at Home, Returning from a Long Trip West," *Chicago Herald*, December 12, 1890, 6.

821. "The Ring," *St. Louis Post Dispatch*, December 27, 1890, 8.

822. "Jackson and Corbett to Fight," *Chicago Tribune*, December 30, 1890, 5; "Jackson and Corbett Will Fight," *Chicago Tribune*, December 31, 1890, 6; "Scienced Fighters," *Morning Call*, December 30, 1890, 1; "Jim Corbett's Father Will Appeal to the Grand Jury," *Oakland Tribune*, January 7, 1891, 6; "What Corbett's Father Says," *Morning Call*, January 02, 1891, 2; "Champion Snowden," *Morning Call*, January 03, 1891, 2; "Corbett Will Fight," *Morning Call*, January 03, 1891, 2.

823. "Fighting Notes from 'Frisco," *Boston Daily Globe*, December 17, 1890, 5; "Fitzsimmons-Dempsey," *St. Louis Post Dispatch*, January 4, 1891, 24; "Billiard Tournament" *Morning Call*, January 08, 1891, 2.

Chapter 11 – Jackson and Corbett to a draw - (1891)

824. "Losers and Winners," *Morning Call*, January 15, 1891, 1.

825. "Corbett In Town-What the Golden Gate Pugilist Has to Say," *Daily City Item*, January 7, 1891, 2; "The Coming Mill," *Daily City Item*, January 10, 1891, 2.

826. "Fight Talk," *Times-Picayune*, January 13, 1891, 6. Jackson was a guest of the Manhattan Club, an organization of black members.

827. "Bound For New Orleans," *Chicago Tribune*, January 12, 1891, 6.

828. "Going to the Fight," *St. Louis Post Dispatch*, January 8, 1891, 10.

829. "The Great Ring Fight," *St. Louis Post Dispatch*, January 12, 1891, 8.

830. "Other Contests," *St. Louis Post Dispatch*, January 12, 1891, 8.

831. "Last Edition-Dempsey Knocked Out," *Chicago Tribune*, January 15, 1891, 1; "Dempsey's Defeat, It Came Like a Thunderclap on the Pugilistic World," *St. Louis Post Dispatch*, January 15, 1891, 10; "Fitzsimmons Victory," *Ogden Standard*, January 17, 1891, 4.

832. "Dempsey's Fall," *Morning Call*, January 15, 1891, 1.

833. "Great Fitzsimmons," *St. Louis Post Dispatch*, January 16, 1891, 5; "After the Fight," *Times-Picayune*, January 15, 1891. Reports said that Davies got up early and met with Fitzsimmons and Carroll and secured a contract.

834. "Fitzsimmons Victory," *{Ogden} Standard*, January 17, 1891, 3; "Sporting Notes," *Pittsburg Dispatch*, January 17, 1891, 6; "Now With Parson Davies," *St. Paul Daily Globe*, January 18, 1891,6; "Sporting Notes," *Salt Lake Tribune*, January 20, 1891, 8.

835. "Game Until the End-Dempsey's Fight Against Big Odds-"Parson" Davies Explains etc.," *Chicago Herald*, January 17, 1891, 7.

836. "Gossip About the Boxers," *Sun*, January 25, 1891, 10.

837. See note 309 above at 114.

838. "Sullivan Thinks Slavin Will Be a Soft Snap for Him," *Los Angeles Times*, January 19, 1891, 5; "Corbett in Town," *Inter Ocean*, January 18, 1891, 2; "Pugilist Corbett in Town," *Chicago Herald*, January 18, 1891, 6; "Ring Talk," *{Sacramento} Record-Union*, January 19, 1891, 1. Corbett met Sullivan that night.

839. "Corbett's Fight with Jackson-the Former Not Afraid of the Australian's Fists-Great Match Promised," *Chicago Herald*, January 19, 1891, 6.

840. See note 309 above at 118.

841. Fields, Armond, *James J. Corbett, A Biography of the Heavyweight Boxing Champion and Popular Theater Headliner* (McFarland & Company, Inc., 2001), 39-47.

842. "Theaters and Music," *Brooklyn Eagle*, February 1, 1891, 13.

843. "Hyde & Behman's Theater," *Brooklyn Eagle*, February 3, 1891, 4.

844. See note 852 above at 44.

845. "Kilrain and Godfrey Sign Articles of Agreement," *Morning Call*, January 30, 1891, 2.

846. "The Fitzsimmons and Carroll Row," *St. Louis Post Dispatch*, February 12, 1891, 12; "Fitzsimmons on Carroll," *St. Louis Post Dispatch*, February 14, 1891, 8.

847. "Fitzsimmons on the Stage," *Idaho Statesman*, February 7, 1891, 1.

848. "Hitters and Wrestlers," *Bloomington Bulletin*, February 6, 1891, 3.

849. "Bob and Jimmy Are out Carroll and Fitz Part, the Australian Being Engaged by A Chicagoan, *Inter Ocean*, February 7, 1891, 1; "Slugger Fitzsimmons at Chicago," *Morning Star*, February 15, 1891, 3.

850. "A Lone Hand. Fiztsimmons Signs a Contract on His Own Behalf, And Leaves Carroll etc.," *Times-Picayune*, February 7, 1891; "Bob and Jimmy Are out-Carroll and Fitz Part, The Australian Being Engaged by a Chicagoan," *Inter Ocean*, February 7, 1891, 2; "Fitzsimmons Gets An Offer," *St. Louis Post Dispatch*, February 6, 1891, 8.

851. "Fitzsimmons Means Business He Offers to Fight Pritchard Burke or Toff Wall in England," *Philadelphia Inquirer*, February 13, 1891, 3

852. Advertisement, *Chicago Tribune*, February 15, 1891, 3.

853. "Corbett Is All Right," *Chicago Tribune*, February 10, 1891, 6.

854. "Fitz Comes to Town-Talk on Himself by the Lank Un," *Chicago Herald*, February 14, 1891, 7.

855. "Fitzsimmons Tours The Land," *Chicago Tribune*, February 14, 1891, 6.

856. "The Ring," *St. Louis Post Dispatch*, February 16, 1891, 8.

857. "Fitzsimmons Means Business He Offers to Fight Pritchard Burke or Toff Wall in England," *Philadelphia Inquirer*, February 13, 1891, 3.

858. "The Champion Fitzsimmons," *Evening Herald*, March 6, 1891, 1.

859. "Are Evenly Matched," *St. Louis Post Dispatch*, March 30, 1891, 5; "Big Money for a Flight-Astoria's Athletic Club Offers a $17,000 Purse to Hall and Fitzsimmons," *Inter Ocean*, March 25, 1891, 6; "Hall Posts a Forfeit," *Inter Ocean*, March 28, 1891, 6; "The Prize Ring," *Record-Union*, March 30, 1891, 1.

860. "Pugilism In Farce Comedy," *Chicago Tribune*, April 6, 1891, 3.

861. "The Ring," *St. Louis Post Dispatch*, April 14, 1891, 8.

862. "Odds and Ends of Sports," *Sun*, April 07, 1891, 4.

863. "Anxious to Fight Fitzsimmons," *Pittsburg Dispatch*, February 08, 1891, 7.

864. Advertisement, *Chicago Tribune*, February 15, 1891, 3.

865 . "Theatrical Gossip," *Inter Ocean*, February 15, 1891, 12.

866. "Corbett's Programme," *Inter Ocean*, February 18, 1891, 2.

867. "An Offer to Daly," *Inter Ocean*, February 19, 1891, 2.

868. "Pugilistic Events," *Omaha World Herald*, February 1, 1891, 16; "The Pugilists," *Carroll Sentinel*, February 27, 1891, 2.

869. No Headline, *The {Ogden} Standard*, March 3, 1891, 4; "Parson Davies Here," *The {Ogden} Standard*, March 1, 1891, 5; "The Ring," *St. Louis Post Dispatch*, March 5, 1891, 10.

870. "Pugalistic 'Parsons'," *Salt Lake Herald*, March 01, 1891, 3.

871. "Corbett Passes Through," *Standard*, March 5, 1891, 1.

872. "The Parson Gone," *Standard*, March 4, 1891, 1.

873. See note 309 above at 126-127.

874. "Corbett and His Malaria," *Morning Call*, March 06, 1891, 2.

875. "Coming From Australia," Morning Call, February 06, 1891, 2; "Clever Fighter," *Morning Call*, February 18, 1891, 2; "In Demand," *Morning Call*, February 21, 1891, 1; "The Ring," *Morning Call*, March 08, 1891, 10; "Amusements," *Record-Union*, March 17, 1891, 2; "A Brutal Exhibition," *Morning Call*," March 18, 1891, 1; "Jim Hall at Portland," *Morning Call*, March 20, 1891, 8; "Fitzsimmons Challenged," *Record-Union*, March 23, 1891, 1; "The Ring," *St. Louis Post Dispatch*, March 24, 1891, 10; "Hall-Fitzsimmons," "Paper-Fighting Pugs," *Morning Call*, March 28, 1891, 1; "Hall-Fitzsimmons," *Record-Union*, March 31, 1891, 1

876. "In the Boxes," *Record-Union*, March 30, 1891, 1.

877. "Kilrain and Godfrey," *St. Louis Post Dispatch*, March 13, 1891, 8; "The Ring," *St. Louis Post Dispatch*, March 14, 1891, 8; "Kilrain Wins A Fight," *Chicago Tribune*, March 14, 1891, 3.

878. "Talk of the Town," *Oakland Tribune*, March 16, 1891, 1.

879. "Godfrey in Ogden," *Salt Lake Herald*, March 21, 1891, 3.

880. "The Prize-Ring," *Morning Call*, March 30, 1891, 1; "Are Evenly Matched," *St. Louis Post Dispatch*," March 30, 1891, 5.

881. "Refused The Money," *St. Paul Daily Globe*, April 01, 1891, 1; "Talk Is Cheap," *Morning Call*, April 04, 1891, 1; "Clark Wants A Fight," *Chicago Tribune*, April 3, 1891, 6.

882. "The 'Parson's' Return," *Inter Ocean*, March 27, 1891, 6; "Parson Davies' Tribute to the Colored Pugilist," *Salt Lake Tribune*, March 28, 1891, 1.

883. "Hall-Fitzsimmons," *Record-Union*, March 31, 1891, 1.

884. "Sporting Notes," *Salt Lake Tribune*, April 2, 1891, 6.

885. "The Middle-Weight Mill," *Salt Lake Tribune*, April 6, 1891, 1.

886. "Brevities," *Daily Nevada State Journal*, April 7, 1891, 2.

887. "The Australian Pugilist," *Salt Lake Herald*, April 09, 1891, 3.

888. "The Australian Champion," *Salt Lake Tribune*, April 9, 1891, 3.

889. "Jim Hall Shows His Science in the Ring," *Ogden Standard*, April 10, 1891, 4; "Hennessey Not In It," *Salt Lake Tribune*, April 11, 1891, 3; "Pugilist Jim Hall," *Salt Lake Herald*, April 11, 1891, 1.

890. "Local and Other Briefs," *Salt Lake Herald*, April 12, 1891, 2.

891. "The Ring," *St. Louis Post Dispatch*, April 13, 1891, 8.

892. "Laughs At Fitzsimmons," *Chicago Tribune*, April 18, 1891, 6.

893. "Jim Hall to Arrive to-Day. The Latest Pugilistic Wonder from Austrian Probably Looking for a Fight," *Chicago Herald*, April 17, 1891, 5.

894. "Dixon to Arrive Today," *Chicago Tribune*, April 18, 1891, 6.

895. "Investigating The Astoria Offer," *St. Louis Post Dispatch*, April 22, 1891, 10; "Ready to Make a Match," *Chicago Tribune*, April 22, 1891, 5; "The Sporting World," *St. Louis Post Dispatch*, April 23, 1891, 12.

896. "Fitz in Early Days-A Former Manager Tells of Confidence and Suspicion," *Philadelphia Inquirer*, May 27, 1897, 4.

897. "Stopped By The Police," *Chicago Tribune*, April 28, 1891, 6.

898. "Peter Jackson Not Badly Hurt," *Chicago Herald*, April 5, 1891; "Peter Jackson Injured," *Morning Call*, April 05, 1891, 8; "General Sporting Notes," *St. Paul Daily Globe*, April 06, 1891, 5; "Peter Jackson Injured," *Galveston Daily News*, April 19, 1891, 19; "Athletic Sports," *Morning Call*, April 21, 1891, 8; "Sports of All Sorts," *St. Louis Post Dispatch*, April 17, 1891, 5; "The Ring," *St. Louis Post Dispatch*, April 19, 1891, 18.

899. "The Ring," *St. Louis Post Dispatch*, April 19, 1891, 18.

900. See note 309 above at 126-127.

901. "Jackson's Condition," *St. Louis Post Dispatch*, April 14, 1891, 8.

902. "Field of Sport," *Morning Call*, April 07, 1891, 8; "Jackson's Condition," *Oakland Tribune*, April 8, 1891, 8.

903. See note 309 above at 127.

904. "Meet in Fort Wayne Siddons and White Spar to Night etc.," *Chicago Herald*, May 9, 1891, 6.

905. "Chicago Sports Will Attend a Trainload of White Siddons Admirers Going to Fort Wayne," *Chicago Herald*, May 7, 1891, 5.

906. "Sporting Notes," *Salt Lake Tribune*, May 10, 1891, 8.

907. "Speaks of Sports-Hall-Woods," *Omaha Daily Bee*, May 12, 1891, 2.

908. "Sporting Events," *Salt Lake Tribune*, May 12, 1891, 5.

909. "The Sparring Match," *Ogden Standard*, May 16, 1891, 1.

910. "Still They Come," *Morning Call*, May 15, 1891, 2.

911. "Declared It A Draw," *Chicago Tribune*, May 22, 1891, 2; "Neither Man Hurt," *St. Louis Post Dispatch*, May 22, 1891, 1.

912. "Jackson and Corbett to Receive $2,500 Each," *Daily Nevada State Journal*, May 23, 1891, 2; "The Proper Thing," *St. Louis Post Dispatch*, May 23, 1891, 8.

913. "The Ring," *St. Louis Post Dispatch*, May 25, 1891, 10; "Mirror of Sport," *St. Louis Post Dispatch*, July 12, 1891, 6.

914. "Corbett Will Not Fight," *St. Louis Post Dispatch*, May 26, 1891, 8; "Jackson Willing," *St. Louis Post Dispatch*, June 1, 1891, 5.

915. "Sporting Arena," *St. Louis Post Dispatch*, June 7, 1891, 11.

916. "A New Boxing Club," *Morning Call*, June 12, 1891, 2; "The New Athletic Club etc.," *Pittsburg Dispatch*, June 06, 1891, 8; "The New Boxing Club," *Morning Call*, June 12, 1891, 2.

917. "Sporting Notes," *Pittsburg Dispatch*, June 04, 1891, 8.

918. Advertisement, *Tacoma Daily News*, June 2, 1891, 3.

919. "Jim Hall's Manager. 'Parson' Davies, the Well-Known Sport Once More in Portland," *Oregonian*, June 8, 1891, 6; "Parson Davies And His Charges Jim Hall and Billy Woods in the Athletic Tournament Today, *Oregonian*, June 7, 1891, 2.

920. "Parson Davies' Gossip-Another New Orleans Club Takes Up Boxing Matches," *Chicago Tribune*, December 10, 1899, 20.

921. "Athletic Tournament," *Oregonian*, June 8, 1891, 2.

922. "Echoes from the Distant Past," *Montana Standard,* December 11, 1938, 41.

923. "Out For Blood," *St. Louis Post Dispatch*, June 14, 1891, 11.

924. "Miscellaneous Sporting News-Can Hardly Wait," *Omaha World Herald*, June 14, 1891, 7.

925. "'Wonder' In Town," *St. Paul Daily Globe*, June 14, 1891, 6.

926. "Knocked Out by Billy Woods," *Chicago Tribune*, June 16, 1891, 6; "The Ring," *St. Louis Post Dispatch*, June 16, 1891, 3.

927. "Odds and Ends," *St. Paul Daily Globe*, June 17, 1891, 4.

928. "The Ring," *St. Louis Post Dispatch*, June 23, 1891, 8.

929. "Fight Or Fake?," *St. Louis Post Dispatch*, July 20, 1891, 8.

930. "Plans of 'Parson' Davies He Will Not Get Married but Will Arrange Several Prize Fights," *Chicago Herald*, June 19, 1891, 7.

931. "New Articles of Agreement Signed for Their Coming Fight," *Chicago Tribune*, July 3, 1891, 6.

932. "Jim Hall Training Hard," *Chicago Tribune*, July 3, 1891, 6; "Thinks Hall Will Win," *Chicago Tribune*, July 7, 1891, 6; "Sporting Men Beginning to Look More Favorably on Davies' Man," *Chicago Tribune*, July 12, 1891, 4.

933. "Hall is Confident in the Best Possible Condition Kline Has Treated Him in a Common Sense Fashion," *Chicago Herald*, July 19, 1891, 5.

934. "Goes to Bed Early," *Chicago Tribune*, July 10, 1891, 6 (Davies says that rumors are absurd).

935. "Jim Hall As A Sprinter," *Chicago Tribune*, July 14, 1891, 6.

936. "Quiet Gentlemanly Fellows," *St. Paul Daily Globe*, July 05, 1891, 7.

937. "Fighters In Training," *Chicago Tribune*, July 10, 1891, 6.

938. "Hall In Seclusion," *St. Paul Daily Globe*, July 22, 1891, 1.

939. "Badly Punished," *Morning Call*, July 22, 1891, 1; "The Story of A Day," *St. Paul Daily Globe*, July 22, 1891, 4; "No Match For Martin," *Chicago Tribune*, July 22, 1891, 2.

940. "Proclamation Against The Fight," *Chicago Tribune*, July 22, 1891, 2; "Before The Governor," *St. Paul Daily Globe*, July 22, 1891, 1; "Enforce The Law," *St. Paul Daily Globe*, July 22, 1891, 4; "How It Was Fought," *St. Paul Daily Globe*, July 23, 1891, 4; "Law and Order Triumph," *Chicago Tribune*, July 23, 1891, 2; "Slanders St. Paul," *St. Paul Daily Globe*, July 25, 1891, 2; "The Law And Order League," *St. Louis Post Dispatch*, July 28, 1891, 8.

941. "No Fight After All," *Daily Argus News*, July 23, 1891, 1; "The Ring," *St. Louis Post Dispatch*, July 25, 1891, 8; "No Boxing In Minnesota," *St. Paul Daily Globe*, July 25, 1891, 6.

942. "To Arrest Fitzsimmons," *Chicago Tribune*, July 21, 1891, 6.

943. "The Parson Is Back," *Inter Ocean*, July 26, 1891, 3.

944. "Corbett-Hall Match at Battery D," *Chicago Tribune*, August 2, 1891, 4; "Hall And Corbett Spar," *Chicago Tribune*, August 6, 1891, 5.

945. "Acting Takes Less Courage," *Morning Call*, July 31, 1891, 7.

946. See note 45 above at 61-62.

947. "Talk of the Stage World," *Evening World*, August 12, 1891, 2.

948. "Ryan Bests M'Millan," *Chicago Tribune*, August 10, 1891, 6; "The Ring," *St. Louis Post Dispatch*, August 10, 1891, 8.

949. Magee, Dorothy M. & Bright Future for Mt. Clemens Committee, *Centennial history of Mt. Clemens, Michigan, 1879-1979* (Mt. Clemens Public Library, 1980), 84.

950. "Two Pugilists In Town," *Ogden Standard*, December 8, 1891, 10.

951. "Stabbed Jim Hall," *Pittsburg Dispatch*, August 25, 1891, 6.

952. "Romances Of The Ring-The Parson etc.," *Trenton Evening Times*, April 23, 1916, 23.

953. "Parson Davies Dead," *Referee*, September 22, 1920.

954. Marx, Jack, *Australian Tragic: Gripping Tales from the Dark Side of Our History*, (Hachette Australia, 2009).

955. "The Parson Slashes Jim Hall," *Ogden Standard*, August 26, 1891, 1; "Hog Sticking Time," *Fort Worth Gazette*, August 25, 1891, 2; "Jim Hall the Pugilist-Stabbed by His Trainer," *Argus* [Melbourne], August 27, 1891, 5; "Jim Hall and His Trainer-The Wound Inflicted In Self Defense," *Argus* [Melbourne], August 28, 1891, 5.

956. "He May Not Die," *Daily Nevada State Journal*, August 26, 1891, 2.

957. "Sporting Notes," *St. Louis Post Dispatch*, September 26, 1891, 5.

958. Jim Hall Played with Ryan-Limitations of the Latter Distinctly Shown by the Australian," *Chicago Herald*, September 29, 1891, 6.

959. "Easy Mark for Jim Hall Milwaukee," *Chicago Herald*, October 9, 1891, 7; "The Ring," *St. Louis Post Dispatch*, October 10, 1891, 8; "Four Rounds Fought.-Then the Police Knocked out Both Prize Fighters," *Tacoma Daily News*, October 10, 1891, 1.

960. "Peter Maher's Offers," *Chicago Tribune*, October 28, 1891, 10; "Hall to Maher," *St. Paul Daily Globe*, October 28, 1891, 5 (Davies issued challenge for Hall).

961. "Pat Killen the Victor," *Chicago Tribune*, October 12, 1891, 6; "The Ring-Killen Whips Ferguson," *St. Louis Post Dispatch*, October 12, 1891, 5.

962. Siler, George, *Inside Facts on Pugilism*, (Laird & Lee, 1907), 84-91.

963. "Knocked Out By Death," *Chicago Tribune*, October 22, 1891, 5.

964 . "Pat Killen's Death Partly the Result of a Prize Fight Although He Had the Best of the Match with Fergason," *Chicago Herald*, October 22, 1891, 3.

965. "The Ring," *Chicago Tribune*, October 30, 1891, 10.

966. "Sullivan's Manager In Town," *Chicago Tribune*, November 7, 1891, 6.

967. "General Sporting Notes," *Pittsburg Dispatch*, October 16, 1891, 8.

968. "The Ring," *St. Louis Post Dispatch*, November 10, 1891, 8.

969. "They Will Battle," *St. Louis Post Dispatch*, November 16, 1891, 8; "Slavin Must Fight," *St. Louis Post Dispatch*, November 18, 1891, 5.

970. "Jackson And Slavin Articles," *St. Louis Post Dispatch*, December 17, 1891, 15.

971. "International Tug-Of-War," *New York Times*, November 29, 1891, 3.

972. "Jackson and Slavin Matched," *Chicago Tribune*, November 22, 1891, 6; "The Ring-The Slavin Jackson Match," *St. Louis Post Dispatch*, November 29, 1891, 23.

973. "The Parson's Tug of War," *Chicago Tribune*, December 3, 1891, 6.

974. "Tug Of War The Fad," *Chicago Tribune*, December 6, 1891, 14; "Pulled For Glory," *Chicago Tribune*, December 8, 1891, 6; "Work Of The Tug Of War Teams," *Chicago Tribune*, December 15, 1891, 7; "Tug Of War Tournament Ended," *Chicago Tribune*, December 17, 1891, 7.

975. "'Julius, The Ghost'," *Chicago Tribune*, December 16, 1891, 5.

976. "Julius The 'Ghost,' Is Lamblike," *Chicago Tribune*, December 18, 1891, 3; "Sat On The 'Ghost'," *Chicago Tribune*, December 19, 1891, 3.

977. "Won In Four Rounds," *Chicago Tribune*, December 20, 1891, 7; "A Brutal Fight," *Burlington Hawk-Eye*," December 20, 1891, 1.

978. "Jackson Signs The Articles," *St. Louis Post Dispatch*, December 15, 1891, 12.

979. "Slavin Says He Wants to Fight," *Chicago Tribune*, December 8, 1891, 6; "Slavin And Mitchell Sail," *Chicago Tribune*, December 9, 1891, 7; "The Ring," *St. Louis Post Dispatch*," December 13, 1891, 23; "Tuesday's Fights. Sullivan And Slavin," *St. Louis Post Dispatch*, December 27, 1891, 22; "To-Night's Fights-Sullivan And Slavin To-Day," *St. Louis Post Dispatch*, December 29, 1891, 8.

980. "Without A Backer," *St. Louis Post Dispatch*, December 31, 1891, 8.

Chapter 12 – Staying on Top – (1892)

981. "The Days of Finish Fights," *Winnipeg Free Press*, January 22, 1927, Story Section, 6 (Joe Choynski's article).

982. ""Joe Choynski, Who KO'd Jack Johnson, Taken by Death," *Cincinnati Times-Star*, January 25, 1943, 1 and 17.

983. "Terrier Of California Is Dead," *Cincinnati Enquirer*, January 26, 1943, 12-13.

984. "Sporting Notes," *Morning Call*, January 3, 1892, 9.

985. "Jackson to Stop a Heavyweight," *Chicago Tribune*, January 3, 1892, 5.

986 "Big Salaries to Pugilists," *Montreal Herald*, January 2, 1892, 47.

987. "Personal and General," *Salt Lake Herald*, January 5, 1892, 2; "The Jackson Glove Contest," *Ogden Standard*, January 5, 1892, 5; "The Ring," *St. Louis Post Dispatch*, January 4, 1892, 8.

988. "Davies Goes To Meet Jackson," *Chicago Tribune*, January 8, 1892, 7.

989. "Slavin and Mitchell Coming," *Chicago Tribune*, January 4, 1892, 5; "Slavin's Future In Doubt," *Chicago Tribune*, January 4, 1892, 6; "Slavin Will Fight Jackson," *Chicago Tribune*, January 5, 1892, 7; "Pugilistic Pointers," *St. Louis Post Dispatch*, January 9, 1892, 8; Advertisement, *Chicago Tribune*, January 10, 1892, 28.

990. No Headline, *Chicago Tribune*, January 10, 1892, 5.

991. "The Police Won't Interfere," *Chicago Tribune*, January 7, 1892, 7.

992. "Sporting Melange. Record of a Day in the Athletic World," *Inter Ocean*, January 12, 1892, 6; "Among the Fighters," *St. Louis Post Dispatch*, January 12, 1892, 8.

993. "Had Lively Set-Tos," *Chicago Tribune*, January 13, 1892, 7; "Blood At Battery D," *Inter Ocean*, January 13, 1892, 6.

994. "Jackson and Slavin Meet," *Chicago Tribune*, January 14, 1892, 6.

995. "Jackson's Plans," *Inter Ocean*, January 19, 1892, 6; "Jackson Sends His Forfeit," *Chicago Tribune*, January 17, 1892, 7.

996. "Theaters and Music," *Brooklyn Eagle*, January 17, 1892, 9; "Peter Jackson Down East," *Newark Daily Advocate*, January 18, 1892, 6; "Peter Jackson in Brooklyn," *Arizona Republican*, January 27, 1892, 1.

997. "General Sporting Notes," *Chicago Tribune*, January 24, 1892, 7; "Noted Boxers Will Appear," *Boston Globe*, January 25, 1892, 8.

998. "Corbett-Jackson," *St. Paul Daily Globe*, February 07, 1892, 7.

999. "Corbett Wants to Meet Slavin or Jackson," *Salt Lake Herald*, February 07, 1892, 1.

1000. "Fitz Defeats Maher," *Chicago Tribune*, March 3, 1892, 7; "Down Went Maher," *St. Louis Post Dispatch*, March 3, 1892, 5.

1001. "Fitzsimmons Opponent," *World*, February 14, 1892, 24.

1002. "The Lyceum," *Philadelphia Inquirer*, February 16, 1892, 4.

1003. "It Was All Science-Professor Billy Meclean Spars Three Quiet Rounds with Peter Jackson," *Philadelphia Inquirer*, February 17, 1892, 3.

1004. "Sporting Miscellany," *Boston Daily Globe*, February 20, 1892, 3.

1005. "Thinks Maher Will Whip Fitzsimmons," *Pittsburg Dispatch*, February 17, 1892, 8.

1006. "Sports Give A Show," *Chicago Tribune*, February 2, 1892, 6.

1007. "Next Week's Sparring Events," *Chicago Tribune*, February 13, 1892, 11.

1008. "Police Stop A Fight," *Chicago Tribune*, February 16, 1892, 7.

1009. "Rather Fancies Maher," *World*, February 24, 1892, 3.

1010. Source Citation: Class: BT26; Piece: 24; Item: 91; Source Information: Ancestry.com. UK Incoming Passenger Lists, 1878-1960 [database on-line]. Provo, UT, USA: Ancestry.com Operations Inc, 2008. Original data: Board of Trade: Commercial and Statistical Department and successors: Inwards Passenger Lists. Kew, Surrey, England: The National Archives of the UK (TNA). Series BT26, 1,472 pieces; "Jackson Reaches England," *St. Louis Post Dispatch*, March 5, 1892, 2; "Peter Jackson In England," *Chicago Tribune*, March 6, 1892, 6..

1011. "Our Possible Challenger," *World*, March 6, 1892, 3.

1012. "They're Going To See The Fight," *Chicago Tribune*, February 21, 1892, 6; "Those Big Battles," *Chicago Tribune*, February 28, 1892, 6; "Off For The New Orleans Fights," *Chicago Tribune*, February 28, 1892, 6.

1013. "There Was No Fight," *Chicago Tribune*, March 1, 1892, 7.

1014. "Tomorrow's Big Battle," *Boston Daily Globe*, March 1, 1892, 15.

1015. "General Sporting Notes," *Chicago Tribune*, March 1, 1892, 7.

1016. "The Coming Fight," *St. Louis Post Dispatch*, March 1, 1892, 8; "The Fitzsimmons-Maher Battle," *Chicago Tribune*, March 2, 1892, 7.

1017. Kramer, W. M. and Stern, N. B., "San Francisco's Fighting Jew," California Historical Quarterly, 53 (Winter 1974).

1018. "Fitzsimmons and Hall-'Parson' Davies Still Judiciously Advertising His Australian," *Kansas City Star*, March 5, 1892, 3.

1019. "Olympic Club's New Articles," *Chicago Tribune*, March 20, 1892, 6.

1020. "Pugilistic Pointers," *St. Louis Post Dispatch*, March 4, 1892, 8.

1021. "The Ring-Fitzsimmons in New York," *Times Picayune*, March 21, 1892, 5.

1022. "The Ring," *St. Louis Post Dispatch*, March 24, 1892, 12.

1023. "Sullivan To The Fighters," *Chicago Tribune*, March 6, 1892, 6; "Sullivan's Final Conditions," *Chicago Tribune*, March 8, 1892, 6.

1024. "Corbett Will Fight Sullivan," *St. Louis Post Dispatch*, March 8, 1892, 8; "Looks Like Fight," *St. Louis Post Dispatch*, March 9, 1892, 8; "Sullivan's Money Is Posted," *Chicago Tribune*, March 11, 1892, 6; "Corbett, The Man," *Chicago*

Tribune, March 14, 1892, 7; "Matched For Battle," *Chicago Tribune*, March 16, 1892, 7.

1025. "Fighters Are Very Vociferous," *Chicago Tribune*, March 9, 1892, 6.

1026. "Fred Pfeffer's Case," *Chicago Tribune*, April 11, 1892, 10; Magee, Dorothy M. & Bright Future for Mt. Clemens Committee, *Centennial history of Mt. Clemens, Michigan, 1879-1979* (Mt. Clemens Public Library, 1980), 81-95.

1027. "Hall and Choynski to Appear," *Chicago Tribune*, March 25, 1892, 7; "Hall Is After Boden," *Chicago Tribune*, March 29, 1892, 7; "Hall Says Fitz Is Lying," *Evening World*, March 29, 1892, 1.

1028. "Among the Fighters," *St. Louis Post Dispatch*, March 25, 1892, 12.

1029. "Parson Davies Takes No Stock In Fitzsimmons' Challenge," *St. Paul Daily Globe*, April 1, 1892, 9 (Byline from Louisville, Kentucky).

1030. "The Ring," *Pittsburg Dispatch*, March 30, 1892, 8; "Jackson Quarrels With His Trainer," *Salt Lake Herald*, March 31, 1892, 1.

1031. "Local Heavyweights Meet," *Chicago Tribune*, April 2, 1892, 7.

1032. "Hall Clearly Outpointed Choynski," *Chicago Tribune*, April 3, 1892, 3.

1033. See note 969 above at 138-141.

1034. "Daily Sporting Story," Date: 1912-11-06; *Salt Lake Telegram*, November 6, 1912, 10.

1035. "Hall Coming East," *Pittsburg Dispatch*, April 04, 1892, 7; "Hall and Choynski Arrive the Famous Pugilists Were Accompanied by 'Parson' Davies," *Philadelphia Inquirer*, April 4, 1892, 3.

1036. "The Mighty Sullivan In The Drama Tonight," *Bloomington Bulletin*, April 6, 1892, 1; "Amusement," *Daily Pantagraph*, April 6, 1892, 3; "A Narrow Escape," *Bloomington Bulletin*, April 6, 1892, 1; "The Might Slugger Arrives According to Schedule," *Bloomington Bulletin*, April 6, 1892, 1; "Appearance Of Slugger Sullivan As A Stage Hero," *Bloomington Bulletin*, April 7, 1892, 2; "'The Earnest Actor'," *Daily Pantagraph*, April 8, 1892, 1.

1037. "Jim Hall Stops a Local Pugilist-Jack Flood Proves an Easy Mark for the Great Middleweight," *Philadelphia Inquirer*, April 5, 1892, 3; "General Sporting Notes," *Chicago Tribune*, April 7, 1892, 6.

1038. "Jim Halls' Last Appearance He Will Meet Jack Haughey at the Ariel Club to Night," *Philadelphia Inquirer*, April 6, 1892, 3.

1039. "Choynski and Hall to-Night," *Philadelphia Inquirer*, April 9, 1892, 3; "Hall and Choynski Win Easily," *Philadelphia Inquirer*, April 10, 1892, 1.

1040. "Jim Hall Scores Fitzsimmons," *Chicago Tribune*, April 10, 1892, 4.

1041. "Fred Pfeffer's Case," *Chicago Tribune*, April 11, 1892, 10.

1042. "Jim Hall Says Some Severe Things About Bob Fitzsimmons," *St. Louis Post Dispatch*, April 10, 1892, 24.

1043. "Hall and Choynski," *Morning Olympian*, April 12, 1892, 1.

1044. "The King-Twelve Thousand Dollar for Fitz and Hall," *Times Picayune*, April 19, 1892, 6.

1045. "Hall and Fitzsimmons Matched," *Chicago Tribune*, April 13, 1892, 6.

1046. "As Bottle Holder," *St. Louis Post Dispatch*, April 14, 1892, 5; "'Parson' Davies' Bottle Knocked Connors Out, Peter Maher Couldn't Stand the Jollying of a Consumptive," *New York Herald*, April 14, 1892, 5. "The Parson Wields A Bottle," *Inter Ocean*, April 14, 1892, 6; "'Parson' Davies Denial-He Did Not Strike Connors Who Attempted to Kill Peter Maher," *Philadelphia Inquirer*, April 15, 1892, 3.

1047. "Sporting Gossip," *Inter Ocean*, April 14, 1892, 6.

1048. On April 18, Hall knocked out a fellow named Chris Cornell in one round. The next evening Choynski was supposed to meet a big Boston boxer named Blockey but the Boston man backed out and Jerry Slattery, a celebrity in New York's Bowery was substituted. Slattery had a big following in the area and the theater was packed. The World noted that Choynski had a curious way of fighting that bothered Slattery considerably and resulted in Jerry's head coming in contact with the floor four times in the first round. He went down three more times in the second round until deciding that it would not be polite to keep getting up and was counted out. For his efforts Joe was presented with a massive floral horseshoe. See "General Sporting Notes," *Philadelphia Inquirer*, April 21, 1892, 3.

1049. Charles McCarthy was knocked out in two rounds by Choynski on April 21 and Slattery returned that evening and again knocked out in two rounds, but this time by Hall. Slattery returned for another two round knock out, but this time by Hall. On that day, Davies published a notice stating that due to commitments Hall and Choynski had in Philadelphia the three of them would delay their departure for England for one week to permit appearances through May 2. "Plenty of Blood and Excitement," *Evening Bulletin*, April 23, 1892, 1.

1050. "Leedom Will Box Smith the Former Was Preparing for His March with Jim Hail," *Philadelphia Inquirer*, April 22, 1892, 3; "Choynski Not Ready," *Pittsburg Dispatch*, April 21, 1892, 8.

1051. "The Police Stopped It," *Pittsburg Dispatch*, May 2, 1892, 6.

1052. "The Pugilists In General," *Pittsburg Dispatch*, May 8, 1892, 15.

1053. "The Ring-Parson Davies Reckons Without the Coney Island Club," *Times Picayune*, May 6, 1892, 9.

1054. "Parson Davies in Chicago He Says Hall Will Fight Fitzsimmons in November or December," *Philadelphia Inquirer*, April 26, 1892, 2; "Parson Davies Puts A New Face On Things," *St. Paul Daily Globe*, April 26, 1892, 5; "Hall Won't Fight," *Pittsburg Dispatch*, April 28, 1892, 8.

1055. "The Olympic's Ultimatum," *St. Paul Daily Globe*, May 03, 1892, 5.

1056. "Hall and Fitzsimmons Once More," *Pittsburg Dispatch*, May 01, 1892, 15.

1057. See note 988 above.

1058. "Week of Sports in New Orleans," *Record-Union*, April 25, 1892, 1; "Myer and M'Auliffe Matched," *Chicago Tribune*, April 24, 1892, 2; "The Myer-M'Auliffe Match-Articles of Agreement on Their Way to Chicago, With M'Auliffe's Signature," *Chicago Tribune*, April 29, 1892, 7; "Myer Has Not Yet Signed," *Chicago Tribune*, May 6, 1892, 6; "Fitzsimons and Pritchard,: *Times-Picayune*, April 30, 1892, 3; "The Ring," *St. Louis Post Dispatch*, May 3, 1892, 10; "$87,000 in Three New Orleans Fights," *Chicago Tribune*, May 4, 1892, 6.

1059. "The Ring," *St. Louis Post Dispatch*, April 29, 1892, 12.

1060. "The Ring," *St. Louis Post Dispatch*, April 29, 1892, 12..

1061. "Bob Fitzsimmons is Here the Champion Middle-Weight," *Philadelphia Inquirer*, May 2, 1892, 3.

1062. "The Ring," *St. Louis Post Dispatch*, May 3, 1892, 10.

1063. "General Sporting Notes," *Chicago Tribune*, April 30, 1892, 6; "Hall Off For Europe," *St. Paul Daily Globe*, May 05, 1892, 5; "Gone and Good Riddance," *Duluth News-Tribune*, May 5, 1892, 1; Ancestry.com. UK Incoming Passenger Lists, 1878-1960 [database on-line]. Provo, UT, USA: Ancestry.com Operations Inc, 2008. Original data: Board of Trade: Commercial and Statistical Department and successors: Inwards Passenger Lists. Kew, Surrey, England: The National Archives of the UK (TNA). Series BT26, 1,472 pieces.

1064. "General Sporting Notes," *Chicago Tribune*, May 27, 1892, 7.

1065. "The Ring," *St. Louis Post Dispatch*, May 15, 1892, 5.

1066. "Big Odds On Slavin," *St. Louis Post Dispatch*, May 29, 1892, 8; "The Ring, The Slavin and Jackson Fight To-Morrow," *St. Louis Post Dispatch*, May 29, 1892, 24; "Jackson In Splendid Shape," *Chicago Tribune*, May 23, 1892, 6.

1067. Hall met a fighter named Kit Mahoney in London on May 25 and stopped him in four rounds. Choynski met Mike Horrigon in London on May 24 and knocked him out in the first round. Horrigan was one of the few men Choynski could recall by name. He remembered Horrigan because he "was full of tattoo marks." Joe had a scheduled bout on May 25 with Jack Hart, but the result is not reported. He met Hart again four days later and won in three rounds. In between this matches with Hart, Joe knocked out a man named William Patmore in the first round on May 27. "The Ring," *St. Louis Post Dispatch*, May 18, 1892, 12.

1068. "The Parson's Break With Hall," *Sun*, September 15, 1892, 4; "Jim Hall Arrives," *Salt Lake Herald*, December 11, 1892, 16.

1069. See note 988 above.

1070. "Slavin Is Whipped," *Chicago Tribune*, May 31, 1892, 1; "Jackson's Victory," *St. Louis Post Dispatch*, May 31, 1892, 8; "The Ring, Parson Davies Grows Reminiscent," *Times Picayune*, March 24, 1898, 8.

1071. "Did 'Parson' Davies Win Heavily," *Chicago Tribune*, June 1, 1892, 7.

1072. "Sullivan Is Sorrowful," *Bloomington Bulletin*, June 1, 1892, 7.

1073. "General Sporting Notes," *Chicago Tribune*, June 4, 1892, 7.

1074. "The 'Parson' Cautious," *St. Louis Post Dispatch*, Jun 5, 1892, 16.

1075. "Jackson Is Willing," *Chicago Tribune*, December 6, 1892, 6.

1076. "'Parson' Davies Busy," *Chicago Tribune*, June 6, 1892, 14.

1077. See note 1077 above.

1078. "General Sporting Notes," *Chicago Tribune*, June 20, 1892, 16.

1079. "Parson Davies and His Company to Visit France," *Salt Lake Herald*, June 21, 1892, 8.

1080. "Parson Davies and His Fighters," *Chicago Tribune*, July 10, 1892, 6; "Peter Jackson and Joe Choynski in Germany," *Salt Lake Herald*, July 12, 1892, 1; "Miscellaneous Sports," *Pittsburg Dispatch*, July 11, 1892, 10.

1081. "Gossip Of The Prize Ring," *Brooklyn Eagle*, July 27, 1892, 12.

1082. "The Ring," *St. Louis Post Dispatch*, July 27, 1892, 7.

1083. "Hall May Have to Fight A Gang," *Chicago Tribune*, July 31, 1892, 7.

1084. "On English Soil," *St. Louis Post Dispatch*, August 13, 1892, 8.

1085. "Whipped By Hall," *St. Louis Post Dispatch*, August 20, 1892, 8; "Hall Victorious," *St. Louis Post Dispatch*, August 21, 1892, 7; "Hall Won It Easily," *Chicago Tribune*, August 21, 1892, 4.

1086. "Parson Davies Left," *Chicago Tribune*, August 28, 1892, 5.

1087. "Government Officers Anxious, The Power of the Federal Authorities in Quarantine Matters," *New York Times*, September 1, 1892, 2; "No Foothold Yet Gained; Cholera Gets No Nearer Than Quarantine. No New Cases on the Moravia and None on Other Vessels, *New York Times*, September 2, 1892, 1; "More Victims of Cholera, Four Deaths Yesterday on the Quarantined Ships, etc.," *New York Times*, September 5, 1892, 1.

1088. "General Sporting Notes," *Trenton Times*, August 26, 1892, 8; "Parson Davies Left," *Chicago Tribune*, August 28, 1892, 5. The *Tribune* article includes some accurate and some inaccurate information.

1089. "Olympic Color Line," *Chicago Tribune*, September 1, 1892, 7; "'Parson' Davies Arrives at Quarantine," *Chicago Tribune*, September 3, 1892, 5; "'Parson' Davies Not Held-Set Free from Quarantine, He Makes All Haste to Reach New Orleans," *Inter Ocean*, September 4, 1892, 6.

1090. "Parson Davies; Senator McPherson; A. M. Palmer; Dr. Jenkins; Tammany; Doctor," *Inter Ocean*, September 6, 1892, 4.

1091. See note 988 above.

1092. "How Corbett Will Travel. The Californian Will Go To New Orleans In Luxurious Style," *St. Louis Post Dispatch*, September 3, 1892, 5; "Corbett Will Travel Like a Prince," *St. Louis Post Dispatch*, August 10, 1892, 8; "Corbett's Train Selected," *Trenton Times*, August 10, 1892, 5; "Corbett Will Travel Like A King," *Chicago Tribune*, September 1, 1892, 7.

1093. "Corbett Leaves His Quarters," *Chicago Tribune*, September 4, 1892, 4.

1094. "Corbett At Charlotte," *Inter Ocean*, September 5, 1892, 3; "On Board The Corbett Special," *Chicago Tribune*, September 5, 1892, 2; "Waiting The Big Fight," *St. Louis Post Dispatch*, September 5, 1892, 1.

1095. "The Ring," *St. Louis Post Dispatch*," February 14, 1893, 8. Corbett states that Davies notified him on the way to New Orleans that Jackson was willing to meet Corbett again if Corbett won the fight.

1096. "Corbett's Sudden Departure," *Chicago Tribune*, September 6, 1892, 3.

1097. "Myer Knocked Out," *Inter Ocean*, September 6, 1892, 6. Parson Davies and Joe Choynski listed as a notables present.

1098. "Green-Room Special, That is What They Call the Train That Carries the Sports," *Inter Ocean*, September 4, 1892, 6; "Chicagoans Will See The Fights," *Chicago Tribune*, September 4, 1892, 4. Among those traveling were: Vere Davies, Otto Floto, Henry Glickauf, Bill Bradburn, Bath House John Cullerton, and John Kline. "More Chicagoans Arrive," *Chicago Tribune*, September 4, 1892, 4 Those traveling included: Alderman Powers, Alderman O'Brien, Alderman Morris, John Condon, and Malachi Hogan.

1099. "Extra-Jack Wins," *St. Louis Post Dispatch*, September 5, 1892, 1. Joe Choynski was a second for McAuliffe. "After The Big Fight," *National Police Gazette*, September 4, 1892, 2; "Corbett Welcomed," *National Police Gazette*, October 1, 1892, 2; "Sullivan's Glory," *National Police Gazette*, October 8, 1896, 2.

1100. "George Dixon Whips Skelly," *Pittsburg Dispatch*, September 7, 1892, 7. Carroll, Joe Choynski and Jack McAuliffe were seconds for Skelly.

1101. "Chicago Sports Back," *Chicago Tribune*, September 10, 1892, 2 (Vere Davies says that he went to the fight with his brother Charlie and Warren Lewis. He states that Charlie bet $2,500 on Corbett at 1 X 3 odds.

1102. "Warren Lewis," *National Police Gazette*, October 1, 1892, 10.

1103. "Already After Corbett," *Cleveland Plain Dealer*, September 15, 1892, 5; "Corbett and Jackson," *Boston Daily Globe*, September 14, 1892, 15.

1104. "Corbett and Jackson Will Fight," *Chicago Tribune*, September 26, 1892, 12.

1105. "Pugilistic Pointers," *St. Louis Post Dispatch*, September 22, 1892, 12.

1106. "General Sporting Notes," *Chicago Tribune*, October 7, 1892, 6.

1107. "Pugilistic Pointers," *St. Louis Post Dispatch*, October 10, 1892, 8.

1108. "Frank Glover Is Dead," *Chicago Herald*, September 23, 1892, 6.

1109. Doherty, W. J., *In the Days of the Giants* (George C. Harrap & Co. Ltd., 1931), 80-89.

1110. "Jackson and Goddard Matched," *Trenton Times*, September 27, 1892, 6.

1111. "The Ring," *St. Louis Post Dispatch*, October 1, 1892, 8.

1112. "Choynski Confident," *St. Louis Post Dispatch*, October 17, 1892, 8.

1113. "General Sporting Notes," *Chicago Tribune*, October 5, 1892, 7.

1114. "The Ring," *St. Louis Post Dispatch*, October 28, 1892, 12; "A Good Fight Looked For," *National Police Gazette*, October 15, 1892, 11; "It Will Be A Great Fight," *National Police Gazette*, October 22, 1892, 10.

1115. 1892; Microfilm serial: M237; Microfilm roll: M237_599; Line: 28; New York Passenger Lists, 1820-1957 [database on-line]. Provo, UT, USA: Ancestry.com Operations, Inc., 2006; "Jackson After Corbett," *Trenton Times*, October 28, 1892, 5; "The Ring," *St. Louis Post Dispatch*, October 27, 1892, 8.

1116. "Sporting Notes, *St. Louis Post Dispatch*, November 1, 1892, 8.

1117. "Godfrey Knocked Out By Choynski," *Chicago Tribune*, November 1, 1892, 6; "Choynski Won The Fight," *Morning Call*, November 01, 1892, 1.

1118. "Choynski Defeats Godfrey. Profitable Investment of the Coney Island Athletic Club," *New York Times*, November 1, 1892, 2; "Done In Fifteen Rounds," *National Police Gazette*, November 12, 1892, 10; "Choynski's Recent Victory," *National Police Gazette*, November 19, 1892, 11.

1119. See note 988 above.

1120. Year: 1892; Microfilm serial: M237; Microfilm roll: M237_600; Line: 22; Source Information:

Ancestry.com. New York Passenger Lists, 1820-1957 [database on-line]. Provo, UT, USA: Ancestry.com Operations, Inc., 2006; Original data: Passenger Lists of Vessels Arriving at New York, New York, 1820-1897; (National Archives Microfilm Publication M237, 675 rolls); Records of the US Customs Service, Record Group 36; National Archives, Washington, D.C.

1121. "Fighter Mitchell Jailed," *Pittsburg Dispatch*, October 05, 1892, 1.

1122. See note 988 above.

1123. "Jackson at the Academy. The Australian Heavyweight Spars Four Light Rounds with John McVey of This City," *Philadelphia Inquirer*, November 2, 1892, 3.

1124. "Pete Jackson's Living Hope," *Boston Daily Globe*, November 14, 1892, 16; "Pugilists as Actors," *Philadelphia Inquirer*, November 15, 1892, 3; "The Ring," *St. Louis Post Dispatch*, November 16, 1892, 12.

1125. "Corbett and Jackson Meet-The Champion of the World and the Champion of Australia Shake Hands," *Philadelphia Inquirer*, November 19, 1892, 3.

1126. "Plays and Players," *Boston Daily Globe*, November 27, 1892, 10; "Stage Notes," *San Antonio Daily Light*, November 30, 1892, 3; "At the Play Houses," *Sunday Herald {Bridgeport, Connecticut}*, January 29, 1893, 34; "Amusements-Lost in London," *Lewiston Evening Journal*, January 10, 1893, 5.

1127. "Gossip of the Ring and Field," *Evening World*, November 26, 1892, 5; "Knocked Out," *Morning Call*, November 27, 1892, 1; "Pete Hit Him Once," *St. Paul Daily Globe*, November 27, 1892, 10; "Pete Jackson Resents an Insult," *Weekly Gazette And Stockman {Reno}*, December 1, 1892, 8.

1128. "General Sporting Notes," *Philadelphia Inquirer*, November 21, 1892, 3; "The Lyceum," *Philadelphia Inquirer*, November 29, 1892, 5.

1129. "Jackson Beat Kelliher. The Big Colored Fellow Punched Him at Will for Three Rounds," Philadelphia Inquirer, November 29, 1892, 3.

1130. "Jackson Meets Billy McLean," *Philadelphia Inquirer*, November 30, 1892, 3.

1131. "Jackson to Meet Leedom," *Philadelphia Inquirer*, December 1, 1892, 3; "Leedom Easy for Jackson," *Philadelphia Inquirer*, December 2, 1892, 3; "Jackson Bests Fallon," *Philadelphia Inquirer*, December 3, 1892, 3.

1132. "Joe Choynski Knocks Out Joe Fallon," *St. Paul Daily Globe*, November 27, 1892, 10.

1133. "Smith Easy for Choynski," *Philadelphia Inquirer*, November 22, 1892, 3; "Jack Fallon Knocked Out, Philadelphia Inquirer, November 27, 1892, 3.

1134. "The Ring," *St. Louis Post Dispatch*, November 30, 1892, 10.

1135 "The Ring," *St. Louis Post Dispatch*, December 1, 1892, 16; "Jackson Is Willing," *Chicago Tribune*, December 6, 1892, 6.

1136. "Choynski Coming," *Salt Lake Herald*, December 9, 1892, 6.

1137. "The Colored Slugger-Pete Jackson Talks About Pugilism En Route," *Omaha World Herald*, December 13, 1892, 5.

1138. "General Sporting Notes," *Salt Lake Herald*, December 13, 1892, 5; "Pete and the Parson," *Salt Lake Herald*, December 14, 1892, 5.

1139. "Peter Jackson," *Deseret Evening News*, December 15, 1892, 5.

1140. Big Peter On Parade, *Salt Lake Herald*, December 15, 1892, 6.

1141. Ibid.

1142. Ibid.

1143. "Brevities," *Daily Nevada State Journal*, December 16, 1892, 3.

1144. "Parson Davies In Ogden," *Ogden Standard*, December 22, 1892, 1.

1145. "The Parson In Town," *Inter Ocean*, December 24, 1892, 6; "Maher's Chicago Debut," *St. Louis Post Dispatch*, December 24, 1892, 8.

1146. "Boxing at Battery D," *Chicago Tribune*, December 25, 1892, 4; "Boxing Match Thursday Night," *Chicago Tribune*, December 27, 1892, 7; "Pugilistic Pointers," *St. Louis Post Dispatch*, December 29, 1892, 12; "Choynski and Maher May Fight," *Chicago Tribune*, December 29, 1892, 7.

1147. "Choynski Shows Up Well," *Inter Ocean,* December 30, 1892, 7.

1148. "Choynski's Plans," *Omaha Daily Bee*, January 1, 1893, 2.

1149. "Sparred and Boxed," *Chicago Tribune*, December 30, 1892, 7.

1150. "Corbett In Chicago," *National Police Gazette*, November 5, 1892, 10.

1151. "Pugilism Pays," *St. Louis Post Dispatch*, January 1, 1893, 22; "Year's Prize Fights," *Chicago Tribune*, January 2, 1893, 12.

Chapter 13 – The Stage and *Uncle Tom's Cabin* - (1893)

1152. "Another Fighting Club, *New York Times*, January 29, 1893, 3.

1153. "Choynski and Davis [sic]," *Ogden Standard*, January 1, 1893, 1; "Choynski Is Surely Coming," *Salt Lake Tribune*, January 2, 1893, 1; "Anxious To See Joseph," *Salt Lake Herald*, January 1, 1893, 2.

1154. "Joe Drew A Crowd," *Salt Lake Herald*, January 3, 1893, 8; "Offered a $5,000 Purse," *Salt Lake Tribune*, January 9, 2.

1155. "Choynski and Davis [sic]," *Standard*, January 3, 1893, 1.

1156. "Sporting Notes," *Morning Call*, January 05, 1893, 8.

1157. "Jack Ashton Dead," *World*, January 7, 1893, 10; "Jack Ashton Dead," *Philadelphia Inquirer*, January 7, 1893, 3; "Jack Ashton Dead," *New York Herald*, January 7, 1893, 9; "Telegraphic Notes of Sport," Chicago Tribune, January 8, 1893, 7; "Jack Ashton's Death," *World*, January 8, 1893, 13.

1158. "Sullivan's Fiery Talk," *Galveston Daily News*, December 27, 1892, 2.

1159. "John L. Going Crazy," *Pittsburg Dispatch*, December 27, 1892, 7 (Sullivan appeared before a crowded house); "Windsor Theater," *Evening World.*, December 28, 1892, 3 (Sullivan before a friendly house); "Sporting News and Notes," *Evening World*, December 27, 1892, 2; "Sullivan Speaks," *Tombstone Epitaph*, January 1, 1893, 1.

1160. "Jack Ashton in a Hospital," *Boston Globe*, January 5, 1893, 11; "Our Theaters Next Week," *Evening World*, December 24, 1892, 5.

1161. "Preparations for Jack Ashton's Funeral," *Sun*, January 9, 1893, 8.

1162. "Telegraphic Brevities," *Morning Call*, January 10, 1893, 2.

1163. "Benefit For Ashton's Widow," *St. Louis Post Dispatch*, March 5, 1893, 3.

1164. 'Choynski in Europe. The Prize Fighter Details His Experiences Abroad," *Morning Olympian*, January 5, 1893, 1.

1165. "The Ring," *St. Louis Post Dispatch*, January 11, 1893, 3.

1166. "Pugilism," *Record-Union*, January 9, 1893, 1; "Choynski After A Fight," *St. Louis Post Dispatch*, January 9, 1893, 8.

1167. "Afraid to Meet Choynski," *St. Louis Post Dispatch*, January 14, 1893, 8.

1168. "Pugilism on the Coast," *St. Louis Post Dispatch*, January 21, 1893, 8.

1169. "Peter Jackson, The Colored Champion at Turnverein Hall Last Evening," *Los Angeles Times*, January 20, 1893, 1.

1170. "To Play Uncle Tom," *Chicago Tribune*, January 21, 1893, 7; "The Ring," *Morning Call*, January 22, 1893, 16.

1171. See note 988 above.

1172. "Sporting Notes," *Inter Ocean*, September 8, 1890, 2; "The Oleaginous Parsom [sic]," *Inter Ocean*, October 15, 1890, 2.

1173. "Plays and Players," *Boston Daily Globe*, November 27, 1892, 10; "Stage Notes," *San Antonio Daily Light*, November 30, 1892, 3.

1174. "Big Peter on Parade," *Salt Lake Herald*, December 15, 1892, 6.

1175. "Uncle Tom's Alleged Cabin Coming to Chicago. Is Now on a Red River Plantation, but Will Be Placed on Exhibition--How Mrs. Harriet Beecher Stowe Obtained Material to Form the Character--No Evidence That Her Model Went to the South--Traditions of McAlpin, Alias Legree. Escape of Eliza. Points of Resemblance. Fits the Description," *Chicago Tribune*, November 20, 1892, 12; "At The World's Fair Some Of The Attractions That Are Of Note," *Trenton Evening Times*, December 7, 1892, 7; "At the World's Fair," *Freeman*, February 11, 1893, 5; "What Is to Be Seen At the World's Fair," *Aurora Daily Express*, August 7, 1893, 4. The history of this real cabin had been traced to Nachitoches, Louisiana where the people in that community claimed that the real Simon Legree had been a man living near there named Robert McAlpin. In addition, none other than Frederick Douglas had propossed an opera utilizing all Black members, founded on "Uncle Tom's Cabin," and to be presented at the Chicago Fair.

1176. "Odds and Ends," *Omaha Daily Bee*, February 22, 1887, 5.

1177. See note 988 above.

1178. "The Athletic World," *Wanganui Herald*, March 11, 1893, 2.

1179. Clark, Susan F., "Up against the Ropes, Peter Jackson As 'Uncle Tom' in America," The Drama review 44, 1 (Spring 2000), 157.

1180. Ibid. at 160.

1181. "Sullivan Will Not Fight Jackson," *Toronto Daily Mail*, December 31, 1888, 2.

1182. "Sullivan Won't Notice A Coon," *St. Paul Daily Globe*, December 30, 1888, 7.

1183. "Sporting Notes," *Sun*, May 02, 1888, 3.

1184. "Jackson Wants to Meet Godfrey," *Boston Daily Globe*, May 28, 1888, 2; "General Sporting Notes," *Logansport Pharos*, May 18, 1888, 3; "Colored Heavyweight Champion," *Logansport Pharos*, June 1, 1888, 3.

1185. "The Ring," *Te Aroha News*, July 14, 1888, 5.

1186. "Athletic Mems.," *Sydney Mail*, September 1, 1888, 20.

1187. "Athletic Mems.," *Wanganui Herald*, August 25, 1888, 2.

1188. "The Ring," *Te Aroha News*, July 14, 1888, 5.

1189. "The Mill Arranged For Champions in California," *Morning Oregonian*, July 1, 1888, 2.

1190. "Two Colored Gladiators," *Omaha Daily Bee*, September 9, 1888, 9.

1191. "Colored Fistic Artists," *Morning Oregonian*, September 26, 1888, 8.

1192. "Among the Pugilists," *Herald*, September 2, 1888, 5.

1193. "The World's Champion Pugilist," *Pittsburg Dispatch*, May 08, 1892, 15.

1194. "Saw Himself Fight. Sharkey Witness [sic] the Pictures and Comments on Them. Peter Jackson Showed His Generosity When he Fought His Fist Battle In This Country," *Sandusky Star*, November 16, 1899, 1.

1195. See note 1188 above at 161.

1196. "Cardiff Is Willing," *St. Paul Daily Globe*, January 12, 1889, 5; "Will Tackle Jackson," *Pittsburg Dispatch*, January 30, 1889, 6.

1197. See note 1188 above.

1198. See note 1188 above at 171.

1199. "Peter Jackson In Uncle Tom's Cabin," *Morning Call*, February 28, 1893, 7.

1200. "Fighters In Training," *Chicago Tribune*, July 10, 1891, 6; "Big Peter on Parade," *Salt Lake Herald*, December 15, 1892

1201. "A Talk With Jackson," *Salt Lake Tribune*, April 1, 1893, 6.

1202. "Not Spoiling for a Fight. Jackson Says He is Not Running after Champion Corbett," *Omaha World Herald,* April 21, 1893, 3.

1203. "We Did Not Laugh," *Decatur Daily Review*, January 25, 1893, 4.

1204. "Peter Jackson's Challenge," *New York Times*, February 12, 1893, 3.

1205. "Pugilistic Pointers," *St. Louis Post Dispatch*, January 21, 1893, 8.

1206. "To Fight In March-Men Who Will Take Part In The New Orleans Carnival," *Chicago Tribune*, February 19, 1893, 4.

1207. "Lewis Is Champion," *St. Paul Daily Globe*, March 3, 1893, 1; "Lewis Is The Winner," *Chicago Tribune*, March 3, 1893, 7.

1208. "Would Not Fight-West Prevents Choynski Knocking Him Out," *Morning Call*, February 7, 1893, 2; "Couldn't Knock Him Out," *Record-Union*, February 7, 1893, 1.

1209. Advertisement, *{Sacramento} Record-Union*, February 24, 1893, 2.

1210. "Amusements," *{Sacramento} Record-Union*, February 25, 1893, 1; "Amusements," *{Sacramento} Record-Union*, February 27, 1893, 3; Advertisement, *{Sacramento} Record-Union*, February 24, 1893, 4.

1211. "Choynski Looking For Trouble," *Omaha Daily Bee*, February 27, 1893, 3. This article reports that Choynski was in Chicago on February 26, 1891.

1212. "Random References," *Ogden Standard*, February 25, 1893, 4.

1213. "Thinks Hall Will Win Easily," *Chicago Tribune*, February 26, 1893, 5; "Joe Choynski Talks," *St. Paul Daily Globe*, February 27, 1893, 5; "Pugilistic Pointers," *St. Louis Post Dispatch*, February 27, 1893, 8.

1214. "Thinks Hall Will Win Easily," *Chicago Tribune*, February 26, 1893, 5; "Joe Choynski Talks," *St. Paul Daily Globe*, February 27, 1893, 5; "Pugilistic Pointers," *St. Louis Post Dispatch*, February 27, 1893, 8.

1215. "Our Theaters," *Morning Call*, February 26, 1893, 11.

1216. "Peter Jackson In Uncle Tom's Cabin," *Morning Call*, February 28, 1893, 7.

1217. "Amusements," *Morning Call*, March 2, 1893, 2; "Local Amusements," *Morning Call*, March 10, 1893, 4.

1218. "Corbett's Manager Going to New York," *Chicago Tribune*, February 14, 1893, 7; "The Ring," *St. Louis Post Dispatch*, February 14, 1893, 8. Article states that Mitchell gets the preference because he was the first to challenge the winner of the Corbett-Sullivan match. "Mr. Mitchell Is Here," *New York Times*, February 16, 1893, 3; "Corbett Will Fight," *Chicago Tribune*, February 17, 1893, 7; "Mitchell Eager To Fight," *New York Times*, February 18, 1893, 10; "Mitchell Makes The Match," *New York Times*, February 19, 1893, 3; "Shady Financial Operation Creates Trouble Between the Visitors from England," *Chicago Tribune*, February 22, 1893, 7; "Mitchell Proposes to Meet Corbett in New Orleans to Sign Articles," *Chicago Tribune*, February 24, 1893, 7; "They Have Agreed-Full Text of the Articles of Agreement," *St. Louis Post Dispatch*, February 25, 1893, 8.

1219. "Jackson Money Withdrawn," *{Sacramento} Record-Union*, February 16, 1893, 1.

1220. "Mitchell On Shore," *Chicago Tribune*, February 17, 1893, 7.

1221. "Brutal Slogging," *Morning Call*, February 25, 1893, 8; "Miller Dies From Hawkins' Blows," *Morning Call*, February 26, 1893, 3.

1222. "Jackson's Proposition," *St. Louis Post Dispatch*, March 14, 1893, 10; "Jackson and Corbett," *Salt Lake Herald*, March 14, 1893, 1.

1223. "Jackson Peer of All, Says 'Parson' Davies," *Seattle Daily Times*, December 14, 1910, 19.

1224. "Backing Hall," *Chicago Tribune*, February 27, 1892, 12; "Ryan's Fight Is Off," *Chicago Tribune*, March 2, 1893, 7.

1225. "Gibbons Whips Daly," *Chicago Tribune*, March 8, 1893, 7.

1226. "Hall Knocked Out," *Chicago Tribune*, March 9, 1893, 7.

1227. "Fitz Made Fortune In Whipping Hall," *Nebraska State Journal*, August 1, 1909, C-7.

1228. "Winning On The Fight," *New York Times*, March 10, 1893, 3.

1229. "Theatrical Chat," *Ogden Standard*, March 12, 1893, 12; "Stage Chow Chow," *Ogden Standard*, March 12, 1893, 12.

1230. "Theatrical Chat," *Ogden Standard*, March 5, 1893, 6.

1231. "Theatrical Chat," *Ogden Standard*, March 5, 1893, 6.

1232. "The Parson's Farewell," *Morning Call*, March 20, 1893, 7.

1233. The characters and their roles were: Uncle Tom (Jackson), Auctioneer (Davies), Marks (Stockwell), George Harris (H. S. Duffield), Simon Legree (Clarence Ferguson), Phineas Fletcher (Frank Hatch), George Shelby (Walter Miller), Haley (Chas. Forrest), Tom Loker (Fred Wagner), Sambo (O. T. Jackson), Quimbo (Harry Fisher), Liza (Phosa McAllister), Mrs. Saint Clair (Grace Fielding), Eva (Little Anna), Topsy (Minnie Sheldon), Emeline (Adele Saunders), Chloe (Alice Waters). "Amusements," *Standard*, March 25, 1893, 1; "Theatrical Chat," *Standard*, March 26, 1893, 6; "Jackson and Choynski" *Salt Lake Herald*, March 25, 1893, 5.

1234. "'Uncle' Tom's Cabin," *Standard*, March 30, 1893, 4; "Amusements," *Standard*, March 28, 1893, 3; "Amusements, Peter Jackson As Uncle Tom," *Standard*, March 29, 1893, 3.

1235. "Amusements-Peter Jackson & Co." *Salt Lake Herald*, April 01, 1893, 2.

1236. "The New Peter The Great," *Salt Lake Tribune*, April 1, 1893, 6.

1237 "A Talk With Jackson," *Salt Lake Tribune*, April 1, 1893, 6; "Still After Corbett," *Salt Lake Herald*, April 1, 1893, 6.

1238. "Polite Peter Jackson," *North Adams Transcript*, April 4, 1898, 7; "Jackson at a Ball," *Boston Daily Globe*, January 31, 1908, 9.

1239. "Nye In The West. William Stops Off At Some Places In California. He Sees Peter Jackson etc.," *Trenton Evening Times*, April 1, 1893, 7.

1240. Clark, Darlene and Jenkins, Earnestine eds, *A Question of Manhood: A Reader in U.S. Black Men's History and Masculinity, vol. 2, The 19 Century: From Emancipation to Jim Crow* (Bloomington Indiana University Press 2001), 299. The author also claims that the dispute about the place for the Corbett-Jackson rematch broke out after the parties agreed to a rematch. However, it is perfectly clear that Jackson had said it would not fight in the South within a few days after their first match in 1891. See, "Jackson Challenges Corbett," *Sun*, June 2, 1891,

5 Jackson will fight at the California Club or any other fair club, New Orleans barred.

1241. "Amusements, Uncle Tom's Cabin," *Salt Lake Herald*, March 28, 1893, 5.

1242. "Peter, the Parson, and Joe," *Omaha Daily Bee*, April 16, 1893, Part One, 2; "Clippings From Our Exchanges," *Washington Bee*, April 29, 1893, 1. Quoting from the *Omaha Progress*: "Jackson is a good actor."

1243. "Punches from the Shoulder," *Omaha Daily Bee*, April 24, 1893, 3.

1244. "From Ring to Pulpit," *St. Paul Daily Globe*, April 14, 1893, 1.

1245. "Jackson's Side of the Case," *Omaha Daily Bee*, April 21, 1893, 2.

1246. "The Ring," *St. Louis Post Dispatch*, May 1, 1893, 8; Advertisement, *St. Louis Post Dispatch*, May 1, 1893, 5; "The Ring," *St. Louis Post Dispatch*, May 2, 1893, 10.

1247. "Honors To Peter Jackson," *St. Louis Post Dispatch*, May 4, 1893, 8.

1248. "Parson Davies Posts a Forfeit," *Chicago Tribune*, May 11, 1893, 14.

1249. "Sporting Comment of Interest to All," *Philadelphia Inquirer*, May 7, 1893, 16.

1250. "Scraps of Sport," *St. Paul Daily Globe*, May 11, 1893, 5.

1251. "General Sporting Notes," *Chicago Herald*, May 23, 1893, 6; "Peter Jackson Goes East," *Chicago Tribune*, May 30, 1893, 6.

1252. "Peter Jackson Keeps Mum," *World*, May 31, 1893, 3.

1253. Ibid.

1254. Ibid.

1255. "Held A Poor Hand," *Morning Call*, June 04, 1893, 21.

1256. "Peter Jackson Keeps Mum," *World*, May 31, 1893, 3.

1257. "Jackson In England," *St. Louis Post Dispatch*, June 21, 1893, 7.

1258. "General Sporting Notes," *Chicago Tribune*, June 23, 1893, 6; "Griffo Is After a Fight," *Chicago Tribune*, June 23, 1893, 7; "Griffo In Chicago," *St. Louis Post*

Dispatch, June 24, 1893, 8; "Sporting Notes," *St. Louis Post Dispatch*, June 30, 1893, 5.

1259. "Sporting News," *Trenton Times*, June 29, 1893, 2.

1260. "Choynski Signs The Articles," *Chicago Tribune*, June 25, 1893, 5; "For A Purse of $15,000," *Brooklyn Eagle*, June 25, 1893, 20; "Fitzsimmons And Choynski," *St. Louis Post Dispatch*, June 27, 1893, 6.

1261. "Purse for Choynski and Fitzsimmons," *Chicago Tribune*, July 10, 1893, 6.

1262. "Solly Smith Is Good," *Chicago Tribune*, July 11, 1893, 6.

1263. "Knocked Out By A Chance Blow-John Griffin Whipped by 'Solly' Smith-Corbett to Meet Jackson," *New York Times*, July 11, 1893, 2.

1264. "Solly Smith Is Good," *Chicago Tribune*, July 11, 1893, 6.

1265. "Fight Next June," *St. Louis Post Dispatch*, July 12, 1893, 8.

1266. "Big Match Clinched," *Chicago Tribune*, July 12, 1893, 7; "Fight Next Summer," *Bismarck Daily Tribune*, July 13, 1893, 1.

1267. "Pugilistic Pointers," *St. Louis Post Dispatch*, July 13, 1893, 3.

1268. "Peter Jackson to Arrive Today," *Chicago Tribune*, July 26, 1893, 7.

1269. "Four Bouts In Newark," *Brooklyn Eagle*, July 27, 1893, 2.

1270. "Peter Jackson Ready To Sign," *Chicago Tribune*, July 28, 1893, 7.

1271. "Peter Jackson Here to Arrange a Mill with Corbett," *Chicago Tribune*, July 28, 1893, 7.

1272. "This Evening's Battles," *St. Louis Post Dispatch*, July 31, 1893, 8.

1273. "Many Fights Booked," *Chicago Tribune*, July 30, 1893, 5.

1274. "Jackson and Corbett," *St. Louis Post Dispatch*, September 4, 1893, 8.

1275. "All Around Sport-Peter Jackson's Arrival," *Morning Call*, August 3, 1893, 10.

1276. "Green Had Pluck," *Morning Call*, August 1, 1893, 2; "Corbett Leaves For The East," *Chicago Tribune*, August 2, 1893, 7.

1277. Petersen, Robert, *Gentleman Bruiser, A Life of the Boxer Peter Jackson* (Croydon Publishing 2005), 253.

1278. "Dan Creedon's Power," *Chicago Tribune*, August 14, 1893, 7; "In Fifteen Rounds," *Evening Bulletin*, August 15, 1893, 1.

1279. "Very Glad to Get Home. Spectators in the Arena at Roby Attached by a Mob," *New York Times*, August 16, 1893, 6.

1280. "Sporting Notes," *Morning Call*, August 16, 1893, 4; "Dempsey-Burge Fight Still On," *Chicago Tribune*, August 19, 1893, 6; "Among the Pugs," *St. Louis Post Dispatch*, August 20, 1893, 10.

1281. "Only One Cent Capital," *Salt Lake Herald*, December 14, 1893, 8; "Vagrant Fakirs," *Morning Call*, December 27, 1893, 10.

1282. See note 988 above.

1283. The second season cast was: Uncle Tom (Peter Jackson), Auctioneer (Davies), Marks (Stockwell), George Harris (H. S. Duffield Davies), Simon Legree (Clarence Ferguson), Phineas Fletcher (Frank Hatch Sam Carman), George Shelby (Walter Miller Joe Choynski), Haley (Chas. Forrest), Tom Loker (Fred Wagner Rod Wagoner), Sambo (O. T. Jackson), Quimbo (Harry Fisher William Hart), Liza (Phosa McAllister Ida Warner), Mrs. Saint Clair (Grace Fielding), Eva (Little Anna [Laughlin]),

Topsy (Minnie Sheldon Louise Miller), Emeline (Adele Saunders), Chloe (Alice Waters [not listed]). "Uncle Tom's Cabin," *Newark {Ohio} Daily Advocate*, August 30, 1893, 5; Advertisement, *Newark {Ohio} Daily Advocate*, August 28, 1893, 5.

1284. "Peter Jackson," *Newark {Ohio} Daily Advocate*, September 1, 1893, 8.

1285. Advertisement, *Cincinnati Enquirer*, September 16, 1893, 5.

1286. "Wants A Match," *Cincinnati Enquirer*, September 8, 1893, 2; "Fitzsimmons and Choynski," *St. Louis Post Dispatch*, September 9, 1893, 8.

1287. "Theatricals," *Olean Democrat*, September 12, 1893, 3, Advertisement, *Olean Democrat*, September 14, 1893, 3; Advertisement, *Olean Democrat*, September 15, 1893, 5.

1288. "Local Pencilings," *McKean Democrat*, September 15, 1893, 3.

1289. "Footlight Stars," *{Syracuse} Herald*, September 17, 1893, 2; "Actor and Pugilist," *Syracuse Courier*, September 19, 1893.

1290. "O'Donnell and Choynski," *St. Louis Post Dispatch*, August 23, 1893, 8.

1291. "Pugilistic Pointers," *St. Louis Post Dispatch*, July 13, 1893, 3; "Telegraphic Notes of Sport," *Chicago Tribune*, August 3, 1893, 7; "May Stop The Fight-Arrest of Roby Sports Tonight Now Threatened," *Chicago Tribune*, August 14, 1893, 7; "Denounces Columbian Fights, Old Citizens of Lake County, Ind., Meet and Pass Resolutions," *Chicago Tribune*, August 24, 1893, 6; "Will Stop The Fight, The Governor of Indiana Has Forestalled Monday Night's Sport," *Daily State Register*, September 4, 1893, 1; "Will Roby be Raided? Dominick O'Malley Says That Governor Matthews is Bluffing," *Inter Ocean*, September 4, 1893, 1; "Gov. Matthews Massing Foot, Horse and Artillery at Roby," *St. Louis Post Dispatch*, September 4, 1893, 8; "Troops Around the Arena," *Elkhart Daily Review*, September 5, 1893, 1; No Fight at Roby. Gov. Matthews of Indiana Bests Dominick O'Malley. Troops at the Gates," *Duluth News-Tribune*, September 5, 1893, 1; "Johnny Didn't Fight," *Daily State Register*, September 5, 1893, 1; "Roby Prize, Fight Cases to Be Heard by Judge Langdon," *Chicago Tribune*, September 27, 1893, 6; "Will Be Brought Off South-Plans of the Columbian Club in Case of Defeat Monday," *Chicago Tribune*, September 30, 1893, 6.

1292. "A Determined Governor," *Saginaw News*, September 14, 1893, 2.

1293. Dan Creedon and Tom Tracy had arrived in the United States in late December 1892. Tracy had "Dummy" Mace for the lightweight championship of Australia just before coming to the States. Creedon had fought a draw with Martin Costello in Australia. They were part of a steady stream of Australian fighters but not of the same caliber as Jackson and Fitzsimmons. See, "Big Purses," *Boston Daily Globe*, December 26, 1892, 6.

1294. "Mayor Gilroy Would Stop It," *New York Times*, September 26, 1893, 2.

1295. "Where Law Is To Be Defied," *New York Times*, September 26, 1893, 1; "Who Will Tell Gov. Flower," *New York Times*, September 27, 1893, 1; "Gov. Flower Gives Warning," *New York Times*, September 29, 1893, 1; "The Fight Must Be Stopped," *New York Times*, September 30, 1893, 8; "Will Denounce the Bruisers, Brooklyn Ministers to Preach Against the Prize Fight," *New York Times*, October 1, 1893, 13; "Brooklyn Good Name at Stake," *New York Times*, October 3, 1893, 1; "Thunders of Denunciation, Prize Fight Promoters Attacked from the Pulpit," *New York Times*, October 9, 1893, 1;"Gov. Flower Appealed To," *New York Times*, October 11, 1893, 1; "Mass Meetings to be Held," *New York Times*, October 12, 1893, 9; "Gov. Flower Silent," *St. Louis Post Dispatch*, October 19, 1893, 2; "To Stop the Fight," *Chicago Tribune*, October 20, 1893, 6; "Will Interfere," *St. Louis Post Dispatch*, October 22, 1893, 10.

1296. "Leeds and Ernest," *St. Louis Post Dispatch*, October 9, 1893, 8.

1297. "To-Nights Big Boxing Show," *Brooklyn Eagle*, October 17, 1893, 8.

1298. "At the Playhouse's," *New York Herald*, October 15, 1893, 2; Advertisement, *New York Herald*, October 16, 1893, 1.

1299. "Pugilism and Pathos," *World*, October 17, 1893, 2.

1300. "Music and Drama," *Lewiston Daily Sun*, October 19, 1893, 17.

1301. "Amusements," *Lewiston Evening*, October 20, 1893, 8.

1302. "Joe Choynski's Hard Luck," *St. Louis Post Dispatch*, November 13, 1893, 8; "Choynski Was 'Put to Sleep,' the Pugilist Knocked out and Robbed in a Fourteenth Street Dive," *New York Herald*, November 14, 1893, 13.

1303. "Phew! What Clothes. Pete Jackson on Exhibition, Too," *World*, November 15, 1893, 8; "It is a Good Show of Horses; But Society will Assert Itself at the Garden . . . Peter Jackson in a Silk Hat Makes a Hit etc.," *New York Times*, November 15, 1893, 1.

1304. "Peter Jackson in Town, He Will Meet Corbett Next June," *New Haven Register*, November 15, 1893, 1.

1305. "Entertainments. A Novel Feature in the Oft Played "Uncle Tom's Cabin," *Hartford Courant*, November 13, 1893, 3.

1306. "Peter Now Talks," *{Syracuse} Herald*, December 10, 1893, 3.

1307. "Stage Gossip," *Philadelphia Inquirer*, November 26, 1893, 10.

1308. "The National Peter Jackson," *Philadelphia Inquirer*, December 5, 1893, 2.

1309. "Mitchell's Condition," *Omaha World Herald*, December 10, 1893, 12;

1310. Ibid.

1311. "Uncle Tom's Cabin," *Worcester Daily Spy*, December 15, 1893, 1; "Peter Jackson as 'Uncle Tom' Tonight," *Worcester Daily Spy*, December 14, 1893, 8.

1312. "Another Fight on Tap a Battle Arranged between Joe Choynaki and Steve O'Donnell," *Philadelphia Inquirer*, December 22, 1893, 3; "Choynski and O'Donnell," *Omaha World Herald*, December 24, 1893, 7.

1313. "Pugilist Jackson Talks," *Weekly {Decatur, Illinois} Herald-Dispatch*, December 23, 1893, 6.

Chapter 14 – Disappointment - (1894)

1314. "Have A Clear Field," *Chicago Tribune*, February 12, 1894, 11.

1315. "At Pope's," *St. Louis Post Dispatch*, March 18, 1894, 3.

1316. "Little Change of Affairs In Jacksonville," *Brooklyn Eagle*, January 16, 1894, 8.

1317. "Has A Dead Cinch," *Salt Lake Herald*, January 17, 1894, 1; "Telegraphic Notes," *Daily Nevada State Journal*, January 17, 1894, 2.

1318. "Tally Ho! Overturned Theatrical People Take a Shin after a Midnight Supper and Meet with a Mishap," *Philadelphia Inquirer*, January 22, 1894.

1319. "Jacksonville's Guests," *St. Louis Post Dispatch*, January 25, 1894, 2.

1320. "Confidence in Jackson-Parson Davies Declares He Has a Wonder in the Black Man," *Idaho Statesman*, January 27, 1894, 1.

1321. "Corbett-Jackson Match," *Lowell Daily Sun*, January 26, 1894, 9.

1322. "General Sporting Notes," *Chicago Tribune*, July 16, 1894; "Fitzsimmons," *Daily Kennebec Journal*, January 27, 1894, 1.

1323. "Corbett," *St. Louis Post Dispatch*, January 25, 1894, 1; "Was Not In It," *St. Louis Post Dispatch*, January 26, 1894, 2; "Corbett's Fight-He Unmercifully Hammered England's Great Gladiator," *Lowell Daily Sun*, January 25, 1894, 15.

1324. "Denver Smith and Jackson May Meet Before Jackson and Corbett," *Helena Independent*, January 29, 1894, 1.

1325. "Denver Smith and Jackson," *Brooklyn Eagle*, January 29, 1894, 8.

1326. "After 'Lanky Bob'," *St. Louis Post Dispatch*, February 3, 1894, 8.

1327. "Washington Wants Fight-Tacoma Athletic Club Offer $40,000 for Corbett and Jackson," *Lowell Daily Sun*, January 29, 1894, 9.

1328. "Parson Davies Come to See Brady-The Roby A. C. Offer Denied," *Brooklyn Eagle*, February 1, 1894, 8.

1329. "Chat With the Boxers," *Omaha Daily Bee*, February 4, 1894, 16.

1330. "Peter Jackson Is All Right," *Chicago Tribune*, February 4, 1894, 7.

1331. "Peter Jackson Will Be Ready," *Chicago Tribune*, February 5, 1894, 4.

1332. "Have A Clear Field," *Chicago Tribune*, February 12, 1894, 11.

1333. "Negroes Are Barred," *Chicago Tribune*, February 21, 1894, 11.

1334. "Negroes Will Stay," *Chicago Tribune*, February 26, 1894, 3.

1335. "Insists On A Guarantee-Parson Davies Considering Offers for the Jackson-Corbett Fight," *Brooklyn Eagle*, February 13, 1894, 8.

1336. "Thinks Peter Can Still Fight," *Chicago Tribune*, February 19, 1894, 11.

1337. See note 45 above at 120-21.

1338. "Gentleman Jim," *St. Louis Post Dispatch*, February 25, 1894, 10.

1339. "He Wants To Fight In England," *Chicago Tribune*, March 6, 1894, 11; "Corbett on His Next Fight," *New York Herald*, March 12, 1894, 9.

1340. "Peter Jackson Talks," *National Police Gazette*, March 17, 1894, 10.

1341. "Peter Jackson's Side," *Brooklyn Eagle*, March 9, 1894, 1.

1342. "Pugilist Jackson Pronounced to be in Perfect Physical Condition," *New York Herald*, March 10, 1894, 8; "Jackson In Condition-The Colored Champion Declared to be a Physical Marvel," *National Police Gazette*, March 31, 1894, 7.

1343 ."Peter is All Right. In some Lines He Shows up Better than Corbett," *Wheeling Register*, March 11, 1894, 5.

1344 "Parson Davies Meets Brady," *New York Herald*, March 13, 1894, 8; "The Latest Sporting News," *National Police Gazette*, June 9, 1894, 11.

1345. "Backing For The Jackson Fight," *Chicago Tribune*, March 12, 1894, 8; "In and About Town. Almanac for Baltimore This Day," *Sun*, March 12, 1894, 8.

1346. "Brady in No Hurry," *Chicago Tribune*, March 16, 1894, 11.

1347. "Peter Jackson Tonight," *Decatur Daily Review*, March 17, 1894, 2; "Peter Jackson's Uncle Tom," *Decatur Morning Herald Dispatch*, March 18, 1894, 2; "Peter Jackson, Actor," *Decatur Daily Republican*, March 19, 1894, 8.

1348. "Davies In St. Louis," *St. Louis Post Dispatch*, March 17, 1894, 4; "At Pope's," *St. Louis Post Dispatch*, March 18, 1894, 31.

1349. "Went to See Jackson," *Decatur Daily Review*, March 18, 1894, 2.

1350. "Gov. Waite's Advice to 'Parson'," *Chicago Tribune*, March 24, 1894, 7.

1351. "The Corbett-Jackson Fight. Brady Tells How the Battle May Take Place in London," *Philadelphia Inquirer*, April 11, 1894, 3.

1352. "Says America Is The Ground," *Chicago Tribune*, March 27, 1894, 11.

1353. "Anxious to Hear From Corbett," *Chicago Tribune*, April 2, 1894, 11; "Fight Here," *St. Louis Post Dispatch*, April 3, 1894, 5; "Peter Is Puzzled," *St. Louis Post Dispatch*, April 5, 1894, 8; "Corbett's Farewell Speech," *St. Louis Post Dispatch*, April 7, 1894, 4; "Peter Issues A Defi.," *Chicago Tribune*, April 10, 1894, 11.

1354. "Jackson to Corbett," *St. Louis Post Dispatch*, April 10, 1894, 8; "Corbett Reply to Peter Jackson," *Chicago Tribune*, April 11, 1894, 11.

1355. "Holding Corbett To The Contract," *Chicago Tribune*, April 26, 1894, 11.

1356. "Odd 'n' Ends," *Oshkosh Daily Northwestern*, February 19, 1938, 12.

1357. "Drama and Music," *Boston Daily Globe*, April 29, 1894, 23; "Uncle Tom's Cabin," *Boston Daily Globe*, April 29, 1894, 18.

1358. "The Corbett-Jackson Fight," *Syracuse Daily Standard*, May 1, 1894, 6.

1359. "Jackson Replies to Corbett," *Brooklyn Eagle*, April 30, 1894, 1.

1360. "Jackson Will Go West," *Brooklyn Eagle*, May 8, 1894, 9; "Davies Has All His Money Up," *Chicago Tribune*, May 8, 1894, 7.

1361. "Sporting Notes," *St. Louis Post Dispatch*, May 10, 1894, 13.

1362. "The Fitzsimmons-Choynski Purse," *Chicago Tribune*, May 13, 1894, 4.

1363. "Fitzsimmons-Choynski Match,"*Chicago Tribune*, May 9, 1894, 7.

1364. "When and Where Will Jackson and Corbett Fight?," *Morning Call*, May 20, 1894, 18.

1365. "Corbett Must Decide," *St. Paul Daily Globe*, May 27, 1894; "Peter Jackson May Back Out," *Chicago Tribune*, May 26, 1894, 4. It is not known whether taking down the stakes was Jackson's or Davies' idea but it was probably Davies' suggestion."Parson Davies Wants The $20,000," *Chicago Tribune*, May 27, 1894, 4; "Corbett Cables-The Champion Protests Against the Taking Down of the Stake," *St. Louis Post Dispatch*, May 26, 1894, 4.

1366. "General Sporting Notes," *Chicago Tribune*, June 2, 1894, 7.

1367. "Wants to Meet Griffo," *Brooklyn Eagle*, January 31, 1895, 4.

1368. See note 988 above.

1369. "What Edgren Says," *Fort Wayne Journal-Gazette*, November 4, 1917, 11.

1370. "Choynski's Excuses," *Brooklyn Eagle*, June 20, 1894, 1.

1371. "General Sporting Notes," *Chicago Tribune*, August 9, 1894, 11.

1372. "Jackson's Expenses Are Guaranteed," *Chicago Tribune*, August 21, 1894, 12.

1373. "Prizefighting," *Times Democrat*, August 6, 1894, 4.

1374. "Jackson Will Fight the Machine," *Chicago Tribune*, August 11, 1894, 7.

1375. "Peter Jackson Here," *Chicago Tribune*, August 12, 1894, 5.

1376. "Corbett-Jackson Fight Off," *St. Louis Post Dispatch*, August 14, 1894, 3.

1377. "Peter Says He Is Ready," *Salt Lake Herald*, August 13, 1894, 8; "What Corbett Says," *Salt Lake Herald*," August 13, 1894, 8.

1378. "No Jackson-Corbett Match," *Chicago Tribune*, August 14, 1894, 11; "Corbett and Jackson Jaw," *Fort Worth Gazette*, September 4, 1894, 4.

1379. "Sporting Notes," *St. Louis Post Dispatch*, August 20, 1894, 3.

1380. "Negroes Shot Down," *Chicago Tribune*, September 2, 1894, 6.

1381. "Jackson on Corbett," *St. Louis Post Dispatch*, August 19, 1894, 9.

1382. "Peter Jackson Is Tired," *Brooklyn Eagle*, September 1, 1894, 1.

1383. "Signed Articles-Brady Binds Corbett to Fight Jackson Next Spring," *St. Louis Post Dispatch*, September 9, 1894, 8.

1384. "Jackson Can See No Match Ahead," *Chicago Tribune*, September 1, 1894, 6; "Sioux City Club Scouts Fail," *Chicago Tribune*, September 6, 1894, 8.

1385. "Sioux City-Corbett-Jackson," *Chicago Tribune*, September 8, 1894, 7.

1386. "Jackson Dejected," *St. Louis Post Dispatch*, September 7, 1894, 1; "Well Its Off," *{Ogden} Standard*, September 11, 1894, 1; "Will Never Fight Corbett," *{Ogden} Standard*, September 12, 1894, 1.

1387. "Jackson's Position," *St. Louis Post Dispatch*, September 9, 1894, 8; "Will Not Sign," *St. Louis Post Dispatch*, September 10, 1894, 3.

1388. "Jackson Draws His Stake Money," *Chicago Tribune*, September 13, 1894, 11; "Jackson Takes His Money," *Reno Evening Gazette*, September 12, 1894, 1.

1389. "Jackson Talks," *Fort Wayne Sentinel*, September 14, 1894, 1; "Jackson Interviewed," *Delphos {Ohio} Daily Herald*, September 15, 1894, 5.

1390. "Pugilistic Gossip," *Boston Daily Globe*, September 18, 1894, 5.

1391. "Corbett's Stiff Talk," *Evening Herald*, October 5, 1894, 5.

1392. "Corbett As A Critic," *Chicago Tribune*, November 19, 1894, 11.

1393. "Corbett As A Critic-The Champion Thinks Fitzsimmons a Better Man Than Jackson," *St. Louis Post Dispatch*, January 9, 1895, 5.

1394. "Barry Defeats Leon," *Chicago Tribune*, September 16, 1894, 5.

1395. "Choynski Has Sport," *Chicago Tribune*, September 18, 1894, 8.

1396. "The Fight Is Off," *Winnipeg Free Press*, September 24, 1894, 5.

1397. "Boxers at Work-Ryan and Choynski are Punching the Bag," *Oakland Tribune*, November 1, 1894, 10; "Exercising for their Fight," *San Antonio Daily Light*, November 1, 1894, 5; "Will Fight Sharp," *St. Louis Post Dispatch*," November 2, 1894, 7.

1398. "Woods and Baker," *St. Louis Post Dispatch*, November 6, 1894, 7.

1399. "Dan And His Party," *St. Louis Post Dispatch*, September 24, 1894, 1.

1400. "One Will Win," *St. Louis Post Dispatch*, September 26, 1894, 1; "Creedon Is Beaten," *Chicago Tribune*, September 27, 1894, 8.

1401. "Red Bob to Corbett," *Chicago Tribune*, September 28, 1894, 8.

1402. "Jim Can't Get Away," *St. Louis Post Dispatch*, September 28, 1894, 7; "Still Ignores Fitz," *St. Louis Post Dispatch*, September 28, 1894, 7; "Corbett and O'Donnell Talk," *Chicago Tribune*, September 28, 1894, 8; "Corbett Issues His Ultimatum," *Chicago Tribune*, September 29, 1894, 6; "O'Donnell's Offer," *St.*

Louis Post Dispatch, September 1894, 7; "Fitzsimmons' Reasonable Position," *Chicago Tribune*, September 30, 1894, 6.

1403 ."Red Bob to Corbett," *Chicago Tribune*, September 28, 1894, 8.

1404. "General Sporting Notes," *Chicago Tribune*, September 29, 1894, 7.

1405. "Hall And Creedon," *St. Louis Post Dispatch*, October 12, 1894, 3; "Pugilistic Pointers," *St. Louis Post Dispatch*, October 31, 1894, 2; "Pugilistic Pointers," *St. Louis Post Dispatch*, November 2, 1894, 2.

1406. "Sporting Notes," *Chicago Tribune*, February 5, 1895, 7.

1407. "Corbett And Fitz," *St. Louis Post Dispatch*, September 29, 1894, 3; "Pugilistic Gossip," *St. Louis Post Dispatch*, October 4, 1894, 2.

1408. "Ryan and Dempsey," *St. Paul Daily Globe*, October 6, 1894, 6; "Ryan and Dempsey," *Sandusky Register*, October 4, 1894, 2.

1409. "Pugilistic Pointers," *St. Louis Post Dispatch*, October 13, 1894, 5.

1410. "Woods and Baker," *St. Louis Post Dispatch*, November 6, 1894, 7; "The Sporting World," *Dallas Morning News*, November 7, 1894, 3.

1411. "Jim Hall Will Be In Trim," *Chicago Tribune*, November 11, 1894, 4; "Jim Hall's Condition," *St. Louis Post Dispatch*, November 15, 1894, 7; "No More Boxing in Chicago. Parson Davies' Show Tonight Marks the Windup of Local Sparring," *Chicago Tribune*, November 15, 1894, 11; "Hall vs. Woods and Baker Tonight," *Chicago Tribune*, November 15, 1894, 11.

1412. "Jim Hall Loses Two-Both Baker and Woods Win Against Their Matches," *Chicago Tribune*, November 16, 1894, 11.

1413. "Why Local Boxing Is to Stop," *Chicago Tribune*, November 16, 1894, 11.

1414. "Fitz Hits to Hard," *Chicago Tribune*, November 17, 1894, 3; "Fitz Explains," *St. Louis Post Dispatch*, November 21, 1894, 6.

1415. "From Jail to Stage," *Chicago Tribune*, November 18, 1894, 7.

1416. "Out On Bail," *St. Louis Post Dispatch*, November 18, 1894, 10.

1417. "No More Boxing In Syracuse," *Chicago Tribune*, November 2, 1894, 11; "Riordan's Funeral," *Racine Daily Journal*, November 19, 1894, 3; "Riordan's Death," *St. Louis Post Dispatch*, November 20, 1894, 6.

1418. "Purely An Accident-Parson Davies Exonerates Fitzsimmons of Blame," *St. Paul Daily Globe*, November 18, 1894, 1; Riordan Was Dissipated," *Brooklyn Eagle*, November 18, 1894, 3; "Almost Always Drunk," *Morning Call*, November 18, 1894, 9; "Corbett Says Riordan Was Diseased," *Chicago Tribune*, November 18, 1894, 7.

1419. "Jim Hall Echoes the 'Diseased' Theory-Medical Supervision Advocated," *Chicago Tribune*, November 18, 1894, 7.

1420. "Corner's Verdict On Riordan," *Chicago Tribune*, November 23, 1894, 11.

1421. "General Sporting News," *Chicago Tribune*, November 24, 1894, 7; "Fitz' Indicted-Lanky Bob Must Answer for Con Riordan's Death," *St. Louis Post Dispatch*, January 19, 1895, 2; "Fitzsimmons Will Go When Wanted," *Chicago Tribune*, January 25, 1895, 11; "Fitzsimmons To Answer," *St. Louis Post Dispatch*, January 21, 1895, 5.

1422. "After O'Donnell for Choynski," *Chicago Tribune*, November 24, 1894, 7; "How Parson Davies Got His Name," *Cleveland Plain Dealer*, June 14, 1908, 57.

1423. "With Young Griffo-Kid Lavigne Anxious to Get On Another Go With the Australian," *St. Louis Post Dispatch*, November 29, 1894, 7.

1424. "Davies and Sullivan now Friends," *Chicago Tribune*, December 3, 1894, 11.

1425. "Tommy Ryan Arrives In New Orleans," *Chicago Tribune*, December 9, 1894, 6.

1426. "Fighters At Orleans," *St. Louis Post Dispatch*, December 9, 1894, 11; "All Want to Bet on Tommy Ryan," *Chicago Tribune*, December 13, 1894, 11; "Jack Dempsey In Fine Condition," *Chicago Tribune*, December 14, 1894, 11.

1427. "Bowen and Lavigne," *St. Louis Post Dispatch*, December 15, 1894, 7; "Andy Bowen May Die," *Chicago Tribune*, December 15, 1894, 2; "Bowen Dead-He Never Recovered Consciousness After the Blow," *St. Louis Post Dispatch*, December 15, 1891, 1; "Blow Ends His Life," *Chicago Tribune*, December 16, 1894, 5; "Knocked Out-The Killing of Bruiser Bowen Puts an End to Pugilism," *St. Louis Post Dispatch*, December 16, 1894, 7.

1428. This was not the middleweight Dan Daly of St. Louis. That fighter had died of pneumonia in November 1891. This Dannie Daly was a popular fighter in the Omaha area.

1429. "Tommy White Tells How It Happened," *Chicago Tribune*, December 17, 1894, 11.

1430. "Corbett's Claims," *St. Louis Post Dispatch*, December 21, 1894, 7; "May Fight No More," *Chicago Tribune*, December 19, 1894, 11.

1431. "Parson Davies Send Two Challenges," *Brooklyn Eagle*, December 24, 1894, 3.

1432. "The Dempsey-Ryan Fight," *Brooklyn Eagle*, December 21, 1894, 4; "To Put Down Boxers," *Chicago Tribune*, December 22, 1894, 7.

1433. "Dempsey Agrees to Box Ryan Fifteen Rounds," *Morning Call*, December 26, 1894, 4; "Tommy Ryan Is Getting Heavy," *Chicago Tribune*, December 26, 1894, 11.

1434. At the end of 1894 Eddie Stoddard was representing the formerly great Jack Dempsey and also acting as the matchmaker for the Atlantic Athletic Club on Coney Island. The Atlantic was a new club that was constructing a facility known as the Sea Beach Palace. The creation of a new athletic club became possible as a result of litigation relating to the earlier closing of the Coney Island Athletic Club. That club had filed suit to enjoin authorities from continually interfering in its matches, and a Justice of the Supreme Court of New York had entered his order enjoining the authorities from stopping all boxing exhibitions and essentially leaving it to the police to decide on a case-by-case basis when a boxing exhibition stepped over the line and became an illegal prize fight. "Barry And Leon Out," *Chicago Tribune*, December 29, 1894, 7.

1435. "Transferred The Fight," *Brooklyn Eagle*, January 2, 1895, 4; "May Let Them Fight," *Chicago Tribune*, January 3, 1895, 11.

Chapter 15 – Tommy Ryan Becomes World Champion - (1895)

1436. "Dempsey's Friends Are Anxious," *Chicago Tribune*, January 5, 1895, 7; "Choynski's Chance," *St. Louis Post Dispatch*, January 5, 1895, 10.

1437. "The 'Parson's' Party," *St. Louis Post Dispatch*, January 11, 1895, 5.

1438. "Ryan and Dempsey," *St. Louis Post Dispatch*, January 14, 1895, 6; "Ready For The Big Fight-Ryan And Dempsey Are Both Confident," *Brooklyn Eagle*, January 18, 1895, 4; "Ryan And Dempsey-Both Pugilists in Good Condition for To-Nights Battle," *St. Louis Post Dispatch*, January 18, 1895, 6.

1439. "Reasons Why Dempsey Lost the Fight," *Brooklyn Eagle*, January 19, 1895, 4.

1440. "Ryan Given The Bout. Officials Stop His Match With Dempsey In The Third Round," *Chicago Tribune*, January 19, 1895, 7; "Dempsey's Sad Downfall. Was Not in Condition to Meet Ryan. The Contest A Farce," *New York Times*, January

19, 1895, 6; "Dempsey Was Disgraced-The Once Famous 'Nonpareil' a Pudding for Tommy Ryan," *Chicago Tribune*, January 19, 1895, 7.

1441. "General Sporting Notes," *Chicago Tribune*, February 9, 1895, 7. Choynski will to fight the Harlem Coffee Cooler). Other attempts to match Choynski are discussed in the following articles: "Choynski's Chance," *St. Louis Post Dispatch*, January 5, 1895, 10; "Jackson and Mitchell," *St. Louis Post Dispatch*, January 23, 1895, 5; "Creedon and Choynski," *St. Louis Post Dispatch*, February 4, 1895, 5. Davies trying to match Joe with any man in England except Jackson.

1442. "Pugilistic Pointers," *St. Louis Post Dispatch*, January 23, 1895, 5; "Creedon And Choynski," *St. Louis Post Dispatch*, January 31, 1895, 4.

1443. "Fistic Schemes of Parson Davies," *Chicago Tribune*, February 11, 1895, 8.

1444. "'Parson' Davies' Fighting Plans," *Chicago Tribune*, February 17, 1895, 5.

1445. "Live Sporting Notes," *Kansas City Daily Journal*, February 22, 1895, 2.

1446. "The Ring-Corbett Wanted a Guarantee for the Bag-Punching," *St. Louis Post Dispatch*, February 19, 1895, 8.

1447. "Davis [sic] Is Heard From," *St. Louis Post Dispatch*, March 1, 1895, 7.

1448. "Foxy Parson Davies," *St. Louis Post Dispatch*, February 22, 1895, 7.

1449. "Parson Davies' Trip to England," *Brooklyn Eagle*, February 23, 1895, 4; "General Sporting Notes," *Chicago Tribune*, February 24, 1895, 7; "Among the Fighters," *St. Louis Post Dispatch*, February 28, 1895, 8.

1450. "The Ring-'Parson' Davies Has Completed His Arrangements in Chicago," *St. Louis Post Dispatch*, February 25, 1895, 8; "Choynski and Tommy Ryan," *Chicago Tribune*, February 26, 1895, 11.

1451. "Matches For Ryan and Choynski," *Chicago Tribune*, March 7, 1895, 11; "Referee George Siler-Will Officiate for the Tracey, Ryan, Creedon and Choynski Bouts," *St. Louis Post Dispatch*, March 11, 1895, 8; "Boxing Bouts at Kansas City," *Chicago Tribune*, March 12, 1895, 11; "General Sporting Notes," *Chicago Tribune*, March 14, 1895, 11.

1452. "General Sporting Notes," *Chicago Tribune*, March 13, 1895, 11.

1453. "General Sporting Notes," *Chicago Tribune*, March 15, 1895, 11; "To Bind the Ryan-Burge Match," *Chicago Tribune*, March 18, 1895, 11.

1454. "Declined By Davies-The 'Parson' Refuses a Nomination for Alderman in Chicago," *St. Louis Post Dispatch*, March 11, 1895, 8.

1455. "Rufus Sharp Matched," *St. Louis Post Dispatch*, March 15, 1895, 7.

1456. "In the Days of Finish Fights," *Winnipeg Free Press*, February 19, 1927, Story Section, 11.

1457. "Fighters Arrive in the City," *Chicago Tribune*, March 20, 1895, 11; "Ryan Beats Tracey," *Chicago Tribune*, March 21, 1895, 11; "Tracey Almost Beaten," *St. Louis Post Dispatch*, March 21, 1895, 5.

1458. "No One Is Put Out-Choynski and Barry Have The Best of Their Fights," *Chicago Tribune*, March 22, 1895, 11; "Dan Defeated Also, Choynski Had Creedon at His Mercy and Clearly Outclassed Him," *St. Louis Post Dispatch*, March 22, 1895, 7; "Dan Creedon Has Returned," *St. Louis Post Dispatch*, March 23, 1895, 8.

1459. "Davies Is Poisoned," *Chicago Tribune*, March 25, 1895, 7; "'Parson' Davies Poisoned. Druggist Makes a Blunder and Gives Strychnine as a Grip Preventive," *Inter Ocean*, March 25, 1895, 8; "'Parson' Davies near Death," *Boston Journal*, March 25, 1895, 3; "Parson Davies Ill," *St. Louis Post Dispatch*, March 25, 1895, 8; "The Parson Used Strychnine," *St. Paul Daily Globe*, March 26, 1895, 8;

1460. "Knockout At The Triangle Club," *Chicago Tribune*, March 26, 1895, 11.

1461. "Ryan and Dick Burge to Match," *Chicago Tribune*, March 28, 1895, 11.

1462. "Ryan and Smith to Meet April 29," *Chicago Tribune*, March 29, 1895, 11.

1463. "General Sporting Notes," *Chicago Tribune*, April 1, 1895, 11.

1464. "Ryan's Battle with Jack Wilks [sic]," *Chicago Tribune*, April 2, 1895, 11; "Ryan and Wilkes," *St. Louis Post Dispatch*, April 3, 1895, 10.

1465. Asbury, Herbert, *Gem of the Prairie* (Alfred A. Knopf, 1940), 157-159.

1466. Coughlin had demonstrated his power in April 1894. He was a candidate for re-election in the First Ward and Chicago's independent Democrats ran a candidate named Bill Skakel against Coughlin. Skakel was a friend of the American Labor Movement and later in 1894 would be one of the men who posted bond for Eugene V. Debs when he and other leaders of the American Railway Union were arrested for conspiring to interfere with the United States' mail by urging railroad workers to strike. Coughlin was not impressed with Skakel's labor connections and hired a number of thugs to intimidate voters, attempting to cast tickets for Skakel. In response Skakel then hired his own "workers" to try to keep the polls open for his people to vote. Blood was spilled when a gun fight broke out between the opposing sides. The first shots were fired before noon outside a polling place at 470 Clark Street. A gang of Skakel supporters tried to remove a Coughlin badge from one of his workers. Workers from both sides confronted one another and drew guns. A Black man named Lewis Lather shot a man named John Dee in the shoulder. Dee was the bartender at the notorious "House of David" and a chief lieutenant for Coughlin. Later gun fire also started near a polling place at Taylor and Plymouth Streets where another Coughlin man was shot. Bathhouse retaliated, and throughout the day voters were intimidated by Coughlin's men. More importantly, Coughlin's men working the polls remained in possession of the actual election returns and altered the results at will so that Coughlin remained Alderman. See, "Fight for Aldermen-Each Party Striving to Control the City Council," *Inter Ocean*, January 29, 1894, 5; "Skakel for Alderman. Ex-Head of the Gamblers' Trust out Against Coughlin in the First Ward," *Inter Ocean*, February 9, 1894, 1; "Disorder at Chicago," *{Rockford} Morning Star*, April 4, 1894, 1.

1467. "Council Meets and Adjourns- Aldermen Have but Little Business on Their Hands," *Inter Ocean*, April 4, 1895, 8.

1468. "Stopped the Fight. Alderman J. J. Coughlin Keeps Ryan and Wilks Apart, He Secures Warrants," *Inter Ocean*, April 6, 1895, 4.

1469. "Coughlin Wins Out," Chicago Tribune, April 6, 1895, 7; "Ryan-Wilkes Bout-Warfare Between Chicago Politicians Causes It to Be Stopped," *St. Louis Post Dispatch*, April 6, 1895, 8.

1470. Ibid.

1471. Ibid.

1472. "Hall and Choynski Matched," *Chicago Tribune*, April 9, 1895, 11.

1473. "Mayo and Armstrong to Fight," *Chicago Tribune*, April 29, 1895, 11. Armstrong was born in September 1873 near Rogersville, Hawkins County, Tennessee as the first child of Jeff and Sallie Armstrong. Hawkins County is near the far northeast corner of Tennessee. There were many White and Black families in Hawkins County, Tennessee and several Armstrongs indentified as Mulattos. The White Armstrong families in Hawkins County had been in that area for many generations, having moved there from around Augusta, Virginia. The White Armstrongs were primarily farmers and they were supporters of the Confederate States of America during the Civil War. There were many Black men and women in the 1860 Slave Census of Hawkins County with the Armstrong surname.

1474. "To Arrange for Three Fights," *Chicago Tribune*, May 3, 1895, 11; "Pugilistic Pointers," *St. Louis Post Dispatch*, May 25, 1895, 8.

1475. "Happenings At Asbury Park," *New York Times*, August 4, 1895, 17.

1476 "Choynski Is After O'Donnell," *Brooklyn Eagle*, May 13, 1895, 4.

1477. "Ryan and Smith Both Confident," *World*, May 21, 1895, 9; "Police Stop the Bout,"

Sun," May 28, 1895, 5; "Ryan and Smith Fight A 'Draw'," *Chicago Tribune*, May 28, 1895, 11; "Declared A Draw," *Atlanta Constitution*, May 29, 1895, 7.

1478. "Trainers Often Win for Fighters," *Deseret Evening News*," November 19, 1903, 3.

1479. "Proves a Pugilistic Fiasco," *Chicago Tribune*, April 4, 1895, 4.

1480. "Fads In Pugilism," *St. Paul Globe*, April 11, 1897, 11.

1481. "Aggregation of Sluggers," *Salt Lake Tribune*, June 9, 1895, 3.

1482. "After A License to Fight," *Chicago Tribune*, June 14, 1895, 12; "Police Stop the Fights," *Chicago Tribune*, June 16, 1895, 4.

1483. "John L.'s Big Benefit," *Brooklyn Eagle*, June 28, 1895, 5; "Sullivan's Big Benefit," *{Frederick, Maryland}* *News*, June 28, 1895, 4.

1484. "Ex-Champion Pugilist Dead. Sketch of the American Contests of the English Heavyweight," *Chicago Tribune*, July 11, 1895, 6; "Pugilist Greenfield Dead," *Boston Daily Globe*, July 11, 1895, 2.

1485. "Dempsey's Days Are Numbered," *St. Louis Post Dispatch*, July 12, 1895, 8; "Jack Dempsey Dying, The Ex-Middle-Weight Champion Is Passing Away, *St. Louis Post Dispatch*, October 22, 1895, 2; "Jack Dempsey Gives Up The Fight," *Chicago Tribune*, October 25, 1895, 7; "Jack Dempsey Is No More," *St. Louis Post Dispatch*, November 1, 1895, 6; "Jack Dempsey Has Passed Away," *Chicago Tribune*, November 2, 1895, 6.

1486. "Sporting Miscellany," *Boston Daily Globe*, July 7, 1895, 7.

1487. "John L. Talks Through His Hat," *Lebanon Daily News*, July 16, 1895, 4.

1488. "Amusements," *Bangor Daily Whig And Courier*, July 23, 1895, 2.

1489. "Smith And Ryan Matched To Fight," *Chicago Tribune*, July 24, 1895, 5; "Ryan-Smith Match Is Arranged," *Chicago Tribune*, July 25, 1895, 5.

1490. "Boxing Gossip," *Sunday Herald*, July 21, 1895, 9.

1491. "Choynski's Opinion of Hall's Defi," *Chicago Tribune*, July 31, 1895, 4; "Jim Hall Is Anxious For A Match," *Chicago Tribune*, July 31, 1895, 4.

1492. "General Sporting Notes," *Chicago Tribune*, August 2, 1895, 4; "Choynski Gets Another Chance, The Parson Arranges to Match Him Against Godfrey and Joe Accepts," *Chicago Tribune*, August 10, 1895, 7.

1493. "Dixon and Leonard Box To-night," *New York Times*, August 19, 1895, 5.

1494. "Dixon And Leonard Arrested," *New York Times*, August 20, 1895, 5; "Pugilists Start A Riot," *Brooklyn Eagle*, August 20, 1895, 4; "Dixon And Leonard Are Arrested," *Chicago Tribune*, August 20, 1895, 4; "Sports Placed Under Bail," *St. Louis Post Dispatch*, August 20, 1895, 5; "Dixon and Leonard Arraigned," *New York Times*, August 21, 1895, 8; "Holds Dixon and Leonard," *Chicago Tribune*, August 22, 1895, 4. Tom O'Rourke and Parson Davies were both discharged.

1495. "General Sporting Notes," *Chicago Tribune*, September 25, 1895, 6.

1496. "Parson Davies' String of Fighters," *Chicago Tribune*, September 26, 1896, 6.

1497. "For John L.'s Benefit," *Chicago Tribune*, September 28, 1896, 6; "Stand By Culberson-Parson Davies Thinks the Legislature Will Prevent the Fight," *St. Louis Post Dispatch*, September 28, 1895, 5.

1498. "Talk of the Sports," *Chicago Tribune*, September 30, 1895, 5.

1499. "'Parson' Davies Drops Into Town," *Chicago Tribune*, October 8, 1895, 5.

1500. "Choynski Anxious To Meet Maher, Will Endeavor to Arrange a Contest During His Visit to Pittsburg," *Chicago Tribune*, October 9, 1895, 5.

1501. "Choynski and Maher to Fight," *Chicago Tribune*, October 11, 1895, 5; "Twenty Round Draw," *St. Paul Daily Globe*, October 13, 1895, 6; "Skill and Hard Hitting," *Sun*, October 13, 1895, 9.

1502. "Creedon Wins His Go With Craig," *Chicago Tribune*, October 16, 1895, 5.

1503. "Madden And Barry Meet Monday," *Chicago Tribune*, October 20, 1895, 7.

1504. "Won In Four Hot Rounds," *San Francisco Call*, October 22, 1895, 5; "Barry Wins In Four Hot Rounds," *Chicago Tribune*, October 22, 1895, 7.

1505. "Clarke's Stand On The Fight," *St. Louis Post Dispatch*, October 18, 1895, 9.

1506. "Corbett Will Wait For His Rival," *Chicago Tribune*, October 26, 1895, 7.

1507. "Called A Coward And Cur," *San Francisco Call*, October 29, 1895, 5.

1508. "Sporting Notes," *St. Louis Post Dispatch*, October 29, 1895, 5.

1509. "Chicago Sports Stay At Home," *Chicago Tribune*, October 31, 1895, 2; "Drunk and Loquacious," *San Francisco Call*, October 31, 1895, 3.

1510. "Parson Davies on the Wing," *Marion Daily Star*, October 31, 1895, 1; "Hot Springs Law," *St. Paul Daily Globe*, October 30, 1895, 1 & 5.

1511. "Hot Springs Budget," *Galveston Daily News*, November 1, 1895, 2.

1512. "Maher Scares Jim Out," *Chicago Tribune*, November 1, 1895, 7.

1513. "Froth and Vaporing," *San Francisco Call*, November 1, 1895, 1.

1514. "The Governor Wins," *San Francisco Call*, November 3, 1895, 3.

1515. "Return of the 'Parson's Party," *Chicago Tribune*, November 4, 1895, 4; "John Says, The Ex-Champion Very Much Disgusted With the Fiasco," *Fort Wayne News*, November 4, 1895, 1.

1516. "Parson Davies' Party," *Galveston Daily News*, November 5, 1895, 2.

1517. "Return of the 'Parson's' Party," *Chicago Tribune*, November 4, 1895, 4.

1518. "Peter Maher's Prospects," *St. Louis Post Dispatch*, November 14, 1895, 14.

1519. "Sullivan To Receive A Benefit," *Chicago Tribune*, December 2, 1895, 5.

1520. "John L.'s Dream," *St. Louis Post Dispatch*, December 10, 1895, 7.

1521. "Tickets Largely In Demand," *Chicago Tribune*, December 11, 1895, 8; "John L.'s Last Appearance," *Chicago Tribune*, December 14, 1895, 7.

1522. "Not His Last Appearance," *Chicago Tribune*, December 15, 1895, 7.

1523. "Found Dead in a Yard," *New York Times*, December 22, 1895, 8; "Was Sister of 'Parson' Davies-Woman Identified Who Was Horribly Mangled in New York,"

Inter Ocean, December 26, 1895, 1; "'Parson Davies' Sister Body of a Woman Murdered in New York Has Been Identified," *St. Louis Republic*, December 26, 1895, 9;

1524. "She Is Davies' Sister-Discovery of the Identity of a Murdered Woman-Found Horribly Mangled Last Saturday in the Rear of a Building-Her Relationship to the 'Parson' etc.," *Chicago Tribune*, December 26, 1895, 8.

1525. "Dead, Her Head Crushed," *World*, December 22, 1895, 7.

1526. "Parson Davies' Sister," *World*, December 26, 1895, 10.

1527. "Talk of Quadruple Alliance," *Chicago Tribune*, December 27, 1895, 4.

1528. "Not Parson Davie's Sister," *World*, December 27, 1895, 9.

Chapter 16 – Times Changing – (1896–1897)

1529. "Wants Palmer and Dixon Matched. 'Parson' Davies tells of His Earlier Experiences with Pugilists. Barry Is the Greatest of Bantams," *Chicago Tribune*, February 8, 1897, 8.

1530. "Amusements," *Inter Ocean*, December 8, 1895, Part 4, 37.

1531. "Takes A Benefit Saturday," *Inter Ocean*, December 11, 1895, 4; "Offers Sullivan an Interest," *Inter Ocean*, December 16, 1895, 4.

1532. Advertisement for the Academy of Music, *Inter Ocean*, December 20, 1895, 8.

1533. "City Brevities," *{Rockford} Daily Register Gazette*, December 24, 1895, 3 (The play will be in Rockford December 30, 1895); "'The Wicklow Postman'-Ex-Champions Sullivan and Ryan to appear with Parson Davies," *{Rockford} Morning Star*, December 27, 1895, 2; "John L. and the Goat," *{Rockford} Daily Register Gazette*, January 4, 1896, 4; "Put Up, Connors," *Inter Ocean*, January 11, 1896, 4 (Davies has returned from Milwaukee after a week long run of the Wicklow Postman); No Headline, *Sterling Standard*, January 23, 1896, 4; Miletich, Leo N., *Dan Stuart's Fistic Carnival* (Texas A&M University Press, 1994), 118.

1534. "Sporting News," *St. Louis Post Dispatch*, January 6, 1896, 5.

1535. "Ryan Want to Box Joe Choynski," *Chicago Tribune*, November 6, 1895, 8; "Maher-O'Donnell Fight, *St. Louis Post Dispatch*, November 9, 1895, 5.

1536. "Tommy Ryan Talks," *St. Louis Post Dispatch*, January 12, 1896, 11.

1537. "Jim Hall And Joe Choynski-First Big Fight of the New Year Scheduled for To-Night," *St. Louis Post Dispatch*, January 20, 1896, 8.

1538. "Sporting Notes," *St. Louis Post Dispatch*, January 15, 1896, 5.

1539. "Choynski's Great Fight-He Defeats Jim Hall At Maspeth In Thirteen Rounds," *Brooklyn Eagle*, January 21, 1896, 10. ; "Choynski's Great Victory," *St. Louis Post Dispatch*, January 21, 1896, 5.

1540. "Knocking Out Maher and Jim Hall," *Winnipeg Free Press*, January 29, 1927, Story Section, 47.

1541. "Choynski's Great Victory," *St. Louis Post Dispatch*, January 21, 1896, 5; Joe Choysnki Wins the Fight," *Chicago Tribune*, January 21, 1896, 8; "Was The Fight On The Square," *St. Louis Post Dispatch*, January 22, 1896, 10; "Choynski Arrives In The City," *Chicago Tribune*, January 23, 1896, 8.

1542. "Noted Old Fighter is Dying in a Hovel," *Oshkosh Daily Northwestern*, March 10, 1913, 3; Pugilist Jim Hall Found Dying, *New York Times*, March 11, 1913, 9.

1543. "Australian Middleweight Has Answered Last Bell," *Racine Journal-News*, March 25, 1913, 18.

1544. "Knocking Out Maher and Jim Hall," *Winnipeg Free Press*, January 29, 1927, Story Section, 47.

1545. "Battle End In A Draw," *Chicago Tribune*, January 31, 1896, 8.

1546. "Sporting Notes," *St. Louis Post Dispatch*, February 1, 1896, 5.

1547. "Sporting Notes," *St. Louis Post Dispatch*, January 28, 1896, 5 (Davies has retained the Opera House at El Paso); "Fistic Program All Arranged," *Chicago Tribune*, January 28, 1896, 8; "Barry's Opponent Johnnie Murphy," *St. Louis Post Dispatch*, January 30, 1896, 5.

1548. "Lived a Killing Pace," *Reading Eagle*, February 16, 1896, 8.

1549. "Fell Off The Train," *Daily Illinois State Register*, January 30, 1896, 6.

1550. "John L. Sullivan Falls From A Train, He Is Badly Battered and Cries as His Wounds Are Dressed," *New York Times*, January 30, 1896, 1.

1551. "Falls From Fast Train," *Chicago Tribune*, January 30, 1896, 8; "Does Not Remember The Fall," *Chicago Tribune*, January 30, 1896, 8; "In A Bad Way," *St. Louis Post Dispatch*, January 30, 1896, 1; "John L. Is In A Bad Way," *Chicago*

Tribune, January 31, 1896, 3; "Sullivan Is Better," *St. Louis Post Dispatch*, January 31, 1896, 5.

1552. "Sullivan Improves," *Daily Illinois State Register*, February 1, 1896, 5; "Sullivan Not Out of Danger," *Chicago Tribune*, February 1, 1896, 7; "John L. Sullivan Rounding To," *Chicago Tribune*, February 2, 1896, 7; "John L. Sullivan Better," *New York Times*, February 2, 1896, 10; "Greatly Improved," *St. Louis Post Dispatch*, February 2, 1896, 10; "John L. Sullivan Recovering," *New York Times*, February 3, 1896, 1; "Sullivan Is Gaining," *Daily Illinois State Register*, February 4, 1896, 6; "Sullivan Able to Join His Company," *New York Times*, February 6, 1896, 5.

1553. "Sullivan To Leave To-Day," *Daily Illinois State Register*, February 5, 1896, 6; "Sullivan Departs," *Daily Illinois State Register*, February 6, 1896, 5; "Choysnki Is Unable To Leave," *Chicago Tribune*, February 5, 1896, 8.

1554. "'Parson' Davies The Noted Pugilistic Manager Is On His Way to Texas," *St. Louis Post Dispatch*, February 2, 1896, 10.

1555. "Dramatic Brevities," *San Francisco Call*, February 2, 1896, 22.

1556. "The Dallas Theater," *Dallas Morning News*, February 2, 1896, 4.

1557. "John L. Sullivan Improving," *Dallas Morning News*, February 4, 1896, 4.

1558. Advertisement, *San Antonio Light*, February 2, 1896, 8; Advertisement, *San Antonio Light*, February 4, 1896, 8;

1559. "John L. Sullivan Going to See the Fight," *Sun*, February 5, 1896, 4; "Sullivan To See the Fights," *New York Times*, February 5, 1896, 6.

1560. "John L. En route," *Oakland Tribune*, February 10, 1896, 12.

1561. "Dwyer Money for Fitz," *Chicago Tribune*, February 4, 1896, 8.

1562. "The Sports Make a Statement," *Daily Illinois State Register*, February 9, 1896, 1.

1563. "Bill To End The Fight," *Chicago Tribune*, February 6, 1896, 8; "Barred By Uncle Sam," *Chicago Tribune*, February 7, 1896, 8; "Makes The Bill Law," *Chicago Tribune*, February 8, 1896, 7.

1564. "Agree To Fight Friday," *Chicago Tribune*, February 18, 1896, 8; "Fight Seems To Be Sure," *Chicago Tribune*, February 19, 1896, 8; "Will Fight To Win," *Chicago Tribune*, February 20, 1896, 1; "Prospects Grow Brighter," *Chicago Tribune*, February 20, 1896, 2; "Maher Is Ready," *St. Louis Post Dispatch*, February 20, 1896, 5.

1565. Kelly, Fred Charters, *George Ade, Warmhearted Satirist* (The Bobbs-Merrill Company, 1947), 98–99; Miletich, Leo N., *Dan Stuart's Fistic Carnival* (Texas A&M University Press, 1994), 166-167.

1566. "Off For The Big Fight-Fitzsimmons, Maher, and a Few Spectators Leave El Paso," *New York Times*, February 21, 1896, 6; "Off For The Fight," *Chicago Tribune*, February 21, 1896, 1 (Davies will hold the watch for Maher); "One Blow Settled It," *Daily Illinois State Register*, February 22, 1896, 1; "Won With A Punch," *Chicago Tribune*, February 22, 1896, 1.

1567. "Kinetoscope People Are Losers," *Chicago Tribune*, February 22, 1896, 2.

1568 . "Special to the World," *World*, February 20, 1896, 3.

1569. "New In A Nutshell," *Arizona Republican*, February 23, 1896, 5; Advertisement, *Los Angeles Times*, February 21, 1896, 1; "About the Theaters," *Los Angeles Times*, February 23, 1896, 24.

1570. "Disgusted Sports," *Reading Eagle*, February 16, 1896, 2; "Boxing Should Be Protected," *St. Louis Post Dispatch*, March 9, 1896, 5.

1571. "Sullivan Declares Himself," *St. Louis Post Dispatch*, March 6, 1896, 5; "Talking Through His Hat-John L. Still Claiming Something He Never Possessed," *Chicago Tribune*, March 7, 1896, 7.

1572. "Parson Davies Arrives," *San Francisco Call*, March 7, 1896, 7.

1573. Advertisement, *San Francisco Call*, March 8, 1896, 23; "Amusements," *San Francisco Call*, March 9, 1896, 7; "At The Playhouses," *San Francisco Call*, March 9, 1896, 7; "Midweek Theater Notes, *San Francisco Call*, March 13, 1896, 14.

1574. "John L. Sullivan Is A Sick Man," *Chicago Tribune*, March 11, 1896, 7; "John L. Sullivan's Denial," *St. Louis Post Dispatch*, March 7, 1896, 5.

1575. "Sharkey and Greggains," *San Francisco Call*, March 12, 1896, 16; "Sharkey Was Too Strong," *San Francisco Call*, March 13, 1896, 11.

1576. "Amateur Boxing Bouts," *San Francisco Call*, March 19, 1896, 8.

1577. "The Boxers-Choynski's Chances of Whipping Sharkey," *San Francisco Call*, March 21, 1896, 10.

1578. "Latest News Concerning the Doings of Sportsmen, Athletes and Boxers," *San Francisco Call*, March 25, 1896, 8.

1579. "Choynski and Kid M'Coy To Box," *Chicago Tribune*, March 13, 1896, 8; "Sporting Notes," *St. Louis Post Dispatch*, March 19, 1896, 7.

1580. "Ryan Knocked Out-'Kid' McCoy Finished Him Decisively in Fifteen Fierce Rounds," *St. Louis Post Dispatch*, March 3, 1896, 5; "Knocked Out At Last," *Chicago Tribune*, March 3, 1896, 8.

1581. "Police Stop The Bouts," *Chicago Tribune*, March 22, 1896, 4.

1582. "Jimmy Barry's Hand Again 'Off'-Bantam Champion's Bad Luck with the Fist Which Whipped Madden," *Chicago Tribune*, March 30, 1896, 8.

1583. "Boxing And Police-The Corporation Counsel Construes Their Power Under the Horton Law," *World*, September 23, 1896, 10; "Clipper Fights Stopped," *World*, October 8, 1896, 11; "Boxing Bouts Stopped," *New York Times*, October 9, 1896, 12; "As To Boxing Contests," *New York Times*, October 11, 1896, 7.

1584. "The Boxers-Choynski and Sharkey In Good Trim for Thursday Night," *San Francisco Call*, April 11, 1896, 10; "Sharkey And Choynski," *San Francisco Call*, April 16, 1896, 7; "Tom Sharkey A Winner-Choynski Failed to Stop the Sailor in an Eight-Round Bout," *San Francisco Call*, April 17, 1896, 11; "Mauling An Amateur," *Salt Lake Tribune*, April 17, 3; "Choynski Challenges Sharkey," *Daily Nevada State Journal*, December 4, 1896, 2.

1585. "Sully's Last Night," *Butte Weekly Miner*, April 16, 1896, 6.

1586. "As Popular As Ever," *Ironwood News Record*, March 28, 1896, 3.

1587. "Plays and Players," *St. Paul Daily Globe*, April 19, 1896, 19; "Plays and Players," *St. Paul Daily Globe*, April 26, 1896, 22; "The Theaters," *St. Paul Daily Globe*, April 29, 1896, 4; "John L. On Old Age," *St. Paul Daily Globe*, April 30, 1896, 5.

1588. "Minneapolis Globules," *St. Paul Daily Globe*, May 9, 1896, 5; "Minneapolis Globules," *St. Paul Globe*, May 12, 1896, 3;

1589. "Temple Theater," *Alton Evening Telegraph*, May 15, 1896, 3; "The Wicklow Postman And John L.," *Alton Evening Telegraph*, May 16, 1896, 5.

1590. Advertisement, *Kansas City Daily Journal*, May 10, 1896, 12; "Amusements," *Omaha Daily Bee*, May 31, 1896, Part I, 8; "May's Last Day of Sport," *Omaha*

Daily Bee, May 31, 1896, Part III, 19; "Amusements," *Omaha World Herald*, June 2, 1896, 8.

1591. "Cock Fight on the Stage Eral Game Birds Used In The Wicklow Postman John L. Sullivan and Paddy," *Sioux City Journal*, June 1, 1896, 8;

1592. "Sport," *Sioux City Journal*, June 7, 1896, 5.

1593. "John L.'s Drunk," *Davenport Daily Leader*, June 8, 1896, 6.

1594. "Pugilists Make A Flying Visit-John L. Sullivan and Paddy Ryan En Route to Pittsburg," *Chicago Tribune*, June 8, 1896, 4; "John L.'s Last Appearance," *Inter Ocean*, June 3, 1896, 4; "Haymarket," *Inter Ocean*, June 7, 1896, 37.

1595. "John L. Sullivan Quits-Ex-Champion of the World is a Total Wreck," *St. Louis Republic*, June 14, 1896, 5; "Sullivan Quits The Stage," *Pomeroy Herald*, June 18, 1896, 2; "End of John L.'s Stage Career," *Burlington Hawk Eye*, June 14, 1896, 8.

1596. "Sullivan's Ring History," *Hammond Times*, November 5, 1957, 14.

1597. "Fight Ends In Draw," Chicago Tribune, June 25, 1896, 7; "Creedon And Choynski," *St. Louis Post Dispatch*, June 25, 1896, 6.

1598. "Choynski and Maher Matched," *Marion Register*, July 1, 1896, 3.

1599. "Joe And Parson Part Company," *Chicago Tribune*, July 10, 1896, 7.

1600. "In Short Meter," *Cedar Rapids Evening Gazette*, July 20, 1896, 6.

1601. "Hopkins' South Side Theater," *Chicago Tribune*, July 5, 1896, 36; Advertisement, *Chicago Tribune*, July 5, 1896, 36.

1602. "Hopkins' South Side Theater," *Chicago Tribune*, July 19, 1896, 31; "Hopkins' South Side Theater," *Chicago Tribune*, July 26, 1896, 34; Waller, George A., *Moviegoing in America: a sourcebook in the history of film exhibition*, (Blackwell Publishers Ltd., 2002).

1603. "Maher Cannot Arrange A Match," *Chicago Tribune*, July 24, 1896, 8.

1604. "Corbett Reasserts His Belief," *Chicago Tribune*, August 16, 1896, 6.

1605. "Maher and Choynski," *San Francisco Call*, July 27, 1896, 12; "Clubs and Fighters," *San Francisco Call*, July 28, 1896, 10; "Will Fight In New York," *St. Louis Post Dispatch*, July 28, 1896, 5; "Maher and Choynski," *San Francisco Call*, July

29, 1896, 11; "Choynski and Maher to Meet," *Chicago Tribune*, July 30, 1896, 8; "The Two Fighting Joes," *San Francisco Call*, August 7, 1896, 12.

1606. "Sporting League Formed," *St. Paul Globe*, July 31, 1896, 5.

1607. "Tom Sharkey is Here-Man Matched Against Corbett Reaches Chicago," *Inter Ocean*, August 1, 1896, 4; "Talks Of His Fight," *Chicago Tribune*, August 1, 1896, 6.

1608. "Armstrong Knocks Out Mayo-Parson Davies' Protégé Has An Easy Time Of It," *Chicago Tribune*, August 3, 1896, 8.

1609. "Sharkey Leaves For Detroit," *Chicago Tribune*, August 4, 1896, 8.

1610. "White And Smith Are to Fight," *Chicago Tribune*, July 31, 1896, 7.

1611. "White and Santry Arrested," *Chicago Tribune*, August 10, 1896, 8.

1612. "Tommy White and Dixon Matched," *Chicago Tribune*, August 8, 1896, 7; "White Leaves For New York," *Chicago Tribune*, August 25, 1896, 8.

1613. "Sullivan and Sharkey-Twain to Wind up a Boxing Show in New York," *Inter Ocean*, August 7, 1897, 4; "Sharkey Will Box in Chicago," *Inter Ocean*, August 9, 1896, 11.

1614. "Sharkey To Meet Sullivan," *Brooklyn Eagle*, August 14, 1896, 5.

1615. "Parson Davies is Back," *Inter Ocean*, August 14, 1896, 4.

1616. "To Give An Athletic Exhibition-'Parson' Davies Will Tour Indiana with a Company," *Chicago Tribune*, August 1, 1896, 8.

1617. Advertisement, *Fort Wayne News*, August 18, 1896, 4; Advertisement, *Fort Wayne News*, August 20, 1896, 4.

1618. "John L. Is Here-Parson Davies and His Band of Pugilists in the City," *Fort Wayne News*, August 22, 1896, 1; "John L. Was Here," *Fort Wayne News*, August 24, 1896, 2.

1619. "The Boxers' Corner," *St. Louis Post Dispatch*, January 29, 1899, 18.

1620. "Sharkey Arrives Tonight Naval Champion to Box at the Alhambra Theater," *Inter Ocean*, August 25, 1896, 4; "Sharkey's Boxing Well Received," *Chicago Tribune*, August 27, 1896, 8.

1621. "Sharkey To Meet Sullivan," *Brooklyn Eagle*, August 14, 1896, 5; "Big Fellows Galore, A Great Galaxy of Heavy Weights at Madison Square Garden," *Philadelphia Inquirer*, August 23, 1896, 23.

1622. "This Is A Good Thing," *St. Louis Post Dispatch*, August 30, 1896, 10; "Tom's Coy Admission-Sharkey Says That He Knows He Can Whip Corbett," *St. Louis Post Dispatch*, August 31, 1896, 5.

1623. "Sullivan And Sharkey Don Gloves," *Chicago Tribune*, September 1, 1896, 8; "Sharkey And Sullivan," *St. Louis Post Dispatch*, September 1, 1896, 5.

1624. "Parson Davies Not Done," St. Louis Post Dispatch-The Smooth Psuedo-Cleric Will Not Quit Pugilism," *St. Louis Post Dispatch*, September 21, 1896, 5; "Fight Topics From Chicago," *Philadelphia Inquirer*, September 22, 1896, 5.

1625. "Fight Declared A Draw," *Chicago Tribune*, September 26, 1896, 8; "Tommy White Is Clever," *Brooklyn Eagle*, September 26, 1896, 5; "White Fought Well," *Inter Ocean*, September 29, 1896, 5; "Harry Gilmore Is Home Again," *Chicago Tribune*, September 29, 1896, 8.

1626. "White Leaves The 'Parson'," *Chicago Tribune*, October 1, 1896, 8.

1627. "Tommy White Is In The City," *Chicago Tribune*, October 13, 1896, 8.

1628. "Would Abolish Fight Managers," *Racine Journal-News*, June 14, 1920, 12.

1629. "Managers Are Jokes, Remarks Tommy Ryan," *Post-Standard*, June 30, 1910, 11.

1630. "In The Prize Ring," *St. Paul Globe*, November 1, 1896, 16.

1631. "Boxers Ready For The Ring," *Brooklyn Eagle*, November 15, 1896, 16.

1632. "Maher And Choynski To Meet," *Chicago Tribune*, November 16, 1896, 8.

1633. "Maher Wins The Fight," *Chicago Tribune*, November 17, 1896, 8; "Choynski Knocked Out," *St. Louis Post Dispatch*, November 17, 1896, 6; "Roosevelt Pleased With the Fight," *World*, November 17, 1896, 2; "'Slugging Matches' Revived, *New York Times*, November 18, 1896, 4.

1634. "Passing Of A Champion," *Chicago Tribune*, January 14, 1900, 19.

1635. "Choynski Disregards Instructions," *Philadelphia Inquirer*, November 18, 1896, 4; "Falls Before Maher," *Inter Ocean*, November 17, 1896, 5.

1636. "Slavin Soon Quits-Australian Lasts Only Four Rounds at New York," *Inter Ocean*, November 24, 1896, 5; "Slavin Gave Up," *St. Louis Post Dispatch*, November 24, 1896, 5.

1637. "Call The Fight A Draw-Spectators Decide The Mace-Donovan Contest," *Chicago Tribune*, December 15, 1896, 5.

1638. "In The Days of Finish Fights," *Winnipeg Free Press*, February 12, 1927, Story Section, 7.

1639. "Corbett to Meet Fitz," *Chicago Tribune*, December 18, 1896, 8.

1640. "Bennie Falk's Bet," *St. Louis Post Dispatch*, December 5, 1898, 7.

1641. "Broadway A. C. Bouts," *Brooklyn Eagle*, December 21, 1896, 12; "Chicago Pugilist Wins," *Chicago Tribune*, December 24, 1896, 8.

1642. "Maher And Choynski At Pittsburg," *Chicago Tribune*, December 27, 1896, 7.

1643. "Beating All Comers-Barry, Maher and Choysnki Boxing in Pittsburg," *St. Louis Post Dispatch*, January 3, 1897.

1644. "A Liberal Boxing Law-St. Louisans Want to Adopt New York Statute," *St. Louis Post Dispatch*, January 11, 1897, 5; "The Old And The New Law-Proposed Legislation to Govern Boxing in Missouri," *St. Louis Post Dispatch*, January 24, 1897, 10; "Frisco Rejoices," *St. Louis Post Dispatch*, January 30, 1897; "Fight Bill Is Signed-Governor Of Nevada Makes The Measure A Law," *Chicago Tribune*, January 30, 1897, 7.

1645. "Pick Corbett To Win," *Chicago Tribune*, February 8, 1897, 8.

1646. "Dick Roche Here," *St. Louis Post Dispatch*, January 1, 1897, 5.

1647. "Duffy Is Dead," *St. Louis Post Dispatch*, January 4, 1897, 5; "Duffy Dies From His Injuries," *Chicago Tribune*, January 5, 1897, 8; "How Duffy Died-An Account of the Fight Which Ended in Death," *St. Louis Post Dispatch*, January 5, 1897, 5.

1648. "Not Killed By The Blow," *Syracuse Daily Standard*, January 1, 1897, 1.

1649. "Fitz Signs To Fight," *Chicago Tribune*, January 5, 1897, 8.

1650. "Parson Davies Will Make A Determined Effort," *National Police Gazette*, January 16, 1897, 11.

1651. "Barry and Kelly Draw," *Chicago Tribune*, January 31, 1897, 7.

1652. "Sullivan and Ryan to Meet," *Chicago Tribune*, February 3, 1897, 8.

1653. "Another Fistic Carnival, Davies Will Try to Pull Off One in Nevada," *St. Louis Post Dispatch*, February 10, 1897, 5; "Davies' Carnival At Reno," *Brooklyn Eagle*, February 11, 1897, 12; "Fight To Be At Carson," *Chicago Tribune*, February 11, 1897, 8; "Another Fight-Denver Ed Smith and Joe Choynski to Have a Go," *St. Louis Post Dispatch*, February 21, 1897, 10.

1654. "Jimmy Barry And Ward Are Matched," *Chicago Tribune*, February 21, 1897, 7; "Get Up a Match," *Chicago Tribune*, February 23, 1897, 8.

1655. "Jimmy Barry Get The Decision," *Chicago Tribune*, March 2, 1897, 3; "Chicago Colored Giant Wins Easily," *Chicago Tribune*, March 7, 1897, 5.

1656. "Parson Davies' Special," *Salt Lake Herald*, March 11, 1897, 2; "Parson Davies' Great Attraction," *{Colorado Springs} Gazette Telegraph*, March 7, 1897, 5; Advertisement, *{Colorado Springs} Gazette-Telegraph*, March 8, 1897, 5 (Davies' company to appear March 12, 1897); "Parson Davies En Route To Carson," *Chicago Tribune*, March 9, 1897, 3; "Parson Davies' Special," *Salt Lake Herald*, March 11, 1897, 2; "Parson Davies and His Pugilistic Stars," *{Colorado Springs} Gazette Tribune*, March 11, 1897, 5; "Parson Davies; Cripple Creek," *{Colorado Springs} Gazette-Telegraph*, March 11, 1897, 8; "Parson Davies in Denver," *{Colorado Springs} Gazette-Telegraph*, March 12, 1897, 2.

1657. "Celebrated Pugilists Here," *Salt Lake Herald*, March 15, 1897, 7.

1658. "World Honors At Stake," *St. Paul Globe*, March 17, 1897, 1; "Bob Gets Pay For The Fake," *San Francisco Call*, March 12, 1897, 3; "Sullivan Wants To Challenge," *Chicago Tribune*, March 17, 1897, 2.

1659. "Crowds Leave For Carson-Much Hubbub in Chicago Over The Departure of Special Trains," *St. Louis Post Dispatch*, March 13, 1897, 5; "Start For the Fight," *Chicago Tribune*, March 14, 1897, 3; "Exodus of the Pugs," *Morning Herald-Dispatch*, March 13, 1897, 1; "Exodus of the Sports," *Salt Lake Herald*, March 14, 1897, 1.

1660. "Events in Council Bluffs-No Brass Band and a Crowd to Greet Parson Davies' Special," *Omaha World Herald*, March 15, 1897, 3.

1661. "Sullivan Backs Corbett," *Daily Register Gazette*, March 16, 1897, 1; "Coming to the Fight," *Reno Evening Gazette*, March 16, 1897, 1; "John L. Picks Corbett," *{Syracuse} Evening Herald,* March 16, 1897, 6; "John L. Grows Boastful," *San Francisco Call*, March 16, 1897, 3; "The World's Champion," *Daily Nevada State Journal*, March 18, 1897, 1; "Eight Specail Cars Leave Denver," *Plain Dealer*,

March 17, 1897, 3; "Account by Ingalls Describes His Trip to the Scene of the Fight," *Kansas Semi-Weekley Capital*, March 19, 1897, 3.

1662. "But One Man In It," *San Francisco Call*, March 17, 1897, 5.

1663. "EXTRA 4:30 A. M. – Fitzsimmons Wins In Fourteen Rounds-Cornish Defeats James J. Corbett for the Pugilistic Championship of the World in a Hot Contest-Stiff Blow Near the Heart Dies the Work," *Chicago Tribune*, March 18, 1897, 1.

1664. "Fighters Are Ready," *Kansas City Journal*, March 17, 1897, 5.

1665. "Second Day Feast On the Big Fight," *San Francisco Call*, March 19, 1897, 16.

1666. "Parson Davies' Colored Hercules," *San Francisco Call*, March 20, 1897, 9; "Fitzsimmons At the Chutes," *San Francisco Call*, March 22, 1897, 12.

1667. "Chicago's Only Champion Fighter," *Chicago Tribune*, March 31, 1897, 8.

1668. "Anthony and Barry," *San Francisco Call*, March 29, 1897, 9; "Barry and Anthony Matched," *St. Louis Post Dispatch*, March 30, 1897, 5.

1669. "Choynski and 'Denver Ed' Matched," *Chicago Tribune*, April 6, 1897, 8; "Big Offers Alleged for Sharkey-Maher," *Chicago Tribune*, April 13, 1897, 8.

1670. "The Maher-Sharkey Fight," *San Francisco Call*, March 26, 1897, 8; "Maher In Training," *Salt Lake Herald*, March 26, 1897, 1.

1671. "'Jimmy' Barry In Good Condition," *Chicago Tribune*, April 20, 1897, 8; "'Frisco Sports Excited," *St. Louis Post Dispatch*, April 21, 1897, 5.

1672. "Davies and Barry Reach Chicago," *Chicago Tribune*, May 7, 1897, 6.

1673. "Ring and Glove," *San Francisco Call*, April 13, 1897, 9.

1674. "Davies As A Boxing Club Manager," *Chicago Tribune*, April 21, 1897, 8; "'Parson' Davies Is In Charge," *St. Louis Post Dispatch*, April 21, 1897, 5.

1675. "Choynski and Fitz," *San Francisco Call*, April 22, 1897, 5; "Choynski Challenges Fitz-Parson Davies Formally Issues a Defy for a $5,000 Finish Fight," *St. Louis Post Dispatch*, April 22, 1897, 5.

1676. "Barry Defeats Anthony," *Chicago Tribune*, April 24, 1897, 4.

1677. "Great Fun At The Ring Side-Barry Gets The Bantam Decision Over Anthony-Two Smokys Put Up A Farce," *St. Louis Post Dispatch*, April 24, 1897, 5; "Pugilistic Pointers," *Chicago Tribune*, April 27, 1897, 8.

1678. "Off with His Pugilists-Parson Davies Leaves San Francisco for a Tour of the East," *Tacoma Daily News*, April 27, 1897, 4; "Gans and Leonard Meet," *San Francisco Call*, April 28, 1897, 11.

1679. "Corbett and Chovnski-The Fine Italian Hand of 'Parson' Davies Makes Its Appearance," *Kansas City Star*, May 10, 1897, 3; "Choynski and Corbett-Parson Davies Trying to Bring Them Together for a Twenty Round Go, *Philadelphia Inquirer*, May 11, 1897, 4.

1680. "Amusements," *Omaha World Herald*, May 4, 1897, 3; "Davies And Barry Reach Chicago," *Chicago Tribune*, May 7, 1897, 6.

1681. "May Fight 20 Rounds For $10,000," *Chicago Tribune*, May 11, 1897, 4.

1682 "Choynski And Smith Tonight," *Brooklyn Eagle*, May 10, 1897, 5; "Choynski to Meet Smith Tonight," *Chicago Tribune*, May 10, 1897, 4; "Denver Smith Fights Foul," *San Francisco Call*, May 11, 1897, 3; "Smith A Foul Fighter," *Chicago Tribune*, May 11, 1897, 4; "Choynski Won On A Foul," *Brooklyn Eagle*, May 11, 1897, 4.

1683. "The Days of Finish Fights," *Winnipeg Free Press*, January 29, 1927, Story Section, 7.

1684. "Davies Discusses The Fighters," *Chicago Tribune*, May 14, 1897, 6.

1685. "Sharkey Has A Competent Trainer," *Chicago Tribune*, May 17, 1897, 4.

1686. "Armstrong Shows Improvement," *Chicago Tribune*, May 25, 1897, 4.

1687. "Armstrong to Box in Chicago," *Chicago Tribune*, May 27, 1897, 5.

1688. "Armstrong Praises Tom Sharkey," *Chicago Tribune*, May 30, 1897, 7; "Choynski Threatens Fitzsimmons," *Chicago Tribune*, June 2, 1897, 5; "Saved George Siler A Speech," *Chicago Tribune*, January 31, 1898, 4.

1689. "See Armstrong and Barry," *Chicago Tribune*, May 31, 1897, 4.

1690. "Police Raid The Fight," *Chicago Tribune*, June 10, 1897, 5; "Want No More Fights-Police Ordered To Stop All Slugging Matches In New York," *Chicago Tribune*, June 17, 1897, 4; "No License For Sullivan And Fitz-Brooklyn Authorities Meeting," *Chicago Tribune*, June 30, 1897, 4.

1691. "Had A Cork Leg, But Was A Boxer," *Chicago Tribune*, July 2, 1897, 6; "Pugilists Arrive in Chicago," *Chicago Tribune*, July 5, 1897, 5.

1692. "General Sporting Notes," *Chicago Tribune*, July 2, 1897, 6; "Well Known Pugilist Dead," *Republic*, July 12, 1895, 5; "Sporting Notes," *Chicago Tribune*, July 13, 1897, 4.

1693. No Headline, *St. Louis Post Dispatch*, January 17, 1898, 5.

1694. "Lesson Of The Ring-Eight Years Ago Sullivan And Kilrain Fought," *St. Louis Post Dispatch*," July 8, 1897, 9.

1695. "General Sporting Notes," *Chicago Tribune*, July 9, 1897, 4.

1696. "Jimmy Barry's Trip," *Chicago Tribune*, September 27, 1897, 4.

1697. "Hopkins Hunting a Theater," *Chicago Tribune*, July 9, 1897, 4.

1698. "Will Hold A Boxing Carnival-Parson Davies and Tom O'Rourke Form A Partnership and Will Locate at Reno," *Chicago Tribune*, July 31, 1897, 4; "Brady's Big Carnival," *St. Louis Post Dispatch*, August 3, 1897, 5.

1699. "General Sporting Notes," *Chicago Tribune*, August 5, 1897, 4; "Choynski and Armstrong Spar," *Chicago Tribune*, August 7, 1897, 9.

1700. "Peter Jackson Coming Here," *Philadelphia Inquirer*, August 17, 1897, 4.

1701. "Jeffries and Choynski Matched," *Salt Lake Herald*, August 1, 1897, Part One, 9; "Pugilistic Pointers," *Evening Times {Washington, D.C.}*, August 4, 1897, 6.

1702. "Notes of the Boxers," *Chicago Tribune*, September 8, 1897, 4.

1703. "Ryan and M'Coy-The Former Gets Big Bob Armstrong to Assist Him in His Training," *St. Louis Post Dispatch*, August 31, 1897, 7.

1704. "Syracuse Tommy Ryan," *St. Louis Post Dispatch*, September 9, 1897, 7; "Police Stop Fight-Sensational End to the McCoy-Ryan Encounter-Siler Calls It A Draw-Honors Between the Men About Even at the Close-Was Jobbery Intended? Indications That Ryan's Backers Planned for Interference," Chicago Tribune, September 9, 1897, 5; "Discussed By Referee Siler-Says It Is Untrue That He Saw Kelly-His Early Talk with McCoy," *Chicago Tribune*, September 11, 1897, 6; "Dan Creedon Talks-He Has Something to Say About the Recent Meeting Between M'Coy and Ryan," *St. Louis Post Dispatch*, September 11, 1897, 5; "Fight Brings Scandal-Syracuse Police Officials Are Openly Accused," *Chicago Tribune*, September 11, 1897, 6; "The M'Coy-Ryan Fight-Followers of the Ring Do Not Think as Well Now of the Kid," *St. Louis Post Dispatch*, September 10, 1897, 7; "Honest John Kelly-He and Jimmy Carroll Shed Light on the McCoy and Ryan Mill," *St. Louis Post Dispatch*, September 14, 1897, 6; "M'Coy And Ryan Mill," *St. Louis Post Dispatch*, September 21, 1897, 7.

1705. "Big Bob Armstrong," *Chicago Tribune*, September 12, 1897, 5; "Corbett to Aid the Miners," *New York Times*, September 13, 1897, 5; "Box For The Miners-Big Crowd Sees the Fighters at the Armory," *Chicago Tribune*, September 14, 1897, 4.

1706. "Creedon Is Coming-Colonel Hopkins Will Make It An Occasion Long to be Remembered And the Parson Will Assist," *St. Louis Post Dispatch*, August 26, 1897, 8; "Big And Little Pugs-All Are Coming to Help Creedon's Reception and Benefit Along-Choynski and Happy Dan," *St. Louis Post Dispatch*, September 4, 1897, 5; "Creedon And Tracey-St. Louis Two Star Pugilists Will Come In From the East This Evening-That Reception to *Dan," St. Louis Post Dispatch*, September 10, 1897, 5; "To Meet Dan Creedon-Joe Choynski, The Prince of Heavyweight Boxers, Will Come From Chicago," *St. Louis Post Dispatch*, September 15, 1897, 5.

1707. "What Armstrong Is Like," *Syracuse Standard*, September 20, 1897, 2; "McCormick Ready for Battle," *Philadelphia Inquirer*, September 25, 1897, 4; "Santry Benefit On Tonight," *Chicago Tribune*, October 15, 1897, 4.

1708. "Uncle Sam's Big Warships Prepare to Threaten Cuba," *Chicago Tribune*, September 15, 1897, 1; "On Verge Of War-Assistant Secretary Roosevelt So Tells Officers of the Naval Militia," *Chicago Tribune*, September 22, 1897, 1; "Navy Is Made Ready-Uncle Same Putting His Ships on a Fighting Basis," *Chicago Tribune*, November 27, 1897, 1; "Yellow Jack At New Orleans," Chicago Tribune, September 10, 1897, 1; "Yellow Fever will Not Down," *Chicago Tribune*, September 11, 1897, 4; "Five New Cases At New Orleans," *St. Louis Post Dispatch*, September 14, 1897, 1; "March Of The Fever," *Chicago Tribune*, September 15, 1897, 2; "Panic Due To Fever," *Chicago Tribune*, September 16, 1897, 1; "Yellow Jack Invades Illinois," *Chicago Tribune*, September 20, 1897, 1; "Colored People Not Immune," *Chicago Tribune*, September 23, 1897, 3; "Yellow Fever In New York," *Chicago Tribune*, September 23, 1897, 3; "Death List Grows," *Chicago Tribune*, September 26, 1897, 3; "Ravaged By Plague," *Chicago Tribune*, October 3, 1897, 3.

1709. "All For Dan's Sake," *St. Louis Post Dispatch*, September 16, 1897, 7.

1710. "Jackson Is Here," *Chicago Tribune*, September 19, 1895, 5; "Jackson And Choynski," *Chicago Tribune*, September 19, 1895, 5.

1711. "Corbett A Sick Man," *St. Louis Post Dispatch*," September 27, 1897, 5.

1712. "The Color Line Drawn," *St. Louis Post Dispatch*, October 11, 1897, 5.

1713. "Only Short Bouts-Mayor Harrison Will Not Permit Twenty-Round Goes," *Chicago Tribune*, October 13, 1897, 4.

1714. "The Parson's Plans-Charles E. Davies In St. Louis and Representing the Boxers-Joins the Press Club Boys-And May Give a Royal Entertainment With Them in the Coliseum," *St. Louis Post Dispatch,* October 20, 1897, 5; "Col. Hopkins In Town-He Has Something to Say About the Creedon-McCoy Battle," *St. Louis Post Dispatch*, October 21, 1897, 7.

1715. "Boxing Start Inauspicious-Mayor Harrison's Alleged Idea of the Conduct of Sport Not Being Carried Out-Other Gossip," *Chicago Tribune*, October 25, 1897, 4.

1716. "Tracy and Griffo Matched," *Chicago Tribune*, November 2, 1897, 4; "He Stopped Smiling," *St. Louis Post Dispatch*," November 8, 1892, 5.

1717. "The Big and Little Pugs," *St. Louis Post Dispatch*, November 1, 1897, 5; "Choynski Challenges Ryan," *Brooklyn Eagle*, November 1, 1897, 10.

1718. "Brave Young GriffoThe Great Lightweight Arrives From Chicago This Morning," *St. Louis Post Dispatch*, November 9, 1 897, 7; "Young Griffo In St. Louis," *Chicago Tribune*, November 12, 1897, 6.

1719. "Tracy And Griffo-The Two Great Lightweights All Ready for Tonight's Battle," *St. Louis Post Dispatch*, November 18, 1897, 9.

1720. "Griffo And The Trolley Car," Chicago Tribune, November 19, 1897, 5; "Young Griffo Hurt in a Collison, *Brooklyn Eagle*, November 19, 1897, 4.

1721. "Griffo In Disgrace-The Australian Pugilist Makes A Sorry Spectacle of Himself," *St. Louis Post Dispatch*, November 19, 1897, 7; "Young Griffo Is In Prison," *St. Louis Post Dispatch*, November 21, 1897, 8; "Griffo And Franey," *St. Louis Post Dispatch*, November 22, 1897, 5; "Griffo Ordered to Leave," *Chicago Tribune*, November 23, 1897, 4.

1722. "Griffo And Lavigne," *St. Louis Post Dispatch*, November 24, 1897, 5.

1723. "Still On A Big Drunk-Griffo, the Pugilist, Has Another Very Lively Time at Chicago," *St. Louis Post Dispatch*, November 25, 1897, 6.

1724. "The Colonel And The Parson," *St. Louis Post Dispatch*, December 1, 1897, 5; "Griffo Swears Off-Signs the Pledge and Starts West After Lavigne," *Chicago Tribune*, November 28, 1897, 7; "Griffo on Earth Again," *St. Louis Post Dispatch*, December 16, 1897, 12.

1725. "Tommy Ryan Arrives Tonight," *Chicago Tribune*, November 27, 1897, 4.

1726. "Match Walcott And Tracey," *Chicago Tribune*, November 30, 1897, 4.

1727. "Ryan Not Yet Here-'Billy' Stift's Opponent Expected This Morning," *Chicago Tribune*, November 29, 1897, 4; "Ryan To Meet Stift, Twelve Round Boxing Event Tonight at Battery D," *Chicago Tribune*, November 30, 1897, 4.

1728. "Decision For Ryan-Police Stop the Match with Stift in Six Rounds," *Chicago Tribune*, December 1, 1897, 4.

1729. "Joe Choynski And Jeffries," *Chicago Tribune*, November 30, 1897, 4; "Choynski's Friends-They Are All Betting That He Will Defeat Jeffries To-Night," *St. Louis Post Dispatch*, November 30, 1897, 7.

1730. "Choynski And Jeffries Draw," *Chicago Tribune*, December 1, 1897, 4; "They Fought A Draw-A Rattling Battle Between Choynski And Jeffries Last Night," *St. Louis Post Dispatch*, December 1, 1897, 5; "Jeffries' Showing Was Good-Now Has Some Claim to Class Among the Top Notchers-Choynski's Defense Has Improved," *Chicago Tribune*, December 2, 1897, 4.

1731. "May Fight Tonight-Jimmy Barry Is Scheduled to Meet Walter Croot," *Chicago Tribune*, December 6, 1897, 4; "Jimmy Barry Wins," *Chicago Tribune*, December 7, 1897, 6; "Walter Croot Is Dead-The Fight for the World's Championship Has a Fatal Ending-Jimmy Barry Kills His Man," *St. Louis Post Dispatch*, December 7, 1897, 6; "Boxer Croot Dead-Jimmy Barry's Fight in London Ends Fatally," *Chicago Tribune*, December 8, 1897, 6; "English Bantam Weight Dies," *New York Times*, December 8, 1897, 4; "Jimmy Barry Is Exonerated," *Chicago Tribune*, December 12, 1897, 6; "Barry Remanded on Bail," *Chicago Tribune*, December 15, 1897, 4.

1732. "At the Ringside," *Trenton Evening Times*, December 15, 1897, 6; "M'Coy The Favorite," *St. Louis Post Dispatch*, December 16, 1897, 12; "Picking The Winner," *St. Louis Post Dispatch*, December 17, 1897, 8; "Fit For The Fight," *Chicago Tribune*, December 17, 1897, 4; "Fight Won By M'Coy," *Chicago Tribune*, December 18, 1897, 3; "Going to the Walcott-Tracy Fight," *Morning Herald*, December 19, 1897, 4; "Expect A Fierce Go," *Chicago Tribune*, December 21, 1897, 4.

1733. "Notes of the Boxers," *Chicago Tribune*, December 12, 1897, 6 (Davies is arranging bouts at Battery D); "He Distrusts M'Coy . . . Fighters Lose Battery D), *Chicago Tribune*, December 14, 1897, 4; *City of Chicago v. Ward*, 169 Ill. 392 (1897).

1734. "Court Stops A Mill-Battery D Decree Restrains Tracey and Walcott," *Chicago Tribune*, December 22, 1897, 4.

1735. "Fight Next Monday-Walcott and Tracey at the 'Winter Circus'," *Chicago Tribune*, December 23, 1897, 5; "To Fight Tonight-Walcott and Tracey Meet at the Winter Circus," *Chicago Tribune*, December 27, 1897, 4.

1736. "Draw In Each Bout-Tracey and Walcott Share Honors at Winter Circus," *Chicago Tribune*, December 28, 1897, 4.

1737. "The Chicago Police," *Chicago Tribune*, January 6, 1898, 5.

1738. "Choynski and M'Coy," *St. Louis Post Dispatch*, December 30, 1897, 6.

1739. "Jimmy Barry Is Acquitted," *Chicago Tribune*, December 22, 1897, 4.

Chapter 17 – New Orleans – (1898–1908)

1740. "Parson Davies-The Astute Diplomat of Fistiana in Buffalo-An Entertaining Talk-Famous Authority on Sporting Topics Discusses Recent Big Figth and Other Ring Affairs," *Buffalo Courier*, November 11, 1899.

1741. Ibid.

1742. "Passing of A Champion-George Dixon, Although Beaten, Retains His Popularity-Successful Career of Many Years of 'Little Chocolate'-'Parson' Davies Does Not Believe That Terry McGovern Is Superior to the Colored Man at His Best-Governor Roosevelt and the Repeal of the Horton Law-Dixon's Age Tells-Roosevelt at the Fights, *Chicago Tribune*, January 14, 1900, 19.

1743. "Parson Davies in Town," *St. Louis Post Dispatch*, January 3, 1898, 5.

1744. "Tom Kelly's Opinion," *St. Louis Post Dispatch*, January 9, 1898, 27; "Parson Davies' Plan," *St. Louis Post Dispatch*, January 10, 1898, 5.

1745. "The Ring-Parson Davies and Hopkins Here," *Times Picayune*, January 10, 1898, 7; "Mack's Melange," *Times Picayune*, January 16, 1898, 9.

1746. "The Play Houses of Old New Orleans," *Times Picayune*, March 28, 1898, 9.

1747 . The extent of the syndicate's involvement in New Orleans is explained in detail by Dr. Claudia Anne Beach in a dissertation she submitted to the Graduate faculty of Texas Tech University in 1986. Her dissertation focused on the career of Henry Greenwall, a theater owner and manager in both Texas and New Orleans. In the late 1890's Greenwall managed the Grand Opera House in New Orleans.

1748. "The $100,000,000 Theatrical Syndicate," *Times Picayne*, July 28, 1907, 44.

1749. "David Bidwell Dead," *New York Times*, December 19, 1889, 4; "Mrs. David Bidwell. Remembered by Her Employees," *Times Picayune*, January 1, 1891, 3.

1750. "Mrs. Bidwell's Theaters-The New Deal With Jefferson, Klaw & Erlanger," *Times Picayune*, September 17, 1892, 3; "Amusements- The New St. Charles Theater, *Times Picayune*, September 18, 1892, 6.

1751. "Mrs. David Bidwell, Laid to Rest Yesterday In The Tomb With Her Husband," *Times Picayune*, May 18, 1897, 14.

1752. "The Bidwell Will Declared Valid," *Times Picayune*, August 2, 1898, 3; "O'Malley's Record Will Rest For Awhile Now," *Times Picayune*, April 13, 1906, 5.

1753. "Dr. Pratt's Theaters," *Times Picayune*, January 23, 1898, 8; "Jefferson, Klaw & Erlanger Theaters," *Times Picayune*, January 30, 1898, 22. "O'Malley's Record Will Rest For Awhile Now," *Times Picayune*, April 3, 1906, 5: There is additional discussion of the Tri-State Amusement Company in: "Fight On In Theatricals-Big Vaudeville Combination Has Been Formed," *St. Louis Post Dispatch*, November 27, 1898, 9.

1754. "New Temples of Thespis," *Times Picayune*, January 30, 1898, 4.

1755. "Klaw & Erlanger's Theaters," *Times-Picayune*, March 27, 1898, 22; "Klaw And Erlanger's Theaters-The Architect's Description of the Tulane and Crescent Theaters," *Times Picayune*, March 20, 1898, 3.

1756. "Ruhlin And Bendorf," *St. Louis Post Dispatch*, January 14, 1898, 5.

1757. "As to Boxing in Chicago," *St. Louis Post Dispatch*, January 15, 1898, 5.

1758. "M'Coy's Typewriter," *St. Louis Post Dispatch*, January 17, 1898, 5.

1759. "Tracy And Douglas-Arrangements Complete For Their Meeting In The Oriental Theater," *St. Louis Post Dispatch*, January 20, 1898, 5; "As To Bob Douglas," *St. Louis Post Dispatch*, February 2, 1898, 5.

1760. "Tracy and Douglas Matched," *Chicago Tribune*, January 21, 1898, 5.

1761. "The Bantam Weights," *St. Louis Post Dispatch*, January 21, 1898, 5.

1762. "Davies Is Misrepresented-O'Rourke's Action in Sending for Julian Late at Night Wrongly Ascribed to the 'Parson'," *Chicago Tribune*, January 20, 1898, 4.

1763. Ibid.

1764. "The Bag Punchers," *St. Louis Post Dispatch*, January 22, 1898, 5.

1765. "Armstrong May Meet Maher," *Chicago Tribune*, January 25, 1898, 4; "Purse for Barry and Sammy Kelly," *Chicago Tribune*, January 29, 1898, 7.

1766. "Bouts At The C.A.A.-Armstrong and Childs the Feature Tomorrow Night," *Chicago Tribune*, January 28, 1898, 4; "Six Bouts For Tonight," *Chicago Tribune*, January 29, 1898, 7; "Knocks Out Big Bob. Frank Childs Spoils Armstrong's Reputation," *Chicago Tribune*, January 30, 1898, 6; "Completely Knocked Out-Bob Armstrong Vanquished by a Chicago Pugilist," *Oregonian*, January 30, 1898, 11; "The Ring, Bob Armstrong Knocked Out," *Times-Picayune*, January 30, 1898, 8; "Big Surprise Party-That Is What Frank Childs Gave Bob Armstrong Last Saturday Night," *St. Louis Post Dispatch*, January 31, 1898, 5; "Saved George Siler A Speech-Childs Action in Knocking Out Armstrong Changed Referee's Plans-Boxing Gossip," *Chicago Tribune*, January 31, 1898, 4; "The Boxers Ready," *St. Louis Post Dispatch*, February 3, 1898, 7.

1767. See note 989 above at 112.

1768. "Davies on Armstrong's Defeat," *Chicago Tribune*, January 31, 1898, 4.

1769. "The Ohio Champion," *St. Louis Post Dispatch*, February 12, 1898, 5.

1770. "Choynski And [Tut] Ryan-Their Proposed Battle at San Francisco Has Been Declared Off," *St. Louis Post Dispatch*, February 4, 1898, 5.

1771. "Mack's Melange Composed of Comment on the Most Important Current Sporting Events. Parson Davies and Choynski at Sixes and Sevens," *Times Picayune*, February 13, 1898, 12.

1772. "Choynski And [Tut] Ryan-Their Proposed Battle at San Francisco Has Been Declared Off," *St. Louis Post Dispatch*, February 4, 1898, 5; "Choynski After 'Kid' McCoy," *Trenton Evening Times*, February 5, 1898, 6.

1773. "M'Coy and Choynski-The Kid Says O'Rourke Proposed A Fake Fight Between Those Two," *St. Louis Post Dispatch*, August 2, 1898, 5.

1774. "Tommy Tracey Here-The Crack Lightweight Arrives in St. Louis from Chicago This Morning-Comes to Meet Bob Douglas," *St. Louis Post Dispatch*, February 1, 1898, 5; "As to Bob Douglas," *St. Louis Post Dispatch*, February 2, 1898, 5; "The Boxers Ready," *St. Louis Post Dispatch*, February 3, 1898, 7.

1775. "Tracey Fails to Win," *Chicago Tribune*, February 4, 1898, 4; "Recognized At Last-St. Louisans at Last Tip Their Hats to Young Bob Douglas," *St. Louis Post Dispatch*, February 4, 1898, 5.

1776. "A Big Boxers' Trust-That Is What the Chicago Athletic Clubs Have Just Formed," *St. Louis Post Dispatch*, January 28, 1898, 5; "A Prize Fighters' Trust-Parson Davies Coming East With a Great Scheme in View," *Brooklyn Eagle*, February 12, 1898; "Boxing Club Trust in New York," *Chicago Tribune*, February 13, 1898, 7; "Parson Davies' Plan. More About the Scheme for a Prize Fighters' Trust," *Brooklyn Eagle*, February 14, 1898, 4.

1777. "Cyclist Jimmy Michael," *St. Louis Post Dispatch*, March 1, 1898, 5; "Dave Shafer Here-Jimmy Michael's Trainer Arrives Here from Chicago," *St. Louis Post Dispatch*, March 2, 1898, 5; "The Welsh Rarebit-He Is Not Here and Will Not Be Here Until To-Morrow," *St. Louis Post Dispatch*, March 3, 1898, 6; "Jimmy Michael In St. Louis," *St. Louis Post Dispatch*, March 5, 1898, 5.

1778. "Barry And Ritchie Matched," *Chicago Tribune*, March 7, 1898, 9; "With Sporting People," *{Washington D. C.} Times*, March 11, 1898, 6.

1779. "Everhardt Is To Box Here," *Chicago Tribune*, March 8, 1898, 5; "Mack's Melange-McCoy and Bonner," *Times-Picayune*, March 13, 1898, 12; "Boxing Bouts For This Week," *Chicago Tribune*, March 14, 1898, 9; "Mack's Melange," *Times-Picayune*, March 30, 1898, 10; Advertisement, *Times-Picayune*, March 24, 1898, 5; "McCoy Talks of His Bout With Bonner," *Times-Picayune*, March 24, 1898, 8.

1780. "The Ring-The St. Bernard Club's Claimants," *Times Picayune*, March 19, 1898, 8; "The Ring-St. Bernard Athletic Club Building Strengthened," *Times Picayune*, March 20, 1898, 8; "There Is A Way To Stop A Prize Fight-Sheriff Nunez Finds Even a Simpler Scheme," *Times Picayune*, March 29, 1898, 7; "Mack's Melange-Composed of Comments on Current Sporting Events- Parson Davies and the McCoy-Bonner Contest," *Times Picayune*, March 27, 1898, 9.

1781. Advertisement, *Times Picayune*, March 25, 1898, 6; "The Boxers' Corner, *St. Louis Post Dispatch,*" March 27, 1898, 15.

1782. "Attorney General Asks An Injunction To Restrain the St. Bernard Club From Bringing Off the McCoy-Bonner Fight in Its Arena," *Times Picayune*, March 26, 1898, 8; "Threatened Rebellion By Prize Fighters," *Times Picayune*, March 29, 1898, 4.

1783. "There Is A Way To Stop A Fight.-Attorney General Cunningham Consults With St. Bernard," *Times Picayune*, March 28, 1898, 8; "M'Coy And Bonner," *St. Louis Post Dispatch*, March 28, 1898, 6.

1784. "M'Coy and Bonner-Their Fight at New Orleans Stopped by the Authorities," *St. Louis Post Dispatch*, March 29, 1898, 5; "Prevent M'Coy-Bonner Fight," *Chicago Tribune*, March 29, 1898, 7.

1785. "Davies to Turn Actor-Well Known Sporting Manager Going on the Stage," *Fort Wayne News*, April 5, 1898, 1; "About the Boxers," *Boston Daily Globe*, April 8, 2.

1786. "Another Big Match," *St. Louis Post Dispatch*, April 12, 1898, 5; "Talk Among the Pugilists," *Chicago Tribune*, April 20, 1898, 4.

1787. "Last Editon-5 Extra-Over 250 Live Lost On The Battleship Maine," *St. Louis Post Dispatch*, February 16, 1898, 1; "Extra-3:30 A. M.-Main Is Blown Up In Havana Harbor," *Chicago Tribune*, February 16, 1898, 1; "Is It War With Spain?," *St. Louis Post Dispatch*, February 17, 1898, 2.

1788. "Last Edition-War-Proclaimed To The World-Notice to All Nations That the United States Has Instituted a Blockade of Cuban Ports-Dewey May Fight First Battle-Sampson's Guns Threaten Havana," *St. Louis Post Dispatch*, April 17, 1898, 1; "War Has Begun-Spain Throws Down the Gauntlet at Madrid by Dismissing the American Minister-Uncle Sam Takes It Up," *Chicago Tribune*, April 22, 1898, 1; "Illinois Ready to Respond-Call of President McKinley on a Basis of 100,000 Men Would Take the Prairie State's Entire Militia," *Chicago Tribune*, April 22, 1898, 7; "Madrid Shouting For War-Delirious Conduct of the Populace in the Spanish Capital Throughout the Day and Night," *Chicago Tribune*, April 23, 1898, 2; "Spain Now Declares War," *Chicago Tribune*, April 25, 1898, 1.

1789. "Attractions for the Week," *Chicago Tribune*, May 8, 1898, 43; "Attractions for the Week," *Chicago Tribune*, June 5, 1898, 37.

1790. "Boxing Bouts Are Postponed-'Parson' Davies Decides to Hold the Fights Scheduled for May 9 at a Later Date," *Chicago Tribune*, April 25, 1898, 9; "'Parson' Davies' Bouts June 2," *Chicago Tribune*, May 11, 1898, 4.

1791. "Corbett to Box in Chicago," *Chicago Tribune*, May 18, 1898, 4; "Corbett May Box Here," *Chicago Tribune*, May 22, 1898, 7.

1792. "M'Coy A Hot Favorite," *World*, May 20, 1898, 10; "M'Coy And Ruhlin," *Chicago Tribune*, May 20, 1898, 10.

1793. "Parson Davies in Town," *St. Louis Post Dispatch*, May 23, 1898, 5.

1794. "Fighters in Hard Training," *Chicago Tribune*, May 28, 1898, 4; "Boxing Bouts At Tattersall's," *Chicago Tribune*, May 29, 1898, 7; "On Deck Once More," *St. Louis Post Dispatch*, May 30, 1898, 5; "Tattersall's Bouts Tonight," *Chicago Tribune*, June 2, 1898, 4.

1795. "Boxers in The Dark-Lights Go Out at 'Parson' Davies' Entertainment," *Chicago Tribune*, June 3, 1898, 4.

1796. "Fights Lost On Fouls," *Chicago Tribune*, June 4, 1898, 7.

1797. "Bernstein Wins Defeats Eddie Santry in a Twenty Round Bout," *Philadelphia Inquirer*, July 23, 1898, 4; "Bernstein Whips Santry, The New Yorker Always the Better Man at Close Quarter's but He Gets His Knocks," *Sun*, July 23, 1898, 8.

1798. "Watts an Easy Mark," *Trenton Evening Times*, August 6, 1898, 6; "Jim Jeffries Outclasses Armstrong with Broken Hand Second Ten-Round Fight with O'Donnell off Californian Injured," *Philadelphia Inquirer*, August 6, 1898, 4.

1799. "Sharkey at the Lyceum," *Philadelphia Inquirer*, August 25, 1898, 7.

1800. "Sports in Short Metre," *Philadelphia Inquirer*, November 22, 1898, 4; "Tom Lansing May Die from Knockout-One Time Sparing Partner of Jim Corbett Almost Totally Paralyzed as a Result," *New York American*, November 26, 1898, 7; "Pugilist Ill-Tom Lansing, Trainer of Corbett Almost Entirely Paralyzed as Result of Fight," Boston Journal, November 27, 1898, 6; "Puglist Lansing Dying from Blow," *Evening Times*, January 21, 1899, 3; "No Action to be Taken," *Kansas City Journal*, January 24, 1899, 5.

1801. "Boxers' Corner," *St. Louis Post Dispatch*, April 10, 1898, 15.

1802. "Multnomah Club Gets Tommy Ryan," *Oregonian*, August 27, 1911, 4.

1803. "Big Jim Jeffries, He Will Try And Put O'Donnell and Armstrong Out To-Night," *St. Louis Post Dispatch*, August 5, 1898, 5; "Jim Breaks His Left Arm," *San Francisco Call*, August 6, 1898, 4; "The Boxers' Corner," *St. Louis Post Dispatch*, September 18, 1898, 28.

1804. "Odds and Ends of Sporting Chatter," *Philadelphia Inquirer*, August 8, 1898, 4.

1805. "Ryder's Sporting Letter," *St. Paul Globe*, May 13, 1900, 6.

1806. See note 66 above at 38, 50, 120 and 126.

1807. "General Sporting Notes," *Chicago Tribune*, August 31, 1898, 4.

1808. "The Hotels," *Times-Picayune*, September 1, 1898, 6.

1809. "Notes," *Times-Picayune*, September 1, 1898, 7.

1810. Compare: "The New Theaters-The Klaw-Erlanger Co.'s Beautiful Temples of the Drama-The Crescent Theater," *Times-Picayune*, September 25, 1898, 19; and "A Very Important Decision," *Times-Picayune*, October 26, 1898, 4; "Railroad Combinations," *Times Picayune*, November 10, 1898, 4; "A Louisiana Law Against Trusts," *Times Picayune*, June 2, 1899, 4; "Law Against Trusts," *Times Picayune*, June 4, 1899, 15; "The Fight Against The Trusts," *Times-Picayune*, June 6, 1899, 4; "Anti-Trust League Hold A Meeting," *Times Picayune*, June 8, 1899, 2; "Why Trusts Are Dangerous," *Times Picayune*, June 12, 1899, 4.

1811. "With the Boxers," *St. Louis Post Dispatch*, June 30, 1900, 5.

1812. "Poor Old Peter Jackson," *St. Louis Post Dispatch*, August 18, 1898, 9; "All Kinds of Sport," *Kansas City Journal*, August 21, 1898, 5.

1813. "St. Charles Theater," *Times Picayune*, September 11, 1898, 8; "Amusements," *Times Picayune*, September 12, 1898, 5.

1814. "'Parson' Davies' Niece Dies," *New Orleans Item*, May 1, 1904, 8.

1815. "Crescent Theater," *Times Picayune*, September 25, 1898, 8.

1816. "No Thanks-Parson Davies Declines to Manage the Corbett-McCoy Match," *St. Paul Globe*, October 6, 1898, 5.

1817. "Mack's Melange Of Comment on Important Current Sporting Events-Sailor Sharkey and Kid McCoy etc.," *Times Picayune*, January 1, 1899, 24; "A Big Fistic Carnival," *St. Louis Post Dispatch*, January 8, 1899, 5; "M'Coy Is Favorite-Over in England They Are Betting The Hossier Will Beat the Sailor," *St. Louis Post Dispatch*, January 4, 1899, 5; "Few Bets on the Fight-M'Coy is Still a Slight Favorite With the Plungers," *Chicago Tribune*, January 8, 1899, 7; "Before The Battle-It Is Even Money and Take Your Pick on Sharkey and M'Coy Everywhere," *St. Louis Post Dispatch*, January 9, 1899, 5.

1818. "Chat of Ring and Diamond," *Hamilton Daily Republican-News*, January 7, 1899, 8; "Big Fight Tonight," *Daily Iowa Capital*, January 10, 1899, 1; "Thomas Sharkey Defeated McCoy-The Battle Was a Hot One from the Beginning," *Times-Picayune*, January 11, 1899, 8; "He Played Possum-That's What Sharkey Did Tuesday Night With Kid McCoy," *St. Louis Post Dispatch*, January 11, 1899, 5.

1819. "Boxing Shows Too Numerous-Mayor Harrison Threatens to Call a Halt-'Parson' Davies Reaches Chicago," *Chicago Tribune*, January 28, 1899, 4.

1820. "Corbett And Sharkey," *Chicago Tribune*, February 1, 1899, 7; "Confirms Corbett-Sharkey Match," *Chicago Tribune*, February 2, 1899, 4; "Sharkey Says He

Will Win," *Chicago Tribune*, February 3, 1899, 4; "Tom O'Rourke In The City-Sharkey's Manager Posts a Forfeit for the Fight With Corbett-Boxing Gossip, *Chicago Tribune*, February 6, 1899, 9

1821. "Julian And O'Rourke," *St. Louis Post Dispatch*, February 9, 1899, 4 (Carter Harrison has vetoed the Corbett-Sharkey match); "Boxing May Be Discontinued-Row Among the Promoters Imminent in Consequence of Sharkey-Corbett Permit Being Refused," *Chicago Tribune*, February 10, 1899, 4; "J. J. Corbett and the C. A. A.," *Chicago Tribune*, February 11, 1899, 7.

1822. "Sharkey at Mt. Clemens," *Chicago Tribune*, February 23, 1899, 10.

1823. "The Base Ball Season is Open," *Racine Daily Journal*, April 29, 1899, 8; "The Ring-Sharkey's Survey Of The Field," *Times Picayune*, April 30, 1899, 8; "Sharkey and Vaudeville at the Academy of Music," *Times Picayune*, May 1, 1899, 13; "Amusements-Academy of Music," *Times-Picayune*, May 2, 1899, 8; "The Ring-The Gymnastic Club Stag," *Times Picayune*, May 5, 1899, 8.

1824. "About the Boxers," *Boston Daily Globe*, April 7, 1898, 15.

1825. "New Boxing Rules," *Sandusky Star*, April 10, 1899, 4.

1826. "'Old Drury' Is In Ruins-St. Charles Theater Burned to the Ground at Midnight-Mysterious Fire Started Near the Stage etc.," *Times Picayune*, June 5, 1899, 1; "The Destruction Of The Old St. Charles," *Times Picayune*, June 5, 1899, 4; "St. Charles Theater Burns-Landmark at New Orleans Destroyed by Fire at Midnight-Leased by J. D. Hopkins," *Chicago Tribune*, June 5, 1899, 1.

1827. "O'Malley's Record Bing Made Plain to Public," *Times Picayune*, March 30, 1906, 3.

1828. "'Parson' Davies-Thinks the Fire Was of Incediary Origin," *Times-Picayune*, June 5, 1899, 1.

1829. "O'Malley Still Having Hard Time With His Witnesses," *Times-Picayune*, April 3, 1906, 11; "A Thousand Dollars For Each Incendiary," *Times Picayune*, June 6, 1899, 2; "The Police At Work-And Think They Will Be Able to Find Some Light," *Times Picayune*, June 6, 1899, 2; "Pratt Plans A Fine New Theater," *Times Picayune*, June 7, 1899, 11.

1830. "Parson Davies Going," *Times Picayune*, October 2, 1908, 5.

1831. "O'Malley's Record Being Made Plain to Public," *Times Picayune*, March 30, 1906, 3 (O'Malley's testimony regarding suggestions that he burned the Saint

Charles); "O'Malley Still Having Hard Time With His Witnesses," *Times Picayune*, April 3, 1906, 11; "O'Malley's Record Will Rest For Awhile Now," *Times Picayune*, April 13, 1906, 5.

1832. "Notes of the Boxers," *Chicago Tribune*, June 6, 1899, 6.

1833. "St. Louis Boxing Club-'Parson' Davies Will Start A New Pugilistic Organization," *Time-Picayune*, June 27, 1899, 8; "Dixon And O'Rourke Arrive," *Chicago Tribune*, July 3, 1899, 5; "Boxing In St. Louis," *St. Louis Post Dispatch*, July 15, 1899, 5.

1834. "World of Sport," *Sandusky Star*, June 29, 1899, 1.

1835. "Amusements," *St. Louis Post Dispatch*, July 9, 1899, 39.

1836. "No Boxing In St. Louis," *Kansas City Journal*, December 18, 1898, 5; "Fined For Abetting Boxing Match," *Omaha Daily Bee*, December 18, 1898, Part I, 11.

1837. "With The Boxers-Manager Whitney Says the Santry-Dixon Mill Will Positively Take Place," *St. Louis Post Dispatch*," July 30, 1899, 8.

1838. "Dixon-Santry Fight Tonight," *Chicago Tribune*, July 14, 1899, 4; "Dixon Draws Crowded House-He Wins the Decision from Santry at the Star Theater in an Interesting Fight," *Chicago Tribune*, July 15, 1899, 7.

1839. "The Heavyweights," *St. Louis Post Dispatch*, July 13, 1899, 9; "Boxing In St. Louis-Parson Davies Arranging To Bring Dixon Here," *St. Louis Post Dispatch*, July 15, 1899, 5; "With the Boxers," *St. Louis Post Dispatch*, July 16, 1899, 15; "Dixon And Santry-All Preparations In Progress For Their Contest," *St. Louis Post Dispatch*, July 27, 1899, 8; "Dixon's Birthday," *St. Louis Post Dispatch*, July 29, 1899, 7.

1840. "Davies And Dixon-The 'Parson' And The Champion In St. Louis-Dixon to Meet Santry Here," *St. Louis Post Dispatch*, July 17, 1899, 5.

1841. "Leon Hard At Work," *St. Louis Post Dispatch*, July 19, 1899, 5; "Kid M'Coy In Town," *St. Louis Post Dispatch*, July 31, 1899, 8.

1842. "With The Boxers," *St. Louis Post Dispatch*, July 16, 1899, 15.

1843. "With The Boxers-Manager Whitney Says the Santry-Dixon Mill Will Positively Take Place," *St. Louis Post Dispatch*, July 30, 1899, 8.

1844. "Dixon-Santry Fight Postponed," *Chicago Tribune*, August 1, 1899, 4.

1845. "Santry's Stock Up," *St. Paul Globe*, August 16, 1899, 5.

1846. "M'Coy And O'Rourke," *St. Louis Post Dispatch*, August 1, 1899, 6.

1847. "Dixon And Santry-They Left For New York On Tuesday Evening's Train," *St. Louis Post Dispatch*, August 2, 1899, 8; "With The Boxers-Next Friday Night: Dixon and Santry will Meet in New York," *St. Louis Post Dispatch*, August 8, 1899, 5.

1848. "Sharkey May Win-Parson Davies Thinks Well of the Sailor's Chances," *St. Louis Post Dispatch*, July 18, 1899, 7; "With The Boxers," *St. Louis Post Dispatch*, August 9, 1899, 7; "With The Boxers," *St. Louis Post Dispatch*, August 21, 1899, 5; "With the Boxers," *St. Louis Post Dispatch*, September 3, 1899, 14); "Douglas And Smith," *St. Louis Post Dispatch*, September 8, 1899, 7.

1849. *The Picayune's Guide to New Orleans* (The Picayune, 1904) 109.

1850. "Parson Davies' New Venture-He Purchases the Crescent Billiard Parlor in New Orleans," *St. Louis Post Dispatch*, August 19, 1899, 5;

1851. "O'Malley's Record Will Rest For Awhile Now," *Times Picayune*, April 13, 1906, 5.

1852. "At A Glance," *Newark Daily Advocate*, November 1, 1899, 2; "St Louis's Annual Horse Show," *Los Angeles Times*, November 1, 1899, 5; Obituary, *Hartford Courant*, November 1, 1899, 2.

1853. "With The Boxers," *St. Louis Post Dispatch*, August 24, 1899, 9.

1854. "Choynski And Ryan," *St. Louis Post Dispatch*, August 29, 1899, 7.

1855. "With The Boxers-Something About Them and Their Plans," *St. Louis Post Dispatch*, September 21, 1899, 12; "Form A Fight Trust," *Chicago Tribune*, September 21, 1899, 4; "Sporting Clubs Have Formed A Trust," *San Francisco Call*, September 21, 1899, 5; "Form A Pugilistic Trust," *Salt Lake Herald*, September 21, 1899, 3; "A Pugilistic Trust-Leading Athletic Clubs of New York Have Combined," *Kansas City Journal*, September 22, 1899, 5.

1856. "Amusements," *St. Louis Post Dispatch*, September 24, 1899, 44 (Hopkins to have the Rough Riders at Athletic Park); "Parson Davies' Wild West Show," *Chicago Tribune*, October 5, 1899, 4; "Ropers and Rough Riders-Aggregation of Dextrous Horsemen and Wild Animals to Entertain Crowds at Tattersall's," *Chicago Tribune*, October 29, 1899, 8; Advertisement, *Chicago Tribune*, October 29, 1899, 40 (Texas Rough Riders and Ropers at Tattersalls); "Give A Rough

Riders' Show-Pickett Throws a Steer, Using Nothing Except His Hands-Exhibitions with Wild Horses, *Chicago Tribune*, October 30, 1899, 4.

1857. "Sports At New Orleans-This Winter Will See A Revival of Pugilistic Contests," *Chicago Tribune*, October 8, 1899, 19.

1858. "The Mirror of Justice Held Up to D. C. O'Malley," *Times Picayune*, March 29, 1906, 3; "O'Malley Record Being Made Plain to Public," *Times Picayune*, March 30, 1906, 3.

1859. "Mr. Davies' Statement," *{New Orleans} Times Democrat*, October 12, 1899, 4.

1860. "A Duel On Camp Street-Dominick C. O'Malley and Colonel C. Harrison Parker Empty Their Pistols in a Bloody Encounter," *Times Picayune*, October 11, 1899, 1; "Editors In Fierce Street Encounter-D. C. O'Malley and C. H. Parker, of New Orleans, Seriously Wounded-O'Malley Belittled Parker-Duel the Result of a Cartoon in New Orleans Evening Item etc.," *Atlantic Constitution*, October 11, 1899, 1; *{New Orleans} Times Democrat*, October 11, 1899, 1; "Parson Davies' Story-He Gives His Version of the Shooting Affray," *{New Orleans} Times Democrat*, October 11, 1899, 2; "Colonel Parker's Condition," *Times Picayune*, October 11, 1899, 5.

1861. "Street Duel in New Orleans," *New York Times*, October 11, 1899, 1.

1862. "Who Began the Shooting," *New Orleans States*, October 11, 1899, 1.

1863. "A Duel On Camp Street-Dominick C. O'Malley and Colonel C. Harrison Parker Empty Their Pistols in a Bloody Encounter," *Times Picayune*, October 11, 1899, 8.

1864. "A Duel On Camp Street-Dominick C. O'Malley and Colonel C. Harrison Parker Empty Their Pistols in a Bloody Encounter," *Times Picayune*, October 11, 1899 at 11.

1865. "Long Tom Shaw-Dean- A Bookmaking Legend," *The Times-News*, July 19, 1978, 17; "Shaw, Dean of Bookmakers, Handled 200 Million Bucks!," *The Milwaukee Journal*, June 21, 1944, 32.

1866. "Parker-O'Malley Case Again Continued," *Times Picayune*, December 16, 1899, 3; "Neither Col. Parker Nor O'Malley Heard," *Times Picayune*, December 29, 1899, 11.

1867. "Favors Boxing League," *Chicago Tribune*, October 15, 1899, 19.

1868. "New York Fight Gossip," *Chicago Tribune*, October 29, 1899, 19.

1869. "Jeffries Is Improving Rapidly," *Chicago Tribune*, October 20, 1899, 4; "New York Fight Gossip-George Siler On The Jeffries-Sharkey Postponement," *Chicago Tribune*, October 22, 1899, 23; "Easy Day For Fighters-Jeffries Takes Light Exercise, Sharkey on Horseback," *Chicago Tribune*, October 27, 1899, 4; "Big Fight Next Friday-Jeffries and Sharkey to Meet for Heavyweight Honors," *Chicago Tribune*, October 29, 1899, 20; "Winner Hard To Pick," *Chicago Tribune*, November 1, 1899, 6; "Big Fight Is On Tonight," *Chicago Tribune*, November 3, 1899, 4.

1870. "Notes of the Fighters," *Chicago Tribune*, November 1, 1899, 6; "Davies Likes Sailor's Chances," *Chicago Tribune*, October 29, 1899, 20.

1871. "Jeffries Gets The Decision-Wins from Sharkey After Twenty-five Rounds of Hard Fighting at the Coney Island Club," *Chicago Tribune*, November 4, 1899, 1.

1872. "Sharkey Says He Is Robbed," *Chicago Tribune*, November 4, 1899, 1; "Woes Of Referee Siler-Man Who Umpired Big Fight Replies to Sharkey," *Chicago Tribune*, November 5, 1899, 17; "Early Fight Unlikely," *Chicago Tribune*, November 9, 1899, 9; "Siler Gives the 'Why'," *Chicago Tribune*, November 12, 1899, 17.

1873. "Parson Davies. The Astute Diplomat of Fistina in Buffalo. An Entertaining Talk. Famous Authority on Sporting Topics Discusses Recent Big Fight and Other Ring Affairs," *Buffalo Courier*, November 11, 1899.

1874. "Peter Jackson Is In Hard Lines, 'Parson' Davies Comments on the Colored Fighter's Misfortunes," *Chicago Tribune*, November 6, 1899, 9.

1875. "The Ring," *St. Louis Post Dispatch*, December 9, 1899, 5.

1876. "Saw Himself Fight-Sharkey Witness [sic] the Pictures and Comments on Them-Peter Jackson Showed His Generosity When he Fought His Fist Battle In This Country," *The Sandusky Star*, November 16, 1899, 1.

1877. Id.

1878. "Notes of the Fighters," *Chicago Tribune*, December 6, 1899, 6.

1879. "Peter Jackson Seriously Ill," *Chicago Tribune*, December 24, 1899, 19.

1880. "Mecca Of The Sports-New Orleans Will Be Lively During The Winter," *Chicago Tribune*, December 3, 1899, 20.

1881. "With the Boxers," *Chicago Tribune*, December 12, 1899, 7.

1882. "With the Boxers. The Jeffries-Sharkey Pictures to be Exhibited Here To-Day," *St. Louis Post Dispatch*, December 24, 1899, 14.

1883. "Referee George Siler. He Is Here in the Interest of the Sharkey-Jeffries Pictures," *St. Louis Post Dispatch*, December 22, 1899, 7.

1884. "Referee Geo. Siler-He Talks About The Jeffries and Sharkey Mill-Why Sailor Rushed Things etc.," *St. Louis Post Dispatch*, December 18, 1899, 5.

1885. "Bancroft May Go South," *Hamilton Daily Republican-News*, December 29, 1899, 7.

1886. "To Keep Sharkey Busy," *Chicago Tribune*, April 8, 1900, 19.

1887. "'Parson' Davies' Boxing Budget-He Still Picks McCoy and Dixon to Win-Story on Felix," *Chicago Tribune*, January 1, 1900, 9; "M'Coy A Winner In Five Rounds-Peter Maher Is Knocked Out at the Coney Island Sporting Club," January 2, 1900, 4; "M'Coy Praises Maher-Says the Irishman was Never so Fast Before," *Chicago Tribune*, January 2, 1900, 4; "Parson Davies' Letter-Comment on the M'Coy-Maher and M'Govern-Dixon Battles," *Chicago Tribune*, January 7, 1900, 19.

1888. "'Kid' M'Coy Again In Training-Resumes Work at Muldoon's After Resting Three Days," *Chicago Tribune*, January 6, 1900, 7; "M'Coy Fights Choynski-Battle Twenty-Five Rounds In New York Tonight," *Chicago Tribune*, January 12, 1900, 8; "M'Coy's Victory Is Undeserved-Choynski Loses a Remarkable Three-Round Contest at Broadway Club-Blunders of Officials-Mistake in the Time and Failure to Hear Bell Save the Hossier Pugilist-One Spectator Falls Dead," *Chicago Tribune*, January 13, 1900, 4; "Choynski's Defeat-M'Coy Hit Him So Hard He Refused to Leave His Corner-Broadway Club Queer Fight-It Lasted Only Three Rounds, but in That Time the Hossier Was Knocked Down Four Times," *St. Louis Post Dispatch*, January 13, 1900, 5.

1889. "M'Govern-Dixon Fight Tuesday-Little Fellows Are Ready for the Championship Battle at Broadway Club," *Chicago Tribune*, January 7, 1900, 17; "M'Govern Whips George Dixon-Wins the 118-Pound Championship in Eight Rounds at Broadway Club-Hard Fight From Start-Colored Man Weakens Under Terrific Punishment and O'Rourke Throws Up the Sponge," *Chicago Tribune*, January 10, 1900, 5.

1890. "From Governor Roosevelt's Message," *World*, January 4, 1900, 3: See also, "Horton Law Still On The Books," *World*, March 31, 1899, 8; "Devery Strikes

At Big Fight. . . Warns the Public In A Statement that Horton Law Will be Rigidly Enforced," *World*, June 7, 1899,1; "To Investigate Gardiner," *New York Times*, November 22, 1899, 5; "Horton Sparring Law Amendment," *New York Times*, January 3, 1900, 3; "Two Bills to End Prize Fighting," *World*, January 4, 1900, 3; "He Thinks The Fight Was A Fake," *Chicago Tribune*, January 11, 1900, 4; "Passing Of A Champion," *Chicago Tribune*, January 14, 1900, 19. This article written by Charles E. (Parson) Davies-Davies and he recalls Roosevelt's position on boxing and his message to the New York legislature. "Horton Law In Danger-Unexpectedly Strong Opposition to Fight Measure Develops," *Chicago Tribune*, February 6, 1900, 4; "To Knock Out The Horton Law-The Repeal Bill May be Passed By The Assembly," *National Police Gazette*, March 3, 1900, 10; "Blow to Prize Fights-Repeal of Horton Law Recommended by Code Committee," *Chicago Tribune*, February 8, 1900, 9; "Another Nail In Horton Law-Assault of Referee White Adds Opposition to Boxing Privileges," *Chicago Tribune*, February 11, 1900, 17.

1891. "Parson Davies' Comment," *Chicago Tribune*, June 17, 1900, 19.

1892. "The Double Cross-Kid M'Coy Said to Have Given His Friends That," *St. Louis Post Dispatch*, January 6, 1900, 5.

1893. "Methods Of The New York Ring-Policy of 'Sure Thing' Promoters Will Be Ruinous Says George Siler-Long List of Swindles-McCoy-Choynski Affair Only One of Many Similar Frauds in Pugilism-Repeal of Law Probable," *Chicago Tribune*, January 14, 1900, 17; "Brady Says Siler Is Wrong," *Chicago Tribune*, January 17, 1899, 4; "Tom O'Rourke Angry-He Replies Warmly to the Recent Insinuation of Siler-The Jeffries-Sharkey Mill," *St. Louis Post Dispatch*, January 18, 1900, 12.

1894. "Says Siler Dislikes The Irish-Senator Timothy 'Dry Dollar' Sullivan Calls the Referee an A. P. A.," *Chicago Tribune*, January 19, 1900, 4; Cartoon, *Chicago Tribune*, January 21, 1900, 17. The text of the cartoon reads: "Referee Siler: 'Now, before I give my decision I must ask a few questions. What is your nationality, Mr. Schmit?" Schmit: 'I was a German.' Siler: 'And yours, Mr. Mulligan?' Mulligan: 'Oi'm Irish, begob.' Siler (to Mulligan): 'Well, you lose.'").

1895. "Literature of the 'A.P.A.'; Circulated Secretly by Men Who Fear to be Known," *New York Times*, May 26, 1894, 1.

1896. "The Days of Finish Fights," *Winnipeg Free Press*, February 5, 1927, Story Section, 7.

1897. "Billiards-The Pool Handicap," *Times Picayune*, January 3, 1900, 8; "Billiards-Contest At The Crescent, *Times Picayune*, January 4, 1900, 7; "Billiards-Cleveland Wins The Handicap," *Times Picayune*, January 6, 1900, 8; "Jeffries' Next Fight," *Chicago Tribune*, January 28, 1900, 19 [By Charles E. (Parson) Davies]; "Arrange A Novel Fight," *Chicago Tribune*, February 4, 1900, 20 [By Charles E. (Parson) Davies].

1898. "Sharkey A Wonder-Quick Victories Over Goddard and Jeffords," *St. Louis Post Dispatch*, February 20, 1900, 6.

1899. "Gov. Roosevelt Meets Sharkey-Tells the Sailor He Would Like to Spar with Him," *Chicago Tribune*, February 22, 1900, 4; "Sharkey And The Governor," *St. Louis Post Dispatch*, February 25, 1900, 14.

1900. "Fighters etc.," *Atlanta Constitution*, February 24, 1907, 34.

1901. "Arrange A Novel Fight-Choynski and Joe Walcott to Meet on Feb. 23," *Chicago Tribune*, February 4, 1900, 20; "Choynski-Walcott Match Next-Easterners Think the Colored Man Is Entirely Outclassed," *Chicago Tribune*, February 19, 1900, 4; "With The Boxers-Plenty of Gossip About the Choynski Walcott Battle," *St. Louis Post Dispatch*, February 26, 1900, 5.

1902. "Walcott Is A Winner, Barbadoes Negro Gets Decision Over Choynski," *Salt Lake Tribune*, February 24, 1900, 2; "Walcott Wallops Joe Choynski-With All Physical Qualities Against Him the Colored Welterweight Wins," *Philadelphia Inquirer*, February 24, 1900, 10; "Joe Walcott's Victory," Chicago Tribune, March 4, 1900, 18 [By Charles E. (Parson) Davies].

1903. See note 66 above at 76-77.

1904. "War of the Poolrooms-History of the Trouble that Threatens Local Racing," Chicago Tribune, March 25, 1900, 20; "Blow To Prize Fights," *Chicago Tribune*, April 1, 1900, 19; "O'Malley's Record Will Rest For Awhile Now," *Times Picayune*, April 13, 1906, 5; "With the Boxes," *St. Louis Post Dispatch*, April 15, 1900, 23 9.

1905. "Parson Davies' European Trip to Take a Team of Prominent Fighter Across the Big Pond," *Philadelphia Inquirer*, January 28, 1900, 14; "Boxers to Go to Europe-Parson Davies Negotiating to Take O'Rourke's Aggregation to the Exposition," *Fort Wayne News*, March 9, 1900, 7.

1906. "Parson Davies Going Blind," *Evening World*, March 4, 1901, Night Edition, 6; "Parson Davies Hopeless-Will, According to a Friend of His, Soon be Totally Blind-Has Stricture of the Optic Nerve," *Boston Daily Globe*, March 4, 1901, 5; "Parson Going Blind-Charles E. Davies, Well-Known Sporting Man, Losing

His Eyesight," *Philadelphia Inquirer*, March 5, 1901, 7; "Parson Davies Gallus as Ever, *Philadelphia Inquirer*, March 16, 1901, 6.

1907. "With the Boxers-Gov. Roosevelt Signs the Bill That Kills Boxing in New York," *St. Louis Post Dispatch*, April 3, 1900, 7; "Roosevelt Signs Lewis Bill-Congratulates Author of the Repeal of the Horton Law," *Chicago Tribune*, April 3, 1900, 6.

1908. "'Parson' Davies' Chat," *Chicago Tribune*, April 15, 1900, 19.

1909. "'Parson' Davies Here," *San Antonio Daily Light*, April 10, 1900, 5.

1910. No Headline, *St. Louis Post Dispatch*, August 24, 1900, 3.

1911. "Will Fight For Sporting Laws-Admirers of Boxing in New York Have Started an Organization," *Chicago Tribune*, May 19, 1900, 6.

1912. "Parson Davies Comment-Peter Jackson's Surprising Criticism of American *Fighters," Chicago Tribune*, June 17, 1900, 19 [By Charles E. (Parson) Davies].

1913. "Hope For A Fight Law-Louisiana Legislators Considering a Bill Favoring Pugilism," *Chicago Tribune*, June 24, 1900, 20 [By Charles E. (Parson) Davies].

1914. "Young Griffo In Shape," *St. Louis Post Dispatch*, July 7, 1900, 5.

1915. "'Paddy' Ryan, Ex-Champion, Dead," *New York Tribune*, December 15, 1900, 4; "Death of Pugilist Paddy Ryan," *Chicago Tribune*, December 15, 1900, 8; "Pugilistic Career of Paddy Ryan-Fought his way to Prominence by Thrashing Tough Canal Men-Sullivan was his Undoing-Before the Battle at Mississippi City, Miss. Ryan was Considered the Premier in the Fighting World," *The {St. Louis} Republic*, December 18, 1900, 4.

1916. "Frank Childs Is After Johnson-Ready to Accept the Memphis Colored Man's Challenge," *Chicago Tribune*, January 10, 1901, 8; "Scanlan Is Here," *Galveston Daily News*, January 14, 1901, 3.

1917. Roberts, Randy, *Papa Jack: Jack Johnson and the Era of White Hopes* (Simon and Schuster 1985), 12 and 24.

1918. "Both Arrested-After Bout. Joe Choynski's Right in Pit of Jack Johnson's Stomach Ends Pretty Contest in Third Round," *Boston Daily Globe*, February 26, 1901, 5; "Arrest Men After Knockout-Choynski and a Texas Negro in Custody at Galveston," *Chicago Tribune*, February 26, 1901, 8; "Sporting News of the Day Briefly Told," *St. Louis Post Dispatch*, February 26, 1901, 7 (Refers to Johnson as "Jim" Johnson); "Choynski Is Still in Texas Jail-Not Relieved by Failure of Grand Jury to Find a True Bill," *Chicago Tribune*, March 9, 1901; "Texas Fighters Are Released," *Chicago Tribune*, March 23, 1901, 6; "Joe Choynski In A Texas Jail-Liable to Spend five Years in Prison for Prizefighting in Galveston," *National Police Gazette*, March 23, 1901, 7; "The Ring-Refused To Indict Choynski and Johnson," *Times Picayune*, March 31, 1901, 8; "Grand Jury Indicts Choynski," *Chicago Tribune*, May 30, 1901, 6; "No Indictment of Fighters," *Chicago Tribune*, June 2, 1901, 7.

1919. "Medal For 'Parson' Davies. Grand Lodge of Elks Present Him With a Past Exalted Ruler's Jewel," *National Police Gazette*, April 20, 1901, 7; "Testimonial to 'Parson' Davies," *New Orleans Item*, March 24, 1901, 10.

1920. "Boxing In New Orleans," New Orleans Item, April 19, 1901, 8.

1921. "The Ring-Boxing In New Orleans," *Times Picayune*, April 19, 1901, 8 (Dan Creedon and his backer talk to Parson Davies about making a match for the fall); "Mack's Melange Of Comment on Important Current Sporting Events and People. Wrestling Match Between Sharkey, *Times Picayune*, June 2, 1901, 12; "Sharkey Loses At Wrestling-Pugilist Is Thrown Twice by Jenkins at Cleveland After a Hard Struggle," *Chicago Tribune*, June 12, 1901, 6; "Mack's Melange Of Comment on Important Sporting Events and People-The "Old Times," *Times Picayune*, June 23, 1901, 11; "Dan McLeod Won-Tom Sharkey Defeated in a Wrestling Match at Buffalo," *Times Picayune*, July 4, 1901, 4; "Wrestling-Parson Davies Sees Sharkey In Training," *Times Picayune*, July 15, 1901, 8.

1922. "Sharkey and Schonfeldt to Wrestle," *New Orleans Item*, July 3, 1901, 6; No Headline, *New Orleans Item*, July 15, 1901, 6.

1923. "Sharkey Willing to Wrestle Schoenfeldt," *Times Picayune*, June 28, 1901, 8; "Schoenfeldt and Sharkey," *Times Picayune*, July 4, 1901, 8; "Schoenfeldt in Shape for Sharkey," *Times-Picayune*, July 18, 1901, 8; "Prof. Schoenfeldt Dangerously Hurt, Falling Through a Basin at the West End Club," *Times-Picayune*, July 21, 1901, 2; "Schoenfeldt Doing Well, But Has a Long Siege Before Him Yet," *Times-Picayune*, July 22, 1901, 10; "Prof. Schoenfeldt Well, And Will Soon Resume His Negotiations With Sharkey," *Times-Picayune*, August 1, 1901, 3.

1924. UK Incoming Passenger Lists, 1878-1960 [database on-line]. Provo, UT, USA: Ancestry.com Operations Inc, 2008; Original data: Board of Trade: Commercial and Statistical Department and successors: Inwards Passenger Lists. Kew, Surrey, England: The National Archives of the UK (TNA); Series BT26, 1,472 pieces.

1925. "Pugilism. Parson Davies on a Continental Trip," *Times Picayune*, August 15, 1901, 8; "The Ring-Parson Davies to Start a Boxing Club in London," *Times Picayune*, August 28, 1901, 8.

1926. "Croker Wins Victoria Cup," *Chicago Tribune*, June 30, 1901, 18.

1927. Connable, Alfred and Silberfarb, Edward, *Tigers of Tammany, Nine Men Who Ran New York* (Holt Rinehart and Winston 1967), 206-209, 220-230.

1928. "Croker's English Stable," *New York Times*, December 22, 1901, 17.

1929. "Buys Seaside Home for Wealthy Briton-Chris Buckley Negotiates Deal for Valuable Seaside Property," *San Francisco Call*, April 21, 1901, 17; "No Longer Croker's Aide," *The Minneapolis Journal*, December 2, 1901, 9; "Croker's Racing Partner Here," *New-York Tribune*, December 22, 1901, 10.

1930. "Croker's Trainer Retires," *Galveston Daily News*, December 1, 1901, 6.

1931. "Croker's Friend Nagle Very Ill- 'Just Write Out that I Leave Everything to Richard Croker to Dispose Of as He Thinks Best," *World*, September 12, 1901, 7.

1932. "Joe Walcott's Ambition," *Bath Independent*, September 21, 1901, 8.

1933. "Boxing Is At a Low Ebb-'Parson' Davies Writes of Sport in England," *Chicago Tribune*, December 22, 1901, 17 [By Charles E. (Parson) Davies]; "Current Sporting Gossip," *The {New York} Sun*, December 26, 1901, 8.

1934. "News And Notables At Local Hotels-Parson Davies Tells of Things in London Town," *Times-Picayune*, January 5, 1902, 12.

1935. "'Parson' Davies In America-Tells of Boxing Game in England-Effort to Hold Finish Fights at Parisian Club," *Chicago Tribune*, December 26, 1901, 6; "Parson Davies Back Home Again," *Kansas City Star*, December 27, 1901, 3.

1936. "Sharkey Again," *New Orleans Item*, December 14, 1901, 9.

1937. "M'Coy Champion of England," *The Saint Louis Republic*, October 27, 1901, Part I, 13; "Pugilism," *Salt Lake Herald*, January 1, 1902, 7.

1938. "News Notes," *Semi-Weekly Interior Journal*, January 7, 1902, 1.

1939. "Gossip of London," *Dallas Morning News*, October 27, 1901, 2; "M'Coy to Start Boxing School," *Bay City Times*, November 3, 1901, 2; "Contract for Beaumont Oil," *Dallas Morning News*, January 5, 1902, 16.

1940. "Little Bits of Sport," *New Orleans Item*, December 30, 1901, 6.

1941. "News And Notables At Local Hotels-Parson Davies Tells of Things In London Town," *Times-Picayune*, January 5, 1902, 12.

1942. "Parson Davies Talks," *New Orleans Item*, January 6, 1902, 1.

1943. No Headline, *New Orleans Item*, January 30, 1902, 7.

1944. "Jim Hall Has Lung Trouble," *Chicago Tribune*, January 6, 1902, 6; "Sporting Notes," *Grand Rapids Press*, January 6, 1902, 4; "Jim Hall Is Dying," *Omaha World Herald*, January 6, 1902, 2; "Jim Hall, Once Famous Pugilist, Faces Death with Smile and Jest," *Duluth News-Tribune*, January 6, 1902, 1.

1945. "Asleep Again," *New Orleans Item*, February 6, 1902, 6.

1946. "Retired Fighter Aldermanic Candidate," *St. Louis Post Dispatch*, January 13, 1902, 3.

1947. "Young Griffo Nearly Frozen-Is at the County Hospital in a Serious Condition etc.," *Chicago Tribune*, February 3, 1902, 6; "Young Griffo May Lose His Big Fists," *Gazette-Telegraph*, February 3, 1902, 3; "Young Griffo Insane," *Dallas Morning News*, February 7, 1902, 6; "Griffo's Condition Bad," *Salt Lake Telegram*, February 4, 1902, 7; "Griffo Goes To An Asylum," *Chicago Tribune*, February 7, 1902, 6.

1948. "Drawing Color Line. Parson Davies Wonders if Fear Has Anything to do With It," *Salt Lake Tribune*, April 27, 1902, 11.

1949. "Will Be Merry Jousting. Great Sporting Tournament at the King's Coronation," *St. Paul Globe*, January 12, 1902, 9 (A coronation belt will be offered); "Carnival of Sports," *Salt Lake Herald*, January 12, 1902, 4; "Coronation Year Sports," *San Francisco Call*, January 12, 1902, 30; "Coronation Boxing Tournament," *Washington Times*, February 10, 1902, 6; "Yankee Fights for Coronation-National Sporting Club's Commissioners On Way," *Evening World*, March 07, 1902, Night Edition, 8; "Plans for Monster Meet," *New-York Tribune*, March 09, 1902, 10; "Erne to Box Abroad," *Washington Times*, April 13, 1902, 6.

1950. "Want Big Fight In London Club-National Sporting Organization Offers Purse to Jeffries and Ftiz-$15,000 And Expenses," *Chicago Tribune*, April 19, 1902, 5; "Fitzsimmons Stops Working-Leaves Training Quarters, but Still Hopes for Match with Jeffries in England Next June," *Chicago Tribune*, April 11, 1902, 13; 6; "Public Wants Jeff and Fitz," *Chicago Tribune*, April 6, 1902, 9.

1951. "Fitz Seems To Hold Whip Hand-Cornishman Can Afford to Dictate Terms for Location of the Big Fight," *Chicago Tribune*, March 23, 1902, 9. This article is accompanied by a photograph of Jeffries and his family and pets.

1952. "Fitzsimmons Is Soon Coming West-He Is Trying to Arrange For a Heavyweight Boxing Partner," *Oakland Tribune*, April 29, 1902, 3; "In the Sporting World," *Oshkosh Daily Northwestern*, April 30, 1902, 3.

1953. "Siler's Talk of The Ring," *Chicago Tribune*, June 15, 1902, 12.

1954. "Root Knocks Out Stift," *Chicago Tribune*, April 27, 1902, 9.

1955. "Sporting in General," *Hamilton Daily Democrat*, May 28, 1902, 6; "Eddie Kennedy's Friend to Fight in England," *The Pittsburgh Press*, June 13, 1902, 14; "Temple Fights On Monday," The Pittsburgh Press, July 30, 1902, 10 (Match to fight ten rounds with Dido Plumb); "Boxing," *Bridgeport Herald*, October 5, 1902, 23.

1956. "Other Good Bouts," *Boston Daily Globe*, July 21, 1902, 4.

1957 ."Boxing Tournament Is All Arranged," *Daily Morning Sun*, May 30, 1902, 4; "Coronation Fights Arranged,-Amateurs and Professionals to Contest at National Sporting Club," *New York Times*, May 30, 1902, 6; "Ryan and Sullivan Sail," *The St. Louis Republic*, June 1, 1902, Part II, 17; "Coronation Sports Open," *Salt Lake Herald*, June 22, 1902, 7; "Block and Ryan Will Fight Tonight," *The St. Louis Republic*, June 23, 1902, 5.

1958. "Bat Masterson Sues for Libel-Confesses to Gambling But Denies Cheating Elder Snow," *The Pittsburgh Press*, July 7, 1902, 10; "Gang Of Westerners Captured By Detective, Brace Gambling Outfit Seized in Their Rooms-Bat Masterson, the Famous Ex-Marshal, One of the Prisoners-Victim Said to Have Lost $17,000," *New York Times*, June 7, 1902, 1; "Masterson Laments Loss Of His Pistol-Was Confiscated, But He Hopes to Get It Back at Auction Sale, *New York Times*, June 8, 1902, 23.

1959. "For Merry England," *New Orleans Item*, May 19, 1902, 8; "Off to Merrie England; Parson Davies Did Not Take Any Boxers With Him," *New Orleans Item*, May 28, 1902, 10; "Sporting in General," *Hamilton Daily Democrat*, May 26, 1902, 8; *The St. Louis Republic*, June 9, 1902, 8; "General Sporting Gossip," *Evening Times*, August 19, 1902, 6; "Armstrong Back to American," *Akron Daily Democrat*, August 27, 1902, 6; "Parson Davies' Pugs Return from England," *The Pittsburgh Press*, August 19, 1902, 10.

1960. "Siler's Talk of the Ring-Big Fighters Getting Ready for Their Battle-Jeffries and Fitzsimmons-Near End of Two Months' Training-Are Reported Fit to Go to a Finish on the Night of July 25-Rumors of Trouble with Champion's Left Arm-Jack Root and Gardner to Meet Again- etc.," *Chicago Tribune*, July 13, 1902, 12.

1961. "Both Men Ready," *Boston Daily Globe*, July 21, 1902, 10.

1962. "Parson Homeward Bound," *New Orleans Item*, August 20, 1902, 6; "Fitzsimmons' Age," *New Orleans Item*, September 3, 1902, 6; "Pair of Sportsmen Back Home Again," *New Orleans Item*, October 10, 1902, 2.

1963. "Here, There, And Everywhere," *New Orleans Item*, September 10, 1902, 8.

1964. "To Look After Broad," *New Orleans Item*, October 27, 1902, 6.

1965. "Parson Davies Is Pained," *St. Paul Globe*, October 30, 1902, 6.

1966. "Parson to Go on Stage," *Atlanta Constitution*, December 29, 1902, 2.

1967. "President Ebbets Denies A Transfer," *Washington Times*, January 3, 1903, 5.

1968. "Wants Fight In Salt Lake," *Salt Lake Tribune*, January 10, 1903, 8; "Parson Davies Challenges Corbett or McGovern for Kid Broad," *Times Picayune*, April 2, 1903, 10; "Mack's Mélange Of Interesting Boxing Gossip," *Times-Picayune*, April 9, 1903, 15; "Mack's Mélange Of Interesting Boxing Gossip-Terrance McGovern, Defeated, Returns Home and is Welcomed, *Times Picayune*, April 12, 1903, 14.

1969. "Mack's Mélange Of Interesting Boxing, Wrestling and Rowing Gossip-Jim Corbett at Champion Jeffries' Heels," *Times-Picayune*, December 28, 1902, 14.

1970. "Athletic Tournament To Be Given," *Galveston Daily News*, April 25, 1903, 3.

1971. "Pugs May Mix for Veterans," *Atlanta Constitution*, April 25, 1903, 9.

1972. "The Reunion Committee Makes More Arrangements," *Times Picayune*, April 25, 1903, 4; "Thousands Here For Reunion," *Times Picayune*, May 19, 1903, 1.

1973. "The Capital of the Confederacy," *Times Picayune*, May 20, 1903, 1.

1974. "Yanger to Fight Broad at Louisville Tonight," *The St. Louis Republic*, May 02, 1903, 9.

1975. "Kid Broad and Billy Maharg at the Washington Club," *Philadelphia Inquirer*, April 5, 1903, 12; "Jeffries in Town-Champion, Accompanied by Parson Davies, Looks All to the Good," *Philadelphia Inquirer*, April 6, 1903, 10.

1976. "Yanger Willing to Meet Kid Broad," *St. Paul Globe*, April 9, 1903, 5.

1977. "The Southern Athletic Stag Has Some Fine Features," *Times Picayune*, April 23, 1903, 12.

1978. "Mack's Mélange Of Interesting Boxing Gossip-Jack Root's Triumph Over Kid McCoy a Natural Result," *Times Picayune*, April 26, 1903, 14; "The Ring," *Times Picayune*, April 30, 1903, 10.

1979. "The Ring-Kid Broad to Meet Schneider Here To-Night," *Times-Picayune*, May 8, 1903, 10.

1980. "Schneider Lasts A Round In Front of Kid Broad," *Times Picayune*, May 9, 1903, 10.

1981. "In the Roped Arena," *Deseret Evening News*, May 30, 1903, Last Edition, Part Three, 23.

1982. "Broad May Meet Herrera," *Salt Lake Herald*, May 14, 1903, 7; "Sporting Notes," *Deseret Evening News*, May 16, 1903, Last Edition, Part Two, 12.

1983. "About the Boxers," *Boston Daily Globe*, May 15, 1903, 8.

1984. "Mowatt and Broad Prove Well Matched-The Kid Has the Best of Eight First [sic] Rounds-But Mowatt More Than Redeems Himself at End," *Times Picayune*, May 30, 1903, 10.

1985. "Broad Reaches Butte-Boxer and His Manager Arrive from Chicago to Begin Training at Once," *Anaconda Standard*, June 4, 1903, 11; "Ring Gossip For Pug Fans," *Salt Lake Herald*, June 7, 1903, Last Edition, 4.

1986. "Started Rough House," *Salt Lake Tribune*, June 14, 1903, 7; "Broad and Herrera Mix on Street," *Salt Lake Herald.*, June 14, 1903, Last Edition, 4.

1987. "Herrera's Win Popular Here," *Salt Lake Herald*, June 15, 1903, Last Edition, 7; "Doings in the Roped Arena," *Deseret Evening News*, June 20, 1903, Last Edition, Part Three, 18; "Kid Broad Knocked Out By The Mexican," *Fort Wayne Journal-Gazette*, June 14, 1903, 3.

1988. "Mexican Proves a Quick Winner from Parson Davies' New Protégé for the First Time in the History Board is Sent Down and Out etc.," *Anaconda Standard*, June 14, 1903, 10; "Led From the Sneak Again," *Salt Lake Tribune*, June 14, 1903, 7; "Broad Knocked Out," *San Francisco Call*, June 14, 1903, 34; "Broad Finally Done For," *St. Paul Globe*, June 14, 1903, 7.

1989. "Calls Herrera A Demon," *The Pittsburgh Press*, June 17, 1903, 12.

1990. "Parson Davies Returns from Butte," *Times Picayune*, June 20, 1903, 4.

1991. "Davies Lost $2,500," *Evening World*, June 17, 1903, Night Edition, 8.

1992. "The Ring-Tom Cody Comes To Town," *Times Picayune*, June 30, 1903, 10; "Tommy Mowatt Here to Meet Cody To-Night," *Times Picayune*, July 1, 1903, 10; "Tommy Mowatt Is Given The Verdict-Tom Cody Goes Half the Distance in Fine Style," *Times Picayune*, July 2, 1903, 8; "Mack's Melange Of Interesting Boxing Gossip etc.," *Times Picayune*, July 5, 1903, 14.

1993. "Another New Theater-The Old Wenger Place to Be Converted Into a Modern Playhouse," *Times Picayune*, May 29, 1903, 4.

1994. "Trocadero Theater's Future," *Times Picayune*, July 3, 1903, 5.

1995. "Advocates Big Boxing League," *The Pittsburgh Press*, July 21, 1903, 10.

1996. "Jeffries Wins In Tenth Round, Corbett No Match for Heavyweight Pugilistic Champion in Fight at San Francisco-Seconds Save Count Out-Give Signal of Surrender After Their Man Is Made Helpless by Two Terrific Blows in His Stomach. Beginning of the End. Where Corbett Is Deceived. Jeffries' Surprising Speed. Adopts Ryan's Advice, etc.," *Chicago Tribune*, August 15, 1903, 1; "Jeffries Is Still Champion," *Daily Nevada State Journal*, August 15, 1903, 1.

1997. "The Ring-Broad Here for Southern's October Stage," *Times Picayune*, October 6, 1903, 10; "The Ring-Broad and Herman in Training," *Times Picayune*, October 11, 1903, 15.

1998. "The Ring-Nobody Anxious To Meet Kid Broad," *Times Picayune*, October 18, 1903, 14.

1999. "The Ring-The Broad-Callahan Match Arranged," *Times Picayune*, November 3, 1903, 11; "The Ring-Callahan and Broad Monday, *Times Picayune*, November 8, 1903, 14; "Callahan-Broad Bout Proves Lively-Callahan Best at Long Range by Long Odds, But Broad the Hardest Puncher in Close Quarters," *Times Picayune*, November 10, 1903, 11; "The Ring-Comment on the Callahan Contest," *Times Picayune*, November 11, 1903, 11.

2000. "Parson Davies Here," *The Times Dispatch {Richmond, Va.}*, November 17, 1903, 9.

2001. "News And Notables At The New Orleans Hotels," *Times Picayune*, November 25, 1903, 10.

2002. "Poolroom War in New Orleans," *San Francisco Call*, December 3, 1903, 10.

2003. "Kid Broad Defeated," *Seattle Daily Times*, November 18, 1903, 5.

2004. "News And Notables At The New Orleans Hotels," *Times Picayune*, November 25, 1903, 10.

2005. "Broad and Mowatt to Meet Thanksgiving Eve," *Times Picayune*, November 15, 1903, 14; "The Ring-The Mowatt Broad Match, *Times Picayune*, November 17, 1903, 10; "The Ring-Southern Athletic's Big Stage," *Times Picayune*, November 21, 10; "Mowatt Will Arrive Today to Meet Broad Again," *Times-Picayune*, November 23, 1903, 10; "Mowatt Defeats Broad This Time, And the Fighting Conductor Gave Doubt No Room etc.," *Times Picayune*, November 26, 1903, 12.

2006. "In the World of Sport," *Oshkosh Daily Northwestern*, December 9, 1903, 8; "In the Sporting World," *Oshkosh Daily Northwestern*, December 18, 1903, 8; "Sporting," *Racine Daily Journal*, December 19, 1903, 8; "'Kid' Broad Defeated," *The {Syracuse} Evening Herald*, December 19, 1903, 8.

2007. West, Tommy, *The Long, Long Trail in The World of Sports*, (s.n. 1918), 62 – 63.

2008. Ibid.

2009. Ibid. at 65 – 68.

2010. "Eddie Hanlon to Fight Kid Broad Before the San Francisco Athletic Club," *San Francisco Call*," January 21, 1904, 10; "Broad Starts for This City," *San Francisco Call*, January 22, 1904, 10 (Parson Davies wires that Broad left New Orleans yesterday); "Broad Thinks He's A Winner," San Francisco *Call*, January 26, 1904, 8; "Broad Starts Training Work," *San Francisco Call*, January 27, 1904, 10; "Referee Still to be Chosen," *San Francisco Call*, January 28, 1904, 10; "Californian Fighter Is Made A Warm Favorite," *San Francisco Call*, January 29, 1904, 10 (Parson Davies wires instructions to Broad); "Eddie Hanlon Fights Cleveland Man to a Standstill in Decisive Fashion," *San Francisco Call*, January 30, 1904, 11.

2011. Ibid. 2011, at 71.

2012. "Prize Ring Weights May Be Readjusted," *St. Paul Globe*, January 10, 1904, 14.

2013. "To Regulate The Boxing," *Atlanta Constitution*, February 8, 1904, 17; "Talk New Weights-By Which to Classify The Pugilists," *Evening News*, March 17, 1904, 9.

2014. "The New Bijou," *Times Picayune*, January 25, 1904, 6.

2015. "New Orleans In The New Century," *Times Picayune*, January 10, 1901, 3; "Urge a War on Mosquitoes," *Times Picayune*, May 29, 1901, 13; "Progressive Union. The Directors Devote Another Evening to Discussing Managers, But Will Postpone the Selection," *Times Picayune*, January 19, 1902, 9; "Personal And General Notes," *Times Picayune*, April 9, 1902, 4; "Reunion Committee To Hold Its First Meeting Wednesday Afternoon," *Times Picayune*, November 2, 1902, 28; "Blanchard's Tribute," *Times Picayune*, July 27, 1904, 1.

2016. "Guide To The News," *Times Picayune*, December 7, 1903, 2.

2017. "Summer Amusements-Jake Wells Secures West End as Well as Athletic Park," *Times Picayune*, February 18, 1904, 4; "Proposals," *Times Picayune*, February 27, 1904, 7.

2018. "Saved The Swan-About All of the Old Athletic Park to Remain, except the Ground," *Times Picayune*, March 21, 1904, 11.

2019. "Summer Amusements-Jake Wells Secures West End as Well as Athletic Park etc.," *Times Picayune*, February 18, 1904, 4.

2020. "Bandmaster Paoletti Secures Contract for West End," *Times Picayune*, March 25, 1904, 5; "Jake Wells Here," *Times Picayune*, April 17, 1904, 4; "Opening Night at Athletic Park," *Times Picayune*, May 3, 1904, 12.

2021. " 'Parson' Davies' Niece Dies," *New Orleans Item*, May 1, 1904, 8.

2022. "More Bidders Rumored For The West End Lease," *Times Picayune*, July 26, 1904, 4.

2023. "News And Notables At The New Orleans Hotels," *Times Picayune*, August 31, 1904, 6; "Parson Davies' Schemes," *Deseret Evening News*, August 20, 1904, Last Edition, Part Two, 18.

2024. "Athletic Park Fire-Does Several Thousand Dollars Damage to Casino Stage," *Times Picayune*, August 21, 1904, 5.

2025. "News And Notables At The New Orleans Hotels-Jake Wells Inclined to Abandon New Orleans," *Times Picayune*, September 11, 1904, 16.

2026. "Athletic Park Fire Incendiary-Parson Davies Says Several Attempts to Destroy the Casino," *Times Picayune*, September 26, 1904, 8; "Incendiarism Active Out At Athletic Park-Some Suspicious Signs Being Discovered in the Katzenjammer Castle, Though No Fire Results," *Times Picayune*, September 28, 1904, 4; "Athletic Park Fires-A Large Reward Likely to Be Offered for Detection of Incendiaries," *Times Picayune*, September 30, 1904, 4.

2027. "Civil District Court . . . New Suits," *Times Picayune*, February 15, 1905, 7.

2028. "The Opening of the Lyric Theater," *Times Picayune*, November 21, 1904, 10.

2029. "John L. Goes West-Big Fellow Gets A Good Business Chance," *Boston Daily Globe*, September 7, 1904, 21; "John L. Sullivan Deserts Boston," *Evening World*, September 7, 1904, 8; "Some Off-Side Plays," *Chicago Tribune*, September 11, 1904, 1; "Ring Spendthrifts," *Evening World*, September 23, 1904, Evening Edition, 12; "Langford's Rapid Rise," *Boston Daily Globe*, September 27, 1904, 22.

2030. "Takes A Tip From John L.," *Oshkosh Daily Northwestern*, September 24, 1904, 12.

2031. 'Talk of Turf War-Parson Davies Thinks Corrigan Win in the Jockey Club Fight," *Galveston Daily News*, January 15, 1905, 4; C E Davies, Arrival Date: 6 Jan 1905, Age: 43, Male, American, Port of Departure: Havana, Cuba, Ship Name: Chalmette, Port of Arrival: New Orleans, Louisiana National Archives' Series Number: T905_6: New Orleans, Louisiana. Passenger Lists of Vessels Arriving at New Orleans, Louisiana, 1903-1945. Micropublication T905. RG085. Rolls # 1-189. National Archives, Washington, D.C.

2032. "The Fate of the Lyric," *Times Picayune*, January 11, 1905, 7.

2033. "Lyric Theater," *Times Picayune*, April 2, 1905, 4.

2034. "Cuban Theatrical Circuit," *Times Picayune*, April 30, 1905, 4; "Lyric Theater," *Times Picayune*, April 13, 1905, 4.

2035. "Sullivan-Mitchell 'Willie' Green Succeeds in Matching Two Great Has-Beens etc.;" *Salt Lake Telegram*, April 15, 1905, 9; "Sullivan and Mitchell," *New York Times*, April 16, 1905, "John L. Sullivan Matched-Former Champion Will Fight Charley Mitchell of England in May," *Washington Post*, April 16, 1905, 9; "Pugilist Never Has-Beens," *Galveston Daily News*, April 23, 1905, 22;

2036. "Lyric May Yet Change Hands," *Times Picayune*, April 27, 1905, 12.

2037. "Sullivan and Mitchell Still Talking Fight," *Anaconda Standard*, May 10, 1905, 7; "Poor Old John L. Wants to Fight Once More," *San Francisco Call*, May 10, 1905, 10; "Is After Mitchell-John L. Sullivan Would Meet Old-Time Opponent-No Match With Burns Yet, *Oregonian*, May 12, 1905, 7; "Sullivan and Mitchell," Naugatuck Daily News, May 19, 1;

2038. "John L. Sullivan to Fight Charley Mitchell," *The Times Dispatch*, May 19, 1905, 1.

2039. "Parson Davies To Direct Affairs," *Oakland Tribune*, August 5, 1905, 2; "Sporting Notes," *Titonka Topic*, August 24, 1905, 6.

2040. "Wants Kelly to Fight Gardner," *Salt Lake Tribune*, September 3, 1905, 24.

2041. "Davies And Corbett Buy New York Hotel," *Daily Nevada State Journal*, June 20, 1905 2.

2042. "Jim Corbett A Boniface-He and Parson Davies to Take Tom O'Rourke's Hotel Delevan," *New York Times*, June 13, 1905, 5; "Tom O'Rourke Will Sell to Jim Corbett-Deal on for the Transfer of the Delevan Hotel," *The Hartford Courant*, June 13, 1905, 1.

2043. "Too Much Hot Air Needed At Tavern-Tom O'Rourke Says He's No Handshaker," *Washington Times,* June 13, 1905, Evening, 8.

2044. "Injunction Stops Corbett-From Running O'Rourke's Delevan With 'Parson' Davies," *New York Times*, June 16, 1905, 16.

2045. "Lyric's Season-Parson Davies Returns and Makes Announcements," *Times Picayune*, August 14, 1905, 4.

2046. Ibid.

2047. "Off Season Gossip," *Times Picayune*, July 30, 1905, 31.

2048. "Erlanger Threatened to Crush Me---Belasco; Playwright Tells of Stormy Interview in Manager's Office. Stood it for Money Reason, Business Kept Him from Striking Syndicate Member, He Testifies—Got Miss Crosman Away from Him," *New York Times*, April 8, 1905, 8; "Belasco Shakes Fist and Threatens Klaw. 'I'll Send You to Jail for Conspiracy,' He Shouts in Court. Admit Syndicate Agreement," *New York Times*, April 11, 1905, 2; "Sam Shubert Will Meet With Klaw & Erlanger," *Chicago Tribune*, June 17, 1905, 1; "May Fight Theater Trust-The Shuberts Eventually to Form New Syndicate-Belasco to Join," *The Pittsburg Press*, June 17, 1905, 2; "New Syndicate of Theaters-Belasco, Shubert and Fiske Complete An Alliance-Discrimination by the Trust Will be Fought by Publicity of Methods and Presentation of New and Worthy Attractions-Make-up of Circuit, *Los Angeles Times*, June 21, 1905, 14; "Shuberts Cut Loose From the Syndicate; Formally Announce Their

Independency of Klaw & Erlanger. Have Booked Belasco Shows. The Break Started by Their Refusing to Agree Not to Extend Their Circuit," *New York Times*, July 15, 1905, 7; "Theater Managers Win In Speculator's Test; Right to Impose Conditions on Sale of Tickets Is Upheld. Court of Appeals Decides Daniel Frohman Believes That the Ruling Disposes of the Metcalfe Suit Also," *New York Times*, December 6, 1905, 11.

2049. "Theater Talk-'Parson' Davies Returns From the Fountain Source-The Shuberts Have an Eye on New Orleans, Including a Prospective New Theater," *Times Picayune*, October 11, 1905, 8.

2050. "Shuberts After Greenwall And His Texas Circuit-They Want Lease While He Insists on Sale-Sarah Bernhardt to Play at Greenwall Theater Here," *Times Picayune*, December 15, 1905, 5.

2051. "News And Notables At The New Orleans Hotels-Parson Davies Offers to Bet Independents Will Be at the Lyric-Cuban Fever Mainly Among the Immigrants," *Times Picayune*, December 19, 1905, 12.

2052. "Edgrens Column-Graphic Undoing of the Second Undoing of the Once Invincible Mistah Dixon," *Evening World*, September 21, 1905, Evening Edition, 2; "Dixon Is Soon Out," *Boston Daily Globe*, September 21, 1905, 1.

2053. "At The Wake of 'Little Chocolate'-Tommy Murphy Chief Mourner," *Evening World*, September 21, 1905, Evening Edition, 2; "Dixon Knocked out in the Second Round the Former Featherweight Champion Was No Match for Tommy Murphy," *Pawtucket Times*, September 21, 1905, 2.

2054. "Athletic Park-To Be Transformed into an Amusement Fairyland," *Times Picayune*, February 04, 1906, 29.

2055. "News and Notes of Sport," *Palestine Daily Herald*, February 26, 1906, 6.

2056. "Parson Davies, Baseball Magnate," *Sun*, February 12, 1906, 8.

2057. "Parson Davies-Stricken With Blindness After A Meeting In His Office," *Times Picayune*, February 23, 1906, 13; "Charles E. Davies Stricken-the 'Parson' Refereed the Famous Sullivan-Corbett Fight," *Kansas City Star*, February 23, 1906, 7.

2058. "Starbeams," *Kansas City Star*, June 6, 1906, 6.

2059. "Parson Davies May See Again," *Evening World*, March 26, 1906, Final Results Edition, 9.

2060. "The Old Time Ring Figures-Most Have Passed Away, And Their Successors Don't Meaure Up," *Salt Lake Tribune*, Mar. 18, 1906, 30.

2061. "McGovern to Fight Here," *New Orleans Item*, March 29, 1906, 6; "Purse for Nelson and McGovern," *The Lima Times Democrat*, March 29, 1906, 7; "My Fight M'Govern Again," *Syracuse Herald*, March 30, 1906, 16; "Sporting," *Racine Daily Journal*, March 30, 1906, 14.

2062. "'Parson' Davies to Return Shortly," *New Orleans Item*, April 14, 1906, 9; " 'Parson' Davies Says He Is Soon Coming Back Home," *New Orleans Item*, April 20, 1906, 6.

2063. "Brief Messages of Comfort," *Times Picayune*, April 25, 1906, 3.

2064. "Parson Davies Goes On Stage," *Los Angeles Herald*, June 10, 1906, 18.

2065. "Giant Machnow Looms Large in the Lower Bay," *New York Times*, June 17, 1906, 17.

2066. DeArment, Robert K., *Bat Masterson: The Man and the Legend* (University of Oklahoma Press, 1989), 374-376.

2067. "Giant Tries To Kiss The President's Hand," *New York Times*, June 21, 1906, 7.

2068. "Biggest Man In The World Meets The President," *Washington Post*, June 21, 1906, 27; "Biggest Man In The World," *Harrisonburg Daily News*, June 22, 1906, 4; "Davies Calls on Pres. Roosevelt," *New Orleans Item*, June 27, 1906, 8; "'Parson' Davies Introduces 'Biggest' Man to 'Greatest' Man In World," *New Orleans Item*, July 2, 1906, 6.

2069. "Masterson Starts Panic-Encounter With Two Westerners Clears Out a Café," *Washington Post*, June 21, 1906, 21; "Wild West at Waldorf," *New York Tribune*, June 23, 1906, 1; "Only Hot Air, No Guns, Fired In Hotel Row," *Evening World*, June 23, 1906, Final Results Edition, 5; "Bat Masterson In Hotel Fight," *The Pittsburgh Press*, June 23, 1906, 10.

2070. "Schubert's Agreement," New Orleans Item, June 19, 1906, 1; "Baronne Street Theater To Be Named The Shubert, And Will Present Main Independent Attractions, With Stock Company at Lyric-Parson Davies Brings the News, and Describes Interview With Roosevelt by Himself and the Russian Giant," *Times Picayune*, July 21, 1906, 4; "Shubert Deal Closed, And Independents Have Ten Years' Lease on Fine Theater," *Times Picayune*, December 12, 1906, 7.

2071. "Makes Improvements," *New Orleans Item*, August 13, 1906, 7; "Lyric To Open-Parson Davies Announces the Stock Company's Start," *Times Picayune*, August 26, 1906, 23; "Good Joke," *New Orleans Item*, September 15, 1906, 10; "Werner Treasurer of Lyric Theater," *New Orleans Item*, November 1, 1906, 10; "New

Shubert Theater-Handsome Playhouse Being Made Ready for Opening," *Times Picayune*, December 20, 1906, 12; "Shubert Opening-Brilliant Programme Arranged for New Theater To-Night," *Times Picayune*, December 29, 1906, 4.

2072. "Parson Davies Danger-Struck By Streetcar and Considerably Hurt-But Managed to Roll Out of Wheels' Reach In Time to Avoid Death," *Times Picayune*, December 12, 1906, 22.

2073. "Parson Davies Hurt by Car," *The Item*, December 22, 1906, 5; "Parson Davies Struck by New Orleans Car," *Washington Times*, December 22, 1906, Last Edition, 8

2074. "Parson Davies Protest-Against Increasing Tax on Theater, for Politicians' Benefit," *Times Picayune*, January 4, 1907, 7.

2075. "Lyric Theater," *New Orleans Item*, January 21, 1907, 2.

2076. "Things Theatrical-A Number of Changes Billed for Next Season," *Times Picayune*, March 26, 1907, 13.

2077. "Shuberts Next Season-Parson Davies Says It Will Be a Good One," *Times Picayune*, April 19, 1907, 11.

2078. "The White City Opening," *Times Picayune*, March 24, 1907, 36; "White City Growing And Will Be Ready For Opening in April," *Times Picayune*, March 29, 1907, 8; "White City Wet-Rain Postpones Opera Opening for a Week," *Times Picayune*, April 27, 1907, 7; "Amusements-White City," *Times Picayune*, May 4, 1907, 17.

2079. "Parson Davies Here On A Pleasure Trip," *San Francisco Call*, June 23, 1907, 37.

2080. "Important Question of Referee for Match Will Be Discussed by Managers Tonight," San Francisco *Call*, June 25, 1907, 7.

2081. "Clever Lightweight Eager for Return Bout," *San Francisco Call*, July 15, 1907, 5; "Nolan Insists That Referee Must Not Place His Hands On Referee But Must Let Them Fight Themselves Free From Clinches," *San Francisco Call*, July 23, 1907, 10.

2082. "Parson Davies Ill-Forced to Take to His Bed With an Attack of Rheumatism," *Times Picayune*, August 8, 1907, 18; "Parson Davies Ill," *The Pittsburgh Press*, August 9, 1907, 19; **"Parson Davies Ill But Not Seriously,"** *Washington Times*, **August 8, 1907, Last Edition, 10.**

2083. "Siler Testimonial," *Deseret Evening News*, August 13, 1907, Last Edition, 6;

2084. "Parson Davies Near Death," *Salt Lake Tribune*, August 16, 1907, 18.

2085. "Davies Will Conquer in Battle for Life," *New Orleans Item*, August 21, 1907, 19.

2086. "Parson Davies Thriving On Milk," *New York Times*, September 15, 1907, S1.

2087. "The Genuine Milk Cure," www.oldandsold.com-articles06-eat-37.shtml.

2088. "Russian Lion Is Eighth Wonder," *Los Angeles Herald*, February 16, 1908, 17.

2089. "'Parson' Davies On Stage," *Atlanta Constitution*, March 26, 1908, 26.

2090. "Parson Davies Back On the Job," *Washington Times*, September 16, 1908, Last Edition, 12

2091. "Parson Davies Going-Famous Sporting Man Closes Out His Local Interests-Will Take a Long European Trip and Then Settle on the Pacific Coast," *Times Picayune*, October 2, 1908, 5; "Parson Davies To Travel In Europe," *New Orleans Item*, October 2, 1908, 7.

2092. "Rialto Gossip," *Los Angeles Herald*, October 6, 1908, 6.

2093. "Parson Davies Going-Famous Sporting Man Closes Out His Local Interests-Will Take a Long European Trip and Then Settle on the Pacific Coast," *Times Picayune*, October 2, 1908, 5.

2094. "Parson Davies Going To See the Foreign Wreslers Perform," *New Orleans Item*, March 30, 1909, 8.

2095. "Lehmann Real Estate in Trust for Creditors," *Times Picayune*, January 1, 1908, 13.

2096. "Athletic Pak [sic] 1906 Failure," *Times Picayune*, October 6, 1909, 5.

2097. "Hunting Grounds And Fishing Camps-Disagreeable Weather Again Spoils Sport. Ducks Seem Plentiful," *Times Picayune*, December 14, 1909, 6.

Chapter 18 – It's a Great Country – Ours - (1909–1920)

2098. See note 2 above.

2099. "Parson Davies Tells Of Golden Age For Sports," *Oakland Tribune*, January 10, 1915, 36.

2100. "Parson Davies Dying-Taken Quietly to the Home of His Sister in Chicago," *Times Picayune*, May 26, 1901, 11; "Parson Davies Probably On Death Bed At

Present," The Pittsburgh Press, May 28, 1909, 10; **"Parson Davies Starts Last Fight for Life,"** *Columbus Daily Enquirer*, **May 30, 1909, 4.**

2101. Chicago City Part, Ward 13, Cook County, Illinois, 1910 U. S. census, Age 39 (Anita D. Wilson), Enum. Dist. 661, Sheet #9A; Chicago, Ward 13, Cook County, Illinois 1920 U. S. census, Age 49 (Anita Wilson), Enum. Dist. 786, Sheet #13A; Illinois Statewide Death Index, 1916-1950 - Davies, Anita Marie, Certificate #6005523, February 17, 1927.

2102. "Dying-'Parson' Davies, Manager of Great Fighters, Playing His Last String Out," *The San Antonio Light & Gazetter*," June 8, 1909, 9.

2103. "Charles E. ('Parson') Davies, Noted Chicago Sportingman," *Coshocton Daily Times*, August 8, 1909, 6.

2104. "Parson Davies Ill," *San Francisco Call*, February 23, 1910, 12; "Parson Davies Ill In Chicago," *New-York Tribune*, February 23, 1910, 9; "Parson" Davies Growing Weaker," *Belleville News Democra*t, February 23, 1910, 6; "Parson Davies Is Critically Ill," *Janesville Daily Gazette*, March 3, 1901, 1.

2105. "'Parson' Davies Ill in Chicago," *New York Times*, February 23, 1910, 10.

2106. "Parson Davies Is Through," *Idaho Statesman*, July 17, 1910, 7.

2107. "Career of Parson Davies," *Idaho Statesman*, July 24, 1910, 6.

2108. "Parson Davies Ill," *Salt Lake Telegraph*, July 18, 1910, 10; "Parson Davies Not Dying, But Is Coming to Chicago-Veteran Sportsman More Cheerful than Ever When Asked About Rumor of Stroke of Paralysis," *Chicago Tribune*, July 19, 1910, 11; "Parson Davies Still A Live One," *The Pittsburgh Press,* July 19, 1910, 19; "Parson Davies Said to be Dying," *Reno Evening Gazette*, July 19, 1910, 6; "Parson Davies Improving," *Washington Post*, July 19, 14.

2109. "Parson Davies Improving," *Washington Post*, July 19, 1910, 9; "Skidoo Wins Bookie's Coin," *Chicago Tribune*, July 21, 1910, 11 (Davies will arrive today from New York); "Billy Delaney Talks Fight," *Chicago Tribune*, July 27, 1910, 11.

2110. "'Parson' Davies Suffers Relapse," *New York Times*, July 28, 1910, 7; "Parson Davies in Weak Condition," *Washington Post*, July 28, 1910, 14; "Davies Suffers Relapse," *Racine Daily Journal*, July 30, 1910, 7.

2111. "Pertinent Sports Paragraphs," *Des Moines Daily News*, March 4, 1911, 8.

2112. "Negro Is Shrewd Financier," *Chicago Tribune*, October 2, 1901, C4 (Davies is back in New York).

2113. "Parson Davies Dying, Alone and Friendless," *Duluth News-Tribune*, March 12, 1911, 3.

2114. "Sport Topics," *Waterloo Evening Courier*, May 1, 1911, 2.

2115. "Parson Davies and John Rogers Off for Ireland; Rogers Says They'll Return With Next White Hope," *New Orleans Item*, May 1, 1911, 7.

2116. "Parson Davies Returns-Veteran Sporting Man Still Suffering From Paralysis," *New York Times*, October 30, 1911, 13.

2117. "Parson Davies Returns," *New York Tribune*, October 30, 1911, 4.

2118. "Parson Davies in Failing Health," *Oakland Tribune*, May 26, 1912, 25.

2119. "Parson Davies Ill and Poor," *Olean Times*, August 7, 1912, 7.

2120. "Whites Vs. Blacks Won't Meet Again-Parson Davies Says These Pugs Have Come to Parting of the Ways," *New Castle News*, January 3, 1913, 15.

2121. "Parson Davies Says Negro Boxers Will Be Eliminated by Promoters-Veteran Manager, Who Handled Peter Jackson, Says White and Colored Boxes Will Never Again Contest for a Title-Boxing Authorities Are Following Example Set by Organized Baseball," *Winnipeg Free Press*, January 4, 1913, 22.

2122. "Is McCarty Now Heavy Champ? Experts Inclined to Disregard Black Pugs in Awarding Title," *Atlanta Constitution*, January 12, 1913, 9; "Parson Davies Is On Right Track," *Times Picayune*, January 12, 1913, 14.

2123. "Newspaper Decision Plan is Sorriest Ever Thinks 'Parson' Davies, Now Here," *New Orleans Item*, March 22, 1913, 9. :

2124. "Notable Improvements On Buildings During Year," *New Orleans States*, November 2, 1912, 41.

2125. "Were Hall's Old Friends-Charley Mitchell and Parson Davies Both Critically Ill," Piqua Leader-Dispatch, March 17, 1913, 1; "Were Hall's Old Friends, Charley Mitchell and Parson Davies Both Critically Ill," *Coshocton Daily Times*, March 19, 1913, 6; "Australian Middleweight Has Answered Last Bell," *Racine Journal-News*, March 25, 1913, 18.

2126. "Parson Davies Awaits The End," *Fort Wayne Journal-Gazette*, December 13, 1913, 32.

2127. "Parson Davies Tells of Golden Age of Sports-Grand Old Man of Sportdom Awaits End With Gameness and Resignation," *Oakland Tribune*, January 10, 1915, 36.

2128. Ibid.

2129. "The Greatest of Glove Fighters-The Callow Youth and his Views-What 'Parson Davies' Thinks of Peter Jackson and Co.," *Referee*, January 27, 1915.

2130. "Wilson Signs Balls For War Fund Bid," *Muskegon Chronicle*, June 29, 1918, 10.

2131. Vere D [sic "R:] Davies, Chicago, Ward 34, Cook County, Illinois, 1900 U. S. census, Age 44; Vere R. Davies, Amberg Township, Marinette County, Wisconsin, 1910 U. S. census, Age 47, Vere R. Davies, Amberg Township, Marinette County, Wisconsin, 1920 U. S. census, Age 55 ; Carrie L Davies and son Leroy C., Mt. Clemens, Ward 3, Macomb County, Michigan, 1910 US census, Age 39.

2132. Amberg Historical Society, *Amberg The First 100 Years, 1890-1990*; J. Downing, *John Downing's Amberg Recollections*, (1996).

2133. "Dempsey Like Cardiff-Old Ones And Those of To-Day: Chat With Parson Davies," *Referee*, September 18, 1918.

2134. "Elks' National Home-Application for Admission," October 10, 1918.

2135. "B. P. O. Elks National Home ---- Medical Record," November 13, 1918.

2136. "Old Timers Would Not Guarantee to Receive Large Sums-Parson Davies, Veteran Manager, Takes a Wallop At Promoter Tex Rickard," *Wilkes-Barre Times*, August 22, 1919, 29.

2137. Commonwealth of Virginia, Department of Health-Division of Vital Records, Certificate of Death No. 14781, Chas. E. Davies, June 28, 1920.

2138. "Death Takes Parson Davies; Known Over Sport World," *Chicago Tribune,* June 29, 1920, 14; "'Parson' Davies Dead," *New York Times*, June 30, 1920, 18; "'Parson' Davies Dead," *Schenectady Gazette*, June 30, 1920, 11.

2139. *Cincinnati Times*,

2140. "Spink Tells About 'Parson,'" *Reno Evening Gazette*, July 28, 1920, 9.

Index

CPSIA information can be obtained
at www.ICGtesting.com
Printed in the USA
BVHW020433090223
658190BV00006B/192